The Clouded Hills

Flint and Roses

The Sleeping Sword

Brenda Jagger was a Yorkshirewoman who was married with three daughters, and lived, for the latter part of her life, near Bradford. She worked in Paris and Dundee and later in the north of England as a probation officer. Her work with 'wayward girls' and the study of her own family, increased her interest in the female situation and helped her to create the compelling women's characters which appear in this book.

Brenda Jagger

The Clouded Hills

Flint and Roses

The Sleeping Sword

BLACK CAT

First published in Great Britain as individual
volumes by Macdonald & Co (Publishers) Ltd
London & Sydney

Reprinted as a single volume 1988 by
Macdonald & Co (Publishers) Ltd under
the Black Cat imprint

ISBN 0-7481-0195-0

Printed in Hungary

Macdonald & Co (Publishers) Ltd,
3rd Floor, Greater London House,
Hampstead Road, London NW1 7QX

a member of Maxwell Pergamon Publishing Corporation plc

Photoset in North Wales by
Derek Doyle & Associates, Mold, Clwyd

Contents

The Clouded Hills

1

My grandfather, Samson Barforth, built himself a house on the hill above Lawcroft Fold so that on summer evenings, in the company of the woman who was not my grandmother and not entirely the housekeeper she claimed to be, he could look down on the valley he had made his own. And although a more patriotic Englishman never breathed, he was ready enough to admit that he had made a pretty penny out of Napoleon.

He had lit a bonfire of thanksgiving, true enough, to celebrate the Duke of Wellington's victory at Waterloo, but the long French wars, with the constant need for men and for uniforms of good Yorkshire cloth in which to clothe them, had brought prosperity to Barforth looms; and even as he had raised a glass of his best claret to drink the Duke's health, he would not have been sorry, perhaps, to see hostilities start up again, somewhere else. And when the great Duke had entered Parliament and shown himself opposed to Free Trade my grandfather had put his claret away and said hard things about national heroes who, when the battle was over, could think of nothing to do but uphold laws which would keep the price of bread high.

'They've got no place in peacetime, these generals,' I'd heard him grumble to the woman who was not my grandmother, this shocking Mrs Stevens, half his age and far too pretty for anyone's good. 'No place at all. Why should a man suppose that because he knows how to win a battle he knows how to do anything else? Can you tell me that? No, no, of course you can't. But I can tell you, Mrs Stevens, that if the price of bread goes up again there'll be hunger in the cities. And I've noticed, time and again, that when hunger comes, trouble is never far behind.'

And because, as everyone at Lawcroft Fold knew, my grandfather was always right, there was hunger – other people's hunger – through those guarded years of my childhood, men clamouring in our mill yard for higher wages as the price of a loaf continued to rise, and the landlords – encouraged, my father insisted, by the Duke of Wellington and his aristocratic cronies – refusing absolutely to let in the cheap foreign corn that would make everything right.

'Perhaps he doesn't eat much bread, the great Duke,' my grandfather snorted, too angry sometimes to be consoled even by the fluid, feline Mrs Stevens. 'But he grows corn now, I reckon, since we've given him a two-hundred-sixy-three-thousand-pound estate to thank him for saving us from the French. So maybe we shouldn't blame him for feathering his own nest. And what about those gallant redcoats of his, those veterans of Waterloo that he's pensioned off, coming here with their two pounds in prize money in their pockets, looking for work and grumbling when they can't get it or aren't fit for it? What about them, filling my weavers' heads with their fancy notions of liberty and equality that they learned in France?'

But as I played quietly in my grandfather's garden through my warm childhood summers, my sparkling, fur-cloaked winters, not even the prospect of those hard-eyed veterans hungrily prowling our hills had the power to disturb me, for what could a handful of soldiers do – how could the Duke of Wellington himself hope to prevail against Samson Barforth?

My grandfather had been a merchant in his young days, travelling to Lincolnshire with a string of packhorses for the sheep shearing, choosing his wool with care to suit the requirements of the worsted trade, driving a hard bargain, and then coming home again through the deserted Pennine ranges to distribute his stock. First he would go to the combers, who would draw out the long fibres into the creamy coils necessary for worsted yarn; then to the spinners and weavers, working, each man at his own loom, each woman at her own spinning wheel, in their cottages. And, since he was a man who could always see where money was to be made, I suppose it struck him early on that instead of merely carrying the wool and taking his commission, it would be more profitable to retain ownership of it himself, through all its processes, and employ the less enterprising cottagers to weave it for wages.

A hard life, certainly, with much of it spent in the saddle, since it took four spinners in those days to keep one weaver occupied with yarn, and the villages were not grouped companionably together but scattered in hostile, desolate places, stony tracks breaking off suddenly before outcroppings of rock, identical stretches of moorland and steep, faceless hillsides, where a man could wander, lost, for days on end and an injured man might never be found at all. A solitary life, too, both for him and for my grandmother, who could not accompany him on his rough journeyings, and since she knew quite well that many of the village girls were bold and bonny, and that travelling men were not famous for their ability to resist temptation, it may have been partly for her sake that he paused one day at the place called Lawcroft Fold to consider the old corn mill and the fast-flowing stream that refreshed the valley bottom.

He had noted the dampness of the grey moorland air, the grey-peaked hills that tore the rain clouds apart – a guarantee that no waterwheel, in this barren land, need ever be still – and laying down his packs and calling his horses to a final halt, he had purchased the entire property: the mill and the millhouse, the land and the water rights that went with it; he had swept out the dust of the miller's last lean years and transformed himself into that new species of employer, a man who demanded that his workpeople should come to him – not he to them – at a given hour and should remain until they had his permission to leave.

The hills around Lawcroft Fold – bare, brown uplands, waterlogged in winter, wind-raked at all seasons – were still alive in those years with a close-fisted, independent breed of men who lived hard and perhaps not too long but who lived as they pleased and had no mind to make changes. They had their handlooms and their spinning wheels, a weekly piece of cloth to be woven as and when it suited them and carted away every Friday to the Piece Hall in Cullingford and offered for sale. They had an acre or so of land apiece, on which to keep a pig and a cow and to grow such crops as could survive the raw northern air and the poor soil. To men like these, who took orders and wages from no one, my grandfather as an employer was not welcome. But perhaps, being as thrifty of emotion as of everything else, they only began to hate him when he introduced into the valley, with great secrecy and some danger, a number of new machines which, by spinning an eventual eighty threads at a time instead of one, were destined to be the assassin of the spinning wheel.

My grandfather had brought in soldiers to preside at the installation of his machines, while men with hammers in their hands had prowled outside his gates, determined to smash the fiendish inventions that would deprive their women – the spinsters – of work. There were many among them who saw the new spinning frames as a threat not only to earnings but to family life, since a woman who is anchored all day to her wheel, in her own house place, surrounded by her children, has neither the time nor the opportunity for mischief. But let her be idle or send her to a man like Samson Barforth who would put money into her hands, then neither husband nor child could ever know real peace of mind again.

Everyone had heard about the gangs of women employed in the coal mines, strapping, brawling creatures beyond any man's control, crawling half naked down the tunnels with a candle in their mouths and a chain between their legs, dragging a coal cart behind them, in the company of men who were not their husbands: the Law Valley was unwilling to expose its own women to such misery and such temptation.

Samson Barforth was stoned one night as he rode across Cullingford Moor. His windows were broken. He was shunned by the local gentry, who resented his use of the river water to drive his mill wheel to the detriment of their own ornamental fountains; he was shunned, too, by the inhabitants of Cullingford, the nearby market town, who from self-interest and snobbishness followed wherever the gentry led. But my grandfather, being a Barforth, knew that right was on his side, and he experienced no difficulty whatsoever in overlooking abuse and even assault when there was a profit to be made.

'They'll soon see reason,' I could imagine him saying to my grandmother, in the days before Mrs Stevens. 'They can't beat progress, and they can't beat me.' And so it was, for the weavers, momentarily encouraged by the abundance of mill-spun yarn which kept their own looms occupied, were slow to notice the expansion of my grandfather's business, his use of the surplus yarn to weave pieces of his own, so that quite soon he was able to describe himself not only as a spinner but as a full-scale manufacturer of worsted cloth. By the time it was realized that his pieces, being as good as anyone else's but more plentiful and in more regular supply, had attracted the best customers, and that he had no yarn to spare, it was too late.

The old corn mill grew and gave birth to other, sounder structures. A solid, stone house was built for my grandmother – an uncompromising, square-cut pile with a door firmly in the middle, two windows on either side of it, two windows above, and a stone-flagged kitchen, where my grandmother baked her own bread, trussed her own chickens, made soap

11

and candles, and bullied her maids, and where my grandfather added up his accounts and learned to call himself a rich man.

Labour, of course, was always scarce, for no Law Valley man would willingly submit himself to the prison of factory life, and so my grandfather, looking further afield, began to construct rows of cottages around the mill yard: identical two-roomed boxes soon filled by the mass of agricultural labourers who, driven off the southern farmlands by the loss of their free pasture, were drifting rootlessly North, and by the perpetually starving Irish, who would take any man's wages. And when all else failed, it was always possible to strike a bargain with some parish priest or other who, only too glad to empty his poorhouse, would send pauper children by the cartload from as much as two hundred miles away – little abandoned mites too young, some of them, to remember their parents or their proper names, bound as apprentices for a term of fourteen years, boys and girls alike, at the end of which time my grandfather would give them a decent suit of clothes or a good gown, and if they had done well, employment as a free operative in his thriving enterprise.

A long, low dwelling was built to accommodate them, right in the mill yard itself, and when Parliament, at the instigation of Robert Peel, himself the son of a calico printer, decreed that such apprentices should be taught their letters and numbers and a little religion, and that boys and girls should sleep separately and no more than two to a bed, my grandfather obeyed the law, as many others did not, by dividing his apprentice house in two, building a school and hiring a schoolmaster, whose duty it was – my grandfather being of the Methodist persuasion when he could be persuaded at all – to walk the children the weekly five miles to the Church of England the law had specified.

My grandmother, a giantess of my childhood, her stern, well-creased face always surrounded by oddly contrasting butterfly caps of lace and satin ribbon, did her duty strictly by these parish children – valuing, no doubt, their contribution to her ever-increasing comfort – and saw to it that they had an abundance of hot oatmeal twice every day to sustain them through the boom times, when their labour was often required from five o'clock in the morning until eight o'clock at night. And, her favourite colour being blue, she dressed them identically for church on Sundays: dark blue gowns for the girls, dark blue jackets and cord trousers for the boys – even the schoolmaster, in a good blue coat – all of which must be removed on their return from divine worship, since Sunday was often a convenient day for the cleaning of machines.

There were masters, of course, who were less gentle. There had always been tales in the valley of beating and strappings, of infants savagely mauled by the machines or by an overseer's spite, of men who, when their businesses failed, drove their apprentices to the middle of some lonely moor and turned them loose like a litter of unwanted pups to fend for themselves. But my grandmother had always been indignant of such goings-on, my grandfather scornful.

'Bad business,' I'd heard him say. 'Any fool can see that. Treat them right and they'll work. Treat them wrong and they'll run away, and then you'll have to spend time and money catching them or fetching a fresh lot to take their place. And these parish priests drive a hard bargain. Bad business.'

Even when my grandmother died – furious because she had let it be known she wasn't ready and hated to be defied – there had been the sloe-eyed Mrs Stevens to call a doctor to a sick or injured child and to make sure that the 'brats' overseer' was a man of Christian principle and not too rough. But the day of the parish apprentice was over now, for, since the steam engine had been tamed to take the place of the waterwheel and the mills were no longer tied to the banks of rivers, and since fresh famine in Ireland had brought yet another flood of hungry, hardy workers to our shore, the once pleasant town of Cullingford had spread like a giant weed garden, new streets of low, already grimy houses rushing outward to meet the fast-growing ring of factory gates, the black-belching stacks of prosperous factory chimneys; and there were free children in plenty to fill our sheds, kept in order and kept awake by their own hardhanded mothers. The ministrations of the Barforth ladies were no longer required, and although this new breed of factory children seemed smaller and paler than the ones we had fed and housed ourselves – living, as they did, in those mean streets where no Act of Parliament could compel their mothers to put them no more than two to a bed or to teach them to be Christians – there were, at least, more of them, and the work was done just the same.

Mrs Stevens gave her mind now to her pickles and preserves, my mother to her embroidery, and by the time I was sixteen, with Waterloo already far behind us, I was too secure, too convinced of Barforth right and might to be greatly concerned that once again there were soldiers in our mill yard, doing little, it seemed, but lounging and laughing and ogling the maids, but ready, at my grandfather's command, to defend the installation of yet more machines, the new power looms that would force the last hand weaver from the freedom of his cottage workshop or would starve him to death.

The introduction of these power looms, of course, to men like my grandfather, was entirely logical. Since we had spinning machines, it followed as naturally as night follows day that we must have a weaving machine of some sort to keep pace with the vast quantities of yarn we could now produce. But the hand weavers, already losing their struggle to compete with the factories, seeing their earnings cut and their standards falling, seeing their precious freedom eaten away, could not be expected to take so reasonable a view. And since the landowners had once again increased the price of bread and it was rumoured that the younger weavers had taken to drilling with firearms on the moor on warm nights – instructed, one supposed, by those reckless, penniless veterans of Waterloo – trouble was expected and, being looked for, might well be found.

My father, I knew, would have delayed the coming of the new looms, for, never having known poverty as my grandfather had, he was often inclined to take an easy way and was less urgent, less fixed of purpose. But although the mills were now supposedly in his charge, my grandfather's vision was still acute, his ambition still thirsty, and when he had stumped down from the Top House and ordered, 'Get the looms in, and get the military,' my father had not chosen to disobey.

They were alike in many ways, big men in youth who turned heavy in middle life, vigorous and full-blooded, hearty of appetite, except that my father, being a copy of the original mould, was somehow a little less, his needs more easily satisfied; and perhaps we all knew that it was my brother Edwin – taller, at twenty-four, than either of them – who held first place in my grandfather's heart.

'The Boy,' he called him, in an entirely different tone from the one in which he referred to me as 'the Girl,' and it was Edwin who had gone to fetch the soldiers and the engineers and who had spent long hours in the sheds deciding, with my grandfather, where the new looms were to be placed.

'The Boy knows what he's about,' my grandfather told Mrs Stevens, who, in her turn, made sure we all heard it, and when my brother concluded that nothing would suffice but the building of an entirely new factory, a stone temple of progress and profit, my grandfather chortled his delight.

'We'd best knock this old heap down,' Edwin announced, 'before the new looms do it for us. No shoring up and making do. If we're to do the job at all, then we'll do it right.' And as his vision began to extend to four storeys, six storeys capable of housing not merely the dozen looms on order but five hundred more, I saw my grandfather take on colour, my father fade, and I remembered that, somehow, it was always my father – never my brother – who would find his horse surrounded by muttering hand weavers, always my father who bore the brunt of some woman's hysteria, who was jostled and threatened and asked if he would be satisfied when the hills were full of walking skeletons.

'Ignore them,' my grandfather said.

'Ride them down,' my brother advised.

But my father could do neither, and there were times when I would have offered him sympathy, had I dared.

'One can see their point of view,' I had heard him tell my mother, speaking low in case my grandfather, from the Top House, should hear him; but unlike Mrs Stevens, who drank in my grandfather's every word, my mother rarely listened to anyone and hardly ever to her husband.

'Isabella,' he said quite harshly, 'does nothing trouble you?'

Smiling vaguely, she murmured, 'Why yes, dear,' and went back to her embroidery.

My mother was a beautiful woman, but beyond the facts of her dark, glossy hair, perfectly oval face, and startling grey velvet eyes, I knew little about her and had never found the way to ask. She was the scent of lavender through my childhood, by no means aloof, since aloofness is a cold thing, a positive thing, and she was far too elusive for that; a woman who gave no orders and made no demands, who always answered, 'Why

14

yes, dear. Of course, dear,' but who was, just the same, as private and separate and elegant as a cat.

My father had caused her portrait to be painted soon after their marriage, showing her in the narrow, Grecian-styled gown of those days, a silver ribbon casually holding her tumbled curls, a dark shawl draping her bare shoulders, her eyes half closed, languorous, her smile making promises it had evidently not been in her nature to fulfil. And standing before it as a child, I had thought her the most exquisite creature in the world and had been amazed that my father did not seem to love her as much as he could have done and that my grandfather did not love her at all.

It is not given to many children to understand the reasons for their parents' marriage, but I knew – because, being a girl and generally ignored, I overheard a great deal and assumed far more – that it was, perhaps, the sole occasion on which my father had gone against my grandfather's wishes. Not that my mother had been in any way ineligible, for, as Miss Isabella Baxter, a master cutler's daughter from Sheffield, she had had a little money and some gentility, and there had been others besides my father who had wanted her. It was simply that the Barforth wives had always been plainspoken, sensible women, useful rather than beautiful, the kind who knew and kept their place, dull perhaps but safe, their feet firmly planted on the ground, and my grandfather had given loud and quite ferocious warning that Miss Isabella Baxter could make no man feel secure. He, too, it seemed, had noticed the languorous smile, the gracefully leaning figure that could entice a man from his duty, encourage him to squander time and energy that should be given to business – the true purpose of a young man's life – and not to pleasure, which should be left for later. But my father, properly enticed, had persisted, and even my mother, for perhaps the first and last time in her life, had made a stand, declaring that she would have no other, and had eventually gone to church to marry him in a cloud of silk gauze and lace that had shocked the Law Valley.

But somehow they had not been happy. Perhaps my father's romantic impulse had not endured. Perhaps my mother's expectations had been too high. Perhaps he had believed she would be changed, on her wedding night, by some mysterious alchemy into the uncomplicated, four-square wife a Barforth really required, while still retaining her exceedingly complex charm; and his disappointment may have caused her to retreat from him, to become even less a Barforth as he, in time, became more. And although my father never spoke a word against her, growing merely a little more morose every year, my grandfather would tell anyone who cared to listen – and when had Mrs Stevens been unwilling? – that he found her lovely face and her skill at fine needlework poor compensation for her feckless, aimless ways and her sad inability to raise her children.

My brother Edwin, it is true, had come roaring into the world like an infant Hercules, and I, despite my inferior sex, was no weakling, but between us and after us a half dozen little Barforths had lived a few sickly months apiece and since such weakness could not possibly have come from him, my grandfather believed most fervently that it came from her.

15

I went, often enough, to put flowers on that little row of Barforth graves: brothers Samson and William, sisters Isabella and Emma, Sophia, and a shadow called Lucy I could just remember and who had caused my grandfather to curse and grumble when he was told that her birth would be the last.

'So it's over now, is it?' he'd said. 'That's the best she can do? Two out of eight and no more to follow. Small return, son William, I call it, for what she's cost you. Well, one learns to make the best of what there is to hand, that's the great thing, and at least there's the Boy. Yes, I've got my stake in the future. I've got the Boy. And I reckon the Girl can be made to stir herself, when she's an age for it, and bring us a good man into the house, somebody to stand by Edwin when we're gone. And who knows, William lad, if your Isabella should really prove as delicate as they say – well, I reckon you'll take a solid woman next time, one of our own kind who'd strengthen the stock, because there's the mills to think of and we need every hand we can get.'

There was no open quarrel between them, for my mother quarrelled with no one, while my grandfather was so habitually sharp-spoken that he often seemed angry with the world in general rather than with her in particular. But her sweet, absentminded smile caused the knotted veins at his temples to swell; her way of talking – very soft, very low, and saying nothing – brought the fierce, mottled colour to his cheeks, and it irked him greatly that my father would not join him and hate her too.

'Aye, lad, it's a bad business,' he would say sometimes, heavy with sympathy, sly with complicity. 'You'd best let the Girl come up to Mrs Stevens and see the proper way to go on, for she's too quiet by half, your Verity. The Boy, now, he's an open book, but it strikes me your girl could turn whimsical and deep. You'd do well to watch her, lad, for we can risk no more of it.'

'She's well enough,' my father said, not altogether defending me, not absolutely denying his wish for a more comfortable wife, and I understood that, as my mother's daughter, I was suspect too and that if I wished to be acknowledged as a Barforth, I would be obliged – unlike my brother – to prove my worth.

They gave me gold earrings the day I reached sixteen, a fan on ivory sticks, white kid gloves, a puppy from my brother's yellow crossbred bitch, a strand of coral, a tortoiseshell comb, to put up my hair; and that evening, in the midst of admiring my presents and instructing me on how the puppy should be fed, my brother casually, defiantly, told us it was time he took a wife.

'Yes, dear,' my mother said. 'Naturally.'

Edwin, who was more inclined to share my grandfather's point of view than I, flushed angrily, stung by her roundabout but effective way of reminding him what a menace he had been, these past few years, to maids and mill hands, and to the farm girl over at Farncliffe Craggs who, last winter, had borne his child.

'You have the young lady in mind then?' my father said quickly, flushing, too, for Edwin had spent the day at the Top House, talking of power looms and weddings, it seemed, with his grandfather, not his father, missing a generation as he was far too apt to do. And as he saw his authority thus whittled away, my father's bitterness escaped its fetters and found its tongue.

'It's a matter not to be taken lightly, and as I know your nature, lad, you'll need a sensible, thrifty woman with her feet on the ground – a woman who wants what you want and understands why you want it – one of your own kind, Edwin. Romance is all very well but it's not hard-wearing, and honeymoons are soon over.'

But my mother, who was thought to hear nothing, notice nothing, and who certainly did not appear to think herself insulted, although I thought it and suffered for her, lifted her elegant head from her needlework and said lightly, 'But he's to marry his cousin, Hannah Barforth, surely? Isn't that what he arranged with his grandfather – or his grandfather with him – long ago?'

'Shall you dislike it very much, Mamma?' my brother asked her, cooler, harder than my father, caring little for the whims of any woman, his cousin Hannah among them. And, my new comb holding my hair in the smooth chignon of womanhood, I was irritated suddenly, quite unbearably, by his smug assumption that Hannah not only would take him but would be very glad to do it.

'Well,' I said, stiff-necked with the unaccustomed weight of upswept hair and tortoiseshell, 'before we like it or not, we'd best know if you've asked her yet. She may not like it overmuch herself.'

And I have never forgotten him, standing brown-skinned, brown-eyed in the sunshine, convinced beyond all question of his ability to take the future by the throat and force from it anything it should be foolish enough to deny him.

'She'll like it very well,' he said, laughing me to scorn. 'There's no doubt about that, or I'd not ask her at all. I'd give no woman in the world the chance to say she'd turned me down. I'll ask her tomorrow, when the new looms come in, and you can dance at my wedding, Verity Barforth, if you can learn to keep your hair from falling down – and maybe you'll catch yourself a husband while you're about it.'

And because I knew he was as irresistible and indestructible as my grandfather, and because I was at an age when weddings were very much on my mind, I believed him and laughed too.

2

They brought the looms in the night, a line of quiet, sluggish carts escorted by soldiers, my brother Edwin at the head of them, leading his army as bravely as any Iron Duke. And although there was a sullen crowd in the mill yard the next morning, they parted, muttering but cowed, to let my grandfather through when he rode down from the Top House to make sure his overlookers and that strange new breed of men called engineers were setting all to rights.

17

'They'll be in production by the end of next month,' he announced bluntly as he strode back to his horse, glaring at anyone who seemed inclined to argue; hoping, perhaps, that somebody would. And that afternoon my cousin Hannah came to call, knowing, no doubt, that Edwin planned to speak to her and having her answer ready.

She was very tall, my cousin Hannah, and very determined, a Barforth to her fingertips, clever, self-assured, and exceedingly handsome; and if she was still single at twenty-three it was only because she had made up her mind long ago to marry my brother, who, in fact, had always been willing, although my grandfather had not.

No doubt my grandfather had dreamed of someone truly exceptional for Edwin, a girl who combined the practical good sense he had valued in his own wife with Mrs Stevens's persuasive charms; a girl with money, too, and expectations – a millmaster's only child, perhaps, who would inherit her father's business and give it to Edwin. And while Hannah could not be faulted in looks or behaviour, she was something of a poor relation with a family history not unblemished, whose dowry, if there was a dowry, would only be small. Yet Edwin could be stubborn, and my grandfather was eager to see the start of a new generation, to which Hannah might well make a cheerful, sensible, healthy mother; and as she walked into the house that flowery May morning, rather more stately than she should have been in her dull, green gown with its narrow flounces, I had no doubt that she was soon to be my sister.

She was not, strictly speaking, so nearly related to me as she seemed, being the daughter of my father's cousin – another broad, brown-eyed Barforth who had once been in a reasonable way of business at Low Cross Mill not far away. But my uncle, Tom Barforth, who could have lived comfortably on the profits of his weaving sheds, had attempted to live grandly and had kept a mistress in Leeds, spending time with her when he should have been at his mill; quite naturally, he had not prospered. His wife, Aunt Hattie, had been a pretty woman and may even have been good-natured in her younger days, but the constant cheese-paring economy that had been necessary to support his extravagance, her having to wear her own petticoats to shreds while he continued to patronize an expensive Leeds tailor, had soured her disposition and lowered her spirits. With ruin staring them in the face, I had heard, neither she nor my uncle had fought too hard against the fever which had carried them off three years ago, leaving Hannah and her brother and sister to manage as best they could.

'Poor souls,' Mrs Stevens had said mistily on her way back from Aunt Hattie's funeral. 'Poor lambs. Whatever will become of them?'

And, indeed, the situation had seemed so hopeless that Hannah's brother, my cousin Joel, had been expected to sell out, salvage what he could, and take employment. My father, I believe, had even made a tentative offer to take him on at Lawcroft, although my grandfather, who disliked Joel, had declared gruffly – and very likely in Joel's hearing – that Australia would be near enough. But my cousin Joel – who undoubtedly, in face and manner, was much like his father – was cast

18

more truly in the Barforth mould and, taking off his own well-cut jacket, rolling up the sleeves of his fine cambric shirt, had set himself to prove the Law Valley wrong. Although Low Cross Mill as yet was far from prosperous, debts had been paid and men no longer avoided Joel in the street in case he should ask for credit, while Hannah, a far more efficient, housekeeper, it seemed, than her mother, kept a good fire in their hearth and plain but wholesome food on their table, and saw to it that Elinor, the youngest member of the family, was as well turned out and well behaved as any girl should be.

'Remarkable young people,' Mrs Stevens often declared, thinking no doubt of Joel, who knew how to charm when it suited him. 'They should be an example to you, Verity.'

Yet, in spite of their admirable courage and tenacity, there was often a harshness about them both, a resentment of their own poverty, a certain contempt for those of us – myself and Edwin included – who had never known hard times, that made me ill at ease.

My mother, had it occurred to her, could have sent her carriage for Hannah that morning, knowing that she and Joel would wish to see the new machines and that Edwin certainly wished to see Hannah, but my mother's arrangements were as insubstantial as her smile – her feelings for Hannah perhaps more definite than she cared to show – and when she saw the sisters, Hannah and Elinor, coming through the gate from the mill yard and up to our door, she looked, for a moment, quite puzzled, as if she could not quite remember their names, except that it was Barforth.

'Oh – yes, dear,' she said. 'How nice – really – how pleasant.' And her voice, without in any way losing its sweetness, reduced Hannah – flushed with her expectations of being the future mistress of this house – to the level of a chance acquaintance who should really not have come in unannounced.

But almost at once my brother Edwin, who had been on fire all day about the looms and had been longing for Hannah to come and tell him how brave and farsighted he was, strode into the parlour, the warm tones of his nature dispelling my mother's coolness; and as he clasped Hannah's hand eagerly in both his own and told her, 'The looms have come,' we all knew he was actually saying, 'Now, at last, will you be my wife?'

'Yes,' she replied, 'they've come. And you had no trouble. I knew you would have no trouble, once you were determined and let them know it. Oh, Edwin, well done, Edwin. Joel has looked in at the mill to see how the engineers are progressing, and I wondered – could I, do you think, go and take a look, too?'

'I came up on purpose to fetch you,' he said, beaming broadly, immensely gratified by her interest and her praise. 'We'll go now, straight off, because I want to talk to you on the way. And then, Mother, if you're agreeable, we're all to meet at the Top House by three o'clock, to take a glass of something, and a bite of something, too, if I know anything about Mrs Stevens. If you're agreeable, that is, Mother, and you've nothing planned for dinnertime – nothing that can spoil?'

'Oh no, dear,' she said, as if the thought of dinner, which we took regularly at four o'clock, had not so much as entered her mind. 'What could I have to spoil?'

But Edwin, determined not to upset his great day, took Hannah's arm in a firm, possessive hold – glad, perhaps, to feel her so solid, so real – and with a nod and a half smile in his mother's direction led her away.

I walked up to the Top House some time later with my cousin Elinor, a girl of my own age, who, unlike the serious-minded Hannah, had few interests in life just then beyond ribbons and ringlets and the contemplation of her own delicate, china-doll prettiness, which did not come from the Barforth side of the family at all.

Hannah and Joel, Edwin and my father all had something of my grandfather about them: 'black Barforths,' with his hooked nose and uncompromising jaw, and even I, although my oval face and smaller features came from my mother, had the dark Barforth eyes, the heavy, chocolate-coloured Barforth hair. But Elinor was pink as a new rose and as fragrant, very much as my Aunt Hattie must have been as a girl; extraordinarily dainty, impossibly vain, with hair of a pale, silvery fairness and eyes a cloudy tint somewhere between blue and green, her slender figure, even at fifteen, elegant in her meagre finery.

My cousin Hannah had one good gown for summer, another for winter, and a sensible bonnet which she wore day in, day out, needing no other decoration than her grand Barforth self-esteem, but Elinor, by ingenuity and skill with her needle and a little unashamed begging from her richer relations, contrived always to appear fresh from the hands of some fashionable city dressmaker. New muslin flounces would appear on the hem of some old dress of mine; a satin bonnet I had long discarded would acquire an ostrich plume taken from a cap of my mother's; a dashing straw hat, freshly crowned with spring flowers and the sauciest knots of ribbon, would be revealed, in whispers, as something for which Mrs Stevens had seen no further use. She would cut herself a wicked little spencer jacket from an evening cloak looted from my grandfather's attic, a sash and matching reticule from the lining, while her pursuits of fans and gloves and costly little bits and pieces was so shameless, so very much like the terrier who gnaws and worries and refuses to let go, that she rarely came away empty-handed.

But today, although her pink muslin dress was worthy of comment, her appearance seemed momentarily to have slipped her mind, and even my enthusiasm for the roses in her chignon and on her sash and the little posy of rosebuds and ribbons dangling from her arm failed to distract her fully.

'I had them from the minister's garden,' she said absently.

'Had them? You mean you took them?'

'Oh – yes, so I did. And why not? Hannah sent me to call – and I had no wish to go – and as I was coming away through the garden, there they were, the first of the season, just the thing for this gown. And I knew he'd never notice. Even if he had, I'd have picked them by then, and he'd hardly have expected me to put them back.'

'But what did you say to Hannah?'

'About the roses? That the minister is a Christian gentleman, which is true, surely? And that he gave them to me, which should be true if he's really a Christian. And if I'd asked him, I daresay he wouldn't have known how to refuse, so I've saved him the trouble, which you could almost say was very good of me.'

But even this example of her own cunning, her skill in playing the featherbrain to outwit her scrupulously honest sister, was not enough to lighten her mood, and as we picked our way up the stony little path to the Top House, she suddenly caught my hand and said urgently, 'Verity, let's hurry.'

'But why? We're not late.'

'No – at least, I suppose not, since I never know what time it is. I leave it to Hannah to tell me. But, Verity, just the same, even if we're not late, let's hurry.'

And glancing nervously over her shoulder at the mill and the millhouse, black in the valley below us, she whispered, 'There were men, you see, on the road as we came down to the mill, and I thought they meant to block our way, and Hannah thought so too although she kept saying, "Nonsense, Elinor, nonsense. Walk straight on." And so I did, for I meant to keep close to Joel. And it was no nonsense either, because they shuffled around us quite horribly, and even Hannah looked scared, which of course she wasn't, because she told me so. Anyway, Joel told them to move aside, and so they did, although some of them were quicker about it than others. But it was the muttering, Verity, and the scowling, and they were all so miserable – all of them, and all those others too, because I looked back, even though Joel told me not to – and they were all over the hillside, little groups of five or six everywhere, just staring down at the mill as if they hated it – staring like trees seem to stare sometimes, although Hannah said I was being fanciful, because trees have no eyes. But that's just the point: they haven't, and yet sometimes they still seem to see – and you'll know, Verity, how baleful they can be. Yes, that's what they put into my mind, fanciful or not – blind trees watching us. It must be the looms they hate, I suppose, and Joel said they were madmen to think they could stand in the way of progress. Although I don't know much about progress – well – if it means they're to lose their livelihood and their homes and live on the parish, then I daresay they don't think too well of it. But I could see what he meant about them being mad. Oh, Verity, do ask your mother to send us home in the carriage, because she won't think of it, and Hannah won't beg – and do please ask her in good time before dark – Verity?'

'Well, of course I'll ask her,' I promised easily, by no means alarmed, since Elinor would say almost anything to beg a ride in a carriage and her fears were usually no more than a means of making herself noticed. 'And if the horses have gone off somewhere or if she doesn't want them to go out again, then you can stay the night with me.'

But to spend the night at Lawcroft Fold, when she had seen it under siege, menaced by that dark human ring of trees, was not at all to her liking, and, as she caught my arm, her eager little hand touched its fear into my skin, sharpening my tongue.

'Oh, Elinor, such a fuss. And what a goose you always are. Trees, indeed. Weavers, that's all, having a grumble about the looms, and what more can they do but that? There's Edwin and Joel, and the soldiers down at the mill, and there's my grandfather. Do you think my grandfather – of all people – would let anyone harm us?'

He was waiting in the garden of the Top House, a gnarled old tree himself, sitting on a bench from which he could see the whole vast, stone-clad outer garment of his enterprises; his mill, his chimney stack, his school, his chapel, the grey tentacles of Cullingford that were creeping ever nearer, the millhouse he had built for his wife, the Top House, built for himself and his final indulgences, the grey smoke of prosperity, rising from the town, blowing eastward today, so that above his head there was even a patch of blue sky, a hopefully glimmering sun.

'So you've come to see me, Verity Barforth, have you?' he said. 'Good. And where's your mother?'

And looking behind him, I saw that my father's eyes were asking me the same question.

Edwin was there already, and my cousin Joel; and although they were superficially much alike, I judged my brother to be the pleasanter, easier man and knew somehow that Joel, for all his show of friendship, did not really like Edwin at all, considered him, in fact, to be a pompous fool and intended to get as much out of him as he could when they became brothers-in-law.

Joel Barforth was twenty-eight that year, somewhat leaner and considerably darker than Edwin, a man who had been wild in his youth – much addicted to cards and bare-knuckle prizefighting, to fancy wines and spirits instead of plain, honest ale – and although, on his father's death, he had shouldered his responsibility in true Barforth fashion, Law Valley men still treated him with suspicion. In an area where a man's worth could often be measured by the engine grease and dirt ingrained beneath his fingernails, my cousin Joel's hands were always scrupulously manicured; and if, as a child, he had been notoriously threadbare, having been obliged, like his mother, to pay for his father's extravagance, his garments now were always well chosen, well pressed, his boots highly polished, his cravat so elaborately arranged that the Law Valley often wondered how he could find the time. He was, I suspected, shrewd, hard, keen, cunning, one of the truest Barforths of them all – more like my grandfather, even, than Edwin – but my grandfather did not like him, had refused assistance at the height of Joel's troubles which he could easily have afforded to give, and even now when Joel had proved his ability to survive, was inclined to treat him scornfully, giving him no opportunity – when Edwin was there – to shine.

Certainly no one could accuse my brother of wasting time on dress, for it was very clear that even on his betrothal day, with a dozen coats to choose from, he had taken the first one that came to hand: peacock blue, as it turned out, with a yellow waistcoat and checked gamekeeper's cravat, a poor showing indeed beside Joel's plum-coloured coat and dove-grey trousers, his white, artfully tucked and pleated shirt, the snowfall of his cravat that proclaimed the sartorial gulf between them. And although I could like him no better for it, I understood well enough why Joel so disliked my brother.

Edwin, with no effort whatsoever on his part, would inherit Lawcroft Fold, while Joel, at considerable personal sacrifice, would be lucky to hold on to his few leaking, broken-down sheds at Low Cross. Edwin had only to express the desire and instantly his grandfather had ordered power looms, soldiers to guard them, a new mill to put them in, leaving Joel to endure his scorching, unsatisfied ambitions. Edwin, at twenty-four, was to marry the girl of his choice, while Joel, four years older, could see no end to his courtship of a certain Miss Rosamund Boulton, who had agreed to wait but could not be expected to wait forever.

He had no greeting for me beyond a slight, formal nod, for I had no part in his schemes for the future. It was very much in his interests, I knew, to marry his sister Hannah to my brother, and his sister Elinor to any man with a few hundred a year who would have her, thus relieving himself of expense and responsibility and bringing him a step nearer to marrying his own handsome Miss Boulton. But I could be of no use to him in that, and, giving Elinor a look which clearly told her to behave herself, he turned back to his conversation with my grandfather. And I was aware that behind his deference he was as bitter and seething as a bad November, acknowledging my grandfather's malice and returning like for like.

Sitting gracefully on its shelf of landscaped greenery cut from the otherwise bare hillside, fragrant among its beds of lavender and carnations and feathery foreign greenery, the Top House was not a place I greatly cared for. No one could fault its elegance or its comfort, or feel anything less than admiration for its airy, high-ceilinged rooms, moulded in blue and white and gold, and furnished in a lightweight, light-coloured style Mrs Stevens believed to be French and which I had always thought too insubstantial for my grandfather. But Mrs Stevens, who knew all the arts of pleasing men and practised them lovingly, had scant regard for the opinions of women and none at all for those of young girls; and although my brother – and even my father – often came here to be cosseted and flattered and to sample her excellent mulled wine, she had a way of making me feel unnecessary so that I was never sorry to leave.

But Hannah, the chosen bride, who would be mistress of Lawcroft, when her time came, in a far more positive way than my mother, was not to be neglected – certainly not by Mrs Stevens, who knew my grandfather was not immortal and that she would have her living to earn when he was gone – and it was no surprise to me to see her and Hannah whispering together, Hannah straight and tall and just a little ill at ease, Mrs Stevens a soft breeze fluttering around her, murmuring of stolen kisses and wedding bells and the recipe for her special syllabub, a secret she would entrust to no one else.

23

She was a slender, boneless woman, Mrs Stevens, moving in a constant aura of rose water and gentle, obliging laughter, a superb housekeeper whose larder shelves were a temptation of savoury pies and pickles, custards and cheesecakes, her kitchen ceiling festooned with glazed, exotically flavoured hams, garlanded with spicy sausages, and, in season, festering with illegal game from Lawcroft Moor. Her seedcake and spice cakes were famous, her apple jellies miraculous, her bowls of potpourri quite unique, her smile extremely caressing, yet I did not like her, my mother did not like her, and I was relieved to see my cousin Hannah draw back a little, as if she found the older woman's perfume too cloying, her manner altogether too winsome for her age and her station.

But Mrs Stevens was too experienced a campaigner to be unduly dismayed and, quite certain that Hannah would need an ally in time when she came to share a home with my mother, she gave my cousin's arm a final, loving squeeze and came floating towards me with an air of such deliberate secrecy that everybody turned to listen.

'Verity, dear,' she whispered, knowing how well whispers carry, 'it is well past three o'clock. Does your mamma mean to honour us, or has it slipped her mind?'

'I was just wondering the same myself,' Edwin muttered, heavy with his great news. 'She'll be in the garden, I shouldn't wonder, talking to the flowers or watching the grass grow. Well, I've got something to say and I've a mind to say it now –'

'You'll wait,' my father told him, 'until your mother comes.'

But Edwin looked through my father to my grandfather, and seeing the pain in my father's face, I said quickly, 'She'll be here presently. She told me so.'

'Aye, she told you so and promptly forgot all about it, or else she never meant to come at all, which is more likely. She knows well what I have to say, and why she can't bring herself to like it I'll never know. No – and she'll never explain either. She'll smile and say, "How very nice," and I tell you, there are times when it's too much – when it won't serve –'

'Edwin,' my father said dangerously, 'I told you to wait and you'll have the manners to do it, and keep a civil tongue in your head while you're about it.'

'Oh, dear,' Hannah murmured, moving swiftly between them, angry in her turn with my mother for keeping Edwin waiting, angry with my father for taking his wife's part against his son, yet intending her role to be that of peacemaker. But her intervention was not needed, for at the same moment, my grandfather rose lumberingly yet quite majestically to his feet.

'Say your piece, lad,' he ordered bluntly, as if my father were not there at all. 'It's past three o'clock and there's meat on Mrs Stevens's table too good to spoil. Let's hear you.'

I saw, like fragments of stained glass, my father's jealous hurt, my brother's satisfaction at getting his way and his certainty of getting it again, their mutual hostility, and the cold, sardonic gleam in my cousin Joel's eyes as he watched the Barforth ranks so sadly split asunder.

'Well, it's no secret, I reckon,' Edwin said, his strong brown fingers reaching out for Hannah and claiming her with an enthusiasm that touched us all and may have given her actual pain. 'It's time I was wed – high time – and there's no other lass I'd want for a wife but Hannah. They told me to choose a sound woman, one who'd look me in the eye and see things my way, and there's no woman anywhere more straightforward. She'd never keep me waiting and keep me guessing – no, I know where I am with Hannah. And that's what I have to say. We've known a long time how things were likely to turn out between us, and today I told her it was time we got it settled, and so we did. She's to be my wife as soon as she likes – the sooner, the better – and if anybody don't care for it, then it's all the same to me.'

'Oh, Edwin,' Mrs Stevens sighed, 'how beautiful. Oh, Edwin – and Hannah, too – how very moving. We all of us wish you well – all of us, I'm sure.'

As if at her signal, there was a surge of congratulations, of back slapping and kissing, Edwin preening himself like a gigantic, slightly embarrassed peacock, Hannah mindful of her dignity yet conveying to him with every glance, every movement of her square, capable hands that she would be everything he wished, hard-working mistress of his house, enduring companion of his bed, mother of his dozen sturdy sons, with nothing elusive about her, nothing to intrigue him, nothing to plague him or to remind him in any way of his mother. And when the kissing was done we went into Mrs Stevens's high-vaulted, deep-windowed dining parlour to gorge ourselves on her chicken pie, her hot new-baked bread, her almond creams, and my grandfather's wine.

My grandfather sat heavily at the head of his festive board, eating little, gazing with a certain sentimental satisfaction at Mrs Stevens as she performed her intricate little domestic ballet around the table, coaxing the men to partake of this and that, to try just a little more of the other, leaving the women to fend for themselves, not really caring whether they were served or not. The engaged couple remained side by side, stiff with self-conscious happiness, Hannah's smile deliberately cool, her eyes excited and hot, her hand, I thought, still in Edwin's, concealed by a fold of Mrs Stevens's lace cloth. But my father, after some brief discussion with Joel, hovered restlessly a moment or two before retreating to the window seat to stare moodily out of the window which would give him the best view of the path my mother would be bound to take; and when Mrs Stevens offered him a wedge of her chicken pie and a murmur of sympathy I missed neither his irritable gesture of dismissal nor my grandfather's frown.

'We'll drink to the future,' my grandfather said very loud, his glance flickering over my father, leaving him and settling on Edwin. 'Yes – Edwin and Hannah – the future. Let's have the champagne, Mrs Stevens, and while we're about it I'll give you something else to drink to. Now that we're all assembled – all of us, that is, who choose to assemble – I have this to tell you. The new looms will be in production by the end of next month, with more of them on the way and more on order, and it's only fitting that there should be a new mill to house them. Yes, Edwin, I saw my builders yesterday and when it's done, lad, when it's six storeys high, we'll pack it full of every newfangled device those engineers can offer us, so long as there's a profit to be made. That's it, lad, eh? Power and profit, progress, if that's what you like to call it. And it's all to be yours, lad, one day, yours and Hannah's.'

'By God,' Edwin said, his eyes on fire, his knuckles showing white as his fingers crushed themselves around Hannah's wrist, heedless of the pain he must be causing her and which she, gritting teeth behind her smile, bore like some unflinching shield-maiden of old.

'Oh yes, to the future,' sighed Mrs Stevens, her eyes resting for an instant on my cousin Joel, speculatively, appreciatively, remembering the tales she'd heard of his wild days, imagining for a self-indulgent moment how things could be if she were younger, Joel richer, while he, who could afford to neglect no opportunity, raised his glass to her very slightly, his eyes quite caressing but the brain behind them, I thought, working out exactly what he'd do in Edwin's place and concluding, no doubt, that he'd do it better.

'The future?' my father said, asking a question, his voice toneless, tired. And I would have gone to his side had not Elinor, by no means pleased that it was Hannah's future they were all discussing and not her own, suddenly whispered in my ear, 'Well, if that's the best your brother can do I don't envy Hannah. What a proposal. I shall expect something more romantic than that, especially the first time.'

'And who's going to marry you?'

'Somebody – somebody special. And lots more will want to and be dreadfully upset when they can't.'

'Oh yes, to be sure – hundreds,' I told her lightly, knowing her portion would be even smaller than Hannah's; so small, in fact, that it may not get her married at all. But Elinor, who knew as well as I did that marriages were composed of settlements and vested interests, acreage and who one's father happened to be on good terms with at the time, had enough faith in her own undeniable charms to be able to set these matters aside.

'Oh, I'll get married soon enough,' she announced airily, 'and I know exactly how it will be. I'll have strawberries and champagne for breakfast on my wedding morning, to start off with, and after that I'll sit with my toes on the fender whenever I feel like it. I'm going to have a perfectly lovely time, Verity. I've quite made up my mind to it. Let's both have a lovely time – let's go and ask Mrs Stevens for some more champagne.'

But my father suddenly caught my eye, frowned as if I had somehow displeased him and, instead of following Elinor, I crossed to the window and looked out, hoping to see my mother and knowing I wouldn't.

'Now then, miss,' my father hissed straight into my ear. 'Why didn't she come with you? Didn't I tell you to walk up here, by three o'clock, with your mother?' But he well knew the injustice of expecting me to compel her when he had never found a way to do it himself; and frowning again, he patted my arm – sorry, in his heart, that because of her, and because I had her face, he could not altogether love me.

26

'She'll come,' I told him. And seeing that I had annoyed him further with my sympathy, I said quickly, 'Father, Elinor wishes to go home in the carriage. May I tell her yes?'

'Why not?' he said, not caring. 'Just as you please.'

But Hannah, whose ears were in every way as sharp as her eyes and her tongue, was suddenly upon us, flushed with indignation that anyone should be asked to get their horses out on her behalf. 'There is absolutely no need,' she said, rude almost in her wounded pride. 'My sister pampers herself; I'm always telling her so. If her feet hurt, then I'm sorry, but the exercise will do her good.'

But Elinor could be braver, sometimes, than one supposed, was always far shrewder than most people gave her credit for, and her doll's face crumpling with a most becoming distress, her cloudy eyes turning in helpless, tearful entreaty – unerringly – to my grandfather, she whispered, 'But it's not that, Hannah. You know – quite well – that I'm afraid.'

'Afraid.' Immediately the Barforth men stood tall on their earthbound, well-shod feet. 'Afraid? How's this?' And as the tale came spilling from Elinor's lips, protest was loud and, for a moment or two, quite ugly.

'If anyone's harmed you –' Edwin threatened, while Joel, just as threateningly, answered him, 'There was no harm done. I can look after my sisters, I reckon.'

'Oh dear, dear me,' Mrs Stevens murmured, floating between them. 'The poor, poor lambs. And yet there is absolutely nothing to fear. Mr Barforth has said so, and I am sure you can believe him. Mr Barforth has lived through times like these before, and, my dears, he knows. You may all be easy.'

'I'll be easier in a month from now, when the looms are running – if they ever are,' my father said suddenly, astonishingly. 'It's true, what the lass says. There are men on the hillside. I've seen them myself, spoken to them myself, and by God – and I don't care who hears me says it – they have my sympathy. A sheep allows itself to be slaughtered, but a man – well, perhaps I'd fight before I'd see my children starve or put them out of work for a man like me. Yes, so I would, and there's no one here who wouldn't do the same.'

'My goodness,' Mrs Stevens exclaimed, outwardly thunderstruck but inwardly very well pleased to see my father's final fall from grace, for he was handsomer, easier than my grandfather, a man of her own age, and it was my belief that she'd once offered herself to him and been refused. But if she had expected my grandfather to show his anger she was disappointed, for he knew a deadlier trick than that; lifting himself heavily to his feet, he put one hand on Edwin's shoulder, the other on Joel's, his gnarled, old man's fingers gripping them with the tenacity of thirsty tree roots that will not be denied.

'We'll walk a little, lads,' he said. 'Take the air. Maybe we'll go and have a look at these men who choose to set foot on my land. Maybe we'll remind them that my permission's required – you and me, lads. And if you've no stomach for it, son William, then I expect you'll be going home to your wife – if you can find her.'

And it was then that my mother, suddenly, was among us, leaning gracefully in the doorway with hardly more substance than a shadow but with something in her that reduced Samson Barforth's magnificence to meanness, Mrs Stevens's caressing charm to the antics of a bawdy house, my brother and Joel and my cousin Hannah to callow, grasping youngsters who had not altogether remembered their manners.

'Isabella,' my father said sharply, and although I think he meant to say, 'Where have you been?' the words came out, 'Are you all right?'

'Why yes, dear,' she told him. 'Should I be otherwise? Mrs Stevens, do allow me to congratulate you on your table. Is that your famous syllabub and your excellent lemon cheesecake? Delicious – everyone says so – but no, I eat so little – just a sip of wine and a whisper of a macaroon – so kind. Yes, I was sewing, and the time simply slipped away – you'll understand how that can happen, being such a busy woman yourself – and then there was the man – Oh, did I forget about the man? I do believe so. A man came into the garden as I was about to leave and called me back – quite a rough person, I must confess. Ira Agbrigg, he said his name was, and I have no reason to disbelieve him, for he kept on saying it over and over, "Ira Agbrigg, ma'am, that's my name," so I am drawn to conclude he is working for a reward. Ah yes – he bade me to tell you that the men are no longer on the hillside and in the woods – not that I ever imagined they were – but that they are all gone to Lawcroft Green. Three hundred of them, he said – a meeting of protest, he called it – and that I was to tell you they are in deadly earnest, that the talk is of desperate measures. Oh dear, three hundred, which perhaps means two hundred, since he was clearly much alarmed and may not have counted right. But even so, there are no more than a dozen soldiers. Ah well, one must hope that it will rain.'

'Rain, Isabella?' my father said, bewildered.

'Rain,' my grandfather echoed, his jaw thrust pugnaciously forward, his face so swollen and mottled with rage that Hannah, mindful of her new duties, planted herself directly in front of my mother and said loudly, 'Rain, Aunt Isabella? Why rain?'

'To put out the torches, dear,' she said reasonably, sweetly. 'For if they have torches, as Mr Ira Agbrigg said they did, then one can only suppose they are coming to burn the mill – which is quite shocking, of course, and most unwise, but quite easy to do, one supposes, since raw wool is greasy, I believe, and easily set ablaze. Dear Mrs Stevens, you have turned quite pale; and Hannah, too. But surely, didn't I hear you just now telling each other that there is nothing to fear – so little, in fact, that my husband may just as well come home to his wife, if he could find her – which, of course, he couldn't, since I am here.'

Like everyone else, I had no idea whether she spoke in great malice or great innocence; whether she wished to hurt my father or defend him. But one thing I did know, and perhaps it was to alter the whole course of my life; I had thought of my mother as a weak woman, helpless in the face of Barforth disapproval, and I had thought of strength in terms of loud Barforth voices, a hard male fist, a dark Barforth eye. Yet now I had witnessed a new kind of strength, as quietly, airily, almost dreamily my mother dismayed and defeated them all.

3

My grandfather, needless to say, was the first to recover.

'So it's damned Luddites again,' he announced quite cheerfully, a gleam in his eye that may have been satisfaction, since he was a man who not only enjoyed a fight but always expected to win. 'Aye, Luddites. I thought we'd got rid of that particular breed of vermin way back. When was it? Must have been 1812, I reckon – when you were just a baby, Verity lass – when we all got letters signed "General Ludd," saying how they'd murder us unless we rid ourselves of our vile machinery. It was the shearing frames they didn't like in those days, and, damn me, if they didn't mean business. Aye, those Luddite hammermen thought they were heroes all right, smashing down honest men's doors to get at the frames, their pikemen and hatchetmen coming behind; and what they couldn't break they'd burn. Damned heroes – forty thousand men they said they'd got, ready to crush us and crush the King with us unless he toed their line – and set up King Ludd in his place, I reckon. And that was enough – after a fire or two – to scare the smaller manufacturers into giving way. But then they went up against William Cartwright at Rawfolds, over in the Spen Valley, and he was ready – he'd brought in the soldiers and posted lookouts; he'd even set spiked rollers on his stairs and a tub of oil of vitriol on his landing in case they broke in. Not that they did. A round or two of musket fire, that's all – killed a couple of them and wounded a few more, and off they went – scattered them and made them think again. Most of them had had enough by then, I reckon, which is why the ringleaders turned sour and murdered William Horsfall not long after. Aye, I remember Will Horsfall well – a plainspoken man with a decent business over Huddersfield way – and he was ready for them, too. Even had a cannon in his mill yard, as I recall; not that it did him much good, since they waited for him one night when he was riding home over Crosland Moor and shot him out of his saddle.

'Damned Luddites, with their oaths and ceremonies and their hammers – swore eternal brotherhood, they did, and how they'd suffer hell's torment before they'd turn traitor. And all it took to break them, in the end, was money.

'I'm ready to admit there must have been hundreds – thousands – hereabouts who knew their names and faces, gave them shelter and money and never would have turned them in. But we only needed one greedy man – just one – and when we offered two thousand pounds for the names of Horsfall's murderers, we found him. And that was the end of it, son William, grandson Edwin. We rounded them up, sent them to York to be hanged, and the rest soon went skulking off home. And if the

Law Valley remembers them at all, it remembers how hard it was for their women and children to manage without them; it remembers that the machines came in just the same – that it wasn't worth dying for. And these men today aren't real Luddites, I'll be bound. They'll have sworn no oaths nor bound themselves blood brothers. They're just common rioters, without leadership or discipline, and they'll turn tail soon enough. Come, then; we'll all go down to the millhouse and see what's to do.'

But Mrs Stevens, for once, was not of the same mind.

'I must put that child to bed, really I must,' she suddenly cried out, making a dash at the considerably startled Elinor. 'Can't you see she's about to swoon?'

Although Elinor had no intention of swooning and began to say so, Mrs Stevens would have none of it.

'The child can barely keep her feet,' she insisted feverishly, 'which is hardly to be wondered at. But don't concern yourselves. Go and do what must be done, and I will take care of her. A child of her years – and her sensitive disposition – must not be exposed to scenes of violence. It could do her lasting harm – I only pray that the mere thought of it has not harmed her already. But don't let it distract you from your purpose. You may all safely leave her with me.'

And making it abundantly clear that with a sick girl on her hands no one should count on her for very much else, she shepherded the unwilling Elinor away.

We left then in a tight procession that gradually lengthened and separated, my mother gliding effortlessly ahead with no apparent thought of danger, my father stumping behind, heavier of foot, heavier of spirit, unable as always to catch her. Behind them came Hannah, straight-backed, calm, refusing to hurry, walking with a deliberately measured tread since one never knew who might be watching, preparing herself for her new role as my brother's support and inspiration in time of trouble.

But Edwin was not so self-possessed. His immediate instinct had been to stride on ahead, to bar the gate – his gate, his mill, his looms – with his own body if required, but my grandfather could not easily walk alone and, peevishly brushing aside my father's offer to help – 'Look to your wife, son William, ere you lose her again' – he held out an imperious arm to Edwin, the other to my cousin Joel.

'These lads will see me right,' he said, leaning heavily, I thought, on Joel; taking pleasure, perhaps, in crushing his sleeve since he had always mistrusted a dandy and knew that if this coat should be damaged Joel would not find it easy to get another.

'You'll have your work cut out to watch that pretty jacket of yours today, Joel my boy,' he said gleefully, his old man's malice rising into a chuckle. 'There'll be a stain or two on it by nightfall, I shouldn't wonder – and grime under your fingernails, for once, millmaster, if they get to burn the sheds. And what are you doing there, Verity Barforth – mooning about, taking all in and saying nothing, like your mother. Why don't you come and give me your arm and set your brother free? It won't have crossed your mind, girl, that he's eager to get to the fray – that he takes after me.'

And, panting, wheezing, working himself up into a mighty rage – hating me for my youth and my inferior sex, hating Joel for his keen wits that must always be a threat to Edwin, hating my father for obeying him and hurrying after his wife, hating his own body for its weakness when his spirit was eager to take a hundred rioters by the throat – he sank his gnarled old fingers into my arm and came stamping home.

For I believe the millhouse, in his heart, was his home, built when he had been a solid workingman, for a workingwoman without pretensions, who had been content to sit in her stone-flagged kitchen, within sound and scent of his machinery, and had required nothing more for her comfort than the one square parlour, cheerfully allowing him to use the other downstairs room as a countinghouse and, sometimes, a storage space for raw wool. They had stacked wool upstairs, too, in my grandmother's day; in the back spare bedrooms, in the attics, anywhere a corner could be found, and although she was long dead and he had been glad enough to move on to the graces of the Top House and Mrs Stevens, whenever he came here he instinctively looked for her and was not pleased to find my mother in her stead.

'Well then – well then,' he said threateningly, shouldering his way through the door. 'And where's this Ira Agbrigg of yours, Isabella? Spirited him away, have you?'

But Ira Agbrigg was waiting, cap in hand, a thin, pasty-faced, weak-eyed man somewhere around thirty, shabby and shamefaced, a strange blending of terror and determination washing over him as my grandfather and my brother closed in, eager for anything he could tell them and perhaps willing to pay for it but not much liking a traitor, just the same.

'Let's have it all again, lad,' my grandfather ordered. Out it all came: the mutterings and the resentments, the panic, the gnawing, hopeless fears of the cottagers, which, without leadership, might have remained impotent.

'So there's a ringleader, then?' my grandfather said excitedly.

And so, it seemed, there was: Jabez Gott, a young Law Valley man who had been 'away' – in prison, one supposed, for some conravention of the 'gag acts' prohibiting political assembly; a man whose father had been transported to Australia for disobedience, whose brother had been slaughtered by a British sabre on the Manchester battlefield of Peterloo, whence he had gone to demand the right to vote; a man who had lived some time in Lancashire, where the machines had taken a firmer hold, and who had seen starvation for himself. A wizened old man of twenty-two, Jabez Gott, whose eighteen-year-old wife had died in pregnancy, from lack of nourishment, and who openly avowed that he had nothing more to lose. And he it was who, assembling a group of like-minded men around him, had convinced the steadier minds of the Law Valley that soon they would have nothing to lose either, and had gathered up their fear and moulded it, like iron, into a weapon.

'Jabez Gott,' my grandfather said. 'Never heard of him – but I'll keep the name in mind. It's always as well to have a name.' And taking Edwin and my father and Ira Agbrigg with him, he went off to the kitchen to find the only chair remaining from my grandmother's day and to make his plans.

I sat down in my accustomed place by the hearth, knowing that nothing would be required of me. Hannah sat very stiff and straight at my side, puzzled and rather hurt that nothing had yet been required of her. Joel, all too obviously excluded from the war party, stood by the hearth, tapping his foot against the fender. My mother calmly took up her embroidery, and for a long time there seemed nothing to do but listen to the rasping of my grandfather's voice in the next room, the excited rise and fall of Edwin's, the low restrained muttering of my father, as they extracted more names from Ira Agbrigg, whose voice could not be heard at all.

'Poor Mr Agbrigg,' my mother said, looking up from her stitching. 'He is betraying his friends, you know, and is very much ashamed, although I am sure he has his reasons. He may have told himself it will prevent bloodshed and he may believe it – and, for his sake, we must hope your grandfather will remember him. Oh dear, I forgot the name of the man who delivered William Horsfall's murderers to justice – do you remember, just now, your grandfather was telling us they had offered a two-thousand pound reward? I remember the occasion, too, and it is quite certain that the man, whoever he was, did not receive his money. He died in extreme poverty, I believe, and had been made very miserable a long while before, since no one would speak a word either to him or to his family. They cut him off completely – exiled him – which, of course, he must have expected; he would, no doubt, have moved away, if he had received his money. But, as I said, he did not.

'Joel dear, since one can never be certain what the day may bring, if you should care to change your coat, I feel sure Edwin will have something more suited to the occasion. In fact, I am sure of it, since my son is not very particular. If it eases your mind, dear, do take it off and let me find you another.'

But Hannah, always suspicious of my mother, always resentful at any reference to her poverty, cried out, 'Aunt Isabella, really – how can you suppose – how can you? – that Joel would consider his dress at such a time?'

Sensing, perhaps, the angry tears burning behind her eyes, knowing how mortified she would be if they came to be shed, her brother turned from his contemplation of the hearth and gave my mother a smile that was superficially charming, totally false.

'I really don't know why I shouldn't,' he said calmly, very coldly. 'Most kind of you, Aunt Isabella, but I believe I'll decline. Somebody will have to go and fetch a magistrate, you see – I reckon Edwin's grandfather will be out in a minute or two to tell us so – and if I'm to ride into Cullingford, or out of it, or up to Patterswick to bring the squire, then I'd feel – easier – in my own clothes, Edwin's taste not being the same as mine.'

'Just as you please, dear,' my mother said, amusement hovering at the corners of her mouth.

Although my grandfather was never a comfort to me, I was relieved – as I saw Hannah start to bristle – when the door burst open and the room filled up again with his towering, demanding presence.

'That's it, then,' he snorted. 'Just like last time. Three hundred, this fellow says, assembled on the green, with at least half of them ready to come here and take issue with me. Now then, lads, here's what we'll do. Son William may stay here to guard the women, and as for you boys, one of you can come with me to the mill yard to make sure those redcoats know how to earn their sixpence a day and the other can fetch a magistrate. Edwin, which is it to be?'

'I'll stay. It's my place,' Edwin said, and then he frowned suddenly, for there was glory to be had, too, in riding hard and alone across the troubled hillsides, in going out to meet danger unaided instead of waiting for it, tamely, behind a line of redcoats, at home. And his inability to be in two places at once caused him evident frustration.

'Shall I stay?' he asked himself out loud.

My cousin Joel, still lounging by the fireplace, answered for him. 'Oh, I expect so. You stay and review your troops, Edwin – much the best thing – and leave the rest to me.'

'And what do you mean by that, exactly?'

'Anything you like to make of it.'

'Something low and dirty, I'll be bound,' Edwin snarled then, as Hannah made a sharp, horrified sound and half rose to her feet, he turned towards her – remembering after all, that it was her betrothal day, that Joel was her brother – and said, not altogether apologetically, 'Well, I'm sorry for that, Hannah, because the last thing I want to do is upset you, and I know life hasn't been easy. But it's not my fault I've had the advantages. There's no cause for me to be ashamed because I'm rich and likely to get richer – never been ashamed of anything in my life. And if I was as poor as a church mouse I'd be damned before I'd go about envying other people. And if I was envious I'd make damned sure I didn't show it.'

'Envious?' Joel said, his long, lounging body as taut now as Hannah's, the white-lipped anger in him reaching out for Edwin, who was very ready to meet it. 'Envious? Just tell me that again, cousin Edwin.'

'Yes, gladly, cousin Joel. Can you look me in the eye and say you don't wish those machines down there were yours?'

'Well now, cousin Edwin, I might look you in the eye and say they'd do better if they were.'

And as the two of them moved together, perfectly prepared to thrash each other in my mother's parlour, my grandfather's arm shot between them like a bar of iron.

'You'd say that, would you, Joel Barforth?' he said very quietly. 'Well – for the moment I reckon I didn't hear you. But if you've got yourself into an evil frame of mind, so much the better. You'll get the chance to work it off, I shouldn't wonder, before the day's through. Now go and tell them to saddle you a horse. And you, Edwin lad, come with me.'

The day had clouded over, easing itself now towards evening, and as my mother immersed herself once more in her sewing and Hannah continued to stare down at her tightly clasped hands, her loyalties badly torn, I settled myself on the window seat, my eyes drawn to the mill. The soldiers were still there, taking their ease, but otherwise the yard wore its everyday face: the comings and goings of carts piled high with bales that, from loose corners, shed scraps of wool like dandelion puffs on the night air; other carts heavy-laden with finished pieces, setting off on the rutted, bone-shaking road to Leeds or to the canal which, sluggishly, slowly, carried our goods to Liverpool and the sea.

The sheds would soon be emptying, bringing the yard briefly alive with the busy sound of wooden clogs on stone, the patient outline of female heads covered in the fold of a shawl, the jauntiness of cloth caps set at an angle on wiry, north country curls, leaving behind the engineers and loom tuners, who had an interest in defending the machines, and the soldiers. And who knew how many of our own operatives would go quietly home and how many would find their way to Cullingford Green, to join brothers and fathers and cousins, torch in hand. Could we really be sure that the soldiers, who must have friends – sweethearts even – among the weavers, would risk too much on our account? As the shadows lengthened and deepened, I felt obliged to ask myself if I was brave, and found no answer.

My life, until today, had been as outwardly bland as the long coils of wool combed ready for spinning, perfectly smooth, cloud-textured, cream-textured, and if, inside me, I had encountered a few tangles, if now and again I resented my grandfather's supreme authority, if I could not always believe my brother to be totally in the right, if I wanted my father to love me and my mother to love my father, none of that had been terrible. If I had sometimes felt out of tune with myself, sitting in my mother's cool shadow, realizing I had not inherited her skill with a needle, at least the chair had been comfortable, the fireside warm. I had been safe. Yet now, through the spring twilight, a harsher world beckoned to me – a world where Jabez Gott's wife, a girl not much past my own age, had died of pregnancy and starvation, where Jabez Gott's brother had been massacred at the place called Peterloo near Manchester when soldiers like the ones now lounging in our yard had ridden with drawn swords into a peaceful crowd who had assembled merely to demand a small measure of parliamentary reform, and left more than a hundred men, women, and children bleeding on the ground.

How would I feel tonight if Jabez Gott's brother should die all over again, outside my window, leaving his blood on the cobbles of Lawcroft Fold? How *should* I feel?

My grandfather, I knew, would be triumphant, considering it no more than every Jabez Gott deserved. My mother would make some cool, pointed remark and drift back to her embroidery. Hannah would say, 'Well done, Edwin.' Mrs Stevens would comfort us all with cakes and wine. And I, being a good girl, would eat those cakes, speak when spoken to, give them the answers they expected to hear, not because I feared them but because to be different, in the house of Samson

Barforth, was to be alone. But I could not rid myself of the impression of a pair of eyes, flickering somewhere behind my own: huge lack-lustre eyes in a hollow face which may have belonged to the wife of Jabez Gott or to a dozen girls I had seen tramping the hills, a child straddling their hips, going nowhere, wanted nowhere. And forcing myself into their wasted shapes, putting stones beneath my own bare feet and the tugging stranglehold of a child's arms around my neck – a child myself, as they were, bearing other children – I shivered.

'Are you afraid?' my father said, appearing suddenly beside me.

When I nodded he touched my arm briefly, timidly almost, since he had shown me little affection in the past and found it awkward now.

'There's no need. They'll not seek to harm you. They're not savages, just men who see their world coming to an end and who very likely know there's not much they can do about it. Nothing except make a stand, that is – a protest – and when that's all a man has left, who can blame him? Jabez Gott may believe he can set the world to rights by burning Lawcroft Fold, but the men behind him – or most of them – know it can't be as easy as that. They know we'd build again – for somebody will always build, somebody must build – and if they follow Jabez Gott at all it's only to make their voices heard – as men should be heard – because they're too proud to go under without a cry. They know it's over. Before the factories cornered the markets, Verity, there wasn't a cottager of my acquaintance who made less than thirty shillings a week, and now some of them are living on as little as four shillings – or not living, exactly, but keeping body and soul together, taking the outwork it pleases us to give them for as much as we're pleased to pay. They had meat, Verity, when I was a lad, and white bread, and the occasional bottle of rum, but now it's oatmeal and potatoes, and when there's none of that they'll stew nettle broth, aye, and tell you it's tasty and wholesome if you happen to enquire. Poor devils, it's their tragedy to be caught in the wrong place at the wrong time; to have been born when their traditional way of life is ending, when events are moving too fast to do anything but sweep them away. Your brother and your cousin Joel tell me there won't be a handloom in the Law Valley five years from now. Well, they're young men, and hasty, and I'd say longer, a fair bit longer, but it has to come just the same. They'll hang on, for they're a tough breed and stubborn, and not all the millmasters will turn against them. Old Ben Hobhouse, over at Nethercoats, don't care for power looms, but old Ben won't live forever, and his son is likely to be as hasty as mine when the time comes for him to take over. No, they'll be squeezed out – starved out – and even the most pigheaded among them is going to end up using his handloom for firewood one of these bad winters.'

'But if we expand, Father, like Edwin said, they can work for us, can't they – in the mill?'

'Can't they?' he said, staring past me to the mill and the bare hillside beyond it. 'I'm not so sure. When your brother builds the new factory he's dreaming of, he'll put a high stone wall around it and a big iron gate, and if you'd been a free, stubborn man all your life, you may not care to hear the clang of those factory gates shutting behind you every morning. If you were a countryman, of course, you'd find it easier, because you'd be accustomed to pulling your forelock to the parson and the squire. But a lad born in those cottages grows up to be his own master, and he'd find it hard having to doff his cap every time he met your grandfather, or Edwin – or me – crossing the mill yard. In fact, he'd find it so hard that I doubt he'd do it at all. He'd more likely turn sour and disobedient and hard to handle. No, they'll keep on doing outwork as long as we'll allow it, but I don't think they'll work for us in the mill – not this generation. And I'm not sure we'd take them.'

'But what then, Father? What else can they do?'

'I don't know, and it troubles me. I think a whole generation may just pass away. Some of them will die, a few will move on, but most of them will strive and struggle for pennies – they'll eat nettles when they have to, and grow old and bitter, I shouldn't wonder, until their children are old enough to be earning. Because the new generation will come to us. And even then, I don't know – I don't know. This afternoon, at the mill, your cousin Joel got his hands on the new looms, and he wondered if a man's strength would be needed for their operation. It seemed to him that a woman would suffice, and women, you know, don't swing Luddite hammers, and they'll accept what's offered them in the way of wages far more readily than a man, especially when they've got children to be fed. So we may prefer to fill our sheds with women. And have you considered the Irish? They've been pouring into Cullingford by the cartload these last few years, since the potato crop started to fail – big, strapping wenches who could make two of most of ours. And everybody knows the Irish will work for less.'

'Are the weavers right, then, Father?' I asked timidly, badly wanting to know, and he made an angry movement, a regretful movement.

'No, of course they are not. One cannot – one should not – stand in the way of progress. In that, at least, I am in agreement with my father and my son. The weavers have no more right to forbid us our machines than we are entitled to deprive them of their means of existence. We should lean towards each other – realize we are of the same species, not alien beings snarling at each other like packs of rival hounds. We are laying up bitterness, Verity, for the future – a cesspit of bitterness – Jabez Gott and your grandfather both – for at the extremity of their views they are both equally wrong.'

But here, it seemed, he had said too much and, giving me a puzzled look, wondering why on earth he was unburdening himself to his daughter, he patted me once again, rather clumsily, on the arm and went away.

My grandfather spent a long time in the mill yard, pacing up and down in front of the soldiers, telling their officer how to handle his men in exactly the same fashion as he often told the parson how to manage his church, the banker his bank; and even if his presence caused the men to straighten their shoulders and button their tunics, they were still an unkempt, ill-favoured assembly and numbered no more than a dozen.

36

'One hesitates to expect too much of them,' my mother said, nodding pleasantly to the officer, who had caught her eye through the window. 'Perhaps one should consider why they enlist in the first place – meagre pay and meagre rations, and a public flogging every time they misbehave. I doubt if anyone really picks them up when they fall in battle – not all of them, at any rate.'

And, watching the blend of scorn and embarrassment on Hannah's face, I wondered how they would contrive to live together, how I would contrive to live between them, and the arrival of Joel and the magistrate was welcome.

He was Squire Dalby of Patterswick, a man of aristocratic temper and broad acres, a believer in the perfect authority – so far as his tenants were concerned – of the Established English Church, an ardent supporter of the Corn Laws, which had brought hunger to the cities, a subscriber to the view that since God had fixed every man at birth in the place He wished to see him, it was no less than sinful to try to change it. Although he stood for law and order and would have been as ready to hang a child for stealing a shilling as a grown man for slitting his neighbour's throat, he had no liking for upstart manufacturers who, now that they had made their dirty money, were demanding extravagant privileges like seats on the Bench and voices in the House of Commons, which belonged – by law and by Divine Right – only to landed gnetlemen.

'Having a spot of bother, are we, Barforth, dear fellow?' he asked my grandfather, making small distinction, it seemed, between Samson Barforth, who owned the machines, and Jabez Gott, who was out to break them. Yet he accepted a glass of wine and a slice of the seedcake Mrs Stevens had hastily sent down from the Top House – assuming my mother's larder to be bare – while the sight of my mother herself, in her light green gauze, her shawl sliding gracefully around her shoulders, appeared to afford him immense pleasure.

'Have we met, madam – surely?' he murmured, quizzing glass at the ready, taking no more trouble to conceal his appreciation than if she had been a milkmaid. Even when my father and my grandfather intervened, for different reasons, he continued to talk to them and look at her.

'Will you not come into the kitchen a moment, Aunt Isabella?' Hannah asked, altogether shocked by the squire's free and easy manner.

'Why, dear?' my mother replied, her grey velvet eyes quizzical and amused. 'What have I to do there?'

And Hannah had no choice but to leave her alone.

'One would expect her to leave the room for her husband's sake,' I heard her mutter to Joel, but my cousin, who had scoured the hillsides on his way to fetch the magistrate, had weightier things on his mind than a little middle-aged flirtation and, striding forward, hastily gave his opinion that the yeomanry should have been called out, and a few stout special constables, to make a show.

'Have we not done enough then, lad, in your opinion?' my grandfather enquired with deceptive mildness. 'You'd do more, would you, if it all belonged to you?'

37

Hostility would have flared again between Joel and my brother had not Squire Dalby, with a mighty yawn, indicated his total lack of interest in the squabbles, the values, or the opinions of the lower classes.

'Sheep – that's what the trouble is,' he announced somewhat surprisingly. 'Sheep. They don't really want to break your machines, Barforth. Never would have thought of it if some damned Jacobin hadn't come and put it into their heads. Train them in France, you know, these professional revolutionaries – Roman Catholics and atheists every one of them, and damn me if I know which is the worst. France, that's where they go, these malcontents, and when they've got themselves enough liberty and equality, back here they come to spread the word. Not your machines they're after at all – don't care a fig for your machines. It's the rule of law they're out to smash – King and Constitution, that's what they're after – and it won't do, Barforth. Every man was born to his allotted place – I know mine and I expect you know yours – and there's no getting away from it. Find the ringleaders, that's all you have to do. Find the damned Jacobins and send the sheep home.'

It was perhaps a tribute to my grandfather's strength of will that he accepted this landed gentleman's advice in a silence that was malicious, resentful, but absolute.

We were ready, or so we kept telling each other, but suddenly everything outside was quiet: an ordinary evening, deepening, cooling, so much like yesterday that riot, arson, bloodshed receded, became tinged, if only faintly, with ridicule. The soldiers were still waiting in the yard; the engineers and loom tuners and such of our operatives who had elected to stay – Ira Agbrigg among them – were waiting, too, all of them uneasy, some of them afraid, fortified at regular intervals by mugs of ale sent down by Mrs Stevens, who still declined to come herself.

Then, when we had almost stopped looking for them, when all the tension of the day which had frayed our nerves and made us so peevish began to seem unnecessary, then, at that moment, there they were, not violently and clamorously with the great parade of torches we had expected, nor the raucous shouts of hate, but simply there, a dark wedge of silent men, appearing as if they had been there all the time and had only now become visible. Silent and dark, dream figures, lacking substance, so that I was slow to recognize the sound of glass shattering on the cobbles, the bark of musket fire, and unwilling to believe that they were stoning the mill and that the soldiers had fired their warning shots – one hoped – into the air.

I no longer knew if I was afraid. The day had lasted so long, so wearied me, that I simply wanted it to end. With my mother and Hannah, I followed our menfolk as far as they allowed us, to the limit of our garden gate, and watched, listened, drifted a little way from reality, since it all seemed so strange and I felt so tired.

I heard the bulldog rasping of my grandfather's voice, some muttered reply: a wavering, I thought, of ranks, as those who had perhaps not meant to come so far hung back, while others stood their ground. Sheep, Squire Dalby had called them – these ordinary, decent men who, if given the choice, would always prefer right to wrong, good to evil, and who now, feeling the cold, the peril, would have been glad to go away. But not one could fail to recognize the wolf hunger in the men who stood in front, shoulder to shoulder: the true, sworn brotherhood, their thin, taut faces yellow-pale in the moonlight. I understood dimly that although they numbered no more than nine or ten, their intensity, their total fixity of purpose could be well-nigh impossible to resist. If one of them had come whispering to me of injustice and exploitation – a man who was fierce and frail, pitiful and formidable all at once – perhaps I too, had I been poor and uncertain, would be standing there now, somewhat against my will but fascinated, mesmerized, clutching a shawl around me, with a hatchet or a meat cleaver hidden beneath it. And although I knew they were wrong and foolish, and that if it was justice they sought this was not the way to obtain it, it troubled me deeply that I lacked Hannah's certainty, that unlike her and Edwin and my grandfather – or Jabez Gott – I could not tell myself we were absolutely right.

One man, I saw now, had detached himself from the crowd: a thin, youngish man with narrow shoulders clothed in dark corduroy, a shock of sandy hair, hands that seemed made of veins and knuckles – Jabez Gott, no other – making uncoordinated gestures that spoke, somehow, of nerves frayed beyond endurance, of emotions that were running wild, out of control, like a horse that terrifies its own rider. But his voice failed to reach me as, talking excitedly to the men at his back, pleading with them, I thought, to remember the pledges that had been made, he strove to rally them. I wanted desperately to hear him, not because I hoped to hear anything profound or even sensible – for I did not – but because his violence, his hot, fierce energy reminded me of my grandfather, as he might have been had Fate kept him poor. They were alike – this thin, ragged young man, that heavy, self-centred old one – alike in their need to set their mark on the world, to displace the air around them, and surely they should be able to understand each other?

But Squire Dalby had not come to listen, required no explanations. Advancing as near as he could, quite fearlessly, he drew himself up to his full height, which was not considerable, and bellowed, 'Silence for the making of this proclamation.'

And because he was the squire – even in the Law Valley men knew what that meant – there was a hush, a shuffling of feet, a doffing, in some cases, of caps.

'Now then,' he said, his eyes on the chimney stack, 'I imagine you all know me and what I'm about to do. I'm not sure just why you're here, and maybe some of you are not too sure about it either, but the law doesn't allow these little get-togethers, I'm afraid. And since I represent the law – yes, be very sure of that – it is my duty, as a properly authorized person, to send you all to your homes so that I may go to mine. I am come to read the Riot Act to you, my good fellows, and you must take heed, for once it is read, unless you obey it to the letter, such of you as are apprehended will be adjudged felons, and the penalty for that, as you well know, is death. And if we don't hang you – and I see no reason why we shouldn't – at the very least you'll face transportation to Australia, which I daresay amounts to the same thing.'

And taking a mighty breath, he pronounced tonelessly, tediously, the words which, by their own weight, had crushed the fighting spirit of mightier crowds than this.

'Our Sovereign Lord the King chargeth and commandeth all persons, being assembled, immediately to disperse themselves, and peaceably to depart to their habitations, or to their lawful business upon the pains contained in the Act made in the first year of King George, for preventing tumults and riotous assemblies. God Save the King.'

I thought, perhaps we all thought, that it would be enough, for even before the squire had finished speaking men had begun to slip away; not many at first, but enough to unsettle the ones who had wanted to fight it out, who had believed in their own desperation and hate, and although I could not hear their mutterings, I knew they were saying, 'What good can we do if we hang?' and 'Who'll feed our bairns if they send us to Australia?' and 'If we make this sacrifice, make martyrs of ourselves, how long will it be remembered? For them it was over.

But the sandy-haired man – Jabez Gott, surely? – and the half dozen around him were beyond the fear of hanging. As they tried frantically to rally their mates, my heart tore for all of them: for the ones who turned dully away and the ones who hysterically persisted; for my father, standing ashen-faced and sick-hearted; for my brother, looking puzzled, not having expected to be so moved; and for myself, standing somewhere in the wasteland between them, belonging nowhere.

'Desperate measures,' I heard Jabez Gott shout. 'Desperate measures. Remember what we vowed – what we promised.' And then, 'Cowards!' he shrieked. 'It's always the way – always the way. I'm not the first man to look over my shoulder and find no one behind me. But I'll leave my mark – make sure I'm not forgotten. I've not come this far – made this sacrifice – to go away empty-handed.'

But it was over. No more than a handful of men stood around him now, unwilling to leave him but wanting to take him away with them rather than stay, and we all expected him to go. The soldiers had already relaxed their guard, the engineers had crept gratefully back inside the sheds to sample more of Mrs Stevens's ale, Squire Dalby and the Barforth men were already walking back towards the house, making a summer Sunday stroll of it, congratulating themselves and each other. And perhaps it was the loud, self-satisfied note of Squire Dalby's laughter that entered Jabez Gott's mind and pushed it over the edge of reason.

The strolling group had almost reached the gate.

'Well done, Edwin. Oh, well done,' I heard Hannah say; and I heard Squire Dalby answer her, his eyes on my mother, 'No more than one expected, my dear. Just a little talking-to, that's all it ever takes.'

And then, because they were all looking at each other, admiring each other, perhaps I was the only one who saw Jabez Gott break jerkily away from his mates; the only one who saw his yellow-pale face growing, taking on features and textures as it came nearer; the only one who saw the blank eyes, the tears spilling down his cheeks, the thin mouth twisted with the all-consuming, unreasoning need to destroy.

So appalled was I, so fascinated, that my scream of warning came too late.

'Barforth swine!' he shrieked, scattering them with the force of his madness. 'Swine – slayers of the innocent! I said desperate measures – I said it – and you'll never forget me.'

Screaming now with the hysteria of a sacrificial victim – the role he had cast for himself – he dragged a pistol from under his coat and, mistaking his true enemy, pushed my grandfather aside and fired straight into my father's chest.

4

I saw it happen, not once but over and over again through that first unspeakable night, over and over through the months that came after, through the years, the image fading for a while, almost deserting me, and then, when I thought myself free of it, returning to spread tentacles of horror through every recess of my mind.

I saw my father's chest break open and his life pour out of it. I saw Jabez Gott, making no attempt to flee, tear open his shirt, baring his own scrawny chest to the sacrificial knife. I saw the soldiers advance to the slaughter and Jabez Gott begin to bleed. I saw his mates running like hares in every direction, with the soldiers and my cousin Joel after them, their shouting and clattering and the bark of their muskets growing to a sea-roaring in my ears. I saw my brother Edwin sink his head in his hands and Hannah stretch out a hand towards him, wanting to go to him, I think, and finding that her feet had taken root. I saw Squire Dalby, his elegant coat spattered with blood, move to my mother's side, and heard his startled exclamation as, with a long, sighing whisper, consciousness drained out of her and she folded bonelessly to the ground.

I remember, after that, only fragments of the night: the soldiers carrying my father back to the house, only pretending to be careful since they knew he was dead; my mother telling them to lay him on his bed and then, sitting at his side, drawing the bed curtains around them both, shutting herself away with him until the doctor came to tell us what we all knew and to help her to make him decent.

I remember my grandfather stamping, shouting with a gigantic fury which was partly grief-inspired, since he had lost his only son, partly shame-inspired, since they had quarrelled and it could never now be mended.

'You'll get them all, every one of them,' he kept on saying. 'Round them up and hang them. And anybody who gives them shelter is as guilty as they are – isn't that so, Squire? Twelve men. I saw twelve men with that mad devil, and I'll see twelve men hang. If it's the last thing I do, I'll hang them all.'

41

I remember Hannah, determined as always to do the right thing but doing it awkwardly, wanting to give comfort but unable to hide her disapproval of those tight-drawn bed curtains, her conviction that my mother's insistence on remaining in such close, solitary confinement with a dead man – albeit her husband – was somehow not quite right.

I remember Edwin, not really knowing what to do with himself, the master of the house now, ready to accept his responsibilities but surprised, I thought, at his own tears.

And then I remember myself, drifting like a shadow from place to place, feeling cold and far away, with that loud sea-roaring still in my head, preventing me from hearing or answering when anyone spoke to me.

'Your father is dead,' I kept on telling myself, but they were just empty words that rattled in my mind, so that even when morning came and I had slept a little, my birthday puppy sharing my bed, I would not have been surprised to see him crossing the yard, returning from the mill for his breakfast and his mug of ale.

Downstairs, in the thin, cool light of early morning, nothing seemed changed. In the kitchen I met the same gleaming copper, the same black-faced, evil-tempered stove as yesterday, the same stout countrywoman, our maid Marth-Ellen, baking the day's bread, red-faced with her exertions. There was the same supercilious black cat, the same lazy tabby, my brother's yellow bitch getting up stiff-legged from the hearthrug, my own gangling, enthusiastic puppy, Marth-Ellen calling to me from her breadboard to 'get that little demon out of here.'

The same. Except that my body was tight with tears I could not seem to shed; except that I was cold and could not warm myself, and there were sea waves still, rolling around my head, washing me away from too close a scrutiny of the truth. And when, suddenly, those sea waves receded, I was, for a moment, most appallingly empty, a hollow shell through which a sharp wind was painfully blowing, bringing me, one by one, a procession of images I did not wish to see.

'Your father is dead,' I told myself once more, and, abruptly, the harsh daylight was an assault on my eyes, unbearable, horribly bright.

He had given me a kitten once, long ago, bringing it up from the mill in his pocket and allowing me to find it there, laughing at my delight, pleased perhaps to have stirred the quietness of me to such excited laughter. And now he gave it to me again, the dainty three-cornered face, the velvet striped body nestling in the palm of his broad Barforth hand, my own face eagerly upturned, wanting him to kiss me, wanting to nestle against him, too, yet unable – afraid of a rebuff – to tell him so. And so, through the years, uncertain of his affection, I had half reached out my hand and, fearing he would refuse to take it, had drawn it back of my own accord.

'May I sit beside you in the carriage, Father,' my mind had asked, my feet wanting to carry me across the yard to him, to tug at his sleeve, to jump on his knee, but I had not spoken and he, impatient with my silences, my pleading, uncomfortable eyes, had driven off without me.

And so we had continued.

'Am I pretty, Father?' I had needed to know on the day of my first ball gown when, back from the dressmaker's, I had come demurely downstairs, white-taffeta'd, blue-sashed, hopeful.

And although he would have answered, 'Aye, the prettiest girl I've ever seen,' whether he meant it or not, it was so important to me, I so badly wanted it to be the truth, that I had not asked.

And now, no longer a child, I knew that in his solitude he had needed my love, anybody's love, and still I could find no way to release the tumult inside me, the bitter, futile grieving. A dome of glass, it seemed, like the ones they place over dried flowers, had descended over me; smooth glass, untroubled to the casual eye, while, against the inner side, my emotions beat frantic hands, unable to show themselves. And, one by one, as the memories and the pains had come to me, they trooped back again to lock themselves away in my heart, growing heavier as they remained unspoken.

'She's well enough,' he had said of me to my grandfather, and so it remained; 'well enough,' no more than that, and even then, feeling at last the relief of tears, I could not support the easy sympathy of Marth-Ellen and Mrs Stevens, both of them so willing to comfort me, and rushed out into the garden to find a secret corner in which to cry.

Yet, outwardly, I must still have seemed calm, earning myself a nod of approval from Edwin when I served him his breakfast, and when Hannah came down from the Top House, where she had spent the remainder of the night, I was able to answer her questions and follow the drift of her advice.

'You should go to your mother,' she told me. 'Indeed, you must go to her, Verity, for it can't be good for her, it can't be right, sitting all this while behind those curtains with – It is most odd and I have asked Edwin to send for the doctor again, except that he has not time to go himself and the stableboys are afraid to meet a felon on the way. Joel shall go presently, but in the meanwhile you must do what you can, Verity. Take her a tray of tea and then persuade her to come down or at least to go to another room. And when she is feeling stronger, there are things which really must be done. I appreciate her loss – indeed, I feel deeply for her, considering my situation with Edwin – but your grandfather and Edwin have suffered, too, and really, it is always best, however tragic the circumstances, to keep oneself gainfully employed. I don't wish to put myself forward, but no matter how painful it may be, one has certain duties that simply cannot be set aside. There is mourning to be got ready, for one thing, and since it is the master of the house who has died, the servants should be put in mourning too. Luckily, Elinor and I have plenty of black crepe left over from our own parents, but in your case – well, the most economical way, of course would be to dye the dresses you already have, but I can't really ask them to get a dye tub ready without your mother's permission. And people will be calling or sending to convey their sympathy, and someone must receive them. Really, I am not at all sure what we should do. You are the daughter of the house, but you have only just gone sixteen and may not be up to it – people may not quite like it. Yet if, on the other hand, I do it myself, it may be thought presumptuous, my engagement to Edwin being so recent and no wedding date being set. Verity, do just run upstairs and tell your mother that if she won't come down she absolutely must let me know how she wants things done.'

But my mother had nothing to say to me, and when my grandfather and Mrs Stevens arrived later in the morning she would not speak to them either.

'She was always half cracked,' my grandfather said, stumping his way downstairs, 'and now she's gone altogether. Well, so much the better, for I never liked her – she was never good enough for my son. And now we'll have a fresh start. Where's Edwin, eh, and Hannah? Send them to me, will you, Mrs Stevens, for I'm weary – bone-weary. I'll sit awhile in my wife's kitchen and take a glass of wine, if such a thing's to be found in this house since my wife died. And send the Boy to me, and his lass, and we'll talk of the future. There's no sense now, is there, Mrs Stevens, in looking back? I did what I could, didn't I? And what is there now but the Boy and the future? A good boy, and if the lass has no money to bring with her at least she's straight and plainspoken – at least when she opens her mouth I understand what comes out. So – the wine, Mrs Stevens, and then my lad.'

No more trouble was expected. The crowd had facelessly gone home now, its fighting spirit crushed by the horror of what had occurred. Jabez Gott was dead, and four of his companions with him, shot down by the soldiers; as the day progressed, the others were accounted for one by one, apprehended – with some more timely assistance from Ira Agbrigg – and despatched first to York and then, one must suppose, to the gallows or a prison ship. And when only two remained at large, and these not ringleaders but young lads merely, both of them thought to be badly wounded, my grandfather began to be certain of his revenge.

He had, perhaps, loved my father at the level where love has nothing to do with sense or even with liking, but there was no doubt that he loved Edwin more, and although he would continue to grieve for my father he would not, in the everyday sense of the word, miss him.

'Life must go on,' he announced, waking suddenly from his reverie in the kitchen rocking chair. 'Yes, and renew itself, eh, Edwin? So we'll have a wedding as soon as may be – and a christening as soon as decent – and then another. That's what your father would say to you if he could, and I'm doing naught but saying it in his stead. I've gained a great deal in my life, lad, and lost a lot, for I had other sons, besides your father, who died in their cradles, and you have brothers in the churchyard who should have been standing beside you today. But never mind that. It's weakness, lad, to look back – and folly. What's done is done, and all I want now is to live long enough to see your children grow – that's all I ask. Just make sure, lad, that there'll be a Barforth down there, making those looms turn, after I'm gone, and another to follow him. That's all I want. And now I'll go back to my own house, Mrs Stevens, and my own bed, for I'm not easy here. Edwin, your arm, if you please –'

My father was in his coffin now, a stranger encased in white velvet and polished wood, exposed in the back parlour for all to see, and since my mother chose to remain upstairs, strange and silent behind her bed curtains, I went with Hannah to the kitchen, lending my seal of approval, while she informed Marth-Ellen when and what we would eat. But, indeed, she scarcely needed me, for Marth-Ellen, who had no intention of losing a good place, was more than eager to gain the favour of Edwin's bride, and perhaps her curtsies and her 'Yes, ma'ams' and 'No ma'ams' finally caused Hannah to acknowledge the change in her situation.

While my father had lived my mother had been the mistress of this house and might have remained so for the first twenty or thirty years of Hannah's married life, presiding over Hannah's affairs, choosing her servants, interfering with the upbringing of her children. For twenty or thirty years Hannah could have been little more than a guest in my mother's house, but now, since my father's slow, disillusioned life had spurted out of him so violently, left him too fast for protest or consolation, Edwin would be the master, his wife the supreme domestic authority over us all. And although she was too proper, too kindhearted to admit it, even to herself, I knew that secretly she must be relieved, that eventually she would be pleased.

'Edwin, do take a little more,' she said as we ate our belated meal. 'Your grandfather told us that life goes on and so it does. This custard tart is not excellent, for the nutmeg must have been put in with a coal shovel, but it is sustaining, and we shall improve the quality presently.'

'I've no appetite, lass,' he told her, but he had, and the excited, only half-suppressed light in his eye when she talked of what they would do 'presently' gave me a twinge of such discomfort that I excused myself and went outside.

The evening was cool again, freshening towards rain, the mill silent as a mark of respect for the dead, although I remembered how Edwin – and Joel, too – had made some protest when my grandfather had dismissed the soldiers.

'You'd do well to keep them another night,' Joel had advised, Edwin agreeing, but my grandfather, having already quarrelled with the officer, vowing he'd have no more red-coated scum in his yard, had turned peevish even with his grandson.

'It's over,' he snarled. 'When I say it's over, it's over. Ten of them dead or under guard, two lads dying of their wounds somewhere, and the rest sick to their stomachs of Jabez Gott and his like. They're crushed and finished, and I want no redcoats littering up my yard to remind me of what they couldn't prevent last night.'

And so Edwin had been obliged to content himself with setting Ira Agbrigg to keep his eyes and ears open and, if any further riotous assembly threatened, to let us know.

Life, indeed, for my grandfather, would go on. He would continue to sit on his hillside, I thought, growing richer and harder to manage. Mrs Stevens would continue to pamper him and smile for wages, while here, in the millhouse, Hannah would improve the quality of Edwin's custard,

45

the whiteness of his linen, and would devote her formidable energies to making herself the perfect wife, the perfect mother of Samson Barforth's great-grandchildren. My mother, I supposed, would take up her embroidery again, here or elsewhere, and lead her own life inside her head, as she'd always done. But in it all I saw no place for me. Could I exist, with any degree of comfort, between Edwin and Hannah? Was there any comfort for me in my mother's dream? And, doubting, I felt a vast longing for my father pour out of me like a wail across the mill yard.

And yet the quality of my grieving, even in these few hours, had altered. This morning, in my hiding place by the garden wall, sheltered by the downward drooping of an ancient pear tree, I had wept privately, bitterly, for my father alone: for his loss of life and opportunity, for the terrible waste of him. But now my own life seemed in the night air to swing loose and lonely, with nothing left to cling to.

There was no one, of course, who wished me ill. Edwin was fond of me; Hannah would do her duty; my grandfather, jealous of all his possessions, would guard me vigilantly. But in that dark, solitary hour, I did not wish to belong to my grandfather; I did not wish, in fact, to cling to anyone but to stand and look the world full in the face with my own quiet but not unperceptive eyes and see its colours and textures for myself.

And although I was quiet, certainly, I was neither awkward nor shy. Hannah had thought me too young to receive my mother's callers, but I knew I could have managed everything well enough without her. Hannah would always be deceived by a sanctimonious turn of phrase, a flattering manner, but I, like my mother, often saw beyond phrase and manner to motives and meanings it was not always comfortable to see. Stubborn, my grandfather had once called me, and remembering my cousin Elinor's gay chatterings of weddings, I thought I might have need of that stubborn streak ere long when Hannah, once established as my brother's wife, would very likely consider it her duty to find a husband for me.

Marriage, of course, would come, as marriage came to all girls of my station, but, since Hannah's taste would not be mine, I would have to take good care to prevent her from laying her well-meaning hands on my future.

When my cousin Joel came out of the house and stood a moment in the doorway, lighting the cigar Hannah would not permit him to smoke inside, I was taken unawares, with no opportunity to avoid him. Not that I particularly disliked him. He was, undoubtedly, handsome, capable of arousing a giggling excitement in certain friends of mine who would have been badly scared had he decided to look their way, but he was also a realist and, knowing that well-mannered, well-dowered young ladies were not for him, had never taken the slightest notice of them – or of me. Yet tonight, with my tortoiseshell comb holding up my hair, perhaps I looked old enough, womanly enough, to merit an instant's attention, and glancing at me beneath lowered eyelids with a certain insolence, a certain amusement I did not like, he came strolling down the path to my side.

'You'll take cold,' he said. 'In fact, my sister asked me to tell you so,

46

should I happen to meet you. You've been out in the night air too long, in her opinion, and I daresay she knows what she's about.'

'I daresay. But I believe I'll stay out a while longer.'

'You may suit yourself. I'm off to the Top House to fetch Elinor and take her home. There's no call that I can see to spend another night under Edwin's roof.'

That should have been enough, and, indeed, I think he was about to go. But then, peering at me through the twilight, he said, 'You're not looking too bright, cousin. This makes a difference to you, then, all this?'

'Of course it does.'

'Of course. I hadn't considered. God knows, I wasn't over-sorry to lose my own father, but that doesn't mean everybody else must be the same, and I reckon it's different for a girl. But you'll do all right, Verity; your grandfather will see to that. There's plenty of money to marry you with.'

'I suppose so. I've never thought much about it.'

'No,' he said, laughing shortly, sharply, not looking at me any longer. 'That doesn't surprise me. The ones who think most about money are those who haven't got it. In fact, when you have creditors waiting to dun you round every street corner, it's hard to think of anything else. But that need never concern you, cousin. They'll marry you comfortably – splendidly, in fact, if you can put your grandfather in the right frame of mind. There's Bradley Hobhouse over at Nethercoats, or Matthew Oldroyd at Fieldhead: they've both got good businesses to inherit – just like Edwin – and they'd both be glad to take you. They'd treat you so well you'd never notice the difference.'

And because I was old enough to recognize his bitterness and his impertinence, and to know from where it stemmed, yet still too young to know how to put him in his place, I said quickly, just to say something, 'You'll be getting married yourself now, I suppose.'

'Oh, you suppose that, do you? And what do you know about it – except what Elinor tells you?'

'It's not a secret, is it?'

'No, no, there's no secret, although the lady's father doesn't like to hear much about it. Yes, for your information and Elinor's, I was thinking of getting married, for Miss Boulton has been waiting a fair while. But I have a problem now, you see, that I hadn't bargained for. Your brother was all set to marry my sister tomorrow, if she'd have him, and he still would, I reckon, which would suit me down to the ground. But knowing the way Hannah feels about doing the right thing, she won't take him until he's out of mourning, which could be a year, couldn't it, for a father? And if I have Hannah to support for another twelvemonth I can hardly afford Miss Boulton. And even then, if Hannah went right now, it would depend on my half-yearly profits before Isaac Boulton would listen to me. Well, I know how to balance my books to my advantage – a trick I learned from my father – but I'm not sure they'll look good enough. So you see, things have changed rather, for me too.'

'I'm sorry.'

'Oh, don't be,' he said airily, apparently much amused. 'We can't all have Edwin's luck. Not many men can afford to marry at twenty-four, without somebody else to pay the bills. Most of us have to wait until we're well past thirty – well past forty sometimes – before we can hope to support a wife; and I'm only twenty-eight, so I've got time.'

But had Miss Boulton? I wondered, as he went on through the gate and up the path to the Top House, for she had seemed to me, on the two occasions I had met her, a flighty, not altogether good-tempered girl whose wild-rose prettiness would soon show thorns. Yet Joel, I decided, was well able to manage his affairs without help from me, and although I was cold now and would have been glad to go inside, to do so would have looked like obedience to Hannah and so obstinately I remained outdoors. And when she came to the window, not seeing me in my dark dress with the light behind her, and called out, 'Verity – where are you? Will you come in now?' I got up and, keeping close to the wall, slipped around the side of the house towards the gate leading to the mill yard.

I should not have been there, had no wish to be there, so near the place where my father had died, yet Hannah's voice, still calling behind me, 'Verity, Verity, come in now,' served only to push me farther away. And so it was that I opened the gate, walked a step or two into the yard, and realized, without knowing how or what it signified, that I was not alone.

I had heard no more than a rat rustling, somewhere in the dark ahead of me, a common enough sound, for we had rats in plenty and cats, and stray dogs who got into the sheds in the cold weather, yet this, I knew, was a man; no heavy-footed watchman, no engineer going about his rightful business, but someone nervously running from shadow to shadow, who should not have been there at all.

I should, most certainly, have rushed back through the gate and up the narrow garden, shrieking 'Edwin!' at the top of my lungs, but, in that first instant, I froze, as my mother had frozen at the sight of my dying father; although I tried to move backwards, to Edwin, to safety, my feet refused to take me. Who would come here tonight, I reasoned, but a man with a yellow-pale face and sandy hair, sick with hate and the need for revenge? And although that man was dead, twelve others had stood around him, two of them hiding somewhere in the hills, grieving for their companions and their ruined endeavours. And if I stood in their shoes, would it seem right to me to strike another blow, another gesture of crazy defiance before the gallows or starvation took me? I thought that it would and, remembering my father and the yellow-pale, weeping face of his destroyer, I froze again, fear consuming my mind, clouding my reason entirely. I had only to call out and Edwin would come running to defend his property and his sister, yet an instinct powerful enough to paralyse my tongue bade me keep Edwin away. There had been murder and vengeance already – did I want to see Edwin with blood on his hands?

I would creep back up the path and go indoors as if I had heard nothing – as indeed I would have heard nothing had not Hannah's voice driven me here in the first place – and tomorrow, when it was discovered that a few yards of cloth had been slashed to pieces or a bale of wool broken open and scattered in the wind, we would have no trouble in making up the loss.

But I had reckoned without Hannah's sense of duty towards her lover's fatherless, well-nigh motherless sister, her insistent 'Edwin, that child will take cold. Do please go and fetch her in,' so that he was already outside, making his grumbling way down to the yard, when the far shed began to burn.

It seemed, to me at any rate, just a little thing, no more than a candle flame dancing behind the window, uncertain, unlikely to take hold, and I needed to hear Edwin's bellow of rage as he rushed past me to understand that this was arson, another capital crime for which somebody would have to pay.

'Bloody old fool,' he thundered, meaning, incredibly, my grandfather. 'I told him we'd best keep a guard tonight – and Joel told him – but no, he knows best – he bloody knows best. Go and get Joel, for God's sake – there's nothing in the far shed I'm bothered about, but if it spreads –'

I was about to do his bidding when we both saw the man clearly, bent almost double, running across a treacherous shaft of moonlight.

'Let him go,' I shouted. 'Let's see to the sheds,' but the fire was, indeed, not serious as yet, no blaze of vengeful triumph but a smouldering, smoky thing likely to burn itself out, and he seemed not to hear me.

And once again, I recall no more than fragments – wish to recall no more – just Edwin's strong, eager body bounding forward, rich with confidence in itself and its future, knowing that with his long legs, his powerful shoulders, the well-nourished, well-tended bone and fibre of him, he could easily outrun a felon and hold him fast. And so he did, laughing as he caught him by the scruff of his neck and flung him back against the wall, forcing the narrow head and the yellow-pale face up into the moonlight so that I saw again the hollow eyes, the tears spilling from their corners, a lad who knew his nineteen-year-old life was over.

There was no pistol this time. Perhaps I had thought of a pistol, dreaded it – remembering – so that when the boy broke free and I saw the knife in his hand – a long-bladed kitchen knife, a familiar object – it seemed far less terrible.

'Now just throw that down,' Edwin said reasonably, his mind, I think, already going back to the fire, wondering how far it had spread and why the devil I had not gone yet to fetch Joel, and feeling himself so safe, so totally in control, that when the blow fell the sheer surprise of it may have spared him pain.

There came the sounds of men running – Joel, perhaps, who must have seen the fire by now, bringing the coachman, the stable lads – and, half turning his head, Edwin, still despising his adversary, stumbled, lurched forward into a yellow-pale, scarecrow embrace, a hand with fingers like dry sticks groping behind his neck, pulling him nearer, using Edwin's own weight to force that common kitchen blade through his fancy silk waistcoat and into his stomach.

49

Edwin. My brother Edwin. Why had I never known before that I loved him? And, knowing it now, I threw myself forward, screaming, clawing blindly, aimlessly, ready to put my teeth into the boy's throat and savage him had I been able to hold him.

'I'm sorry!' I heard him scream, his hands biting into my shoulders, trying to free himself of me. 'I'm sorry.'

Even through my madness I could feel the trembling of his body.

'Get away from me! Oh please, get away –' he shrieked, bringing me to the ground. When I still clung to him he tried to scramble away on all fours, wheezing and whining – sobbing, it seemed to me, unless I was the one who sobbed – until at last there was Joel, fiercely swooping, lifting him and tossing him against the shed wall like a rag doll, picking him up again and beating his head against the stone until the doll stopped screaming.

In the harrowing silence, I dragged myself across the cobbles to my brother's side and knelt very close to him, touched his cheek with a wondering hand, as I had never touched him before, smoothed the heavy brown hair away from his forehead, traced the outline of his jaw with my fingertips, straightened his cravat and the collar of his coat, made him tidy and decent.

'Edwin, love, do look. Your mill's on fire. Do look, darling. They'll soon put it out, so you don't have to worry, but do look.'

And I laid my cheek against his cheek, my mouth briefly on the corner of his mouth.

'He's dead, isn't he?' Joel said, dropping swiftly down on one knee. 'Isn't he?'

And looking up, meeting the flash of excitement in his face, knowing him for a predator, I leaned across my brother's body, hiding the jagged, oozing rent in his waistcoat, and, savage in the defence of my own kind, snarled at him, 'Not yet. Not yet.'

5

We buried them side by side in the corner of the graveyard where my brothers and sisters and my grandmother lay, with ornate headstones of gold-lettered, highly polished marble above them – a huge old apple tree shedding its blossoms on the newly dug ground – and even Squire Dalby, a High Churchman who equated Methodists with Jacobins, Roman Catholics, and the devil, attended the memorial service in the squat, square chapel my grandfather had built in his wife's day.

It was a soft pink and blue May morning, with a gentle breeze and new sunshine slanting on fresh green: a day for a young man's pleasures, not an old man's heartbreak; yet broken my grandfather certainly was, and everyone who saw him that day, shivering, shrunken, gave their opinion that he and Edwin would not be long apart.

There had been a great deal of sympathy, a gratifying show of respect, messages of condolence reaching us from manufacturers and gentry

50

alike. The Hobhouses of Nethercoats, our chief competitors in the worsted trade, and the Oldroyds of Fieldhead, spinners of high-quality yarn, had expressed their heartfelt sorrow and their readiness to do anything – within reason – to assist. Mr Rawnsley the banker and Mr Aycliffe the builder had paid us every attention, Mr Aycliffe, who was to have undertaken the building of Edwin's new mill, managing not to ask my grandfather what he intended to do about it now. And we had received floral and verbal tributes from some of Cullingford's oldest residents; the aristocratic Colonel Corey of Blenheim Lane, his cousin, the lawyer Mr Corey-Manning – both of them in some way related to Sir Giles Flood, Cullingford's manorial lord – and an assortment of their female relatives, persons of quality not much given to associating with the manufacturing classes but making an exception in our sad case.

Letters had appeared, not only in the *Cullingford Courier* but in newspapers as far off as Bradford and Leeds, praising my father's achievements, my brother's promise, the noble stand they had both made against anarchy. And, in recognition of that stand and the tragedy our family had suffered in their common cause, the local industrialists had subscribed two thousand pounds towards the repair of our mill. My brother's murderer, much of his body in splints from the damage Joel had inflicted on him, had been sent to York with the others to hang, thus ensuring, it was felt, that mill wrecking, machine breaking was now a lost cause in our area; and although I was glad of that, I found no consolation, as Hannah was later to do, in referring to my father and brother as martyrs.

The road leading to the chapel was lined that day on both sides with black-draped carriages which had disgorged so liberal a helping of top-hatted, black-gloved gentlemen and ladies in black crepe and mourning veils that my grandfather's plain little chapel could not hold them all. And so they waited outside until the service was over, some to see what they could see, some because they thought it advisable to be seen, some touched with genuine regret for my father and brother, others weeping simply at the reminder that they too must come to this. A great crowd, their combined fortunes totalling far more than men not born to riches had ever seen a way to earn before, and, behind them, from the mean streets now surrounding the chapel, shawl-covered heads, a line of Sunday cloth caps – Ira Agbrigg among them – coming also to pay their respects to a man who had been known as a fair master.

I rode in the first carriage with my mother and my grandfather, keeping well away from him, uncomfortable with the enormity of his grief and his blind, blazing fury that God had permitted this dreadful thing to befall him. But he had no time for me – no time for anyone – fixing his eyes on the black plumes dancing on the horses' heads, seeing beyond them, I supposed, to the ruin of everything he had lived for. Edwin had been 'his lad,' 'his pride and joy,' and just as he had monopolized him in life, so he refused to share him in death. No one had loved Edwin as he had, consequently no one else had the right to mourn him so intensely, and when Hannah found herself unable to share his

51

view, he had simply ordered her to take herself off to her own home since she had no purpose to serve in his any longer.

I could not recognize my mother's face beneath the swathes of black veiling on her bonnet, yet even in the anonymity of mourning dress she seemed different from the rest of us; and although she was no tower of strength, no comforting shoulder to lean on, I had leaned on her these last days and she had not entirely let me fall.

She had taken my father's death strangely, but her care of Edwin, during the bitter hour it had taken him to die, had been tender, unexpected. She had not comforted him, since a man of twenty-four with the world at his feet cannot be consoled for the loss of it. She had simply held him in his pain, taken him back to his childhood when she'd had the power to make everything right, and afterwards, when Hannah went into some kind of a fit, choking and shaking, staggering about the room and hurting herself against the walls and the chairs, my mother had calmed her and held her too.

I had required no one to calm me. My cousin Joel had carried me up from the mill yard and put me down in the kitchen rocking chair; and I had remained there, motionless, striving in the most appalling silence of my life to fight my way back to reality through those sea waves which were once again swamping my mind. For a nightmare time I thought myself doomed to spend my life curled up with Edwin's blood still on my hands and in my hair, down the front of my dress. But the sea-roaring ceased, as it had done before; my eyes felt sharpened to an acute, distressing observation of the people around me, an observation totally without pity.

Hannah had wandered by me, ashen, unsteady. I thought coldly, She'll get over it. She should have left well alone.

My grandfather had appeared a moment in the kitchen doorway, gasping, blindly groping, and my thoughts told him, That's right, old man, choke – for it was your pride that killed him, and your spoiling. Don't come to me for pity – don't come to me for anything.

Mrs Stevens and our maid Marth-Ellen had come to peer at me, red-eyed, both of them; uncertain, it had seemed to me, of their own future, for the men on whom they depended were dying. I had not answered them, and when my cousin Joel came in, having changed his soiled clothes and combed his hair, and told Marth-Ellen, 'You'd best see to that child,' her answer had been the simple lifting of her shoulders in a gesture of defeat.

'She'll not let me near her, nor Mrs Stevens, either. Jumpy as a cat with a basket of sick kittens, she is. I've seen it before. It passes.'

But my cousin Joel, as accustomed as Hannah to getting his own way, would have none of that. 'She can't stay here like that, unwashed. Good God, woman, the state of her. Get a can of hot water upstairs in her room, and make her bed ready. I'll fetch her.'

Yet I had no mind, at that moment, to be fetched, and as Marth-Ellen, seeing no reason to take his orders but taking them just the same, had hurried away, I had fastened my eyes on his face, seeing quite clearly his soured ambitions and his present savage hopes, and had discovered that he no longer intimidated me.

'Get up, Verity.'

'I don't think I will.'

'I think you must. Come, love, you can't sit there forever, in such a mess.'

'Why can't I?'

'Well, if you need a reason, because I say so.'

And, my lips parting quite painfully, I had hissed at him, 'Say what you like, Joel Barforth. There's no call for me to take notice of you. You're not the master here – not yet, at any rate.'

And I could have smiled at his sudden recoil, as if a tiny inoffensive sparrow had somehow raised an eagle's beak and bitten him.

But my cousin Joel was a man of experience in the ways of self-defence; had fought his own battles, hard and dirty, all his life and, recovering instantly, had given a short altogether mirthful laugh. 'Ah well, whatever that means, we'll not talk of it tonight, Verity. You're tired, and you've got your mind in a tangle, so come to bed, love, it's the best place for you.'

He had lifted me easily, held me too tightly for protest, delivering me like an ill-wrapped parcel to Marth-Ellen, to hot water and clean sheets and an unspeakable, tormented night from which I had risen, the next morning, my usual, apparently calm self.

And now, today, we were laying them to rest.

There was a respectful hush as we arrived at the chapel, the gentlemen, who had been strolling up and down discussing their dealings at the London wool sales, grouping themselves in suitably regretful attitudes, the ladies who may have been wondering how Hannah Barforth, having lost her bright future, would contrive, at twenty-three, to find herself another, raising wisps of cambric to their enquiring eyes. And, had they allowed it, I would have remained in the carriage, closed my eyes, lost myself in my sea waves, and slept.

My cousin Joel was waiting to hand us down. Although he must have moved very fast to have reached our carriage step – having travelled behind us with his sisters – he looked as if he had been there, sorrowfully, calmly, for a long time. Immaculate as always, correct in every detail of black coat and trousers, and mourning bands, he raised his hat to my mother, put a gentle hand under her elbow to help her down and a protective arm around her shoulders to steady her against the impact of sunlight and curiosity, and then, instead of leaving me to manage my skirts and the carriage step as best I might – the treatment he usually accorded to little girls – he held out a hand to me, too, and lifted me with immense care, his solicitude arousing some sentimental murmuring in the crowd.

'Poor lamb,' I heard a woman's voice say. 'She saw her father shot dead, and then they butchered her brother in her arms. Is it any wonder she can barely keep her feet?'

'Aye,' a deeper voice grunted. 'I'd not like a lass of mine to go through that. The shock could turn her head and she'd never be right again.'

And a deeper voice still. 'She'll be right enough. She's a Barforth.'

But then, as my grandfather's mottled, irate head appeared in the carriage doorway, there was a collective intake of breath, a certain drawing back, for although many of them had come to see him weep – thinking it high time Samson Barforth's luck ran out – he was so terrifying, so awesome in defeat that malice and curiosity took flight and silence fell.

He stood for a moment, feet planted foursquare on the ground as they always were, sharp eyes passing from face to face, taking note of absentees as he used to do every morning in the mill yard, daring them all, it seemed, to wonder what he meant to do now with his mill and his money when there was no one but a scatterbrained woman and a half-grown girl to come after him.

I saw his mouth twist itself into a grimace which could have been the sardonic laying down of a challenge – or a barrier to tears – and then, as he took a step forward, an old, desolate man, unutterably bitter, adamantly alone, my cousin Joel came swiftly to his side.

'Take my arm, sir,' he said and, for a moment, it hung in the balance, my grandfather being much inclined, I thought, to push Joel away peevishly. But then he paused, considering, his expression cunning and vindictive, making no secret of his hatred for this healthy young man who was alive when Edwin was dead.

'Aye,' he said, after a long, baleful moment. 'Happen I will take your arm, lad – happen I will, for as long as it suits me.' And putting his hand on Joel's elegant, well-brushed sleeve, deliberately crushing the fabric as I had seen him do before, he leaned his full weight against him and went into his chapel to pray.

There were refreshments afterwards, some of the mourners having come some distance – one or two even from the other side, the cotton side of the Pennines – and requiring a plentiful supply of Mrs Stevens's ham and pickles and curd tarts to sustain them on their journey home. As we reached our door, the lady herself was there to receive us, come down from the Top House in her black silk dress and to bathe us all in warm smiles, some of us receiving rather more in the way of her tender care than others.

Hannah, I noticed, who had moved through these last few days like a statue carved in granite, was no longer a particular favourite, being allowed to sit and stare at the carpet as much as she pleased. My cousin Elinor had never counted for very much in any case, but my own importance, it seemed, to Mrs Stevens as well as to my cousin Joel, had increased enormously.

'The dear child has suffered a grievous shock,' she kept on murmuring to the sober, frock-coated gentlemen who were trying not to enjoy their food too heartily or to admire Mrs Stevens herself too openly in the eagle-eyed presence of their wives. And I found that my teacup was constantly being refilled, my plate piled high with slices of seedcake and gingerbread she declared she had made specially for me.

'Clever Mrs Stevens,' my cousin Elinor said, managing even in a plain black gown that was far from new to look extremely pretty. 'She thinks

54

your grandfather can't last much longer and knows that when he dies there's no one he can leave his money to but you. So when you're rich, Verity, and you turn out your wardrobe, do remember me. You'll not want those tortoiseshell combs when you can afford ivory and pearls, will you, and I mean to put my hair up now. Hannah said I was to wait until her wedding but – well – she can hardly expect me to do that now, can she, when there's absolutely no guarantee ... Heavens, I could still have my hair hanging down my back when I'm thirty, at that rate.'

Elinor's life, of course, was but little changed by the loss of my father and brother. She had spent the night of the riot snugly ensconced at the Top House with Mrs Stevens and had witnessed nothing; now, despite her good intentions, she was growing bored with the white-lipped, rock-hard grief in Hannah that she could not share.

'She should cry more. It would do her good,' was Elinor's verdict, but Hannah had fought all her life against the passionate side of her nature, the part of her which longed now to make some grand, tragic gesture, some pagan expression of mourning like the cutting and burning of her own hair on the funeral pyre. And caught in the straitjacket of her self-discipline, she held herself aloof, with no suspicion, I supposed, that had she left well alone – had she not fussed and fretted about the hour of my bedtime and sent Edwin to look for me – by the time my brother had seen the fire, the felon would no longer have been in the yard to murder him, and she herself would still have been the future mistress of Lawcroft Fold.

Yet such speculation was profitless and unkind, particularly since I was the one destined to take her place. And if that was hard for me to contemplate, my grandfather appeared to find it well-nigh impossible.

'I have no appetite, Mrs Stevens,' he said on his return from the chapel, and turning his back on Cullingford's elite, he retired to a bench in the garden and sat there like some ancient image of weathered stone, his eyes fastened on the mill.

'Oh dear,' Mrs Stevens asked us more than once, 'what am I to do? He should not be out there alone. He will take cold.'

But no one cared to tell him so and, gradually, his friends and neighbours, his keen-eyed competitors, his suppliers and his customers, his minister and his doctor came, one by one, to press my mother's hand and take their leave. And Mr Olroyd the spinner, Mr Aycliffe the builder, Mr Hobhouse the worsted manufacturer, who all had sons of a similar age, paused a while and made themselves pleasant to me.

'Leave him be,' Joel said, glancing out of the window, hard-faced again, his suave sympathy all gone. 'He has things to ponder, I reckon. Leave him to get on with it. We'll be off ourselves now, Aunt Isabella, but you know where to find me at need. Don't hesitate to apply.'

Even when Joel's hired carriage had rolled away, my grandfather continued to sit and stare at his mill, at his school and his chapel and the long grey rows of his workers' cottages, at the seeds of an empire he had believed would grow and prosper and carry his name into the future – his immortality which would now have to be put up for auction, sold for the profit of a young, unwanted lass.

'Mrs Barforth, can you not speak to him?' Mrs Stevens pleaded, not wishing to hasten his end until she had had the time to negotiate for herself a new beginning, but even as my mother was shaking her head, taking up her embroidery, there he was, glaring at us from the doorway, continuing out loud the conversation he had been having with himself all day.

'So that's it, then,' he announced. 'Yes, that's it – and I'm not broken yet – no. They can think what they like but I'm not finished. I've been down before – never so low as this, but I've been down. And I've always got up again. Life goes on – yes, that's what I said, and I stand by it. Life goes on. And there's one thing we can do now – the sooner, the better. We'll be getting you married now, Verity Barforth. What do you say to that?' And, beckoning imperiously to Mrs Stevens, he stamped away.

I woke late the next morning, and somnolently, unable somehow to bring my ideas together, content simply to lie down on the rag rug by the kitchen fire, my brother's bewildered yellow bitch pressing close beside me, not understanding where Edwin was, I suppose, and sensing something of him in me. And I remained there for a long time, listening to the bitch breathe, thinking of nothing.

Marth-Ellen came and went, leaning over me to tend her oven, never thinking of telling me I was in her way. And as the room began to fill with the basic fragrance of new bread, the slow simmering of broth in the iron pot above the fire, I drifted very far, to a place where no effort was ever required, where nothing ever changed, where – like the dog – it was enough to feel the fire on my skin, to exist at the level of food and shelter and air to breathe: enough, I think, to be alive. Although I knew I would eventually be forced to wake, I chose to delay it, chose not to ask myself why my mother had been summoned to the Top House so early and was so long in coming home.

I dozed a little, rising only to the bare surface of wakefulness when she tapped my shoulder – her eyes rimmed, I noticed, with dark shadows, her own sorrow showing clear in this unguarded moment – and even then, knowing she had something important to say to me, I could only lean drowsily against the dog, ready to drift away again from all complexity, to hide myself in a warm nest of sleep.

But Mother could be sharp when she wished, and quick to make her point for all her apparent vagueness, and sitting down in the fireside chair, the old, creaking rocker with its knitted cushions where Marth-Ellen sat – and my grandmother used to sit – to do her mending, she sent Marth-Ellen away and said, 'Well, since you are so lazy I won't move you. What I have to say will sound as well here as in the parlour. And I must confess it has come a little sooner than I expected and caught me unprepared. Listen carefully, Verity. Someone has asked – this morning – to marry you.'

'Someone?' I said, still drowsy, intent somehow or other on the shading of the dog's coat, the rich gold of her back fading to cream on her legs and belly.

'Verity, are you listening to me?'

'Yes, I'm listening.'

But it neither surprised nor alarmed me that someone had asked to marry me. Amazingly, I did not much care. I wanted merely to be left alone with the dog and the firelight, and I have often wondered if they understood the state of shock I was in and used it for their purposes.

'Well then,' she said, 'since you are listening – I think you must have been long aware that the question of a husband would soon arise, and that even had your father lived, your grandather would have done the choosing. Tell me, dear – there is no one, is there, no young man who seems more agreeable to you than the others?'

'No.'

'Good. I thought not. I told your grandfather so, and I am glad to be right. Does it surprise you that it is your cousin Joel who has asked for you? At your grandfather's suggestion, I imagine, although I feel sure he would have asked in any case.'

'Why should he do that, Mother?'

'Oh, Verity – my dear,' she said, her hands making a fluttering movement, as if they were looking for her embroidery. 'I think you must know – for I believe you know a great deal behind your quiet eyes – that there would never have been the slightest difficulty in getting you creditably married. Your dowry is far from inconsiderable, and your family connections alone are of great value in the Law Valley. But now, dearest, with Edwin gone, there is far more to you than a mere dowry. Have you not thought of that?'

'Oh yes,' I told her, still not greatly caring, still, incredibly, much inclined for sleep. 'I understand all that. But Joel was to marry Miss Boulton, surely, of Cullingford?'

'Ah yes,' my mother said, smiling. 'Yes, indeed. Certainly there is a Miss Boulton. But their understanding seems to have been only between themselves. Her father had not given his consent, not been properly applied to, so there is no actual commitment – the lady has no cause to sue for breach of promise. He assures us of that. And I think you know, Verity, as well as I do, that your cousin Joel would give a hundred Miss Boultons for the one remaining Miss Barforth.'

'Yes,' I told her, feeling the firelight on my face again, knowing that somehow I would have to rouse myself, have to admit that this was urgent, that it mattered, that it was real. 'Yes, I know about Joel. I know what Joel wants. Why does my grandfather want it?'

'Because he is a dynast. Do you understand what that means? He wants to live forever through his descendants, to be constantly reborn in a line of young Barforth men exactly like himself. Well – we all have our dreams – and it rather looked as if he was going to be cheated of his. Life or Fate or God, perhaps, seemed to have dealt him a blow from which he could not recover – from which many people frankly hoped he would never recover – and now he has found a way to remedy it. That is the heart of the matter. You are all he has left. You cannot run the mill, like Edwin, but, hopefully, you may bear children who can – not Edwin's

57

children, of course, but with something of Edwin in them, the nearest he can get to Edwin. Not just exactly what he had dreamed of, I admit, but his own flesh and blood nevertheless. And although your cousin Joel would be completely out of the question for a Miss Barforth of Lawcroft who had a brother still living – would have been branded a fortune hunter had he ever dared approach you – in these altered circumstances he has much to recommend him. He is a good businessman – possibly better than Edwin and certainly more ambitious than Edwin – and a Barforth, too, which means the name would be carried on. And since his own affairs are in a sorry state, through no fault of his own, he would owe everything to your grandfather – an excellent arrangement from your grandfather's point of view. Far better than marrying you to a Hobhouse or an Oldroyd, who would put his own family's interests first and would not allow him a free hand with your children.'

'And what must I do, Mother?'

She sighed, eased her position slightly, showing no surprise in finding me so docile.

'You must answer for yourself. Certainly no one will drag you to the altar by the hair, but, Verity, my poor Verity, your grandfather has set his mind on this, and I wonder if you have the strength to openly defy him? I must confess to you that I have not. I have never stood my ground and told him what I would and would not do. And on the few occasions when I have tried – well – I have had no success. The only time your father and I held to our purpose was when your grandfather opposed our marriage, and in that I am forced to admit he was right. Affection always existed between us – a kind of affection, at any rate – but we were not suited. And so, you see, a marriage of convenience may succeed as well as any other kind; better, perhaps. Your cousin is handsome and not without experience, and he is only your senior by some twelve years – not a great deal, Verity, for you must know that your grandfather would have no hesitation in giving you to a man of forty or more should it seem good to him.'

'Then you think I must take him.'

'I think you must take somebody.'

'And if I dislike him and refuse him – will you stand by me?'

'I would like to,' she said, her grey velvet eyes holding mine. 'Truly I would like to, as I would have liked to stand by your father – oh, so many times. But it did not seem to be in my nature. You may imagine how much I regret it. But at least I have the self-knowledge to warn you – should the need arise – that I am not to be relied on. And I must tell you, too, that it is not my plan to remain in this house. My service, you see, is over, Verity dear. The Barforths have no more need of me, and I am free. I shall find myself a little nest, not too far away, which you are very welcome to share – naturally – should you find yourself at liberty. I think we could do very well together, you and I, if we were left to our own devices, and certainly I shall be left alone now. But not you, dear. You are of great importance to your grandfather at present, and I can think of nothing which would make him release you. Well, I suppose it is my duty to be more precise and so I will say this to you. Unless your cousin Joel is positively hateful in your eyes – and I know of no reason why he should be – then I think you should listen to him. He will be waiting in the parlour already, I imagine, for he was to follow me down from the Top House in half an hour, and I told him to walk straight in. Verity – your grandfather is thinking of his own interests, not yours – we both know that. But in this case I think your interests may be one and the same. And now that he has found a way out of the snare Fate set for him he will not allow himself to be thwarted by you. He would make your life unbearable, child, for he is a vindictive man, and I don't know who would protect you, since I cannot.'

I got up slowly, feeling light and easy as if I had floated somewhere just a little away from my own body: a spectator, listening as my mother persuaded some other daughter – not me at all – into marriage with a cousin and a stranger.

'Did you really love my father?' I asked, surprising myself. And not expecting an answer, I was even more surprised when she said quietly, 'I told you, there was always affection between us – love, if you like – but in our case it was not enough. We loved without liking, without really approving of each other – or it may be that because we were in love we expected too much of marriage. Yes, you would be astonished, Verity, if you knew how madly I loved your father once, when I was young – an experience I would certainly never wish to endure again. Verity dear, I am not at all sure that love is even a good thing. Friendship – light, warm friendship – yes, that, I think, must be delightful between a man and a woman. But to love with passion can be most painful, and it may not suit your nature any more than it suited mine. Dearest – will you go now and talk to your cousin?'

And knowing that neither she nor my grandfather, nor Joel himself, had for one moment expected me to refuse, I nodded my head.

'Thank you,' she said, and when I looked up in amazement, she smiled.

'Yes, Verity, thank you – for being reasonable, for doing what your grandfather and I both believe, for different reasons, to be the right thing. Thank you for making it easy for us, I suppose. Well then, go quickly, for your grandfather is impatient to have things settled, and I see no point in delay. Joel is precisely aware of your position and his own, so there will be no awkwardness – but, just the same, darling, extract a proper proposal from him. Make sure he asks you very nicely, for, considering all you are bringing him, I feel you are entitled to that.'

He was waiting in the parlour – Joel, a man I had known all my life but did not know at all because he had never noticed me – and now, through the sea mist in my brain, I was curious to discover how he would master the situation, how he could possibly speak of marriage to me without appearing pompous or ridiculous or quite simply greedy.

But as my mother had said, he was not without experience, and coming towards me, he said quickly, 'Your mother has spoken to you, then?'

'Yes.'

'She has explained – everything – fully?'

'She has.'

'And what have you to say to me?'

'I thought you had something to say to me?'

'Ah yes,' he said, his mouth lifting at the corners with a wry amusement, a consciousness of his own false position that I perfectly understood. 'You're going to put me through it, are you?' that smile said. 'Going to get your money's worth? Well, and why not? I don't blame you. In your place I'd very likely do the same.'

For a moment, I was tempted to follow my mother's advice, to be coy and capricious, as any girl, surely, at such a moment has a right to be; tempted to force him to some explanation of his motives and to ask him how it was that he could so easily give up Miss Rosamund Boulton. I wanted to see, I think, just how far he would go; if, at the fear of a refusal, he would spin some wild yarn of an affection for me he had felt obliged to conceal, or if, letting his reckless, insolent grin flash out, he would confess himself eager merely for my inheritance and dare me to complain.

But finally, the idea of making him play the lover seemed too grotesque, too dangerous, since it would surely annoy him, and later, when he was my husband and in total control of my life, he would not remember it kindly. And so, setting the pattern of our future lives together, choosing the way not of submission but of common sense – having long known the peril of asking for more than could be easily given – I offered him my polite smile of everyday and said, 'Shall we walk up to see my grandfather, since he is expecting us?'

'Is that your answer to me?'

'Why, yes – at least ... Yes, that's my answer.'

'Good,' he said, his eyes narrowing, the brain behind them busy with his shrewd calculations. 'Excellent.'

Then, almost boyish with relief, more nervous, it seemed, than I, occupied with my own nerves, had supposed, he added quickly, chuckling through the words, 'You don't want me to go down on my knees, then, hand on heart?'

'No, I surely don't.'

'Thank you,' he said, laughing no longer. 'Really, Verity, thank you, for being so reasonable. Your grandfather said you'd be a good girl, but then, old men don't understand these things. And I wasn't sure. You'll be all right with me, you know. I reckon you could have just about anybody, the way things have turned out, but I can look after your affairs better than Bradley Hobhouse, and although Matthew Oldroyd knows what he's doing, he's a shade too careful of his coppers and it's not what you've been used to.'

As I smiled again, polite and friendly – a reasonable girl who understood how these things were done – he put in, perhaps without meaning to say it, 'And, Verity, you are – pretty, you know, really very nice.'

My grandfather was waiting, not for an answer, since there had been no question in his mind, and seeing him in his doorway, tenacious and eternal as a thirsty old tree, his roots deep in the hillside, I knew how impossible it would have been to disobey. Not even my father had been able to do that, not even Edwin, and as I submitted to his sharp-cornered, dusty embrace, I knew that at least he was offering me an established place in the only world I knew. And the night following my father's death, when I had determined to stand on my own feet, seemed very far away.

'Capital,' my grandfather said, twisting my ear with the rough affection best bestowed on a dog. 'You'll make a good little wife if you put your mind to it, and Mrs Stevens will tell you how to go on if your mother can't explain aright. Capital. They thought I was beaten – I could see them yesterday, wondering how much I'd take for the mill, telling themselves they'd bide their time until the business was run down and I was desperate. Aye, let them wait. Let them wait forever.'

Later, when Joel had gone away – having explanations to make, I supposed, to his sisters and to Miss Boulton – my grandfather, full of claret and self-satisfaction, winked his shrewd, sharp eye at me and said, 'Don't worry, lass. I've taken his measure, and he'll treat you right. He knows which side his bread's buttered, yon lad. And he's a hungry man. I never liked him, I admit it. While Edwin lived I kept my eye on him, to make sure he never got in Edwin's way. But that's all changed now. I've told him, if he frames himself, if he shows me he can handle the business, then it's his – or yours, which amounts to the same thing. And if he can't, then I'll sell it over his head. That's what I told him, and it won't harm him to believe it. But it won't come to that because he wants it too bad, he's too hungry for it, and by God, I'll make him earn it before he's through.'

And chuckling, wheezing slightly with his wicked glee, he clasped me in another acrid, uncomfortable embrace and sent me back down the hill a bride.

6

In matters of religion my cousin Hannah's interests tended towards the organization of parish affairs rather than anything of a mystical or emotional nature. She was, of course, a Dissenter, as we all were, since no Law Valley manufacturer worth his salt would join the common herd on the hard back benches of the Established Church while the squire and his lady sat in well-upholstered state in front. No Hobhouse, no Oldroyd – certainly no Barforth – would listen meekly to the parson whose job it was to preach obedience to the squire, contentment with one's humble lot, and to warn against the mortal sin of nurturing ideas above one's station. Such things would do well enough for farm labourers, tied to their cottages and to the squire's whim, but some of these energetic West Riding clothiers had, in their youth, heard the Wesley brothers preaching at the pithead, in the foundry yard, on the edge of a ploughed field, anywhere a congregation could be brought together, and had taken more comfort there than among the squire's aristocratic splendours. Although the first plain chapels such men had built were becoming more elaborate now that money was in good supply and there was an undoubted tendency for the manufacturers themselves to sit in front, their operatives crowding behind, at least the sermon was about industry and thrift, the virtue of not being late for work in the morning – the virtue, in fact, of work for its own sake – and the Hobhouses and the Barforths were well pleased.

Hannah, too, believed in all these things, was always industrious, had no choice but to be thrifty, and, preferring good deeds to good intentions, had deeply involved herself in the Sunday School movement, the movement for the abolition of the slave trade in our colonies, missionary societies and Bible societies, the tedious visiting of deaf old ladies and the sick. She was also far too convinced a Christian to grudge her brother the good fortune which should have been hers and, whatever her private torment, had congratulated me on my engagement with immense composure – had ventured, even, to express her pleasure that we would, after all, be sisters. But on one point she was adamant. Due to my recent loss the wedding must be delayed at least a twelvemonth, and from this view she would not budge.

The rules of conduct, she argued – the rules of decency – were perfectly clear. One remained in mourning and, as far as possible, in seclusion, three months for a brother or sister, six months for a mother or father, a full year for a husband or wife. And since I had lost a father and a brother, in such shocking circumstances, she felt the customary six months should be doubled to twelve, and that no bridal arrangements could be made until then.

'Certainly I mean to observe the full twelvemonth,' she informed me tartly, considering herself, in her heart, I think, to be a widow.

But my grandfather, a man of an older, bawdier generation, held firmly that once one had put a man under the earth with the best headstone one could afford above him, the rest was nonsense. No amount of black armbands and crepe veiling would bring Edwin back, and, ignoring Hannah – disliking her now quite openly and unjustly because she reminded him too sharply of his loss – he stipulated that I should be married as soon as my mother could have me ready.

'Three months at the most,' he said, calculating that at that rate he could have his great-grandson in the spring of the new year.

And so, as May and June dissolved in the blue sun-flecked air of high summer, I spent my days walking the moorland paths above Lawcroft Fold with my brother's old yellow bitch and my own gangling puppy, careless of Hannah's newfangled notion that it was improper for a young lady to walk out alone. And when it rained, I sat on the hearthrug, dreaming into the empty grate or watching as my mother's pale, narrow hands transformed lengths of batiste and muslin and cambric into the intricately tucked and pleated nightgowns, the frilled and embroidered petticoats I would need for my marriage.

62

There were trips to Cullingford, too, where feathers and fringing and lace could be obtained, packages to be collected at the Old Swan yard, where the coaches from Leeds and Manchester swept in and out several exciting times a day. Every afternoon, there was a sewing woman, come all the way from Cullingford Green, to stitch me into the crepe de chines and gauzes, the taffetas and the brocades that would equip me to be a wife. There were vast discussions about the width of a skirt, the number of flounces to be added to its hem, intense consultations over the merits of cashmere and silk crepe shawls, the right shade of blue for a hooded velvet evening cloak, the amount of ribbon and lace that would make a bonnet dashing without being ostentatious, whether gigot sleeves were still in or had gone, sadly, out, so that the marriage seemed to be far more concerned with fabric and design than with Joel.

Indeed, I saw little of him, for it was more to his advantage to woo my grandfather, who had the power to call the wedding off, than the young bride, who had not, and his visits to me, made either on his way to the Top House or back from there, were brief, his mind too full of warp and weft, profits and percentages, for romance.

'Only think of it – getting married to old Joel,' Elinor said with sisterly irreverence. 'Only think of that.'

But thinking of it was precisely what I could not do, and it seemed best to take each day as it came, allowing myself to be manipulated this way and that by the sewing woman, allowing Elinor to root through my cupboards and submitting to her judgement when she told me, 'You can't possibly want this yellow muslin now, Verity; it's not at all the thing for a married lady, so I'd best take it off your hands. Oh – and you have the slippers to match, don't you, and the little bonnet with the pansies on the brim. I'd best take them, too.'

We could not, of course, be married in my grandfather's chapel, the Dissenting clergy not then being empowered to conduct the ceremony of marriage, and so we went to the ancient, smoke-grey parish church, erected by some distant four-hundred-year-old ancestor of Sir Giles Flood, lord of the manor of Cullingford. It stood at the top of the steep cobbled street called Kirkgate, dominating the town, its steeple – which once, in Oliver Cromwell's day, had been hung with wool packs to protect it from Royalist cannon – standing graceful and beautiful against the skyline, a swan among a duck pond of factory chimney stacks. And I was driven there on a hot August morning, in an open carriage, wrapped in my bridal veils, my grandfather sitting in grim self-satisfaction at my side.

My mother had kissed me that morning, a cool butterfly's wing against my cheek, one of the ingredients of that kiss certainly being goodbye.

'You will be glad to know that my own plans are very nearly complete,' she had told me almost a week before, as she sat at her sewing. 'Squire Dalby has offered me a cottage on his estate at a most moderate rent. A charming little house with a walled garden, just one room and a dining parlour with two bedrooms over and two attic rooms over that – ample for me to manage with a man and a maid. No horses, of course, and no accommodation for them, but it is very near the village and people are very kind. I expect you would lend me yours, at need, and Squire Dalby has kindly promised his gig, although naturally one does not wish to presume or to create too much obligation. Yes, dear, I think it will suit me very well – and it will suit your husband too, I make no doubt, for no man can really relish the idea of setting up house with his wife's mother.'

And so I understood that when I returned to the millhouse as Joel's wife, I would be alone.

I wore a white dress with a high, ruffled collar, a bell-shaped skirt ending in twelve rows of deep, lace-edged frills, swansdown and orange blossom and white satin roses to hold my veils, high-heeled slippers that raised me to the middle of Joel's ear – and the middle of my grandfather's ear too, which surprised me since I had always thought him such a giant of a man.

'You look well, lass – very well,' he said as we paused in the church porch; grudgingly, I thought, since I may have looked too much like my mother. And then, with his hard hand firmly on mine, he marched me down the aisle, darting glances of triumphant venom at the Aycliffes and the Oldroyds and the Hobhouses there assembled, their heads uncovered, their backs stiff with disapproval since there was not an Anglican among them, and, in any case, this wedding was all too sudden, would have given rise to some unkind speculation and a discreet scrutiny of my figure had not my grandfather's intentions been so well known.

Not even my grandfather had expected Hannah to walk behind me with flowers in her hands and a smile painted on her aching lips, but Elinor was part of my bridal procession, startlingly fair in pale blue gauze, as unlike her brother in appearance as it was possible to be, although they were like enough in vanity and self-seeking.

I suppose I was pretty too that day, as all brides seem to be, for there was a hush as I entered the church, and then a murmur: a tribute, perhaps, to the frailty of young girls who are brought to the altar by hoary old men and handed over to strangers.

And then there was Joel, waiting at the altar, as beautiful in his way as Elinor, with a white rose on the lapel of his dove-grey jacket, a white brocade waistcoat, a drift of white sea foam for a cravat, his black hair vigorously curling, one brown hand taking mine instantly as my grandfather released it, his grip smoother, perhaps, but just as firm.

I had not often heard the wedding service before, being the first of my generation to marry, but as with so many of life's rituals, I had not really pondered its meaning, and, in my case, many of the words did not apply. I could obey Joel, certainly; in fact, I would be well advised to do so, but I wasn't sure just what was meant by honouring him, and as for love, perhaps it was not essential; he had not asked me for it in any case. Yet I made my vows easily enough and, as I did so – as I became his wife – my property and my expectations passed from me into his charge, so that when his turn came to make the promise 'With all my worldly goods I thee endow,' he was already in possession of the wherewithal to keep it.

I had entered the church door an heiress who, had I been of full age, would have been able to dispose of my fortune at will, to sign contracts, to enter into agreements, but from the moment our vows were spoken, everything I had or earned or came to inherit belonged automatically to him; and he was not even called upon to guarantee that he would be kind.

He could leave me, if he chose, without in any way forfeiting the use of my money. But I, unless I gained his consent, could never live apart from him. He could take my goods and chattels and sell them without my consent; he could clothe his mistress – if he had one – in my silks and satins, give her my jewels. He could remove my children from my care whenever it suited him; in fact, he could do anything he pleased with my property and my person, since now, as a married woman, I had no legal identity of my own. And if, occasionally, there were a duchess or some other powerful lady who sought a divorce, a special Act of Parliament was first required, and I could not imagine His Majesty's government concerning itself with the wrongs of a Mrs Joel Barforth of Lawcroft Fold.

My marriage, like every other marriage I had ever heard of, would be for life, and if the law now chose to ignore me, at least I knew my grandfather would not. And I smiled very pleasantly as I walked back up the aisle, particularly at Emma-Jane Rawnsley, the banker's daughter, and Lucy Hobhouse of Nethercoats Mill, both of whom had sworn to be married not only before me but before one another as well.

Due to our recent tragedy there was no elaborate reception, no need to hire the Market Hall in Cullingford as we would have done in happier times – just a wedding breakfast prettily served by Mrs Stevens, with a lace-covered table festooned with flowers, cake and champagne and colourful, frothy confections that left no memory on my tongue. There was my mother, her mourning dress set aside for the day, wearing pale lilac, her mind apparently elsewhere as Mrs Hobhouse of Nethercoats and Mrs Oldroyd of Fieldhead tried hard to discover on what terms she really stood with her new landlord, the squire. There was my grandfather, planted foursquare at the head of the table, his eyes gloating, gleaming, as they rested on Mr Aycliffe the builder, who was still wondering about the contract for the new mill, or on Mr Hobhouse, his chief rival, who had hoped, no doubt, to get me for his son Bradley and to see Barforth looms making money for Nethercoats.

There was Bradley Hobhouse himself, a young man I had known all my life, making eyes at my cousin Elinor, ignoring his mother's determined efforts to push him towards Emma-Jane, the banker's daughter, plumper than Elinor but considerably richer. And there was Hannah, with a mourning brooch made of my brother's hair set in gold at the neck of her dress, her face pinched as if by cold, smiling as if her mouth hurt her; Hannah speaking sharply to Elinor for flirting with the Hobhouse boy, and then disappearing altogether, to be discovered by Mrs Stevens, as I heard later, on the attic landing crying her bitter tears.

Finally, after a bee swarm of good wishes and some heavy-handed teasing, when my stomach was a little queasy from Mrs Stevens's

65

subtleties and too much champagne, it was evening and I was left alone to contemplate the harsh reality of getting into bed with my cousin Joel.

Since the mill had a prior claim on his time, there was to be no wedding journey. We were to have the Top House for a day or two while my grandfather and Mrs Stevens paid a visit to Leeds; and my grandfather's ornate bed, with its ocean of pillows and bolsters, its heavy fringed canopy, and the gross, unbidden whispering in my head of what he and Mrs Stevens did there, were enough to unnerve me.

'Don't think about it, dear,' my mother had murmured on leaving, having taken an unusual amount of champagne herself. 'It's not as if there was anything you had to do – any skill that you might lack. Not a bit of it. He will know what he's about, and at the very most you have only to follow his lead. And these tales one hears – you know, of brides who go mad with shock or have their hair turned white – well, darling, one never actually meets anyone to whom that happened, so I rather think we may discount it altogether. Naturally you may show surprise, because it is all rather surprising at first, I must confess – but not terrible, not fatal. I speak lightly, Verity my dear, because I find it the best way. My own mother told it to me quite differently, for she had a finely developed sense of the dramatic, and I found it no help at all. Take things lightly, Verity, as I try to do. I think you will find that whatever happens – however badly one is made to feel – the very best defence is to seem not to care.'

Although I understood her meaning, for there was enough of her in me for that, the long wait my husband imposed upon me, leaving me sitting bolt upright in that giant, alien bed while he smoked a cigar and then another, surely, in the room below, added nothing to my composure. The suspense, I thought, would be far more likely to drive me mad than the other – a matter I understood mainly from a few farmyard observations and which I thus expected to last no more than a moment – and when at last I heard Joel's step on the stair and he came into the room, alien himself in his richly patterned dressing gown, his face very dark in the candle flame, I felt more relief than alarm – pleasure, even, at the thought that soon now I would be allowed to go to sleep.

I expected, I think, an immediate assault in the dark, but, leaving the candles burning, he sat down on the edge of the bed, ready, it seemed, at this unlikely moment, for conversation.

'Well then,' he said, a smile just lifting the corners of his mouth, 'so it's done –'

And because he was my wicked, grown-up cousin, experienced in the ways of the world, it did not occur to me that, sitting there in my best embroidered nightgown with my hair hanging loose again in little-girl fashion as he used to see it, I seemed so familiar to him, so very nearly a sister, that he was nervous, too.

'Yes,' he said, his smile flashing out suddenly, its wry humour directed, I suppose, at us both. 'So here we are – and you must be quite terrified, I suppose.'

'No, I'm not.'

'Oh, my word – are you not? Or do you simply mean to be brave, grit your teeth and endure all the amazing things I shall do to you – for I suppose they will amaze you. You can't have the slightest notion –'

'Yes I do,' I answered stoutly, stung by his condescension; unaware in my total ignorance of physical desire, that the prospect of doing those things with me – his little, sad-eyed cousin – was proving far more difficult than he bargained for.

'Oh no you don't, I'd put money on it, for your mother will have told you nothing – not dear Aunt Isabella. One wonders if she even knows herself.'

And although I could vouch for that, not really being too certain of what he meant, I insisted tartly, 'I'm not such a goose. I'm not blind either, and Edwin said things sometimes – to the stableboys when he forgot I was by.'

'Ah well, in that case, if Edwin said things, what can I possibly tell you?'

And, remembering against my will his eyes watching Edwin die and knowing I must not, at any cost, remember it – never – that it was absolutely essential for me to obliterate it totally, at once, I said quickly, to cover the forbidden images with words, 'I know Edwin had a child, two or three years ago, from a farm girl, and I know how much my father had to pay.'

But my sole example of worldliness did not impress him.

'Oh, so you know that, do you,' he said coolly. 'Well, I reckon my sister Hannah knows it too, although she'd die before admitting it. Just think, Verity, if that child had been a boy instead of a sickly girl, you might not be here tonight. Your grandfather might well have decided to adopt Edwin's child – whether his farm-girl mother had liked it or not – and then you'd have been left in peace. Only think of that. I wonder if it's what they mean by destiny?'

'Oh – I don't know anything about that. And anyway, what does it matter? I am here, aren't I?'

'Now I'm not denying that,' he said. 'Not for one moment.' And getting up, he walked to the window, looked out, came back to my bedside, and, putting the tips of his fingers experimentally on my shoulder, ran them down my arm and back again to my neck, tracing the outline of my ear, concentrating perhaps so hard on his own reaction that he missed the rigidity of my body, the flush of embarrassment staining every part of me.

'You really are very pretty, you know,' he said musingly. 'Listen – I won't pretend I've looked at you too closely in the past, because – well, you were always forbidden fruit where I was concerned. If I'd come near you before, they'd have chased me off mighty quick and that would have ruined Hannah's chances. So I didn't look, and you're not a flirt to put yourself in a man's way; just a quiet smile, a "Good evening, cousin Joel" – a deep one, like your mother, I've heard tell, and that doesn't displease me. Your grandfather may not think much of your mother, but she's got style, Verity, a fine, high-stepping style – Dalby's noticed it all right – and I can see you'll be the same. Never flustered, never at a loss for words, but always soft-spoken. You'll make an elegant woman, Verity; the kind other men will look at and say, "By God, he must be doing well to afford her." And I like that.'

And his voice trailing away, his hand clenched itself in a movement of impatience and then went quite roughly into my hair.

'I should wait,' he said. 'I should be patient and give you time. I know it, and I know I won't do it. Verity, I can't tell how innocent you are, or how sly – because my sister Elinor has never been so dainty as she looks – but one thing you can't know about and that's need. How could you? It's not a feminine thing, need. It's a man's demon and it's been biting me too long now. Listen, Verity, they'll have told you certain things about me, or you'll have heard them talking – I've had my wild times, I admit it, but they ended – because my father was wild too – and I've been obliged to deny myself pleasures to which I'd grown accustomed. I'm not making a confession, because I'm not ashamed – oh, damnation take it, how am I to make myself clear without putting you to fright. Have you any idea at all of what I mean?'

'Oh yes – yes,' I told him, anxious now to have it over and done with.

But he shook his head, knowing quite well, I suppose, that Verity Barforth, at sixteen, whose experience of the world stopped short at the limits of the Law Valley, had small chance of understanding the split in his nature between the part of him that found it well-nigh incestuous to desire her and the part of him that was ready, most ardently, to desire any woman.

'I don't believe you,' he said. 'But let's see – let's just see what progress we can make from here.'

To begin with, as my mother had said, although his stroking hands on my arms and shoulders were strange to me and his tongue, parting my lips, took me by surprise since I hadn't realized a kiss was quite like that, it was not pleasant perhaps but not terrible. Something, I thought, to which I could grow accustomed. 'Not really alarming at all, until I realized he had shrugged himself out of his dressing gown and was naked. And the shock of being clasped in that nude embrace released a flood of images in my mind – of my grandfather's weathered, old man's body in this very bed with Mrs Stevens, panting and grunting as Joel was beginning to do – images that flicked my already uneasy stomach to nausea.

'Take off that nightgown,' he muttered.

When I began to protest and ask him how he dared, he almost snarled, 'Take it off. It makes you look like a child, or a damn nun waiting to be crucified. Take it off.'

'Then put out the candles.'

'Not I. I'm no peasant to make love in the dark.'

'Good heavens – you mean to look at me?'

'Aye. And if you want to spare yourself the sight of me you'd best close your eyes.'

And so, my eyes tight shut, I pulled my mother's finely stitched cambric over my head and delivered myself up like a sacrifice, my head swimming again with the obscene posturing of my grandfather, revolted beyond any appreciation of Joel's skill or the realization that, while not for one moment forgetting his own pleasure, he made a decent effort not to hurt me.

But he would have done better perhaps, that first time, had he been less skilful, had he simply taken me without expertise, merely with a little kindness, instead of giving way to his rich enjoyment of the female body, his determination that every one of his senses should be satisfied, that every part of him should be replete – not only hands, mouth, and loins but eyes and nostrils, and the mischievous curiosity that led his tongue to explore the whole surface of my skin, the curves and crevices at which I rarely looked myself.

And so the act I had believed would be so quickly over prolonged itself, rising in intensity as his teeth possessed themselves of the lobes of my ears, the point of my shoulders, and my breasts, not painfully but compellingly, so that I knew I was being devoured, that he was taking me slowly, inch by inch, inside himself, and that I would never be whole again. And because no one had ever spoken to me of pleasure, because I had learned that this whole process was designed to give men satisfaction and to make women pregnant – and my grandfather certainly required me to be pregnant – I grew more bewildered with every caress.

I had been ready for discomfort and embarrassment. Nothing had prepared me for Joel's lingering enjoyment. In my total ignorance of sensuality, I became so desperate for a conclusion that the final pain of penetration was not unwelcome, since that much at least I understood, and even Joel's body nailed shuddering to mine, his long, inexplicable groaning, were not so much a shock as a promise of release.

'Don't fret,' he told me when it was over, turning away from me and breathing hard. 'Women aren't supposed to like it – ladies, that is, at any rate. And if a woman don't care for it with her husband she's not likely to look elsewhere when he goes off to Norfolk for the wool clip. So don't fret, Verity.'

Yet even I, through the fear and ignorance that had been the breeding ground of my disgust, even I could tell that although his agile brain had accepted the shortcomings of our situation, his restless, experienced body had not been satisfied.

7

Those first months of marriage were awkward but polite, dominated completely by my grandfather, who, sitting on the hillside above us – baleful, all-powerful – had every intention of making Joel earn his keep.

He was in the mill yard every morning at five o'clock, watch in hand, eyes peeled for latecomers – as my father, but not always Edwin, had done – since time is money, and no one should be allowed to waste anything that belonged to a Barforth. He spent his days in the sheds, constantly answering my grandfather's summonses to the Top House to explain himself, and his evenings, more often than not, in the countinghouse, checking through old accounts, poring over old ledgers, building up a meticulous picture of Samson Barforth's commercial past and what he, Joel Barforth, could make of the future. And from the very first their ideas on that future were in conflict.

My grandfather, in fact, did not require ideas from Joel. He wanted, quite simply, a caretaker for the next generation, someone to hand over the business intact to a new Edwin, as he had planned to give it to the old; he had no desire, now, for change. And, indeed, since the attack on our mill interest in power looms had declined generally in the Law Valley, not from intimidation but from what was seen as sound common sense.

'I see no reason for it,' Mr Hobhouse of Nethercoats had announced. 'The most I ever pay a hand weaver these days is seven shillings and seven pence a week, and when I can get my job done as cheap as that, what do I gain with expensive new machines – paying these fancy engineering fellows to look after them when they break down, and having to reinforce my sheds to take the weight and the vibration – that's all I get – that and the risk of getting shot at one night on my way home. There'd have to be money in it, lads, a deal of money, afore I'd risk that.'

And although my grandfather could see the possibilities of power weaving as clearly as Joel – or as clearly as Mr Oldroyd of Fieldhead, whose spinning machines could produce more yarn than the handlooms could accommodate – he was determined now, it seemed, that everything at Lawcroft should remain as it was, a monument to Edwin Barforth's memory rather than a steppingstone to Joel Barforth's greater glory.

On his return from Leeds, after our wedding, he had immediately required Mr Aycliffe the builder to attend him at the Top House and, without Joel's knowledge, had cancelled all arrangements for the construction of a new mill.

'No use for a new mill when there's nothing to put in it,' he'd said to Joel, 'for I've cancelled the new looms, while I was at it. I reckon you've got enough to be going on with, my lad. More than you ever dreamed you'd get your hands on, I'll be bound. So let's see how you tackle it – let's see you keep it turned over, nice and steady – the way my son William used to do.'

But if my father had been content with the position of workhorse, scapegoat, Joel was not. As the near-bankrupt owner of Low Cross he had been obliged to struggle from one day to the next, delighted merely if he could meet his commitments; but now that he was acutely aware of the changes in the world outside the Law Valley, of so many new inventions and hitherto unheard-of opportunities, my grandfather held the purse strings and had the power, at any time, to sell the mill or simply close it down, those limits could not be passed, and Joel, with a venomous fury lurking behind his eyes, was obliged to smile, to persuade – to beg, even – when it would have suited him far better to fly at my grandfather's throat.

Our area was famous for the manufacture of calamancoes and shalloons, heavy worsted cloth that, with care, could last a lifetime.

'A Barforth calamanco,' my grandfather was fond of saying, 'can last a woman all her married life and still have enough wear in it to serve her daughter when she's gone.'

And when Joel remarked that although this may have been all very well in the old days, perhaps the younger generation of women would not wish to wear the same garment so long, my grandfather was not merely scornful but very much annoyed.

'You'd cut the quality then, would you, lad,' he snorted, 'to make a quick penny? Aye, and that's your father coming out in you, fast and flashy – turn anything off his looms, your father would, if he thought he could sell it. But I notice his customers never came back twice.'

'There's no question of that, sir,' Joel said, keeping his temper, although I felt the snap of it. 'It's a question of supplying what's needed, and in these days, when there's more cash in hand for luxuries, when people get about more and new fashions are coming over all the time from France, it strikes me that women aren't looking for something they can keep a generation. And where's the sense in producing plain, hard-wearing cloth you can't sell? Lightweights are going to pay better, sir, in the future; I'm convinced of it. Fancy lightweights – power-woven.'

'Aye,' my grandfather snarled. 'Fancy lightweights for fancy ladies. You'd know all about that, I reckon – millmaster – like your father before you.'

And I knew – Joel knew – that had Edwin put forward this idea it would have been hailed as a flash of brilliance: 'Damn me, but the Boy knows what he's about,' instead of 'Keep your fancy ideas to yourself, millmaster, or bear in mind what they did to your father.'

Yet Joel, quietly, with the assistance of Ira Agbrigg, the weaver who had brought us news of the riot, began experimenting with lightweight worsteds at his own mill, Low Cross, a matter which, when it came to my grandfather's attention, provoked the most serious argument they had yet had.

In the first place the employment of Ira Agbrigg did not please him.

'Damn the Judas,' he had said, having spotted him in the crowd at Edwin's funeral. 'Give the fellow a guinea and send him on his way.'

And the fact that Joel had not obeyed but had made use of him – and illicit use at that – would have been enough to raise a storm.

But Low Cross itself was really the heart of the matter, for my grandfather could tolerate no division of loyalties and grudged every second of Joel's time that was not spent at Lawcroft Fold.

'You'll get rid of it,' my grandfather ordered. 'Get rid of it. I told you before you were married that I'd carry no deadwood. Sell it if you can, knock it down if you can't, and I'll have no more tales about buyers who don't come up to scratch. I've never seen any of those buyers of yours – don't believe in these buyers. Well, you can save yourself the trouble of inventing another, for I'll find a buyer myself.'

71

'I must ask you not to do that, sir.'

'What!' my grandfather yelled, stung by the quiet insolence of Joel's manner. 'Ask me? Tell me, more like, and I'll take no orders from you. I'll have that muckheap sold up, lock, stock, and barrel, this time next month, if it's the last thing –'

'Hardly without my consent, sir.'

And seeing the veins swell on my grandfather's forehead, seeing his purple mottled colour, I cringed, looked away, and held my breath.

'So that's it,' he whispered. 'Your consent. And what have *you* to say to anything? You'll consent whenever it suits me, you young scoundrel, and be glad to do it – and if you don't it's not only Low Cross I'll put under the hammer.'

But even the ultimate – the everyday threat – could not deter Joel on this occasion.

'Low Cross is my sisters' home, sir. And the sale of it, as it is now, will hardly provide them with another.'

'Aye, your sisters – and what do you care about your sisters? It's your looms and your damned fancy worsteds you're thinking of, my lad; sneaking there and wasting time with that Judas – time that belongs to me, time I bought and paid for, like I bought and paid for you –'

'Very likely, sir – but, nevertheless, my sisters do live in the millhouse.'

'Then get them married,' my grandfather snarled, altogether beside himself, knowing, I suppose, that he could not really deprive Edwin's intended bride of a home and he had no intention of offering her any alternative. 'Get them established – get rid of them – tell them to look lively and take themselves off to the marriage market. And when they've gone, Low Cross goes with them.'

And so Low Cross was given its reprieve, and Ira Agbrigg with it, my grandfather having forgotten him, it seemed, in his rage against Joel, but there were to be no power looms, no fancy lightweight worsteds, no changes.

'Your time belongs to me, lad,' my grandfather reminded him grimly, frequently, and even on Sundays, when the mills were quiet, he watched Joel carefully, chuckling, I think, when he saw him go down to the empty sheds rearranging them in his mind, taking possession, making complex calculations to suit the day when his time would be his own again.

I existed between them, hardly noticeable in the glare of their mutual hostility, sole mistress now – since my mother's departure for Squire Dalby's hamlet of Patterswick – of Lawcroft millhouse, the place where I had been born, expected, suddenly, to answer Marth-Ellen's questions about the pickling and the preserving, the contents of larders and closets, expected to know what my cousin Joel might wish to find on his plate at dinnertime.

To begin with, there were often dramas, for, unlike my father and brother, who required food simply to be hot and plentiful, Joel had a complicated appetite, a carry-over from his wild days, when he had tasted – in Manchester, I suppose – the new style of cooking from

France, brought over by the refugees from Napoleon's wars. And although Hannah had certainly never provided such delicacies – believing that the sense of taste, along with all the other senses, was better suppressed than encouraged – his new responsibilities had increased his expectations, and he openly found Marth-Ellen's plain roast meats and batter puddings dull.

There were dramas, too, about the polishing of his boots and the laundering of his linen, for Marth-Ellen had a heavy hand with a goffering iron, and his shirt frills were rarely to his liking.

'Hannah did them for him when he was at home,' Elinor confided. 'For mercy's sake, don't let her know I told you, for it was always a great secret, but our poor old Bertha could never do anything right for him, and we couldn't afford anyone else, so Hannah did all the goffering and the dainty work. Poor Hannah, standing for hours in the kitchen, all hot and flushed and her hair coming down – no wonder she was ashamed of it. So come on, then, Verity, I know you're a married lady now and I'm just a silly chit from the schoolroom, but you are going to tell me things, aren't you? I'm absolutely relying on you, for Hannah won't say a word – although now I come to think of it she may not be too sure about it, either. So do tell, Verity – there's really no one else. And – while we're on the subject – whatever happened to Rosamund Boulton?'

I had, of course, nothing to say on the subject of Miss Boulton, since no one – least of all Joel – had thought fit to inform me of her reaction to his marriage. If she had loved him, then no doubt she had cried; if not, then by now she was probably already in careful pursuit of another lover – in either case, there was nothing I could reasonably do about it.

But Joel's domestic grievances were another matter, and although I was still awkward and uncertain in his nightly embraces, I found no difficulty in slipping into Marth-Ellen's kitchen to whip him up a syllabub liberally laced with brandy, according to Mrs Stevens's famous recipe, nor hardship in taking a leaf from Hannah's book and using my own agile wrist and patient disposition to manipulate the goffering iron. And gradually I began to discover not only how to cope but even, sometimes, to get my way.

I was surrounded by natures far more aggressive and urgent than mine, gigantic tempers which flared and fumed and threatened, against which my own protests could not be heard. And so, when my grandfather bellowed, 'Get rid of that damn dog of Edwin's, it ain't healthy and it's got fleas,' or when Hannah, grimacing over a slice of Marth-Ellen's gingerbread, informed me, 'Do you not think, Verity, that this house is getting too much for a woman of Marth-Ellen's age? In your place I would send her to Patterswick, to your mother, and hire myself a pair of clean young girls,' I made no attempt to defend either my dog or my maid.

'Why, yes,' I said smiling, allowing no opportunity for argument. 'Yes, I'll do that – presently.' And I did nothing.

I found, too, that such things as badly polished boots could easily be remedied – that housekeeping, in fact, was not the mystery Mrs Stevens

73

chose to make it – and since I became almost immediately and most obligingly pregnant, no one, so far as I knew, had any cause to complain. I did not ask myself if I wanted a child, since that had been the sole purpose of my marriage, nor did I expect any great show of delight from Joel, who wanted Lawcroft for himself and not for a son who, in this early life at least, would be monopolized – and spoiled – by my grandfather. But the Top House greeted the news with predictable joy, Mrs Stevens floating down the hill at once to make my grandfather's requirements known. I must sit with my feet on a stool, must take large, nourishing meals to build his great-grandson's bone and fibre, must walk no farther than the garden gate. And here, once again, I scored a small triumph.

'Do you know, Mrs Stevens, I think you had best go back and tell him that it would not be wise to coop me up like that for the next six months or so. Tell him I am the type to go into a decline unless I have my day's supply of fresh air, and what would happen to his great-grandson then? Tell him you can read all the signs, and he will believe you.'

'Why, Mrs Barforth,' she said, 'how sly –'

But my grandfather had been out of sorts lately, and, always anxious for her own future when his began to seem uncertain, she did my bidding, ensuring that I was allowed to take my carriage exercise with my cousin Elinor, the only other person I knew with time to spare.

Elinor, of course, was waiting, too; she had been waiting six out of her sixteen years for the man who would become her husband, and although her early dreams of some young landed gentleman had been modified to close consideration of the Hobhouses and the Oldroyds, she was determined, at all costs, not to be left on the shelf.

Certainly, her situation, in the upheaval that had swept over us all, had not changed for the better. If Hannah had married my brother, Elinor's position, alone with Joel and possibly Miss Boulton, would have been difficult but only temporary, for Hannah would have moved heaven and earth, and my brother Edwin with it, until a suitable match for her sister had been found. Edwin, with his liberal allowance, could have added something to Elinor's portion; enough, at any rate, to make her interesting – not, perhaps, to a Hobhouse, but to some small tradesman who would know the value of the Barforth name. But my grandfather, deeply suspicious of Joel, put very little ready money his way, while Hannah had not only lost her taste for weddings but, whether she realized it or not, was in no hurry now to part with her sister and face life alone.

Not that anyone had asked her to do so. At my wedding Elinor had experienced no difficulty in attracting the notice of the square-cut, bull-necked Hobhouse boy, nor in having her thigh surreptitiously stroked by the portly, pious Mr Oldroyd, whose ailing wife had not yet obliged him by falling sick enough to die. But when that lady finally did succumb to one of her many maladies, her husband would remarry carefully, to his profit. And when it was time for the Hobhouse boy to take a wife, it would be Emma-Jane Rawnsley, the banker's daughter, or plain Amelia Oldroyd of Fieldhead, his mother invited to tea, not Elinor.

'There has to be somebody,' she told me. 'Somebody will see me, somewhere, and realize he absolutely can't live – yes, yes, I've been reading novels again, which Hannah doesn't approve, but it must happen like that now and again, surely, or how would they know to put it in all the stories?'

And so, since to be admired she had first to be seen, I went over to Low Cross two or three times a week in the good weather, although plumper and more breathless as time went by, and took her for a drive.

The millhouse at Low Cross was one of the pokiest and dingiest I had ever seen: a dark, square box, not set apart like ours behind its high stone wall but tacked on to the mill itself, so that no more than the thickness of a single wall separated my cousins from the clatter of looms and the coarse conversations of their operatives. The ceiling was low and oppressive, the windows, in an effort to keep out dust and grime and the shouted obscenities of wagon drivers, tiny and always tight-shut, while the door opened directly onto the yard, exposing the Low Cross young ladies to stares and sniggers, which they had long learned to ignore. Not a house in which I would have cared to live; no fit place, indeed, for Hannah, should she ever find herself alone, and often enough, when Elinor, hearing the sound of my carriage, came tripping across those soiled cobbles as if they were a summer meadow, I felt certain that her prettiness and her determination would have their reward. And when I thought of Hannah, my heart sank.

We went, of course, invariably to Cullingford, which was not, in that first year of my marriage, the grim city it later became, having still something of the country town about it: a market square with an old grey-white cross, and two old coaching inns at either side of it – the Old Swan, where one could take the coach for Manchester or Liverpool any morning of the week, and the thriving, bustling Wool Pack, where coaches were coming and going all day to Wakefield, York, Halifax, Bradford, and Leeds. There was the old Market Building on the Wool Pack side of the square, the upper floor of which could be hired for dances, concerts, or weddings, while the ground floor was devoted to the sale of vegetables and cheeses and the unsightliness of the meat and poultry trade. On the other side, the Old Swan side, the Piece Hall stood in all its ancient glory, its gates still opening promptly at eight o'clock every Thursday morning to admit those who had woollen goods for sale and those who wished to buy.

From Market Square one could still see patches of green on the hills that encircled the town; one could still wander pleasantly up the steep, cobbled slope to Millergate to buy a bonnet or a fan, stroll to the top of Kirkgate, even steeper and stonier, to inspect the fine stone tracery of the parish church, or spend an exciting half hour at the bottom of Sheepgate, where crumbling old warehouses stood with their feet in the canal and one could find low, sinister-fronted shops where carved ivory and intricately tooled leather were offered for sale. There were mean streets too, an unsavoury crisscrossing of alleyways behind the main thoroughfares where once-decent houses, now in decay, had been divided up to accommodate a faceless multitude. But they kept themselves aloof, it seemed, and although the streets were alive, on market days, with top-hatted commercial gentlemen come to do business at the Piece Hall or at the Old Swan, where additional piece rooms were provided, it was not difficult to remember that Cullingford had once been little more than a convenient place to cross the stream, a village lost in the isolation of bare, impenetrable moorland, where no stranger ever came.

My grandfather and others like him – the Hobhouses and the Oldroyds, the Aycliffes – had brought prosperity to Cullingford: I was well aware of that. It was, without doubt, because of them that the coaches came and went, that the inns were flourishing and the name of Cullingford was known outside the Law Valley, and yet they did not altogether belong here, nor really anywhere else.

The old divisions of society had been easy to understand. There had been the king and, under him, his dukes and earls and other noble lords; and, beneath them, a multitude of country squires – all drawn together by common interest and inclination into a ruling class, supported by the parsons, who, more often than not, were younger sons of the noble houses. In the countryside there had been the peasants, tied to the farmers, who, in their various ways were tied to the squires; in the towns, small shopkeepers and tradesmen plying their crafts with an apprentice or two, minding their own business; and, in the cities, a mob, having no rights, much given to unlawful assemblies which, occasionally, had to be put down.

But now this sudden machine age had produced a new breed of men: men without either pedigree or prestige, who had discovered other roads to wealth besides the possession of broad ancestral lands or the wielding of a sword, and who were fast becoming too rich and too clamorous for the gentry to ignore.

Yet they still continued to ignore us. Some twenty years ago, I knew, an Act of Parliament had been obtained 'for the lighting, paving, watching and improving the town of Cullingford,' a measure which required the appointment of a Board of Commissioners, all to be leading citizens, men of substance and good character. Yet, although the increase in trade, brought about by the manufacturers, had made the Act necessary and most of them were men of substance and exemplary behaviour, not one place on the board was made available to them. The appointments had gone to Sir Giles Flood, lord of the manor of Cullingford, although few of us had ever seen him, to his son and his son-in-law, to his cousin Colonel Corey of Blenheim Lane, to Colonel Corey's cousin, the lawyer Mr Corey-Manning, and to others who had property in the town but were not well known here.

And it may not have been any great consolation to men like my grandfather that so far all the commissioners had achieved was the lighting of the better streets, the removal of a number of hog styes and muckheaps, and the employment of a few quite elderly watchmen who, patrolling the town with their lanterns and rattles – when the weather was not too inclement – added little to our security.

The landed gentry, with their protective agricultural policies, their belief in the natural harmony of castle, altar, and throne, had no intention of allowing power to fall into the hands of a pack of greedy, upstart manufacturers who would allow cheap foreign corn into the country to feed their operatives and would foul the countryside with their chimney stacks and their chapels. And although one could sympathize with their determination to hang on to their privileges – just as one could sympathize with the workers who, by smashing the machines, were trying to hang on to theirs – one could not expect men like my grandfather, wedged uneasily between, to be content.

Yet, on my afternoon drives with Elinor that spring, there were no outward signs of conflict, unless it was that I, not yet seventeen, was too preoccupied with my approaching motherhood to notice it, and that Elinor had no time to spare for any miseries but her own.

· 'I'll be an old maid' was the burden of her song that lilting April, as she sat beside me in a cast-off dress she had transformed beyond recognition, my old tortoiseshell combs in her fine, fair hair. 'Yes, I can see it coming. I'll be an old maid and I won't be good at it. Hannah, now, she won't take it too badly, because she had Edwin and she can say her heart is in his grave – and, really, that sounds very fine. I wish I could say the same. But by the time your grandfather dies and Joel can afford to give me a portion, then I'll be too old to care. Or Hannah won't let me go.'

'Nonsense,' I told her, feeling her shiver and seeing, through her eyes, the image of Elinor Barforth, beautiful, enchanting, made for life and love, withering to waste. But she would not be consoled.

'No,' she insisted, her chin unusually resolute, her cloudy blue-green eyes swimming with her easy tears. 'I'll turn sour – if I let it happen to me, and there are times when I think I'd do anything to get away. Yes, Verity – think of it – sitting with Hannah in that dark hole, day after day, pretending not to do the ironing – hating it – getting plain, getting old – while Emma-Jane Rawnsley squeezes herself into a wedding dress, for she's as fat as a sow, and Lucy Hobhouse calls in her carriage to bring me a piece of her bride cake. No, I won't have it, Verity. I'll do something – get away somehow – I'll fall in love with somebody unsuitable and run off with him, and even if they bring me back in disgrace, or he abandons me and I have to crawl back, at least I'll have had something – I'll be a fallen woman, and that's better than being an old maid. And if I can't do that, then I'll marry beneath me, even if it means living in a cottage and doing the washing and not having a nursemaid. Even that – why not? – it's what Rosamund Boulton means to do. Oh well, I daresay I shouldn't talk of her to you, and I daresay you won't be interested to know, but she's always thought well of herself, and when Joel cried off she thought there'd be plenty of others. And so there were, Master Matthew Oldroyd among them, but when it came to marriage her dowry's not much better than mine and it wouldn't do. So now she's angling for a farmer out in Wensleydale, just an acre or two and a cow and no society. Dreadful – but before I'll sit at Low Cross waiting to die with Hannah, I'll do the same. You don't understand, Verity. You've got Joel. You may not like him – in fact, I don't always like him very much myself – but he's a husband.'

But by the time I took her back to Low Cross that day, her tears had dried, her china-doll face was composed again, and her manner was that of a carefree young lady entering her baronial hall. It was only as I waved her goodbye that I began to wonder why, for the last hour, I had felt so unwell.

The sun was warm, certainly for an April day, the road stony and the carriage badly sprung, but I was not one for vapours and it came as a surprise to me when, walking from the stables to the house – for we had no carriage drive – earth and sky rushed suddenly together, crushing me between them to a momentary blackness. And when the day returned, I was again surprised that the face peering anxiously into mine was not one I knew but one which I had seen before – thin, yellow-pale, and so sickeningly reminiscent of Jabez Gott that I almost fainted again.

'Who are you?' I gasped, but he did not feel his identity to be of much concern.

'Agbrigg, ma'am,' he said without explanation. 'See, there's your Marth-Ellen coming running. Here, lass, help your missus into the house and I'll go fetch the master.'

'No,' I said desperately, assuming he meant my grandfather, the last person in the world I wanted by me now. 'You'll do no such thing.'

But he was off, hurrying stoop-shouldered towards the mill, and I was relieved when, some time later, Joel appeared.

'What ails you?'

'What should ail me? I'm starting the baby, I suppose.'

'Is it time?'

'It could be. I'm not sure. Who was that man, the one who came to fetch you? He called you the master.'

'Yes,' Joel said, smiling. 'He would. That's Ira Agbrigg – a good lad. Your grandfather calls him Judas.'

'And he calls you the master?'

'So he does. A forward-thinking lad, Ira Agbrigg. Believes in the machine age, like I do, and he knows your grandfather don't much like him. But he's not after affection. He wants to rise in the world, and he'll cling to my coattails so long as I'm going in the right direction – upwards. Verity, are you in pain?'

'No,' I said fiercely, refusing to be in pain, realizing now, when it was too late, that I did not want a baby after all, that I was too young, that I would not know what to do with a baby, that I was afraid of dying. 'No, no, I'm not in pain. And if I am, then it's not what you think, not what I said. I've eaten something, that's all.'

'I reckon I'll send for the doctor, to be on the safe side, and your mother.'

'If you want to give them the trouble of coming all this way for nothing, then you can suit yourself.'

And as he turned to go and issue the necessary commands, I shrieked his name. 'Joel!'

'Yes. I'm here.'

And he reached me, it seemed, in one stride, just as the pain which had been tiger-prowling somewhere at the small of my back struck out again in a knife thrust that almost forced me to my knees.

'By God,' he said, much alarmed, as strong men often are by these female processes. 'Sit down. Here, let me help you to the rocking chair, and then wait, just wait, while I get somebody on the road to fetch the doctor.'

But, clinging to him, tugging him back towards me, half laughing because I could see he feared I would give birth then and there and that for once in his life he would be helpless, and half crying because there was now no doubt that I would give birth sooner or later and was still unwilling, I said quickly, my tongue breaking loose from all restraint, 'No, no, there's no hurry. It goes on for hours – days. It goes on forever. Listen, do listen for once, my grandfather made me have this baby, and if it kills me don't let it go to the Top House. Promise me. If I die take the baby to my mother, keep it away from him.'

'You'll not die,' he said, the pugnacious set of his jaw warning me he would be furious – with me, with death itself – if I did. But having made up my mind to it, I was not easily dissuaded.

'How do you know? Unless you think you're God, like he does! Promise me.'

'All right. You'll not die because you're a Barforth and you've got too much to live for, but I promise. Trust me.'

'I don't know that I do.'

And putting his hand under my chin, not pinching it now in that smug, cousinly way of his but holding it steady, holding me steady, so that I could look at him, he answered, 'Now just you listen to me, Verity Barforth. He may be your grandfather and he may think he owns you – and that he owns me, too – but he's an old man and I reckon we can let him keep his delusions. You're my wife, Verity, and no one – understand me, no one – harms my wife, nor my child, nor anything else that belongs to me. Not so long as I'm alive, they don't, and I'm good for a long while yet. Now, do you trust me?'

And in this one case, if in no other, I did.

'So it's a bargain then,' he said, holding me now very close with a firmness that reassured, a gentleness that surprised and calmed me. 'Now will you let me fetch the doctor?'

But, my hands wildly twisting together around his neck, I could not let him go, and picking me up, he carried me into the hallway and up the stairs, calling out instructions as he went; and he lay me down, once again with that gentle firmness, on my bed.

'Joel, don't leave me. Don't leave the house, especially when my grandfather comes. Don't let him send you to the mill.'

'He'll send me nowhere, and if you don't want him here he won't come, I'll see to it.'

And smiling at my shocked expression – for how could anyone, even Joel, refuse entry to my grandfather – he slid an arm beneath my

79

shoulders, supporting me against his chest, and my labouring body took comfort in his lean, hard strength, my panic subsided. But when, after a brief respite, the pain struck again and I sank my face, gasping, into his shoulder, his arm tightened and his own face, when I could open my eyes to see, had turned pale. And when I said weakly, 'Oh, Joel, I fear I am crumpling your jacket,' both his arms came around me and he replied, 'You may tear it to pieces if you will, if it eases you.'

'I think I shall not do that.'

'No, but, Verity, sweetheart, I didn't know you felt like this about your grandfather. I thought you were ...'

'What? On his side, against you?'

'Aye, that's one way of putting it. It's not so? You've no love for him, have you?'

'Heavens, I've never thought of loving or not loving. I'm just afraid of him, that's all.'

'There's no need for it. Verity, look at me. I can take care of you. And I don't promise what I can't perform. Only a fool does that and I'm nobody's fool.'

And taking me once more in his arms – his compassion astonishing me as greatly as his sensuality had done on our wedding night – he held me, rocked me, stroked my hair to give me comfort, and stroked the small of my back to ease my pain, guarding me from my fears and from my grandfather, until the doctor came.

8

My son was born the following day, arriving, when he finally made up his mind to it, without too much fuss, and, lying back among my pillows, luxuriating in my body's release from bondage, I thought, I shall have peace now, and was, very soon, disappointed.

'I imagine you will call him Edwin,' Hannah said stiff-lipped, her colour very high. 'It would seem most appropriate – and I feel sure everyone expects it.'

'Oh, my little Samson,' cooed Mrs Stevens an hour later, bending over the cradle. 'My darling little Samson – his great-grandfather's pride and joy. I suppose he is to be Samson – surely?'

'There'll be no Edwin and no Samson,' Joel told me, ominously quiet, not looking too closely into the cradle but claiming what was in it as his own, just the same. 'You may name him as you please, since you had the trouble of bearing him – except that he'll not be an Edwin, nor a Samson either.'

And he strode away, leaving all explanations and recriminations to me.

'My goodness,' my mother murmured, 'such a fuss. I would suggest William, for your father, except that with so many high tempers and high expectations to contend with, perhaps it wouldn't be wise. Maybe one should look outside the family. What do you say to Augustus, or

Alexander, since he is certainly destined for greatness? Or why not name him for St Blaize, the patron saint of wool combers. That may satisfy them all.'

And so he became Blaize Barforth, a tiny, angry scrap in the family cradle, his tight little face bright red, his hair a true Barforth black; an amazing creature – a baby – and, as I had foreseen, I did not know what to do with him and was appalled at his crying, horrified by his helplessness. Puppies I understood, and older children who could tell me what ailed them, but this newborn human, who could not hold up his head, defeated me, filled my whole mind with the worst anxiety I had ever known, so that I lay awake that first night – and for many nights after – my ears straining through the dark, listening, agonizing, in case he should cease to breathe.

'My dear,' my mother told me, 'he is perfectly well. He cries from hunger, which indicates a healthy appetite.'

But my mother had lost six of her eight babies and, quite feverishly, I did not trust her. Nor did I trust the nurse she had found for me in Patterswick; a strong, solid; clean-looking girl, I was forced to admit, but her eyes were small and crafty, pig's eyes, and how could I be sure she would not drug my baby with laudanum to make him sleep or let the kitchen cat get into his cradle and smother him?

I could not have said, at that stage, that I loved him, for he was still a stranger, oddly unconnected with the heaving burden I had carried inside me for so long. I was, quite simply, afraid for him and, had I been permitted, would have taken him into my bed, into my arms, like a mother cat in her basket, and put my claws into anyone who tried to touch him.

But I was not, of course, permitted to do that, for touching him appeared to be the prerogative of all comers: my grandfather, snatching him from the cradle at every visit, whether he was sleeping or not, and holding him up to the light; Mrs Stevens, appearing whenever she had an hour to spare to wake him and then rock him back to sleep; Mrs Hobhouse and Mrs Oldroyd, when they came to call, claiming the right to pick him up and examine him a moment or two, comparing him with their own children, and scraping my nerves to shreds.

But eventually a morning came when I was no longer altogether astonished to find him still alive; when the nursemaid suddenly had a kind smile to compensate for her pig's eyes and a firm but gentle hand as she put my noisy, healthy son into my arms; a morning when I was concerned, once again, with my own face in the mirror and delighted with the new lightness of my body; when I rediscovered my appetite for hot chocolate and new bread and remembered that, in a day or two, I would be seventeen.

My grandfather went to Lincolnshire soon after to visit old friends of his wool-buying days, and, taking advantage of the fine weather, I made myself free of the Top House garden, installing myself there, under the flowering cherry trees and the budding lilac, my son on one side of me, my dogs on the other, while Mrs Stevens, who had never had a child –

81

nor a real husband either, for that matter – advised me on the care and upbringing of mine.

'Bear with her,' my mother advised me one sparkling afternoon when, after a veritable lecture on infant feeding, she had gone inside to prepare our tea. 'She is only safeguarding her position, after all, for your grandfather suffered a severe chill through the winter and has not entirely recovered his strength. Do you know, it struck me only the other day that, really, he is quite a small man, when I used to think him so large. And since, of course, I know perfectly well he stands over six feet high, it can only mean that he has lost a great deal of flesh. And no one can blame poor Emmeline Stevens for wondering what she will do when he is gone.'

'Will he not provide for her?' I said lazily, not really caring, watching my son's miniature fists flailing in the sunlight, his miniature rage at his failure to reach the pink and white blossoms dancing overhead, barely listening until something in her manner warned me she was using Mrs Stevens as a bridge for something else.

'Oh, I hardly think so, not adequately at any rate. I often wonder, you know, about women like Emmeline Stevens. They think themselves so clever and fine, but really their position is most precarious. They can inherit neither a man's property nor his prestige when he dies, and during his lifetime have little more of him than the side of his nature his wife is perhaps glad enough to be without. Not a pleasant existence, and bear in mind that, with no marriage contract to protect them, they can be cast off the very moment they fail to please, without a shred of reputation left – which is very much the same as dismissing a maid without a testimonial. And, of course, they invariably are cast off, for men may desire them but they are never respected, and desire is so fleeting, you know – only respect endures. But Mrs Stevens, I imagine, will survive, for she is no novice and knows the pitfalls of her profession. She was in service once, at a great house somewhere in Derbyshire – a very pretty little parlourmaid she must have been – and I often think she would have done far better had she listened to the young gardener who could have married her instead of setting her cap for her master, who, of course, felt obliged to dismiss her once his passion had cooled. And that has been the way of it ever since. She is quite accustomed to being discarded, our Mrs Stevens – except that, each time it happens, she has grown a little older. And what can it cost you, dear, to be patient?'

'Was I sharp with her? I didn't mean to be.'

'Not very sharp – I merely wondered if her way of life was so distasteful to you that you could not bear her. There have been others before her, of course, for your grandfather has always been an exceptionally lusty man. I believe all the Barforths are so. Certainly your Uncle Thomas – Joel's father – and I must honestly confess to you that your own father made very many visits to Leeds about which I chose not to enquire. I took the view that they did not really concern me – that such things are in a man's nature – a view I know your grandmother shared. For even your grandfather was most discreet during her lifetime. He has many faults, but he took great care never to embarrass his wife. She knew, you see, that he valued her, as his wife, above everything else, and she felt herself in no way threatened – in no way insecure. Men do not discard their wives as they do their mistresses – and I have every reason to believe your grandmother was an exceedingly happy woman.'

Silence for a moment, then the sounds of the dogs panting in the sun, the child stirring in the warm, safely padded world of his cradle, birdsong somewhere among the cherry trees. A holding in of breath, a reluctance to move myself towards understanding, a reluctance to feel.

And then I said carefully, 'Mother, is there something you want to tell me about Joel?'

'No, no,' she said. 'Absolutely nothing, for I know nothing about him. I merely took the opportunity to express an opinion, for we had so little time for conversation before your marriage. I sent you into the world all unprepared, my dear, and here you are, a mother already, so there is nothing I can tell you on that score. And as for the other – your husband may become a model of fidelity, but if he should not – if he should conform to the family pattern – Oh dear, how hard this is to express without appearing insensitive – but these fiercely energetic men, these competitive men with their hunting instincts so finely developed, these greedy men, if you like, who cannot bear to have anything pass them by – And when they are so often away from home ... My dear, if it happens it will probably mean very little to him and should not unduly distress you. It is necessary to treat these matters with sense rather than feeling – believe me – and after all, you did not marry through a sudden fit of emotion. If now, dear, you can become friends, use friendship as a foundation on which to build; then I think you will be well served. I set great store by friendship, Verity; I believe I once told you so. If I could choose I would always prefer a friend to a lover.'

'And can you choose?'

'At my age I think I can. Squire Dalby and I are friends.'

'Do you mean to marry him?'

'Oh, my dear, hardly that,' she said, the trill of her laughter easing the load between us, 'even if he would have me, which seems unlikely. His wife has been twenty years in her grave, and he has a son and a grandson waiting to inherit – I can't think he would embarrass them with a worsted manufacturer's widow, at this late stage. No, no – friendship, that is my aim. Warm but peaceful friendship – no demands, no jealousies – free, open friendship. You would not believe how delightful it can be.'

Mrs Stevens served tea in the garden, and afterwards when my mother had returned to her friend the squire, I continued to sit awhile under the blossom trees, wondering if Joel would be unfaithful and concluding that he would; concluding, since my mother would not have mentioned it otherwise, that he already had. And what did I really feel about it? Would it indeed be pointless to have any feeling at all, since I had no power to prevent it? Certainly I could throw hysterical fits as his mother had often done; I could whine and complain to my friends, as she had; I could even go to my grandfather, who, although he might privately consider male adultery to be a far more trifling offence than being late at the mill, would defend me. He would even use it as an additional rod with which to scourge Joel.

'So there's more of your father coming out in you, lad, is there? And there's a short answer to it. If you can afford a harlot's bills, then I'm paying you too well, and since it's my money and my time you're spending, I'll have to cut you down to size.'

The truth was that events had moved far too quickly for me. Only a year ago, this very month, I had sat in this same garden with my cousin Elinor, two little girls beneath anyone's notice, while Hannah had dreamed of her wedding, Edwin of his power looms, and Joel had brooded over how he was to settle his father's creditors. And now, a year later, Edwin and my father were gone, I was Joel's wife and the mother of his son – and I had only just stopped being sixteen.

Joel had given me a bracelet for my birthday, a thin twist of gold; he had even fastened it around my wrist and kissed my hand with a casual gallantry I found decidedly pleasant, until he had spoiled it all by pinching my chin and ruffling my hair in his old cousinly fashion. He had kept his promise and remained beside me through my long hours of labour, leaving only a moment or two before our son was born when the midwife, shocked and somewhat unnerved by his presence, had shooed him away. And afterwards, when I had been weak and tearful with relief, he had filled my room with flowers and kept his temper – certainly for my sake – when my grandfather, declaring them unhealthy, had demanded that they should all be taken away.

'Flowers,' my grandfather had snorted. 'Damn things belong in a garden – or a whorehouse. They'll take up the air and choke the bairn. Flowers – I reckon that's another of the damn fool notions you've picked up from your father.'

But Joel, quietly and with, for him, immense patience, had replied, 'My wife was glad to receive them, sir. She's tired, you see, which is hardly to be wondered at, and I've no mind to upset her. In fact, I don't see my way to denying her anything right now that could give her pleasure.'

And although my grandfather had grunted and grumbled and stamped his feet all the way downstairs, I had kept my flowers.

Nor had he been impatient to reclaim his conjugal rights. A month, the midwife had told me, was as much as most men allowed their wives before they came pestering again, but Joel had shown no such unmannerly haste.

'Don't fret,' he had told me, that firm hand gentle once more beneath my chin. 'A brute I may be on occasion, but not the kind to risk putting you through this agony again in a hurry. Take your time, get your strength back, and when you're ready just let me know.'

When, touched by his consideration, I had shown myself ready sooner than I might otherwise have done, he had treated my newly healed body almost with respect and, for a while thereafter, had taken such care as he could not to impregnate me again. And remembering the midwife's harrowing tales of women forced to go on producing one child nine months after the other, I had been intensely grateful.

In exchange for that and for his support and protection, his casual, tolerant affection, could I acknowledge his physical appetites to be greater than mine; his physical curiosity, as a man, in need of more variety than mine, as a woman, and accept it as natural for him to supplement the deficiency elsewhere? Presumably both my mother and my grandmother had done exactly that and retained their dignity, while Joel's mother, who had not accepted it, had become a shrew, a hysteric, and a nuisance. Did I, in fact, see such acceptance as a basis for the friendship my mother had talked of? I thought I did not. Was there no way for us to approach each other – for I was willing to admit I had much to learn, if he would be prepared to teach, and to admit that I, too, had skills and knowledge that he lacked – and surely the fact that we shared a roof, an inheritance, a child, must mean more to him than any chance encounter? And if, sometimes, I still saw his face looking down at Edwin, his ambition leaping towards the mill, the looms, the heiress, before the breath was out of my brother's body, I would try to forget. And if I could lock that memory away, surely he could bring himself to look at me and realize that my hair was no longer in pigtails, my eyes no longer so quiet as they used to be. But my thoughts were sketchy and could not have been put into words, and how could I, barely seventeen, make Joel sit down and listen while I outlined my scheme for a better future?

How did I visualize that future? What did I really feel for the man I was still sometimes surprised to call my husband? He was, without doubt, hard and calculating, but these were traits of which my Law Valley heart could not wholly disapprove, and I had admired him, often enough, for his sharp, sardonic wit, the fierce energy that took him, after a day of gruelling labour, to Low Cross, where, in flagrant disobedience of my grandfather's wishes, he would work long into the night, repairing, adjusting, operating with his own hands the looms that wove his experimental fancy worsteds. I had seen him ride home at dawn, dirty and drained, with more than an hour to spare before Lawcroft demanded his presence again, and had seen the narrow, glittering anger in his eyes, instantly suppressed, when my grandfather, noting his fatigue, had made some scathing hint of an evening spent in wine and cards.

'Watch him, lass,' he would tell me at such times. 'I can see his father in him, plain as day.'

But it was not my uncle Thomas Barforth but Samson Barforth himself I could see in Joel, and my grandfather's iron qualities in this younger, handsome man were not displeasing. And he was handsome. There was nothing now in his long, hard body that I found offensive, nothing to shock me when he strode naked across my bedroom floor with a branch of candles in his hand, the flame turning his skin to amber and darkening his eyes and his vigorously curling hair, adding brilliance to the sudden flash of his teeth as he gave me his bold pirate's grin.

Yet the fact remained that we had not chosen each other. We had been brought together to fulfil my grandfather's desires rather than our own and, being very much aware that Joel desired other women and had sacrificed a woman he may even have loved whereas I had desired no one, sacrificed nothing, I was afraid to expect too much. Had he spoken to me of love on our wedding night I would have been offended, and yet now the possibility of love between us stirred, tantalized the fringes of my mind, and then I paused and grew cautious as I remembered his casual fingers pinching my chin, his teasing voice calling me 'little cousin,' 'sweet cousin' sometimes, but 'cousin' just the same. And on the occasions when a more intense feeling had arisen or had started to arise – when I had become 'sweetheart,' 'little love,' occasionally 'darling' – I could not forget how he always turned it away with a laugh and called me 'cousin' all the more.

I was woman enough now to know what troubled him. He had seen me growing up alongside his sister Elinor, a little girl at a time when he, twelve years my senior, had already started to think of women. It was surely not to his discredit that the mental barrier which prevents men from desiring their sisters had made it difficult for him, in the early days, to desire me.

But could that barrier now be crossed? Certainly I had never regarded him in any way as a brother. Throughout my entire childhood I had seen him as a man full-grown, a potent, predatory male, and had listened with rapt attention whenever his mother, my Aunt Hattie, had come whispering his misdeeds to my own mother.

There had been a married lady in Harrogate, of good family, older than Joel, who had ruined her reputation for his sake; an irate husband who could not be expected, Aunt Hattie feared, to take the matter lightly. There had been an actress in Leeds, a singer of bawdy music-hall songs, with no reputation to lose but every intention, according to his mother, of ruining Joel's health. There had been another actress, who had cost him money he could not afford, a mysterious woman whose source of income was never named, who had made him scandalous gifts of clothing and encouraged his taste for fine wines. There had been a frenzied episode in Manchester with a young widow, whose letters, when my Aunt Hattie had finally managed to read them, had made her blush. And there had been Rosamund Boulton.

He was a sensualist then, my cousin, my husband, but no despoiler of virgins. A man with a taste for women of character: mature, forceful beauties beside whom I must appear tame indeed. Although I had a fair enough opinion of my own character, privately considering myself to be as honest as anyone else and a shade more intelligent than some, and although my face and figure did not altogether displease me, I knew I lacked the flamboyance, the variety, the experience to which Joel had grown accustomed.

Not that I believed he ever deliberately hurt me. I had not forgotten his compassion in the hours before Blaize was born. I knew he was fond of me and pleased with me more often than not; and I knew, dimly, that I should perhaps be grateful he had not attempted to use his skill and charm to turn my seventeen-year-old head and make me fall in love with him. He had not amused himself with my untried, uncertain emotions as some men could well have done. He had done nothing, in fact, by Law Valley standards, about which I could reasonably complain. And, at the end of the day, I could do no more than admit the wisdom of my mother's words. If Joel took a mistress, if he already had a mistress, it would mean very little to him. Whatever it meant to me – if it made me angry, or if I were stung by the injustice of it; if it gave me a sense of failure or futility, or even if it hurt me – my best defence would be to pretend that I did not care.

Elinor deserted me somewhat that fragrant May, being little inclined to sit and marvel at the infant Blaize when Emma-Jane Rawnsley was fast reaching an understanding with Bradley Hobhouse's mother, if not with Bradley himself. And so she took her carriage drives with Emma-Jane, keeping her eyes peeled, to the great annoyance of Mrs Rawnsley, who knew quite well what Elinor was up to, even if Emma-Jane did not. But Hannah paid me regular visits, growing more stately than ever in her plain brown taffeta, her mauve silk, the mourning brooch of Edwin's hair always on her collar, and although she was not fond of babies in the physical sense and appeared most ill at ease on the few occasions Blaize was allowed on her knee, she was his godmother and took her responsibilities seriously.

Indeed, an afternoon with Hannah was always a serious business, for she was more engrossed then ever in the Sunday School movement, spending a full eight hours every Sunday at Ramsden Street Chapel, near Low Cross, where poor children were taught first to read and then to read the Bible, and spending considerably longer than that in explaining to the minister how best to organize his congregation. Ramsden Street Chapel, it seemed, depended very largely on Hannah's support; it would, I feared, be very likely to crumble and fall down should she ever desert it. So accustomed was I to her feuds with various old ladies who dared to question her advice and, on one or two occasions, had gone so far as to accuse her of bullying the minister, that when, one afternoon, she broke off in mid-sentence and said, 'Verity, I believe you are acquainted with Mr Morgan Aycliffe,' I assumed he was chapel business too.

Only her silence, the tension vibrating inside her as it sometimes did in Joel, made me look at her and realize that, whatever it was, it was personal, vital, enormous.

'Am I? Mr Aycliffe the builder? Oh – just barely acquainted with him, Hannah, although I think my father knew him well. I understand he is in a very large way of business, and he was to have built Edwin's mill –'

'Yes,' she said, her cheeks, always highly coloured, flooding with crimson. 'He has told me so.'

'You are acquainted with him yourself, then?'

'Yes,' she said harshly, angry suddenly, as if it were none of my business; furious, I think, at her own tongue-tied, girlish confusion. 'You may recall, some eight or twelve weeks ago, that a Dr Blackstone came to Ramsden Street to speak to us about the abolition of the slave trade?

Certainly you recall it, for I remember telling you how pleased we were at the attendance. Mr Aycliffe was there. No, he is not a member of our congregation, but we had extended our welcome to everyone, and he was there with Mr and Mrs Rawnsley, who presented him to me and asked me to take tea with them afterwards, which I thought most kind. Mr Aycliffe was impressed by the speaker and remarked how well the meeting had been organized, which caused me some embarrassment when Mrs Rawnsley failed to restrain herself from telling him I had been the organizer. In short, we had some conversation about abolition, and about Sunday Schools – which he considers a good thing – and since then we have met several times, under the supervision of Mrs Rawnsley – and once in the street, by chance, when I saw no harm in pausing a moment, since Elinor was with me. There was no harm, surely?'

'Surely not.'

'His wife died a year ago,' she said, flinging the words at me as if they were stones. 'Naturally he has observed the full mourning period, as I have. In fact, he came out of black armbands only ten days ago –'

And, understanding that she was drowning in embarrassment, pleading to be rescued and too proud to cry for help, I said quickly, 'And has he spoken to you?'

She looked, for a moment, quite horrified, very much on the brink of tears, but instead of weeping she straightened her back and said resolutely, 'I think you know what your brother and I meant to each other. I will not dwell on it. And I daresay you are very much shocked to hear me mention Mr Aycliffe – or anyone – when it has been little more than a year. And I would like you to understand that it is in no way the same – that my feelings, as such, are not involved – merely that we appear to have a great deal in common, a certain similarity of thought –'

'But has he spoken to you – of marriage?'

'No,' she said, her chin very firm. 'But unless he had that intention – taking into account his strict code of conduct – I do not think he would have approached me at all. And he has singled me out most particularly. Mrs Rawnsley herself has remarked on it – she is always remarking on it, which is really why I felt obliged to tell you.'

'And if he does speak to you? Will you take him?'

'Oh – as to that – The correct procedure would be for him to speak to Joel, and I am undecided as yet. I can only say he is a good man who champions a great many charitable causes, and I could be of use to him in that. And he has had much suffering, with which I am well able to sympathize. His wife died of some lingering malady of the nerves which greatly distressed him, and he has a most unsatisfactory child. Perhaps I could help him there too.'

'Hannah,' I told her, 'the Aycliffe boy is hardly a child; he must be well turned twenty – easily twenty-two.'

But the idea of a stepson very nearly her own age did not seem to deter her, and at the end of an hour I was in no doubt that however thoroughly she had convinced herself that this marriage could be no more than a Christian duty, in reality she was as eager to escape the mill yard of Low

Cross as Elinor. While the prospect of allying herself to the rich, highly regarded Mr Aycliffe, of being a married lady able to dispense charity instead of receiving it, filled her with a wild delight.

'I'll tell Joel,' I promised, and, when I did, his answer was immediate, triumphant.

'By God, Verity, if she can land Morgan Aycliffe she'll do well for herself – and for me. How far can we rely on it?'

'Far enough, I think. He must have made his intentions fairly clear if Ramsden Street Chapel is taking notice.'

'But he could still cry off. Is there a way to fix him?'

'Hardly,' I said, remembering that not even Rosamund Boulton had found a way to fix her man; and just possibly catching the drift of my thought, Joel gave a short laugh.

'No, I suppose not. No way Hannah would be prepared to take, at any rate. So – what's to be done? How does an old stick like that go about his courting?'

'I don't see what we can do. But if he's serious, then I suppose he'll do something himself. He could call on me, I suppose. He must know she comes here a great deal, and if he calls to see me, then he has a chance of seeing her – and you.'

'That's it,' he said. 'He'll call. And when he does, take care your grandfather knows nothing of it. I don't know what Morgan Aycliffe's worth but being his brother-in-law would do me no harm if I ever had to go cap in hand again to Rawnsley's bank. And if he's even considering marrying her – knowing there's nothing much to come with her and I've not much to add to it – then he must have confidence in me. And that wouldn't please your grandfather. Is that Marth-Ellen of yours fit to serve him tea, if he comes?'

'I'll see to it.'

'Yes,' he said, 'I believe you will.' And, in a high good humour, he reached out his hard hand and, with a cousinly gesture of affection, pinched my chin.

The millhouse had been designed for the convenience of a millmaster who wished to keep an eye on his operatives, not for the entertaining of guests, and so, in anticipation of Mr Aycliffe's call, I had them clear the front parlour of the paraphernalia of housekeeping, got out my wedding china and washed it myself, supervised the preparation, every teatime, of wafer-thin bread and butter, the polishing of silver spoons, dressed myself carefully, daintily, brought flowers into the house, created as best I could an atmosphere of tranquillity and grace that would, surely, induce romance. But I could have spared myself the pains, for romance seemed to be neither in Morgan Aycliffe's mind nor in his nature.

I had seen him a hundred times before, but, because his life had no bearing on mine – and because he was of another generation – I had never noticed him, and, when he finally rode up to my door and got stiffly, almost huffily down from his tall roan, it was as if I were seeing his thin, grey face and his long, grey body for the first time. He was somewhere between forty-five and fifty, with a back so stiff that I wondered, with a seventeen-year-old's inclination to giggle, how he would ever manage to sit down, and then watched, with the respect he easily inspired, as he folded himself neatly into a chair, with his long, rather bony hands placed precisely, one on each knee.

'Dear Mrs Barforth,' he said, his voice somehow dry and bony, too, 'I feel this visit to be sadly overdue. Indeed, I have long meant to call with my congratulations on the birth of your son. My word, what exquisite roses, the very first of the season – such a tasteful blending of colour –'

Watching him closely, only half listening to the easy, oily flow of his voice, I had the same impression of suppressed energy that Joel gave me, except that in Morgan Aycliffe's case, the suppressing was by his own hand, as if his own virility made him uneasy. And it occurred to me that he may not be so straitlaced as he seemed.

His clothes, it was true, were of a clerical sobriety, sombre in the extreme, but the fabric was expensive and the cut excellent; the watch chain across his dark, unpatterned waistcoat was solid gold, and the black onyx ring on his finger elaborate and costly, his fingers themselves many years away from any actual contact with bricks and mortar. And, in those first few moments, I did not find him a comfortable man.

But, like most men of business, he knew how to make himself pleasant, and, having paid my bread and butter the compliment of eating it and allowing me to send for more, he crossed one leg with meticulous neatness over the other, pressed the tips of his skinny fingers together, and commenced the true purpose of his visit, the delicate business of presenting his credentials as a prospective bridegroom without in any way committing himself should his intentions change or the lady herself prove unworthy.

A cautious man, Mr Aycliffe, and a lonely one, he told me; the more so since he and his late wife had enjoyed a rare harmony, which had made his bereavement doubly hard to bear. He had kept his wife's room exactly as it had been in her lifetime, her toilet articles remaining just as she had left them, her pincushion and embroidery frame in their accustomed place. He had not really expected, he told me, to recover from so tragic a blow, but, needless to say, there had been his business to consider, contracts to fulfil, workmen to be kept in employment, and, recognizing his responsibilities, he had not shirked.

'Life must go on,' he said, and I had the impression, most discreetly conveyed, that for Morgan Aycliffe life was going very well indeed.

He did not, of course, mention the soundness of his financial position, although his references to his good relations with Mr Rawnsley the banker were enough to convince me of that. But, knowing Hannah's connection with Ramsden Street, he confessed to me, with a rueful smile, that his own religious views were somewhat unusual. He was, in fact, a little of one thing, a little of the other; a Dissenter, I concluded, when he was among Dissenters, yet a man who, aware of the privileges conveyed by the Anglican Church, saw no reason to shun them. Not that he, personally, wished to attend the universities of Oxford and Cambridge – open only to Anglicans – yet his instinct was always to be on the winning side, to keep his options open. A subtle man, then; a clever man who, although he would not say so, and no doubt for vastly different reasons, was as eager for marriage as my cousin.

'My wife was a most unworldly person,' he told me, 'one who preferred the security of her own home and was never plagued by curiosity as to the hurly-burly of life outside. Her anxieties were all of the kitchen and the store cupboard, and it was my pleasure and my pride to be able to shield her from other cares. She has been sorely missed.'

'I daresay your son has been a comfort to you,' I said, and, his lips parting in the smile of an indulgent father, he replied, 'Yes, indeed. We stand very close together, Crispin and I, although sons, my dear Mrs Barforth, as you will soon discover, have minds and wills of their own. An excellent boy, Crispin – something of a dreamer, and with his mother's delicate disposition, but a fine son. I had him trained an architect, you know, at some inconvenience and expense, but he has no head for the building trade – he dreams of building castles instead of houses for honest working folk to live in. But that's his mother in him, for she was often fanciful, and he'll learn. She indulged him, I fear, almost to excess, for he was her pride and joy, and although the effects of her pampering on his character have not all been for the best, I could deny her nothing in her later years. And so my son has been somewhat spoiled, I confess. Yes – spoiled – but we are, little by little, setting ourselves to rights. I hope you may come to know him, Mrs Barforth.'

'I hope so too.'

'Most kind,' he said, beaming his approval, taking my hand on leaving with a fulsome warmth that was clerical in feeling and left me in no doubt that he would come again.

And, while I was mulling him over, my door opened and Elinor came into the room, complaining bitterly because the Rawnsleys and the Hobhouses had set her down in the top road, above my grandfather's house, so that she had been obliged to walk and had mud on the hem of her dress.

'The old cat,' she said, referring to the highly suspicious Mrs Rawnsley. 'She could have set me down at the door. She could see that roan horse as plain as I could – obviously a gentleman's horse – and she wasn't even curious. All she wanted was to send me walking down the hill; putting me in my place, I expect she calls it. And it's not my fault if people look at me instead of her fat Emma-Jane. Three gentlemen raised their hats to me today in Market Square – complete strangers – and I didn't smile at them first, whatever Mrs Rawnsley says. Well, so he's been to declare himself, has he? Aycliffe, I mean. What do you think to him?'

'I'm not sure.'

'Well, I'm sure,' she said, and, swinging her reticule in one hand and her frilled parasol in the other, she spun round slowly in a dancing movement, her skirts billowing like the wings of a yellow butterfly, showing off her beauty and grace, her lightness of heart, until she stopped moving and I saw the tense, resentful anger in her face.

'I'll tell you what I think, Verity. It's disgusting, sermonizing and sighing and making eyes, and his wife not cold in her grave –'

'Well, not too warm either, darling, since he wore black for a twelvemonth –'

But my attempt at lightness did her no good, and stamping her small foot, her cheeks scarlet with her doll's anger, she almost shouted, 'I'll tell you about him. He's old and stale and his wife hated him. Lingering malady of the nerves, he calls it, but the truth is, he frightened her to death. And his son hates him, too. They say his son wouldn't speak to him at the funeral and not for a long time after. He's rich and he's mean and he's old and what I want to know is, if Hannah marries him, what is going to happen to me? You haven't thought of that, have you? No. No one has. Let's get Hannah married, that's the great thing – let's get Hannah settled. But there's me, Verity. What's going to happen to me?'

9

Joel had expressed his ignorance of Morgan Aycliffe's exact worth, but, in the days that followed, he hastened to inform himself and was well pleased with the answers. About Mr Aycliffe's building enterprises we already knew, since he was responsible for the newer part of Cullingford, somewhat larger than the old, but Joel, after a few visits to the Piece Hall and the Old Swan and other hostelries where businessmen were wont to congregate, was able to track down hints of Aycliffe involvement in canals, turnpikes, and coal mines, of inherited money and money still to inherit, which filled him with a pure and lasting delight. And, Law Valley men being notoriously close-mouthed, much inclined to 'hear all and say nowt,' we knew such hints were to be relied on. Admittedly the existence of a son, the spoiled, fanciful Crispin, was something of a drawback, since, when the time came to carve up his father's estate, he would be bound to take the lion's share.

'He could live somewhere between ten and twenty years,' Joel calculated happily. 'Call it fifteen – which would bring Crispin well into his thirties, with Hannah's children, if she has any, still too young to have got their hooks into the business. Well, I'd like it better if there was a chance of Hannah's getting the lot, but there's plenty for all, I reckon, and I'll have it in writing from him, once we get started, that she's to be well provided for.'

And so, on the whole, it was decided that no better brother-in-law could possibly be found.

'He's old,' Elinor declared, wrinkling her nose. 'Never mind, Hannah, you'll be a widow that much sooner. So, if you think it's what you want – if you think it's worth it – then I'm happy for you.'

But Hannah, too nervous, I think, to bother with Elinor, took refuge in dignity and refused to quarrel.

'You are all making a great fuss,' she said, 'and I hope you will not be too disappointed if it comes to nothing – for I have by no means made up my mind.'

But she had, and because I knew how intensely, how dreadfully, she was longing not for the man himself but for the smooth, gold ring that would liberate her from the restrictions Cullingford imposed on its spinster ladies, I gave Mr Aycliffe the most encouraging of welcomes when he called, and, since he could not call at Low Cross, where there was no adequate chaperone, I invited Hannah and Elinor to stay with me. And although, as May entered into a warm June, he had not yet proposed, each visit committed him a little further, each slice of seedcake made it more difficult for him to withdraw, and the irrepressible Elinor was soon talking of bridesmaids' dresses and giggling at the thought of calling Morgan Aycliffe brother.

'I'm determined she shall have a decent wedding,' Elinor told me. 'No poky little affair in dove grey with a new feather in her bonnet. I shall persuade her into white satin if it's my last day's work – because she'll never wear it afterwards and I can easily cut it up and make it over again to fit me. And I think I shall wear white, too; not satin, because I'll have the satin in any case – something gauzy and lacy, with frills caught up with blue ribbon. And my hair in a great big Apollo knot with a white rose in the middle. And Bradley Hobhouse will see me floating down the aisle and he'll look at Emma-Jane Rawnsley's buck teeth and he'll know he can't live without me, no matter what anyone has to say to it. Yes – and when they threaten to cut him off with a shilling I shall plead with him to give me up, of course, knowing quite well he won't. And then I think they'd better forgive us and let him make an honest woman of me, because I would like a proper wedding in the parish church with all the bells ringing. Yes, that I would.'

She laughed, dancing around the room again, enraptured by her own imaginings, and then, her dainty feet returning abruptly to earth, she sighed. 'Ah, well … I just wish Hannah and her old gentleman would hurry themselves up. They just sit there, in the parlour, and talk about the condition of the poor and how to go about freeing the slaves in the West Indies. And if it's left to her they'll go on like that forever. All he needs is a little push – I told her so last night and I thought she meant to slap me, she was so put out. But it's true. In her place I could get him to propose in ten minutes, and so could you, I reckon. She thinks these feminine wiles, as she calls them, are beneath her, but I don't think it's wily: I call it common sense. And what about this famous son of his that he keeps promising to bring with him and never does? It strikes me that Master Crispin Aycliffe may not altogether like the idea of a new mamma and a parcel of little brothers, all wanting a share of the Aycliffe estate. And I can't say I blame him. I wouldn't like a new mamma of my own age. Just think of it – if you can bear to. It's perfectly disgusting.'

'Hannah doesn't think so. And, after all, Crispin Aycliffe is a man with his own life to lead. He may not even live in the house with them. He may get married, or go out to the West Indies and begin freeing the slaves. Perhaps you should smile at him, instead of Bradley Hobhouse, when you get your white gauze …'

'Yes,' she said, suddenly extremely serious, concentrating so hard on this new possibility that all else was forgotten. 'Yes, of course. I could marry Crispin Aycliffe, couldn't I? Is it legal, Verity, do you suppose, for a girl to marry her brother-in-law's son? It doesn't sound legal and, with my luck, he'll adore me and it won't be. Do you think our minister would know? Oh, I do wish Hannah would stir herself. All she needs to do is be a little more approachable – she needs to give him the eye, in fact, and she'd have a fit if she heard me say so, although it's perfectly true. I could show her how to do it in a trice – I was born knowing how to do it.'

And as Morgan Aycliffe appeared just then at the parlour door, with Hannah behind him, Elinor caught her sister's eye, her own eyes sparkling with a look that said, 'Come on, Hannah, this is how it's done. Just you watch me,' and, stepping forward into a shaft of sunlight, she gave the sober gentleman a smile of such studied enchantment, such innocent, fascinating mischief, that he took a step backwards, most hurriedly, towards the safety of Hannah, startled and, it appeared, considerably displeased.

But at least our wish to meet the elusive Crispin was soon gratified, for, a few days later, Mr Aycliffe invited us to dine, not at the comfortable hour of the late afternoon we were used to, but at the fashionable city dinnertime of six o'clock, a notable departure from tradition in the Law Valley.

I wore, for the first time, the long velvet evening cloak my mother had given me before my marriage and, under it, a gown of cream-coloured crepe de chine, cut with a simplicity that had pleased Joel, while Hannah's brown silk, equally simple, had seemed to him too plain. But there was no doubt at all that Elinor was looking her best in a gown the colour of sharp, fresh lemons, a confection of gauze over silk which she had persuaded me to buy against my better judgement, feeling it to be too pretty for my nature, but which, after a change of ownership, having been shortened and tightened and further embellished with knots of satin ribbon, was perfect for hers.

'I've quite decided about the son,' she whispered to me as we were setting out, intensely serious beneath her teasing, scatterbrained manner. 'I've quite stopped thinking of Bradley Hobhouse. I called on Emma-Jane the other day, and he was there, and really, I could see he's just the kind to do as his mamma tells him. So if he did run away with me he'd only run back again. Now I've been making enquiries about Mr Crispin Aycliffe, and they say at Ramsden Street Chapel that he will do anything if he thinks his father may not like it. And if I got myself married to Crispin before the old gentleman had a chance to marry Hannah, I suppose he wouldn't like that at all.'

'But have you even seen him, Elinor?'

'No. Have you?'

And it seemed suddenly strange, very strange indeed, that in a town like Cullingford, I had not.

'They say in Ramsden Street,' Elinor murmured, lowering her voice to a thrilling whisper, 'that his mamma would never let him play with the other boys in case he took cold or skinned his knees. And they also say, my dear – and do listen carefully to this because it is really quite special information, and Hannah would have the vapours if she knew I knew – they also say that since his mamma died, he drinks.'

And she put her head on one side like a graceful little monkey which, having just performed a trick, is waiting for a reward.

The Aycliffes lived in the select area of Cullingford known as Blenheim Lane, a narrow, leafy thoroughfare beginning with the ancient, venerable home of Colonel Corey, cousin to Sir Giles Flood, our ground landlord, and ending with the new, elaborately stone-fronted houses and the self-conscious gardens of men for whom the need to live in their factory yards no longer applied. Mr Thomas Rawnsley the banker lived here, with his plump daughter, Emma-Jane, Mr Corey-Manning, the lawyer, and his sister, Mrs Roundwood, her husband being the owner of our newspaper, the *Cullingford Courier and Review*. There were some smaller houses, too, all in a row, belonging to a Corey widow and a pair of Corey-Manning spinsters; their upstairs windows, surely, giving them a view of the Fleece Inn, where, in the absence of an adequate courthouse, Colonel Corey sat, in his capacity as magistrate, whenever there was a poacher or a debtor to be put away, or the father of a bastard child to be forcibly reminded of his obligations. And in a discreet position in the middle of the lane stood the Aycliffe dwelling, as tall and grey as the man himself, set well back behind its ornamental iron gate, in a pool of tree shadow.

The hall was dimly lit, cool and hushed as a chapel, except that the panelling, fragrant with beeswax and almost black in colour, was of a quality unknown in Ramsden Street, while the staircase, growing from the centre of the hall and branching to left and right, had bannisters like ribbons of ebony, carved here and there with fruit and flowers.

Mr Aycliffe was there to greet us, narrower than ever in his black evening clothes, offering us a thin, faraway hand, and it was immediately apparent to us all that his money was older than ours, that he had progressed from the stage of accumulation to that of display.

The house, I supposed, was not comfortable in the chintzy flowery way of Mrs Stevens, but its subdued elegance spoke to my nature, its uncluttered drawing room, furnished with the gleam of silver against dark walls, the graceful swan-curving back of a fragile sofa, a fragile chair – so different from the millhouse, where chairs were designed to take the weight of a heavy, tired man – delighted my eye. And it took me a breathless moment or two to realize that its perfection was also oppressive, a setting for the jewel of a man's success rather than a home.

I could not imagine a woman leaving her embroidery on that sofa, nor a boy growing up here, surrounded by so much silence, so many frail and lovely porcelain figurines, so many pieces of fine enamelled glass displayed in black lacquer cabinets or set out on small tables of dark, polished wood. And, indeed, among the first awkward spurts of conversation and the even more awkward pauses, we were all aware that the boy, the wayward son, was nowhere to be seen.

Hannah, her emotions gathered into a spot of colour beneath each cheekbone, sat in silence. Elinor frankly stared, admired, coveted, while

Joel – who also had it in his nature to spend money on objects that could neither weave nor spin nor reproduce their kind – hid his own covetousness by a slight air of nonchalance, as if he were used to seeing such treasures every day of his life.

But I was not, and, my eye alighting with pleasure on the two black basalt urns, one on either end of the marble mantelshelf, I said, 'How lovely. They are – Wedgwood – are they not?'

'Yes,' he replied, his thin mouth sketching a smile, rather as if it grudged the effort. 'My urns – very true – you will not have seen their like in these valley.'

And after his contemplating them for a moment with a gloating that was in no way austere, an expression of intense annoyance suddenly pinched his face.

'Good heavens, they are not straight,' he muttered, so absolutely furious that, thinking he had detected some major fault in their construction, I half expected to see them shatter to ruin and was relieved when, crossing to the fireplace with a rapid step, he moved the urn on the left a fraction to one side so that it exactly matched the position of the one on the right.

'I cannot bear it,' he told us, 'when things are set awry. It should be a simple matter for the girl, when she dusts, to put my things back as she found them. I am not asking her to devise artistic arrangements of her own, not asking her to think – Yet I have never had the good fortune to employ a servant who could understand how painful it is to me when I see my possessions in disorder. The beauty of a pair of vases is that they should be a pair, standing in harmony with each other. If they are disarranged but a half inch it irritates me, offends me, like a false chord in music – a matter which even my wife was quite unable to comprehend.'

It was at this mention of his mother's name that Crispin Aycliffe walked into the room.

He was, as we had supposed, perhaps twenty-two, with a narrow, finely moulded face which could, one day, grow lean, and hair, shading from pale brown to honey fair, cut in feathery layers across a high forehead; his light bone structure gave no great impression of strength, although there was nothing in that first glance to indicate the invalid, the recluse, or the drunkard. He looked, in fact, very much the carefully brought-up young gentleman who, his family fortunes having been made a generation or two ago, had escaped the toil of the factory yard, and he would have been handsome enough, in his pale, insubstantial fashion, to please anyone had his expression not been so peevish, so frankly bored.

'Good evening,' he said, bowing with false dancing-school courtesy to me and Hannah and Elinor but not looking at us.

'Good evening,' he said to Joel, offering him a disinterested hand.

'Good evening,' we replied, Hannah stiff with nerves, Joel with a certain grim amusement, not caring a fig for being disliked if there were a profit to be made. But Elinor, seeing nothing beyond his cool civility, caught her breath and blinked in delighted surprise – for what was the bullnecked Bradley Hobhouse to her now? – and, as Crispin Aycliffe turned away, she gave to his father, somewhat by mistake, a smile that held all the sparkle of crystal in candelight. And once again, Morgan Aycliffe's thin mouth pinched its disapproval, his eyes, for an instant, looked hunted, as if this display of girlish charm was every bit as abhorrent to him as a pair of ill-matched urns.

We went into dinner then, Mr Aycliffe giving me his arm, Hannah walking stiffly with Crispin, Elinor with Joel, her feet barely touching the ground and her mind, I thought, on a fast coach for Gretna Green, the only one of us to be unimpressed by the pale green damask of the dining-room walls, the mahogany sideboard inlaid with satinwood, the long table, its surface polished to the sheen of glass, the epergne and candelabra of embossed silver, the cost, the value.

There was a portrait, well lit by a branch of candles, of the lady who had died, according to Hannah, of some lingering malady of the nerves, and, according to Elinor, of fright occasioned by her severe spouse. But her painted face looked calm enough, as if she bore him no grudge, and, noting the pearls painted around her throat, I knew that Joel – and possibly Hannah, too – would be quick to assess their worth and wonder what had been done with them now.

'I have no daughter,' Mr Aycliffe said, startling me, since I thought he had read my mind and was about to tell me the whereabouts of his wife's jewels. Although he simply meant to apologize for the lack of a hostess, the point was clear to us all. He had no daughter and consequently his wife's pearls would be available, surely, to her successor, unless, of course, his son should, in the meantime, marry a lady capable of making her claim.

A manservant attended us, an ageing, anonymous black shape, but a manservant, not a girl. And, having expected the food to be anonymous too – in keeping with our host's deliberately clerical manner – I was surprised by the collops of veal in a buttery, peppery sauce that lingered on the tongue and by the wine that was not clerical at all. Mr Aycliffe did, indeed, apologize for the variety and abundance of the wine, suggesting that it was done for our sake since he knew my grandfather kept a good cellar, but, although he drank less than Joel and considerably less than his son, his dry fingers curved themselves with a collector's appreciation around the long, ornamented stem of his glass and his tongue savoured the bouquet with a lingering pleasure that – whether he liked it or not, and whether Hannah liked it or not – could only be called sensual.

But perhaps Hannah was less shocked by this new aspect of her lover than she might have been. Certainly all this caressing of his possessions – the possessions themselves – had, at first, seemed strange to her, and being strange had seemed wrong, but she had no deep-rooted objection to comfort, having preached the merits of the frugal life from necessity rather than conviction, and the image of herself presiding at this luxurious board did not displease her.

And certainly Mr Aycliffe's conversation was altogether beyond reproach.

'Yes,' he said, raising his glass to admire the effect of candle flame on the dark red liquid, 'as you know, I am much concerned with the Sunday School movement, although there has been criticism – ah yes, a great many people have explained to me the dangers of educating the labouring classes. I have been warned that it can serve no purpose but to make them discontented with their lot, and, naturally, I would be the last man alive to ignore the folly of educating anyone beyond his station. But that, you see, is where my critics are in error, for how much better to educate these young men ourselves, carefully choosing the information that can be of use to them, than to have some radical hothead come along and unsettle them with nonsense – and dangerous nonsense too. We teach them to read the Bible, to be industrious, right-minded, and grateful, and I think no one can refuse to acknowledge the valuable service we perform.'

And, as he had clearly paused for some sign of appreciation, we gave it to him, murmuring, 'Most valuable,' 'So very right,' all of us except the son of the house himself, who continued to stare at the wall, his fine face unutterably bored – drinking, I thought, more than he should and eating little – the fingers of one long, well-tended hand tapping irritably on the table.

'I suppose you must agree with your father?' Elinor asked indiscreetly, saying the first thing that came into her head to attract his notice.

And, his eyes going through her again, past all the primrose fairness she was so willing to offer, he said, 'Oh indeed I must,' and returned, quite rudely, to his wine.

But Elinor – who had conquered Bradley Hobhouse and knew of no reason why she should not conquer the world – was not to be put off, and, believing the best way to impress one man was to show herself off to another, she turned to Morgan Aycliffe, not because she wished to flirt with him but because he was the only other man in the room beside Joel, and even Elinor could not flirt with her brother. But her effect on Mr Aycliffe was once again unfortunate, bringing back that pinched expression to his eyes, that thinly quivering distaste to his nostrils, so that I felt bound to intervene with some dull little remark about Charity Schools – charity in general – which won me a flash of blue-green anger from Elinor's eyes and Mr Aycliffe's gratitude.

We left the gentlemen alone soon after, knowing our manners, and returned to the drawing, where, presently, the faceless manservant brought us tea and coffee in cups of a terrifying fragility, and little cakes coated with almonds.

Feeling the tight agony of Hannah's nerves, I said, 'It has all gone very well.'

'Oh, I do hope so.'

'Of course it has,' Elinor trilled, and, getting to her feet, began a dancing, twirling promenade around the room, her skirts flying so close to the objets d'art so perfectly displayed on their low tables that I painfully held my breath. 'Of course it has – of course – it's as good as done. He just wanted to see if you matched his statues and his vases, and how best to place you – an inch to the left, an inch to the right. Well, let's give him something to think about.' And as she came to a halt by the mantelpiece, her wicked hand shot out and set the black basalt urns quite roughly askew.

'Stop her,' Hannah said desperately, too horrified to move, and, jumping up, knowing how destructive her mischief could be, I slapped Elinor hard across the arm and sent her back giggling to her place.

'Put them back,' Hannah said. 'Put them straight. Please.'

But somehow I couldn't get it right.

'Is that it?'

'No.'

'Oh – I can't do it. Is that it?'

'No.'

'Oh – heaven help us, there's somebody coming.'

And the door opened, bringing Crispin Aycliffe to my side.

'Allow me,' he said. 'Oh no, don't be alarmed – my father is not directly behind me. He is still at the table with your husband pretending he don't care for the port, so we have ample time. Now then, I have often heard him say four inches from the edge of the mantel shelf, four inches from the Meissen bowls – so, how does that seem? Is that it?'

'I think so. I think it will do.'

'Yes – although I cannot suppose it will do for him. But don't be concerned for that. It is fairly safe to assume that when a man rearranges his vases as much as my father does, he enjoys it, so you have actually afforded him a pleasure. Will you take a little more coffee or tea? I was told to entertain you, and you must really give me the chance to be obedient.'

'No, nothing more, thank you,' Hannah said, her stomach too cramped with anxiety, I thought, to cope even with tea.

But Elinor, still mischievous and giddy, accepted as eagerly as if he had promised her a pearl in the bottom of her cup and, stirring in her sugar, said, once again indiscreetly. 'Was that your mother in the dining-room – the portrait, I mean? She must have been a very lovely lady.'

'Oh, I wouldn't say she was lovely,' he answered, his face completely without expression. 'Not a bit of it. That likeness was taken long ago, before this malady of the nerves you will have heard about. She became very wasted, very spoiled – not lovely at all the last time I saw her.'

His light, sardonic eyes moved slowly from Elinor's face to Hannah's and remained there.

'How terrible,' Hannah said, her voice barely under control, knowing how pointedly she had been reminded that, in his view, his father had not waited overlong to find a replacement.

And without meaning to speak at all, I heard my voice say, 'I am so sorry for you.'

'Are you?' he said, the fine arch of his eyebrows raising in surprise, taken aback, as I was, yet ready enough, I think, to say more, to ask me why, had not Joel and Mr Aycliffe come back just then. At the sight of

99

his father, he gave me a slight inclination of his head and withdrew not just his body to a far corner of the room but his personality with it, the kind of escape I had often seen my mother make.

A difficult young man, certainly, who would be a sharp thorn in Hannah's side; a dangerous, complex enemy to her peace of mind, who would have no reason to listen if I tried to explain that Hannah meant no harm, that she was a good, sensible woman who should be allowed her chance in life. A young man who was unlike anyone I had every met, who aroused my curiosity and my compassion. Yet, driving home that night, more than half asleep, I had room in my head for only two things, the pinched face of Morgan Aycliffe, entering the room after dinner, noticing at once that his urns had been tampered with again, and the realization that throughout the entire evening he had not addressed one word directly to his son.

We did not see Mr Aycliffe for some days after that. His half hour alone in the dining room with Joel had provided him with an ideal opportunity to speak his mind, but he had not done so, and when his absence extended to three days, five days, we began to be puzzled and alarmed.

'He's decided you don't match his furniture,' Elinor said with wicked glee. 'You're too tall to fit on the mantelpiece and you're the wrong colour for the hall table.'

But at the end of the week, on the eighth day, a note was delivered announcing Mr Aycliffe's intention of calling that afternoon, if Joel could spare an hour of his time. Hannah and Elinor, as it chanced, had driven over to Patterswick to visit my mother, and I made sure I was in the kitchen when Mr Aycliffe arrived, coming out at the end of an hour only to peer from the window to take note, from his manner and Joel's, that all had gone well. And so, going back into the kitchen to supervise Marth-Ellen's cakes, I was unprepared for Joel's voice yelling. 'Verity – come quick,' and downright alarmed when I found him in the front parlour shaking with laughter.

'Joel – what is it? Whatever is it? Didn't he propose?'

'Oh yes,' he said, wiping his eyes and then succumbing again to those undignified whoops of delight. 'He proposed all right. By God, Verity, he proposed. The damn fool has asked me for Elinor. Yes, you may well stare, for I did the same. I thought he had mistaken the name and told him so, which didn't please him. But no, it's Elinor he wants. Elinor. Damn me, I always knew he was the kind to have one hand on a prayer book and his other up a housemaid's skirt, but I never thought he'd lose his head this way. The fool – I ask you – with all his urns and his vases and his Napoleon brandy – has there ever been such a fool?'

10

It was, of course, perfectly disgraceful – scandalous, even – and, beneath my immediate pity for Hannah, I too could feel laughter stirring, for I did not like Morgan Aycliffe and would not be sorry to see him discomfited.

But then, as Joel began to whoop again with his unkind mirth, suspicion bit into me and I said, experimentally, hopefully, 'So that's the last we shall see of Mr Aycliffe.'

'Oh – hardly that.'

Altogether aghast, I sat down, shuddering slightly as the ludicrous image of Morgan Aycliffe in a nightshirt suddenly burst into my mind, sickening me.

'Joel – you can't possibly … Oh, Joel, you can't consent.'

'Why can't I?'

'Because Hannah –'

'Hannah has nothing to do with it anymore,' he said, laughter draining out of him, leaving him hard and hurtful in the face of my opposition. 'If he can't have Elinor he won't come back for Hannah, you can be sure of that. He didn't find it easy – believe me – standing here, asking me for my seventeen-year-old sister. He knew exactly what I was thinking, and what everybody else is going to think – and say, behind his back – and he didn't like it at all. But he did it. That's how mad he is for her, and if he don't get her he'll bolt – so Hannah's lost her chance either way.'

'So you consented.'

'I did.'

'And Elinor? You mean to force her, then?'

'Force her? What the devil makes you think I'd have to force her?'

And, as that grotesque image of the grey-faced widower in his night attire once again danced into my mind, I cried out, 'Because she won't take him willingly – you know she won't.'

'I know no such thing,' he said, and as he looked at me keenly, recognizing the disgust in my face, I saw his temper snap and felt it reach out for me with a crouching snarl, designed to hurt.

'You don't understand us at all, do you, Verity – me and Hannah and Elinor? Won't take him? She'd give her eye-teeth for him – yes, yes, yes, indeed she would – for him and for the dress allowance he can give her and for the pearls he can put around her neck, and for her own carriage so she can stop begging rides in yours and Emma-Jane's. That's what's been biting her these last few weeks, because she thought Hannah was going to get all that, and she'd be left on the shelf. And if he's not pretty, then neither is Bradley Hobhouse, who's just younger, and that don't last. But how could you understand, Verity, when there's always been your grandfather to put his hand in his pocket every time you had a whim or a fancy? So don't judge what you can't comprehend. Elinor would do anything to get out of the hole her father left her in – as Hannah would.'

'As you would?'

'I reckon so,' he said, the sting of his anger so venomous now that I turned and walked away from him, finding, to my own surprise, that by the time I had reached the refuge of my bedroom and bolted the door, I was in tears.

It was his affair, then; his and Elinor's and Hannah's, the three of them together. Deciding to take no part in it, I called my dogs and, walking up the path past the Top House, followed the track beyond my

101

grandfather's garden that led to the open moor. And when the dogs had had their run and my shoes were full of stones, I sat with Mrs Stevens, drinking tea and watching, from my grandfather's hillside perch, as the carriage returned from Patterswick and stopped at the millhouse, and Hannah and Elinor went inside.

'I'll take some more tea, Mrs Stevens, if you please,' I said, and sipped it slowly, allowing the time to pass – an hour at least – before I saw Joel come out of the house and walk across the yard to the mill. And then, after having another slice of gingerbread and calculating that the coast would be reasonably clear, I took my leave, entering the millhouse cautiously by the kitchen door and hurrying up the back stairs to find Liza, the nursemaid, and give Blaize his supper.

I put my son to bed, sat for a moment enjoying his total contentment, and then went back to my own room, hoping for solitude, but it was not long before there was a discreet knock and Elinor's fair head appeared enquiringly around the door.

'I expect you are very angry with me,' she said, walking flat-footed like a little girl across the floor and sitting, hands neatly folded, in front of me, waiting for her scolding.

'You mean to take him, then?'

'Oh yes, indeed I do.'

And when I began to ask her how she could, she made a decisive movement with one hand that reminded me very strongly of Joel.

'How could I not? And I didn't steal him from Hannah, no matter what anyone has to say. I never even thought of him, for he seemed positively to dislike me, except that I suppose he did that on purpose, to stop himself showing that he liked me too much. Or so Joel says, anyway.'

'And what of the things you said? That he was old and stale and that he frightened his wife to death?'

'Oh that,' she said, half sighing, half laughing. 'Well, I talk a great deal, don't I, and mean less than the half of it, you know that, Verity. But I am not so stupid – really. Sometimes it's better to appear stupid and go prattling on because otherwise who would ever notice me? Emma-Jane can afford to have buck teeth and never say a word, because half the men in Cullingford owe money at her father's bank. But I'm a poor relation, and all I'm entitled to say is "Please" and "Thank you kindly." And, you see, if I did that, then I'd be treated like a poor relation, which is even worse than being one, and I made up my mind long ago not to let that happen. Joel and I, you know, we're both the same; we'd do anything for money. I sometimes wonder what we'll ever find to strive for once we have it. So I'm not stupid. I know Bradley Hobhouse would never run off with me, Verity – and, far worse than that, I don't think I'd have the courage to go in any case. And that's quite terrible, you know, when you think how just dreaming about it has kept me going. So I have to do the best I can. And Mr Aycliffe must love me enormously, wouldn't you think, to risk the gossip, because they won't take kindly to it at Ramsden Street, I can tell you.'

'Elinor,' I said very slowly, 'if I catch you flaunting yourself, just once, in front of Hannah, then I shall slap your face until it swells, even if it should be on your wedding morning.'

'Oh, Verity,' she said, laughing, rubbing her cheek with a hand not entirely steady, 'how fierce you can be in your quiet way. But Hannah can defend herself, you know, and you may save yourself the trouble of slapping me, for she has done it already. She flew at me like a spitting cat and boxed my ears soundly, I can tell you, with Joel not lifting a finger to stop her. But listen, Verity, Hannah doesn't love him, you know, and now it makes no difference to her whether I take him or not – except that if I don't take him there'll be two old maids at Low Cross instead of one. And I'm not cut out to be an old maid, I've told you that often enough. I can't go on prattling and dreaming forever, and what else can I do? I don't care for the chapel and good works like Hannah. I don't want to teach Sunday School, and I can't manage, somehow, to feel sorry for the slaves when I'm not free myself. And those sugar plantations and cotton plantations are so far away. I can't even begin to imagine them. But I can imagine myself, Verity, in a few years, if I stay at Low Cross. And there won't be another Mr Aycliffe.'

'But he's so much older than you, Elinor, and so stern.'

'And so rich. And I'll be good at being rich. He likes beautiful things. Didn't you see him, the other night, with his statues and his fine wines. I won't help him with his Sunday Schools, like Hannah, but I can look pretty – that's what Joel told me to do: to look pretty and keep my mouth shut. And that must be what he wants. There must be two sides to his nature, I suppose: the serious side that wanted Hannah and the fancy side that wanted me – and my side won. Oh, Verity, don't be too cross. I'm going to have such a lovely time. Strawberries and champagne for breakfast, just like I always told you, except that I'd stopped believing it and now it's coming true. Hannah will get over it, and you don't want to spoil it for me, do you?'

'No, I don't. But, Elinor, do you really understand about marriage – I mean?'

'Oh,' she said airily, 'about kissing and being in the same bed? Well, it's not such a mystery.'

But Elinor's mother had been dead a long time, and because I could not imagine Hannah explaining in any great detail, or even fully understanding the details herself – and because Morgan Aycliffe was repulsive to me and I assumed he must repel her, too – I said rather primly, 'There's a great deal more to marriage than kissing.'

'Oh yes,' she said, 'a great deal more, and I won't be the first to live through it. We kept dogs, Elinor, like you, and pigs, and I've heard my mother say many a time that men were just the same.'

I did not expect Hannah to appear at breakfast the next morning, but it was Elinor who shirked, Hannah sitting straight-backed at the table while serving buttered toast and honey to Joel, when he came up from the mill, as if nothing of any importance had occurred. And I was aware of the bond between the three of them: a shared determination, bred of their shared poverty, that no personal sacrifice was too great if the interests of their family would be served; a bond which prevented Hannah from blaming either of the other two, although I knew she was mortified, horrified, sick at heart.

She had wanted that marriage herself, desperately, but now, having boxed her sister's ears and called her a thieving minx, after a night of self-torture and humiliation, she was almost awe-inspiring in her calm.

'I have a great deal of plain sewing to do,' she told me when Joel had gone back to the mill. 'I will take it upstairs and sit in the window. The light is better there.'

'Yes, of course.'

And then, visibly drawing herself together, she said, 'Naturally you will have heard that my sister is to be married?'

'Yes, indeed.'

'Yes – and I daresay you may have been surprised, although you must admit that there has been nothing in any way improper. When a gentleman becomes a regular visitor at a house where young ladies are to be found, he must eventually declare himself – we all know that to be the rule – and since Mr Aycliffe has declared himself, I can see no occasion for talk – gossip – you will know what I mean. Certain acquaintances of ours – Mrs Rawnsley, for one, and Mrs Hobhouse, I daresay, since they are always together – have expressed the view that Mr Aycliffe's interest was in my direction. But that was no more than supposition – I always said so, you have heard me say it – and I should not like it if they were to – to –'

'They will not,' I told her, knowing she meant 'to commiserate.' And, watching the proud, painful squaring of her shoulders as she picked up her work basket and walked away, I made up my mind to see Mrs Rawnsley and Mrs Hobhouse as soon as I could, and to suggest to them, without exactly telling a lie, that Mr Aycliffe may well have proposed to Hannah first and been refused.

My grandfather, as expected, was not pleased at this piece of good fortune which had come Joel's way. He had ordered him to get his sisters married and out of Low Cross, certainly, but he had had a shopkeeper or a schoolmaster in mind, not another financial giant like himself who could encourage Joel's habits of independence and disobedience. Although he might well have given Elinor the wherewithal to settle herself nicely into a dairy or a schoolhouse, he now elected to give her nothing. But Mrs Stevens, for whom weddings were occasions of great heart-searching, came down from the Top House whenever she could, to help with the trousseau, and, once again, it seemed that marriage was a purely feminine matter, a choice between lilac gauze and sky-blue satin, with which the bridegroom – once he had been securely attached – had nothing to do.

My mother came quite often too, adding her fine stitching to the growing pile, and, while Hannah undertook the plain sewing of the household, my mother, Mrs Stevens, Elinor, and I sat in the stone-flagged kitchen – Blaize gurgling in his cradle beside us –

concealing ourselves behind the companionable hum of our voices and the plying of our needles, with fashion books strewn all about us and a pot of tea constantly brewing by the fire.

It was, of course, to be the best trousseau ever seen in the Law Valley, for Joel would not have his sister go out a beggar, and even though Morgan Aycliffe was willing to take her on promises alone, he would at least give her the means to cut a dash. And since cutting a dash was a matter well understood by both Joel and his younger sister, we were busy indeed.

'Oh, do stay just a little longer, Mrs Stevens,' she would plead. 'Just fit me into this yellow silk again, for I've a dreadful feeling I measured wrong last time and it needs another inch off the hem. And if I don't know for sure it will nag me and nag me, and I'll never sleep tonight. And you will come tomorrow, dear, dear Mrs Stevens, won't you, because you are so good and clever –'

And Mrs Stevens, whose burden was growing every day heavier as my grandfather's temper grew shorter, his constitution weaker, would smile through her fatigue – for a Mrs Morgan Aycliffe was a different matter entirely from a Miss Elinor Barforth – and promise to come if she could. Indeed, she rarely failed, for, as my mother had once told me, she had her future to consider, and her attentions both to Elinor and to me were most marked.

'Dear Mrs Barforth, dear Miss Elinor,' tripped from her tongue like summer rain, and, whenever there was a dispute between us, which happened not infrequently, her tact was altogether a work of art.

'I think Mrs Barforth is right, Miss Elinor, my dear, because this pattern is certainly gay – excessively so, Mrs Barforth, as you say. But then, glancing at it again, although it wouldn't do for Mrs Barforth at all, since she likes simple, elegant designs which suit her so well – perhaps on Miss Elinor, who is in quite another style – So pretty. What do you think?'

And, holding up a length of sprig muslin, having called me elegant and Elinor pretty, she would leave the decision to Fate, or to my mother, on whose taste we could all rely.

Yet there were times when Elinor's bubbling excitement and Hannah's rigid control were hard to bear, and times when Joel's odd blending of self-satisfaction and ill temper distressed me. Could it be that, after all, he had his doubts about giving his sister to this dry, difficult man? Was his conscience indeed stirring, while ambition and self-interest forced him to ignore it? Yet we were the same age, Elinor and I, and capable of making the same judgements, and although I was often overwhelmingly anxious on her behalf, I could detect nothing in her own manner but unsullied delight.

Even when she heard the news of Emma-Jane Rawnsley's engagement to Bradley Hobhouse, she merely chuckled and said, 'Poor Emma-Jane. She will have his mamma to contend with, and I hope she may find a way to deal with her, for I am sure I never could. If she thinks she is to be mistress of Nethercoats she will have a rude awakening, for Mrs

Hobhouse is quite the most managing woman I ever met, and I should not like her putting her long nose into my cupboards. Well – thank goodness there is no mamma-in-law in Blenheim Lane to bother me.'

But did she ever give a thought to other things in Blenheim Lane that could bother her: to the silence, to those perfectly spaced basalt urns, to Mr Aycliffe himself? And had she considered how Crispin Aycliffe, who had been hostile to a stately woman like Hannah, must feel now that his mother's place was to be taken by a girl of seventeen? Had she considered that his presence could prove far more disturbing than any mother-in-law?

We dined once again at the Aycliffe house – Joel, Elinor, and I – this time with Mr and Mrs Rawnsley as fellow guests, neither Hannah, who had not been expected, nor Crispin Aycliffe, who most certainly had been, choosing to appear. The next morning, unable to stand Hannah's extreme politeness, her absolute refusal to ask how the evening had gone although she was longing to know, I called my dogs – in whose company I was never ill at ease – and took my familiar walk past the Top House and out to the moor.

It was high summer then, the sky behind me yellow with the slow penetration of sunlight through the pall of factory smoke, but I turned my back on the town, striding quickly away from it to a point where the tufted upland grass was sharp-scented and even the sky shredded, first to a cleaner grey and then to blue.

Hannah, I knew, did not approve of my lonely ramblings; she had even spoken to Joel about my breach of convention, the necessity for a suitable companion, but he had made nothing of it, and that morning, leaning against the wind, letting the dogs run free – the puppy now as big as her mother and not always ready to obey either of us – my mind was so full of the bare, brown curve of the land, the nearby music of moorland water, the tangy freshness of space and solitude, that I failed to recognize Crispin Aycliffe until he spoke my name.

I had seen him approach in the distance, a man walking a horse, a dark-green-coated figure that could have been anyone, and I had thought only to call up my young dog, who would be very likely to snap at the horse's legs. But it was the old bitch who came obligingly to heel, the young one pausing for an instant, flighty and nervous, dancing away, and then pausing again, taunting me to give chase.

'They are very large dogs, Mrs Barforth,' a man's voice said, 'for a lady.'

The wind striking me a capricious blow, whipping the ribbons of my sunbonnet into flight and my hair into disarray, I looked up and saw him, hat in hand, smiling, his mouth no longer sulky, his face almost boyish without its studied boredom.

'Should you be walking here, Mrs Barforth, quite alone?' he asked, and, knowing that his father shared many of Hannah's narrow views, I shook my head.

'No, I daresay I should not, for I always go home with stones in my shoes, but someone must walk the dogs.'

106

'Your dogs?'

'Yes – at least the young one is mine, and the old one belonged to my brother, so I may say she is mine now too.'

'Your brother Edwin?'

'Did you know him?'

'Oh – barely. We shared a term or two at the grammar school, but I cannot say we were friends. You are not in the least like him.'

'I suppose not. But do you often take this road, Mr Aycliffe? It seems a little out of your way.'

'Indeed it is,' he told me, his eyebrow making its fine, quizzical arch, 'since it leads only from Cullingford to Lawcroft Fold, and then on to nowhere. I was coming to pay you a visit, to apologize to you and to Miss Barforth for my absence at dinner last night. At least, I intended to come, but somehow my horse rode on, until your house was behind me – so I dismounted and I am walking back.'

'Why? In case you should ride past us again?'

And for an odd, uncomfortable moment, I saw him in that sombre, beautiful house, hiding his bruised feelings behind that quizzical, insolent lifting of the eyebrow, that sardonic curving of his mouth, while his father ordered him to saddle up and ride over to Lawcroft without fail to pay the visit that common courtesy demanded, that filial duty absolutely required.

'The girl is to be my wife, and you will go to her, as you should have done a month ago, and you will say everything that is proper, everything that is due to her as my intended, everything that is due to me as your father. I am not answerable to you, boy, but you are answerable to me, and you would do well not to forget it.'

And because he was indeed answerable, because his father held the purse strings and would not hesitate to drawn them tight, he had ridden over to Lawcroft, looked down at it from the moorland road – sick, I thought, with anger and disgust – and ridden on, needing a moment more of clean air and space to equip himself for the ordeal of taking Miss Elinor Barforth's tiny hand and declaring himself ready to love her as a son.

'It would seem,' he said quietly, 'that I gave serious offence by my failure to dine –?'

'Not to me, certainly.'

'Possibly not. But to your husband and to – your cousin?'

'Oh, as to them, they are both quick to take offence and quick to recover.'

'But you will nevertheless accept my apology?'

'Of course.' And, feeling again the abhorrence in him that prevented him from even speaking Elinor's name, I quickly added, 'And I will convey it to my cousin. She is not at home today, but she will gladly forgive you. You may tell your father so.'

'Oh,' he said, 'thank you,' his hand adjusting something at the horse's head, his attention apparently elsewhere, until my young bitch, planting herself at a safe distance from the flying hooves, set up a howling that caused the fine bay animal to shiver. It was not until my flighty young dog had gone dancing off into the wind and his horse stood, sullen and offended but peaceful again, that he looked at me very carefully and said, 'Is Miss Elinor Barforth really not at home?'

'Well ... yes, as it happens, she is at home, but she is very much occupied with my mother and our housekeeper, and I know they don't wish for a visit from anyone today.'

'And is it so very obvious that I don't wish to pay one?'

'Yes,' I said, my eyes drawn directly to his face. 'And there is no reason in the world why you should apologize for that. I perfectly understand why.'

'Do you?' he said, his eyes half closing with a weary gesture I had observed in him before. But he was not ready yet to accept my sympathy, and when his eyes opened there was no weariness in them any longer, but keen, cool sarcasm, tinged unmistakably with spite.

'And why is that, Mrs Barforth? Do you imagine I object to my father's choice of a second wife?'

'I think it can scarcely please you.'

'Oh, but it does. It pleases me enormously.'

And when I shook my head he laughed, not pleasantly, a snap of malice once again in his face.

'You are quite wrong, Mrs Barforth – so very wrong, believe me. I am delighted – totally enchanted – with Miss Elinor. And if there is something undignified or questionable in the spectacle of a man of my father's years cavorting with a child – and I imagine she is very much a child – then, well, that delights me even more. I am not, as you may have noticed, particularly attached to my father, but even I – Mrs Barforth – in my worst moments – could never have devised so complete a punishment for him as this. They have the very greatest chance of unhappiness I think I have ever observed, and if you knew me better you would understand that I could hardly object to that.'

But it was too much, too personal; I was too aware of the hurt in him, smarting beneath his cruelty, too ready to sympathize, and I said stiffly, 'Mr Aycliffe, we do not really know each other, and you should not speak to me like that.'

'No,' he said, instantly the courteous young gentleman minding his manners, his smile rueful and charming, expecting to be forgiven. 'Of course, I should not. I know that very well, and yet I allowed myself the liberty – indulged myself – because, well, you feel so very sorry for me, don't you, and so I knew you would forgive me. I have taken advantage of your kind heart, you see, just as I used to do with my mother, for it is quite true that I have been very much indulged. Have I really offended you?'

'No. But I must be getting back now.'

'Then I have offended you.'

'No, not in the least.'

'Then why must you hurry back to Miss Elinor – who is not at home? But, of course, if you must, then I am sorry for it, especially since we may not have the chance to talk again.'

'Why is that? Are you going away?'

'Yes,' he said, smiling. 'Indeed I am, and you may tell me how glad you are of it, if you wish, for your cousin's sake. I am going to France and, hopefully, to Italy, in pursuit of architectural knowledge – not forever, alas, but for long enough to prevent my sour face casting a gloom over the start of your cousin's marriage. Naturally I shall attend the wedding, for it would be thought odd in Ramsden Street otherwise, but I shall leave straight after. I am at pains, you see, to spare my new mother the slightest degree of awkwardness.'

'No, you are not,' I said sharply, speaking to him very much as I would have spoken to my brother Edwin, and, throwing back his narrow head, he burst into a peal of real, uncomplicated laughter.

'You think I am merely feeling sorry for myself, then?'

'I don't know about that, and perhaps you have good reasons. But this is not of my cousin's making, you know. She is young and her life has not been easy, and really, when it comes down to it, she can only do as she is bid.'

'Yes, indeed,' he said, suddenly very serious, gentle almost. 'You are right, of course. How terrible to be a woman. I have often thought so. God knows, I am not so free as I could wish, but a woman has no freedom at all. And, worse than that, she knows she never can be free. I think that would drive me mad. There is always someone pursuing you, isn't there – father, brother, husband, children, eating your time and energy and believing they have a right to it, allowing you no rights at all. I find it terrible, and yet I have done it myself, for I laid all my burdens on my mother's shoulders, no matter how weary she was. And if I take a wife I shall doubtless do the same. But you are quite right, Mrs Barforth; your cousin is not to blame, and you clearly would not wish to see her made miserable.'

'Indeed I would not.'

'And I have worried you on her account. Please forgive me. The fact that my father and I cannot live in peace together does not exclude the possibility of his being at peace with someone else. I have a bitter nature, I think, and often I make too much of things. Your little cousin may be exactly what my father needs, and, in that case, she will do well enough.'

I turned and walked forward, towards Lawcroft, my back now to the thin blue sky, my face to the smoke, and he fell into step beside me, his horse following with supercilious grace while my old yellow bitch pressed close to heel, the puppy continuing her frenzied ballet on the borders of the track. It was late afternoon, the earth heavy with the accumulated heat of the day, the town a charcoal sketch in the distance, the roof of the Top House just visible now, beckoning me home to a world where the uncomfortable truth was rarely spoken. And, looking up at Crispin Aycliffe, accepting his presence lightly and naturally, as if I had known him as long as Edwin, I said, 'Was your mother very unhappy?'

'My dear Mrs Barforth, whyever should you think of such a thing?' he said, his brows raising again in that defensive arch of sarcasm. 'My mother was surely the happiest creature alive, for she had everything any right-minded woman could desire; I have heard my father tell her so a hundred times. A house in Blenheim Lane, her carriage, pearls ... My word – happy? I should say so.'

And I could only hope that if these grand possessions had not sufficed for the first Mrs Aycliffe, they would surely content the second.

We strolled the rest of the way to the Top House in silence, and, as he bent over my hand, I told him, 'I shall envy you when you go to France. I have been to Leeds and twice to Sheffield to visit my mother's family, and if I get to London before I die I shall consider myself well-travelled. So I shall think of you, when you are looking at your palaces and your churches.'

'Yes,' he said, 'do think of me. Who knows, I may even find a beautiful princess looking down at me from one of those palace windows and come home with a royal bride to dazzle Ramsden Street.'

And so there was laughter at our parting, a surface gaiety, draining abruptly out of me and causing me to speak sharply to the dogs as he rode away. He would go to France and Italy; Joel, to London or anywhere else he chose; Elinor would go to Blenheim Lane, which in her eyes was as exciting at Samarkand, and Hannah, surely, would grapple with her disappointments and wrest something out of life, while I would stay here, neither happy nor unhappy but smiling, maintaining order, keeping the peace, and being quiet, reasonable, and serene. And for one brief moment of fierce intensity – a moment I did not relish at all – I wondered when life was going to begin.

11

They were married on a cool September morning that spoke of summer's end, Elinor in a cloud of white gauze over satin, looking like some frail creature of air and moonlight as she entered the church on Joel's arm, followed by two little girls, cousins from her mother's side of the family, whose presence spared Hannah and me the embarrassment of being bridesmaids. And I suppose, when one accustomed oneself to the stark contrast of dainty, fairy-tale bride and long, grey, withered groom, that it all went very well.

Hannah was there, of course, smiling through her ordeal, clothed in brown silk and the grand mantle of her Barforth dignity – the brooch of Edwin's hair on her collar again – and a fine gathering of Hobhouses and Oldroyds and Rawnsleys attended, brimming with good wishes and curiosity. The professional classes, too, were represented: Mr Corey-Manning the lawyer, bringing his spinster sister, and Mr and Mrs Roundwood of the *Cullingford Courier and Review*, arriving, a bare second before the bride, with a cousin of theirs, Dr Overdale, who, having recently moved to Blenheim Lane, was fast establishing himself as Cullingford's most expensive physician.

My grandfather had agreed to come, declaring himself eager to see Aycliffe go to his doom, but somehow he had not found the energy, was not up to it, although Mrs Stevens was there, and my mother, on Squire Dalby's arm, their appearance causing considerable excitement among the 'manufacturing' ladies, who, having no good opinion of Isabella Barforth, would, nevertheless, have given a great deal to make the squire's acquaintance. And occupying a pew near the back of the church were Mr and Mrs Isaac Boulton with their younger, married daughter Catherine and their elder, still single daughter Rosamund, who had been abandoned by Joel for my sake.

'You will not mind my asking the Boultons,' Elinor had said. 'It would seem odd to leave them out, for we have known them forever. I have stayed at their house often enough, and Rosamund, who is so clever with her needle, has always helped me with my dresses.'

Although I had agreed that it would seem most odd if they were not included and that I knew of no reason why I should mind, I found myself looking closely at this girl, a woman now of twenty-five or twenty-six, who, by waiting for Joel, trusting him, had landed herself, it seemed, firmly on the shelf. She was tall and well proportioned, with bright, almost bold dark eyes and high colour in her cheeks, her dark hair fashionably arranged beneath a dashing military bonnet, her hands hiding themselves in a feathered muff dyed to the exact blue of her gown. She looked smart, self-possessed, capable, the kind of girl who could dance all night and be first downstairs, fresh as a daisy, the next morning. Quick-tempered, perhaps, and flirtatious; disappointed, certainly, although she did not show it, and I would have been less than human had I not wondered what she thought of Joel now, what he thought of her. And, pondering her situation, I saw Crispin Aycliffe nodding to me from the other side of the aisle.

'Good morning, Mrs Barforth,' he said quietly.

'Good morning, Mr Aycliffe,' I replied.

And I found I had clenched my hands tightly, gripped by an uncanny, unnerving sensation that of all the people here assembled this pale young man was the only one who knew me; the only one, besides myself, who was entirely real.

There was champagne later, Elinor still in her blissful dream, her husband, and his son, too, looking as if they felt the cold, and it was not long before he whisked her away on the honeymoon I could scarcely contemplate, escorted to the coach by Messrs Hobhouse, Oldroyd, and Rawnsley, who, for one night at least, would gladly have been in his place, while Hannah, free at last from the obligation to smile, broke a plate, kicked my old bitch, and reduced Marth-Ellen to tears.

I had given a great deal of thought to a wedding gift, settling finally on a dessert service, complete with sauce tureen and ice pail, decorated with painted roses in more shades of pink than I had believed possible. And driving to Blenheim Lane to present it, after their return, I think I expected to find Elinor sunk in shock and despair and bitter regret.

'Is Mrs Aycliffe at home?' I enquired of the manservant, nervously preparing myself for a denial, but instead of the door of the room we had been brought up to call a parlour but which was now a drawing room

111

burst open and Elinor herself, ringlets and ribbons dancing, came tripping out to greet me.

'Oh, darling, how marvellous,' she said, without really looking at the china dishes, which had been purchased, in any case, to impress her husband. 'Wilkinson will put them somewhere, and then Mr Aycliffe will put them somewhere else when he comes home. Wilkinson, do see to it, and then tea, please, in the drawing room, with lots of cakes.'

And I concluded, from the faceless Wilkinson's almost imperceptible shudder, that the first Mrs Aycliffe had never presumed to take tea with friends in the drawing room, among all the precious glass and porcelain – or, indeed, had perhaps never invited friends at all.

'Are you well?' I asked her, puzzled, because although she looked well, it hardly seemed likely. But Elinor had a certain toughness, a certain coarseness, in her nature that not only enabled her to find her husband's marital endeavours amusing but made her quick to appreciate the power his desire gave her.

'My dear, he'll do anything for me,' she said, letting me see the new ring on her hand and the wide gold bracelet around her arm. 'Anything – I have only to ask – and all because he just wants to look and look at me. My dear, you can't imagine – I thought I'd be quite frightened, but he's so careful. I suppose it comes from handling all this porcelain. And do you know, that's exactly how he makes me feel – precious porcelain. I'm not even to worry myself about the housekeeping. We have Wilkinson and Mrs Naylor for that, and a host of girls ... I'm just to sit here, looking pretty, and whatever I want I just have to ring for it. When he comes home, he'll just gaze at me all evening – I don't even have to think of clever things to say. And he gave me champagne on my first morning too – oh my, I'll never forget it – although I do wish strawberries had been in season.' And she broke off, giggling not in the least coyly.

'You find it all quite – pleasant, then?'

'You mean ...? Oh well, naturally, one has to make a fuss at first, because it's expected, but, as they say, one doesn't die from it, and I think I may well endure ten minutes of puffing and panting for all this. In fact, I believe one could actually get to like it if – well – I do, that's all.'

With a younger man, I thought, a handsomer man. And, not realizing he was in my mind, I asked, 'And what of Mr Crispin Aycliffe?'

'What of him? He's gone. Didn't you see his sour face at the wedding? Looking down his nose at everything as if there was a bad smell? Well, he's gone to France, where there probably is a bad smell, and if he never comes back I shan't be sorry. Although he will come, of course, because my husband needs him to look after the business and our other financial affairs. Oh my – did I really say that? Our financial affairs – how absolutely splendid that sounds. Anyway, that's why we need Mr Crispin.'

A princess, I thought, looking down from a palace window, pink towers and spires, rose-tinted sky and water; and it suited him. A rich and royal bride coming back to Cullingford to put Elinor's nose out of joint. And because that suited him, too, I found myself smiling; I was glad that he, at least, if only for a little while, was free to find his own way.

'Perhaps he won't come back,' I told her. 'Perhaps he'll make a rich, exciting life for himself somewhere and have a new adventure every day ...'

'Or they'll hang him,' she said, quite viciously, ringing her bell for more tea and then, when it arrived, leaving it to go cold as she took me upstairs to see her silver-backed brushes, her scent bottles, her trinket boxes, but not as yet, I noticed, that marvellous double strand of her predecessor's pearls.

Yet she was well and I was glad of it, as one must be glad for anyone who sees a dream come true, and if I was uneasy, perhaps it was only because I disliked the idea of describing it all to Hannah when I got home. But the necessity, as it happened, never arose, for, as I descended from the carriage, Ira Agbrigg, that bringer of evil tidings, was standing there, cap in hand, his odd, lashless eyes respectfully lowered as he handed me a message from Mrs Stevens that my grandfather was ailing.

I had known, I suppose, that he would die eventually, sooner rather than later – as Mrs Stevens had known it – but knowing is not believing and we were both of us unprepared and terrified, she at the loss of her livelihood and I at the loss of this supreme authority who, by standing between me and the lesser authorities of father and husband, had offered me the possibility of appeal. 'Father says you may not,' they had told us as children, and both Edwin and I had always answered, 'But Grandfather says we may.' And it had always sufficed.

But now the doctor – the smart new Dr Overdale from Blenheim Lane – decreed that it would be a matter of days, a week at the most, and felt obliged to defend himself by repeating the warnings he had given on his previous visits about the effect of the wine and the food and – although he did not exactly say so – of Mrs Stevens on the overweight, overage bulk that was still, although only barely, Samson Barforth.

'He has had these attacks before,' Mrs Stevens told me desperately. 'Five or six these last two years, and he has always recovered. Dear Mrs Barforth, surely, there is hope?'

But I did not think so and she did not think so; and, as she moved sadly away, I was aware for the first time of age in her face, the tiny lines around her eyes, the slackening of her jaw now that her mouth was not smiling, the sheer fatigue of a woman who has turned forty and dares not admit it.

My mother was sent for, Hannah and Joel came, but my grandfather, waking from his drugged sleep to the realization of his end, was not reconciled. Death was just another enemy to be grappled with, and when he understood that he could not defeat it, that it had mottled his cheeks and clogged his chest for the final time and that soon it would be at his throat, he lay back in the ornate bed where I had spent my wedding night and consoled himself by hating us all.

'You were the ruin of my son, Isabella Baxter,' he growled at my mother. 'You took him from spite and broke him, and now you lead a

113

harlot's life – playing the whore for Dalby like Emmeline here plays the whore for me – except that she's a silly whore and I'll wager you're a sour one.'

And when Mrs Stevens, tears streaming down her face, leaned forward to adjust his pillows, he struck her quite hard, making himself cough again, and told her to take her fool's face out of his sight.

'What good are you to me now?' he shouted. 'And I'll not have your weeping and wailing – that's not what I paid you for and I don't want it. You'd cry as much for a sick cat, woman – damnable, stupid woman. Get out. Get out, now. I don't want you, haven't wanted you for a long time. Get away. I want my wife.'

And that, after ten years of her devotion, was his goodbye to her.

Nor would he allow Joel in the room with him.

'Tell him to wait downstairs,' he snarled, 'like the lackey he is. He knows where to find the will afterwards – that's all that bothers him – and so he can wait. Maybe he reckons I'm taking too long and he'd like to slip up here and hold a pillow over my face – aye, he'd like that right enough. I should never have let him have the Girl. I should have given her to Morgan Aycliffe's lad, as I intended. Aye, you didn't know that, did you, Verity? Aycliffe spoke to me and I was agreeable, but then Edwin died and I didn't want Aycliffe's bony hands on my mill. No – but I tell you this – if I'd strength left I'd go down now and fire it myself, just to spite yon lad downstairs. That I would – just to spite him.'

And then, for a long, aching time, he was quiet.

I thought he would not wake again, for his breathing became shallow as the night wore on, and his face chalk white where the purple mottling had not touched it, but death was neither so simple nor so clean, and towards morning he awoke, his eyes shooting fiercely open but his body limp and feeble and needing care. Even then there was another long day, with the September sunlight slanting in through the drawn curtains, hardly sweetening the foul air, Mrs Stevens somewhere outside, pathetically hovering, and Joel waiting for his inheritance, while my mother and I sat one on either side of the great bed, hypnotized by the shallow breathing that seemed sometimes to stop and then, by the sheer effort of will, started painfully up again.

The doctor came, shook his head, made his murmurings, and then went downstairs to wait with Joel, who, after all, would be the one to settle his fee, and even then, as the night fell again, my grandfather did not die, his body and soul welded together, it seemed, by his determination to keep Joel waiting a while longer.

'Would you like to rest?' my mother offered, and, when I refused, she fell asleep gracefully, her head resting on the chair back, her hands folded.

Perhaps I dozed, too, for suddenly I was wide awake, aware that the candles had burned low, that something was wrong and I was to blame.

And then he whispered, 'Verity.'

'Yes, Grandfather.'

I had to come close to hear him, for his voice was dying before him, the

114

touch of his hand as it grasped mine like crinkled old paper that would flake and shrivel in the fire.

'I don't like him,' he said. 'Yon Joel – he's like me, I know it, but I don't like him. But I've left him the mill for your sake. I could have cut him off, sent him to the devil – but you're his wife and you'd have had a poor time of it then. So I've left you everything, Verity, which is the same as leaving it to him since you can't touch it while he lives – and he'll live. By God, he'll live. I should have given you Aycliffe's lad – cut my losses and married you as I'd intended – but I wouldn't be cheated, you see. I thought I could have Edwin again. Thought I could – but no – and it doesn't matter now – damn it – doesn't matter.'

And slowly, the room became empty, terrifyingly, totally still.

'I think,' my mother said, quite coolly, 'that he has gone.' And, reaching forward, she unclasped his hand from mine and then smoothed my hand with both of hers, washing his dead touch away.

'Poor man,' she said with no expression whatsoever in her face. 'He admitted defeat in the end, and I shall try not to be glad of it. He absorbed so many people's lives – your father's certainly – and there is no doubt that he was a selfish man. I used to hate him so dreadfully. Yes, Verity, really hate him. I used to long for his death. Yet here it is, and, as he said, it doesn't matter now. Go quickly, dearest, and tell your husband and our poor Emmeline. She at least will shed an honest tear.'

And, bending over him, with a steady, almost impersonal flick of her wrist, she closed his eyes.

Hannah and Mrs Stevens were in the darkened hall, Hannah maintaining the solemn face she believed to be death's due and Mrs Stevens sobbing quietly for those ten years of devotion that were ended now and for the next ten years which might well prove lean indeed. But before I could speak, the parlour door flew open and Joel, pushing them both aside, took me by the shoulders, his fingers gripping hard, as if he felt the need to shake the news out of me.

'He's dead, isn't he?' he said, the same words he had used on another occasion, the same excited glitter in his eyes, and when I nodded, although his lips didn't move, I heard his mind say, 'Thank God for that. I though we'd have the old devil to shoot.'

Mrs Stevens sat down, just that, with no apparent intention of ever getting up again, and although my mother was to pass the night at the Top House, Hannah, considering them both somewhat featherbrained, decided to stay too. But Joel dismissed my offer to remain with them and I soon found myself walking down the stony pathway beside him.

It was a crisp night, the sky twinkling with cold stars, the air coming down from the moor spicy with autumn, and, as I let it wash over me, I was aware of my own aching weariness and a certain silence within me that should have been grief. But there was no silence in Joel and once we were out of earshot – the black bulk of the mill just discernible below us in the night – his hand closed around my arm with the effect of an iron claw.

'Did he say anything about his will? Has he left it to you – as we agreed?'

'Yes – everything.'

And, as he came to an abrupt halt, his tension and his triumph poured out of him with the effect of a long, shuddering sigh, telling me that until this moment he had not been certain.

'Right,' he said. 'That's it, then. The first thing I do tomorrow is talk to my brother-in-law Aycliffe about building. And as soon as we get the old devil underground I'm away to Lancashire for the best power looms I can find, and a man who can adapt them to suit my purpose.'

But the mention of power looms chilled me, and I whispered, 'Won't there be trouble?'

'Machine breaking? I reckon not. Ira Agbrigg keeps me well informed and there's no Jabez Gott now to stir them up. I doubt they even need reminding what he looked like, swinging in the Castle Yard at York, but if they do Ira Agbrigg can take care of it. There'll be no trouble.'

'Will we move to the Top House?'

'Yes – not that I relish it, with your grandfather's mark all over it – not when I've a mark of my own and the wits and the guts to make it. But the mills and the machines comes first, and the Top House will serve until I've cash to spare. And I need the millhouse at Low Cross for Ira Agbrigg, since I've a mind to make him manager there, and he has a wife and a parcel of brats to come with him. So there's Hannah to fit in at the Top House, too.'

Although the prospect of accommodating Hannah made my heart sink, the face of another woman – even more in need of a home – swam into my mind.

'What will happen to Mrs Stevens?'

'Mrs Stevens? What should happen to her?'

'Well, something – surely?'

'Oh, as to that,' he said, shrugging his total indifference to her fate in a manner I found displeasing, 'women of that sort should know what they are about. I believe your grandfather may have left her five hundred pounds, and I daresay she feathered her nest, these past ten years, at his expense. More fool her, if she didn't.'

And, remembering my mother's light voice telling me, 'She is quite accustomed to being discarded, our Mrs Stevens,' I was suddenly very angry. I had disliked her because I had seen her as part of my grandfather, had laughed at her honeyed wooing of every man she met, her cloying, transparent self-seeking, but the reality of her – her no longer being young; knowing that when her beauty finally faded and her five hundred pounds was done, she could well be faced with the stark choice of the brothel, the workhouse, or the street – that reality touched me very deeply. Emmeline Stevens, the woman who no longer mattered to the men who had used her once her usefulness was done – men like my grandfather and Joel, for they were alike, who took women for a variety of purposes, to satisfy a range of appetites, as they would take any other commodity. And her plight convinced me of two things: that no woman could really grow accustomed to being discarded and that it was no particular virtue on my part but merely an accident of birth which prevented me from standing in her shoes. And I made up my mind that

116

when we moved to the Top House I would ask her to stay.

I went home then, feeling the cold, leaving Joel to contemplate his new possessions a while longer, but I was still at my toilet table, brushing the tangles from my hair, when he came into the room, carrying a tray with a bottle and glasses, and a branch of triumphant candles.

'Champagne,' he said, vibrant, victorious, and totally joyful.

'Champagne?'

'Yes – champagne for a funeral. Shocking – but then I'm not always a hypocrite, you see, Verity, and I'm a free man tonight. He was a bad old devil, your grandfather – I know that, you know that – and maybe I'll be the same at his age – so, if you outlive me, you have my permission to celebrate my passing with champagne, and good luck to you – you and my son together. But this is my time now – just starting – and I'll do the celebrating.'

And lifting his glass to the light a moment, he smiled at it, saluted it almost, and drank greedily, his whole body rich with enjoyment.

'You'll drink with me?'

'Yes.'

'Good. But then I knew you wouldn't refuse. You always give me what I want, when I want it – don't you, Verity? Always so good and polite – except that I'm not a polite man, girl, and tonight I'll need more than that. Tonight your politeness won't be enough.'

'Whatever do you mean?' I said, withdrawing from him.

And, laughing at my obvious perplexity, he refilled his glass and swallowed the wine once again with powerful, full-throated pleasure.

'I'll tell you, Verity. I thought he'd never die, that old man. I thought he'd live to plague me until I was old myself and soured by the burden of him – too old and dry to care. But he's gone and I'm in my prime, and, by God, I like it. I need to revel in it, Verity; I need to burn the pleasure of it out of me tonight, so I can show a decent, sober face tomorrow, when I stand by his coffin. And I need you to revel with me.'

'I don't – I don't know – I don't think –'

'No, you don't know, and you don't think, and maybe you can't – maybe it's not in you. But it's a challenge, if nothing else, and that's always been my style. I like to fight and I like to win, and what I win I value – so let's see, shall we, what we can do with you, to stop you saying, "Yes, Joel," like your mother used to say, "Yes, William," and for the same damn reasons – because it's easier to say yes and get it over with. Come here.'

But my body had turned completely cold, as awkward and tense as on our wedding night, and, stung by his mockery – and perhaps to give myself a little time – I cried out, 'Well – you may talk about challenges, but you didn't put yourself out to win me before we were married. You let my mother do your proposing for you, and you were grateful enough to me for not making a fuss.'

'Ah yes,' he said. 'That hurts, does it? That makes you cross? Good. Your grandfather was the challenge that day, sweetheart, not you. And now it's your turn – now that I've got time to spare. Yes, yes, I was an unfeeling brute. Get angry with me – very angry – lose your temper, Verity.'

'No, I will not.'

'Oh yes you will – just think about my making you take Hannah to live with you, and what she thinks should be done with your dogs.'

'What about about my dogs?'

'Didn't I tell you ...?'

'Joel –'

'Ah well – it's not the moment – but Hannah says it's not right for a lady to have dogs that size. And I have to admit – gun dogs – something odd about gun dogs, I'm bound to agree. So get yourself a pair of spaniels, if you like, and as to the others, perhaps Hannah's right. Perhaps I'll tell you to get rid of them.'

And whether it was true or merely some part of the strange game he was playing, it was an exercise in power – between me and Hannah? between me and Joel? – and I knew I'd have to fight; I knew, incredibly, that I wanted to.

'I won't do that, Joel.'

'Won't you, by God.'

'No, by God.'

And I could not miss the snap of excitement in his eyes, the heat in his fingers as they closed around my wrist and pulled me towards him.

'You'll defy me, then?'

'I'll defy you.'

'And if I take the brutes out now and shoot them? What then? You know I could, and would.'

'I know.'

'And ...?'

'Don't, that's all.'

'My word,' he said, his eyes flickering over my bare shoulders. 'Defiance, and disobedience. Rebellion, then?'

'If you like.'

'Oh, I do, I do.'

'Leave me be,' I shouted, struggling in his arms, realizing he was hurting me, although I could feel no pain, and suddenly, as his mouth came down on mine, a great, uncomplicated, wholehearted fury welled up inside me, liberating me utterly from the restraints of common sense. Sinking my teeth into his lower lip, I twisted both my hands into his hair and tried hard to get my knee into his groin, to hurt him any way I could, so that, overbalancing, we fell together onto the bed, Joel freeing himself, laughing, catching my wrist and pulling me against him.

'That's it, darling,' he said. 'Come on, stay angry a while longer.'

Howling now with the birth of most uncharacteristic temper, I began to strike out, hitting him anywhere, not hurting him at all, I suppose, since he went on laughing, but needing to strike, welcoming the fierce release of energy that quickened my breath and the glorious loss of dignity.

'Damn you,' I threw at him, seizing a pillow and vainly battering him with it. 'You think you're so marvellous ...'

'I do,' he said. 'Come, I'll show you.'

Taking hold of the pillow, he tugged it sharply forward and then, as I fell on top of him, turning swiftly over so that I was beneath him, our mouths snapping and biting at each other a moment longer, before my body, of its own accord, acknowledged its need and made no effort to escape when he eased his weight away and, casting his eyes over the entire length of me, put his mouth delicately against my stomach and let it travel upwards, inch by lingering inch, to my mouth, which, for the first time, and most astonishingly, was waiting.

'It's called pleasure, Verity,' he said, his breath teasing my ear and the base of my throat. 'Why leave it all to me? In your place I'd make damn sure I got my share. When I touch you like this I'm telling you you're beautiful – it's the best way I know. Since I reckon I'm not ugly, you can tell me that, too, can't you, in the same fashion?'

Pleasure, alien to my nature, yet there it was, in his skin, in the intricacy of his bone and muscle beneath my fingers, in the earth-scent of him, in the flaunting challenge of him. Pleasure in my own skin, too, rising up in breathless expectation from every pore, so that my body expanded in the glow of it, languorously stretching, languorously sighing itself towards him until, quite suddenly, something stirred hesitantly, almost secretly, a tiny threat waking, growing, its tendrils coiling, delicately spreading. And as I intently bent my whole mind on that tiny thread of joy, determined not to lose it, not to frighten it so that it would shrivel away to its birthplace at my body's core, he said, 'Shall I stop now?'

'What …?'

'Shall I stop? Let you go to sleep?'

'No! Don't – please, Joel.'

And afterwards, when the threads had joined together into my body's first sensual rejoicing, when I had clung to him and cried aloud with ecstatic amazement, he lay smugly on his back and told me, 'You'll know now what I mean by need. Ah yes, I've got you now, Verity. You'll miss me, girl, next time I'm away. You'll be sending to the Old Swan to see what time my coach gets in, and getting yourself ready. And I'll bring you perfumes, the next time I'm in London – the kind my sister Hannah doesn't approve of – and you'll wear them for me.'

But for all that he had shown me of the nature of need and pleasure, for all he had spoken of challenges and triumphs and the gifts he would bring me, he had made no mention at all of love.

12

We took possession of the Top House as soon as my grandfather had been decently carried out of it, and there, almost exactly nine months later, my second son, Nicholas, was born. My daughter, Caroline, followed fourteen months after that, her birth proving so difficult, so unlike the other two, that Mrs Stevens – who could be relied on to know such things – warned me that, for a while at least, there would probably be no more.

My recovery from that third confinement was slower, too, and I spent the summer of my daughter's birth sitting in the garden of the Top House, as my grandfather used to do, looking down on the recently completed six-storey mill Morgan Aycliffe had built for Joel from a design supplied by his son Crispin, large enough to accommodate upwards of eight hundred power looms, and which had cost £80,000 of my grandfather's money.

'Yon lad's overspending himself,' declared Mr Oldroyd of Fieldhead, who had the reputation of being ready to cut a currant in half.

'I reckon old Samson Barforth would turn in his grave if he knew,' muttered Mr Hobhouse of Nethercoats, who still maintained, with some violence of language, that power looms had no place in the future.

But neither Mr Aycliffe the builder nor Mr Rawnsley the banker appeared to share that view, and within two years of my grandfather's death, Joel's commercial standing in Cullingford was high. And when the new looms began to come in, slowly but very surely replacing the old, there was a grumbling and a growling but little more, for Cullingford was by then in a state of explosion, surging out from its centre to swallow every available stretch of green separating it from the surrounding villages, and then swallowing the villages themselves, so that one could no longer tell where Cullingford ended and Fieldhead, Thornwick, or Lawcroft Fold began.

At the start of the century there had been only two mills of any size in the region of Cullingford, ours and the Hobhouses', but now, less than thirty years later, as other men besides Joel saw the advantages of this new machine age, there were already fifty, with the prospect, it seemed, of fifty more, the monstrous belching of their chimneys fast discolouring the rows of back-to-back cottages with which Morgan and Crispin Aycliffe had covered the fresh grass, had driven away the memory of birdsong.

And the town in which I had grown up, comfortable little Cullingford with its 13,000 souls, was now a sprawling, black-faced, uneasy giant, where some 43,000 people earned – or did not earn – their bread.

In the streets around Joel's other mill, Low Cross – Simon Street and Saint Street, Gower Street – the tall houses designed for the original, quiet inhabitants of a sleepy market town had been reduced to anthills where the Irish – in perpetual flight from famine – crowded five and six and ten to a room; a wild, foreign people, alien in speech and religion, not understood and so mistrusted. And every day saw the arrival of the landless agricultural poor – on foot, most of them, their possessions and their children on their backs – coming North in search of work.

Although there was work, not all were fit for it, not all would take it, and there was always resentment brewing beneath the grime, always the possibility of another Jabez Gott somewhere in the tenements of Simon Street or those rows and rows of dingy, identical cottages thrown up by the Aycliffes.

120

It had happened, I suppose, as my father had foreseen: for the hand weavers in general, even when hunger began to bite, would not take work in the factories, and those who did could neither settle nor give satisfaction. Accustomed to working very much as they pleased, to staying up all night Monday and Tuesday to finish the week's work by Wednesday, making Thursday and Friday into a holiday if it suited them, they – like the farm workers, with their habit of following the seasons – could not adapt to the steady flow of work required day in, day out, by a machine. When the sun shone and they had enough cash in hand to meet immediate requirements, many of them quite simply would not appear; others would come in the afternoon when they had finished digging their allotments or tidying their hen runs – and when the millmasters retaliated by keeping wages low to ensure regular attendance and by imposing fines on latecomers, it was not understood. But, as Joel had seen from the start, a woman – a very young woman – had strength enough to operate a power loom, and, although women and children had always worked in the mills, increasingly now men were required only for the skilled work of loom tuning or the heavy work of loading and lifting. And since hand weavers were usually small men with no spectacular endowment of muscle, the hard labour – at Lawcroft and on Mr Aycliffe's building sites – was reserved for men of farming stock and the Irish.

'Bloody thieving Barforth bastard' was scrawled one morning on the garden wall of the Top House, but Joel, who drove a smart, high-perch phaeton down to the mill these days, with a glossy grey mare between the shafts, did no more than smile, remarking that perhaps Hannah's Sunday Schools were not such a good idea after all if this was what came of teaching the poor to write.

But Hannah's Sunday School was more than ever her pride and joy, her control of Ramsden Street Chapel as absolute as Joel's control of Lawcroft, and although she was not popular with the entire congregation, as he was not liked by all his operatives, there were few who cared to disobey either of them. Hannah, of course, had not welcomed her move to the Top House – certainly not in the dreadful capacity of spinster sister-in-law, and certainly not with Mrs Stevens remaining as housekeeper – and she had made her feelings immediately clear.

'You are surely not thinking of keeping that woman on,' she had told me the day of my grandfather's funeral, when Mrs Stevens, only an hour earlier, had wept with gratitude in my arms. 'For it would be thought most odd – the whole of Cullingford being aware of the terms on which she stood with your grandfather. I must ask you, Verity, to consider my own position in this, for I really cannot be expected to associate so closely with her.'

But, from necessity, they got along well enough, tolerating each other as they tolerated my dogs and my children, and there could be no doubt that, as a housekeeper, Mrs Stevens had no equal in the Law Valley.

The Top House, enormous for my grandfather alone, was less spacious now, but there was an adequate drawing room and dining room for the entertaining of guests, a back parlour for my day-to-day living, and a small oak-panelled room behind it where Joel could retire with his newspapers and his accounts and the cigars his sister found so offensive. There were my grandfather's lofty bedchamber, new-furnished and new-painted, two cosy rooms for Hannah and Mrs Stevens, and two cosy rooms to spare; the attic floor was pleasantly converted to nurseries, with space for the nursemaid Liza, my old Marth-Ellen, and the girls already in Mrs Stevens's employ. We had the garden, the carriage drive, the stables with rooms above them for the coachman, and his lads, and although it was not enough for Joel, it had, at least, the bones of the gracious living he required – a step, no more, in the direction he wished to take.

He had been, to begin with, a hungry fighter, goaded by pride and poverty, ferocious in his energy and his desires, and now, with Lawcroft at his feet, his appetite had not abated. He had his phaeton now, sure enough, to take him down to the mill, but he was there, in the mill yard, every morning at five o'clock as he had always been, to see the engines come on; there, at the mill gates, to see the first of his operatives arrive; there to see the last of them leave, letting them know that if their hours were long, his were longer. He was there in the sheds, too, throughout the day, appearing without warning, unerringly locating the source of trouble or idleness, making it abundantly clear to all of them, from managers and overlookers to weavers, spinners, and even the young 'piecerners' and 'scavengers' who twisted together the broken threads and retrieved the waste, that there was no job at the whole of Lawcroft that he had not done himself at one time or another, no job he was not prepared to do again, if the need arose. And it was well known in the Law Valley that men who had worked for Bradley Hobhouse and even for Matthew Oldroyd, neither of whom were fond of soiling their own hands, had a rough ride when they came to work for Joel.

Yet his wages, to men who understood his requirements, were good and his treatment of those wise enough to know he could be neither fooled nor flattered was fair.

'Don't tell me why you *can't* do it,' he would demand of a loom tuner faced with the apparent wreckage of a machine or a shed manager with an impossible delivery date to meet. 'I can think of a hundred reasons why not. What I want from you are the reasons why.'

And, more often than not, the machine was mended, the goods went out on time, a bonus was paid, the successful man's name entered into the credit side of Joel's memory.

'I don't ask the impossible,' he told them. 'If I can do it, so can you.'

For the ones who could not there was no alternative but to go, cap in hand, to the likes of Hobhouse or Oldroyd.

'You don't suit me' was all Joel ever told them, winning himself no popularity in the town, nor in the Piece Hall either, where other manufacturers grumbled that he had enticed their best men away with money and sent them his dregs.

He had supervised, or so it seemed to me, the laying of every brick during the building of the new mill, accepting no delays, refusing to deviate an inch from his original plan.

'It won't suit me,' he said bluntly to Morgan Aycliffe whenever that wily gentleman suggested some little time-saving alteration. 'It might suit you, since I daresay you'll charge me the same whichever way we do it, but it won't suit me. I ordered what I need, and I reckon that's what I'll have, if you please, Mr Aycliffe.'

Nor did he expect those around him to be idle, and I was quick to learn which tasks he considered appropriate to a wife. He did not require me to be skilled in the making of soap and candles as my grandmother had been, nor, particularly, in the art of fine needlework or the correct arrangement of garden flowers, but he demanded far more than Morgan Aycliffe, who could content himself with a pretty face, and more than Bradley Hobhouse, whose placid Emma-Jane talked of nothing but her children and her squabbles with her mother-in-law. Joel wanted, expected, a wife who could grow with him; who could provide a setting for the things his money could buy; who could cope efficiently, without assistance from him, with the administration of a large household, improving the quality of life's surroundings with a skill and taste as new to Cullingford as the power looms themselves. And so, having Mrs Stevens to do my cooking, Liza to take the donkey work out of minding my children, I set to work on my social graces and my mind until, quite soon, when Morgan Aycliffe spoke of Sèvres and Meissen, I could answer him with Minton and Derby, and when Crispin Aycliffe spoke of Wordsworth and Coleridge, I knew they were poets and not cotton spinners from across the Pennines. And, by reading Joel's newspapers, I knew about the Corn Laws and the vexing question of parliamentary reform.

And I had my own, quite separate pleasure, my long, moorland ramblings through grey-veiled, cool spring mornings, saffron-yellow summers, biting, steel-tinted winters, with a dog sniffing close at either side, a sudden, soot-coloured bird rising up startled in my path, an awareness of small creatures, busily nest-building, life-building in the damp, roughly springing grasses, the interlacing of old trees. And, as those seasons blended and re-blended, first one toddling child, then another, emerging from the cocoon of babyhood to explore the wide, amazing world of the Top House garden.

I was not, it seemed, a woman who could take much joy in pregnancy, unlike my friend Emma-Jane, who had become pregnant on her wedding night, or thereabouts, and who viewed her body's basic biology with great pride, making it the constant subject of her conversation. Pregnancy to me had been a loss of freedom, a small invasion, but motherhood I found to be quite otherwise, and although I did not constantly wish to increase the quantity of my offspring, I was well pleased with those I had.

I had thought babies to be all alike, until the unique miracle that was Blaize. For a while, I pitied other women with their quite ordinary children. Then in the months before Nicholas came, I had worried in case this second child should be no more than a pale copy of the first. And it had taken me a day or so to accustom myself to adoring this new variation of the Barforth face, to understand that I could love them both, differently yet equally.

There was little more than a year between them, with their identical dark Barforth curls, their insistent Barforth voices making their requirements known from the start, and then the wonder of two Barforth natures growing together yet quite separately. Blaize was the winning one, the artful one, his hair fading from black to a deep brown, his eyes the same smoky grey as my mother's. He would always get his way by a sweet, guileful smile, would always bide his time, while Nicholas, the true 'black Barforth,' ebony-curled and amber-skinned, the handsome one, was ever resolute and impetuous.

Blaize from their earliest nursery days would say, 'I don't think I'll do that'; Nicholas, scowlingly, standing his ground, would declare, 'I will not do it.' And far more often than not, it would be Blaize, bowing gracefully with the wind, transferring adult tempers to his belligerent brother, who would obtain the favour, the forgiveness, who would avoid whatever task he had not wished to do, while Nicholas would end in angry, pent-up tears, taking his own punishment furiously, proudly, and even his brother's if I were not there to intervene.

'You can't deceive me, Master Blaize,' I would tell him, my heart bleeding for my younger son, understanding very well the pride that made him hide his weeping face in a corner, that made him pull away from my consoling hands. 'I know what you're up to, Blaize Barforth, getting your own way with Liza, blaming everything on your brother. You'll not get your way so easily with me.'

But Blaize would smile his pointed smile, so like my mother's, his clear grey eyes as innocent as hers, something behind their untroubled surface telling me that for all my scolding it was his unquestioned belief that I loved him best. 'Oh yes,' those eyes told me, 'I know you have to defend him, but he's only Nicholas and I'm Blaize.'

The enormity of his self-esteem, his complete certainty that the world properly belonged between the palms of his brown, Barforth hands, seldom failed to move me to laughter.

And then there was Caroline, my daughter, the female born of my own female body, without whom I would not have been complete. My daughter – beautiful from her moment of entry into the world, with black silk hair and eyes the colour of a midnight sky, an enchantment who, on the battleground of the nursery floor, knew of no reason why she, a girl, should not be the conqueror.

'She's very strong, and very noisy,' the nursemaid Liza told me, with less than wholehearted approval. 'She'll take some quietening down, ma'am, I'm telling you, when the time comes.'

But the time had not yet come when it would be necessary to explain to her that a young lady must be meek, with the appetite of a bird and motionless as a lily, and so when she put her fist into Blaize's mocking eye, stole Nicholas's pudding, and raced them both, shrieking, around the garden, I refused to listen when Liza clicked her tongue, when Hannah said, 'That child, Verity, really she gives me the headache,' refused to wonder when Joel, who rarely noticed his children, announced, 'That one should have been a boy.' We no longer took our dinner in the middle of the afternoon. We had luncheon now, at midday, which, by pushing our dinner hour into the realm of moonlight and candlelight, enabled us more easily to entertain and wear our evening clothes, as the landed gentry had ever done. And if Mrs Hobhouse and Mrs Oldroyd, who believed the gentry had no morals, did not quite like it, family pressures soon obliged them to follow suit. While Mrs Aycliffe – my cousin Elinor – liked it very well, and although her husband did not permit her to give large parties, fearing possible damage to his porcelain, she could be counted on to sparkle at any gathering of mine.

I gave a dinner one warm evening for no better reason than to show off the new pale blue watered silk on the drawing-room walls, and the new pale blue chairs to match, which toned well, I thought, with the deep red velvet sofas we had purchased the year before. And, as usual, Elinor was the first to arrive, coming early – before her husband – to chat and chirrup and arrange herself advantageously in the light, so that the next person who entered my drawing-room door would see her perfect pose and might lose the desire to look at anything else.

Strawberries and champagne, perhaps, were no longer served for breakfast in Blenheim Lane, the honeymoon and the first intensity of her husband's enraptured gazing being long over, but the glow of his possessions still warmed her and the pleasure of curling up, kittenlike, with her vast saucer of Aycliffe cream still appeared to suffice. And even the arrival, one after the other, of two little girls and a series of miscarriages to follow had barely disturbed her blissful dream.

The children, who could clearly never be admitted to the hushed Aycliffe drawing room, had been from birth so absolutely confined to the nursery, to the back stairs, to a world apart, that Elinor, when they were brought down to her for ten minutes at teatime, treated them carefully, with a faint air of surprise. Children, certainly. But her children? Incredible. And it was always with relief that she gave them back to Nurse.

But tonight she was clearly agitated, and since painful emotion in Elinor was usually associated with her stepson, I settled myself to listen, and was not sure I would be able to sympathize.

Crispin Aycliffe had indeed spent some time in France but had soon been called home again. His designs had been required for Joel's new mill at Lawcroft, for an extension the Oldroyds were building at Fieldhead, for those rows of uncouth cottages, and although he went away again whenever he could, his father – especially now that the other children were beginning to arrive – had no intention of dispensing with his services. Morgan Aycliffe, perhaps, had never looked too closely at his infant daughters – had certainly never wanted them – but they were a responsibility and a burdensome one at his age. They had to be provided for, as Elinor had to be provided for, and having lost his own inclination for the building trade – preferring to pass his days in financial manipulations of a more subtle nature and his evenings gazing at his porcelain and his wife – he began to rely more and more heavily on his son. Crispin was needed at home, and at home he must stay. But he remained unwillingly, fretfully, and in everything but his professional capacity as an architect he was a most unsatisfactory son. Or so Elinor had told me, and so she was about to tell me again.

'I am come early on purpose to say they will be late,' she said. 'And if they come at all I shall be astonished, for they have had such a set-to. He has not slept at home for three nights, so where he has been sleeping you may well imagine, and you know my husband cannot abide such a thing. And when he came in this evening – looking exactly as one would suppose – he laughed and said he would gladly go away again if his appearance gave offence, and that it would suit him well enough to take rooms somewhere and spare us the sight of him altogether. Well, and I wish he would, but my husband will not hear of it – he thinks people would talk and say it was because of me. A young man's place is at home, he says, until his wedding day – which means I shall be burdened with him forever, for he will not look at the girls my husband proposes, and the girls he does look at – well – you will know what I mean. And he will not leave without his father's consent, because of the money. So – there they are, having their set-to in Blenheim Lane, and your dinner spoiling. And what about Hannah? If Crispin does not come we shall be odd numbers at table, and Hannah will very likely refuse to dine.'

But the sound of new arrivals wiped all thoughts of Hannah, and of both Aycliffes, from Elinor's mind and she was altogether composed, dimpling with delight, as the Hobhouses were shown in, the more so when she realized that Bradley's wife, her old rival Emma-Jane Rawnsley the banker's daughter, was dressed, like herself, in yellow.

'Oh, look, Emma-Jane,' she said wickedly, 'look how alike we are.'

Patting her own gauzy, primrose skirts into artful disarray, she went skipping across to Emma-Jane's side so that all of us – especially Emma-Jane's husband – could see that if Elinor were a primrose, Emma-Jane could only be a full-blown, well-fleshed dandelion. But if he still retained a taste for primroses – as he may well have done – he was a Law Valley man, with his priorities in good order, and before he had finished shaking hands with Joel, I knew his acquisitive eyes had tracked down every new item the room contained, and calculated its worth.

Not that Bradley was himself short of money, his father's recent death having made him the master of Nethercoats and the several hundred handlooms it contained. And if Joel had been an easier man, Bradley – notoriously easy himself – would have been ready enough for friendship and praise; he might even have taken his advice about the power looms he was now anxious to buy. But Joel was not easy, and I suppose Bradley knew, as my next guest, young Matthew Oldroyd of Fieldhead knew, that he had little respect for men like themselves – and my brother Edwin – who had never had to struggle.

And as they stood one on either side of him on the hearthrug, downing their sherry and ready for their dinner, talking yardage and how much one could expect to get for it, I sat with Emma-Jane and Elinor, and Lucy Oldroyd, who had once been a Hobhouse, and waited nervously for the Aycliffes.

Hannah came into the room, in her favourite brown silk, looking very aloof and very handsome, and received a nod and a faint smile from Emma-Jane and Lucy, a good enough greeting for a spinster lady of no particular fortune and autocratic temper.

'Is you husband not well?' she asked Elinor, rather as if she were about to add, 'And is it any wonder?' But just then, as I was about to slip away and warn Mrs Stevens that we might be less than ten at table, we heard the doorbell again and the Aycliffes, father and son, were among us.

'Oh, there you are,' Elinor said, obviously startled. 'And not a minute too soon.'

But, ignoring her, they took my hand in turn, the father first and then the son; their lips spoke courteous words without meaning, their mouths smiled, and no one would notice – except Elinor and me – that throughout the entire evening, and tomorrow evening, and very likely the one after, they would not address a single word to each other.

'Oh dear,' she whispered, pressing her hands together. 'I can see it was very bad. They have been talking about her – his mother – and my husband will not forgive him for days and days. Oh dear – the dreadful boy, if only he would get married and go away. There must be someone, Verity – someone respectable – that he could take a fancy to. And if not, then I hope he runs off with a married woman and disgraces himself entirely, so that I may be rid of him.'

We had dinner then, Mrs Stevens's favourite soup rich with its liaison of eggs and cream, turbot and ducklings and spicy fruit tarts, wine from my grandfather's cellar, by no means exhausted yet; and the table decorated with garlands of rosebuds at every corner, with a vast arrangement of ferns and fruit and flowers in the centre.

'My word, this is very nice,' Morgan Aycliffe said accusingly, raising his glass to the light, admiring the crystal as much as the golden, altogether impeccable liquid it contained. 'Very nice indeed, Barforth – mighty well done.'

For the first time that evening Joel glanced at me, from the other end of the table, seeing the woman I had created to fit his requirements, the sensible, quiet little cousin grown up to be a sensible, self-possessed wife, wearing his diamonds in my ears, his silk on my back, a woman other men would look at – as he had told me on our wedding night – and say, 'By God, he must be doing well to afford a woman like that.'

As I took the ladies to the drawing room after dinner, leaving the gentlemen alone, I wondered as I passed Crispin's chair how he would amuse himself: if he would merely drink his port and stare at the wall or if, quite casually, he would toss some hot, controversial stone into their pool of conversation, making the sluggish, after-dinner waters sizzle. Catching my thought, he looked up and smiled, his eyebrows making their fine arch, and, as clearly as if it were happening inside me, I knew that his head ached, that those three nights of low company had soured his stomach and his spirits, that if there had been pleasure he could no longer remember it.

'Verity?' Hannah enquired from the doorway, puzzled, thinking I had found something amiss with the table.

Shaking my head, I hurried away.

'I hope they will not be too long,' Emma-Jane said, taking up the whole of a red velvet sofa with her wide skirts, not really caring how long they were since men were of little interest to her now that she had one of her own. But Elinor, who cared a great deal, sighed and shook her head.

'Then you will be disappointed, for I expect they will be hours – discussing their dirty politics – how long it is going to take the poor old King to die and when he does will the new one agree to extend the franchise – and if he does, who is to get the vote and who is not. And for my part I'm weary of it – absolutely – so that I don't care if they give the vote to the sheep and pigs, or shoot the Duke of Wellington, as Mr Aycliffe seems to think they should, or ask the Pope to come and sit in the House of Commons.'

'Lords,' I said, well used to Elinor's vagaries. 'I expect he'd feel easier in the Lords.'

But Hannah, always ill-tempered at dinner parties, especially when the gentleman invited to partner her was the neglectful, moody Crispin Aycliffe, said tartly, 'The franchise is of great importance, Elinor. Think a little before you speak, and then perhaps you'll understand that Cullingford – with upwards of 40,000 people – must have its own Member of Parliament. It is really quite vital.'

'Oh, stuff,' Elinor told her. 'And if we get him, he'll end up in Sir Giles Flood's pocket – or in my brother Joel's – and even if he doesn't, what exactly can he do for me? Will he build us a suite of assembly rooms like they have in Bradford and Leeds, so we can give real balls occasionally instead of having to make do with the market buildings and all those foul smells from the shops underneath? Oh, no, he'll just try to get the Corn Laws done away with, if he's Joel's man, so they can bring the price of bread down and Joel can pay lower wages. And if he's Sir Giles Flood's man he'll try to keep the Corn Laws in so the farmers can charge what they like. And, whatever they do, I don't care, because I'm in the family way again and I don't expect to survive it.'

'Oh, darling,' I said, laughing, 'how nice – and you'll survive.'

But this news, which should have been of interest to both Lucy and Emma-Jane, met with a sudden, stiff silence, a blank staring into space that was caused by the presence of Hannah, a single woman, before whom it was improper to speak of anything remotely connected with the marriage bed. And their quite spiteful determination that Hannah – who was far more intelligent than either of them – must be excluded from any kind of adult conversation, must be kept totally in the dark, was somewhat amusing but considerably unkind.

Yet there was nothing very much wrong with either Emma-Jane Hobhouse or Lucy Oldroyd. They were neither malicious nor angelic,

128

neither brilliant nor stupid, just ordinary women who enjoyed the good things of life and wanted more of them but were not uncharitable, Emma-Jane being mainly concerned with her pregnancies, Lucy with her apparent inability to become pregnant at all. They were, I supposed, happy, yet, thinking of Bradley Hobhouse and the penny-pinching Matthew Oldroyd, I could not imagine why. Clearly then, marriage to them was not about personalities but about position, security; nor was it about surprises, since neither Lucy nor Emma-Jane would ever wish to be surprised. It was enough for them that the days should follow one after the other, comfortable, cushioned, peppered with identical joys and sorrows, their calm broken by nothing more serious than a tiff with their mother-in-law or a chipped plate; enough that nothing should be asked of them that they did not immediately understand; enough for them to say, 'I am Mrs Bradley Hobhouse or Mrs Matthew Oldroyd. And this is my house, my son, my new blue chairs.'

I am Mrs Joel Barforth, I thought, with no identity apart from him. Mrs Joel Barforth. Not Verity any longer, but a serene, cool-eyed woman – Mrs Joel Barforth – who could discuss porcelain and poetry and politics, who knew the names of dozens of French sauces and how they should be served and which wines should accompany them, who understood pleasure and need, now that her body had matured – and was sophisticated enough, even, to understand that sometimes her husband took his pleasures elsewhere. And since I had accepted the limits of our relationship, there was no reason – surely? – why I should not be happy, too.

'It is because of my condition they are so cross,' Elinor whispered to me, and, seeing my blank expression as I emerged from my reverie, she hastened to make herself clear. 'My husband hates me to be pregnant, you know that. The alteration to my shape offends his eye, and he finds it indelicate in other ways. He will not come near me for months before, and months after, for which I am not at all sorry, although it makes him very nervous and prickly as a porcupine. And then, people tease, you see, and congratulate him as if it was a miracle at his age – which only serves to remind him that I am young and he is not, for which I am not at all to blame. And Crispin, of course, is thinking of himself, for if I should have a boy his own position is threatened. My poor Prudence and Faith can cost him no more than a dowry apiece, but a little brother would put his long nose out of joint. And so you see, there I am, between the two of them. And when my husband dies I have no idea what will become of me, for that odious Crispin will turn me out with nothing but my petticoats if he can find the way. Oh dear, how hard it is. I think I am going to cry.'

But, as her lower lip began to tremble, the double doors opened, bringing the gentlemen back to us again, and instead of weeping, she gave them all a brilliant, welcoming smile.

'I expect you will have noticed,' she murmured to me a while later, 'that Bradley Hobhouse has not spoken a word to me all evening, which, in Emma-Jane's place, I would find most suspicious, considering the way he has been looking – and looking – oh my. I can only hope my husband is still too furious with his son to notice, or I shall have to answer for it. And it is not my fault, after all.'

But, blessedly – for I was tired now of false smiles, false conversations – it was almost over, and quite soon Mr Aycliffe had Elinor in her cloak, allowing her just a moment to display the swansdown lining before he bade her, quite sourly, to stir herself since tomorrow would be a busy day.

'Aye, busy enough,' Bradley Hobhouse yawned, stretching his luxurious, weighty frame, with no intention, I thought, of making that grim five o'clock trek to the mill yard now that his father could be none the wiser. But Matthew Oldroyd, whose father was still hale and hearty enough to kick him out of bed if need be, made a sign to his Lucy that she understood, and all three carriages were brought round to the door.

'Goodbye, and thank you, Mrs Barforth,' Crispin Aycliffe said as I accompanied them into the hall, his hand very cool – a boy's hand almost, narrow and lightly boned; a scholar's hand, perhaps, although I knew nothing of scholars.

'Goodbye, Mr Aycliffe. I think your father is already in his carriage – waiting.'

'Oh, then he should wait no longer, for I believe I may walk.'

'Oh – do you think so?'

'Yes,' he said, smiling, understanding my concern and not offended by it, enjoying it even. 'I think so.'

And taking his hat, he went outside, still smiling, and walked, quite slowly, past the Aycliffe carriage.

'Good night, sir,' he called out, tipping his hat at a jaunty angle, making no reply when, from the dark interior his father hissed rather than spoke the one word 'Crispin,' making the name itself into a threat, a dire warning. 'You try me too far, boy,' that furious whisper said, and the insolent tilt of Crispin's hat replied, 'Not far enough, sir – not yet.'

Hannah went quietly to bed and, when we were alone together, Joel said, 'Well – envy. I like it. They'd be content with what I have, here and now, Bradley and Matthew. They'll call it success if they can hold on to what their fathers leave them. And so I make them uneasy when they see I'm not satisfied. They get to wondering where they'd be without Nethercoats and Fieldhead behind them, and the answer is right back on the muckheap. I feel good tonight, Verity –'

'I'll – er – go out for an hour,' he said. 'It strikes me I'd best drive over to Low Cross and see what the night shift are doing. There's a piece I'm waiting to have a look at, and I reckon it should be off the loom by now.'

And because he had taken the trouble to explain himself instead of simply telling me, 'I'm off,' and going, I knew he was lying.

'I'll go up to bed, then,' I said.

Nodding agreement, he reached out a casual, cousinly hand – yet again – and pinched my chin. 'Yes, love, go to bed. It's a long way to Low Cross in the dark – there and back again.'

'So I may expect you when I see you?'

'I reckon so.'

'Yes – good night, then.'

'Good night, Verity.'

And when they brought his phaeton to the door, I refused to lift a corner of the heavy velvet curtains or the shrouding, confining lace to see in which direction he drove away. I refused to listen to hoofbeat or heartbeat, or anything but the calm shell of myself which assured me that – like my mother and my grandmother before me – I understood, I accepted, I was not threatened. 'If it happens,' my mother had said, 'it will mean very little to him.' And I had no intention of asking myself – not tonight, not ever – what it meant to me.

13

That same year – my twenty-second – saw the death of the King, our fourth Hanoverian George, an event not much regretted except, perhaps, by his Prime Minister, the Duke of Wellington, who was left with the hushing up of a royal scandal or two and the certainty of a general election.

He had been a man of appetite, King George, accustomed to breakfasting on pigeon pie and champagne, with brandy, hock, and laudanum to follow; and a great lover of other men's wives, although he had locked his own out of the Abbey on his coronation day. His only child, Princess Charlotte, having died in childbed, he was to be succeeded by his brother, the Duke of Clarence, a fussy, well-meaning old gentleman who, it was thought, in his eagerness to please might listen not only to the Duke of Wellington but to the clamorous voice of Reform.

And Reform, of course, was the only answer, for although some of us were very rich that year and some of us very poor, we all had our grievances. We were not content.

In the countryside, men turned into landless labourers by the enclosure of common pasture and driven to despair by a series of harsh winters had taken to burning hayricks and breaking the threshing machines that were rendering their muscles obsolete. In Ireland, there was unrest: a growing Catholic demand for freedom from Protestant England, trouble in the streets, and the Lord Lieutenant – the Duke of Wellington's brother – attacked in his box at the theatre. Here in the newly industrial North, the hand weavers were tightening their belts, withdrawing into the bitter, resentful brooding of men who want to work and cannot, supported in many cases entirely by what their wives and children could earn in the mills. And since the millmasters, in their determination to keep their sheds full all day, every day, adhered to their policy of low wages, those earnings were rarely sufficient.

In France, there was revolution again, a bloodless, businesslike affair this time, exchanging one king for another, not to suit the convenience of a haughty aristocracy or the demands of a radical people but due

131

entirely, we were led to believe, to the calculations of cool-eyed men of business. And whenever there was revolution in France its unsettling effects were felt here, too, not only among the London mob and the northern political unions – notoriously easy to unsettle in any case – but among businessmen of our own, who, now that the accumulation of money was less difficult, less of a challenge than it had been, were beginning to appreciate the attractions of a new challenge – political power.

In that troubled year of 1830, there was no one, it seemed, who wished matters to continue just as they were – no one, that is, except the Duke of Wellington and his following of country squires, our own Squire Dalby among them – for even the aristocratic Whigs, that party of impeccably born grandees, were ready for change, if it could help them to oust the Iron Duke from power.

Reform, then, of Parliament, was the only answer, for, in a country where a mere fraction of the population had the right to vote, no effective change could otherwise be brought about. Parliament existed, we had been told, to serve the interests of property, not of individual people, but the trouble was that since the original boroughs had been created, 'property' had shifted somewhat – had moved North, for the most part – so that towns which had once been flourishing were now almost deserted, while others had transformed themselves from hamlets at a river crossing to thriving centres of human endeavour. And although these dwindling old boroughs had lost their importance and their population, they still retained the right to send a representative to Parliament – ready to support the agricultural interest – while the new industrial towns were not represented at all.

The county of Yorkshire as a whole, the largest in England, sent only two members to Westminster. The ancient city of York had a member of its own, and the city of Hull, along with a dozen other antique boroughs, many of them remote country places by now and in the pocket of some great landlord who would bestow them on promising young men of his own choosing who would be guaranteed to handle matters his way. But Leeds, Bradford, Sheffield, Wakefield, Halifax, Huddersfield, Cullingford were not enfranchised; they had no one in Westminster to speak for them, and now that trade was expanding, now that Yorkshire cloth was becoming a new wonder of the world and Yorkshiremen were anxious to secure that world very much as their oyster, the matter was growing urgent.

The issue of Reform became so sensitive, so vital, that in November of that year, the Duke of Wellington's government was defeated, three months after an election victory, an event for which the great Duke was himself entirely to blame, having risen to his feet and informed the nation that the extension of the franchise was so abhorrent to him that he would not countenance it at any price.

Not only would he refuse to bring forward any such measures himself, he told a shocked House, but he would consider it his duty to oppose them when proposed by others. In the Duke's opinion our electoral system was perfect, the distribution of votes just as it should be, since he and all his friends had one and, apart from the soldiers in his army, he had probably never met anyone who did not. But, as with many old men, however distinguished, the ducal eyes were focussed on the past, and his apparent conviction that votes should be reserved for gentlemen was his undoing. A fortnight later his resignation was in the hands of our new, uncertain King William, who was perhaps not too sure about Reform himself, while the manufacturers of the Law Valley – who were very sure – began meeting quietly to discuss what a Member of Parliament of their own would be worth to them, and how best to use him.

'Sir Giles Flood will be sure to have his man ready,' Morgan Aycliffe lectured us one evening when we had gone to dine with him and Elinor, who was looking unwell. 'Yes, Sir Giles still thinks of Cullingford as an extension of his own stable yard, and as soon as the Reform Bill goes through he'll have his man ready – his son-in-law, or one of the Dalbys, or some bright spark from London who won't even trouble to make a speech at the hustings. So we must prepare, Barforth; we must make absolutely certain that the first member for Cullingford will speak for us – will be one of us ...'

And seeing the scornful tilt of Crispin Aycliffe's smile and the not altogether kindly amusement in Joel, I understood that Mr Aycliffe was ready now – with a son who could be trusted with the mundane details of the building trade, if not its profits – to pass on to higher things. He was not only willing to stand for election himself, he most ardently desired it; he longed, in fact, for the pomp and circumstance of it and would be mortally offended should his candidature be set aside, and yet, unprepared to expose his emotions, he wanted not merely to be invited but to be coaxed, wooed even, and was relying on Joel to do him this service.

But Joel, in matters of emotion – as I could have told him – was not to be relied on, and, taking a lazy sip of wine, his nostrils quivering with what may have been appreciation of its bouquet but was more likely suppressed mirth, he answered, 'Aye, he'd best be one of us, but I don't know who'd care to tackle it. I certainly wouldn't, so anyone who is thinking of asking me would do well to think again. Not much in Bradley Hobhouse's line either, although I daresay Emma-Jane may fancy a trip or two to London.'

And here, Elinor, whose pregnancy was not going just as it should and who had not really been listening, caught the words 'trip to London' and said eagerly, 'I can't think why you don't go yourself, Mr Aycliffe, for it would suit you – and it would suit me. Yes, Morgan, you must be our first member. I've absolutely set my mind on it, and you've talked of it so much that I can tell you want to – don't you?'

And as her voice thinned to astonishment and faded away, perhaps only Morgan Aycliffe's son was not surprised at the effect of her indiscretion. I had seen Mr Aycliffe's disapproval before, had seen him pinch his face and set his entire body into rigid lines of outraged dignity, but I had not seen his temper, which, suppressed like· all his other feelings, was a twisted, fearsome thing when it broke free.

'Mrs Aycliffe,' he said in no more than a whisper, 'do not, if you please, address me by my first name in public.'

That was all he said, but that whisper chilled me, speaking as it somehow did of punishment – not by violence but by a long, cold, suffocating silence in the days to follow when he would not address a single word to her.

'Oh dear,' she muttered. 'If I've said something amiss, then I really don't know –'

'You've said no more than we were all thinking,' Crispin Aycliffe cut in swiftly, getting up from the chair where he had been lounging, apparently half asleep, and coming to stand face to face with his father. 'Naturally you must sit for Cullingford, sir – if the Bill goes through. That's my opinion, and I feel sure Mr Barforth will endorse it.'

And as he raised his glass, with his eyes, very cool, very steady, on his father, Joel got up, too, glass in hand, and said, 'We'll drink to it, then. You can have my vote, Aycliffe – if the Bill goes through.'

'Oh, don't worry about the Bill,' Crispin told him, his eyes still holding his father's. 'There'll be a Bill all right. The country wants reform, and so our leaders – because they want to stay our leaders – will give it to us. But what kind of reform it will be I couldn't say. Just enough, I imagine, to satisfy those with the power to make a fuss – should they not be satisfied. You'll get your member for Cullingford, you can be sure of it, but they'll fix the property qualification so high that not more than a thousand of you, out of the 43,000 in this town, will have the right to elect him.'

'And what,' Morgan Aycliffe said, speaking again in that chill whisper, 'is amiss with that?'

'Nothing, sir, if you happen to be among the thousand.'

'As I will be – as *you* will be.'

'Quite so.'

And all the time their eyes were locked together, the ferocity of whatever was between them drinking up the air so that I could hardly breathe.

'You must excuse my son,' Morgan Aycliffe said, his thin lips sketching themselves in a completely mirthless smile. 'It is well known that young men who travel abroad, at their father's expense, often pick up disease, and my son has succumbed to the germ of revolution. He subscribes to the dangerous, the comic notion that every man should have the vote, without property qualification – without any qualification at all. Yes, you will be shocked, Barforth, for so was I when I first became aware of it, and I only mention it now since your wife – and certainly my wife – can hardly comprehend the extent of his folly, the implications and the threat to their own persons. Yes, he sympathizes with the penniless, you see, since he is penniless himself, more often than not, by the fifteenth of every month. You should beware of him, Barforth. He would give the vote to the operatives in your factories, and I cannot think you would take kindly to that.'

But Joel, whose only creed was to buy in the cheapest market and sell in the dearest, had small interest in political speculations of so wild a nature and no interest at all in Aycliffe's tantrums with his son. When he opened his mouth to reply, I think that he almost yawned.

'Well, as to that, he may do so any time he has a mind, for, if they got the vote, they'd have sense to know they'd have to use it my way. So, since I can count my operatives just as surely as Squire Dalby and Sir Giles Flood can count their tenant farmers, you'd be putting upwards of a thousand votes in my pocket, thank you very kindly.'

'And if they voted against you they'd lose their jobs, just as Dalby's tenants would lose their smallholdings?'

'Well, I reckon that's what they'd expect, and I reckon they'd not be disappointed.'

'And the fact that there would be a certain similarity of conduct between yourself and the squire, to whom you are politically opposed, does not concern you?'

'Concern me?' Joel smiled, automatically reaching out for the cigar he could not smoke here, in the Aycliffe drawing room, although it was permitted in mine. And he seemed so large, suddenly, so dark, and Crispin so light, so easily broken, that my mind urgently whispered, 'Don't hurt him.'

'If you mean,' Joel went on, 'that we both know how to take care of our best interests, me and the squire, then I don't see anything to concern me in that. I don't blame Dalby or Flood or the Duke of Wellingtom himself for keeping a hold on their privileges – because nobody will take mine away from me, you can rest easy on that score.'

'Yes, I feel sure I might. And yet you would deal harshly with the privileges of others, if they happened not to accord with your own?'

'Wouldn't you?' Joel asked him, easily, tolerantly, more inclined for amusement than anger. 'Surely – if it came to it – wouldn't anybody? Take the Corn Law, for instance. The Duke of Wellington and his associates, the Dalbys and the Floods and the rest of them, are farmers – corn growers – and who am I to blame them for wanting to keep the foreign corn out and their own profits high? I'd do the same if I stood in their shoes. But from where I stand, I want the foreign corn in, so that my operatives can afford to eat without pestering me for higher wages. So I have to support Lord Grey. He's likely to give me what I want not because he cares about my wages bill but because he wants the Duke of Wellington's job. That's what it comes down to – not so much conviction as common sense. They may cut each other's throats at Westminster any day they please, but what I do believe in – most sincerely – is that I shall take good care they don't cut mine.'

'Ah yes,' Crispin said, smiling too. 'I think we may all rest assured as to the continued good health of your throat. And I admire your honesty, at least, Mr Barforth. You don't pretend to hold any deep political conviction, or any kind of conviction at all – as some do.'

But this was too much for Morgan Aycliffe, who, suspecting his own convictions – or supposed lack of them – to be under attack, suddenly inserted himself into the conversation like a knife blade, too angry now for good manners, driven most painfully against his will to break his lifelong commandment that Aycliffe linen, dirty or otherwise, should only be washed in the strictest privacy.

135

'There will be no universal suffrage,' he hissed, as if it were an entirely personal matter, a misdemeanour of Crispin's he was determined to put a stop to. 'It is an indecency – a madman's dream.'

And the locking of eyes, the clash of wills began again.

'I believe you are wrong, sir.'

'I believe I am right.'

'That is your privilege.'

'What right has a man to say how a country should be governed unless he has property in it?'

'Because he is a man, sir. And because government should be concerned with people, not exclusively with possessions. Because we are Christians, sir, or profess to be, and have learned about brotherhood.'

'Easy to say, my lad, when you possess nothing and never show yourself in chapel.'

'As you say, sir.'

And as Crispin walked across to the decanter to refill his glass, Morgan Aycliffe threw at him, in that hideous whisper, 'And you drink, boy – you drink.'

'Yes, sir,' Crispin said coolly. 'So I do.' And raising his glass to his outraged parent, he saluted him, smiled, and drank it down.

'I am not well,' Elinor said, scrambling to her feet. 'Mr Aycliffe, I am not at all – as I should be. Oh dear, oh dear – Verity, will you come upstairs with me? I am not well.'

Although her interruption was timely and she did indeed appear very much out of sorts, her husband did no more than give her his permission to withdraw, showing no disposition at all to comfort her.

I did not expect to see Crispin Aycliffe again so very soon, for it was not his habit to pay polite calls or take tea with ladies, but the following afternoon brought him to my drawing room, a rueful smile on his lips and his air that of a naughty schoolboy who can usually wheedle his way back into anyone's good graces.

'I am come to make my apologies, Mrs Barforth.'

'I wish you would not. There is no need.'

'I think there must be. Can you deny that I behaved badly?'

'Oh – quite badly – very badly, if you like. But if you had good reasons – if it helped – then it doesn't matter.'

And when he began to say something, hesitated, and then seemed unwilling to continue, I said quickly, 'I was not offended. I am not going to pretend otherwise. And that is the end of it. May I give you some tea?'

'No – no, thank you – no tea. But if I may sit with you a while – for the polite interval …?'

And already I knew that if he never took another step towards me but remained on the edge of the blue satin chair, a yard away, he was still too close.

'Is my cousin Elinor quite recovered?'

'I have not seen her today. She must have remained upstairs.'

But we were not talking about Elinor at all; we were simply talking, using words because only true friends – true lovers – can really be silent

136

together, and we could be neither. Yet words do not always obey the tongue. It was certainly unwise of me, instead of making some remark about the inclement weather, to ask him, 'Do you truly dislike your father?'

And it was unfair of him, perhaps, to lean forward so eagerly and give me an honest answer. 'In my better moments I do. It's far easier, you see, to dislike him – as he dislikes me – than to feel sorry for him.'

'Will you tell me why?'

'I would tell you anything, Mrs Barforth. My father dislikes me for many reasons, some of them very simple. Because my uncle – my mother's brother – has recently made me a small allowance – not a great deal but enough to permit me to be mildly disobedient. Because I am sinful, as he calls it, and not ashamed by it, while he is not sinful at all – since it is not sin in marriage, surely? – and is frequently alarmed by his own desires. Those are the simple reasons, but mainly, I suppose, it is because I remind him of my mother.'

'And she was – she was unhappy, I suppose?'

'Oh yes, quite dreadfully. I think the very foundation of my childhood was her unhappiness, for I was always aware of it. I used to hurry home from school when I was quite a little boy, convinced that something terrible had happened to her – and often enough I would find her weeping or could see that she had heard me coming and had tried to calm herself. I felt quite unable to stay away from the house for too long, in case she needed me – in case she was in danger ...'

'And was she in danger?'

'Physical danger? No, of course not. My father is not a violent man – not with women and fine china, at any rate – and he would never have lifted a finger against her in anger. It was his disapproval she feared, and unfortunately she could do nothing right for him. In his opinion she was a most unsatisfactory woman – as I am a most unsatisfactory son – and eventually she began to believe him. She lost faith in herself, since he had none in her, and when that happened, she began to fade.'

'But what did she do to displease him?'

'Oh, a hundred little things that his eyes magnified out of all proportion – the incorrect arrangement of his vases, a glove left on a chair, a careless word, so that eventually she would hardly open her mouth in his presence. She was, I think, naturally high-spirited, even a little scatterbrained, rather like your cousin Elinor, except that she lacked Elinor's resilience, Elinor's tough Barforth fibre. She was warmhearted and sensitive and perhaps not too brave. Her spirit bruised easily, you see, and my father found her unhappiness insulting. He could not admit that it stemmed from him. There had to be another reason, and so he decided she was not well, an invalid prone to odd fancies. He isolated her from old friends and from the possibility of making new ones; he isolated her most luxuriously, but it was a prison just the same – and so, in a way, he suffocated her. He gave her everything he believed she ought to have, except light and air, and so she withered. And he was angry with her, so angry that she withered even more. He was angry the

137

day she died, and so was I. I still am. There's no more to it than that, except that, I, too, find it hard to breathe in his atmosphere.'

'And what will you do? Will you go away again?'

'Oh, I hardly think so,' he said with a forced nonchalance, his familiar, sardonically arched brow. 'How could I possibly be spared now that my father is acquiring a taste for the political life, which has never been cheap. He will need me to keep a sharp eye on his interests – and even on his wife – while he is away at Westminster. No, no, my father needs me, and I am very good, you know, at my profession. I believe I know how to squeeze together more human souls per acre than any other man in the Law Valley, which may not have been the purpose of my architectural studies abroad but is certainly most financially rewarding. My cottages may fall down in a year or two, I admit, and I have never pretended, even to the poor devils who have to live in them, that I could not do better. But they are cheap, you see – unsanitary, ugly, but cheap. And our profit margin is very high.'

'I'm sorry.'

'Why? Because I'm ashamed of my work? Yes, I am ashamed of it – it's the same feeling my father has, I suppose, every time he feels the urge to get into bed with his wife, which is perhaps one of the reasons I pity him.'

'Mr Aycliffe, I don't think you should –'

'No, of course I should not speak to you like that – not to a lady – a lovely lady – but you understand me, Mrs Barforth. Don't you?'

And because I did, because I could feel my heart pounding, the air entering and leaving my lungs, because I could hear the stirrings of that uncomfortable identity inside me which claimed the right to hope and feel – to comfort this man if I wanted to comfort him, to say, 'Yes, I understand. Go on. Share your pain with me. Let it create a bond between us. And then, when it doesn't hurt any longer, who knows?' – because of that, I knew it was time to send him away. All my choices had been made for me, long ago, by others. I had no rights, no personal hopes. I was the wife of my husband, the mother of my children; I could have no identity beyond that, and I must tell him so.

But, after all, it seemed he did not need to be reminded, for he got up, clearly preparing to take his leave, and I got up, too, nervously extending a hand.

'Once again you will have to forgive me,' he said. 'Perhaps I am too sensitive to climate – I see a great deal of misery around me, in those fine new slums I have created, and I tend to absorb too much of it. Mrs Barforth, did you know that my father once spoke to yours, or perhaps to your grandfather, about a marriage settlement between you and me?'

'Yes – yes, I knew –'

'And that I – because it was my father who had proposed it – turned sulky and would not agree to meet you … No, you couldn't know that, nor how bitterly I regret –'

'Mr Aycliffe.'

'Yes, Mrs Barforth.'

I could not, for a moment, remember the words which meant 'I think you had better go' and, remembering, found my tongue heavy and awkward when I forced it to speak.

'Yes,' he said, 'I think you are right. I will leave at once – naturally –'

And when he had gone I sat down, folded my hands, closed my eyes, and sought for silence with immense determination.

14

I did not wish to see Crispin Aycliffe again, of that I was very certain, but to avoid him would not only have appeared odd, it would have meant avoiding Elinor, too. And since her pregnancy was not going as it should, I continued to call at Blenheim Lane and so continued to meet him there, and elsewhere, and to show him the neutral civility of caution, the preservation of oneself from unnecessary pain.

'Good morning, Mrs Barforth,' he would say to me. 'Are you well?' And I would answer, just as coolly, 'Very well, thank you. And you?' And that was all.

But Elinor, sickly and depressed – fanciful, as her husband had begun to call her – aware, perhaps, that he no longer gazed at her quite as he used to, was inclined to blame Crispin for all her ills and would greet me every day with some fresh example of his spite.

I would find her, more often than not, in her bedroom, curled up on a sofa surrounded by the lotions and potions of sickness, the odds and ends of idleness with which her husband had forbidden her to clutter his drawing room. Her hair would be hanging girlishly down her back, her thickening body hidden, as best she could, in a swathe of lace and frills, and before I had taken off my bonnet, her tale of woe would begin.

'Well, and I am glad to see you, for no one has even glanced at me the whole morning. They brought me my tea and toast at nine o'clock and since then I could have died and would have been quite cold by now. Yes, and I am obliged to sit up here because he fears my medicine glass may spill over on his carpet or that I shall put it down on his satinwood table and it will leave a ring ... And if I am not well enough to go downstairs tonight, will he come and sit with me? Yes, when he's eaten his dinner and read his paper and quarrelled with his son – yes, and when he does come in he'll straighten all the bottles on my table and tidy up my books and my needlework before he even asks me how I am. And then he'll sit like a cat on hot bricks, without a word to say about anything but that abominable young man. It's Crispin's fault. It's Crispin who makes him so nervous, and if I lose this child and myself with it, then I shall know who to blame. Oh, there was such a set-to the other night, Verity, and right outside my bedroom door, in the corridor where everyone would hear them. He had come home very late – indeed I think it was almost morning, for it was quite light – and since he has to pass this door to reach his own, my husband heard him and, oh my goodness, Verity, the things they said to each other. I suppose he was not quite sober – for

139

my brother Joel was never sober when he came home so late, except that my father was never there to see – and my husband called him spendthrift and feckless, and then they began about the allowance he has from his uncle, and how my husband had tried to put a stop to it. And then my husband told him he was not fit to have it, since all he did was squander it on revolutionary newspapers and women of bad character. So there they were, going at it hammer and tongs, until my head ached, and I could hardly look Mrs Naylor in the eye the next morning when she brought my tea, because she must have heard them, too. He wants me to lose this child, I'm sure he does. He doesn't want a half brother with a half share in the business. That's why he's always provoking me, and provoking my husband – or else he wants my husband to throw him out so he can say it was because of me, and ruin my reputation. Yes, I do believe he does, for I have heard my husband say to him a hundred times that he will not let him go. "You will stay here, boy, and do your duty until I decide your duty is done." That's what he tells him. Oh dear, what an odious creature he is. And to think that when I was younger and didn't understand things so well, I wondered if he might marry Hannah. I used to think any husband was better than none, but I'd have her stay single all her life before I'd see her take him.'

But Hannah had made some slight arrangements of her own, Ramsden Street Chapel having acquired a new minister that year, a square, plain-looking man of thirty-five, red-haired and most distressingly freckled but more than ready to appreciate Hannah's administrative talents. At about the same time, on a visit to my mother, she had made the acquaintance of the new incumbent of Patterswick Church, a pale, rather beautiful young man who, experiencing some difficulty in communicating with his parishioners – his accent being vastly different from theirs – had been most grateful for Hannah's advice. And so, between the two of them – the forceful Methodist Mr Brand and the beautiful, timid Anglican Mr Ashley – her days, somewhat to my relief, were full.

'She won't marry them,' Elinor told me. 'It's Ashley she likes best and Brand she thinks she ought to like best, and so she'll hover between the two and miss them both. And really, one wonders, isn't that the best part – the courting, when you're always nice to each other and you've got your own bed to go home to? Ah well, if I die having this baby she can marry Morgan Aycliffe after all – if it's legal.'

But, towards the end of November and the sparkling, frosty beginning of December, there were times when she decided she might well live a little longer and, since her husband did not like her to appear in public once her pregnancy began to show, my services were often required.

'You may go to your brother's house and nowhere else,' Mr Aycliffe told her, requesting me privately to invite no other company when she was there – for Bradley Hobhouse had sniggered the last time he had seen her in that condition and would certainly do so again – but Elinor, like Joel, would always take a yard for every inch one gave her and saw no reason to deny herself the excitement of our winter lectures on the slave trade.

We were, of course, dedicated opponents of this pernicious traffic, both in the sugar plantations of our own dominions and the cotton plantations of America, and, to renew our enthusiasm, we would be visited from time to time by some reverend gentleman or other lately returned from the West Indies, who would regale us with all the horrors of human degradation. Sometimes there would be exhibits, bullwhips, thumbscrews, leg irons – now and again with blood still on them – and there would be tears from most of us and indignation from us all, and Lucy Oldroyd, more often than not, would be carried outside in a dead swoon. And for a few days afterwards we would feel chastened and would count our blessings and be kind to one another, until the West Indies and America began to seem very far away and we very small, and we slipped back into our everyday selves again.

Speakers, of course, varied. Some of them were pompous, some tedious, some downright embarrassing in their emotion or their enjoyment of the sin and shame of it all. Some were forthright and sincere; a few dwelt rather too lovingly on the fine female bodies put up naked for auction. A few, like Mr Richard Oastler of Huddersfield, that great champion of Abolition, were magnificent, never to be forgotten. But whatever the quality of the oration, the experience, in the dull, grey wasteland of our northern winter, did us good, and as we arrived at Ramsden Street schoolhouse that December evening, although we had heard it all before and knew, in fact, that the battle for Abolition was almost won, excitement was not lacking.

And perhaps Elinor was doubly content because, at the last moment, she had almost been prevented from coming at all for lack of the male escort her husband considered essential. Mr Aycliffe, who was himself a leader of the Abolitionist cause in Cullingford and who had been expected to take his accustomed place on the speaker's platform, had been obliged, quite deliberately I thought, to cancel; while Joel, in response to Elinor's frantic note, had merely shrugged his shoulders and gone off to his Oysters Club, a group which met supposedly for political discussion but mainly for the sampling of oysters and cold punch in the best room at the Old Swan. And having resigned myself to an evening in Blenheim Lane, making soothing murmurs to Elinor's well-nigh continuous complainings, I had been surprised to find her dressed and smiling, standing in the hall on tiptoe with eagerness.

'Don't take off your cloak,' she said, 'for Crispin is to escort us, which is very kind of him, except that I believe he is doing it mainly to annoy his father, who doesn't wish me to go.'

'Then perhaps you should not go.'

'Nonsense,' she said. 'Nonsense. He didn't expressly forbid it. He just said it was impossible since I had no one to take me. And now that Crispin has actually offered, I don't see how I can be blamed.'

And Crispin, handing us into the carriage, his face once again a mask of weariness and boredom – a stranger – said coldly, 'Oh, you may rest easy on that score, Mrs Aycliffe. I shall take the blame entirely – I think we shall both make very sure of that.'

It was not far to Ramsden Street, a bare quarter of an hour of close confinement with a man who should not have cared for me enough to be unkind, whose presence or absence should have meant nothing to me. Yet I was aware of every breath he took, aware of the fresh scent of lavender on the surface of his skin and the odours of a living body beneath it, of blood flow and pulsebeat, of the texture of nerve and muscle, the texture of the heart; while, entirely divorced from logic or common sense or the natural desire to prevent myself from shame or hurt, my fingertips desired to touch him, my skin desired to be touched by him – glowed, expanded, basked almost in that desire. And I was terribly afraid.

There were a great many carriages already in Ramsden Street: the Hobhouses', bringing Emma-Jane and her mother-in-law; the Oldroyds', bringing Lucy; a single vehicle carrying a collection of the Corey and Corey-Manning widows and spinsters – Anglicans, every one of them, but willing to stretch a point on this occasion. And as we entered the schoolhouse there were other people, sitting on the back row of chairs: small shopkeepers and tradesmen and clerks in their best corduroy jackets and Sunday boots, and Ira Agbrigg, the mill hand who had come to warn us the night my father died and who, having attached himself to Joel's shadow, was now the manager of the small but thriving Low Cross Mill, Joel's old home.

But prosperity, I noticed, had not touched him outwardly, for, sitting self-consciously in the middle of the room – in a kind of neutral ground well behind the millmasters' families but in front of the clerks and grocers, the old-clothes dealer and the pawnbroker, who doubtless remembered him of old – he was still a thin man, bones and angles and anxieties taking refuge beneath a good winter coat. And because I understood the gnawing unease from which he suffered – for he was no longer a mill hand, would never be a master, was mistrusted by his old associates and despised by the new – I paused and spoke to him.

'How do you do, Mr Agbrigg, and where is Mrs Agbrigg this evening? Is she not well again?'

He had married a woman even thinner and paler than himself, a sad-eyed, lashless little mouse who, almost annually it seemed, brought forth another child, a whimper of humanity that sometimes lived and just as often did not.

And, as I passed on, leaving him flushed and grateful, Crispin Aycliffe whispered, 'That was most generous of you, Mrs Barforth; most condescending. You have made the poor fellow very happy.'

The platform party was already assembled, the Reverend Mr Brand looking extremely plain, extremely serviceable; the visiting speaker too bearded and bewhiskered and buttoned up in his dark clothes to have any identity other than 'the speaker'; and Hannah, having organized the meeting, having booked the speaker and paid his expenses, supervised the placing of the chairs, the proper arrangement of books and pamphlets, cups and saucers, and the collection plate, feeling justified tonight in putting herself forward.

This was, after all, her Sunday School. Hers was the voice which decided every issue; hers the voice which settled every crisis, from the number of pupils to be taught and the nature of that teaching to the quality of tea to be served at evening meetings and the exact purpose of those meetings themselves. Hannah it was who dispensed charity and patronage, who sorted out the 'good poor' who could be helped from the 'bad poor' who deserved their poverty and should be allowed to get on with it. And although there were still a few old ladies who resented her authority, who attempted to stage a revolution from time to time and occasionally deserted altogether to the Baptists or the Congregationalists, I could think of no occasion on which she had failed to get her way.

'See how she enjoys it,' Elinor whispered, settling herself in the centre of the front row. 'The new minister is quite in her shadow, just as if this was her own drawing room and he the husband with nothing to do but pay the bills. And, only think, she doesn't even have to order his dinner, you know, or worry about his ill humour, for he will never be ill-humoured with a woman who is free to go or stay as she pleases. No, no, he'll be sweet as pie, for he'll not risk losing Hannah to the Baptists, you may depend upon it.'

The Reverend Mr Brand rose to his feet and, asking for silence, introduced the speaker by name and reputation, managing to make some reference to Hannah's skill and devotion to her Christian duty as he did so; and, my mind registering no more than Hannah's careful lack of expression and Emma-Jane Hobhouse's quick, peevish frown – for she, too, was a Christian lady, pregnant and overburdened, doing her duty in quite another way – I found myself unable to attend, unable to care.

There had been slaves hereabout, I knew, in my grandfather's day: young African women brought to a lonely farmhouse in the Dales by men who had been answerable to no one and obliged to make no explanations when the women had disappeared. They had been murdered, Emma-Jane Hobhouse declared, raped and most horribly murdered, for one could still hear their ghosts on winter nights wailing for freedom. And suddenly I heard the echo of that cry in my own heart, for was I not bound, in my way, more tightly than any cotton picker, any harvester of sugarcane, since they, at least, had the hope of freedom? And I was aware of Crispin Aycliffe again, lounging in the chair beside me, his legs stretched out with an ease that was quite insolent, his eyes half closed.

'I have seen little children torn from their mothers' arms,' the speaker was saying. 'Infants torn from their mothers' breasts, human souls shackled in cold iron, beaten and abused so that you may take sugar with your tea – sugar, my friends, a luxury unable to sustain life itself but for which lives are sacrificed ...'

And although it was true and terrible and must be stopped, I had no easy tears like Emma-Jane and Lucy and Elinor, no flush of indignation like Hannah, nothing but a vague, aching sadness and, behind it, the cool voice of reason, telling me there was more to slavery than sugar, bidding me to remember the cotton mills just a few miles away across the Pennines, kept alive by slave-picked cotton from America. And I knew, had Joel and I been born those few miles farther west, that our prosperity – and Hannah's – would have been based on slavery, too.

Yet there was nothing to do but endure until the bearded speaker had recounted his full catalogue of horrors, leaving us hushed and shocked and weeping, and Mr Brand took the floor again to suggest that, in the absence of Mr Morgan Aycliffe, his son, Mr Crispin Aycliffe, might wish to say a word or two in the speaker's praise.

'Why, yes,' Crispin said, without surprise, hardly shifting himself from his position of insolent ease. And then, as the congregation turned towards him with courteous attention – since, after all, his father had contributed most generously to the cause – he got up, smiled, stretched himself a little, and smiled again.

'Dear sir,' he said with perfect, dangerous politeness, 'I have found you a most accomplished speaker, and a most tactful one, for in the midst of all your emotions you never once fell into the trap of reminding us that were it not for the cotton mills next door to us, in Lancashire, the plantations of the American South could serve no purpose and thousands of miserable African slaves could be set free. And since we all of us have friends and relatives who spin cotton for a living – and a mighty good living it is, too – we are grateful to you for not troubling our consciences with that.'

And as he gazed coolly around the room, where the women were busy dabbing their eyes and gathering together their shawls and gloves and the men were wondering how much or how little they should drop into the collection plate, and if they could now evade Miss Hannah Barforth's eagle eye and slip outside to smoke, perhaps only the speaker, the minister, Hannah, and I were aware of what he had really said.

Don't, I thought urgently, willing him to hear me. Don't do this, Crispin, for if you shame your father like this he will manage to hurt you for it. And, for an instant, as he began again, I was reassured, and then almost instantly appalled.

'I had the honour recently,' he went on, 'to spend an evening in the company of Mr Richard Oastler, a name you will all know and must certainly respect, since he has done more perhaps than anyone else in our area towards the abolition of colonial slavery. I found him to be – as I had expected – a most honourable, most pleasing gentleman, and perhaps I can do no better, on this occasion, than quote some of his own words.'

'Yes, yes,' Mr Brand said, inexpressibly relieved at this mention of Richard Oastler, that eloquent champion of the oppressed. 'Please do so, Mr Aycliffe. They could be none other than well received.'

But, as Crispin reached into his pocket and brought out a neatly folded sheet of newsprint, I saw the alarm in the speaker's face and his hand hastily clamping itself on Mr Brand's arm, warning him of danger. And I saw that it was too late.

'I have in my hands,' Crispin said, still speaking coolly, lightly, 'the copy of a letter written by Mr Oastler to the editor of the *Leeds Mercury* some few weeks ago, and which may interest you – alarm you. I will not bore you with the whole, nor will you be likely to ask for more. Very well, he begins – and I must stress again that these words are Mr Richard Oastler's, not mine. "It is the pride of Britain that a slave cannot exist on her soil." '

And here, as Crispin paused, there was an obedient murmur of agreement, for this was exactly what Mr Oastler could have been expected to say.

But Crispin's voice went on, light, impersonal, and gradually silence fell, a hushed, uneasy, unwilling attention. ' "The pious and able champions of Negro slavery should have gone further than they did, or, perhaps, to speak more correctly, before they travelled so far as the West Indies, should at least for a few moments have directed their attention to scenes of misery, acts of oppression, and victims of slavery even on the threshold of our homes. Let the truth speak out. Thousands of our fellow creatures and fellow subjects, both male and female, the miserable inhabitants of a Yorkshire town, are at this moment existing in a state of slavery more horrid than are the victims of that hellish system, colonial slavery." '

'Mr Aycliffe,' Hannah said, very angry, on her feet now, her body tense.

And, giving her a slight bow, still smiling, he said, 'Miss Barforth,' and carried one: ' "The very streets" – and I quote Mr Oastler again – "are wet with the tears of innocent victims at the accursed shrine of avarice, who are compelled not by the whip of the slave driver but by the equally appalling thong or strap of the overlooker, to hasten half dressed to those magazines of British infantile slavery – the worsted mills in the town and neighbourhood of Bradford." Yes, yes, I do agree, as I am sure you have all noticed, that Mr Oastler is talking of Bradford, all of ten miles away, but we have worsted mills in Cullingford, too, and so it is reasonable to assume that we have a slave trade of our own. May I continue?'

'You had better not,' Hannah said, her fists tightly clenched, but there was, after all, only so much that a spinster lady, in these circumstances, could do, and pausing a moment to allow the frozen silence to bite, he smiled at her once again.

'I cannot agree, Miss Barforth, really I cannot, for I have heard you on many occasions – you and my father – express the depth of your admiration for Mr Richard Oastler. I have even heard you call him an inspiration to this your favourite cause, and I feel that in your heart you will be glad to give him a hearing. Listen then. "Thousands of little children," he tells us, "both male and female but principally female, from seven to fourteen years of age, are daily compelled to labour from six o'clock in the morning till seven in the evening, with only thirty minutes for eating and recreation. Oh, listen," he bids us, "to the sorrowing accents of these poor Yorkshire little ones." And he continues, "If I have succeeded in calling the attention of your readers to the horrid and abominable system on which the worsted mills in and near Bradford are conducted" – and I think that we here in this room are near enough to Bradford to feel ourselves included – "then I have done some

145

good." There is just a sentence more. "Christians should act and feel for those whom Christ so eminently loved and declared that of such is the Kingdom of Heaven. I remain, yours, etc., Richard Oastler, Fixby Hall, near Huddersfield, September 29, 1830."

'And since Mr Oastler's information derives from his friend Mr Wood of Horton Hall, himself a manufacturer of some substance, we may assume it to be correct.'

Silence again – of shock, almost of disbelief – a general averting of eyes, of pretending it had not happened at all or, if it had, one had not noticed it oneself – rather as if he had performed some act of gross physical obscenity. And then Hannah, too furious now for dignity, looking more like Joel than I had ever seen her, leaned forward across the speaker's table – Mr Brand and the speaker seeming almost to cower behind her – and hissed, 'You would not dare say these things if my brother or some other man of standing were here to oppose you.'

'But I have said nothing, Miss Barforth,' he told her, still elaborately polite. 'These are Mr Oastler's words, not mine, and if there are those in this hall – and I believe there are – who have laboured in the mills themselves as children, perhaps you will allow them to judge.'

And, bowing again – to Hannah, to Elinor, to the speaker, to Emma-Jane Hobhouse, but not to me – he walked quite slowly down the aisle between the rows of seats and went outside.

He was waiting for us, of course, in the carriage, for he would not abandon his father's wife, in her condition, to be taken home by strangers, and he had been obliged to wait some time, since the meeting had not been easy to disperse and Hannah, who was to come back to Blenheim Lane with us, had at first refused to ride with him. Even now, although Elinor allowed herself to be handed into the carriage with something like a giggle, Hannah refused to be touched and seated herself.

The night was very cold, a threat of snow hovering beyond the dark, the ground iron-hard, and, as the horses strained to take us up one hill and down another, the panting of their overburdened chests and the creaking of harness were the only sounds. We sat in sharp-edged silence, Hannah's anger cooling now, like molten iron, to a point where she could fashion it into a weapon, and, suddenly, without condescending to look at him, she said loudly, 'Mr Aycliffe, I have to tell you that you have behaved abominably.'

'Yes, of course you do.'

'And I must also advise you of my intention to inform your father of what has occurred.'

'Yes, of course you must.'

And not another word was spoken.

Mr Aycliffe had not yet returned when we reached Blenheim Lane, and as we were shown into the hushed splendour of his drawing room, the walls seemed to close around me like a tomb, the richly furnished burial place of a king, perhaps, but a tomb nevertheless, a place of concealment for the dead, and taking a nervous step or two, I spun round to Hannah, already seated, and asked her, 'Is this necessary? Is it even wise? Should you not consider Elinor and her condition – and the effect further quarrelling could have on her?'

'I hope I know my duty to my sister.'

'I wonder if you could be mistaking it.'

'Indeed. I am not quite certain what you mean by that, Verity. And I must tell you I find your own attitude surprising. I expected to see some indignation in you, for my brother's sake, since he was clearly among those singled out for attack.'

'Well – that may be so, but I think your brother is quite capable – like Mr Aycliffe – of handling his affairs without my assistance.'

'Are you accusing me,' she said, getting to her feet, 'of interference – of meddling? Are you suggesting that I am acting from spite?'

And the honest blaze of her indignation defeated me, convincing me that Hannah, in the pursuit of what she sincerely believed to be right, could not be diverted.

'No, Hannah, you are not spiteful, but I still wonder if, for Elinor's sake, we should try to keep the peace – to make the incident seem less rather than more?'

'Oh, don't worry about me,' Elinor cut in, installing herself by the fire, more animated than I had seen her in a long time. 'I feel quite well – almost new again – and Crispin must want his father to hear about it, otherwise he'd hardly have done it in Ramsden Street – would you, Crispin? – and I'm sure he'd rather hear it from Hannah than from Emma-Jane.'

My stomach twisting with anxiety, I walked out into the hallways, thinking I heard a carriage, and, turning, found Crispin behind me in the half dark.

'There is nothing you can do,' he said quietly. 'Don't try to defend me, Verity – Verity. No one else will, and you can't stand against them all.'

And, stupidly, the sound of his voice speaking my name – saying 'Verity' instead of 'Mrs Barforth' – pierced some unwanted source of emotion inside me and brought me close to tears.

'Are you really so unafraid as you seem – so careless of what your father will say to you?'

'Oh no,' he said. 'No one is quite so careless as that. I care rather more, I think, than he will ever believe. I am bound very tight, you see, and so I must cut deep to be free.'

'Free? To do what?'

'More than I have yet done. More than talk – and dream. More than build ratholes for men to live in. More than that. You would do the same, I think, Verity, if you could.'

And I have always thought he meant to touch me, and that I would not have resisted, had not Hannah appeared in one doorway and his father, almost simultaneously, in another.

'I heard the carriage,' she said, feeling even now the need to explain her presence in the hall when, as a guest, she should have kept to the drawing room, but the pallor of Morgan Aycliffe's face, the inexpressible

147

disgust written clear across his thin features, reduced her to silence. And as he came slowly through the door, walking as if his limbs hurt, Crispin said, 'I fear you are too late, Miss Barforth. My father, it seems, has met someone on the way who has performed your task for you.'

Mr Aycliffe paused, carefully divested himself of cloak, hat, and gloves, handing them without haste to his manservant, and then, going past us into the drawing room without so much as a glance at Crispin, said tonelessly to Elinor, 'I will bid you good night, Mrs Aycliffe.'

'Oh, but I am not in the least tired. I wish to –'

'I will bid you good night.'

'Oh why, sir?' Crispin said. 'She merely wishes to witness my downfall. Surely you can indulge her in that.'

And, as they at last faced each other, it was clear that the older man was straining himself to his limits to keep his self-control while the younger, by any means at his disposal, was determined to break it.

'I will deal with you presently, boy – privately. When my wife is safely abed, and these other ladies removed from your insolence.'

'Oh – as to that – I am not sure I have a mind to be dealt with, sir. In fact, I think I may walk into town and take the air.'

'You will do,' Morgan Aycliffe said dangerously, 'exactly as I bid you.'

'I wonder.'

'And I do not wonder. You will come when I call you and go where I send you, because you can afford to do no other. You owe me obedience. It is your debt to me and I shall demand payment in full.'

'And if I refuse the debt, I wonder how you will set about collecting it.'

And pressing back against the wall, I saw that even Hannah was afraid, and understood that we were witnessing a kind of murder, a deliberate amputation of the last shred of affection that bound them together.

'Go to your room, boy. Go now. Stay there until I call you. And remember you have no mother now to throw herself between us –'

'No, sir, I have no mother, and I will not go to my room just now. Not until I have told you that you and I must part, sir – sadly but finally.'

'No,' Morgan Aycliffe said. 'Never. I am not a fool, boy. I know you do these things to provoke me and drive me to the point of dismissing you, but you have not succeeded. You will stay here, in my house. I am your father. I am entitled to your support and your labour.'

'Why, sir? To provide dowries for your daughters and an easy life for your widow when you are gone? No – no – I think not. And do not threaten me, sir, with changes in your will, for you mean to disinherit me in any case when my usefulness is done. I know that very well. And so do you, Father, so do you, even though you may not yet have called your lawyers, even though you may not even have admitted it to yourself. Admit it now. Acknowledge the pleasure it would give you on your deathbed, knowing you had worn me out in your service, when all the time you had left your fortune away from me. And perhaps I have no mind, Father, to let you die so happy. Nor have I a mind to stay and watch you drain the life out of that silly child over there, as I saw you drain it from my mother –'

148

And, at last, it was enough. I saw Morgan Aycliffe's face dissolve and then re-form itself again into a living snarl, as far beyond his control as the arm that, raising itself, struck his son hard across the mouth.

'Oh dear,' Crispin said. 'I wish you had not done that. You have not hurt me, Father, do not think it. I merely regret it for your sake. You have struck me often enough before and I realize it pains you far more than it pains me, as you have always told me – yet you have always recovered. No doubt your little wife will know how to console you.'

It was Hannah who put herself between them, who said, 'This is too much,' and who led the suddenly helpless Mr Aycliffe away.

I took Elinor upstairs, without gentleness, without sympathy, and bundled her into her bed, refusing to answer when she gurgled, 'That looks like the end of it, then. He's going. And I hope you don't blame me for being glad, for you can see what a brute he is, and that he would never have treated me fairly. Silly child, indeed. Well, I may be silly, but I'm here, in my warm bed, and who knows where he'll sleep tonight. Do stay, Verity. Talk to me a little, for I'm too excited to rest.'

But, barely staying to bid her good night, I hurried to the top of the stairs and waited, hiding myself away like a child at a party spying on her mother's guests. Hannah came across the hall, a glass in her hand, opened the drawing-room door and went inside, shutting herself in most decidedly with the man who had not, in the end, chosen her as his wife. The old manservant appeared, a heavy bag in his hand, placed it by the hall table, and went away again. And then, 'Crispin,' I whispered through the gloom, using his name at last, and went running downstairs to him.

'Where will you go?'

'Oh somewhere – not far – don't worry. I shall be quite safe.'

But, in the dreadful turmoil of my nerves, his safety seemed in doubt, his father's malice a thin winding sheet to bind him and choke him, and I said urgently, 'Did you have to make him so angry? Could you not simply have packed your bags and gone?'

'Yes,' he said gently. 'So I could. I have done it before. And he could give out that I was travelling abroad for my health or on his business, as he has done before. And sooner or later someone would come to tell me that he is getting older, his strength is failing – he is in need – and I would have come back. As I have done before. And so, this time, I have been monstrously rude to him before witnesses, two of whom will not keep silent. I have given him the opportunity to present himself to his little section of the world as a wronged father, and I think the role will suit him. Certainly no one will blame him for what has happened tonight, and that is what matters to him, you see. He is as susceptible to guilt as some people are to the measles, and now that he no longer needs to feel guilty on my account – for Miss Hannah Barforth will soon convince him I am not worth it – he can let me go. There will be no reprisals, Verity, but I am so very glad to see that you care.'

'Oh – as to that –'

'Yes – as to that –'

149

And carefully, very carefully, he touched my cheek with the very tips of his fingers.

'I am not in love with you, Verity – at least, I have tried not to be. But I think I could love you – very much, very much – if you would allow it. And you would not allow it, would you?'

'I cannot allow it.'

'No – quite rightly.'

And, seeing the strain in his face, the immense fatigue, I knew that none of this had been done lightly, with a shrug and a quizzical lift of the eyebrow, as he had pretended.

'I really will be safe, you know. I have a small allowance from my uncle – the famous fifty pounds a year my father swears has led me into mischief – and so I shall not starve. Verity, will you tell me to leave. I am finding it very hard to say goodbye.'

'Yes, you had better go. Much better. Goodbye.'

And as he walked away, into a bitter night, a harsh December that had already begun to murder the poor, the homeless, the weak, I knew poverty myself, for the first time – poverty of the heart – and weakness, and the terrible conviction that I too had lost my rightful home.

15

The Duke of Wellington, his government defeated, was gone now to sulk in the House of Lords and to make gloomy predictions that any extension of the vote would open the floodgates of revolution. But the spirit of disobedience was abroad again, and it was not only the industrialists who cried out for Reform.

'Cullingford must have the right to elect its own member to Westminster,' Mr Aycliffe thundered whenever anyone was near enough to hear him, and although he merely meant that a small section of Cullingford, comprising Joel and Bradley Hobhouse and a few trustworthy managers and shopkeepers and tradesmen should have the right to elect Morgan Aycliffe, support was now coming to him from lower sections of society, from curly-headed Law Valley men with cloth caps and callused hands who said, 'Aye, let the millmasters take on the squires so that when our turn comes we'll find it that much easier to take on the masters.'

Reform, then, had become a matter of time, of degree. Wellington and his government had been ousted for denying it, and his chief opponents, Lord Grey and Lord Russell, who during their long time in opposition had been regularly promising it, had no option now but to perform; and so, in March of that year, 1831, Lord John Russell entered the House of Commons, where one third of the constituencies represented were controlled outright by one hundred aristocratic landlords – nine of them by the Duke of Newcastle, whose members called themselves his ninepins – and lay before it his scheme for improvement. Boroughs with less than 2,000 inhabitants were to be disfranchised completely; those with less than 4,000 were to elect one member only, instead of two, thus creating plenty of spare seats for allocation to the northern towns. There would be rather fewer members than before, and, the vote being extended to all men in the boroughs who occupied, as owner or tenant, property worth ten pounds a year, there would be half a million new, somewhat well-to-do voters to elect them.

Naturally, under this system, some would fare better than others, in London, and even in Manchester, where rents were higher, a ten-pound property qualification did not imply any great social standing, but in Leeds and Bradford, in Halifax and Huddersfield, in Cullingford, where rents – and wages – were very low, enfranchisement was mainly a middle-class, purely masculine affair; for although there were extremists like Crispin Aycliffe who demanded one man one vote, no one, in my hearing, had suggested offering the vote to a woman. And had anyone done so, the result would have been laughter.

Not exactly revolution, one might have thought – in fact, I did think so, although no one asked for my views – but there were many who saw it very differently. The industrialist Joel Barforth could hardly challenge the authority of a Lord Grey or a Lord Russell, both sprung from the ancient nobility, secure in the accumulated wealth and privilege of generations, but he could challenge a smaller country squire like Eustace Dalby – even a bigger one like Sir Giles Flood – and, fearing a transfer of power from themselves to this new, cunning, aggressive race of millmasters, the squirearchy was quick to take alarm. Forces were mustered. The Duke of Wellington, speaking from his wife's deathbed, reaffirmed his view that responsible government could not be carried out to suit the whim of public opinion, that this Bill was simply a prelude to further Bills which would eventually sweep away the House of Lords, the Church of England, the monarchy, the last vestiges of decent society. But the Whigs were in no position to retreat, and, when the Bill passed its second reading in the Commons by only one vote and seemed certain to be thrown out by the Lords, the Whig Prime Minister, Lord Grey, demanded that Parliament be dissolved and a new general election fought solely on the issue of Reform.

'The Bill, the whole Bill, and nothing but the Bill' was the battle cry of the election that April. In London, the Duke of Wellington's city residence, Apsley House, was attacked by a Reform mob, his windows smashed and his railings torn up, while his duchess lay dead inside. In the southern counties, where distressed agricultural labourers were still burning hayricks and getting themselves hanged for it, it was felt that some change, any change, would be welcome. The Reform Bill would not cure all ills, but it would be a step forward, which, at the very least, was better than standing still. Many people, if questioned, would not, perhaps, have known exactly what they expected from it, but in the industrial towns of the North, this second generation of manufacturers were in no doubt at all. They needed a voice – a great many voices – in Westminster, to smash the abominable Corn Laws and advocate free trade, to make laws to suit the North for a change, instead of the

151

agricultural South. And so clamorous were they for Reform that their operatives, seeing perhaps that at this stage there was little in it for them or merely finding the habit of opposing the employers too strong to break, turned their backs and gave their attention to men like Mr Richard Oastler, who, in that election month of April, ignored the burning issue of Reform altogether, requiring instead that all candidates should support the introduction of a ten-hour working day.

But the Reforming Lords Grey and Russell received the mandate they had requested, sweeping back to Westminster with a majority that made the proposal of a second Reform Bill inevitable. And while Squire Dalby prepared to sell his estates while he still could in order to go abroad – before someone suggested the setting up of a guillotine in Cullingford Marketplace – and my husband, and the husband of every woman I knew, went down to the Old Swan to toast the new era – their era – in champagne, I sat with my cousin Elinor in the darkened room considered appropriate for such occasions and watched the birth of her third child.

Nothing, from the start, had gone entirely right with this pregnancy. It had made her very sick and very stout, had puffed up her ankles and her face, had hidden her pretty, pointed chin and her dainty features, had taken the lustre from her hair and depressed her spirits, so that for the last few weeks, from a combination of self-disgust and the certain knowledge that her husband no longer found any pleasure at all in gazing at her, she had taken to her bed and cowered there like a sick animal.

'There is a concoction of chamomile flowers and mullein leaves I know of,' Mrs Stevens had offered, 'which will put the shine back into your hair.' But so low had Elinor sunk that even this could not cheer her.

'What does my hair matter,' she said, 'when I am going to die, in any case. Everybody knows the third child is the dangerous one – the killer – and I only hope it is a boy so that my husband may be spared the ordeal of marrying again and inflicting this nastiness on someone else. Now, is that not noble of me, Verity – to think of others at such a time?'

But her attempt at humour – and nobility – merely reduced her to fresh tears and when, in the fearsome dark – with her husband not yet returned from the Swan – she gave birth to another tiny girl and did not die, she simply turned her face into the pillow, weeping now from sheer weakness, and refused even to look.

'Give it to its nurse,' she said when the midwife tried to press the fragile bundle upon her.

And seeing the woman's shocked expression and not wishing to hurt her feelings – nor to give her an opportunity to gossip – I took the child myself – not a pretty child but just a red, angry scrap of wails and creases – and, because it had not asked to be born, rocked it and held it tight.

'You have another daughter,' I told Morgan Aycliffe much later, while Elinor slept, and although his disappointment must surely have been great, his face registered no more than a kind of thin disdain.

'Tell me, Mrs Barforth,' he said, carefully removing his gloves, 'is it – in your opinion – a strong child?' And when I said that it was not, he refrained, quite visibly, from exclaiming, 'Good. Good,' letting me know, wordlessly, that although a son might have served him as a replacement for Crispin, a daughter – a third daughter – could not be welcome. 'Perhaps she may not survive,' his pinched, thoroughly weary expression told me. 'Perhaps it would be as well if she did not.'

But the little girl, although she lay suspiciously still for a day or two, managed to cling to life – as is often the way with females – and was soon installed in the nursery at the top of the house with her sisters, to be cared for by Nurse and suckled by a placid, heavy-breasted farm girl, who, between them, spared Elinor the necessity of seeing her at all.

And Elinor, in fact, still had no desire to see her, and not much inclination, even when the first month was over, to leave her bed.

'Oh yes,' she told me, 'they keep bringing her down to me and thrusting her under my nose – and I make the right noises because it is easier to pretend than to have them nagging me and whispering to each other that I am unfeeling. But, to tell the truth, she looks exactly like the other two, and I can see nothing to go into raptures about. And what does my opinion matter, in any case? It is my husband who will decide what is to be done with them. I shall have nothing to say to it. They are calling her Cecilia, by the way – Hannah suggested it, although I can't think why, since I know of no one of that name in our family. Prudence, Faith, and Cecilia – well, good luck to them. No, Verity, I do not wish to get up today. Hannah has been bothering me about it all morning, but if I know nothing else at least I know when I am comfortable.'

Even Hannah, who still reigned supreme at Ramsden Street Chapel and whose opinions did not pass unheard at Patterswick Church, who could bend both the Dissenting Mr Brand and the Anglican Mr Ashley to her will, met defeat at the hands of this passive little sister who, when asked to get up, simply closed her eyes and went to sleep, or, when forced to her feet, declared herself to be dizzy and fell back into bed again.

'She must be made to accept her responsibilities,' Hannah declared, but there was a growing feeling in Blenheim Lane that not much could be expected in the way of responsibility from the second Mrs Aycliffe. And when tiny Cecilia began to vomit and whine and grow tinier than ever, it was Hannah who lay in wait for the wet nurse and caught her ruining her milk by swigging gin; Hannah who spared Morgan Aycliffe the unpleasantness of dismissing the woman – who was drunk and abusive – by doing it herself; Hannah who found a healthy replacement and had her safely in the Aycliffe nursery before the next feeding time.

'What an entertainment we have had this afternoon,' Elinor told her husband on his return, 'for the wet nurse was drunk, and there was such a set-to – such a deal of huffing and puffing that I had to get up and watch the fun.'

But his reply was no more than a gradual tightening of his features, that look of thin disdain so habitual with him and, as her voice began to ebb away and her gaiety with it, he merely said, 'I am appalled.' And I couldn't tell if his contempt were directed solely at the nurse, at Elinor, or at himself.

The days of his enraptured gaze – the days of strawberries and champagne – were so totally at an end that even their memory, I think, distressed and amazed him. And if he could not forgive himself for the sensual impulse that had led him to propose to the pretty young sister instead of the sensible older one, he could not forgive Elinor – it seemed – for inspiring it. The difference in their ages alone did not disturb him too much, for Hannah was herself very much his junior and, in a world where women were apt to die young anyway, in childbed or from the strain of raising large families, a man could be forgiven for taking one who could be expected to last. It was simply that, his passion having cooled, Elinor had nothing else to offer him but a vivacity he found unseemly and a fertility that filled him with dread. He had fallen victim to lust, he had been tempted and had succumbed, and now, saddled forever with this prattling child, he felt he had been cheated. Lust, it seemed, was not splendid, as he had hoped, but untidy. It was a clutter of knitting needles and medicine bottles in his drawing room; a drunken country girl, her breasts swollen with sour milk, stumbling across his threshold; it was a nursery full of little girls who, one day, would surely escape their place of confinement and lay sticky fingers on his porcelain, who would defile his Wedgwood and his Coalport, his dignity and his purse. And because Elinor was lust, who had played him this foul trick, had lost him his son and failed to provide him with another, he chose to turn his thoughts in other directions, to the parliamentary career which would enable him, more than ever, to avoid her.

'You may inform Mrs Aycliffe I will not be dining at home this evening,' he would tell his housekeeper as she presided over his solitary breakfast, and Elinor, much relieved, would plan her day around her own whims and fancies, her callers and her growing number of aches and pains.

'I am not quite well this morning. No, no, I really don't know what ails me – a little dizziness, a slight pain behind the eyes. I could get up, but it hardly seems worth it since I shall only go back to bed again. And, I ask you, what is there to get up for? They can all manage splendidly without me. When I make the effort and go downstairs in the evenings I can do nothing right, for my husband has been so morose since Crispin left. And was that my fault? I suppose it was. Just as I am to blame for having girls instead of boys.'

Crispin. Although at the command of good sense I decided not to think of him, only the surface of my mind obeyed. I continued, as I had always done, walking my dogs every morning on the moorland road above the mill, taking tea with Emma-Jane and Lucy, submerging myself in the life of my household, the lives of my children, inviting my husband's friends to dine. I engaged a nursery governess on Hannah's recommendation: a well-starched Mrs Paget to supplement the services of my nursemaid, Liza. I taught my six-year-old son Blaize to read, and was astonished – and made much of it to Emma-Jane and Lucy – when I discovered my five-year-old Nicholas had somehow taught himself. I brushed my daughter's hair at bedtime, enchanted by its fragrant, sable

154

coils, and told her the stories my old Marth-Ellen had once told me, rejecting the new books of moral fables given to me by Hannah.

I promised Caroline a kitten for her birthday that year – a gift my father had once made to me – and took her, hand in hand, down a country lane in search of the old woman who kept white cats and usually had a litter to dispose of. Although all through the bumpy drive, jumping up and down beside me in the carriage, she had talked of a white, fluffy kitten – 'Snowy,' she'd said, calling out to the passersby. 'We're going to fetch Snowy' – when we finally located the low stone cottage and found a basket alive with all the colours of a casual feline mating, she had been so enchanted by deep tiger stripings, a little black-and-white patchwork body, a pair of transparent eyes saucily winking from a head the texture of grey velvet, that I, enchanted with her, had understood the impossibility of making a final selection and had allowed myself to be convinced that if she had a kitten, then Blaize and Nicholas should have one too. And giving way to her pleas of 'It's only fair, Mamma,' and her very plausible fears that if we left them behind their wizened owner would be more than likely to drown them, I had come away with the striped tabby for Caroline, the grey for Nicholas, the black-and-white for Blaize, arriving home to a frozen welcome from Hannah, to a sharp reminder that Mrs Paget, the governess, was averse to animals in her nursery; to Nicholas, who demanded the black-and-white cat because Blaize had it; to Blaize, who privately not caring much for cats at all, hung on to it because Nicholas wanted it; while Caroline, cutting through their dispute with an imperious hand, declared that since they did not know how to behave, she would have all three.

'They'll be mine,' I told them, 'every one, before the month's out, unless you learn to care for them properly.'

'Oh, I'll look after mine all right,' Blaize said.

'And so will I,' Caroline told me. 'Better than him.'

Yet by the end of that first month, after a great deal of boasting from Blaize that his cat would soon be big enough to eat the other two, after a great deal of petting and ribbon tying from Caroline, who considered hers the prettiest, I found only Nicholas beside me when I put out the daily saucers of milk, the fish scraps and meat scraps; only Nicholas to concern himself and go hunting with me whenever one of the mischievous trio could not be found. And, as so often before, my heart bled for him when, having accepted their food from his steady hand, the fickle creatures stalked away to jump, purring and flirtatious, on the lap of my other son, the careless and charming Blaize.

I found peace in the smooth unwinding of my days. I drove to Patterswick to visit my mother, sorted linen, made potpourri with Mrs Stevens, ordered new clothes, and experienced pleasure, sometimes, when my husband made love to me – sometimes not – and irritation whenever he reached out that cousinly hand to pinch my chin. And when, from time to time, it seemed that my last meeting with Crispin Aycliffe had been the only real thing that had ever happened to me, I closed my eyes to it, closed my mind to it, and hurriedly went about my daily tasks.

It would have been easier, of course, had he gone away altogether, but

Mr Richard Oastler's letter to the *Leeds Mercury* had created a mighty stir in our community, and by so publicly associating himself with it, Crispin had become involved. He had gone from his father's house to spend a few days at Fixby Hall, where Richard Oastler was employed as steward by its owner, Squire Thornhill, and where, Mr Oastler having diverted his considerable energies from the slave trade to the cause of oppression nearer at home, Crispin was introduced to the Huddersfield Short Time Committee, headed by Mr Oastler and dedicated to the shortening of the industrial working day.

And instead of going on from Fixby Hall to London or to his uncle, on whose favour he must now depend, he had come back to Cullingford, where a Short Time Committee of our own was forming, and had taken lodgings at the Red Gin, a public house of ill repute somewhere in Simon Street. He was often to be seen in the company of Mark Corey, an illegitimate son, rumour had it, of our gallant Colonel Corey of Blenheim Lane, who, unlike his supposed father, was a revolutionary, a ne'er-do-well, and owner of a scurrilous weekly newssheet, the *Cullingford Star*.

'The Bill,' then, 'the whole Bill, and nothing but the Bill.' But to Richard Oastler and Mark Corey and Crispin Aycliffe, and to a multitude of workingmen – and a multitude of other men who had no work – it was not the Reform Bill but the Ten Hours Bill that mattered. Since the masters would not reduce the working day voluntarily, they must be forced to do it. The factory children – and the women, too – must have legal protection. And although there had been Factory Acts before, which had made very little difference to anyone, at the mere hint of further legislation the manufacturers reacted very much as the Duke of Newcastle had done when, criticized for evicting tenants from one or other of his nine constituencies because they had not voted his way, he had replied, 'Have I not the right to do what I like with mine own?'

It was not that all millmasters were the savage demons it suited the *Cullingford Star* to have us suppose, for, like any other, they varied from the very good to the very bad, with a great many in between who were sometimes one thing, sometimes another. There were men like Bradley Hobhouse, who, from indolence rather than any definite streak of cruelty, set a target of production for every day and allowed his overlookers to achieve it in any way they pleased. And since the time-honoured Law Valley method for keeping factory children awake was to strap them or duck their heads in a cistern of cold water – and since the accident rate at Nethercoats, from exhausted children falling into the machines and having their clothes, their hair, and sometimes their limbs torn off, was unusually high – Emma-Jane wore a very long face when the town, suddenly, became flooded with copies of Richard Oastler's letter, one of which found its way into her carriage and one, wrapped around a stone, through her parlour window.

At the other end of the scale, there was Mr John Wood, the worsted manufacturer from Bradford, who had contributed £40,000 to Richard Oastler's campaign and who, in his own mill, provided baths, and seats

156

for his operatives to rest on, and allowed them half an hour for breakfast and a lordly forty minutes for dinner. And somewhere among them was Joel Barforth, expanding faster than anyone, still building larger premises that would need more hands, more women, more children, more overlookers greedy for their bonus if production was kept up and certain of their dismissal if it was not. And if these overlookers, who needed the money, worked little girls of eight and nine for seventeen hours a day to earn it, and strapped them to keep them on their feet, I knew that Joel, unlike Bradley Hobhouse – who preferred not to look – would be well aware of it.

'I ask them to do nothing,' he announced, when pressed, 'that I have not done myself. I worked at Low Cross with my father from seven years of age, and when my mother set her mind on sending me to school I walked there, five miles, summer and winter, and back again, and then worked half the night when we were short-handed. And I'll tolerate no interference in my affairs. I'll allow no spineless government official into my factories, telling me what I can and can't do, any more than I'd allow him into my wife's bed.'

And Emma-Jane Hobhouse, who was dining with us, rushed to agree. 'Really,' she said, 'I believe this Richard Oastler is merely out to make mischief or to get his name in the newspapers again, now that the slave trade campaign seems almost over. Poor man, one could almost pity him, for he is only the steward of Fixby Hall, not the squire, and having been so idolized for his work for Abolition, is quite beyond his station; one can see that he doesn't want to sink back into obscurity. But why should we be made to suffer for it? And I tell you this, if this horrid Ten Hours Bill ever came to pass, we should not be the only ones to grumble at it. Ten hours of work sounds very fine, but has he stopped to wonder how people are to manage on ten hours' wages? If we stopped our engine at the end of ten hours and sent everybody home, most of them would stand outside the gates and beg to be let in again. And if parents were unwilling to send their children to work, what on earth could we do to force them? They couldn't manage without their children's wages, that's the truth of it – my word, we've all seen women dragging their children to work by the ear or chasing them into the yard with a possing stick. Really, Mr Oastler should confine himself to what he knows, like managing Squire Thornhill's estate, for if he has all this time to spare for our affairs, one can only assume he neglects his own.'

But Emma-Jane was troubled in her conscience, and every morning, as I walked out with my dogs, I found myself pausing on the path above the Top House and looking down at the mill, enclosed by its high stone wall set with black iron spikes and a massive iron gate. I was never awake these days to hear those gates clang shut at half past five precisely, separating the early risers, who deserved their day's pay, from the latecomers, who did not. But I would be on the path sometimes by half past eight, breakfast time, when the gates opened again for a quarter of an hour and the latecomers would be let in, reprimanded, fined, while others, who had already been at work a full three hours, would come out into the yard for a breath of soot-flecked air, a slice of bread and dripping, and to make water before the engine came on again, when they would need permission to leave their looms.

There would always be a line of children outside the gate, tiny girls five or six years old with bundles in their arms which could have been rag dolls but which were babies, coming to the mill to be fed. And, gradually, a woman would detach herself from the crowd, suckle her baby, hand it back to its five-year-old nursemaid, and go hurrying away, with two or three of her older children about her, to her labour. And although I wanted to deceive myself, my eyes refused to lie and I saw how small these children were, how crooked, how pale, how many threw one leg inwards as they walked, how many had one shoulder higher than the other or were bent at both knees from straining bones that were still soft.

Children had always worked in the mills, and I had never questioned it. My grandfather and my father both had employed them, and before that they had worked for their own parents, in the cottages, where the whole family had laboured hard to produce their weekly piece. Country children went gleaning at harvestime and fed pigs and chickens on bitter winter mornings; city children cleaned crossings, made lace, swept chimneys, and were expected to fend for themselves as soon as they were able and were expected to leave home, in many cases, and go into service at twelve or younger to make room at the family table for new little ones. No one had ever told me that childhood was a time of idleness, for even I, as a little girl, had been required to mend linen, to help with pickles and preserves in season, to make myself generally of use. And at least, as Emma-Jane put it, the factory children were spared the burden of having to learn to read and write. But that troupe of pale dwarves filing listlessly into the mill – twisted bodies that, if they grew at all, could only become twisted men, scarred women – got into my dreams, lodged themselves somewhere behind my eyelids, so that they were never altogether out of view.

'Naturally,' Hannah said, 'although Mr Oastler is guilty of gross exaggeration, there is abuse. The Hobhouse mill leaves a great deal to be desired. And Bradley Hobhouse should be made aware that if he allows young persons of both sexes to mingle together so freely, without adequate supervision, then promiscuity can be the only result. It has been brought to my notice that some of his overlookers are men of most unsavoury repute and since factory girls mature so rapidly – due to the heat in the sheds, one supposes – Well, I have heard of two cases of girls from respectable families in Ramsden Street who have been most vilely led astray by their employment at Nethercoats. Someone should speak to Emma-Jane before the *Cullingford Star* gets to hear it and we are all made to suffer.'

But the flaunting factory queens of Hannah's imaginings never crossed my path, while the sad-eyed, crook-shouldered boys and girls I did encounter showed no signs of the energy required for seduction. They were, quite simply, too weary, and it seemed to me that the scorching heat of the sheds instead of maturing them would be far more likely to wither their vital impulses away.

Yet how could I, the wife of Joel Barforth, protest? How could I do more than keep silent when, in that glorious reform year of 1831, Mr Michael Sadler, the member for Newark and formerly an importer of Irish linens in Leeds, lay before the House his bill for the protection of young persons in factories and for the regulation of the working day? If the bill became law it would be illegal to employ anyone under the age of nine, although in the absence of any official registration of births, this would be difficult to enforce and the old Law Valley attitude – if they're big enough, they're old enough' – would still apply. Young persons between nine and eighteen would be permitted to work no more than ten hours a day from Monday to Friday and a mere eight hours on Saturdays.

And, in the general protest, I kept a determined silence. When the proposals of Sadler's bill were issued in pamphlet form by Crispin Aycliffe – firmly established now at the *Cullingford Star* – and distributed throughout the mills, my silence deepened and extended itself, so far as possible, to my mind.

'Don't think for one moment that Crispin Aycliffe cares about the factory children,' Hannah said hotly. 'That young man has joined Oastler's campaign merely to annoy his father. He knows perfectly well that when Cullingford is enfranchised Mr Morgan Aycliffe will stand for election, and his aim now is to embarrass him. That young man is not an idealist. He is simply malicious.'

And when, one afternoon, we met Crispin Aycliffe face to face as we were crossing Market Square and he was coming perhaps from the Red Gin, Hannah refused to acknowledge his bow, stared through him, and seemed ready to walk through him had he not stepped aside, her hand gripping my elbow like a vice, so that I was bound to follow. And that night, plagued by the memory of his smile that had said, 'Don't worry. I know you have to pretend to hate me,' I looked closely, cruelly, in my mind's eye, and admitted that every morning when I set out with my dogs I longed to see him coming towards me through the mist. And, terrified by the intensity of that longing, I decided I would walk my dogs on the moorland path – in the place where he knew he could find me – no more.

I was Joel's wife. That was my reality, and all else was illusion. And although I had been too young and too dazed on our wedding day to understand the vows I made, I knew they could not be broken. In my heart, perhaps, I could neither love nor honour him, but my only hope of living in peace was to pretend that I did.

As so often before, it was Elinor who tested my resolve.

The possibility of her husband's election as Cullingford's first Member of Parliament had at first meant little to Elinor. But once the implications had been pointed out to her – prolonged visits to London, even a house there – she had taken on a new lease of life.

'I must have something fit to wear,' she announced, finding no difficulty at all in jumping out of bed now that she had something to get up for, and when I called again it was to find her upstairs, certainly, but surrounded by lengths of satin and silk brocade, lace and beads and feathers, and by a tall, dark woman I almost recognized.

'No, no,' Elinor called out. 'No need to ask me how I am, for I am very well. Tell me, how do you find this blue brocade? That is more to the point, for Rosamund here swears it matches my eyes, and I'm afraid it turns them green. Oh, Verity, you are acquainted with Miss Boulton, are you not?'

And although our acquaintance could not be a happy one since she, being still single, could not be expected to forget that Joel had deserted her to marry me, we bowed and smiled and talked at some length about fabric and design and the pleasure she took in creating gowns for others to wear.

I calculated that she must be around thirty now, a slender woman who would, in ten years, be gaunt and elegant rather than beautiful; with a great deal of charm but little softness in her dark face; a woman who had tried to marry several times since Joel and who now, her family's affairs not having prospered, was obliged to supplement her income with her needle.

'I make a great many wedding gowns,' she told me. 'When Estella Corey, Colonel Corey's daughter, married last spring, she wore one of my creations and ordered her entire outfit from me for her London season. Oh yes, I am kept very busy in Blenheim Lane.'

And, knowing what was expected of me, I murmured, 'You must make something for me, when you have the time to spare.'

'With great pleasure, Mrs Barforth – and for your little girl too, should you ever require it. And dare I ask you to visit me in my new premises? Yes, I am about to embark on a new venture: a shop for the sale of ready-made children's clothes of the very highest quality. The latest London designs and a few ideas of my own to make them really exclusive. The very first shop of its kind in the area; and, depending on its success, I mean to add ladies' wear, bonnets and shawls, slippers, fans, perfumes, all the little luxuries I am sure you are accustomed to sending to London for. Why go to so much trouble and have such a long wait and then find they have sent the wrong colour or that it was not really what one had in mind when it can all be obtained here, from me, in Millergate. Oh, I am so excited, Mrs Barforth, so full of plans –'

And noting down Elinor's instructions, making a quick sketch of something she declared could be safely left to her judgement, she picked up her fashion books, her pin-cushions, the tools of her trade, and hurried briskly away.

'Well, and I don't know why she should be so abominably pleased with herself,' Elinor muttered, suddenly very cross. 'Always running here, running there, in and out of everybody's houses, tittle-tattling as she goes. Well, she may think herself very clever, but she wearies me, that's all – just wearies me.' And her small, smooth fingers flexing themselves as if they needed something to break, she gave way to a sudden, spiteful impulse, her mouth turning hard and crafty as she said, 'And perhaps she is clever at that, for her new shop is really very smart – all powder-blue velvet and little gold chairs – and knowing the price of property in Millergate and the kind of stock she intends to carry, I'd dearly like to know where the money is coming from. A partner, she says, smug as a cat in a cream pot, but who? Yes – what I would give to know that.'

Silence for a moment, a brittle thing, easily passed over. But I was in no mood suddenly for social conventions, and instead of replying, 'Who indeed?' and talking of something else, I said slowly, quite pleasantly, 'I doubt you would give a great deal, Elinor, since you must know already.'

'Oh,' she said, startled. 'And what do you mean by that?'

'I mean that if someone has invested money in Miss Boulton's shop, then it is probably Joel, and if you didn't think so – or know so – you would not have mentioned it to me in the first place.'

'Verity,' she said, her cheeks flooding with pink, her eyes with tears, for she was fond of me and wished me no harm. 'Verity, I'm so sorry. I don't know why I said that. I felt so miserable suddenly – seeing that woman so full of energy when I have none at all, and seeing you so serene – and now I feel so wicked and so – so – dreadful –'

And, for a moment, it was dreadful, for this was a name I knew, a face I knew, no anonymous expensive woman in London or Manchester. This was different – frightening.

'It doesn't matter,' I said.

'Oh, but, Verity, it does matter.' And, fearful now, knowing that her brother Joel would not take kindly to this gossip, remembering what a clever, vindictive enemy he could be, she whispered, 'What are you going to do? You won't ask him, will you? Tell him?'

'Oh – what should I do? I imagine I'll order a dress from her, and one for Caroline, for if the franchise comes, there'll be parties and dinners, and we must look our best. And I have to agree that it will be most convenient not having to send to London every time one wants a decent cashmere shawl.'

'Don't you care at all?' she asked, still speaking in that sad little whisper, her face, emptied of its vivacity, seeming quite plain.

'Oh – as to that – what good would it do me to care? And since it would be foolish, I fully intend not to put myself in the trouble.'

'You can order your emotions – just like that?'

'Well – so it seems. Or perhaps I simply behave as if I can.'

'How like your mother you are, Verity.'

'Yes. I believe so.'

'But I am not,' she said, her hands clenched into those futile fists again. 'I am not. I thought I was so clever once, Verity – being a woman, getting all this without having to work for it, curling up on a cushion like that girl in the nursery rhyme and eating strawberries and cream all day. But I didn't know how the long the days are – I just didn't know ... He doesn't want me now, Verity; he just thinks about politics and makes me feel I'm in his way – makes me feel a nuisance, a failure. And he wants that election so badly it's making him peevish, making him ill. Don't you think he looks ill?'

Her next question hovered unspoken between us, for how could she say such a thing, how could I listen to it? Yet her mind spoke, and mine heeded.

'Do you think he'll die soon, Verity? Do you think he'll die and set me free?'

16

September brought the coronation of our new King William, a less than wholehearted event, perhaps, since he was elderly and ailing and arrangements had already been made for a Regency in case he should die before his niece, twelve-year-old Princess Victoria, had reached eighteen. But we gave a dinner, nevertheless, loyally toasting him in champagne, and, the Reform Bill being almost won, it was suggested that evening, around my dinner table, that a committee be formed to erect a hall in some suitable part of Cullingford, where the nation's great events could be celebrated in style.

'It will not be easy to find a site,' Morgan Aycliffe said dryly, as if it mattered little to him in any case. 'However, on reflection, there may be one possibility. Not cheap, of course, but central – most convenient – and the committee, I feel sure, would not wish to pinch pennies.'

Nor, it seemed, should we wish to economize on the question of architecture.

'You will be wanting a room large enough for dancing, I imagine,' Morgan Aycliffe said wearily, finding it all a great nuisance. 'And a reading room and a lecture hall too, one would suppose, and if one is to follow the fashion of Leeds and Bradford and add a billiard room – well – the cost, of course must escalate accordingly. The Bradford Public Rooms, too, I fear, are sadly ornate, a deal of fancy stonework and ironwork, which can never be cheap and may be thought unnecessary – unless, of course, it would grieve the ladies should we seem to lag behind. Yes – ballroom, lecture hall, reading room, billiard room, adequate facilities for the convenience of patrons and the preparation of refreshments, a reception hall with a staircase – for I fear the ladies will expect a staircase of decent proportions where guests can be received – and a retiring room. Hmmm, yes, I doubt it could be done for less than ten thousand pounds, although, of course, I cannot commit myself to an estimate made off the cuff.'

And although everyone knew that Mr Aycliffe had certainly worked out his figure carefully in advance and would lose nothing by it, no Law Valley man would blame him for that.

The money was to be raised in thirty-pound shares, each share conveying a vote on its owner and ladies being permitted to vote by proxy. And since Joel, by speedy purchase of shares, had placed himself, perhaps from force of habit, in a position of command, the Assembly Rooms became yet another outlet for Hannah's fierce energies.

'If we are to do it at all,' she announced, quoting an old Barforth maxim, 'then we must do it right,' and, taking Mrs Stevens with her as chaperone – at some inconvenience to me – she set off on a visit to inspect the public buildings of Bradford and Leeds, returning with copious notes, drawings, and measurements, and a few warnings.

'Naturally I do not wish to put myself forward,' she told the more important members of the committee, assembled once again informally in my drawing room. 'And, given my religious commitments, I do not think anyone can accuse me of encouraging frivolity. The Reverend Mr Brand, I must admit, does not approve of dancing, but I am inclined to feel, like the Reverend Mr Ashley, that in moderation it can do no harm. And the practice of giving charity balls, as they do in Bradford, is a most practical and pleasant method of doing good. I must point out, however, that should we hold such functions the price of the tickets must never be lower than one guinea apiece, and that the tickets themselves should only be purchased at the invitation of a committee member. Naturally not even this system is foolproof, and undesirable elements will, from time to time, slip through the net, but if it is strictly adhered to one may at least have the satisfaction of feeling one had done one's best. It is also the custom in Bradford to admit visiting businessmen on a yearly subscription basis, and I must tell you that this custom, although exceedingly popular with the young ladies, is not entirely without risk. In the main these men are of good standing and place too high a value on their business connections in the town to seriously misbehave. But very little is known about some of them, and, in any event, one would in no way wish to be accused of organizing a marriage market. However, that must be left for others to decide. Now, as to the question of design ...'

And, with a few well-chosen phrases, Hannah, excessively demure yet somehow totally dominating in her eternal brown silk dress with the mourning brooch of my brother's hair still on its collar, demolished Morgan Aycliffe's dreams of a highly ornate, highly priced Gothic palace quite beyond recall.

'I believe we should think along simple, classical lines,' she announced. 'Doric columns, elegance rather than ostentation. I happen to have with me a drawing ...'

And, anticipating no more difficulty with this group of hardheaded businessmen than her two devoted, obedient parsons gave her, she produced a neat sketch almost from thin air.

'Here it is,' she said. 'Most competently done, and, besides its artistic merits, perhaps Mr Aycliffe could tell us if it is feasible, if – should we have cause to celebrate enfranchisement this year – it could be ready in time. And then, of course, there is the matter of decoration, curtains and floor coverings and furnishings – and colour. White walls, I fear, are unwise, for they soil so quickly and give off so much glare. I think one must have a little more imagination than white. I may go to Bradford again for a second glance.'

But soon there was less cause to hurry for, on October 8, after passing successfully through the Commons, the Second Reform Bill was thrown out by the Lords, resulting in riots in most of our major centres of population, a new bitterness in the conflict between industrialists and

163

squires. In Cullingford the windows of the Coreys and the Corey-Mannings, our most prominent representatives of the gentry, were broken, an event not entirely lacking in prestige since the Duke of Wellington's London house shared the same fate. There was a great deal of arson, too; the Duke of Newcastle's Nottingham home and a large proportion of the city of Bristol went up in flames, while the traditional November 5 bonfires were livened up that year by effigies of unpopular bishops – twenty-one of whom had voted against the Bill – burning away beside Guy Fawkes and the Pope.

Troops were called out and a great many people died – some of them for their convictions, some of them by mistake, not a few because they were too drunk to get out of the way. Yet they could all have saved themselves the trouble, for the government was in no mood to give way, and, in December, a Third Reform Bill was placed before the Commons, not much different from the first, while our Whig Prime Minister, Lord Grey, made it clear that if the Lords persisted in refusing it yet again, he would ask the King to create enough new Reform-minded peers to push it through.

The main problem, of course, was the Duke of Wellington, who, when the Bill showed its monstrous head for the third time in the Lords, rose to his feet – too deaf to hear criticism or protest, too proud to care even if he had – and duly talked it out, bringing us closer to revolution than we had ever been.

The government resigned, leaving the King with no one but the Duke of Wellington with courage enough to try to form another. There was an immediate run on the Bank of England, as industrialists like my husband withdrew their funds in obedience to the Radical slogan 'To beat the Duke go for gold' and, in addition, declared that they would pay no taxes until they had their way. In the northern cities, men of a more violent nature – who saw middle-class freedom as a steppingstone to their own and who fully shared the Duke of Wellington's view that once Reform had begun there would be no stopping it – began to barricade the streets. Suddenly the country was on a war footing, class against class, and once again, as in the year my father died, there were tales of armed gangs drilling in the woods and of soldiers sharpening swords that would not all be used – if matters came to that – against the mob.

I did not expect myself to be attacked, for I could see no profit to anyone in that, but so ugly was the mood of the streets, so haphazard the violence brewing beneath the very cobbles, ready to slay as indiscriminately as the typhoid, that I stayed close to home, confining my children and my dogs to the garden. Yet when I did walk out, drawn once again to the pathway above the mill, I could still see that faceless bee swarm of women in the mill yard, waiting with the patience of weariness and need for the gates to open, totally submissive, as men know women must always be submissive when there are children to be fed. And I wondered just what the Reform Bill meant to them.

I had accompanied Hannah often enough, these past months, on her missions of mercy in Patterwick for her Reverend Ashley, and in the

164

grey-faced, mean-spirited alleys behind Ramsden Street, where the gutters ran foul with sewage water and the occasional rotting carcase that had once been dog or cat. And although I could do no less than admire her zeal, I returned always unsatisfied, for Hannah visited only the 'good poor,' carefully selected by her two reverends, who could be trusted to behave decently before a lady and who, if they failed to act upon her advice, at least knew how to thank her for it. And, indeed, Hannah's advice was, in most cases, perfectly sound. She was undoubtedly justified in advising a young mother that her eight or nine small children would do better if they showed clean faces and clean pinafores to the world, although with their living in one of Morgan Aycliffe's two-room cottages, where the sole source of water – a solitary tap in the middle of the grimy street – was only turned on for an hour or two every day, she did not state how this should be achieved.

'I think,' she lectured, gently but firmly, 'that eight children – or is it nine? – are quite enough, for there is no more space, either upstairs or downstairs, for another mattress, and your older boys and girls are getting too big to sleep together. It is high time you thought about hanging a curtain to separate your bedroom, half for your husband and yourself, half for your daughters, while your boys must use the floor downstairs as best they may. My sister-in-law may have some curtaining fabric to spare – oh good, Verity, I felt sure you would – and if Mrs Stevens could make it up and we could supply some brass rings and a rod – yes? I think we may make all decent, in that case. But really, my dear, there must be an end to it – large families are all very well for those who can afford them, but you must remember that you cannot.'

And although the young woman gave her most fervent agreement, it was not kind of Hannah, in my view – since she had not specified just how further pregnancies could be avoided – to be so cross when, on a subsequent visit, she found the girl with tears in her eyes and a tenth child already showing under her none-too-clean pinny.

'It was him, not me,' she said, gesturing towards the mill, where her husband was employed. 'He had a drink one Friday night and that was it, wasn't it. What could I do?'

'Nothing,' I told her, but Hannah, with whom all men, even my brother Edwin, had been careful, did not believe that any woman could be taken against her will or could give herself, knowing the consequences, merely to avoid a black eye and a few foul phrases.

'I will ask Mr Brand to speak to the husband,' she said as she came out of the dim, acrid little hovel into the wet and littered street. 'But I am beginning to feel we are wasting our time in this case. If they had restrained themselves to begin with and settled for two or three children at the most, then they could have done well enough, but now they seem to have set their feet on a downward path. And if the husband is drinking his wages, I can see nothing but the workhouse at the end of it.'

And so the young family was transferred, with one blink of Hannah's eyelids, from the list locked firmly in her mind marked 'deserving' to a second list marked 'feckless, ungrateful, not worth the trouble.'

Yet there were many others, pensioned-off servants of Squire Dalby's and old weavers of my grandfather's day, all of them existing meagrely in tied cottages, who welcomed Hannah's visits, glad of the soup and cakes, the knitted blankets and shawls and the sound of another human voice she brought them, and were by no means unwilling to doff a cap or sketch a creaky curtsy at her comings and goings.

'What a marvel she is,' the Reverend Ashley often told me. 'Take care of her, Mrs Barforth, I beg you, for I cannot imagine how the parish ever managed without her.'

'A fine, noble lady,' the Reverend Mr Brand thundered at me. 'The very finest it has been my privilege to meet.'

Yet neither the pale, beautiful Mr Ashley nor the plain, vigorous Mr Brand proposed marriage, and when I wondered why – being anxious to get her settled in her own home and away from mine – my mother surprised me by declaring it was because Hannah would not permit it.

'I cannot speak for Mr Brand,' she said, 'since I barely know him, but our Mr Ashley would marry her rather than lose her. Oh yes, yes, I am well aware that he would prefer to remain single, for he is indeed somewhat too frail for the married state, but if Hannah wanted him he would not know how to resist. She would need to do no more than make her wishes known. Yet why should she limit herself to Mr Ashley and his hundred pounds a year when, by marrying neither, she can have the better part of both? Yes, yes, I know how sorry you feel for her, because of Edwin and Mr Aycliffe, but only think, dear, how easy her life must be. She has the devotion of two men without any obligation whatsoever, and as to children, if she feels the lack of them, I imagine she can help herself to her sister's. Elinor would not miss a child or two, or even three, and how convenient for Hannah, to be spared the ordeal of actually bearing them.'

'And you think that would be enough for her?'

'Oh, my dear,' my mother said, laughter trilling out of her like birdsong, 'it would have been quite enough for me.'

But in Hannah's case, as I watched her stooping to pass the doorway of some low cottage, a heavy basket on her arm, or standing straight-backed, straight-souled, before a committee or a Sunday School class, or before Morgan Aycliffe himself when he explained to her – not to Bradley Hobhouse or to Joel – why the Assembly Rooms were not rising fast enough, I was not sure. My mother had learned to be content with life's surface – as I was learning to do – but Hannah, like Joel, needed to be in the battle itself, wielding pike and gun, and even precise control of Mr Ashley and Mr Brand was not enough.

Her nature, like Joel's, craved the stimulus of constant challenge – a craving so intense that she became physically ill, with headache or toothache, when it remained unsatisfied – and, again like Joel, she was constantly, restlessly in search of new worlds to conquer and hampered, at every turn, as he was not, by her sex. Naturally she could not offer herself for election should the franchise come, but she could support the man who did – Mr Aycliffe or another – and although her feminine

166

modesty would not allow her to utter one word in public on his behalf, she could assist him in the composition of speeches and articles that were stylish and tasteful and contained nothing which could be used against him at a later date. She could not herself preside over the meetings of the Assembly Rooms Committee; she could merely preside over the president, her brother, who found it amusing to impose his sister's wishes on Hobhouses and Oldroyds and Corey-Mannings, and on Mr Aycliffe himself. She could not, as my mother had suggested, bear children, but her orders were the only ones to carry weight in Elinor's nursery, and it was Hannah who decided when little Cecilia should be weaned, when a doctor should be called to diagnose Prudence's spots or Faith's cough, and how much fresh air and sunshine should be allowed to all three. And eventually, although her official home was still with me, she had her own room in Morgan Aycliffe's house and her regular place at his table, directly beneath the portrait of his first unhappy wife, with his second unhappy lady welcoming the intrusion since she was thus spared the necessity of conversation.

'I have put some of my thoughts on paper about the free trade issue, Miss Barforth – jottings, merely – and would be glad of your opinion,' Mr Aycliffe would casually murmur. And she, some time later, would reply, 'Most concisely put, Mr Aycliffe – a masterpiece of verbal economy. Should you wish to make a fair copy I would be most honoured.'

'Ah – the honour would be done to me, Miss Barforth. And should any little irregularities of style present themselves to your notice, by all means feel free ...'

'What a good thing he did not marry her,' my mother said after dinner one evening in Blenheim Lane, 'for they could never have had so immaculate a relationship had she been his wife. Had he married her he would have been obsessed with his obligation to desire her body – or his lack of it – but, as it is, he is free to value her mind, while poor Elinor must bear the burden of the other side of him. But what about the son – that most interesting young man? I have heard he is associating with anarchists and atheists and the landlady of the Red Gin. Can it all be true?'

And I was bound to say it was. Perhaps I had looked for Crispin this past year as I had walked dutifully beside Hannah, my charity basket on my arm, through those foul courtyards cobwebbing their way behind Ramsden Street; perhaps I had hoped for him, wanted him to appear suddenly through the constant yellow-grey gloom of those back alleys. But he was never there, and I had taught myself that his life, like mine, was full and had no room for strangers.

And I could not doubt that his life was full, for – setting aside the rumours concerning his relations with his landlady – his work with the Short Time Committee and his contributions to the *Cullingford Star* had made him a great hero to some of us, a great nuisance to others, and his name and face so well known that I was often obliged to hear others discuss him, although I did not discuss him myself.

'He's a grand lad, young Mr Aycliffe,' my maid Marth-Ellen told me, having heard news of him from her sister, who lived in Simon Street. 'Do anything for anybody, he would – give you the shirt off his back if you asked him for it. Fetch a doctor, he will, any time of the day or night – and pay, sometimes, I reckon, since not even old Dr Turner goes to Simon Street these days unless he gets his money in advance. And when there was no money to bury Maria Flaherty – her next door to my sister's granddaughter – and nobody bothered about her because she was sodden with drink and killed herself with it, just like it killed her man last winter – they say it was Mr Aycliffe who put his hand in his pocket for the funeral and kept an eye on the bairns until her sister could be got to take them. Aye – Maria Flaherty – and she was a filthy young slut at the best of times. They think a lot of Mr Aycliffe in Simon Street.'

But Hannah judged differently.

'Don't think for one moment he cares about the factory children,' she continued to insist. 'He has still no other motive than malice towards his father.'

And perhaps, to begin with, her judgement had been partly true, for Cirspin had never pretended to be noble and was not above taking his revenge. But he had lived now, for more than a year, in an alleyway somewhere behind the Red Gin, a typical, short, narrow street of identical two-room houses thrown down on a patch of clay and engine ashes, with a dung heap at one end and a swill tub at the other, put there by a pig farmer who would pay a penny or two for the communal slops. For more than a year he had viewed misery not from Hannah's lofty if well-intentioned heights but at the range of his nostrils and the pores of his skin. He had woken in the night to the whimpering of the woman next door, separated from him by a paper-thin wall, as she gave birth to another unwanted child; and he had listened to her bitter complaints and then her wail of anguish because the child, after all, was dying and there was no money for a doctor. He had grown accustomed to the sound of distress and the violence that it breeds; to the men – and the women – coming home from the gin shop and the beerhouse, needing to break something or one another, taking sex as they took combat and strong drink because these, at least, were desires that could be satisfied and one had to do something to feel alive.

He had seen the children too, staggering home like sleepwalkers every night, drowning in grime and dust and fatigue; misshapen old men of nine or ten, some of them, who whined and shivered all night in their sleep from the ache of limbs that would never be straight again. He had heard them in the morning too as they were shaken awake in the cold dark and pushed out into the street to begin again on that treadmill of heat and noise and toil, going round and round like mice on a wheel until some of them fell off and were whirled away forever.

There was a girl that year at the Hobhouse mill who, when her sister became entangled in the machinery, tried to pull her out and had her own arm torn off, both sisters bleeding to death before they reached the infirmary.

'The girl fell asleep at her work,' Emma-Jane told me defensively.

'And although it's tragic and horrific and I'm very sorry, I don't see how Bradley can be blamed for it. The overlooker should have kept her awake, that's what he's there for, after all. I've told Bradley to dismiss him, as a gesture, because, after all, if he lets the girls fall asleep, one can hardly feel any confidence in him.'

But we learned some days later, through the agency of Mark Corey's *Cullingford Star* – from the pen of Crispin Aycliffe – that these girls, being the sole support of an ailing mother and six infant brothers and sisters, had, since the age of eight, been in the habit of getting up at half past three in the morning to walk several stoney miles to Nethercoats, where, in temperatures of seventy-six degrees, they endured fourteen hours of hard labour, returning home as they had left it, in the pitch dark, arriving sometimes with cracked and bleeding feet, and frequently much bruised about the shoulders from the overlooker's strap.

'Is it any wonder,' the article concluded, 'that such girls become lethargic? It would seem more a matter for wonder that one of them possessed the courage, or the humanity – in so inhumane a world – to attempt to save the other from destruction, thus destroying herself in the process. And if anyone should ever pause to enquire – which seems unlikely – why the machinery was not turned off at once, one must remember that someone, possibly with a bonus to earn, may not have understood the hurry.'

And beneath Crispin's skilful, dramatic words, the Hobhouses' discharged overlooker was allowed to have his say.

'Yes, I have a strap to beat them with,' he agreed, 'although that's mainly for the boys. I just give the lasses a clout, more often than not, across the ear, and that does the trick. Yes, the mothers complain sometimes, or some of them do, but they've been bairns themselves, like I have, and they've had their share. They know, same as I do, that if the masters want to employ bairns, there's only one way to make them work. If they stay awake they stay alive, and what's best – a clout or two, or a lick with a strap, or happen a right good kicking, or going round the shaft and ending up dead? What do they expect? The masters bring the bairns in, and if they don't attend to their work they hold the rest of us up from doing ours, and then the masters complain. And if there's any other way but the strap, then I'd be glad to know it, because I'm always sorry afterwards – every time, I'm sorry.'

'Despicable man,' Emma-Jane Hobhouse almost sobbed, without making it clear whether she meant their former overlooker or Crispin Aycliffe. 'Making it out that it's all Bradley's fault, as usual, and it's not, because he didn't make those girls get up so early and walk all that way. Their mother brought them to the mill and begged us to give them work. "Ailing mother" indeed; well, maybe she is ailing, and I don't wonder. But what this obscenity of a newspaper forgot to mention is that there's a father too, who hasn't done a stroke of work for years – no, not a stroke; he just stays in bed all day getting his wife pregnant and sending his children into the mill so he can spend their wages on drink. No, they forget about that.'

But, in the next issue, the *Star* remembered and, in a damning article undoubtedly from Crispin's pen, we were made aware that not all working-class parents were noble or unwilling to sell their children into slavery. There were mothers who wept at the mill gates as they saw their children absorbed into the heat and dust, and fathers who grieved and raged and shouldered as much of the burden as they could. But there were also couples who, living in a permanent state of drunken squalor, bred children solely for the money they could eventually earn, beg, or steal.

'And why should you be surprised at this?' the *Star* thundered, shattering our momentary self-righteousness. 'Why should anyone be surprised when one considers that these same parents were themselves brutalized and abused in childhood – "pauper brats," some of them, brought here when five years old from the poorhouses of the South, to work, eat, and sleep in our mill sheds, knowing nothing, from that young age, but the overlooker's strap and the parson's weekly reminder that it is all the will of God.'

And below was an illustration of an overlooker's black leather thong, set into its short, evil-looking handle, and of a Negro slave, well fed and curly, his chubby hands raised in grief for the diminutive, almost skeletal white child who was about to be whipped.

'This should be put a stop to,' Morgan Aycliffe said, holding a copy of the *Star* shaking between his outraged fingers and recognizing his son's authorship, I imagine, even better than I did.

But Joel, who had never suffered much from embarrassment and was a stranger to guilt, merely shrugged and smiled.

'Then we'll put a stop to it. It shouldn't be difficult. Even a rag like this costs money to produce, and these lads who are producing it – whoever they may be – will hardly have much of their own. So they're either begging it or borrowing it, and all that's needful is to locate their source of supply and block it or cut it off altogether. I'll see to it myself when I get the time, but for now I'll put Ira Agbrigg onto it. A good man, Ira, for secrets. He'll ferret it out, and then you may leave the rest to me.'

But even Ira Agbrigg, just then, had little time for secrets or very much else, as the Reform issue rose, once again, to the boil. This third Bill, introduced in December and passed triumphantly by the Commons, had been thrown out by the Lords, yet again, in May. Lord Grey, having requested the King to create enough new peers to push it through, had been refused and then he had resigned. The Duke of Wellington had been sent for, either to form a government or to stage an aristocratic *coup d'état*, depending on one's point of view, but it was soon clear that his efforts, however valiant, could not succeed. He could find no one really willing to stand beside him and, by the middle of the month, the Reforming Lord Grey was back again, informing a possibly nervous monarch that he must either agree to the creation of new peers and get the damnable bill into the Statute Book or suffer the consequences. And since there could be little doubt that those consequences might well include not only the loss of his throne but the loss of his head, he had no alternative but to agree.

The Third Reform Bill became law on June 7 in the year I was

170

twenty-four, the Duke of Wellington and one hundred of his supporters –
who could not bring themselves to vote in favour – saving the royal face
somewhat by abstaining altogether so that the wholesale distribution of
new peerages would not be required. Bradford, Leeds, Halifax,
Manchester, Sheffield, Cullingford were all enfranchised. The middle
classes, the industrialists, the master tradesmen, the shopkeepers, the
better-class householders, those who paid a minimum rent of ten pounds
a year – even Ira Agbrigg, former mill hand and now manager of Low
Cross – were all free.

But I was a married woman, for whom, like infants and idiots, the law
allowed no freedom, and, like the other women of my class, I turned my
mind to silks and satins – for the Assembly Rooms and the Reform Bill
were completed together, and we were to give a ball.

17

Morgan Aycliffe and Hannah between them had created for us a classical
palace of culture and entertainment, faced by fluted Greek columns and
long, shallow steps; a swan of a building, preening itself among a
collection of lesser barnyard fowls, the old shops and warehouses
clustered around it. It had a square hallway, elegantly marbled in black
and white, with a staircase rising majestically from it to reach a broad
landing where guests could be received and ushered through the double
doors to a long, high-ceilinged apartment, the lecture hall and ballroom,
lit by the most magnificent chandelier Cullingford had yet seen, a
waterfall of crystal donated by my husband in my name, to the
mortification of Emma-Jane Hobhouse, who, having already provided
the blue velvet curtains – and made a great song and dance out of her
generosity – could not, with decency, increase her offer. Nor could she
grumble, being pregnant again and not really fit to be seen, when it was
decided that Elinor and I should act as hostesses at the great Reform
Ball, Lucy Oldroyd, being of a retiring disposition, having declined,
while Hannah, who had certainly earned the honour, being single and,
consequently, out of the running.

I had no idea how much she minded. The Assembly Rooms had
undoubtedly risen as much by her efforts as by the exertions of Morgan
Aycliffe's bricklayers. Hers had been the tenacity of purpose, the vision,
the determination to thwart even Emma-Jane, who had really wanted
green velvet curtains and had been prevented from supplying them only
when Hannah had told her that blue would go better with the chairs.

'What chairs?' Emma-Jane had asked, looking blankly around the
empty room.

'The chairs Mr Aycliffe has asked me to order on his behalf,' Hannah
explained calmly, finally, so that Emma-Jane, instead of demanding that
the order be altered or cancelled, said, 'Oh, I see,' and waited, quite
meekly, until the straight-backed blue-and-gilt chairs were delivered and
she could match her curtains accordingly.

171

Yet, on that grand gala opening Hannah would have no choice but to stand behind me and her younger sister, behind Emma-Jane, even – unless Nature provided the young Mrs Hobhouse with some other way, that evening, of occupying her time – and although it would be the duty of every man present to pay attention to me, Joel Barforth's wife, very few would trouble to notice his unmarried, undowered sister.

'Perhaps she should marry the Reverend Mr Ashley for the occasion,' Elinor suggested languidly. 'Even his hundred pounds a year would guarantee her a place in the receiving line, if that's what she wants. Although what she'd do with him afterwards, I really couldn't say.'

But Elinor, surprisingly, had lost her own enthusiasm for balls lately, and although there were some mornings when she was ready to take the Assembly Rooms by storm and others when she would arrive, mischievous as a kitten, merely to disagree with anything Emma-Jane Hobhouse proposed, there were other occasions – many occasions – when, quite abruptly, in mid-speech, mid-air, her vivacity would drain away, leaving her blank-eyed, peevish, not knowing where to put herself.

'I'm not well,' she would declare. 'I'm tired.' And, with no more excuse than that, she would walk out of tea party or luncheon party, walk out of church – once in the middle of a Hobhouse christening – or, if she happened to be in her own house, would retire upstairs, leaving her startled guests to their own devices.

'I had a headache,' she would tell me, 'and that's that. Yes, it may have given offence, but I can't be expected to know in advance how I'm going to feel. I'm just not brave, that's all – or stupid. I know Hannah would sit downstairs and smile no matter how much her head ached – and I expect you'd do the same. But why? Why should I put myself through agony for Emma-Jane Hobhouse, or for anybody else for that matter? It's just not worth it. And if they do it for me, then that's their business, and I surely don't appreciate it.'

But whether or not she meant to attend the Assembly Ball – and I found it hard to believe that Elinor, of all people, would be able to stay away – she ordered a sky-blue satin gown from Rosamund Boulton for the occasion and made substantial purchases of fans and silk gloves, ivory combs, and a great many other things she did not need.

I went with her to that new, smart-as-paint little shop in Millergate, with Rosamund Boulton's name in pink above the door, and, since everyone else I knew had commanded their ball gowns from her, I did the same, allowing her to dissuade me from my original white silk to a quite different idea of her own.

'I could see you in this light green, Mrs Barforth – a very cool, elegant shade which would certainly become you, for one should dress to suit the personality as well as the face and figure. And since, with your dark colouring and your height and slenderness, any shade would suit you, I feel we should concentrate on a general impression of poise – serenity. Do try this green, Mrs Barforth.'

And, as she swathed that length of silk crepe around me, smiling, professional, totally self-possessed, I understood how much Joel meant to her, that she would rather strangle me than dress me but would dress me, just the same, if she could, in the one colour she knew Joel disliked.

A small triumph, which I almost allowed her – a woman turned thirty still so achingly in love with the man who had abandoned her at twenty-three – and then could not allow, so that as she threw the fabric across her counter and began to measure, I called out, 'One moment, Miss Boulton – may I change my mind. I think the white, after all.'

'Oh,' she said, hating me, her scissors hovering. 'Just as you please, Mrs Barforth, of course – although I must say I'm surprised.'

'Yes, but you'll do it for me, Miss Boulton, won't you, as I've asked – and I'm sure it will be beautiful.'

But I could not trust her, and although I attended the fittings and let her mould the dress on me, I went privately to the best needlewoman I knew, my mother, and spent quiet, mellow afternoons in her house at Patterswick, watching her ply her needle as I had done all my life, her tranquillity touching the seeds of my own, so that, in her presence, I was at peace. She made me a dress of cream-coloured gauze over a foundation of embroidered silk, a delicately worked tracery of cream on cream, with billowing, transparent sleeves and a skirt as light as a summer cloud, and when I took it home and hung it beside the white brocade Rosamund Boulton had made too tight across the bodice, I forced myself to think of her with Joel and to assess just what it meant to me. And I had not anticipated how completely I would fail.

She had wanted him once and had been willing to wait for him against her father's advice. He had wanted her, too, but not enough to forgo the Barforth inheritance for her sake. They had met again, perhaps not too long ago, when all her subsequent attempts at matrimony had failed, and if he had put money into her business – and I was sure he had – then she was his mistress by now, had been his mistress before the loan, would continue to be his mistress for as long as it gave him satisfaction. And did I care? Should I care?

He's with her now, I told myself that night when he failed to appear at dinnertime; he's gone to the Old Swan for his oysters and his punch, and then to the shop, to her, just about halfway between the Swan and home. I saw him letting himself in through the back door, enjoying the deception and the knowledge that she had been waiting for him, longing for him, all day as his wife never seemed to do. I imagined him taunting her, talking business, making her wait a while longer, when all the time he could sense the heat in her, the need. I stripped him in my imagination, took off his expensive coat and fine, cambric shirt, which, even in a moment of passion, he would fold carefully on a chair back, remembering the days when such garments had been beyond his means. I looked at the long, hard curve of his back, the breadth of his shoulders, the scattering of dark hairs on his chest and arms, the skin that could look like amber in the candlelight, the arrogance and power and beauty of him. And then I stripped her too; I made her thinner, perhaps, than the truth of her, angular but ardent, wanting pleasure, knowing how to give it. I put her in his arms and found, to my amazement, that I could go no

173

further, not from anguish of the heart but from the sheer physical refusal of my brain to function. At the precise moment of their joining together something inside me that controlled the source of my imagination snuffed out and the coupling did not take place. They still lay there, somewhere in the back room of that smart new shop, but they were unreal – as I was unreal – dolls merely, and when I tried to bring them and myself to life, I encountered nothing but fog and confusion.

And so I had two ball gowns, two pairs of satin slippers, two feathered fans – one white, one cream – yet I almost missed the dance itself, for two weeks before the great event I miscarried a child I had only vaguely begun to suspect, thereby annoying my husband, who, though by no means a fond father, was not pleased to see Bradley Hobhouse with five sons and another on the way when he had but two.

'Oh my,' Elinor said, coming to perch at my bedside, 'if you are going to be ill, then I had better be ill too, for I really cannot stand at the head of that staircase alone.'

But Joel required the presence of his wife at the Assembly Rooms on that memorable, sultry summer night, and since it did not seem to cross his mind that I could fail, I got up and, in reply to his brusque 'Are you all right?' replied that I was very well.

'You are a little pale, dear, and a little hollow in the cheeks,' my mother told me, 'but it suits you – it makes you look mysterious and just a little sad, which men will always like since it appeals both to their protective instincts and to their curiosity. And if Mrs Stevens can do up your hair very high on the crown of your head, then it will make the hollows deeper, and you will seem sadder and sweeter than ever. Can she do that?'

She could and did, forming a heavy, intricate coil threaded through with cream rosebuds after rinsing my hair in her special lotion of aromatic vinegars and herbs and brushing it to a fine shine.

'Beautiful,' she murmured, cooing over me, patting the folds of my cloudy, gauzy skirt with affection, for I was her pet and her treasure these days, the recipient of all her cossetting as my grandfather had once been. And although I knew that these loving gestures were merely the tools of her exhausting trade – that of making herself pleasant to strangers – at least with me she could allow her own cheek muscles to sag a little, her ankles to swell in the heat; she could take her nap in the afternoons; she could be, in fact, a comfortable, gossipy, middle-aged woman. And she was grateful.

Joel came into the room as she left it, impressive as he always was in evening clothes, and, looking me up and down, he said decisively, 'Yes. I saw it in your cupboard and thought it plain, but you'll make the others look overdressed, and that's good – that's good, Verity. You may like to wear these with it.'

And he took, quite casually, from his pocket a necklace of cream-tinted, velvet-textured pearls and held them out to me.

It was a complicated piece, three strands worn high around the neck with a fourth hanging halfway to the waist, a diamond droplet at its

174

centre, and, putting it on, I stood for a moment before my mirror, entranced by its sheer loveliness, quite breathless but not precisely grateful. He would not ask for the jewels to be returned to him tonight, when the dance was over, as Morgan Aycliffe did, nor would he keep them hidden away under lock and key and oblige me to beg his permission to wear them, as Elinor had to do. On the contrary, he would be glad to have me wear them as often as I liked since the reason for their purchase was not only to give me pleasure but to show the world that in this glorious Reform year of 1832, when Bradley Hobhouse was known to be losing money through his own mismanagement and Matthew Oldroyd was not making quite so much as his father before him, Joel Barforth was a man who could offer his wife toys such as these.

And so, turning myself this way and that to see the lamplight probing the velvet heart of the pearls, the wild heart of the diamond, I murmured, 'Thank you, Joel,' without really looking at him.

'That's what I like,' he said, laughing. 'I give her a fortune in jewels and she says, "Thank you, Joel" – no more than that.'

'What would you like me to say?'

'Oh, exactly what you did say – it's enough. After all, if you'd been a boy, you'd have had the mill, wouldn't you, and the money, and I'd still have been scratching a living at Low Cross, so there's no need for raptures.'

And he would have been married to Rosamund Boulton, I thought, shivering suddenly, so that I reached for my shawl and told him quite crisply that we must not be late.

I took my place at the head of the stairs without too much apprehension, for although I was to receive guests they would mainly be the people I had known all my life, and such strangers as there were could only be the Leeds and Bradford equivalents of the Hobhouses and Oldroyds, and the party our manorial lord, Sir Giles Flood, had warned us he would bring.

We had not, in fact, expected Sir Giles, since he was rarely seen in Cullingford itself, preferring to transact his business with us from the safe distance of his hunting box in Leicestershire or his town house in Belgravia. But our recent enfranchisement could not have escaped him, and although he could have no hope of winning the newly created constituency of Cullingford – being as dedicated to the landed interest as the Duke of Wellington himself – his presence here tonight indicated that he meant to put a candidate in the field.

'It is merely to annoy us, don't you see?' Elinor whispered as we mounted the staircase together. 'Mr Aycliffe is definitely to stand as representative for the manufacturing interest, and because the squires are so piqued about the Reform Bill getting through, they have decided to take up this business of the ten-hour day. And although Richard Oastler and Michael Sadler seem really to care for the factory children, I am very sure Sir Giles Flood does not. He only wants to get back at the manufacturers for daring to push the franchise, so he will put up his own candidate – someone not to win but just to make a nuisance of himself and force my husband to spend more of his campaign funds than he need have done. Anyway, that is what my husband says, and it sounds very complicated – and very likely – but what I really want to know is where did you get that dress and why are you not wearing the one Rosamund made you? She will think you most unkind and I – well – I think you are sly.'

But her spirits were too high that night to be much affected even by the sight of my pearls – finer than the ones she was allowed to borrow, now and then, from the shrine of the first Mrs Aycliffe – and standing beside me on the landing, taking an occasional little skipping step in her excitement, she seemed her old, irrepressible self again.

Below us, the hall, lit by another Barforth chandelier, was like a rose garden, with vast arrangements of pink and white blossoms lining the walls, twining themselves around the columns, climbing the staircase, while every long, shallow step was crowned with a bowl or a basket of flowers. In the rooms behind us, my household staff and Elinor's and Emma-Jane's, along with an army of hirelings, were standing, we hoped, at their posts beside the buffet tables, while below us and to our right, in what would be the reading room, a full-scale supper was to be served. The orchestra, selected by Hannah, was in its place, and her blue-and-gold chairs waited to receive the happy, the excited, the disappointed, the footsore and the weary, while I, as the first carriages began to roll by, remembered I had barely touched my dinner and that I would be obliged to stand here a very long time.

'Thank God I am not a duchess,' Elinor muttered as the first self-conscious arrivals began to drift upstairs. 'Imagine having to do this three or four times a week in the Season. One is bound to get a headache after an hour of it – in fact, I can feel mine coming on already.'

But this kind of entertainment, as well as the Assembly Rooms themselves, were new to Cullingford, and after our having talked of little else for weeks, our having spent the day laying out gowns and gloves and pelerine, and the afternoon wiring our ringlets into place, the temptation to come early and actually see for ourselves was too great. By ten o'clock Millergate, Market Street, and Kirkgate were blocked with carriages and the rose-garden staircase had become a multicoloured moving tapestry, with a gigantic communal smile, a collective hand reaching for mine, and a voice – my voice – repeating, without any assistance from my brain, 'How nice to see you. How very nice to see you. We are so glad you were able to come.'

The Hobhouses and the Oldroyds arrived in a cluster, strong colours, warm laughter, Emma-Jane feeling herself sufficiently close to me to be frankly jealous of my pearls, Bradley saying, 'Hmmmm, well – they must have cost a pretty penny,' and then bolting away to the refreshment room, as if he thought Emma-Jane might suddenly demand the same. And after them came the stream of lesser people, the newly enfranchised 'ten-pounders' who had reason to celebrate – our own managers among them, some of them shaking my hand with a brash self-confidence, some with a studied charm that reminded me of Joel in his younger days, while

Ira Agbrigg's thin, silent wife turned so pale when I spoke to her and her eyes became so terrified that I would not have been surprised to see her turn and run for cover like a cornered vixen.

My mother and Squire Dalby brought Hannah with them, the Reverend Mr Ashley walking a pace or two behind, looking delicate and pale and very well pleased, since the Reverend Mr Brand, who did not approve of dancing, could not be here. Indeed, Mr Brand's objections had been so strong that he had attempted to dissuade Hannah from coming herself, but 'I shall take no harm,' she had told him, and, as she came striding towards me, her mind clearly on the hundred last-minute details she assumed I had forgotten, I did not doubt it. She looked competent, eagle-eyed, regal, a grand personage who deserved a second, respectful glance and something rather better than a hundred-pound-a-year country parson dangling at her skirts.

'Why are you wearing flowers in your hair?' she asked me, plainly considering my cream rosebuds an insufficient headdress for a millmaster's wife, and answering her, I was unaware of Rosamund Boulton until she was standing before me, holding out her hand, her smile freezing on her lips as she saw my gown.

She had come with her father, her married sister, and her brother-in-law, a respectable family party which would only be noticed for the challenging, almost desperate beauty of Rosamund herself. She was in gleaming, dazzling white satin – chosen to put my white brocade in the shadow – a dress she had moulded to her body to accentuate every long, lithe curve of it; a bold, provocative outfit which would not please many women but would draw the eye of every man. There were red roses at her waist and in her hair, and a long feathered fan swishing nervously, irritably in her hand, belying a restlessness beneath the sophisticated, professional charm that would appeal to these Law Valley men, who, like Joel, could rarely resist a challenge.

'Why, Mrs Barforth, how delightful you look ...'

'Thank you, Miss Boulton, and so do you.'

'But that dress, Mrs Barforth – if I have ever seen anything so exquisite I really can't remember when.'

'How kind,' I said, making no explanation, wondering why I was being so cruel when I did not hate her, when it would be so easy for me to say, 'It was a gift from my mother – totally unexpected,' and relieve her mind of the agony of wondering why I had set aside the dress she had made me herself.

Did I know about her and Joel? And if I did, could I put a stop to it? Would he abandon her all over again to please me? Those questions, I knew, would haunt her throughout the dance, would torment her until she could snatch a few words with him, ask him, warn him, plead with him, annoy him, since he would not take kindly to her fears and jealousy tonight. And, knowing this, understanding the how and the why of it, I kept silent and let her go.

Sir Giles Flood and his party, quite naturally, were not expected until the last, and when a breathless lad came running upstairs to tell us their

177

carriages were in the street, I knew a moment of alarm, quickly suppressed, since Sir Giles Flood was but another arrogant, overbearing, rich old man, and I had known plenty of those. But perhaps I was unprepared for the size of his party, the size of the man himself – a full six feet and a half, or so it seemed, of aristocratic ennui – a manorial lord indeed, his cousin, Colonel Corey, whom I often saw in Blenheim Lane, faded to insignificance beside him. Colonel Corey's daughter, Estella, was there too, now the wife of a dashing Captain Chase, who had come in full-dress uniform; and, behind them, a half dozen young men and several young ladies, none of whom could possibly be Lady Flood.

'My dear Mrs Barforth,' Colonel Corey said, coming towards me, bringing a rich odour of brandy and cigars, a certain bluff geniality, with him. 'My word, this is all very nice – and very nice of you to have us too – very civil, enemies in the camp, eh? But we won't worry about that tonight. Are you not acquainted with my cousin, Sir Giles? No, I imagine not, for you would have been in the schoolroom the last time he came among us. Giles, dear boy, let me present Mrs Barforth to you. You won't regret it.'

'Mrs Barforth?' the lord said, offering me two limp and languid fingers by way of greeting. 'Now then – let me see – there's a Samson Barforth somewhere, as I recall – pushy kind of a fellow – he'll be your husband, ma'am, I reckon?'

'My grandfather,' I told him, my nerves jangling but my voice quite cool. 'He died some years ago.'

'Did he, by Jove,' he said, and as he glanced down at me, his lordly lips began to twitch slightly at the corners with the birth of a smile.

'Very happy to make your acquaintance, Mrs Barforth,' he said, the two limp fingers becoming a hand, holding mine far too long with lordly privilege, until his cousin, Colonel Corey, who appeared eager to hold my hand too, said, 'Don't frighten the girl, Giles,' and elbowed him aside.

'Good evening, Mrs Chase,' I said, very much amused. 'Captain Chase.' And then, assuming that I knew no one else, I paused, waiting to be introduced, and found myself holding out a hand to Crispin Aycliffe.

'My goodness,' Elinor said, forgetting both her manners and the impression she too was making on our ground landlord. 'Oh my goodness.'

But Sir Giles's arrival had brought the entire Assembly Rooms Committee out onto the landing, Morgan Aycliffe and Joel among them, and, in the shadow of Sir Giles's august presence, there was nothing to do but smile.

'Mrs Barforth,' Crispin said to me, bowing formally over my hand.

'Mr Aycliffe.'

But Elinor gave him the very tips of her fingers, gingerly, as if she thought her husband might snatch them away again, while everyone else – except Lucy Oldroyd, who was too softhearted to snub anybody – managed, in the confusion of that overcrowded landing, not to greet him at all.

178

'I'm sorry,' Emma-Jane hissed into my ear. 'I don't want to make a scene, but I really can't speak to him. After all those vile things he has written about us I don't know how he can show his face – upsetting me when I'm like this ...'

And Bradley, his mouth dangerous, muttered into my other ear, 'Let him talk out of turn just once, Verity, and I'll take him outside and thrash him. By God I will.'

'I feel cold,' Elinor breathed, pressing close beside me, using my body to shut out the sight of her husband making some tight-lipped, grey-faced remark to Mrs Chase, his mouth moving as if every word gave him pain. 'Don't you feel cold, Verity? I feel cold – perhaps I'll just slip away and get my shawl.'

But our manorial lord, having dined exceedingly well, required now to be entertained, and, reaching out a commanding hand, he clasped my elbow and led me into the ballroom, the crowd parting before us with a docility I found astonishing and which he did not notice at all.

'Let's get things going, eh, Mrs Barforth – breathe a little life into the proceedings,' he said, and, taking me to the centre of the room amidst a light flutter of applause, bowed and clicked his heels, knowing, with the supreme self-confidence of those born to greatness, that the orchestra would at once begin to play a waltz.

And because there was nothing but Crispin in my mind, the fact that I was dancing with Sir Giles Flood, who had every intention of flirting and making love to me if he could – since he was known to be obliging in that direction – bothered me not at all. I could be in no doubt that had Crispin come alone, without the protection of Sir Giles, he would have been asked to leave; he would have been hustled roughly downstairs and booted out into the night as likely as not. And why was he here? What connection had he with the Floods and the Coreys, other than his association with Colonel Corey's bastard son Mark? Had he known them in London, or in France? And would they stand by him if Bradley Hobhouse took too much wine and turned his threat into a promise? And if Bradley made trouble, who would stop him, for although Law Valley men were not barbarians they were not too sophisticated to enjoy a rough and tumble; and, if it came to it, I knew that even Joel would be ready to take off his jacket, provided there was someone to hold it for him, and use his fists. And I did not want Crispin hurt – not by anyone, but most of all not by my husband.

'Creating quite a stir, our young Mr Aycliffe, don't you know,' Sir Giles said, clearly well satisfied, and, sensing my interest as a man experienced with women can always do, he grinned broadly, 'Ah, I see you are wondering about him too – just what he's doing here with me and my cousin and those young sprigs. But he's a bright young man, young Aycliffe; exactly what we need. A champion of the people, no less, and it's the people we're after, you see – the little people who haven't got the vote this time but are bound to get it sooner or later – and when they do it won't be our fault, you know. No, no, it was the present government who lowered the drawbridge, and when that happens everybody is sure to get in sooner or later. And if one can't keep them out – if one can't beat them, m'dear, one joins them. No more than common sense, I should think. Yes, the industrialists will take this constituency in September, make no mistake about that, but we'll put up a fight, make our impression, not on today's voters, but on tomorrow's – all those poor devils who work in your mills, m'dear. How long is it? Fourteen, seventeen hours a day? Can't be allowed, you know; simply not decent – no wonder this Ten Hours Bill appeals to them. Never heard of it myself, I must confess, until young Mr Aycliffe let me know about it, for which I'm entirely grateful, since it sounds like a very good thing to me. And with Mr Aycliffe himself to spell it out for us, I don't see how we can fail. No, the millmasters can win this time, but I'll see a man of my own as member for Cullingford before I'm through, for when all's said and done, m'dear, it is my manor and you can't deny me my entitlement to have my say.'

'You mean Mr Crispin Aycliffe is going to stand for office?'

'Well, in a manner of speaking, I rather think he is. Young Captain Chase, my cousin's son-in-law, is my official candidate, for he needs a job of work to do and I'm inclined to keep these things in the family as much as I can. But he's from the South – Godfrey Chase – don't understand the natives, and they can't make head or tail of him – but with Crispin Aycliffe there, you see, to answer the questions and make the speeches, young Chase has no need to open his mouth at all. And if he does, we can rely on Crispin to tell him what to say. Aycliffe for the industrialists, m'dear, and Aycliffe and Chase for the squires. Well, if that don't confuse them, I'll be surprised, for it confuses me.'

And there it was, the whole story; concise, obvious, quite dreadful. Morgan Aycliffe for the manufacturing interest, to enable him to get away from his wife; Crispin Aycliffe for the gentry, for his nuisance value and to interpret for the real candidate, Captain Chase. And my first thought was: Poor Elinor – poor little girl. They'll crush her between them.

18

I danced next with Colonel Corey, while Sir Giles took Elinor; then Mr Corey-Manning the solicitor, Mr Lucius Attwood the brewer, Mr Roundwood, the owner of the *Cullingford Courier and Review*, with Dr Overdale, and with a multitude of other worthy men who wished to dance with their hostess as good manners required and then to retire to the refreshment table as quickly as they could. And, on each occasion, when I had been complimented on my looks and the appearance of the rooms, I was asked if I had heard about Crispin Aycliffe.

'Interesting times ahead,' Colonel Corey told me. 'Fine, young man, our Crispin – met him through a relative of mine – not anyone I expect you'd know, Mrs Barforth – just a young man of my acquaintance. But yes, he'll be a great help to my son-in-law. In fact, I doubt if the captain could manage without him.'

Mr Attwood the brewer, who had a troublesome son of his own, considered the whole affair to be criminal and thought that Crispin should be publicly flogged at the cart tail as they'd known how to do in the old days.

'Used to tie their wrists to the tailboard of some old wagon,' he said with relish, 'and then we'd drive it slow from the Old Swan to the Bee Hive at the top of Millergate, flogging all the way, with a gang of urchins chucking stones and dung and anything else they had a mind. And when a lad had been through that he soon found the way to mend his manners. We had more respect in those days, and more gratitude. Youngsters knew what they owed their fathers, and how to pay it. And now look where we've got to – a lad like Crispin Aycliffe, who looks as if he couldn't knock the skin of a rice pudding, turning against his own class and setting out to make a fool of the man who raised him.'

And, spluttering with indignation, Mr Attwood forgot the dance was over and went on holding my hand, muttering furiously, until Matthew Oldroyd came to claim me.

Whirling around that polished floor, dazzled by the play of light from Joel's chandelier, clasped in one set of middle-aged arms after another, I found that I needed no more than a fraction of myself to smile and play the polite game of question and answer, leaving the rest free to observe, to taste the atmosphere around me. And it was not sweet. I saw Elinor raise a hand to her lips to stifle a giggle and then, her husband's eyes on her, back away towards the double doors, seeking escape. I saw the huddled outrage of the Hobhouse and Oldroyd ladies, a closing of ranks, stone-cold stares and hastily drawn-in skirts as Crispin Aycliffe passed by. I saw Rosamund Boulton edging towards Joel, raising an enquiring eyebrow, possibly the only person in the room who was too intent on her own affairs to care, or even to have heard about the Aycliffes. But Joel, although well aware of Morgan Aycliffe's position, had no intention of allowing it to spoil his evening. After all, no one would be heckling Joel Barforth at the hustings. Appearing not to see Miss Boulton – although I imagine he saw her very clearly – he strolled across to the manorial party, standing every inch as tall as Sir Giles Flood, and, having made himself generally pleasant – having nodded with a certain grim amusement to Crispin – he began a lighthearted but prolonged conversation with the real Tory candidate, Colonel Corey's son-in-law, Captain Chase. And Miss Boulton knew as well as I did that Joel's interest in the gallant captain extended no further than his wife.

She was fair and sharp-featured and somewhat distant in her manner, Mrs Chase – Estella Corey, who had ordered her wedding gown from Rosamund Boulton; a girl of twenty, perhaps, who knew her own worth, since her mother had been a Flood, and whose languid airs and graces contained their fair share of Flood arrogance. Not a beautiful girl, not even pretty with her pale, watery eyes and her abundant teeth, but a thoroughbred, a challenge, the kind of girl that Joel, in his Low Cross days, had never dreamed of being able to afford – which would, in itself, be enough. And as he bowed over Estella Chase's limp, well-bred hand and led her into the dance, I saw Miss Boulton's face stripped, just for a moment, of the smile, the wit, the brilliance, the bold sparkle, and become a brittle mask of anguish.

But then there was Morgan Aycliffe, appearing in the doorway, looking very much as he always did, a long, grey, mournful man, no stranger to distress, and Hannah, striding purposefully towards him with the Reverend Mr Ashley trailing far behind. Planting herself before him, shielding him from the public view, she began to talk earnestly, telling, him no doubt, that the shame was Crispin's, not his, and that if any awkward questions should be asked she would be glad to deal with them on his behalf.

Crispin did not approach me. By now, my mother and Squire Dalby had joined the Floods in the charmed circle of chairs they had installed near the refreshment table – where, for the rest of the evening, until they left immediately after supper, they remained, drinking quantities of claret and champagne, talking and dancing exclusively with each other – a party within a party – Estella Chase breaking the rule only to dance again with Joel. Crispin sat with apparent ease among them, with one of Sir Giles's young ladies on either side of him, and gradually, since most people were intent on enjoying themselves and it was a personal matter anyway, everyone but his father and Hannah and the hot-tempered Emma-Jane managed to forget him.

Supper was served downstairs on a long table covered with white damask and a multitude of expensive dishes – veal, chicken and oyster patties, cold roast turkeys and hams, trifles and creams and mountainous ruby-coloured jellies, a veritable feast – with Emma-Jane Hobhouse installed in an armchair at the head of it, placidly eating one plateful for herself and the next for the baby, kicking quite visibly inside her.

'I cannot help thinking that Mrs Hobhouse would have done better, in her condition, had she remained in the security of her own home,' I heard Morgan Aycliffe say to Hannah and, meeting his cold, fastidious eyes and the protective blaze in Hannah's, I understood that sympathy would not be well received by either. Clearly, for both of them, it was a case of what could not be mended must be ignored and since one could not take one's only son by the throat, call him 'Judas,' and sink a carving knife into his heart – as Mr Aycliffe may well have liked to do – the next-best thing was to pretend that he did not exist at all.

'Elinor has gone upstairs,' Hannah told me, 'to the retiring room, to rest.' Then, as Mr Aycliffe went off to fetch her a glass of lemonade, she lowered her voice and said, quite crossly, 'She says she is unwell, but I have just been to see her, and there she is, curled up on a sofa, chatting away to Emma-Jane Hobhouse's maid and your Mrs Stevens – having her forehead rubbed with rose water and her supper brought up on a tray. And when I told her I thought she should come down she said, "Oh, I'm comfortable here, and I've seen everything I want to see downstairs – it wasn't really so exciting, was it, as one might have thought." Do you know, Verity, it's my belief she's actually bored – bored, when this awful thing has happened to her husband – and I can't tell you how much it grieves me to see my own sister with so little sense of

– well – duty, responsibility. She should be here, shouldn't she, at his side – not leaving it to others. Oh dear, Mr Ashley is over there looking quite forlorn, trying to make conversation with Miss Boulton – and why she should be in such a sulk I can't imagine. Do go and rescue him, Verity, for women of her sort positively intimidate him – and my conscience would not allow me to leave Mr Aycliffe just now.'

But Miss Boulton, her smouldering, snarling temper just barely under control, intimidated me too and, escaping from Hannah, I let the crowd engulf me, carry me into the hallway and up the stairs towards the ballroom, where I concluded – from Miss Boulton's state of mind – that Joel was dancing with Estella Chase again. But before I reached the doorway a couple standing close together in a corner of the landing caught my eye: a girl I didn't know who had clearly just been paid a compliment, her young face looking upwards, beginning to smile, displaying the inviting curve of a young neck and shoulders, and Crispin smiling down at her, aware of the invitation. And my whole body suffered such a pang of sheer physical anguish that I rushed forward, quite blind, heedless of anything but my need to get away, not to look, not to know that he could and did desire someone else.

This, I thought wonderingly, is jealousy. This is the suffering you wanted to feel for Joel and could not. This is what Rosamund Boulton is feeling. And it was as terrible to me as that first clawing agony of childbirth, which, in my panic, I had thought would never end. I had expected to die, then, in the hours before Blaize was born and, for a brief moment, I expected to die now. But one does not die so easily and, biting my lip, breathing for an instant as deeply as I could, I made my eyes see again, forced them to pick out of the haze before me the slender, azure shape that was my mother, the stumpy black and white of Squire Dalby, the brittle, arrow-fine silhouette of Estella Chase, her eyes interested, calculating, her own thoroughbred curiosity aroused, as Joel led her back to her chair.

'My dear,' my mother said, hurrying towards me, 'what is it? You have turned quite pale.' And because she thought my concern was for Joel and Mrs Chase, I smiled and was calm again – so calm that even when Crispin came through the door alone and stared hard at me, questioningly, I did not flinch.

'You will not endear yourself to your friends by dancing with me, Mrs Barforth,' he said, 'but perhaps you will not mind that.'

'Dear Mr Aycliffe,' my mother answered him in her vague, ever accurate way, 'I do not think my daughter is much inclined to play the great political hostess. I think we may safely leave that to the Duchesses of Devonshire and Newcastle, who are not likely to show their faces in our Assembly Rooms.'

And, having reduced it to its proper size – having shown me how to defend myself should anyone criticize – she drifted away.

The ballroom was quite empty, most people not having yet returned from supper, Hannah and Mr Aycliffe safely out of sight, Joel in conversation again with Captain Chase, talking through the husband to

183

the wife, too intent on searching out a response in this difficult, unusual woman to notice me. There were a few couples dancing, young people escaping to each other while their chaperones were eating, and Rosamund Boulton, who had followed me upstairs and was now sitting beside her father, venomous and painful with her jealousy, her eyes clawing Joel's back as he displayed his peacock arrogance, his stallion vitality, to Estella Chase. Ira Agbrigg was there too, sitting stiff and uncomfortabale in his new clothes beside his terrified wife, always on hand, one felt, should Joel need him. And, as I began to wonder if they had been too shy to go down to supper and if I, as hostess, should make sure they were fed, the music started up, Crispin touched my arm, and everything but that ceased, entirely, to exist.

'Do you think I was wrong to come here?' he said.

'Yes – if all you meant to do was hurt your father.'

'And you think I am wrong to involve myself in the election – to try and win it for Captain Chase?'

'That depends.'

'On what?'

'Do you really care about the factory children, Crispin?'

And my use of his name, because it came so naturally, made the pressure of his hand on mine seem natural too.

'Oh – as to that – do I care? Not every day. I could consign them all to the devil quite cheerfully, many a time, and take the train and be rid of them. I find caring to be a great encumbrance. A man is well advised to avoid it – except the lucky ones among us, that is, who manage to care only for themselves.'

'You mean – men like my husband?'

'Yes, of course I do.'

'Then you should not say it, not to me.'

'Of course I should not. I should not be dancing with you, either. I have taken an unpardonable liberty, for when the dance is over I shall walk away quite freely and you will be left to explain to your family, who will not be pleased with you. Verity, do you still walk your dogs on the moor in the early morning?'

'No – no, I don't – at least, hardly ever. But never mind that. What do you really mean to do, Crispin – really – with yourself, and your life?'

'Oh,' he said, 'do I want to be a politician, you mean?' And, laughing, he whirled me around for a moment in a silence altogether without strain, since our minds and our bodies were still talking to each other.

'No, I think, on the whole, I would rather not. It is just that – how can I explain it, Verity? You must know my father well enough by now to realize that I was raised in almost total silence. Yes? And because of that, perhaps I need to make a noise in the world. And if I am to make a noise it may as well be a useful one, may as well serve a purpose. Not the best of motives, maybe, but as good as another – and honest, I think, since I have nothing to gain by it. I have no care for my soul, as my father has, since I am not acquainted with such things, and society allows me better ways of working out my frustrations than it does your cousin

Hannah. Yes, I have seen her many a time, picking her way through the back alleys, looking as if she had a peg on her nose, and you with her. No, no – how could I have spoken to you? She would have come between us at once to protect you from my contamination – and she would have been right. Verity, will you walk your dogs tomorrow on the top road?'

'No.'

'No, of course not – but if you should be there, around nine o'clock, and you should happen to take the path that forks to the right past Lawcroft –'

'I never go that way.'

'Naturally – it is much too solitary, and I imagine you could not walk so far as the flat stones beyond the ridge, the ones that fan themselves out like a skirt, that the locals call Old Sarah. It is a very rough pathway, almost no pathway at all, and there is always mist on such high ground, before the sun gets up. Where may I leave you – since the music has stopped? Shall I take you back to your husband?'

But I saw now as the music drained out of my mind, as the room became real again – such a petty, tawdry little room, such a sham – that Captain and Mrs Chase were taking their leave, were already out on the landing, with the Hobhouses and Hannah and a wedge of solid, vindictive Law Valley faces glaring at us, blocking Crispin's path to safety. And fear touched me.

'No, no. Go quickly now. The Floods are leaving and you must not stay here without them.'

'But I cannot abandon a lady in the middle of a dance floor. And what can you possibly suppose they would do to me?'

'I don't know – no more than jeer at you, perhaps, or snub you, which breaks no bones –'

'Exactly. And if I am to be a politician I must accustom myself to jeers and snubs, you know.'

'Oh yes, I daresay you must, but not now – please. Oh dear, your father has come in and is standing where you cannot possibly avoid him.'

'Supposing, of course that I wish to avoid him,' he said, and holding my hand a moment in both of his, he bowed and walked quite slowly through that hostile crowd, as I had seen him do once at Ramsden Street, straight towards his father. But those who were hoping to see blood or tears or both were doomed to disappointment, for there was nothing in the slight inclination of Morgan Aycliffe's head to speak of outrage or humiliation and nothing in Crispin's equally slight acknowledgement of the greeting that spoke of insolence.

'Good evening, sir,' Crispin said.

'Good evening,' his father answered, and, bowing again, the older, greyer man walked forward, smiling his taught smile, into the illuminated room, and the younger went lightly downstairs, both of them faithful, for the moment, to their family creed of silence.

I came home in the lilting, magical light of the summer dawn, a rose-tinted sky warming the smoky town, yet even at that hour there were people in the streets, black, bent outlines, shawl-wrapped for protection, not from the cold of the season but from the cold of fatigue; a sudden crowd of children appearing like a flock of starlings with enough energy left to stare at the carriage, to hurl a random stone. But I had no pity that night, no curiosity, no awareness of anything beyond myself and the strange conviction that my whole life had shrunk from its full twenty-four years to the few hours I had spent with Crispin Aycliffe. The years had been long and smooth, slipping easily one into the other; years of reason and good sense, quiet pleasures, quiet sorrows, effortlessly acquired, easily forgotten. And although I knew I would have to be content with them again – for I was neither wanton nor brave – my life suddenly appalled me.

It would last, I thought, another twenty, another thirty years or more, and then, at the end of it, what could I find to say of myself should anyone enquire? Would it content me, on my dying day, to know that I had been sensible, logical: that I had never deliberately harmed anyone? Would it be enough to know that I had never suffered because I had never allowed myself to feel?

'Verity, I have something to say to you,' Hannah announced abruptly,leaning towards me from the corner of the carriage. 'And indeed, I am very sorry to have to say it at all. But you should not have danced with Mr Crispin Aycliffe.'

'Should I not, Hannah? And why is that?'

'You must know very well why,' she said, perfectly ready to be angry, since I was, after all, only her little cousin, no matter who had married me, and she assumed Joel, in this case, would be on her side. 'His behaviour during this past year cannot have escaped you – those articles of his accusing better men than himself, your husband among them, of malpractice, which is easy for him to say when he has nothing to do himself but sit about in gin shops and alehouses. And then, to appear tonight, among the very people he has so much maligned, with no other motive than to taunt his father – and you must agree he could have had no other motive than that. Your encouragement of him appeared odd, Verity. It attracted notice, and not very favourable notice at that. Needless to say, Mr Aycliffe himself did not speak a word against you – but others, unfortunately, were less charitable.'

'And I am sure you defended me very ably, Hannah.'

'Naturally – as I would always defend my own family. But, since I had no idea at all as to what possessed you, it was not an easy task.'

'Well, I am sorry for that. I was merely doing my duty as a hostess, or so I thought – and I suppose I remembered about the prodigal son and how he had been welcomed home in the Bible, and imagined I was doing right. And to refuse him would have seemed quite odd, you know, for I had already danced with Sir Giles Flood and with Colonel Corey and Captain Chase, all of them in the same party – of the same persuasion.'

'It is not at all the same,' she said, furious now because I was being frivolous and devious, my mother's daughter, who had done a great deal of dancing, it seemed, while she, who had organized the proceedings, had hardly danced at all. 'It is not Crispin Aycliffe's politics I am

186

complaining about – since he has none, in any case – but his nature. Sir Giles Flood remains loyal to his background. Crispin Aycliffe has betrayed his. He is a snake in the grass, no more and no less, and if you are unable to see the damage he has inflicted, and intends to go on inflicting, on his father, then I must assume you have deliberately closed your eyes.'

'Small chance,' Joel said tersely, his legs stretched out on the seat, 'of closing mine with this racket going on.'

But Hannah, although she depended on Joel for her daily bread, was not afraid of him and had no intention of curbing her tongue for his sake.

'My opinions may count for little,' she said acidly, 'but it is my right and my duty to express them. And in my view, Mr Aycliffe was entitled to the support of his friends this evening – entitled to a certain rallying round in which neither of you chose to participate. And since he is, after all, our brother-in-law, he must have felt it deeply. I am sorry for that, and so, I imagine, is he.'

The carriage having come to a halt outside our door, she got down without assistance and strode inside.

'She is, as it happens, quite right,' Joel said, helping me down, and I nodded, grateful to her now, in fact, since her anger, and my need to defend myself, had cushioned the true cause of my malaise.

'Yes. I do know that. Unfortunately she tends to say the right thing in the wrong way, often at the wrong time, so that instead of seeing the error of my ways I simply lose my temper.'

'Temper?' he said, laughing, throwing a casual arm around my shoulders. 'Temper, Verity? I can't imagine it. I've seen you cool and a shade sarcastic, but honest-to-God temper – no, not you, love. Not that I'm complaining about your way of saying things – far from it, for I've never heard you speak a word that wasn't to the point; I've never seen you put a foot wrong.'

And, drawing a deep breath of pure, uncomplicated satisfaction, he held me against him, pressed my head against his shoulder, and ruffled my hair, not so much as a lover but as a conqueror, a man full entitled to take liberties with a woman who knew the art of keeping other men at bay.

'You were perfect tonight, Mrs Joel Barforth. If I hadn't seen you growing up here, at the millhouse, I'd have thought you very definitely out of somebody's top drawer, and I might have been curious, wanting to find out a lot more about you. And that's exactly how I want my wife to be. Make them curious, Verity; look expensive and hard to please, keep them guessing ...'

But once upstairs, when my pearls were locked away in the jewel case he had given me for the purpose – large enough, I noticed, to accommodate his future generosity – and my lovely dress was neatly bestowed in its cupboard, his mood of warm approval altered, quickened to the restless excitement I knew of old, which would end, surely, in a great unleashing of sensual revelry. And, lying back on my pillows, waiting, I was more inclined than I had ever been for his caresses. I wanted him quite suddenly, quite desperately, to make love to me. I wanted to be repossessed; wanted him to burn away the emotion I had felt tonight for another man, in the heat of our legally coupled, eternally coupled bodies; wanted him to drown my newborn heart-searching in a floor of physical pleasure. I wanted, at the end of an hour or so, to be limp and bruised and exhausted, my body so submissive, so grateful, so satiated, that there could be no thought left in me anywhere of Crispin Aycliffe.

I wanted my body to be enslaved and mesmerized by Joel's body; wanted to be so totally overwhelmed by rapture and the certainty of its renewal that I could forget the hope of love. I wanted, in fact, to be safe.

'Why don't you come to bed?' I asked him. 'Do you mean to pace the floor all night?'

But if there was invitation in my voice he did not hear it and, flinging himself down beside me, his weight disarranging my pillows, he reached out not for me but for a cigar, inhaling the tobacco with unashamed greed.

'Your sister would have something to say to you – and to me – if she knew you smoked in bed.'

'I daresay, but then my sister can be narrow in her ideas, we're both agreed on that. What did you make of the Floods, Verity?'

'Which one of the Floods?'

'Whichever one you fancy.'

But the fancy was his, not mine, and lying so close beside him, I could feel the huntsman's blood stirring in his veins as he remembered Estella Chase's cool eyes and languid hands, the supercilious airs and graces that had intrigued him at the dance. And it seemed to me, noting the wry amusement tilting his mouth, wrinkling the corners of his eyes, that only decency prevented him from saying to me, 'She has an eye for me, our high-toned Mrs Chase. Didn't you see her, making out she wasn't looking and then looked, hard as she dared, under her eyelids?' And, because I had seen it, and because Rosamund Boulton's hungry, despairing eyes seemed only to have added spice to the challenge, I said coolly, 'Sir Giles was very much as I expected, and Mrs Chase, too, although she is quite plain.'

'Aye,' he said, his mouth more amused than ever. 'So she is, although she doesn't know it. And a woman who thinks so well of herself must have her reasons. Plain as a pikestaff and thinks she's an empress – doesn't it make you wonder?'

'Not much.'

But my coolness, like my invitation, escaped him, and, angry now and fearful, with Crispin Aycliffe swimming resolutely back into my thoughts, I knew a moment of fierce refusal, when it was impossible to continue lying here so close to him with the spectre of another woman, another man hovering between us.

'I'm tired, Joel,' I told him, sliding deliberately against him as I pretended to settle down to sleep, inviting him now in a fashion he would not overlook.

'Are you, by God? We'll see about that,' he said, throwing back the bed covers, his hands and his mouth good-humoured before they became urgent. He was fond of me, pleased with me, generous and tolerant, with an easy affection that he never questioned, that gave him no pain, especially now that I had obliged him by growing into the kind of woman he had always intended. Yet when it was over, when my limbs had quivered with joy and continued to throb with the memory of it, the inner core of me was not possessed, not protected, neither satiated nor enslaved but as tumultuous as if he had never touched me at all. And, frozen by the warm air of that summer morning, I lay for a long time awake while the careful fabric of my life, so painstakingly, sensibly constructed, tore itself to shreds around me, warning me that I might never again be truly at peace.

19

I had never experienced difficulty in getting out of the house early in the morning, to go walking with my dogs, yet on the morning after the ball my entire household – except its master, who had left, as usual, for the mill – seemed to block my way.

'My dear, you cannot get up,' Mrs Stevens told me, determined not to be robbed of the hour of gentle backbiting she had clearly promised herself. 'You were not in bed until the small hours and you must rest – naturally you must – until luncheon at the very least. I doubt if Mrs Aycliffe will get up all day, and Mrs Hobhouse certainly will not, for she was delivered of another boy not three hours ago. I heard it from the laundry maid. Another boy – yes, that makes six – but never mind, dear, you may have a dozen yet, and there's not one of hers so bonny as Master Nicholas nor so artful as Master Blaize.'

And when Mrs Stevens had been disposed of, Master Blaize and Master Nicholas themselves came to me with a demand for justice, with Liza following behind with demands of her own. There had been toothache in the night, Caroline so noisy and demanding in her pain that she had disturbed everyone's rest, and now, peevish from lack of sleep, Blaize had pulled the tail of the grey cat and then Caroline's hair; Nicholas, in defence of the kitten rather than his sister, had slapped Blaize, who, as was only to be expected, had slapped him back. In the resulting affray, a bowl had been overturned, and there was porridge on the nursery floor, murder in Liza's heart, and broken china.

'I can't do anything right with them,' Liza muttered, peevish herself and bristling when Mrs Paget, the governess, flowed smoothly on the scene, so well starched even at this hour that I wondered if she ever went to bed at all.

'Please don't concern yourself, Mrs Barforth,' she told me, eternally smiling. 'Liza should know better than to bother you with trifles. They do show off so, madam, when you are here. Each one wishes to impress you, which is only natural.'

189

And although I knew she meant for me to run along until teatime, when she would bring them all brushed and starched for my inspection, I had it in me that day to remind her that they were, after all, my children and sent her away.

I took Caroline on my knee, sitting in the nursery rocker as I used to do in the cosier days before Mrs Paget came and, holding her hot, tousled little head against my cheek, murmured wordlessly to her, letting her delay me, crumple my dress, disarrange me, so that I would set out too late for temptation or would not go at all. And when Nicholas, still furious about his cat, planted himself before me and said accusingly, 'Why are you talking secrets to her?' I pulled him against me and whispered nonsense into his ear, combing his dark curls with my fingers.

The boys were both at school now, and although Blaize, sitting cross-legged and mischievous on the window seat, would have remained there all day in delicious idleness, Nicholas had always been aware of the passing of time, like any true Barforth, and was soon restlessly tossing his head beneath my hand, unwilling to be late.

'The carriage will be waiting,' he said, conscious, it seemed, even in childhood of the cost of carriage horses and aware that it did them no good to stand fretting in the heat any longer than they had to.

'Let it wait,' Blaize answered him. 'It's our carriage.'

And, to Blaize, it was 'our' school too, since it had not taken him long to discover that the grammar school very largely owed its existence – and the headmaster, Mr Blamires, his career – to the donations it pleased Joel and Bradley Hobhouse and Matthew Oldroyd to give. And that being the case, he had no more fear of the redoubtable Mr Blamires than he had of my maid Marth-Ellen.

I had taken them both, three months ago, to present them to Mr Blamires, with Blaize unashamedly holding my hand and Nicholas walking resolutely alone. As Joel's wife, I had been treated with immense courtesy and had listened with equal courtesy to the man who had once given Joel the smattering of Greek and Latin he had never used again, and promised to do the same for his sons, who also would have small use for it. But young gentlemen must, at least once in their lives, translate a sentence or two of Virgil, a line of Plato, and so they now set off every morning, making the journey by carriage that Joel had made on foot, the immediate difference between them being that whereas neither had any aptitude for the classics, Nicholas cared more than he need have done, and Blaize cared not a scrap.

'What's the good of it?' was Blaize's opinion, tossing his books carelessly into a corner. But failure of any kind having a bitter taste to Nicholas, I opened his books myself, struggling one lesson ahead of him, finding sometimes that Blaize, leaning carelessly against my shoulder, would, with a flash of brilliance he never troubled to sustain, breathe life into those dead sounds, laugh with delighted surprise at his own cleverness, and stroll away.

I would have kept them at home that morning after the dance. I would have been glad to notice a rash, to hear a cough; would have been glad of

190

any excuse at all to tuck them up in bed and imprison myself in watching over them. But Nicholas was soon straining at my leash; even Blaize showed a perverse willingness to comb his hair and straighten his collar, race Nicholas for the best place in the carriage. And when they had driven off, and Caroline had curled up and fallen peacefully asleep – no longer needing me, either – I found the dogs waiting, puzzled and hopeful, on the driveway, and was most painfully aware that it was still but a quarter past eight o'clock.

There was, as Crispin had said, a mist on the top pathway. It swallowed the dogs as they ran ahead of me, so that I was constantly obliged to call them back. And I was startled by each sudden appearance of their wet, dark gold shapes, by every shift of air and cloud that could but did not reveal Crispin Aycliffe coming towards me. He would not, of course, be there. I did not expect him; I had embarked on this long, uncomfortable expedition simply to prove the lightness of his intentions. Yet when I reached the ridge, panting a little from the roughness of the ground, and saw him leaning against the pile of rocks known as Old Sarah, the ill temper in his face, his mouth as tight-drawn, almost, as his father's, startled me and made me angry, too.

'Good morning,' I threw at him through the grey cowl of rain-decked air. 'Not that it's good, and not that you seem overjoyed to see me.'

'No,' he said, getting up, his face still set and closed. 'I was hoping you wouldn't come – sure you wouldn't come. It would have been far easier.'

And, as he came towards me, the dogs, catching my temper, converted it to danger, so that the old bitch bristled, baring her teeth, and the young one, not designed for heroics, cowered behind me, stretching her neck, and began to howl.

'You'd best make them behave,' he said, smiling at last, and when it was done and they had gone running ahead to sniff the puddles and taste the morning, he told me, still quite roughly, 'Hoping you wouldn't come has nothing to do with wanting – you do see that, don't you? I've been up here a long time, waiting, long before there was any hope of seeing you, because there seemed no point in being anywhere else. And I think I may have gone on sitting here all day if you hadn't come, cursing you and being grateful at the same time. Can you understand that? I don't even know you very well, Verity, yet I can't see beyond you. You block my way to other things that are well within my reach. And I have to resolve it now, one way or another, since you are here and I don't believe you would have come lightly.'

'No, not lightly, although I don't know just why I came at all. And now I think I had better go away again.'

'Better?' he said. 'Yes – much better, not that you will – not that I'd allow it. These things don't happen so tidily.'

And, catching my wrist, he spoke my name sharply and pulled me into his arms.

'Don't,' I said, just as sharply, awkward now and bitter because this was only what any other man would do, seizing his opportunities, and if this feeling – this hope – should curdle and turn sour it would leave me with nothing I cared to remember. And when he would not obey, the mist got into my mind, coiling itself around my precious common sense, so that I heard myself cry out, 'Stop it. Not this way. Don't take me – that's what Joel does. Can't you let me give something, freely, for a change?'

'Verity,' he said, his voice shaking. 'Oh my darling – absolutely – when?' And the enormity of what we had both said affected my nerves so strangely that I laughed, and, after a startled moment, he laughed too.

'Before you tell me when,' he said, ruefully but easily now, his arm almost companionably around my shoulders, 'perhaps we should consider where, for we can give nothing to each other in this high wind. And I do not suppose you would come to my lodgings, would you?'

'You know that I would not – not now, at any rate. Perhaps never. Crispin, what are we saying to each other? What are you asking me to do? And why am I even listening to it?'

We had come back to the rocks again, instinctively seeking shelter from the wind and, as we leaned together against the stone, he took my hand, kissed it, and then slid both arms around me, holding me gently and lightly as my body knew it had always wanted to be held.

'Verity – my Verity – I am as scared of this as you are. I have all my life wanted one deep, intense relationship, one total commitment – and it shouldn't be with you, my darling – certainly it should not. Yet everything brings me back to you. And it is no easier for me, no simpler, than it is for you. No man in his right mind would choose to love a woman who is not free.'

'If you love me.'

'If? Yes, perhaps you are right to doubt it. And that is what we have to discover, surely – for if all I am to you is an adventure, and all I really feel for you is desire, then we shall soon know it. And don't frown at me and wrinkle your nose when I mentioned desire, for I am not ashamed of it – no – and you should feel no shame, either. It is not the whole of love, but love wouldn't be entire without it, Verity, and I don't mean to conceal my desire for you.'

'Perhaps we should pray that that is all it is, then – just desire.'

'I daresay. But don't speak of it so contemptuously – just desire; don't underestimate it. And don't worry about it, either. Don't be alarmed, for I am not asking you to desire me – not until you want to, until you can. I won't hurry you. I have harmed you enough by bringing you this far. Believe me, I know very well that I should have gone away months ago, without speaking to you; that even now I should leave you in peace – shouldn't I?'

'Oh yes,' I told him, combing his fine, flyaway hair back from his forehead with my fingers, my body utterly content with him, dangerously at ease. 'Of course you should leave me in peace, just as I should refuse to see you again. We both know what we should do, there is no difficulty about that. And what puzzles me most is why I am no longer terrified.'

'Are you not?'

'No – at least, I think I would be if I could really believe it. It all seems

192

so unreal that it doesn't trouble me – not yet. Crispin, I don't know what time it is. I simply feel it is time for me to go.'

'Yes, of course. Will you kiss me goodbye?'

'Oh no – much better not.'

But, face to face in the shelter of the rock, the mist torn apart now by shreds of sunlight, I put my hand carefully on his cheek and my mouth carefully, carefully, on his, as one would kiss a sleeping child, lingering to retain the odour and texture of him in my mind, to carry his lightness, the cool delicacy of him home with me to cherish, to sustain me, in case I should never see him again.

'Thank you,' he said, very quietly, and as I called my dogs and walked away from him over the roughly springing grass, I was happy – blindly, rapturously happy as children are in the blissful days before they learn of consequences and folly, of guilt and retribution, when it is enough to hold a single, perfect hour in the hand and call it good. I was happy and alive, the blaze of my joy, the sheer richness of its transforming me into the Barforth I had never really been, as powerful as my grandfather – as powerful as Joel – until the shadow of his house fell over me again and drew me in.

'My dear, you are wet through,' Mrs Stevens called from the gate. 'Do hurry, for it is about to rain again – and Mr Hobhouse has called to announce his new son, although we knew it already, and Sir Giles Flood has sent roses, a mass of them, which I have put in the hall with the card well displayed. An excellent card, perfectly plain – a gentleman's card, which Mrs Hobhouse would be delighted to have on her mantelpiece – and Mrs Aycliffe too, I shouldn't wonder. No, he has not sent flowers to either of them, for I enquired most particularly of his coachman. Do hurry, dear, and take off those wet shoes, for there has been such a set-to upstairs. The governess came to ask me for a drop of brandy since Caroline has had toothache again, and Miss Hannah happened to be nearby – and Miss Hannah has strong views against giving spirits to children, as you know, and has never been shy of expressing them. And Mrs Paget is simply not a woman who can be spoken to in quite that way. You had best see her at once, for I am sure she means to pack her bags, and Mrs Hobhouse would take her gladly, you know, now that she has six children to look after, and her Mary-Jane has got so old.'

For a moment, her words flowed through my mind without meaning; they were addressed to another person, at some other level of understanding, and not to me.

Mrs Paget, who had no intention of leaving, allowed me to persuade her to stay, largely, she implied, because she knew I could never manage my unruly children without her. Hannah, by no means pleased with me and my haphazard domestic arrangements – even though she herself had recommended Mrs Paget to me in the first place – took herself off on Assembly Rooms business, church business, her charity basket on her arm; and when I had admired my roses, and spent an hour consoling my daughter and separating my warring sons, when I had eaten my luncheon, I drove over to Emma-Jane's to pay my compliments and deliver an embroidered shawl and lace cap for her child.

I had not expected to be shown upstairs, but Emma-Jane, six times a mother now and with a peasant resilience she saw no reason to conceal, was not averse to company, and although her nurse, intent on dramatizing the occasion, whispered to me, 'No more than a few moments, ma'am, if you please. I dare allow no more than that,' I found Emma-Jane sitting up in bed surrounded by pillows and plum cake and all the clutter of a hearty teatime.

'Well, and so I have done it again,' she told me, her mouth full of fruit and spice and brown sugar. 'Another boy – nothing but the best for my Bradley. And look at him, not a day old yet and strong as a little bull already. He's the image of my brother, Ben, which won't suit my mother-in-law, although if he was fair and blue-eyed and skinny she'd still insist he looks like Bradley. That was the first thing she said this morning, after he was born. Not "Is he well?" or "Are you well, Emma-Jane?" but "Oh, my word – he's my little Bradley all over again." Well, her little Bradley stands six feet tall and weighs upwards of sixteen stone, so I'm bound to think her cross-eyed. But do have a slice of cake, Verity, or a macaroon – yes, I know I'm not eating for two anymore, but what else is there for me to do, sitting here in bed for the next three weeks, for Nurse won't let me set a foot to the floor until then. I can't help it if I don't feel frail when I ought to. I'll be as fat as a pig when I do get up, but that doesn't matter, does it, after you're married. Nobody expect a mother of six children to have a shape, after all. But he's a bonny baby, isn't he? And, do you know, Verity, lying here with nothing to do but think about it, I really believe I'd like a girl next time.'

Next time, I thought, looking in the cradle at the scowling little face and inhaling the milky, powdery odour of the newborn. And remembering my own miscarriage, only a month ago, I was possessed suddenly by a great surge of panic, a total dread of being pregnant again, a refusal to accept – as Emma-Jane seemed happy to do – that this was my sole purpose, that I had no choice.

'He's beautiful,' I said, knowing I had not said enough, but the cooing and gurgling Emma-Jane thought proper to the occasion – and which she herself had lavished most generously on my own children – was beyond me that day, and it was a blessed relief when Nurse came, full of her own importance, to shoo me away.

Mrs Stevens had accompanied me, having some business to transact with Emma's housekeeper, and while I waited for her in my open carriage, watching the slant of the August sun on the dark, square house, the dark-leaved shrubbery around it, thick hedges and bushes relieved only sparsely by a dull purple, an uncertain yellow, Bradley himself – who should have been at the mill – came to join me.

'Yes,' he said, answering my congratulations, 'six boys – six workers and not a dowry to find. You'd best watch out, the rest of you, for the town will be alive with Hobhouses ere long, and if they're like me and have six apiece, then it's a dynasty I'm founding.'

But his smug, entirely natural satisfaction in his own virility went no deeper than a layer or two of skin, a roll or two of the fat which his massive frame could still carry with dignity; and as Mrs Stevens came hurrying across the carriage drive – making a great show of not wishing to keep me waiting, although, truth to tell, it did not worry her at all – he leaned towards me and said hurriedly, much too casually, 'I hear Joel has made an offer for Sam Carter's mill at Tarn Edge.'

'Oh – I don't know, Bradley. He may have done.'

'Yes, and a mighty big offer at that, since Sam Carter never gave anything away.'

'I imagine so.'

'And I expect Joel will throw all the handlooms out and put power in – not that I blame him for that, although it means more men out of work and I can't take them. I doubt if Matthew Oldroyd can take them, either. I hear tell Joel wants the Carter place for some new lustre cloth – something to suit the fine ladies who have too much money to spend – and that sounds like Joel, eh? Won't say a word about it himself, but they're saying plenty at the Piece Hall and the Old Swan – they even say he's to start building again.'

'I really don't know, Bradley.'

'My word, I should say not – and if you did you wouldn't tell me, of course you wouldn't. He once blacked my eye, Joel, when we were youngsters, you know. I knocked his coat off a peg when we were at the grammar school, fooling about, as lads do, and kicked it around the floor a bit, never thinking it was the only one he had. And he damn near killed me. Your brother Edwin tried to separate us, and damn me if he didn't go for Edwin as well – took the pair of us on and smashed us both into the ground – not because he was bigger than us, or tougher – it couldn't have been that – so I reckon it was because he was angrier. It wasn't a lark to him, like it was to us; he didn't care how much we hurt him so long as he could hurt us back – and by God, he hurt us. Headmaster gave him a fair flogging afterwards – reckon he couldn't sit down for a month – nobody ever touched his coat again, I can tell you. And now I reckon he'll have more coats than any man in the Law Valley, although he's short on sons, Verity – and that won't do, my lass. A man in his position, with all those mills to run, needs sons, so you'd best put your mind to it, girl.'

And planting a kiss on my cheek, managing, as he always did, to disarrange my bonnet, he helped Mrs Stevens up beside me and stood on the carriage drive – a man who had never really been angry, never been hungry – waving, smiling, until were were far away.

I was not inclined to return home, and so we drove, inevitably, to town, down Blenheim Lane, past Colonel Corey's handsome, mellow home, and the Fleece Inn across the way, where he still sat as a magistrate, for lack of more dignified accommodation, to the dread of poachers and debtors and fathers of bastard children for many miles around. There was no need to hurry past the Aycliffe house, since Elinor would still be in bed, but I was glad to see her curtains drawn just the same. I was relieved when the good houses petered out, giving place to the bad, which, in turn, brought us to Kirkgate and Millergate, a smart

195

new shop with Rosamund Boulton's exhausted face at the window, the Piece Hall and the Old Swan, enjoying its last spurt of glory now as a coaching inn, since the railway was coming every year a little nearer, Morgan Aycliffe having already chosen a site and set about evicting the inhabitants to make room for a station and, eventually, a station hotel.

It was a Friday afternoon, and, Thursday being payday, the streets were full of men with money in their pockets who would not go back to work until the cash ran out; men who had been gloriously drunk last night, less gloriously today, who would snarl and prowl tomorrow at the stale tag end of pleasure, until there was nothing else to do but go home to be cursed and clouted by their wives, to push one brood of children out of the door and set about making another.

There were children too in the streets, as there always were; children locked out of their homes while their mothers were at work, children abandoned altogether or just wandering, the infants who had not yet been sent to the mills straighter, chubbier than their wizened seniors but puny just the same, pasty of face and foul of tongue, splashing their feet in the sewage channels and pelting filth at passing carriages.

'One should do something about those wretched creatures,' Mrs Steven said tartly, clearly having deportation to Australia in mind, but, leaning forward to smile at one ant cluster of tousled and receiving giggles and vulgar gestures in reply – for these were not my cousin Hannah's worthy causes who had had their hands and their imaginations washed in Ramsden Street – I thought of Crispin, who had chosen to live among them, and smiled.

And from Crispin my mind went to his friend and now, apparently, his associate, the Tory Member for Newark, ten-hour working day had found scant favour in Westminster, resulting in nothing more definite than the appointment of a Select Committee empowered to make further enquiries. But Michael Sadler, addressing the House of Commons in March, when the agitation for parliamentary reform had been at its height, had shocked even that sophisticated body by displaying one of the black leather thongs, a necessary tool, it seemed, of the West Riding overlooker's trade. The House heard of the heat and dust of the sheds, the stench of grease and gas and sweat, the deformities, the degradations, and, when it refused to act – since the manufacturers could always find enough doctors and parson to swear that such things toughened the body and purified the soul – the Short Time Committees decided to act for them.

There had been a massive Easter pilgrimage organized by Richard Oastler and his friend, the fiery Parson Bull, curate of Bierley; Mr Oastler himself marching out of Huddersfield with brass bands playing, to meet contingents of Short Timers from all over the West Riding, who had gathered in Leeds. I was not sure how many came, for the number varied depending on who was telling the tale and no one could guess how many fell by the wayside, for it was twenty-two miles from their starting point to the Old Castle Yard in York and many of them were ill-shod, undernourished, poorly equipped to handle the rough overnight going

196

and the continually pouring rain. But a great many, certainly, were there the next morning to stand around Mr Oastler in the Castle Yard and to exchange with him that burning promise which had been the main purpose of the ordeal: Our children shall be free.

And although newspapers like the *Cullingford Courier and Review* and the *Leeds Mercury* had made fun of the whole affair, suggesting that Oastler saw himself as a king dispensing justice to a grateful populace, their very malice brought the plight of the factory children and the activities of the Factory King to the attention of many who had been unaware of them before. My maid, Marth-Ellen, told me that when Oastler returned home, after that Easter day, having walked a total of ninety miles, the soles of his feet peeled away as he removed his boots, a small matter, which in no way delayed his journey to London, to give evidence before Mr Salder's committee.

Parson Bull had gone to London, too – and Crispin Aycliffe – armed with the names and circumstances of hundreds of families whose children were deformed from stooping and straining in the mills. They had taken with them a few terrified examples of oppression: the girl from a Leeds poorhouse who had pulled her six-year-old bones out of place by dragging heavy baskets; the boy who, at the age of eight, had such pain and weakness in his legs that he had to be carried a mile to the mill, every morning, by his brother and sister, all three of them getting a beating if they were late. The committee heard of the ten-year-old child who was tied to an iron pillar and beaten by his overlooker, then gagged and forced to run round and round a loom, past this same overlooker, who would sometimes strike him and sometimes not. They heard about the fourteen daily hours of labour, the appalling accidents, the promiscuity, the tub in the yard which was all some factories had by way of privies, for men and women alike. They heard how impossible it was, in such circumstances, for parents to educate their children; to do little more than put their exhausted, unwashed bodies to bed on Saturday night and wake them in time for work on Monday morning. They heard of fathers who, unable to find employment themselves, were refused Poor Relief unless they agreed to send their children to the mills; of fathers who were heartbroken and bitter at the harm they were forced to do to their own infants; of fathers who would sell their children's souls for a drop of gin.

And all this in a Christian land, the richest, most progressive nation in the world; all this beneath my feet, inside my nostrils, behind my eyelids, sleeping inside me, as I had slept myself until Crispin had opened my heart; and my eyes, of their own accord, had opened too.

He had said nothing to me that morning of his visit to London, his meetings with Michael Sadler; the devout politicians, the battling churchman Parson Bull; with Richard Oastler, the land agent, the countryman whose flamboyance and sincerity could so move and uplift city crowds. He had said nothing to me about the pathetic scraps of humanity who had told their harrowing tales to Sadler's committee, nor how he and Oastler and Parson Bull had persuaded them to speak, had soothed their fears of retribution from their employers, had fed them and consoled them on the bewildering journey to London and back again. He had said nothing of all that, but I understood now that he had half hoped I would fail him not merely because of the dangers and distresses inevitable in an affair with a married woman but because he had no real room in his life now for personal affairs at all. Perhaps, as Hannah said, he had joined Oastler's campaign in the beginning to obstruct his father – in fact, I felt fairly sure he had – and I believed, as he had told me at the dance, that there were indeed many times when he wished he could walk away from it all and be free again. But I did not think he would walk away, and I wondered – with sorrow and affection and a whisper of jealousy – if he had already found his total commitment, his intense relationship, in a way he had not bargained for.

Yet I had done nothing from which I could not withdraw. I had not committed adultery and could see no likelihood of ever committing it, since the moment of wild passion necessary for an act so contrary to my education could hardly take place on a stretch of public moorland and I knew that to visit his lodgings in secret, or find some other place of concealment, would be totally beyond me. And so we could not be lovers, from lack of opportunity and from a certain incredulity inside me that made the idea seem almost laughable. Men committed adultery, and women like Rosamund Boulton who had little to lose; women like Estella Chase, perhaps, with enough noble blood to despise the conventions. Our late Queen Caroline had done it, and there were plenty of factory girls who, in times of unemployment, would take to walking the streets. But what had that to do with me? Was it even what I desired?

I tried to see myself in bed with Crispin – tried to find a bed to put us in – tried to see myself dressing hurriedly in some unfamiliar place, rushing home breathless and fearful, lying, covering my tracks, perpetually ill at ease. And I could imagine no love strong enough to survive such furtive, hasty couplings, such shoddiness. Yet, even so, I knew I was no longer prepared to set aside the one real relationship life had offered me. I was entitled to something, surely – entitled to claim a small measure of love and freedom, so that at least, later on, I would have something to remember. And I understood now, even more clearly, why I had almost suffocated at Emma-Jane's bedside and trembled at the sight of the cradle, knowing that I could have a dozen children yet and that my own fertility would prove to be my jailor.

'And was it a pretty baby?' Mrs Stevens asked, catching my thought.

Leaning towards her confidentially, making sure of her attention – knowing full well she was hoping to hear some spicy detail of Bradley Hobhouse's sexual appetite, reputedly prodigious – I said, 'Very pretty – like all babies. But, do you know, Emmeline dear, I've just been thinking it over, and it strikes me that I'm in no hurry to have another child.'

'Ah well, dear, that I can understand,' she said, suddenly very interested in the shop front, the passersby. 'But one takes what God sends.'

'Do you think so?'

'My dear – of course I think so. And we all know what a lottery it is, how some of us bring forth every springtime and think nothing of it,

198

whereas others go for years and years with never a one.'

'Oh, come now, Emmeline,' I said, warning her by my unaccustomed use of her first name that although my tone was light, I was not in jest. 'Can it really be such a lottery as all that? You lived with my grandfather for ten years, and with other men before him, and you don't look to me like a barren woman. Was it really chance, Emmeline?'

'Dearest,' she said, colouring slightly, 'my situation was never, in any way, similar to yours. You should be aware that one of the things a man values in his wife is her fertility, and one of the things he values in his mistress is her lack of it.'

'Then there *is* something – I knew it – something one can do?'

'Verity,' she said, and I could see she was both shocked and alarmed, 'what are you asking?'

'Not a great deal – Emmeline dear. You have brewed me potions to make my hair shine, and perfumes, and tooth powders, and tonics to make me strong. I have conceived four times already – is there no way of ensuring me a little rest?'

'No way that is certain – and, Verity – please, dear – your husband has a right to his children. I think it could be considered criminal in a wife to deny him knowingly – certainly he would think so. Why, Mr Hobhouse was saying just now that you need more sons, and I am sure Mr Barforth would not quarrel with that.'

'But I would quarrel with it, Emmeline,' I said, and, taking her by the wrist, I fixed her with a stare I knew she could not withstand for long. 'It is my body, Emmeline. They call it "labour," and so it is, hard and dangerous; and they call it "confinement," and it is that too. And my body has laboured and been imprisoned four times, and, for a little while, that is enough. We are not all made the same. I cannot lie in bed and stuff myself with cake for three weeks every year like Emma-Jane and talk about my "next one" like she did, with her new baby less than a day old. You had better help me, Emmeline – really – you had better.'

'Oh dear,' she said. 'Oh, Verity – how is it that you have become so hard? You were never so hard ...'

'No – not hard enough. But I am still sensible, Mrs Stevens, and so are you. And you will help me, dear. You know you will. What else can you do?'

'There is more of your grandfather in you than I thought,' she told me. 'Your grandfather and your mother blended together. My word. My goodness – yes, of course I will help you, Verity – naturally dear, anything you say.'

And we completed the rest of our drive in silence, having much, I believe, to consider privately.

20

It would end, I decided, with the fine weather, when the hazy, amber mornings of October choked themselves in November fog and sleet; when the white-cold of December and the nasty, sodden miseries of

January and February made it impossible for us to linger on the moor. And by the time spring came again he would be too engrossed with his Ten Hours Committee and I would be pregnant, perhaps, with Joel's child, since Mrs Stevens could only offer me help, not certainty. He would have thought better of it, or forgotten, and I would be in no state to remind him. But, before the snow came, I went out as often as I could to Old Sarah's Rock, allowing him each time to possess a little more of me, wanting him to possess the whole, so that when he told me, 'You'll come to my lodgings, Verity – yes – yes, you'll come soon,' I was beginning to believe him. And although I was often afraid, I felt no shame since, of the three of us, the only one who really enjoyed his life was Joel.

Joel had taken exception, certainly, to the findings of Michael Sadler's committee, but he saw it merely as a nuisance, not as a threat.

'Let them legislate,' he said, 'if they will – if they can – which I doubt, for Parliament, after all, is composed of men of affairs who are more likely to see things my way than Richard Oastler's. And there's always a way round it. If I have a likely lad who wants to work more than the law allows, what's to stop him putting in his ten hours at Lawcroft and another four or five, or as much as he likes – or as much as I like – at Low Cross? And even if our Mr Michael Sadler has thought of that, I doubt he can find a way to stop it. And I don't whip my employees. I don't even whip my horses, or my wife. Do I?'

And, pinching my chin, he went breezily on his way, too busy with the purchase of Carter's mill at Tarn Edge and his pursuit of Estella Chase to wonder about my sudden interest in Reform.

The Ten Hours Bill, if it ever came, was to be set aside, then, at Lawcroft, an obstacle, like all others, that Joel would not long allow to block his way. But one evening towards the end of October he came striding into the house, his face so black with rage that I, who had seen his rages often enough before, stood hastily back from this one, knowing it to be different. And then, because it could concern my meetings with Crispin, I hurried after him, carefully opening the study door he had slammed so violently shut and stood for a moment on tiptoe, wondering if I could weather the storm.

'What is it, Joel? Has something – gone wrong?'

'Wrong? Oh no, no – what could be wrong? In my superbly run enterprises how could anything go amiss? One of the old sheds at Low Cross has burned down, that's all – early this morning.'

And, for a moment, I was infinitely, blessedly, relieved.

'Oh – but it didn't spread? It wasn't a big fire? For we saw nothing –'

'No. It didn't spread, and if you had seen smoke on the horizon, would it have concerned you? There's a deal of smoke hereabouts, and mill fires are common enough. And the shed was due to come down anyway.'

'So it wasn't serious?'

'Did I say so? No, it wasn't serious, or shouldn't have been – except that there were fifteen children inside.'

'Oh, Joel – no, Joel –'

'Oh yes – locked in, I might add, and nobody could find the key –'

As I struggled against nausea his fist came crashing down on the table and he snarled, 'That bloody Agbrigg. He'll make Low Cross pay, he tells me – and so he has – but there's cheap labour and cheap labour, and if he has to bring in Irish brats by the dozen from God knows where – if he has to take in waifs and strays from off the streets and let them doss down in the old sheds – well – I warned him, no trouble, nothing that the *Cullingford* bloody *Star* can get hold of. And so he has to lock them in at night – for their own good, he tells me – to keep them off the streets or stop them from entertaining men on my woolsacks, or some such bloody nonsense. He wants to keep them respectable – playing the parson, doing his own bit of reform – and so he locks them in and goes off to a prayer meeting and lets them burn themselves to death. God knows what the real Reformers are going to make of that.'

I sat down in the deep armchair by the desk, suddenly very cold, as if the ice of an intense winter had entered the room, a living presence, blue-lipped, skeletal, making me shiver.

'They were all girls, then? Young girls?'

'Yes – twelve-year-olds, I reckon – fourteen, some of them, maybe.'

'And some of them younger?'

'Agbrigg says not. And I intend to believe him.'

And he sat down, too, on the other side of the desk, took a cigar from the heavy silver box and inhaled deeply once and then twice, his eyes narrowing against the smoke; he was intensely shaken, I thought, and unwilling to admit it, determined to show nothing but the indifference of a Matthew Oldroyd, the defensive bluster of a Bradley Hobhouse. And I was surprised, puzzled – oddly disturbed – to see that he felt more than that, to realize that, whether he liked it or not – and he did not like it – he could not view this tragedy impersonally, that those fifteen 'operatives' had acquired fifteen quite separate faces – young faces which, because they mattered more than he felt they should, had weakened him.

'Are there no relatives?'

'Not yet, though no doubt they'll appear should I decide to put my hand in my pocket. And maybe I would. I've paid compensation often enough before, looked after the widows and orphans and doctors' bills, which no law in the land obliges me to do and which is more than the Hobhouses have ever done. But then, if I do it now and some clever devil from the *Star* gets to know about it and mentions my name to Richard Oastler – says I'm buying silence, or easing my conscience – No, no, no – if they get their Bill through and try to enforce it they can't inspect every mill in the country. They'll pick out the names they know and come ferreting in what they hope are the right muckheaps. And I won't stand for it.'

'And are they all – all –?'

'Dead? Twelve of them. They took the other three to the infirmary, but they can do nothing –'

'Dear God –'

'Yes. Quite so. An accident, Verity – we all know about accidents.

201

We've grown up with them. And my record's good. I have twice as many employees as the Hobhouses and only a quarter of the accidents – except that now I've had fifteen in the same place at the same time. Where you have machines, you have injuries – it's bound to happen.'

'Yes, I suppose so. Where you have machines – and children –'

'And what is that supposed to mean?' he snarled, his hot temper flowing swiftly around the other things he was feeling and did not wish to feel, obscuring them from his view. 'I don't need a lecture from you on factory children, by God, I don't. And I didn't invent the machines. I haven't got it in me to invent anything. All I know is how to use whatever comes to hand. I can recognize a need and work out how to fill it at a profit – that's all. And if anybody says one word – just one word – about my methods and my motives, then I'll put another corpse in the graveyard. And if you have nothing better to do than sit and stare at me, you can just take yourself off, girl.'

But the quick, defensive flaring of his anger, was soon over and, when I made no move to leave, he said quietly, 'You'd best pay a visit to Agbrigg tomorrow, for he's taking it badly – thinks I may use him as a scapegoat, I expect, if it comes to it.'

'And would you?'

'Very likely. But, as it happens, I don't see the need for it. But go and talk to him, just the same, for he'll appreciate it. And take Hannah with you, for he's of an Evangelical turn of mind – an odd sort of fellow, really. And when he tells you he locked those girls in to keep them straight, you can believe him.'

It was not a duty I wished to perform, and so, to get it over and done with, I set off early the next morning, Hannah, large with her good intentions, beside me. And perhaps it was only in my imagination – since mill fires, truly, and fatal accidents with them were very common – that ordinary passersby, working girls who were usually eager to stare at a lady's carriage, avoided my eye. And although I had made up my mind, long before we reached Low Cross, that I would not look at the gutted shed, it loomed on the edge of my consciousness from the moment of our arrival like the reeking pit of a nightmare into which one is bound to fall.

Low Cross – where Hannah and Elinor and Joel had been born and brought up – had never been a favourite place of mine, sunk in its stagnant little hollow much too near the centre of town, drawing its work force from nearby Simon Street, where, nowadays, in houses that dripped with damp and shook with the passing of every cart, the Irish were packed in six or seven to a bed. It was here that men murdered each other, sometimes, on Friday nights; here that the fevers started in the hot weather, and where not everyone could hope to survive the winter. It was here that one's eyes smarted from the stink of garbage and sewage, from the streams and gases rising out of the canal – strong enough, it was said, to blacken silver, strong enough, certainly, to take the breath away. It was here that the unpaved, rutted alleyways, sodden with cess water, swarmed with mongrel dogs and mongrel brats, snapping and snarling together in raucous harmony. A malodorous, unmannerly place, these days, Simon Street – home of the Irish and Ira Agbrigg and the Red Gin – a place where no lady, not even Hannah with her charity basket, any longer dared to tread. Yet today, as they opened the mill gates for us, the familiar clamour seemed hushed, and once again I felt hostility, a menace of silence telling me I would do better to take myself and my sleek, well-nourished carriage horses and go away again.

The millhouse, too, was as gloomy as I remembered it, its windows tightly sealed against soot and noise, sun and air, its low-ceilinged parlour painted a dingy brown, which Joel – since it had sufficed for his mother and his sisters – had seen no reason to change. Yet, for the Agbriggs, who had raised eight of their eleven children in two rooms at the mean end of Sheepgate, it may have seemed spacious enough. Not that there were eleven children now, the processes of nature having reduced the number to some five or six, all of them straight-limbed enough since their father's rapid promotion in Joel's service had taken the older ones out of the mill before too much harm had been done, the younger ones having escaped it altogether. But they were puny just the same, fleshless and bony as if it took more than one generation of good feeding to make up the loss, their eyes deep-set in faces that had the pallor of an old candle, and quieter, I thought, than healthy children ought to be. And it was as well that their father, seeing the carriage, came hurrying across the yard to greet us, for his wife, sitting in her dim, dark brown parlour, her curtains drawn as a mark of respect for the dead, seemed unable to say a word.

'Ann, we have guests, Ann,' he urged her quite gently, almost with pleading. 'Mrs Barforth is here, and Miss Barforth, the master's sister – Ann. Ann, love.'

But she could manage no more than a wan smile, her eyes no longer terrified as on the night of the dance but completely dull, dark smudges merely in a face so lifeless that it was hard to believe she could really see anything at all. And it was her son, a boy of about twelve, who set chairs for us and asked if we would take tea.

'No, no,' Hannah said, torn between the natural emotion of seeing her old home again in the hands of strangers and her quick response to human distress – her fingers itching, I imagined, to set this poor woman to rights. 'You are not well, Mrs Agbrigg, which is not to be wondered at – in fact, you are not well at all. Mr Agbrigg, your wife is clearly not herself – would she not be better in her bed?'

'I have tried, Miss Barforth,' he said humbly. 'And young Jonas here has tried. And neither of us can move her.'

'Then how long has she been sitting here?'

'Since early morning, ma'am. She was all night at the infirmary with the bairns we sent there, and when she came home she sat down and has not spoken since. What shall I do, ma'am?'

And, rising to her feet, hovering between genuine compassion and a strong desire to investigate the Agbriggs' domestic arrangements, which she did not expect to be satisfactory, Hannah said, 'You may leave her to me, if you will, for this will not do, you know. If she has been up all night she must rest, and even if she cannot rest she must not sit here, in full view of the curious. Come, Mrs Agbrigg, we will go to your room. Your son – Jonas, isn't it? – will come with us to help you climb the stairs, since I have every reason to know they are dark and steep, and then, when you are quite comfortable, we will have some tea. Mrs Agbrigg.'

'Ann,' her husband said, pleading again, 'go with the lady, love. Go with the lady.'

And Ann Agbrigg, hearing them both, I think, at a great distance, rose very slowly to her feet, the habit of obedience – even in shock – being too strong to break, and meekly, with head bowed and hands patiently folded – the posture of a mill girl waiting at the gates – followed Hannah from the room.

'I am truly sorry, Mr Agbrigg,' I said, uncomfortable at being alone with him, for although he was the most respectful of men, there was still, beneath the sober frock coat, the gold watch chain, the careful attire of respectability, something desperate and strange about him, the same hunger I had seen in the men who had killed my father and my brother, that blending of fierceness and frailty I had found so moving and so terrible.

I knew little about him. He was simply Ira Agbrigg, who had attached himself to Joel, a small opportunist clinging to a great one. Mr Agbrigg, he was called now, and in Simon Street men doffed their caps to him; a member of Ramsden Street Chapel, a pillar of the community whose son – this same, sharp-eyed Jonas – attended the grammar school with Blaize. A resourceful, useful man, Joel said, although the roughness of his speech still closed many doors to him and, in Joel's view, his thin, tired wife would hold him down.

'That's what comes of marrying young,' Joel had said. 'He should have waited – found himself a woman who could keep up with him – instead of losing his head over the first mill girl who caught his eye. Strikes me she'd be happier in a back-to-back in Simon Street, which is where she came from, and that's a pity. He can't like it, the way he strives his guts out to improve their standards, when she can't even improve herself.'

And, knowing how Joel would have treated a wife who could not 'keep up,' I had expected to see the same impatience and resentment in Ira Agbrigg too and was surprised by his evident deep concern.

'She takes life hard,' he told me. 'Always has. Worries over silly things – feels uneasy all the time, for no reason. And this has been too much for her. We've lost six children out of eleven, Mrs Barforth, and I'm not complaining about that because I know plenty who've lost more – some who've lost every one they had – but Ann took it bad each time, and now it's all come back to her. She's grieving for the bairns who died here last night, and for her own bairns all over again – and trying not to blame me for it all, I shouldn't wonder, because she won't want to blame me – never wanted to blame me for anything. Am I to blame, Mrs Barforth?'

'Oh, Mr Agbrigg – I really don't think –' I began, not knowing what I thought.

But the tragedy which had clogged my tongue had served to loosen his and, forgetting his awkwardness and his humility, he burst out, 'Can't you understand why I locked those girls in, Mrs Barforth? You can see what it's like in this neighbourhood – Simon Street, Gower Street, Saint Street? You're a lady but you must know what goes on here – they say every other house is a knocking shop and I've no reason to think otherwise. And those girls were no better than any others. An extra shilling was riches to them, and if I hadn't kept my eyes open they'd have gone out to earn it any way they could, and ended up diseased and in the family way – ruined. Mrs Barforth, you should have seen them when they came here – oh, they came in dribs and drabs, not in cartloads like in the old days when the parish priests used to send us up here, in consignments, a hundred at a time. Dribs and drabs, it is now. Some of them were turned out into the street by their own kin, to fend for themselves, because they were taking up too much room or because the mother had a new man in the house and the girl was getting bonny; some of them orphaned and wanting to keep out of the workhouse; some of them in danger from their own fathers when they were drunk. It must be hard for you to understand, Mrs Barforth, just what it's like to be homeless and rootless, how a twelve-year-old girl can be alone in the world, except for the village constable and the poorhouse overseer, and the brothel keepers in Simon Street. But I understand – that I do – and so I let them sleep in the old shed, not as part of their wages – although I expect Mr Barforth thinks I should have deducted something – but just to give them a roof over their heads. And when they started getting out at night and made a disturbance in the yard, I locked them in, not to keep them at their work as people are saying but to keep them off the streets. I wanted to do some good, not that I'll be believed, because even if they don't go so far as to accuse me of murder, they'll make out I had vile intentions of my own – young girls and a man with a sick wife – it's easy to say. I'm not liked here, and I know it. They don't care to see one of their own get on. They don't mind the gentry having money, because that's inherited – got without effort – but when a man like themselves rises above the average it makes them feel bad – makes them wonder why I can do it when they can't, and they don't like that. Not that I am one of their own, if the truth be told.'

And, seeing my surprise, realizing that by his speech I had taken him for a Law Valley man, he shook his head and smiled.

'No, ma'am, I'm not a native of these parts, although just where I did come from I couldn't rightly say. I was brought here, in a consignment, when I was too young to know my right name or age, or where I was coming from. I was a parish apprentice, ma'am, and before that I'd been in a poorhouse somewhere – left on the doorstep, I reckon, by my mother, whoever she may have been, and she may have been no older than some of those bairns who died here yesterday. I grew up in the sheds, Mrs Barforth; we all did, all my consignment – eating, sleeping, working in the same room, boys and girls together, dossing down anywhere on sacks and heaps of waste, bound until they said we were twenty-one. And of the hundred who came up with me I doubt there's more than a dozen alive today – and I may be forty, ma'am, or thereabouts, and they could be no older. Well, I had no name, like I told you, so they called me Agbrigg because that was the village my overlooker came from, and then later, when I thought I'd better have a Christian name like everybody else, I called myself Ira, after one of the Hobhouses, because I thought it might bring me luck. And so it did. I never got crooked in my limbs, ma'am; never bowed at the knees like most of them, and though I've got strap marks across my back, at least my back itself is straight – I don't really know why. And then I met my Ann, which was luck enough for any man, and I made promises. I said we wouldn't starve, that I'd take her out of the weaving shed and put a decent roof over her head and keep it there – and so I have, and more besides.

'I knew I had to do more than just grumble, more than just envy folks that had more than me, if I wanted something of my own, and so I went to Sunday School – got myself washed and tidied up and spent my days off learning to read and write instead of at the cockpit and the pithouse like my mates. And once I could read I was free. I saw what the machines could do, Mrs Barforth; I saw the changes they'd bring, just like your husband did, and that's why I brought your mother that warning. It wasn't treachery. It was common sense, because you can't stand in the way of progress. I know that – and you must know it – but they don't know it down there in the yard, Mrs Barforth, and you can't tell them. All they see in me is a crawler, a greaser, a sneak, doing his master's dirty work – and it's hard for my Ann. I can stand it, but she's got no friends now, you see. Her old mates don't trust her anymore, and she's not one for solitude like me. She doesn't talk much but she likes to feel part of things, and it's hard for her now when her old neighbours pass her in the street – it's hard for the children, too. My Jonas – my eldest – is a clever lad, doing well at school, and Mr Barforth tells me he can find a place for him – a good place – for which I'm grateful. And I can afford to keep the girls at home to help their mother – there's no call for them to go out and earn a penny, I'm proud to say. But they get beyond my Ann sometimes, talk about things she's never had the chance to understand, and they get out of patience when they think she's slow – especially Jonas. And she's mighty fond of Jonas. She takes that hard, too.'

'I'm sorry. If there is anything I can do –'

'Why no, ma'am,' he said, remembering, with visible discomfort, that I was Joel's wife. 'Nothing at all – beyond the honour of this visit, for which we are most grateful. But you have not had tea, Mrs Barforth – you must take something before you go. Yes, yes, indeed you must.'

And, solely to please him, because I knew he would fret about it otherwise, I drank the weak brew he eventually managed to serve me, and kept on repeating, 'How delicious. How very refreshing,' until I felt a perfect fool.

'That young woman must pull herself together,' Hannah told me as we drove away. 'With five children to think of she cannot afford to indulge herself by going into a trance. You won't believe this, but they have no maid, just a woman who comes in to scrub. Can you imagine that? Naturally they can afford it – I have some idea of the wages my brother pays, and they could easily manage a cook and a parlourmaid and a skivvy, and at least a man outside. Mrs Agbrigg never had a word to say, but the boy was quite talkative – a good sensible boy, young Jonas Agbrigg – and from what he says it strikes me that although his mother insists she wants to do the work herself – and may even believe it – the truth is that she doesn't know how to handle servants and is afraid to try. And it won't do, you know. In the first place it looks odd for a man in his position not to have servants, and she'd be far happier in herself once she'd made the effort. She feels she's letting her husband down – which, of course, she is – and the cure for that is to assert herself, convince herself that Mrs Ira Agbrigg is worth something and need stand no nonsense from anyone.'

And although she was – as so often – quite right, I could not help wondering if Hannah's strong medicine would do more harm than good.

I drove next to the infirmary at the top of Sheepgate somewhat to Hannah's dismay since public hospitals, designed for the accommodation of whores and vagrants, victims of gin-shop brawling and others who could not afford to be decently cared for in their own homes, were not greatly to her taste. But I had made up my mind and, having first sent the coachman inside to enquire, I found it impossible to remain in the street and, jumping down, went through the door and into what could have been the sparsely decorated hallway of an ordinary dwelling house.

Inside there was a sweetish, unpleasant odour and the impersonal shabbiness of a public building no one had thought to beautify, and, having expected a great hustle and bustle, some official instantly on hand to ascertain my business, I was amazed to find myself alone but for two young men lounging against the stair rail, one of them a stranger and the other Crispin Aycliffe, who, with a cool, formal nod of his head, seemed to be warning me to keep my distance.

And I would have gone willingly back into the street, dreading these inevitable chance encounters, the necessity for falsehood, had his companion not made a sudden move towards me, an excited flash of recognition in his face.

'Your conscience troubling you, then, Mrs Barforth, is it?' he said, rougher than Crispin, smaller but fiercer, a fighting cock of a man with the flamboyant good looks one glimpsed sometimes at a fair. A gipsy lad in a good coat and an exceedingly fancy waistcoat, not at all the kind of man I would have expected to speak to me.

'I beg your pardon?'

'Conscience, Mrs Barforth – or your husband's conscience? You've come, with your basket of goodies, have you, ma'am, to ease the last moments of the dying. Very commendable, except that you're too late, I fear. They've all gone – all fifteen of them – so there's nothing left for you to do but buy them a headstone – something really splendid, with a nice inscription, I should think.'

'That's enough, Mark,' Crispin said very quietly. 'We're not campaigning against women.'

But the man – Mark Corey, certainly, of the *Cullingford Star* – his face quite ghastly, having just come downstairs from viewing those nightmare bodies, was devoured by a need to strike out at someone, anyone, and he paid no heed.

'Are we not?' he said, speaking rapidly as if he had so much to say, so much protest inside him, so much outrage that he must rid himself of it or choke. 'Are we not campaigning against them all? She's Joel Barforth's wife, isn't she? And what objection has she ever made to living on his blood money – and living well? Can she be innocent, Crispin – really – or even decent, when she lives with a man who picks twelve-year-old girls up from the streets, locks them in his sheds, and throws the key away? Maybe she's just never thought about it, Crispin, so ask her, tomorrow, in your article – and all the others like her – and see if she can reply –'

'Easy, Mark,' Crispin said, for indeed the man was very close to tears. 'Easy, old friend,' and, as they clasped hands and drew close together, the understanding between them excluded me, their absolute certainty of being right defeated me, a woman who could see fragments of right and fragments of wrong everywhere.

'I'll take you to your carriage,' Crispin said, his hand giving Mark Corey's a final, reassuring squeeze, and turning, walking quickly outside – running away – I could not speak to him, had no idea at all what I could possibly – ever – say to him again.

'Well, I did warn you,' Hannah told me as our carriage clattered smartly up the hill, away from the town and the silent, shawl-clad figures standing around the infirmary door. 'And now I suppose you have got yourself soundly insulted, for you must know who that young man was. No, no, not Mr Crispin Aycliffe, we all know about him. That was Mark Corey, who calls himself the editor of the *Star*, which he calls a newspaper. And, indeed, I hardly think he has the right to call himself a Corey for that matter. He may be a natural son of Colonel Corey's – although the colonel himself has never said so – but that would not make him a Corey, would it? However, somebody paid for his education, for he was at the grammar school with Crispin Aycliffe, and then they tried to make a churchman of him, which was clearly doomed to fail. He went to France, of course, as they all do, to get their revolutionary ideas, and since then he has been persecuting us with his dreadful newspaper. I know all this because Mr Morgan Aycliffe has told me.'

'But you know so many things, Hannah.'

'I am not stupid,' she said robustly. 'And one thing I do know, and that is why Crispin Aycliffe and Mark Corey were at the infirmary. They are going to write an article about the fire, not because of Ira Agbrigg – for who has heard of Ira Agbrigg? – but because they believe they have found something to use against Joel. And whether it is the truth or a lie will in no way concern them. And so if Mr Corey insulted you just now, you must let Joel know of it so that he can take appropriate action – so that people may understand they are dealing with a bully and a liar, not some kind of avenging angel.'

But when we returned to the Top House to find Joel most unusually at home in the middle of the day and he demanded, 'How did you get on?' for the first time in my life I took refuge in assumed frailty and answered, 'Oh, I am not quite well, Joel. I have been too long in the heat and dust and my head aches. Hannah will tell you about it. I think I must really lie down.'

21

The *Cullingford Star* made its appearance some two or three days later, a shoddy publication printed on coarse paper, as different as could be from Mr Roundwood's *Courier and Review*, which, on the whole, told us things we were glad to know, such as the progress of Mr Morgan Aycliffe's political campaign and the brilliant success of our Assembly Ball.

The *Courier*, predictably, had reported the fire at Low Cross as a tragic accident, finding it unnecessary, in an area where industrial fires were common, to indulge in speculation about keys and what may or may not have been the reason for those locked doors. But the *Star*, which some kind soul pushed under our door in the early hours of the morning, not only speculated, it accused, assassinated, presented, with a pen dipped in venom, a picture of man's brutality to his own species that curdled the blood.

No relatives of the dead girls had yet been found. No proper record existed of their names and ages. And so who were they? And were there others, confined somewhere in a slavery baser than any West Indian plantation? How many young persons from Simon Street and Gower Street and Saint Street were missing from home? And since, as always there were dozens, hundreds, unaccounted for, had they perhaps been taken into captivity? Was this, then, how profits were made? Had a certain well-known local industrialist found a speedier way to amass his millions? Had it come to him one night around the second magnum of champagne that instead of paying low wages he would do better to pay no wages at all? And so a picture was built up of Ira Agbrigg scouring the Simon Street area in the dead of night like a vampire, looking for vagrants, the little lost children, the straying lambs, to lure them back to Low Cross, lock them up, and work them until they dropped.

One was asked to consider a Roman galley with soldiers patrolling the benches with whips, pausing here and there to unshackle a dead oarsman and toss him overboard while a replacement was fastened in his place. And on the deck of such a galley would be a cold-eyed, cold-hearted gentleman who saw nothing amiss with using the bodies of his fellow creatures to speed his transportation, consuming them as casually as a present-day engine consumed coals. And the readers of the *Star* were asked to pity such a Nero, to understand that such a man, so devoid of humanity, would surely bring about his own destruction. They were asked to bear in mind the tale of King Midas, who, having requested of the gods that everything he touched should turn to gold, found that his food and drink became metal on his tongue, and his wife a golden statue in his arms, and that such a man was doomed to spiritual decay, a vast inward rot, and was certain to putrefy in the midst of his splendours.

'You will take action against them, of course,' Hannah said, handing the paper back to Joel as if it were a dead rat, her nostrils revolted by its imagined odour, and, taking it from her, folding it carefully, he put it in his pocket and smiled.

'I don't know that I shall, not direct action in any event, for if I put them out of business, I'm Nero again, aren't I, and they're martyrs to their cause. And every cause needs its martyrs – my word, yes, the more the merrier – so I doubt I'll oblige them in quite that way.'

'But you won't simply ignore it – let them get away with it?'

'Did I say that? I don't think I did, you know.' And, pushing back his chair, he said to me, 'And how is my wife this morning? Does your head still ache? You'd best not sicken just now, my girl – unless you're breeding again – for we've a funeral to go to tomorrow, and if you're not there some fool is going to swear I've turned you to gold.'

And, seeing through his eyes, I had a vision of Rosamund Boulton encased in precious metal in her shopwindow, and of Estella Chase hardening in places since she was perhaps not yet entirely possessed; and I understood the content of his smile.

My old bitch was not inclined for exercise that day, preferring the comfort of a hearthrug to the first snap of cold in the autumn air, but the young one did not fail me and went loping ahead, knowing her way by now to Old Sarah's Rock. There was a fine veil of rain in the air, a pale grey sky with a patchy grey mist beneath it, and the ground was so heavy with water that the hem of my dress became unwieldy, my progress unsteady, my spirits as dark as the bare fold of the land before me, cowering at the approach of winter. And when I came upon Crispin, standing in the shelter of the rock, Mark Corey's words were there, like poles in the ground, between us: 'Can she be innocent?' And because nothing, to me, had ever been entirely black, entirely white, I knew there was no answer.

'Well,' he said, 'you are looking at me very strangely, and so you must have read the *Star*. Is he going to sue?'

'No.'

'I thought not. And you are angry with me?'

'Am I?'

'Verity,' he said, throwing back his cloak and opening his arms and his mind towards me in a gesture that always moved me, always drew me irresistibly towards him like a homecoming, a return to the source of my true self. 'Verity, Verity – I am sorry for what happened at the infirmary – sorry for what Mark said to you – but he doesn't know you and you don't know him, which is a pity, for you would like each other.'

'Do you think so? Would he permit himself to like me, when I have gorged myself for so long on bloody money?'

And I did not know why I had spoken so sharply when the last thing I wanted – the one thing I could not bear – was to quarrel with him.

'Don't,' he said, growing sharp in his turn. 'Don't, Verity. Mark Corey may not please everyone on first acquaintance, but he has strong feelings, sincere emotions, and after the horror we had just seen – after that – he was not in command of himself and neither was I. And because of that horror – to ensure that it never happens again – can you blame me, Verity, for my need to strike out? Yes, yes, I know my words were inflammatory – a deliberate play on the emotions – a savage personal attack on a man I happen to dislike for very private reasons – I admit it freely. But there was enough truth there to justify every syllable of it – and if you had seen those girls you would understand why. Verity, we must settle this between us, for it is not the end of it. I know how awkwardly you are placed, but I could not bear it – and I must tell you this – if you tried to defend him.'

I disengaged myself from his arms and walked a step or two away from him, knowing how easy it would be to offer him my wholehearted support, to say, 'Yes, Crispin, tell them anything – take any atrocity you can and enlarge it, invent it, anything, because the end justifies the means.' And so it did, for the children had to be protected; I knew that now as well as he. A way must be found, somehow, anyhow, to allow them their childhood, to guarantee them shelter and time and space in which to grow and, when childhood was done, an opportunity to live with dignity. But was it not too easy, too obvious, to fasten one's hatred on Joel and others like him, to imagine that curbing him or removing him would solve everything? Did we, in fact, know how to recognize our oppressors, or were we all oppressors, all self-seeking, all of us to blame? An accident of birth had made Mark Corey a radical and Joel Barforth an industrialist, just as that same accident could so easily have reversed the roles of my grandfather and Jabez Gott. And how many, I thought, even down there in the mill yards, once their own needs were satisfied, would lift a finger to help others? Not many, it seemed to me, not many, and although it made none of it right, it made it difficult, a maze of human good and ill through which I could not find my way. And concluding that our salvation could only come from inside ourselves – from a maturing of our own greedy, childish, grasping, frightened human hearts – and because I saw no possibility of such a universal change, I wondered why I could not tell Crispin an easy lie, settle it as he wanted it settled, and think only of myself and him.

'I am not making excuses,' I told him. 'It is just that I know someone else who saw those girls, someone who went to the infirmary with them and stayed there until they died, and who has barely spoken a dozen words since.'

'Mrs Agbrigg?'

'Yes. I think it unlikely she ever learned to read, but she has a clever son who can read for her. And if he doesn't tell her about your article, then someone else will.'

'Yes,' he said. 'I know. I met her at the infirmary, and however sorry I'm inclined to feel, I can't afford it, Verity. She's a nice woman, but her husband did lock that door, and because that door was locked those children died. Verity, it's as clear-cut as that, isn't it?'

'No, Crispin. Nothing could ever be so clear-cut as that – not to me. I would want to know why he locked that door. He says it was to keep them off the streets, and although I don't say he was right nor that it was right for them to be there – because that certainly wasn't right – what I do believe is that he was trying to do the best he could, as he saw it.'

'Agbrigg? My God, Verity, the man's a positive disease. They detest him at Low Cross.'

'Only because he's so close to Joel, and they detest Joel.'

'Exactly.'

And suddenly it was no longer a question of Low Cross or the *Cullingford Star* but our own personal triangle, its spikes threatening now to impale us.

'I cannot bear to hear you defend him,' he whispered, his face blanched with jealous anger, as perhaps mine had blanched with fear. Yet instead of throwing myself against him and vowing that I detested Joel as heartily as anyone at Low Cross – as Crispin wanted me to do, as I wanted to do – I said, much too calmly, 'I am not defending him. I know what Joel is – after all, he is my cousin. I have known him all my life. And even if I wanted to defend him it would be a waste of time, since he doesn't care what people think of him.'

'No, he doesn't care what men think of him, that I grant you, but where women are concerned – You know he has other women, don't you?'

'Stop it, Crispin.'

'Why? You do know, don't you, about Miss Boulton? And Mrs Chase now, too, it seems, according to Mark, who is, after all, her half brother –?'

'Yes, I know. It doesn't seem to matter.'

'It matters to me – because he has you too.'

And, covering his face briefly with his hands, he shuddered, quite violently, a movement of distress that banished all my hesitation and brought my arms around him.

'So that's jealousy, is it?' he said, smiling, nuzzling his head against mine. 'I thought I was above it, you know, but I'm not, and it hurts. What are you going to do for me?'

And when I merely held him tighter he laughed, making a joke of what we both knew to be the most urgent thing in our lives.

'I know what you can do. You can come and live with me, on my fifty pounds a year, in my attic at the Red Gin. How would that suit you?'

'In some ways it would suit me very well.'

'Yes – or I could move away from here and find responsible employment, in London perhaps, for I am, after all, an architect not without talent and there is money to be made. I could earn the wherewithal to keep my own carriage and a cook and a parlourmaid, and all the little niceties we've both been accustomed to. And you could spend your days waiting for me to come home and saying, "Yes, dear. Quite right, dear," every time I expressed an opinion, like my mother used to do. And we could feel very triumphant because Mrs So-and-So had left a card, or very desperate because she hadn't. Would that suit you better?'

'It would hardly suit you at all.'

'I suppose not, and I might not even be very good at it. I have often wondered if I could ever turn sour, like my father, if I began to feel out of place with my life. Perhaps there is enough of him in me for that. So what now, Verity?'

What indeed? The sky, I noticed, had clouded over, and there was a chill wind sighing across the surface of the moor, bending the stiff grasses: a dull, clammy morning, promising more rain, heralding a cold ending of the year. And feeling the numb misery in him, knowing what he was steeling himself to say, I knew it would be an act of love to say it for him.

'Perhaps we should not meet again – not for a while, at any rate.'

'That is not what I want, Verity.'

'Oh – I think, in a way, it is. There are too many things standing between us, and I think you are afraid to find me more of a Barforth than you imagined – or that circumstances may force me to become so. I think you are afraid I may turn you away from the path you have chosen – and I think you may be right.'

He leaned, for a moment, quite heavily against the rock, and my own body, too, was weak; a great weight, it seemed, was pressing against my forehead, a certain bewilderment that I, who was not brave, had found the courage to say these things.

'How clear your eyes are,' he whispered, 'and how small you make me seem. I am no more reasonable, you see, than any other man. I knew you would dislike my article, yet I wanted you to lie to me and call it brilliant. I wanted you to be unquestioningly on my side. I need that exclusive devotion, and yet I am not prepared to give it. I have found something to do with my life, and it seems I cannot part from it. I am a poor creature sometimes, Verity, for it is not in me to say goodbye to you.'

And it was a blessing that my dog came suddenly careering back to me and, rearing up, clapped muddy paws on my shoulders, almost overturning me.

'Foolish animal, you are quite wet through – get down, be still. I had better take her home, for she is shivering and the moor must be running with water. Silly girl, you have no sense at all.' And, brushing my hands against my cheeks, I said unnecessarily, 'It is coming on to rain,' knowing that the sudden flurry of raindrops would offer me some concealment if I began to cry. 'Crispin, I had better run, for Mrs Stevens is obsessed with the weather and she is likely to send the carriage for me, as far as it can come.'

'Yes, of course. Of course – Verity –'

'No,' I said, wildly perhaps, for me. 'No' – forbidding him to hold me back, refusing absolutely to listen, and, obsessed with my determination that we must part this way, as loving friends, I turned and fled, unaware until I reached the road again that my dog had not followed me and then leaving her, for the first time, to find her way alone. And that day I truly understood how necessary it is sometimes to fall ill, how the only way to survive is to draw the bed curtains and creep inside the sheets, remaining motionless, untouchable, until one can bear to face the daylight again.

And I had need, in the days that followed, of all my strength, a full measure of my reason.

To begin with there was the funeral: fifteen small, plain coffins, and a multitude of silent figures lining the way to the churchyard, crowding into the church, so that, walking past them to a front pew, I had a panic sensation of drowning, could feel them surging forward in a great wave to overwhelm me. But they had nothing with which to harm me but their silence, and when the short, awkward service was over, every face I looked at turned away from me, every eye avoided mine.

Hannah was there, and the Agbriggs – Ann Agbrigg invisible beneath her mourning veils – and Mark Corey, standing in a corner of the church porch, giving Joel a look of hatred and contempt to which Joel replied by coolly tipping his hat. But not even Mark Corey could dispute the evidence of the relatives, who, appearing in some miraculous fashion, had no complaints to make, and everything would have gone smoothly had not Mrs Agbrigg suddenly paused on her way to the carriage and fluttered to the ground with no more substance about her than a silk scarf in the wind.

'I feared it would be too much for her,' Hannah told me, pulling off her gloves briskly when we reached home and looking around her for the appearance of the tea tray. 'Mr Agbrigg says she didn't wish him to face the ordeal alone, which is very commendable, but it is a pity, just the same, that she could not keep her feet. It may have given a false impression, which would do her husband more harm than good.'

But, by nightfall, we learned Mrs Agbrigg was suffering not from remorse but from a fever contracted, it was thought, at the infirmary when she had kept watch at those nightmare bedsides.

'They took a vagrant in that night,' Hannah said, managing to be well informed even at this crisis. 'An Irish girl from heaven knows where, quite filthy, complaining of dizziness and pains in the head, and then they let her go or she simply went away leaving her fever behind her. Poor Mrs Agbrigg. I hope she is strong enough to bear it – I do indeed. I have sent Marth-Ellen to enquire if anything is needed in the way of linen or remedies, for the Agbrigg girls are barely old enough to understand the doctor's instructions and they have no other woman in the house. Marth-Ellen has taken soup, too, which I am sure you do not mind, Verity, and I think it would be as well to send her tomorrow – every day, in fact, for I am not at all sure they know how to manage on their own.'

But, by the end of the week, Marth-Ellen, too, had taken to her bed, burning and freezing in turn, her head wrenched apart by an iron claw, she told me, a knife blade somewhere in her chest.

They never gave the fever a name. We had had cholera and typhus, and our seasonal epidemics of diphtheria and smallpox, and we could all recognize the consumption that withered away so many women and the choking coughs that carried off our babies. But some ailments which came to ravage us, nailing us to our beds and then abruptly departing, had no name and were called, simply, fever. And this was one of them. First it came upon the Agbriggs and the teeming dens of Simon Street,

214

where one lived or died according to one's own strength, since a doctor was rarely called there; then Marth-Ellen, bringing the sickness into my house; then Lucy Oldroyd and, and a child of Elinor's, and three of Emma-Jane's; then the Reverend Mr Brand, who lay alone in his house for two days until Hannah went to look for him; and then, early one morning, my governess, Mrs Paget, begged me to come and look at Nicholas.

Fretfully tossing his covers, he was lying in bed, red and cross, hurting, he told me, just hurting. But by afternoon he was cooler, demanding food and entertainment and making a great fuss, and it was Blaize who lay flushed and much too quiet, shivering with cold although his skin burned to my touch.

'Don't alarm yourself unduly,' the doctor told me. 'Such a strong child – a little Hercules – his body should make light work of this. It is not so, you understand, with nursing mothers, and new babies, with the old and the weak and such like. But a fine little chap like this should fight his own way through. Moisten his lips a little if you cannot make him drink, keep him warm, say your prayers – there is nothing more, at this stage, one need do but that.' And I understood he was telling me there was no cure, that some lived and others did not, and I would have to wait and see.

I sat down at the bedside, pressing my hands together, striving to be calm, and remained there, sometimes with Hannah, sometimes alone, for the rest of that day and night and the day that followed, obsessed with the need to make him drink, cradling his painful little body against my shoulder, appalled at the fierce, dry heat of him as the fever glazed his eyes, swallowed the roundness of his cheeks and pinched them into the bare bones and hollows of sickness.

'He must sweat,' Hannah said, knowledgeable in the progress of the disease since she had already nursed Marth-Ellen and Mr Brand. 'He must drink – and he must sweat.' And I knew she was hurt when suddenly I pushed her capable, well-intentioned hands away and declared I could manage alone.

'Call me when you need me,' she said, deeply offended, deeply concerned, for this was her brother's house, her brother's child, and she had never had much faith in me. But Joel was away in Manchester, knowing nothing of Blaize's condition, and there was no appeal.

'I will look in every hour,' she told me, 'for you will need to sleep eventually, Verity. And although your devotion is commendable, I have to tell you that it lacks good sense. Make no mistake about it, he is very unwell and your experience of nursing has not been great.'

And although, once again, she was quite right, panic had made me stubborn and I meant to have my way.

But a moment came that second night when, jerking myself awake from a momentary doze, I was heartened by a fine beading of moisture on his brow and then became almost immediately terrified by the sudden drenching of his body, sweat dripping from him like the layers of a candle. Having done all the other things the doctor had required, having dabbed his forehead with cologne and his lips with water, I went down on my knees and tried to pray. But my conversations with God had always been conventional, impersonal, and even through the raw reality of my grieving, I could think of nothing to say.

I knew well enough that few women expected to raise all their children. My own mother had buried six, Joel had lost two elder brothers and a number of sisters, Emma-Jane Hobhouse was the sole survivor of five; I myself had attended the funerals, throughout my childhood, of a dozen of my playmates carried off by measles, by typhoid fever, by a strange, nameless wasting away. 'You're too fond of those bairns, missus,' the old woman from whom I had bought the kittens had told me. 'And in the long run it doesn't pay. Keep your distance, lass, or you'll end by laying up grief for yourself. I had thirteen once and now never a one; half in the graveyard, a pair at sea, the rest God knows where.' Yet now, when it seemed that my turn had come, I was not resigned.

I had loved him for seven years, first as an extension of my own body and spirit and then for himself: Blaise Barforth, unique, unrepeatable. Now, as he lay melting before my eyes in that dreadful sweat, the full horror of his loss struck me a mortal blow from which I knew I would not heal. I had lost my father and my brother, had seen them struck down, bleeding, but the anguish I had felt then was nothing compared to this. I had known, even when that sorrow had been at its height, that I would learn, however painfully, to live with the memory of it. But now, frantic and blind with panic, I would have torn out my own life willingly if somehow I could have injected it into my son.

I could not bear to lose him, could not contemplate a world without his cool, mischievous smile or his unshakeable belief, even when I so often seemed to favour his brother, that I loved him best. And in this moment I did love him the best.

I heard my voice, or perhaps only my thoughts, promising, 'Let him live and I will try never to think of Crispin Aycliffe again.' And in case I weaken, I will allow myself to become pregnant again, which will please Joel and punish me enough in itself.

Having made my bargain, I rested my head on my son's counterpane and, for a very long time, wept.

I slept too, as Hannah had said I would. Then, waking with blind eyes in the darkness and certain, in that first conscious moment, that he was gone and I had let him die alone, I experienced the most intense gratitude of my life when I found him not only alive but sleeping more naturally, sweating still but better than before.

I got up clumsily, my body cramped and aching, and, going over to the washstand to rinse my face and hands, I heard the door open. Hannah, I thought, hoping to find me asleep. Without turning round, I whispered irritably, 'He's much improved – and I can manage perfectly well. I'm quite all right.'

'Good,' Joel said. 'I'm delighted to hear it.' So astonished was I to hear his voice that I answered sharply, ungraciously, 'What are you doing here?'

'Well, and where should I be?'

216

'In Manchester, surely, until Friday?'

'Yes, except that I had a message to say that I was needed at home.'

'Not from me.'

'No,' he said, coming slowly into the room. 'Apparently not from you.' And standing by the bedside, looking down, he murmured, 'He is my son, you know, after all.'

'Yes,' I said, sitting down suddenly, lulled by the miraculous rise and fall of the child's breathing, my son who was also Joel's son. 'Yes, he is, and he even looks like you. I thought not. I thought it was Nicholas who had your face; and Caroline, both your face and your manner. But he's like you. And like me, too, like my mother ...'

'Well,' he said sharply, although the hand he closed abruptly over mine was surprisingly unsteady, 'isn't that just as it should be? Part of me and part of you. But you say he is better, truly?'

'Yes, yes. I see you have no more faith in me than your sister.'

'Verity, Mrs Stevens met me at the doorway and pleaded with me to make you go to bed. You can trust me, surely, to sit with him until the doctor comes?'

'Oh yes, indeed, but I think I will stay with him myself, just the same.'

And so, obstinately, since I could hardly stand, barely see, I remained guarding my child as I had done on the day he was born, until the doctor came. Only then would I allow Mrs Paget to relieve me and Mrs Stevens to put me to bed.

I slept a long time, the whole of a crisp autumn morning, the amber beginnings of an afternoon, waking to find my room awash with sunshine and Joel, standing at the window, asking me if I could eat breakfast, luncheon, tea?

'Yes, all of them, I think. But first, Blaize ...?'

'Yes, he's mending. And the other two are showing signs of nothing but wickedness, which Hannah says is normal.'

'Hannah would.'

'I daresay, but what shall I ask them to bring you, my lady? Will you have a tray and eat in bed?'

And when it came and I had devoured hot muffins and gingerbread, and Joel, sitting at my bedside in his shirt sleeves, had most surprisingly poured my tea, he said, 'Tell me something – do you dislike my sister?'

'No, as it happens.'

'And what does that mean?'

'Oh, there are times when I feel that I want to dislike her, but actually I don't.'

'I'm glad,' he said, his hand closing once again over mine, startling me. 'Because if you did dislike her I'm afraid you would have to endure it. No, no, I'm not trying to set her above you or any foolishness of that kind, and I'm well aware that she is high-handed and obstinate and fond of her own way, as I am myself. But when my father died, Verity, with his affairs in such a tangle, Hannah stood by me like a rock, and I have no mind to forget it. You don't know what it means, Verity, to owe money, to watch the lads you were at school with change direction when

217

they see you coming in case you want to borrow – or to go into the Piece Hall and find them all too busy to talk to you. They were all waiting to see me fail, Verity, and, by God, they'd have enjoyed it, because not one of them could have got himself out of the mess I was in – certainly not Bradley Hobhouse, or your brother Edwin, either. And I was doing it. Even without your grandfather's money, I was doing it. Low Cross was beginning to come straight, and I'd have got on all right. I'd have managed – me and Hannah – you do see that?'

'Oh yes,' I told him, passive, yawning, still too full of sleep to care what I said. 'You'd both have done well. She would be married now to my brother, and you to Miss Boulton, and we'd have been obliged to go on sending to London for our shawls and fans.'

'Quite so,' he said, standing up, his face suddenly very keen, very careful, and then, with neither guilt nor swagger nor anything else in his voice, he asked me, 'You know, then, that I financed Miss Boulton's shop?'

'I do.'

'And what conclusion do you draw?'

'Oh – that your financial arrangements are not my concern, unless you choose that they should be.'

'How very reasonable,' he said, again expressionless. 'And how like you. You may take it that my conscience troubled me on her account, for reasons we both know of and have never had any reason to discuss. Do we have any reason to discuss it now?'

'I don't think so.'

'Neither do I.'

And as he leaned towards me, the warm, male scent of him, the odours of wine and tobacco that lived on the surface of his skin, the good, red blood flowing vigorously underneath reminded me of the bargain I had made, that if Blaize lived I would conceive another child. And although the vow itself had lost its urgency – for he was alive and I would soon convince myself he would have lived in any case – the need for a barrier between me and Crispin Aycliffe seemed more than ever vital.

'You know that I've bought Carter's mill at Tarn Edge, don't you?' he said. 'Yes, of course you do, and I've bought a ten-acre site just beyond it, because I reckon we've lived here long enough, Verity, in Samson Barforth's house. I want a decent house of my own before I'm forty, and once I've got the mill altered to suit me, it strikes me we could landscape a few of those acres and build ourselves a palace while we're about it. What do you say?'

'Yes,' I told him, understanding simply that from Tarn Edge I could not walk my dogs on Lawcroft Moor, would be spared the agony every morning of denying myself the chance to look for Crispin; and, drawn together by this new enthusiasm and by our realization last night of what it could mean to lose a son, there was a brief companionship between us.

'Well – the mill first, of course – business before pleasure or there'll soon be no pleasure at all, as Bradley Hobhouse is starting to discover. And then I'll have a house my sons can be proud to live in when they're grown.'

218

'And your daughter.'

'Naturally, my daughter, and with the dowry I can give her she'll be able to marry wherever she likes. They'll be clamouring for that girl of mine, and not just manufacturers, either – landed gentlemen, titled gentlemen, why not? She could have any one of the Hobhouse boys, but what could they give her except money, and I can give her plenty of that – she'll be used to that – so a title may be the only thing left for me to buy her.'

And as he grinned down at me, making light of it yet meaning it just the same, there was something about his nakedly expressed ambitions that made him seem younger, less sinister, unless it was that I was older and no longer so intimidated by this wicked, handsome cousin, twelve years my senior, who had always looked down his nose at little girls.

'Lady Caroline – good heavens,' I said, sliding lower into my nest of pillows, knowing how easily his sensual curiosity could be aroused, refusing to be troubled by his faithlessness since I myself was faithless, now, in spirit.

'My word, Verity – if I thought you were the kind of woman who'd invite a man into her bed in the middle of the day, I might just take advantage of it.'

'Are there such women?'

'Ah well,' he said, nudged into remembrance of Miss Boulton, his eyes careful again in the strong daylight. 'And if there are, they have nothing to do here, between us, surely? Are you growing up, cousin?'

'That – or growing old. And don't call me cousin.'

'What a shrew,' he said, taking my chin between his hard, pinching fingers. 'What a scold. It's no bad thing we're cousins, Verity – that you've always been a Barforth. If you'd been a Hobhouse you'd have been nagging me by now to do something for Bradley, thinking about Nethercoats instead of Lawcroft. But, in our case, your interests are exactly the same as mine, and that's what binds people together – that's what counts. Other things can be very pleasant – friendship, for instance – but, however warm it is, however interesting, it's here today and gone tomorrow and only a fool puts his faith in it. Friendship has no bones. But property in common, blood in common, children in common – there you have the real bricks and mortar of life. And you're at the very centre of it, Verity. So, sweet cousin, does anything worry you?'

'Nothing,' I told him. 'Nothing at all.' And although he was offering me a reassurance I did not need, since I felt perfectly secure of my place in his life, I was ready once more to accept it.

'I'm sorry,' he said gruffly, having little experience of apologies. 'Sorry you didn't feel the need to send for me when you thought Blaize was dying, that you were so surprised to see me after Hannah sent the message in your place.'

'I'm sorry, too.'

And briefly, as our eyes met, we reached out, hesitating, on the borders of an unknown pathway that could lead us beyond the barriers that had always held us apart, but both of us, I think, nervously aware of the risk, afraid of failure.

'They are my children,' he said. 'I may not appear to notice them, for my father never noticed me, unless it was to call me to help him load a wagon or get him up the stairs when he was drunk. But they are my children. They'll never see me drunk and incapable, and when I make them work it will be to their advantage more than mine. I'm saying – I don't know – they're my children and yours ... And, by God, if we'd lost that little demon it would have hurt me.'

Although he could not have spoken the words, I understood his half-acknowledge thought and answered it, for in the event of that loss we could have turned neither to Estella Chase nor to Crispin Aycliffe but only to each other in our grieving.

22

I conceived another child and almost immediately miscarried, as I had done earlier that year, but as Blaize continued to thrive, I decided that my bargain with God could now be considered null and void, and I returned to the contraceptive practices that even Mrs Stevens privately thought wicked.

But others were less fortunate than Blaize. Elinor's little girl recovered and the Reverend Mr Brand, dragged from the jaws of death by Hannah's iron will alone, it seemed, but my old Marth-Ellen, in her sixty-eighth year, died almost apologetically, as if she had left behind a pile of ironing to be done. And, following her coffin back to Patterswick, her native place, I could not forget that it was Hannah who had sent her to the Agbriggs, the source of the infection, and I was bitter and unfriendly towards her for days.

The Hobhouse child survived, although he was sickly afterwards, causing Emma-Jane so much anxiety that she, too, miscarried the girl she had set her heart upon and had such trouble conceiving again that she came to our versatile Mrs Stevens for remedies which I begged should not be confused with mine.

Lucy Oldroyd recovered her health, and Rosamund Boulton's married sister, and the housekeeper to the Corey-Mannings – those of us who were well fed and had the means, in that raw November, to warm ourselves. But in Simon Street, where the diet was oatmeal porridge and weak tea, there was a great deal of dying, a terrible blending of sorrow and anger and apathy, of those who wished to burn down the whole world for vengeance and those who were simply too tired to care, of those who went quietly, almost gladly, and those who wished to take Ira Agbrigg – or Joel Barforth – with them.

Ann Agbrigg recovered, too, slowly and quietly as she did everything, but perhaps the fever, after whetting its appetite in Simon Street, had become more virulent, greedier, when it reached her children, for they were among the last to be infected, all five of them at once, presenting a volume of nursing care so completely beyond Ann Agbrigg's strength that Hannah, who had never lacked courage and knew no one else would be likely to help the vampire of Simon Street, went to Low Cross and undertook it herself. And I cannot imagine how she found the words to inform Ann Agbrigg, not yet risen from her own sickbed, that although the eldest boy, Jonas, and a girl, Maria, seemed likely to recover, the other three, in the space of two days, had passed from sleep to death as imperceptibly as the pale guttering of a candle.

The Agbrigg funeral was the most terrible I had yet attended, Ann Agbrigg, dead herself in all but the movement of her limbs, being supported by the two children who were all that were left to her after she had suffered the painful, hopeful agonies of childbirth eleven times. And although they were whispering in Simon Street that this was divine retribution, I doubt if she was aware of it, for her eyes seemed quite blind, her vision very far removed from the things she could not bear to see, her mind turned inwards or backwards or simply refusing to function at all. She shed no tears, made no moan; she was simply there, obediently standing and sitting as she was bid, and it was her husband, fully conscious of his loss, who really needed the support of young Jonas's arm.

He had aged ten years, Ira Agbrigg, in that harrowing week, and had lost flesh I had not thought he possessed to lose, so that now the skin, stretched tight across his yellow-pale face, looked as if it could split, pierced by his cheekbones and the awkward, painful movement of his thin lips. Yet, for all that, he thanked me for my presence at the cemetery and for my graciousness in returning to his home to drink tea and eat a slice of seedcake I assumed Hannah had provided.

'Miss Barforth has been an angel of mercy,' he said. 'It overwhelms me to think of it – such a fine lady concerning herself with us. She sat up all night with Maria, telling me to take my rest since I had my business to attend to on the morrow. And both Jonas and Maria owe their lives to her. My wife could not – cannot – she is not recovered yet. Mrs Barforth, you have seen her – she won't speak to me, or can't, and doesn't seem to hear me – she couldn't believe, could she, what they are saying? – about punishment for those bairns who died in the shed? The doctor says she's numb with shock and it will wear away, but if it should not –? Everything I've ever done has been for her, Mrs Barforth, and if she can't see it, doesn't want it, what good has it all been?'

Yet we had other things, quite soon, to distract us from our grieving, for December brought us two events of great moment: the first elections ever to be held in Cullingford and the engagement of my cousin Hannah to the Reverend Mr Ashley, Anglican parson to my mother's ever-devoted, High Church, High Tory squire.

I had not expected her to choose Mr Ashley, particularly since her attention to the Reverend Mr Brand during his bout of fever had thrown them into such close contact that certain ladies in Ramsden Street thought their marriage not only imminent but essential; while Joel, sharing my astonishment, was seriously displeased, considering a hundred-pound-a-year parson no fit mate for his favourite sister. But my mother, growing younger, it seemed, with the passing of each tranquil

221

day and utterly content to sit gracefully on life's fence and observe, with gentle irony, those of us who still played life's games, saw little occasion for surprise and none at all for haste.

'Do not,' she told me, 'make plans as yet to give her bedchamber to Caroline, for we cannot expect a speedy conclusion. Mr Brand, I feel sure, would have insisted on marriage within a six-month, and indeed I am amazed that he has managed to stay unwed so long. But Julian Ashley, my dear, is the very man for betrothals and will not mind how long it lasts – forever, if that should be what Hannah has in mind. And, you know, dear, even a betrothal gives some status, at very little cost. She will have no more to do than come over here two or three times a week, which is what she does anyway, put some order into Mr Ashley's affairs, and then rush off to do the same for Mr Morgan Aycliffe, and Mr Ira Agbrigg, neither of whom, it seems, can rely on their wives. It may well be, dear, that someone – at Ramsden Street perhaps – has dropped a hint that her interest in those two gentlemen could be sentimental as well as charitable, and in that case, what better way of killing the rumours than to get herself engaged to a third. She will have to sacrifice Mr Brand, I suppose, since he can hardly allow the promised wife of another parson to meddle in his parish affairs. But Mr Brand may have made himself too pressing, you know. He may have seized what he thought were opportunities when she went to nurse him – for parsons are men, after all, like the others – and I think that would have frightened her away. At least she can rely on Mr Ashley, for he will not even recognize his opportunities, much less take advantage of them. Odd, isn't it, how things turn out. When they were both girls I thought Hannah plain and awkward and imagined she would become gaunt in later life, ungainly, while Elinor had the kind of loveliness one knew would never fade. Yet here they are, Hannah, in her thirties now – as Edwin would have been – striding through life like an Amazon queen, and Elinor, so much younger, looking quite extinguished. How sad, she was so vivacious, that little one, so full of herself, so appealing. Her loss of spirits pierces my heart. One must hope to see her bloom again if her husband goes to Westminster, for surely he will take her with him?'

And simply by putting the question, my mother acknowledged that she had her doubts, for Morgan Aycliffe's political ambitions had a certain bachelor, even monastic quality about them, and what troubled me most was that Elinor, who should have been on fire to go to London, seemed not to care.

'Oh, he tells me nothing,' she said. 'If I am to go I shall be informed of it, and if I am to stay he will arrange the housekeeping with Mrs Naylor and all the rest with this Mr Adair who has come to manage his business. And it is all the same to me.'

Yet, knowing Elinor, I could hardly believe her.

'You will not want to know us when you have your fine house in Belgravia,' said Emma-Jane Hobhouse, pregnant again and so huge that it surprised no one when she later produced her twins, increasing the total of her sons to eight. And when Elinor turned her head away, too listless to reply, I found myself making excuses on her behalf, explaining that since Mr Aycliffe's parliamentary duties could occupy him no more than half the year, there seemed little point in going to the expense of a second family home, when everyone knew a gentleman alone could manage perfectly well in two rooms with a manservant and an occasional cook.

But the election had first to be won and, through November and December, a new fever mounted, centred on the respective campaign headquarters, situated at the Bee Hive and the Old Swan.

We had won the right to return two members, the industrialists putting Mr Morgan Aycliffe and a somewhat faceless cousin of Mr Lucius Attwood the brewer, a Mr Thirlwell, into the field, our manorial lord, without any hope of winning – for the nuisance value only – offering us Captain Chase assisted by Crispin Aycliffe, whose expenses, it seemed, were being met by Colonel Corey, father of the radical editor Mark Corey and cousin of Sir Giles Flood. And instantly the town was divided between the manufacturers and those who wished to gain their favour, who were solidly behind the party which had given them the franchise, and the gentry and the workers, combining together to support the Duke of Wellington or, as the workers saw it, the party of Richard Oastler, which advocated factory reform.

Mr Aycliffe, immensely dignified in dark grey Cullingford – one hoped Barforth – cloth, made few promises in his speeches, pledging himself simply to support Lord Grey, the Prime Minister, to whom we owed our freedom, and his meetings would have been sober and probably very dull had he not been heckled constantly – not by Crispin, who knew that a father-son conflict would not win general favour, but by the highly excitable Mark Corey himself, who, surrounded by a group of like-minded friends and an outer ring of tough-grained, determined Short Timers, demanded to know Mr Aycliffe's views not only on the Ten Hour Bill, to which he was necessarily opposed, but on any other subject that seemed likely to embarrass him.

The question of allowing Methodists and members of other non-Anglican groups to attend our ancient universities was not touched upon, since Mr Aycliffe – representing a 'millocracy' that was largely non-Anglican – would be bound to support it. Nor was he challenged on the Corn Laws, since their repeal would be to the advantage of both Mr Aycliffe and the average workingman, and to Mark Corey himself for that matter. But, with his hands in his pockets and his tongue in his cheek, Mr Corey, in all the flamboyant splendour of his scarlet waistcoat and his spotted gamekeeper's neckcloth, made his appearance whenever Mr Aycliffe was due to speak, cutting through the candidate's well-chosen words – chosen, in many cases, by Hannah – with the very questions he did not wish to answer.

Would Mr Aycliffe support the abolition of stamp duty on newspapers so that the workingman could afford to read them? Clearly Mr Aycliffe would not, although, surrounded by a mighty gathering of those same workingmen, he clearly did not like to say so. Would the honourable gentleman support the abolition of the death penalty for offences other than murder or treason? What, in fact, were the candidate's views on crime and punishment? Would he put a stop to flogging in the Army? Would he work for the emancipation of the Jews – many of whom were settled in Leeds and might well bring their skills and culture to Cullingford – so that they could enjoy the same rights as a Methodist? Did he believe in the secret ballot, so that no man, squire, parson, or manufacturer could influence the vote of another? And when Mr Aycliffe had made his clipped, noncommittal replies, taking great care to offend no one, since there was no telling which way the wind would be blowing next year or even tomorrow, he would stand on the steps of the Piece Hall, or wherever he happened to be – looking so dry, so grey beside Colonel Corey's mischievous, quite beautiful bastard son – and submit himself to questions from the crowd, those toughs from Simon Street, and Gower Street and Saint Street who, although not entitled to vote themselves, felt perfectly free to pelt him with abuse and garbage and to smash the windows of the Old Swan, an occurrence so many times repeated in that election month of December that in the end the landlord made do with wooden shutters and the glazier's bill somehow found its way to us.

Crispin's main task, of course, was to introduce Captain Chase to the mass of workingmen not yet empowered to vote; no easy matter since the captain's cultured accent could neither be understood nor be taken seriously, giving rise to such gales of laughter that eventually he stopped speaking altogether, leaving Crispin free to put forward his own quite revolutionary ideals. Captain Chase imagined he was promising a measure of factory reform. Crispin Aycliffe made it clear that if every man in the mill yard, every man in the country, had his vote, then promises would be unnecessary. With the vote in his pocket the workingman could demand his freedom, not beg for it, and dismissing the ten-pound franchise as an insult, he declared that the only qualification should be a man's status not as a householder but as a Briton.

Yet this doctrine, while appealing to the Simon Street masses who could not hope to own property – and, I confess, to a married woman like myself, who could own nothing, either – did not find favour with everyone. There were men – overlookers' sons, maybe – who, by hard work and sacrifice and with perhaps not too many brothers and sisters to bar their way, had raised themselves a little above the rest, escaped from Simon Street to the new stone terraces of Sheepbridge Lane – men who, one day perhaps, by their own efforts, would be ten-pound householders and who saw no more reason to share their privileges than Sir Giles Flood would have done.

Nor was the vote itself considered such a prize if, after all, they would be obliged to use it to suit the masters rather than themselves. And although Crispin's explanation of the secret ballot was clearly of interest to some of them – shabby, keen-eyed lads with the wit to plan ahead, who wanted more out of life than a jar of ale every Friday and a quick tumble on a pile of waste with any mill girl who was willing – there were others who, accustomed to living from day to day, went about drunkenly and foolishly declaring that if they got the vote they'd be glad to sell it to the highest bidder.

The vote, then, in a town where only approximately a thousand out of a population of 43,000 were entitled to it, was seen at present as a middle-class issue; and although some of these workingmen were ready to demand it and fight for it, while others would not trouble to use it if it was theirs, they were all agreed that there was little one could do about it this December. Radicals like Crispin Aycliffe and Mark Corey might say what they pleased about the rights of man, but neither of those gentlemen had a half dozen children to feed through the winter, and although in general Cullingford men were quite ready to use their fists, when the time was ripe, and firearms if necessary and available, not all of them were.

But Crispin, surrounded by his escort of Short Timers – those rugged, dedicated men who knew exactly what they wanted and were willing to fight for it, sacrifice for it, today, right now, as long and as hard as they had to stood daily on the Piece Hall steps, with Captain Chase smiling benignly at a safe distance behind him, and spoke about the factory children. And this, at least, unlike the franchise, was immediate, urgent, possible; this concerned them all.

And when Crispin threw at them, 'Do we want a ten-hour day for women and children?' they thundered back, 'Aye, that we do.'

'And who is trying to cheat us of it?'

'The masters – Barforth, the robbing bastard.'

'Who who will help us?'

'Oastler – and Sadler – Richard Oastler, the Factory King.'

'And what do we need to help Richard Oastler? What do you need to help our Factory King?'

'The vote,' they screamed, suddenly seeing the sense to it, wanting it now, this minute, not next year or the year after when we could all be dead. And although Colonel Corey, who was paying Crispin's expenses and who had no difficulty at all in understanding the West Riding accent, must have seen this as a serious misuse of his money, Crispin was carried shoulder-high around Simon Street, while the Red Gin was the only hostelry in town to keep its windows intact.

Our own windows, needless to say, were less fortunate; a well-aimed brick landed squarely on my dinner table one evening, accompanied by a scattering of glass that entirely missed the industrialist, Joel Barforth, slightly injuring instead the sympathetic parson, Mr Ashley, Hannah's timid fiancé. But some days later, as Joel drove his phaeton into town at a spanking pace, stones were thrown at his horse's legs, causing the valuable animal to bolt, foaming and dangerous, down Sheepgate, where a street market was being held, overturning fruit stalls and vegetable stalls and a swill tub or two as it went; it was brought under control at last by a Joel Barforth who, forgetting his dignity, had reverted to the wildness of his younger days and, jumping down from his damaged vehicle, smashed his fist into the first grinning face he saw.

'Bloody thieving Barforth bastard' appeared once again on our factory walls, in letters a foot high, put there, one supposed, by persons well known to our dogs and our watchmen, since neither had complained, and although Joel was quick to recover his temper and continued to drive his phaeton to town, I took out my carriage, those last few days, only to deliver my sons to school and to fetch them home again.

Polling day dawned cold but dry and clear, greeted by the ringing of church bells and the clamour of the singing, parading crowds who, since they could not vote, intended at least to enjoy themselves. And when the Old Swan and the Bee Hive had both been pelted with stones and filth by a grubby, cheeky gang of boys whose only political conviction was to do as much damage as they could, and all the bunting, blue and orange alike, had been torn down and made away with, the candidates themselves became fair game.

A bombardment of eggs greeted Mr Morgan Aycliffe at his first appearance of the day, considerably injuring his self-esteem, although the same lads, having raided somebody's hen run, dashed immediately across town to throw the remainder at Crispin and Captain Chase; while the third candidate, the colourless Mr Thirlwell, was for a long while, prevented from setting out at all by a gang of Simon Street toughs who had invaded his lawn.

But the result was never in doubt, and anyone with the most rudimentary knowledge of arithmetic could have worked it out.

Mr Aycliffe and Mr Thirlwell between them would share the votes of the manufacturing interest – the mill-masters themselves, their managers, the tradesmen and better-class shopkeepers who served their needs; while only the Coreys and the Corey-Mannings and a few shopkeepers situated in the Simon Street area, who wished to avoid trouble, would vote gentry. Dr Overdale, who attended gentry and manufacturers alike, would, of course, be in something of a dilemma, while the town's innkeepers were, in some cases, unreliable, having made promises, with professional geniality, in both directions. But, on the whole, there were no surprises, other than Mr Boulton, Rosamund's father, who, against his own best interests, voted for Captain Chase, in protest perhaps at the party of the manufacturers, one of whom had seduced his daughter, while one or two others, torn between their private conviction and pressures from Simon Street or Lawcroft or Blenheim Lane, found it wiser to fall ill or be called out of town and not vote at all.

And, waiting at home as a woman should, far more concerned for my old dog – Edwin's yellow crossbred bitch – who had died early that day, than for the House of Commons and all who sat therein, I was not surprised – not even very interested – to learn that Morgan Aycliffe had topped the poll, Mr Thirlwell following discreetly behind, and Captain Chase, for all Crispin's efforts, barely visible in the distance.

Joel sent me a message to join him at the Aycliffes', with a case of champagne – and Hannah – and we dined there, very late, very lavishly, but with little real enjoyment, for I was still grieving for my dog, and Mr Aycliffe himself was plainly weary, suffering perhaps from a depression of the nerves that often comes when some great object has been achieved.

'What a triumph,' Hannah told him on arrival. 'And so richly deserved.'

And for Hannah Mr Aycliffe's thin lips did sketch a smile. But to the rest of us he was merely polite, having invited us only because the circumstances required it; because victories must be celebrated with due pomp; because, after all, he was a 'public man' now and knew his responsibilities. Yet, for all his attentions and courtesies, it was all done so joylessly, the performance of an arduous duty rather than a pleasure, that it would have been better had it not been done at all.

'Mrs Barforth, I believe this pâté is to your liking, do take a little more.' But, as always, I was so deeply aware of the staggering value of his china that the scrape of my knife on the exquisite Wedgwood plate seemed sacrilegious and I had no appetite.

'I think we may consider the day fairly won,' he told us, leaning back in his carved oak chair, his thin, dry fingers caressing the stem of his glass in a way I found unpleasant, perhaps because I knew how rarely these days he caressed his wife. 'Yes, a triumph for good sense. A victory. And, for me, a new beginning.'

'You will excuse us, I am sure,' Elinor said abruptly, having no mind, it seemed, to sit placidly by while he gloated over a beginning in which she did not play a part. 'You may take as long as you like over your port.'

And while Hannah slipped upstairs to count the children and interrogate their nurse, I went with Elinor to her too elegant drawing room to take coffee, appalled, as I always was, by the fragility of the cup.

'Is Faith quite recovered from the fever?' I asked, merely to start a conversation, and she answered listlessly, as she had been doing all day, half listening, uncaring.

'Yes, I believe so.'

'And you? You seem worn out.'

'Yes, so I am. Quite worn out.'

'From what?'

'Oh – from doing – doing nothing, I suppose. And don't you know that it is the hardest thing of all – doing nothing, all day, all night – passing the time. I find it a weary business, at any rate.'

And then, after a short but heavy silence, an uncomfortable thing, she said, 'I am not to go with him to London, you know. It is quite definite.'

'Oh – I'm sorry, Elinor.'

'Yes. I daresay. Mrs Naylor is to look after me and the glass and the china. Nurse is to look after the children. Mr Adair is to look after the business and see to the household bills – to tell me how much I may spend and what I may spend it on.'

And, before I could think of anything which might console her, she hissed suddenly, quite viciously, 'I am to have no money, Verity; no allowance. I am to apply to Mrs Naylor for pin money, who will then apply to Mr Adair, since it is not proper for me to approach him direct. I am to sit here all day and listen to the clock ticking my life away. I am fit

227

for nothing else, you see – not even for breeding. He is leaving me, Verity, don't you see that? Oh, very politely and correctly, as he does everything, and in such a way that no one else will even notice. And, of course, I shall have everything he thinks I require – and I shall certainly have the children, since he can't wish to bother with them himself. But I am to be abandoned, Verity, just the same – cast off. Fat Emma-Jane can keep her husband, and mousy little Lucy Oldroyd, and you – but not me. And I was the pretty one, wasn't I? The prettiest of you all? Isn't that so, Verity – can you deny it?'

'No – you were the pretty one, Elinor. You still are.'

'I hate him – hate him. Do you know that?' she whispered, shuddering with the violence of her emotion, and, jumping to her feet, she picked up a tiny porcelain shepherdess, not unlike herself, and dashed it wildly against the fender. And then, as the delicately painted face and the frilly, lace-edge porcelain body disintegrated, I saw my vivacious, impossible, lovable cousin Elinor crumble with it.

'Oh dear God,' she said. 'Dear God – dear God –' And watching her trembling with fright, cowering away from the consequences of her action – knowing she would not be pardoned – I remembered her as she had been on the night, seven years ago, when she first came here to dine, dancing and swishing her skirts around this same room, not caring a fig for Mr Aycliffe and his porcelain, while Hannah and I had trembled. And I was saddened beyond belief.

I heard their feet crossing the hall – her husband's and mine – and, swiftly gathering up the pieces, I went hurrying to meet them.

'Oh, Mr Aycliffe, I do not know how you will ever forgive me, for I have done a dreadful thing –'

'Surely not, Mrs Barforth.'

'Oh, I do fear so.'

And I held out to him the evidence of Elinor's crime.

'It is not usual for me to be so clumsy, but I caught it with my skirt as I was passing … Oh dear, naturally I will replace it –'

'Such generosity,' he said, his voice empty of all expression, 'is quite beyond you, ma'am. It cannot be replaced. Please think no more about it.'

And although that was all he said, I knew that I had been accused of a heinous offence, judged and condemned, and that if he lived to be a hundred he would never find it in his heart to forgive me.

23

There was no doubt that Joel was getting richer, a fact which could not hope to find favour with everyone, and when his purchase of Tarn Edge became common knowledge and speculation arose regarding his plans for the splendid ten-acre slope of Tarn Rise, Emma-Jane Hobhouse chose to settle the matter by calling to enquire.

'I hear you're building a new house, Verity?'

228

'Yes – so it seems.'

'And what about this one? Is it to be sold?'

'I really couldn't tell you.'

'No? Well, it reached my ears that Joel was thinking of making it over to Hannah as a wedding gift, which I can only put down to foolish gossip since everybody knows a house of this size to be quite beyond Mr Ashley's means. No, no, I said, when I heard it, if Hannah Barforth chooses to marry a parson, then it follows that she wants to live in a parsonage – doesn't it stand to reason?'

But Hannah, as my mother had foreseen, was in no hurry to marry at all and replied to Joel's cutting enquiries as to time and place, and her exact plans for Mr Ashley's hundred pounds a year, with a simple 'When I'm ready, brother.'

Mr Brand had gone out of her life now in a considerable huff, but Mr Morgan Aycliffe, following his departure for London, communicated with her far more frequently than with his wife, and to compensate her for the loss of Ramsden Street she now had the Agbriggs, parents and children, whose affairs required a great deal of attention.

Ann Agbrigg had not recovered her health. She was simply there, a presence in a chair by the window, giving no trouble, eating what was set before her, managing, with some help from her daughter, to keep herself clean and tidy, but no more than that, a shadow who could neither appreciate her husband's success nor understand the sorrow she caused him.

'Poor man,' Hannah said, fairly often, clearly puzzled by his attitude. 'It is quite pathetic to see them together. People think of Mr Agbrigg as such a hard man and yet, before his wife, he reminds me of nothing so much as a hopeful dog with a bone. And when he lays it at her feet and she doesn't even notice I do believe he hides in a corner and cries his eyes out. Poor little woman. I see no possibility of a change, but they are so glad of my visits that I can hardly fail them, and left to themselves they have no idea how to carry on. They are doing their parlour in a lighter shade – did I tell you? My suggestion, of course, since they think of nothing for themselves, and I always did find those dark browns and greens altogether depressing and often wondered what my mother was about to select them in the first place. And Maria is to go to Mrs Turnbull for lessons. Mr Agbrigg had placed her with a most unsuitable woman, some person advertising herself as a teacher of deportment and needlework and French and who had no samples of her own work to show me when I called, and failed to pronounce one word of a foreign language in my hearing. You see how gullible he is? Mr Agbrigg had taken her for a lady and dared not question her word. Well, I questioned it, and now Maria is with Mrs Turnbull, an old acquaintance of mine, who keeps an excellent establishment. Not a brilliant child, of course, Maria; a little mouse, which is what one would expect. The boy, Jonas, however, is really very quick and doing very well at the grammar school. I had a word with Mr Blamires, his headmaster, the other day, and he is really quite impressed with young Jonas – which is rather more than he could say for Blaize, who seems to have divided his time there so far between sulking and fighting.'

'He has only been there a little while, Hannah.'

'Yes, and I imagine Mr Blamires is well aware of it, although in view of Joel's position in the town, and his generosity, he would not say so. I am very fond of Blaize, as you must know, but he can be very high-handed at times, and I almost wonder if you have been too tender-hearted, and my brother too busy, to check him as you should. And Nicholas, I believe, is just the same. I wondered, too, Verity, now that the boys are at school, should you not give some thought to Caroline? Mrs Paget is all very well when it comes to washing and dressing and doing up her ringlets, but in matters of education – and discipline – I find her a trifle lax. Caroline should now be embarking on some regular course of study, and my friend Mrs Turnbull could help you there. She is constantly receiving applications from suitably skilled ladies, many of whom are willing to enter private employment, and Elinor has taken on a Miss Mayberry, with whom we are all well satisfied. Do think it over, Verity. Caroline may have a great position waiting for her in the future, and you would not forgive yourself if you failed to prepare her for it. Have a look at Miss Mayberry when you are next at Elinor's and hear what Elinor has to say for her.'

But Elinor, when applied to, had little interest in governesses or anything else.

'Miss Mayberry? Oh, she's well enough. She lives upstairs with the children and brings them down, now and then, at teatime to wish me a good afternoon in French. And when I decide to take them for a drive she comes, too, because Mrs Naylor wouldn't trust me alone, I suppose – and occasionally she lets Prudence in here just before dinner and makes the poor child pick out a tune on the piano. It's supposed to be a treat, although I don't quite know who is being treated since it turns the child chalk-white and makes her sick afterwards, and I confess I don't enjoy it. But, naturally, they know best – Miss Mayberry and Nurse and Hannah –'

'If you think it makes Prudence ill, why don't you forbid it?'

'Oh, my dear,' she said, making a languid, rueful gesture. 'Do you know, one evening I quite made up my mind to do just that – I almost did it. But then – well – the fuss and the ill temper and Hannah being sent for next morning to tell me I'm failing in my duty – and convincing me, as she usually does. And then having to apologize to Miss Mayberry and having her running around me for a week or two asking my permission for every little thing, because I'm sure she doesn't want to lose her place. No, no, in the end it seemed best just to look away and think about something else, and then applaud prettily and say, "Well done, Prudence. Well done, Miss Mayberry." Much better – and, of course, there is one consolation, because Mrs Naylor cannot bear to see the children in the drawing room – she hovers, my dear, in absolute agony, even now when there's nothing much left for them to break. What she'd really like is to put the whole room under dust covers, but since my husband did leave the furniture I assume he meant me to sit on it – and sometimes I think I actually prefer the room this way.'

Although I had been deeply shocked at first to see the drawing room denuded of its treasures, Mr Aycliffe having taken his favourite pieces to London with him and placed the rest in the safe custody of the attic, I had to admit that I was more comfortable now, more inclined to linger. The polished, inlaid tables carried nothing more awe-inspiring these days than dried flowers under glass, a china milkmaid and ploughman, an apple women, rosy, rustic children and an assortment of dogs and lambs and bright yellow chicks, the purchases of Morgan Aycliffe's earlier years, long since outgrown but which Elinor, discovering them packed away in an old tea chest, had arranged to suit her own uncritical eye. And, on her good days, when Emma-Jane Hobhouse came to tea and compared her own, rapidly expanding waist with Elinor's girlish nineteen inches, or Daniel Adair, her husband's manager, remembering her husband's age and how attractive she would be as a widow, almost turned himself inside out to impress her, then Elinor was at ease in her drawing room – mistress, at last, of her surroundings.

But not all her days were good and far too many afternoons I would find her prostrate on her couch, not knowing what ailed her except that she was weary – weary – Weary to death and without care as to when it came.

'The trouble is,' Hannah said, 'that she will not stir herself. She could be busy now with her husband's affairs. Someone must go about the constituency and assess its mood so that he may be informed as to what people are saying and thinking. And since Elinor cannot, or will not, then I feel obliged to undertake the task myself. Oh yes, I know it is not my place and may give rise to gossip, but if Mr Aycliffe should ever lose his seat for lack of information which Elinor could have supplied, it would not go well with her. And while I do not wish to see her in distress, I do feel that a man in public life should be able to rely on the support of his close relations, and that Mr Aycliffe has been most unfortunate in that respect.'

Unfortunate indeed, but Elinor, surviving every one of Hannah's lectures, continued to fluctuate between a lethargy so stifling that she could barely trouble to raise her hands and periods of intense activity when she would have herself driven furiously around town, inviting everyone she met to tea, and spending her husband's money as fast as his manager, Mr Adair, would allow.

'I do not need another evening gown,' she would say to Rosamund Boulton, 'but since I am here, I may as well have a look – and yes, you may make me up that sky-blue satin, and the black one, Rosamund dear, while you are about it, for it will make a perfect foil to my husband's first wife's pearls. No, no, there is no need to take my measurements. My waist is still nineteen inches, which Emma-Jane considers scandalous at my age, for I am almost twenty-five and should rightly look like an old crow by now. Well, one day I shall turn thirty, I suppose – like you, Rosamund – but in the meantime have you nothing to age me? For when

I go to London someone may mistake me for my husband's daughter, and we cannot risk that. But never mind, for we can always send my sister Hannah in my place.'

But such outbursts were often followed by a sick melancholy that I could not dismiss, like Hannah, as mere childishness.

'Leave her to wallow,' Hannah advised, 'which is what I mean to do, for if I stay I shall box her ears.'

But solitary brooding, in my view, was not the medicine she required, and one summer night she kept me talking very late in Blenheim Lane, holding my hand and chatting, not of her present sorrows, but of our shared childhood, so that travelling home in the warm dark I was heavy and sentimental with a past that had always contained Joel.

Yet where was Joel tonight? A mile away, perhaps, or two, but no closer to me than Morgan Aycliffe to Elinor. And was my life, as a woman, less empty than hers? Admittedly, Joel had not physically abandoned me. He was here, in my daily life, in my bed more often than not, and it did not wound me if, when he took me in his arms, he thought of the aristocratic Estella Chase or some other chance-met adventuress, since I invariably thought of Crispin. But, for all my good sense and my desire for peace, for all his talk of our shared interests, could it really suffice? And, knowing that it could not, I prayed suddenly, quite fervently, that I could be like Emma-Jane Hobhouse, engrossed with her own fertility and the tittle-tattle of everyday life, a woman at peace in this man-made world.

Was I, in fact, the freak of nature, Emma-Jane the norm? And if she were the breed of woman society required, should I not try to resemble her, to cover my body and my mind in layers of her complaisant, contented fat so that I too could doze in the afternoons with my mouth open, and argue for weeks about what constituted a perfectly baked apple tart? Or should I admit that, in a world where Emma-Jane personified success, I was doomed to failure and, having come to terms with that, should I withdraw, like my mother, and watch that unbalanced world pass by? Pondering these questions, I was not immediately aware of the tumult in the streets.

Polling day now was six months past, but Cullingford, having enjoyed its first taste of political upheaval, was not unwilling for more, especially since the December electorate had not favoured the cause of the factory children. Crispin Aycliffe's policies had been soundly defeated in Cullingford; a Mr George Banks, a convinced Ten Hours man, had fared no better in Bradford. Richard Oastler, the Factory King himself, had been rejected by Huddersfield, while Mr Michael Sadler had failed to secure re-election at Leeds, leaving the Ten Hours Movement without a voice at Westminster. And that – or so Bradley Hobhouse and some others declared – was the end of that; or should have been, until battling Parson Bull of Bierley made the journey to London and persuaded the intense, deeply religious Lord Ashley to take up the Ten Hours cause. Lord Ashley had never seen a factory child or been aware, at any conscious level, that such abuse existed, but the Reverend George

Stringer Bull had found no difficulty in persuading him to reintroduce Sadler's Bill to the House.

'Damnable interference,' Bradley Hobhouse had muttered. 'And what does this Lord Ashley know about my weaving sheds? Do I go and tell him when to plant his corn, or whatever he does on his estates? Ten hours, indeed. It takes me ten hours to cover my overheads, and I need five more, at least, after that, to show a profit. And if I lose, they all lose.'

But Joel merely shrugged and replied, 'We'll not lose. We've got honourable members and our own, now, haven't we, at Westminster, and what did we elect them for but this? So let Morgan Aycliffe and the rest of them earn their keep or when they pass the begging bowl round again they'll get nothing from me.'

And so it was, for although the Ten Hours bill was given a first reading, the newly elected industrial members knew what was expected of them and, drawing solidly together, had little difficulty in convincing the House that Sadler's committee, however moving and horrendous, had been too one-sided to justify legislation. Evidence had been heard from mill hands and midwives, parsons and idealistic land agents, from victims and their sympathizers, but the manufacturers themselves had not been allowed to state their case. And once again it was thought better to delay, to gather more facts, to appoint a Royal Commission this time instead of a mere Select Committee like Sadler's, which, instead of shipping cartloads of wrecked humanity to London, would come North, to interview masters and men in their native surroundings and see for itself.

These commissioners, as it turned out, were gentlemen of the very highest integrity, but in that summer of 1833, to the mass of workpeople, who had learned to expect very little from gentlemen – honourable or no – they seemed no more than the tools of a government willing to play the masters' game. And when Richard Oastler, still smarting from his defeat at Huddersfield, thundered out his warning that the commissioners were coming to cheat the people, not aid them, the simmering brew of discontent came once more to the boil.

For months past, ever since it was known that the commissioners would be coming, the air had somehow tightened, and I had grown so conscious of eyes peering at me suddenly from beneath a shawl, shooting me quick glances from the shading angle of a cloth cap, watching, speculating, that for the first time I began to share Emma-Jane's fears of intruders in the night, of shadows that became strangling hands, raping hands, and I dreamed again, often, of that gaping hole in my father's chest and of my brother's dead face.

The Hobhouse mill, I knew, was watched night and day by silent relays of Ten Hours men, determined that Bradley should make no attempt to clean up his sheds or install decent privies before the commissioners came; and Tarn Edge, where building was taking place, had been singled out, not openly like Nethercoats, since Joel was a harder, trickier man than Bradley, yet so thoroughly that I could no

233

longer visit it without that nightmare sensation of eyes in my back, of someone pale and twisted with little to hope for and little to lose watching me just beyond the edge of my sight.

And when the commissioners arrived they were met by bitter crowds who harassed and hustled them, and by Oastler's partisans, the hard-faced Ten Hours men, who followed them from town to town on horseback, a grim escort they found impossible to shake away. There were mass meetings and processions. In Bradford so many threats were made against them that Mr John Wood had felt obliged to refuse them entry to his mill since he could not guarantee their safety. And, returning from Elinor's that summer night, brooding on my personal demons, I had forgotten that the enemy, as they were called, had reached Cullingford and that Joel, even now, was in consultation with them – over dinner, one supposed – at the Old Swan.

Naturally, in this atmosphere of suspicion and hostility, it had been impossible to entertain them at home, to the chagrin of Mrs Stevens, who, like Joel, had great faith in the effects of well-seasoned sauces, well-chosen wines and cigars; and so, in his superbly cut evening clothes, a heavy gold ring on either hand, a pearl in his necktie, a gold-topped ebony cane, and a black silk hat, Joel had gone down to the Old Swan to assure the honourable gentlemen that, unlike Mr Wood, he was able to offer them his protection in Cullingford, no matter where they wished to go. And I cannot imagine they doubted him.

But now, abruptly, I was aware not only of disturbance around me, to which I was no stranger, but of wood smoke pricking my eyelids, reminding me, in my reverie, of bonfires, Guy Fawkes and November, until, with a start, I woke up to an airless, over-warm July.

'What is it, Thomas?' I called out.

Busy with the restless horses, who were no fonder of wood smoke than I, my coachman, who had served my grandfather and still thought of me as a chit of a girl to whom not much respect was due, merely grunted, as if I should have seen for myself. 'Trouble. And there'll be more unless I turn these brutes around.'

But Blenheim Lane was not only very long but very narrow, the trees in full summer leaf joining hands in places overhead, and having passed the Fleece, whose yard would have given us a turning space, there was nothing to do, in the growing crowd, but continue forward.

I heard Thomas curse as the horses – which he had always thought too high-bred and fancy for a carriage, too much of Joel Barforth and not enough of Samson – became fractious at the scent of fire; and, as I leaned out again, he shouted, as my grandfather would have done, 'Get in with you, lass. You don't want them to recognize your face tonight.' And, whipping, cursing, furious at being saddled with the responsibility of his master's wife when he didn't much care for the master and it was my own fault anyway for gadding about at night instead of staying at home as a decent woman should, he set off again as best he could.

I had no hat, no cloak, just a knot of ribbon in my hair and a light summer shawl, a gauzy complement to a dress which seemed suddenly too bright, a clean fresh lemon that could not hide in a corner, which could identify me: 'That's Joel Barforth's wife. Stop the bitch.' And because I knew it could happen – that they could drag me about the streets by the hair, abuse and defile me – because my father's life had bled away through that hole in his chest and they had impaled my brother on a kitchen knife six inches long, I was afraid.

Kirkgate and Millergate, as we lumbered down their steep, cobbled sides, were a mess of abandoned carriages and broken shop fronts, littered with stray dogs and cats and stray children gorging themselves on the scattered pickings of Mr Wilmot's grocery, Miss Timmins's bakery, the Fearnley sisters' tea and coffee shop, places I knew and could barely recognize now in the tumultuous dark. And, at the bottom of Millergate, where it joined Market Square, we were forced to halt.

They had built a bonfire in the Old Swan yard, a huge, smoking pile beneath the windows of the supper room where the commissioners, and Joel, had gone to dine. As a great tongue of flame leaped suddenly into the air, I heard them shouting Joel's name and saw him appear at the window, open it, and with the cool arrogance that made him so detested and so feared, lean against the window frame with the nonchalance of a spectator at a show.

I saw the firelight pick out the gold buttons on his waistcoat, the flash of those white teeth against his dark face as he made some remark to the men in the besieged room with him; I saw faces looming out of the crowd, leering, grinning, hating, unreasoning, beyond any appeal I could make to them, functioning now not as men and women who could know pity and good sense – although they would know it again tomorrow when it could be too late for us all – but as part of a crowd that kill and maim with no more responsibility than a raindrop must feel for the devastation of a storm. In the morning it would not be their fault. In the morning someone else would have thrown the stone, wielded the knife, tossed that burning piece of wood through the Swan door. In the morning some of them would not even remember what it had all been about in the first place, while others, remembering, would be sorry or ashamed; and others still, feeling that not enough had been achieved, would be ready to start again. But now, with the calm that extreme fear sometimes brings, I recognized that I was trapped and that, since I could not rely on Thomas and could not reach Joel, I would have to save myself. And as the crowd parted to let a solid wedge of Ten Hours men come through, I clasped my hands and held my breath, like a child who, by closing his eyes, hopes he will not be seen.

I did not at first recognize what they were carrying on their shoulders, there in the tossing, uncertain torchlight, and when I did the shock alone carried me to the far edge of panic. And although I told myself that the thing they were holding aloft was not Joel – for he was still there at the window – it was so sickeningly real, the cut of the coat, the elaborate shirt frill, the width and height of him, that part of my mind refused to believe it was just a doll. And as they paraded their effigy once, then twice around the inn yard – giving Joel time to recognize himself, should he need it – and then heaved it savagely into the fire, my mind, for one brief, harrowing moment, caught the odour of flesh burning, the agony of a man screaming soundlessly through the flame. And, drenched as I was by that torrent of hate, it seemed to make no difference that Joel's living face was still at the window, looking down.

I tried to look away and could not; I tried to close my eyes and could not do that either, and so, like everyone else, I watched the doll burn, saw the legs disintegrate, the chest open to disgorge heaven knew what garbage as the expensive coat shredded away and the shirt frill, the face, the tall silk hat were devoured, one by one. And because the hate was there, because they truly desired him to suffer this torment, it was real again and terrible. And when it was over, when the doll lay in ashes and symbolic murder had been done, all eyes were raised to that long upper window, where Joel was still leaning, glass in hand, against the sill.

'Bloody thieving Barforth bastard,' they shrieked at him.

And, looking down, smiling – that white flash of perfect teeth against his amber skin – he raised his glass to them in cool salutation, drank, bowed, and went inside.

And most strangely, in the great howling and screaming that went up around me, the brandishing of torches and shaking of fists, I found that I was smiling too.

But there still remained the matter of my own safety, and in that sea of faces swamping the square, spilling out into the adjoining streets as water does in confined spaces, I could see no help, no hope at all. I doubted if any of these men would offer violence, in the normal way of things, to another man's woman – although they would all indulge occasionally in a rough and tumble with their own – but this was not a night for normality, for remembering how ashamed one would feel afterwards, and when the fire began to burn low and Joel, after all, had not burned with it, I would be a natural target for their frustrations. No one, I thought, had recognized the carriage as yet, so intent were they on the Old Swan and the men inside it – and, indeed, there were many vehicles in the square, cut off as I was from escape – but eventually, quite soon, although some would drift away back to their homes or to the ale-houses, the bitter ones, the hurt ones, the ones perhaps who had nowhere else to go, would stay and, seeing the carriages as a symbol of life's injustice, would vent their hate against them. And I had no mind to sit in a fragile box on wheels while they pelted me with stones and filth and the maddened horses, plunging out of control, jolted me to destruction.

'You'd best get down, missus,' old Thomas grunted, appearing suddenly, his head close to mine. And when I could do no more than stare at him, appalled by the very idea I had had in mind, he said, quite furiously, 'Come on, lass. They don't know your face so well, but they know mine and they'll remember in a minute or two whose horses I drive. And if you're sitting behind me they'll soon work out who you are and I can't be responsible for what they'll do to you. These aren't mules, you know, these fancy high-steppers, and if they lose their heads there's more than you to get hurt.'

236

And when I went on staring, he picked up the carriage rug and threw it at me.

'Put this round you, lass, and get down – get down. Get into the Swan if you can, and if you can't then get to the back of the crowd and make for the top of Millergate. And if you don't see me there, knock on a door – there's decent houses at the top end of Millergate – and get somebody to take you in, or take you home, or send a message. And look sharp about it.'

No one, for a very long time, had told me to 'look sharp,' certainly not a coachman whose sole concern should have been my safety. But, realizing he did not mean to abandon Joel's mettlesome horses here, where they could trample a dozen other women underfoot – women far closer to him in background and temperament than I – I nodded, swallowed hard, wrapped the rug awkwardly around me, and got down.

Millergate, I thought, Millergate, and shockingly, having lived here all my life, I had no idea where Millergate was, so little notion of which way to turn that I simply moved blindly away from the carriage, thinking that anywhere, surely, was better than here. No one spoke to me or tried to stop me, no one deliberately blocked my way – for, after all, without my carriage and my fringed parasol, my deep-brimmed satin bonnet, who was I anyway? But I had never been in a crowd before, had never experienced the accidental jostlings and pushings of strangers, had never inhaled the stale breath and sweat of people who were unknown to me, and I found it terrifying.

Millergate, I thought again. Please, Millergate, for indeed there were houses there with little gardens and decent front doors, a maid to give me tea and a man to take a message home. But Millergate swam away from me, came back a moment, and then was not Millergate at all but some narrower place, unlit, malodorous. And when I turned back there were too many people behind me, too many eyes, so that, keeping my head down, I blundered again and was truly lost.

Yet to be lost here, in my native town, was ridiculous and, pressing close to the wall, I paused a moment, forcing myself to reflect. These could only be the alleyways that cut between Millergate and Kirkgate, glimpsed a thousand times as I drove by, and if they were foul and damp, dens of vice and dens of disease, at least they were short. I had only to keep on walking in the same direction and eventually a paved, gaslit thoroughfare – Millergate or Kirkgate, I no longer cared which – would open out before me. I had only to keep on walking – no more; I must, in fact, keep on walking, and, hurrying forward, my useless satin slippers paddling through murky water, I felt my identity shred away from me and knew real terror. I was just a woman alone in the streets at night, fair game for any man, and the fear of being recognized as Joel Barforth's wife no longer seemed important. I was appalled now merely by my own helplessness, by being a woman who could be forced into a corner, abused by unwashed hands and coarse mouths, held down by the scruff of the neck as dogs hold bitches. And with the spectre of so much degradation reaching out to touch me through the hot dark, I rushed off sightlessly again, my breath catching painfully in my chest, meeting nothing but blank walls, a pathetic mouse – scurrying through tunnels that engulfed me, until at last a hand caught my wrist and an unknown voice said, 'Mrs Barforth.'

'No. No I'm not. Let me go.'

'Wherever to, God love you, for you haven't an idea in your head as to your direction. I saw you get down from your carriage and you've been going round in circles ever since.'

Oddly enough, the fact that the stranger was a woman did nothing to console me.

'Just let me go, that's all, whoever you are – out of my way. I don't know you.'

'No. But I know you, sweetheart,' she said, tightening her grip on my wrist. 'You're high-and-mighty Barforth's wife, all right, not a doubt about it. Lost your carriage, did you? No, no, don't try to take a swing at me, Miss Verity, because you're not up to it. I'd have you down in the muck before you knew what had hit you.'

And then, dragging me close against her, her face almost touching mine, she muttered, 'Don't think I want to do this, because I don't. I don't care what happens to you – however bad it is, you'd deserve it – and you'll get it, my lass, soon enough, if you stay here. The lads are still mostly down at the fire, but they'll be back ere long and they'd gobble you up alive, little lady, make no mistake about it. So I've got to take you to Crispin, darling, haven't I, because if I leave you here and he finds out about it, he'll lose his good opinion of me. And I wouldn't want that to happen. So come on, love, come to Crispin. It's what you want, I suppose, same as he does – and if you're even half a Barforth you won't be slow to take your opportunities.'

And fascinated, overpowered, with no more will to resist than Ann Agbrigg, I followed her.

24

I had never seen the Red Gin at close quarters before; I knew of it simply as the haunt of brawlers and malcontents; of godless, rootless men and immoral women – of whores. Now, with my hand firmly in the grip of one of these – a bareheaded, brazen creature swinging her hips, tossing her long black hair – I found myself walking down a passage as narrow and unpleasant as a greasy ribbon and then mounting a rickety, littered back stair to a room I most certainly should not have entered.

'Wait here,' she said. 'I'll fetch him.'

Although I heard her turn the key in the lock and had no guarantee that she had really gone for Crispin, I sat down almost like a well-behaved child at school, with no thought of escape.

There was a lamp burning on a scarred wooden table, bare floorboards, bare walls, a narrow iron bedstead, a kitchen chair, books in tidy piles, writing materials: the bare essentials of existence. A monk's cell, I thought; obsessively neat – where Morgan Aycliffe, not Crispin, could have taken refuge to scourge his soul. And, from the inn below it, the noise of unkempt revelry seeping through the floor, the tight-packed anthill of the street across the way, of the room next door, the intimate functioning of strangers' bodies constantly within range of eye and ear and nostril, no longer separated from me by the thickness of stone walls, an acre of rose garden, a carriage drive. And although it was troublesome, it was in some ways a protection.

He was a long time in coming but when the door finally opened I could see he had been running.

Unprepared for the emotion in him and the emotion in me leaping forward to meet it, I said, quite harshly, the first words that entered my head. 'Who was that woman?'

And because he had not expected me to say that, it steadied him, gave us both a breathing space.

'She is Dinah McCluskey, the landlady here. She told me what happened, and, Verity, your coachman should be whipped. He should never have left you to make your way alone.'

'Oh, he was thinking of the horses, I expect, for they would cost a great deal of money to replace, whereas women come cheap enough. Only think, if the horses had been damaged, Joel would have been obliged to send to Tattersalls in London and pay out a thousand guineas or more. And what could I cost? Just a rather splendid headstone, and he wouldn't even have to go out of Cullingford to replace me. So Thomas knew what he was about.'

'Verity,' he said, 'are you – quite well?'

'No. I think I am probably hysterical but I expect I shall be able to contain it. And if I did have a fit, would it matter – here? Would anyone trouble to enquire?'

'I am very sure they would not. In fact, you could scream your head off and no one would dream of interfering. It would simply be assumed I was beating you – which all women deserve from time to time and some of them enjoy – and if you opened the window and shrieked, "Murder," they would only suppose you deserved that too.'

'I am in your power, then.'

'No,' he said, his voice losing its forced lightness, his face tightening. 'You are not in my power. You know that very well. I think you must stay here awhile, for there is still an ugly-tempered crowd in the streets, and then I will arrange for you to be taken home. I have nothing to offer you but brandy, I am afraid, and even Dinah may· have difficulty in finding tea at this hour.'

'Brandy, then. It won't harm me. It kept my grandfather alive during his last years – or so he said – and he was never wrong.'

The glass he gave me was of fine-cut crystal, incongruous in those meagre surroundings, and the brandy may well have been superb, although, as I crossed the room and stood by the window looking down at the putrid alleyway, it burned, then numbed my tongue. And I knew that whatever happened between us would be of my choosing; he would

239

remain cool and polite, convincing me, perhaps, of his indifference, if the woman, Dinah McCluskey, had not said to me, 'Come to Crispin. It's what you want, I suppose, same as he does.'

'Were you in the square?' he said quietly. 'Did you see the burning?'

'Yes. And I saw Joel salute the crowd afterwards. I don't know what I should have felt about that, but actually I was proud of him.'

'I'm sorry.'

'You shouldn't be. I've told you before – he's my cousin. I understand him. My father would have been shocked and upset, and my brother would have blustered and tried to break a few heads – and got himself killed all over again. But my grandfather would have done exactly as Joel did, and whether you liked my grandfather or not – and I didn't like him at all – you had to admit that he was magnificent. I don't always like Joel too much either, but that has nothing to do with being proud of him, of giving him credit for courage and audacity – or for wishing he was on your side. Because he'd do a lot more for your cause than Mark Corey – if he believed in it, or if he could see a profit in it.'

He smiled, ruefully, unhappily, his face very pale in that uncertain lamplight; thinner, I thought, the fine, fair skin creasing at his eye corners, the eyes themselves a paler blue, as if they had been washed by fatigue. And, knowing beyond question that I loved him, I wondered why I had made my voice so hard, why it seemed so essential to explain that I had an odd, unlikely respect for Joel, too.

'Barforth pride,' he said, trying to make his voice light again. 'Is there no end to it? I have never seen you so fierce.'

'I daresay, and you may well see me fiercer, for I want to know how that woman was aware of a connection between us.'

'Because I told her of it.'

'Crispin, for heaven's sake, how could you do that?'

'Because she is kindhearted and intelligent and can be trusted to listen when the brandy talks and to keep quiet about it afterwards. She is exceedingly common, I grant you, but if she had not followed you from Market Square, I dread to think what might have befallen you. You should be grateful.'

'So I am, grateful indeed. What did you tell her?'

'Would there be any purpose in repeating it?'

'There may be.'

'Verity,' he said, his voice no more than a whisper, his eyes closing briefly as if, suddenly, his head ached. 'Don't do this to me again. Don't come so close to me and then disappear in my hands like smoke – not again. It may hurt you, too, but it crucifies me, Verity.'

'What must I do, then?'

'Nothing, for nothing has changed. I am no more able to support you than I was before – less able, for the election cost me dear and I am in debt for every penny. And now that my face is well known, and my opinions, people apply to me for assistance and I am rarely able to refuse. If we ran away together we would have a merry procession following us, your husband and my creditors – you may as well know it.'

240

'Yes – yes. I know it. Now tell me what you have said to Mrs McCluskey.'

He walked a step or two away from me and back again, catlike in his tense, delicate testing of the air around me, making a valiant effort to persuade himself not to touch me, not to attempt my downfall, reminding himself how much I had to lose, vowing he would do nothing to harm me even if I, foolish woman that I was, seemed so strangely willing. And his resolve made me smile, for I knew – in my mood of foolishness and strangeness – that he could not keep it.

I had asked him, long ago, not to take me, to allow me the chance to give, and now, watching his painful hesitations, his longing to commit himself and his fear of commitment struggling inside him for mastery, it struck me that for the first time in my life I was free. No one – except Crispin and Dinah McCluskey – knew at this moment where I was, and if people were searching for me they would not look here. Liberty, brief perhaps, but liberty just the same, and what did brevity matter since life itself was short and uncertain and I could have been killed down there in the street or could have died six months ago of the fever. And suddenly, basking in a newfound strength that had all the warmth and fragrance of sunshine, I saw no shame in acknowledging not only my love but my desire for this frail, beautiful man, not only the matching of our minds but my body's sheer, basic need to possess him, to give itself into his possession.

'I can't ask you to be my mistress,' he said, a schoolmaster lecturing me, lecturing himself. 'Can I? Not again. I asked you once and you gave me no reply – there could be no reply, I understand that, and so we parted.'

And, reaching out my hand and winding an arm around his neck, I told him, 'I'm not so sure. I think it was because you feared I would persuade you into some little villa and make a respectable man of you. But now, since your creditors would not allow that in any case ...'

'Verity, don't laugh at me. I love you. I don't always know why, and God knows I've tried not to, but I love you.'

'And I love you.'

And in those first moments, our delight had the wondrous, almost innocent quality of children discovering the scents and shades of the world, a slow wandering through enchantment as his hands gently removed, one by one, the pins from my chignon, his mouth smiling and tasting, his nostrils deeply inhaling, as I shook my hair loose against his face. We had waited a long time, yet now there was no hungry falling upon each other, no cause at all for haste. And standing a breath away from him, I understood at last the pleasure of display, no longer submitting my body to a man's eyes but offering it, pausing at the unfastening of each tiny pearl button, raising my arms above my head with a rich, sighing content as my bodice fell away, glad of the lamplight on my bare shoulders and the contours of my breasts, proud suddenly that those breasts were still smooth and firm, that my legs, emerging from the froth of my petticoats, were long and slender at the ankles, loving my own body at that moment, beneath the caress of his gaze, because he loved it.

And even then, when the fine, lightly boned moulding of him, the fragile blond skin with its silk-scattering of fair hair, had moved me to an immense, wondering tenderness, we gazed a while longer until, with the very tips of his fingers, he touched my forehead and my cheeks, my mouth, the outline of my ears and throat, the length of my breastbone and thighbone, while I, stretching my arms above my head again with that same languorous sighing, turned slowly round, my body ready now to dissolve in his, to flow over him and into him like a rich, unhurried stream.

The bed was hard, with a lumpy pillow and a sctachy blanket, and there were still the street noises, still the raucous merriment of whores and drunkards from below, squalid and wicked, if any of it had been real. But it did not concern me, for the real world had become very small and I had nothing to do in it but devote myself to the pleasures of Crispin Aycliffe, pleasure far more complex and delicate and nervous than the forthright explosions of male joy to which I was accustomed. I was, in that hour, his most devoted and willing slave, lost and bemused with adoration, wanting nothing but the rich reward of his skin against my skin, the lightness of his bones beneath my fingers, so drunk with giving that my own pleasure took me by surprise and left me too mindlessly content to remember that I was now an adultress, who ought to be ashamed and truly afraid.

'Truly,' I told him, breathless and laughing, wanting him again already in my mind, knowing he needed to be reassured, 'truly that must have been perfect.'

And he smiled. 'Of course. Did you think that I could ever be less than a perfect lover?'

And then, leaning over me, his elbows one on either side of my head, his smile gone, he said quickly, 'I was never more nervous in my life – terrified of offending you or hurting you or not pleasing you enough. Love me, Verity.'

'I do.'

'More than you love anyone else?'

'Easily – but then, who else do I love?'

'Your children,' he said, sitting up. 'You love your children.'

'Yes, I do.'

'I have seen it in your face, sometimes, when you look at them. Your tenderness has moved me.'

'That displeases you?'

'Dear God, no. It delights me, except ...'

'Yes – except?'

'Except that I am honest enough to care that our love could harm them, and base enough to know that I will not sacrifice it.'

And brushing my hand the length of his tense, anxious back, an indulgent, comforting gesture that was not unmaternal, I told him, laughing at him, loving him, 'Crispin Aycliffe, you have spent years of our lives trying to entice me into your bed, and now that you have me I do believe your complicated nature is looking for reasons to regret it.'

'Ah – then you must hold me in your arms a while longer and smooth my fears away, for I am soon melancholy, particularly when I have been very joyful. I need a great deal of cosseting and spoiling, Verity – I warn you.'

And so, taking him in my arms, his head nuzzling against my shoulder, I turned his fine, fair hair around my fingers, dropped light, quick kisses on his eyes and ears and chin, the hollows and angles of his delicately moulded face, kissing the hurt child in him that was still lost in the dark until the man awoke and he made love to me again quite briefly but with an assurance that enabled him to open his eyes in the moment of pleasure and smile.

It was time, then, to go and, disengaging myself from with the infinite care one bestows on objects of enormous value, enormous frailty, I got up and stood for a moment, surveying the bare little room – the monk's cell – smiling at the cheap, ugly furnishings, the damp patches on the walls, the scarred boards underfoot, as if they were priceless treasures.

'I thought this would be the worst part,' I told him. 'Getting up, getting dressed, hurrying out into the street – I thought it would seem sordid – that I wouldn't be able to bear it. Yet here I am, doing it, and the only thing in my mind is that I love you.'

'Thank you,' he said, getting up, the rueful smile back on his lips. 'I believe you said that to put me at ease, because you knew I would be worried about it, too. You will come to me again, Verity?'

'Yes. I don't know where – for I don't know that I could possibly come here alone without discovery – but I'll find somewhere. People think me placid and easy to manage but, in fact, when I am determined, I can generally get my way. Now – you will have to help me with these tapes and these infernal little buttons – and I do not think I can do up my hair alone.'

We dressed without embarrassment, wound my hair into a plain but convincing knot, laughed at the frothy burden of my petticoats and their awkward fastenings, and instead of the shame, the dry-mouthed dread of discovery that I should have felt, my mind refused to be distracted from its rich glow of remembered happiness.

'You have committed adultery,' reason accused me, and my conscious mind replied, 'Next time I will bring a big, deep-brimmed bonnet so that I can simply cram my hair inside it and run.'

'Adultery is a crime,' reason said. 'Before God and before the law. And it is not the same law for a woman as for a man. Society excuses a man, but an adulterous woman is worse than a leper. And Joel, whatever he may do himself, would hurt you if he caught you.'

But my mind, raising an impatient finger to its lips answered, 'Hush – don't interrupt – don't annoy me – don't distract me from looking at him, from remembering, from planning how I can come to him again.'

And then, standing at the door and seeing Crispin in the good blue coat he had worn at the hustings, growing shabby, I noticed, at the lapels

243

and the elbows – reminding me of the debts he could surely never repay on his fifty pounds a year – I asked him, 'Crispin, how long have I been here?'

'Well, I have never been a man for the exact time, especially since I let my watch go, but it cannot be less than two hours.'

'Dear God –'

'No,' he said, quite sharply. 'Don't ask God to help you. You can rely on me for this. You are not accustomed to deceit, but I served a long apprenticeship. My mother taught me to lie, for my father surrounded us with so many rules that the only way we could breath was to deceive him. And so I know what I am about. You cannot walk home in those foolish slippers, which saddens me, since I would enjoy a long stroll in the moonlight, and unless we happen to meet your coachman on the way, the only thing for it is to go to the Swan.'

'Will Joel still be there?'

'Oh, I imagine so. He will have cause to celebrate his own triumph, for it is not every man who is elevated to the level of Guy Fawkes. Oh yes, he will still be there – and he will be very much obliged to me, I imagine, for rescuing his wife.'

As a spasm of discomfort, a prickly, unpleasant thing, briefly crossed my mind, he put a hand under my chin, forced my head up, and made me look at him.

'Do you doubt me already? Do you think I have made love to you only to humiliate your husband? Do you think he even entered my head just now? And if you tell me he entered yours you will mortally wound me.'

We walked, hand in hand, down the rickety staircase, the greasy passage, into the alleyway, picking our way through noise and stink and litter, and, with his arm around me, my whole body was still dazzled by his nearness, throbbing with a blissful, butterfly joy that extended no further than every footstep, every single intake of breath. Enchantment and then, too soon, the glimmer of gaslight, the windows of the Swan beckoning in the distance, so that I paused in the shadows, my feet growing heavy and unwilling to tread a paved road again, and the outline of the square, the Market Cross, the Piece Hall that I knew so well striking me as alien, hostile, dangerous.

And in the moment before we entered that illuminated space, tension gripped him suddenly, painfully, and he said, 'Tell me, Verity – tell me –'

'I love you.'

'And then – and then? More than that –'

'I love you best – much more than anyone else.'

'Than anyone?'

'Yes, yes – more than I could ever love anyone.'

'Thank you,' he said, the taut pressure of his nerves sighing out of him. 'So – come then, my darling, I'll take you across the way to the Swan and teach you how to lie.'

The square had emptied now, a light wind tasting of ash and the memory of burning stirring the debris underfoot, reminding me of a ballroom, forlorn with departed gaiety, but the Swan still sat there in its accustomed place, humming and glowing with good cheer, ready to cater all night long to the appetites of those who were prepared to pay. Walking now a polite distance away from me, with no greater familiarity than a solicitous hand beneath my elbow as I negotiated the mess in the inn yard, Crispin saw me safely bestowed in a back parlour, procured the landlady to attend me, and then, with apparent coolness, mounted the stairs to find Joel and inform him of my plight.

'Barforth, dear fellow, if I might have a word – yes, I daresay I am the last man you expected to see here tonight, and no – very civil of you, but I won't take anything just now. The fact is – well, your wife – no harm done as it turns out, although there could have been – by God, there could have been. Caught up in that little spot of bother, it seems, on her way home from your sister's – my stepmother's. Damned coachman couldn't see his way through, took fright and made her get down. Some fool's notion of picking her up at the top of Millergate, if she ever got there, which of course she didn't. Exactly, Barforth – that's the very word I'd have used myself. Found her in Cropper Alley – yes, that's right, Cropper Alley – could have been the great Wall of China for all she knew. Absolutely worn out and a bit shaken, but luckily I got to her before anybody else, and she's downstairs with Mrs Parkin. What you do to your coachman, of course, is your own affair, but I expect you'll be taking Mrs Barforth home.'

And hearing the light, drawling note of his voice as they came downstairs together, my mind turned rogue again and I was very near to laughter.

'By Christ, Verity,' Joel said from the doorway, appalled, I think, by the mud-splattered hem of my dress, my fouled slippers, my bare, quite dirty feet at ease on Mrs Parkin's good stool. And I thought: How big he is – how dark – basic colours, black and red and great bands of gold – compared to Crispin, behind him, turquoise and lilac and misty, muted shades blending his personality together like a spring evening.

But I said, with great composure, 'Yes, I am in a state, which is hardly to be wondered at, and I would like very much to go home.'

He had, of course, been drinking for hours, was as drunk as he ever permitted himself to be, but he was steady on his feet and decisive in his movements as he turned away from me to Crispin, wanting to be rid of him, I thought, since he had no mind to scold me, or whatever he meant to do, before strangers.

'I am very obliged to you, Aycliffe.'

'Oh, my pleasure – really – absolutely my pleasure, you may believe me.'

As they shook hands and Crispin bowed slightly towards me in leave-taking, I was aware once again of laughter welling up inside me and stifled it instantly, knowing that if Joel heard it and ever discovered the cause he would kill me for it.

And why, I wondered, did I have so little care for that? Why did I refuse, obstinately, to bow myself with shame and terror when my position was both shameful and terrifying?

'You are quite sure,' Joel said, coming towards me, 'that no one harmed you – quite sure?'

'Why, yes. No one spoke to me at all. I was pushed and jostled a little but no more than anyone else, and I hope you do not mean to blame me for it. I stayed late with your sister because she was in her miseries again, and when Thomas told me to get down and walk to Millergate, I could see the sense to it.'

'Sense? There was no sense at all. He should have brought you here or stayed where he was until the crowd dispersed, or forced himself a way through – they'd have stood back soon enough when they saw it was either that or being ridden down. But, in any case, you are not to blame – bedraggled little sparrow that you are – and I will deal with Thomas later. Come now, I'll take you home.'

'There's no need to take me. Just send a message and they'll come to fetch me. Don't leave your guests on my account.'

'My guests will do very well without me for an hour or two. Just throw those shoes into Mrs Parkin's fire, for I'll not have them in my phaeton, and we'll be on our way. Come – if you had less than six inches of mud on your skirt I'd carry you, but – evening clothes costing what they do – you'll have to manage as best you may.'

But he lifted me a step or two, just the same, across the splinters of charred wood, the brim of what had been a silk hat wedged grotesquely among them, warning me all the while to keep my muck away from his trousers, and, as he tossed me up into the phaeton, I was still happy, still blissfully, gloriously lost to reason. I felt intensely alive, rich and beautiful and clever, my senses and appetites sharpened so that colours seemed brighter, sounds clearer, champagne or spring water equally delightful, and I could have rolled myself in the summer grasses, as young animals do, from sheer joy of living. And, my mood extending to Joel, I wondered if he felt this exultation when he had been with a woman he desired; and then, abruptly, I pitied him, for Joel, who wanted to possess the whole world, had surely never possessed this. Joel, I was quite certain, had never been in love in his whole life. How could his restless desires, his conquests and his triumphs compare with the emotion I was feeling now?

Poor, magnificent, all-powerful Joel. And pitying him – still too dazed with joy to understand that I had cause enough to pity myself – I could feel the reserve I had always felt towards him melt away and I could accept him, value him, exactly as he was.

'Thomas goes in the morning,' he said, taking a corner dangerously, setting the dust flying. 'Or he goes tonight, if I catch him.'

'Oh, he'll not mind that. He's old and ready to go to Patterswick to live with his sister – and he's heartily sick of me.'

'Is he, by God.'

'Yes. I was in the square, Joel. I saw the bonfire, and I saw you raise your glass to them afterwards.'

'Did you?' he said, his smile flashing out as it had in the inn yard. 'And what did you think of that, little cousin?'

Smiling too and closer to him in some odd, quite terrible way than I had ever been before, I answered, 'I'll tell you, cousin – I thought I had never liked you so well before in my life.'

25

My mother, being desirous of inspecting the site of our new property at Tarn Edge, had arranged to meet me there the following day and to take me back to Patterswick with her for tea, an expedition which should have given me ample opportunity for a private conversation had not Hannah announced at breakfast, 'I think I had better come with you, Verity. In fact, I think Mr Ashley would expect it of me on such a pleasant day.'

While I finished my tea and toast and ran upstairs for my bonnet, our numbers were again increased, first by Elinor driving up at a spanking pace and calling out, 'My miseries are entirely gone. What – are you going to Patterswick? Excellent – I'll join you, for I hear you had an adventure last night and you can tell me on the way,' and then by young Jonas Agbrigg, who, coming to return a book Hannah had lent him, eagerly accepted her offer of a drive.

'You can take Jonas up with you, Verity, and I will ride with Elinor,' Hannah decided. Since the introduction of Jonas Agbrigg filled Blaize, then Nicholas, then Caroline with an overwhelming desire to come too, I set out surrounded by children while my two cousins followed behind, in the Aycliffe carriage, most comfortably alone.

It was a day of great heat, a blue and gold sky, a thirsty land gasping between the intense reds and yellows of summer flowers, the moorland spiky and crackling underfoot although I had not walked there that morning. And still – my crime already a day old, my body having accommodated Joel's waking desire that morning quite automatically, my mind making little of it, my mouth having smiled and lied as I repeated the story of my escapade to Hannah, to Mrs Stevens, to Elinor, as I would go on repeating it to the many who would ask – still I was happy. And if this mindless, girlish bliss – these symptoms of first love – were ridiculous in a woman of twenty-six, three times a mother, then I was content to be ridiculous. And if they were dangerous – as they undoubtedly were – then, when the time came, I would suffer. And, amazed, amused even at my own recklessness, I smiled at every passerby, even at young Jonas Agbrigg beside me in the carriage, and asked him, 'How is your mother, dear?' although I did not like him and knew that, to him at twelve years of age, his ailing mother was an embarrassment, a nuisance.

'She's very well, ma'am,' he answered dourly, although I knew she had taken to wandering lately, suddenly not being there when, just a moment ago, she had been quietly in her accustomed place.

'A tremendous anxiety,' Hannah had told me. 'She was on Cullingford Green two days ago and had to be fetched home on a tatter's cart, and last week Mr Blamires of the grammar school met her on the road above

Lawcroft: she had no idea where she was going – was ready, in fact, to go anywhere with anyone, like a stray dog. Fortunately Mr Blamires recognized her and took her back to Low Cross, but eventually she is bound to encounter someone who will be differently disposed and one trembles to think what may happen then. For her own safety she ought to be restrained – no, no, not with chains, you silly goose, although it would come to that, I fear, if her husband could not afford to care for her at home. I mean simply that they should lock her door and bar her window, but Mr Agbrigg will not hear of it. He looked as shocked as you when I suggested it. Yet what else is to be done? Is she to be left to walk under somebody's horses, or into the canal – for I declare she has no more sense of danger than a toddling child – or to fall into the hands of some villain who would take advantage of her? It would give me no pleasure to turn the key in her door, but I assure you that, when I consider the alternatives, I would force myself to do it.'

As I looked at Ann Agbrigg's clever son, scuffling with my own children for what seemed to them the best place in the carriage, I wondered if it had shamed him when Mr Blamires, his headmaster, had brought his mother home, and if he too would be willing to turn that key.

The surviving Agbrigg girl, Maria, was of little interest to Hannah; a quiet little thing who could do nothing more exciting than sew a straight seam. But the boy Jonas, as plain as his sister, as long and angular and yellow-pale as his father, had a sharpness of intellect – altogether above his station – which had quickly claimed her notice.

A graceless boy, Jonas, sullen and secretive, who had fallen foul of his teachers in the early days until Mr Blamires – most discerning of headmasters – had taken Hannah aside and confided in her that Jonas, far from having difficulty in keeping up with his socially superior classmates, had so far surpassed them that, in some cases, even the masters were finding it impossible to keep up with him.

'Mr Blamires was quite taken aback,' she in her turn confided in me. 'Naturally, every master dreams of having a brilliant pupil, but considering the thousands of pounds the Hobhouses and Oldroyds – and the Barforths, of course – have given the school, the poor man was very much alarmed at seeing all the prizes go to an Agbrigg. I sympathized, of course – who would not? – but I was quick to make Mr Blamires aware that no suggestion of holding Jonas back could find favour with me. After all, one never knows what a boy like that may do in the future – what heights he may reach – and how would one feel then if one had not encouraged him?'

Since that day, Hannah had set herself the task of encouraging Jonas Agbrigg as much as she could, earning herself a place perhaps in his memoirs should he ever achieve greatness, while he had attached himself to her good graces with a willingness that made me suspect he was neither so unworldly nor so unpolished as he seemed. A calculating child, I thought, unlike my own sons, who lived like greedy butterflies from one sunbeam to the next, unlike my daughter, who thought the world existed for her pleasure, unlike my own children altogether, who were, just then, causing the alien Jonas so much discomfort with their jostling for position that Hannah called out, 'Verity, can you not keep those children in order? They will have Jonas out on the road ere long if they are not checked.'

'It's our carriage,' Blaize said, clear-eyed and innocent, knowing Hannah could not hear him.

'It's our road as well,' Nicholas muttered, compelled to go one better, not caring whether Hannah heard him or not.

'And I don't like him,' Caroline declared. 'He smells.'

And although the odour Jonas exuded was that of good, cheap soap, nothing to be ashamed of, the look in his pale, slightly uptilted eyes would have worried me had she been older or more available to his spite.

My mother was waiting for us at Tarn Edge, in Squire Dalby's open landau, chatting to Daniel Adair, the Aycliffe manager, who may have had business on the site or may simply have made it his business to be there, since he was a man who enjoyed an audience, particularly of women. And as he helped us down and began to tell us where my drawing room would be and to explain the proposed width and magnificence of my hall, it struck me that one did not often see an Irishman, in these parts, in such a perfect state of health.

He was a man of thirty-five, not tall but square-cut, powerful, with a perpetually smiling mouth and a merry eye, quick to spot its own advantage; a man who, having been instructed by Morgan Aycliffe simply to run the business at a profit and no questions asked, could be relied on, one felt, to feather his own nest with a kind of good-humoured rapacity that would make him popular even among those he robbed. And although he very likely believed that young women were fit for nothing but bed and breeding, while old ones should be firmly anchored to washtub and kitchen stove, nothing could have exceeded the gallantry of his escort, the courteous tilt of his head as he listened to Hannah's questions, the clarity of his replies, the twinkle in his eye as he let himself be discovered looking at Elinor and me, and even my mother, in a way that said, 'Naturally I could never presume to touch, for I'm just a common man, but I'd like to – I'd really like to.'

I stood a little apart, for I had been here often enough before and knew the dimensions of the house, the distance from the mill, how a high stone wall and a future circle of trees would screen me from the unpleasantness of factory life; how, in fact, the firm of Morgan Aycliffe, master builders, would assist me to turn my back on the factory altogether by giving my front windows a view of open fields and a stretch of unblemished sky above them. I knew that I was to have a thick hedge of rhododendrons around my wall, sweet-scented shrubs and half an acre of roses to take the factory smells from my air, a paddock for my children to race their ponies with another wall around it, massive gates and a gatekeeper, and more trees to ensure my privacy. I knew it was to be not just a house, or a home, but a palace for an industrious industrial prince, with myself, his gracious, perfectly mannered consort, inside it.

And I knew I would be that consort. I would give him everything he asked of me, as I had always done, because I could see no other way. I would be obedient and sensible and crafty, and what I could not have by right, I would get, like any other bondswoman, by stealth.

'What are you dreaming of?' my mother asked, gliding up to me in her fluid fashion. Then, catching the drift of something in my face with which she did not wish to involve herself, she said quickly, 'I have the feeling Hannah is in no hurry to see the completion of this house. I suppose your removal from Lawcroft must force her to consider her own position. If she intends to marry Mr Ashley she should certainly name the day, for there seems little point in moving up here with you only to remove again to Patterswick. Mr Ashley is entirely at her disposal – would not dare, I imagine, to be otherwise. Will she marry him, do you think? They tell me Mr Brand has entered the lists once again. Is he, after all, likely to succeed?'

Indeed, Mr Brand, fully recovered from the fever by now and fully aware of what Hannah's loss was costing him in time and effort, had taken to calling on me lately, planting himself squarely in my drawing room at teatime, or any other time he could find an excuse to call, and bewailing not Hannah's engagement to Mr Ashley but her conversion to the Church of England which it entailed.

'It is her soul, Mrs Barforth – her bright, pure soul.'

Yet I didn't think that Mr Brand, as he swallowed his tea and his emotion, was really thinking of Hannah's soul. He wanted her in bed with him, I believed, and the mother of half a dozen red-headed, earthbound children just like himself, and if she meant to become a parsonage wife at all – and I had yet to be convinced of it – I thought she would be more comfortable with him than the ethereal Mr Ashley.

But – and I could not have explained this to Mr Brand – it was not really Mr Ashley, at the moment, who stood between them, nor Morgan Aycliffe, either, but the simple matter of Jonas Agbrigg's education.

'Jonas must go to Oxford or Cambridge,' she had decreed. 'His calibre demands it.' And since only members of the established Church of England were eligible for these ancient seats of learning, it followed – in her view – that Jonas must give up his Methodism and be received, by Mr Ashley, into the Anglican fold.

'It seems to me quite pointless,' she said, with true Barforth logic, 'to allow these fine points of religion to ruin an entire career. I am convinced our Lord never intended it, for if one fails to help oneself when the opportunity arises I do not think one should expect anyone else to make up the deficiency. I have explained to Mr Agbrigg – who has very simple views on religion and is far more humble with the clergy than he has need to be nowadays, considering what he is earning – that he has no need to attend the Anglican church himself, simply to allow Jonas to do so. I have offered to take him with me to Patterswick, provided I may continue to use your carriage, which should cause you no inconvenience since you have the use of Joel's on Sundays, and Mr Ashley will, of course, be only too pleased to receive him as soon as I have convinced the father.'

And so, until Jonas's confirmation had taken place, or until another enthusiasm came along, Mr Ashley had little to fear.

'Oh, I fancy she will be moving up here with us,' I told my mother, and she gave me her vague, pointed smile.

'Yes, I fancy you are right – in fact, I imagine we will all stay very much as we are. Only look at Elinor – skipping along beside Mr Adair and allowing him to believe she is laughing at his witticisms although, in fact, she is merely thinking that she is looking her best today and is not listening to him at all. Poor child, her husband will not die so very soon, you know, for these melancholy men who find life such a burden can be relied on to live forever. Only think what an attractive widow she would make – I am certain Mr Adair has thought of it – with her own enchanting face and figure and all Mr Aycliffe's money, since one supposes he has disinherited his son, and Elinor's children are all girls. A temptation for any man, and Mr Adair appears very ready to be tempted. Well – I am sure he can be very rough when he is not being very charming, and once he got his hands on Elinor and the business he would probably cheat her daughters of their dowries and would take no notice at all of Elinor's headaches. But, at least, he would not be melancholy, so perhaps there would be no headaches – perhaps we should see her blossom again as Mrs Adair. How sad – for she will be Mrs Aycliffe, I think, not perhaps until her dying day but until it is too late for blossoming. Poor lamb, perhaps she would do better to concentrate on being Mrs Aycliffe, since it is so clearly her destiny – and stop trying to share it with her sister – since I can see nothing else for her.'

As we got back into our carriages and Mr Adair waved us a hearty goodbye, I wondered, all the way to Patterswick how much my mother knew – or guessed – for the advice she had thought appropriate for Elinor could just as well have applied to me.

There was very little to distinguish Squire Dalby's village of Patterswick from a dozen like it, a cluster of grey stone cottages housing his dependants, the paler grey of the church, a few farms squatting among the folds of the land, my mother's house with its ivy-covered wall, its garden mossy and overgrown, it low, oak-panelled rooms dim and cool at all seasons, haunted by a scent of hyacinths that had lingered from generation to generation, the squire's own ancient dwelling just a leafy, shady walk away.

And there, in my mother's flowery, chintzy parlour, an apple-cheeked country girl served us tea, with a silver kettle and basin, on rose-patterned china, and chocolate cake and angel cakes and sticky gingerbread, to which Blaize and Nicholas and Caroline helped themselves raucously, the plates emptying before Jonas Agbrigg's lashless eyes until Hannah delivered her sharp protest and my mother sent the girl for more.

But Jonas, it seemed, had no appetite; he was almost embarrassed by the confectionery Hannah heaped on his plate and was sitting so awkwardly that Blaize, quick to spot his opportunities, needed only to jog his elbow slightly to send that plate flying, the chocolate cake landing squarely, creamy side down, on my mother's pale, decidedly costly rug.

'Oh dear,' she said. 'What a pity. Do have another slice.'

251

But Hannah, who had seen Blaize's wicked elbow as well as I had, put her own plate down smartly and enquired in a voice not to be ignored, 'Verity, do you intend to let that pass?'

'What, dear?'

'I think you know very well.'

And when, unwilling to make more of the incident than I had to, I continued to look vague and to sip my tea, she turned furiously, very directly, to the culprit himself.

'That was an extremely wicked thing to do, young man. You have damaged your grandmother's carpet and upset a fellow guest.'

'Not me,' Blaize answered innocently, rudely. 'I didn't drop my cake. It was him.'

'Because you pushed him.'

'No, I didn't,' Blaize told her.

'No, he didn't,' Nicholas told her too, his eyes less innocent, the set of his jaw declaring his readiness to do some pushing on his own account.

'He didn't, either,' Caroline said, quite certain that her opinion must settle things once and for all.

And, finding the whole thing ridiculous and futile, taking note of Hannah's mounting fury and Elinor's barely stifled yawn, I got up and shooed my sons outdoors.

'You did push him, didn't you?' I told Blaize, blinking at the impact of the strong sunlight. And, blinking too, he smiled, his eyes very nearly on a level with my own.

'Oh yes, of course I did. I know you saw me, and I knew you wouldn't give me away to Aunt Hannah.'

'Indeed – well, it wasn't kind of you, Blaize. He may not be a likeable boy, but he's had a sad life, and apart from that, as your Aunt Hannah told you, he is a guest.'

'I didn't invite him.'

'That makes no difference. Neither did I.'

'And you don't much like him either, Mamma. I know you don't. And even if you did, you'd still be on my side.'

'Don't be too sure.'

Yet it was true and, as his easy self-assurance inclined me, as always, to laughter, I felt a chill whisper of warning inside me, repeating Crispin's words, 'I am honest enough to care that our love could harm them.' And sickeningly aware that it was true, I peered keenly at Blaize, his smoky eyes inviting me to share his mischief, and at Nicholas, standing on my other side, darker, deeper, his feeling for me more intense, perhaps, than his brother's, and I knew that no part of my love for them, or for Caroline, had changed. I would love them every day of my life. And I wished them to be free and whole and individual. But would they, even when they no longer needed or desired my day-to-day caring, extend the same understanding to me? Could they ever accept that my love for a man who was not their father removed nothing from my feeling for them?

Blaize perhaps, who would be worldly, I thought, when he was grown,

252

might come the closest. But Nicholas, insecure enough to be jealous, would suffer, would clench his fists and bite back his tears, and I could not be sure what Caroline would make of me.

'I am base enough to know I would not sacrifice it,' Crispin had said, and I could not sacrifice it either.

'Where have you gone, Mamma?' Blaize said, cutting through my reverie.

And smiling, flinging an arm around each of them, I answered, 'Oh, not far.'

We were to visit the squire after tea, and because an invitation to Dalby Hall was such a rarity, even Elinor found the energy for a brisk walk to the lodge gates, with my children, having been reprimanded once again by Hannah, racing around her, while Hannah herself, taking the sullen young Agbrigg with her, went off in search of her fiancé.

'Come, dear,' my mother said, clearly not wishing to be alone with me. 'We should go up to the Hall, too. The squire has company already – his grandson and his daughter-in-law, who always upsets him – and since he has nothing to do in the summer, when there is no hunting and shooting, he spends a great deal of his time drinking and he may not even recognize Elinor so late in the afternoon. I think I may be needed to make things smooth.'

But I had come expressly to talk to her, as she seemed to know very well, and I shook my head.

'Elinor will manage the squire well enough, Mother, and there is something I wish to tell you.'

'Are you quite sure, dear,' she said, looking round for her embroidery in her old, vague manner. 'Quite sure? Things tend to become so real, I find, when one talks about them. Perhaps if you just think about it a little longer – whatever it is – it may become less urgent –'

'I doubt it.'

'Then after tea, dear – when the squire is settled and Elinor can occupy herself flirting with his guests, and the children can play with the puppies, if young Master Agbrigg ever condescends to play – or if he is even a child – Did I tell you about the puppies, ten of them – five black and five yellow? I wondered, in fact, if you would care to choose one to replace your poor old bitch – Edwin's old yellow bitch –?'

'Mother …'

'Be very sure, Verity.'

'Yes. I am in love with Crispin Aycliffe, Mother, and he with me.'

'Oh dear,' she said, executing several quick, apparently accurate stitches in the cushion cover she was making. 'Oh dear.'

And then, laying down her work, folding her hands, she gave me her tranquil faraway smile and moved her shoulders in the faintest sketch of a shrug.

'That strikes me as most unfortunate. Yes, I caught a spark of something between you a long time ago, I confess it, and when I heard that he had rescued you last night so romantically, I wondered … But, Verity, why have you told me this? Surely, I ought not to have been told?'

'Because I need you, Mother. It did not end last night, and I may need an alibi, a meeting place, and, in the final instance, a refuge. I think you owe me that, Mother.'

'Owe you?'

'Yes, since you persuaded me, when I was very weak, into a marriage which suited your convenience more than mine. If you had allowed me time to recover from my father's death and Edwin's, I might have remembered the kind of man Joel is, and shown more defiance.'

'Oh no,' she said, taking up her work again. 'No, no, Verity. Let us remember things as they actually were. If I had allowed you the time you speak of you might have defied me – which I doubt – but you would not have defied your grandfather for long. You know that perfectly well, child.'

'Yes, of course I do.'

'And have you been so very unhappy with Joel?'

'No. Neither happy nor unhappy – just sensible.'

'Quite so – whereas Crispin Aycliffe has not been sensible at all. Apart from the fact that he threw away his inheritance in a most reckless manner – you may or may not know that he is considerably in debt to Colonel Corey and to others, I believe.'

'Yes, I know that.'

'Then what future does he offer you?'

'None. He has chosen his own way of life, and I know I cannot share it.'

'But do you at least hope for a change – do you feel able to persuade him into more profitable attitudes?'

'No – at least, I hope he will change but I am sure he will not.'

'Then why, darling? Why take this dreadful risk at all?'

'Because I want something, Mother – something in my life before I'm old – something of my own choosing – something I want, not something somebody else thinks I should have. And he's all I've ever wanted. Wanting nothing was pleasant in its way, very safe and warm and rather superior at times, but I can't go back to it now. I've lived on half feelings and lived very well, but it was a kind of emotional virginity, and like the other kind, once it's gone then that's the end of it.'

'I see,' she said, very gravely for her, and, sighing deeply, looked down at her hands.

'Verity, my dear, I suppose you realize that Joel would never – absolutely never – be prepared to allow you the freedom he permits himself.'

'Yes, I realize that.'

'Nor would his own moral shortcomings even incline him to tolerance. Dearest, I believe he would treat you most savagely and vindictively should the occasion arise. And the sad thing is that no one would blame him. The law would allow him to do just what he pleased with you, and all your friends, even the women – especially the women – would declare it no more than you deserved. It is not precisely a stoning to death these days for an adulteress, but something very like it. And his own adulteries, which appear to have been many and various, would win you no sympathy. You would simply be told that it is different for men. Dearest, I believe he is fond of you, in his way, and that would only make him worse.'

'Well – and I believe I am fond of him too.'

'And just as determined, I see, as the rest of them – the Barforths.'

'I fear so. I have grown up, Mother. You cannot manage me any longer by drifting away into your embroidery, for I will follow you and involve you – for, as I have said, you owe me this.'

She got up, still light in her movements but very slow; crossing to her window, sheltered by its tiny, diamond-shaped panes and its widely frilled chintz curtains, she looked out a moment at the sunshine, not to warm herself, I think, but to check her security.

'They are right,' she murmured, 'the ones who say it is different for men, for they designed the world by themselves, for themselves, and although you and I can well imagine what it is like to be a man – an individual who claims the right to work and speak for himself and who does not bear children – I doubt if there is one among them who knows how it feels to be a woman. They make me smile, these radicals like Mark Corey and your Mr Crispin Aycliffe, when they talk of freedom, for what do they know about it when they cannot even imagine a servitude from which there is no escape. A man who is thrown into prison knows his cell has a door, and a man imprisoned by poverty can strive and hope for better days. But we are born slaves to our own fertility, and how does one escape from that, especially since nature has bound us further by equipping us with emotions, so that we generally love the children we bear? I have had eight children, Verity, a task which has eaten away seventeen years of my life, years of great weariness and some pain, when I simply functioned at the level of any other breeding, nursing animal and had no time to ponder on my humanity or my intellect, no time at all for what men call the finer things of life. Wasted years, I might add, since you are the only one left alive. That is the full tale of my life, Verity. I have had eight children, some half dozen miscarriages, and I can do fancy needlework. You may engrave that on my tombstone when the time comes, for there is no more.

'Clever women are not happy women in our society, my dear, you must know that, for although men may greatly desire us, they do not, in general, like us. And if some totally effective means of avoiding pregnancy should ever be found, many men would rise up against it in horror and call it sin, simply from the fear of setting us free. "Keep her pregnant and you'll keep her out of mischief," they say, and what they really mean by mischief is not infidelity but independence, their own unwillingness to lose us as domestic servants and to compete with us in other fields of endeavour. You were always far more intelligent than your brother Edwin. I believe your cousin Hannah could manage Lawcroft every bit as efficiently as Joel. But if you were given the opportunity of real work, real responsibility, would you be willing to devote so much time to the niceties of your husband's dinner or his shirt

255

frill? Would Hannah be so tireless in her arrangement of the altar flowers, or so happy to compose Morgan Aycliffe's speeches and allow him to pass them off as his own? Naturally not. It takes a very clever man, Verity, to accept intelligence in a woman – a very clever man, indeed, to value it. Mediocre men will always feel threatened by it, will need to console themselves by clinging to their man-made myth that woman is no more than a kind of high-grade cow. And, since the majority of men – and women – seem to be quite mediocre, they will keep you down. And, if you deviate from their rules – my dear, they will slaughter you.'

'Yes, Mother. But I have no skill for fine needlework, you see. And I am not totally lost to reason. I will obey the rules. I will be deceitful and cunning, and I will tell lies to my husband very cheerfully, as he tells lies to me. And he will believe me because it suits him to believe me. There is no question of elopement or open scandal, Mother. I am not a romantic girl. I could, perhaps, persuade Crispin to give up his social ideals and come away with me – for Joel would not actually murder me, and although he would be unpleasant, it would in no way break his heart. And if I refused to come back to him and went on refusing long enough I think he would let me go, for his vanity would not allow him to live with an unwilling woman. I would be poor, of course, but reasonably secure, for Crispin would never desert me, even if he wanted to. And when he began to blame me for forcing him into a mould he did not like, we would still be polite to each other – bored, perhaps, and sad, but polite. And I will not do that to him. I know how fragile love is, Mother. It is not likely to last long in this harsh climate. And when it is done I shall not ask you to help me again.'

The afternoon, outside her window, had deepened from dancing noontime gold to a rich, quiet amber, draping itself warmly around her apple trees, wrapping the sleepy, nodding heads of her lupins, the musky, full-blown faces of her roses, in a gentle haze, encircling the whole house and garden with fragrance and serenity. And I knew she would not refuse me.

'Well then, since I cannot dissuade you, and you seem to know your peril, what must be done?'

'I wish simply to know that I may rely on you at need – although you once told me that you were not reliable.'

'Ah yes. But I was weaker then. Your grandfather was still alive, and although I never vanquished him, no one else has seemed so very terrible to me since he has gone. I tremble for you, Verity. You see yourself clearly now, and Crispin, but afterwards he will go on his way – merrily or sadly – but he will go free, and you – You say love is fragile and I hope you may be right, for how could you ever bear it if it should last?'

'Was that the church clock?' I said. 'Striking four? We should really go and rescue the squire from Elinor, and his ancestral hall from Blaize and Nicholas.'

And, knowing there was nothing more to say, she caught up her bonnet and her shawl, gave me mine, and, glancing affectionately around her flowery little room, smiled to herself, glad, I suppose, that among her portion of life's misfortunes, she had never found herself – or, at least, not for a long time – in love.

26

The factory commissioners stayed some days among us, conscientiously compiling and comparing facts, interviewing anyone who would speak to them and ignoring the Ten Hours men – still dogging their footsteps – who would not.

'I have no idea what happens inside my sheds,' Bradley Hobhouse informed them, 'any more than I know what goes on in my wife's kitchen. I do know how much my machines are capable of producing, for it is my business to know that, but the rest is up to my shed managers. If you call a man a manager and pay him a manager's wages, it's only common sense to let him manage, wouldn't you think? That's what I think, at any rate, and so if you require personal details regarding my employees, I must refer you to my managers. Good morning to you, gentlemen.'

'The parents of the children in our employ do not complain,' Matthew Oldroyd, the worsted spinner, offered. 'In fact, we have children thrust upon us – more than we can take – and indeed, since we are primarily engaged in spinning, I fail to see how we could continue without them, for only very small children are able to go under the machines to join the threads when they break. And if the threads are not joined the yarn cannot be spun. I assure you it is not heavy work, and although I do take very small children – smaller than in the weaving sheds – I do not know where they would go otherwise, for their parents would never think of sending them to school. They would be left to roam the streets with nothing to eat and every temptation to steal, and I cannot think they would be better off. Here, at least, they are warm and dry. And if their mothers are employed here too, as is usually the case, they may find each other at dinnertime. Deformitiees? Yes. Some of our children are crooked but I do not know that they were straight when they came to us. Some of them are not crooked. We have a great many attractive youngsters in our employ. Promiscuity? That is hardly my concern, sir, unless it takes place on my premises, which it does not – or very rarely. I believe some of our girls become pregnant before marriage; others after. And yes, some of their babies die, some do not. I could not say how many, or for what reason. Beatings? Do you reprimand a schoolmaster, sir, for flogging his pupils? I have had many a flogging myself, as a boy, and took no harm from it. Vast numbers of children cannot be allowed to run wild, sir, among machinery. They must be kept in hand and kept awake –'

And every overlooker who was interviewed muttered sullenly, 'We have our own wages to think of. If the bairns don't frame we can't frame neither.'

And every parent said, 'We need the money.'

257

But Joel personally escorted the commissioners around Lawcroft and Low Cross and Tarn Edge, and he told them simply, 'I am here to make a profit. That is my sole purpose. I did not build these factories with the charitable aim of providing employment for those who could not find it elsewhere. My aim, unashamedly, is to make money for myself and my family, and, assuming that my employees are similarly motivated, I pay good wages and provide better facilities than anyone else in the Law Valley. And, once again, I do this not from charity but from common sense, since any man or woman works better if he, or she, is decently treated. And since my operatives come here for the same reason as myself – money – I imagine they must be well satisfied. There is no process in my mills, gentlemen, from the meanest and dirtiest to the most complex, that I cannot do and have not done myself. And if the profit is mine, then I take the risk to go with it. I could lose everything overnight, as you well know, and there would be no Royal Commission appointed to look into my well-being. I would be considered capable of taking care of myself, and so I am – so is any man worthy of the name. Yes, gentlemen, I do employ children; girls mostly, who, by the time they are twelve or thirteen, are often the main wage earners of their families, capable of supporting their parents in some cases. And since a reduction in their working hours would mean a corresponding cut in wages, I cannot think they would welcome it. Is there promiscuity in my sheds? Not while the engines are running, gentlemen, I do assure you. How would I be personally affected by a ten-hour day? You will have been told, of course, that we take ten hours to cover our overheads and require the remainder for our profits. Well, if you have heard that you have been talking to badly organized men, for I can sometimes make my profits before the rest of them are out of bed. No, the ten-hour day in itself does not alarm me, although you must bear in mind that when you speak of ten hours for women and children, the men are involved too, since it would not pay me to keep the engines running for the men alone. However, that will in no way prevent me from fulfilling my orders and keeping my customers satisfied, for, no matter what conditions prevail, an industrious man can always make his living.'

The commissioners, however, when all had been said and done, found that there was room, indeed, for improvement, and eventually the gist of their report found its way into the *Cullingford Star*. They had evidence enough, they declared, that the children employed in factories worked the same number of hours as the adults, the effects of this labour producing, in many cases, permanent physical damage. They had been made aware that such children, by reason of those long hours, were unable to receive any kind of education and would be too exhausted to profit by it if they did. They had noted too that at the age when these children entered the mills and were exposed to such massive injury, they were not free agents but were sent there by parents or guardians who took full possession of their wages. Consequently, in their opinion, a case was more than fully made out for the interference of the law.

But even that was not enough, for when, after much wrangling in the

House, legislation was at last introduced that same year, it was not a Ten Hours Bill, or anything like it. Children between the ages of nine and thirteen were to work no more than forty-eight hours a week and were to be given some elementary education during working hours; young persons of thirteen to eighteen were not to exceed sixty-nine hours, while children under the age of nine were not to be employed at all. And, to give the Act some bite, four factory inspectors were appointed and given the awesome task of enforcing it. But it was by no means the sweeping, cleansing instrument of reform that had been looked for, and men so far apart as Joel Barforth and Richard Oastler himself were quick to spot its inadequacies.

The length of the adult working day was still at the good pleasure of the masters. The mills would be open, engines running and looms turning, twenty-four hours of the day if necessary, so that youngsters who wanted to work, or were being forced to it by needy or greedy parents, could be shunted from mill to mill, to do their eight hours here, another eight hours there. It would be an astute or remarkably lucky inspector who managed to plug such a loophole as that.

And although Mr Oastler talked hotly of strikes and how he would teach the factory children of any master who broke the law to wreck the spindles with their grandmothers' old knitting needles, I knew of no millmaster who paid much heed to him.

'It has been most cleverly done,' Crispin told me, bitter with disappointment. 'The situation was becoming ugly and so, to take the heat out of it, they gave us something. Not enough to satisfy those of us with sense to see into the future, but enough for those who, never having had very much anyway, didn't expect a great deal. And so now, although the Ten Hours men know they've been cheated, the troops have gone home. And not even Oastler will be able to get them out again in a hurry.'

A perfect opportunity, perhaps, for me to say, 'What will you do now, Crispin? Surely – isn't the fight over? Can't you think of yourself now – and me?' But I had learned already that for a man like him there would always be another battle, the interval between being no more than preparation for the fray.

We met, that summer, that beautiful, deep-gold autumn, once again on the moor, only one dog now frisking around us in the fragile early mornings, the hazy evenings. And because I had always walked my dogs that way, and had always been so sensible, so good, so beyond reproach, no one suspected me. But it was never enough. The undulating landscape, the sudden outcroppings of rock, sheltered us, offered us an illusion of safety, but I could not give myself to him on the hard ground and could not – absolutely could not – visit him again at the Red Gin. And so, instead of sin or heartbreak, guilt or fear of retribution, our main preoccupation was where to go to make love.

For a blissful September fortnight there was an empty cottage of Squire Dalby's, just over the rim beyond Patterswick, so that I could leave my carriage at my mother's and go hurrying through the sweet-scented afternoon – a little stroll before teatime – to throw myself laughing and breathless into his arms – and return while the kettle was still boiling. Sometimes there was an apartment belonging to Mark Corey, the back room of a leather-goods shop in Sheepgate, reached casually through the shop door; the merchant was paid to look the other way when I arrived, with my face well hidden beneath the bonnet or shawl, my carriage being sent to deliver calling cards and messages with instructions to collect me in Millergate in an hour's time. And finally, there was a hut beyond Old Sarah's Rock, belonging once again to Mark Corey, with a bare, flagged floor, a chair and table, and a bed with a thin mattress that was an agony to my nerves, my dignity, the small of my back.

'Oh, darling – wait a second – is someone there?'

'No, no – only the dog, scratching.'

'Oh, the dog – if anyone sees her, they'll know –'

'Know what? That we're making love, or trying to, at this hour of the morning? No one would ever believe it. Law Valley men make love at night, in the dark, and they think everybody else must do the same, so we're quite safe.'

'Hardly that. And you're a Law Valley man yourself.'

'Sometimes I wonder. Perhaps I'm a changeling, left on my father's doorstep in a basket. Darling, don't you want me at all?'

'You know very well that I do, or you wouldn't ask.'

And, with great, good-humoured gentleness, he would coax me to that hard, unlikely mattress and ease me beyond awkwardness to a dreamy, hazy state where my body could float effortlessly into love.

'I know you can't be at ease here,' he told me, 'but I need you this way, to reassure myself. I even like to see you shiver and make that little grimace of distaste when you first come in here, because then I know you must love me very much to come here at all. How much, Verity?'

'More than you deserve.'

'Ah, yes – but that won't do, you know. You have to say how much, or I'll go away hungry, and won't manage to sleep or eat, and you'll worry –'

'All right. I love you – entirely – quite dreadfully.'

'And it hurts you – when you don't see me?'

'Oh yes – badly.'

'Good,' he said, rolling over on his back, laughing at himself and yet sighing at the same time, with a content I knew would not last for long.

'What a spoiled child you are, Crispin.'

'Oh yes – I was a spoiled child once. And what an ideal state that was. It suited my nature exactly. I have been trying to get back there ever since.'

'Well then – and don't I spoil you enough?'

'Will you come to my lodgings?'

'No. And why should you want me to? It is scarcely more comfortable there than here.'

'Because it is a barrier, and I want you to cross it. It may help me to cross a few barriers of my own. Will you come?'

'Not yet.'

And on that point alone he could not move me.

But in everything else my only aim was to please him, not in the servile sense of making him pleased with me but in giving him pleasure, in coming to understand the shades and humours of his mind and body, in nurturing and nourishing them and making them grow. My own body could not always find pleasure on that narrow mattress, could never achieve it at all in the furtive little room behind the leather shop, but my ability to fulfil his needs and quench his constant thirst for reassurance, to ease the tight tangle of his nerves so that he sighed, and wept sometimes, with physical satisfaction, had an acute, altogether special pleasure of its own. And the difference between my lover and my husband was that whereas Joel needed women, Crispin needed me.

Yet his uneasy nature had other needs beyond my strengths and skills as a woman, and although his concern for flesh-and-blood humanity may have been, to begin with, a reaction against his father, a man whose dust-dry emotions were reserved for glass and china, having found his cause he would not use it merely to strike attitudes, as the flamboyant Mark Corey sometimes did. He would not – as Mark Corey could well do – rise to prominence one day as a radical politician and become almost indistinguishable from the grandees it was his business to oppose. He would not, in fact, be successful in any way that I could understand success. Yet, since all the things I had been taught to desire had always been within his grasp, the choice had been deliberate, and I was bound to accept it.

'If I am to be of any use to these people,' he told me, 'then I have to understand them. I have to know not what I want them to have but what they want themselves. I have to know what it feels like to be them. And I can only do that if I am myself cold when they are cold, if my nostrils are offended by the same smells, if I am exposed to the same dangers – and even then it is not enough, since I am not imprisoned in misery as they are. I am an educated man. I can walk away from it, back to the affluence my education could bring me. And because there is no way for me to actually feel the hopelessness of a man who was born in Simon Street and knows himself condemned to die there, I can simply observe it at close quarters and write about it in Mark's paper. Little enough, but I have started to receive invitations now to lecture up and down the country, to groups who had no idea such harsh conditions existed anywhere in this Christian land of ours – which is little enough too, Verity, but something – a drop in the ocean, but that's what oceans are made of, surely?'

And so he continued to live, precariously, above the Red Gin on his fifty pounds a year, borrowing when his allowance did not suffice and, more often than not, giving the money away.

'Yes,' he said sweetly, 'I know you think me irresponsible. It is simply that I was brought up to believe money grew in my father's pocket, and I cannot rid myself of my lordly attitudes.'

But to the Barforth side of me debt was a far more shameful thing than adultery, and I would never pass an opportunity to scold him.

'Crispin – Crispin – you have lent money to half of Simon Street, from what you tell me – and how many do you think are even grateful?'

261

'Very few. None, perhaps, since they will never be able to repay me and they must find it a great nuisance, feeling obliged to cross the street to keep out of my way.'

'Then why do you do it?'

'Why not? I am not looking for gratitude.'

'Of course not – but they use you, Crispin. All this rent that cannot be paid and these doctors who will not come without the money in advance. Yes – yes – I know that happens – but does it happen every time? Do they always use your money for that, or does it go in drink?'

'Not all of it. Some of it, of course. But sometimes, Verity, all that is needed to separate life from death is a shilling. Imagine that. One can buy a life for a shilling – a sick life, admittedly; usually a very young one. And if I have a shilling, and I must confess there are occasions when I don't – Verity, don't fret, I am only really in debt to Colonel Corey, who obliges me because of Mark. And Mark is into him for thousands.'

'I daresay. But he is Mark's father, after all – or so one supposes.'

'One supposes correctly.'

'Oh, I don't care about that. He's not your father, at any rate, and how do you mean to repay him? Obviously he expects it. He has made you sign for it, hasn't he?'

'Yes, yes – but he knows quite well I shall have nothing until my uncle dies. It was all arranged on that understanding, and he's not a bad old stick, Verity. He has money to burn and what could he possibly gain by prosecuting me for debt? If he gets me locked up there is no way in the world I can ever repay him, since my uncle would probably disown me, and it would upset Mark no end, which matters to the old boy. He's always been ready to do anything for Mark, except marry his mother, of course, which is only out of consideration for his daughter, Estella Chase, who doesn't mean to share her inheritance with a stepmother. And if you're wondering what would happen if Mark and I fell out, then don't, because we've known each other too long for that. Verity, if I frittered it all away on extravagant living, then I'd allow you to be angry, but I don't.'

'No,' I told him, sharp with anxiety. 'One can see that. Isn't it time you had a new coat? You've worn that one so long I can't remember you without it – and it's getting thin at the elbows.'

'Is it? Yes, I believe you're right. I suppose Joel has dozens and dozens of coats, hasn't he, all spotless and well brushed and not a button missing anywhere? Odd, isn't it, the way things work out sometimes. He only had one coat when we were all at school, and I remember standing in the crowd while he very nearly massacred Bradley Hobhouse for tramping on it. I was quite a little boy then, of course – younger than Joel and Bradley – and every morning my mother dressed me up in something fresh and new, and every night my father inspected me from top to toe to make sure I'd kept myself clean. And the dramas we had about a mud stain, or a loose thread – you can't imagine.'

'Well, that must have been a great nuisance for you, but you can't wear that coat much longer because it will soon fall apart. Crispin – you wouldn't …?'

'No,' he said, very decisively for him. 'Darling, the amount of pin money you receive may be magnificent – in fact, I'm sure it is – so magnificent that you simply don't know what to do with it, and I'd be doing you a service if I took some of it off your hands. But no, you must not give me things – really, you must not.'

'What nonsense. If you were rich, you would give me presents, wouldn't you?'

'Certainly. I pass sleepless nights wrapping you in sables and diamonds and cloth of gold – which does nothing to help my insomnia, quite the reverse.'

'And yet you will not allow me to buy you a simple coat?'

'I will not.'

'Is that logical?'

'No. But is it logical for you to refuse to come to my lodgings? Verity, I shall wheedle and cajole, I warn you, and grow angry and shed a few tears, so you had better come now and save us both the trouble.'

And I could not tell him, for perhaps I did not know, that my hesitation was in part due to his bold, black-eyed, exceedingly common landlady, Mrs Dinah McCluskey, who had told me, at our brief meeting, how much she valued his good opinion.

But in all other ways my life flowed on, that summer and autumn, with astonishing serenity. I supervised the affairs of my household; I engaged a governess, a music teacher, and a drawing master for Caroline and found Mrs Paget a place with Emma-Jane, who, with nine sons already and the likelihood of nine more, would need a nurse for many years yet. I spoke, sensibly I thought, to the headmaster, Mr Blamires, about the progress of Blaize – who did not appear to be progressing in any useful direction – and of stubborn, surly Nicholas. I spent lazy, gossiping afternoons with Mrs Stevens, lulled by the beckoning tones of her voice. I discussed pregnancy with Emma-Jane and the lack of it with Lucy Oldroyd, took tea with the Reverend Mr Brand and conveyed his messages to Hannah, leaving her in no doubt that she was sorely missed in Ramsden Street. I took my carriage exercise up and down the town and smiled warmly at Colonel Corey whenever he raised his hat to me. I gave dinners for Joel's colleagues, friends, enemies, anyone he wished to use or make envious or impress. And when Squire Dalby came to tell me that he wished to marry my mother I gave my consent and was instructed by Joel – who could see the advantages of having a squire as a father-in-law – that I should do my utmost to persuade her.

Morgan Aycliffe came home in the autumn, thinner and greyer but wearing his new authority well, a sombre, deep-purple aura about him that, after six months at Westminster, spoke already of state secrets, the crushing burden of high office.

'He should have been a Roman Catholic,' my mother said, 'for he would have made an excellent cardinal. One can imagine him, so sleek and sinister, flitting among secret passages with vital documents concealed in his sleeves and a great ruby ring with poison in it too, I shouldn't wonder. Oh dear, perhaps it is just as well that cardinals are not allowed to have wives.'

And indeed, I could detect no signs of improvement in his relations with

Elinor. He had acquired, certainly, something of the professional politician's automatic charm of manner, enough at any rate to supply me and Emma-Jane and Lucy, the wives of his principal supporters, with such details of the London scene he thought would please us. We learned of the animosity between the King and the Duchess of Kent, mother of Princess Victoria, the royal heir, and her determination to act as Regent should he die before Victoria became eighteen. We learned of the savage disposition of the King's brother, the Duke of Cumberland, and how it would suit him if Victoria never reached eighteen, so that the young princess lived in constant fear of kidnap or murder or worse.

We learned, too, that the present government, which had given us the franchise, could see stormy waters ahead – very stormy – yet the exact details of tempest, flood, or act of God were not considered fit for ladies, could only upset us, and were reserved strictly for our husbands – who would be unlikely to tell us – and for Hannah, whose nervous system, while remaining ladylike, was evidently considered by Morgan Aycliffe to be superior.

'He can never marry her, you know,' Elinor said one evening as we sat alone in the drawing room. And as her dainty, pointed face crinkled with smiles, these last few bleak years seemed to have been wiped away from her, and she was her old, irrepressible self again.

'What a thing to say, Elinor, when he is married to you.'

'But that is exactly why he can never marry her. A man cannot marry his wife's sister, even after her death, which seems rather unfair since what difference can it make when one is under ground. But, at least, they have nothing to gain by murdering me, have they?'

And although the trill of her laughter filled the room – adorned again, I noticed, by some of its more valuable objets d'art – I remembered my mother's airy description of secret passages and poisoned rings, and I shivered. Not that I believed Morgan Aycliffe capable of putting down a stray dog with his own hands, much less murdering his wife, but that could make it no easier for Elinor – the pretty one, who had expected so much from life – to know that this old, grey man, having once lost his head on her account, considered her now simply a nuisance and a bore.

Yet, that night, it did not seem to trouble her greatly and, noting that she had the late Mrs Aycliffe's pearls around her neck again and a new sapphire on her hand, a new sky-blue satin gown from Miss Boulton, an air of pert assurance, a certain awareness of her own worth that the Barforth side of me recognized and approved, I wondered if she had at last come to terms with her situation and herself and elected to make of it the best she could.

As to my relations with my own husband, I cannot think that he, at least, was aware of any change. He was extremely occupied that year, with his new mill, his new lightweight cloth, the branch line to Cullingford, which was soon, it seemed, to materialize and make him – the possessor of abundant railway shares – an even wealthier man. He was busy with engineers and architects, designers and craftsmen of all kinds, who swarmed thick as August flies at Tarn Edge. And when he

264

was at home, he discussed footage, acreage, mileage, profit, and – since profit was happiness and he was determined to be happy – the necessity of making more.

I saw Rosamund Boulton too, often enough, at her shop, and judging by her forced smile and her strained, tight-lipped courtesies, I suspected that profit was all Joel cared to discuss with her these days too. And profit there certainly was, for Miss Boulton's business was thriving, spilling over into the shop next door, where she had opened special departments for the sale of shoes and shawls and garments of a more discreet nature, direct – or so she said – from France. But affluence did not appear to suit her, for she was often ailing, prone to unexplained backaches and headaches and attacks of ill temper, relying more and more on her fresh-faced young assistants to spare her the necessity of making herself pleasant. And, although Estella Chase had gone to London in the spring and remained there long after her husband came North for the grouse, Joel was himself in London two or three times that year, in Liverpool and Manchester more than he need have been, I thought, if railway business had been the only attraction, and, glimpsing Miss Boulton's face in an unguarded moment, I concluded she knew rather more about that than I.

'So your husband has gone away again,' Elinor said to me one morning towards the end of the hot weather. 'Well, mine will be off again before long, and I shall not grieve over it, for I find Mr Adair much easier to manage.'

And, patting her skirts and her ringlets, preening herself as she had done as a girl but with an allure now that belongs only to a woman, she put her head close to mine and murmured through a half sigh, half laugh, 'While we are on the subject of Mr Adair – and naturally I would say this to no one else, Verity – I do believe the foolish man has taken it into his head to fall in love with me, which is quite impertinent when one remembers that five or ten years ago he was nothing but a common bricklayer. Yes, only think – my husband left me in Mr Adair's charge because I could not be trusted with the spending of my husband's money, and now all I have to do is flutter my eyelids and sigh when the bills come in – which never succeeded at all with my husband – and Mr Adair has not a word to say. Not to me, at any rate, although certainly explanations must have been made to my husband – and good ones too, since he has not reprimanded me either. And that, you know, is certain proof that Mr Adair is clever and cunning as well as most obliging. I must thank him – if I happen to remember it – when I see him again.'

'Not too warmly, I hope.'

'Good heavens, no, Verity, dear – a bricklayer? Hardly. But enough to put him firmly on my side, for there is something else … Oh well, I really shouldn't tell you this, but since I am going to anyway I had better tell you now, at once, and all that can happen to me is that I will have longer to feel guilty about it.'

'Oh dear, Elinor –'

'No, not yet. I have done nothing yet, but Mr Adair is not the only one

265

who has been paying attention to me lately. It is Bradley – Bradley Hobhouse – and there is no need to stare, because you know very well he would far rather have married me in the first place, if his mamma had not made such a fuss about money. Well, he has been looking at me again – exactly as he used to – which is hardly surprising when one looks at Emma-Jane, who reminds me of nothing so much as a cottage loaf.'

'Yes, so she does, but then Bradley is no feather either.'

'I should say not,' she said, chuckling quite greedily. 'But he carries it well, Verity. He eats and drinks and sleeps, he's fat and good-humoured and easy, he's pleasant … Oh, don't be alarmed, I'm not thinking of running away with him again. He can barely afford the family he has, much less take on a second, and poverty would suit neither one of us. It's just that, on the days when he has been looking at me, I feel better than on the days when he hasn't – unless Mr Adair has been looking, which, just now and again, rather makes me tingle inside and makes me wonder – oh, quite wicked things. It does me good, and that's enough – really – quite enough. For now, at any rate.'

Take care, I thought, yet I was not the one to speak to her of the sanctity of the marriage bed, to remind her of loyalty and true dealing, when I had seen precious little of either, when I was myself, in fact, entirely true to no one.

Life, it seemed, was movement, transition, and a time would unavoidably come when I would be forced to take a step backwards or forward, to open a door, to say goodbye to Crispin or not say goodbye to him. And since I could not, at that moment, visualize, much less solve, the problems of our remaining together, I chose not to think of them at all. I would allow myself this season of good weather, this time of youth which, having eluded me at sixteen, had come to me now, ten years too late. And when the days cooled and clouded over, when the moor was wind-racked and rain-scoured with November – when winter deprived us of our hiding place – then would be time enough for contemplation.

27

Ann Agbrigg died that winter, an early casualty of the cold weather and her own careless wanderings, having too little interest in life, perhaps, to cling to it. She died in complete silence, a death merely of the body, the spirit having long since withered. And, standing at her graveside, I understood her husband to be far beyond consolation.

'Naturally, I went to them at once,' Hannah told me, 'and although Mr Agbrigg eventually arranged everything as I suggested, he was quite strange. She had been dead for some hours when I arrived and he was still sitting at her bedside, in the dark, and was quite sharp with me when I covered her face and sent him away. One simply cannot afford to brood, especially when there are children to be considered, and I must admit I was shocked to hear Mr Agbrigg say he would gladly give his children twice over to have his wife back again. Oh, I know people are apt to say wild things at such times, but Mr Agbrigg was quite calm, quite matter-of-fact about it, and, with everything considered, I cannot excuse his behaviour to Jonas. I have always known Mr Agbrigg to be a hard man, but to accuse Jonas of being glad of his mother's death – relieved, he said, because now she could embarrass him no longer in front of Mr Blamires, nor hold him back from his grand ambitions – well, I find that hard to forgive.'

'But it's true, Hannah – surely?' I said, remembering young Jonas Agbrigg's careful, crafty eyes, and she shrugged, making an impatient movement with her hand.

'Well, of course it's true. She would have been an embarrassment and a hindrance to him. I know that and you know it, but Jonas, who has an excellent disposition, could have no such feelings about his own mother, and it was wrong of his father to suggest them to him. She was a hindrance to her husband, too, whether he likes to think so or not, for she had no notion as to the management of her household affairs, and if Joel means to make him manager at Lawcroft, as I believe he does, the poor woman would never have settled here. She would have gone wandering back to Simon Street at every opportunity, and I suppose what is making him so bitter is that he knows quite well he should not have taken her away from there in the first place. He must have been aware of his own capabilities, even as a young man when he first went courting, and he should have chosen a girl who had it in her to grow with him.'

And so Ann Agbrigg was laid to rest by a husband too bitter for tears, and a month later, Ira Agbrigg, the parish apprentice, who knew neither his real name nor his exact age, was appointed manager at Lawcroft and invited to occupy the millhouse where, long ago, he had come to tell my mother of his workmates' intention to riot.

'We should do the house up for them, don't you think?' I suggested to Hannah, expecting her to take care of it herself, but her own affairs were coming to a head just then and, glancing up at me from her breakfast-time correspondence – a great deal of it to do with Mr Aycliffe – she said absently, 'Yes, for Mr Agbrigg will not dare to change anything – or will not think of it. If you can prevail upon them to get some good chintz covers for their parlour chairs you will do them a service, Verity. And Jonas should have Edwin's old room, I think, for the fireplace there is the only one that does not smoke, and he will need a good fire to study by. And speaking of Jonas – and since I imagine you will be having a good sort-out before you move to Tarn Edge – there is a bookcase in the back spare bedroom doing nothing at all. If you should care to make Jonas a present of it he would be much obliged. In fact, if you are agreeable, I will arrange for it to be delivered at once, since Tarn Edge is nowhere near completion and Jonas must have somewhere to put his books.'

But, in fact, our move to Tarn Edge could not really be so far distant as Hannah envisaged, for, under Mr Daniel Adair's expert eye, the walls were growing into the recognizable shape of a house, each brick, each pail of mortar advancing the moment when Hannah must name her wedding day. Certainly Mr Ashley expected it, and Mr Brand lived in dread of it; even Joel, whose scathing eye had seen from the start that Mr Ashley would never become a bishop, was reconciled, had already made some grudging financial promises. And when Mr Ashley was offered the living of Redesdale, some fifteen miles away, Patterswick Church being required now for a relative of Squire Dalby's, we knew there could be no more delay. She would have to marry him now and content herself with the affairs of one parish, or she would have to break with him and expose herself once again to the onslaught of Mr Brand and the sheer inconvenience of the single life.

'I thought in the spring,' she told me at Christmastime, having already made an excursion to Redesdale, with my mother as chaperone, to inspect the church and parsonage and to ascertain the disposition of the local squire's lady – a feeble creature, it seemed, too occupied with her dozen or so children to give Hannah much trouble. 'Yes, Easter,' she said, quite decidedly.

And so Mr Ashley ate his Christmas dinner at my table, in peaceful, placid silence, willing to fetch and carry and smile when one asked him to, willing to be married or not to be married, offering no opinion of his own even on the vexing question of Irish church reform, which, Mr Aycliffe declared, could well bring the government down in the new year.

Elinor was there too that Christmas day, and her three little girls, three dolls identically dressed in blue satin frocks and lace pantalettes, three pairs of round blue eyes and three heads of elaborately wired ringlets, shading from light brown – Crispin's colour – to Elinor's pale, silvery gold. Three little mouths too, which never spoke a word since Morgan Aycliffe believed that if children must be seen then they should not be heard, and he was much inconvenienced all day by the noise my own children made, by Caroline's constant bids for attention and the sorry spectacle of Blaize and Nicholas coming to blows for no better reason than an inborn desire for combat.

'He started it,' Nicholas shrieked, probably quite correctly.

'Well, come and finish it then,' Blaize taunted, grinning wickedly, bracing himself to receive the full weight of his brother's irate body which knocked the pair of them to the ground in a pummelling, biting-and-scratching back-alley tumble which was every bit as lethal as it looked. And when Joel, who had not been unacquainted with back alleys in his younger days, took them both by the scruff of their necks and booted them through the door with instructions to go and kill each other somewhere else, Morgan Aycliffe's horror at the prospect of damage – not to young bones, which would heal, but to the hall furniture, which would not – was so great that Hannah took him away to the library for a soothing discussion on church tithes and whether or not we should send troops to Portugal.

'They're just boys,' Caroline explained with infinite condescension to her Aycliffe cousins, who had no experience of the species. And since

268

there were times when I too found boys somewhat trying, I settled the four little girls around me and for half an hour told them the fairy tales of my own childhood, my old Marth-Ellen's legacy to me.

Faith and Cecilia, the two younger Aycliffes, curled up beside me in the big chair, barely listening, lulled simply by my voice and a physical contact to which they, raised entirely and impersonally by nurses, were unaccustomed. But Caroline, who had heard the stories before, was concerned largely with her dress – the cloud of pink gauze over silk she had found on her bed that morning – her new coral beads, her newly pierced ears, threaded temporarily with silk ribbon, with the doll wearing an exact copy of her own party frock, its dark ringlets tied up, like hers, with pink velvet. And Prudence, the eldest and plainest of my nieces, was clearly unimpressed by the quality of my entertainment; did not, perhaps, set much store by fairyland at all.

'That can't be right, Aunt Verity,' she said suddenly, frowning at her narrow, immaculately shod feet. 'If the princess was so silly as to keep getting herself caught over and over again by that dragon, and then putting everybody to so much trouble to rescue her, I don't see how she could have been a good queen. She should have helped herself more.'

'Oh, darling, yes, but it's just a story.'

'Well,' snorted Caroline, who would, without doubt, have made an excellent queen, 'I'd like to see you set about fighting a dragon.'

'I would,' Prudence said, her chin resolute, 'if I had to.'

'No you wouldn't. You'd run. You'd run screaming for your mamma.'

But the idea of running to Elinor for assistance was so foreign to Prudence that, frowning again, concentrating hard, she was about to justify her claims to courage when Caroline, not altogether enjoying the sight of Faith and Cecilia nestling so cosy on my knee, announced scathingly, 'Well, no silly old dragon would ever catch me.'

'And if he did,' I told her, tugging at a stray ebony ringlet, 'then he'd soon bring you back.'

And Caroline, saucily grinning, believing herself, like Blaize, to be my favourite child, made a sudden leap forward to fling her arms around my neck, roughly dislodging Faith, who bore it stoically, and Cecilia, who started to cry, bringing the Aycliffe nanny, who was never far away, instantly to her side.

'Dear me, Miss Cecilia, you've crumpled your frock, which I can't wonder at, sitting so gracelessly. And Miss Faith. Young ladies keep their backs straight, my dears, and their knees firmly together, and never, never do they allow their own backs to touch the backs of the chairs in which they are sitting.'

And with her pale eye telling me that, with my shoulders comfortably supported by cushions, I was setting something less than a good example, she took her charges away.

'Verity, dear,' Elinor said, slipping her arm through mine, 'shall we have a headache, you and I? We have nurses for the children, and Hannah for my husband. Joel is bored with all of us, and Mr Ashley will not even notice we have left him alone. Come upstairs and let me tell you how Bradley Hobhouse took quite five minutes to help me into my cloak last night at the Assembly Rooms, and how Mr Adair positively swelled up – yes, just like a toad – with jealousy. Oh, I can't tell you how much I liked that, Verity. Do come upstairs, because I want to talk and talk and talk about it, and we'll be quite wicked, shall we, and ask Mrs Stevens to bring us a bottle of wine, or two. This coming year is going to be good to me, Verity. I can feel it.'

We celebrated the new year – Elinor's year, as she kept on insisting – with a charity ball at the Assembly Rooms, a glittering, fancy-dress affair, the proceeds of which, with tickets at two guineas each, would be considerable – to be used for the relief of our ever-increasing poor. And although few of the men, if any, would condescend to fancy dress, believing their evening clothes to be quite fancy enough, competition among the ladies was murderous.

'They will all dress up as queens,' my mother told me when I asked her advice. 'Depend upon it – and heavy queens too; a dozen Elizabeths, with ruffles and stiff brocades, and as many Mary Stuart and Good Queen Phillipas, so very well wrapped up in wimples and long sleeves. And they are right, of course, since most of them will not suffer from being wrapped up a little. Now you, Verity, I wonder – since, Elinor in the mood she is in, will certainly do something spectacular – have you thought of what you mean to do yourself?'

'I rather hoped you would do it for me.'

'Yes,' she said, smiling, well content with herself these days, since a proposal of marriage from a High Tory squire, even if she had no mind to accept it, was no mean achievement for a woman of her age and origins. 'That is what I supposed. In fact, I have a small idea … Should we, perhaps, give some thought to the Empress Josephine, Napoleon's lady?'

'Should we? And how was the Empress Josephine?'

'Oh, light as thistledown, in transparent muslins and gold sandals, with bare feet with gold lacquer on her toenails – Grecian and wicked. Quite a simple costume to arrange, since I have the very dress you need upstairs in one of my boxes, a dress I brought with me when I married, and of which your father's mother did not approve. Shall I fetch it? I have the gold sandals too.'

'And the lacquer? Surely not, Mother?'

'Why, yes,' she said, making her face very innocent. 'Times were much freer when I was a girl, you see, for we still had our wicked Prince Regent, who was very much in favour of painted toenails. Unfortunately, once again, your grandmother did not approve of mine, and by the time she died I had rather passed the season for such things – so you may reap the benefit of it. Your husband may not approve, of course, for you will be rather more naked than he is accustomed to see you in public, but the surprise may be no bad thing. Few husbands actually looked at their wives, I find, unless they have a reason to do so, and it does no harm, now and then, to provide a reason.'

And her tone was so airy, so totally without guile, that I knew she had something very specific in mind.

Yet the dress, when it came out of its wrappings, was an enchantment, high-waisted, narrow, the merest sketch of a sleeve leaving arms and shoulders quite bare, the muslin so light that the feeling of nakedness was at first shocking, and then, as I moved so weightlessly, so pleasantly without my petticoats, altogether exhilarating. And although I doubted if, by wearing it, I would inflame Joel's lasting passion, which, in turn, would banish Crispin from my mind – as my mother clearly hoped – the thought of fluttering Emma-Jane's feathers – and Hannah's – was too much to resist.

I took the dress home with me, with the shoes and the gold paint, and I added my pearls. I arranged my hair in a casual Regency tumble as my mother had shown me – a boyish head almost, with a woman's body all too visible beneath the shimmering fabric, bare painted feet so outrageous that even Mrs Stevens, who, in her day, had paraded her nakedness every bit as daringly as this, became quite nervous.

'What will Mr Barforth say?'

And, indeed, as he came into my bedroom, busy with his shirt studs, I believe that, at first glance, he thought I was still in my petticoat and, thinking more of his own appearance than mine, was about to tell me to hurry. But the unusually heavy perfume – also borrowed from my mother – catching his nostrils, bade him look again, and Mrs Stevens had her answer, for what he actually said was 'By Christ, you don't mean to go out dressed like that, do you?'

'The Empress Josephine did.'

'Aye, I daresay. But not in Cullingford.'

'Don't you like it?'

'Yes,' he said as I turned away from the mirror to face him, letting the diaphanous, shimmering material float against my body. 'I like it. In fact, I like it so much I'm forced to the conclusion that it's not decent.'

'Well, before you judge it indecent, I'd best tell you my mother wore it as part of her trousseau – and the young ladies of her day wore them damp so they'd cling even more. Come, Joel, you're old enough to remember narrow gowns like these.'

'So I am,' he said slowly, the tolerant good-humour draining out of his face, leaving him irritable and strangely displeased. 'So, I believe you have a shawl, at least, and you'll surely have need of one. The biggest, I reckon, you can find.'

The frowning strangeness of him – reminding me not of Joel Barforth at all, but of the pinched, tight-lipped prejudices of a Morgan Aycliffe – sent an unaccountable, altogether wicked delight coursing through me, causing me to twirl and sway once again, close to the lamplight.

'Of course I have a shawl, and I shall wear it like this, just slipping off my shoulders, like the Empress Josephine. Whatever can be wrong with that?'

'Not a great deal,' he said, most amazingly angry. 'Except that every man who sees you like that is going to be well aware that the rest is worth seeing. I'm surprised that it doesn't trouble you.'

'And I'm surprised that it should trouble you.'

271

And possessed again by that demon of wicked delight, I draped myself under the lamplight, threw out one hip slightly so that the fabric clung to the outline of leg and thigh, revealing one scandalously painted foot, and asked him, 'Would you like me to take it off?'

My reward was a bitten-off exclamation of anger, the nervous clenching of a fist, and a certain tightening and darkening of his whole face.

'Get your shawl,' he said in the voice he used to issue notices of dismissal at Lawcroft and Low Cross. 'And before we set out may I remind you that because you have dressed yourself up like an adventuress there is no need to assume the manners of one. Your shawl and your fan, then, if you don't mind – we're late already.'

And throughout the drive to town, as I sat beside him wrapped in dark blue velvet, my hands clasped inside a swansdown muff, he did not speak a single word.

The Assembly Rooms were most festively ablaze, spilling long shafts of light out onto the road, where a good number of the poor for whose benefit we were assembled had gathered to jeer and stare as we disported ourselves on their behalf; then crowed with delight when the Hobhouse horses, just in front of ours, slipped on the frosted cobbles and Emma-Jane, massive now both in pregnancy and out of it, required three men to help her down.

'You'll have to get rid of them,' she told Bradley furiously, not making it clear whether she meant the populace or his none too sprightly, none too well-matched greys, and taking my arm and Joel's, she allowed us to lead her up the shallow steps into the black-and-white-tiled hall, leaving her husband behind to see how much harm had been done and how best it could be patched up.

She had dressed herself as an ungainly Elizabethan, in a huge, red velvet skirt with a white ruff squashing the soft flesh under her chin and puffing out her cheeks: a hot, heavy costume that would exhaust her before the night was done. And filled suddenly by a sheer, wicked delight, determined to enjoy myself whether Joel approved of me or not, I let my cloak slip from my shoulders, handed it to the retiring-room woman, and, lifting a deliberately languid arm – as the Empress of the French would surely have done – adjusted one of my boyish, kittenish curls.

'Verity,' she said, a most alarming flush mottling her heavy cheeks, 'just look at you, Verity Barforth. If I didn't know better I'd think you were nineteen.'

And there was anger in her, and accusation, for how could I flaunt myself like that, how dare I be thin and rich when she was fat and they were beginning to lose their money?

'My word,' Bradley Hobhouse muttered, flushing in his turn as we went to join our husbands on the stairs, his eyes flickering eagerly over me from top to toe. But Emma-Jane would have none of it.

'Take my arm, Bradley,' she ordered, her plump cheeks quivering. 'You know very well that I'm to be careful on the stairs. You know what

272

the doctor said, and I'm only here at all because you wanted to come and didn't feel right about turning up without me.'

And although Joel smiled at her offended back, his eyes were not angry but watchful, calculating, and still he had no word to say.

There would be no possibility, I knew, of seeing Crispin that night, for he was in the Midlands, on a lecture tour of country towns, staying in pleasant wayside inns and the homes of the local gentry and flirting, no doubt, with some squire's daughter, exposing me to the raw misery of knowing that nothing held us together but our combined desire, that nothing compelled him to return to me – the misery, indeed, of knowing that it would be logical, merciful even – better for him, better for me – if he did not return at all. And perhaps the shimmering cobweb of a dress and my scandalous painted feet were no more than steppingstones to help me walk away from the spectre of his loss.

'Verity,' Hannah said, a severe Mary Stuart in plain black silk and white widow's cap, looking more like a nun than a queen, 'that dress is really very skimpy. Put your shawl higher up around your shoulders and it will not seem such a bad fit.'

But pale Mr Ashley, quiet and clerical and anonymous as ever, blushed like a girl and looked another way.

I did not expect Mr Aycliffe's approval and was not disappointed, although Mr Daniel Adair, an indispensable member of the Aycliffe entourage nowadays, let his merry Irish eyes roam over me with an appreciation that was altogether wholesome.

'You're a fine woman, Mrs Barforth,' those eyes said, 'and there's nothing in the world pleases me better than that.'

Elinor was enthusiastic, vocal, generous in her praise. 'Go home,' she said, stamping a tiny, saucy foot. 'Go home at once. Nobody is going to look at me now – off with you.'

But, as she well knew, she was in no danger of being overlooked. She had come as Marie Antoinette, her costume modelled on one of her husband's china figurines, her favourite sky-blue satin with an enchanting lace apron, cascades of lace at sleeve and hem, the first Mrs Aycliffe's pearls wound tight around her throat, a high white wig that gave her pointed face the translucence and delicacy of porcelain. She had lace at her wrists, too, knots of it on her shoes, lace ribbons floating from her high-piled coiffure, a wide lace sash set with fresh flowers; she was, in fact, so very much the dainty feminine ideal men dream of that even Joel – who had had no word of praise for me – put a brotherly hand under her chin, turned her face towards him, and said, 'Very nice – and if you could stop chattering for five minutes, I'd say very nice indeed.'

The room was hot and bright and very full, a jungle of potted plants lining the walls, the musicians earning their fee strenuously, a ball like the dozens I had attended here since the opening night, with hostesses fussily trying to outdo each other and the hostesses before them, and mothers bringing their daughters to market, offering them proudly, sadly, desperately, to men who knew exactly how much each one was worth; women like Emma-Jane, whose desires had shrunk to a cup of tea and a soft armchair to drink it in; like Hannah, who despised herself for needing a man at her side; and like Elinor, who, having made up her mind to live again, unashamedly wanted them all.

'Well now,' Joel said, turning to me at last, 'will the Empress Josephine condescend to dance?'

And as we moved away through that mass of anxiously stitched, anxiously compared costumes, born of ideas which had seemed so bright at the time, so totally original until one met a dozen like them on the stairs, I saw Elinor hesitate a moment between Bradley Hobhouse and Daniel Adair, and, as she made her choice, I saw Emma-Jane flop down indignantly into a chair and Mr Adair walk scowling away.

I went to sit by Emma-Jane when the dance was over, submitting myself to the details of her latest baby's feeding, how James was almost as tall now as Thomas and little Freddie was talking and walking much sooner than the others. But she was anxious and angry, feeling the heat, hating me in my airy dress yet needing me, since not even the progress of Freddie, her favourite child, could distract her from the spectacle of Freddie's father dancing a second time with Elinor.

'I'm not well,' she said in a bewildered fashion, for she was quite unaccustomed to jealousy. 'I shouldn't be here at all. I can feel my ankles swelling, which is what the doctor said would happen. Will you tell my husband, Verity, that I am indisposed?'

And getting up, knocking over one of the spindly, gilt-legged chairs in the awkwardness of her suffering and of her vast velvet skirts, she rushed off to the retiring room, where someone would have a smelling bottle and a stool for her swollen feet, and sympathy for a woman who had always unfailingly done her duty as a wife.

'Emma-Jane is unwell,' I told Bradley when the moment came, but, shrugging those bulky, lazy shoulders, he merely swept me into the dance.

'Aye, she's breeding again and shouldn't have come. She'll throw up a time or two, I reckon, and be as right as rain after. You're looking grand, Verity – you and Elinor – what a pair you are – although I can't take to that manager of Aycliffe's, that bog-trotter, whatever his name is – Adair? Well, makes no difference to me what he calls himself, because they all look alike and they all sound alike, but if he speaks sharply to me again I'll flatten him.'

Yet Mr Adair, when he danced with me some time later, having lost Elinor once again to Bradley, had enough finesse to conceal his annoyance, understanding that the last thing a lady wishes to discuss with her partner is another lady. And so Mr Adair, with enormous charm of manner, kept his eyes on my face, no matter how much they wished to go looking for Elinor, and even when we collided with her and Bradley during a waltz and she allowed the impact to throw her briefly into Bradley's arms, he refused to be distracted from his task of convincing me that I alone was beautiful. A clever man, Mr Adair, I thought, who would not pursue his employer's wife without encouragement – no matter how old and frail her husband appeared to be – who would need

274

to be very sure before he made a move, and it occurred to me, if not to Emma-Jane, that Elinor's sudden interest in Bradley might be less obvious than it seemed.

Yet Bradley it was who took Elinor to her champagne supper at midnight, sitting on the floor at her feet while his wife and Elinor's husband remained quite forgotten, Emma-Jane in the hands of the retiring-room woman, Mr Aycliffe in consultation with a group of his electors.

Rosamund Boulton was not present, although her handiwork was much on display, but Estella Chase, lately returned from almost a year in London, arrived a little before midnight, in some indeterminate costume of dull green crepe which, although I could not have put a name to it, suited her very well. She looked careless, haughty, a stalking thoroughbred too sure of herself to worry that her back hair was coming down, extending a limp, not particularly well-manicured hand to the many who rushed to present themselves to this second cousin of our manorial lord, although it was clear she remembered no one by name and saw no reason to try.

But my mother, who had been dining that evening with the Coreys and could be a Dalby any time she had a mind, was unimpressed, and slipping her arm through mine, she said, 'Dearest, do you remember Mrs Chase? Yes, yes, dear, I am sure you do if you try. Colonel Corey's daughter? Colonel Corey, I believe you know my daughter, Mrs Barforth?'

'Indeed I do,' he said. 'My word, indeed I do.' And because of the money he had lent to Crispin – because he might even know that Crispin and I were lovers, since his son, Mark Corey, knew it – my mind was too busy to assess the glance Estella Chase exchanged with Joel until it was over.

He danced with her once, no more, keeping his polite distance, saying little, taking her back to her father and making his bow. Yet after that he danced with no one else, taking his stand by the refreshment-room door and helping himself from time to time at the punch bowl, a spectator with eyes half closed, watching her dance with other men and watching me too in a way to which I was not accustomed, which made me uncomfortable, half afraid, with his mouth hard, his expression morose and unfriendly.

'Has your husband's dinner disagreed with him?' my mother murmured, but before I could properly reply – before I could tell her that the shimmering, cobweb of a dress had not succeeded – there was a hand on my arm and a whispering voice advising me that Mrs Hobhouse was really quite unwell and had asked for me.

She was, in fact, on her feet when I reached the retiring room, colossal with rage, purple at the injustice of a world where she, who had never done anything wrong, who had been a devoted wife and mother, could be forgotten – simply forgotten – while a silly, mincing chit like Elinor Barforth, who had married that disgusting old man for money when she had failed to get her hands on Bradley, should be floating on air, the centre of attention, with Bradley – so at least a dozen people had told her – sitting at her feet.

'Didn't you tell him I'm not well?' she shrieked at me. 'I've been here for hours – hours – and what is he doing? Has anybody brought me my supper? I could starve and nobody would care?'

And as the retiring-room woman and I attempted to calm her, Elinor, who had certainly followed me and overheard the whole, came tripping into the room, fanning herself with a dainty, quiet cruel hand.

'My word,' she said, 'you do look seedy, Emma-Jane. Quite green.'

'Spiteful little cat,' Emma-Jane hissed, lunging forward to strike a wild blow which did little harm. 'You've always been jealous of me – always wanted whatever I had. Well, if I lose this baby you'll be to blame.'

'Oh, as to that,' Elinor said, the trill of her light laughter somehow filling the room, reminding me, if no one else, of those far-off days when she'd had to beg a ride in Emma-Jane's carriage and say 'please' and 'thank you' for an unwanted length of cotton, 'I wouldn't dwell on that, Emma-Jane. I expect you could spare a baby or two. You'd hardly miss it.'

'Wicked,' Emma-Jane said, a sob in her voice. 'Wicked girl –' And, coming between them – Emma-Jane weeping bitterly now and Elinor shaking with glee – I took my cousin by her lovely, tipsy shoulders and bundled her from the room.

'That, Elinor, is enough. The poor woman is quite hysterical, and you don't really want her husband, do you?'

'Of course I don't want fat Bradley. Fat Emma-Jane can keep him. But it's nice, isn't it, Verity, to know I could take him if I wanted him? So nice. Take him and ruin him, because he knows I'd be no good for him, that he can't afford me, and yet he still couldn't resist … Verity, don't be cross with me. You've had the men at your feet tonight too, so you must understand. They own us, after all, don't they, and this is the only way we can strike back – make them desire us until it hurts them, and then run away. That's the game, dearest, isn't it? I'm no fool. I'll keep on running, keep on smiling and promising and then saying no. What else have I got to do – how else can I tell the difference between being awake and being asleep?'

'Oh, Elinor,' I said, despairing suddenly for both of us. 'Elinor, what a world this is.' And there, in the narrow landing by the retiring-room door, we flung our arms around each other, careless of wigs and laces and fine muslins, careless of prying eyes, and hugged each other tight.

'My word, how very moving,' a hard, sarcastic voice told us, startling us both since we had heard no one approach, startling me even more when I saw the taut, ill-tempered lines of Joel's face, with something written between them which I could not in any way decipher.

'You were a long time gone,' he said, tight-lipped. 'And it crossed my mind to wonder what the devil … However, now that I've found you, I have to say that this whole affair is quite tedious, and we can be on our way.'

'Oh, but it's only half over.'

'No, no, Mrs Barforth. I've ordered your carriage and so I'd say it's quite over.'

276

'Well, I'm sure I don't care either way. Good night then, Elinor. I'll call tomorrow.'

'Good night,' she said, looking nervous, tearful, her hand sketching an almost childish gesture of farewell as I went off to retrieve my belongings and then hurried to meet Joel, awaiting me in the hall.

Jealousy, could it be that? But jealousy of my affection, suspicion, or a more primitive reaction, the basic instinct of a predatory male who, while making free with other men's wives, does not wish anyone to gaze too closely at his own? Jealousy. And if jealousy meant fear of loss, as I understood it, then would losing me mean more to him than an assault on his pride? And if he cared more, or differently, than I had believed, if my light-headed flaunting of myself in my mother's old gown had indeed aroused something in him, stripped me finally, in his eyes, of my aura of girlhood, of our too close kinship, if it had done that, then surely I must go as far as I could to meet him.

'I am base enough to know I would not sacrifice it,' Crispin's voice said to me from far away, an echo of our first lovemaking, but it was clear to me now that the sacrifice would soon have to be made, and would have to be made by me, not only for my children's sake but for Crispin's too. He could not exist forever waiting, wasting his talents and himself, at the Red Gin.

And, if my husband held out his hand to me I would have no right to refuse. Nor would it be wise to question his motives. Perhaps he had seen me tonight as a desirable woman who could at last challenge and excite him. Perhaps it was simply that, having had enough of philandering, mellowing now that his middle years were within view, his mind was turning to a deeper relationship, finding less satisfaction in chance encounters. But, whatever it was, I must accept it, must work with him to nurture it, must no longer be afraid of the potent male in him which I had always felt unable to satisfy. I must admit to myself, finally and forever, that I too had held back from him, unwilling to risk my emotions with a man who had aroused such storms in other women, who had so casually broken hearts and reputations. I must now take that risk, must give in order to receive.

'Joel,' I called out, holding my cloak snugly around me, covering my offensive nudity, 'I'm here.'

But as we walked out into the crisp night, there were two carriages at the door, our own and Colonel Corey's, with Estella Chase waiting peevishly to be handed inside.

'I will bid you good night, Mrs Barforth, Mr Barforth,' she said, each word a sharp-edged stone flung in Joel's face, her own face pinched with cold fury.

'Good night,' he answered brusquely, almost pushing me into the carriage, his intention to ignore her so plain, so rude, that even the coachmen must have known that there had been harsh words between them, even the coachmen must have pitied the poor little wife who seemed so unaware of the tension crackling and snarling from one to the other.

Jealousy? Of what? I had wondered. Jealousy of whom? Had it really been my lovely, gleaming gown, my painted feet, my posturings in the lamplight, or – as so often before in Joel's life – had it not concerned me at all? Had he wished to leave early on my account, thereby annoying this haughty woman who had counted on having him to herself? Or was he taking me home merely because he had had a tiff with Mrs Chase, who was leaving too? And although I had no answer I was no longer so ready to make a sacrifice.

<h1 style="text-align:center">28</h1>

I do not think it had been part of Daniel Adair's original plan to make love to Elinor. At their first acquaintance she had been a frail, capricious woman with no will of her own and very little spirit, and although it may well have occurred to him that her frequent bouts of ill health were rooted in emotional and sexual dissatisfaction, I believe he had no intention – while her husband lived – of attempting a cure. Daniel Adair, crafty and ambitious, lighthearted and warmhearted, a man for laughter rather than tears, would have been content to bide his time, for Morgan Aycliffe, by the look of him, could not last forever, and Elinor, as a wealthy widow with no sons to demand their share of the Aycliffe fortune, would be a glittering prize. Naturally, Mr Adair would have made some attempt to possess himself of her affections well in advance of her husband's demise, since there would be other bees in plenty circling the honeypot, but a woman may give her affections without risk, provided she does not give her body along with them, and Mr Adair, who could afford to buy his pleasures, was in no hurry.

But Elinor's fresh awakening to herself as a woman, her remembrance of the power her beauty gave her over the men who desired it, her delighted, determined skill in making them desire it the more, put a different face on things. Elinor the ailing little mouse, Elinor the featherheaded spendthrift, could be easily dealt with by a resourceful man, easily frightened or flattered into good behaviour, but Elinor the enchantress of other women's husbands – Elinor who, if left to herself, would certainly get into trouble and might, like Crispin before her, lose the Aycliffe inheritance altogether – such an Elinor was a threat to Mr Adair's schemes and, I have never doubted, a temptation to his own vigorous sensuality.

Perhaps Elinor had not intended him to make love to her, either. Her body, accustomed to serving an old man's hurried, awkward demands, was completely ignorant of sexual fulfilment. To her the sexual act had first seemed a joke, then a nuisance, then an ordeal to be got through as quickly as possible whenever it could not be avoided altogether; and it was a man's admiration she required – a man at her feet, not in her bed.

But when Morgan Aycliffe returned to London for the start of the parliamentary session in February, she allowed Daniel Adair to kiss her one afternoon – feeling herself perfectly safe simply because it was afternoon and fornication, she believed, could only take place at night – and, finding the experience decidedly unusual, quite unable to understand why a man's mouth on her mouth, could have such a strange effect on the pit of her stomach, she was unable to stop thinking about it, unable to rest until he had kissed her again. And even then it was a game. They dined together that night, making Elinor's account books their excuse, the Aycliffe housekeeper hovering between them, and afterwards, in the library, supposedly going through those conveniently muddled accounts, she bolted the door and offered him her mouth again, then her bare arms and shoulders, and found, to her amazement, that even by pressing herself into his arms she could not get close enough, that her thin silk gown was a barrier, as solid as a brick wall, which she could not tolerate. And so she tore the barrier down, fell on him, starved and parched by her ten dry years, and then, when her limbs had flooded with a pleasure she had not believed in, she lay purring blissfully against his shoulder, submissive and bemused, convinced beyond all question that no one but Daniel Adair could make this marvellous thing happen to her. And, in those early days, all that mattered was that he should make it happen again and again, with no thought of what could come after.

It was a wonderful spring that year, fragile, pale blue mornings, lemon-yellow afternoons, cool, hyacinth-scented evenings, opening the moorland pathways, freeing me from winter restraints, so that once again I could walk out to Old Sarah's Rock and the hut beyond it. I knew we had survived the winter mainly because Crispin had gone away at the start of it, to the Midlands and then to London, putting real distance between us, which had been far easier to bear than the few impossible miles from Lawcroft to the Red Gin.

It had offered us the opportunity to drift apart, an opportunity we should have taken and had, perhaps, meant to take, but as I pushed open the creaking door on that first blustery March morning and saw him there, still in his old blue coat, the winter months evaporated and we had never been separate.

'What I dream of,' he said, 'is waking one morning and finding you there, knowing you've spent a whole night beside me. Now, is that too much to ask – one poor little dream?'

Yet he had other dreams in his head just then, having spent the winter with men of his own kind in an immense exchange of ideas and ideals, culminating in his meeting with the radical politician Francis Place, who, although he was not to publish it for some time to come, had already worked out the themes of his People's Charter.

'Being with him was a revelation,' Crispin told me, his face thinner than ever from his December diet of good conversation. 'I can't tell you how exciting it was, listening to him expressing the views I've always shared and never quite put into words. I kept thinking: Yes, of course, I know that. I've always thought that, except that I'd kept it in the background of my mind until he released it, with just a few simple words. It was almost like falling in love – recognizing yourself in another person, as I did with you – or suddenly realizing one has a religious vocation. He

279

drew all the loose threads together for me – after all, he's been a professional politician for a long time and he can speak convincingly and persuasively as they all do – but the feeling of actually finding a man one can believe in was quite overwhelming. And quite astonishing too, since I thought I was the cat who walks alone and had no great capacity for belief in anything except my own personal bits and pieces. It makes one feel far less lonely.'

'Good. I'm very glad for you.'

'Darling – are you jealous of an old Westminster warhorse like Francis Place? Then I shall believe in him all the more.'

'Yes, yes – but what does he believe in? What shocking things are you going to be advocating in next week's *Star*? You had better tell me, so I may keep it away from Hannah, for she upsets herself very much and goes on and on at breakfast time. Is it very revolutionary?'

'My word,' he said. 'I am more powerful than I supposed, if I can disturb Miss Hannah Barforth's tea and toast. Yes, I fear it is quite extreme and will appeal to no one in Cullingford but the residents of Simon Street. He believes, as I do, that government should be concerned with the individual, not with property, and so he advocates one man one vote, as I have always done, whether or not that man possesses a penny to call his own.'

'Definitely a measure for Simon Street.'

'Quite so. And to avoid the spectre of the millmaster standing over the new voter with a whip in one hand and an eviction notice in the other – my word, what a picture, I must get someone to sketch it for me, and include it with my article – well, the way to avoid that, of course, is to have a secret ballot. My father – and your husband – would merely say we were giving the common man the freedom to sell his vote three or four times over, and naturally, some would do that. But the majority would vote as they saw fit. Wouldn't they?'

'Yes, yes, I suppose so – they would vote for Mark Corey instead of your father.'

'They could even vote for me.'

'For you? How can you stand for Parliament yourself? You have no money.'

'Exactly. I could not support myself in office, and, in Francis Place's opinion, I shouldn't need to. He wishes to abolish the property qualification for Members of Parliament and to pay them salaries like any other professional men.'

'Oh well – I see now why you believe in him.'

'Because it is to my own advantage? Yes, and why not, if I feel I have some contribution to make? But aren't you shocked at the idea of men like me filling the House of Commons – men without property put there by the mass of the people who have no property, either? Doesn't it excite you?'

Irritated perhaps by his enthusiasm, I gave him a typically Barforth answer. 'Why should it? What advantage could there possibly be to me?'

'None,' he said dryly. 'None at all.' And then, understanding that this

280

fine flaring of his opportunities, this opening up of new vistas, could hardly be pleasing to me, shackled as I was to Cullingford, he put his arms around me so gently that for a moment my heart stopped and I feared he was about to bid me goodbye.

I went home determined to be glad for him, for if Francis Place should ever find the means of throwing open the parliamentary career to men like Crispin, then his future could be bright indeed. And what did it matter that I would remain here, with no real future of my own, a part of Joel's destiny, since that was my fate in any case? But that afternoon, taking my usual drive with Elinor, I found myself struggling against a murky, altogether uncomfortable envy, for her love was still a newborn miracle and mine, perhaps, was coming to an end.

Next morning, having reached the same conclusion, Crispin was pale with anxiety as I walked towards Old Sarah's Rock. He began immediately to talk about nothing, a great rush of words weaving themselves skilfully, whimsically around my good intentions, telling me that our parting, like all painful events, would come in its own good time and that there was nothing I need do about it today.

He was, of course, more deeply in debt than ever, for no one seemed to pay for either his lectures or the journeys they involved, while the *Cullingford Star* and certain residents of Simon Street could be relied on to devour his meagre allowance well before the month-end. And although he would not take a penny from me, declaring no gentleman ever borrowed from a lady, his ban did not extend to all members of my sex.

He had borrowed, quite substantially, I knew, from a spinster aunt somewhere in Wensleydale, and there was always his bold-faced landlady, Mrs Dinah McCluskey, widow of the terrible, seventeen-stone landlord of the Red Gin, who had died, some two years ago, in a brawl involving her honour.

'She's a good soul,' Crispin said cheerfully. 'And pretty well fixed since her husband died. She doesn't mind if I'm behind with the rent. It pleases her to have what she calls a gentleman living in her attic, and I amuse her too.'

'I daresay. She couldn't be in love with you, could she?'

'Well, I honestly don't see why she couldn't, except that I'm a trifle lightweight for her taste. Her husband was a mighty man, and there are one or two just like him at her beck and call. And I cannot even dazzle her with my learning since she sees very well that I fail to make a decent living by it. If she were a man, you know, and loved you as I do, she would run off with you whether you liked it or not. And when your husband came to repossess you she would make short work of him too.'

And I saw no point in protesting that I was no mere object, to be repossessed like a bale of dress goods, since that was my condition exactly.

Yet my awareness of defeat corresponded with a great flowering of Elinor's spirit, a lovely reaching out that put peach bloom and rose bloom in her skin, gave depth to her voice and the colour of her eyes,

281

thrusting her from her prolonged, neurotic girlhood to a wonderful, gold-tinted maturity. And I watched, with sympathy and envy, as she passed from her trance of sexual desire to that far more perilous state of love.

'What do you mean to do?' I asked her, as my mother only last summer, had asked me. 'What future is there, Elinor?'

As I spoke the words, my mother's voice came to me from that same long-past season warning me – or warning Elinor through me – that melancholy men like her husband, to whom life appears a burden, are usually very slow to lay it down.

'I shall be patient,' she said. 'What else is there? I shall be sensible for the first time in my life – and patient.'

'You mean you will wait for your husband to die?'

'Yes,' she said, settling herself down against the blue velvet upholstery of her carriage, her eyes quiet, her face totally serene, as if the death of Morgan Aycliffe was as natural to her as the blending of one season into another. 'That is exactly what I shall do. Does he deserve more of me than that?'

'And will Mr Adair wait too?'

'Oh yes – can you doubt it?' she said, her eyes sparkling with mischief, her mouth gentle with the knowledge and acceptance of the man she loved. 'Of course Daniel will wait, Verity. I am not such a goose – I know how much the money – Morgan Aycliffe's money – means to Daniel. I know that is why he flirted with me in the first place and worked so hard to make me rely on him. I know, darling. But that is not the way of things now. He loves me now, Verity.'

And I had no cause to disbelieve her, for Elinor had always been lovable, and now, glowing with these new, vibrant shades of womanhood, she would have been hard for any man to resist. And Daniel Adair, at least, was not a cold man. Ambitious and hardheaded, certainly, but with a reckless side to him and a romantic side, with a heart that could be moved to love and persuaded to faithfulness.

'He will probably cheat your daughters of their dowries,' I told her, quoting my mother again. 'And he may beat you when you misbehave. But I think you'll be happy – I hope so, at any rate, Elinor. I do hope so.'

'And you'll continue to receive me when I'm plain Mrs Adair, and Emma-Jane Hobhouse turns up her nose at me because my mother-in-law was a washerwoman?'

'I will.'

'Even if Joel condemns me for giving Daniel control of the business, instead of him? Because he won't be able to stop me, Verity – there'll be nothing anyone can do to stop me.'

And clasping my hand suddenly with a fierce, desperate grip, she closed her eyes and said, 'Pray that it happens, Verity, for if I pray myself I may give offence, and then it could all go wrong. Please, Verity, it's not that I want him dead, it's just that I want to be alive myself, which doesn't sound quite right, but you'll know what to say. I don't shock you, do I? It's not my fault, dearest; surely it's the law to blame, and those who made it – the ones who allow no escape from an unhappy marriage but death. No divorce, no separation without the husband's consent, just death – his or mine. I could have died, last year, many a time, without even weeping for myself, and he wouldn't have wept for me, either. But not now. I have never felt so strong, Verity. I wake up in the mornings – and you know how frail I used to be in the mornings – and now I could fly. Really I could; straight through the walls and away above the smoke. And I can't lose that feeling, can I? I can't let anything stand in its way.'

No escape from an unhappy marriage but death, yet I had never thought of Joel as anything but overpoweringly alive, a vital force dominating the lesser lives around him as my grandfather had done. And when I tried to place myself in widow's weeds, with Joel's money – my money – in my hands, and the freedom to dispose of it, and myself, as I thought fit, my mind faltered. I could not, in fact, even contemplate Joel's death, much less welcome it, and when I attempted to force myself, I was shaken, totally appalled.

Yet a great distance had opened up between us lately, a coldness that made him difficult of access and difficult to please. He was an irritable presence at table that summer, behind a newspaper, a drift of cigar smoke on the stairs, a closed study door.

Apart from his infidelities, of which I was supposed to know nothing, he had never treated me unkindly. He had been unfailingly generous, had made me lavish gifts, never questioned my spending, had praised me and protected me. But now, since the night of the dance, his easy, tolerant affection had gone.

'Is it veal again? Do we eat nothing else at this house?'

'But, Joel –'

'Damnation – I'm sick of it.'

'Then what would you like to eat? You have only to tell me.'

'The housekeeping is your affair, madam, and I'd hope, after all these years, that you could get it right.'

And when, the following evening, there would be beef or lamb, salmon or pheasant from Dalby Hall, all of it succulent, well seasoned, well garnished, he would eat in a silence I found more unnerving than his complaints.

Nor did his displeasure confine itself to the dining room. It came to bed with us too, invading an area of our lives upon which I preferred not to brood. I had feared, after Crispin's first lovemaking, that my body would be unresponsive to Joel and had been amazed, had wondered about myself, when this had not always proved to be the case. Yet now there were nights when Joel would take me roughly, without skill, deliberately denying me pleasure he had once been so determined to arouse; there were other nights when pleasure eluded us both, when his mood would fluctuate alarmingly from annoyance to something I dared not call tenderness, from an urge to blame me for my inadequacies to an even more alarming urge to apologize, almost, for his own. And at such times, as tense and awkward as I had been on my wedding night, I was confused, intrigued, often very afraid.

283

'Does he suspect you?' Crispin asked, looking out over the dry, summer moor as if it made no difference.

'No. I am sure he does not. He wouldn't brood about that, not Joel ... Crispin, it's time, isn't it? Isn't it?'

'No,' he said, hands playfully on my shoulders.'Not yet. I don't know why, but not yet. Just a little longer, Verity. I have a strange feeling something may happen to help us.'

But as I walked back alone that morning towards Lawcroft it seemed far more likely that something would happen to destroy us, or to destroy me, at any rate, since, if the storm broke, I would warn Crispin, somehow or other, to make his escape. And so heavy-laden was I by this certainty of my doom that I was not surprised, just terribly afraid, when Joel's phaeton, which should have been at Tarn Edge or Low Cross, swept in through the gates and hurtled sickeningly towards me.

It could, of course, be nothing more than a spot of engine grease on a shirt cuff which brought him home, to change it for a fresh one, but my whole guilty body flooded with a blind panic that, ironically, became my own punishment, the cause of my heartbreak.

'Dear God,' I heard myself whisper, and my dog, my companion of these ten years, pressing close to my side, caught the spark of my fear and, before I could stop her, went streaking off down the drive towards the man and the carriage, the hooves and the wheels that menaced me.

He made, I think, an effort to avoid her, for his horse had cost him several thousand guineas and he had no mind to break its legs, nor his own, by taking a tumble. But my bitch, who had been a coward all her life, having found her courage, persisted, snarling at those long, lethal legs, snapping through the flying dust and stones and curses, the screaming, rearing horse, as the phaeton swayed, righted itself, and went clattering on, leaving behind a twitching sprawl of yellow limbs.

She was dead when I reached her, blessedly, for I could not have borne the helpless, bewildered ending of a good beast who has never heard of heaven, much less learned to hope for it. But even without that, it was too much and I was myself amazed at the grief that forced me to my knees on the gravel beside her, and unlocked a flood of tears I thought would never end. She was dead and, putting my face against hers, paying her the only tribute I could, I saw, on the insides of my eyelids, my brother Edwin, who had given her to me on my sixteenth birthday, a hundred years ago. And remembering him, my tears flowed faster than ever, my sobs became clamorous, painful, hurting not only my chest but my ears.

I neither knew nor cared what had happened to Joel, whether he had overturned or bolted, or simply driven on regardless, but suddenly his boots were there, and his hand clenched around his driving whip, Joel standing over me as he had done once before, when my brother was dying in my arms. But he had been excited then, exhilarated by the violence of the night and by another man's murder he knew he could use to suit himself, whereas he was angry now and disgusted and more than ready to be unkind.

'Get up,' he said. 'Get up – get up. It's a dog, no more. It's not one of your children lying there. It's a damned dog.'

And when I couldn't get up, could in no way explain to him that I was weeping again for my brother and my father, for Elinor and for myself – for him too, perhaps, in some recess of my mind – he hauled me to my feet and snarled, 'Stupid girl – you have no one but yourself to blame. If you can't control your damnable animals then you shouldn't keep them.'

'I could control her.'

'The devil you could. Well, that's an end to it, and I'm not sorry. You can stay at home in the mornings now, like other women, for there'll be no more dogs – hear me? – no more. Do you hear me?'

'I hear you.'

'And if you bring one into the house behind my back I'll shoot it – understand?'

'I understand.'

'Now get inside,' he said, at a point of fury where he would have struck me, I think, had not the grooms and the gardener and Mrs Stevens all come running. 'Get inside, before they all see what a disgrace you are. Get your work basket and sew, like your mother, or sort out your linen cupboard – do something women are supposed to do. Get inside.'

And recognizing my peril, I ran.

But I was bereaved, brokenhearted, inconsolable, not even wishing to be consoled, since I could tell no one what that nervous, obliging animal had meant to me. And although I grieved for her own sake, her death had also been the symbolic ending of my love for Crispin, a brutal amputation performed, just as symbolically, by Joel. I had no dog now, no reason to walk to Old Sarah's Rock, and I would never have another, for even if Joel would permit it, no other dog could ever take the place of that foolish, faithful yellow bitch, given to me so casually by Edwin on the last day but one of his young life.

I dreamed of my brother that night, my sleeping brain, in the moment he fell mortally wounded across my knees, giving him Crispin's face, so that it was Crispin I mourned, cradling his body in my arms, hard gravel underneath my knees, until he became in turn my dog, my brother again, and I awoke suffocating in the heavy dark, my ears straining for a new anxiety. And there it was, the noise outside my door, a clumsiness that could not be Joel, who always entered silently in the night, whether he had been drinking or not, or who, if he wished to wake me, did it decisively, with a branch of candles in his hand. And because I had been dreaming of violence, of that kitchen knife in my brother's chest – in Crispin's chest – I sat up and waited, trembling, with no thought of escape. A sacrifice.

But then as the door was shouldered open and I saw the familiar silhouette, the height and breadth I recognized, I called out 'Joel?' enquiringly, wondering what ailed him.

'Who else?' he snapped. 'Damnation – take the filthy things from me, for I must be out of my mind.'

And suddenly, in the darkness, something landed on my chest, an amazing, squirming tangle of limbs and sharp claws and cold noses that gradually, a tail here, a bright saucy eye, an eager little tongue there, became not one but two puppies, one gold and the other a dark brown chocolate. I don't want another dog, I thought. No, I don't want either of you. But the feel and the smell of them enchanted me, and within seconds I was laughing – and crying – fighting them off and hugging them, squealing myself now as their sharp excited puppy teeth made free use of my bones.

'You said I couldn't have another dog.'

'Yes, and I meant it too. And then I got to thinking how it was your brother who gave you that crossbred bitch, so now you have two from your husband. Purebred, the very best gun dogs money can buy; wasted on you, I reckon. And I'd be obliged if you'd keep them out of my way, and make damn sure they're reliable before we move to Tarn Edge. Now, get them out of my bed, Verity. Fifteen miles I had to go for the little brutes, to Keighley and back, with half a bottle of brandy inside me or I might not have gone at all. I'm tired.'

'Thank you, Joel,' I said. 'Thank you very much.'

And by the time I had settled them down in my old dog's basket by the kitchen fire, laughed at them, cried over them, and hurried back upstairs, he was almost asleep.

'They're beautiful, Joel,' I said, my hand on his shoulder.

In that state of half sleep, half unknowing, he turned his head against my shoulder and murmured, 'Of course you're beautiful – I've always thought so.'

And I have always believed that, had it not been for Elinor, the coldness between us would have been over.

29

In July of that year, the Prime Minister, Lord Grey, resigned, an event leading, some weeks later, to the return of Morgan Aycliffe, who, like others, had come home to test the mood of his electorate should the Whig government topple altogether. And the day of his homecoming brought me a hastily scribbled note from Elinor, begging me to dine with them.

'Bring Joel if you can, but if he is engaged come yourself, with Hannah or alone – please, please, don't fail.'

But when I arrived in Blenheim Lane, with Joel and Hannah and even the Reverend Mr Ashley in tow, whatever panic she may have felt at facing her husband again had subsided, and she greeted us calmly, warmly, displaying, in fact, so much self-possession that even Mr Aycliffe himself seemed impressed.

'How very nice,' she said, 'that we are all together again,' and as she shepherded us gracefully into the dining room I saw her husband's eyes slowly assessing her, wondering, perhaps, if this new, mature Elinor was a fit mate for him after all.

'The beef is excellent, Mrs Aycliffe,' he told her, obviously if pleasantly surprised, and, leaning back in her chair, eating little herself, she acknowledged his compliments with immense composure, surveying us all quite lovingly, as if, in the overflow of her heart, she had more than enough tenderness to spare.

'Really – quite delicious, my dear,' he said, and she nodded, smiled very slowly, a woman at last, serene and perfectly balanced and beautiful: a worthy partner of any man's labours.

She showed, that evening, a most enchanting courtesy to all of us, listening with a rapt attention she certainly could not feel as her husband and mine talked of business and politics, drawing from Mr Ashley the tale of the badly repaired parsonage at Redesdale, which had occasioned yet another delay in Hannah's marriage, showing more affection to Hannah herself than I had seen in years.

'My little girls will be your bridesmaids,' she declared. 'Prudence and Faith in pink and Cecilia in white, I think, since she is so much smaller – and it will all be quite perfect. We shall have such pleasant summer days together, Hannah, for I will often bring the children to visit, and Jonas Agbrigg may come with us any time he likes. I know you will wish to keep yourself informed of his progress and if I keep an eye on him you may worry less. Everything is going to work out so well, darling – everything – I feel it.'

'Are you all right?' I whispered as the confusion of leave-taking enabled us to have a private word, and, smiling once again, as if her great inner joy would be more than enough to sustain her, she pressed her cheek briefly, lovingly, against mine.

'Oh yes. He is here, but he will go away again.'

'And you can endure it?'

'I must. After all, I have endured him for ten years, and I think I may endure a little longer. If he comes to my room tonight – and it is not at all certain that he will – I shall not think of him at all. I shall think of Daniel, and by closing my mind to everything else I shall survive.'

'I do believe my little sister is growing up at last,' Joel remarked as we drove home. 'Tonight she really looked like Mrs Morgan Aycliffe, and damn me if Aycliffe didn't think so too. He'll be taking her back to London with him, I shouldn't wonder, which may not please all of us – eh, Hannah? – but you can't deny it's where she ought to be.'

And if Hannah understood his hint that her influence with our first Member of Parliament might be coming to an end, she ignored it.

But perhaps it plagued her just the same, thinning out her sleep as other anxieties thinned mine, so that we both slipped abruptly into wakefulness when the hammering started, the terrible night-wailing of some desperate creature, gone mad or pursued by violence, or by justice, to our door.

'Stay here,' Joel commanded, reaching hastily for a dressing gown. 'There's no telling who it may be.' But I think I knew, and I was there, in the hall, with the servants and the hastily lit candles, the excited, delighted yelping of my puppies, as he opened the door and Elinor, with

287

only a thin cloak over her nightgown, ran inside, a hunted creature brought to bay, cowering from everything that moved until she saw me and fell, panting and wet through, into my arms.

'God Almighty,' Joel said blankly, and Hannah, her lips chalk-white – for only tragedy of the first magnitude could cause a woman, even Elinor, to run half naked through the night – demanded, 'The children? Mr Aycliffe? Are they dead?'

And standing there with her collapsed body slumped against me, not even listening to the words she was pouring into my ear, I said, 'No. Send the servants away, Hannah – Joel – immediately.'

And when they had done it and come to stand one on either side of me, hard-eyed now and suspicious, I told them, 'She can't talk to you now. I shall take her upstairs and put her to bed.'

'What lunacy is this?' Joel said.

'What disgrace?' Hannah echoed, and drawing Elinor closer to me, I said, 'She has left her husband, or he has turned her out – and, either way, I shall take her upstairs, for she is not even half conscious and you will get nothing from her. Wait for me in the study. I will be down presently.'

And I suppose it was because they were so unaccustomed to receiving commands from me that they obeyed.

Mrs Stevens had lingered on the first landing, knowing her own usefulness in times of crisis, and together we dried Elinor's feet and the tangle of her hair, found her a fresh nightgown, a clean, lavender-scented bed, hugged her and kissed her and told her the pain would go away, the fear would go away, although we all knew otherwise. And gradually we pieced together the tale I, at least, already knew, that she had held firm, sure of herself and her ability to safeguard her future, until the moment he had put his hands upon her. And then, sickened by the conjugal rights her new maturity had encouraged him to reclaim, she had at first refused and finally, when he persisted, had lost her head and told him all.

'I couldn't,' she said simply. 'I thought I could. Until the instant he got into my bed I was sure of it, for I'd been doing it all these years, but after Daniel, it wasn't the same. For a moment or two I was mad with terror, quite mad, as if Daniel was my husband and Morgan Aycliffe was an intruder, a criminal. And so I said things, and he knew. He's an old man – he smells old, feels old. I couldn't.'

And, throwing pitying arms around her, Mrs Stevens murmured, 'Yes, darling, I know, I know.'

They were waiting for me in the study, Joel leaning against the fireplace smoking. Hannah sitting straight-backed, rigid with shock and shame and some honest anger that this would damage her own relations with Mr Aycliffe. And both of them, brother and sister more alike now than ever before, turned hard, accusing eyes on me as I came into the room, having clearly weighed me in their personal balance and, as Hannah had always expected, found me wanting.

'So,' Joel said grimly, 'are you in a position now to make explanations?'

288

'If you like.'

'Like? No, I don't like this at all – none of it, for I never heard of a woman who left her husband, and Aycliffe would not turn her out without good reason. There is another man, then?'

'Of course there is,' Hannah cut in, her fists clenching and unclenching with suppressed fury. 'What else, what else? Yes, indeed, and I think, Joel, that you would do well to require your wife to be frank with us, to inform us of the man's identity, since we cannot doubt she knows.'

And, meeting her eyes, nodding slightly, he said, 'Verity?' – the quiet menace of his tone making me well aware of the thin ice on which I stood.

'It is Daniel Adair,' I told him, wondering why I was so calm, why I remained unafraid when, abruptly turning his back, he gave the short, unpleasant laugh that warned of danger, while Hannah, white then red again, became so tight with anger that I felt the strain of it in my own bones.

'Yes,' she said, 'a bricklayer. How apt, how typical. One would expect better judgement from a kitchen maid. And while we are speaking of judgement, Verity.'

'Indeed – are we speaking of that?'

'I fear so. And I find it an unpleasant task to be obliged to question your own. May one ask when you first became aware of this – this criminal association? For everything in your manner tells me that you knew of it long before tonight.'

'Yes, I knew. I knew from the beginning.'

'Of course you did. And failed, for reasons I am sure my brother will find hard to understand, to take any responsible action. Failed to inform either him or myself, as you should have done.'

But Joel, swinging round to face us, instead of taking me to task as I had expected, dreaded, said harshly, 'Leave that. For now, at any rate. We have Elinor to deal with first, and Aycliffe. And I'm damned if I know what's to be done.'

Hannah, the sister who had never yet failed him, met his eyes again, her answer ready.

'There is only one thing to be done, Joel, and, with your permission, there is no need for Verity to be involved in it. We must take her back, now if possible or early tomorrow morning, before it becomes the common gossip of the town. If anyone saw her running through the streets in that lunatic fashion, they will hardly have believed the evidence of their eyes. I think we can shut our own servants' mouths and feel reasonably confident that Mr Aycliffe will know how to do the same. But the longer the delay, the greater the risk. Come, Joel.'

'And if he won't have her?'

'It is very much in his best interests to do so. There may well be a general election before the year is out, and he cannot be allowed to ruin his career. He cannot afford a scandal, for although he is the victim in this case the *Cullingford Star* would not take that view. He will be well aware of that, once it is pointed out to him, once Elinor has been prevailed upon to plead for pardon.'

'He will not pardon her,' I said very softly.

Again she spun round to me, her eyes ablaze. 'No, and I do not expect it of him. No one could expect it. It is merely necessary for him to behave as if he had.'

'And she will not plead with him, either. Not tonight, at any rate.'

'What do you mean by that?'

'I mean that she will not be going home tonight. She will be staying here, as my guest.'

'You have no authority,' Hannah said, spitting out each word like an angry cat. 'No authority to offer her shelter under my brother's roof.'

'Rather more authority than you, Hannah, I think.'

And as she snapped her mouth tight shut to hold back her outraged words, Joel said coldly, dangerously, 'You will apologize for that, Verity, to my sister.'

And still I was not afraid.

'Presently, Joel. But Elinor is your sister too, is she not? And I wonder why you are so ready to send her back to that spiteful old man who does not really want her, who has not wanted her for a long time, without even hearing what she has to say.'

'She will have no choice,' he said. 'If I deny her shelter, and the decision is certainly mine, where else can she go?'

But having found my courage, like my old yellow bitch who had not hesitated to charge a horse and carriage for my sake, I knew I could go on.

'I think there must always be a refuge, Joel, if one looks hard enough. She could go to my mother, at Patterswick, I believe.'

'And if I forbid you to take her there?'

'Then she may go alone, if she is determined and sure of her welcome, for my mother is entirely free to offer hospitality as she pleases. And no one but Elinor's husband may legally compel her to return, should he so desire.'

Amazingly, instead of giving vent to his temper, he stared at me for a moment and then turned his back again, the fingers of one nervous hand drumming against the mantelpiece, one irritable foot tapping against the fender.

'Joel,' Hannah said, 'we are not obliged, surely, to listen to this foolishness?'

And then, realizing that Joel was listening only to his own thoughts, refusing to communicate with either one of us, she turned again to me.

'Does it surprise you that my brother is at a loss for words? Setting aside all moral issues, you may be certain that if Elinor persists in this madness her husband will know how to defend himself. He will admit no financial claims, and she will never see her children again.'

'Ah, no. But then, how much does she see of them anyway, with the nurses and governesses you have found for them, and the house so full of precious china they are hardly made welcome in it. Do you really believe she would miss them?'

'It is her duty to miss them,' she thundered. 'And finally, one way or another, she must learn to do her duty. Joel, we are wasting time here. We should go back to Blenheim Lane at once.'

But, inexplicably, Joel's back was still turned, his eyes apparently held by the fan of pleated paper that filled the summer hearth. Finding it easier to address his lounging shoulders than scowling, brooding face, and hoping, I think, in some recess of my mind that he would finally turn to me in sympathy and understanding to take my part instead of Hannah's, I began to speak quickly, knowing that her claims on him were very strong and that she would not allow me much time.

'She is your sister, Joel, and entitled to your support. She may be foolish and capricious, and difficult, I admit it, but she was seventeen and young for her years when that man married her. She thought marriage was a new silk dress and sleeping late in the mornings, and now, when she knows what it could have been, she's in despair. All I ask is that you talk to her when she's calmer, treat her like a woman for the first time in your life and give her the opportunity to defend herself. She has been badly treated too, you know. Yes, Joel, you know she has.'

When he still would not answer me, when even the slight movement of his hand and his foot ceased, shrouding him in a choking silence. Hannah shot him a puzzled, reproachful look and then spoke the words she had expected him to say.

'Yes, indeed. Very badly. A beautiful home full of well-trained servants. Three healthy children. A decent, intelligent husband with a successful commercial career behind him and what may well be a brilliant career in politics at his feet. Nothing in the world to do but issue her commands and spend that man's money. And she betrayed him!'

'It does not surprise me, Hannah.'

'I daresay.'

'And if he is honest with himself it should not surprise Mr Aycliffe, either. He will not be so heartbroken, you know, for he has never loved her.'

'I dispute that. I know him better than you do, and had he not entertained the deepest feelings for her he would not have married her.'

'What nonsense, and you know it. He married her on a sensual impulse, probably quite foreign to his nature, which he has regretted every since, for once it was satisfied he had very little use for her. And that was his own fault, Hannah, not Elinor's, for he was old enough to have known better. And so was Joel, for that, when he consented to it. But she was not. Well, I suppose he is not the first man to lose his head in middle life over a girl young enough to be his daughter, and one can sympathize with that. But there was no need for him to turn peevish, to neglect her when he no longer found her exciting in his bed. Hannah, he has virtually ignored her these past two or three years, and however well-intentioned your motives, you have encouraged it.'

'How dare you say that to me.'

'It seems I dare. What did he expect when he went off to London and left her alone? He deserted her – yes, yes, that is the right word, deserted her – because she bores him and ages him, reminds him of what a fool he once was, and because he feels uncomfortable with the children and is afraid of having more. Yet no one blames him for that. He is coldhearted and selfish. Whether you are prepared to admit it or not, if you are strictly honest, you must know that her loss would not grieve him. And I also think, Hannah, that you should question your own motives. Why are you so determined to send her back? Is it Elinor's relationship with Mr Aycliffe that you are so anxious to save, or your own?'

She raised her hand then, fist clenched, to strike me, I think, but the habit of dignity was too strong, and lowering it, twisting her hands together, she hissed, 'Be careful, my girl, very careful, unless you would have us question your own morals, as I have always questioned your mother's.'

And her scathing 'my girl' was, finally, too much.

'If you are making comparisons, Hannah,' I said very clearly, making sure she heard and understood, 'then you have not far to look, for your father was an alley cat where women were concerned, and your brother is the same, with no more consideration for me than your father had for your mother. And Edwin was like them. He would have led you a merry dance, my girl, and you would have had no time then for passing moral judgements on matters you barely understand. You seem to think Elinor lewd, but she has in fact bolted from her husband because she simply cannot bear him to touch her. One can hardly call her sexually depraved for that.'

'Joel,' she said, just the one word, an appeal not only for help but an expression of how deeply she had been wounded, a cry which brought him instantly round to face her, the sister who had so valiantly shared his hard times, whose own life was still far from easy. And I could not tell from the tense, tautly etched mask of his face what it had meant to him to be called an alley cat, whether he had heard or cared, whether he would punish or laugh, whether he would astonish me by asking if he had hurt me, and by being ashamed. Yet I did know, with a sudden flow of feeling that softened me, weakened me, that I had been hurt and that, should he ask for pardon, I would not refuse it.

'I will go to Blenheim Lane now,' he said, his eyes holding Hannah's bending her to his will as perhaps only he could do, ignoring me entirely. 'I may do better, man to man, alone. And until we know his intentions Elinor keeps to her bed, here, under my roof, with no one but yourselves and Mrs Stevens near her. And as for what is between the two of you, you must settle it as best you can.'

He let the door slam shut behind him, and we stood there for a moment, Hannah and I, facing each other, imprisoned in her anger and my newborn freedom from restraint, which had made me cruel.

'I do not like you, Verity,' she said.

'That is your privilege.'

'Yes, and do not think that my brother will ever take your part against me, for he will not. Not in the long term. I stood by him when our father died, and he knows, had Edwin lived, that the Barforth inheritance would have been mine. My loss has been Joel's gain, and he remembers that.'

'Indeed. But the Barforth inheritance belonged to neither of you,

Hannah. Samson Barforth was my grandfather, not yours. The inheritance was mine.'

'Which is why my brother married you.'

'So it was. And you, Hannah, would do well to forget my marriage, and Elinor's, and give some thought to your own.'

'Do not presume to advise me, Verity. I am older than you and have a great deal more sense –'

'But you are a spinster, Hannah, which ignores sense and seniority – and it does not suit you.'

And as her hand shot out at last to hurt me, I caught her wrist and, amazing myself that I could hold it so tight, could so obviously give her pain, I told her, 'I do not dislike you, Hannah; in fact, sometimes I like you very well, and what you think of me makes no difference. But, for your own good – and stop pulling away from me, for I shall hold on until I have done – for your own good, concentrate on your own life and let other people get on as they think fit. Marry Mr Ashley, if you must, although I think Mr Brand would suit you better. But marry someone, for you are no more able to exist alone than Elinor.'

There was, after that, a great deal more, a vast rooting out of grievances, of all the times I had slighted her or mocked her, my odd, unreliable nature that made me so difficult to live with, my inability to appreciate the awkwardness of her situation, such a torrent of resentment that, in the end, Mrs Stevens flowed smoothly through the door, coaxed Hannah away with the little murmurs and gestures of sympathy she had used with my grandfather, and then came back to tell me Elinor was at last asleep.

'Poor child, she imagines Mr Adair will come tomorrow to take her away.'

'And you do not think he will?'

'Oh, dearest – hardly. What do you think?'

'I think he will not come, either.'

'Oh dear,' she said, 'dear, dear – and he will not prove us wrong, you know.'

And patting my cheek, she went sadly away.

I sat then, for a long time, alone in the study, watching the daybreak, the door slightly ajar, so that when Joel returned I could see him before Hannah, yet when he finally came, I had fallen deep asleep and woke with a mighty jolt, his hand on my shoulder.

'It's five o'clock,' he said, dropping heavily into a chair. 'I should be on my way to the mill.'

'You surely won't go this morning?'

'I surely will. I'll lose a day's business on the day I die, I reckon, but not before. So – since I can hardly flatter myself that you waited up to see me safe home – you'll be wanting to know about our brother-in-law Aycliffe.'

And it amazed me that after all I had said he could speak to me so naturally, that he could speak to me at all.

'Yes – will he take her back?'

'Oh, I think something may be arranged. He was very much mortified and felt obliged to speak at length about the wrong done him, and about the sins of the flesh in general. And one can only allow his position to be devilish awkward, for he has lost both his wife and his business manager, and I think, in the long term, he will feel Dan Adair's loss the keenest.'

'Oh,' I said, aware of his shrewd eyes on my face, knowing that although he had spoken lightly his keen brain was probing mine, assessing me, making its calculations. 'Well, poor Mr Aycliffe, for his notions of propriety will never allow him to reinstate Mr Adair, whatever he plans for Elinor.'

'Quite so. However, he means to solve the issue for the moment by returning immediately to London, although if a general election comes, he will have to make up his mind to face her.'

'And Elinor?'

'May stay with us until his further instructions, although he will not contribute one penny to her upkeep while she remains from under his roof, nor may she take anything from his house but the barest personal essentials his housekeeper will put together for her. And she is on no account to see her children.'

'And how are we to explain her presence here?'

'Ilness, and the need to be cared for in his absence.'

'What illness?'

'Good God, how am I to tell? Women are always ailing, and you and Hannah between you can think of something.'

But he did know, had agreed to it, even though he did not like it, and, recognizing the flaring of his temper as a cover for his unease, I said quite coldly, 'There is only one illness which would suffice. A malady of the nerves, like the first Mrs Aycliffe, so that if she persists in refusing to live with him he can give out that she is mad. Joel, how could you agree to that?'

'I agreed to nothing,' he said irritably, flicking open his heavy, silver cigar box and then, changing his mind, going to the door and calling into the silent hall for tea, knowing someone would hear.

'Listen, Verity – and there's no reason why I should even explain this to you, no reason at all why I should put up with your damned insolence. I got her the best deal I could. He would have been well within his rights to demand her immediate return, and if he had and she'd bolted again, and gone on bolting – well – nobody is going to blame a man for locking up a wife like that. But I'm giving her time to compose herself, which is what you asked of me, so that when she does go back she can do it right. Get your feet on the ground, girl, for there's a lot of money at stake. He must be sixty now, or more, and feeble, and when he's gone I want Elinor to have the enjoyment of his money, not see it tied up in those girls' dowries to be handed over to strangers. She's had ten years of him. She's earned her fair share, and she wouldn't thank you, in the long run, if you talked her out of it. She's my sister, after all, as you've pointed out to me more than once tonight.'

The door opened to admit the tea tray, borne by a girl who, not having

294

yet been chastised by Hannah, still showed her curiosity. And when she had gone and he had drunk one cup straight down and poured another, he told me with elaborate nonchalance, 'By the way, he asks that Hannah shall supervise his household while he is away.'

'Should that surprise me?'

'Verity, if you think I forced Elinor's marriage on her, then you have a short memory. She was more than glad to take him.'

'Yes, I remember. She talked a great deal about strawberries and champagne. I remember that very well indeed.'

'Well then – I know as well as you do that he should have married Hannah. I imagine he must know it himself. But how could I have told him so at the time?'

'You couldn't. And if you had not consented he would still not have married Hannah. I know. And if what I said to Hannah tonight offended you, then I am sorry, but she was very rough with me and I saw no reason to take it meekly. I am not sure what I have done to earn her dislike – in fact, I don't think I knew, before, how very heartily she does dislike me.'

'You are mistress of Lawcroft, that is all,' he said, going to stand by the fireplace again, fatigue showing now in the droop of his shoulders. 'It is a position she expected to fill herself – would have filled – and she has always thought herself far better suited to it than you. Just as she has always considered herself a far more suitable Mrs Aycliffe than Elinor.'

'She may be right – on both counts.'

'Perhaps. Verity –'

'Yes.'

'Yes, indeed. By God, I don't know why I should talk to you at all. You said a hard thing of me tonight, Verity. No, no, I don't dispute it. I am not a sound man with women. I never have been – nor was my father. My mother did not take it well, and I had forgotten that she sometimes brought her troubles to your mother, and that you may have overheard.'

'Yes, that is how little girls learn about life, by poking and prying, since no one will actually tell us anything. Elinor knew all about it too, but Hannah denied it – decreed that her father was incapable of such bad behaviour and that her mother was worried simply about the war and the state of trade.'

He smiled, very briefly, his face for just a moment almost kind.

'Yes, Hannah would say that. But, at least, one knew what my mother's feelings were. They were distressing and something of a nuisance at times, but one recognized them, whereas with you, I have never been certain – was not certain until tonight, when you admitted it, that you even knew at all. And I have still no idea – not the faintest idea – what it means to you – if indeed it means anything. And I want to know, Verity – I'm damned if I know why, since I shall continue to suit myself in any case – but I insist that you tell me.'

'My word,' I said, getting up too, feeling very light, as if by a simple effort of will – this wonderful will I had discovered hiding inside me – I could transform myself into air and elude him, elude anyone who sought to hold me down.

'What is this, Joel? You have got everything in the world you have ever wanted. Are you running short of things to want?'

'And what the devil do you mean by that?' he said, his face scowling again, his fist clenching nervously against the mantelpiece.

'I mean, having stirred the emotions of so many other women, do you want mine too? Do you want my jealousy? Think carefully, Joel, for it would be a great inconvenience to you. As you say, you would go on just as you are, no matter how many scenes I made. And I cannot think my hysterics would amuse you for long.'

Once again he turned his back, as he had done several times during the long night, unwilling, it seemed, to expose more of his own feelings than he had to; and when he spoke, after a silence I bore with astonishing calm, it was to the empty hearth, the fire screen, the cold, uncomplicated marble.

'You were a child when we married, Verity. I was a man with my appetites already formed. And you grew up slowly. For a long time I was ...'

'Bored with me?'

'Careful, I should have said – careful with you.'

'And I was most grateful. Will you not at least change your coat before you go down to the mill, for you have had a long drive?'

'Damnation,' he said, a mere whisper addressed once again to the mantelpiece. 'They should have named you Isabella, for your mother. You are not going to tell me, are you, whether I have wounded you or disgusted you or simply made you laugh – whether you hate me or you couldn't give a damn.'

'Oh, Joel, what an idea – hate and disgust. My word, such strong language –'

'Be careful,' he hissed. 'I warn you – take care – for I am not squeamish with women either, and I could find it in me to hurt you.'

But the door had opened again and Hannah looked in, dressed and with her hair done, but seeing me, she disappeared at once, taking his violence and whatever lay beneath it with her.

'It's late, Joel. The servants are all up.'

'Yes. I'll take a rasher or two of bacon, I think, before I go out again. Is there likely to be any new bread?'

'I'll find out.'

'Good,' he said, turning round, showing me his everyday face, the shadows under his eyes no deeper than when he had spent the night in town. 'And by the way, I thought I'd have a word with Dan Adair while I was about it.'

'Oh yes?'

'Oh no, because I couldn't find the fellow anywhere. Went to his lodgings, and one or two other places, and there wasn't a trace. His landlady wouldn't talk because she'd been paid not to, and being Irish, she'd rather take his money than mine, but it looks to me as if somebody at Aycliffe's got word to him and he's blown – halfway across the Irish Sea by now, I reckon.'

And while I wondered how I would find the words to tell Elinor, he calmly selected a cigar, lit it, and, narrowing his tired eyes against the smoke, said, 'And if you haven't realized what a damn nuisance that is, I'll tell you, for without Adair there's no guarantee we'll have Tarn Edge ready in time. And I don't like it – not one little bit – when people let me down.'

30

Hannah set off that morning with Joel, bidding him leave her in Blenheim Lane so that she could see for herself the direction of Morgan Aycliffe's mind; and, returning some four hours later in the Aycliffe carriage, she was by no means pleased to find Elinor's door bolted against her.

'You will hardly deny me the right of access to my own sister,' she told me, her eyes hard, her tone as cold as December river water, and when I answered that it was not I but Elinor who denied her, she did not choose to believe me.

'You may think me meddlesome,' she said, holding herself as if her very spirit was stiffly corseted, 'but your view is not shared by my brother-in-law, Mr Aycliffe, who has seen fit not only to confide in me but to request my services as a go-between. There are certain matters which must be communicated to my sister, and, if she really cannot face me, then I trust there will be no objection if I slip a note under her door?'

But neither Hannah nor Morgan Aycliffe himself had any real meaning for Elinor that morning as she sat at the window of my best spare bedroom, docile and drowsy as an invalid, her hands patiently folded, her nature folded too, half asleep, until Daniel Adair should come to claim her. She was waiting, in fact, for a faithless man to prove his fidelity; for a self-indulgent man to put her interests above his own – waiting, I thought, for a miracle.

But, since miracles could certainly occur and no one had expressly forbidden her to write to him, I provided pen and paper and, quite openly, ordered her short, possibly heartrending letter to be taken round to his address. And while we waited for a reply, which I, for one – and possibly Elinor too – did not expect, I marvelled at her calm.

'He will be very angry with me on the surface,' she said, 'and very frightened underneath. He was so poor, you see, as a child – poor in a way we can't begin to understand – and so a house in Blenheim Lane, and all that goes with it, seems like paradise away. Yes, he will be very cross, and very worried about how to make a living, and about what my husband could do to him – for he has always taken Morgan for a vindictive man, but as soon as I speak to him, explain to him, then I shall make everything right. I have not always been rich myself, which he fails to take into account. I managed for years to do up my own buttons and laces, and my own hair. And you surely remember the skill I had with my needle?'

297

And when she had repeated it all for me for the third time I understood she did not believe a word of it.

Emma-Jane Hobhouse called that morning, having heard a whisper from her parlourmaid, who had a sister in Morgan Aycliffe's service, but Hannah reached the drawing room before me and by the time I arrived Emma-Jane was in full possession of the facts as Hannah had chosen to display them – not lies, since Hannah never lied, but a simple distortion of the truth, for everybody's good.

'Naturally I would not say this to everyone,' she was telling an eagle-eyed Emma-Jane as I entered the room, 'but we have known you all our lives and I imagine you have always thought her highly strung – one minute up in the air, the next wallowing in the mire – our mother was much the same, excitable and delicate; it was always either laughter or tears with nothing in between, and such natures, while delightful, are often fragile. And, as you know, she recovered very slowly, if at all, from the birth of her last child. Not all women are blessed with your amazing resilience, Emma-Jane – those beautiful healthy boys, one after the other, my word. But you will remember how my sister became – well, rather odd, very nearly a total invalid, after Cecilia was born? Yes, yes, of course you do, for you often remarked it, and I have even heard you wonder if it was her failure to give her husband a son which made her so morose. And you may well have been right, Emma-Jane – you may well have been remarkably astute – for these things prey on the mind and depress the spirits, giving rise to swings of mood and temper which must, eventually, result in a certain fraying of the nerves. Well, my sister's nerves are very frayed. I am at liberty to say no more than that. You may think it sudden, Emma-Jane, but we have long seen it coming, and if you think carefully you will realize the many occasions lately on which she had not been herself. Yes? I felt sure of it. No, no, we did not think our local doctors competent to prescribe in such a case. Mr Aycliffe has returned to London for the express purpose of consulting a specialist. Yes, indeed, it is a tragedy; the poor man has lost one wife, has been obliged to disown his only son, and now finds himself with three daughters to provide for, and a wife who is just a shadow – a mere shadow of herself. And on top of that there has been some trouble with the business. Yes, I don't properly understand it, but on his return from London I believe Mr Aycliffe found his affairs in a terrible state – oh my goodness, I couldn't begin to comprehend the details, and no one has mentioned the word 'embezzlement' in my hearing. I only know he has discharged his manager, or, at least, it may even be the man has run off in the night, which sounds unlikely – and would certainly be an admission of something or other. But that is what I have heard.'

When Emma-Jane had gone away, happy to spread the word and even happier to contemplate Elinor in a state of mental decay, Hannah turned to me and said very coldly, 'Do not imagine that I accuse Mr Adair falsely of theft, since he has stolen another man's peace of mind, nor my sister of insanity, since that is the only charitable view I can take of her present behaviour.'

298

Joel came home at noon and, calling me into his study, put Elinor's letter to Daniel Adair into my hands.

'You knew she had written this?'

'Yes.'

'Splendid. Absolutely first-rate, Verity. Tell me, are you part of a conspiracy to ruin my sister, or is it merely that you too have lost your wits?'

'I saw no harm to it since I knew he would be gone. You said yourself he would have bolted ...'

'Yes, and so you allowed her to send this pathetic nonsense to his lodgings, to that landlady of his who was plainly sired by a vulture, and who has just extracted a hundred pounds from me for its return.'

'Oh,' I said. 'Oh no.'

And then, looking at him keenly, I said, 'No, Joel. I don't believe you.'

'And why not?'

'Because you would not have paid. You would have found something to threaten her with in return – and how much could it take to frighten a lodging-house keeper? I believe I could do it myself.'

'Aye, I don't doubt it. But Aycliffe would have paid and Elinor would have paid – a year from now when she is safely back where she belongs – and gone on paying to safeguard her good name. Because a year from now she'll value her place in the world, and she'll be terrified of anything that could remind her husband of the past. She'll have to earn her keep in Blenheim Lane after this – haven't you the sense to see it? – and love letters, my girl, are an indulgence quite beyond her means. Are there any more, do you think? Adair said not. But then, what else would you expect Adair to say.'

'Mr Adair? You saw him, then? He has not gone away after all?'

'Ah no,' he said, his mouth curving with a grim, altogether malicious humour. Opening his cigar box with a leisurely hand, he lit a cigar and inhaled deeply, enjoying his body's response to the tobacco and to the pleasure of making me wait.

'Oh, he bolted all right,' he said at last through the fragrant smoke. 'About as far as Leeds, I reckon, before he got to thinking what a pleasant little thing she is, my sister, and that if she'd had the good sense to bring her jewellery away with her, he might as well come back and dry her tears.'

'He does care for her, then?'

'So it would seem – moderately, at any rate, although five hundred pounds in his pocket and certain promises soon cured him of it.'

I sat down, oppressed not by fatigue but by an immense grey vapour of sadness, wreathing itself around me like the tobacco smoke encircling Joel's self-confident head, his complete certainty that every man could be bought, every woman sold, if the price was right.

'That was handsome of you,' I told him. 'But what if he takes your money and your sister as well?'

And because that was exactly what he would have done himself, he smiled.

'No, no. I thought of that and allowed for it. Five hundred pounds will tide him over, and certainly it was more than he expected, for he knows and I know that I could have had him for less, but it can hardly guarantee his future. He can't go back to Ireland and live like a lord on five hundred pounds – not for long, at any rate – and, if I read him aright, his ambitions are just a little larger than his capabilities. He needs someone to show him the way – like Ira Agbrigg did – and I like hungry men, Verity. I can use hungry men. If he lies low until Elinor is safely home, I may just decide to take him under my wing.'

'And he trusts you?'

'Of course not. But he wants what I can give him, and he knows that if he goes off with my sister he has no chance with me at all. And apart from making that grand gesture and giving him five hundred pounds more than I need have done, I let him know just how and why he could serve me. He can consider the five hundred pounds a retainer if he likes – nothing to do with love letters at all. That's what I'd do in his place. He's not wedded to the building trade, and he's just the kind of footloose charmer I need to sell my lightweight cloth in warmer climates than these. And, in a year or two when Aycliffe's gone, and Elinor has claimed her reward – who knows? If she should still have an eye for him then, which I doubt, I'll gladly look the other way.'

'And where exactly is he now?'

'At the Swan, waiting for me and the afternoon coach. He has a sister in Liverpool – or a woman, at any rate – who can give him bed and board, and since I have business there myself, I may as well use him as a travelling companion. And the more people who see us, the better, for if the dog had really seduced my sister – as somebody may be putting about – then I'd be far more likely to knock him down than ride with him to Liverpool, wouldn't I? So you may talk some sense to Elinor, and then, when I come home in a day or two – and if Hannah has done her work well with brother Aycliffe – we may all be at peace again.'

But, Elinor, it seemed, was at peace already, not with the wholesome serenity of true content but with an apparent refusal to face up to her situation that was as difficult to grapple with as a handful of thin air.

'Poor Daniel,' she said, when I gave her back her letter and told her how it had been obtained. 'I suppose he could do no other, for Joel is very overbearing, and if he insisted on offering money I know my Daniel is not the man to refuse. So, we are to go to Liverpool. Well, I confess I had not thought of Liverpool, but one place is as good as another, and I expect you will be relieved to see the back of me. Dear Mrs Stevens, do run downstairs for me, for I am certain I heard the door, and if there is a letter and it is left too long on the hall table, my sister is sure to waylay it. Naturally she will burn it unopened, for although Hannah may feel free to destroy my letters she would never dream of reading them. Do hurry, Mrs Stevens – and hurry back. Verity, I fear Hannah will be a great problem, for she got in here just now while you were with Joel, and she has the strangest notion that I must return to Blenheim Lane – to my husband. Well, I laughed a little at that. I couldn't help myself, for the very idea of our being together again is quite comic. After all, he didn't want me to begin with – hasn't wanted me for ages – and he couldn't possibly forgive me now. Even Hannah agreed that he couldn't forgive me. My going away can make no difference to him, except that it will save him money,for I have always been so spendthrift and careless. He can still be a Member of Parliament and have his apartment in London, and he can even put the good china back in the drawing room when I am not there to break it. It is not as if he cared for me, Verity, for he does not. You know that, don't you? So I shall sit here, if I may, as quietly as a little cat, until Daniel comes to fetch me away. Was that the doorbell again? Mrs Stevens has been an age – do you suppose there is a letter and she and Hannah are having a tussle over it? Verity, do run downstairs and see, for Mrs Stevens is afraid of Hannah and lacks the authority. You are the mistress of the house, after all, and if she has taken my letter and you ordered her to give it back, I hardly see how she could refuse. Oh, Verity, darling, do hurry, for if she tears it I may never get all the pieces together again, and if she should burn it – for I suppose there must be a fire in the kitchen, even in this heat – Oh dear, oh dear, run, darling. Was that the door again?'

But there was no letter, no word, and when at last she had succumbed to a soothing potion of Mrs Stevens's and fallen fast asleep, I went thankfully outside, into the over-abundant summer garden, my mind requiring solitude and my lungs very much in need of air.

There was a hazy light across the lawn, with roses full-blown, ready to spill their petals at a touch, velvet butterflies and velvet flowers, so soon to wither, and it seemed my cousin Elinor was no better equipped for survival than they. At best the rose petals would be gathered and dried for potpourri, butterflies snared and spiked, their wings pinned for display, a small crucifixion that no one called cruel, since butterflies and flowers – and dowerless women – have no purpose but to decorate, and no voice to complain. And, seeing Elinor pinned butterfly-fashion in Morgan Aycliffe's drawing room or pressed like a dead flower between the harsh pages of his will, Joel's will, Hannah's will, anyone's will but her own, her defeat, which the surface of her own mind still refused to recognize, struck out at me, suffocating me, so that I knew I needed Crispin to help me breathe again.

And what really prevented me from going to him? Yesterday it would have seemed impossible, but last night I had spoken words to Joel and Hannah which had seemed impossible too, and I had not been made to suffer for them. And feeling once again that sensation of lightness, as if my body could dissolve into the gold-flecked, soot-flecked air and float away, I went back to the house, ordered the carriage, and calmly changed my clothes.

And all it took, like most things in life, was determination and desire. Joel was on his way to Liverpool to spend a night or two on the town, I imagined, with Elinor's lover. Hannah had gone yet again to Blenheim Lane, where the requirements of her small nieces could be relied on to occupy her for some time. And it was simple enough to stop my carriage outside Rosamund Boulton's smart, rapidly expanding shop and get down, murmuring something about a fitting, while the carriage went on to Nethercoats to take a present of fruit and flowers to Emma-Jane and her tenth bouncing baby, with instructions to return for me in an hour. I even went inside and made some small purchases, leaving the parcels behind to be collected presently, and then, crossing the dusty, empty street, found, without difficulty, without chance encounters, the dim, narrow shop front of the ivory seller Crispin had told me of, whose back door would give me access to Cropper Alley and the Red Gin.

Coming from the glare of the street the shop was cool, empty, quite dark, the shopkeeper as wrinkled and squat as his oriental carvings, showing neither surprise nor interest in my readiness to put money in his hands for the privilege of seeing Mrs Dinah McCluskey. But he sent a boy to fetch her just the same, ignoring me while I waited, ignoring her as she came striding in, swinging her hips and her long black hair, not even looking up as she said, 'Well – would you believe it,' and led me away.

The alley was worse, in the hot daylight, than I remembered it; fouler, slimier, the creaking stairway at the back of the inn narrower, noisier, the woman behind me bolder, her black eyes inquisitive and scornful.

'Are you sure he's at home?' I asked her, feeling the need to say something, and, sensing that I had no idea how to address her, her smile deepened.

'Oh yes. He's in all right. I know what goes on in my own house – not like some folks, eh, love?'

And knocking smartly on his door, she gave me a familiar pat on the shoulder, her enjoyment huge and crude and possibly dangerous.

He was sitting at his worktable, reading, writing, as I had always imagined him, his student's face pale from lack of air and sleep, his shirt open at the neck and sleeves, his shoulders very thin beneath the cambric. And for a moment, because he was completely astonished and I was completely overjoyed, we were speechless and foolish with our emotion.

'Verity, there has to be a reason.'

'Yes. I needed you.'

'Something has happened?'

'Yes. But not to me. I just needed you.'

'Then here I am. Come in and close the door. That's all you've ever needed to do.'

His arms closed then around me, cool and light; no rock to lean on, no bulk with which to defend me, but a clear honesty that did not seek to twist me or crush me into any shape other than my own.

'What would you change in me, Crispin?'

'Nothing. And you?'

'Nothing.'

'Surely, you'd make me thrifty and sensible – and ambitious?'

'No. An impractical dreamer, just as you are. I love you. Spendthrift and too ready to borrow money from men you think can spare it. Naïve sometimes, and other times too clever by half. I love you. Proud of your own complex, spiky, uncomfortable character, because the last thing

302

you'd want to be is simple and easy. Innocent and cynical at the same time. The only person I've ever trusted, although basically your disposition is too nervous to be reliable. I love you.'

'Darling – have you come to say goodbye?'

'I don't know. But it seems natural to be here. Is it possible that it's all happened before? That we've been going round and round in circles for an eternity, because I've kept on making the wrong decision – thinking it was all so impossible when all I ever needed to do was come in and close the door like you told me? No, no, don't be alarmed. It's not the sunstroke. I feel quite well. You said I would come here sooner or later, didn't you? How nice for you, to be always right.'

'Are you going to tell me your reason?'

'Oh – I had one, or two, that seemed very pressing when I started. But now that I am here, I think it is mainly that I want to make love to you.'

'Oh yes – yes, please do. In fact, perhaps that's exactly what I need, to be bullied, taken –'

'Yes,' I told him, pushing him gently towards his meagre, impeccably folded bed. 'Sometimes you need to be a little boy again because you didn't get it right the first time.'

And once again I had dissolved in air, once again I was impossibly light, totally powerful, for I knew of no one who could put chains on the wind, which blew in whatever direction it chose and, being invisible, had only to stand still to evade its pursuers, had only to bide its time.

But afterwards, with my head on his bare, brittle shoulder, I said, 'My cousin Elinor has left your father.' And I waited, praying he would be compassionate.

'Oh – so that's it. I believe I'm sorry.'

'For her?'

'Yes, but then, I was always sorry for her. For him too, oddly enough. Perhaps I've grown up sufficiently now to stop hating him. Presumably she has a lover?'

'Yes, Daniel Adair.'

'His foreman?' he said, unable to suppress a grimace of distaste. 'Surely she could have made a better choice than that.'

And sitting up, drawing my knees to my chin and clasping my arms around them, my back arched slightly away from him, I shook my head.

'What choice? I don't think she made a choice at all. He was there. She's reached a point in her life where she desperately needed to fall in love, and so she fell in love with him. Choice? What could Elinor know about choice? You have no sisters, Crispin, and so you can't know how they bring us up. Choices are for boys, not girls. You have the bother of wondering what to do with your lives, but we know, right from the start. Find a husband, they tell us; a rich one, if you can, and if not, any husband, any man at all who's willing to put a ring on your finger. And when you've got him, cheat him. My old maid Marth-Ellen told me that many a time and I never heard my mother contradict her. And I can remember Elinor's mother, my Aunt Hattie, doing her mending at Low Cross and telling us, "There are good men and bad men, girls. If you get

303

yourself a bad one blind him in both eyes, if he's good just blind him in one. If you spend five shillings, tell him it cost you ten and pocket the difference. That's the only way to live with a man, although even a bandy-legged tinker is better than no man at all." So don't blame Elinor for running down the aisle to your father. She was only doing what she'd been raised to do. She didn't even understand why he wanted her. It just seemed a miracle to her that he did. It's not her fault, surely, that she grew up just a shade too intelligent to settle for being a painted doll? Choice. She began life as a nuisance to her father – as I did – because she was a girl and he wanted boys to help him in the mill. She was pushed into marriage by her brother, who wanted a useful connection. She was used by your father, who would have done better to work off his passions in a brothel. And now her helplessness appalls me. They will parcel her up – Joel and your father – and put her wherever it suits them best. They will discuss her and dispose of her as if she had no more comprehension than a carriage horse. And there is nothing she can do about it. You talk of your factory children, Crispin, who are put out to labour by their parents when they are too young to be called free agents, and you complain because it is the parents who profit from that labour. But what about young ladies? They marry us off before we are old enough to make a fuss, and to keep us docile they teach us nothing – nothing, Crispin – that we could ever use to earn a living and set ourselves free. They create a fashion for useless silly females, and that is what we become – useless and silly, so that if childbirth doesn't kill us, or milk fever, we die slowly of boredom. And, like my Aunt Hattie said, even that's better than being a spinster, since everybody knows spinsters die from frustration and shame.'

He put his hand on my shoulder, very gently, let it travel down my spine and back again, and then clasped his fingers loosely round my wrist.

'I am a man, Verity. Do I oppress you?'

Taking his finely chiselled face between my hands, I kissed him and quite suddenly laughed.

'No. I suppose you are just as bad as all the rest, but I chose you, which is a different matter. And I need you.'

'You have me,' he said, lying on his back and sighing with apparent content, boyish and rather frail as he often was in moments of emotion. 'Indeed you have me.'

And as I bent over him, claiming him, it was of no importance to me whatsoever that my carriage must already be waiting, the horses fretting, the driver wondering, beginning to worry. I was here, by my own choice, and I would leave, in the same fashion, as I chose. And whatever befell me next month, or next year, I would depend on no one for my salvation. I would choose to defend myself, no object of passivity and pity like Elinor but a woman who understood that, in the final instance, there is always an alternative – that if nothing else, at least one may claim the right to refuse.

31

I had not thought my relations with Hannah could worsen, but in those last hot August days, our bitterness became a solid presence, a sharp-clawed hand slicing through our good intentions, so that the entire household became irritable and cautious, the maids clumsy, the children fractious, Joel more prone than ever to eat his dinner at the Swan.

'Ah well,' my mother said airily. 'At least she will have to get married now, dear, since she clearly cannot continue to live with you in this fashion. Yes, I feel she has made all the alterations to Redesdale parsonage one could expect the squire to tolerate, so there is nothing left for her now but to name the day – although whether it will be Julian Ashley or George Brand, I am not yet certain.'

And indeed, Mr Brand once again entered the forefront of our lives when Hannah, realizing with what ease anyone could dispose of Mr Ashley, requested him to visit Elinor and if he could not coax her then to terrify her into decent behaviour.

But even the evangelical Mr Brand, the veins in his mighty neck swelling, his voice throbbing with passion as he spoke of hell's eternal bonfire, had little effect.

'Poor man,' she said, watching him from her window as he went away with tears in his honest eyes. 'He really cares, doesn't he, that I shall spend eternity roasting away. Oh dear, do run after him, Verity, and explain in your own clever fashion that I should actually prefer it, so long as it was with Daniel, to lying in the cold ground with the worms, and my husband. Do run and tell him, for he looks so sad.'

But Hannah, who had been biding her time, appeared quite suddenly in the doorway, filling it entirely, not with her height alone but with the awesome, outraged quality of her anger.

'I don't know you,' she said, her eyes fastening themselves on her sister, ignoring everything else. 'I don't recognize you. Have you no shame?'

And Elinor – who had never openly defied Hannah before – desperately seized the remnants of her courage and rushed shrilly to the attack, a downy little canary making its pathetic assault on an eagle.

'Well, and if we are talking of shame, what of you – for I know you have taken my letters.'

'What letters?' Hannah said, briefly puzzled, and then, understanding, she smiled as Joel often did before striking a blow. 'Letters. There have been no letters, silly goose, and there will be none. He is in Liverpool, with Joel's money in his pocket, praying for you to make up your mind to go home again, so that he can repair the harm you have done him. The man cannot afford you, even if he wanted you – which is by no means certain – it is as simple as that. You have robbed him of one career and unless you come quickly to your senses you will rob him of another. I think you should know that Joel has made him a business proposition which depends entirely on your return to your husband. So, little sister, if you care for the man at all – as you keep on insisting that you do – you should go home, should you not, to your husband and children, so that the man may be prosperous again, and happy. Surely, if you love him, you should desire his happiness – and his prosperity – shouldn't you? I am very certain he desires to be prosperous himself.'

'No,' Elinor said, backing away, her face ghastly, and, running to the window she leaned out, dragging the warm air into her lungs like a woman suffocating, drowning.

'No, Hannah,' she whispered, her tiny hands clinging to the window frame as if she thought we meant to prise her loose by force. 'No – no – you don't understand. I can't go back. Hannah, you can't know what it is, what it feels like. It makes me sick, Hannah – sick, now, even thinking about it. I could endure it once, but not now. If you condemn me to that, Hannah, then you condemn me to death – I warn you.'

'Nonsense – theatrical nonsense,' Hannah snorted,although she moved forward just the same, as I did, towards that wide, high, empty window, in case Elinor should really be desperate enough to harm herself. But Elinor, feeling our approach, stiffened like a trapped animal and slid bonelessly to the ground; and there, clutching her stomach, she was so distressingly and agonizingly sick that even Hannah was alarmed and, for a day or two, much kinder.

Yet when the doctor had been called – and Emma-Jane Hobhouse had been made aware of it – and Elinor, after a series of restless nights, had recovered sufficiently to take a reasonable bowlful of Mrs Stevens's special broth, the same problems still remained and Hannah – well aware that Morgan Aycliffe might yet refuse to receive his wife, even if she could be persuaded to return – set to work again.

'How busy she is,' my mother murmured. 'How utterly untiring. I feel certain that Elinor's house has never before been so well ordered, nor her children so excellently administered. I saw them the other day, taking their carriage exercise with their dear aunt, all of them dressed so exactly alike, and so impeccably neat and tidy that had they not looked so expensive they could have been charity children – eyes downcast, hands folded in their little laps, not a word for the cat – you will know what I mean. And although I intended this in the kindest possible fashion, what a convincing schemer our Hannah has turned out to be. Really, she is so very believable, for everywhere I go lately people are commiserating with me on the collapse of Elinor's health. "Poor child," they say, "so young – but then her mother's nerves were always uncertain and these things run in families." Naturally I look solemn and nod my head in agreement – for I dare do no other – but the odd thing is that I cannot remember your Aunt Hattie ever being so delicate. And that is rather strange, since I knew her far better than Mrs Hobhouse and Mrs Oldroyd did, who have both spent hours recently reminding me of her spasms and her palpitations – all of which I have quite forgotten. Well – I do remember one occasion when she took to her bed and was too ill to see anyone – yes, I remember that well enough – but when Emma-Jane mentioned it I didn't like to confess that it was not altogether the mysterious malady your Aunt Hattie – and Hannah – said it was but merely that your uncle – Joel's father – had given her a black eye. Tell me, dear, are you going to hide Elinor away forever? She would be welcome, you know, to come to me at Patterswick. She could sit in my garden, in the sunshine, quite safely, for I always hear a carriage at least a mile away and could whisk her off to bed at the very approach of Emma-Jane.'

But Morgan Aycliffe, from his bachelor apartment in Westminster, had made it clear that he could tolerate no breath of scandal. His wife might lose her health and her sanity if she chose but not her reputation, and so, throughout the fine weather, she remained on a chaise longue by the bedroom window, becoming gradually so lethargic that she could barely make the effort to brush her hair, could see no point – just as in the days following the birth of her last child – in getting dressed since she would soon be going to bed again, and, in any case, had nothing fit to wear because her husband, having sent her the very barest of essentials, had locked her wardrobe door and hidden the key.

'I'm so tired,' she would say. 'So very tired,' and, closing her eyes, she would allow an afternoon, a day, a week, to slip away from her like water.

'Oh – how wonderful. Is it really Tuesday? Do you know, I thought it was Monday.' And, gradually, there was no more talk of letters, no mention at all of Daniel Adair.

She slept, grew pale enough to convince the sharpest, shrewdest observer she was ailing, and became vague and uncertain, so that the few who did see her – our maids, who gossiped to other people's maids – were able to add substance to Hannah's hint of a nervous collapse, creating a climate of sympathy, rather than ridicule, for Morgan Aycliffe.

'Poor man,' they said, remembering that his first wife had been odd too. And before anyone had time to wonder if the gentleman himself could be in any way to blame, Emma-Jane Hobhouse, still smarting from Elinor's brief flirtation with Bradley, spoke up in his defence.

'He was too good to her,' she declared. 'He had her waited on hand and foot, put no limit on her spending, never said a harsh word about the bills she ran up. And now look at him, living in those poky rooms in London, doing his best to safeguard all our interests, and worrying himself sick, I shouldn't wonder, about her and those poor children. She hasn't seen them, you know, not once since she fell ill – not that she ever saw much of them in any case. In fact, my Bradley always says he doubts if she can tell them apart. Well – poor Mr Aycliffe. Thank goodness there's always Hannah. I don't know what any of the Barforths would do without Hannah. We all know that Joel relies on her far more than on Verity, who always has her head in the clouds.'

And when this was gleefully repeated to me by Lucy Oldroyd, who wanted to be everybody's best friend, I could have laughed and cried, for Hannah was soon to leave me, and although I was glad of it, I knew I would miss her.

I was, just then, extremely occupied, for the house at Tarn Edge, with or without Daniel Adair, would be ready for occupation by Christmastime, and it seemed that every coach brought me curtain samples, carpet samples, sketches of plasterwork and marquetry and hand-painted Chinese wallpaper, or mysterious packages that, spilling sawdust and straw and splitting fingernails, opened to reveal an exquisite piece of Sèvres or Meissen, some treasure of Wedgwood or Coalport, ordered by Joel without asking – without apparently caring – whether they suited me or not.

I was on my knees one morning, unpacking a potpourri vase, my fingers gloating over the cloudy design of roses and pink-draped, pink-limbed dancers, when the skirt of Hannah's serviceable brown morning dress came swishing across the floor towards me and, looking up, I saw by her iron composure that she had something of importance to communicate.

'For the new house?' she said, indicating the vase with her foot.

Nodding, I got up, brushing a clinging wisp of straw from my sleeve, bracing myself, perhaps, since the new house could hold little interest for Hannah, who surely did not mean to live in it.

'Yes, I think it is one of a pair, so no doubt we shall be having another delivery ere long.'

'Oh, more than one, I believe, for when my brother starts spending there is no end to it. But you will be wanting to know my intentions ...'

'Joel will want to know,' I said sharply, desperately. 'You should talk first to Joel, surely – if you have come to a decision.'

But Hannah in her mood of cold dignity was far more alarming to me than in the heat of her anger, and, sensing my reticence and her own power, she smiled.

'I think that is for me to decide. You, at any rate, Verity, will hardly beg me to stay.'

'You have decided to go, then?'

'I have. And before I do, I must warn you that this change in my own affairs will in no way lessen my attempt to put my sister's house in order. I am determined to see her restored to her rightful place before my own marriage, if possible, but if not, then very soon after. And I would like to make it very clear that if you persist in encouraging her in her foolishness, then you and I cannot be reconciled. Mr Aycliffe has indicated to me in a recent letter that he has managed to overcome his scruples – his natural repugnancy – largely due to my own efforts in preventing gossip. And I will not have those efforts wasted, Verity. I have prepared the way for Elinor's return to respectability, at some cost to myself, since I have not enjoyed putting about these tales of her mental instability, whatever you may think to the contrary. And yet, instead of helping me, as I might have expected, you have taken an attitude that I fail to understand. And I am not the only one, Verity, for Joel does not understand you either, and is most seriously displeased – almost ill at ease, whenever I mention your name. I do not wish to part from you on these terms, Verity, but in your present state of mind you give me no choice.'

I walked slowly to the open window, as Elinor had once done, but my

308

motive was not escape, merely a desire not to be overheard; and, ascertaining that there was no gardener snipping off dead roses on the path below, no maid gathering the petals for the myriad of purposes of Mrs Stevens, I came back again knowing I had little chance of convincing her.

'Hannah, let me say two things to you – first of all, there is no reason for you to leave us unless you really wish to do so. Tarn Edge will be very large, you know, with space enough even for two women who do not always see eye to eye. But marriage – if that is what you decide on – may give you a clearer understanding of Elinor's troubles, and I must ask you to face the fact that she may never bring herself to overcome them. Morgan Aycliffe has the legal right to compel her to return, but you know, as I know, that he will never use it. He would never inflict on himself the humiliation of a captive wife. And I will not allow you, or anyone else, to bully her into thinking she has no choice. Yes, yes, Hannah, I know how sincerely you believe you are acting for her own good. I know you have always been well-meaning, even when you have been most misguided. But in this case you fail to take into account the strength of her physical repulsion – a subject on which you cannot be well informed. You accuse me of not helping you with her, but what help could I give other than turning her out and closing my door behind her so she has nowhere else to go but Blenheim Lane? Well, I have housed stray dogs and cats many a time and so I think I may do the same for your sister. And when you are married and settled at Redesdale, I doubt that Mr Ashley would make any objections to your receiving her there, for he is a Christian gentleman, after all.'

And instead of the indignation, the moralizing, the fresh reproaches I had expected, her face flooded with a scorching crimson, the most painful colour I had ever seen, and she said harshly, 'Did I mention Redesdale – or Mr Ashley?'

'No – no –'

'No, I did not. In fact, it would be most improper in me to do so, since I put an end to my relations with Mr Ashley quite ten days ago.'

'Oh – I'm sorry – at least, I suppose – but then, I have often thought Mr Brand may be more suited –'

'Mr Brand,' she said, clasping her hands together, that dreadful colour still hot and fierce in her cheeks. 'Mr Brand has been your candidate all along, has he, Verity? And your mother's too, I gather, from something she said to me the other day. It will displease you then to know that Mr Brand has engaged himself to a Miss Mayfield from Halifax, a nice enough little woman – which, really, is hardly my concern, since I must now tell you that when his period of mourning is over, sometime in the winter, I have promised to marry Mr Agbrigg, a promise I most assuredly will not break.'

And so shocked was I that I began to laugh until, seeing her face, I froze and said weakly, 'Oh no, Hannah – no, no, Hannah – you can't do that – really, you can't do that.'

She seized my wrist with her hard, unrelenting hand and dragged me as

309

close as she could, dominating me with her height and indignation, with the veneer of Barforth grandeur and Barforth fury that still remained.

'And why not? My sister fell in love with a bricklayer, did she not? Then why should I not do the same with a mill hand – although he is far from being a mill hand now.'

'You can't mean that, Hannah – surely – not love –'

'Can't I? Why can't I? Are you brooding on physical repulsion again, Verity? Mr Agbrigg may repel you but it doesn't necessarily follow that he repels me. Perhaps I am not so nice in my notions as you and Elinor – perhaps I can't afford to be. Unless, of course, it turns out that I have rather more in my head than this eternal business of repulsion. Yes, yes, he's far from handsome and exceedingly rough-spoken, I grant you, although the speech, at least, can be remedied – a pauper brat from nowhere, who doesn't even know his real name, but a man who has risen by his own efforts – hindered, not helped, by those around him – and who could rise much further.'

'Good God, Hannah, rise where? He's the manager of Lawcroft Mill –'

Her temper flaring, she pinched my wrist hard, meaning to hurt, and with a powerful movement of her arm and shoulder pushed me away.

'Yes, he's the manager of Lawcroft, and what will Julian Ashley ever be? What will George Brand ever be? Love. Of course I don't love him. I don't love anybody. I've gone beyond that. I'm simply at a point in my life where I must marry someone. I must have an establishment of my own – must – absolutely must – and I won't confine myself to the limitations of a parson's wife. What is it, Verity? Do you want to see me at Redesdale, walking behind the squire's lady, mending and making do and being glad of your castoffs, and Elinor's? Or with George Brand, who'd take me off to some pest hole in Africa as a missionary, once he got his hands on me? Or would you really like to see me stay here and grow old and dependent on you – the poor spinster sister who does the plain needlework and has her dinner upstairs with the children when there are guests? Oh no. I was cheated of the life I should have had, Verity – the life that was given to you in my place – and now I must do the best I can for myself. I would have married Julian Ashley, make no mistake about it, or George Brand – one or the other – as soon as I was sure there was no better alternative. Oh yes, Verity, Mr Agbrigg may be plain and common and what of it? Mr Adair was handsome and common and I never heard you object to him.'

I was appalled now, beyond any hope of concealment.

'Hannah, Hannah – how will you live – oh, Hannah, take care.'

'I will,' she said, still flushed but growing hard again. 'Very good care. I shall live in the millhouse, where I would have lived with Edwin. There will be a great deal of gossip, of course, and Emma-Jane Hobhouse may not invite me to dinner, but you will defend me, I feel sure of it, just as you have defended Elinor. I have always had certain ideas about the millhouse, as you know, and in my hands it will become very comfortable – really, most pleasing. And this town is growing, so rapidly, that ere long we shall be a fully fledged city with our own council, our own mayor

– and I see no reason why the first Lord Mayor of Cullingford should not be Mr Agbrigg. Newcomers to the area will know nothing of his origins, and others will forget. They will think of him simply as a Cullingford man of business, well-to-do and well connected, and I do not think anyone could dispute my suitability for the position of Mayoress. I may never be so rich as you and Elinor, but I shall be immensely respected. I shall be important in this town, Verity. People will know my name and court my favour. People will stand back to let me pass. And I shall have one tremendous satisfaction. I shall have a very clever son, for with proper guidance, I do not think there are any limits to what Jonas could achieve. Now then – I do believe I hear Joel's carriage? Yes, I thought I had timed things aright, for he mentioned at breakfast time he would be back around midmorning. I would be obliged to you, Verity, if you would give him my news. Naturally I do not expect him to be pleased and so I will wait upstairs until his first reaction has cooled. Perhaps you will come up presently and let me know?'

But Joel, on hearing that his favourite sister was to marry Ira Agbrigg, largely, it seemed, because she wanted to be Lady Mayoress and mother to the unpleasant Jonas, was so incensed that, not caring who heard him, he strode into the hallway and bellowed her name loudly up the stairs.

'Yes, Joel?' she said, coming as slowly as she dared, and snarling something under his breath, he took her roughly by the elbow and pushed her into the study.

'I'll turn him off,' I heard him growl at her. 'I'll have him out of Lawcroft and out of the valley by nightfall.'

Hannah must have expected him to say that and, not feeling my presence to be required, I went out into the garden, putting distance between myself and such a lava flow of true Barforth rage.

I must have walked more slowly than I had intended, for it did not seem long before Joel was out on the gravel drive in front of the house, shading his eyes from the sun and calling, 'Verity, where the devil are you?'

He was still very angry, very ready to hurt, but his temper was in control now, an invisible menace chained to his will, although the horse, standing between the shafts of his phaeton, caught the spark of it and, shivering, began to toss her showy chestnut head.

'Is Hannah – all right?'

'All right? I wouldn't say that. I'd say she's as cracked as the other one. I'd say they're a pair of prime idiots, my sisters. And I'd say Agbrigg's a deep one – one I'll have to watch. Agbrigg – my God – how can she do this to me?'

'Can you stop her?'

He pulled on his driving gloves, his hands independently angry, I thought, because it was no longer possible for a man in his position to take a whip to a disobedient woman; nor was it likely that the shrewd Ira Agbrigg would oblige, as Daniel Adair had done, and part with his bride for five hundred pounds.

'I could make it damned awkward for her. I could take his house and his job and see he didn't get another hereabouts. But the world doesn't stop at the end of the Law Valley, and they've calculated I won't do it anyway. She's not Elinor. She might just go with him – calculating again that I'd fetch them back. And he's useful to me. He knows a lot about my business. It's always been at Low Cross, remember, that I've experimented with my new cloth and my new machines, where we've adapted and adjusted, and I don't really want my trade secrets put up for auction, do I? That's been part of their calculations too.'

'So you'll give them your blessing?'

'Hardly. Listen, Verity, go and see Agbrigg this afternoon. Find out just where he stands in the matter, for it strikes me it was all Hannah's idea. He still talks about his wife as if she were waiting for him at home with the kettle on instead of in her grave, and, for the life of me, I can't believe it ever entered his head to make love to my sister. So, if he's unwilling, or uneasy, if she's bullied him into it, then I want to know, because then I can bully him out of it and still keep him on at Lawcroft. Understand? I'll be at Tarn Edge around four o'clock. See me there.'

The millhouse at Lawcroft was cool and quiet as always when I arrived, my old home invaded by strangers, one of them, the boy Jonas, coming out to greet me, his pale, narrow face and slanting, colourless eyes informing me that he was aware of the situation and gloried in it. And as he went off to the mill to fetch his father, with shoulders hunched in the fashion of one who spends much time stooping over his books, I understood that whatever private reservations Mr Agbrigg might have about taking a Barforth wife, young Jonas had no doubts at all that a Barforth stepmother was just his style.

The surviving Agbrigg girl, Maria, hastily installed me in the parlour, much smaller than I remembered it and overcrowded now with the old horsehair sofas and ungainly schoolroom chairs of the Agbriggs, but just the same it was the room where my brother Edwin had announced his intention of marrying Hannah, where Joel, on my own betrothal day, had congratulated me on my good sense, the room where I had last spoken to my father.

'Will you take some tea, Mrs Barforth?' Maria Agbrigg enquired, a prim, plain little mouse unlikely to inspire more than casual kindness in Hannah and declining the complication of cups and saucers, I was almost tearful with memory – with the perilous, painful game of wondering what might have been – when the door opened to admit my new prospective brother-in-law.

He had first come to his house as a hungry young man, cap in hand, to lay information against his workmates, desperate enough for anything that would release the trap of his poverty. And I saw now that, beyond the dark frock coat and well-pressed, well-cut trousers, beneath the cambric shirt and the sober but expensive necktie, he was still dissatisfied. He had lost his poor, sad Ann and nine of his children, and with them, perhaps, the last thread of gentleness in his nature, the last whispering hope of any real personal joy in life. But Ann's favourite son still remained – and one of her daughters with Ann's thin, fair hair and a

312

touch of her frailty. I needed no more than ten minutes of Mr Agbrigg's time to realize he knew exactly how useful Hannah wanted to be to Jonas, how useful she could indirectly be to Maria, and that he had no intention of denying them their opportunities. Perhaps the idea of her as a woman had not even occurred to him until she decided that it should, but once the offer had been made, once it was all there before him, he would not let it go.

He had always felt the deepest admiration for Miss Barforth, he told me, keeping his eyes on the carpet. He believed her to be a truly marvellous woman and had no hesitation at all in placing his future, his children's future, in her capable hands. He was, of course, well aware of the vast social gulf between them. She was far above him and would always remain so, he would never dispute that, nor would he dispute the right of anyone to be surprised – annoyed – at her decision to marry so far beneath her station. But – and here he did, for a moment, glance palely at me and then away again – no one could deny that he was hard-working, which counted for a great deal in the Law Valley, and good-living, which may count for rather less but which, in a matter of this kind, was surely of value. Nor was there any question of financial gain on his part, since Miss Barforth had no fortune and no expectations and would be more likely to empty his pocket than fill it. Their decision to marry had been taken logically, he felt, and carefully, and since Miss Barforth was now a lady of some maturity and immense determination, one could safely credit her with the ability to know her own mind.

A speech, I thought, which bore Hannah's signature as clearly as those delivered from the hustings by Morgan Aycliffe, Hannah's voice speaking through her half-willing, half-eager bridegroom, saying, 'I am thirty-four years old and single, and I will do as I please.'

'She is very fond of my boy Jonas,' Ira Agbrigg said as he handed me into my carriage, speaking his own words now, as if he thought some kind of emotion appropriate to the occasion. 'Thinks she can make something of him.' And I drove away quite sadly, hardly knowing what I could say to Joel.

The afternoon was fine, the treetops already gold with approaching autumn, a thin, blue sky hazing to saffron on the horizon, the road to Tarn Edge shorter than usual since I was in no hurry, and empty of anyone who could delay me from reaching the spot where Joel's house was rising from the ground like a small cathedral.

The outer shell was completed now, the graceful Gothic spires giving height and presence to massive stone walls which sprouted, in every possible crevice, a midsummer profusion of carved fruit and vines and mythological heads of tangled hair. The front entrance was wider, had more steps, more columns, more ironwork on the heavy oak door than the Assembly Rooms in Cullingford; the hall, still bare, was several square feet larger and had more doors opening from it; the sweep of the staircase was grander, climbing upwards to a landing as wide as the millhouse parlour, and a mighty window of ruby and emerald and sapphire glass. Joel's house, the shop front of his achievement and success, with Joel's phaeton already standing on the uncompleted drive, and another carriage I didn't recognize, a smart equippage with a coachman lounging moodily, thirstily perhaps, at the horses' heads.

Joel's house, smelling of new plaster and new paint; vast, empty spaces, a cool refuge from the dusty, sticky day, the silence shattered, not unpleasantly, by the unseen tapping of a workman's hammer, a saw slicing busily through wood, a house beginning to come alive. Bare boards under my feet, a happy clattering as I ran upstairs, a willingness to lose myself in these unknown rooms to furnish them, in my mind, not merely with chairs and tables, but with Blaize and Nicholas and Caroline, with my puppies' excited yelping, with Mrs Stevens stirring her broths and her medicines and her perfumes, with Hannah bringing her clever, spiteful Jonas and her embarrassed husband to call, with Elinor, drawing her chaise longue to the window, forgetting about the letters that never came, forgetting everything, perhaps, except that she was weary. And, with a sudden acute pang that took my breath away, I did not know if I would ever live here and forgot, for a terrifying moment, what I was doing here now, forgot my intentions and aspirations, my very name. And, closing my eyes, I could see nothing but an alleyway leading to the Red Gin and could hear a voice – not Crispin's, my own perhaps – telling me I had only to open the door.

But it was the window that came first to my hand, the new frame lifting jerkily to fulfil my need for air, and, leaning out a little, breathing greedily, gratefully, I saw Joel coming across the as yet unlandscaped garden, with a bare-headed, long-limbed woman I recognized as Estella Chase.

I had seen her last at the Assembly Rooms, arriving late with the Coreys and the Corey-Mannings and my mother, looking at Joel in a way I understood, letting her long, narrow hand linger on his arm, displaying her lean, thoroughbred body so that it would linger in his mind. And I saw that now, recently returned once again from London, she was doing the same, offering enough of herself, as she swayed close to him and then away again, to arouse – or re-arouse – his appetite. And although there was no reason in the world why I should not have called out to them, waved from the window, and gone tripping downstairs to greet them, I drew back a little and kept silent, even when they paused almost directly beneath me.

'We are dining with the Floods tonight,' she said, 'which is always a vast production, so I must be on my way. But now I have let you know I am home again, perhaps we shall not be strangers?'

'Surely not,' he told her, ready enough, I thought, to let her go since there were stonemasons and carpenters awaiting his instructions and the claims of his house, just then, were more important, more exciting, than any woman.

'Let me take you to your carriage,' he said, holding out a hand to steady her across the rough ground.

It was then, I think, that he looked up and saw my face at the window, my eyes somehow connecting with his, so that we were still looking at each other when he drew the surprised Estella Chase into his arms and kissed her very slowly, so that I could see the tip of his tongue against her lips, her own tongue flicker greedily to meet it, the excitement of her body nailing itself to his, which may not have been excited at all.

'Joel – darling – I thought you'd forgotten.'

'How could I ever do that?'

'Easily – wicked as you are. I'd quite decided to forget you.'

As she lifted her face once again for his kiss I found myself pressed hard against the bare wall, invisible now to them both, fists clenched, every nerve in my body clenched, it seemed, against the onslaught of my anger, the roaring, red-flecked Barforth fury which now, pounding inside my body, needed violence to be at peace.

I'll hurt him, I thought. I'll hurt him badly. He'll pay me for this.

Through the painful clamping of my teeth on my lower lip, the clawing of my own nails against my palms, hurting myself and willing him to feel the injury, I heard my mother's cool voice telling me how it could be done. He had kissed that woman without desiring her, simply to wound me, hoping to wound me, and so there would be no wounds, or none that he could see. I would not delight him with tantrums, nor flatter him with jealous tears. I would give him what his vanity least desired, my indifference, and, hurrying, running almost, I left that bare room behind me, reaching the landing, the stairs, flew down the hall, paused to catch my breath, and, walking through the heavy, iron-studded door, met them head on as they came around the side of the house.

'Ah, there you are,' Joel said, his face quite blank although I could feel the calculation behind it, the cruelty, the eagerness for my reaction.

'Yes, dear,' I replied, with no idea at all how I made my voice so calm and bright when everything beneath the surface of my placid skin was trembling. 'Here I am. Here you are too, and Mrs Chance. It is Mrs Chance, isn't it? How nice to see you again.'

'Chase,' she said. 'My name is Chase. Oh yes, Mrs Barforth, I was driving by, and having heard you are building a palace, I could hardly restrain myself from taking a look.'

'Of course you could not restrain yourself, Mrs Chase. I do so perfectly understand. Well then, now that you have let us know you are home again, perhaps we shall not be strangers.'

And it could not have possibly escaped her that I had quoted the very words she had used to Joel a moment ago.

'Oh,' she said, her pale eyes staring. 'Quite so. But, heavens, the time. I really must fly, Mr Barforth, Mrs Barforth.'

We watched the carriage drive away in a taut silence.

'It won't please her,' he said, 'that you forgot her name, or appeared to.'

'If that is supposed to worry me, then I find I can hardly bring myself to care.'

'So I see. That surprises me, Verity. I don't think I've ever known you to take the trouble to dislike anyone before, and whatever can Mrs Chase have done to deserve the favour?'

And growing hard suddenly, I answered, 'I merely find her type of woman tedious. She has a great opinion of herself but, really, if it were not for her London gown and her London manner, I doubt if any man would give her a shilling.'

'Ah, so you think her a light woman?'

'Yes, when I think of her at all, which is seldom.'

'That I grant you,' he told me, coming to an abrupt halt. 'She is a light woman. And what I want to know now, Verity, is why that should bother you? My sister Elinor is a light woman, too. We both know that, and yet you were a tigress in her defence. Really, I continue to marvel at it.'

'Elinor has nothing to do with it.'

'Has she not? And has she nothing to do with this change in you?'

'What change? I am not changed.'

'Are you not?'

'No, I am exactly as I have always been, and if you think otherwise, then it can only be that you have never looked.'

'So, I neglect you, do I? Have you any particular complaint to make?'

And because I could hear, beneath his words, the voice of his will urging, 'Fight me, Verity. Come, girl, bite me, scratch me,' and because I had found another, infinitely more subtle way to bite him, I said with all my mother's deliberate vagueness, 'Why no, darling, absolutely not. What an idea.'

But as we went back to the house, side by side, civilized again and cool, to talk of floor coverings and wall coverings and Ira Agbrigg, I was not sure who had won or why the battle had been fought at all. I only knew I felt sick at heart, desolate and bereaved and exceedingly weary, and that I did not wish my life to continue in this way.

32

In September, after a day in the saddle clearing his land of foxes, Squire Dalby felt a pain across his chest which, growing more and more acute, not only confined him to his bed for six weeks of glorious hunting weather but, by reminding him of his mortality, increased his determination to marry my mother.

'It is all because of his heir,' she told me when I drove over to visit them both. 'It is his grandson who inherits from him since he has lost his son, and as he has never seen eye to eye with his daughter-in-law, who has married again, he feels that she and her husband will turn me out of my cottage as soon as he is dead. Dear man – the world is full of cottages, and although I tell him repeatedly that I have money enough for my needs, he simply cannot bring himself to believe it. He is totally convinced that the young squire will order me out of Patterswick with threats to set his dogs on me if I return, and he will not be persuaded that I would simply move to Redesdale or Floxley, or even come to you.'

'Perhaps you had better marry him, then.'

'Well, dear, I think I must consider it – in fact, that is the very least I can do after all his kindness. My dear old Dalby has convinced himself he is not long for this world and it is his gallantry, alongside his whim to annoy his daughter-in-law, which inclines him to take me for a wife. But, between ourselves, I think with proper care, he may live a long time yet, and although I had made up my mind never to marry again, I think I might not altogether dislike the position of squire's lady.'

The wedding took place at Patterswick in the middle of November, in a church somewhat fittingly decorated with the richly tinted blooms of autumn, although my mother, coming down the aisle on Joel's arm, looked young enough to cause some consternation on the bridegroom's side of the church, where certain elderly Dalbys, having been informed that the bride was a widow and a grandmother, seemed unable to believe their eyes.

She was attended, once again quite fittingly, by a procession of children, Caroline and the three Aycliffe girls in white, flouncy dresses and pink sashes, Caroline in a temper because she had wanted a blue sash or a yellow one or, failing that, a pink dress, anything to make her stand out from her Aycliffe cousins.

'It is my grandmamma,' she had said, mutiny writ large across her scowling Barforth brow. 'She's only their mother's aunt, which makes them her second nieces, and that's nowhere near as close as me. I should come first, by myself in a pink dress, and they should just bunch along behind me – they're narrow enough to get down the aisle all three together, side by side.'

And Caroline, flying off in a rage at the denial of what she considered a perfectly reasonable request, was not to know that if Hannah had had her way, the Aycliffe girls would not have been there to trouble her at all.

'It is quite out of the question for them to be bridesmaids at such a time,' she had declared. 'Altogether ridiculous when one considers the state that family is in.'

But Hannah herself was in something of a state just then, having suffered greater humiliation than she had anticipated at Cullingford's reaction to her new engagement, led by Emma-Jane, who, conveniently forgetting that Hannah had jilted both Mr Ashley and Mr Brand, expressed great astonishment at the lengths some spinsters would go to in order to get themselves off the shelf.

'I was never so shocked in all my life,' she told me gleefully, looking better than I had seen her in years. 'I wonder Joel doesn't put a stop to it. But then he and Mr Agbrigg have always been so close – always whispering secrets together – and I suppose they're just like Lucy Oldroyd and me. We can't afford to have a fall-out because we know too much about each other. But, just the same, it's going to be awkward for you, isn't it, having him in the house, using your first name and making your children call him uncle. Naturally the rest of us can get out of inviting him, but I don't see how you can avoid it, Verity. Oh dear, you poor thing, you do have my sympathy. Thank goodness we won't have to come to the wedding, because I should cry, all the way through – I wouldn't be able to stop myself.'

Having this to contend with, Hannah was perhaps less vigilant than usual in the matter of my mother's bridesmaids, allowing herself to be take by surprise when my mother, bypassing her authority, wrote directly to Mr Aycliffe in London, informing him of her marriage to a gentleman of considerable local importance and requesting that his daughters should attend her.

'Permission granted,' she told us, floating into my house one morning with a letter in her hand. 'Mr Aycliffe congratulates me on my forthcoming marriage and although he doesn't quite say it – and I didn't quite say it either – he appears to agree with me that a refusal to allow his daughters to be my bridesmaids would appear not only churlish but rather odd. And Mr Aycliffe does not wish to appear odd. I must invite Elinor too, you know – to avoid that slight suggestion of oddity – for if we are to play happy families we must do it right. Yes, absolutely, I must invite her, and I see no cause for alarm, Hannah. We can hardly hope to see Mr Adair on a white charger come to carry her away. And since neither the Hobhouses nor the Oldroyds will be there, I think we may manage her tolerably well. You had best get her a new gown, Verity, for unless her husband agrees to release her clothes, she will be a sorry sight.'

But Morgan Aycliffe had no intention of putting into his wife's faithless hands the costly silks and satins she had extracted from him, fearing, one supposes, that she would sell them to finance her escape or wear them to attract another lover.

'Mr Aycliffe's instructions have been most explicit,' his housekeeper, Mrs Naylor, informed me when I called, keeping me standing in the hallway with such scant courtesy that I understood she did not regard me as her master's friend. 'Undergarments and nightgowns he told me to send on to her, her hairbrushes – except the silver-backed ones – such toiletries as I deemed necessary, and a change of outer garments suitable for day wear – all of which I have done. I have made a list, Mrs Barforth, which I submitted to Mr Aycliffe for his approval, and I would be glad to go through it with you. I believe you will find she has received everything to which Mr Aycliffe considered her entitled, and without his further instructions you must see that I have no authority whatsoever ...'

And leaving that hushed, shadowy house behind, feeling a mad urge to stand in the high-walled, box-hedged garden and shout some bawdy popular song at the top of my voice, I drove straight to Millergate, purchased a length of sky-blue satin, a deep-brimmed bonnet trimmed with white ribbon-roses and a dashing white feather, and set Mrs Stevens to ply her needle.

Mr Aycliffe, of course, was far from pleased with my mother's interference in his affairs, and although he could not withdraw his grudging consent to his daughters' attendance at the wedding, he did specify – most decidedly and most peevishly – that they must have no conversation with their mother.

'Ah well,' my own mother murmured, 'that should be easy enough, for I do believe I have never heard any one of them say more than "please" and "thank you" in their lives, which is hardly conversation.'

Yet, on the day I took them to Miss Boulton's to be fitted for their wedding clothes, my own talkative Caroline did not have things entirely her own way. And when her refusual to wear a pink sash like her cousins became shrill and persistent, Miss Boulton was so sharp with her, so unprofessionally tart, that I could only conclude she was in the throes of one of her nervous headaches, or that the presence of Joel's child made her uneasy.

'I still won't wear a pink sash,' Caroline continued mutinously, knowing that Miss Boulton, however irritable, would hardly go so far as to slap her.'I don't want to look like them.'

It was Faith, the tallest and prettiest of Elinor's children, who stepped forward and said with an unusual measure of sweet reason, 'But you'd never look like us, Caroline. We're all fair and you're dark, and you're inches taller. You don't need any old sash to make you stand out.'

Joel Barforth's daughter, however, had not been entirely convinced even then; she had gone on scowling and muttering, pretending not to understand Miss Boulton's instructions to raise her arms, turn this way and that, stand still, so that the irate dressmaker was easily forgiven when she stuck a pin – accidentally or not – in Caroline's thigh, imagining to herself, perhaps, that it was Joel – or Estella Chase – she was attacking.

But Rosamund Bolton's skill had not faded with her hopes and her good looks, and the four children who followed my mother to the altar of Patterswick Church could not have looked prettier. They came demurely in pairs, Caroline first with Prudence, the eldest of the Aycliffes, whose fine, light brown hair and thin, pointed face reminded me achingly of Crispin, honey-blonde Cecilia and silver-blonde Faith walking behind, Caroline a head taller than any of them, stronger, infinitely more alive, her dark ringlets a rich, true black against the foamy white dress and the satin sash which, as Faith had said, she did not need to make herself noticed.

Joel's daughter. And Joel himself a step or two ahead of her, giving the bride away, playing the gallant son-in-law to perfection as he raised my mother's hand to his lips, relinquished her to her elderly but ardent squire, and then stepped into the pew beside me.

The church seemed surprisingly full, although it did not take a multitude to fill it, Dalby servants and tenants sitting self-consciously at the back, the Dalby heir, young Master Felix, and his mother, in front, Colonel Corey, who was cousin to Squire Dalby as well as to Sir Giles Flood, immediately behind them with his daughter, Estella Chase, a scattering of sporting gentlemen and their ladies shuffling their feet in the pews in between. On the bride's side of the church, Joel and I, a handsome couple, occupied the front pew with our handsome sons, Blaize in dark blue velvet, Nicholas in chocolate brown, Elinor and Mrs Stevens behind us and, behind them, Hannah, impeccably turned out in brown silk with cream lace at her throat, an acutely uncomfortable Ira Agbrigg on one side of her, a much gratified Jonas on the other, the girl, Maria, squeezed into a corner, almost out of sight.

319

The inclusion of the Agbriggs had given rise, quite naturally, to a great deal of discussion since Joel, while making no move to prevent the marriage, had not precisely given it his blessing.

'You may take it that if Mr Agbrigg is not asked, then I shall feel obliged to stay away,' Hannah informed me in Joel's hearing, but when he refused to commit himself either way – refused to discuss anything with me these days other than the most essential domestic issues – my mother, who had championed Elinor, felt it only right to help Hannah too and, driving down to the millhouse, had delivered to the Agbriggs their invitations herself.

'Yes, you may thank me, Hannah,' she said. 'I really am a very good-natured woman, although your brother may not think so, for he scowled quite ferociously on hearing what I had done. However, since he failed to make his wishes clear, I do not see how we are to blame. And on the day, you know, when he has bestowed his mother-in-law on a Dalby of Patterswick, he will be too well pleased to make a fuss.'

And Joel, for all his scowling, had nodded quite civilly to Ira Agbrigg on his way down the aisle, nodded to Colonel Corey too, and to the other hunting, shooting gentlemen who believed, one and all, that money could only come respectably from land, highly delighted, as my mother had said, at this breach in their ranks. Certainly they had their privileges and their pedigrees, certainly they had never soiled their hands with engine grease and hard cash as he had, but perhaps a time was coming when a man's best pedigree would be his bank balance, and when that day dawned Joel Barforth would tower head and shoulders above them all.

I saw Estella Chase glance at him from the corners of her eyes and saw her mouth curl with remembered satisfaction, a woman who was not really my enemy, since she probably never thought of me at all, and, remembering the killing rage I had felt that afternoon at Tarn Edge, I turned my mind hastily away from her to my mother, who, in her swathes of ivory lace, was making her vows.

And it would not do, for I had stood in a church very like this one, eleven years ago, making those very same vows to my grown-up cousin, and I had kept none of them, he only one. We had never loved each other, or even considered the possibility. He had neither cherished nor worshipped me; I had neither honoured nor obeyed him. But he had endowed me with the worldly goods which had been mine in the first place and continued to so endow me when his own skills had caused them to multipy. And, increasingly, our marriage had become a financial arrangement, a commercial enterprise which, after the move to Tarn Edge, would no longer necessitate the sharing of a bed. I was to have my own magnificent, bay-windowed apartment, separated from his by a dressing room as big as the bedroom we now shared, so that when he came home with the dawn, or did not come at all, there would be no explanations to make. Not that I ever asked. Not that he ever offered to tell. But, at Tarn Edge, in the civilized, sophisticated manner of Captain and Mrs Chase, I would be unaware of his comings and goings unless I chose to enquire. And it was a symptom of the disease between us that I would not, could not make those enquiries.

But I could question myself and increasingly did so. What, indeed, could I ever mean to Joel? To begin with, I had been Edwin Barforth's well-mannered, well-dowered sister, not intended for fortune hunters such as he. With Edwin's death I had been a prize he would have given his right arm to win. But I remembered, now, hearing these marriage vows all over again, the awkwardness of our wedding night, and understood, as I had not understood then, how difficult it had been for him to overcome the barrier a man feels with a woman who is almost a sister. He had done no more than his duty that night. And could it be that now, when I had given him three children and seemed unlikely – unwilling – to produce more, he had decided that our sexual duty towards each other was done? Was he, in claiming freedom for himself, allowing me mine? Was he saying to me, 'I require your skills as a hostess; I required you to preside over my social engagements and my domestic comforts, and the education of my children. I require you to wear my pearls and diamonds and my furs so that the world may know me as a rich and generous man. But I do not require you as a lover and, in that respect, you may please yourself, as I shall, provided you are discreet and I never come to hear of it.'

A provocative, tempting thought, and a dangerous one too, for Joel, beneath the London sophistication of his dove-grey coat and trousers, the pearl in his necktie, the scented oil on his hair and the scented lotion on his skin, was still a Law Valley man, raised in a world of double standards, where enjoyment was a male preserve, sin a strictly female matter. In the Law Valley, only men made love for pleasure; respectable women did it because it was their duty, harlots because it was their trade, and it seemed to me perfectly possible that however skilfully Joel played the gentry's games, no matter how real his satisfaction in winning a thoroughbred like Estella Chase, she was, in the private recesses of his mind, no better than a high-class whore. And although he could enjoy a whore – respect her, even, if she extracted enough of his money – he would expect his own wife – in true Law Valley fashion – to be beyond reproach.

Joel may not want me himself – surely he did not want me? – but he would allow no one else to have me, would give no one the opportunity to laugh at him as he was himself all too ready to laugh at Captain Chase. Yet when I had thrown his adulteries in his face, he had made no real defence, had not threatened and blustered and lied as I had expected. And why had he deliberately forced me to watch him kiss Estella Chase? Had he wished to taunt me, or test me, or had it simply been a way of saying, 'This is what I am. We both know it, so now let us be honest about it. Let us be cousins again, in our private lives, and go our separate ways.' And why, since that afternoon, had he barely addressed a word to me, and not very civilly? Why had I felt that murderous rage, that dreadful unleashing of the Barforth side of my nature when, increasingly, I had little room in heart or mind for anyone but Crispin? And, most of all, if Joel was really offering me this compromise and I accepted it, how long could I remain intact? How long before my love for Crispin deteriorated into excitement and I became – like Joel – a self-indulgent adventurer?

Yet what else could I do? I went now, whenever I could, sometimes quite recklessly, to the ivory shop, to Dinah McCluskey, who cleared my way through the alley to the Red Gin. I had opened Crispin's door now a dozen times and then closed it behind me, yet I always opened it again, my mind becoming so fragmented that, inside his room, I was a girl in love who saw nothing but him, yet the instant my foot touched the creaking stairway leading back into the alley, I became a woman with a dinner-party menu to plan, a parcel to meet from the afternoon coach, a chipped vase which must be returned and replaced, a child to be fetched home from school. And I knew my danger, for he was involved now, more than ever, with political ideals which could well take him out of the Law Valley, and unless I could discover the mad courage to go with him, I would be forced, as a final act of love, to release him.

My mother left the church, Mrs Dalby of Patterswick now, to a joyous pealing of bells, my daughter Caroline preening herself on the church porch as people came rushing to congratulate the bride, seeing herself, I thought, one day leaving some vast cathedral on the arm of a prince, her Aycliffe cousins walking behind her like a flock of quiet, sad-eyed doves following a peacock. And for a while we all stood in the churchyard in the autumn sunshine, remarking on my mother's incredible youthfulness, the incredible good fortune of the squire, at his age, to get so lovely a wife, the incredible good fortune of the bride, with her common, commercial background, to get herself so gentlemanly a husband.

'How like your mother you are, Mrs Barforth,' Estella Chase murmured to me, offering two totally disinterested fingers by way of greeting. 'My father and I were both much struck by it.'

But her father, the once upright and genial Colonel Corey, much altered now by recurrent bouts of illness, looked too frail in the cruel November daylight to have much interest in anything but the cosseting of his failing limbs, and it was largely on his account that we cut our observations short and drove back to the Hall.

Squire Dalby's house was very old, quite small now to my eyes, which had grown accustomed to the budding splendours of Tarn Edge, but so very old, so overlaid with the births and deaths, joys and sorrows of so many lives, that beside it Tarn Edge was as yet no more than a costly pile of stones. To begin with, there had been a pair of towers, built for defence against Scots and Lancastrians and Parliamentarians, as well as the private feudings of ancient Dalbys, who, in quieter times, had added rooms as it pleased them, a hall with a gallery, a cobweb of corridors and terrifying stairways, creaking boards and sagging, bulging walls which even to the insensitive could have contained a secret chamber and the bones of a captured enemy, a mad relation, a faithless woman.

But today all was light and harmony, the stone-flagged hall decorated with harvest fruits and autumn branches, the fragrant crackling of logs in the plain stone hearth that had nothing to adorn its mantelpiece but an array of pewter jugs and dishes which may have seen service in Cromwell's time. There was a massive, iron-bound oak chest, a colossal oak sideboard, much scarred and knotted, a number of narrow wooden chairs offering no comfort, a table almost as long as the room itself, bearing a wedding breakfast clearly intended for men who had spent the day in the open air, in the saddle. A harsh, tough-grained, somewhat arrogant setting, in no way softened by the light of the window occupying almost the whole of one wall, its panes set with the armorial bearings of the local nobility who had allied themselves with the Dalbys, the Ramsdens of Huddersfield, the Tempests of Bradford, the Wintertons of Floxley, the Floods of Cullingford, the de Greys of Redesdale, and, in the centre, the device of the Dalbys themselves, to which my mother could only add her wit and charm.

By no means overawed, she floated serenely among her guests with a word and a smile for everyone, and, watching her, my father's face rushed swiftly into my mind and out again, leaving tears in my eyes.

'Do go and talk to the Agbriggs,' she murmured, laying a cool, happy hand on my arm, 'for no one else will, and Hannah is beginning to look fierce. And, dearest, do tell Elinor that if she wants a half hour or so alone with her children it can easily be arranged.'

But Elinor, when the offer was conveyed to her, shook her head, her eyes dull and disinterested.

'No, no. Thank your mother kindly, but, really, why embarrass the poor things? They are timid enough in any case, and heaven knows what Mrs Naylor has been saying to them lately. No. Let them run and play in the garden while they can.'

And when, worried at her apathy, I tried to urge her, she tossed her head and bit her lip, with something of her old impatience.

'What on earth can I find to say to them? What possible good can I do? They are girls, don't you see? Girls – like you and me and Hannah were once girls – and I don't think I want anything to do with girls. They'll get married – their father will see to that – and I don't think I want to know about it. And, after all, the last thing they need is my example, for who could call my life a success? No, no. I'll just go and talk to my sister. Poor Hannah, I never thought she'd need my help, but now there is something I can do for her. I'll go and say kind things to Mr Agbrigg – who really doesn't like us very much, you know – and I'll flatter his clever son, which is easy enough even for me. Look, the children are doing very well. I do believe Faith is actually skipping, which I never saw her do before. Let them be.'

Skipping indeed, silvery ringlets flying, forgetting everything but her enjoyment of the fresh air and her own unaccustomed freedom of movement, Prudence and Cecilia and Maria Agbrigg joggling along behind, grouped around Caroline, who was explaining something, organizing something, studiously ignoring her brother and Felix Dalby, who, with another boy – a young Winterton of Floxley – were hatching secrets nearby.

323

'What an attractive child your daughter is – so unusually self-possessed,' someone murmured to me, and meeting the brilliant, altogether false smile of Lady Winterton of Floxley Park, I remembered the rumour that her estates had been sadly burdened by extravagance and misma-nagement, and realized that Joel's boast of being able to offer his daughter a title one day had not been idle.

'And are those your sons, Mrs Barforth? Such sturdy little men and such a comfort – such a stake in the future – when there is property to be looked after. I am so rarely in Cullingford – I find it so sadly altered from the quaint little market town of my childhood. My cousin Giles Flood's town, we always thought of it, although it seems rather to be your husband's town now. When I next come over I wonder if I may leave my card?'

And I knew that the effort it had cost this woman – a Flood and a Winterton – to beg an invitation from me, a mongrel millmaster's daugh-ter, would be an additional satisfaction to Joel.

'Well, dear,' I could imagine her saying to her balding, rather chinless spouse, 'if Estella Chase can sleep with the man, I think I can bring myself to take tea with his wife. They have money to burn, dear. Money they can't possible know what to do with, and it could almost be an act of charity to show them. She is quite a presentable little thing – quite well-spoken. One has no need to be ashamed of her. And one must assume her daughter will have a fortune. Naturally, dear, I quite agree, one cannot possibly want to marry such people, but one can hardly doubt how badly they would like to marry us – and in that case, they must be made to pay for the privilege.'

'They are girls,' Elinor had said, only moments ago. 'They'll get married – their father will see to that – and I don't think I want to know about it.'

But smiling, giving this arrogant, overbearing woman the answer she wanted to hear, I reached out in my mind to Caroline – tossing her dark ringlets for the Dalby boy and the Winterton boy to see – and I wanted urgently to know about her future, to stand between her and the mistakes I had already made, to stand beside her when she made mistakes of her own.

And leaving Lady Winterton behind, I walked quickly down the garden, understanding from the arrogant nonchalance of my son Blaize and the scowling pugnacity of my son Nicholas that unless I acted quickly they would very likely turn on the heir to Floxley Park, the heir to Dalby Hall, and knock them both down.

33

We moved to Tarn Edge at the end of the month, an enormous exodus, leaving the Top House unsold, untenanted, a prize Joel would bestow where and when he chose – on Hannah, perhaps, if she could find her way back into his good graces; or, if she did not, on some ambitious stranger it might please him to promote over Ira Agbrigg's head.

Both Hannah and Elinor made the move with us, Hannah clearly as a temporary measure, since her wedding date was already set, her authority already supreme at the millhouse; Elinor perhaps as no more than a fleeting visitor, since the fall of the Whig administration that November and the likelihood of a general election meant the return of her husband to Cullingford and an alteration of some sort in her affairs.

I had expected Mr Aycliffe to be seriously displeased at Hannah's engagement, shocked even, but he had written warm letters of congratulation both to her and to Mr Agbrigg, proving to me at any rate that, valuing Hannah's friendship as he did and having suffered at the speculation it had sometimes caused, he not only considered the protection of a husband more convenient but was well suited to see her marry a man who would be unlikely to complain whenever he – Morgan Aycliffe – monopolized her time. And since the engagement had also served to bring Hannah and Elinor much closer together, it seemed that Hannah would manage to arrange things in her own way.

My own time, just then, was eaten up by the demands of Tarn Edge, consumed entirely by the interviewing and engaging of new staff, the arrangement and rearrangement of furniture and ornaments, the sheer administrative burden of such a household. Mrs Stevens – a friend now rather than an employee – had gladly relinquished her housekeeper's keys, contenting herself with the care of my social commitments and other small matters between overselves, and every morning, in her place, there was a stately Mrs Richmond to offer me the day's menus and to guide me – since she had seen service with a baronet – in the way my husband wished me to go. We had a butler now, who had taken great pleasure in bringing me Lady Winterton's calling card on a silver tray, and a pair of good-looking footmen – a danger, most likely, to the maids, who, unlike my old Marth-Ellen, who had never hesitated to speak her mind, were trained, according to Mrs Richmond's aristocratic notions, to keep out of my way.

A lady, it appeared, did not concern herself with the names and faces of her staff. She wished simply to be served efficiently, unobtrusively, by willing but anonymous hands, and required her house to be immaculately maintained but had no desire at all to see the work being done. And so I grew accustomed to lavender cotton uniforms and white starched aprons whisking themselves out of any room I happened to enter, or disappearing into empty bedrooms to avoid passing me in a corridor; accustomed to being on speaking terms with no one but the head parlour-maid, who served my tea, immaculate in her black silk dress and white cap and ribbons, and pretty, cheerful Sally, who did my hair and looked after my clothes.

And I believe that until the house was ready, fully furnished and fully staffed, even I had not realized the extent of Joel's success.

'I'll have a decent house before I'm forty,' he had told me, and now, at something less than that, he had built Tarn Edge, a monument to the power of machines and his own courage and ability to use them.

'It must be like living in the Assembly Rooms,' Emma-Jane Hobhouse told me. 'Don't you feel strange, sometimes?'

And Lady Winterton, driving over one bracing December morning with my mother, expressed her envy by ignoring the house altogether. 'What a lovely day. And how fresh the air is. One would hardly think oneself so near to town.'

But both Nethercoats Mill and Floxley Park were in decline, and their owner's pique could do no more than flatter us.

The house was set on a slight rise of the land, the grounds falling away from it like a wide, tiered skirt of lawns and flower beds and elaborately clipped box hedges, their intense dark green broken by the sudden white gleam of a garden statue. There was a summerhouse, a covered, trellised walk festooned by hanging baskets of ferns and blossoms leading from it to a stretch of quiet, lily-studded water. There would be a carpet of daffodils in the spring, forsythia, lilac, massed hedges of rhododendron shading from the palest pink to a royal purple. There would be roses and carnations to come after, a mighty oak, a dreamy willow, evergreens to see us through the winter, glass houses for rare plants and blooms so that at all times the house could be filled with flowers.

The hall now was richly, darkly panelled, the stained-glass landing window casting an almost medieval light on the life-size bronze stag at the foot of the stairs, the longcase clock of elaborately carved mahogany, the marble nymph, set in a fluted recess, brand-new yet managing somehow to give an air of dusty antiquity, as if she had been but recently unearthed from some Grecian hillside.

The drawing room, its huge bay windows turned away from the mill – only two miles distant – was a clear forty feet by twenty, its high ceiling a marvel of gold and blue mouldings, bearing the weight of two chandeliers, offering between them the shimmering, dancing light of eighty candles. The fireplace, backed by a gilt-framed mirror that rose almost to the ceiling, was pure white marble; a French clock in ormolu and enamel stood in the centre of the mantelpiece with a pair of flowery, rococo vases by Sèvres on either side.

There were wide velvet sofas, their weighty feet sinking into the carpet, balloon-backed, cabriole-legged chairs, ormolu-mounted, inlaid cabinets of dark wood, glass-fronted to display the fine porcelain of Coalport and Meissen and Sèvres we had collected with small knowledge but growing enthusiasm. Delicate, linen-fold panelling covered the lower half of the walls, with more moulded plasterwork above it, a neutral, ivory-coloured background for the heavy-framed Italian landscapes Cullingford could barely understand and the scantily robed pagan nymphs and shepherds it could not understand at all.

The dining room was high-ceilinged too, its carved wooden walls almost black against the oval portrait of Caroline in a white dress and pink-fringed shawl, Blaize and Nicholas in jewel-coloured velvet jackets, my own bare shoulders, framed in a cloud of gauze, my pearls painted in exquisite, lustrous detail, the likeness to my mother beyond dispute. The dining table was very long, very highly polished; the sideboards, along two walls, were carved with cupids and grapes and acanthus leaves, and set with shelves and niches for the accommodation of crouching bronze animals, crystal lamps, silver, and more porcelain, each costly object doubled by the tall mirrors behind. The windows were shrouded with heavy, dark velvet, and the double doors leading to the book-lined, leather-upholstered smoking room were of decorated oak, this smaller room, which would be Joel's private sanctum, leading in turn to a wide terrace with steps directly into the garden, so that he could take his guests and their cigars into the fresh air on summer nights.

I had a sitting room of my own leading to the same terrace, chintzy and light, with all the feminine clutter of worktables and writing tables and a pianoforte covered with an embroidered shawl, which I had never learned to play. Apart from these rooms, my own creamy, lacy bedchamber, and Caroline's smaller version of the same, the rest of the house was almost unknown to me.

The kitchens, undoubtedly, were superb, crammed with every modern device, but kitchens were for cooks, as schoolrooms were for governesses, housekeepers' rooms strictly for housekeepers, and Joel's room, with its capacious half-tester bed, its vivid oriental rugs, its much-talked-of recess that contained his private bathtub, was altogether for Joel. I would not enter without an invitation.

Needless to say, the house brought Joel no popularity. Law Valley men, if they had money, did not spend it on bronze lions and paintings of near-naked women. Nor did they indulge themselves with the suspicious, very nearly effeminate habit of taking hot baths. Law Valley men invested their spare cash in far more solid propositions than fine porcelain, or they hoarded it. They washed in cold water, in a bedroom they shared with their wives, and now that Joel had chosen not only to play the sultan in his personal habits but to consort with the gentry as well, he was regarded with growing alarm. Not only were the feelings of Law Valley men truly lacerated at this squandering of hard-earned wealth, but what on earth would happen if their own womenfolk should expect them to do the same?

The Reverend Mr Brand, catching the drift of public opinion and still smarting perhaps at Hannah's defection, was quick to preach a sermon on the subject of criminal extravagance. Emma-Jane Hobhouse, whose ten little boys were bursting Nethercoats at the seams, continued to let me know she could never bring herself to live in such a mausoleum. Little Lucy Oldroyd, who had plenty of money and could hardly blame me for her husband's aversion to spending it, lectured me gently about the simplicity and humility of a truly Christian way of life, hinting at the discomfort she felt in my opulent surroundings when there was such poverty and deprivation in the world. But none of them ever refused my invitations and, between them and my host of new acquaintances, my time was rarely my own.

It was not only the Wintertons and the Dalbys who 'took me up' that year, for Cullingford was going through yet another stage of rapid growth, manufacturers and merchants moving in from all parts of the area and beyond with the capital to buy up old factories or build new ones; men of energy and ambition who were quick to appreciate Joel's achievement and sophisticated enough to allow him his hot baths and his painted nudes, and for whose wives I was a natural social target.

327

I took tea now not only at Floxley Hall but in the elegant new villas multiplying at the continuation of Blenheim Lane. I dined with charming, gruff-voiced men of supposedly Germanic origin, whose wives sometimes spoke little English at all but who, far from despising our pictures, were often artists themselves, devoting hours to their canvases, to the pianoforte or the violin, to matters other than the eternal production of babies and hot dinners. And if Emma-Jane Hobhouse considered their tastes decadent, their religious practices decidedly suspicious, I for one, was fascinated, immensely encouraged, happy almost, on the days when I could convince myself that Crispin would love me forever and that Joel would not care.

Estella Chase's father, Colonel Corey, who had looked so frail at my mother's wedding, died at the beginning of the winter, making Mrs Chase a wealthy woman, and it was at his funeral that I first saw Morgan Aycliffe again, standing grey-lipped, hollow-eyed, enormously long and thin in his tightly buttoned black coat at the back of the church. And later, in the wind-raked, bitterly cold graveyard, when he raised his hat to me, I had no choice but to approach him, grateful that Crispin, who had known Colonel Corey well – who had been, in fact, considerably in the old gentleman's debt – was not there.

Mr Aycliffe had come back, of course, for the general election, having decided to risk himself at the hustings once again, and, for a moment, he talked gravely to me about the King's dismissal of his Whig ministers in November and his sending for the Duke of Wellington, who had refused to do more than act as caretaker until Robert Peel could be fetched home from abroad. And now, even though Peel had chosen rightly to go to the country, Mr Aycliffe doubted that there would be any clear decision.

'We are a deeply divided nation,' he told me, but although he said little else I understood that, politics apart, he had heard how Cullingford was building again, new factories and new houses, more worker's cottages, more terraces for overlookers and craftsmen, more managerial villas, more palaces for those who wished to rival Joel. And then there was the matter of his wife.

Elinor locked herself in her room the evening he called to see Joel, but he made no attempt to molest her, and when he left it was Hannah, momentarily back in favour, who was called into the smoking room to receive her brother's confidences. But, knowing them all as I did, I required no great wit to see through the net they were weaving.

Six months had passed since Elinor's attempted elopement and now we were at the end of our excuses. Now she must either recover from her illness or die of it, and, recovering, must either return home or be cast out into permanent exile. And although Mr Aycliffe no longer desired the lady's fair body – had perhaps rather passed the season for such things altogether – and had nothing but abhorrence for the foolishness and depravity of her nature, he was prepared to admit the awkwardness, at this time, of fighting an election without her. The recent increase in Cullingford's population had brought new voters, new ideas, and his success was no longer the foregone conclusion it had been two years ago.

This time he needed to win the support of strangers and he was decidedly nervous at the idea of the vicious Mark Corey and his own ungrateful, lying son presenting him to these newcomers, in the pages of the *Cullingford Star*, as a man who had ill used his young wife. Not, of course, that there had been any ill usuage, but in a world where it was considered more amusing to believe a sensational lie than the plain truth, it seemed best on the whole to remember his Christian principles, raise up the fallen woman, and take her home. And, having done so, he felt that Joel would have no hesitation in recommending him to his new friends, both as a politician and as a master builder.

So he was ready to take her back, and Joel, who knew the value, in these days of expanding trade, of a friend at Westminster, was ready to let her go. Nor, I imagine, was he prepared to tolerate the interference of his meddlesome wife, for, a day or so after Mr Aycliffe's return, Elinor was whisked away on a long-proposed visit to my mother, leaving me anchored to my social engagements at home.

'Just a few days in the country,' Hannah told Emma-Jane brightly. 'She is much improved and we have high hope of her being able to stand up to her social obligations during the election. But you will see for yourself at my brother's party on the twentieth. Yes, yes – of course she will be there.'

And I could only conclude that Hannah, who went regularly to Patterswick, knew far more than I.

'Are you sure?' I asked when Emma-Jane had gone.

Shrugging, Hannah answered coldly, 'Has it ever been in doubt? My sister will be here, at your grand reception, on her husband's arm – not only willingly but gladly.'

And to avoid unnecessary argument, I refrained from reminding her that since we were giving the reception partly to present Morgan Aycliffe to his new electors and partly to refresh the memories of old ones, her prediction, for Mr Aycliffe's sake, had best be correct.

I had spent the whole of one dreary day in my sitting room with Mrs Stevens, writing cards of invitation, an anxious morning or two with my new housekeeper, Mrs Richmond, but her training in a baronet's household enabled her to view the feeding and entertaining of a hundred or so Law Valley notables with no particular alarm. And when she presented me with a list of all the things I had been meaning to bring up with her, and more than a few others which had not even entered my mind, I realized that she required no more of me – that Joel required no more of me – than a warm smile and a welcoming murmur on the night and a gown that would be remembered even if my conversation was not.

I bespoke my outfit this time from Rosamund Boulton – refusing an offer from my new friend Mrs Mandelbaum to take me to Leeds, a suggestion from Lady Winterton that I might like to try her dressmaker in York – for Miss Boulton had looked unhappy lately, as well as ill-tempered, and perhaps Hannah's wedding dress, already on order, had done little to ease her mind.

My confidence was not misplaced, for she designed for me a stunning confection the colour of old ivory, its wide skirt almost entirely covered with pearl beads stitched, by the several embroideresses now in her employ, into dainty outlines of flowers. There were pearls too on the foamy, lacy sleeves, a thick, gleaming band of them at the shoulders, thinning to a mere scattering at the elbows, a tracery of pearls and lace along the low neck, and an imaginative cluster of pearl-studded, ivory roses for my hair. Admiring its shimmering elegance, aware of the bustling, thriving shop around me, I wondered what case Miss Boulton really had – when she was so clever and so prosperous – to be so morose?

I took the dress home with me and tried it on again, arousing great enthusiasm in Mrs Stevens and Sally, my recently acquired maid, but when I mentioned it to Joel he either did not hear or did not think it worth an anwer.

'I thought Miss Boulton looked most unwell today,' I told him and then retreated instantly into some safe discussion of Caroline's music lessons, since Rosamund Boulton could lead to Estella Chase, to infidelity, to that dressing room separating my bed from Joel's like a thick, spiked wall, real issues, real decisions, unanswerable, unthinkable just now, when I had not yet discovered the extent of my courage or whether, indeed, I was brave at all.

'I find this all decidedly odd,' my mother told me, having driven over to discuss Elinor and discovering instead, after a quick glance at that dressing room and some shrewd questioning, that my own marriage was in a more perilous condition than she had thought. 'I have no objection to separate rooms. In fact, I find the arrangement most civilized. But no man gives up his conjugal rights without good reasons, and it is no more than prudent to ascertain exactly what they are. In matters of this sort it is essential that a woman should know just where she stands, for, all else considered, my love, if you were to become pregnant now you would find it most awkward. Yes, yes, you may have discovered the uses of sponges soaked in vinegar and certain ointments – Mrs Stevens's harlot's tricks, in fact – but none of them are totally reliable. I merely mention this in passing, since if I were to be put to the torture I would hardly know how to describe either your hopes or your intentions. But, dearest, since the subject has arisen, is it not time now to let Mr Crispin Aycliffe go? I perfectly understand the superior quality of your love, but think, dearest, think well, is it not time now for you to withdraw and give him the opportunity to fall in love with someone else? Painful, of course, even to contemplate the possibility, and he would certainly swear to you that he could never love again. But life is not really like that, Verity, and you should not stand in his way. Can you, in all honesty – in all sanity – tell me I am wrong?'

I could not. Yet the elections, in which Crispin was deeply involved, enabled me once again to put off my decision, his conversation now being political rather than romantic, our time together considerably reduced. He had spoken out this time no longer as a Tory, no longer exclusive in his support of Richard Oastler and the local issue of factory reform, but as a radical, an out-and out revolutionary, who advocated

330

with passion that every man, no matter what his status, should have the vote. And when he was hissed and jeered and asked how he could justify the folly of putting power into the hands of an ignorant, gin-soaked populace who could not run their own meagre affairs, much less govern a nation, he had answered simply, 'Educate them.'

Dreams, of course, according to Morgan Aycliffe, since one half of the people didn't wish to be educated and the other half was incapable of it, yet Crispin continued to speak, whenever a crowd assembled to hear him, somewhat to the embarrassment of the official Tory candidate, a portly, excessively good-natured gentleman who, while wishing to stress the alliance between the Tories and the workers, had no desire at all to incite them to riot.

But, whenever I drove through town that December on my many errands and my vastly escalating social duties, I saw groups of workmen carrying Tory banners calling for action against the abominable alliance of the Whig grandees and the middle classes, and although these men still lacked the votes to drag the manufacturers down they had muscle in plenty to attack, once again, the windows of the Swan and, on polling day, to persuade certain voters to abstain.

'We won't win,' one of them told me, thrusting himself in my way as I came out of Miss Boulton's shop, my maid Sally behind me, her arms full of parcels. 'We won't win this time, but we'll win in the end. And then it'll be God help the likes of you. It's you who'll be carrying the parcels then, and this lass here who'll be wearing your silks and getting into your fine carriage. Go and tell your husband that, Mrs Barforth.'

Had I been close enough to Joel just then even to tell him that much, he merely would have replied, 'They may knock down what I've built up – like they did in France – but they'll need me, or a man like me, to build it up again.' And, as usual, I could see right – and wrong – on every side.

On the fifteenth of December, five days before my party, his election campaign already at its height, Morgan Aycliffe declared his intention of driving to Patterswick to see his wife and, meeting no opposition from Joel, who had spent an hour with his sister the day before, or from Hannah, who had gone to Dalby Park with him and remained there, I ordered my carriage and went off to give Elinor warning.

'Ah yes,' my mother murmured, hurrying to greet me across the uneven stone paving of the great hall. 'It is today, then? I think she is quite ready.'

And going upstairs to one of the dark, low-ceilinged bedrooms which Squire Dalby had seen no reason either to carpet or to decorate since his great-grandfather had not, I found my cousin sitting on the hard, ancient bed, her few remaining possessions set out around her.

'Today?' she said, no longer the whispering, sobbing girl of six months ago, no longer the lethargic, blank-eyed creature of a fortnight past, lacking the energy to raise her hand, but a woman I had never really seen before, hard-eyed and resolute, almost unfriendly, the impertinent tilt of her head telling me that neither my sympathy nor my impotent good-intentions would be welcome.

331

'Well then, one day is the same as another, and, as you see, I can be ready in five minutes. I have only these few petticoats and everything else I may carry home on my back. Five minutes ...'

'Elinor, is this really what you want?'

'And what else is there?'

'Joel –'

'Joel will not give me a penny. He told me so yesterday. I may do as I please, he says, may take Daniel Adair or anyone else who wins my fancy, once I have made sure of my husband's money. But, until then, I am to go home and behave myself. And one has to admit the sense of it.'

'And if you refused, Joel would not see you starve – whatever he says –'

'Ah no, I am well of aware of that. But we are not talking of starving, are we, Verity. We are talking of living, and my ideas on the subject are very exact, very large. I find, after all, that I would like the keys to my wardrobe back again, and my carriage to drive. And Joel has arranged all that for me, has been most specific about the way I am to be treated and the pin money I am to receive. You should not have given yourself the trouble of coming all this way to see me, Verity, when tomorrow I will be back in Blenheim Lane. Hannah is here, and she is to come home with me and spend a day or two, until I find my feet. Really – you are not needed.'

And crossing to the window, she turned her back to peer through the dull, diamond-shaped panes.

'Will my husband be very long, do you think?'

'No. Half an hour behind me on the road. But, Elinor, tell me, is it part of the bargain between your husband and mine that you and I shall no longer be friends?'

'No,' she said, her back still resolutely turned. 'No one has asked me that. No one has spoken of you at all. It is just that – I don't want your sympathy, Verity. I find it – inconvenient.'

'How is that?'

'Because you remind me, more than anyone else, of what a fool I have been. And I do not wish to be reminded. Because I confided in you the whole of my silly, sloppy, worthless little romance, and whether or not you smiled at me behind my back, it suits me to think you did. I dislike you because I dislike the memory of myself as I was six months ago. And I dislike you most of all because now you would like to see me do something heroic and altogether extraordinary, like somehow managing to support myself instead of returning to the only man who appears willing to do it for me. You want me to live up to all the threats and promises I made, and I dislike you for wanting that – and myself for not being able to do it. I think you are probably my best friend, Verity, which is another cause for dislike, since I can't help feeling I have disappointed you.'

We sat in silence for a while, one at either side of the bed, her few meagre petticoats between us, the dark December afternoon outside the window threatening rain, the empty Patterswick road offering us suddenly the sound of hooves and wheels.

'I think he is coming.'

'Yes. But he will spend a little time first with my mother. Elinor – what is really in your mind?'

And as she made her answer, the rain tore itself loose from the skirts of a vast grey cloud, the room becoming too dark for me to see her face.

'Oh – what has always been there, I suppose. I shall recover, presently, and learn to stop despising myself. But I have been a great fool. I had only to wait, as Daniel Adair told me. "Just you wait," he used to say. "Bide your time and you'll have it all," which meant, of course, that he intended to have it all away from me as soon as he could. Well, now I shall do just that, and when I have it, I shall share it with no one. It strikes me that the world is full of Daniel Adairs, and when I am free I shall be able to pick and choose. My husband may not leave me his entire fortune, or he may tie it up so that I shall only have the spending of a part. But there will be enough – my brother will see to that. I shall have my horses and carriage, my clothes, and I shall be courted for what I have and for what my daughters have. In the meantime I shall be fully occupied. I shall be waiting for my husband to die. I shall devote my time, right gladly, to that.'

The sound of hooves now was immediately below us, Mr Aycliffe's spare, grey figure visible on the gravel, feeling the cold, I thought, and grateful of my mother's offer of hot, spiced wine; a man too burdened, perhaps, by the demands of politics and commerce to be unduly troublesome to his child-wife, who was no longer a child.

'Well,' she said, getting to her feet, smoothing her hair and rearranging the folds of her skirt. 'I had best go and present myself as a penitent and get it over. Tears, I suppose, will be very necessary, and I may swoon a little – yes, indeed I may, for I would like to wear the first Mrs Aycliffe's pearls to your party and it will take a great deal of humility to achieve it. Don't look so sad, Verity. Don't ask yourself how I shall endure. I shall stare at the ceiling and think of the sky-blue satin dresses as I have done these ten years past – as I should have done on the accursed night I ran away. And he, no doubt, will think of the votes and the contracts Joel has brought him, and remind himself that I am cheaper than a proper whore. Don't worry. My mother detested my father, and you and Hannah are not in love – not with your husbands, at any rate.'

And reaching out her arm quite blindly before her, she pressed the hand I slipped into hers, opened the door, and, composing herself as the supplicant she was about to play, walked very quietly down the corridor, down the stairs, going meekly as a nun to judgement.

34

Tarn Edge on the night of the reception was everything one had hoped for, luminous with candlelit crystal and silver, fragrant with hothouse blooms and the spicy, tantalizing odours of fine wines and foods designed to please not only the palate but the eye. There was to be no dancing, this being a serious occasion, an opportunity to discuss vital economic and social issues with Morgan Aycliffe, Member of Parliament for Cullingford, as well as to marvel at the wealth and good taste – or criminal folly and extravagance, according to how one looked at it – of Joel Barforth, his chief supporter. But seriousness had never been a bar to Law Valley appetites and, had these not been adequately catered for, few would have scrupled to ask the reason why.

Refreshments of an insubstantial nature – claret, sherry, a magnificent ice-cold punch, tea and coffee for those whose constitution or whose religion forbade them anything stronger – were to be served from the arrival of the first carriage to the moment the last one rolled away. While somewhere around midnight we were to serve a mammoth champagne supper of salmon and game, Frenchified pâtés and intricate savoury moulds that some would find irresistible and others indecent. There would be ices too, for the ladies, high-peaked mountains of cream stuffed with nuts and cherries, an epergne overflowing with fruit and ferns like a horn of plenty, and to enable the gentlemen to retire in peace to the smoking room for their brandy and cigars, there would be a pianist, come all the way from Manchester on my new friend Mrs Mandelbaum's recommendation, to entertain us.

I had written on the bottom right-hand corner of my cards of invitation: 'To meet Mr Morgan Aycliffe,' lacking the confidence to include his wife's name, but they were among our first arrivals, Mr Aycliffe self-conscious and stern, Elinor looking at last like a politician's wife. There had been no time to acquire a new sky-blue satin gown but she had filled in the low neck of an old one with layers of creamy lace, removed a great deal of the trimming from the skirt, transforming a once dashing outfit into something infinitely more demure. The silky cascade of her hair had been tamed, its ringlets and wildly curling tendrils smoothed into neat wings coming from a centre parting to cover her ears and form an elegant but subdued coil at the nape of her neck. And although the first Mrs Aycliffe's pearls were around her neck again she seemed to have no awareness of them, no intention at all of flaunting them at Emma-Jane. She looked as if she had been very ill indeed, would be quite likely to fall ill again, but unlike the old days when the merest hint of a headache would have taken her to bed, she remained for the whole of that long night at her husband's side, listening intently as he explained his policies, smiling when he smiled, leaving him only when his political duty called him to the brandy bottle, and hers, it seemed, was to sit between Hannah and Emma-Jane and pay polite attention to the music.

Emma-Jane, of course, so plump now that it was hard to tell whether she was pregnant or not, did not believe a word of Elinor's illness and was completely convinced, as little, sharp-eyed Lucy Oldroyd was convinced, there had been something very much amiss. But there was nothing they could prove. And although, in normal circumstances, they would not have worried overmuch about that, Bradley Hobhouse, increasingly concerned about money, might have pointed out to Emma-

Jane that if he ever needed to borrow, then Joel Barforth was probably the only man who could afford to lend. Matthew Oldroyd, who had been twice fined recently for employing underaged children in his spinning mill, might have warned Lucy that it would be as well to keep on the right side of their Member of Parliament. And perhaps neither of them really had the nerve to question a situation which my mother – Squire Dalby's lady – had so readily endorsed. Certainly, in their minds, they knew Elinor had had a lover, but Emma-Jane had never heard of Daniel Adair, Lucy's imagination extended no further than the holding of hands beneath a carriage rug, a few kisses and sighs, and, as the evening wore on, even Hannah's vigilance began to relax.

'I think everything is going very well indeed,' she told me, her eyes on Ira Agbrigg, terribly stiff in his brand-new evening clothes but having no difficulty, among all these strangers, in finding someone to talk to him. Bradley Hobhouse, who had been drinking, Hannah thought, before he arrived, had indeed pushed past Mr Agbrigg on the stairs and Matthew Oldroyd had asked him how he did. But George Mandelbaum lately come to us via Manchester and Hamburg, was pleased enough to make the acquaintance of Hannah's fiancé, and since Mr Mandelbaum would undoubtedly be of importance in our community, I thought that Hannah's social and civic ambitions could well be realized one day.

'Mr Agbrigg looks quite presentable in his new clothes,' my mother murmured. 'Really – is it possible that he came to me once, cap in hand, clogs on his feet, and his elbows out of his jacket, to inform against his friends? And now he is almost too smart. You will have noticed, I suppose, that Sir Charles Winterton's coat is decidely short in the sleeves – one can only suppose he had it from his grandfather, like the rest of his goods and chattels.'

And, indeed, the contrast between the neat-as-a-new-pin Mr Agbrigg and the carelessly-thrown-together Sir Charles Winterton was reflected everywhere, creating a gulf between the newly rich, the 'machine-rich,' and these landed gentlemen and their languid ladies who did not feel the need of fine clothes and expensive French furniture to prove their status. Even little Lucy Oldroyd, not noted for her extravagance, had a decent diamond on her finger; even Emma-Jane had encased herself in a length of gold-embroidered purple satin that would not have looked amiss on a queen. But Lady Winterton, whose dull green gown inspired me with thankfulness that I had refused the services of her dressmaker, wore no jewellery but an antique ring which might have been improved with cleaning, while her hands, although proclaiming her a noted horsewoman, would have profited from the attentions of a clever maid.

Estella Chase was not there, being still in mourning for her father, but Mrs Elizabeth Flood, daughter-in-law of our manorial lord Sir Giles, who had looked in for a disdainful five minutes and stayed until well after supper, had only a single strand of pearls around her throat – the remainder, one supposed, having gone to satisfy her husband's passion for cards and Arabian stallions – and wore a gown we all believed we had seen before.

But, undoubtedly, it was going well. Those who wished to meet Morgan

Aycliffe met him; others, like the Tory gentry, who wanted nothing to do with a Whig, contented themselves with costing up the contents of the drawing room and wondering between themselves what kind of fortune Joel was likely to give to Miss Caroline; whether, perhaps, the demands of one's ancestral estates could justify the bestowal of a niece or possibly a younger daughter on Mr Blaize or Mr Nicholas Barforth. Others, who wished merely to eat and drink, gossip, see and be seen, found their desires more than adequately catered for.

I moved from room to room, murmuring, smiling until my cheeks cracked, accepting glasses of champagne and, moving away, setting them down again untouched. Hours of rich food in my nostrils had taken my appetite away; false conversations had planted themselves on my tongue, so that I no longer needed to think as I spoke, functioning perhaps as career hostesses must, with an automatic brilliance far removed from reality.

'You're beautiful,' Bradley Hobhouse told me, meaning it, although most women seemed beautiful to him through the brandy fumes so often in his head, and when one thought of Emma-Jane ...

'You are looking extremely well,' Morgan Aycliffe said peevishly, having had rather too much of pretty women for his taste these last few years.

'Stunning,' Sir Charles Winterton proclaimed, while my new stepfather, Squire Dalby, grew quite sentimental and shed a few tears because he had not known my mother at my age.

But Joel, his eyes sweeping brusquely over my lovely, lustrous gown, had merely reached into his pocket and tossed at me, as casually as he had once tossed me my pearls, a thick rope of gold, elaborately twisted and set with diamonds, which now was an unaccustomed weight on my arm.

I had thanked him – quite meekly, I think, having nothing else to say – and, nodding, smiling a little, he had walked past me on business of his own, giving me no clue as to his meaning. The bracelet, I supposed, had cost a great deal of money, since Joel would not have bought it otherwise, and, as with my pearls, he would not ask me what I had done with it tomorrow morning. He would not require me to return it to him for safekeeping, would not grumble if I wore it in the garden when I exercised my dogs. The bracelet was mine, although I had not asked for and did not greatly care for it, manacling my wrist and weighing me down, for it was heavy, as this house was heavy, as Joel's apparent indifference to me, which should have been light, was heavy. And I could see no point in further resistance. I was Verity Barforth and would never be any other, and I must go to Crispin as soon as I could and tell him so. I must admit to myself that he could be happy without me; that I, without him, could be reasonable again, sensible and safe. And when I was older, quieter, surely it would not matter so much? Surely I could immerse myself in my children's lives, as other women seemed able to do, and remember him in small, permitted doses, with pleasure? Surely it would be enough to know that, recognizing his need for freedom, I had willingly, lovingly, set him free?

At three o'clock in the morning, four o'clock in the morning, when the Aycliffes and the Wintertons and other respectable people had long since ordered their carriages and gone home, the house was still full of the hard-core drinkers, some of them in small scatterings, here and there, most of them in the smoking room in various stages of intoxication. Bradley Hobhouse, who had taken Emma-Jane safely back to Nethercoats as soon as she had eaten her supper and then come back alone, was asleep now in a deep leather armchair, his legs a peril to unsteady passersby. A young Winterton cousin had collapsed neatly on a sofa; a certain young lady, her matrimonial prospects now somewhat impaired, had been obliged to retire to a spare bedroom, to the mortification of her mamma, who, quite understandably, refused to leave her side. But my presence now among men who were turning bawdy or nasty or stupid with drink was not required and, approaching a much-mellowed Joel, I asked him, 'I could say good night now, I think?'

'Yes,' he said, a warm hand on my shoulder, his body richly at ease, the wine inside him, it seemed, inclining him to a universal goodwill. 'Go to bed now, if you wish. In fact, I'll light your way, madam, as a husband should.'

He led me from the smoking room and up the stairs, which had no need of bedtime candles, his hand still on my shoulder, leaning against me a little as if his balance was no longer altogether accurate. And, having rarely seen him so completely in his cups, I smiled up at him, finding it natural, appealing almost, that he had drunk so deeply to his own triumph.

'I think it has gone very well. Are you pleased?'

The deserted corridor was like a strip of cool water flowing above the tumult downstairs, hushed and dark. His hand lingered about me in the beginning of a caress, an indication, perhaps, that once again there could be peace between us, deceiving me so totally that even when he straightened, held himself erect and well away from me, hawk-faced and keen, no longer drunk at all, I did not begin to be afraid.

'I walked up here with you to thank you,' he said, each word coming by itself, distinct and dangerous. 'For a husband should thank his wife, should he not, Verity, when she has served him well?'

'Oh – as to that –'

And still I was not afraid, but ill at ease.

'What is it, Joel?'

'Why, what should it be?'

'You seem strange. Have I done something amiss?'

'I wonder. But we'll come to that later. I am here merely to thank you, as I said, for a job well done. It went well tonight, very well. Everyone says so. And I am glad to see you still so faithful to my interests, however unfaithful you may be to me in other ways.'

For a moment in that narrow, empty space, his words danced like sharp needles over the surface of my skin, piercing a slow passage to my brain.

'Do you hear me, Verity?'

And although my mind, recovering its courage, answered, 'Yes, I hear you, and you have only yourself to blame,' my tongue was too heavy, too cold either for protest or for defence, my body lost in a wild snowdrift of fear. Yet I knew that from the very beginning this moment had been waiting, biding its cruel time, certain of its own strength and my utter powerlessness, and, pressing my back against the wall, adopting the stance of any other trapped and terrified animal, I could hear my breathing labouring in my chest, hurting.

He took a step or two backwards and then slowly walked towards me, halting a bare inch away. 'You dirty bitch,' he said, his faced quite blank. 'So it's true, then.'

And, holding me with one hand, he hit me twice across the face, viciously and accurately, so that my neck muscles wrenched in agony and my head, reeling backwards, struck hard against the wall.

'It's true, isn't it? Say it. Damn you, Verity, say it. It's written on your face clear enough, but I'll hear it, one way or another. Are you unfaithful to me? Say it?'

Appalled by that terrible blankness in his eyes, I understood that to allow him to shake a confession out of me would be to cheapen everything I had felt, tarnish everything I had valued, and lifting up my head and my voice, I whispered, 'It's true.'

'Yes,' he said. 'I know. I've known these past six weeks, known and not known. So it's true. And the man's name?'

'You must know that too.'

'Of course I know it, and where you meet him and for how long. Of course I know. Now say it.'

'He's not to blame; he didn't force me.'

'No, by God, but I'll force you. His name.'

'Crispin. Crispin Aycliffe.'

'Yes, Crispin Aycliffe. You breathe it to me like a prayer, but it won't help you, neither of you. Now get to your room and wait until my guests have gone and I have time for you. Get to your room, damn you. Get out of my sight before I indulge myself and thrash you.'

My maid was waiting, sleepy but determined to do her duty, and it was easy to let her undress me and brush my hair, somehow possible to answer her chatter with a nod and a smile as she got out my jewel case and locked away my pearls and my new bracelet. But when she had gone I took off my nightdress and put on a dark wool gown suitable for morning, twisted my hair into a low knot similar to Elinor's, the best I could manage unaided, afraid I think, of appearing in any way naked before him, afraid of losing control and rushing outside in my bedgown like Elinor. And sitting, hands folded, waiting as he commanded, I was frightened most by my own veneer of outer calm, my body encased, as so often before, in glass. So had I been on the night my father died, and on the next night when they had murdered my brother. So still and quiet that no one had noticed my agony. And so was I now, drugged by my determination to bleed unseen, to retain intact those fragments of myself which neither Joel nor my grandfather, in some ways not even Crispin,

338

had been able to dominate. Yet now, perhaps, I would be obliged to sacrifice that ultimate freedom for Crispin's sake, would be obliged to plead and implore forgiveness, like Elinor. And the taste of the sacrifice was cold ash on my tongue. Joel would require vengeance, as my grandfather would have required it, and somehow I would convince him that, as the blame had been mine, the punishment must be mine too. So I would even incite him to punish me, so that, free of the need to hurt, he might even reach some measure of understanding.

I heard the carriages leaving, one after the other, until even Bradley Hobhouse had been poured into his equipage and rolled away. I saw the sky lighten with the start of a cold morning and heard Joel, I thought, in his own room; I held my breath for a moment, waiting for the dressing-room door to finally open, but he did not come and I had to wait a half hour longer before one of Mrs Richmond's faceless maids came to summon me downstairs.

He was sitting behind his desk in a high-backed chair, a coffee tray with one cup, a honeypot, and the remains of a crusty loaf before him. He had changed his clothes, shaved, breakfasted at his leisure, a man as alert and refreshed as if he had slept soundly the whole night.

He said, master to maid, 'You had best sit down, although there is not a great deal I want to say and I shall not keep you long. Have you anything in particular to say to me?'

And chilled by his complete self-possession when I had prepared myself for the scorching heat of his anger, my mouth turned dry, my stomach lurched uneasily.;

'Perhaps all I can say is that I thought, sometimes I was almost certain, that you knew.'

'And condoned it? Then you understand nothing of my nature. I was very far from suspecting you, Verity. I wondered at your motives for defending Elinor. But I decided it was because I had neglected you, and Hannah had interfered. And there was a moment when I was almost pleased to think you cared enough to complain. Yes, just think of that. You've contrived to make something of a fool of me, Verity, for a man believes, generally, what he wants to believe, and I didn't want to believe you false. That's why you had to tell me yourself. I believe it now.'

'Why tonight, with the house full of people?'

'Why tonight? The opportunity presented itself, as opportunities always do, if one bides one's time, a lesson my sister Elinor has learned to her cost and somewhat too late.'

'I am not Elinor. It is not at all the same.'

'Ah no, naturally. Her sins are mean and slightly ridiculous; yours are splendid. That is always the case. But the fact of the matter is that you are exactly the same – you less greedy perhaps, less simple, less easy to manage, but still birds of a feather.'

And, seeing no reason to be meek now that I had nothing more to lose, I said, 'Yes, birds of a feather, all of us, following our family traditions.'

He brought the flat of his hand down on the table with a mighty slap, setting the coffee tray jangling, warning me that he had it in him not only

339

to hurt me badly but to enjoy it.

To divert him, remembering that he could also hurt Crispin, I said quickly, 'May I know who told you?'

'Does it matter?'

He got up, strode irritably to the fireplace, threw his cigar into the fire, restraining himself, I thought, from immediately lighting another, and then, as if the whole conversation had suddenly wearied him, sat down again, staring at his cigar box, drumming his fingers against it.

'I heard it from Estella Chase,' he said, still contemplating the massive gold-and-onyx box. 'And she had it from her half brother, Mark Corey – a friend of Aycliffe's.'

And, each word cutting like a drop of ice water through the thick silence, I answered, 'In fact, you heard it from your mistress.'

'So I did. She has nothing to do with you.'

'Oh – I should think about as much as Crispin Aycliffe has to do with you.'

He pushed back his chair, got up again, putting distance between me and the abrupt, unleashed snarling of his temper, taking a cigar with him this time and lighting it from the fire, inhaling deeply before he returned to lean against the desk, in command of himself again, and to look down at me.

'I have kept my distance from you for more than a month,' he said, his lips hardly moving, his eyes dark slits in the gloom, narrowly glittering. 'I waited deliberately until I had mastered my impulse to flog you – not because I care about giving you pain but because a woman with a cut lip and a black eye is a pitiful spectacle and I have no mind to see you the object of pity. You are going to suffer, I suppose, but you'll suffer in private. There'll be no one to say, "Poor soul, poor lamb," because no one will even know.'

'Very well, Joel, I'll suffer. I've always known there was a good chance of it. But tell me first, what have I done to you that you haven't done to me? What has Crispin done to you that you haven't done to Godfrey Chase and heaven knows how many others?'

'Nothing,' he said, his eyes still slitted with rage, but his mouth was hard and cold and sarcastic. 'And what has that to do with it? Are you asking me for justice? I'm not interested in justice – only in reality. I'm no blustering hypocrite, Verity. Have I said a word about sin and shame? No, no. I've talked about surprise, because I didn't think you had it in you, and I've talked about anger – but as for guilt or remorse, I don't give a damn. I don't want you on your knees begging my pardon – like Elinor with Morgan Aycliffe – because all you're likely to be sorry about is getting caught. And, I repeat, let's see things as they are and forget any high-flown notions of justice. I outwit my competitors, but that doesn't mean I admit their right to outwit me. And no matter how much of a fool I make out of Godfrey Chase, no man – understand me – no man does the same to me. You should have known that, Verity, indeed you should.'

And my fear, at the moment, must have been so apparent that he smiled.

'What do you mean to do?'

'To you? Or to your paramour? I could take a horsewhip to him, I suppose, if I wanted to. No one would blame me and he wouldn't know how to defend himself. I reckon Dinah McCluskey could stand up to me better than him.'

'You know her, then?'

'Of course I know her. Everybody knows her. She was the biggest whore in the Law Valley before McCluskey took her on. But rest easy, for if I thrash him even Bradley Hobhouse could work out the reason, and that wouldn't suit me. I don't mean to give them the satisfaction of seeing me down, and what a satisfaction it would be, eh, Verity? Barforth with his mills and his money and his fancy new house – high and mighty bloody Barforth, with a wife who takes her petticoats off for a nobody like Crispin Aycliffe. No, no, Verity. You'll not do that to me. We'll keep it between the two, or three, or five, or six of us, I reckon. I can fix Dinah McCluskey and Mark Corey, and I can fix you too, my girl.'

And I knew that if I was ever to make a plea for my freedom, for my right to decide the course of my own life, for the simple right to be heard, it would have to be now.

'Joel – let me tell you –'

'Nothing. Tell me nothing.'

'Joel, you have to listen to me – try to understand how I think and feel. And you have to know you can't order me to stop feeling as I do –'

'Have I tried to?' he said. 'You haven't been listening, Verity. Perhaps I don't care how you think and feel. In fact, you may think and feel exactly as you please. It's your behaviour I can and will control. Why discuss it any further? You will do as you have always done, Verity. You will look after my house and my children and my guests – all of which you do very well. Nothing will change, except that, until further notice, you may consider yourself safe from my physical attentions – and of course you will not see Crispin Aycliffe again, nor receive messages from him, nor even open any letters he sends you. Is there anything else?'

'Yes,' I howled, jumping up, my whole body clenched tight with outrage. 'You can't dismiss me like that. You have to listen to me, hear my reasons. You have to stop treating me like a child or like an employee. I'm a living woman with a brain as good as yours, and you can't lock me away.'

But, once again, I should have known him better than to imagine he would threaten anything he could not enforce, and perhaps I was not too surprised when he opened a drawer and threw a sheaf of papers heavily onto the desk.

'But I can.'

'And who will you have as my jailer? You are not always at home to watch me yourself. Who will do it for you?'

'No one. No one could. I appreciate how clever and resourceful you are – be sure of it. And who should know better than I that if a woman wants to misbehave she'll do it, one way or another. Fear of the law never stopped a hungry man from stealing a loaf of bread, nor a hungry woman from stealing an hour or two in a strange bed. However, in your case, I have the means to remove your appetite. You remember Colonel Corey, do you?'

'Why yes. What has he –'

'And you know that he was the father of Mark Corey, as well as of Estella Chase? Not a satisfactory young man, Mark Corey – illegitimate to begin with, and sour about it. Upset Mrs Chase a great deal when he insisted on calling himself Corey instead of Smithers, or whatever his mother's name really was – although the colonel was too fond of him to complain, which upset Estella even more. Spend-thrift too, our Mark, always in and out of trouble, so the colonel not only made him an allowance but lent him fairly weighty sums from time to time – most of which lost itself in that newspaper of his, and created more bad blood than ever between him and Mrs Chase.'

'And –'

'Yes, you are looking worried, Verity. Are you already a step or two ahead of me? These documents were Colonel Corey's property – Mark's debts, in fact, and a few paltry sums advanced to one of his cronies. A hundred or two here and there, a thousand, perhaps, in all, which is the same as a million when you're living on fifty pounds a year and can't pay it. You do follow? Yes, I thought you would. This money is now owing to Colonel Corey's estate, or was, until Mrs Chase made me aware of it, when I purchased the debts from her – Mark Corey's and Crispin Aycliffe's – to relieve her of the unpleasant duty of calling them in. If Mark Corey cannot pay me he will go to jail, and in any case, it will be the end of the *Cullingford Star*, something that has been in my mind for a long time. And what happens to Crispin Aycliffe is up to you. He doesn't strike me as particularly robust, and life in a debtor's prison is very harsh. A year or two of that and he could well find himself prone to the same nervous ailments as his mother – unless the jail fever or the rats got him first.'

And we both know there was nothing more to say.

I sat for a while, very quietly, looking down at my hands, my breathing shallow, sections of my mind closing themselves down – sections I would not need again, sections of emotion and energy that could only be a burden to me in this shrinking world – and then, nodding slightly, I asked him, 'What must I do?'

'Nothing. Look after your housekeeping. I will convey to him your regrets that the affair is over, and what more is there to be said? You will do nothing to displease me in the way of writing or receiving letters – I feel I can rely on that, unless, of course, you wish to see the poor devil in jail, in which case you have only to say the word. No? Well then, we may continue with our rich and happy lives – or, at least, I shall. You will want to sleep now, I suppose, for you look quite done in.'

As I stood up and walked to the door he stubbed out his cigar with a vicious grinding movement and said, 'Thank you, Verity – no hysterics, no excuses – most sensible of you. Really – most reasonable. And if you

342

are thinking, like Elinor, of waiting for me to die, I shall take my time about it, I warn you – my own good time.'

'Yes, Joel,' I said and went away.

35

Morgan Aycliffe was re-elected a week or so later with a comfortable majority and returned, quietly triumphant, to Westminster, leaving Elinor again installed in Blenheim Lane. But this time, instead of Daniel Adair to keep an eye on her, there was a long-nosed, sharp-featured Mrs Hardisty, an Aycliffe cousin, officially Elinor's companion but, in reality, her keeper.

'Dear Maud,' Elinor called her, and she was soon accepted as Elinor's shadow, a voice counting the hours of Elinor's day, a keen eye and ear checking the content of her conversations and to whom they were addressed. Not a bad woman, certainly, but too decided in her opinions for comfort, and determined to have her way not from any love of power but because she could not believe any other way to be right. And Elinor, with her new, hard-earned wisdom, chose neither to rebel nor to submit but channelled the unsuspecting lady's energies to her own good purposes.

'Dear Maud will see to it,' Elinor would say, good and quiet as a little nun, hiding the malice in her eyes as 'dear Maud' hurried upstairs to reprimand a child or a disobedient parlourmaid, went through accounts and menus, or submitted her weekly report to her cousin.

'Dear Maud, do lower the blind – the sun is in my eyes,' and Maud, barely distinguishing Elinor from Faith or Prudence or Cecilia – finding privately, in fact, that Prudence had more sense, Faith a more open disposition – would click her tongue, put down her work, and tug irritably at the offending blind.

'Is that enough?'

'Oh – yes, Maud dear – enough for now, except that the sun will move in a quarter of an hour, I suppose. And what shall I do then?'

But at Maud Hardisty's direction, she wrote a stilted, dull little letter every Friday morning to her husband and had begun to embroider for him a pair of braces, which, if nothing else, created the right impression when Emma-Jane and Lucy came to call.

But our immediate preoccupation that winter was Hannah, who, having won Joel's consent to her marriage, if not his approval, was determined to do the thing in style.

'Surely, it will be a private family affair?' Emma-Jane asked me, oozing with sympathy. 'Bradley and I were talking of it just the other night, and we imagined she would just slip into church quietly with you and Joel and Elinor, and no one else the wiser. Naturally I'll call on her afterwards with a bride gift, but as to witnessing the thing take place – no, no. I can't think she really wants any of us to do that.'

But such a hole-in-the-corner affair had not so much as entered

Hannah's mind. She meant – had meant from the start – to make her vows in the parish church, high above the town, surrounded by flowers and bridesmaids and all the pomp and circumstance that my brother Edwin would have brought her. And, when George and Rebecca Mandelbaum accepted Hannah's invitation with pleasure, when it was realized that Squire Dalby would go wherever my mother led, and that even Lady Winterton, who, insofar as manners and appearance were concerned, could see little difference between one common man and another, was willing to attend, Emma-Jane's resolve began to weaken.

And so, once again, I sat in Rosamund Boulton's fitting room with Elinor and dear, inevitable Maud, while five little girls – Maria Agbrigg this time with Caroline and the Aycliffes – were pinned into their wedding finery.

The dresses were to be of white spotted net over white satin, and from the first there was trouble, not only with Caroline but with Hannah herself, who, for all her thirty-four years, was a virgin bride and felt entitled to make a greater show than my mother, a widow with three grandchildren to her credit. Her own outfit was a masterpiece of restraint, lace the colour of pale, milky coffee on a foundation of cream brocade, high-necked, tight-sleeved, the skirt enormously wide, regal rather than virginal; and the prettiness she could not feel appropriate to herself she wished to see in her bridesmaids, but Rosamund Boulton, looking harassed and nervous, not at all well, somehow could not get it right.

'No, no, Miss Boulton, those frills are far too narrow – not at all what I have in mind. We are dressing bridesmaids, after all, not charity children for a Sunday outing. I want these net skirts to have the appearance of clouds – fluffy clouds on a March day, not scraggy little things all limp with rain – and I don't care how many yards it takes. And on the satin underskirts, if you could stitch a few white flowers, quite large ones so they can be seen through the gauze. And I want the bonnets absolutely covered with flowers, very small ones, white and yellow, to give the effect of crocuses. I don't want to see any fabric at all, just flowers, and lace inside the brims. You can do that, I suppose, Miss Boulton?'

'Oh, by all means, Miss Barforth,' Rosamund Boulton said sourly, no longer on her knees with pins in her mouth as she used to be but standing straight-backed and eagle-eyed while her minions pinned and tucked in her place. And in consideration for her all too obviously aching head, I felt obliged to take my outraged daughter home when, having herself pointed out that five little girls cannot walk in pairs, she discovered that Maria Agbrigg – not Caroline Barforth – was to head the procession, carrying Hannah's prayer book on a pillow of silk and lace.

Maria, of course, her colourless, lashless eyes quite terrified, would have given way; her father, had be been consulted, might not have wished her to put herself forward either and might well, in fact, have been better pleased with the quiet ceremony Emma-Jane had suggested, but Hannah, with the unwavering support of her protégé, Jonas, was unprepared to give an inch. And although Caroline, already a Barforth to her fingertips, pointed out that since her father was paying for the wedding she ought to play a main part in it, not only were the lace pillow and prayer book allotted to Maria but also a deeper-brimmed bonnet and a few extra flounces at the bottom of her skirt, to mark her status as attendant-in-chief.

'I thought you might like to get claret colour for Blaize and Nicholas,' she told me. 'I know the velvet suits they had for your mother are as good as new, but people do remember, and my brother would not thank us if we seemed to be penny-pinching. A really deep, rich claret – I have seen exactly the right shade – would suit them very well since they are so dark – with white lace collars.'

But Blaize, entering his eleventh year, wanted a proper broadcloth coat and trousers like his father, and Nicholas wanted whatever Blaize wanted, only bigger, more of it, and the claret velvet gave rise to a great deal of muttering, the lace collars to downright mutiny.

'No,' Nicholas said, squaring up to Hannah, his black eyes narrowing as Joel's did with rage. 'I won't wear that. I'll tear it up.'

But Blaize, a little older, broke free suddenly from the first level of childhood and, assessing his aunt's mood, gave her a charming, calculating smile which also held something of Joel.

'I'll wear mine, Aunt Hannah, don't worry. I won't spoil your day.'

But, on her wedding morning, Blaize's collar had somehow disappeared, could neither be found nor replaced, and only Nicholas – whose collar had been removed for safekeeping – appeared in lace.

The evening before the ceremony Hannah spent an hour with me in the small sitting room, rendering an account of herself like a housekeeper quitting her situation rather than a woman about to become a wife.

'I have turned out all my drawers and boxes,' she said, 'and arranged with Mrs Stevens what is to be given to the maids. You will find everything in order.'

And as the February wind gathered strength behind the windows, drawing us together in the comforting circle of firelight and candlelight, I told her, 'Hannah, I wish you well with all my heart. If this is right for you, then I can only be glad.'

'Right enough,' she said, holding out her capable, square-tipped hands to the fire, and prone these days to sudden surges of emotion I found hard to control, I lightly touched her arm, knowing my question would not be well received.

'Hannah, if you could have your life over again – arrange it as you pleased – marry anyone you pleased – tell me, which man would you choose?'

'You are thinking of your brother,' she said coolly, taking up the poker and stirring the logs to a fiercer blaze. 'And that is only natural. I have thought of him myself often these last few weeks, and shall continue to think of him, especially as I shall be occupying the house where he was born. Unfortunately I am experiencing some difficulty in remembering his face.' And, replacing the poker carefully in its stand, she clasped her hands together, her face soft and rueful yet without any weakness.

'We should be friends again, Hannah.'

'Yes, of course we should. And I will answer your question. If I could have the ordering of my life, I doubt if I would marry any man. I would be a man, like my brother Joel. I'd manage his mills and drive his phaeton and take myself off to London whenever it suited me. I'd get some real work to do, take on some real responsibilities, instead of running petty parish errands and feeling myself grow as small-minded as they are themselves. I'd grapple with real issues. I'd be a Lord Mayor, if I could. I'd take Morgan Aycliffe's constituency away from him and go to Westminster myself. And, obviously, since no woman can do any of these things, I'll content myself with the next-best thing and marry someone who can.'

'And – affection, Hannah? What of that?'

'Love, you mean? Well, I had that with Edwin and he would have made me into an Emma-Jane. Oh yes, and that was what I wanted at the time – ten children and all my linen cupboards in good order – but I shall do better now. Don't worry about me, Verity, for I am not so shortsighted as you seem to think. I am well aware how deeply Mr Agbrigg regrets his wife, and that marriage with me is more of an honour, in his view, than a pleasure. But I have nothing to fear from him. According to the law, a wife passes under her husband's authority and discipline, but in our case my husband would do nothing to offend my brother Joel, and I rather think the authority will be mine. And make no mistake about it, he may regret his dear Ann and tell himself he is marrying again so soon for the good of his children, but he wants to progress – he wants to be a mayor and an alderman and anything else I can devise. He is not doing it all for them.'

And rubbing her hands once again over the fire, she said, 'Ah well – we have a busy day tomorrow,' and went for the last time to her solitary bed.

We got up the next morning to grey skies, a high wind playing havoc among the remnants of last year's leaves, but by breakfast time there was little more than a thin curtain of rain misting the treetops and, as the decorated bridal carriage drew up to the door, a patch of white appeared among the clouds, not sunshine but an indication that the sun, at least, was there, somewhere on high.

'But who on earth is going to sit on the bridegroom's side of the aisle?' Emma-Jane had wanted to know. 'He has no relatives – or so one supposes – and it will all be most unbalanced – most odd.'

But there were managers now, of the various sections of Lawcroft and Low Cross and Tarn Edge, a new class sandwiched between ourselves and the workers, who were prosperous enough to make a decent show and shrewd enough to keep on the right side of Ira Agbrigg and his Barforth wife. And so the bridegroom's pews were adequately filled, young Jonas – to the disgust of certain other youthful gentlemen – looking immaculate, if not handsome, in a plain grey coat and dark trousers, and his sister, Maria, playing her part to perfection.

The wedding breakfast was at Tarn Edge, the usual cold collation of hams and tongues and turkeys, which, apart from the champagne, was also standard Law Valley procedure for funerals, and apart from one regrettable, predictable occurrence, there seemed nothing to mar the day.

'Who's this, then?' Blaize asked, his eyes on his brother's lace collar. 'One of the bridesmaids gone astray?' And underestimating Nicholas's fury, he found himself on the ground, rolling and pummelling and spitting curses neither of them should have known, until Joel's well-shod foot kicked them apart.

But Hannah remained serene, between her newly acquired son and daughter, accepting congratulations with the air of one who has allied herself with an earl, confident that Joel, with his commercial instincts, would make the best of things and decide to settle matters her way. Distinctions, of course, were still being made. Jonas and Maria would call Hannah 'Mamma' but there was no question, yet, of an Uncle Joel. Ira Agbrigg, although my permission had been granted, could not persuade his tongue around my Christian name and would continue, perhaps indefinitely, to address his employer as Mr Barforth or sir when the occasion required. Yet Morgan Aycliffe, who had made a special journey from London to bring Hannah his good wishes and a Wedgwood dinner service that had considerably upset Emma-Jane, seemed able to recognize a future Lord Mayor when he saw one. And it was no secret that Joel, no matter how distant his manner, would continue Hannah's allowance and had not yet given the Top House away.

She would, as she had said, do well enough within the limits she had set herself, and when it was over and she had gone down to the millhouse – the demands of Barforth enterprise permitting no time for a wedding journey – I was surprised how acutely I missed her. She had been a buffer between me and Joel, another person always at the table, so that conversation of some kind was possible, and her absence, giving rise to silences I could not endure, compelled me to fill the house with guests, bright people, dull people, kind, cruel, or downright half-witted people, anyone at all so that Joel and I need never be alone.

Springtime brought me the undulating carpet of daffodils the gardeners had promised, lilac and birdsong, clean-washed blue skies, my young dogs yelping their high spirits among the new grass. There were picnics that June by the lily pond, tables set out under the willow tree, starched maids bringing baskets of party food from the house while Elinor's 'dear Maud' shredded her nerves and ours with her dread of bee stings, grass stains, wet shoes, horrific tales of children drowning in ornamental garden water. There were carriage drives to ruined abbeys, one agonizing Saturday-to-Monday at Floxley Hall when Lady Winterton, with more guests than she could easily accommodate, had offered us a double bed and we had slept back to back, or Joel had slept and I had lain uneasily awake.

But there had been no harsh word spoken, simply a strange brand of politeness that at best was cool, at worst had the touch and texture of black ice. We existed under the same roof, spoke to each other carefully, whenever necessary, a business arrangement, a form of life imprisonment that aroused no pity since no one but ourselves – and a few others – were even aware of it.

'I will convey to him your regrets that the affair is over,' he had told me, but I did not know when or how the information had been conveyed, or received, how Crispin had replied, and when a boy thrust a letter into my hand one day in town, I took it home, as I had promised, and gave it unread to Joel, not in meekness but because I did not trust him and, with Crispin's life in my hands, could not risk another trap.

There were other letters after that, reaching me in various ways, all of them delivered promptly to Joel, who, without any discussion, slid them into a desk drawer instead of burning them, so that I was not surprised when, one morning, I saw them bound up together and was required to write a covering note, explaining their return and asking Mr Aycliffe to trouble me no more. And after that – on the very day that Mark Corey was arrested for debt – the letters ceased.

I was, perhaps, eight miles from the Red Gin but I could have been in China, and, hedged around now by servants, children, friends, no longer a girl who could walk her dogs alone to Old Sarah's Rock or anywhere else, I attempted to come to terms with my private isolation, tried hard to convince myself that, having always known the penalty, I must not shirk now that I had been required to pay it. And I managed, generally, to be calm, until the thought of the barren years ahead sickened me and turned me cold.

And what would Crispin do with those years? Sometimes I could endow him with a rich, full life, with political or literary status and a wife and children to share it with him. But at other times, the hurt child in him tugged at my mind, rekindling my need to protect him, a far more primitive, more overwhelming emotion than I had felt for my own sons. Blaize, I knew, would always have his way. Nicholas would take life by the throat and squeeze what he wanted out of it. Like Joel, they were strong, deep-rooted evergreens, their growth undiminished by summer heat or winter gale. They would prosper and multiply for their own satisfaction, whereas Crispin, without their tough fibres, was less attached to life, might not take the trouble to succeed alone. He needed, as he had often told me, an exclusive relationship; he needed, in fact, to be loved, as Joel apparently did not – as Blaize and Nicholas might not – and the thought of the harm I had done him was not easy to bear.

I would never try to see him again, I knew that, but one flowery, sun-flecked afternoon when I had taken my children and Elinor's to Patterswick, I saw Dinah McCluskey swinging her brazen hips towards me down a quiet lane, and my need to know how Crispin was – just to know that much – became to acute for caution. I didn't ask myself how she came to be in such a place, alone and bareheaded, walking as if the lane belonged to her and everyone else should be ready to make way. I simply knew that Joel was safely away in Liverpool, that there was no one else to observe me here but 'dear Maud', who was too hotly in pursuit of my scampering children and Elinor's, too alarmed by the dangers lurking in this placid countryside, to notice what I did.

As she came abreast of me, keeping her eyes downcast, leaving the decision to me, I called out, 'Good afternoon, Mrs McCluskey. What brings you here?'

'Oh, you've decided to know me, have you?' she said. 'And what about that woman over there? I doubt she'll want to know me. But never mind. You can tell her I'm a gipsy hawking pegs.'

'She doesn't matter.'

'Happen not. But before she comes and pokes her nose in – well – how are you, Mrs Barforth?'

'Well – and you?'

'Oh, middling.' And tossing her head, her eyes bold and black as any gipsy's, she laughed. 'But you'll be wanting to know about Crispin?'

'Oh yes – please. Did you come here to find me?'

'I did.'

And pushing the gleaming tumble of her hair back from her forehead, she paused and smiled again, enjoying her power, knowing I would go down on my knees to please her.

'Well – he took it bad, Mrs Barforth. He knew it was bound to happen, but when it did he wasn't ready. You should have told him yourself, really you should, instead of sending your husband. That wasn't nice of you.'

'He came himself, then? I didn't know.'

'Of course he came himself,' she said sharply, scornfully. 'You wouldn't expect him to send his foreman, would you, or his butler?'

'I'm sorry.'

'So you should be. Well, we used to see a lot of your husband in the old days before he was your husband, when he couldn't afford the prices at the Swan. But that was the old days and I wasn't going to let him get near Crispin. "He's out," I told him. "Gone to Manchester on the Flyer," and when we'd had our few words, he says to me, "Right, Dinah. Tell him my wife sends her regrets. Explain to him she's seen the error of her ways, and let him know if he can't quite understand why, then I'll be happy to call again and go through it with him myself." First off, of course, all Crispin was bothered about was if he'd hurt you. But I sent somebody to have a look at you and you seemed all right. "Leave it," I told him. "Let it go. Don't put anything down on paper." But he had to write those letters you didn't answer, and when Mark Corey was arrested we understood why. I reckon it was Mark who told his sister about you and Crispin, and she told your husband. Well, Mark should have kept his mouth shut, and I'll tell him so if I ever see him again, but there's no forgiving the spiteful bitch for what she's done to him. He's her brother, after all, wrong side of the blanket or not, and she could spare him that thousand or two, after what she's raked in from her old man. Crispin went very quiet after they took Mark – very quiet. Shut himself away upstairs, thinking things out, I reckon, and it struck me he might decided to go away. After all, there's no money now to run the *Star*, and to tell the truth I'm about ready to move on myself. But no. He comes

349

downstairs with some scheme to raise the money to buy Mark out – not that it's likely to work, because Crispin has the best will in the world but no sense where money's concerned. And then he asked me to come and see you.'

She paused again, letting her eyes roam over the smiling summer fields, the leafy branches twining their arms over our heads, very obviously disliking her task, having promised to perform it for Crispin's sake but with no confidence in the message – whatever it might be – and with no faith in me at all.

'Mrs McCluskey, please. What is it?'

And I think I knew how much she wanted to stride away from me, leaving me in ignorance of the request, telling him that she had delivered it and that I had refused.

'He wants you to go away with him,' she said harshly. 'He says it will take time but he thinks he can arrange it. First he'll have to make peace with his father, which will take some crawling, but he thinks the old man would be glad to do it, now that Dan Adair's gone, and would agree to pay his debts. Then, of course, being Crispin, he says he'd have to work for the old man awhile, put his affairs in order for him before he'd feel right about taking a job in London or wherever. But, if you'll agree to wait for him, that's what he's ready to do. He doesn't think your husband would bring you back once you'd actually gone. He says it's pride with Barforth, not heart, and that rather than make a fool of himself running after you, he'd snap his fingers and set up a stable of high-priced hussies in your place. Anyway, that's what he's ready to do for you – give up everything he cares about, which he reckons is only fair, since you'll have to give up a few things too. That's what he asked me to say.'

I walked a step or two away from her, needing badly to be alone, needing the whole world to fall silent so that I could contemplate unhindered the intense joy and the intense sorrow of what she had just told me, this act of love and sacrifice, this challenge, this whispering of hope where there had been no hope at all, growing to a wild sea-roaring in my ears. And then Dinah McCluskey came up behind me and put her shapely but rough-textured hand on my arm.

'Well then, Mrs Barforth, I've given you his message, like I promised – two days and two nights it took him, staring out of his window, to make his mind up to it, so the least I could do was deliver it. So now I'll go back and tell him you said you'd like nothing better, but it can't be done. That's what you want me to say, isn't it?'

'Is it?'

'Oh yes, I think so, Mrs Barforth. You've got too much to lose, love, just think about it – those fine children tumbling about over there in the field, for one thing. You'd never see them again. And what about him, Mrs Barforth? Oh yes, he means every word he says and he'll do everything he's promised, if he gets the go-ahead from you. But I reckon, at the bottom of him, he'd as soon go to jail as go back to his dad. Can you make up to him for that?'

'Can you?'

350

'Happen I can.'

'I doubt that, Mrs McCluskey – indeed I do.'

'Why?' she said. 'Because I'm a common barmaid? That doesn't upset him. He thinks there's romance in the working class – and dignity – and he's right, except that he forgets we're good and bad same as everybody else. And if you put a bonnet on me, you know, and gloves, and a high-necked frock, I'm not so bad. I'd pass, in a crowd, as a lady.'

'You don't imagine he'd marry you?' I asked her, astounded, wounded, hating her, terrified of her.

And her voice throbbing now with urgency, she put her face too close to mine, offending me with her breath, the healthy fresh-air odour of her skin, the tang of spirits and tobacco clinging to her clothes.

'I don't know. But if he did he wouldn't regret it. You may have a lot of feeling for him, Verity Barforth, but I doubt you can give him what he really needs. Haven't you read him aright yet? He wants a woman who can be wife and mother to him at the same time, and you can't be either. Content yourself with what you've got, and leave him to me. I'll have no man but him, and no child but him, and although I don't doubt he'd take some persuading to it, it would be the best thing for him in the end. My life's been hard, Verity Barforth. They sent me to your grandfather's mill when I was five, and I was on the streets at twelve, peddling my wares for pennies, and then for shillings when I got a bit wiser, until Jack McCluskey set me up behind his bar and then married me. Big, beer-swilling ox that he was – drinking his profits – finished up a raving madman, seeing spiders in his soup and thinking I was trying to kill him. Swore he'd kill me first and damn near did more than once. Well, if I could survive Jack McCluskey, nothing else is going to put me down, and there's nobody can take advantage of Crispin if I'm there to look out for him. I've had no bairns of my own, you see. An old woman aborted me with a knitting needle when I was thirteen, twenty years ago, I reckon, and there's been no sign of anything since then. So he can have that side of my nature too. You should step aside, Mrs Barforth – really you should – and give me the chance to show him he needs a woman like me.'

There was a rustling in the hedgerow, some small field animal busy about its own concerns, a bird persistently singing, children's voices rising in the distance to a pitch of high excitement, a quarrel brewing, Maud Hardisty's wail of terror at the prospect of torn trousers, a grazed knee which could lead to certain blood poisoning and heaven knew what else; a chill little wind suddenly rose up from the grass, bending the clusters of buttercups, the fragile pink-tipped daisies, and breathing down my spine. And I saw that the children and Maud Hardisty were coming towards me very fast.

'So?' Dinah McCluskey said, 'I'll give him your regrets, shall I?'

'No.'

'No. What do you mean, no? Have your wits about you, girl? What else can you say?'

But rounding on her, loathing her, I said, 'Tell him I need a little time – not a lot – but time. Tell him I have to think it out – as he did himself –

for his sake. Tell him that, left to myself, I'd come away with him in my petticoat, but that I have to be sure it's right for him.'

'Damn you,' she said, her hand fastening around my wrist like a talon fallen from the sky. 'Selfish bitch. You know it's not right for him. But you'll play with him, won't you? Use him like your husband uses his women. You're tarred with the same brush, all you bloody Barforths.' And pushing me savagely against the hedge, she strode off.

36

I went home, exercised my dogs, spent a bedtime hour with my children, sat at my dinner table, with Joel's rope of diamonds around my arm, and tried to imagine myself otherwise. I tried to root out the self-seeking element from my love, to hold it up and examine it in a strong light. I thought of courage and punishment, and remembered the texture of Caroline's hair, her squeals of protest when the brush caught in the tangles. I thought of solitude, a deserted landscape, an empty, pale sky, and chatted to my guests. I slept, much later, in an uneasy cocoon of dreams where Crispin's face, emaciated almost beyond recognition, peered at me from behind his father's shoulder. 'I couldn't get away,' he said, and, as Morgan Aycliffe stepped gleefully aside, I saw Crispin's body, manacled, shackled, hideous, and Elinor, frantically laughing, pointing. 'We feed him twice a day,' she shrieked. 'And he sleeps in the countinghouse. What more can he need?'

I woke to a break in the weather, rain lashing my window, a listless morning of headache and tension, unable to decide on the lighting of a drawing-room fire, much less the course of my life, and Crispin's, and Joel's, an afternoon with Joel himself unexpectedly home, dressing almost at once to go out again; an early evening, fine and still, bringing news that reduced some things to their proper size, gave stature to others.

I was crossing the landing at the head of the stairs when, looking down, I saw Mrs Stevens and Mrs Richmond with their heads together, recognized the signs, and, going downstairs, was at once detained by Mrs Stevens's hand on my arm.

'Oh, Mrs Barforth – such a terrible thing. It is Miss Boulton. I fear she is dead.'

'What? Rosamund Boulton?'

'Yes, poor soul – poor, tragic soul.'

'But how? – She has looked ill lately, but so suddenly –'

'Yes, dear, so ill – we have all remarked it,' Mrs Stevens began, meaning to break the news gently, but Mrs Richmond, who was little concerned by the death of a dressmaker and knew of no reason why it should concern me, said flatly, 'There was no illness. She cut her wrists, it seems, with a kitchen knife. Quite shocking, and I am not at all sure if they will bury her in hallowed ground, or if they ought to.'

'Oh dear – dear me,' I heard Mrs Stevens say. 'Come, dearest, come and sit down.'

And while I stood, both hands clenched on a chair back, too frozen to bend my body into the chair, she hurried away, brought me a smelling bottle, hurried away again to contact her sources of information, and returned an hour later with the whole pitiful, atrocious tale.

Miss Boulton, it appeared, had slashed her wrists early that morning in her room above the shop and had lain there behind the door until her father, quite by chance, had called with some message from home.

'Poor man,' Mrs Stevens said, tears in her eyes. 'She was still alive. In fact, she was still breathing an hour ago, but her family have been told there is no hope. Oh dear – Verity – dear Verity – I am afraid she was pregnant, there is no doubt about it. And although she has bled massively from her severed veins, they say it is the miscarriage that will kill her.'

I didn't know where Joel was and would not have dared send for him if I had, and so I waited, my sitting-room door ajar, for the sound of his phaeton, and then hurried to meet him in the hall, seeing at once from his face that I was too late, that he already knew. And when he walked past me without a word, I waited a moment, followed him, and entered his bedroom for the first time.

He was sitting in a tall armchair by the fireplace, staring into the empty grate, an unlit cigar in his hand, his face, which this morning had held all the arrogance of a man in his prime, suddenly showing the years, the strain of commercial combat, the strain of philandering, the accumulated lack of sleep. He looked spent, emotionally bankrupt, and, never having seen him in pain before, I hesitated, not knowing how to comfort him and surprised that I felt so strong an urge to try.

But before I could speak a word his narrowed eyes shot open and he almost shouted, 'Well, you will be wanting to know if the child was mine.'

'Oh no – what does it matter?'

'It matters to me. And it mattered to her, because if I had been the father there'd have been no need for this. I'd have paid – and handsomely. Why not? I've been sending money to your brother's bastard ever since he died. I can afford one of my own. I'd have set her up somewhere, away from the gossip – made life easy for her. She knew that. But the child wasn't mine – couldn't have been – and, as you say, it makes no bloody difference because I'd have seen to her all right in any case. All she had to do was come and tell me – no more than that.'

But how could she have admitted to him, I thought, when he had twice deserted her, that she had allowed herself to be used and then abandoned by another lover? And, kneeling on the rug beside his chair, not quite touching him, I said, 'Joel, were you ever in love with her?'

And it was very far from anything he could bear me to say.

'Go to hell, Verity,' he said, so calmly that, the tone of his voice bearing no relation to his meaning, I was unprepared for the swift pressure of his hands on my shoulders, dragging me to my feet and hauling me backwards against the wall.

'You'd best leave me,' he said. 'Just go – for God's sake, leave me alone.'

And glancing at his sombre face, I fled.

I sat, then, in my little back parlour, watching the evening come on, listening as the clock counted the seconds, droplets of time hurrying away, all of them in the same direction, forwards, never backwards to that vital moment of decision when one could choose again, differently, when one could lay down the knife, reject a lover's advances, when one could hope again. And I did not know how far back the fault lay. If my brother Edwin had not died, Rosamund Boulton would not be dying now; she would be Mrs Joel Barforth of Low Cross, harassed, perhaps, and hard-pressed for cash, ironing Joel's shirts herself to save a maid, pinching and scraping to make a decent show when her sister-in-law Hannah came down from Lawcroft to tea. And I, perhaps, would have been in Blenheim Lane, keeping the peace between Crispin and his father, while Elinor might well have been the spinster in Rosamund Boulton's place. And would this different settling of the kaleidoscope have made us happier, better, or would we now, from the inherent discontent of our natures, simply be calling our grievances by other names?

Perhaps I heard the doorbell, perhaps I was merely expecting someone, some new dimension to the catastrope, so that when my door opened and Mrs Stevens, considerably shaken, told me, 'Mrs Barforth, it is Mr Boulton,' I was shaken too but not greatly surprised.

He was standing, an ordinary, elderly man, just within the empty hallway, the look of a good tradesman about him, serviceable, with big-knuckled hands, stooping a little at the shoulders; Rosamund Boulton's father, who had warned her from the start that Joel Barforth would bring her nothing but trouble and who, ever since the opening of her shop – knowing, one supposed, whose money had been used to launch it – had made a point of never being in the Piece Hall at the same time as Joel and had avoided, quite openly, shaking his hand or meeting his eye. I remembered, too, that, at the election, he had voted most surprisingly Tory, unwilling to share even the politics of the man who had first seduced his daughter.

Yet he was here now, on the eve of what must surely be his daughter's death, and despite his hesitant expression, the air of a man somewhat overawed by his surroundings, when he asked for Joel my instinct was to deny, quite amazingly to protect.

I said, much too quickly, 'Oh, he's away, Mr Boulton. He's in Manchester and won't be back until Monday morning. Mr Boulton, please, what can I do for you?'

'Nothing, lass,' he said. 'I'll wait.'

'But, Mr Boulton, surely not until Monday ...?'

And as I stood there, transparent perhaps with pity for this man I did not really know, and with my new, astonishing need to defend the man I knew too well – who, surely, had no need of aid from me – Joel appeared at the head of the stairs. He wore no jacket, his shirt open at the neck, his

354

sleeves unfastened, and, pausing a moment, drawing a resolute breath, he made a slow descent, walking, I thought, as a man goes to the gallows.

'I'm here, sir,' he said. 'Just arrived. Will you come this way?'

And they went into the smoking room and closed the door.

I could not let them go alone but I dared not follow. Nor could I have explained my fears, but Joel would do him no harm, and he was an old man, tough and wiry, but no threat to Joel, in full, vigorous prime. And although Joel had done Miss Boulton much wrong, her father must know, since I knew and others knew it, that their affair had long been over. Yet how much resentment had her father nourished, how much shame had he felt seeing her name above that shop doorway, hearing the rumours? How many suitors, perhaps, had she turned away because of her passion for Joel, so that ultimately her father could see no one but Joel to blame for her disgrace, the tragedy of her ending? Joel may not have been the father of her child, but what could that matter now to Mr Boulton?

Why was he here? And why was I so afraid? Was it simply the air of death around him that had unnerved me or was it Joel's own guilt-ridden distress that drew me down the corridor, my hand reaching out for the smoking room door, knowing I must not enter yet finding that my fingers had somehow turned the handle, that a strength I had neither summoned nor suspected propelled me inside and closed the door behind me, my body leaning against the carved wood so that no one else could follow.

And what my eyes told me was, quite simply, not to be believed. Joel was standing by his desk, his head bowed slightly, reminding me more than ever of a man mounting the scaffold. Mr Boulton stood close beside him. Then I saw the knuckles clench, the old man's body hunch forward as he drew the driving whip from his boot and raised it, hissing through the heavy air.

'Oh, Mr Boulton,' I heard my voice cry out. 'Mr Boulton. No, Joel, don't hurt him.'

But Joel, who could so easily have wrenched the whip away, after an instinctive movement of self-defence stepped backwards, his whole face losing its colour again.

'Mr Boulton –' he said, no more than that, and then, as the lash caught him again, knocking him back against his desk, I saw his jaw muscles clench, his eyes close, and knew that he meant to submit, to allow this desperate, crazed old man to take his revenge.

A stripe of red appeared, suddenly, across Joel's chest, the fine cambric of his shirt shrivelling away at the shoulder, showing more red beneath. And then, through the hissing and whining of the whip, the dreadful beast-panting of his pathetic assailant, a whole cobweb of crimson patterning the front of him, smudging as the blood began to flow, his chest seemed to open, as my father's had once done, and the astonishment on his face was my brother Edwin's astonishment when an adversary as weak as this one had plunged a carving knife into his gut.

Joel's hands clenched white-knuckled on the chair back as he submitted to the traditional horsewhipping of adulterers and despoilers

355

of women, his dark face shocked and set with determination neither to cry out nor to fall down until it was over. And I was proud of him. I felt his agony with him, groaned for him, and was proud of him, until a moment came when the deadly singing of the whip jolted me into calling out foolishly, 'That's enough. Stop it at once.'

Yet it was sufficient, for, miraculously, the hissing stopped, the air ceased to vibrate, and the old, grey shape dwindled suddenly, folded into a chair, an old, big-knuckled hand hanging loosely from either knee, two eyes staring, blank and blind, from a face that had no life, no colour but that of cold ash. And as I peered closely at him, Joel's face came to me, his breath rasping with a sound I thought splintered bone might make, his words not entirely the ones I had expected. 'Look after him,' he said. 'Don't let him go. He's not responsible. He could harm himself.'

And lowering himself into the tall leather armchair where he so often sat to administer the affairs of Lawcroft and Tarn Edge, he slumped forward, tattered and bleeding, across his desk top.

'Look after him, Verity.'

But Mr Boulton, sinking into some terrible, grey twilight, was as limp now as seaweed, sodden and spent, incapable of movement, let alone of flight, and I could think of nothing to do for him but leave him in peace.

'He's well enough. Let him rest awhile. But you, Joel, oh, Joel, stay there a moment, while I send for the doctor.'

'No,' he muttered, trying to get up but then falling back into the chair with a thud that squeezed fresh blood through his shirtfront, sending a thick slug-trail of it leaking down the back of his hand. 'No doctor.'

'What ...'

'No doctor, Verity.'

'But you must have a doctor – you're bleeding.'

'No, no! For God's sake, Verity, if you fetch a doctor somebody is going to know about it, and work out why, and they've had enough to bear, the Boultons, without this. He's got to live in this town, the poor devil, afterwards, and his wife ... It's got to be kept quiet somehow. God knows how, for I can't think straight, not yet. Help me, Verity.'

And there it was. 'Help me,' he said, and realizing that at last he was speaking to me as a woman capable of decision and enterprise, a woman whose strength he recognized, whose comfort he undoubtedly needed, knowing myself to be fascinated by that need, uncertain of it yet confident beyond question of my own ability to fulfil it, I nodded my head very slightly.

'Yes, we'll manage it. And, Joel, I think you must resign yourself, for a little while at least, to doing as you are told.'

And through all the weariness and pain I saw his grin flash out, drawing from me an answering smile.

Concealment, of course, was essential even here, for I knew none of the servants well enough to trust, and although Mrs Richmond was perhaps too grand for gossip, her disapproval could only hinder me. But Mrs Stevens, I knew, would not fail me, and finding her waiting in the corridor, whispering to her as much as she required to know, I left her to

356

administer brandy and any other assistance she could think of to Mr Boulton, bidding her lock the door, while I, bringing Joel's jacket, helped him into it, supported him up the stairs to his bedroom, and there, where hot and cold water and clean towels were already waiting at this hour, began slowly, delicately, to cut away his shirt.

'Mind the carpet,' he said weakly as the blood began again to flow. 'It's worth a fortune.' But the separation of torn cambric and torn skin, the prising loose of the finely matted hairs on his chest caused him such agony that only when it was done and he lay back in his chair, stripped and nauseous and still bleeding, did he glance down at the upholstery and mutter, 'Christ, look at the mess. They'll never get these stains out of the leather.'

He was badly but cleanly cut across the chest and shoulders, raw weals raised thick along his back, one hand split from wrist to palm, a long, slashing wound on the shoulder, not deep but persistently oozing with red, seeping through the towels to my hands and sleeves, soaking the front of my dress.

'You need stitching,' I told him, 'and I can't do it.'

'Then bandage me tight.'

And so I did, padding him well under the linen strips, binding him round and round to the point of suffocation almost, so that he was glad, I think, to lie down on his bed while I rolled up the stained towels and hid them away, threw the rose-tinted water out of the window, disguised, if not altogether obliterated, the damage to chair and carpet, and then, crossing the forbidden barrier of the dressing room to my own bedroom, disposed of my own soiled garments, washed, dressed in something appropriate to the hour should anyone call, should the servants or the children see me, and hurried downstairs again, damp and inwardly shaking, greatly unwilling to leave him even for a moment, to check on Mr Boulton, to assess the damage to the smoking room and Mrs Stevens's ability to repair it, and to retrieve the whip.

I carried it upstairs with me, wrapped in a towel I had fetched downstairs for the purpose, meeting Mrs Richmond on the way.

'Ah, madam,' she said, her eyes fastening on the towel draped artlessly over my arm, 'may I take that for you?'

'No, thank you.'

And although she could require me to make no explanations, she had no intention of letting the matter rest there. Not that she was particularly curious, nor even cared very much what I was up to. But as my housekeeper, she felt it essential to her dignity to be well informed, to have an answer for any impudent little parlourmaid who may have seen Joel staggering upstairs in his greatcoat, leaning heavily against my shoulder.

'Is everything all right, madam?'

'Why, yes, Mrs Richmond, perfectly – except … Well, to tell the truth – and I see no reason for not telling the truth, since I am exceedingly vexed about it – my husband has been drinking, Mrs Richmond, which, for a man in his position, is quite shocking, and I do not at all wish the whole world to know it. Please tell the staff he is not to be disturbed on any account. Naturally he will not be dining. I will take something on a tray later, and if he is recovered enough to join me I will let you know. I am simply thankful that we have no guests tonight.'

'And the gentleman downstairs with Mrs Stevens?'

'Oh I do not think he will be dining. He is an old and rather dear friend of Mrs Stevens's, and it appears they have something to discuss of a private nature. Really, I should leave them alone.'

And I did not care whether or not she believed me, only that she should behave as if she did.

Joel was still lying down when I got back to him, desperately uncomfortable beneath those tight bandages but breathing more regularly, sufficiently recovered to ask for brandy and raise himself to drink. Yet, even so, his first urgent whisper took me by surprise.

'Verity, can you get me dressed, do you think?'

'I suppose so – not that I would –'

'But you must. Get me an evening shirt and a waistcoat. In fact, get me two waistcoats so I can put one on top of the other and then if the bleeding starts again it can hardly show.'

'Joel, are you raving?'

'Very likely, but I'm expected at the Swan.'

'What of it? I have only to send a message.'

'Aye, and have them saying I daren't show my face because of what's happened at the Boultons' – and worse than that if it gets about the old man was here. I told you, he has to live in this town afterwards – and his wife is in poor health already. So get me my clothes, and another brandy while you're at it.'

'I'll do no such thing.'

He closed his eyes, keeping his temper, learning very slowly to cope with weakness when he had built his life on undiluted strength; and, opening them again, it seemed he had discovered frailty's chief weapon, a smile.

'Verity, I can do it without you, one way or another,' he said quite sweetly, defying me gently and with humour as Blaize did. 'No matter how you try to stop me I'll get up and dressed, order the carriage – I'll do it and you know I'll do it. I'm asking you to make it easy for me. And if I kill myself you'll be a rich widow that much sooner.'

But I was a Barforth too, capable of calling his bluff, and it was not until he heaved himself to his feet, took a few dizzy steps towards his closet, endeavoured quite drunkenly to put on a shirt, that my awareness of his pain unnerved me and brought me to his side scolding but ready to help his desperate, guilt-ridden enterprise.

'I think you are quite mad. You will do Mr Boulton no good if you collapse on the Swan floor.'

'I'll not do that,' he muttered, struggling one-handed with his cravat, looking likely to collapse there and then. 'It's a calculated risk, like all the other risks I take. These slashing cuts look worse than they are, and a little blood goes a damn long way. If he'd stabbed me just two inches

358

deep I might not have bled much at all but he could well have murdered me. But all he's really done is break the skin. I'll show my face, buy my round, and then come home again. But I'll go – choose what, choose how – I'll go.'

'Then I'll come with you.'

And, seeing the surprise in him, the beginnings of gratitude, I clicked my tongue with false impatience, not ready yet for either.

'Yes, Joel, I have been thinking it over, and if you persist in this pigheadedness, then I shall be pigheaded too. What is to happen to Mr Boulton? You have not considered that, have you? Well, we cannot leave him downstairs forever, nor can we turn him loose to find his own way home, so someone must go with him. And since you cannot, and I would not lay such a burden on Mrs Steven's shoulders, then clearly I must do it myself. I will have them get the carriage ready – unless, of course, you have any thoughts of driving your phaeton – and we will leave all three together. I will put you down at the Swan, take Mr Boulton home, see him safe, and come back for you. And you may stop frowning, Joel, for there is no other way it can be done.'

'I cannot ask you to go to the Boultons',' he said, still frowning. 'Good God, Verity, I cannot ask you to do that.'

And I replied, quite tartly, 'You have not asked me.'

I feared, at the last moment, that Mr Boulton might make some difficulty, but he was still faraway, still docile, willing to go wherever Mrs Stevens required, and it was Joel who hesitated at the carriage step, wincing, and needed my arm to make bearable the ascent. And as the coachman, far too conscious of Joel's reputation as a whip, set off at a cracking pace, he winced again, and I with him, my body feeling each jolt twice over.

'I will come back for you in an hour,' I told him as the Swan at last drew near. 'Perhaps sooner, but I will wait an hour before sending in for you. Are you in pain?'

'Soreness mainly. I believe I am on the mend.'

'I doubt it. Don't drink too much. You have lost blood and eaten nothing. Bravery is one thing, bravado another.'

'I am not playing the hero, Verity.'

'I know.'

'And do you know how sorry I am to have exposed you to this? I think I have never been sorrier in my life, nor more conscious of what I owe you.'

He got down from the carriage somehow, using his bandaged right hand to account for his clumsiness, his awkwardness of gait.

'Damn glass broke in my hand,' I heard him say to Bradley Hobhouse as I drove off, hurriedly, before my passenger's empty eyes and vacant face were recognized, before my own impulse to get down too became too strong to master.

'Mr Boulton,' I said gently, 'where may I take you? To your own house, or to the shop?'

But one place was as good as another to him just then, and, basing my judgement on Mrs Stevens's information, I drove straight to Millergate to find a lamp burning in the window above the shop, the doctor's gig outside, a harassed woman in the doorway who, seeing us, came running out considerably dishevelled and sharp-tongued with relief.

'Father, how could you? We have been looking everywhere. How could you, with Rosamund as near death as anyone can be. No, she has not gone yet, but it can only be moments – How could you? Go in now, for mercy's sake, and ease her mind, if she can still hear you. Go quickly now – unless you are too ashamed.'

And as his younger daughter's scolding pierced the fog in his brain, he blinked, shook himself like a wet dog, and went inside.

I had no intention of staying after that, no thought of anything but escape from this familiar place, rendered alien and terrible by death, from this woman in whose destruction I had surely taken part – the woman I had taunted, years ago, by wearing a dress she had not made for me and who had suffered such biting agony that same night when Joel had first looked at Estella Chase. But her sister, Mrs Bramley now, I thought, came swiftly back into the street, stationing herself between me and the carriage;.

'I am obliged to you, Mrs Barforth, for bringing my father home. He disappeared, earlier on, when we were much distracted – when we thought my sister had actually passed away – and my mother has been frantic since then. Mrs Barforth, has he –? Mrs Barforth, I hope he has caused you no trouble.'

'None at all. He was merely wandering – just wandering. I think he is much shocked and requires care.'

'Yes,' she said, a tall, thin woman, neat and nervous, not unlike her sister. 'My whole family needs care, just now, every one of them, and since it all devolves on me – since I am the only one near enough in my right mind to make decisions ... Come in, Mrs Barforth – come in a moment – please – for I have just this instant reached a decision, and there is something I must say to you.'

37

I was back at the Swan within the hour, as I had promised, reaching down from the carriage, both hands outstretched – playing the happy lover – to help him in, conscious of the hot, grateful pressure of his fingers, the cold sweat beading his brow, the cavernous sigh coming from the very depths of him as we rolled back up the hill towards Tarn Edge.

'Did it go well, Joel?'

'Aye, well enough. You'll allow that I've always been an adequate liar. And you, Verity –?'

'The same – well enough. She's still alive, and they think now that there is reason to hope – not certainty, but hope.'

'Thank Christ,' he said and, incredibly, in the flickering, treacherous moonlight, I saw that he was crying.

Mrs Stevens was waiting in the hall, hands twisted anxiously together, her eyes compassionate, whispering to me that, in the smoking room she had made all tidy – not perfect but sufficient – and I took him upstairs, walking once again as a lover, my arm around his waist, his arm around my shoulders. And when I had undressed him, washed him and bandaged him again, put him to bed, he said, 'Stay with me.' And so I sat down beside him, noting the greyness of his face, its gauntness against the white pillows, his eyelids blue-veined, black-smudged, his cheeks scoured into hollows, looking as Blaize had looked on that night of fever.

'Will you bring me a cigar?' he asked, hesitant almost, as if I were a stranger, and as I brought it, he groaned suddenly and said, 'I have to do something for her. Whether she lives or dies, I have to do something for her. Verity, what can I do?'

'You can settle Mark Corey's debts and get him out of jail.'

'Mark Corey. Dear God –'

'Yes – Mark Corey.'

And leaning back against his pillows, very weakly, almost imperceptibly, he laughed.

Some time later, when his eyes were closed and my eyelids were aching for sleep, I was jerked abruptly to wakefulness by his whisper, coming at me like a bee sting through the dark.

'Does she want him, Verity?'

'Her sister says that she does.'

'Then she could have raised the money herself, to buy him out – surely?'

'Not without your being aware of it, since she'd have had to take it from the business, and she knew how much you wanted to close his paper down. And then he knew nothing of the child, for it seems matters had come to an end between them, or nearly so. She thought his eyes were roving in another direction, and so why should she set him free for someone else –? At least, that is what her sister says. And perhaps she didn't want to beg. Perhaps she didn't want to say, "I have paid your debts so now you must marry me," I can understand that.'

'Aye,' he said quietly. 'But he'll marry her, just the same.'

'Joel – how can you? If he's not willing?'

'I'll make him willing. I'll make him damn glad. I'll get him out of jail and I'll get him down the aisle – or my money will, his newspaper will. Settling his debts won't be enough. He'll need money if he wants to print that bloody filthy rag again, and now that his father's gone, I see no alternative for him but to take a well-dowered wife. And since I'll be supplying the dowry, I reckon I can pick the bride. He'll see the sense to it. He'll take what I offer and slander me in his first edition. Why not? I'd do the same.'

'Joel – Joel – how can they be happy, if he doesn't want her –?'

And setting his jaw, he snarled, 'I don't give a damn for what he wants. If she wants him, then she'll have him. The rest is up to her.'

The next morning, blessedly, was Sunday, bringing me no need to dissuade him from going down to the mill. He had passed a quiet night, his bandages were clean, his flesh ridging painfully together, long, raw scars, uneven and ugly, but no longer seeping his life away; mending, he said, as I washed and bandaged them again and laid my hand across his brow for signs of fever.

'I'll live,' he told me, and because there was a question in his voice which asked, 'Are you glad? Are you sorry?' I became immensely occupied with towels and soiled linen, and hurried fussily away.

He spent the morning and afternoon in bed, staring moodily at the ceiling, endlessly smoking, but he allowed me to cancel an engagement to dine with the Mandelbaums, using my own sick headache as an excuse, and came downstairs in the early evening, appearing suddenly in my sitting-room door, to the consternation of Mrs Stevens, who, after one swift glance at his face and then at mine, picked up her work basket and fled.

'So,' he said, sitting down carefully, 'and what has our dear Emmeline to tell us today? She'll have had her spies working overtime these last twenty-four hours, I'll be bound.'

'She says Miss Boulton seems to be mending – slowly – although it is still not certain. They had Dr Overdale first of all, from Blenheim Lane, who does not approve of suicides and said there was nothing to be done. But then they sent for the new young doctor who lives in Simon Street, where suicides are ten a penny, and I suppose experience tells. That is what Emmeline Stevens says.'

'Verity, do you pity her?'

'Mrs Stevens?'

'Verity, for God's sake, I am not talking of Mrs Stevens.'

'Miss Boulton, then? Yes, I pity her intensely. I believe I have always done so. Shall I ask them to light a fire in here, for I think I feel a chill –'

'Verity,' he said, so violently that the effort hurt him and he pressed a hand briefly to his chest. 'Verity, will you talk to me – not of fires and the weather – talk to me?'

And I was at a loss to understand the feeling of power – of elation – that possessed me.

'I don't know, Joel, for you have never talked to me. You have given me instructions and reprimanded me sometimes, and you have teased me – pinched my chin and ruffled my hair in that abominable manner – and called me "reasonable" and "sensible" often enough. But I don't think one can call that conversation.'

'Maybe not. If I talk to you now, will you listen?'

And when I nodded he hesitated, at a loss himself in this new situation, faced – as I was – with a person he had known all his life and never known at all.

'I have to explain –'

'There's no need, Joel.'

'There is a need, dammit, I have to explain, and don't hide yourself away – don't disappear into a cloud like your mother. Listen to me. The father of the woman who had been my mistress for years whipped me last night because he believed I had ruined her – and he was right. And we

362

can't let that go by without comment – can't lose it in discussions about lighting fires. You must want to know something more about it. At the very least you must be curious.'

'I asked you something about it last night and you wouldn't answer.'

'No,' he said. 'I couldn't answer. You asked me if I'd ever loved her, and I don't know what that means. I wanted her once, badly enough to marry her, since that was the only way to have her, but I let her go readily enough when I got the chance to marry you. I expected her to get married herself fairly soon after, and so did she, and if she had that would have been the end of it. I never gave her a thought for a long time, and then, one day, I called in Blenheim Lane to see Morgan Aycliffe, and there she was, on her knees, dressmaking for Elinor. Well – I'd like to say my conscience troubled me – and in a way it did – but when I made her my proposition about the shop I knew what I wanted out of it for myself. And if she'd turned me down I can't say for certain, if I'm honest, that I'd have gone on backing her. But she didn't turn me down – far from it – and for a while I can't deny that it was exciting – everything, her jealousy even, was exciting – mainly her jealousy. I liked her to love me. I liked to watch it – test it – and even when sleeping with her lost its excitement and was no more than convenient, I still liked her to love me – until it became a nuisance. And then I told myself she was doing well in the shop and that I'd nothing to reproach myself for. So – there's your answer – I like her to love me?'

'And Estella Chase?'

'Estella Chase loves Estella Chase. She's peevish and tricky and unreliable and curious. That's been the basis of my relations with her – curiosity – and I reckon it's been long satisfied.'

And as the evening deepened, the house quietened, leaving us completely alone, I asked, 'Why are you telling me this, Joel?'

And he, leaning slightly forward, his eyes hesitant again, replied, 'Because I want to talk about you. I want to clear them out of our way, and tell you –'

'No, Joel. Not now. You're grateful now, and still weak –'

'Yes, Verity. I've spent the day and most of last night thinking about it, and there are things you have to know.'

'But it's not the moment – can't you see? You're tired, I'm tired –'

'I couldn't touch you, Verity, in the beginning – do you know that? – without a damned, stupid feeling that it was wrong ...'

'Yes, yes, I know. I understand. You've told me and now, please, don't talk so much. It's not good for you. You'll start the bleeding again.'

'I felt I was harming you, Verity, and it troubled me that I cared. I was a man who'd had other women, and you were so untouched.'

'It was so long ago – it's over.'

'I felt I'd never penetrated you, Verity – you were like smoke in my hands. I couldn't hold you, and it maddened me, many a time.'

'Oh – as to that –'

'And I never lost that uncertainty. That's why I kissed Estella Chase that afternoon. You'd talked so calmly about my infidelity – so bloody calmly – and so I wanted you to see it – I thought that might make a difference. You wouldn't tell me what you felt, or didn't feel – and so I had to know. And finding out was painful. I didn't think a woman could hurt me, until that afternoon, when you came sailing out of the front door with a smile on your face. I wanted – oh, God knows what I wanted –'

'You wanted to see me sick and shaken and trembling – as I'd been two minutes before – that's what you wanted. You wanted me to love you, like Rosamund Boulton, but what were you prepared to feel for me – your new challenge?'

'I don't know. Is it true – that you were shaken?'

'Yes. And it's true I've grown up, Joel.'

'I know it. I couldn't have got on without you last night, and today, thinking it over, I know there is no one but you I could have asked to help me, no one else I would have cared to ask.'

'Hannah?'

'No, not Hannah, Verity.'

'And is that supposed to mean something?'

'Perhaps I'm thanking you. Perhaps I'm saying we can't go on as we are?'

But emotion in Joel, the slight trembling in his voice as he spoke those last words, held the terror of all things that are totally unknown, and I got up, walked away from him, feeling a desperate need for escape, to say, 'I am not quite well. I must go upstairs,' managing only to reach the window before he came and stood behind me, not touching me, although the warmth of his body, the odours of his skin touched me, separately, quite distinct.

'Verity – do you still care for Crispin Aycliffe?'

'Yes.'

And his sigh entered me, fanning out inside my body, warm, alien air, invading, possessing.

'Verity, if – and I say if – I were to allow you to see him – just see him, as you did before – live with me and see him – would you agree? Would it be a solution? Don't answer all at once. Think about it, for your answer matters to me.'

And, unbelievably, I swung round to him and said irritably, 'Oh, do go and sit down. Why on earth must you walk about so? I can feel your chest hurting. Do sit down.'

He obeyed me, crossing the room slowly to the fireside chair, watching me from lowered lids as I followed him, sat down too, my hands folded one inside the other, quietly, my breathing shallow, everything in me suspended somehow – waiting, waiting – letting the minutes flow by in silence until they measured half of one hushed hour, my body still tight-curled like a bud – waiting, waiting – to open and know itself.

'Why did you make me that offer, Joel?'

'Because –'

'Tell me the truth.'

'Yes. There's no trap, Verity. It seems that after all my philandering,

I'm just a poor devil who doesn't want to lose his wife. That's what it comes down to.'

'That – or you want to reward me. A husband for Miss Boulton, a lord for Caroline, a lover for me.'

'You could be kinder, Verity, than that,' he said, and raising both hands, pressing them hard against my eyes, I felt tears stinging behind my eyelids, their first dampness on my fingers.

'I'd abide by it,' he said. 'God help me, but I'd keep my word. I don't say I wouldn't try to win you away from him – I don't deny there's a part of me that believes I could – if you'd let me try. I'd do it.'

'Why?'

'God knows. I'd do it, that's all. I'm as amazed as you are and it's taken me all afternoon to bring myself to admit it, but I'll do it. I don't say I love you – maybe I just think I could love you. Maybe I want to love you – and I'd go to the devil before I'd say that to anybody else. I don't want to love anybody else. And I'm a man who takes risks, you know that. If we keep on as we are he'll be between us for the rest of our lives. And it was only a game when I told you I didn't care how you thought or felt, only how you behaved – a charade, like it's been a charade these past six months, you must know that. I've always cared – selfishly, maybe, because I've always thought I could leave you for later, that you'd be here waiting – growing up – ready for me when I'd tasted everything else. And I miscalculated the time. I left it too long. And the power of the law and the power of my money can't keep you – not the way I want you. So if you want to see him, see him – stay with me and see him. Maybe I'm giving you a licence to hurt me. I reckon I've hurt you often enough.'

'Yes, you have.'

'That's not an answer.'

And once again time flowed between us, soft waves of slow-dropping water. Silence. And then: 'Is it a licence to hurt you, Joel, or a calculated risk – the calculation being that I won't use it?'

'Whatever you like,' he said, the strain of the day very clear now in his face, staining his eyelids, engraving lines I'd never seen before from mouth to chin. 'There's no reason why you should trust me, God knows. If you think I'm making a grand, empty gesture, then I can't blame you. If you think it's all just because I can't bear to lose, then I can't blame you for that either. But I've made the offer. It still stands. What do you say?'

And this time the silence was airless, tense, the lowering quality of a hot summer sky straining towards thunder, until I said, 'No. I say no,' and the storm receded.

'Why not? Tell me.'

'Because I cannot accept so false a life – you with your lovers and me with mine. I thought six months ago, that I could. I thought you were making me this same offer when we began to sleep apart – and even then I was uneasy with it. Adultery does not suit me, as it suits you. I could never take a lover, as you take a mistress, for pleasure. It would not satisfy me, and I don't know – I don't know – how much it satisfies you.'

'What do you want then?'

And for a long moment I looked down at my folded hands.

'I believe I want to be married, or not to be married. One thing or the other. And if I am married then I will be faithful to my husband and expect him to be faithful to me. I want my husband to be my lover and my friend – my dearest, closest friend. I want him to rely on me for the support and guidance it is in my nature to give, as I will rely on him in the areas where he is best able to guide me. I want him to trust me, and I want to trust him. Whatever happens to me during my days, however small or comic or momentous, I want to feel an immense urge to run and tell him of it, to share it with him, and I want him to feel the same urge towards me. I want us both to feel that no pleasure, not one of life's experiences, can be fully realized unless the other is involved – the good alongside the bad. I want his weaknesses and his faults as well as his strengths. I want him, as he is, a whole person, and I want him to want the whole of me. If I am married then I will refuse the fiction that I have only a woman's role to play and he only a man's. We must be two of a kind, the same species, giving the best that is in us to each other. That is what I want – if I am married.'

'Yes,' he said, leaning back heavily in his chair, his eyes closing on a great tide of weariness. 'And you are not talking about me – don't think I don't know it. And if you are not married?'

'Would you allow me – not to be married?'

'Allow it? No. But I don't know, any longer, if I can altogether prevent it. I should make another grand gesture now, should I not – another calculated risk? I should tell you to leave me, give you the money and the goods to make yourself comfortable – the calculation being that my generosity would touch your heart and you'd say, "Poor Joel, he must love me to distraction. I'd better stay." Yes, that's what I should do, but I find the risk too great – it scares me, Verity.'

And he was smiling now, ruefully, wistfully, drawing a smile from me, reminding me, for no reason I could name, of the man who had sat in the window of the Old Swan and raised his glass to the howling crowd below; the man who had driven fifteen miles one night and back again to throw my puppies at me in the dark; the man who, bleeding across his desk top, soiling his good shirt and his precious carpet, had said, 'Verity, see to Mr Boulton'; the man who later, that same night, had said, 'Verity, help me.'

'Do you dislike me, Verity?' he asked now, and I shook my head.

'No. I have never done that. If you had troubled to pay attention to me when I was young – because you are handsome and clever – I would probably have fallen madly in love with you and you would have broken my heart. Because if I had loved you then, when I was young and awkward and didn't know how to handle it, you would never have thought of loving me.'

'I am thinking of it now.'

'But you don't know for certain that you can. Joel, would you allow me to visit my mother – while you are thinking about it – so I can think too?'

'I don't want that.'

366

'No. But will you allow it?'

And for the final time that night silence entered the room and stood between us, its arms outstretched, holding us apart, the busy ticking of the clock a hammer beat, speeding my pulses and the beat of my heart.

'Yes,' he said at last, each word a dead weight on his tongue. 'Go to Patterswick.'

'Thank you. And I think – with your permission – that I would like to take Caroline too. May I do that?'

Although I believe his mouth opened to say, 'No. Never,' the words came out, laboured, unwilling. 'Yes. Take her,' his lips closing on the last word, biting back whatever remained in him to say.

Yet later, through all my tears and confusion, my thoughts of love and freedom, of grand gestures and calculated risks, it did not escape me that he had at no time offered to release Crispin's debts.

38

And so my life narrowed, adapted pleasantly to the small, cosy doings of Patterswick, to my mother's daily inspection of her flower garden, her tranquil afternoons when I, drowsy with sunshine and indolence, would watch her ply her needle. There was a pony for Caroline, the squire not understanding why we were here but happy if it made my mother happy, spending his last, good-humoured years in perfect harmony. And for a week, or two, then three, I wanted no one, was no longer afraid of decision but was content to let it grow naturally inside me, strengthening as my restful body strengthened in the sun and air, the tautness of my nerves relaxed, became well oiled and smooth with resolution. And gradually the things which had appeared impossible became not simple but well within my capabilities. I found the key to myself and knew, above all, that I was my own person. I discovered Verity Barforth, hiding inside me, and learned to value her.

At the end of the third week my mother spent a day in Cullingford, so clearly wishing to go alone that I made no move to accompany her. The next morning, as we breakfasted together, she had a whole parcel of news to impart. Mark Corey was out of jail, busily retrieving his printing presses. Miss Boulton had gone to Scarborough, with her mother and sister, to convalesce. At the millhouse Hannah was brisk and purposeful, giving the impression of a woman at least ten years married, while a suggestion had been made that Elinor should spend part of the winter in London, in a rented house large enough for her to entertain. My dogs were noisy and mischievous, Mrs Stevens very tender, Nicholas had blacked his eye, Blaize had been most charming to his grandmamma, both of them were dining now, every evening, with Joel, who had upset the governess by allowing them a sip of brandy. Emma-Jane Hobhouse was pregnant again. Lucy Oldroyd, who was not pregnant, was thinking of adopting a child.

'Oh, and one other thing,' she said airily. 'I think you must expect a visit about midmorning, I imagine – from Mr Crispin Aycliffe.'

'Mother, what is this? What have you done?'

And her face as she turned it towards me was as clear-eyed and innocent as the face of my son Blaize in his blackest moments of mischief.

'Well, my dear, I have meddled a little, I must confess, which is not at all my habit, so I feel sure you will excuse me. I have merely given him the money to pay his debts, that is all, for I am quite certain Joel does not mean to release them, and it struck me the other day how much easier you would find it if you were perfectly free to make up your mind. This way, my love, there is no pressure and no excuse. You can never say to yourself afterwards, "I was forced to it. I had no choice." Now you can all choose, quite freely. I do not wish to influence your choice, dear. I merely wish you to know that it has been entirely up to you, and as for the money, I am well able to afford it, for my dear Dalby will not let me spend a penny of my own. In fact, he still persists in believing I am quite penniless, although he knows quite well I am far from that. Well, dear, your Mr Aycliffe must certainly have gone to see Joel last night to redeem himself, and then he has only to look to the hiring of a horse and ride over here, so I think we may safely expect him in an hour. If you wish to run upstairs and tidy your hair, I will not detain you.'

Crispin came promptly, as soon as he was able, the same frayed blue coat, the same intense feeling of harmony swaying me as I stood by my mother's parlour window, a warm tide of feeling carrying me towards him, although my body did not move. And we stood for a while without speaking, content simply to be under one roof together.

'I am free now,' he said. 'I have paid my debts.'

And no one else existed anywhere. We were alone, body and spirit blending together as rivers blend at their joining place, a complete and final moment of love, as I told him, 'The time has come now, hasn't it? As we always knew it would. Perhaps we can both bear it now.'

We walked for a while then, in the garden, although I saw nothing of the flowers or the grasses, nothing at all that I recognized but his face, his hand loosely clasped around mine, felt nothing but the same childlike wonder of our first night together which had been leading us gently, irrevocably ever since to this moment of goodbye. And I would not speak the word, had no need any longer of my voice to reach him.

I knew his destiny now, and I would not diminish him. I would believe in him and in myself. We had come together scarred and hesitant and full of need, but now, at our parting, we were free and whole, no longer self-seeking but self-sufficient, aware of the strength and the harmony within ourselves. We had healed each other, discovered our true selves within each other.

'Will you go now, Crispin?'

'Yes.'

And then: 'Verity, I must know, before I leave, how your life will be.'

'I shall be well, Crispin, and free. That is your gift to me.'

And my eyes did not see him go. My hand did not relinquish the clasp of his hand, although for one brief moment I shivered and felt the cold.

My mother came to me afterwards, held me for the first time in our lives, although I was not weeping, stroked my hair and made little murmurings over me as I did sometimes with Caroline.

'You have not harmed him, dearest,' she said. 'Don't think it, for one learns so much from sorrow. In fact, without it, we can learn very little at all, and he will know now how to use his knowledge well. Other women will fall in love with him, of course, but now, because of you, he has no need to fall in love again himself. I believe your memory will suffice to set him free as he so ardently wishes to be free. He may do great things now, or he may not, but you, darling, what now?'

I slept through the night, waking to a sun-drenched sky and my mother calling, from the pathway below my window, to bid me a good morning.

'I am gathering roses for the parlour,' she told me, 'since Lady Winterton is invited to tea. I mention it merely in case you should wish to avoid her.'

'I don't greatly care to see her. But if I decide to avoid her where could I go?'

'My dear,' my mother said sweetly, with perfect innocence, 'the thought had already crossed my mind, I confess it, and I really couldn't say.'

We breakfasted together as usual, Caroline, rapidly adapting to country hours, having risen with the lark and set off long ago to race her pony in the meadow. Sipping my tea, enjoying my mother's efficient grace as she lifted the lid of the honeypot and passed me a jar of her rose-petal jam and her home-churned butter, I asked her, as I had once asked before, 'What must I do, Mother?'

'Ah,' she said, her narrow elegant hands pausing a moment above the toast rack. 'As to that, my love, I have a notion you will do exactly as you think best.'

'And will you help me?'

'How may I do that?'

'Well, you have set Crispin free.'

'So I have. I have paid his debts, which, of course, will allow him the freedom to incur more, if he chooses. But you must know that my purpose in so doing was to widen your alternatives – not his – so you would be free to consider – well – the alternatives I mentioned.'

'Are there really so many?'

'Oh, I imagine there are always at least two: to do something or not to do it. You will know what I mean.'

Lady Winterton arrived at the earliest possible moment at which one could decently expect a tea kettle to be on the boil. Sitting down in her brusque manner, her hands, which had clearly done their share of stable work that morning, immediately busy with the cream jug, the sugar tongs, the chocolate cake, she fixed me with her inquisitive, arrogant eye and said, 'You are still here, then?'

'Yes, indeed.'

'Well, you know your own business best, of course, but I wonder that your husband can spare you for so long.'

369

And she was only prevented from asking me more, having not quite shed the habit of interviewing manufacturers' wives as if they were housemaids, by my mother's smooth intervention with a dish of almond slices Her Ladyship was unable to resist.

But the almonds and the apricot preserve served only to delay her curiosity, not to abolish it, and it was soon apparent that, having almost decided to marry her son to my daughter's dowry, she considered my affairs, matrimonial or otherwise, very much her concern.

'You will be going home presently, I daresay.'

'I daresay.'

'Yes – and what is this I hear. Mrs Dalby, about your old cottage? Mrs Chase informs me that you are having it done up, quite extensively improved, and I was bound to notice, as I drove by just now, that she is right. What is afoot then, Mrs Barforth? We wondered, Mrs Chase and I, if you were planning a little country retreat for yourself, or if Mr Barforth intended to use it for a hunting box, which surprises us, since there is ample room here at the Hall.'

And when, in all honesty, I could give her no information about the cottage, and my mother, very intent on her tea kettle, would not, she swallowed her almond slices in a great huff and went away unsatisfied.

We walked down to the village later that day, Caroline frisking ahead of us, a pair of the squire's half-grown hound puppies at her heels, my mother leaning gently on my arm, not in frailty but because she had acquired during her second, comfortable marriage the habit of being protected.

And with the sweet-scented air of the country evening in our faces, the fast-dropping twilight draping itself all around us in an illusion of privacy, I said, 'So they are gossiping about me already.'

'I fear so.'

'And are you really improving the cottage, Mother?'

'Why, yes, dear. I have walked down here with you on purpose to view it.'

And the cottage already in sight, we strolled silently to its wooden gate and the garden, where the roses my mother had planted in her early widowhood were still blooming, the honeysuckle riotously spreading, her lilac trees and cherry trees and apple trees still offering leafy shade.

'See,' she told me. 'All is clean and fresh inside – the walls new-papered – just a few chintzy covers, I think, on these chairs, and anyone could be perfectly at ease ...'

And as Caroline raced upstairs in a wild spurt of exploration, the hound puppies rooting and sniffing outside, I asked her, 'Why, Mother?'

'Oh, just a question of choice, dear. You chose to set Crispin free, as I hoped you would, and now you may choose your own freedom, or something altogether different. This little cottage of mine could serve any one of a dozen needy Dalbys or it could be yours, just as you wish. And whether you take it or not, you will always know that you could have taken it. And I was always extremely happy here.'

'But you married again.'

370

'Ah yes. That is what I chose to do.'

'And Joel?'

'What of him? Joel is not at all my concern. Are you strong enough to see him now?'

'I must see him eventually.'

'Yes, and you must have your answer ready, for he is a clever man, your husband. Shall I let him know.'

But Caroline, tumbling downstairs, excitedly repossessing this cosy corner of her childhood, 'her' cottage now, 'her' meadow, 'her' pony, 'her' squire, who would pluck the moon from the sky at her asking, spared me the necessity of reply.

My mother made another journey to Cullingford early the next morning, clearly to see Joel, although, on her return, I asked no questions and she offered me no information. And, expecting him in a day or two, late in the evening or on a Sunday – for when had Joel Barforth ever lost a half a day's business on my account – I was surprised to see him that very afternoon, his phaeton tearing up the gravel, entering the house like an invader, an imperious hand held out to me with a blunt request to 'Come out into the garden. This crumbling old pile gets me down.'

'I don't know why I am here,' he said, striding irritably among my mother's roses. 'God knows if I'm right or wrong. I don't understand myself anymore, and I've never understood you. It's just that I felt I ought to come. I've been on tenterhooks to come ever since Aycliffe threw his money at me the other night.'

'And you took it?'

'Of course I took it. Whyever not? You're thinking of grand gestures, are you? Well, that's one I wasn't prepared to make. A paltry thousand pounds I didn't need and he's desperate for, all he has in the world, I reckon. Oh no, I may not be able to stop him seeing my wife, but I'll be damned before I'll pay him.'

'Am I your wife, Joel?'

And stopping in his tracks, he put hard, heavy hands on me, forcing me to stop too.

'He was here, wasn't he?'

'Take your hands off me, Joel.'

'What did you say to him?'

'Take your hands off me, Joel, if you want me to say anything more to you.'

And I saw the anger blazing in his eyes, cooling slowly at the command of his reason, which also, just as slowly, unlocked his fingers from my arms.

'All right. What did you say to him?'

'We spoke privately.'

'Dear God, what am I coming to? You'll have to tell me more than that.'

'Well I'm here, with no immediate intention of leaving. And he won't be coming again.'

371

Triumph first. 'You sent him away?'

And then a growl of suspicion. 'What do you mean – no immediate intention of leaving? You've no damn fool notions of staying here indefinitely, have you? Verity – I want you to come home.'

'Yes. But you didn't answer my question.'

'What question?'

'Am I your wife? I said I would be married or not married. And you know very well what I mean.'

We walked for a moment in silence, Joel's eyes brooding darkly on the roses, not seeing them, although their colours moved me to a new awareness of life – a certain excitement growing inside me – their perfume tanalizing my nostrils, making me giddy, a girl again walking in a garden with this powerful, handsome man who had not wanted me as a girl, who had given me no opportunity to want him.

'I could say anything,' he told me, 'to get you back. Words come cheap enough. I could say any damn thing I thought you wanted to hear, whether I meant it or not. Could you tell the difference?'

'Oh – who knows? Let's try, shall we?'

And his lowered lids snapping wide open, he said, 'Verity, are you flirting with me? You'd best take care, for I'm in deadly earnest.'

'Tell me.'

'What? I'll tell you how I've lived these last three weeks. I've tried. I've dined at home every night with my sons, which hasn't always been a pleasure, and I've missed my daughter. I've counted my successes, and, commercially, they've been enormous. I've made my million several times over, and every night, these three weeks, I've felt like a poor man. I've missed you, Verity – yet I've spent so little time with you lately that the reason couldn't be simple. And so I reckon I've been missing what I think we could have together now – what I want us to have. And so I've done certain things to please you. I've given Hannah the Top House, and I've convinced Morgan Aycliffe he'd best take Elinor to London and treat her right if he wants to keep on the right side of her. I've made my peace with the Boultons and put Mark Corey back in business. And I've put the children at Low Cross on ten hours a day, with Lawcroft and Tarn Edge to follow if it's a success, which has made me the most hated man in the Piece Hall – again – and is going to make them hate me worse if I do it, as I think I can, without loss. So you've made a philanthropist of me, Verity. I even had a letter from Richard Oastler congratulating me on having seen the light – leading the way – impudent devil, good as told me I hadn't turned out nearly so bad as he'd thought me, and when he writes again I reckon he'll be asking for my contribution to his campaign funds. And they'll take a dim view of that at the Piece Hall – although I've yet to see what the *Cullingford Star* will make of me now.'

'Oh yes – I can't wait for the first edition.'

'I've missed you, Verity.'

'Yes –?'

'What do you want me to say now?'

'I expect you'll think of something.'

372

And taking my wrist again, this time very lightly, he held me in his arms and kissed me, in a rose garden, as he should have done years ago, and then kissed me again, most urgently, no longer in any way my cousin.

'Will you marry me, Verity?'

And there, in full sunlight, face to face, we laughed wholeheartedly.

'Really marry you?'

'Yes. I understand your requirements, madam.'

'And can you fulfil them?'

'I do believe so. And if I fail it won't be for want of trying.'

'Well then – I'll let you know, Joel.'

'What! What do you mean, you'll let me know? You can't say that to me, dammit!'

'Joel – I'll let you know.'

'Devil take you,' he said, his tension relaxing, his mouth beginning to smile. 'Very well – very well, I deserve that – or do I? Just don't be too long. Shall I come for you tomorrow?'

'Joel –'

'Yes – yes, I understand – you'll let me know. I'll go now, while my temper holds. Will you excuse me to your mother – tell her I'll be over to see her presently.'

I watched him leave, waved to him as he disappeared through the flying gravel, the haze of the mellow afternoon, and then I walked back through the glowing roses, smiling, languorous, wanting to stretch myself in the scented air like a cat, sleekly purring. And in the doorway my mother was waiting, smiling too.

'I see you left him no appetite for tea,' she said. 'Ah well – you will be going home, then, tomorrow?'

And walking past her, my smile growing, spreading from my lips until my whole body seemed to be smiling, I told her, 'Yes, I suppose I may go home tomorrow – unless, of course, you would care to lend me your carriage, in which case – perhaps – I think I will go tonight.'

Flint and Roses

'For she's made of flint and roses'

John Davidson

1

My mother had been a light-hearted seventeen on her wedding day, my father a stern, fastidious forty-nine, and although no part of their marriage contract required her to be broken-hearted at his death some twenty years later, it was generally assumed that without him she would not know which way to turn.

Possibly she had not loved him – in view of his age and his gloom and his autocratic disposition many people would have been surprised if she had – but she had certainly depended upon him. He had been much more to her than a husband. He had been her teacher, on whose judgment of matters ranging from the care of her immortal soul to the choice of a parasol, she had unquestioningly relied. He had been her guardian, taking care never to expose her to the dangers of going out alone, keeping a supply of sensible, solid women on hand to accompany her about the town when he could not. He had been, beyond all doubt, her master, whose decisions had been considered absolute.

'Poor Elinor,' they said when his illness first struck. 'She will not have the slightest notion how to face the world on her own.' 'I fear he has gone, madam,' the doctor told her, positioning himself to support her should she crumble and fade away then and there at his feet. 'Oh dear!' she said. 'Oh dear – how terrible! I think I had better be alone!' And going downstairs, as gentle and unassertive as a captive dove, she stood for a moment in the centre of the darkened drawing-room, and there, fancying herself unobserved, began to spin out her skirts in a billowing, carefree dance – my father's pampered, submissive little wife no longer, but a girl who had once been poor enough to marry an old, austere man for his money and to regret it.

She had been Miss Elinor Barforth of Low Cross Mill, daughter of a careless father who, at a time when the cloth trade was thriving and other men making their fortunes, had committed the sin of extravagance, which had inevitably led him to the far greater sin of poverty. Instead of harvesting his profits and ploughing them back into his weaving-sheds, Grandfather Barforth had spent them on fancy waistcoats and fancy women, and at the time of her marriage my mother had had little to recommend her but her slight, dainty figure, the pale blonde ringlets framing her porcelain complexion, the unusual blue-green colour of her eyes – qualities not much valued in a wife by the hardheaded Yorkshiremen of our industrial, industrious Law Valley. And in our town of Cullingford, where a man's worth was measured by his standing in the Piece Hall and at the Cullingford Commercial Bank, she must have been astonished and intensely grateful when my father, Mr Morgan Aycliffe, had offered to take her as his second wife, without a dowry.

My father had been well-to-do all his life. The son of a master builder he had inherited a business so well established that his own hands had never been obliged to trouble themselves with bricks and mortar. He had been, not brilliant perhaps, but shrewd, a man who knew the value of being in the right place at the right time and how to get there, so that at a moment when the steam-engine, the spinning frame, the power-loom had brought vast industrial expansion to the North – a vast influx of humanity with it – my father had been on hand to fill the bare, West Riding landscape with the six-storey mills, the towering chimney-stacks, the warehouses, the unkempt sprawl of workers' cottages which had transformed the pleasant townships of Bradford, Halifax, Cullingford and Huddersfield into grim-visaged factory cities.

There had been two textile mills in Cullingford when my father built himself a house in the then almost rural tranquillity of Cullingford's Blenheim Lane. Twenty-five years later, when he had buried his first richly dowered wife and engaged himself to marry my mother, there were fifty, most of them constructed to his designs by gangs of Irish navvies he had imported for the purpose, while Blenheim Lane itself, at its lower end, was malodorous with factory smoke, raucous with factory operatives, emerging only as it climbed the hill out of town as a fit place for a gentleman to reside. And having inherited one fortune and made another, having married a first wife for profit and a second for pleasure, he had turned, in his later years, to the fresh delights of power.

Cullingford, in the year I was born, had no politicians, since politics had been designed for gentlemen, for those who owned the land rather than those who scratched a living from its soil or defaced it with their foul-belching commercial enterprises. Government – always – had been aristocratic, an affair very largely of the southern, agricultural counties, where one solitary but noble gentleman might control the votes of half a dozen constituencies. And while the North remained a bleak, forgotten upland where hill-farmers precariously raised their sheep and cottagers wove the fleeces into cloth, taking a week, perhaps, to produce one coarse, laborious piece, there had been no one to complain. But the steam-engine and the power-loom put an end to that, my father being one of the first to join the campaign for Parliamentary Reform, demanding that our new-born industrial towns, crammed with so many new-born millionaires, should no longer be forced to accept the rule of country squires, that Parliament should cease to be a meeting-place for landed gentlemen and listen to the voice of the belligerent, possibly vulgar, but increasingly prosperous North.

'Cullingford must have the vote,' my father had insisted, finding no lack of millmasters and ironmasters, worsted-spinners and brewers to support him, and, when the vote had been obtained, he had secured election himself and served Cullingford's interests most faithfully until the day he died.

Yet for all his gifts of public oratory, my father was an almost completely silent man in his private life, his one pleasure being the refined but solitary pursuit of rare china and porcelain, items of Sèvres and Meissen which he displayed in the glass-fronted cabinets of his drawing-room, promising unmentionable doom to any child depraved enough to touch. But the temptation, in fact, seldom came our way, for my father, who was not fond of children in any case, could rarely bring himself to admit us to his drawing-room, preferring, when absolutely

378

necessary, to meet us on our own ground, upstairs in the nursery wing devoted to our care.

There had been a son of his first marriage, a most unsatisfactory young man, who, having objected to a stepmother younger than himself, had been banished from hearth and home, his name erased from the family Bible, from the last will and testament, from our memories. And I cannot think that, at his time of life, my father had welcomed other children. Yet we existed, not even boys who could have been groomed to help him in his business or succeed him at Westminster, but girls who would be very likely to cause him trouble, would certainly cost him money. Daughters, and since the only profit a man can expect to make from a daughter is the acquisition of a useful son-in-law, we were, from our earliest days, moulded deliberately for that very purpose, not by our mother, whose sole task in life was to entertain her husband, but by such nannies and governesses as were considered best qualified.

The guidelines of our education were very clearly set down. Respect for authority first of all, since a girl who learns to obey her teachers and her father will extend the same wide-eyed, unquestioning docility to her husband. Punctuality next, since gentlemen do not wish to be kept waiting – every morning of my childhood finding me up and dressed by six o'clock to begin a day irrevocably divided into tidy, busy hours, controlled by the nursery clock which could tell me far more precisely than any governess exactly when I must put my sketchbook away and take up my embroidery frame; the very moment when I must cease to play my scales and begin the daily chanting of French verbs and English prayers, without listening to either.

We were taught to sing and to smile; to speak without really saying a word; enough mathematics to appreciate the value of our dowries; enough religion to make us understand that God, having created us weak and female, had also designed us for the convenience of man, an arrangement it would be sinful even to question. We were taught to be innocent by the simple procedure of removing from our sight, our grasp, our hearing, anything which might arouse our curiosity. We were taught to be industrious in private – mending our own stockings and petticoats – but to be idle in public, displaying a piece of cobweb fine embroidery in languid hands, since a woman who has no work to do herself offers proof of her husband's ability to pay servant's wages. We were taught to dress for the occasion, to be appalled by a crumpled glove, a shower of rain, to go into maidenly raptures at the sight of newborn kittens without daring to ask how it was they had appeared so suddenly in their basket, since no one is quite so innocent as all that and we knew the question would be termed 'improper'. We were the perfectly mannered daughters of Morgan Aycliffe – as bereft of individuality as our mother – who would go to our bridal beds, in due season, as quietly as we had gone to our piano practice: obedient, punctual, innocent, accomplished, and very bored.

No difficulty was ever anticipated with my younger sister Celia, who was tense and timid, and most anxious to be married. Nor with my elder sister Prudence, although her keen, disciplined intelligence often caused my father to regret she had not been born a boy. Celia was fashionably small, fashionably demure, far more concerned, at fifteen, as to when she could reasonably expect her flowery wedding-veil, her hour of bridal glory, than with the identity of the bridegroom himself.

My sister Prudence was taller, less amenable, her eyes a shade too watchful, her wits too sharp to find favour in a world which did not encourage cleverness in women. But there was a certain air of efficiency about her which, my father believed, might attract the eye of someone with a large household to manage, a certain elegance which, if properly nurtured, would make her the kind of hostess much sought after by the socially ambitious male.

Celia, it was hinted, would go to an industrialist, a newly rich man of the Law Valley who could give my father solid support at election time. Prudence would make a political marriage, a promising newcomer to the Whig party, perhaps, who might well attain the Cabinet appointments my father had missed. But I was somehow more difficult to place in my father's mind, and it seemed – for reasons of which I was not then aware – that he was inclined to be ill at ease with me.

Coming between my sisters in age, I resembled my mother closely in some ways and, quite sadly, in others was her direct opposite. I had inherited her pale blonde hair, except that mine, unlike her silken curls, was straight and heavy, difficult to manage, its weight defeating the bonds of pins and ribbons, so that there was usually a ringlet tumbling down, stray coils escaping from underneath my hat, loose tendrils taking flight at the very moment it was essential to be neat. My eyes were blue enough, I suppose, to please anyone, except that they were short-sighted, often clouded over with the boredom that caused me to be inattentive to my teachers, neglectful of my studies, retreating from the strait-jacket of my father's reality into a far more pleasant world of my own. And worse than that, perhaps, since it could not be corrected, from the age of fourteen I had started to grow, outstripping Prudence, who was herself quite tall enough, winning no favour with my father, who in the last months of his life had been seriously displeased to find my eyes on a level with his own.

Naturally he would succeed in finding me a husband, for like my sisters I would have a dowry of twenty thousand pounds and a share of his estate, half of which was to be held in trust for us during our mother's lifetime. But clearly I worried him, causing him to conduct long discussions with our governess, Miss Mayfield, as to the nature of my crimes, the list – as he grew weaker and I grew stronger – appearing more alarming every day. I had left my sketchbook on the hall table, and when accused of untidiness had answered carelessly, 'Oh heavens, Miss Mayfield, I suppose so.' I had sat all morning, my needlework in my hands, without taking a single stitch, so deep in my forbidden day-dreams – and of what was I dreaming? of whom? – that I had answered her reprimand with a shrug, an unmannerly. 'Gracious me, Miss Mayfield! I doubt it will cause the sky to fall.' But on the afternoon I spent ten sinful minutes gazing at myself in a mirror, deciding that my pale eyebrows were insipid, and was caught later trying to darken them with a solution of Chinese ink and rosewater, my father, nearing the end of himself, shuddered quite visibly and informed my mother, 'I had best speak to Joel about that girl, for you will never manage her, Elinor.'

And that same day he sent for my mother's brother, Mr Joel Barforth of Tarn Edge, appointed by the terms of his will to watch over us, and warned him, one supposed, that although Celia would always be obedient and Prudence reasonable, he could only speak with regret of his troublesome daughter Faith.

'She is perhaps just a trifle scatterbrained,' my mother had suggested, her voice dove-gentle as always, her eyes downcast, not wishing to question his judgment, merely to soften it.

'She is insolent,' he had said, 'and disorderly. And worse than that, she is vain.'

And those were the last words I ever heard him speak.

His funeral service in the parish church high above the town was extremely well attended, for my father had not only served the political interests of Cullingford's manufacturers for more than a dozen years, but had possessed a hard-headed grasp of commercial affairs which had made him a valued, if not a popular man.

As Morgan Aycliffe, master builder, he had been responsible for the erection of Cullingford's magnificent Assembly Rooms, for every factory of size in the district, and for the grandiose villas of the men who owned them. He had built square-shouldered, no-nonsense chapels for Dissenters, gracefully spired churches for those who kept the established worship of the English realm, a college for Roman Catholics, another for Quakers, had commenced construction of a station and a station hotel in readiness for the day, surely not long distant, when Cullingford would be joined at last by branch line to Leeds.

Nor had he neglected the lower sections of our society, for it had often been pointed out to us as an example of his shrewdness that every one of the mean, narrow streets cobwebbing from one set of factory gates to another, tight-packed with their low, two-roomed workers' cottages, had been designed by him. And I had heard him declare with pride that he knew how to squeeze in more families per acre than anyone else in the County of Yorkshire.

As Morgan Aycliffe, Member of Parliament, he had spoken warmly in support of Free Trade, had denounced the Corn Laws which, by forbidding the import of cheap corn and keeping the price of home-grown grain high, had worked to the advantage of the landowners and against the industrial interest he had been elected to serve. He had opposed, unsuccessfully, the introduction of factory inspectors and the passing of laws to control the number of hours our local industrialists – most of them our relatives and friends – could oblige women and children to work in their weaving-sheds. He had laboured hard to prevent the introduction of the Bill forbidding the employment of children under the age of nine, arguing that tiny bodies were essential to the spinning trade, since only they could crawl under the machines to mend the broken threads, and that the parents of such child-operatives were in dire need of their wages. And on his last appearance in the House he had spoken out bitterly against the proposed introduction of a ten-hour working day, an unpardonable intrusion, he had declared, into the business affairs of his constituents, and no help at all to the labouring classes who would be thus obliged to exist on ten hours' pay.

And so, as we drove at the head of his funeral procession on that chill January morning, up the steep cobbled streets that would take him to his final rest, the churchyard was surrounded by closed carriages, the church itself most flatteringly overcrowded with substantial, silk-hatted gentlemen and their ladies, come to pay him their parting respects.

The worsted manufacturer Mr Hobhouse of Nethercoats was there, with his wife and the eldest of their fourteen children; the banker Mr Rawnsley, with whom my father's credit had always been high; the worsted spinner Mr Oldroyd of Fieldhead, a widower himself, who had already called at our house to offer his private sympathies to my mother; the foreign-born, exceedingly prosperous Mr George Mandelbaum, whose wife, her emotions nurtured in a warmer climate than ours, actually shed a tear. There were manufacturers and professional men from Leeds and Bradford; the Members of Parliament of both those cities; a scattering of our local gentry, who although they had disapproved of my father's politics were finding it expedient these days to cultivate the newly rich. And, as a final honour, there was a carriage bearing the coat of arms of Sir Giles Flood, lord of the manor of Cullingford, although that noble and decidedly disreputable gentleman did not come himself.

'What a sad loss!' they said. 'Poor fatherless children! Poor Elinor! No one could be surprised to see her follow him by the month end. Good heavens – only think of it – we must all of us come to this. How terrible!' They lowered his coffin into the hard ground. 'He was not a *young* man,' they said, 'older than me, at any rate.' It was done, and I went home with Prudence and Celia to serve glasses of port and sherry to my father's mourners, who had their own ideas as to what he had been worth and – if they happened to be the parents of sons – couldn't help wondering how much of it, besides that twenty thousand pounds apiece, he had left to us. He was gone, there was no doubt of it. I had seen him go. But throughout the whole dreary afternoon I failed to rid myself of the sensation of his eyes still upon me, that he would suddenly appear, his cold face pinched with disapproval, and demand to know what these people were doing here, cluttering up his drawing-room, setting down their glasses on his immaculately polished tables, their careless hands and wide skirts a danger to his porcelain; his presence so real that I wondered if my mother, sitting so very still, looking so very frail, was aware of him, too.

But the Hobhouses and the Oldroyds, the Mandelbaums and the Rawnsleys, the gentlemen from Bradford and Leeds and Halifax, having done their duty, were not disposed to linger; and, approaching my mother one by one to mutter their self-conscious sympathy, were soon heading either for home or the Old Swan in Market Square, to drink hot punch and transact a little business so that the entire day should not be profitless. And soon there remained in my father's drawing-room only my mother's family, the Barforths, who had once been poor and now were very rich, my father having no one of his own beside ourselves and the son of his first marriage, whose name I had never once heard on my father's lips.

I had been acquainted with wealthy and powerful men all my life – indeed my father had allowed us to be acquainted with no other – but it was generally acknowledged that my mother's brother, Mr Joel Barforth of Tarn Edge, of Lawcroft Fold, of Low Cross – the three largest textile mills in the Law Valley – was of a far higher order than any of these. For, rising above the legacy of debt and disgrace his father had bequeathed him, he had been the first man in Cullingford – perhaps the first man in the world – to see the advantages of the new, power-driven machines, and to possess the courage to exploit them.

Following the slump in trade after our wars with Napoleon, when most manufacturers had been shaking their heads and keeping a tight hold on their purses – muttering that the 'old ways' were best – Joel Barforth, then a young and reputedly reckless man, had filled his weaving sheds with the new machinery, turning a careless back on the hand-loom weavers who came to complain that he was taking their living away, shrugging a careless shoulder when they threatened his devilish innovations with hammers and his property with fire. He had spent money which the Hobhouses and other well-established residents of the Law Valley had considered criminal folly on a new breed of men called engineers and designers, purchasing their inventive and creative skills to make Barforth cloth not the cheapest, certainly, but the most efficiently produced, the very highest quality available, not merely in Cullingford but in the world. And because he had seen no reason to be modest about his achievements, because he had strolled into the Piece Hall in Cullingford as if he owned that too, and had greeted with no more than the tilt of a sardonic eyebrow the news that his competitors – with their faith in the 'old ways' – were not all doing well, he had not been popular and many had wished to see him fail.

But now, with scarcely a hand-loom weaver left in the Valley, Uncle Joel had passed far beyond the possibility of failure, his factory at Tarn Edge alone, I'd heard, capable of producing five thousand miles of excellent worsted cloth every year, his order books permanently full, his authority in the town of Cullingford very nearly complete.

Yet, as I watched him that day sitting at ease beside his serenely elegant wife, too large a man for my father's fragile, brocade-covered chairs, I somehow feared his influence less than that of his sister – who was my mother's sister too – our Aunt Hannah.

Uncle Joel was too splendid, I thought, too remote to concern himself in any great detail with the comings and goings of his orphan nieces, or, if he did, would do it with style, with the same breadth of vision he extended to all his enterprises. But Aunt Hannah had always been a source of authority in our lives, a woman of immense determination on whose judgment my mother frequently relied – a woman, we were given to understand, who deserved our respect and consideration because her life, unlike my mother's, had always been hard.

She had kept house for Uncle Joel during his early struggles, had sacrificed her youth to his convenience, and then, when neither he nor my mother needed her, had married late and somewhat unsuitably, reaping no advantage from her brother's subsequently acquired millions. Yet her husband, Mr Ira Agbrigg, who had been a widower with a half-grown son at the time of their marriage, was now the manager of Lawcroft Fold, perhaps the most important of the Barforth factories, a man whose quiet authority was acknowledged in the textile trade, and it was the long-held opinion of Mrs Hobhouse and Mrs Rawnsley that, if Aunt Hannah could learn to content herself with a manager's salary, she would do well enough indeed.

But it was not in her nature to take second place to a Mrs Morgan Aycliffe, her own sister, nor to a Mrs Joel Barforth, her own brother's wife, both these ladies younger, and in her view considerably less able, than herself, and although she was ready enough to borrow our carriage-horses and to help herself to the surplus products of the Barforth kitchens – unable, she said, to tolerate waste – I had always recognized her as a great power.

Uncle Joel, no doubt, would wind up my father's business affairs, or keep them ticking over as he thought fit, but unless my mother, who so far as I knew had never made a decision in her life, chose now to stir herself, it occurred to me that the minutiae of our daily lives – of far greater importance to us than building land and railway shares – would be left to Aunt Hannah.

Uncle Joel, apparently disinclined for conversation, planted himself on the hearthrug dominating the fire, and reaching for his cigar-case – although I did not think that even he would dare to smoke here, in my father's drawing-room – allowed his gaze to rest speculatively on my father's glass-fronted cabinets and his intricately inlaid, expertly polished tables, each one bearing the treasures of Sèvres and Meissen, Minton and Derby, that my father had cherished far more than his children.

I saw Aunt Hannah's husband look down uncomfortably at his feet, his sense of propriety telling him it was time to leave, his sense of reality reminding him he would need his wife's permission to do so. I saw my Uncle Joel's wife, kind Aunt Verity, smile with tolerant, tranquil understanding at her husband, well aware, I thought, of his urge to light that forbidden cigar, and of the commercial instincts which were now leading him from force of habit to assess the value of my father's porcelain.

And for a while there was no sound but the busy crackling of the fire, the ticking of the ormolu and enamel clock standing, as it had always done, at the very centre of the mantelpiece, a black basalt urn perfectly placed at either side. But Aunt Hannah was not given to prolonged meditation, and, fixing my mother with an irritable eye, announced, 'Well, then, Elinor – it's a bad business.'

'Yes, dear. So it is.'

'Indeed. And he'll be sadly missed, for heaven knows how we'll find another Member of Parliament to serve us so well. I suppose the by-election must be quite soon?'

'Yes, dear. I suppose it must.'

'And I wonder if you have given any thought to a suitable memorial?'

'Oh – my word! Should I do that, do you think, Hannah?'

'I think it will be expected of you, Elinor. A headstone will hardly suffice, you know, for so distinguished a man. No – no – something altogether out of the ordinary. And it strikes me that if the worthies of this town could be prevailed upon to subscribe towards the building of a concert hall, then there would be every reason in the world to name it after your husband. Now what do you think to that?'

'That would be splendid, Hannah.'

'Well, then – if you agree, of course – a committee could easily be formed for the purpose, and in view of Mr Aycliffe's services to the community I can anticipate no difficulty. Really, it would be most appropriate.'

And as my mother continued to smile, a placid little woman who had no objection to monuments or concert halls or anything else so long as she was not required to stir from her own warm corner, my Uncle Joel, that most awe-inspiring of gentlemen, grinned suddenly, as mischievously as a schoolboy, and said, 'Aye – most appropriate. And if the firm of Morgan Aycliffe should undertake the construction work, then I'd think it more than appropriate. I'd think it shrewd.'

And with an air of enormous unconcern – master in his own home, master, now, it seemed, in ours – he selected a cigar, lit it and inhaled deeply, bringing home to me by that one simple, almost contemptuous gesture that my father, who had not permitted tobacco in his house, much less his drawing-room, was dead indeed.

'Joel!' Aunt Hannah said, quite horrified. 'Good heavens! – what are you thinking of? Not in *here*.'

But, standing in the centre of the room, his bulk overshadowing the memory of the narrow, silent man whose ghost he had so easily laid to rest, he did no more than shrug his powerful, expensively covered shoulders.

'If Elinor don't like it, I reckon she can tell me so.'

'Elinor?' Aunt Hannah cried out, the hint of nervous tears in her voice causing me to wonder if she had indeed cared for my father as sincerely as she pretended. 'Elinor has nothing to say to it. This is Morgan Aycliffe's house, as you very well know, and when did Elinor ever have any sense of what's right, or any sense at all? It's not decent, Joel – the poor man is scarcely in his grave. And it's the porcelain – you know the care he took of his porcelain and how he feared the tobacco would stain it.'

'Ah yes,' my mother murmured, perfectly serene in the face of this

385

tirade. 'The porcelain – the famous, beautiful porcelain. There is a word to say, Joel, is there not, about the porcelain?'

And rousing herself suddenly she smiled at me, and at Prudence, and at Celia, and sent us off to bed.

We had rooms of our own now, below the nursery-floor, identical toilet tables swathed in white muslin, narrow, white-quilted beds, nothing to distinguish one from the other except that Prudence and Celia maintained their possessions in immaculate order while I, alas, did not. And as Celia bade us a sedate good-night, hurrying off to dream, with total fifteen-year-old contentment, of the twenty thousand pounds which would secure her the wedding, the christening, the smart new villa of her heart's desire, I joined Prudence for a moment at her fireside, neither of us ready to be alone.

We had not loved our father. He had not required it, and it had occurred to neither of us to do so. Unlike Celia, who had felt secure beneath the wing of his authority, we had been oppressed by it, yet now there could be no sense of relief, no real hope of broadening our narrow spirits, our restricted horizons.

Possibly – without my father to run to – our governess, Miss Mayfield, might prove a trifle less invincible. We might, with some contriving, be at last empowered to pay calls and receive them without her eagle-eyed supervision, to write letters without submitting them for her inspection, to hold conversations out of her hearing. We might, indeed, be allowed to choose our own gowns – within reason – to make the momentous decision between lace or ribbons, a bonnet crowned with feathers or with a satin rose. And it was the measure of my father's defeat that only one of his three daughters could content herself with that. Celia would do well because she wanted only what it was right and proper for her to have. Prudence would find life hard, since she wanted to make up her own, female mind as to its direction. I had no idea what I wanted – except that I had not met it yet, except that it was not to be found in Blenheim Lane.

'What of the porcelain then?' I enquired carefully. 'Is it to go to our brother, do you imagine?' And having lived in fear of those frail treasures all my life – for if someone's skirt had ever dislodged one of them it would certainly have been mine – I added, 'Well, and I shouldn't mind.'

'Nor I,' she answered, continuing to stare into the fire, her face, in its tight concentration, more like my father's than ever. 'Indeed, it is only right that he should have something, especially when one considers that if he had not quarrelled with father he might have had it all. But he is a man. One supposes he is able to take care of himself. I should like to worry about him, but I have other things on my mind. I am far too busy wondering whether it will be a Hobhouse or a Rawnsley they will purchase for me with my twenty thousand.'

'Perhaps mother will still give you a London season, as father planned.' But Prudence, her mouth hard and sarcastic, although she had not wanted to go to the London marriage-market in any case, shook her head. 'Oh no. Mother will do exactly as she is told. You know how she is, with her "Yes, dear – no, dear" except that now she will be nodding and smiling to Uncle Joel instead of father. And although I am sure Uncle Joel means us no harm and would add to our money rather than cheat us of a single penny – and believe me, there are uncles who *would* cheat us – well, he won't take the trouble to send us to London. He knows he has to get us married, and he'll do it, but he won't be as careful as father. He'll accept anyone who offers, so long as he's respectable – anyone Aunt Hannah draws to his attention – just to get the job done. And all mother will say is "Yes, dear. How very splendid". What a poor, silly creature she is, Faith. Was she always like that, do you suppose, or was it father – twenty years of father – that turned her into a porcelain doll? I have a nightmare sometimes that I could be the same.'

I kissed her lightly, knowing she did not really like to be touched, knowing there was no lasting comfort I could give; and, crossing the landing to my own room – wondering about that porcelain doll, that dainty puppet who had waltzed so blissfully the night her puppet-master died – I became once more an unseen, unwilling witness.

Below me in the darkened hall Uncle Joel and his wife were taking their leave, and as Aunt Verity stooped to kiss my mother's cheek and then moved away my uncle paused a moment, cigar in hand, its unaccustomed male fragrance shocking and attracting me, so that I paused too, looked down, and then, afraid of discovery, was obliged to remain.

'There's a lot of money, Elinor,' I heard him say. 'Not bad, eh, for twenty years' work, however tedious. And you're still young enough, like I said you'd be. The world's wide and you can afford to enjoy it now if you'll bide your time. All I ask of you is to wear your widow's weeds like a good girl, as long as it's decent, before you start spreading your wings.'

And smiling up at him, neither docile nor helpless, but radiating an enchanting, altogether wicked sparkle, she threw both arms around his neck, and standing on excited tiptoe hugged him tight.

'Yes, Joel, a twelvemonth of black veils, isn't it, for a husband? Then lilac and grey for a year after that. I'll do it, don't fret yourself, for I've no objection to black. But it strikes me no one could really blame me if I went off to wear it in a sunnier climate. The northern winter, you know, and my tendency to take cold – in fact my doctor may positively insist upon it.'

'Aye, I reckon he might.'

'Italy, I thought, or southern France – for a while, Joel. I've earned myself that, surely? Hannah can see to the girls – and Verity – for the whole world knows me as a woman who couldn't be trusted to arrange a tea-party, much less a wedding.'

'So they do. Just promise me you'll arrange no weddings of your own – in Italy and France.'

'Oh Joel,' she said, hugging him again, her face glimpsed behind his shoulder, vivid and alive. 'I think you can be sure of that. No weddings for me, darling, not until I'm old at any rate. And I'm not old – oh, no – *that* I'm not.'

And standing in the doorway she waved her hand, a free-flowing, graceful movement of her whole body, stretching herself in the crisp, night air – without a shawl, without a chaperone – until his carriage was out of sight.

2

My mother took to her bed the very next day, suffering, they said at first, from the effects of fatigue and sorrow, which, combined with the biting January wind – the prospect of a raw February, a howling March to follow – could well settle on her lungs. And so it was left to Uncle Joel to inform us that my father had bequeathed his entire collection of porcelain to Prudence, thus causing much distress to Celia, who did not care about the porcelain, but, being the youngest, the smallest, the only one who had really believed in father's teachings, would dearly have loved to be singled out.

'It's worth thousands,' Aunt Hannah declared accusingly, as if Prudence had been a scheming parlourmaid. 'Thousands and thousands – and to a girl not yet nineteen. Good heavens! I can hardly think it wise. Naturally there can be no question of removing any part of it, Prudence – in fact you would do well to think of yourself merely as a guardian until such time as you are married and your husband can take proper charge of it.'

But an hour later, having thought the matter out, I noticed she was kinder to Prudence than usual, for this legacy would make her the most marriageable of us all, and we had no need to be reminded that Aunt Hannah's stepson, Jonas Agbrigg, was in need of a rich wife.

Nor was I surprised, some three weeks later, to find myself accompanying my mother to Leeds, the first stage of her journey to London and abroad in search of the softer climate she had convinced our family doctor she required, and then returning with Prudence to Aunt Hannah's house, where Celia – who also suffered from the cold – was waiting.

There had been some suggestion, hotly contested by Aunt Hannah, that Prudence should accompany my mother, a further suggestion that we should all three remain in our own home, under the combined supervision of our housekeeper, Mrs Naylor, and Miss Mayfield, our governess, whose duties, now that our education appeared to be over, were becoming vague. But although our house had been kept open and a somewhat tearful Miss Mayfield assured that there would always be a place for her therein, Aunt Hannah had insisted that, for a week or so at least, we were to be her guests. And as I sipped her weak tea and ate her scanty slices of bread and butter on that first afternoon, I felt it was by no means all she would insist upon.

My aunt's house at Lawcroft Fold was old and plain, a square, smoke-blackened box hugging the hillside above Lawcroft Mills, owned by her brother, managed by her husband; her windows, although she contrived to ignore it, offering a view of the factory buildings crouching in the valley, the high, iron-spiked factory wall, the huddle of workers' cottages around it; her morning rest disturbed by the hideous five o'clock screeching of the factory hooter, the clanging shut, a precise half-hour later, of the massive gates.

Yet the house itself was decently proportioned, a solid oak door at the centre, two high square rooms on either side, a sufficiency of bedrooms, the front parlour – for the benefit of Aunt Hannah's guests – offering a brave show of plum-coloured velvet upholstery, a busily patterned carpet that would not show the years, a jungle of bright green foliage in ornamental pots, a great deal of fancy needlework – embroidered firescreens, cushion covers, table-runners, tapestry pictures in heavy frames – done with immense skill by Aunt Hannah herself to conceal the lack of the Meissen and Sèvres and the antique silver to be found in such abundance in Blenheim Lane.

But, in complete contrast, her back parlour was achingly clean, exceedingly bare, and for that interminable week or so I was obliged to spend my mornings in that cheerless apartment, assisting with the household's plain sewing, submitting myself to the tyranny of hem-stitch and blanket-stitch, the bewilderment of button-holes, at which I did not excel, and to spend my afternoons at the front of the house, my chair well away from the fire, listening, speaking when spoken to, as Aunt Hannah issued tea and instructions to the ladies she had involved in her works of charity – colleagues in their opinion, assistants in hers – and who, because of her desire to spare her own elderly carriage-horses, were obliged to come to her. And it was a constant proof of her natural authority that these ladies, the wives of owners not managers, although they disliked and resented her, and frequently threatened among themselves to rebel and ignore her, could be reduced after ten minutes of her company to obedience.

She had as always a dozen schemes afoot. There was her plan to educate orphan girls for domestic service and then to 'place' them in the houses of her friends; her longstanding efforts to provide blankets and good advice for such poor families as she deemed worthy; her determination that our local manufacturers should open their hearts and their bank accounts to Cullingford's need for a concert hall – since Bradford had one – and that it should be named after my father. But most of all that winter her mind was occupied by the proposal that Parliament should be petitioned to grant Cullingford its Charter of Incorporation, with the right to elect our own mayor and town council – not, one felt, because she was really troubled by the inefficiency of our present parochial system of local government which had failed to pave the streets or provide an adequate water supply – in some cases no water supply at all – to the poorer sections of the town, but because she intended her husband, Mr Ira Agbrigg, to be our first mayor and herself his mayoress.

Mr Agbrigg could not bring her riches, but he could, at her prompting, offer her prestige; and since there were others who felt they had a greater claim to civic honour, it suited her, when Mrs Hobhouse of Nethercoats Mill and Mrs Rawnsley, the banker's wife, came to call, to remind them that her nieces were the daughters of the late Morgan Aycliffe M.P., her brother Mr Joel Barforth himself.

'Naturally my brother is most anxious for the Charter to be granted,' she would throw casually into the pool of conversation, her keen eyes assessing the ripples she had created. 'He feels local government to be altogether essential – since who better to ascertain our needs than ourselves – although he was telling me the other day that the office of mayor will really be most arduous.' And here she would smile directly at Mrs Hobhouse, whose husband was not noted for his energy.

'And of course the mayoress will have her duties to perform,' she would murmur, glancing sidelong at Mrs Mandelbaum, the wool-merchant's wife, who was of a retiring disposition, hated crowds, and, when she was nervous did not speak good English.

'But will your brother not wish to take office himself?' Mrs Rawnsley, the banker's wife, once asked her.

'Ah, no,' Aunt Hannah replied, 'his time is too fully occupied; but he will certainly put forward his nominee.'

And since Mr Rawnsley's bank would have been hard pressed to support the withdrawal of Barforth favour, his wife had no more to say than 'Oh, yes – quite so. Assuredly Mr Barforth's views will be listened to.'

'Naturally,' Aunt Hannah told her kindly, enjoying her moment of power as hugely as if she had already instructed Uncle Joel to transfer his funds, as if she really believed he would obey her. 'I could not say at this stage just who that nominee may be. But I think we can all agree on the soundness of my brother's judgment and his desire to serve the best interests of the community. Now then, ladies, if we could turn our attention to this little matter of a concert hall –'

And having reminded them – humble manager's wife that she was – of her grand connections, the intricate financial web which bound most of them to her brother, the extreme eligibility of her sister's daughters, which was a matter of some importance to those with marriageable sons – she would without once mentioning her husband's name, pass on to other things.

We had not of course expected to be pampered in Aunt Hannah's house, for although her husband's salary was known to be ample – my Uncle Joel being generous to those who gave him value for money – her charitable and social activities, her insistence on living, at least on the surface, as a Barforth rather than an Agbrigg, proved an evident financial strain. The future mayoress of Cullingford could not refuse to contribute substantially to the charitable foundations she had herself brought into being – could not, in fact, give less than the women she had bullied into giving anything at all. She could not refuse invitations to dine from ladies of substance whose husbands she intended to cajole into supporting Mr Agbrigg's candidature, and, having accepted, she was obliged to invite them in return. When she did, her table must have its share of crystal and silver, and no one must be allowed to suspect that she had herself prepared the sauces and desserts which were far beyond the skills of the ageing kitchenmaid she called her cook. But in the more private areas of her home she could keep a watchful eye on coals and candles, could employ her own half-trained charity children as maids, reserving just one presentable parlourmaid for the serving of drawing-room tea. 'Ah – what have we here, I wonder?' she would ask at the appearance of her tea-tray, her smile half-amused, half-sarcastic as she served, with immense composure, the gingerbread and chocolate cake, the apple-curd tarts and cheese muffins she had baked herself only a few hours before.

Yet from the start of our visit, although Celia and I were obliged as usual to do our own mending and keep our own rooms in order, thus freeing her servants for the downstairs dusting and polishing that would '*show*', she extended such leniency to Prudence that Celia, who was easily offended, soon began to complain.

'She wants you to marry Jonas,' she said, her face sharpening as it always did when there was a marriage in the offing. 'Well, that's what comes of being father's favourite and getting all the porcelain. But I suppose it's only right you should get married first, you being the eldest – and they say Jonas is very clever.'

And when Prudence, seriously annoyed, declared that marriage was not greatly on her mind, Celia, who feared nothing in the world so much as being left on the shelf, calmly replied, 'That's nonsense, Prudence. Of course you're thinking about marriage. It's the one thing everybody thinks about – and you should be quick about it, so Faith and I can have our chances.'

I had been acquainted with Jonas Agbrigg all my life, or for as much of it as I could remember, yet all I really knew about him was the much-vaunted fact of his academic brilliance. He had, it seemed, shown from the very first a flair for learning far in advance of his years and his relatively humble station. At the grammar school, long before Aunt Hannah's marriage to his father had given him a degree of social standing, he had easily outdistanced the sons of the local 'millocracy' on whose generosity the school depended and had been something of an embarrassment even to certain schoolmasters who had found themselves hard-pressed to keep up with him. He had shown himself, indeed, to be so universally gifted that Aunt Hannah, whose pride in him was boundless, had been unable to decide just where those gifts could be best employed. She had to begin with planned to make a churchman of him, dreaming perhaps of bishoprics, archbishoprics – of herself installed as hostess in some ecclesiastical palace – until a certain tartness in his manner, a decided lack of saintliness, had inclined her to consider the law. And now, having returned from the University of Cambridge, an opportunity had been purchased for him, with the help of Uncle Joel, in the legal practice of Mr Corey-Manning, a neighbour of ours in Blenheim Lane, who was – according to Aunt Hannah – exceedingly fortunate and immensely grateful to have obtained his services.

Jonas was a young man of twenty-four, pale and expressionless, a taller, better-nourished version of his father, although he had not inherited Mr Agbrigg's stooping shoulders and big-knuckled, work-scarred hands. Jonas's hands, on the contrary, were long and lean and perfectly smooth, with never so much as an ink-stain on his carefully – by Cullingford's standards almost effeminately – manicured fingers, and, although he dressed plainly, he was at all times immaculate, and far too conscious of it for my comfort.

I could, if I put my mind to it, understand that we had not always been kind to Jonas. During our early childhood, when the boys and girls of the family had been allowed to play together, my Uncle Joel's sons, Blaize and Nicholas Barforth, had mocked him quite mercilessly for the care he took of his clothes, being completely careless of the damage they inflicted on their own. Their sister, my cousin Caroline, possessing from birth a fine appreciation of the social order in which a mill-manager's son had no more importance than a groom, had often snubbed him and encouraged us to do the same.

'Oh, it's only the Agbrigg boy,' Caroline would announce. 'He won't want to play.'

And Jonas, his long, uptilted eyes scowling, would walk off, making us somehow aware that in his view our games were infantile and each one of us a bore.

Even now, although he was always scrupulously polite, he was not a comfortable young man, his return home each evening bringing a certain tension, which stemmed in part from the surprising coolness between him and his father, a circumstance of which Aunt Hannah herself seemed unaware.

'Good evening, sir,' Jonas would say.

'Evening, lad,' he would receive in reply; and, brought up on Aunt Hannah's extravagant hopes for her stepson's future, it astonished me that his own father should have no more to say to him than that. Yet Mr Agbrigg, his thin face quite haggard in the lamplight, a faint odour of raw wool often discernible about his clothing, would eat his supper in silence every evening, his shrewd, narrow eyes registering nothing as Aunt Hannah requested Jonas to give us his opinion of the day's news, expressing no opinions of his own, and then, folding his napkin with those big, work-hard hands, would say simply, 'I'll be off back to the mill, then, to see the night-shift come on.'

My Aunt's ambitions for Jonas, of course, were of a far higher order than those she entertained for his father. Mr Agbrigg, self-educated but unpolished, his speech still retaining the broadness of the West Riding, could be pushed just so far and no farther. He was without doubt exceedingly well-respected in Cullingford's Piece Hall, where men were more concerned with cash than with culture, and would be a popular mayor with our town's largely unlettered population. But Jonas, with his academic distinction, his neutral accent, his chilly determination to succeed, could do Aunt Hannah credit in the eyes not only of Cullingford but of the world.

She knew exactly what she wanted for him. To begin with, when his childless employer, Mr Corey-Manning, decided to retire, Jonas must be in a position to take over the business. Then, with a well-established legal practice behind him, a year or two's experience as a town councillor, a member of this committee and that, the way to Westminster, my father's old seat on the Whig back-benches, a Cabinet appointment – Whig or Tory mattered little to Aunt Hannah – would be open.

But even Jonas's talent, even his genius, could not hope to succeed without the cash in hand to buy Mr Corey-Manning out when the time came, without a sufficient income not only to fight a decent election campaign but to maintain himself in office when he succeeded; and, since Aunt Hannah had no money to give him and Uncle Joel could not be relied on forever, the only course open to him was to marry someone who could.

Naturally he would leave the choice of a wife to his stepmother, and she had selected Prudence for a number of reasons: largely, of course, for the dowry and the porcelain, partly because Prudence herself was exactly the kind of efficient, energetic girl who would help a man to go forward, rather than hold him back; but also because her alternatives were limited to the three of us. Jonas, she well knew, would never be permitted to approach a Miss Mandelbaum or a Miss Rawnsley, whose fathers – like ours – required something a little more solid in a son-in-law than ambition, self-confidence and a university degree, which in their experience had never been an essential ingredient in the making of fortunes. But my father was dead, and, having only my mother, her own younger sister, to contend with – in Aunt Hannah's view no contest at all – she began her campaign with vigour and a lack of scruple which enabled her to drop the most transparent hints to Mrs Hobhouse of Nethercoats Mill, who had ten sons of her own, that Prudence was spoken for.

But Mrs Hobhouse, who had clearly informed herself how much my father's porcelain would be likely to fetch at auction, was as fond a mother as my aunt, and the next time we called at Nethercoats, Prudence found herself burdened with another suitor in the hearty, heavy shape of Freddy Hobhouse, the eldest of the ten equally heavy Hobhouse sons.

'Prudence is such a dear girl,' Mrs Hobhouse enthused, beaming as she saw how obediently Freddy was plying my sister with tea and muffins; while Aunt Hannah, knowing that Freddy, who should have been at the mill at this hour, had been specifically summoned to his mother's drawing-room for the purposes of seduction, sat straight-backed, her mouth very hard.

'Yes,' she said. 'As you know, she is a great favourite of mine. A parent must be impartial, but I think an aunt is entitled to her preferences.' And later, as we drove home, Freddy, a warmer man than Jonas, having spent longer than necessary in arranging my sister's portion of the carriage-rug, Aunt Hannah enquired tartly if in view of her recent bereavement Prudence thought it proper to pass her time in flirting. To which my sister, with a cold fury equal to her father's, her fastidious nostrils quivering in exact imitation of his, replied that she did not understand Aunt Hannah's meaning; and that if she had understood it, she felt certain it would have given her much offence.

'The Hobhouses,' Aunt Hannah announced at dinner that evening, speaking directly to her husband, 'are in a sorry state indeed. It saddens me, every time I go over there, to see the worsening of their affairs – for they are worsening, Mr Agbrigg, are they not? My word, when I think of Nethercoats as it used to be, in old Mr Hobhouse's day – And when Bradley Hobhouse took it over from his father it seemed as solid as a rock. Certainly Emma-Jane Rawnsley, as she was then, thought so, or she would hardly have married him. But Bradley has never been a man of affairs, too easiful, too apt to leave it all to others. I have heard my brother say so many a time, and although Emma-Jane is a good soul, she is not a strong character either. Well, as to how Nethercoats may provide a living for those ten boys, and dowries for those four girls, I haven't a notion. And neither has Emma-Jane. They have made room for Freddy and Adolphus, but the younger boys will be forced to take employment elsewhere, which is a great pity, don't you agree, Mr Agbrigg? Really, one can only tremble for their future.'

But Freddy Hobhouse, completely untroubled by that future, attended the parish church the following Sunday, an act almost amounting to a declaration, since the whole world knew the Hobhouses to be Methodists; and afterwards, in the churchyard, he gave Prudence his arm as she picked her way over the frozen ground, having first elbowed the physically and socially inferior Jonas aside.

'Can't have you coming a cropper, Miss Aycliffe,' he announced with all the breezy self-confidence of a man who has always known where his four square meals a day are coming from, and as I followed them I couldn't fail to miss the taut yet perfectly controlled anger in the arm Jonas offered to me, nor the pouting outrage of my sister Celia, left to pick her way across the ice without any man's arm to lean on.

It was perhaps just as well that Uncle Joel's wife, Aunt Verity, took note of the situation and rescued us.

'They must come to me now,' she said at the end of the second week, and although Aunt Hannah was not pleased, Aunt Verity, after all, was Mrs Joel Barforth of Tarn Edge, and she was obliged to agree.

'Very well, Verity. But I must ask you to remember that they are still in full mourning and should not be taken out a great deal. In fact they should not really go out at all – their father was most precise in such matters.'

But Aunt Verity's beautiful, silk-upholstered, silver-mounted carriage was at the door, her fur rugs swiftly wrapped around our knees, and within the hour we were installed before a happily crackling fire, our feet on velvet stools, while this younger, kinder aunt asked nothing of us except that we should be at ease.

Uncle Joel's house at Tarn Edge was scarcely a dozen years old, and, although it was but a mile or two distant from the largest of his mills, the windows of its principal rooms were turned away from the scowling city skyline with its fringe of chimney stacks to offer a view of old trees, thinning as they climbed the hillside, to sharp-scented, sharp-tufted moorland.

The house itself, a Gothic structure of spires and ornamental towers, had always been something more than a mere dwelling-place, for, unlike most Law Valley men, who preferred to confine their surplus cash in bank vaults or invest it in objects large and solid enough to announce their own value, Uncle Joel saw no shame in self indulgence. And so, as a tribute to his own unflagging energy, he had built himself a palace, its treasures displayed not with the glass-fronted, locked-away care of my father, but with a nonchalance that some called arrogant, others magnificent.

The vast hall was medieval in feeling, a life-size bronze stag guarding the foot of the stairs, a gigantic stained-glass window at their head, casting its ruby and emerald light on a wealth of intricately carved panelling, dappling the limbs of a white marble goddess and attendant nymphs standing in splendid – some said shocking – nudity on the wide landing. But these sombre glories apart, the rest of the house was as light and pastel-tinted as a summer garden, blue velvet or honey-coloured velvet underfoot, blue silk walls rising to ceilings that were moulded in blue and white and gold, and set with the brilliance of crystal chandeliers; while in the ballroom, recently added for my cousin Caroline's convenience, a dozen windows opened directly on to a broad, paved terrace, a landscaped acre of roses, a trellissed walk, a lily-pool.

No one at Tarn Edge House ever gave a thought to the household's plain sewing except an elderly woman employed for the purpose, while at all hours of the day one could encounter a cheerfully starched maid running upstairs with hot water or a deliciously laden tray. At Tarn Edge, certainly, no one counted coals or candles, nor cared how many times the horses were got out, and had I found my uncle's presence less overwhelming I would have been well content.

He was undoubtedly a handsome man, massive of build, exceedingly dark of hair and commanding of eye; but, accustomed as I was to my father's narrow, stooping shape, my uncle's very maleness, the rich odours of wine and tobacco hovering about him, his luxury and freedom of speech, all, in their various ways, alarmed me. My father's authority had been a chilling but restrained whisper, Uncle Joel's a mighty bellowing at the foot of the stairs whenever his sons, as often happened, were delaying his departure for the mill. For my uncle, in the fiftieth year of his age, still chose to be at his factory gates most mornings at half-past five o'clock, watch in hand, to check the punctuality of his employees, the stamina of his managers and his children; and the greatest source of discord at Tarn Edge was that my cousins, Blaize and Nicholas, were rarely of like mind.

'Get yourselves down here, damn you,' I grew accustomed to hearing him shout. 'We've a business to run, and God help it when it gets into your idle hands. But so long as it's mine – so long as I'm paying your bills – you'll jump when I tell you – damn you!'

And my cousin Nicholas would run scowling down the stairs, as big and dark and angry as his father, his waistcoat undone, hastily shrugging on his jacket, while my cousin Blaize would come sauntering behind at his leisure, his own brocade waistcoat correctly fastened, his curly-brimmed beaver hat and light-coloured kid gloves nonchalantly in his hand. From my room at the front of the house I would hear the crunch of wheels on the gravel, the growled commands of my uncle as he mounted his carriage, and would watch, sometimes, from my window, as my cousins on their thoroughbred bays raced each other for the lodge gates – Nicholas, hatless more often than not, bound for Lawcroft Fold to be instructed by Mr Ira Agbrigg into the intricacies of textile machinery; Blaize, his hat tipped at a rakish angle, heading for the smart new suite of offices at Tarn Edge, to be initiated into the religion of profit, the mortal sin of loss.

My uncle was known throughout the West Riding, with some justice, as a man who had everything. No business enterprise of his had ever failed, but, in addition to that, at a time and in a place where men took wives for convenience, he had married a woman who was not only graceful, sweet-natured, and most pleasing to look at, but who actually loved him, was loved by him, displaying an open delight in his company which I, moulded by the long silence that had been my parents' marriage, found intriguing, something, I suspected, to be envied. And it followed, perhaps, quite naturally that this handsome, affectionate couple should have fine children: Caroline and Nicholas, the younger son, being as dark and immediately striking as their father; Blaize, the elegant, careless first-born, a shade or two lighter and finer, his mother's child, who would, one felt, float effortlessly through life protected from misfortune by the power of his unique, altogether disarming smile.

On countless occasions during our childhood I had seen that smile flash out, melting the hearts of any irate adult from maidservant or gardener to Aunt Hannah herself, so that, knowing Blaize to be the real culprit, the one who invented the mischief for others to perform, they were nevertheless conquered by that impish charm, and somehow or other ended by meting our their punishments to the well-meaning but stubborn Nicholas. And although Blaize was decidely less handsome than his brother, his light grey eyes in no way to be compared with Nicholas's eyes, which were almost black, his straight, chocolate-coloured hair nothing to Nicholas's ebony curls, his face quite unremarkable until it was illuminated by his smile, he had been born, it seemed, with so much easy assurance, a total conviction that everyone must notice him first and like him best, that so indeed it was.

'Yes, of course I'll do as you ask – why not?' Blaize had declared almost daily throughout our childhood and then, with everyone off their guard, had done exactly as he pleased.

'That's nonsense,' Nicholas had declared. 'I won't do it,' proceeding to stand his ground, black eyes scowling, as he took his punishment, and quite often Blaize's punishment as well.

It was Nicholas, straightforward, obstinate, who on every occasion growled out: 'I don't see why I should apologize when I'm not sorry.' Blaize who, gracefully shrugging his shoulders, declared himself quite ready to be as apologetic as anyone pleased, after which he would do whatever it was he had apologized for all over again. It was Nicholas who, disliking any kind of failure, had worked hard at school and had managed somehow to win a reputation as a difficult, argumentative lad, prone to use his fists; Blaize who, barely working at all, was remembered as a likeable, witty young rascal who could have done wonders had he condescended to try. And all my life I had been dazzled by Blaize, who was never defeated, never dismayed, for whom life seemed a carefree, cloudless summer day; and – being often in disgrace myself – had felt an immense sympathy for Nicholas.

Yet both these cousins, having strutted through my early years like young Lords of Creation, were separated from me now by the unseen barrier surrounding all marriageable girls, and it was their sister Caroline who, finding Prudence too serious and Celia too young, dominated my time.

'I know Faith is in mourning,' she explained to her mother, who was not in any case too severe about such things, 'but no one could possibly criticize her for going around with me.' And quite soon I became not only Caroline's best friend but her property.

'We are to drive to town this morning,' she would announce, walking into my room long before breakfast. 'And then, when I've done my shopping, we are to call on the Mandelbaums, which is a great bore, since the Mandelbaum boy wants to marry me. But you can chat to him, Faith, because it would be much more sensible of him to want to marry you. Manufacturers again and their wives at dinner tonight, I'm afraid – really, you'd think father would see enough of them elsewhere – but we can escape to the landing sofa afterwards, and I shall rely on you to protect me from the Battershaw boy, who wants to marry me too, according to his mother. Battershaw's Brewery, Faith – of course you know them – they make thousands and thousands a year with their light ales. Mrs Battershaw was telling me, which I thought very vulgar of her. So what do you think I should wear this morning? Come on, Faith, you're quite good with clothes – the blue velvet pelisse with the swansdown trim and the bonnet with the white feather? Yes, I thought about that too, except that my dear friend Arabella Rawnsley has had one made just like it – or as near as she could manage – and I really can't drive down Millergate looking like a Rawnsley. Hurry up, Faith, and we'll go to the Swan and see if the mail coach is in, for I'd like to know just where my parcels from London have got to. Really, you'd think they could deliver on time, since they must know there's absolutely nothing fit to buy in Cullingford.'

A young queen – my cousin Caroline – who required a lady-in-waiting, and I suppose I had always known that, however rich I might one day become, Caroline would be richer; whatever marriage I might make, Caroline's would be grander. And I was happy enough to drive with her at least twice daily from Tarn Edge down the leafy slope of Blenheim Lane, the steep, cobbled track called Millergate that took us via the even steeper, stonier Sheepgate directly to Market Square, flanked at one side by the Old Swan, where the London coach still clattered in each afternoon, and at the other by the ancient Piece Hall, a relic almost of a bygone age, when the handweavers had come down every Thursday from their moorland cottages to offer their heavy worsteds for sale. The old market buildings had been removed now, at my father's instigation, the fishmongers and the butchers, the butter and cheese sellers concealed, in these prosperous times, behind an elaborate stone façade, an Italianate structure which had won my father much praise. His Assembly Rooms – his greatest architectural triumph – were visible too from Market Square, a smoke-grey building in the classical style, Doric columns and graceful proportions contrasting and partly concealing the weed-garden of warehouses crumbling on the canal bank behind it, their cellars foul with floodwater, their floorboards sodden and dangerous with half a century's rain.

And if nothing in our main shopping area of Millergate was worthy of purchase, that did not prevent us from looking, touching; did not prevent me – since I was, as Caroline had said, quite good with clothes – from combining two lengths of silk, a little ribbon and lace into a confection which more often that not would find its way into our carriage.

'Miss Aycliffe has taste,' they said of me in Millergate, implying, I suspected, that since I lacked the striking dark eyes and black curls of Miss Barforth, I had need of something to see me through. Yet, although I was myself condemned to wear black at least until the month of June, I enjoyed not only the colour and texture of these rich fabrics, but the advantage this instinctive sense of dress gave me over Caroline, who had the advantage of me in every other way.

'What about this, Faith?' she would say, throwing a length of purple velvet across her shoulder.

'Oh, no, Caroline – at least, not until you are a duchess.'

And while she tried on something else, pouting, shrugging, but doing as I told her just the same, I took advantage of those large, dressmakers' mirrors to discover that even a mourning dress might be improved by a high ruffled collar which could make a long neck seem longer, that a black frill so near the face made a pale complexion paler, fair hair a shade or two fairer, that a strategically placed lamp or a branch of candles could even turn that heavy, unruly hair of mine to silver.

'What are you doing, Faith?'

'Thinking about myself, Caroline. When you're not beautiful – when you're tall and fair, and small, dark women are all the rage – it takes thought.'

Of all the Barforths, Caroline was the one who most resembled Uncle Joel, being possessed of the same energy and endurance that had made him his not altogether unblemished fortune. Like him, Caroline would always head directly towards her goal, demolishing rather than climbing any obstacle foolish enough to block her way, and her problem lay not so much in deciding what to do with her life – since she believed she could do anything – but in what she would like to do best.

Marriage, of course, would be her eventual destiny, as it was the destiny of all female creatures who got the chance, but Caroline's marriage, like her London gowns and her French gloves and parasols, would need to be of a quality and a rarity not easily found in Cullingford. No 'Battershaw boy', no 'Mandelbaum boy' would suffice for Caroline Barforth, and it was a contradiction of her nature that, although she was fiercely proud of her father and more than ready to enjoy his colossal fortune, she preferred never to refer to the means by which that fortune had been made.

Money, to the Barforths and the Hobhouses, to the Oldroyds and the Mandelbaums, was equally desirable from whatever source it came, but Caroline, with all the money she could ever require so readily to hand, had turned her mind to finer things, having learned quite early of the few landed gentlemen who had so far come her way that the only wealth they really valued was tied up in ancestral acres, ancient names and traditions, which Barforth looms could not provide.

Her father was certainly a great power in Cullingford: his influence could make itself felt in the commercial circles of Bradford and Leeds, and even in London; but to the sporting squires who came north to hunt foxes, course hares, shoot grouse and pheasant – to the disreputable, almost penniless Sir Giles Flood, lord of the manor of Cullingford – Mr Joel Barforth was no more and no less than a tradesman, a man to whom one might nod in passing but whom one would not expect to receive through one's front door. And, since she was a true Barforth, wanting whatever was difficult, whatever the world told her she could not have, I believed that Caroline had set her obstinate heart not only on entering those noble front doors, but on being well received inside, on becoming, as her brothers had always called her, not Mrs Battershaw, or Mandelbaum, or anything at all, but Lady Caroline.

'I suppose your sister Prudence will settle for Freddy Hobhouse,' she told me one wet afternoon as we sat on the landing sofa. 'Because, after all, even if Nethercoats is going down, he can always build it up again, and she could hardly consider the Agbrigg boy. She'll have a nice little house and a nice little mill, and I can't think that Freddy will be hard to handle. And you and Celia will get just the same. Yes, it's all quite simple for you. I envy you, Faith, really I do – because I can't see myself in a mill-house at all. And they are mill-houses, aren't they, whatever one does to them, full of millmasters and brewmasters, talking wool and light ale. Good heavens! – I couldn't bear that.'

Responding to her shudder with a smile, wondering what her father would say should he hear her refer to Tarn Edge as a mill-house, I failed to notice Blaize until he flung himself lightly down beside us and drawled, 'Don't fret, Caroline. If a manufacturer is beneath you, we can always get you a lord. We could even try for Sir Giles Flood, for they say he has an eye for little girls since he turned eighty.'

'And that,' Caroline said, squaring up to him, 'is enough of that.'

399

'Oh – I don't know.'

'Well, *I* know. And furthermore, brother dear, shouldn't you be at the mill?'

'Of course. I'm just a manufacturer after all – where else should I be?' And, stung by the mischief in his subtle, smiling face, the composure she knew to be her best defence faltered, and she snapped. 'Yes, a manufacturer. And not even a good one, father says.'

'Ah well, if *father* says –'

'Yes, he does. And there's no need to look so smug. He says you're a fly-by-night, whatever that may mean.'

'Oh, you know,' he said, very much amused. 'You know very well what it means. And so I am. But you can rest easy. I'll settle down, eventually, and work – not so hard as Nicholas, I grant you, but hard enough, so that when you marry your lord we'll have the money to pay off his mortgage and his gambling debts.'

'You'll do no such thing.'

'Well, and if we don't, love, you'll have a poor time of it, for why else would a lord marry a trademan's daughter?'

'My father,' she said quite viciously, her jaw clenching with the effort to hold back her temper, 'is not a tradesman. And I'd like to hear you call him so, Blaize Barforth, to his face. Not that you ever would, for with all your airs and graces you're still afraid of him, and so is Nicholas. You can grumble, the pair of you – Nicholas thinking he knows more about cloth manufacture than father, and you pretending you don't care – but you'll always do as he tells you, just the same. And so you should, when you consider his position and everything he's done for you.'

'Quite so,' Blaize murmured, less mischievous now, although a slight smile still touched the corners of his lips. 'He's done a great deal for me. He's made a manufacturer of me, which is very splendid, provided that's what I like to be.'

'Like it!' she snorted, the duchess giving way now to the child I remembered, who had never scrupled to use her fists – fierce and determined Caroline, with her belief, apparently by no means dead, that the Barforths were the greatest people in the world. 'Like it? And what has liking to do with it? You'd better like it, for if you let him down I'll never forgive you. He's spent his whole life building Tarn Edge and Lawcroft Fold and Low Cross, and he's entitled, Blaize – he's *entitled* –'

'Entitled to what? My gratitude?'

'Yes, so he is. Your gratitude, and your labour.'

And suddenly I saw a new Caroline emerge, or perhaps simply the old one, the real one, stripped of her genteel pretensions – a girl who, had she been born of an earlier generation, would have laboured herself alongside her men, a hard-headed, tough-fibred girl of the West Riding, who would have brewed nettles for food when times were bad, who would have endured and overcome as those older Barforths had done, and who surely in her heart must secretly despise the airs and graces of that class above her own to which she now aspired.

'My word,' she muttered, 'If he could pass the mill on to me I'd take

400

care of it for him. I'd be down there every morning, just like he is, to see the hands arrive on time and make sure the managers don't rob me. I'd –'

And, as she paused breathlessly, painfully aware of her self-betrayal, Blaize smiled. 'Dear Caroline – good heavens! – you'd be a manufacturer yourself if you did that. Can you mean it?'

'Damnation!' she said, a word I had never heard on female lips before, clenching her fists in a gesture of total fury she jumped to her feet and swept away as regally as she could contrive.

'That was not kind of you, Blaize,' I said serenely, no stranger to Barforth tantrums.

'No – but then, she'll forgive me, you know, since I am, after all, her favourite brother.'

'Are you?'

'Oh, yes – I do believe so. And it does her good to remember how proud she is of father. Poor father, I suppose he wishes she had been born a boy, for he declares I am not much use to him, and he cannot get on with Nicholas.'

'Is it true that you don't like to be a manufacturer?'

'Gracious me!' he said laughing. 'You look as shocked as if I had declared myself a Roman Catholic or a Socialist. Do you know, I am not really sure whether I like it or not – and certainly I like the money it brings. My brother Nicholas likes it well enough. You wouldn't catch him coming home in the middle of the day to change his clothes and slip over to Leeds, as I mean to do.'

But here, it seemed, he was wrong, for as he lingered a moment on the sofa – asking me if there was anyone I had in mind to marry, asking how Prudence would manage to dispose of Jonas without being disposed of herself, most painfully, by Aunt Hannah – there was a step on the stair, and Nicholas came into view, a man decidedly in a hurry, his neckcloth a little awry. Seeing us, he stopped, stared, his eyes narrowing as if it surprised him, did not altogether please him, to find his brother sitting there in such merry, easy tête à tête with me. But in the moment before I allowed myself to be flattered, I remembered that all their lives these two had wanted, instantly, anything which seemed to attract the other, had fought each other murderously for trifles, from the simple habit, bred in them by Uncle Joel, of competition, of proving, each one to himself, that he was first and best.

'Do I believe my eyes?' Blaize said. 'Brother Nicholas deserting his sheds in the middle of the day?'

'Aye, you can believe it, since I was there all night. And even I feel the need of a clean shirt after sixteen hours.'

And as Blaize got to his feet and sauntered away, looking as if the mere thought of a sixteen-hour stretch at the mill fatigued him or bored him to death, Nicholas sat down in the exact spot his brother had vacated at my side.

'Blaize hasn't been teasing you, has he?'

'Oh, no. He's been teasing Caroline. He overheard her saying she didn't care for manufacturers and then trapped her into admitting she'd be the best one in the Valley – if she'd been a boy.'

He smiled, no sudden, luminous brilliance like Blaize, but a slow, almost unwilling release of mirth that tilted his wide mouth into a smile, soon over, as if smiles, like time and money, were valuable and should not be squandered.

'Maybe she would. Better than Blaize, at any rate.'

'Is he so bad?'

'Bad enough. He could manage all right if he wanted to. He knows how to go on. He just doesn't care.'

'But you care? You like being a manufacturer, don't you, Nicholas?'

'Ah, well,' he said, leaning back against the red velvet upholstery, 'I haven't got my brother's imagination. I've never thought about being anything else. It's there – a good business ready and waiting – and only a fool is going to turn away from that and go into something else just for the sake of making changes. Blaize is no different when it comes down to it. He may not want to be a manufacturer but there's nothing else he wants to be either, and since he's nobody's fool I reckon he'll take his share of the business when it comes to us. I'll just have to make sure he does his share of the work.'

And he smiled at me again, by no means a man flirting, but a man who was willing to confide in me his shrewd assessment of his brother's character, his belief in his own good sense and ability, which would be enough, when it came to it, to bring Blaize into line.

'You're all right are you, Faith – I mean, here, with us?'

'Yes, I'm very well.'

'I'm glad to hear it.'

No more than that. He got up, offering only a half-smile now, his mind already returning to whatever problem had detained him so long in the sheds, leaving me alone on the landing sofa. The house was very still, Aunt Verity out visiting somewhere, a hushed, lamplit tranquillity settling almost visibly around me as the early winter dark came peering through velvet-shrouded windows, the distant crackling of a dozen log fires keeping the cold at bay. Nothing had happened, Nicholas Barforth had sat down beside me, had spoken a few unremarkable words, given me his slow, quite beautiful smile, not once but twice, his hair very black against the red velvet sofa-cushions, the handsome sullen boy changed into a handsome, hard-headed man, his voice still somehow or other in my ears. Nothing had happened at all. Yet I couldn't rid myself of the belief that at last – without my father to frown at it, without Miss Mayfield to spy on it – my life was about to begin.

3

I was in no hurry to return to our tall cool house in Blenheim Lane and the chaperonage of our now considerably diminished Miss Mayfield. But Celia, feeling herself slighted by Caroline's attentions to me as she had felt slighted at Lawcroft Fold by Aunt Hannah's attentions to Prudence, soon began to fancy herself unwell, and although I suspected that had Caroline offered to drive her to town, or Blaize spent a minute or two with her on that red velvet sofa, she would have made a most rapid recovery, my cousins did not oblige, and there was nothing for it but to take her home.

Miss Mayfield, ready to do anything that would justify her continued employment, put her to bed, consoled her with herb-scented pillows and raspberry-leaf tea, dabbed at her forehead with aromatic vinegars, murmuring to her, no doubt, that she would soon have a husband to protect her from neglectful cousins, spiteful sisters, from the world's ills with which Miss Mayfield herself, a spinster lady of no fortune and some forty-five summers, was obliged to cope alone.

And although, just occasionally, I was aware of my father, stooping beside one of his cabinets, moving a fragile Meissen shepherdess a fraction nearer to her shepherd, an ivory-limbed nymph nearer to the light, his face pinching with its sudden ill-temper at the sight of a pair of Minton pot-pourri vases set a hairsbreadth askew, I found that if I stared at him hard enough his shadow would fade, that if I drew back the curtains to let in the sun he would go away, leaving me to enjoy this incredible luxury of having no one to please but myself.

Mrs Naylor, our housekeeper, had her own work to attend to; Miss Mayfield, that fire-breathing schoolroom dragon, sadly reduced now to a scampering little mouse without the prop of my father's authority, was too afraid of losing her place to make any real attempt to control us. Until mother came home we were, quite incredibly, free, Celia having nothing to distract her from the imaginary music of her wedding-bells, Prudence, no longer held in bondage by her embroidery frame, beginning gradually to assume command, ordering tea to suit her own convenience, not Mrs Naylor's, making free use of the carriage in all weathers, at all hours, whether the coachman liked it or not, crisply ordering Miss Mayfield to 'Tell Mr Jonas Agbrigg I am not at home', whenever he happened to call.

'Oh dear – dear me, Miss Prudence, this is the second time you have refused to receive him, and I could tell he was quite peeved about it. And what will Mrs Agbrigg say, for you are to dine at Lawcroft tomorrow and cannot avoid seeing Mr Jonas there.'

'Well then, my dear,' Prudence told her, clearly disinclined to listen to her nonsense. 'You must write a note to Lawcroft explaining that I am not well enough to dine.'

'Poor Miss Mayfield,' I said as she hurried away, flustered and tearful. 'She lives in terror that Aunt Hannah will accuse her of incompetence when mother comes home. Poor soul! I hardly think mother will turn her away, but how dreadful – at her age and with those nerves she is always complaining of – to be obliged to find another situation.'

But Prudence's fine-boned, fastidious face held little sympathy.

'Then she should have taken care long ago to avoid such a position.'

'She has no money, Prudence. She is forced to depend on someone.'

'Exactly,' she said, biting off the word like a loose embroidery thread. 'I am glad you call it depending on someone rather than earning a living, for that perfectly describes her situation here.'

'Father thought well of her.'

'Yes, for she suited his requirements. She is a gentle-woman, you see, possibly a shade better-bred than we are, since her father was a clergyman and her mother an attorney's daughter. She was educated to be an ornament, and when her family fortunes declined and she could find no one to marry her, there was nothing else to do but hire herself out as a governess, so she could pass on her ornamental knowledge to others. She knows nothing, Faith. And neither do I. And I think that is why I am so hard on her. She has crammed me with embroidery stitches until they have turned my stomach. She has tittle-tattled about flowers and ferns until I can no longer bear the sight of either. She has marked my arithmetic correct when I have deliberately done it wrong to catch her out. And it strikes me that her notions of grammar change with the waxing and waning of the moon. She is ignorant, Faith, and so are we, which is just as it should be. Girls are meant to be ignorant, you know that, so they hire ignorant women to make sure of it, to stop us from asking awkward questions later, when we are married. Doesn't it worry you, Faith, that you know so little?'

'I try not to let it show.'

'Well,' she said flatly. 'It does show. And when Jonas Agbrigg looks down his long nose at me and reduces his conversation to the simple words he thinks I can understand – well – I can't blame him, can I, however much it maddens me. And when Freddy Hobhouse offers me his arm and his protection I could laugh and cry at the same time, because he may be a man but – oh dear – he's so simple. Believe me, the idea of spending a lifetime honouring and obeying a mutton-head like Freddy has a comic side to it.'

'You mean to refuse them both, then?'

'I don't know what I mean to do. And I am in no hurry to decide. I have nothing against marriage – really, in some cases, one can see that it could be quite delightful. But to marry now, when I have seen nothing, when I know nothing – oh no. Why on earth should I end all my opportunities in that fashion? Celia may be ready to shut herself up in some man's drawing-room and never come out again – and really I think it would be the best place for her – but it wouldn't do for me. Not yet, at any rate. It strikes me that I could have rather a pleasant life, here, for a year or two, as a "daughter-at-home", for I think I can find the way to manage mother when she comes back again. Yes, indeed. At the end of a year or two I might have made something more interesting of myself than a china doll.'

'You don't think of – falling in love?'

'Why?' she said. 'Do you?'

And because there was no doubt of it and because it was as yet too precious, too uncertain to be held up to the light of day, I smiled, shrugged, pretended to hear carriage-wheels suddenly on the drive, and hurried to investigate.

The spring of that year saw the opening of Cullingford's branchline to

Leeds, an event occasioning much excitement and rejoicing among the manufacturing classes who most urgently required this new, rapid method of moving their goods, and among those of us who, with the price of a railway ticket at our disposal, were now provided with easy access to Liverpool and London and the heady temptations of 'abroad'.

For twenty years and more, the rutted, bone-shaking turnpike road from Cullingford to Leeds had been slowly sinking beneath the weight of carts heavy-laden with 'finished pieces, a slow, perilous, inadequate beginning of their journey to the markets of the world. For almost as long, the canal – an even more leisurely process – had been a stinking, festering disgrace, unable to accommodate the requirements of a trading community which in forty years had eight times doubled its size.

Industrial machinery – the steam-engine, the spinning frames, the power-looms – had changed Cullingford from a nondescript market town of cottage industries, peaceful pleasures, to an uncoordinated, explosive sprawl where men like my Uncle Joel had first devised and operated the factory system, herding the sudden influx of work-hungry field-labourers and bread-hungry Irish to work together under one roof, arriving at an hour convenient not to them but to him, taking their departure only when the specified daily quota was done. And every new invention, while bringing prosperity to some, had been the destruction of others. The spinning frames had forced Law Valley women to abandon their domestic wheels and take employment with men like the great worsted spinner Mr Oldroyd, of Fieldhead, who expected long hard labour for his wages. The power-loom, which required only the hand of a woman or a child to operate it, had forced Law Valley men to chop up their hand-looms for firewood during the hungry winters when there was no work, leading them eventually to take employment, if they could get it, submitting, not always willingly, to the tyranny of the mill and the millmaster, the stringent discipline of my Uncle Joel's factory clock.

Cullingford, I knew, was a snarling, perilous place whenever trade was bad and resentment high, its streets uneasy with ill-fed men, who having spent their childhood working at the loom, had been discharged more often than not as soon as they grew old enough to ponder such matters as social justice or an increase in their wages, their employment taken by women who were concerned only that their children should be fed. And if our town was graced by the elegance of Blenheim Lane, millmasters' palaces and the bright new villas of their managers, I could not be unaware that in the Irish quarter of Simon Street and Saint Street whole families were living without light or water, without heat or hope, without anything I would be likely to recognize as food.

But even they, it seemed – the unemployable, the malcontents, the desperate, the weak, Irish and English, Catholic or of any other denomination – would benefit from the introduction of the railway, since this efficient means of transport, capable of carrying great numbers of people at a time, could be used to persuade them to emigrate, a fund for this purpose having already been started, to which Uncle Joel had contributed a thousand pounds, although he had not stated, in my hearing, just where he wished to send them nor what he proposed they should do there.

Uncle Joel, like my father, had always believed in the railway, although there had been great opposition to it from the very start. Those with a financial interest in the canals or the turnpike roads had declared it from its conception to be a great evil. Landowners, appalled at this desecration of the countryside, had soon convinced themselves and each other that the foul belching of trains would abort their cattle, fire their corn, distract their labourers from their proper duties. A few political notables, the Duke of Wellington and our own manorial lord, Sir Giles Flood, among them, had issued dire warnings that the railway would assist the working classes to congregate and air their grievances, or to receive visits from radical hot-heads who could explain to them what their grievances were.

Yet, as inevitably as the power-looms, the railways had come snaking up and down the country, joining city to city, market to market, until Cullingford men could no longer tolerate that bone-shaking turnpike to Leeds, and Parliament had been petitioned for the granting of a Cullingford and Leeds Railway Bill, presenting engineers and investors alike with so many set-backs, such a quantity of digging and tunnelling through the sharp-sided, stony hills with which Cullingford was surrounded, so severe a plague of navvies, making their camps on the wasteland beyond Simon Street, brawling and drinking their wages, that our more sober citizens had found themselves in agreement with the Iron Duke, while others had feared the project would never end.

In the April of the year my father died – too late for him to realize his profits from the station and the station hotel – the Cullingford line was officially opened, the first train setting out at ten o'clock of an uncertain, misty morning, laden with cigars and champagne and over a hundred of our town's most substantial gentlemen, on its long-awaited journey to Leeds, that flatter, smoother town whose main lines to London and Liverpool would set Cullingford free.

I had written a careful letter to my mother, still sojourning abroad, suggesting she might care to witness the great event, hoping, in fact, that she could be persuaded on her return to put an end to our period of mourning. But, without exactly saying she would or would not come, she did not appear and I was obliged to content myself with my eternal high-necked black dress, and to subdue as best I might my envy of Caroline's dashing blue and gold stripes, which I had chosen for her, and the graceful coffee-coloured flounces of Aunt Verity's lace.

I drove to the station in the Barforth landau, our own carriage following behind with my sisters and Aunt Hannah who, as always, was anxious to save the legs of her own carriage-horses and unwilling to risk them in a crowd. But we arrived almost at the same time, picking our way together through the flag-strewn station yard, a good half of its surface invisible beneath the marquee, erected overnight to house the massive luncheon of duck and turkey and thirty prime Yorkshire lambs provided to refresh the travellers on their return; every other available

406

inch of space being crammed with carriages and carts, with tall silk hats and plumed bonnets, with clogs and cloth caps and shawls, with 'good' children clinging sedately to parental coat tails and 'bad' children swarming everywhere, unsupervised and dangerous, unsettling the horses and the tempers of the coachmen, a sticky-fingered, mud-spattering menace to frock-coats and skirts alike.

The platform, to which we were admitted by invitation only, was a jubilation, more flags festooning the track on either side, two brass bands playing martial music in strident competition, the engine itself a brand-new marvel boldly striped in red and black and gold, already quivering with its own terrifying capacity for speed, its iron-clad ability to endure as no carriage-horses could ever do. And although I had made the coach journey to Leeds on several occasions in my father's austere company and boarded the London train, I knew that this engine was different and felt as thrilled – briefly – as the mill-urchins who, slipping unbidden on to the platform, were being almost good-humouredly cuffed away.

We had no mayor as yet to shake the driver by the hand, but Uncle Joel, whose dress-goods would dominate the freight trains and who had a great many railway shares in any case, was well equipped to perform the office; quite ready, should all run smooth, to remember the man's name and offer some suitable recompense. And, as the early veils of mist lifted, leaving only the pall of smoke which hung continually over our city – smoke to which we were well accustomed, of which we were even fond, since it was a visible announcement that our mills were working to capacity, that we were prosperous – the pale spring sun broke through, glinting on trumpets and drums, on gold watch-chains and busily waving Union Jacks, catching the sparkle of Aunt Verity's diamonds, the lustre of Hobhouse and Mandelbaum pearls, the well-nourished smiles on those several hundred faces, as if the elements too wished to share our self-content.

Without doubt, we had ample reason for contentment, for we, but a generation or two away from the weavers cottages and a life of toil and trouble with never a penny to spare, had invented, developed, operated the machines which had altered the fabric of our society. We, some of us rough-spoken and still hard-handed, all of us hard-headed, had built the factories at which the landed gentry shuddered, had made the fortunes at which they were amazed, since no commoners before us had been able to compete with their affluence, had dared to demand a share of their privilege. And now this railway track, this engine, was ours, not theirs, made necessary and possible by the yarn we spun, the cloth we wove, by the industry and enterprise, the thrift, the stamina, the self-discipline of which we were so justly proud.

Everyone, of course, among that favoured platform-party, had desired to ride on Cullingford's first train; many had been disappointed; and we had talked of little else for weeks past. My Uncle Joel's place had never been in question, nor that of Messrs. Hobhouse, Mandelbaum, Rawnsley and Oldroyd, whose claims were almost as well substantiated.

Sir Giles Flood of Cullingford Manor had been approached and had disdainfully refused, but his cousin, Sir Charles Winterton, who had property in Cullingford and debts in just about every other city in the West Riding, and whose son, 'the Winterton boy', had now placed himself among the multitude of those who wished to marry Caroline, had been less proud. Mr Corey-Manning, the lawyer, had eagerly accepted the invitation, despite his age and Aunt Hannah's loud-voiced opinion that he would do better to stand down in favour of Jonas, although with Uncle Joel's help she had secured a seat for Mr Agbrigg, a triumph, she felt, which would assist immeasurably in his mayoral campaign.

The landlord of the Old Swan, our most important coaching inn, was to make the journey – a gesture, one felt, of recompense for the loss of business he would be bound to suffer when those fourteen coaches which set off every day from his inn yard became passengerless, obsolete. But competition for the remaining seats had been so murderous that when Uncle Joel proposed taking his two sons, Mr Rawnsley his five, and Mr Hobhouse all ten of his, each gentleman had been limited to one son apiece – the eldest – to which restriction all had grudgingly agreed.

Freddy Hobhouse, then, was to go, and Jacob Mandelbaum, young Jack Rawnsley and Benjamin Battershaw of Battershaw's Light Ales; and, to represent the next generation of Barforths, my cousin Blaize, a decision which had given rise to sharp words between Uncle Joel and Nicholas, who was exceedingly interested in trains, and between Nicholas and Blaize, who, while openly avowing his total indifference, seemed determined to make the trip if only to annoy his brother.

'Such a fuss,' Caroline told me, wrinkling a fastidious nostril at the first whiff of engine smoke. 'They agreed eldest sons, so eldest sons it must be, and one can hardly blame Blaize for being born first. It's not a question of whether one wants to go; it's a question of privilege. If one gets a good offer, one takes it – it's as simple as that. I wouldn't have stepped down, if I'd been invited, for anybody.'

But Nicholas, standing at the footplate with his father, seemed to be bearing his disappointment well enough, holding an animated, probably very technical, conversation with a group of railway employees, his dark eyes keen and interested, the first sight of him causing my stomach to lurch in a most shocking fashion, so that the whole of that raucous crowd was instantly reduced in my mind to a set of nondescript, wooden images; and Nicholas Barforth. And, for the life in me, I could not have said why.

The moment of departure, it seemed, was very near, drawing – as the favoured few began to climb aboard – an ear-splitting, cheek-bulging crescendo from the bands, a great whistling and steaming from the train, a tremor of anticipation that interrupted even Aunt Hannah's conversation with the wife of our new Member of Parliament, whose good offices she was clearly seeking on her husband's behalf. There was a flutter of applause from correctly gloved, ladylike hands, a certain feeling of relief, since the spring weather was unreliable, the sky clouding over, and we had been standing rather a long time. A few flags began to wave;

Mrs Hobhouse took out a sentimental handkerchief and, for reasons unknown, dabbed at her eyes. My sister Prudence, anxious to avoid an invitation from Aunt Hannah to go back to Lawcroft with her – and Jonas – was already whispering a request that I should give up my place to her in the Barforth carriage, when Uncle Joel, instead of boarding the train, came striding towards us, cigar in hand, the crowd, who knew a man in a rage when it saw one, parting before him as he made directly for his wife.

'Where's Blaize?' he demanded, and Aunt Verity, the only person in the world, I think, who could have met his onslaught with so serene a smile, replied. 'Darling – I couldn't say.'

'He told me he was coming in the landau with you.'

'Why no, dear. I was to call for Faith and had no room to spare.'

'And he knew that? Yes, of course he did. So where is he, then?'

'Joel,' she said softly, very urgently. 'Does it really matter?'

And, responding, it seemed, to her appeal, his jaw clenched suddenly, his whole powerful body stiffening with the effort to hold back his temper, not out of any consideration for the onlookers, the gossip, the fear of spoiling this great day; but for his wife's sake.

'I try, Verity,' he said. 'Believe me, I try not to let them provoke me – the pair of them – but by God, sometimes, they go too far.'

'I know, darling. They seem determined to prove just how far they *can* go. Don't worry about it now.'

'We'll wait then,' he snapped and, striding back to the engine, exchanged a few words with Mr Hobhouse who had put his head enquiringly out of a window, and then paced for a moment or two along the platform, glancing first at his watch and then at the brand-new, impudently ticking station clock.

'We'll wait,' I saw his mouth say to the startled railway officials who were now running after him, much concerned with their own watches, pausing apologetically at the windows, every one of which was now filled by an important, impatient Law Valley head, while, on the platform, although the bands continued to play, flags were lowered uncertainly, enquiries made. Had the engine broken down, then, before it had started, which would suit the landlord of the Old Swan if no one else? Had a tunnel caved in somewhere along the line, as a certain wise-woman of Simon Street had predicted it would? – and even if it hadn't, Mrs Hobhouse suddenly discovered that she would be easier in her mind if Freddy, obediently installed beside his father, did not go after all. Or was it just Mr Barforth, as usual, insisting on having everything his own way?

'Oh dear,' Aunt Verity murmured, a certain rueful amusement in her voice.

'What ails the man now?' Aunt Hannah demanded loudly, taking the opportunity to prove that, however powerful her brother might be, she, at any rate, was not afraid of him.

'Nicholas,' Caroline called out imperiously, beckoning him to her side. 'I expect this is something you've cooked up together – you and Blaize – so if you know where he is you'd better say so.'

'I don't know anything about it,' he said flatly and, meeting his angry

409

eyes, I felt a quick upsurge of satisfaction, not only at his closeness but because, if Blaize could not be found, then surely Nicholas would be allowed to go instead.

It would last, I thought, but a moment longer, for even Mr Joel Barforth in full fury could not be oblivious of that engine steaming and straining at its leash, of the smiles slipping from even the most amiable faces; could not compel a hundred of Cullingford's most prosperous citizens to postpone their journey while he sent to fetch his eldest son; could not neglect the hundred others, waiting, on what now threatened to be a rainy day, on the platform in Leeds. And clenching his watch in a hand that shook with frustration – the unpalatable, amazing truth that he, of whom the whole of Cullingford stood in terror, could not always control his sons – he strode back to Aunt Verity, glaring first at her and then at Nicholas.

'Good God, Verity, this is intolerable.'

'I know. You must go without him, Joel. And there may be a good reason.'

'Aye – he may have taken a fall from that thoroughbred mare I bought him and broken his neck. But it's not likely.'

'I do hope not.'

'No – and he'll not be at the mill either, so engrossed in his work that everything else has slipped his mind. I can guarantee you that.' And turning to Nicholas he said curtly, his voice amounting to a snap of the fingers. 'All right, lad, you've got what you wanted. Get on board in his place.'

That, of course, should have been the end of it. Had Nicholas been less a Barforth, he would have jumped immediately on board, chuckling at his own good fortune and the retribution which must surely be in store for his brother. Had Uncle Joel been less a Barforth, he would have issued the invitation a shade more graciously, since in his heart he was probably just as willing to take Nicholas as Blaize, and had indeed tried his best to take them both. But – unlike Blaize and Aunt Verity, who would always bend, most gracefully, with the wind – they were true Barforths, hard and unyielding, who would take the wind by brute force if they could, to suit their own purposes, or die in the attempt. And, as Uncle Joel began to turn away, considering the matter closed, Nicholas said very quietly, 'I don't think I can do that, sir.'

'Don't you, by God!' his father answered him, his lips barely moving, and, as those nearest to us began to press closer, eager to witness the stag-antlered combat of the Barforth males, which was becoming a legend in the Valley, Aunt Verity put a hand on her husband's arm, her whole body flowing towards him in urgent, loving intervention.

'Not here, Joel. Please, darling –'

But, realizing that he could see nothing now beyond his conflict with Nicholas, a man like himself, too stubborn in his pride to care for retribution, I cannot believe she hoped to prevail.

For a very long time – or so it seemed – with curious, envious, malicious Cullingford buzzing and bustling all around them, they stood and measured one another, a raw contest of wills that tightened the air.

410

'You'll get on that train, Nicholas.'

'Hardly, sir.'

'Nicholas – you'll do it.'

'I don't see how I can, sir. Eldest sons – that's what you decided. No exceptions, no matter what the circumstances – that's what you told me when I asked. And I'm needed at the mill because it won't run itself. You told me that, too.'

And knowing of old that he would have to haul Nicholas by the scruff of his neck into that train – and wondering, perhaps, if at fifty years of age he could still manage it – my uncle snarled something very low, doubtless very obscene, and, with a gesture that struck terror certainly into my heart, strode away.

No one spoke to Nicholas as the flags began to wave again, the train to draw slowly out of the station, Mr Hobhouse beaming jovially from his window. Mr Mandelbaum from his. No one spoke to him as he shouldered a way for us through the crowded station-yard to our carriages, although we all spoke heartily, quite falsely, to one another.

'I am so glad the rain has kept off,' Aunt Verity said.

'Yes, I knew it would,' Aunt Hannah replied. 'I had quite made up my mind to it.'

'It would have ruined the marquee otherwise,' I offered, trying to play my part.

'I think I have taken cold,' Celia whimpered.

'Nonsense,' Prudence told her. 'It is only that you like to think so.'

Caroline, taking off her gloves and putting them on again with great deliberation, no doubt to stop her hands from fastening around her brother's throat, said not a word. But when we were settled in the carriage, and Nicholas, for whom no place could be found, stood alone at the step raising his hat to us. I was unable – whether he had been right or wrong – to do other than call out 'Good-bye, Nicholas', earning myself a smile from Aunt Verity and a glare of pure contempt from Caroline.

We were to dine at Tarn Edge that evening, three little blackbirds in our mourning dresses among the peacock splendours of Aunt Verity's guests, arriving to find her as serene as ever, Nicholas and Blaize showing no obvious scars, even Caroline smiling again at everyone but the Winterton boy on her right, and the Mandelbaum boy attached just as firmly to her left.

Dinner at Tarn Edge was always a formal occasion. We were met in the hall by an array of servants who removed our cloaks as reverently as if they were of the finest sable, escorted to the drawing-room door by a butler as suave and benign as any bishop, who, having known us all our lives, invariably announced us as if we had been the most opulent of strangers: 'Miss Aycliffe. Miss Faith Aycliffe. Miss Celia Aycliffe'; and we would advance straight-backed, mindful of our lessons in deportment, across what had often seemed to me an acre of blue and gold carpet, to shake hands with our host and hostess. There would be a hushed half-hour then, a quick appraisal of gowns and jewels, while Aunt Verity made soft-voiced introductions and my uncle, majestically

411

circulating, informed each gentleman which lady he must take in to dine.

He led the way that evening with Lady Winterton, who, as a representative of the landed gentry, must be considered the most distinguished lady present, and probably thought herself the only real lady there at all. Blaize took Miss Rebecca Mandelbaum, Nicholas Miss Amy Battershaw of Battershaw Light Ales, a circumstance which did not please me, even though Amy Battershaw – a close friend of Celia's – was sallow and silly, and one did not expect the son of the house to be wasted on a cousin. Prudence went in with Jonas. I accompanied Freddy Hobhouse, whose mother, despairing perhaps of Prudence, had decided that my twenty thousand pounds without the porcelain, would suffice; while Celia, who had first declared herself too ill to come at all and then wept copiously because we had not begged her to change her mind, was left to a younger Hobhouse boy, an arrangement not at all to her taste – since Adolphus Hobhouse could entertain no thoughts of marriage until Freddy should be settled – and which would cause her to grumble all the way home that, once again, she had been slighted.

Caroline accompanied the Winterton boy, Aunt Verity his father, Sir Charles, a distinction perfectly understood by all, for although the Wintertons were known to be losing their money, the rest of us to be making ours, they were the possessors of that one commodity beyond our reach, the privilege of pedigree. Winterton land, no matter how sadly mortgaged, had been handed down to them through generations when Barforths and Hobhouses alike had been no more than common weavers. There had been a Winterton at Waterloo commanding a regiment when Uncle Joel's father had been struggling, at the then almost bankrupt Low Cross Mills to keep himself above the precarious level of the ordinary working man. No Winterton had ever soiled his hands with trade, had ever bought or sold anything but acreage, bloodstock, the occasional work of art; whereas my Uncle Joel even now would not hesitate to roll up his fine cambric shirtsleeves and dirty his own hands whenever the need arose, nor to buy and sell anything, provided he could do so to his own advantage. And although the present Sir Charles, while privately considering my uncle to have no more social standing than a village blacksmith, was ready to dine at the Barforth table, ready, even, to permit the common, trading blood of the Barforth daughter to mingle with his own, if the price was right, he was nevertheless a landed gentleman to whom our grandfathers would have instinctively doffed their caps, and we were still, I believe, a little in awe of him.

Uncle Joel's dining-room, like everything about him, was on the very grandest scale, panelled from wall to ceiling in wood that had the sheen and colour of ebony, its sombre expanse broken by gilt-framed, oval portraits of Aunt Verity and Caroline, and by a row of long windows draped ornately in white muslin and velvet of the richest, darkest red. The table, set between two ebony-coloured sideboards, was a masterpiece, a foamy white lace cloth garlanded with ferns and mosses, trails of ivy from candelabra to candelabra, primrose-tinted candles gleaming on silver and crystal, pyramids of spring flowers, daffodils and pale narcissi, the delicacy of violets, the bold, brave stripings of the tulip. And for the space of two hours, while Freddy Hobhouse, forgetting that the principal duty of a dinner-partner is conversation, crunched his way through salmon and whitebait, beef olives, quails and plovers, creams and sponge cakes and tarts. I sat and thought, mainly of Nicholas.

Sitting beside Amy Battershaw – how was it that I had once thought her a pleasant enough girl? – he was assisting her, quite correctly, in the arduous task of dining. He had made sure she was comfortably seated, had himself retrieved her gloves when she had somewhat wildly abandoned them, had indicated her menu-card, hiding, in its silver-filigree holder, among the forest of crystal bordering her plate, and then, knowing her to be short-sighted, had read it aloud to her, suggesting – as a son of the house who knew the specialities of his mother's cook – which dishes she might like to attempt. But Miss Amy Battershaw, whose governess, like ours, had taught her that a lady's appetite must be no bigger than a sparrow's, had most likely taken the precaution of stuffing herself with muffins and gingerbread before leaving home, and in the approved fashion could manage nothing but a morsel of this, a spoonful of that, a simpering, fluttering sip of champagne.

Odious girl, I thought, allowing my own champagne glass to be refilled to the brim, glancing from Miss Battershaw to Rebecca Mandelbaum, who was playing the same charade with Blaize; and only a look of pure horror from my sister Celia, whose appetite was indeed very small, stopped me from accepting a second helping of chocolate cream.

Odious girls, all of them, dressed-up little dolls – and badly dressed at that – too much beribboned and curled, too sugar-plum sweet, too good to be true! Surprised at my own savagery, when only last week I had been perfectly happy to take a carriage drive with Amy and had thought Rebecca's performance at the piano most skilful, I realized quite abruptly that, just as the male population had become divided between Nicholas and those who were not Nicholas, so had the world's females grouped themselves into those who might, and those who might not, take him from me.

Not that I in any way considered him mine. Not that I had so far considered anything but the odd sensation his presence brought me. Certainly I had not yet paused to ask myself why I had chosen to care for Nicholas, who was without doubt every bit as stubborn and quick-tempered as everyone said, instead of for Blaize, who was charm personified, or for any other man. I had not asked myself if, perhaps, it could be nothing more than an extension of my childhood sympathy for the younger brother who had always had to work harder, play harder, than his dazzling senior to obtain the same degree of praise. I had asked myself no questions at all. But how many of us, at seventeen, care overmuch for reasons?

The meal ended, leaving no more than a vague impression of excellence on my tongue, and rising in obedience to Aunt Verity's signal

I returned to the drawing-room, where coffee was already waiting, accompanied by baskets of cakes for those of us – like Miss Amy Battershaw – who had not wished to eat too heartily in the presence of gentlemen. But Caroline, quickly bored by any gathering of women, soon made a signal of her own which took us both upstairs to our cosy, confidential sofa.

'That's better,' she said, 'for I cannot bear to hear the old hens tittle-tattling. I expect you saw Lady Winterton keeping a place for me beside her? – well, and so she might, for her Francis is becoming very persistent, and for all her title and breeding she is pushing him at me just as eagerly as Mrs Battershaw her Benjamin. Well, as to Francis Winterton, maybe I shall and maybe I shan't. But what is certain is that it won't be until I've convinced father to give me a proper London season and a trip to Paris. And it won't be difficult, especially now that I'm altogether his favourite child.'

'There was bloodshed, then – when your father got back from Leeds?'

'As you might expect.'

'And they are both in disgrace?'

'Oh yes, except that Nicholas caught it the most, as he always does – and I can perfectly understand why. Really, Faith, there's no reason for you to look so surprised, since it was Nicholas, after all, who shamed father in public. My word, it seems Mr Hobhouse spent the entire journey giving father advice on how to bring up sons, and you can't expect him to forgive Nicky for that. And, of course, the whole point of the exercise was that Blaize never intended to go in the first place. He doesn't care about trains, but, if he'd said as much and offered to give up his place to Nicholas, father would just have gone on muttering about eldest sons only and refused to allow it. So he played their game, like he always does, and then, when the time came, he just wasn't there. He knew Nicholas would be at the station and that father would offer to take him. It was his way of making Nicholas a present. And Nicholas knew it very well – oh yes – and so did father, because Blaize is always doing that kind of thing. It's his style exactly. All Nicholas had to do was jump on board and by the time they got home father would have forgotten all about it. But Nicholas, of course, had to stand there growling back at father just to prove to himself that he dare, going too far as always and then too stubborn to back down. Hasn't that always been his way? And you've always felt so sorry for him. Faith – I can't think why, since he's perfectly able to fend for himself.'

We came downstairs together, Caroline walking a step or two ahead in her determination to be first at the drawing-room doors, since she could not be certain I would stand aside to let her pass. But as she made her entrance I felt an all too familiar movement at the back of my head, the dread sensation of hairpins coming loose, and, judging my plight too urgent for the upstairs journey to Caroline's bedroom, took refuge in the back parlour, situated at the end of the passage behind the stairs. There was a mirror there, high above the mantelpiece, a degree of privacy, since only an *habitúe* of the house would be likely to use this room, and, standing on the fender, my skirts swinging perilously towards the grate and the small fire appropriate to a spring evening. I had shaken my hair loose, combing through it with hurried, unkind fingers, when the door opened, snapped shut again, and Nicholas stood there, scowling at my back, the set of his jaw and the irritable, down-drooping line of his mouth saying to me very clearly, 'Good God, is there no peace in this house?'

'Faith, what on earth are you doing here?'

And, from an excess of wanting to be warm and encouraging, my answer came out cold, clipped, and distant. 'As you see, my hair is coming down, which is a great nuisance.'

'I do see that. And unless you get down from that fender you are bound to set your skirts on fire, which would be an even greater nuisance.'

'Really – do you think so?'

'I am sure of it.'

'Well then, I will just have to take my chance and prove you wrong, since I need the looking-glass.'

'Evidently,' he said, as curt and sarcastic as he always was in the face of mild annoyance, of foolish young girls who intruded on his desire for a moment's peace and quiet, and disregarded his good advice. But nothing, now, would induce me to leave my precarious perch until my task was done, no matter how right he was, no matter how anxious I had now become about the small but vigorously burning fire. And having good reason to recognize stubbornness when he saw it, he said quickly, 'Look here, Faith, do get down. There have been disasters enough today. You could spare me another, for if you roast they will surely manage to blame me for it.'

'Oh, if it is yourself you are thinking of, I will get down at once. I should not wish to cause you a moment's unease.'

'That is very good of you.'

'So it is. And I have finished now in any case, without so much as a scorched hem, so I will say good-night to you, Nicholas.'

'Yes, Good-night.'

But as I got down from the fender and faced him, knowing, behind the protective shield of my hostility and my cool Aycliffe manner, that in ten minutes' time, back in the drawing-room, I would be grief-stricken and furious at this lost opportunity, something penetrated the fog of his ill-humour, drawing through it his unwilling, rueful smile.

'Oh dear, poor Faith! Will you never learn to manage your hair? I have seen you like this many a time when we were children, spilling hairpins. And do you know, I believe we once sat behind you in church, Blaize and I – do you remember? – at somebody's wedding? – and undid your hair-ribbons?'

'Yes, I remember. I'm not likely to forget it, nor the scolding it earned me afterwards.'

'Well, I'm sorry for that. You could have said it was our fault, you know. I reckon that's what we expected you to do. I thought only boys were brought up not to tell tales, and that girls were allowed to tittle-tattle as much as they pleased. Caroline always does.'

'Perhaps she has a lot to tell tales about.'

'Aye,' he said, his gloom shredding clean away, to be replaced by a most decided, most unexpected grin. 'I reckon she might.'

And it was unfortunate that we were still smiling at each other when the door was thrust open again and Uncle Joel, wreathed in cigar-smoke and bad temper, stood there seeing, not a pair of cousins alone together by chance, reminiscing of a shared childhood, but a young man, his earlier misdemeanours by no means forgiven, who had now committed the further crime of neglecting his mother's guests in the company of a marriageable and apparently flirtatious young lady. And until I saw it in his face I had truly forgotten the enormous damage that a few moments alone with any young man could inflict upon my reputation.

He came into the room, shutting the door behind him, sealing it with his powerful, impenetrable presence, and stood for a moment in silence, his hard face so furious and yet so satisfied that I knew he wanted to think ill of us and would not listen to reason.

'Father –' Nicholas said, his own face hard too. Yet the fact he had spoken at all betrayed his alarm, and I knew through my own, dry-mouthed panic that, whatever we were to be accused of, he would be made to suffer for it the most.

'It occurred to me,' my uncle said, 'that you had been a long time away. And I ask myself why I am surprised to find you in these circumstances.'

'I think you mistake the circumstances, sir.'

'I think I do not.'

'I insist that you do.'

'You are in a position to insist, are you?'

'Possibly not. But just the same, I must ask you to hear my explanations.'

'I do not choose –' Uncle Joel began, but, seeing the black, snarling anger in his face which did not mean to be cheated of its outlet, and the answering snarl in Nicholas, more than ready to offer the combat his father clearly required, I took a hasty step forward, knowing full well that this, being an extension of what had occurred earlier at the station, had very little to do with me, but compelled nevertheless to intervene.

'Uncle Joel – please – my hair was coming down, which happens to me often enough. I came to use the looking-glass –'

'And my son followed you.'

'He certainly did not. He was not even pleased to see me.'

But it had not been a question, merely a statement of what he intended to believe, and I was appalled when Nicholas, raising his shoulders in a careless shrug, announced suddenly, 'Of course you are quite right, sir, as always. I did follow her here, with the most questionable of motives, which unfortunately for me she did not share. So I am entirely to blame and I think you may allow Faith to return – unscathed – to her sisters.'

'Oh Nicholas,' I said, 'Nicholas'; and for a moment there was nothing to do but watch, fascinated and terrified, as they stood quite still, jaws clenched, mouths down-drawn with their fierce, knife-edged anger, a clashing of identical wills, my own will flickering feebly between them, pale and insignificant perhaps, but persistent, since I was half a Barforth too.

'Back down, Nicholas,' my will pleaded. 'Please – back down, as Blaize would do. There's no shame. He wouldn't think ill of you. In fact I believe he'd like to back down himself and can't. Do it for him, because he's older, and it would be easier for you.' And when I saw that he would stand his ground, not yielding an inch, totally regardless of consequences – as his father would have done at his age – I murmured, 'Uncle Joel –', striving to remind him that he couldn't really thrash his son in the hearing of his wife's guests, and that, if he did, many of them would be only too pleased about it.

'Quite so,' he said, apparently reading my mind, an iron lid almost visibly descending over his temper. 'Well then, for the present, my lad, you had best go back and show your face in the drawing-room. And you'd best look pleasant while you're about it, for I'll not have your mother upset again. And as for you, young lady, your father had a word to say to me on your account before he died. I well remember it, and it strikes me I may have a word of my own for your mother – should she ever decide to come home.'

And turning abruptly, letting the door slam shut behind him, he was gone.

I was for a dreadful moment consumed entirely by embarrassment, hot and sticky with it, painfully aware that this could in no way endear me to Nicholas, who would be very likely to save himself from further awkwardness by ignoring me entirely.

'Don't worry,' he said quietly, not looking at me, staring instead at the square of carpet his father had just vacated. 'He will say nothing to your mother, nor to anyone else. By the time he reaches the end of the passage he will have realized how trivial his behaviour has been, and he may well make himself very pleasant when he sees you again. He may even buy you a present to make amends, for that is how I got my chestnut mare, and Blaize his bay. You are quite safe.'

'Oh heavens – I don't care about that.'

'But I care about it. I don't wish to upset you, Faith. And as it happens neither does he – not really. You were just there, at a time when he neded an excuse to be angry, and he has a great talent for making the most of whatever he finds to hand.'

'I'm not upset. I'm just sorry – and Nicholas, do tell me, you really wanted to take that train today, didn't you?'

'Oh that,' he said, dismissing it. 'That precious train. Yes, of course I wanted to take it. Didn't everybody?'

'Blaize didn't.'

'Only because Blaize likes to be different. And I refused to take his place because I am the jealous younger son who doesn't care to pick up his brother's leavings – and because I wished to annoy my father. Isn't that what Cullingford is saying?'

'Yes, and I wonder that you should have given them the opportunity,

417

especially if you wanted to go.'

'Yes,' he said, very low. 'Why should I deny myself the very thing I wanted? That is what Blaize thought. He meant to give up his place to me from the start. I realize that. He'd gone to a lot of trouble for me, even fixed himself up with an alibi at the mill – some tale of him being needed in the sheds, which takes a lot of believing. But there you are: I was offended, or perhaps I didn't want to be manoeuvred, or I was just pig-headed. And I reckon I'll behave just as badly the next time – we all will. You should go back now, Faith, or Aunt Hannah may be the next one to find us – and she'd really believe what father only pretended to believe.'

'Yes, I'll go back. And you? He said you were to come too.'

'Yes. But we can hardly go back together. Tell him "presently" if he asks, which he won't. Good-night, Faith. You'd better run.'

And for the rest of the evening, while Prudence made her cool replies to Jonas, and Celia tried hard to find someone to care that her head was aching, I sat in silence, contemplating the fact that, whether it had been for good or ill, something real, something that far exceeded the expectations of my milk-and-water girlhood, had entered my life. As I had hoped and prayed, life was beginning, expanding, unrolling itself before me like some vast fabric woven with hope and opportunity, with a hundred brightly shaded threads of possibility, with Nicholas – and I was more than ready.

4

The summer, that year, presented us with two events worthy of mention, the eighteenth birthday of Miss Caroline Barforth and the repeal of the Corn Laws, those hated measures invented by the gentry to be a scourge and an abomination to all commercial men.

Introduced at the end of Napoleon's wars to keep out the cheap foreign corn and protect the landowners, who had been charging as much as they pleased for their own crops while the French blockade lasted, this legislation had caused enormous hardship in the industrial cities during all the years since Waterloo. For when the price of corn rose, the price of bread rose with it, and when the cost of a loaf was high and incomes low, the only results could be hunger, resentment, violence sometimes, in places like Simon Street, when Uncle Joel and others like him refused to pay higher wages and put money indirectly into the pockets of the squires.

Nor had the farmers themselves – or, at least, the smaller ones – benefited greatly, since men reduced to beggary could not pay their price, forcing them in their turn to sell out to the big landowners and to join the ranks of the landless poor, many of whom found their way annually to Cullingford. And, in the year my father died, thousands of men, women and children in the richest, most rapidly expanding country in the world were being kept alive – only just – by the haphazard, not always gentle, hand of charity.

I had grown accustomed to tales of agricultural workers, the very ones

418

who harvested the protected grain, dying of starvation in their cottages; of hand-loom weavers, who in this machine age could not earn the coppers necessary to keep body and soul together, expiring at their looms of the same dread disease. I knew that, whenever the winter was harsh, the spring late and inclement, the summer cool and soon over, producing a poor harvest or no harvest at all, corpses would be discovered under the hedgerows or picked up in our own littered back alleys, the pathetic remains of men who had gone on the tramp to look for work, and had failed.

Free Trade, clearly, was the only answer. My father had fought for it all his political life, and promised it at the hustings in every electoral address. Free Trade, cheap bread, an end to the Corn Laws was the only answer, but our current political masters, Sir Robert Peel – who had not endeared himself to us by re-introducing income tax at the terrible rate of seven pence in the pound – and his closest associate, the ancient, aristocratic Duke of Wellington, who believed that industrialists like all other upstarts should learn to know their place and mend their manners, had proved impossible to convince.

Elected by a party of country squires to serve the interests of country squires – to ensure that Englishmen ate English corn or no corn at all – they had for years resisted all pressures from the industrial towns, and it had taken the tragedy of Ireland, where more than a quarter of the population were entirely destitute and the rest not too much better off, to present a situation where the choice could only be cheap food or the most bloody revolution.

The Irish had long been with us in Cullingford, coming in boatloads and cartloads, barefoot and desperate and alarmingly prone to multiply, escaping from famine in 'Derry and Kildare to famine in Simon Street, since even our weaving sheds – where mainly women and children were required in any case – could not accommodate them all. But, in the year before my father died, the potato crop quite inexplicably began to rot in the fields, bringing hardship to poor men in England, who relied heavily on potatoes for food, bringing panic and chaos to poor men in Ireland, who had no other food on which to rely.

And, as Ireland began its death agony and unrest at home began to simmer – yet again – into a revolutionary brew, the radical leaders making full use of the railways, as the Duke of Wellington had always said they would, to muster their forces together, it became clear – apparently even to Sir Robert Peel – that if the people were to be fed and pacified, then the foreign corn must be allowed to flow.

'Peel cannot do it,' his startled landowning friends said of him in London.

'He will not do it,' we had declared scornfully in Cullingford, for, having risen to power as a staunch protectionist, we knew that his own party would not support him, that his own career was at stake, the flamboyant, fast-rising Mr Disraeli having already dubbed him a turncoat and a traitor, even the Duke of Wellington, who disliked reform of any kind and thought the Corn Laws rather a good thing, holding himself aloof.

419

Even then, had the next year's potato crop shown a healthy face, perhaps Sir Robert would have hesitated, modified, compromised, saved his face and his prospects, as indeed we all expected him to do. But the new season's potatoes were as black as their predecessors, and the remnants of the Irish people – those who had neither starved nor emigrated to Cullingford – were living on weeds and nettles and a murderous hatred of certain English landlords who, apparently unaware of the famine, went on insisting that their rent should be paid and issuing eviction notices when it wasn't. And so Sir Robert Peel, well aware that his own career would probably be demanded as a sacrifice, forced his Bill for Repeal of the Corn Laws through a hostile House of Commons, persuaded the Duke of Wellington, who still did not believe in it, to put it before a well-nigh hysterical House of Lords.

'God damn the traitor Robert Peel', they said of him in the agricultural shires, the manor houses, the green and pleasant corners of our land.

'So he's seen sense at last', they said in the Old Swan, the Piece Hall, the factory yard. 'And not before time, either.'

And although Peel himself was forced, predictably, to resign his premiership soon after, the ports at last were open, bread would be cheap again, cheapening the cost of labour with it, and Cullingford cloth – Barforth cloth – could be acknowledged as the marvel it was in every corner of the world.

'We should do something for Sir Robert Peel,' Aunt Hannah announced at the Repeal Dinner – one of many – which she had organized in celebration. 'We asked the poor man for Free Trade, and now that he has given it to us, and ruined himself in the process, it would seem appropriate to put aside our grievances about the income tax and write him a letter of gratitude. In fact, it is no more than common politeness and may do him a world of good – for he can't quite like being out of office. I know I shouldn't like it.'

And, since Aunt Hannah had a draft letter in Jonas's elegant copperplate most conveniently to hand, it was considered, agreed, signed Barforth, Hobhouse, Oldroyd, Mandelbaum – not Winterton, of course, and certainly not Flood, since both these gentlemen would be fully occupied now in trying to sell their corn as best they could on a free market – and dispatched.

'The dear man has sent a most cordial reply,' Aunt Hannah told us a few weeks later, 'although I hardly know what may be done with it, since we have no town hall, no official building of any kind in which to display it'; and it was no surprise to us that when Sir Robert's correct, somewhat stilted letter had been passed from hand to hand, it made its final appearance, neatly framed and pressed, neither at Nethercoats nor Tarn Edge but in Aunt Hannah's own drawing-room at Lawcroft Fold.

My mother returned home for Caroline's birthday dance, descending upon us unlooked-for one afternoon, delighted with our surprise, although I did not miss the faint wrinkling of her nose as she entered the drawing-room, the gesture of one who, having grown accustomed to sunshine and sea-breezes, did not at all relish the taste of stale air again.

'How dark it is,' she said. 'Will the curtains really not open any wider?
No, I suppose not, but then it is so light abroad – France all sparkle, and
Italy so pink and gold, that I had forgotten how grey – Ah, well, that was
yesterday and now I am quite recovered from my ills and come home to
introduce myself to my daughters – for really, girls, we have been sadly
little acquainted. See, I have brought you all a present, lots of presents –'
  And suddenly her magpie hands were full of froth and glitter, pink silk
and blue silk, bracelets and earrings of coral and enamel and tiny
seed-pearls, feather fans and lace fans, and extravagant lengths of
embroidered, foreign-looking brocade.
  'I thought you would want something to wear – I always did so at your
age – and, unless you particularly desire to continue it, it strikes me you
may leave off your weeds now. Six months, is it not? My word, six
months! Well, I must stay in black for another year and more, and then
run through all the shades of grey and lavender, but you are not widows,
after all, but young ladies who are allowed to be vain. Goodness, Faith,
these blue bows and sashes and little rosebuds will do admirably for
Celia, but you are so – so grown, I suppose. Dear girl, no one in Venice
would ever believe you to be my daughter. A sister, perhaps, for you
have my eye and hair colour – which is something very much out of the
ordinary in Venice, I do assure you. And yes – in other ways too, dear – I
believe you are turning out to resemble me.'
  'Hardly, mamma, I am inches taller, and my nose is much too big.'
  'Yes, but such details, you know, do not really signify. A clever
woman learns how to create an illusion.'
  'Father said I was the one most like you,' Celia cut in, tossing her head
to set her ringlets dancing, determined for once in her life to win her fair
share of attention.
  'Yes, dear,' my mother said absently, not even glancing at her. 'You
are a positive enchantment. And Prudence – Good heavens! – you
remind me of someone I have not seen for ages – a relative of your
father's.'
  'She means you remind her of our brother,' Celia said later, imparting
the information because, our brother having been sent away in disgrace,
she could not believe it to be a compliment. But my mother, whose
understanding was sharper than one at first supposed, soon made amends
to Celia by smothering her in all the lace and ribbons she could desire,
and to Prudence by paying her the compliment of leaving her alone,
while she and I soon formed a relationship which hung tenuously but
pleasantly on our shared enthusiasm for fashion.
  'One must develop a style,' she told me. 'One chooses not to copy, but
to be copied – a dear friend in Paris told me that, although I had always
suspected it and behaved accordingly. You are tall and so, since you
cannot shrink, you must make yourself look taller – simple, classical
lines, bold colours or plain white, and no fuss, and a bonnet. I think,
when you are a little older, with a positively towering feather. What fun!
I was never allowed to dress you up when you were small. There was
always a Miss Mayfield to do that. And as for your nose, dear, and the

fact that your mouth is rather wide, you must cultivate an air of feeling *so* sorry for all these poor girls who are cursed with rosebud lips and button noses and dimples. If you appear to like what you have, dear, even if they don't quite like it themselves, at the very least it will make them wonder.'

For Caroline's birthday dance my sister Celia had a dress of palest pink gauze, its flounced skirt strewn with knots of silver ribbon and sprays of pink and white flowers; Prudence a more restrained outfit of pale blue, which, with its touches of cream-coloured lace and her tall, straight figure, gave her a quiet but most decided elegance. My dress was white, a swan, I'd thought dreamily, as our seamstress had pinned the vast skirt into place – 'Too plain,' Celia had told me – a white flower at the waist, another at the shoulder – 'White is for brunettes,' Celia had said, 'everybody knows that' – my hair dressed low on the nape of my neck in one massive coil with a single white rose at its centre, a chignon devised by my mother to look so heavy that anyone who noticed it would be aware that my neck was long and slender, and might miss the fact that my nose and mouth were of a corresponding size. I had pearl droplets in my ears, a broad velvet ribbon embroidered with pearl clusters around my throat, a pair of wide-spaced, worried, short-sighted blue eyes above it, since I was by no means as confident of this unusual outfit as I pretended, feeling in fact as the time of our departure grew imminent that, although these classical lines and colours might be all the rage in Venice, Cullingford was far too accustomed to seeing its young ladies in sugar-pink gauzes and ribbons – like Celia – to be anything other than puzzled.

My mother, who should not have attended a dance at all until her mourning period was over, or, if she managed to justify it on the grounds of family commitment and chaperonage, should have been excessively discreet about it, appeared in a black gown of the most stunning extravagance, cut as low as she dared, its flounced skirt encrusted with jet beads, her blonde head crowned by black plumes and swathes of spotted black net, designed, undoubtedly, to supply Cullingford with gossip for many a long day.

'Aunt Hannah will not approve of that,' Prudence told her as we were about to set off, her light eyes very much amused, but my mother merely patted the black rose placed strategically and most enticingly at her bosom, and smiled.

'Ah well, dear, Aunt Hannah finds so very much of which to disapprove that one may suspect she enjoys it. And if I cannot win her favour then there is always Aunt Verity, who is the most elegant of women and who will not have forgotten the value of a wisp of perfumed chiffon. Yes, girls, you may stare, but I remember your Aunt Verity, in the days before she fell into such a trance of love for Uncle Joel, wearing a gown – my goodness, such a gown! – this one of mine would look staid beside it. Yes, a wisp of perfumed chiffon, no more, I do assure you, with gold sandals on her feet and a gold ribbon through her hair. Lord – how everyone stared, and with good reason: for when a woman uncovers her shoulders and paints her toe-nails one may be sure she intends it to be noticed. And I may have been the only person in the Assembly Rooms that night who understood her reasons; certainly her husband did not, for I well remember how he scowled at her, as black as thunder. Yes, you may find it hard to realize that your aunts – and your mother – have had their share of heart-searchings in their younger days. Ah well, it is long ago now. Everything has been settled on that old score. And I imagine Aunt Hannah may be too preoccupied with your appearance this evening, Prudence, to give much thought to mine. Oh dear, have I said something amiss? If I did not know you to be incapable of such bad manners, I would almost think you were glaring at me.'

'Naturally not, mamma,' Prudence said, her face sharpening. 'May I take it that you have heard something concerning me and Jonas Agbrigg? If so, then I must tell you –'

'Oh no, dear, please tell me nothing. I have every confidence in you, Prudence, and whether you mean to take him or not to take him – well – I am sure you are quite right either way.'

But Prudence, who had grown so brisk and businesslike of late, so very conscious of her rights and so very determined to preserve her new, hitherto undreamed-of liberty, slowly shook her head, detaining my mother with a gesture of authority unthinkable in my father's lifetime.

'No, mamma, that is hardly enough. You must offer me a little more guidance or show me a little more involvement than that. Am I to understand that Mr Jonas Agbrigg meets with your approval?'

'My dear, he is stepson to my own sister, and I can do no more than share her golden opinions. Of course, he has no *money*, but he has the air of a man determined to succeed. I can only tell you that your father believed he *would* succeed – I forget at what – politics, I believe, of which your father was very fond. Power, you know, is very attractive to some men – and to some women also. And, should you *care* to be the wife of a powerful man, Jonas may be a reasonable choice. Freddy Hobhouse will never be powerful, my dear, and he would spend your money far more recklessly than Jonas. He has nine brothers to settle in life, after all, and four sisters to marry, and your dowry, divided among them, would not seem so splendid. But I am sure you know that, dear, and that whatever you decide will be for the best.'

And telling us not to delay, since the carriage was already at the door, she patted her tulle rose once again and tripped away.

'You wanted your liberty, Prudence,' I told her, and she smiled, half amused, half angry.

'So I did. But I believe she could have helped me a little more than that. Clearly Aunt Hannah has let her know that Jonas intends to propose, and she has already given her consent. Well, so much the better, since I don't think he cares for it any more than I do – except that he needs the money – and the sooner it's over and done with the faster he can start angling for you, Faith. Who knows, he may even come after you, Celia.'

'Well, and if he does, I shall not treat him as you have done,' Celia told her in the high-spirited fashion only the subject of matrimony aroused in her. 'I know I am the youngest and that you and Faith think me stupid, but you cannot deny you have blown hot and cold with Jonas – and with Freddy Hobhouse too, for that matter. And that is the surest way to lose them both, and end up on the shelf.'

'Really?'

'Yes – really. And I will tell you something else. You may not have noticed it, Prudence, but both Freddy Hobhouse and Jonas have been making themselves very pleasant to me – oh yes, I know you are "not at home" when they call, and that Faith is always gadding about somewhere with Caroline, so that I am the only one here to receive them. But that does not explain why they have lingered so long, paying me the most marked attentions. To tell you the truth, Prudence, if they were not both half-way committed to you, I believe I could be Mrs Hobhouse or Mrs Agbrigg any time I liked.'

'Indeed?'

'Yes – indeed. You should make your intentions clear, Prudence. I believe people are of the opinion that until you are settled it would not be right to look at us. Aunt Hannah has said as much. And, if Faith don't seem to mind, I can't quite like it – seeing Heaven knows how many chances go by just because you are so hard to please.'

'My word!' Prudence said, once again half angry, half amused. 'Never fear, Celia. I will take whichever one of them should ask me first and endeavour to be married at the month end, just to oblige you. But it is cousin Caroline they are putting up on offer tonight, you know, so you'll just have to stand in line like the rest of us, Celia Aycliffe, and wait your turn.'

The whole of Tarn Edge was illuminated that night, a jewel-casket in the distance, spilling a diamond brightness over the acre of roses, the driveway fringed with widespreading chestnut trees, the sloping lawns; Aunt Verity waiting to receive her guests in a hall that had been transformed into a flower-garden, a profusion of pink and white blossoms apparently growing from the marble at her feet, vast hot-house arrangements on every step of the stairs, exotic plants of an intense crimson, a barbaric orange, jungle-flowers and desert-flowers raising their expensive, exceedingly rare heads among masses of polished foliage.

Everything was to be done that evening in accordance with Caroline's wishes – the proceedings to be conducted, in fact, in the manner of high London society, whose fringes she had once or twice encountered, and whose inner circle she was determined one day to penetrate – and she had really desired to take her stand at the head of the stairs like some Mayfair duchess, an arrangement which, her mother's ballroom being on the ground floor, would have forced us all to climb up the staircase and then down again, a manoeuvre deemed most unnecessary in Cullingford, where we were still suspicious of London ways.

But, this apart, everything was to be the essence of good taste and high fashion, an obedient procession waiting to shake their host and hostess by the hand and to murmur a word of congratulation to Caroline herself, her smooth shoulders rising, strong-boned, amber-tinted, from a tight bodice of white, embroidered silk-brocade, no demurely shrinking young miss but a hostess full-fledged, a triple strand of birthday pearls wound proudly around her throat, diamond and pearl drops in her ears, each ebony ringlet secured with a knot of silver ribbon and a pearl-headed pin. It was, of course, too much. The pearls were too fine and too numerous, the diamonds inappropriate in a girl of eighteen. The silk brocade with its cobwebbing of silver thread was certainly extravagant, or so it would seem to Lady Winterton, whose pearls had been eaten up long ago by the mortgage on her land, whose capable horsewoman's hands bore nothing now but a single antique ring; and to Lady Annabel Flood – the guest of honour, a social triumph for the Barforths – her own jewels and her dowry having fallen early victim to the extravagance of her father-in-law, that old Regency buck, our manorial lord, who even now could not deny himself the purchase of a thoroughbred horse or an enticing woman.

Yet both these ladies arrived most flatteringly early. Lady Winterton – for Lady Annabel's benefit – making a great show of friendship to that tradesman's wife, Aunt Verity; Lady Annabel, who apart from her connection with the Floods was herself an earl's daughter, a person of consequence in her own right, greeting my aunt very warmly, forgetting, it seemed, that she had never before condescended to accept anything from the Barforths but an occasional invitation to take tea.

But now – sacrificing themselves in this vulgar company as English gentlewomen have always sacrificed themselves in the interests of their class and their clan – both these ladies were affability itself, having clearly decided after much heart-searching to hazard their sons in the marriage-stakes: Francis Winterton, placid, disinterested, biddable; Julian Flood, already possessed at twenty-two of his grandfather's rake-hellish quality, which would make him unpredictable and expensive.

And behind them came the Mandelbaums with their musical, dark-eyed Jacob, Mrs Battershaw with her hopeful Benjamin, Mrs Hobhouse of ailing Nethercoats Mill with her Freddy and Adolphus and James, her eyes so dazzled by Caroline's diamonds that my twenty thousand pounds, without the porcelain, grew very pale.

'Good evening,' Caroline said to everyone, 'how do you do?' her smile never wavering, its degree of brightness identical for Mandelbaums and Wintertons alike, extending to Lady Annabel Flood, whose ancestors had arrived with William the Conqueror, no more and no less warmth than to Mrs Hobhouse, who had no ancestors worth speaking of at all.

'Good evening,' to each Hobhouse boy in turn, with nothing in her career-hostess's manner to indicate she had ever met them before, much less boxed the ears of all three, soundly and more than once, in childhood.

'Good evening,' too to Julian Flood, who was indeed almost a stranger, glimpsed only occasionally in church or as he drove his

425

grandfather's curricle at breakneck, arrogant speed through what he still considered to be his grandfather's town, her very refusal to single him out telling me that she was really very flattered – very excited – indeed.

'Good evening,' she said to me, too intent on her own appearance to notice mine. 'I shall pass my partners on to you, Faith, and if they have anything to say about me you can let me know.'

The orchestra, brought over from Manchester at the recommendation of the Mandelbaums, was already playing in preparation for the dance, installed on a raised platform at the end of the long, white and gold ballroom where not too many years ago Caroline and I had run races, our skirts clutched high around our knees. Refreshments, of course, were instantly on hand and would be served throughout the evening, claret and champagne and a tantalizing – possibly unnecessary – variety of cakes being set out in the small dining-room, accompanied by sorbets and ices, an endless flow of tea and coffee, to refresh the dancers and sustain the chaperones until supper-time.

But my mother, unlike the Ladies Winterton and Flood, who had evidently forgotten to eat their dinner, would take nothing but a glass of wine, satisfying her own appetite, I suspected, on the shocked, even hostile stares of Cullingford's matrons, and the stares of quite another order drawn from the widower, Mr Oldroyd of Fieldhead, and a series of other – in my eyes quite elderly – gentlemen as she passed them by.

'By God, can that be Elinor Barforth?' I heard Mr Hobhouse demand of his comfortable wife, forgetting she had been Mrs Aycliffe these twenty years. And his astonishment could not surprise me, for, although she had always been a pretty woman, Cullingford had grown accustomed to see her following demurely in my father's shadow, a tender dove eating passively from his hand, with no hint of the flaunting, diamond sparkle she was exhibiting tonight. And if that sparkle was indecent in a woman just six months a widow, few could deny its allure.

'We will not go into the ballroom until the dancing begins,' she told us 'for although no one may dance with me – poor little widow-woman that I am – I have no mind to sit among the wallflowers. We will wander around a little first and see what we can see, never mind the crowd. And if you are feeling faint already, Celia, then Caroline's nanny will be pleased to take care of you, for I am sure I cannot. I have your sisters to chaperone, after all, and I must not fail in my duty. So run along upstairs, dear, if you feel you must.'

But even Celia, clearly disliking my mother's boldness, believing as she did that no lady should ever put herself forward, should shrink from attention rather than set out to attract it, would not be confined to the nursery on such a night and soon swallowed her complaints.

'Good evening,' my mother said to all and sundry in quite a different tone from Caroline, her twinkling, dimpling smile, her nodding plumage, her artfully exposed bosom telling anyone who cared to look: 'Yes, here I am, Elinor Aycliffe whom you thought to see crushed and helpless without her husband. Yes, here I am, bubbling to the surface of myself, and loving it – oh yes, loving it.'

426

And watching her, understanding each gesture, each nuance of her face from the part of myself which was, indeed, like her, I came near to loving her too.

The ball was opened by Caroline, my Uncle Joel taking her a turn or two around the floor, his eyes very well satisfied but straying from time to time to Aunt Verity, who danced first with Sir Charles Winterton, as the senior representative of the landed gentry, and then with Mr Mandelbaum, reputedly the most prosperous of our merchants. Uncle Joel, abandoning Caroline to the multitude of her admirers, then danced with Lady Annabel Flood; and while these formalities were being observed my heart quickened, as surely the heart of every other girl must have quickened, sitting on those long rows of gilt-legged, velvet-covered chairs, as even Prudence's heart must have skipped a beat at the possibility before us all of disaster, or success.

Yet this was not the first dance I had attended and I knew by the unwritten laws governing such occasions that, even without my white rose and my vast, swan-like dress, without my audacious white velvet ribbon and the air of pity I was trying so hard to cultivate for such females who had failed to grow at least five inches taller than the fashion, I would not lack for partners. Girls who had neither beauty nor expectations might be condemned to spend the evening on that terrible row of chairs, counting the candles and the petals on the flowers, the lace flounces on the skirts of other girls as they danced by, hoping Aunt Verity would notice their plight and conjure up a man – any man – to relieve it. But a Miss Aycliffe, with twenty thousand cash down and the firm promise of more to come, need have no such fears.

Naturally every man present must first offer his attentions to his hostess and her daughter. Naturally Blaize and Nicholas would have been provided with a long list of females – which would not include cousins – to whom courtesy was due. Uncle Joel, his duty dances done, would have time for no one but his wife. But there would be partners to spare, a great many of them, and, as I sat between Celia, who was eager to dance with anyone, and Prudence who was eager to dance with anyone but Jonas, I was forced to admit that the deeper layers of my mind, the ones I could not really control, were entirely occupied with Nicholas.

My preoccupation was not a happy one. I had gorged myself, for a day or two after the incident of the train, on thoughts of him, indulged myself by building and rebuilding in my mind the dark, determined lines of his face, the slight cleft in his chin, the unexpected humour of his smile when it managed to chase his ill-temper away. And, indulging myself still further, I had relived the whole of our encounter, repeated our conversation over and over again, added to it, including the things I had wanted to say or had only thought of much later, as if they had actually been spoken. Yet in the end I had been forced, quite abruptly, to leave the comforting realm of fantasy and to consider, more precisely than ever before, my exact situation and what, if anything, I could reasonably, logically, hope to achieve.

Not even my father's scrupulously contrived efforts to raise his daughters in total innocence had concealed from me that there were various categories of womenkind, for which men had many and equally varied uses. There was the category 'lady', to which I belonged, whose duty it was to be pure of heart and delicate of constitution, designed to arouse the protective, possessive instinct in man; to be kept in luxurious idleness in exchange for the devotion and self-sacrifice with which she would hazard herself – sometimes annually – in the perilous task of childbirth. There was the category 'maidservant', so much stronger and more enduring than the lady that it was difficult to class them as members of the same species, a tireless variety of woman intended for the scrubbing of floors, the laying of grates, the carrying of water and the mangling of linen, her reproductive functions being so little encouraged that she would be dismissed the moment it was suspected they had been put to use. There was that category 'mill-hand', even hardier, capable of fourteen hours a day hard labour in the agonizing heat and noise of a weaving shed, and then another five with wash-tub and scrubbing board at home. And just as gentlemen turned to these tough plants for the practical, daily needs their little orchid-house wives could not supply, so too there was the category 'mistress', a wild jungle-weed, coarse-fibred enough to glory in the rough handling no orchid could be expected to endure.

And I knew, quite simply, that none of this concerned me. No one would ever be likely to ask me to lay a grate or tend a fire, or expose me to the heat and promiscuity of the sheds. I was, most definitely, a lady, created not to be loved but to be married, and even if by some miracle Nicholas could be induced into thoughts of matrimony, his family – which was partly my own family too – would not approve of me.

I may be considered a good match for a Hobhouse or a Mandelbaum, a brilliant one for Jonas Agbrigg, but the Barforths would require some stupendous alliance for all three of their children, and had I been a little older than seventeen, possessed of a greater share of Prudence's common sense, I would perhaps have smiled more convincingly at Jacob Mandelbaum, who liked me, at jovial Freddy Hobhouse, who seemed willing to like anyone, and shut my thoughts of Nicholas away.

'Enjoy yourselves,' my mother commanded, smiling as Jonas Agbrigg bowed stiffly to Prudence, the Battershaw boy first to me and then to Celia, since Freddy Hobhouse had claimed me first. 'Enjoy yourselves, while Aunt Hannah and I sit and tell each other how much better things were in our day.' And, although my appetite for enjoyment was less acute now that its fulfilment depended so largely on Nicholas, I made up my mind to obey.

I was not certain what I hoped for, since I could not hope for Nicholas, except that it was not Freddy Hobhouse, hot-handed, heavy-footed, hugging me in a cheerful polka; nor even Jacob Mandelbaum, serious and supple, who would rather have been playing the violins than dancing. Certainly it was not Francis Winterton, holding me a yard away, talking languidly about Caroline; nor Julian Flood who, having come here to marry one young lady, was reckless and arrogant enough to make himself gallant to another, escorting me to the refreshment-room where his mother, whose financial commitments my twenty thousand pounds could hardly satisfy, put herself instantly between us, walking back with us to the ballroom to make sure we went there, and that I was duly returned to my relations.

It was a dance, the most thrilling of all events permitted to young ladies, fraught with great hopes and great agonies, the making or missing of marriages and reputations, no different from the dozen or so others I had attended, except that it was more splendid. And for the first hour or so everything was just as it should have been. The three immense chandeliers suspended from the high, gold-painted ceiling shimmered and sparkled, the dozen long windows open to the terrace offered a breath of garden-spiced air as one danced by. The violins played their polkas and quadrilles and country-dances, their waltzes, every bit as tunefully as had been promised. The young ladies danced, or most of them did, at least once, provided with partners by Aunt Verity, who, gracefully, tirelessly, circled the room making her introductions. 'Miss Smith, allow me to present Mr Brown who is quite an expert at the polka. Why, Miss White, do not say you are too exhausted to dance, for here is Mr Jones, who would be delighted –'

The older men, having seen their wives and daughters suitably catered for, retired to refreshment-room and smoking-room, the chaperones drew their chairs closer together, sharp-eyed and anxious, some of them, others heavy-lidded with fatigue and the boredom of so eternally discussing the splendid prospects of my cousin Caroline. Aunt Hannah had placed herself firmly beside Mr Fielding, our new Member of Parliament, who was certainly unaware that she intended, eventually, to obtain his office for Jonas. And, while keeping up a steady flow of question and answer, demanding to know the progress of Cullingford's Charter of Incorporation, and when she could expect her husband to be elected mayor, her restless eyes never ceased to check the movements of her adored, adopted son, noting who danced with him and who did not, noting who dared to trespass on his preserves by dancing with Prudence. And her chaperonage, it seemed, extended also to my mother, so that when she returned, not for the first time, from the refreshment-room where the widower, Mr Oldroyd of Fieldhead Mills, had been plying her with champagne, Aunt Hannah leaned forward and snapped, in the exact tone she had used often enough to me and Celia, 'Elinor – do behave.'

Enjoyment was not lacking, but no greater than I had experienced before, nothing I would spend tomorrow in silence remembering. Neither Nicholas nor Blaize would have time to dance with me – although Blaize did smile at me once or twice behind his partner's head, letting me know, by a sweeping glance, that my dress and my hair had won his approval – and gradually the evening began to settle down, to acquire the same bland flavour of everyday, to be entirely predictable, until, having taken a second glass of lemonade with Jacob Mandelbaum and returning to the ballroom, Jacob a step or two behind me, I found myself entangled, just inside the doorway, with Nicholas and Caroline, drawing back as I heard her hiss at him, 'Nicholas, for heaven's sake, you have not yet danced with Amy Battershaw, and she most particularly wishes for it.'

'I daresay. But I have danced with all your other tedious friends, and I think you may allow me a moment –'

'Nicholas,' she said, her voice rising in a way that proved her composure to be less than it seemed. 'Please oblige me in this, for you know quite well Amy Battershaw and I are to travel to Paris together, and, if she should take the huff and decide not to go, then I shall be saddled with some dreary paid companion.'

'Or father will forbid you to go at all.'

'No, he will not. And it is quite odious of you to provoke me tonight when you know quite well how important – Oh, Nicky, for once please do as I ask, for she is sitting there, the silly goose, waiting, and I do believe she has turned someone else away.'

But Aunt Verity, as usual, was at hand; and, flowing between her warring children like cool water, drawing me with her for support, or distraction, she murmured, 'Faith dear, how well you look tonight! That dress becomes you perfectly – don't you think so, Caroline? And Nicky darling, do go and dance with Miss Battershaw – a bore, I admit, but only five minutes of your time – not worth the fuss.'

And he would have gone at once, I think, the corners of his mouth already tilting with a wry, affectionate smile, had not Uncle Joel abruptly intervened.

'What's all this?' he demanded and instantly Caroline – his favourite child, the apple of his powerful, vengeful eye – spun round to him, certain of his support.

'It is Nicholas turning stubborn again, and saying he will not dance with Amy Battershaw.'

'Oh, but he will,' my uncle said, the familiar snap of temper in his eyes. 'He will – and before he's ten minutes older.'

'Dearest –' Aunt Verity murmured, her endearment addressed, I think, to them both, and, not wishing to endure again the backlash of my uncle's anger, I had begun to move away when Nicholas, unable as always to back down, but willing perhaps to offer his mother a compromise, said crisply, 'Of course I'll dance with Miss Battershaw – there was never any doubt about it – but you'll have to extend your ten minutes, I'm afraid, since I am promised to dance first with Faith.'

Instantly – or so it seemed to me – a row of Barforth eyes were riveted to my face, my uncle's hard and suspicious, the thought behind them: 'Ah yes, so it's the Aycliffe girl again, turning out as flighty as her mother'; Caroline's warning me she did not expect her friends to turn traitor and would make short work of any who did; Aunt Verity's alone showing that she retained a sense of proportion and understood that I could only aggravate the matter by a refusal. 'Ah well,' she said lightly, 'I doubt if Miss Battershaw will die of the suspense'; and there was nothing for me to do but give him my hand and wait for the music to begin.

I had longed for this dance, and now – as often happens with the things one longs for in life – it was an embarrassment, an ordeal, a bitter disappointment. I had thought of him so often, not only with the excitement of budding emotion, but with anxiety too, had defended him when Caroline, and Celia, accused him of moodiness and malice, had worried about his stormy relations with his father, remembering all the times I had seen him take his punishment with a stubborn pride that made my uncle's tongue harsher, his hand heavier. Yet now I hoped with unashamed ferocity that Uncle Joel would thrash him and batter him at the end of every disagreement, wished, in fact, that he had broken his back and his spirit long ago.

'You are looking very well, Faith.'

'Thank you.'

And then, as I continued to stare over his shoulder, making it clear that there was nothing more I wished to say, he added quickly, 'Faith – I am sorry.'

'Why? Have you done something amiss?'

'Ah well – as to that – but I did not ask you to dance with me merely to escape Amy Battershaw.'

'My goodness – whatever gave you the notion I could think you had?'

They were playing a waltz, and because I had waltzed with him in my day-dreams since the day Aunt Verity's invitation had been delivered to our door, because I should have been happy – because Celia, if she noticed me, would think me happy – I had never been so miserable in my life, this new, acute sensation of distress, the first real pain I had ever suffered, acting like a hot stone flung into the quiet pool which had so far been my life, sizzling and hurting in its contact with hitherto unruffled waters. And I would have been proud of my composure had I not required every ounce of concentration I possessed to maintain it.

'You are quite right to be angry, Faith.'

'Angry? Heavens, what an idea! I am enjoying myself immensely, Nicholas. It is a splendid party. Everyone says so.'

And sighing, he made no further attempt to talk to me, while I became so stiff and cold that he may have been as glad as I when the music stopped and he could return me to my mother, going off at once to present himself to a much-beribboned Amy Battershaw.

'Well, we are having so much fun,' my mother told me, her eyes extremely bright with mischief and champagne. 'Prudence has danced twice with Jonas and managed to avoid him twice more, largely with the aid of your so very accomplished cousin Blaize. Yes, he knows exactly what is going on around him, dear Blaize – I have always thought so – and I have passed a pleasant half-hour wondering just why he came so artfully to her rescue. I mean, what amused him most? Was it the look on Aunt Hannah's face? Or was it Jonas, who has no look on his face at all? Or did he merely wish to make Prudence admire him, since she refuses to admire anyone else? I am inclined to think that must be it, for he is a little heartless – Blaize. Clever men often are, I find, which makes them no less attractive. However, it makes no difference, since Aunt Hannah has got her safely back again – look, there she is, sitting between Hannah and Mr Fielding, with Jonas standing guard behind her chair. And Celia has been doing remarkably well – she has danced with Jonas and Freddy and Adolphus, and has abandoned all her notions of having a headache.' But my mother's chatter irritated me, since I cared at that moment neither for Celia's triumphs nor Prudence's captivity; and, excusing myself, murmuring something about a hairpin, a handkerchief, I hurried away to Caroline's bedroom, the old, comfortable nanny sitting by the fire surrounded by her stock-in-trade of needle and thread, hairpins and smelling-bottles, ready to mend a torn frill, or a broken heart without too much interest in either.

'You look pale, dear,' she said. 'Drink this'; and I drank something bland and neutral that had an echo of my childhood about it, turning cold and hot and then very cold again, as, ravaged by the strength of my raw, seventeen-year-old emotion, I faced the unpalatable truth, the depth of the pit into which I had so willingly fallen.

I was in love with a man who was not in love with me, which was in itself quite bad enough, but my feeling for him was so unconnected with marriage, depended so little on marriage, that for a moment I was almost as shocked by it as my father would have been. But perhaps my father had not always been so wise – so dry; perhaps he, too, when he had made his unlikely second marriage to my mother, had been driven by needs he chose later to deny.

I did not completely understand the sexual act. For a married woman – according to Miss Mayfield's hints and evasions – it was a duty; for an unmarried woman so unthinkable that it could only be the result of brutal rape, which even then, should she be indelicate enough to survive, would effectively ostracize her from decent company. I had witnessed but one remotely sexual contact between my parents, a faint, uneasy thing, my father's hand hovering, not quite touching, my mother's shoulder, his pinched lips saying, 'Elinor, it is time for bed,' my mother's head turning briefly away, nostrils wrinkling, eyelids lowering to hide the protest she had been unable to suppress; and then, turning back to him, offering her meek, empty smile, nothing warmer than her submission. 'Why yes, dear.' And my feelings for Nicholas had nothing to do with any of that.

But, still gazing into the fire, I began to remember other things, young couples strolling tight-clasped together on quiet evenings, common people, we had been told, who should have been at home preparing themselves for tomorrow's labours instead of 'asking for trouble' in this unseemly fashion. 'Look away, girls.' But I understood that, in this case, we had been instructed to avert our eyes not from depravity but from pleasure, the simple joy – forbidden to us – that two young bodies, two loving, sympathetic minds, could find in each other, a joy that had nothing at all to do with dowries and marriage contracts, the propagation of a man's name and his money.

'Look away, girls.' But no one had forbidden me to notice the softening of my Uncle Joel's face whenever he looked at his wife, the way her hand, very often, would seek his, a certain glow of memory and anticipation between them which, I realized, had sometimes embarrassed my father and Aunt Hannah, and had caused my mother and Mr Agbrigg, Aunt Hannah's plain-spoken husband, to lower their eyes, as if they not only understood very well what that glow meant, but had something in their own lives to remember.

Clasping my hands tight together, giving my whole mind to the task, I understood that everything I desired in life was contained in that warm glance between my aunt and uncle. I was not concerned with social success, like Caroline, nor with social ideals, like Prudence. I had small interest in domesticity, like Celia. I simply wanted Nicholas to smile at me through the lamplight one evening, as his father – who was gentle with no one else – smiled at Aunt Verity; to reach out his hand in a gesture of perfect confidence and understanding, knowing that mine would be there to meet it. And although I was not even acquainted with the word 'sensuality', much less its meaning, I think my body understood it, dimply perhaps, but joyfully, and loved him too.

'And what do you think of my Caroline tonight,' the old servant inquired, not interested in my opinion, but feeling I had been silent long enough. 'A real beauty she's turned out to be – aye, and they're all after her. But she'll take the one she fancies when she's ready, mark my words. Not that she's ready – not by a long chalk – for she's had a taste of London now, and she's pestering to go to Paris, which means she'll surely be going, for I've never known her father refuse her anything. Aye, she'll have what she wants, Miss Caroline. She always was that way, just like her father. And when she gets it, whatever it is, it won't turn out to be good enough. She'll have to alter it, and better it, just like him. Now then, Miss Faith, you'll be going downstairs now, I reckon, so nanny can get on with her knitting. Just a dab of cologne – that's better, eh?'

'Yes, nanny. Thank you.'

But the old woman's evident desire to return to her knitting-needles was frustrated yet again by the abrupt arrival of my eldest sister, who, ignoring nanny's comfortable 'And what can I do for you, Miss Prudence?' said quickly, 'Faith, I am absolutely mortified – indeed I have never been more so in my life –'

'With Jonas?'

'Oh – naturally with Jonas – but mainly with myself. I have amazed myself. I did not know I could be so – oh, I don't know what to call it, weak, I suppose.'

'Good heavens, Prue! You have not accepted him, have you, because you couldn't bring yourself to say no?'

'Indeed I have not – but what I *have* done is almost as feeble. I was to dance the waltz with him that is just starting, and seeing him coming towards me I felt quite certain that instead of dancing he was going to suggest something quite stupid, like a walk in the moonlight, and propose. And instead of facing up to it – for, good lord, it is only Jonas and I am not in the least afraid of him – I suddenly found myself bolting up the stairs like a scared rabbit, exactly the kind of silly, schoolgirl antic I would expect from Celia. Faith, how could I do such a thing?'

'I don't know,' I told her, meaning it, since I had admired her courage all my life, relied heavily on her cool, disciplined powers of reason on the many occasions when my own had failed me. 'Perhaps you thought the place ill-chosen, or that Aunt Hannah would make a scene when you refused him.'

'Did I? And of course she would. But I am not sure it was that. No – he has been so strange all evening – well, he is always strange, but tonight – oh dear, I don't know. And the whole thing suddenly seemed to be so distasteful – so sordid. But this is no excuse. I should have been able to stand my ground. And what on earth am I to do now? He will be waiting in the hall and will expect some explanation. Goodness – how sickening!'

'Then I will go and explain for you.'

'Faith, I can't ask you –'

'You have not asked me. And I am not so fastidious as you are, Prudence. I will simply tell him you are indisposed at the moment, and whether he believes it or not he can hardly say so. And when you come downstairs again you should behave as if you had not been disposed at all – which is no more than the truth – and that will put him off from bothering you again tonight. That is the way these things are done, you know. I'll see to it.' And, delighted at this opportunity to protect her, when all our lives she had looked after me, I went downstairs.

5

He was, indeed, waiting in the hall, positioned at the foot of the stairs where no one could escape him, his eyes no colder than I was accustomed to see them, his thin mouth no more disdainful – the Agbrigg boy of my childhood wearing his dress suit and ruffled shirt a shade too correctly, too much the gentleman, as if he found it hard to forget that his birth did not entitle him to be a gentleman at all. Just Jonas. who, well aware that we had always despised him, might be hurt and angry but hardly surprised to find himself rejected again.

'I am come with Prudence's apologies,' I told him lightly, expecting no difficulty. 'She finds herself somewhat indisposed and asks me to say she cannot dance.'

'Really?' he said, not believing me, but not, it seemed, much caring. 'Nothing of a serious nature, I hope and trust?'

'Oh no. She will be down presently, I imagine.'

And that should have been the end of it; he should have bowed, smiled, offered to escort me back to my mother; I should have accepted his arm, made some slight remark about the splendours of the evening, the excellence of the music and the champagne, and we should have gone our separate ways. But instead, without in any way altering his expression of cool indifference, he murmured, so low that I had to step closer to hear him, 'And do you also imagine that her recovery would be more rapid if I were to make my excuses to Mrs Barforth and take my leave?'

'Good heavens!' I said, laughing, hoping it was indeed a joke, although

I knew quite well it wasn't, 'I don't know why you should think that, Jonas.'

'Do you know anything very much at all, Faith?' he replied so tonelessly, so calmly, that it took me a second to understand his rudeness. But when I did, I knew it authorized me to stop playing the young lady and to answer him back just as rudely as I pleased.

'I shall not ask you to apologize for that, Jonas, since you are probably not sorry. But, as it happens, I am not stupid, and if Prudence is avoiding you then she must have her reasons – and that is not my fault.'

'Did I say so?' he inquired, a lawyer lecturing me, examining me from a lofty, intellectual height, although his pale, slanting eyes were on an exact level with mine, his shoulders not much broader. 'And she has no reason to avoid me that I know of. Why should you think otherwise?'

'Well – I did, that's all.'

'Because you thought I meant to propose?'

'Yes,' I said, considerably startled, yet determined to defend my sister whatever the cost. 'So I did, and it would be most ungentlemanly of you to try to deny it.'

'Really? Why is that?'

'You know quite well why – and will you please stop talking to me like a lawyer.'

'But I am a lawyer, Faith – a very good one, as a matter of fact.'

'I am glad to hear it. And in that case you must know that, having paid attentions to a lady – well, a lady may put an end to such things, a gentleman, once he is committed, may not. Of course you meant to propose.'

'Indeed,' he said, his thin lips sketching a smile that was entirely without humour. 'Naturally you must be right – since a lady can never be wrong – and it is no secret that my mother would like to see me married, preferably to Prudence. But what my mother would like, and what Prudence would like – what I would like myself – cannot always be the same. I think we should let the matter rest there. You may tell your sister so.'

'Yes, I will, and I am glad, at any rate, to see you are not broken-hearted.'

'Are you?'

'I beg your pardon?'

'I said, are you glad to see that I am *not* broken-hearted?'

And, for an instant, his hooded eyes shot wide open, colourless almost, unaccustomed to the light, but leaving me in no doubt that he was deeply offended and had perhaps been so all his life, his habitually neutral expression chilling me now with the kind of anger I had seen often enough in my father, the twisted emotion of a man who, feeling he cannot afford emotion, denies it, conceals it, comes eventually to despise it, and is seriously displeased with himself and anyone else who happens to be nearby on the rare occasions when it breaks free.

Yet Jonas, I felt quite certain, was not in love with Prudence, had in fact presented himself to her in a businesslike fashion which even she had

435

found too cool, too obviously motivated by Aunt Hannah's advice and his own good sense. And I was so intrigued by this show of feeling in a man I had believed entirely passionless that, when he took my arm and obliged me to walk a step or two with him down the passageway behind the stairs, I did not resist.

There were few people in that part of the house, just a servant or two, hurrying soft-footed about their duties with no great interest in a young couple who, by the look of it, wished to be alone. And wondering why on earth he had brought me here – since no matter how pressing his financial needs it was a little too soon, surely, to propose to me in my sister's place – I said primly, 'I would like to go back to my mother.'

'Of course.'

But he was still taut and painful with his anger, its intensity both amazing me and giving me cause for concern, since later, when he returned to his habitual composure, he would not remember me kindly for having witnessed it.

'Tell me something,' he said, his voice clipped and sarcastic, a lawyer again, demolishing the evidence of a witness who was in any case somewhat beneath his notice. 'Obviously my attentions – such as they were – have not found favour with your sister. And since I perfectly agree with my mother that I should marry, and that it should be sooner rather than later, perhaps you will let me know how I have most displeased her. I realize for one thing that I have committed the crime of poverty –'

'That has nothing to do with it.'

'Has it not? Do you know, Faith, in your case I am ready to believe you. There is no need for you to think about money, is there, since you have never been without it. Unfortunately, some of us are less happily situated. I spend a great deal of my time thinking about money. I am obliged to do so, since ambition is expensive and I am very ambitious. I admit it freely. It may seem strange to you that a man of ability and energy cannot progress in this world even half so far as a mutton-head who has a few thousand a year behind him – it has often seemed strange to me – but so it is. I have learned to accept it and accommodate it, since I intend to make more of my life than I suppose a man of my origins has any right to expect.'

'I know nothing of your origins, Jonas.'

'Nonsense!' he snapped. 'You know quite well that my father was a weaver once in your uncle's sheds, and that he first married a weaver, if indeed he troubled to marry her at all. It costs money, you see, to get married. A man can't go to church in clogs and a cloth cap. The parsons don't like it, and there's a little matter of putting something in the collection plate afterwards. So mostly, among the labouring classes, they save their money and don't bother. They just wait until their first child is on the way and then move into the same back-to-back hovel and set about having more. Marriage, after all, is about property, and if a man has no property what difference can it make to him if his sons are legitimate, or even if they're his sons at all? Nobody in Simon Street –

which is where my father came from, where I was born – gives a thought for such things. But naturally it must make a difference to a Miss Aycliffe.'

'Jonas,' I said, shocked, fascinated, beginning now to pity him, wishing I could find the courage to make him stop hurting himself in this way, 'you should not speak to me like this. For one thing, I am not supposed to understand such matters – but, since in fact I do know what you mean, I will tell you that it makes no difference to me at all. And you should not be ashamed of it either.'

'Ashamed?' he flung at me, every line of his over-strung body a snarl. 'Did I say I was ashamed? What have I to be ashamed about? I don't remember Simon Street. I don't remember that day my mother took me into the mill, when I was seven years old, and set me to work. I don't remember going home every night stinking like a pig and getting into bed with God knows how many brothers and sisters who stank worse than I did, because they were older and bigger and had more muck on them. I don't even remember those brothers and sisters, since they died, every one of them except me, because they didn't have the energy to stay alive – or couldn't see the point to it. I don't remember, because by the time I was ten my father had wormed his way into your Uncle Joel's good graces and could afford to take me out of the sheds and send me to school. Your uncle made him manager of Low Cross Mill and gave us the mill-house to live in, which was no palace. They use it now for storage, but after a "one up and one down" in Simon Street it was all too grand for my mother. She couldn't make herself into a manager's wife, you see, and so she lost her wits over it. Started wandering in the end, going back to Simon Street to find her old workmates, who didn't want her any more, and worrying herself sick that she was holding my father back, which she was, and holding me back, since I was at the grammar school by then with all the Barforths and the Hobhouses – like gentlemen all together, except that I was cleverer, a damn sight cleverer – and I couldn't be expected to like it when she turned up at school one day with a shawl on her head and clogs on her feet. Of course I don't remember that either. I don't even remember the way the Hobhouses sniggered, or your cousin Nicholas looked away – most of all I don't remember how your cousin Blaize raised his hat to her and said, 'Good-day to you, madam.' It's completely gone out of my mind. She died when I was about thirteen, and my father had some very hard words to say to me that day – you may have noticed that we don't get on too well together even now. He suggested I'd be relieved to be rid of her, glad that I wouldn't have to feel ashamed of her any longer in front of my friends, although I can't think just who he meant by that. He was quite broken up about losing her, my father, although he recovered soon enough. He married Miss Hannah Barforth no less, the very minute he was out of mourning – for my sake, he said, since she liked the idea of having a clever son and was ready to do great things for me. And if my father, with his accent and the callouses still on his hands, could marry a Barforth – well – I really don't think a Miss Aycliffe should be beyond my reach, do you?'

But, understanding what it meant to him to expose himself in this painful fashion – what it would have meant to my father – I was appalled and fearful and could find nothing to offer him in reply but a whispered, 'Jonas – please – do not –'

'I am extremely sorry,' he said, the whole of him coming to an abrupt halt, his very breathing suspended for a moment as if he needed his entire, doubtless formidable powers of concentration to retrieve the rogue part of his nature which had so disastrously escaped its bondage.

Surely nothing more could now be said? Surely he would take me, in silence, back to the ballroom and would from then on avoid me as much as he could? But, after that moment of total stillness, he turned and stood directly in front of me, closer that I had anticipated, so that, retreating, I found my back against the wall.

'Faith,' he said very quietly, his eyes completely hooded again, something just beneath the surface of him so tense, so watchful, that it caused me to hold my breath. 'I have not proposed to Prudence, mainly because I was unwilling to risk a refusal, for there is no doubt she would have made me an excellent wife. There is a saying that every man encounters three kinds of women in his lifetime, the woman he knows would be good for him, the woman he would like to have, and the woman he can get. Certainly Prudence would have been good for me. My mother made an excellent choice in drawing her to my attention.'

'I will tell her –'

'There is no need. We did not, in any way, commit ourselves. In fact we were both very careful not to do so. The matter is entirely closed. You need tell her no more than is required to set her mind at rest. My mother considers you a great scatterbrain, Faith.'

'Well – she is right again – for so I am.'

'I know.'

And, my back pressed against the wall, the air in that narrow, dimly lit passageway so taut now that it hurt me to breathe, I understood – without in the least knowing how I had reached so shattering a conclusion – this this bloodless man had actually brought me here, not to complain of my sister, but because, incredibly, considerably against his own better judgment, he had wanted to be alone with me; wanted now, although his eyes were still hooded, his jaw set, to kiss me. And, pitying him, yet knowing he could not tolerate pity, fearful of wounding his bruised self-esteem once again, astonished and just a little curious, for I had never even suspected I held any appeal for him, I understood that I must stop him at all costs. For a kiss was far more personal and important than a proposal of marriage, even if the proposal was almost certain to follow after. The rejection of an offer of marriage could be construed simply as the rejection of a man's prospects, a business arrangement which for a hundred acceptable reasons did not suit. But to turn my head away from his kiss would be a terrible thing, something he would find hard to forgive, while to accept it would be dangerous, foolish, unkind. I did not wish to encourage him, certainly, but I did not wish to hurt him either. Nor did I wish to hurt myself, for I had never been kissed before, and although I was quite ready for the experience I didn't want that first, special kiss to come from Jonas.

'I am indeed sorry for the things I said to you just now, Faith – although oddly enough it doesn't disturb me that you should know them.'

'Why should it? I shall not tell anyone else, you can be sure of that. And, after all, we are cousins.'

'Not really. There is no blood relationship between us. Faith – you really are scatterbrained, aren't you, and extravagant too, I suppose, like your mother?'

'Oh yes. Very like my mother. I am not at all a favourite with Aunt Hannah.'

'I know that. But aunts, and mothers, tend to look mainly for accomplishments in a young lady. There are other attributes.'

And there it was, Jonas, who was beyond folly – who could not afford it in any case – committing folly for my sake, bending his narrow head towards me, his thin mouth smiling with a slight, rueful amusement, directed, I supposed, at himself, although I could see no cause for amusement, struggling instead against a panic certainty that, when he finally made up his mind to deliver his kiss, I would push him away, or far worse than that would wound us both by a fit of hysterical laughter. I even closed my eyes, steeling myself to endure, praying for the sophistication that would enable me to wave it gracefully away, to make light of it without awkwardness, to suggest, somehow, that while not taking it seriously I had not found it unpleasant. But such compassionate artifice was not within my capabilities in those days, and when, after a moment, he did not touch me after all, I opened my eyes again to find him staring at me, understanding my dilemma too well it seemed, no softness, no rueful amusement in him any more.

'I believe you wished to return to your mother, Faith.'

'Yes. So I did.'

And, as he escorted me in silence to the ballroom door, abandoning me there quite abruptly, I was not certain from the closed, cold lines of his face if I had acquired a lover or an enemy.

I should, of course, have gone at once to Prudence, was about to turn round and make my way upstairs again, when Celia appeared as if from nowhere, struggling pink-cheeked and breathless towards me through the ballroom crowd.

'Heavens, Faith, what are you thinking of? You have been gone for ages – you and Prudence – leaving me to manage alone. Well, you are to come at once, for mother has taken it into her head to *dance*, yes, with Mr Oldroyd, who must have lost his wits, or is in his cups, for he can only laugh and encourage her. The next waltz, she is saying, and you must come and stop her, Faith, for I could not bear it – only six months a widow, and his wife not dead a year yet. Nobody has ever heard of such a thing. She should not really be here at all and, if she disgraces herself by dancing, then we are all disgraced too. Like mother like daughter, they will say, and who can blame them, for I believe I would say the same myself. Faith – do something – for I have been so enjoying myself and she has no right to spoil it. She's had her life, Faith – it's simply not fair.'

I discovered my mother a moment later, leaning back against her chair, bubbling with a soft, altogether wicked laughter, Aunt Hannah sitting tight-lipped beside her, delivering a most stringent warning.

'You are not in Venice now, Elinor.'

'No, no, dearest – that is all too apparent. But such a fuss, Hannah. Matthew Oldroyd has asked me to dance, which I thought very kind of him, and unmannerly in me to refuse –'

'He did not at all expect to be taken seriously, Elinor, as you well know. He was merely being gallant – or trying to be – in his clumsy fashion, and I never saw a man more startled in my life when you agreed. And where is he now, I should like to know? Gone to find his hat and order his horses, if he has the sense he was born with. Really, Elinor, such things may be permitted in Venice, but they would not be understood here. You should give some thought to your responsibilities, and your age.'

'Ah – as to that –' my mother began, ready, I thought, to put forward some startling theory of her own as to the nature of responsibility. But, happily, all further discussion was cut short by a sudden hush, a tailing off of violins in mid-polka, a standing on tiptoe and craning of necks which could only mean some momentous event was about to take place. And, as the double doors from the drawing-room were thrown open, and Aunt Verity appeared, there was a moment of incredulity, a collective intake of breath, as the tall, military-looking old man walking beside her was recognized as Sir Giles Flood, our manorial lord.

He was not quite eighty, as Blaize had once told me, but perhaps not too far away from it, with a heavy-featured, autocratic countenance, the total self-assurance that is bred through generations of authority, managing, even in the black evening-clothes then in fashion, to have something of the old-style Regency buck about him, who once in rainbow-coloured silks and satins had played whist in high company at Carlton House, and to whom the sinful splendours of Brighton in the Prince Regent's day had not been unknown.

'What a triumph for Verity!' my mother murmured, all other mischief forgotten. 'What an absolute triumph!' For Sir Giles, whose family had held the manor of Cullingford for three hundred years, and who had himself inherited his title at a time when every cap in the Law Valley would be instantly doffed as he passed by – at a time when there had been the lord in his castle, the parson at his altar, the peasants in the fields and the weaver in his two-roomed shack, when every man had been aware of the place to which God had called him and had been ready to keep it – this same Sir Giles had vowed publicly, and very loudly, that nothing would induce him to set foot in the house of any upstart manufacturer.

One could be civil to the breed, he declared, if one happened to meet it, as a gentleman was in honour bound to be civil to his groom or his grocer, but he saw no reason to encourage it, and had delivered many a dire warning to his peers – Sir Charles Winterton among them – against these jumped-up millmasters who with their dirty machines and their dirty money seemed possessed of the amazing and impertinent notion that they were as good as anybody else.

No one had campaigned more vigorously than Sir Giles to keep his manufacturing neighbours well away from public affairs – government, as everyone knew, or ought to know, being the business of gentlemen – refusing to sit as a Justice of the Peace on the same bench as any man who was tainted personally or paternally by trade. He had raised a considerable outcry against the Reform Bill of 1832 which had first allowed the local industrialists to elect their own Member of Parliament – my father – and even now was preparing most viciously to attack Cullingford's Charter of Incorporation, which by sweeping away the ancient, manorial offices of local government would subject the town he still thought of as his personal property to the interference of some low-born manufacturing mayor.

Yet here he was, his hand resting with no apparent distaste on Aunt Verity's arm, and, as he led her into the centre of the empty floor and swung her with amazing vigour into a waltz, the assembled manufacturing company broke quite spontaneously into a round of applause, as if it had been the Duke of Wellington or Prince Albert himself dancing there.

'So it's to be Julian Flood is it – for Caroline?' Aunt Hannah muttered, her head very close to my mother's in perfect harmony. And my mother, unable to take her eyes from that disreputable but lordly figure, breathed, 'Yes, indeed – Joel must be even richer than we thought, or the Floods poorer. Just think of it, Hannah – Caroline at Cullingford Manor. My word, I think Lady Winterton is having a fit, and Lady Annabel Flood is like a cat in a cream-pot.'

Caroline herself took the floor now with Julian Flood, Celia with Freddy Hobhouse, Jonas with some young lady who looked as if she might be worth a few thousand a year, while I, making my way once again to rescue Prudence, still hiding upstairs, found myself face to face with Nicholas, whose request for a second dance drove Prudence and all else entirely from my mind.

He took me very firmly by the hand, very firmly by the waist, and said, his voice equally determined, 'I have to apologize properly to you, Faith. You were in too much of a huff to listen earlier, and I have been waiting my opportunity ever since.'

And I felt such a winging, soaring delight that I could have wished him to do something really dreadful, so that I could forgive him even more.

'There's no need, Nicholas.'

'Of course there is. And you have been looking so distracted –'

'Oh well – that has nothing to do with it. My mother has had a set-to with Aunt Hannah, and, to tell the truth, I am not certain but I think Jonas Agbrigg may have asked me to marry him.'

'Good lord, Faith!' he said, quite horrified. 'Either he has asked you or he hasn't. I hope you are certain as to whether or not you have refused him.'

441

'Oh yes, there is no doubt about that. But I believe I have done it awkwardly, and hurt his feelings.'

'Jonas? Nonsense. He has no feelings to hurt. He's the coldest fish I ever did see. Don't worry about him. It's his pocket, not his feelings, that he worries about, and it's no secret that he's hard-pressed for cash right now, since old Mr Corey-Manning has decided to retire. The old man has bought himself a house in Bridlington and can't wait to get there, didn't you know? Jonas will have to get the money from somewhere to buy him out, stands to reason, or he could find himself with a new senior partner who may not be to his liking. All it needs is for some energetic fellow to come along, with sons of his own to find places for, and Jonas will soon find himself squeezed out.'

'Won't your father help him?'

'I reckon he might. But he'll expect Jonas to have something of his own behind him. There's more to it than just the money for the partnership, after all. If Jonas wants to step into Corey-Manning's shoes he'll have Corey-Manning's social position to keep up – which can't be cheap. More than Aunt Hannah can manage, since she'll need every penny she can scrape together to stake herself as mayoress. They can't expect my father to stand it. He'll listen to a business proposition, I don't doubt, but he's not a charity. He might help, but Jonas will have to do something to help himself, first.'

And, having made our peace, we danced for a while in a comfortable silence, until the music suddenly tailed-off again, a mark of respect for the exit of Sir Giles and Aunt Verity, and a signal that it was supper-time.

'Thank goodness for that!' Nicholas said. 'I thought the old man would never come – and I reckon he didn't really want to, if the truth be known. And since we couldn't start supper without him, and then we had to make sure everyone saw he was here – well, I'm starving. Come on, Faith – you'll have supper with me?'

Instant, incredible joy. 'Oh yes, Nicholas'; and then, remembering my place and his, and that Uncle Joel expected him to earn his keep, 'But won't your father have arranged –? Shouldn't you be taking Miss Battershaw, or someone?'

'Not a bit of it. He's so pleased now with Sir Giles that the Battershaws can all go hang. Come on – before the Hobhouses and the Wintertons clear the board –'

Lady Winterton, indeed, was there before us, circling eagle-eyed around the table, making a most thorough inspection of the cold beef, already sliced and tied back into shape again with satin ribbon, prodding an inquisitive fork into the salmon as if she thought – or hoped – it may have been taken illegally from her river, accepting liberal portions of every dish she passed and wondering out loud if it was really necessary to provide so many.

Sir Giles, with Aunt Verity and Uncle Joel, was installed at a table set apart, screened from the common view by the deft hoverings of butler and head parlourmaid, a dish of oyster patties and a well-iced magnum of champagne to hand, his eldest daughter-in-law, Lady Annabel, offering her erstwhile friend Lady Winterton a slight, immensely superior smile as she came to join him.

'Where is Julian?' snapped Lady Winterton, who always knew the whereabouts of her Francis.

'Oh, somewhere with Miss Barforth,' Lady Annabel – already basking in the possibility that her father-in-law's bills might now be paid – was quick to reply.

'I don't fancy eating in this crowd,' Nicholas announced suddenly, apparently displeased by Lady Annabel's self-assurance as much as by the assembly now jostling and snatching around the supper-table. 'Let's make for the back stairs.' And whispering to a harassed parlourmaid his instructions for a supper-tray, he shouldered a way to the door and hurried me along the same passage where I had walked, an hour ago, with Jonas.

I had sat on these back stairs a dozen times before with Blaize and Nicholas and Caroline, all of us huddled together, children long past our bedtime, watching the dinner-party dishes as they came out of the kitchen, scuffling like puppies for the left-over chocolate creams and ices the maids handed up to us, Prudence and I round-eyed with admiration when Blaize and Nicholas once downed the contents of a forgotten claret jug, Celia tearful with fatigue and the fear of discovery.

Yet it was different now, settling my wide, silk skirts – my lovely swan dress – on the shallow steps, Nicholas lounging on the step below. Quite different, in the half-dark, eating our supper from a tray laden with cakes and champagne, both of us knowing full well that our being here was not entirely innocent, since the conventions which ruled our lives quite clearly forbade us to be alone together at all. Discovery might mean no more than a tolerant reprimand. 'Young lady, you had best go back to your mamma, and we will say no more about it.' But it could also mean accusations of improper behaviour, loss of reputation, and he would not have brought me here unless he was prepared to defend me if the need arose, unless he really found pleasure in my company.

'You are so changed,' he had said to me in my daydreams, but now: 'We are friends again?' he once more enquired, and it sufficed.

'Yes – although you have twice embroiled me with your father, who terrifies me. Doesn't he terrify you?'

'He does not. I daresay he would like to, or perhaps he merely thinks that he should. But he does not.'

'Then you are very brave.'

'Oh yes – a lion. I wonder how Julian Flood will fare at his hands. My father likes a decent return on his investments, so I reckon young Julian had best watch out.'

'You're not pleased, are you, that Caroline should want to marry him.'

He shrugged, his face, in concentration and in shadow, quite dark.

'I've nothing against him – so far as the gentry goes he's right enough, and a sight better than that sickly Winterton. But he *is* gentry and she's not, and yes, I have my doubts.'

443

'But she'd be so good at the manor, Nicholas.'

'I'm not denying it. She wants the manor all right, and the title, but I'm not sure she understands all that goes with it. Blaize now, he could marry a duchess and manage all right, but he's not like the rest of us. Caroline looks like a duchess, but she's a Barforth. She likes money, but she understands how it's made and the men who make it, and I'm not sure she'll ever understand the Floods.'

'They like money too.'

'Aye, or they'd not be here tonight. But they want it for different reasons. Look – I reckon you know how my father has spent his life building up Lawcroft Mills and Tarn Edge and Low Cross? But he'd sell them tomorrow and go into something else – and so would I – if it was to his advantage. The Floods can't bring themselves to part with one useless acre, just because its been in the family for three hundred years. I'm not saying it's right or wrong. I'm saying it's different. And Caroline's not like that. She'd try to run that manor like my father runs the mills, and even if she made the Floods a profit I reckon they wouldn't approve of her methods.'

'They'd take the money, though.'

'So they would.'

We laughed open-heartedly, two people who understood each other, a hard-headed Law Valley man, shrewd and straightforward, who would not always be easy on his woman, rarely romantic, his well-shod feet at all times firmly rooted to the ground; a Law Valley woman, tougher than she seemed, who understood the demands and hazards of his trade, who wanted the things he wanted and appreciated the skill by which they were obtained.

We were alike. We matched, and, as I got slowly to my feet, shaking out my skirts and smoothing my hair with hands that trembled and needed to be occupied. I saw in his face the same narrow-eyed intensity I had seen in Jonas, that spark of awakening and instantly controlled desire that I suppose any man may feel for any presentable woman in a lonely place, but which, far from repelling me as it had done in Jonas, caused my whole body to sway forward, as if it had dissolved in the air between us and was being wafted irrevocably, magically, towards him. And only the fear that is bred into all females who are required to remain virgin – marketable – forced me to pretend that I had stumbled.

'I should go back now, Nicholas.'

'Yes,' he said, for although his own virginity was a long-past memory, offered, one supposed, in approved Law Valley fashion, to the ladies of the Theatre Royal, he knew he would have to be very careful, very sure of his ultimate intentions before making the very tiniest assault on mine.

'I'll take you back. They'll not have missed you, in all the confusion of supper and Sir Giles.'

Yet we had lingered too long, it seemed, for suddenly there was the rustle of a skirt at the far end of the passage, perhaps only the maid come back to fetch her tray, perhaps a stranger who would look askance and go away, perhaps not. I shrank back against the wall, appalled now,

444

when it was too late, by the possibility of discovery and misunderstanding, realizing as so often before that I should have thought of this sooner.

'Don't worry,' Nicholas said, but I think we were both relieved when a voice enquired, 'So – and just what is going on here?' for it was only Caroline, her white and silver skirts blocking the passageway, her face – when I was calm enough to look at it – no longer aglow with triumph but creased with ill-temper and the need, perhaps, of finding someone to blame.

'Oh, it's you,' Nicholas said. 'Thank God for that!'

But clearly something was very much amiss, for instead of laughing and coming to join us on those familiar, friendly back stairs, she continued to stand, hard-faced and glaring – as her father had once done – looking for trouble and almost grateful to find it.

'I asked you a question,' she said. 'What are you doing here, Nicholas?'

'Minding my own business, as you should be minding yours.'

'It is my business,' she snapped. 'This is my party, and I am responsible for the way it is conducted.'

And even then he was not really concerned, for it was just Caroline on her high-horse, as we had seen her many a time, and she would soon climb down again.

'Come on, Faith,' he said. 'Let's find Aunt Elinor.'

But Caroline, suddenly, was a barrier planted before us, refusing even to draw her skirts aside.

'You'll go nowhere, until I've got to the bottom of this.'

'Caroline – why the devil must you always interfere?'

'Don't use foul language to me, Nicholas Barforth.'

'You've heard worse than that – and from your precious father, too.'

'You'll leave my father out of this. He's had more than enough to bear from you. And as for you, Faith Aycliffe –'

'That's enough, Caroline!' Nicholas told her, meaning it; but, placing myself between them – having enough experience of their tempers to know that some form of distraction was required – I said sharply, 'What about me, Caroline?'

'Yes, indeed – what about you? I thought I knew you, Faith, but this is the second time you have been caught alone with my brother. Well, the first time I was ready enough to believe your story, but I'm not sure what to think now –'

And swiftly, before Nicholas could answer for me – knowing that once battle commenced between them I would be unable to make myself heard – I said coolly, 'Well then, Caroline, you may think exactly what you please, for if you can do no better than draw these foolish conclusions then you are as great a goose as my sister Celia.'

'How dare you speak to me like that?' she asked, quite stunned, really wanting to know, and since it was important to me that Nicholas should realize I could defend myself, that I was no simpering, schoolroom miss only too happy to be compromised, I was ready enough to explain.

445

'There's no daring about it, Caroline. You are being quite stupid, and I see no reason why I shouldn't tell you so.'

'Then I'll give you a reason. You are a guest in my father's house, where certain standards are always maintained, and you have behaved shockingly.'

'I have done no such thing, and you know very well I have not. Most likely it is Julian Flood who has done something shocking, by the look of you, for why else are you here, dashing up the back stairs – which happens to be the quickest way to your bedroom. And I won't be the scapegoat for it, Caroline, so you'd best go to nanny and have a good cry.'

There was, of course, the possibility that she would hit me, that Nicholas would roughly intervene, that nanny herself would appear and go running for Uncle Joel, who would then thrash Nicholas, a scene I had witnessed more than once while we were growing up. But realizing, even in her outrage, that the repercussions would be different now – that she was, in fact, quite fond of me and knew I was fond of her – she unclenched her reckless Barforth fist and contented herself with the lesser violence of hissing at me, 'I never thought this of you, Faith. I never thought you'd turn on me. Well, it's envy, I suppose – just envy – and I should be accustomed to that.'

'My word!' Nicholas said, when she had pushed me aside and mounted the stairs, one imperious step at a time, hoping I had not noticed the tears in her eyes. 'Who's the lion now?'

'Yes – but I suppose I had better go after her and say I am sorry – which indeed I am, since I think she is very sorry herself. What on earth can Julian Flood have done to her?'

'Nothing much. Tried to kiss her, I expect, and if she don't like it then she should stop thinking about the manor, since one thing goes with the other. Leave her to it. She'll come looking for you tomorrow to apologize and tell you all about it. But come, Faith – quickly now – for we have been away long enough.'

Taking my hand he hustled me to the end of the passageway and out through a little side-door I had forgotten about, not into the deep midnight I had expected, but a clear, rose-tinted, daybreak.

'Oh, Nicholas – look. I have never stayed up all night before.'

'No, I suppose you have not. Listen, we cannot go in together now. You must go round the side of the house and through the garden-door to the back parlour, and then go through into the hall. Do you remember the way?'

'Oh yes. But what a pity to go in at all.'

'Faith,' he said, 'don't you know the fix you could be in?'

But he was laughing, anxious and amused at the same time, a Barforth who did not wish to compromise me because he did not wish to be compromised himself, but who, with his share of inherited recklessness, of lusty Barforth appetite, was unwilling to miss an opportunity, so that naturally and easily he bent his head and brushed his mouth lightly against the corner of mine; a half-kiss which would have been acceptable

446

between cousins under the mistletoe at Christmastime, no more than that now, perhaps to him; but the most important thing, I believed, so far – the most thrilling – in my life.

'Run,' he said, and I ran, giddy and glowing, through the garden-door, not caring if even Aunt Hannah should be there, since Nicholas had kissed me. The back parlour was empty, the crowd thinning in the hall, music still playing, servants still hurrying to and fro, but an air of impending departure, of cloaks and carriages, of battles already won or lost. Surely I had been missed? Surely there would be the ugliness of questions and recriminations, a dreadful poking and prying into the crystal-clear enchantment I was still feeling, that I believed I would feel forever? But, reaching the ballroom door in a state of considerable alarm, I saw, as often proves the case, that everyone had found their own affairs more interesting than mine. My mother was still lounging in her chair, murmuring wicked replies to whatever Mr Oldroyd, on the chair behind, was whispering over her shoulder; my forgotten, abandoned sister Prudence was sitting patiently beside Aunt Hannah; while a chair or two away from them, Jonas – desperate, hard-pressed, offended Jonas – was most surprisingly deep in conversation with Celia.

6

Aunt Hannah, it seemed, was not so entirely in her stepson's confidence as she imagined, for when he proposed to my sister Celia the following week, during the course of an Assembly Rooms charity ball, she was quite taken aback, and to begin with not greatly pleased.

'Jonas – what *do* you mean?' she said to him when he and Celia approached her hand in hand at the close of the dance. And since she could not believe Jonas capable of impropriety, she turned her formidable Barforth eye on Celia – recognizing a scheming young hussy when she saw one – and ordered. 'You had best go to your mother, young lady, and inform her that I shall have a word to say on your account.'

We took Celia home in a state almost of collapse, weeping in a corner of the carriage and complaining most bitterly that the whole world was against her, that neither Prudence nor Faith would have been treated in this fashion, that she had done nothing wrong.

But the next morning, when Jonas had made it clear that Prudence would not have him, and stressed, no doubt, what Mr Corey-Manning's retirement could mean to them both, my aunt appeared very early in Blenheim Lane to announce herself highly delighted, and to set Celia's mind at ease.

She was prepared within the privacy of the family circle to admit – although not in Celia's hearing – that Jonas's attentions to one sister and his subsequent proposal to another might be thought rather bold, but then, it was well known that young people were impulsive, apt to be carried away by their tender feelings, and so far as the outside world was concerned Jonas – clever, crafty Jonas – had not committed himself to Prudence, and there could be no question that she had been jilted or that Celia was second-best.

It had, of course, been somewhat headstrong of Jonas to approach Celia direct, without first requesting the opinion of her guardians, but, once again, the natural ardours of youth must be held to blame, and before calling on us she had gone first to Tarn Edge and spoken to Uncle Joel – whose consent, by the terms of my father's will, would be necessary – and had made all smooth with him. His niece might be married, he had declared, whenever she pleased, and there seemed little doubt that, in his desire to see her well settled, his assistance to Jonas in a certain matter of business would not be denied.

Aunt Hannah in fact was happy, for now, with the solid capital of Celia's dowry behind him, Jonas had set his foot on the first golden rung of the ladder she had long ago designed on his behalf. Mr Corey-Manning's business would soon be his. He would be a householder, a man of substance and authority, while she, relieved of the anxiety of his expenses, could devote herself entirely to her civic campaign. Jonas himself, one supposed, and for the same reasons, was happy too. Celia, having received her first and presumably her last proposal at the tender age of fifteen – before either of her elder, more highly regarded sisters – could hardly contain her bliss. But when Aunt Hannah had gone to announce her news elsewhere, and Celia, exhausted by rapture, had retired upstairs with Miss Mayfield to discuss her trousseau, Prudence, who had been ominously silent all morning, planted herself firmly in front of my mother, and said, 'You cannot permit this, mamma.'

'My dear, what an odd notion! Why on earth should I wish to prevent it?'

'You know very well why, mamma, for they are totally unsuited. She is not yet sixteen and she is not clever. She has no idea of the consequences –'

My mother smiled. 'Oh, cleverer than you think, my dear, surely – since she knows exactly what she wants in life, as you do not. And as for the consequences, if one gave too much thought to consequences I doubt if one would do anything at all.'

I saw Prudence flex her hands slightly, a movement as nervous yet as fastidious as a cat, expressing her utter dislike of artifice, her rejection of all those – my mother among them – who lived by it.

'Quite so, mamma. But in fact she is being manipulated to suit the interests of others, who are not greatly concerned as to what Celia's own interests might be. And if you do not choose to understand that, then really, mamma – I shall have no alternative but to go and see Uncle Joel.'

'My word!' my mother said, her face dimpling and twinkling with smiles. 'How brave you are! Would you really go to my brother and demand his attention? Why yes, I believe you would, for truly you are so much like your half-brother, of whom we were never allowed to speak. Dear Crispin, so prickly and difficult, and such a great romantic, just as you are, dear – he had such wide, shining ideals. I daresay I am not the only woman in Cullingford who sometimes wonders what has become of him. But never mind that – You would go to your uncle, would you, Prudence? And what would you tell him? That Jonas Agbrigg wishes to marry your sister for her money? He is perfectly well aware of that, dearest. Money is a perfectly acceptable reason for a young man to marry. In fact, when Jonas approached your uncle some weeks ago about this business of Mr Corey-Manning, your uncle himself suggested that the quickest way out of the dilemma would be to find a suitable wife. My brother's generosity is realistic rather than philanthropic, and, although he has great faith in Jonas' ability, he was unwilling to elevate him to a position he could not maintain. His marriage to Celia will provide him with the means to maintain it and will provide her with the wedding-ring which, you cannot deny, is the one thing she desires. My dear, I am not forcing her to the altar. You may think me insensitive, but I can assure you I would never do such a thing. She wants to marry him. You tell me I cannot permit it, but even if you could prevail upon me, and Uncle Joel, and Aunt Hannah, to cancel, then Celia herself would thwart you. I believe you will find, when you are calm enough to talk to her, that she has fallen in love. Oh yes, my dear, and why not? In a few months' time she will be the mistress of her own home, with her own servants to do her bidding and her own horses to be got out whenever it pleases her to drive into town, while you and Faith remain here with me. She will have her own calling cards to deliver, with her own name writ large for everyone to see, while you and Faith will have to make do with your names printed, very small, under mine. And she can do no less than fall in love with the man who has made such wonders possible.'

'I *will* talk to her, mother,' Prudence said, her chin at a mutinous angle. 'I *will* point out to her the sheer folly of it all, the incompatibility of their natures and what it could lead to – and then at least one of us will have made an attempt to do right by her.'

'As you wish, dear,' my mother murmured very sweetly. 'But I cannot advise it. It will merely convince her you wanted Jonas for yourself – which is something she will be well pleased to believe – and, since he did not actually propose to you, did not in fact give you the opportunity of refusing him, she may feel quite justified in saying so.'

We went upstairs together, Prudence and I, hesitating at Celia's door.

'It's my fault, of course,' Prudence said, straight of back, straight of soul. 'If I had done as I ought and allowed him to propose to me, instead of scuttling upstairs in a panic, then he could hardly have gone from me to her a week later. There would have been at least a decent interval, time for her to think. Well, I have never shirked anything before, and I promise you I will never do so again.'

'It was not like you to run away, Prue.'

'No. And if I had seen any possibility of an honest exchange of views between us I would not have done so. If he could have brought himself to say to me "I need your money, Prudence. And in exchange for it I will make you independent of your mother, who irritates you, and of my

449

mother, whose interference you cannot tolerate. Marry me, and I will be rich and you will be free to lead the life of an adult female, not a grown-up child at home" – if he had said that, then I would still have refused him, since there is much in his nature I cannot like, but I would have respected him. I would have given an honest answer to an honest question. But no – I knew he would feel obliged to offend my intelligence by talking of his tender feelings, as he has clearly done to Celia, and that I would have been forced to play out the sickly charade by murmuring something about being honoured by his attentions. I could not do it. And mother, for once, is quite right. Anything I might say to Celia would be instantly misconstrued as jealousy.'

'Mother is often right, Prudence, if one listens carefully. Say nothing. We always knew Celia would take the first man who asked her, and Jonas is not so ... so very much worse than anyone else, is he?'

'Worse? No, I do not think of him as bad. In fact, if Aunt Hannah had not got her hands on him so early and filled him so full of her social climbing nonsense, then he might have been a great deal better. He is very clever, and perhaps he is rather cold by nature, but I think it is Aunt Hannah who has made him so resentful. Whereas Celia – oh heavens, Faith! – Celia is such a goose.'

There was in fact very little amiss with my sister Celia that a few more years of residence in the world would not have mended. She was, quite simply, too young – for which the cure was obvious – too apt to feel herself slighted and to draw attention to herself by falling unwell, natural, perhaps, in a younger child too often excluded from the pastimes and confidences of her sisters. But when I went in to see her that morning, as my mother had said, she had already passed from the smug contemplation of herself as a bride – the very first of her generation to marry – to a state of blissful if self-manufactured love which was undoubtedly giving her immense satisfaction.

'I know he paid attention to Prue,' she told me with genuine concern, since, in the overflow of her own heart, she had no desire to wound others. 'But he explained all that to me. He considers Prue to be an admirable girl, which indeed she is, and when Aunt Hannah suggested she would make him an excellent wife, he was bound to agree. But gradually, during his visits, he found himself drawn quite against his will to me, not realizing the implications until it was too late – and I will confess, Faith, that I had begun to suspect it, for I told you, on the night of Caroline's dance, which way I thought the wind was blowing. Well, I found myself thinking about him too, far more than I should have done, and he was in a positive quandary in case he had committed himself too far with Prudence. Only think of it, he was worrying about upsetting Prudence all the time I was worrying about Prudence upsetting him, which seems so foolish and so sweet now, the way things have turned out. Of course, he didn't mean to propose to me last night. He'd made up his mind that he was honour bound to withdraw a little – cool off, you know, with Prudence, before he could decently approach me. And naturally he thought I was too young and would take fright, and he felt he should be very careful so as not to risk losing me. My word – how sweet! But then, last night, we danced and talked – you know how it is – and is just happened. He was so correct and polite, and then, when I had accepted him, so masterful. I was to leave everything to him – Aunt Hannah and Uncle Joel and everything. Prudence will have chances to spare, you know she will. There is Freddy Hobhouse, who thinks the world of her – and I have seen Jacob Mandelbaum looking at you.'

Clever Jonas, I thought, cold, clever Jonas. There is the woman a man knows would be good for him, he had told me, the woman he would like to have, and the woman he can get. And, his needs being too pressing to risk a refusal from the first, he had thought better of the second and had settled cold-bloodedly for Celia, who in her race to reach the altar would have accepted very nearly anyone. Yet had I really been the one he would have liked? And if so, if I had managed without even noticing it to captivate this man who had certainly not wished to be captivated, whose satisfactions, I believed, came from the manipulation of legal documents and the amassing, in any way he could contrive, of money, then could I not do the same with Nicholas? But, in the bright light of Celia's betrothal morning, I concluded that no more than a fleeting physical impulse, such, I well knew, as a man might feel for a pert housemaid, had inclined Jonas to me, an impulse he had at once stifled and forgotten, returning with relief to his natural habitat of self-interest and ambition, where Celia would suit his purposes just as well.

'I hope you will be very happy,' I told her.

'Oh – assuredly,' she replied, and for the rest of the summer we had nothing to do – were allowed nothing to do – but busy ourselves with Celia's trousseau, Celia's linen and china, Celia's carpets and curtains and her wedding-guests, an occupation frequently tedious but useful sometimes when I needed to stop myself from wondering why these past weeks I had seen so little of Nicholas.

'I shall ask cousin Caroline to be a bridesmaid, of course,' Celia announced grandly, 'and I can hardly avoid cousin Lydia from Sheffield, who used to be my best friend. And then there are the four Hobhouse girls, and my own two sisters, which makes eight in all – and, since I would not like Arabella Rawnsley and Rebecca Mandelbaum to feel left out, I had best ask them too. And I have always been quite fond of Amy Battershaw. What do you think? Although it means asking someone else to make up a pair. I could have Rebecca's sister Rachel, who is rather small, or Lydia Rawnsley – although, since she must be fast approaching twenty-three, perhaps it would not be kind.'

And with that marvellous procession forming in her mind's eye, all these pretty, well-dowered young ladies, the great Caroline Barforth among them, following little Celia Aycliffe down the aisle, she laughed out loud, flushed and almost vivacious in her delight.

'They never expected me to be the first,' she said. 'None of you did. But there it is. Oh, do be careful how you cut out that muslin, Faith, for I shall want at least two dozen petticoats from it, and I have seen a wine-red velvet at Miss Constantine's in Millergate – no, Faith, not for an

451

evening gown. Can you think of nothing but dress? – for curtains. And with cushion covers and a mantel-valance to match I think it would be an improvement in any drawing-room. Please do not look so astonished at me, Faith. You may continue to amuse yourself with ribbons and frills and lace shawls for a while yet, but I am now obliged to turn my mind to more serious issues.'

'Oh yes,' Prudence replied tartly 'Serious issues indeed – is it to be wax flowers or stuffed birds under glass on the hall table? My word, how are you ever to decide?'

But Celia, having so easily achieved the summit of her dreams, was good nature itself, treating us already with the tolerance of an adult towards a pair of quarrelsome children, an attitude she felt quite entitled to adopt, since her marriage to Jonas, arranged for October, when she would be just sixteen, would make her socially older than Prudence and myself, a woman who 'knew', while we remained girls who merely thought we did.

'I cannot bear it,' Prudence told me more than once. 'If she speaks to me in that superior manner just once again I shall box her ears. She is living in a dream. Can you make no attempt to bring her back to reality?'

And, of course, I could not; for Celia, beyond all warnings, continued to float through her betrothal days on a blissful cloud composed mainly, it seemed, of carpet samples and heavy flock wallpapers, mahogany sideboards and red plush armchairs. Jonas – fully occupied by his negotiations with Mr Corey-Manning – appearing content to leave all such arrangements to her.

'After all, she is paying for them,' Prudence snorted as we sat together at our eternal sewing.

'Yes, but she is having such a good time, Prue – surely you can see that? And they may not do too badly together. He will have his business and she will have her furniture. It may suffice.'

'He will have his business, certainly, and he will have ours as well, if he sees half a chance of it.'

'Prudence, whatever do you mean?'

'Only this,' she said, plunging her needle with apparently lethal intent into a fold of fragile spotted gauze. 'He is a man and we are four women alone. At the moment he is no more to us than the stepson of our aunt, whose opinions or demands may count for little. But when he marries Celia he becomes our brother. And if you have not thought of that, then I am quite sure *he* has thought of it, and Aunt Hannah too. Yes, at the moment there is Uncle Joel; but he will not live forever, and supposing I do not marry, or you do not, or that we are widowed? What happens to spinsters and widows, Faith? They remain at home, or they return there, under the guidance of their closest male relative. And in return for the protection of that male relative they devote themselves and their incomes to his best interests – or a way is found to compel them to do so. Women need a man to speak for them in legal matters and in all other matters of greater importance than a tea-party – I am well aware of that – and if I remain single I cannot imagine Jonas allowing me to take my money and live alone, not without a fight. He is a lawyer, remember, and he will know best how to maintain his authority. After all, why should he be content with one dowry, if there is the slightest chance of helping himself to two or three? And the only way I can avoid it is to get married myself.'

Caroline, having completely disregarded our quarrel, was still a regular visitor in Blenheim Lane, still, it appeared, on negotiating terms with Julian Flood, although no announcement had yet been made.

'My word, Celia,' she announced, 'what a regular beehive – I never realized it took such a quantity of muslin and taffeta to be married. And by the way, if it is to be October, my love, then I fear you can't count on me, for I shall be in Paris by then – which is rather a pity – but you'll not miss one bridesmaid, surely, from among so many. The Battershaws are taking me, and I understand the Floods are to be there for part of the time, which will be very pleasant, except that, really, one can see the Floods at home any day of the week, and one may feel inclined – in a strange place – to make the acquaintance of a few strangers. One hardly takes the trouble to go abroad for a family party. Well, Celia, I do wish you every happiness. When I get back from France you'll be Mrs Jonas Agbrigg of – where is it you're going to live? – Albert Place? My goodness – Mrs Agbrigg of Albert Place! It doesn't sound a bit like you.'

'The date could be put back until Miss Caroline comes home,' suggested Jonas's father, the taciturn, hardworking Mr Ira Agbrigg, who, having made a marriage of convenience himself, was apparently not too pleased to see his only son do likewise. 'The lass is young enough, and I reckon my lad can bide his time.'

But Mr Corey-Manning, anxious to hand over his offices in Croppers Court and his goodwill in Cullingford as a whole, and remove himself to the healthier, quieter air of Bridlington, was in a most decided hurry, quick to insinuate that he had had other offers which he could always reconsider. Aunt Hannah, with other schemes afoot, saw no reason for delay. The very house Celia declared she had always dreamed of was miraculously offered for sale. And when my mother announced that she, too, would prefer 'sooner' rather than 'later', October it was certainly to be.

'The house is in excellent condition,' my mother insisted. 'All they need do is select their furnishings and have them carried inside, and as for the linen and the trousseau, it need not be done entirely at home. It is altogether permissible and fashionable, nowadays, to *purchase* such things ready made, and we have these marvellous trains, do we not, to fetch them to us?'

Having no more taste for wedding-fever, it seemed, than Prudence, my mother at once obtained the services of upholsterer, cabinet-maker, plasterer – trades I had not realized she knew existed – went herself to Leeds and Bradford and over the Pennines to Manchester for the items our local shopkeepers could not supply, dispatched a team of scrubbing-women to the newly acquired, four-square house in Albert Place, engaged a cook, a parlourmaid, a pair of Aunt Hannah's charity-girls to do the 'rough', an outside man, who was at once kept busy fetching Celia's parcels from every train. And I knew my mother well enough to realize that all this was being done to suit neither Celia, Jonas, nor Aunt Hannah, but herself.

'You did not know I possessed such energy, did you?' she told me, coming into my room a fortnight or so before the wedding. 'But, since Celia so greatly desires to be married, I may as well give her a little push in her chosen direction. And I will confess to you, Faith, that when I came back for Caroline's party I did not intend to stay even this long. No – no – I required merely to sort out my affairs with Uncle Joel, matters of finance which I make no effort to understand since my brother is so good as to understand them for me, and will not cheat me in any case. And now, my dear, with this wedding almost out of the way, I really do not feel up to another Cullingford winter.'

'So you will go abroad again, mamma?'

'Yes, dear, as I would have gone three months ago had it not been for Celia – although, as it turns out, this marriage relieves me of the obligation to have her suitably cared for while I am away. I have only Prudence and yourself to think of, and Prudence is well content to stay here with Miss Mayfield, who is quite terrified of her and will allow her to do just as she pleases. She will have a married sister, after all and a most efficient brother-in-law who may be applied to in case of need, so there is no impropriety in leaving her behind. You, dear Faith, are to come with me. Now – what do you think to that?'

I sat down carefully on the corner of my bed, thinking, quite simply, of Nicholas – Nicholas – unable to tell her that I could not bear to remove myself from the place where I might see him, although lately I had seen him so seldom, and go to a place where there was no hope of seeing him at all.

'It would be very – pleasant, mamma, except that, perhaps – I think I should stay with Prudence.'

'Now why should you think that?' she said, her smile twinkling across the room to me. 'I am sure Prudence has no particular need of you. Whereas I, my dear, have encountered certain annoyances in travelling alone. I have arranged for us to set off at once after the wedding – you see how masterful I can be when I set my mind to it – for if I stay to see them back from honeymoon I may be obliged to delay even longer for the birth of my first grandchild. And, in any case, dearest, apart from the fact that travel broadens the mind – and heaven knows! a mind raised in Cullingford could not escape being narrow – it would be as well for you to be away from Nicholas Barforth.'

I felt, not only the colour flooding my cheeks and then leaving them – leaving me very cold – but far more than that, a sense, I think, of enormous protest, followed first by the fear of loss, a desperate urge to prevent it, and then the certainty that he was lost already, a terrible feeling, so that I could only mutter, 'Mamma – if you imagine –'

'Oh,' she said, still smiling, 'I do not imagine – I do much more than that. I may not be clever, Faith, like your father and Prudence, nor am I a domestic mouse like Celia, but what I have always been able to do, quite

454

unerringly, is to see exactly what is going on between a man and a woman. It is my one talent. Dearest, I am not being unkind, you know, just sensible. I would be delighted to see you married to Nicholas Barforth. It would be altogether splendid, but there is so much against it – not least the sorry fact that you are ready for marriage and he is not. My dear, only poor men and old men have need of wives. Young men who happen also to be rich can afford to marry late, or indiscreetly, or not at all, but usually they wait and enjoy their freedom until middle age inclines them to sobriety. When they become forty or fifty they may begin to think of the advisability of having sons to assist them in their businesses and to inherit their money – and they require young girls for that. When Nicholas has sown his oats – of which, my dear, he has an ample store, for he is my brother's son, and Joel was not always so steady – it would be too late, my love, for you. I am sorry to put it to you so bluntly, but it is the way of the world, my poor Faith, and I cannot alter it. Blaize is the same, and Jonas, even, would be like them if he could, for why should a man rush to limit himself in marriage when its pleasures are so readily available to him without responsibility – without encumbrance? A spinster is a sorry sight, my dear, but a bachelor who has his youth and looks and money to spend – that is another story. You need marriage, Faith. It is the one career open to you and if you do not succeed in that, then your whole life will be accounted a failure. If Nicholas stays single all his days he may still be acknowledged a dashing fellow. And, in any case, I have good reason to believe he is not ready, and that he knows he is not ready to settle down. The world is wide for him; it is very narrow for you; and you may console yourself, when you are weeping for him tonight, that he would not voluntarily have kept his distance these last few months had he not felt a certain measure of attraction. Had he seen you merely as a pleasant, friendly girl – well – he would have continued to see you, would he not, and dance with you, and take you in to supper, and neither Aunt Verity nor I would have troubled to notice it. But we *have* noticed it, and he, my love, has chosen – for once in his life – to be sensible. So must you.'

'Yes, mamma.'

'Excellent. And you need not be so cast down, for you will find much in France and Italy to distract you. We do not know each other very well, Faith dear, for I will confess that your father had but a poor opinion of me and obliged me to keep my distance from his children – fearing I would muddle your heads with my foolish notions. But I am really quite agreeable, you know, and will try to be a good companion. It is settled then? Of course it is. My goodness – will that confounded wedding-day never come?'

The Barforths gave Celia a magnificent Coalport dinner service; my mother gave furniture and carpets; Aunt Hannah, who could not be outdone on these occasions, gave the drawing-room sofa and chairs; Mr Fielding, the occupant of my father's seat at Westminster, gave a silver salver for the placing of calling-cards; everyone else presented whatever seemed suitable. And, as Celia entered the parish church that brisk

October morning on Uncle Joel's arm, I would not have believed she could ever look so beautiful.

She had always been a pretty girl, but somehow quite unremarkable, a face that did not linger in the memory, often ailing, often, in her own opinion, overlooked; but as she drifted down the aisle to her cool, pale Jonas, pure radiance transformed her, its aura lending her so delicate a loveliness that I could well understand why weddings were occasions for tears. Celia, in fact, was in a state of complete fulfilment, that rare feeling of total self-content where she believed everything she could ever want in life was to be hers. Jonas seemed well satisfied. My mother wept most gracefully throughout the service, and later, at the reception, became so misty with tears that it took several pairs of manly – if elderly – arms to console her. The bridesmaids were much admired, although, in the blue organdie of Celia's choosing, I did not feel my best and was not sorry that Nicholas, having been dispatched to London on his father's business, could not attend.

There was champagne and cake and cordiality, white horses to drive the bridal pair to the station, Celia still radiant – still beautiful – in her going-away dress of powder-blue.

'Well – God bless you, then!' Prudence said, more moved than she'd expected.

'Kiss your new brother, girls,' Aunt Hannah bade us, and, when it was done and we had waved them away, my mother could not return fast enough to Blenheim Lane to pack her own boxes and mine, her eyes every bit as bright and excited as Celia's.

'You are going to have so much fun, Faith darling,' she told me, and, since I was Morgan Aycliffe's daughter, trained to believe that even when one's heart was aching and one's hopes in ashes, one should have the good manners not to embarrass others by letting it show, I answered, 'Yes, mamma.'

And so, the next morning, we were separated for the first time, the Aycliffe girls who had spent their quiet lives identically together going now their separate ways, Celia most incredibly to Scarborough with Jonas, Prudence to Blenheim Lane and the chaperonage of Miss Mayfield, which was no chaperonage at all, myself, quite simply, away from Nicholas.

'Write to me, Prudence.'

'Yes, at least once a week. To promise more would be foolish. Please remember to reply.'

'I don't want to go.'

'No. But when the time comes I expect you won't want to come back either.'

I had made up my mind to be miserable, but I was still only seventeen, and even the train to London, which I wished to find uncomfortable and tedious, became less wearisome after a mile or so – and then the novelty of a hotel bedchamber, a restaurant, my mother's light chatter, no longer mother to daughter but woman to woman, first diverting, then almost exciting.

'We need clothes, dear,' she said, 'in Paris.' And so we had clothes, purchased from a tiny, irritable creature with the face of a beribboned terrier who caused us to wait his good pleasure, no humble seamstress this, but a man of authority who gave to the designing of women's clothes the same dedication and self-importance with which other men built bridges.

'He will not dress you unless he likes you,' my mother murmured, surprisingly nervous. 'And you may not say what you would like. He will tell you what you must have. Be careful, my dear, for when I was last here I saw him turn the wife of an ambassador, and a countess, away.'

A far cry, then, from the dressmakers of Cullingford who would come scurrying to attend us in our own homes, only too eager to dress anybody in anything they had a mind. But when Monsieur Albertini had prowled around me for a tense moment, wreathing me in the smoke from his continual cigar, the entire salon – where even his assistants had the hauteur of great ladies – hushed with the anticipation of his verdict, he came to an abrupt halt, clapped his hands together and, declaring my green crêpe de Chine to be an abomination – 'London? Of course. What else one could expect?' – announced that if I came back in a day or two, and if his inspiration had matured by then, he would create a toilette for which I would shed tears of gratitude.

Yet the one thing I did find – and fairly soon – was that this prancing little ballerina was in fact as shrewd a man of business as any I had met in Cullingford, his taste – and his tyranny – veering always to the expensive, the rare, the unattainable which he – by his genius, his magic – would obtain for 'madame' at a price. And until he explained them to me, I had not fully understood the variety of my needs.

There were his peignoirs, delicate, foamy creations designed for the sipping of early morning tea, the opening of letters and invitations, to be worn in the luxurious, languid hours before one put on one's stays. There was his pelisse – on another plane entirely from the pelisses I had known, and which he advised me to consign to the fire – still a morning dress, but a little more substantial, more elaborate, in which one could receive one's callers. There was his elegant, superbly cut redingote for the afternoon, should madame decide to drive or stroll in the park, the lavishly flounced and embroidered round-dress, should she decide to remain, just as splendidly, at home. There was, most decidedly, his evening dress, its bodice cut low, moulded to bosom and waist, a rich satin which, he assured me, was the exact pale blonde colour of my hair. And then there were the 'little things', as he called them, lace-edged shawls from Cashmere, flowing soft-tinted and supple from shoulder to ankle, fans and reticules and pairs of gloves in their dozens, feather bonnets and frilled bonnets, a dashing military cap with gold tassels and bold plumage, ivory combs to put up my hair by night, tortoiseshell inlaid with mother of pearl by day.

'You will think me extravagant – and somewhat frivolous,' my mother said, surveying our purchases, her own far exceeding mine. 'And so I am. But this is *my* time, Faith – the only time in my life when I have been

457

allowed to do as I pleased, to think what I like rather than what is expected of me – and it may not last for long. Something will force me back to Blemheim Lane, sooner or later – Jonas will set up a caterwauling that I am running through my money and there will be none left for Celia, and Joel will curb my spending. Something will happen to restrain me and restore me to respectability, and, even if it should not, then eventually I shall grow old. So you will be a good-hearted girl, dear, and will not grudge me my special time.'

We remained in France until mid-December, moving south as the winter sharpened to a villa on the outskirts of Rome, marble floors leading one to the other in swirling patterns of blue and purple, walls bright-painted with scenes of a voluptuous grape-harvest, crumbling stone steps leading to a formal garden of clipped box-hedges, stone basins and water-bearing cupids, where a gentleman who had called to renew his acquaintance with my mother kissed the palm of my hand and my wrist and was never seen by me again. We went to Naples to greet the spring-time, then on to Monaco and back to Rome, where another gentleman, more appreciative of my mother's maturity, was waiting.

'Do I shock you?' she asked me. 'I suppose I do. I believe I shocked myself to begin with, but it is quite amazing how quickly one grows accustomed. I do not think I am entirely frivolous. It is just that I cannot nourish myself with ambition, like Aunt Hannah, and did not have the great good fortune to fall quite blissfully in love with my husband a dozen years after I had married him, like Aunt Verity. So I must do the best I can, dear, for as long as I can – surely?'

There were sudden departures in perilous coaches, the caprice of every butterfly moment, strange inns by the wayside – malarial, Aunt Hannah would have named them – beautiful houses placed freely, one supposed, at our disposal by my mother's last year's acquaintances. There were flowery hillsides at noon, with ourselves mounted on donkeys, and red wine and garlic-flavoured cheeses eaten carelessly on the sparse grass in view of a gold-speckled, slumbering sea. Perfumed rooms in the evening, candlelit frivolity, a rose-petal world where men with dark, supple faces – reminding me far more of Blaize than of Nicholas – whispered entertaining nonsense to my mother, and quite often to me.

'It is a very small place, Cullingford, is it not?' she often asked me, and I don't know how it was that I knew – or exactly when I knew – that the suave, eternally good-humoured Signor Marchetti, who had so willingly lent us his Roman villa, was her lover, except that, without witnessing the slightest physical contact between them, I knew it, the realization coming so gradually that when the truth finally dawned it did not even surprise me.

'Paris again,' she announced one morning, and at her restless, magical command there was an apartment built with its feet in the Seine, the soaring façade of Notre-Dame filling our windows, morning promenades shaded by frilled parasols and chestnut trees, a certain Monsieur Fauret escorting us most courteously to the opera, the ballet, to Versailles, offering us his carriage for our drives in the Bois de Boulogne, waiting most patiently as we made our purchases from the couturier, Monsieur Albertini, or from my mother's favourite perfumerie in the Rue Saint-Honoré. He was a slightly built, middle-aged man, this Monsieur Fauret, scrupulously correct at all times in my presence, making his formal bow over my mother's hand.

'Will you do me the honour of dining, madame – and mademoiselle?' But there were occasions when my mother, in her extravagant spangled black gauzes, would set out alone, returning late and oddly languorous, smiling and sighing over the flowers which would arrive the following day. And although she never spoke of love or passion or whatever name she had for it, I knew; and, forgetting such weighty matters as sin and the certain retribution I had been taught must follow, it intrigued me that a relationship between a man and a woman could be so light yet so obviously satisfying to them both.

Naturally, the rules she had chosen to live by – while her special time endured – could not apply to me. My own virtue must remain, not merely intact, but utterly beyond reproach. Yet my fast-growing knowledge of life as a reality, rather than a nursery-tale designed to frighten me into obedience, caused me to examine each one of my girlhood prohibitions, to sort out as best I could the sense from the nonsense, the necessary from the purely repressive, so that I became older, at seventeen, and then at eighteen, than I might otherwise have been. I acquired, with a deliberate effort, a little poise – more than would be thought proper in Cullingford. I applied myself to the art of conversation, the art of listening, the art of making the best of what Nature had given me. I applied myself to the art of forgetting Nicholas Barforth, of reducing him to the provincial young man who had charmed me in the days when I had been a provincial young lady. And I pretended to succeed.

I heard news, erratically, from Caroline, to whom Paris, with the Battershaws, had been something of a disappointment. And although she referred often enough to the Floods, either Julian had made no definite proposal or she, somewhat inexplicably, was managing to keep him at bay. She had spent Christmas Eve at Cullingford Manor, she told me – a sure indication of intent – but then, instead of the announcement I had been expecting, her letter had altered course, recounting that Blaize, as reluctant as ever to spend his time in the weaving sheds, had decided – and was attempting to convince his father – that his talents would be the best employed in selling Barforth cloth abroad.

'He means to wine and dine his way all over the world,' she wrote me, 'with snippets of cloth in his luggage, doing his selling in fancy hotels and restaurants instead of the Piece Hall and the Wool Exchange, like everybody else. Very pleasant for *him*, Nicholas says, although I believe father may be agreeable, for it is true that, unless we know what weight and what design of cloth will suit the tastes and climate of various parts of the world, we can hardly supply it. And Blaize, who can be very pleasant when he likes, will give a good impression of us abroad, which is something to be considered now that so many newcomers are pushing into the textile trade as fast as they can get themselves fixed up with looms.'

459

Strange preoccupations, I thought, in a future baronet's lady, and although she told me that Nicholas, accepting Blaize's challenge, had declared himself ready and able to handle any shipping orders his brother sent home, she omitted to mention if he had danced with Amy Battershaw or Rebecca Mandelbaum at the Assembly Rooms Ball, or if – a dread possibility with which I sometimes scourged myself – he had encountered someone new, whose mysterious allure might tempt him from his cherished bachelorhood.

From my sister Celia I received a fortnightly catalogue of domestic trivia, the devastating effect of sunlight on her dining-room curtains, the inefficiency of Mr Corey-Manning, whose affairs in Croppers Court had been left in such disorder that Jonas was obliged to spend most of his time putting them straight.

Prudence wrote to me dutifully, weekly, as she had promised, her elegant copperplate revealing not only her preoccupation with literature, liberty, and mathematics – her determination to acquire some real knowledge – but a concern my mother found amusing, amazing, for the foul condition of Cullingford's streets and the inadequacy of its water supply. She had made new acquaintances she told me, without describing their faces, giving me the impression that they were serious – I presumed elderly – people, who organised lectures at the Mechanics Institute on subjects designed to improve the minds and the prospects of the more responsible section of the working class; who raised money to re-equip Cullingford's inadequate infirmary, and spent their leisure hours discussing the desirability of cleaning up the Cullingford Canal, the foul vapours of which had been known to blacken silver, or of relieving the squalid overcrowding in Simon Street. And when Cullingford was at last granted its Charter, during my balmy Neapolitan springtime, with authority to elect a mayor, fourteen aldermen, and forty councillors – gentlemen who must be possessed of property valued at a minimum of a thousand pounds or rated at no less than thirty pounds per annum – Prudence filled many pages with her expectations.

Results, she felt, would be less than perfect, since election in many cases had been sought for prestige rather than a desire to be of service, and it seemed unfair to her that from a population of over seventy thousand only some five thousand persons had a property qualification high enough to enable them to vote at all. But the town council would do more, surely, than the old Lighting and Watching Commissioners had ever done – would have to do more, since the councillors had made such a fuss about getting the Charter in the first place – and she could think of no one better, she assured me, than Mayor Agbrigg to lead them.

'We have always seen him as a quiet man,' she wrote, 'the least regarded of all that family, where it was always Jonas's brilliance and Aunt Hannah's determination we were taught to admire. A gloomy man, with just cause to be gloomy, perhaps, since I am now sufficiently in his confidence to have been informed of the hardships and sorrows of his past. But a sound man, who has not taken office for his own glory, nor because his wife wishes her share of it, but because he intends to be useful. I like him.'

460

And, in the manner of Caroline, she forgot, or did not think it worth a mention, that Freddy Hobhouse had proposed to her and offered to wait indefinitely for a reply.

'Dear Hannah,' my mother had murmured that same morning, sentimental with Chianti and sunshine, 'what a great day for her – we shall have our concert hall now, with your father's name upon it, you may be very sure. I must write to her at once, and have something delivered – something quite splendid as a token of our congratulations – for she will need our help now, poor Hannah. I doubt if she can extract much more from Joel, and she will spend every penny her husband possesses to make sure his term of office is remembered, and to pave the way for Jonas to come after him. Goodness – if she knew what this lilac taffeta has just cost me.'

And it surprised us both, I think, for a moment or two, that Ira Agbrigg's first act as mayor was not the drumming-up of subscriptions for that famous concert hall, but an attempt to purchase with public money the privately owned and disastrously mismanaged Cullingford Waterworks Company, so that Simon Street – the putrid district where Prudence, it seemed, in the company of her serious-minded friends, had actually set foot – would no longer be forced to rely on a single stand-pipe, turned on half an hour a day, or the erratic services of a water-cart.

'Good heavens!' my mother said, wrinkling her nose. 'I do not think Hannah will take very kindly to a waterworks as a memorial. Could it be that Mr Agbrigg is not really so tame as we supposed? Ah well, we will go to Switzerland next, Faith – next week, in fact – for they have an abundance of water there. And you may tell dear Prudence that I cannot approve of her visits to Simon Street, nor in the least understand what she can find to do there. In fact I am quite shocked, and not altogether comfortable about yesterday's news that I am to be a grandmamma. No, I realize you were not aware of it, for Celia wrote to me in great secret, considering it improper for young ladies like yourself and Prudence to be informed. However, she describes herself as being in an "interesting condition", which I assume to mean "with child". And that, my dear, is bound to take us home again – in six months or so – since both Celia and our Lady Mayoress will expect me to be in attendance at the great event. Ah well, Monsieur Fauret is going to Martinique in any case. Switzerland, then, and Paris to follow. And I think we had best start saying to ourselves, over and over, how pleasant it will be to see Cullingford again.'

7

We were away just over a year, journeying north again through a raw November, a pall of thick yellow fog obscuring the platform at Leeds, where we changed trains for Cullingford, so that my mother murmured, again and again, 'Heavens, how dark it is! One forgets, every time, how dark – how very meagre.' And, since she had come home merely to await

461

the birth of her grandchild and to review her finances with Uncle Joel, it was as well she could not know that events in Europe would soon prevent her from setting off again.

We were standing all unawares on the threshold of a revolutionary year, when the people of France would rise up once again and replace their ageing king, Louis Philippe, with a new republic, releasing a spark of disobedience which would consume with stunning rapidity the autocratic governments of Italy, Germany, Bavaria, Hungary; a vast earthquake of revolt against poverty and oppression, against the yoke of the Habsburg Empire, the yoke of the landlord and the proprietor, against the old tyranny of the aristocrat and the new tyranny of the industrialist. It was a year which sent hundreds of that desperate class we called the 'labouring poor' to sacrifice themselves in the street-fighting in Milan, in Berlin, in Vienna when the Habsburgs marched in to take it back again; to tear up the paving stones of my mother's beloved Paris, and be slaughtered at their barricades, searching, one supposed, for the liberty and equality which all previous revolutions had promised and then managed somehow to deny. It was a year when our own revolutionaries, the Chartists, would attempt to march on Westminster, bearing a petition of five million signatures, and as many men as they could muster, demanding a vote for every adult male in Britain, and that old revolutionary dream, a secret ballot, to shield him from the persuasion of landlord and millmaster.

Yet we knew nothing of that, standing chilled and travel-weary in the swirling fog of a Leeds November – luckily, perhaps, since my mother, who had grown quieter, sadder with every Northern mile, may well have turned tail and rushed back at once, while the ports were still open, and risked herself at the barricades.

'How dark!' she said again, as Cullingford loomed into sight. 'Midnight at four in the afternoon. Have I really spent my life here?'

And even I – for whom this was a true homecoming, the rest already little more than a summer dream – was briefly saddened by the rain-soaked, wind-raked hills, the chimney-stacks belching their malodorous welcome on the sky-line; by the soot-blackened mass of Cullingford itself as we stepped out of the station, a town not planned for beauty, not planned at all, but thrown down anyhow to suit the convenience of millmasters, a factory here, a nettle-bed of workers' cottages there, even the parish church – which no longer seemed so noble to my travelled eyes – obscured now by the hastily constructed demands of industry.

'The people –' my mother moaned. 'How sad they are!' And so they seemed, bowed heads shawl-wrapped and cowering against the cold, perpetually hurrying, since nothing in these cobbled, narrow streets offered an inducement to linger; closed carriages looming mud-spattered out of the fog, a sudden cough, muffled by the thick air and distance, and then another, a grey drizzle, a factory hooter somewhere mournfully marking time.

'I had forgotten how they cough,' my mother said, shivering. 'I suppose it is the smoke, and those insanitary dwellinghouses your sister speaks of.' And pressing her handkerchief to her face, she walked quickly across the station yard to where our coachman was waiting.

'Well then, Thompson. We're home again.'

'Aye, ma'am,' he replied. 'Dratted train was late.' And we set off for Blenheim Lane.

Prudence was in the hallway to greet us, crisp and neat in a gown that had all her usual quiet elegance, her hair a shade or two darker than I remembered, parted in the middle, drawn smoothly over her ears into a low chignon that gave her narrow face a becoming air of maturity. And although I loved her and had longed to see her again, there was a moment almost of shyness when I knew we had not really missed each other.

For the past year, apart from the ineffectual fluttering of Miss Mayfield, she had been her own mistress, had made her own arrangements, her own acquaintances, expressed her own opinions regardless of effect or consequences, come and gone to suit no one but herself, certainly not her whimsical, capricious mother. But now we must both be 'young ladies at home', and as the house I still thought of as my father's reached out to claim me – so dim and cool, so very still – I could not tell how long it would be before we found each other again.

'My word, you are very smart,' she said, coming to assist with the unpacking of my boxes. But my tales of Monsieur Albertini, the couturier, of Roman gardens and flirtations under Parisian chestnut trees did not interest her, whilst her references to Mayor Agbrigg's plans for drainage and sewage were an astonishment to me.

'And what has become of Aunt Hannah's concert hall, then?'

'Oh, she will have it, I suppose. But Mayor Agbrigg will not be remembered for that. He has sense enough to know that if Aunt Hannah is allowed to busy herself about the concert hall she will not interfere with his own projects. And his projects are admirable, Faith – truly. He will have a great fight on his hands to buy the Waterworks, for the owners do not at all wish to relinquish it. But he will succeed. It is useless, you know, to preach about "cleanliness being next to godliness" to people who are without sufficient water for drinking and cooking, let alone washing. If you live in a street where the stand-pipe is only turned on once a day and you have but one bucket capable of holding water – and you have a family of eight or ten children in your two-roomed cottage – you do not use that water for scrubbing your floors. You boil your potatoes in it, no matter how discoloured it may be, or what nameless particles of filth you find floating in it, and then you drink the potato water. Presumably you make tea with any drops that are left, and then wait – all eight or ten of you thoroughly unwashed – until tomorrow, when the tap is turned on again. It is water they need, Faith, not a sermon – and not a concert hall either. And I am convinced Mayor Agbrigg can provide it.'

'Goodness, such fervour! I do hope so. And what of Celia, and our dear brother Jonas?'

She made a slight movement of her shoulders, a half-shrug of impatience and a little pity. 'I rarely see them. He works. She polishes her silver teapot. I have been too occupied to spend much time with her.'

'Occupied with what, Prudence?'

'Well, I have made an acquaintance or two, you know. I have not been dull. In fact I have been quite daring, for I have even had some correspondence with Mr Crispin Aycliffe, our brother.'

'Prudence, you have not? My word, how very interesting!' And much impressed, since this was a name we had been forbidden to mention, I saw down on my bed, the contents of my boxes scattered everywhere, the distance between us melting away.

'Yes – I discovered that an acquaintance of mine is acquainted with him too – a most odd coincidence – and so I obtained his address and wrote him a line or two about father's death and the arrangements which had been made, since I suppose no one else had troubled to inform him.'

'You mean you offered him a share of your porcelain?'

'Well,' she said, flushing slightly. 'So I did. And I would have made sure he got it, too, whatever the Barforths and the Agbriggs may have had to say – since it is simply sitting there behind those glass cases doing nothing. And he may have been in need. However, he replied most courteously, thanking me but declining, and I have exchanged half a dozen letters with him since then. He has been living abroad but is now in London, married, respectable I suppose except that he is a Chartist.'

'Oh surely, Prue,' I said, fascinated, quite pleasantly horrified, 'he cannot be that? Chartists are revolutionaries and criminals, are they not?'

'Are they? They are demanding one man one vote, which may seem criminal to those who have the vote already. Hardly to those who do not.'

'Well, I have never thought much about it. But who is this new acquaintance then? Is he a Chartist too?'

'Possibly. It is a Dr Ashburn, who comes originally from Cheshire, although he has travelled a great deal and has not been long in Cullingford. He gave a most memorable series of lectures last winter, to which Mayor Agbrigg escorted me, mainly on social issues – starvation and alcoholism and infant mortality, that sort of thing, of which he has ample experience, since he has a great many patients in Simon Street.'

'Good heavens! I thought no one in Simon Street could afford a doctor.'

'They cannot – or very few – and so it is fortunate for Giles that he has private means.'

'Oh yes – Giles, is it? I see.'

'I think you do not.'

'Do I not? Well then, Prue, what is he like, this Giles? Is he seventy-two, and bald, and fat as a bacon-pig?'

She smiled, a trifle unwillingly to begin with, but then with a decided glint of amusement in her eyes. 'No. I think he may be thirty, or not much above it, and he is lean rather than fat. And yes, Faith – since you are clearly wondering – I do see him fairly often. But then, I see Freddy Hobhouse even more, and like him better than I used to, since he has stopped trying so hard to marry me. And I see a number of other gentlemen quite regularly besides – none of whom are seventy-two and bald – including Blaize Barforth, which may surprise you.' And, in my relief that she had not been seeing Nicholas, I said, without meaning to be unkind. 'So it does. I cannot imagine what Blaize may find to amuse him in public health – and sewage.'

But my composed, apparently very contented sister, was not in the least offended.

'Oh, he does not care a scrap about such things. I believe it merely amuses him to observe a young lady who does – since we are quite a rarity. And, when he chooses, Blaize can be very useful. He will work wonders when it suits him – as he did about the new equipment Giles wanted for the infirmary – although he tends to disappear the moment something else comes along to distract him. Well, one must accept him as he is, and get the best out of him when one can. He and Giles Ashburn are great friends – which may surprise you too.'

We went the next morning to Albert Place, where Celia, much altered by her condition, greeted us as if we had never been away, or at least as if she had not really noticed it. And as she drew my mother aside for a whispered consultation about the forthcoming event, of which Prudence and myself were supposed to be unaware, I saw that she, too, had but little interest in our travels.

Everything in Celia's square, immaculate house was just as it should be, her red plush curtains exactly matching her red plush armchairs, her tasselled footstools, her painstakingly embroidered sofa-cushions, the fringed valance hanging from her mantelshelf. Her walls were most fashionably covered with a dark, heavy paper, her floors by a busily patterned carpet of serviceable browns and reds and golds. Her silver teapot was an exact, if smaller, replica of my mother's, the ormolu and enamel clock directly at the centre of her mantelpiece chosen quite clearly with my father in mind, the ornamental plates and jugs and china figurines on the shelves above the fireplace most meticulously arranged, everything, from her profusely carved mahogany sideboard to the leaves of her potted plants, exhibiting a most luxurious polish. But even so, in the midst of the well-ordered, well-sheltered comfort her nature craved, she had her share of complaints.

'Yes – as I told you in my letter, I was obliged to get rid of that kitchenmaid. Aunt Hannah may not have liked it, since she recommended her to me, but her table-top was a disgrace, and her boots – treading dirt into my house – and leaving her pans to soak overnight to save herself the trouble of scouring them. I have seen five girls already and am not entirely satisfied with one. Well, Jonas leaves it all to me, since he has not a moment to call his own. He is always at that dreadful office, slaving away – clearing up Mr Corey-Manning's mistakes. My word, you are very smart, Faith, but you will not wear a light-coloured gown like that more than twice in Cullingford, before the dirt will begin to show. I confess I have lost my taste for fashion since I was married. If I may be tidy and presentable it is all I ask – and all one should ask, I think, since a married woman has so many other matters on her mind, and should not, in any case, make herself conspicuous. You may give my regards to Caroline when you see her tonight, for she never comes near me these days – and I could not, at the moment, risk myself outdoors.'

We drove next to Lawcroft Fold, to pay our respects to our Lady Mayoress, finding her far too occupied by personal affairs and civic affairs – the two being apparently quite interchangeable – to have more than a brief moment for our travellers' tales.

Yes, she believed Paris to be a most interesting city, but were we aware of the scandalous refusal of the Cullingford Waterworks Company to co-operate with her husband? Yes, she had heard that the climate and architecture of Italy was very fine, a land of immense achievement in art and music, but we must surely have heard from Celia how very well Jonas was doing, how, in these days of expanding trade, of contracts and disputes and newfangled regulations, even such substantial businessmen as Oldroyd and Hobhouse, Mandlebaum and Barforth, were showing themselves grateful for his advice.

Mr Corey-Manning, we must certainly remember, had given much of his time to the defending of felons – being a man of a dramatic disposition, more suited, she felt, to the odd calling of an actor than the dignified practice of the law – but Jonas, finding nothing to amuse or challenge him in such petty crimes as were to be found in Cullingford, had chosen, very shrewdly, to concentrate on civil matters, which would bring him to the attention of those who could pay.

'The dear boy,' my mother said vaguely.

'Yes, Elinor, and you will be settling yourself down at last, now that you are to be a grandmamma?'

'Oh, as to that –'

But, happily perhaps, my mother's declaration of intent was interrupted by the arrival of Mayor Agbrigg himself, no less haggard and hollow-chested for his civic dignity, bringing another gentleman with him who, very clearly, did not find favour with my aunt. And as always in a mixed, unexpected gathering, there were shades of greeting.

'I'm right pleased to see you,' Mayor Agbrigg said to my mother, wishing her well when he remembered to think of her at all, which was probably not often.

'Well – and you're looking grand, miss,' to me, his stock attention to any young lady to whom attention was due.

But: 'Now then, lass, how are you today?' to Prudence, really wanting to know, his craggy face warming, something in him suggesting his readiness to take action should she be less than 'very well indeed.'

'And how are you?' she enquired with equally genuine concern. 'You seemed so tired on Wednesday evening at the Institute.'

'Aye – but it was only from listening to old Dr Blackstone droning on. If your Aunt Hannah hadn't kept on nudging me I'd have fair disgraced myself and nodded off.'

'Ah well,' Aunt Hannah said, clearly displeased. 'We can't all be so fluent as Dr Ashburn –' And with the air of a woman acting very much against her will, at the dictates merely of Christian conscience and common politeness, she waved her hand vaguely in the direction of her husband's companion and said coolly, 'Elinor – this is Dr Ashburn. Dr Ashburn – my sister Mrs Aycliffe, and her other daughter, Miss Faith Aycliffe. Prudence you already know.' And it was very apparent that, if she had her way, he would be acquainted with none of us.

I found myself looking at a man of medium height, medium colouring, brown hair, brown eyes – although I could not afterwards remember their exact shade – no sinister revolutionary as his Chartist sympathies might have led me to believe, but slightly, quite finely built, a face that was almost delicate, a great air of quietness about him, a man – certainly a gentleman – who observed life, perhaps, more readily than he participated in it.

'I am delighted to meet you at last,' he told me, his accent quite neutral, giving no indication of his place of birth, his voice rather low, so that one had to listen in order to hear him, but not hesitant, perfectly in keeping with that first impression of inner quietness.

'Dr Ashburn is becoming very famous among us,' Aunt Hannah cut in, her voice, following immediately after his, sounding very shrill. 'He has set himself to teach us the error of our ways. He believes we neglect our workpeople and that your husband, Elinor, provided them with shocking even dangerously constructed houses. He makes us all feel quite ashamed.'

'Now then, now then,' Mayor Agbrigg said easily, obviously well accustomed to this.

'And so we should,' Prudence muttered.

'Should we?' my mother asked lightly. 'Well, I have never examined my husband's houses very minutely, but I do not think I would care to live in one of them. Do you live in an Aycliffe cottage-dwelling, Dr Ashburn?'

'No,' he told her, smiling, completely untroubled by my aunt's hostility. 'I am in Millergate, madam.'

'Oh good – so near to us. You must call – in fact, you must dine, since I believe you call already. Would next Tuesday evening suit you?'

And as he replied that it would suit him very well I glanced at Prudence, finding her surprisingly calm, far calmer than I would have been in the presence of Nicholas.

'You will have come today to patch up our rioters, doctor,' Aunt Hannah said, her sarcasm deepening, her eyes sliding to my mother, who rose, predictably, to her bait.

'Rioters, Hannah? Whatever can you mean?'

'Only that you have chosen an unfortunate time for calling, Elinor, since our local Chartists are coming today – have already arrived, if I am not mistaken – to present their petition to our workers in the mill yard. Yes, you can see them from the window – they have overturned a barrel to serve as a table and are collecting signatures, or are trying to, since I doubt if there are many who can write their names. Well, they went to Nethercoats a month ago and, when Bradley Hobhouse discharged all those who signed, there was a scuffle and a few broken heads. So my husband has taken the precaution of inviting his doctor, I presume.'

'I hope I may not be needed, Mrs Agbrigg.'

'I daresay. But if you are, it will not be the first time. It may interest you to know -- you and my niece, Miss Prudence Aycliffe, who interests herself in these matters – that my brother's wife – your Aunt Verity, Prudence – saw her father murdered down there, in this same mill yard, when she was no more than sixteen, and the night after was at her brother's side when he was done to death – horribly done to death – by felons who called themselves Luddites in those days, Chartists today. I do not forget it – even if others do.'

'Hannah – my dear Hannah,' my mother murmured, her hand going out in a gesture of comfort and affection to her sister, my invincible, immovable Aunt Hannah, who seemed most amazingly close to tears. But the weight of memory between them was clearly burdensome to Mr Agbrigg, who, his face for a moment more drawn than I had ever seen it, blinked hard, needing, I thought, to clear his vision, to shut something away.

'There'll be no bloodshed today,' he said gruffly. 'I'll go down and see to it.'

'I'll come with you,' his wife said.

'There's no need.'

'I did not say there was need. I said I will come with you, as far as the bottom gate. And Dr Ashburn will remain here. The presence of a doctor is an announcement that we expect violence, and so may invite it. He can be sent for.'

She picked up her shawl, wrapped it firmly around her shoulders, and went out of the room, leaving us without a word, her face set and stony, and we gathered instinctively at the window where, positioned as we were so high on the terraced hillside, we could see right over the factory wall to the yard, which appeared, I thought, very much as usual. There were the carts I was accustomed to see in that place, piled high with wool-sacks on entering, with bales of dress-goods on leaving, shire-horses standing massive and patient between the shafts, the usual comings and goings of equally patient women, heads bowed, submissive, slow-moving as herd animals transferring from one place of labour to the other. Nothing in any way disturbing except a knot of men in a far corner, indistinguishable, by their stooping shoulders, their narrow backs, from Mr Agbrigg himself, indistinguishable from the villainous, riotous Chartists who were every bit as hollow-cheeked and meagrely put-together as they.

I saw Aunt Hannah come to a halt at her garden gate, the final vantage point, shielding her eyes from the uncertain winter sun as her husband walked on through the herd of weaving-women, who without raising their eyes made way for him, until, reaching the barrel, he lifted his narrow shoulders in a shrug that said 'All right then, get on with it,' and remained standing there, only his good suit and the glint of his gold watch-chain setting him apart.

'Poor Hannah,' my mother said. 'She would have had a better view had she remained here at the window, but she is making a pilgrimage. She was to have married Aunt Verity's brother, Edwin Barforth, who was murdered down there so long ago. How sad, for I can barely remember him – only that he would have inherited the mill, had he lived, and would have made Hannah so very rich. Mr Agbrigg was here too, that day, when Edwin died – it comes back to me now – and then afterwards the mill was left to Verity, who married my brother Joel, and made him rich instead of Hannah. I see that she has not forgotten it, for she has gone down to the gate so that we cannot see her tears, you may be sure – which cannot be altogether comfortable for her husband. My goodness, how strangely things turn out – how terrifying it all is – for, if that young Luddite had not stabbed Edwin Barforth to death, then I do believe girls, that none of you – and I include your cousins Blaize and Nicholas and Caroline – would ever have been born. With Edwin alive, old Mr Barforth would have had no need of Joel to run the mill and would not have obliged Verity to marry him. She would have married – good heavens, yes! – she would have married your half-brother, Crispin Aycliffe, except that he would not have been your brother since your father, in those circumstances, would never have married me. One young bride in Bleheim Lane was more than enough for him. He would not have burdened himself with two. I might have found a clergyman to take me, or a schoolmaster, and lived out my days in genteel poverty, borrowing Hannah's carriage and begging her cast-off bonnets instead of giving her mine. And Verity – well – she would have had her grand dowry, just the same, and her moment of romance, but I cannot think your brother Crispin would have made a comfortable husband. And all this because of one starving lad down there in the mill yard with a carving knife. I wish you would stop me from running on so, Prudence, or I shall give myself nightmares.'

My mother returned to her chair, somewhat tearful herself, leaving me at the window with Prudence and Dr Ashburn, both their faces intent, concentrating hard on that upturned barrel where the Chartist Petition was laid out, on the men who were standing around it, some of them making the earnest gestures of persuasion, others listening, walking a step or two away and shuffling back again, glancing sidelong at Mayor Agbrigg, who, with that eternally patient ebb and flow of working-women around him – whose signatures were of no interest to anyone – made no attempt to intervene.

'I don't understand,' I said. 'I feel that I should, but I don't know –'

'Hush,' Prudence muttered. 'Be still. It's important.'

But Dr Ashburn, who had perhaps witnessed these scenes often enough to be fairly certain of the outcome, turned to me swiftly and with great courtesy. 'They hope to present their Charter – they call it the People's Charter – to Parliament in the spring, and, since one of its demands is that the right to vote should be extended to every man in the country, they feel that as many working-men as possible – being the class not yet empowered to vote at all – should sign the petition which is to accompany it.'

'Yes, I see that. But why come to the mill, disrupting working hours? They could sign it later, couldn't they, somewhere else, with no fear of Mr Agbrigg taking their names – or whatever it is they are afraid of?'

'My word!' Prudence snapped, as sarcastic as Aunt Hannah. 'That was spoken like a true Barforth, sister. If our cousin Nicholas were here today I imagine he would turn every one of them off for the crime of time-wasting, as Mr Hobhouse did. Fortunately, I suspect Mr Agbrigg arranged for Nicholas to be busy elsewhere this afternoon, which, while it may lessen our entertainment, will at least prevent violence.'

'I do beg your pardon,' I told her, half laughing, but quite ready to defend myself, until once again Dr Ashburn came quickly and with great good humour to my rescue.

'Yes, and I think some of them were expecting to meet Mr Nicholas Barforth, and may even be disappointed.'

'Giles, how can you say that, especially since I know you believe their cause to be just?'

'Indeed I do. But there are some among them who do not object to violence, who will provoke it and use it quite coolly for their own purposes – and who will manage themselves not to be hurt by it. They will tell you it is necessary because the majority of their colleagues are unreliable. And so they are, both unreliable and afraid, since they have known hunger before – as you and I have not – and are so terrified of being hungry again that they will be slow to make a united stand. And, even when they can be stirred to protest, the moment things improve a little they will all go quietly home again. That is why reform is so long in coming.'

'I am sure you are right,' I told him.

'Oh, Faith, you know nothing about it,' my sister replied. 'You are agreeing with Giles now, but when you have listened to Uncle Joel and Nicholas tonight at Tarn Edge you will be saying the same to them. Giles believes that every man, regardless of rank or bank balance, should have the right to decide how he wishes to be governed. The Barforths will tell you it is wrong to extend the franchise to the men in the mill yard because there are more mill-hands than Barforths, and if they all had a vote the mill-hands would win.'

'Thank you, Prudence, for putting it in such simple terms for me.'

'There is a little more to it than that, of course,' Giles Ashburn said, quietly smiling. 'They are asking for a secret ballot so that they may cast their votes without fear of losing their employment, and without fear of intimidation. They are also demanding the abolition of property qualifications for Members of Parliament, and that such Members should no longer be obliged to support themselves in office but should be paid salaries like other professionals. All of which is very revolutionary and quite frightening to many people. Understandably so, in fact since it could involve a considerable transfer of power.'

'He means,' Prudence said, her eyes still on the mill yard, 'that if the

Charter should be granted anybody – anybody at all – even one of those mill-hands down there, could stand for office. All it would take would be brains and eloquence and determination, not money and having friends in high places.'

'And being a man, of course,' I said wickedly, finding, somewhat to my embarrassment, that as Mr Agbrigg turned and walked back towards the house, having avoided trouble by banishing Nicholas, and by his own shrewd, rough-spoken skill, and as Aunt Hannah came back into the room, still sharp and stony but resolutely dry of eye, Dr Ashburn seemed quite intent on watching me.

'You have made a conquest,' Prudence said calmly as we drove off, leaving him on the drive, his hat in his hand.

'No, I have not. He was pleasant to me because I am your sister, that's all.'

'Nonsense. I know him well, and he is not usually so pleasant to young ladies. He does not have the time to spare. Well, if it amuses him to stare at you in that moon-struck fashion, I am sure I do not mind a bit. I merely mention it in case it should worry you.'

'Prudence, I am sure you are mistaken.'

'I am sure I am not. And there is no reason to look so guilty. We are friends, Giles and I – yes, fancy that – friendship between an eligible gentleman and a marriageable young lady. Impossible, you might think, since marriageable young ladies rarely have friendship on their minds. But in this case, I do assure you, it is the exact truth. And I would be considerably startled if he began to gaze at me like that. Mother will say the same – won't you, mother?'

'Yes, dear,' she said. 'So she will. In fact your mother is merely surprised, Faith dear, that you did not notice it yourself. If something should be obscuring your vision – well – ask yourself, my love, does anything in Cullingford seem changed?'

I knew, well enough, that there was no way of telling what meeting Nicholas again could mean to me. I had not pined continuously for him this past twelve month, had, in fact, met several other young men who had charmed me briefly, one image fading under the impact of the next. Yet, as I dressed for dinner that night, more than half convinced – or so I believed – that all I really wanted was to impress him, and Blaize too, with my Continental airs and graces, I became increasingly tremulous on the inside, clumsy and irritable on the outside, so that my hair would not take its usual smooth coil, my lovely blonde satin gown, of which I had such high hopes, seemed at once too much and too little, my nose most certainly too long.

'Good heavens!' Prudence said, slipping unaided into her light green silk, her hair going up without effort. 'It's only Tarn Edge. You're not going to a ball. I expect you want Caroline to turn green, and Blaize, of course, always knows about one's clothes. I wouldn't expect Nicholas to notice – if that's what you do expect – because he'll know by now why Mr Agbrigg sent him to Leeds this afternoon, and will be thoroughly displeased about it.'

I would be cool, I decided, as I crossed the hall at Tarn Edge, glancing with affection at the bronze stag which still guarded the stairs, the vast, stained-glass window still casting its patterns of ruby and emerald and gold on the landing sofa I had once shared with Nicholas. I would be a traveller returned from exotic places, hinting, most discreetly, most skilfully, at my store of new wisdom and experience, giving only a little of myself – as I'd seen these Parisiennes, those Roman ladies do – leaving no one in doubt that there was so very much more.

But I was, in fact, in a state of totally unsophisticated turmoil, dry-mouthed and breathless, and alarmingly, comically disappointed to find that Nicholas was not there.

'Faith – how lovely!' Aunt Verity said.

'Aye, I'll not quarrel with that,' said Uncle Joel.

And while I kissed my aunt, and my uncle bent his head to kiss me – bathing me in his remembered odours of brandy and tobacco, his dark face so very much like Nicholas' – my ears, my nerves, were straining for the sound of his arrival, so that when the door clicked open, and it was Blaize who stood there, my eyes, for an instant, did not see clearly, and I turned to him with all the slow, careful nonchalance I had rehearsed for Nicholas.

'Faith?' he said, his voice containing a slight question.

'Yes, Blaize – how do you do?'

'Extremely well before – better now.'

But such mysterious allure as I had managed to acquire, which had been in some measure appreciated by Blaize and Dr Ashburn, and which had not gone unnoticed by my uncle, was not at all apparent to Caroline, who, coming in behind her brother, announced that dinner would be ages yet and that she and I had ample time for a chat – very evidently about herself – upstairs.

'Well, you have travelled even farther than I, and I must say it suits you,' she said, 'although I am not sure I would like to go abroad again. Mrs Battershaw was sick on the crossing and Amy was such a bore. I was glad to be home again where everybody knows me. And I am glad to see you back too, Faith, for there is no one – really – to whom one can *talk*. I have quite broken off with Amy Battershaw, and Prudence can think of nothing but drains and bandages, which will do very well for a doctor's wife, since I imagine she will take the Ashburn man, don't you, whatever she may say to the contrary? Well, we have plenty of time to talk now, especially if we are to wait for Nicholas, who has been over to Leeds and then gone straight from the station to the mill. There is a lot of extra work at Lawcroft, you see, since Mr Agbrigg became mayor and has his civic duties to attend to.'

'Blaize seems to have finished on time.'

'Yes – Blaize always does, if indeed he has been to the mill at all. He will have found some excuse, I expect, to spend the afternoon drinking somebody's whisky, which seems a peculiar way of going about selling cloth, although oddly enough he *does* sell it. But Nicholas will be in the sheds all right, grinding away. Aunt Hannah is as pleased as punch, as you might expect, never thinking of the inconvenience it is causing to us, especially since father relied on Mr Agbrigg to keep an eye on Nicholas at Lawcroft. And, now that he is so busy with his water-carts, Nicholas may have extra work to do, but can do it as he pleases.'

'And what about you, Caroline? We have been expecting to hear your wedding-bells for months.'

'Ah,' she said, 'yes – I suppose I may be married whenever I make up my mind to it.'

'And you have not made up your mind?'

'Very likely I have. It is just that everyone expects it of me and sometimes I wonder if it is too soon.'

'The Flood boy will not wait forever.'

And, drawing herself up like the empress we had always known her to be, she said, 'That is entirely his affair.'

'Yes, indeed – and if that is how you feel about it, Caroline, then, although it would be a great feather in your cap to marry a Flood, it would be an even greater one to turn him down.'

'You are very bold,' she said, annoyed at hearing her own thought spoken. 'I think we had best go downstairs, for even mother cannot keep dinner waiting forever for Nicholas.'

But then, already half-way to her feet, she said, most unwillingly, 'You are not by any chance acquainted with Matthew Chard? No, I hardly see how you could be, for he has only recently moved north. He is Sir Matthew Chard, in fact, since he has just succeeded his great-uncle at Listonby Park. Yes, the real heir – the grandson – was killed last year out hunting, and old Sir Richard Chard was obliged to send for Matthew, who had never lived much in Yorkshire before. And now he has inherited the loveliest house I think I have ever seen. I went there with the Floods in September – Julian and Matthew hunt together. He is a Leicestershire man.'

'And you like him, this Sir Matthew Chard?'

'Heavens – I have no reason to dislike him. He is perfectly agreeable. Is that the dinner gong at last, Faith? I suppose they have decided not to wait for Nicholas, as we are only a family party and need not go in in pairs. We had best hurry, for father is sure to be hungry.'

But Nicholas was in the hall as I came downstairs, offering me the perfect opportunity to reveal my new self to him at its best advantage, my blonde satin dress rustling on each shallow step as I descended, my fair hair as silver-pale in the lamplight – I hoped – as my mother's, so that, had all gone according to plan, he should have looked up and seen a captivating stranger walking slowly towards him, smiling a cool, mysterious stranger's smile, until quite suddenly she became a girl he had once known and – if Fortune should be on my side – would be anxious to rediscover. But Fortune, it seemed, was entirely absent. I saw him fling his hat and gloves irritably on to the hall table, heard his father's sardonic question, 'What kept you? I suppose we may eat now, Verity, since your son has arrived?' and Nicholas's curt reply, 'Good Lord, I can't come to table like this – straight from the sheds. Go in and I'll join you when I'm ready.'

473

And because I was overwhelmed, quite shattered by the sensation leaping inside me, I said, not coolly but coldly, 'Good evening, Nicholas.'

'Good evening.'

'Are you well?'

'Passably. And you?'

'Oh yes – very well.'

And knowing that my tone had implied 'What a pest you are, Nicholas, to keep us waiting,' and his had answered 'Idiotic girl – I am already late, so why must you delay me?' I went in and took my place at table, my artistry all gone, nothing, any longer, in my head but the one impassioned plea: 'Look at me, Nicholas. Look at me.'

8

Julian Flood proposed for the second time to Caroline a few days later, and was refused in a manner allowing no possibility of a third, thus causing enormous offence to his family, who declared with some justice that Caroline had led Julian on.

'Dreary manufacturing bitch,' he called her one evening, after a brandy or two at the Old Swan, unaware of Nicholas in the far corner until my cousin got quietly to his feet, picked the young lord up by his coat collar and knocked him down again, giving offence this time to Caroline, who, perhaps on account of Matthew Chard, was unwilling to be the subject of a tavern brawl.

'I do not at all wish my affairs to be the talk of the town,' she told me, more agitated than I had ever seen her before, a sentiment quite easily understood since, in refusing one offer – and a brilliant one at that – for nothing more definite than the hope of another, she had taken an immense gamble at which not all of her acquaintances would be sorry to see her fail.

'She is angling after Matthew Chard,' my mother told me unnecessarily, 'and he will not be easily caught.' For Sir Matthew, it seemed, although not a wealthy man by Tarn Edge standards, was not desperately in need of money, could manage – or just about – on his own income and what his grandfather had left him to maintain his three thousand acres of moor, pasture and woodland in reasonable condition. And since he appeared to be a reasonable young man whose tastes were not unduly extravagant, having no racing stable like the Floods but contenting himself with hacks and hunters, his kennels containing retrievers and terriers rather than the Floods' ruinously expensive pack of foxhounds, we concluded that Caroline would have her work cut out.

'I can't think what has possessed her,' was my sister Celia's opinion when I called to take tea in Albert Place. 'One family is just as noble as the other. Cullingford Manor is just as big as Listonby Park, and just as difficult to keep clean, I shouldn't wonder. And frankly these squires all look the same to me – long noses and loud voices. I am surprised at Caroline.'

And perhaps Caroline, who had never expected so foolish and painful an accident as this to befall her, was surprised at herself.

Caroline, in fact, in truth, and quite simply, was in love; concerned no longer with lands and titles but with such idiotic considerations as the light auburn tint of Matthew Chard's hair, the quite unremarkable, but in her eyes miraculous, hazel of his eyes, a certain quality – real or imagined was of no importance – which set him apart from all the other young men she had ever seen. He was taller, a shade wilder than Francis Winterton, considerably less wild and not nearly so handsome as Julian Flood. He entirely lacked the easy charm of her own brother Blaize, the intellectual finesse of Jacob Mandelbaum, even the cold dignity of Jonas Agbrigg. He was, in fact, a perfectly ordinary young squire, a fresh-air man of healthy appetites who asked from life nothing more complex than the pleasure of shooting flying game and running game in season, of riding to hounds four or five days while the weather and the foxes lasted. He was a little arrogant, perhaps, since no one had ever questioned his right to privilege, a little self-centred, since the situation to which he had been born suited his nature exactly, causing him to believe that, if he wanted something, then everyone around him must surely want him to have it too. But Caroline loved him, and being in love myself I was well able to sympathize.

'She has no access to him,' my mother explained, 'She met him through the Floods and they will be unlikely to take her over to Listonby now.'

But Caroline, too inwardly desperate for pride, too truly a Barforth even to acknowledge the possibility of defeat, would have driven unannounced to Listonby herself and taken it by storm, had not Aunt Verity smoothly intervened, inviting the young baronet so regularly to Tarn Edge that his continued presence there became such a commitment in itself that it was understood that, if he had not proposed by Christmastime, then Uncle Joel would feel entitled to demand the reason why.

'It will not be necessary,' my mother said. 'Verity will see to it. If it is upsetting Caroline, then it must certainly be upsetting Joel, and Verity will not allow that. We shall have the wedding, you may be sure of it, if Verity has made up her mind.'

But although I wished Caroline well, and felt sure of her success, I believed that this year in which we stood, and the one to follow, would not be her special time, but mine.

Nicholas called at Blenheim Lane a few days after our return, to deliver some message from his mother to mine, and, despite our bad beginning, lingered an hour in the drawing-room, questioning me about my travels – the first of all our acquaintance to do so – a circumstance made more delightful because I knew full well that he had no real interest in exotic places beyond their profitability as markets for Barforth cloth, which was information I could not supply.

He sat behind me at the Assembly Rooms a week later, listening with unconcealed irritation as our two best-established and most expensive physicians, Dr Blackstone and Dr Overdale, explained that we should regard our town as an object of pride, while Prudence's friend, Dr Ashburn, congratulated us most courteously on the fact that even in London and Glasgow he had seen few slums to compare with ours.

And afterwards, having escorted us home, he remained in the drawing-room so late that, when Prudence had retired to bed and my mother was herself feeling drowsy, she felt obliged to tell him: 'Nicholas, my dear boy, although your company is quite delightful, I would not have your mother accuse me of making a night-rake out of you.'

'Oh lord!' he said, getting easily to his feet. 'Is it really so late? You're such a charmer, Aunt Elinor, you see. You'd make any man forget the hour.'

'You can be quite charming yourself, Nicholas, when you want to be,' she told him, looking very tiny, very fair, beside him as she gave him her hand, knowing perfectly well that he was smiling at me over her head, saying to her and asking me. 'You'll be at the Assembly Rooms dance on Wednesday, I reckon, won't you?'

'Faith, dear,' she told me when he had gone, 'I would not wish you to be encouraged. He is by no means so enraptured by you as Dr Ashburn – who was quite nervous about his lecture tonight because you were there – but yes, assuredly, the fact that Nicholas attended the lecture at all and stayed here so long afterwards – yes, there is something there. But he is a hard-headed young man, Nicholas Barforth, and by the time he reaches home – or the Old Swan, which is somewhat more likely – he will have remembered that in fact he is still reluctant to settle down. It will take a great deal to shake him from that resolve, my dear, and if he should now begin to avoid you then you may feel flattered, for it can only indicate that he is tempted. Flattered, Faith, but not too hopeful, dear. You may be sure I am right.'

And so she was, for the Assembly Rooms dance that following Wednesday proved no more than a miserable ordeal of waiting for Nicholas, who, arriving very late and very clearly from the direction of the Old Swan, lounged in the refreshment room for half an hour, spoke two words to me, and went away again. But the next afternoon when we called at Lawcroft to see Aunt Hannah, he came up from the mill, the coolness we may both have intended to show thawing instantly because, quite simply, we were pleased to see each other.

I had not dazzled him. Beneath my Paris gowns and my high-piled, elaborate hairdressing, which had impressed some others, my body was still too familiar to him to arouse the kind of physical desire which would demand a swift conclusion. It must, I knew, be a much more gradual process than that. But he was pleased – always – to see me, looked for me in any room that he entered and was satisfied when he found me, began to add, at the end of any discussion, 'Oh, Faith will know what I mean.' And so I did.

He called often to see us – as did Blaize and Dr Ashburn and some others – tearing up and down Blenheim Lane in the kind of sporting phaeton his father, who had driven an equipage every bit as lethal in his day, considered no more than a young man's fancy, but which caused great alarm to the more sedate of our neighbours.

'Old Miss Corey-Manning thought I meant to run her down.'

'Yes. I saw from the window. You've done her a kindness. She'll have something to talk about now, for the next six months or more.'

'Aye – Blaize is off to America by the look of it, in the summer.'

'Do you mind?'

'If you mean, do I want to go with him, or instead of him – no, not a bit of it. I'm all right where I am. If he'd take father, I wouldn't complain. I get on well enough with old Agbrigg, but father – well – he should make up his mind. Either he wants me to run the mills or he wants to go on running them himself. He's got to decide. He tells me to use my judgment, tells me he's done his share and it's time he was taking things easy, and then, when I do just that, there he is, like a bolt from the blue, making out I'm going behind his back. You'd think he'd be glad, wouldn't you, to have somebody willing to take over?'

'He is glad, Nicholas. It's just that he's been in control so long, and it's hard for him to let go. And perhaps he doesn't like to admit how much he relies on you. I think you'd be the same.'

He grinned suddenly, a flash of rueful self-knowledge, of pleasure, perhaps, in being able to share it with me.

'Maybe I would. He's not a bad sort – in fact he can be downright splendid at times. If he'd just listen to reason about the combing machines. They're making a fortune in Bradford, Faith, out of the combing machines. It's the last section of the industry to get mechanized, and I don't know what he's waiting for. It's been on the cards for years that somebody was going to come up with a combing machine that would work – it stands to reason. The wool has to be combed before they can spin it, and they have to spin it before we can weave it, and nobody could expect the handcombers to keep pace with us. My father went in for power-looms when everybody said he was a madman, and made his millions, and now, when I put it to him about the combing machines, he gives me the same answers they were giving him twenty years ago. Wait and see. Let them get rid of the teething troubles. I know it means throwing the hand-combers out of work, but that never bothered him before. By God, if I had the capital I'd set myself up as a wool-comber right now – there's plenty of factory property going begging, and I'd still be able to manage Lawcroft, and Tarn Edge as well, if he'd let me. He could come in with me – it wouldn't hurt him. I'd be glad of his advice and his money to begin with, but I wouldn't want him to do any work. I'd pay him back and make him a profit, and it would be *mine*, Faith. You understand that, don't you?'

'Yes, of course I do. And so does he. I suppose he's cautious now because he's older, and he's done what he wanted to do. But he's bound to appreciate how you feel. If you persist – show him you really mean it – then I'm sure you'll convince him.'

'Yes,' he said, leaning towards me, almost taking my hand. 'It's not enough, Faith, just to take over another man's achievement and keep it going. I'll do that – of course I will – and double it if I can. But I want

477

something that I started, something with my mark on it. I want my father to know – and I want the Piece Hall to know – that I can make it on my own.'

'And so you can.'

'Faith, why do I always feel better when I've talked to you?'

He had not said he loved me, had in no way committed himself. But there was something between us. And if it was left alone to grow – if I remained patient and careful, so very careful, never forgetting its fragility – then it would grow, surely, into the one thing in the world I desired? For if Nicholas wanted me, no one could really prevent it. My circumstances had not changed. I was not the great match he could make, but I was good enough – as Jonas had been good enough for Celia – and even if his father objected to the point of casting him out, which seemed most unlikely, my money and his own commercial acumen would suffice. Yet I spun no dreams of elopements and love in a cottage, for Nicholas would have no part in such things. I looked now to reality, to a shrewd, ambitious man who would claim his share of the Barforth mills and have his combing company besides, who would live comfortably, self-indulgently even, as he grew older, and who might – who must – live with me. I knew, without any shame whatsoever, that my body desired his. I knew that our minds matched, that our senses were in harmony. I knew I could make him happy. And I would wait, motionless, in the place where he could always find me, until he acknowledged it too.

Dr Ashburn was also with us a great deal in Blenheim Lane, so quiet, so unobtrusive, that it took a while to recognize his charm, and although I knew I had impressed him to begin with, he was so very much the gentleman, so courteous to everyone, that – my vision clouded perhaps by Nicholas – I managed to convince myself, if not my mother, that his partiality for me did not go deep. Yet Aunt Hannah, retaining a proprietorial interest in our dowries, clearly saw Dr Ashburn as a threat to Jonas's position as head of our family, and since in addition he greatly encouraged her husband's preoccupation with stand-pipes and drainage channels, he could do no right in her eyes.

His visits to Simon Street she saw not as an act of charity – although she was a genuinely charitable woman herself – but a deliberate encouragement of the lower classes to idleness. They would make no effort to pay for medicine or anything else, she declared, once they saw it could be obtained free of charge, while Dr Ashburn's attendance as a physician at certain very private establishments in the same area she considered to be no fit subject for her own ears, let alone ours. Nor could she approve of his work at the Infirmary, although she had herself raised a great deal of money for the old hospital building in Sheepgate to be repaired. But raising money was one thing, personal involvement quite another, and we all knew that hospitals were not for decent people, who would be properly cared for at home, but for vagrants, drunkards, disreputables, who should be moved on as soon as they were sufficiently recovered, to be a burden on somebody else's rates. We all knew that hospital nurses were foul-mouthed, gin-soaked, the dregs of the human barrel, quite ready to supplement their incomes by offering services which were not of a medical nature; that hospital doctors were very young men at the start of their careers, or very old ones whose careers should have long been ended. And since Dr Ashburn was highly qualified and highly acclaimed, having other patients who could afford to pay and were not slow to praise, Aunt Hannah declared him to be sanctimonious.

'Was that Saint Ashburn I saw just now,' she would enquire, 'driving his shabby gig up the lane as if he hadn't a feather to fly with?'

'But it would be foolish to leave a smart new curricle in Simon Street,' Prudence would reply, demure but no less dangerous for all that.

'Indeed, for they would pick it clean and have the horse to market before he had set foot across the first threshold – which is all the thanks he is ever likely to get. Well, every time he sits down at my table – since Mr Agbrigg persists in inviting him – I shudder at the thought of what may be lurking on his coat or underneath his shoes. I wonder, Elinor, that you do not feel the same. Yes, it may all seem very grand to you, girls – these idealistic notions. But your mother and I, having lived longer in the world, have seen it all before and know where it leads to. And, whatever my husband may say, there is something not quite right about that man.'

Yet he was undoubtedly a person of impeccable background, the son of a fashionable London parson and a lady of landed connections in Cheshire, where, following his parents' early death, he had been brought up. His breeding in fact was better than ours, his education infinitely superior, his experience of life wider, since he had worked in many of our major cities and travelled extensively abroad. A gentle, not unattractive man, his quietness spiced with intellectual curiosity, with radical ideals that must appeal strongly to Prudence. And I watched him carefully when, spending time he perhaps could not spare, he would turn to my sister, not eagerly but with a warm attention, as she offered him some article of a medical or social nature, some list of facts and figures she had copied out herself.

'This will interest you, Giles.'

'So it does.' And rapidly scanning every line, he would give no indication that he had – I suspected, seen many of these documents before.

'They would do so very well together,' I told my mother, and because I wanted it to happen, wanted to believe it, it all began to fall neatly, happily into place, a patchwork of glowing colours with each one of us in the very square we desired. Caroline would be Lady Chard, mistress of Listonby Park. Giles and Prudence would surely find each other. Celia already had her flock wallpaper and her papier mâché chairs, Jonas his office in Croppers Court, his growing importance in the community. Blaize had his freedom, had already discovered the way to be a manufacturer in a congenial fashion. I would have Nicholas – perhaps? – surely? – if I held my breath and continued to treat the growing feeling between us with the same care I had seen my father lavish on his porcelain, handling it so gently that it could not break, so firmly that it could not slip away. Surely? And there was so much emotion inside me that I was translucent with it, its radiance spilling out through my skin and my eyes, a joyous overflow of feeling which I could offer most lovingly to everyone. 'Prudence, how cleverly you have done that. Celia, your house is a dream – absolute perfection. Mamma, you look not a minute older than nineteen. Of course he cares for you, Caroline – who would not?'

Matthew Chard declined to eat his Christmas dinner at Tarn Edge that year, his responsibilities as squire anchoring him, he explained, to Listonby. Nor could he risk engaging himself for the day after, since Chards and Floods and Wintertons rode traditionally to hounds on Boxing Day, an occupation which did not allow the making of firm promises. But, depending on the vagaries of the hunt, if they did not draw for an afternoon fox, he might ride over at some unspecified hour to take a glass of wine, possibly with a party of friends.

'Very handsome of him,' Uncle Joel said dangerously. 'And he'd best ride in to make his intentions clear, or he'll ride out again in no doubt at all as to mine.'

And so Caroline spent Christmas day in a sulk, finding no consolation in her over-laden present table when she could have been making herself gracious to Sir Matthew's tenants in the Great Hall at Listonby, while on the morning after she was on such tenter-hooks that her very presence was painful.

Uncle Joel's mills, of course, were back at work by then, his engines having shuddered to a halt at ten o'clock on Christmas Eve, to start up again at five o'clock on Boxing day morning, a circumstance which would take Nicholas and Blaize, if not my uncle himself, to the sheds. But Aunt Verity had secured their early release, unwilling, perhaps, to remain too long alone with the tormented Caroline, and Blaize was already in the drawing-room when we arrived, looking as if he had never seen the inside of a weaving shed, Nicholas coming soon after, galloping hatless up the drive, his neck-cloth askew, calling out from the hall 'I'll only be a minute,' intending the words, I knew, for me.

'Must you make such a racket?' Caroline called after him. 'And you'll need more than a minute to make yourself decent. Not that green jacket again, Nicholas – Blaize, do tell him, for in the distance it looks like nothing but a workman's corduroy. Goodness – who is arriving now?'

But it was only Aunt Hannah, delayed by her husband – since Mayor Agbrigg too had been required at the mill today – but well-pleased with herself just the same, having finally prevailed upon him to call a public meeting to invite subscriptions for the concert hall.

'I have already seen Mr Outhwaite,' she told Uncle Joel, mentioning the name of a local architect once closely associated with my father, 'and we have fixed on a minimum fifteen thousand pounds, to be raised in ten pound shares, do you think, Joel? He has promised to let me have his thoughts on design by next Wednesday at the latest.'

'Twenty thousand,' my uncle said, luxuriously at ease by his fireside, the inevitable cigar in his hand. 'You could do it for less, but if you're going to do it at all, Hannah, then do it right.'

And, as she settled down beside him to discuss her views on the site most likely to be chosen, the suitability of Corinthian pillars, who should be invited to lay the foundation stone, and her husband, having given my mother the latest information regarding Celia, who had not cared to venture out, began to talk quietly to Prudence, I went with Caroline to the sofa on the first-floor landing to await the good pleasure of Sir Matthew Chard and to endure the almost visible agony of her nerves.

He would not, of course, put in an appearance. She had quite made up her mind to it and could offer a dozen excuses. The hunt would be unlikely to pass this way. Having started out in the crisp air of that Boxing day morning, a white haze on the horizon, frost pitting the ground, he would have found himself miles away by noon, too dishevelled and weary to call on a lady, even though that lady would be more than willing to send him home in her carriage and stable his horse most lovingly until he required it. It would be unreasonable to expect him, foolish to regard his absence in any way significant, since, having inherited his great-uncle's position as Master, he had been obliged – absolutely in honour bound – to attend the hunt.

'He may even have broken his neck,' Blaize told her, coming to sit beside us. 'Have you thought of that? He may be lying in a ditch somewhere, gasping out a dying message to his groom. "Go tell my lady that, regrettably, I shall not be dining." Now that, dear sister, has a certain style to it, you must admit.'

But Caroline's mind was too full, too busy straining for the sounds of hooves and doorbells, for real anger.

'Nonsense, he is too good a horseman for that – isn't he? – for he has been riding all his life.'

'So have we all.'

'Oh, not like you,' she said, magnificent even in this absent-minded disdain. 'Not like you and Nicholas on your showy hacks that can take you to the mill yard and back, or to the train. I mean real riding – days in the open country jumping fences – steeplechasing. And when did you and Nicky ever go hunting?'

'Never,' Blaize said with an exaggerated shudder. 'Too hearty for me, I'm afraid.'

'You mean you haven't the courage.'

'No, he doesn't,' Nicholas said, appearing suddenly behind us in the green jacket Caroline had affected to despise, although there was nothing about his grey brocade waistcoat or the neat white folds of his cravat about which she could complain. 'He doesn't mean that at all. He means hunting pink don't suit him, and, even if it did, he'd see no profit in risking his neck or riding down some poor devil's crops to catch what? A fox. There's no money in foxes that I ever heard of.'

And he sat down beside me, not touching me, but his long, hard body making contact, somehow, with mine, a most comfortable homecoming, a sense of naturalness, rightness, that we should be sitting here together.

'You know nothing about it,' Caroline said loftily, rising with ease to their combined bait. 'And why should you? How can one expect it? Blaize will not go hunting because he never does anything at which he knows he cannot excel. But you wish you could, Blaize, even if you won't admit it. Oh yes, you do – you'd love to be the dashing hero, leaping those hedges and lording it afterwards – hunt balls and steeplechases by moonlight – yes, you would, if you thought you'd be any good at it. Whereas you, Nicky – you're just not made for such things.'

'No,' he said bluntly, 'I'm not, and I'll tell you why. I can't afford the luxury of a broken leg. I've got a living to earn, as your father would be the first to tell you, and a man who needs to be in his mill yard at five o'clock every morning can't work up much enthusiasm for steeplechasing at midnight. Now, if there was a profit in foxes I'd chase 'em all right – in a pink coat if that was the best way to do it – and I'd catch 'em too. Except that I'd find an easier way to go about it, or get somebody to invent a machine to do it for me.'

'If you've nothing more intelligent to say than that,' Caroline informed him, 'then I'll thank you to hold your tongue when Matthew comes – he wouldn't understand.'

'*If* he comes.'

'Oh, he'll come,' Blaize said, smiling an altogether false reassurance. 'And don't worry about anything Nicky may say to him, for he'll only think it quaint. And he'll be too busy, in any case, telling you where they found and when they killed, and how many hounds it took to tear the poor beast apart.'

'Foxes,' Caroline said, getting up, 'are vermin. They kill chickens and – and – other things. If you were a countryman, a gentleman, you'd know. And you, Blaize Barforth, if they paid you, you'd tear one apart with your bare hands, unless you happened to have your best jacket on. And you, Nicholas, you'd do it in your evening clothes if the price was right. Not that I care – oh, why must you provoke me – it's not fair – it's simply not fair!'

'I don't think she much cares for hunting either,' Blaize said quietly, as, gathering her skirts together, she swept away from us to find her father, doubtless aware that he, too, would be unlikely to hazard his horses, certainly not his person, for pleasure.

'Then she'd best accustom herself,' Nicholas replied, 'for what else is there to Matthew Chard? He hand-rears his game birds and his foxes for half the year and then slaughters them the other half. And when he's not doing that he is playing whist and faro, which is something else she don't much care for.'

'He's not a bad fellow, Nick.'

'I never said he was. He's not our kind that's all. Put Lawcroft or Tarn Edge in his hands and we'd be in queer street at the end of the month, whereas Caroline – she may look like a duchess, but she'd keep those looms turning, one way or another.'

'So she would,' Blaize said, affection warming his perpetually quizzical smile. 'And she'd wear her coronet too, while she was about it. Dear

482

Caroline, she'll find a good reason for not following the hunt, and if Matthew Chard lives with her for fifty years he'll never know it's because she can't ride. Believe me, once she's Lady Chard she'll know more about horses, from the ground, than the rest of them put together. And there'll be no better stirrup-cups served anywhere in the county than at Listonby.'

We went downstairs then, companionably smiling, pausing before the huge, Germanic pine-tree that dominated the hall, its open arms bravely bearing their load of tinsel and candles, a new innovation this, spreading north from London, inspired by our queen's serious-minded, much-loved Teutonic husband.

'Can it really be comfortable indoors?' I wondered, remembering it, aloof and stately, in the garden a week ago.

'The roots are still there,' Nicholas said, smiling, but Blaize, taking my arm, murmured, 'Let's ask it. A little nearer, Faith – that's right – just there, under the mistletoe.' And, one cool hand tilting my chin, he took the traditional Christmas liberty, his lips, as cool as his fingers, curving into a smile as they kissed me, a fresh, sharp scent about him, a man, as Caroline had said, who performed only those acts in which he knew he could excel; and, in their performance, was truly most excellent.

'Merry Christmas,' he whispered, his cheek brushing mine, 'or should it be Happy New Year? That's better, I think, since it lasts longer. Don't move. We've not done with you yet.'

And, his teasing eyes moving behind me, he said, 'Your turn, brother. It's the only time we can do it and get away with it – supposing one wishes to get away.'

'Blaize,' Caroline called from the drawing-room. 'They're serving tea.'

'I'm coming,' he said, and their voices were very far away, heard through forest trees and water, the other side of a meadow, as Nicholas touched me, not at all as Blaize had done, although perhaps no casual observer would have seen the difference.

It was only a piece of nonsense, after all, this Christmas kissing, a breach in the walls of etiquette and propriety, acceptable between young people at this season, something to be whispered about afterwards. 'I turned quite dizzy – my word, I declare if it had lasted a moment longer, I would have swooned.' Or: 'Odious boy, for it is the second time this Christmas day, and if he comes after me again I shall tell mamma.'

But now there was no swooning, no recoil; a smile, simply, of welcome, as he leaned towards me, a feeling of space condensing around us, his mouth polite at first, as Blaize's had been, and then opening slightly, his hands not touching me since he must have known I would not back away.

'Happy New Year,' he said and kissed me again, holding me now in case the alien sensation of his tongue parting my lips should startle me, unaware, perhaps, in his effort to seem not too urgent, of the giddy overflow of my senses, a joyful movement of my whole mind, my whole body towards fulfilment.

'Good heavens, Nicholas!' Caroline called again, still at the drawing-room door, seeing only his back screened by the branches of the tree, a fold of my skirt, too intent on her own heart-searchings to notice ours. 'We must get tea over and done with, don't you see that? Aunt Hannah is wanting to be off, for Celia is not well and has only Jonas to sit with her. Nicky – what are you doing out there?'

'He's kissing Faith,' Blaize said, appearing beside her. 'What else should a sensible man be doing out there?'

And we went in to take tea together.

The afternoon was drawing in, the early winter dark settling, fog-tinted, behind the windows, a sudden tapping on the glass, half rain, half snow, warning us that no horsemen, surely, would venture to Tarn Edge today.

'Come then, Mr Agbrigg,' Aunt Hannah said, worried as always about her horses' legs on the wet cobbles, especially now, since, with a donation towards the concert hall to find, they could not be easily replaced. 'We'll be on our way then, since I like to take my time going down the hill. I'll see you at Lawcroft tomorrow, Elinor, and the young ladies? Well, Faith at least, since Prudence finds so much else to occupy her these days. Jonas, of course, will look in, although I cannot be sure of Celia. I have told her repeatedly how mistaken she is to shut herself away so much – what she is suffering from is hardly a disease. But she has grown quite morbid, Elinor, and you should really have a word with her. You are welcome to come too, Verity – yes, yes. I know how you are situated at present, but if there are to be storm clouds ahead you may appreciate a change of scene. I leave it up to you. Tomorrow then, at tea-time.' And it was as her carriage was moving carefully away, and my mother, surveying the remains of plum cake and pepper cake and hot mince-pies somewhat ruefully, her stomach still queasy, perhaps, from yesterday's champagne, was about to suggest we should be leaving too, that the drive erupted with hoof-beats again, not the patient plodding of Aunt Hannah's ageing nags, but a wild-riding, hell-raking sound that brought Caroline to her feet and held her in an appalling, quite helpless rigidity.

'Here they are,' Blaize said. 'Young lords at play.'

And, quite abruptly, the hall seemed full of them, their size and their noise, their superb self-command diminishing the towering pine-tree, overpowering the bronze stag, a pink-coated army, mud-spattered and most viciously spurred, an invasion as alarming as if they had ridden their foaming mounts directly up the stairs.

'Boots,' Uncle Joel said ominously, his eyes on the carpet, but young gentlemen such as these, accustomed to their stone-flagged ancestral halls, where such carpets as they possessed hung mouldering on the walls, did not share my uncle's precise awareness of the cost per yard – and mill price at that – of these brand-new, deep-pile floor coverings; would have shown no interest had they been told. And it was a measure of his affection for Caroline that he did not tell them, allowing Aunt Verity to move forward with her smooth 'How very nice of you to call,' separating them into individuals so that we realized, with surprise, they were but four in number, Matthew Chard, Francis Winterton, another man and a girl.

She was not, I thought at that first glance, a person about whom Caroline need be concerned, a thin, breathless figure, laughing and swaggering among the men, every bit as hearty and arrogant, and as dirty, as they. She was nineteen or twenty, auburn hair escaping from her tall hat, the lamplight picking out a hint of red, a dusting of freckles across her nose, a pointed face, wide at the cheekbones, tapering to a kitten's chin, a wide mouth talking, talking, half-sentences unfinished, ending in sudden laughter. She had a riding-habit which had seen better days, a long, flat patch of mud on the skirt, a rust-coloured stain on her cheek, fox-blood, one assumed, proclaiming her the first lady to reach the kill – laughing, I had no doubt, as they had daubed her face with the dismembered tail.

'Glorious day,' she told Aunt Verity, a high, clear voice, the long vowel-sounds of privilege. 'Is that a Christmas tree? I never saw one before. The rage in London, now, they tell me, but I hate the city – and my grandfather is too old-fashioned for Christmas trees. You know my grandfather? Surely? Matthew – do come and explain me.'

And, stretching out her hand to Aunt Verity, an abrupt movement followed by a wide, disarmingly frank smile, she said, 'I am Georgiana Clevedon, and very pleased to make your acquaintance. I am by way of being a cousin to Matthew, or something very like it. My grandfather is Mr Gervase Clevedon, and we have the Abbey – Galton Abbey, although I never remember to call it so, since I cannot really believe there is another like it. There, I have explained myself, haven't I? And you must be Caroline.'

'Indeed,' Caroline said, considerably displeased by this unsolicited use of her Christian name, a liberty to be taken, in our experience, only with parlourmaids. 'I am delighted to meet you, Miss Clevedon.'

But Miss Clevedon, unabashed, held out her grubby hand again. 'Heavens, Miss Barforth! Please do excuse me, for I am sadly lacking in manners. And when I have been all day in the saddle I lose them altogether. Matthew, do come and aid me, for I have blundered. And Perry, do come over here and be presented to Miss Barforth. Miss Barforth, this is my brother, Peregrine – who has no manners either. Although one day he will have the Abbey, so we are glad to excuse him.'

I stood in the drawing-room doorway, near enough to observe, too far away to be noticed or overheard. Blaize and Nicholas standing a step ahead of me, close together; and I was still excited and happy, still very far from the notion that these boisterous, brash young men, this strange young woman, could have anything to do with me.

'Now that,' Blaize said, his eyes narrow with careful appraisal, 'is a very rare bird of the wild wood, brother – very rare indeed.'

'Difficult,' Nicholas replied, his own eyes just as calculating, the hint of coarseness in them both comforting me, I think, since I believed this was the way men looked at actresses and adventuresses, the kind of women, in fact, men did not marry, and who could be no threat to Caroline – no threat to me.

485

'Difficult, Blaize – damn difficult to tame.'

'Couldn't tame it,' Blaize said, clearly forgetting my presence. 'Wouldn't want to. I told you, it's straight out of the wild wood, and there'd be no point any more if you managed to get it to eat out of your hand. But I wouldn't mind a scratch or two making the attempt.'

And then suddenly, as they both at the same moment became aware of me, there was a sharp 'Blaize – that'll do,' from Nicholas, and from the unrepentant Blaize, a laughing, 'I do beg your pardon, Faith. May I hope this is the one time you don't know what we mean?'

But Caroline was now walking stiffly towards us, leaving the much-longed for Matthew in the hall, every bit as offended by his boots as her father, and not greatly pleased with Miss Clevedon, uneasy, I thought, at the state of her riding-habit, and altogether shocked – although she would not have admitted it – by the blood on her cheek.

'This,' she said, with no more than common politeness is my cousin, Miss Aycliffe. And my brother, Mr Nicholas Barforth.'

And I felt a great, nameless relief when he nodded, quite curtly, and merely said, 'Miss Clevedon,' staring with a sarcasm that veered on rudeness at her soiled skirt, the emblem of savagery flaking now against her fair skin.

'And this is my elder brother – Mr Blaize Barforth. Blaize – Miss Clevedon.'

'Yes,' he said, his face alive with the very same collector's excitement I had seen in my father whenever he had brought home some rare piece of porcelain, some totally unexpected find: except that with Blaize it was warmer, would be more quickly over. 'Miss Clevedon – so it is – and you are quite wet through. I suppose there is no likelihood that you may catch a chill?'

'I shouldn't think so,' she told him, her abrupt hand stretching out again, her own expression registering a certain surprise, as if she had not expected a member of the manufacturing classes to possess such charm.

'No – I didn't for a moment imagine it. But do come over to the fire, just the same, Miss Clevedon. I am sure you are above such trifles as the weather, but you must allow the rest of us to be concerned.'

'Blaize,' Caroline said, the flash of her eyes warning: 'Boots – carpets.' But, ignoring her, Blaize took Miss Clevedon's shabby elbow in a careful hand and led her away, glancing at Nicholas in a manner which plainly said, 'I told you. This is a rare one. We'll see, shall we?'

'What an odd creature,' Caroline muttered.

'Yes,' Nicholas said, not listening to her, staring at Blaize, watching too intently, neither comdemning nor excusing, saying too much by saying nothing at all, so that I – as taut as Caroline – nervously enquired.

'What do you think?'

'About what?'

'About Miss Clevedon?'

'Oh – not a great deal.'

And, although he smiled at me then, stayed beside me, walked with me to the carriage, waited bareheaded in the rain to see me drive away,

486

and promised he would come and rescue me from Aunt Hannah the following afternoon – and indeed came – I knew, not that night but soon after, that the special time I had marked out for myself, and which had only started with my return home in November, was already over.

9

The Barforths were invited to Listonby Park for New Year's Day, a meagre enough occasion, Aunt Verity afterwards told my mother, nothing but plain roast meats on the table, indifferent service, a housekeeper, she felt, who would have been more inclined to receive them at the tradesmen's entrance and, in Uncle Joel's opinion, would not have paid their bills too promptly at that. A beautiful house, indeed, the original medieval great hall stone-flagged, oak-ceilinged, the long gallery lined with an impressive array of ancestral portraits and not much else, an early eighteenth-century wing so mellowed, the plasterwork and paintwork so obviously nearing its century, that it had reminded Aunt Verity of the musky beauty of rose-petals approaching decay.

Uncle Joel and Sir Matthew went outside together when the meal was over, to smoke their cigars strolling along the avenue of wych-elms a distant Chard had planted in the park, admiring the sycamores, the gnarled and knotted oaks from an even earlier generation, my uncle taking this opportunity to discover, as he had no doubt expected, that although there was money enough for essentials, Sir Matthew's pleasures, albeit of a less dissipated nature than Julian Flood's, were nevertheless not cheap.

The maintaining of even a provincial hunt like the Lawdale – the feeding of fifty couple of hounds, the salaries of huntsman, whippers-in, earth-stoppers, the upkeep of coverts – would be likely to exceed three thousand pounds per annum, of which his own subscription could not be less than fifteen hundred pounds. His personal stable expenses, without much effort, could cost him two thousand pounds and rising, every year, his private kennels a further five hundred. There was, in addition, the expense of preserving game-birds on his land, their careful hand-rearing and safe-keeping from poachers and predators, so that they could be shot in due season, and by invitation only. And it became clear to them both that in Sir Matthew's costly and time-consuming pursuit of sport, a wealthy and efficient wife would not come amiss.

He proposed to Caroline the following morning, riding over to Tarn Edge immaculately turned-out this time, his boots well-polished and clean, his manner ardent enough to please anyone, being a healthy man more than ready to take a healthy mate. And almost at once, having longed for him, despaired of him, she was no longer sure of herself, riding down, in her turn, to Blemheim Lane to bring me her news, her triumph, and her heart-searchings.

'I'm to be Lady Chard.'

'Oh darling – I never doubted it.'

487

But she had not quite forgiven him for his unruliness of Boxing Day, his inbred arrogance which had seen nothing amiss in trampling mud on her father's floor, the oft-repeated hunting tales which bored her, making her too aware of the very real gulf between them. Yet – apart from the fact that his presence still caused her heart to miss a beat, the fact that, without having the words to describe it or the courage to admit it, his sharp-edged, patrician profile, his lounging body, had aroused her sensuality – she had already won herself a reputation as a jilt by refusing Julian Flood, and could not do the same again. And, when all was said and done – and she said it many times, over and over again – although he was not rich, he had no gambling debts, no creditors waiting on their wedding day to be paid off at the church door, and there was no reason why handsome, energetic Caroline should not be loved for herself.

'He was quite charming,' she told me, 'almost emotional – said he had known at once, seeing me at Listonby, that I belonged there. And, indeed, it is a lovely house. I could do so much with it, Faith. There is a staircase leading out of the Great Hall, carved oak with painted panels on the walls, leading to an enormous room, the size of the Hall itself, not used for anything at all – quite empty – and it would make a splendid ballroom. And the Hall – well, there is nothing much in there now but that huge stone fireplace and a few oak boxes standing around, and a dreadful oak table all scarred and battered. But with some decent floor-covering and a dozen or so deep armchairs and sofas, it would be ideal for house-parties – a log fire in that tremendous hearth at tea-time, can't you imagine it? For that is the thing nowadays – house-parties – since the railways have made it so easy to get about, and one can invite guests from simply anywhere. Bedrooms should be no problem, for although, naturally, I haven't yet seen them, the upstairs passages are like a rabbit-warren, and there must be accommodation to spare. The kitchens, I suppose may be less than adequate, but something may easily be done about that – in fact it must be done, since I am quite determined to entertain. What is the point, after all, of having a house that size unless one means to *use* it? Yes, I shall have to give some thought to the kitchens – and a really good chef who will bring his own kitchenmaids, since people will not come twice unless they are sure of enjoying their dinner. Well – the really good thing about it is that there is no Dowager Lady Chard to pull a long face when I set about making changes.'

'And Matthew?'

'Oh, he will not care a scrap. He was not brought up at Listonby, you see. His real home is in Leicestershire, as you know, and he is not so attached to Listonby that he cannot bear a stone of it to be altered – not at all like the Floods and those dreadful Clevedons.'

And so enchanted was she with her plans for Listonby Park that it was a long time before I could introduce again the name of Georgiana Clevedon, whose pointed face and sudden smile I had been unable to forget.

'Oh, they are connected to the Chards by marriage, I believe,' she said carelessly, 'and I cannot imagine why they think themselves so grand, for that Abbey of theirs is the gloomiest place I ever saw. A quarter of the size of Listonby, and so old – beyond repair, I should think. It was a real abbey once, before whichever king it was who knocked them down – Prudence will know – oh, King Henry VIII, was it? – Well, the Clevedons bought it from him, or he gave it to them for services rendered, a million years ago by the look of it, and they built their house from the abbey stones. In fact part of it still looks like a nunnery – they even have a cloister which they seem to think quite splendid, although it is as cold as a tomb and just as foisty. They have no money, of course, and no hope of any that I can see, for Peregrine Clevedon is the most feckless young man I ever knew, and no woman in her right mind would marry him. And if Miss Georgiana imagines she can save the day by setting her cap at Blaize she will have a rude awakening. Blaize will not think of marriage for a long time yet, and when he does you can be sure he will make a brilliant match, something altogether exceptional. No, the best thing they can do is to sell off their land and their precious Abbey with it, while they still have something to sell – for it would not surprise me to hear any day that it had fallen down.'

We went to Albert Place to see in the New Year, my sister Celia, who had adamantly refused to risk herself outdoors, remaining throughout the entire evening on her sofa, so very much embarrassed by her swollen shape that even the presence of her kindly, down-to-earth father-in-law incommoded her.

'Are you comfortable, lass?' he asked her more than once, wanting, it seemed, to make a show of affection, to move her closer to the fire or farther away from it, some gesture expressive of concern, but she could only reply, 'Quite comfortable, thank you,' the sharpness of her tone implying, 'Leave me alone. Don't draw attention to the sorry state I'm in. Don't stare at me.'

We drank what I felt sure must be an excellent wine, served, in Celia's wedding crystal, on a silver tray.

'All the very best to you, lass,' Mayor Agbrigg said, remembering, this time, not to look at her.

'I have told that girl a hundred times about these glasses,' she answered. 'Jonas, have I not told her that they must be rinsed – really rinsed clean – but no, she dries them with the soap still on them. Jonas, you will have to tell her again, for, in these circumstances, you must see that I cannot.'

'Yes, Celia,' he said quietly, not looking at her either, having no need, perhaps, of vision to know that her lower lip was trembling, her whole face quivering with the approach of fretful tears. 'I'll speak to her in the morning. It can hardly be done now. Please do not cry over it. It is hardly worth so much agony.'

'So you always say. You simply do not understand how these slovenly things upset me.'

'You are quite mistaken, Celia. I understand exactly how much – and how often – you are upset. Are you tired now?'

'Of course I am. I suppose you are thinking I would be better off in bed.'

'Only if that is what you would like.'

But Mayor Agbrigg – the only other man in the room – was obliged to turn his back, making some excuse about mending the fire, before she would allow a completely expressionless Jonas to help her to her feet and lead her from the room.

'Your daughter is very fanciful,' Aunt Hannah said. 'One would imagine no other woman had ever been in her condition before.'

But, before my mother could answer, Mayor Agbrigg, putting down the fire-tongs, said quietly, 'She's hardly a woman, Hannah – just a little lass, scared out of her wits. I hope my lad understands that.'

There was champagne at midnight – no one, now to complain about the glasses, since Celia, we had ascertained, was sound asleep – Mayor Agbrigg, gaunt in the flickering candlelight, raising his glass first to his wife: 'Lets drink to your concert hall, Hannah – the grandest in the West Riding,' and then to Prudence, his quiet smile conveying, 'And we'll pave the streets as well, lass, while we're about it, and shift the sewage.'

There was Jonas, his cool, narrow face giving no hint either of concern for Celia's condition, or of annoyance that she was managing it so badly, bestowing on me and Prudence the customary New Year's kiss, as correct and remote a brother as a husband, playing his role to perfection but with little feeling.

'Happy New Year, sir,' he said to his father.

'Aye – let's hope so,' the mayor replied, and we went home soon after, Mayor Agbrigg accompanying us to be the first foot across our threshold. Aunt Hannah waiting in the carriage while he carried inside the lump of coal for the hearth, the salt for our table, that would ensure our happiness and prosperity to come.

'Happy New Year,' Prudence said to me, later, as we reached her bedroom door.

'Yes, darling – the same to you.' But the radiance inside me had dimmed, leaving me cold, as scared, without exactly knowing why, as Celia, so that like her I needed the refuge, the bolt-hole, of my solitary bed and the release of tears.

We attended the public meeting, called some days later, at the Assembly Rooms, to put forward Aunt Hannah's plans – thinly disguised as her husband's – for the erection of the concert hall.

'What have we got in Cullingford?' Mayor Agbrigg said bluntly, in no way abashed by this gathering of millmasters who could have bought and sold him ten times over. 'We've got the mills and a few decent private houses. We've got the Mechanics Institute and these Assembly Rooms, and the new station, and that's about all. Folks that come here – and they're coming here now from far and wide – are saying Cullingford's not a town at all. They're saying it's not much better than a navvy camp. Now, there's some as don't mind that, and some as do – there's some as don't take offence when they hear tell that Leeds is growing faster, and even Bradford's cleaner. But if we've got the muck, friends, we've got the brass to go with it – enough brass, I reckon, to set it all to rights.'

And although it was not the speech Aunt Hannah would have made herself, having had a great deal to say privately about the need for cultural improvement – preferring her own quotation 'man does not live by bread alone' to Mr Agbrigg's 'Where there's muck there's brass' – the haggard, rough-spoken man she had married undoubtedly carried the day. A joint-stock company was formed, finance to be raised by the taking-up of ten pound shares, any deficiency or any additional costs to be met, it was discreetly understood, by that philanthropic gentleman, Mr Joel Barforth. And henceforth my life was dominated by two issues, the concert hall – Aunt Hannah's insistence on Corinthian pillars, her flirtation with gas-lighting, her apparent disregard as to which orchestras, in fact, would actually play there – and Caroline's wedding.

It was to be in June, not at Listonby as one may have supposed, but in our own parish church, since at this stage it was Cullingford Caroline wished to impress, rather than the Chard tenantry. And so, throughout the bleakest January I could remember, I sat with her in the cosy back parlour at Tarn Edge, toasting ourselves by the fire and talking of what was to be the most splendid ceremony our town had ever seen.

'You understand clothes, Faith,' she told me. 'I've often noted it'; and when the guest lists were put away, the pattern books would come out, samples of fabric, pencil and paper for my sketches.

'I'll go to London. You could come with me, Faith. In fact we could go to Paris, to that couturier you're always telling me of. Why not? Father will arrange it.'

But already in January there was a murmuring of unrest in France, hints that our own malcontents, the Chartists, were on the move again, threatening to carry their demands to Westminster and force them if necessary down the throat of any who were unwilling to listen.

'They'll get nowhere,' Uncle Joel said, lighting one cigar from the embers of another. 'These hot-heads, Feargus O'Connor and the like – they've got the men, and now, with the trains, they've got the means to move them wherever they're needed to demonstrate. But what's a demonstration? They tried to stop the mills from working back in forty-two – went on the rampage both sides of the Pennines, taking the plugs out of the engines so the looms wouldn't turn. And what happened? It was the demonstrators who ran out of steam in the end, same as the engines, except that we soon started the engines up again, and all they really achieved for their "brothers" was to lose them a few days pay. The Chartists will be no different. They may have orators who can tell them they should all have a vote, and that there should be a general election every year so they can practice using it – but they've got no organizers. There's no money behind them. We got the vote in thirty-two because men like me and Hobhouse and Battershaw and Oldroyd threatened to take our brass out of the Bank of England unless they gave it to us. What has Feargus O'Connor got to bargain with? He can call his mob out to break a few windows and throw a stone or two, but once they've rounded up the first half-dozen and shipped them off to Australia the rest will go home again. One man one vote indeed, and a secret ballot so the demon millmaster can't twist their tails on polling day. Well, I can't blame them for that. In their place I'd want the same – except I'm not in their place, and I've no mind to let my millhands choose my government for me.'

491

Yet it was rumoured that the London streets were beginning to be dangerous, that in Cullingford itself the hungry, the unemployed – the residents, one assumed, of Simon Street – were meeting in growing numbers to perform military exercises on the moors beyond Tarn Edge, a copy of the People's Charter in every pocket, a weapon of some kind in every hand, even hungrier men from Bradford, many of whom had been thrown out of work by the combing machines, coming to explain that the same thing was more than likely to happen to them. And, to my relief, it was decided that Caroline must do her shopping at home.

I could not have said that Nicholas neglected me. We met as often as before, talked, smiled, our relationship apparently unaltered. And perhaps it was the very lack of change that troubled me, for, if it did not diminish, it did not grow; and I knew there were times when he held back from me.

'Faith will know what I mean,' he still muttered now and then, but increasingly I could not understand him, was aware simply that something troubled him, my own senses, sharpened by panic, being quick to detect the slow building of a barrier between us, which I could not always bring myself to call Georgiana Clevedon.

I knew him too well for that – or thought I did – for, unlike Blaize, he had never sought the exotic in women, had spoken many times of the need to settle with a partner of one's own kind. He may, from time to time, have enjoyed the convenience of a casual mistress – in fact I knew quite well he had – as exotic or as garish as our local music-halls could provide, but in a wife – and Miss Clevedon, like myself, could only be available to him as a wife – such qualities must surely repel him. Nicholas was practical, shrewd, level-headed enough to choose a woman who was right for him. And since Georgiana Clevedon, 'rare bird of the wild wood' as Blaize had so aptly named her, was so very wrong, I was able for most of the time to convince myself that I was mistaken.

And in the moments when I couldn't – bare, solitary midnights that stripped me of hope and dignity – I concluded that if he wanted her, as he had wanted the actresses of the Theatre Royal, if it was passion, the reckless impulse of sensuality he had not managed to feel for me, then I would wait, closing my eyes and my mind to it, until it was over. I would say nothing, do nothing; I would be, as always, simply here when he needed me, making no demands, ready, like cool water, to heal him if she scorched him, ready to warm him if she proved cold, waiting, until the flame expired, to welcome him home, asking no questions, offering merely the strength of my love for him to lean on if she should weaken him.

But did he want her? Certainly no one but myself thought so, Caroline being too irritated by Miss Clevedon's open encouragement of Blaize, and Aunt Verity, who knew her eldest son rather better, too amused by it, for either of them to connect her in any way with Nicholas. Was it merely my overwrought imagination, my jealousy extending to every woman he met, because I had not, it seemed, succeeded in making him love me? Had he, in fact, given any real indication of regard for her?

None. But I would have been easier, I knew, had he leaned forward to catch a glimpse of her ankle, on her second visit to Tarn Edge, when she had mismanaged her skirt at the carriage-step – something he would have done automatically had it been any other woman – instead of staring stony-faced at the horse's legs, not hers. I would have been easier if, responding to her flighty, familiar manner, he had flirted with her, even treated her coarsely – anything. And I could not have explained, even to my mother, how his show of indifference where she was concerned stabbed me to the heart.

Nor did she appear to want him. Blaize, beyond question, was her choice, and a visit to Galton Abbey at the end of January convinced me that, as Caroline had said, a choice of some kind was necessary, for indeed the estate was much encumbered, the brother deep-dyed in his extravagance, and Miss Clevedon, without doubt, would have to fend for herself in life.

We went first, of course, to Listonby Park, even my mother, unutterably bored now with Cullingford and eager to be off again, twittering with excitement as the house revealed its graceful lines to us through the mist.

'Caroline, my dear – how perfectly lovely!' And so it was, the Great Hall sparse, as Caroline had warned, but noble, the carved oak staircase rising majestically from it, the dining-room and drawing-room – added a mere hundred years ago – of such frail beauty, the baroque plaster mouldings so mellowed from the original white to a delicate cream in places, in others a gentle grey, that I, too, was reminded of fragrant petals at the season's end, and wondered how anything so exquisite could endure.

And when we had taken tea by the crackling, smoking fire – 'I must ask my father to advise me about that chimney' – had paced the Long Gallery up and down to admire the gilt-framed row of Chards, long dead, who would have turned over in agony in their weed-strewn graves had they suspected that any descendant of theirs could marry a tradesman's daughter, we were driven the three miles to the much smaller estate of Galton Abbey, to inspect a house of a very different order.

It stood at a bend of the River Law which had somehow escaped the pollution of our mills, a hurrying, sparkling water still running free beneath a rickety bridge, swirling itself around a row of old stones which the nuns, perhaps, in Tudor times, had used to cross the stream. There was a steep green hillside, ancient trees dipping their arms in the river, and the house, whose stones had heard the tolling of the convent bell, set in a slight fold of the land as if it had grown there, quite naturally, without the help of any man. And although I wanted to find it cold and dismal, like Caroline, I would have been enchanted, had I allowed it.

There was a hall here too, quite small, extremely dark, stone floors, stone walls, stone stairs leading to an open gallery, a feeling of age, a weight of memory and experience so strange, yet so haunting, so much in keeping with Miss Clevedon herself, that I was suddenly, fiercely grateful that only Blaize, not Nicholas, had found time to accompany us.

She received us alone, neither her brother nor her grandfather having returned from hunting, walking abruptly into the room in her inevitable dark green riding-habit, its trailing skirt looped over her arm, two elderly gundogs padding stiff-legged at her side, a pair of greyhounds, a frisk of terriers following behind.

'My word!' my mother said, when the conventional greetings were done, 'I hear you have a cloister – may we risk the encounter of a ghost or two?'

And immediately, without ceremony, we were taken to see the cloister, a dim, empty tunnel leading to no tangible place at all but directly into the past. 'They pulled down the Abbey church,' Georgiana said, 'my great, ever-so-great-great-grandfathers. But they left part of the abbess's house and this cloister intact. I once spent the whole night here, as a child, quite alone, curled up in a blanket, just thinking about it. Don't you find it the most fascinating place in the world?'

'Absolutely,' Blaize said, his eyes ignoring the intricate fan-vaulting and resting directly on her vivid, eager face. And instantly her quite breathless admiration of the stone tracery, the hushed mystery of this ancient place, gave way to a boyish, unabashed chuckle.

'Oh – nonsense – for you are teasing me. Pretending to admire my cloister and looking at me instead. But I am not deceived.'

'Miss Clevedon,' he declared, his hand on his heart, a smile of pure mischief on his lips. 'I am the most sincere of men –'

'He is the greatest flirt the world has ever known,' Caroline said tartly. 'And it is very cold in here – and the air not quite fresh. Matthew, I would like to go outside.'

'So you shall, for I want to have a look at Perry's stable,' Sir Matthew said, aware, one supposed, that quite soon he would have the purchase price of any horse in the county, despite the restrictions my uncle would endeavour to tie into the marriage-contract. But Caroline was nervous of horses, Blaize not obsessive, Miss Clevedon remarkably agreeable to his suggestion that, while his mother and mine returned to the house, we should take a stroll.

'Show me these famous abbey grounds,' he invited her, and so we walked a while in the thin sharp air, my feet and Caroline's uneasy on the stony pathways, Miss Clevedon striding out, her hips as narrow and flat as a boy's, no blood on her cheek today, but a certain translucence, a quick-rising vitality, her hair turning to pure copper at every uncertain shaft of winter sunlight.

She had spent all her life here at the Abbey, she told us, just a few miles distant from Tarn Edge, but as unaware of our existence as we had been of hers. The city, to her, meant London – and that to be avoided whenever possible – the rest mere collections of houses, a strange, restricted way of life she did not care to understand. She had been happy here – every day of her life she had been happy – gloriously content with the company of her brother and her grandfather, and their sporting friends.

And a mere half hour of her company sufficed to make it clear that her brother, Peregrine Clevedon, who was reckless and spendthrift and

494

would have fallen foul of the law more than once had it not been for his family connections, could do no wrong in her eyes, that her grandfather, Mr Gervase Clevedon, was of a nobility and wisdom falling little short of the Deity, that her Abbey was the master-plan besides which the rest of the world's great buildings did not really signify. She was herself a passionate horsewoman, having ridden to hounds six days a week every season since she had turned five years old; and was no mean shot either, although she could not match her brother's record of killing ninety-six pheasants, one smoky Autumn day, with ninety-six shots, eighty grouse with eighty shots, thirty-four partridges with thirty-four shots.

'I believe you pity those of us who have not lived as you have,' Caroline acidly remarked, to which Miss Clevedon gave her sudden, almost startled peal of laughter, tossed her head, as restive and open-hearted as a young colt, and declared that she believed she did.

'But you can hardly expect to live here forever? One assumes your grandfather is not immortal, and that your brother may marry?'

But Miss Clevedon was not dismayed. 'Oh, but it is the Abbey and the estate that matter, you see,' she explained to an increasingly distant Caroline. 'When my grandfather dies it will all be Perry's, and then his children's, and theirs. We will still be here, life-tenants handing into the future what was given to us by the past. That's the great thing. That *is* immortality, don't you see?'

'How comforting,' Caroline said, walking briskly forward, pausing as she reached the river-bank, her eyes critically scanning the fragile bridge. 'Can that be secure, do you think?'

'I daresay it is not,' Miss Clevedon called out, 'but I never use it.' And catching up her skirt still higher, she sprang lightly on to the first stepping stone, and then the second, her boots up to their heels in water, swaying slightly, deliberately, as she flung down her challenge.

'Would someone care to race me to the other side?'

'I hardly think so,' Caroline told her, Barforth fury visibly mounting, since it was clear to her that Matthew Chard, had she not been there to restrain him, would have plunged readily enough into the stream, good, broadcloth jacket best cambric shirt and all.

'I'll venture myself on the bridge,' Blaize offered. 'And rescue you at the other side.'

'There'll be no need to rescue me, Mr Blaize Barforth, I do assure you –'

And they were off, Miss Clevedon leaping, splashing, from stone to stone, her hair coming down in a guinea-gold tangle, her feet kicking up a fine spray as she went, Blaize on the bridge, not hurrying but keeping pace with her, reaching out a hand as they both came to the far bank, allowing her, for just a moment, to pull him forward towards the water.

'I'll give you a soaking yet, Mr Barforth.'

'I think you will not.' And then her quick, gurgling laughter as he tugged her sharply on to the grass and, for an instant, into his arms.

'Matthew, go after them,' Caroline commanded. 'They must not be alone together over there.'

But to Matthew Chard, accustomed to the free and easy hunting society of Leicestershire, the sophistications of Oxford and London, these were the notions of Methodism, of the middle-classes – shopkeepers' morality – and lounging somewhat irritably against the bridge he said, 'Good lord, Caroline what harm are they doing?'

'None, if they come back at once. But if they go up the hill and out of sight that young lady may well find herself compromised.'

'Lord!' he said again, half amused, half wishing, perhaps, that he had gone hunting after all. 'I have been up that hill alone with her a dozen times and thought nothing of it. These things don't signify, I reckon, in good – I mean, in the countryside.'

But before she could give him her opinion of his countryside, knowing full well he had almost said 'in good society', they were back again, Miss Clevedon breathless, almost beautiful, Blaize in no hurry to release her hand. And, smiling at him, fond of him as I was, wishing him well as I did, my treacherous thought still reached out to him: 'Fall in love with her, Blaize. Or make her love you – as you could, if you tried, if you wanted to.'

We started for home soon after, Matthew Chard remaining at Galton to await the arrival of Miss Clevedon's brother, and the house was scarcely out of sight, the superb Barforth carriage-horses making light of the distance, when Caroline, who had remained very cool said to her mother, 'I think you should know that Blaize has behaved very foolishly – in fact, very badly.'

'I wonder,' Aunt Verity said. 'Have you, dear?'

'Yes and no,' he told her, the understanding between mother and son quite complete. 'Badly perhaps. Foolishly – I don't think so.'

'I expect you have been flirting with Miss Clevedon?'

'I have.'

'And enjoying it?'

'Immensely.'

'And she may have enjoyed it too. But is it really wise, dear?'

'Of course it is not wise,' Caroline cut in, 'since the girl is angling for a husband, and he is too blinded to see why.'

'My dear Caroline,' he said, a perfect imitation of her own grand manner, 'I am well aware of her reasons, believe me. Their property is in ruins, the brother is too wild for any woman to marry, and so Miss Clevedon has elected to make the supreme sacrifice. She doesn't like the idea of marrying a manufacturer – my word, she doesn't like it, and it is an indication of her devotion to her family that she is willing to undertake it at all. In fact I am flattered that, in my case, she feels it could be less horrific than she'd anticipated.'

'Then you admit her to be an odious, unfeeling creature?'

'I admit nothing of the kind,' he said, leaning sharply forward, 'for she is every bit as enchanting as I have been telling her these past few weeks. And she is very far from being unfeeling – ver far. I will tell you this, Caroline, she is exactly the kind of girl a man might come to love, quite foolishly, without at all wanting to, you may believe me. She could get inside a man's head, and his skin, and he could find himself quite unable

496

to get rid of her, no matter how much he tried. It would take a warm-hearted man, of course, which puts me out of the running, you'll surely agree?'

'So you have done with her?'

'Have I? Very likely. I am going to London at the end of the week in any case. And if it eases you, Caroline – since this will not shock mother and Aunt Elinor, and Faith may stop her ears – I have a friend in London who intrigues me, perhaps not quite so much as Miss Clevedon, but who is considerably easier of access. So – probably – you have nothing more to fear on her account, and mine.'

'Well, I am glad of that, although you need not snap at me.'

'What is it, Faith?' my mother said, quietly for her. 'Are you not well, dear?'

And, forcing my mouth to smile, an effort made through a sudden weight of weariness, I said, 'No – no – it's the cold, that's all, mamma. Just the cold.'

10

My sister Celia had her child at the beginning of February, a boy some weeks ahead of his time who lived but a moment or two; and it chanced that when her pains started she and I were alone in the house together, Jonas in Leeds on business, my mother and Prudence on an excursion to Harrogate, Aunt Hannah so unacceptable to Celia that I sent at once for Dr Ashburn, not daring to imagine the consequences to myself, and to my sister, if he could not be found.

'It is nothing,' she said, plainly terrified. 'Not at all what you are thinking, in any case.' And, seeing the beading of sweat on her thin, seventeen-year-old face, the utter panic in her eyes, my little sister trying hard, even now, to play the matron, I told her, 'Nonsense. I may be unmarried, Celia, but I have learned that babies do not grow under a gooseberry bush – nor in the doctor's bag, either.'

'Then you know more than I did – last year,' she gasped, biting her lips, allowing me to take her upstairs and hold her hand, her fingers gripping hard, the sheer outrage in her face comic, had it not been so totally appalling.

'Darling – darling Celia – it's going to be all right.'

'All right? It's disgusting!' she cried out, teeth digging vixen-sharp into her lip, 'disgusting – all of it!'

'Oh no, darling, it's natural, isn't it?'

'What do you know about it? You don't even know what I mean. It's horrible, I'm telling you. It's disgusting.'

'Celia – I don't know – but I think you should calm yourself.'

'Why? Why should I?'

'Because I think you should. And the doctor will soon be here.'

'The doctor,' she spat out. 'The doctor – what's a doctor? Another

497

man coming to maul me – dear God! – don't leave me, Faith. I won't be left alone with him.'

But Giles Ashburn, appearing blessedly, almost silently, would not have me stay, disengaging her frantic hand from mine with quiet authority.

'Mrs Agbrigg, I am going to help you and you must help me to do so. Miss Aycliffe, if you will wait downstairs –'

'No!' Celia screeched, thrashing her body wildly again.

'Yes,' he replied, opening the door for me, leaving me with no option, although he had not even raised his voice, but to obey.

Jonas would be here before it was over, I thought, calculating the time of the last train, and my mother, who would come immediately on reading the note I had dispatched to Blenheim Lane. But the afternoon had scarcely darkened. I had been but an hour or two, it seemed, staring into the fire, trying not to heed the muffled sounds overhead, not to dwell on my sister's frailty – my own helplessness – when Giles Ashburn was back again, telling me with his great quietness that although my sister was as well as one could hope her to be, her son, who had been born too quickly, too soon, had not survived.

'There was nothing that could be done,' he said very carefully, uncertain as to how much, if anything, I knew of the process of human reproduction; and, understanding the pains he was taking neither to shock nor offend me, since I might well have to endure it myself one day, I nodded, not wishing to increase his burden.

'May I go up to her?'

'It would be best if she could sleep now, or a while. My nurse is with her.'

'Of course. Was she – much distressed?'

'Not yet. Later, perhaps.'

And conscious suddenly, quite sickeningly, of the tiny, lifeless body which would have been my nephew – conscious of my sister's pain – I cried out, 'It is such a waste.'

'Yes,' he said, still enveloped in his quietness. 'I know. Miss Aycliffe, there is no reason now for you to stay. I shall be leaving shortly, since my nurse can do all that is necessary. May I take you home?'

'Oh no. She may wake, you see – and then there is Jonas. Someone must be here when he arrives – to tell him. He should not be allowed to hear it from a parlourmaid.'

'That is good of you, Miss Aycliffe.'

'Indeed, it is not. But Dr Ashburn, do sit down a moment, for you look quite done in. Will you take something – tea, or brandy?'

'A little brandy would be very welcome,' he said, and, fetching it myself to spare the harassed maids, I returned to find him leaning back heavily against the sofa cushions, a man who seemed younger, more vulnerable, than I had supposed.

'I beg your pardon,' he said, half rising, taking the glass from me and drinking, as I had seen him do before, almost with need.

'Are you quite well, Dr Ashburn?'

'Why yes – quite well, thank you. I have been up all night, that is all. And, to tell you the truth, I am always distressed by death, which may seem strange, since I see so much of it. I had hoped to grow accustomed.'

'I am glad you cannot.'

'Why do you say that?'

'Because to grow accustomed would be the same as growing hard, I suppose.'

He leaned forward, drew a deep breath, of courage perhaps, and said rapidly, knowing the time ill-chosen but unable, it seemed, to prevent himself, 'Sometimes you have been of great help to me.'

'I? But what have I ever done?'

'You have – been there, in Blenheim Lane – where I knew I could find you. The theory that the sight of beauty – of what a man finds to be beautiful – refreshes the spirit, I have found to be most apt.'

It's true, then, I thought. I am not beautiful at all, but he finds me so, which means he is in love with me. I wonder why? He is a clever man, sensitive and serious, distinguished in his way, and I have nothing in my head but fashion and small-talk and Nicholas Barforth. Why should he fall in love with me? And I understood that the happy patchwork I had woven for all our lives was falling irrevocably apart. Giles Ashburn – who could have been so happy with Prudence, I was sure of it, and she with him – loved me and Nicholas did not; and, wanting to spare him distress, hoping that when it came to it Nicholas would try to spare me, I began to murmur the remarks I had been taught to use on such occasions, and he to apologize for his familiarity, both of us talking quickly and saying nothing, until there was the sound of a horse, and Jonas came into the room.

He was, as always, immaculate, the sombre, neutral shades of the man of business, unruffled although he had ridden several miles from the station through a blustery evening, his face registering no surprise, no alarm.

'Dr Ashburn?'

'Yes. Your son was born an hour ago, Mr Agbrigg. Your wife has made a sufficient recovery, but not the child. I am truly sorry.'

'Ah,' Jonas said, his eyelids lowering very briefly, and then: 'I see. I am sure you did your best.'

'I believe so.'

'Shall I go up to her?'

'Yes. She may need you.'

I went into the hall, handed Giles Ashburn his hat and cloak since there seemed no one else to do it, assured him that my mother would soon be here, waited in the open doorway to watch him drive away. And when I returned to the drawing-room Jonas was there before me, standing by the hearth, staring reflectively at the fire.

'You have not been long, Jonas. Is she sleeping?'

'No. She is not sleeping.'

'What then?'

'She is awake.'

'Jonas – if you are telling me to mind my own business, then I must tell you that she is my sister –'

'Yes,' he said, taking the fire-tongs and very deliberately selecting a piece of coal, breaking it neatly, without violence, into even segments and arranging them into a carefully contrived pyramid. 'I will tell you then. She is awake. She has sent the nurse for a tray of tea. I went upstairs because I was told she needed me. I came downstairs again because she does not. Should she need me later, I will go up again. That is all.'

'Jonas – please don't be impatient with her. I am impatient with her myself, often enough, but she is only seventeen, and it has been a – a shock.'

'I?' he said, his eyes still on the fire, his intricate building of the coal. 'I am never impatient. Quite the reverse. I have just been into the kitchen to make certain that her tray, when they take it to her, will be just to her liking. I have reminded them to use a white cloth and I have even held the cup to the light to make certain it is spotless and has no cracks. What more can I do for her, at this moment, than that?'

My sister's unknown little child was buried some days later, Jonas standing chilled but unapproachable at the graveside, my mother and his father shedding a tear, Aunt Hannah looking stern, since she disliked any kind of failure and, although she was sorry for Celia, was beginning to have doubts about her fitness as a future Cabinet Minister's wife.

Celia greeted us on our return from the cemetery, her face like a stone, her body still full of that strange, rigid anger.

'Tea is just ready,' she said. 'I expect you will be glad of it, since the day has turned cold.'

'Thank you,' Jonas answered with scrupulous politeness, taking the cup she offered him, and then, excusing himself once more with great correctness, retiring to his study for the perusal of documents which would not wait.

'I believe it will snow before morning,' Aunt Hannah said, to fill in the silence, to which we obediently chorused, 'Yes, indeed.'

'You are not looking well, Miss Aycliffe,' Giles Ashburn murmured, having looked in for a moment because he had seen our carriage.

'Oh – I am quite all right, thank you'; but in fact I was unable to shake off the chill of the winter graveyard, my bones aching, my chest tightening with the start of an influenza which kept me in my bed longer than it need have done, had I been anxious to rise, thus causing offence to Caroline who wished to consult me about the length of her wedding veil. And even before I ventured downstairs again, it was no secret to anyone that Georgiana Clevedon, having taken more accurately the measure of Blaize, had turned her green woodland eyes and her sudden laughter on Nicholas.

He had danced with her the maximum permitted number of times – three, in fact – at an Assembly Rooms ball, where Miss Clevedon, in an evening gown which Caroline declared managed somehow to look like a riding habit, had given further offence by her complete disregard of the etiquette Cullingford required to see in its young ladies.

'So these are the famous Assembly Rooms,' she had said on arrival, speaking to Julian Flood, but her loud, flat squire's drawl audible to several others. 'My word! I never saw the inside of a counting house, but this must be it.'

While even the comfortable Mrs Hobhouse, having been brought up like the rest of us to consider poverty a sin which, like adultery and associated vices, must be concealed at all costs, had been shocked to hear Miss Clevedon declare herself as poor as a church mouse.

'Oh, I have but the one gown,' she had said when Mrs Hobhouse, trying to be kind, had admired it, 'so I have no bother at all in deciding what to wear – it is simply this one, or if it is not fit to be seen, I cannot go out at all.'

'Lounging,' Aunt Hannah told us, 'at the buffet with the men – behaving, in fact, like a man herself. Thoroughly unbecoming, and I cannot believe any relative of mine could have thought otherwise.'

And so in fact it seemed, for at a town meeting some days later, called by Mayor Agbrigg to discuss the story state of Cullingford's sewers, Nicholas, as astonished as anyone else perhaps, to see Miss Clevedon sitting there, had offered her no more than a curt nod, a cool word, and had left before the speeches ended, making it clear that he desired no private conversation with anyone. Yet Miss Clevedon had remained on her chair, managing at least to keep from yawning – a feat beyond the powers of many – while Mayor Agbrigg had attempted to curdle the assembled blood with tales of overflowing swill-tubs in Simon Street, and Dr Ashburn had put forward his much ridiculed theory that certain diseases, cholera not least among them, may be transferred not only by the touch or the breath of the sufferer, nor by contact with rotting garbage heaps – all of which could be avoided – but by the drinking of contaminated water, which could not. Cholera, Dr Ashburn had declared – quietly, but with immense firmness, Prudence told me – had destroyed sixty thousand English souls only some sixteen years ago, confining itself largely but not exclusively to those areas where sanitation was haphazard, or where there was no sanitation at all. And unless something, in his view, was done about the open sewers of Simon Street, and the local habit of gathering water for domestic usage from any stagnant pool available when the stand-pipe ran out, then it was beyond question that the disease would strike again.

'He was most emphatic in his warning,' Prudence told me, 'and most courageous too, since I know how little he enjoys public speaking.'

And when Prudence refused, despite all my persuasion, to sink to the level of common gossip, I had to wait for Caroline to tell me that Miss Clevedon, having listened patiently to the end, had inquired, once more in that loud, flat drawl, 'Now where is Simon Street? It sounds unlikely and most intriguing, and there is no doubt at all that one has a duty to help the poor. May one go and see it?'

'I suppose you will be wanting tea?' Caroline had replied, compelled to make the offer, she explained, since the girl, after all, was cousin to Matthew Chard, but feeling the coolness of her tone sufficient to ensure a refusal. But Miss Clevedon, with her quick smile, her coltish tossing of the head, had accepted with evident gladness, returning in the Barforth carriage to spend the rest of the day at Tarn Edge.

'I cannot think why Verity and Caroline encourage her,' Aunt Hannah said, coming to sit with me the following afternoon, genuinely concerned, I think, at my slow recovery. Yet Georgiana Clevedon, despite her poverty, was the daughter and granddaughter of landed gentlemen who knew of no reason why she could not visit a manufacturer's household as freely as the cottages on the Galton estate, as freely as Aunt Hannah herself entered the millhouses at Lawcroft. She came and went as she pleased, appearing and disappearing to suit her fancy, not only in Cullingford but inside my head, so that I was never entirely without her, could never lose the impression of that pointed face, hovering somewhere behind my eyes, nor the sound of Blaize's voice telling us how easily even a stubborn man – and quite against his nature – could love her.

'If they would simply leave the matter alone,' Prudence said when Aunt Hannah had gone, 'then I believe it would be no more than a nine days' wonder. Blaize thinks so too. Men are prone to these fancies, and should be allowed, in their own good time, to grow tired of them. That is what Blaize says, at any rate, and since he has fancies enough for a dozen men, then I am inclined to think he is right.'

But the sight of a gentleman's daughter displaying so marked a preference for the son of a manufacturer intrigued Cullingford. The suspicion that the young lady believed her social superiority too enormous to permit any embarrassment – that she was condescending rather than pursuing – gave much offence. And on the very day that I came feebly downstairs, having lost weight and colour, looking hollow, I thought, feeling as if I had dissolved, somehow, into a damp mist and could not take shape again, the drawing-room was full of ladies, half of them well pleased to sympathize with poor, dear Verity Barforth in her troubles, all of them eager to pry from my mother the information Aunt Verity would not give.

'Faith dear, how very unwell you look,' they said to me, reserving my plight, only half guessed at, for later.

'I am very well, thank you,' I went on repeating, my lips feeling stiff and cold, my smile an inward agony, for although my body was still limp, the congestion of my lungs not fully healed, my real sickness, I knew full well, was of despair.

The world had once been kind to me. It had placed me in a comfortable home far beyond the level of those who were obliged to labour. It had given me health and hope and an inclination to laughter; it had given me a nature which required to be loved, and now, without hope of the man I required to love me, I no longer knew what I was doing in the world at all.

'You must take care, dear,' my mother's tea-time ladies told me, each one, on leaving.

'Yes, so I will, thank you, Mrs Hobhouse – Mrs Mandelbaum –' And then, half rising and finding my legs quite fluid, my whole body slipping, somehow, from its direction, I murmured, 'I am not well enough, mother, to go out just yet.'

'No darling,' she said, shaking her head, smiling at me, her voice fainter than I had expected, her face too near to mine and then too far away. 'Go back to bed. Miss Mayfield will sit with you.'

'He has not sent her a note, or a flower,' I heard Prudence mutter angrily, and although I wanted to defend him, I lacked the strength to tell her I had neither expected nor wanted it. For what could he possibly write?

Blaize had sent me flowers in profusion. Giles Ashburn had visited every day. Jonas had called once or twice with cheerful news of Celia, who had been carried downstairs now to her sofa and had even walked, with his assistance, to the window. Even Freddy Hobhouse, using any excuse to see Prudence, had brought me a jar of his mother's famous ginger marmalade to tempt my invalid appetite. But a few lines from Nicholas, saying 'I am sorry to hear you are unwell,' far from reassuring me, would have told me that he did not greatly care. His silence indicated that he was troubled on his own account, guilty on mine, and, even in the weakness of my convalescence, the down-drooping of my spirit. I could not tolerate the thought that I might weigh heavily on his conscience. Whatever happened, I would not be an uneasy memory, to him or to anyone.

Yet hope was not entirely at an end. Nicholas, I heard, had declined an invitation to dine at Galton Abbey, had excused himself from showing Miss Clevedon his father's mills, leaving Blaize to escort her around the sheds, which, she freely avowed, had horrified and depressed her, the sight of so much close-confined humanity inspiring her to thoughts of revolution, the noise and the stench turning her stomach. He was behaving, in fact, like a man tempted, certainly – if the smouldering, brooding glances Amy Battershaw and Rebecca Mandelbaum described to me were anything to go by – but struggling to reassert his common sense. And knowing him to be sensible, I continued fitfully to hope, until the afternoon when Caroline burst in upon me to say that her father had forbidden him to see Miss Clevedon again, at which point I knew there could be little hope at all.

'He has been sneaking off before the engines were shut down,' she told me, flushed with indignation. 'Riding halfway to Galton, and she half-way from there to meet him. Really, the kind of assignation one may make with a housemaid. Well, my father has told him to put an end to it, and he, of course, has said he will not. And even my mother, who will never say a word against him, was unable to stay calm. Yes, we have all told him what we think to it – except Blaize, who was altogether impertinent, saying he should be allowed to get on with it and get rid of it in his own way. A point of view, I suppose, which may serve for a housemaid, but which in this case, is pure folly. Surely you must see that, Faith, for however much we may dislike her, she is a Miss Clevedon of Galton Abbey, cousin to the Chards and the Floods, and with the very

503

highest connections in London, although you would not think it to look at her; and if Nicholas should compromise her and refuse to marry her, then all our reputations must suffer. Blaize may think such behaviour admissible, but the gentry would all band together – including Matthew – to say that one can expect nothing better of a manufacturer. And, quite frankly, although I stress that I detest the girl, I could not blame them. If she were a Hobhouse we should have had her father already on our doorstep demanding that Nicholas name the wedding-day – except that no Hobhouse, and no one else I have ever heard of, would dream of carrying on in this loose fashion. I said so, too, and I believe Nicholas would have slapped me for it, had not my father intervened. "You cannot judge her," Nicholas said, "by your own narrow standards." Yes, he said that, and I thought my father would have had a fit, and it was my mother who had to intervene then, or he would have given Nicholas a thrashing. My word, I have never heard such language as they threw at each other. Well, it is all misery with us just now, as you may imagine, for my father and Nicholas have not exchanged a word since yesterday and my mother is so afraid that Nicholas may walk out one morning and not return that she is wearing herself out, going from one to the other, endeavouring to make the peace. But, Faith – you really do look quite ill. I hope you may be fully recovered for my wedding. You look as if you need a trip to a warmer climate again – like your mother.'

Yet even this escape, which I would have seized gladly, was denied me, for in that same month the French king, Louis Philippe, was driven from his throne by the Paris mob, escaping across the Tuileries Gardens with no time to put on his wig, haunted, no doubt, by the memory of another King Louis, not too long ago, who had lost not only his wig but his head. And as one by one the capital cities of Europe burst into flame and London itself began to simmer, when even in Cullingford Mr Hobhouse was jostled on his way to the Piece Hall, Mr Oldroyd jeered by a ragged, street-corner mob, I understood escape to be impossible and composed myself as best I could, strengthening myself daily, like an athlete, a soldier, to support this constant wounding, the certainty of greater injury to come.

At the beginning of March a stone was thrown at Aunt Hannah's carriage, not causing her horses to bolt, since they were too elderly for that in any case; but the intention had been plain, the missiles aimed not by unruly urchins but by hard and bitter men. And Aunt Hannah may have been displeased at her husband's simple comment. 'They're hungry,' for it had been a severe winter, following a poor harvest, the price of bread still high despite the removal of the Corn Laws, the advantage of Repeal having gone as always, it seemed, to the masters rather than the servants, since wages – paid out to men who had no vote, no power but that of terror and disobedience – were still very low.

'They're hungry.' And now, with the railways and the new penny post to facilitate communications, there were rumours once again of armed risings in the manner of the revolutionary French, the Chartists come to plague us afresh with their demands which only Giles Ashburn, among all our acquaintance, did not consider to be excessive.

504

It was the result, he explained – talking to Prudence, making an uncomfortable effort not to look too often at me – of the reforms of 1832, which had not gone far enough. Much had been promised in the great Reform Year, and much, indeed, received by the middle classes, who for the first time had won representation in a Parliament previously no more than a mouthpiece for the landed gentry. After the Bill of 1832 any man in Cullingford who paid an annual property rent of ten pounds or more could have his vote, to use or to sell as he thought fit, although the absence of a secret ballot somewhat restricted his choices, should he be in the employ of Mr Joel Barforth, or a tenant of Sir Giles Flood. Yet these new voters, Dr Ashburn calculated, had numbered no more than a mere thousand or so in a population of sixty thousand, a solid pressure-group from the middle classes which had sent middle-class men like my father to Parliament to speak for them, in opposition to the gentry and totally neglectful of the troublesome, if labouring, poor.

And having fought so hard for their own right to vote, their own freedom from the ground landlord, the titled farmer, they could hardly be astonished, Dr Ashburn felt, at the Chartists, whose revolutionary demands for one man one vote would make the poor, not necessarily rich, but – since there were so many of them – very powerful.

'Their demands are very logical,' he said, so quietly that it was not easy to realize his opinions were treasonable and, if acted upon, could lead him to the gallows. 'When your uncle, Mr Barforth, fought hard to be represented in Parliament in thirty-two, I am sure Sir Giles Flood thought him quite as much a revolutionary as he now thinks his operatives for making the same demands. There is no cause for astonishment, surely? In fact the Duke of Wellington himself has warned repeatedly that, by extending the franchise even so far, his peers have done no more than open the flood-gates, through which sooner or later the riff-raff are bound to get through. And now, at least, he may have the satisfaction of seeing himself proved correct. The people have finally understood that they can rely on no one but themselves. The gentry will look after the gentry. The manufacturers will look after the manufacturers. Both these groups have made promises to the labouring classes which they have kept only in part, or not at all, or in such a way that no real benefit has been derived. The people, now, have chosen to look after their own interests, and they require the vote to do it. And to spare themselves yet another hollow triumph – the choice between voting for a millmaster or a squire – they require that Members of Parliament should no longer, by law, be men of property. They wish to elect one of themselves, which also seems to be in no way astonishing. Sir Giles Flood may well have considered your uncle too ill-educated and too lacking in political experience to use the franchise correctly once he had obtained it – since he clearly meant to use it against Sir Giles. And, unfortunately, he may have been right, as your uncle is right now, when he says the same thing. But that, surely, is not a reason to deny the franchise. Would it not be better to educate those who are in need of it – which, I imagine, must be four-fifths of our nation – so that everyone may use his vote with responsibility, as seems best to him?'

'Precisely,' my sister said, perfectly in tune with him, 'for our system of education is deplorable. Our boys are taught Latin and Greek and little else, our girls are taught nothing at all, the labouring classes are taught – one supposes – to labour, which sometimes seems better to me than fine embroidery. How I would love to set up a school – do you know that? Yes, if they would let me have my money, I would open a school for girls which would be like no other school in the world – no water-colours, no samplers – real work, Giles. Only think how shocking! I imagine they would attempt to burn me at the stake.'

'Do it, Prudence,' I said. 'Why not? Let's talk to mamma. We could do it together – not even in Cullingford. We could travel together, until we found a place – get away –'

'Not you, Faith,' she said, her voice almost hard. 'You'll get married, you know you will – one day. You can send me your daughters.'

And neither of us could miss the nervous tremor in Giles Ashburn's quiet face, nor how quickly he looked away.

I went out for the first time at the end of that week, braving the sooty March winds to call on Celia who, cutting short my uneasy references to her child, talking solely of a new rosewood card table she had ordered two months ago and which now, being finally delivered, was not at all as desired. And returning home, ridiculously weakened by so brief an excursion, to be told that Mr Barforth – Blaize, I assumed – was waiting to see me, I went alone into the drawing-room, shocked beyond immediate recovery to find Nicholas there.

He was standing at the window, obscured by the half-dark which always prevailed in that room, a silhouette merely against the deep claret of the curtains, although I had no need of light to see his face. And knowing that this, surely, was the moment for which I had schooled myself, my first real encounter with pain, I took off my gloves and my bonnet, slowly, neatly, folded my hands, folded as much of myself as I could grasp and shut it away, before I asked, 'Nicholas?' although the question was neither of his identity nor his intentions.

'Yes,' he said, not moving forward. 'There is something I have to say to you – and quickly, I think.'

'Then say it.'

'I am come straight from Galton Abbey, where I have just asked Georgiana Clevedon to be my wife.'

'Yes, of course.'

And, as the words slipped from my tongue, my mind, too, slipped a shade away from reality, leaving me with an odd sensation that this was not the first time he had said this to me, nor the first time I had so calmly answered. Like a recurring dream it had happened before, over and over again, in the part of my brain which controlled the source of anguish and fear, over and over, a wheel turning me slowly towards him and as slowly away again, so that I had grown accustomed to it, and would not break.

'Faith –'

'Yes.'

'I had to tell you myself. You do see that I had to do that?'

'Yes, I do. I hope you will be very happy, Nicholas.'

'Oh,' he said, striding forward, his face hard and strained, quite pale. 'As to that – I hope so too. Many will think otherwise, but she is a rare person, Faith, truly – I know of no one like her. And I can only pray she may be happy with me.'

'Yes, Nicholas.'

And then, abruptly, his voice harsh, as if the words were forced from him through clenched teeth, he said, 'They will say it is for my money on her part, and on mine because I am stubborn. It is more than that. I had to say that too.'

'There was no need. I knew it.'

'Aye,' he said, a sigh of pure weariness escaping him. 'You always know. You've known, these past weeks, haven't you – known what was happening to me – why I couldn't even come and see you when you were ill? Well, I came, a dozen times, to the end of the street and then went away again – that's the truth – because I couldn't face you. I wasn't sure, until now, that I was even going to do it – it could all have been over, and there'd have been no need to say a word to you about it. You wouldn't have asked me any questions either, would you? No – I know damned well you wouldn't. You'd have made it easy for me – like you're doing now. Christ – I'd better go home.'

But he didn't move, and unable to say more I walked past him to stand with my face to the window, until the sound of the door slamming shut behind him, and the street door after it, released me from that terrible, fierce-clenched control and bent me double for a moment, winded and gasping, as Celia had been at the start of her travail.

'Faith,' Prudence said sharply from the doorway, my mother behind her, and straightening up, sitting down, my voice pronounced what was in my mind, so calmly that in some crazy recess of myself I could have laughed at it.

'He is to marry Georgiana Clevedon. I do not think they can be happy, and I – really – do you know, I wish I could die of it. It would seem easier, except that of course I cannot – no one really dies of these things.'

'How dare he come here!' Prudence said, glaring at the window as if she would have liked to break through it and go after him, a sliver of glass in her hand. 'It is an open acknowledgment that he recognizes there has been something between you – that he has treated you badly. How dare he? He should have had the decency to keep away, and when I meet him again I shall tell him so.'

'Oh no, dear,' my mother murmured, her whole face, it seemed, brimming with tears. 'I must ask you not to do so, for he will have trouble enough. He has Joel yet to face and – oh, Faith, my poor lamb, I should not tell you this, but it may help you to know how she has snared him. Verity was expecting it – oh yes, she was so despondent last night, for it seems he rode over to Galton on Monday and did not return until Tuesday, which did not alarm Verity until she learned that the grandfather had gone away to London, and the brother with him. My dear, they were alone all night together, in that isolated place – no, no, the maids cannot signify on such occasions. And what could he do but make her an offer after that?'

'Ah,' Prudence said. 'It does not surprise me.'

But getting up and returning to the window, concentrating so hard on the last harsh tones of his voice that these other voices, seeking to comfort me, became a nuisance, a mere pestering of flies coming between me and the things I believed, had to believe, I said, 'No. He loves her.'

'Darling, surely not –?'

And, turning to my mother so fiercely that she retreated a hasty step backwards, I repeated his own words, 'Yes, mother. They will say it is for his money on her part, and on his because he is stubborn. It is more than that. He loves her, mother. He believes it, and I believe it – and so must you.'

And at least I had salvaged something. I had kept my faith with him.

11

There was a most terrible, yet in some ways merciful, numbness inside me for a while after that, an absence of sensation which, although I knew it to be unnatural, did not manage to alarm me. I was suspended, it seemed, a little above and around myself, observing my own calm with a certain irony, knowing it could not last, praying only that it would last long enough for me to meet Nicholas again, as I would have to do, until I had seen him married, wished him well, waved his honeymoon train away, at which point, since I could not die and could not run away, I would at least be able to face myself – and Cullingford – again.

His news, of course, had created a predictable explosion at Tarn Edge, Aunt Verity, even, forsaking her tranquillity, pleading with him most tearfully to reconsider, while Uncle Joel had been so moved by his wife's distress that even Caroline had been alarmed at the violence of his anger. Yet, in the end, when his threats of dismissal from the family business and from the family itself had been two or three times repeated, and Nicholas had declared himself perfectly ready to be cast adrift, it had become clear to them all that they did not really wish to part from one another, and so they sat down, more quietly, to discuss what must be done.

Aunt Verity, it seemed, while by no means unaware of Miss Clevedon's charm, simply did not consider her a suitable wife for Nicholas. Uncle Joel, when it came down to it, was still man enough to recognize a 'rare bird' when he saw one, and could have been amused, even captivated by her, had he encountered her as the fiancée of a Flood or a Winterton, or of any man's son but his own. His main objection, after long deliberation, was that he failed to see the profit in such a marriage. In Caroline's case there was a title in the offing, his daughter – whose great-grandmother had spent her days in a weaving shed – elevated to Lady Chard of Listonby, her children in possession of hereditary lands and privileges which money alone could not buy. But, since it would be Peregrine Clevedon, not Georgiana, who would inherit the ancient domain of Galton Abbey, my uncle could not understand in this instance just what he was being asked to pay for.

'Wait a while, lad,' he'd asked, almost patiently for him. 'I know how these things can get in the blood, when you're young. And you're young, Nicky – by God, you're young. Give yourself a chance, lad.'

But Nicholas was of full age, a man with the courage to face life on his own and the skill to succeed, and although, left to himself, my uncle might just have made good his threat of dismissal, seeing no real harm to it providing a door was left open should Nicholas wish to return, he knew the depth of Aunt Verity's feeling for her younger son, and would not run the risk of breaking her heart.

And I suppose it was a shock to him, and to the rest of the Barforths too, when they learned that Miss Clevedon's grandfather was as bitterly opposed to the match as they.

Mr Gervase Clevedon, squire of Galton, was descended by junior line from some of the greatest names in England, having himself married first a viscount's daughter and then the sister of a belted earl, both these ladies bringing little money but immense prestige to the Abbey. Untitled and apparently penniless, he was nevertheless nobler than Matthew Chard: a man whose family creed was a simple one of service to Crown and country, whose own days were spent in the tireless, unpaid administration of local justice, a gentleman whose word had never been questioned because no promise of his had ever been broken, whose decisions, both as a magistrate and a landlord, were invariably in keeping with his own impeccable personal code.

Clevedons, from the beginning of the line, had served. They had never sold themselves, never worked for wages. They had been rewarded by honours, never insulted by the payment of cash, which, even when there had been cash to spare, no Clevedon had ever carried about his person like a grocer. They had served, freely and loyally, and, expecting an equal loyalty from their own servants, had undertaken the care of them in sickness and old age, regarding all those in their employ, the tenants of their farms and their cottages, as members of their extended family.

The butler who served my Uncle Joel at Tarn Edge, who had been imported from London, would be dismissed the very instant he gave less than perfect satisfaction, or would leave without a backward glance to take up a better offer. The manservant at Galton Abbey, who had inherited his father's position, and his grandfather's, would be supported, albeit meagrely, for the rest of his life, and would devote his last energies to anyone who bore the name of Clevedon.

'I work for money,' Uncle Joel said. 'And because I expect others to do the same, I pay good wages.'

'I do my duty,' Mr Clevedon might have answered. 'I am responsible for those born on my land in situations inferior to my own. I hold the land itself in trust for future generations, having received it from those of my name who held it in trust for me. I am true to myself and to all those with whom I have dealings. I offer loyalty and expect to receive it – a commodity which is far beyond price.'

And so, although they were both decent, clever men, they baffled and offended each other, my uncle entirely convinced that all three Clevedons were conspiring to get their hands on his money, Mr Clevedon every bit as certain that the Barforths would crawl on their knees – or ought to – for this alliance with his great name.

Like turns to like, they both said in their different ways. My son needs a sensible woman. My granddaughter needs a gentleman. My son is hard-working, shrewd, where any other man could make a penny he can usually find the way to make two. My granddaughter has been trained to accept the responsibilities of privilege, the duties of a manorial lady towards her estate and its people. She would give those two pennies away to anyone with a hereditary claim on the house of Clevedon, and leave herself starving.

'There may yet be hope,' Blaize told my sister. 'They may argue the terms of the marriage contract too long, until the spark fades, and we shall have no marriage at all.'

But Nicholas, having made up his mind, could not tolerate the delay, and at his threat – made with the calm of complete determination – to simplify matters by taking Miss Clevedon to Gretna Green to be married over the blacksmith's anvil, all opposition ceased.

'Well, at least now I can give some thought to my own wedding,' Caroline told me. 'Honiton lace, I wondered, Faith, for the veil – I believe the Queen had Honiton lace, did she not?'

And, still in that odd state of half feeling, where a pin, sometimes, in my side would not have aroused even a cry, I replied, 'Yes, and orange blossoms on her gown, which in your case would look splendid, Caroline, since you are taller and could have more of them.'

But as the month reached its ill-natured, rain-swept close, my detachment seemed to be like a cloak that slipped, every now and then, from my shoulders, leaving me no protection from the cold. And since I would have frozen entirely had I remained in that torpid state, I awoke, first of all to panic, which, slicing through all my defences, warned me that I could not cope. How could I stand in the Abbey church at Galton and see Nicholas married to another woman? I could not. It was as simple as that. And there were times when the dread of it caught me unawares, a vicious hammer-blow battering away all vestiges of control, so that I had to lock myself away, upstairs, anywhere, to fight it. And if that hammer struck out at me on his wedding day, where could I run, with Amy Battershaw and Rebecca Mandelbaum, and my brother-in-law Jonas watching me?

But I would attend that wedding. I would stand in that church, somehow, without a tremor, and smile. And afterwards, like everyone else, I would go up to Miss Clevedon – Mrs Nicholas Barforth – and I would say all the things I would have said to any other bride.

'I hope you will be very happy,' I forced my lips to speak in grim rehearsal. 'May I say how much I admire your dress? May I call you Georgiana, since we are to be cousins now?'

510

I would do it. And I would do it well, not only for my own pride's sake, but because it mattered fiercely that Nicholas – who had trouble enough and more trouble to come – should not feel troubled by me.

What, indeed, had he done to me? He had not asked me to fall in love with him in the first place. He had made me no promises. He had not compromised me, nor encouraged me to refuse another man for his sake. He had not jilted me, and I was quite wildly determined to give no one cause to think he had.

The truth of the matter was very simple. He had always liked me and had started to like me better. He had recognized me as the woman who would be good for him, but, unlike Jonas, who had settled for the woman he could get – and been glad at the time to get her – Nicholas had found the courage to stake everything on a woman he truly desired. If Matthew Chard had not brought Miss Clevedon to Tarn Edge, or had Blaize proved more susceptible, my patience may well have succeeded. But Matthew Chard had brought her. Blaize, as always, had been too intent on dazzling her to be dazzled himself. She existed. Nicholas did love her. If she was not in love with Nicholas now, I could not imagine it would take her very long to love him. It had happened, and if I was heartbroken and quite desperate at times, if I believed I had lost everything of value in my life, that the essential part of life itself was already over, then that was my concern, and I would be a poor, whining creature if I let it show.

And, growing more and more obsessed by my need to keep faith with him, the quality for which I had been named, it came about that only Blaize and myself had a good word to say for Miss Clevedon.

'Of course you must ask her to be your bridesmaid,' I told Caroline. 'It would look odd, otherwise.'

'Absolutely,' Blaize added. 'I imagine we can make sure she does not come to church in her riding habit.'

While to the assorted ladies of my mother's tea-time, who had heard the strange tales of the Clevedons, but who just the same had a sneaking admiration for a real lord, a real lady, I said, 'Her grandmother was a viscount's daughter,' leaving Blaize to supply the details of a Clevedon who had graced the court of Queen Anne, another who had enjoyed the friendship of the Duchess of Kent, mother of our own, intensely respectable Queen Victoria. And, although these Cullingford matrons knew there was rarely any money in bosom friendships of that nature, they were impressed, nevertheless, and eager to hear more.

'We are doing rather well,' Blaize told me. 'They will all be falling over themselves presently to invite her to their tables.'

'So I imagine.'

'Of course they will not like her,' he said, his eyes, which saw everything, knew everything, looking at me with a characteristic blend of curiosity and kindness. 'But she is not so very dreadful, you know – just different.'

But I had no intention of revealing my heartache to Blaize, whose own heart was too cool, too shallow perhaps for real understanding, consoling myself with the belief that, if I had not managed to deceive him, then at least no one else suspected me. No one else. Yet my mother and Prudence were very kind to me, shielding me, in their different ways, from gossip, filling the gaps of my conversation when, every now and then, my throat was so tight that I could not speak; and Jonas, my brother-in-law, who had been wounded himself, not by love but certainly in his pride, watched me at times, remembering, perhaps, the night of Caroline's dance when I had seen his own composure stripped away.

'You will be the next one to be married, I expect, Faith.'

'Do you think so, Jonas?'

'Oh yes. I think so. I imagine you must see the necessity for it.'

'Good heavens, Jonas! I am only nineteen – not quite on the shelf.'

'By no means – but if you have suffered a disappointment there is really only one way to mend it.'

'What disappointment?'

'Ah – my mother was wrong then? I am delighted to hear it.'

'Jonas – exactly what do you mean?'

'Very little, it seems. My mother had formed the odd notion that you are attached –'

'I am not – absolutely not. It is positively untrue.'

'What is untrue, Faith?'

'What you said.'

'I said nothing.'

'Oh yes you did. You said that I was attached to –'

'Indeed? To whom?'

'To no one.'

'Excellent. I will tell my mother she can be easy. But *had* you been attached to someone – who is to marry someone else – then the best course open to you would be to get married yourself. No one could then say – and there does appear to have been a whisper – that you might possibly be pining away for that unspecified someone.'

'Please don't play your lawyer's tricks on me, Jonas. I am not impressed.' But I wept a long time that night, wounded as I believe he had intended to wound me, well aware that I had not convinced him; and, like all of life's ills, it was small consolation to me that I was not the only one, just then, who suffered.

It had been a hard winter in Simon Street, offering, as a Christmas gift, a hunger that by springtime had festered from hopelessness to rage, making the city dangerous again for those of us who drove out behind sleek carriage-horses, who fed our pet dogs more regularly, more plentifully, than a half of Cullingford could feed its children. There had been unkempt, haggard gatherings on Cullingford Green, Chartist banners held aloft in broad-tipped, big-knuckled hands, a mob, one morning, erupting into the Hobhouse mill yard when the gates were open at breakfast-time, some of them willing to settle, then and there, for higher wages and ready to give a good week's work in exchange; some of them threatening that, with the vote in their hands, there'd be no need to ask for anything ever again, simply to take; others quite openly wanting to burn the mill down.

They had gone from Nethercoats to Market Square, their target undoubtedly the Piece Hall, which, it being market-day, was full of soberly dressed, serious-minded gentlemen of the middle classes, the younger of whom – not having been middle-class for very long – not above using their fists, the elders having plenty to say about how they'd settled these matters in 'their day'. And, in the ensuing hour of street-fighting, the scuffling and cursing, the stone-throwing and window-smashing, the violence had been put down, as always, by violence, by the staves and cutlasses of special constables, the hard-riding of a squadron of dragoons hired for the purpose, leaving a dozen men on the ground, another dozen dragging themselves away to heal or to die – as best they could – in some squalid bolt-hole in Simon Street.

My sister Prudence went to the Infirmary that day, against everybody's orders, to tend the wounded, helping Giles Ashburn to patch them up before they were taken to York to be imprisoned, or hanged, and by April, with the Chartist agitation at its height, the Royal Family – fearing, as so often before, a revolution of the bloodier, Continental variety – had been removed from London for safe-keeping, the Whitehall area garrisoned and provisioned to withstand a state of siege, and two hundred thousand special constables sworn in to obey the Duke of Wellington's command.

'My word, how very stirring,' my mother said, glad of anything to relieve her boredom.

'They're hungry,' Mayor Agbrigg told us once again.

'They're greedy,' Aunt Hannah replied.

'They're inefficient,' said Uncle Joel, greeting with laughter the news that the Chartist leader, Feargus O'Connor, planned to assemble half a million desperate men and march to Westminster to present – or enforce – their petition for Parliamentary Reform; to persuade, in fact, a reluctant government to grant the vote to every working man, or, if they refused, to turn them out and govern in their stead.

'Half a million men, indeed,' my uncle repeated, his bulk firmly planted on my mother's hearthrug, the fragrance of his cigar smoke offending the very memory of my father. 'Yes, half a million, which to the naked eye would look like ten million. Excellent – for if O'Connor could get that half million to follow him then he'd get everything he asked for, and more besides. But where are they to come from? Agreed – we have the railways now, but has Feargus O'Connor offered to pay the train-fare for all those desperate men? Does he have the money? And, supposing they've all been told the name of the meeting-place, has he remembered to tell them how to get there? And, when the day dawns, has it crossed his mind to wonder how many will manage to get out of bed on time, how many are likely to call at the ale-house on the way to the station, and stay there; or how many will have thought better of it? Half a million. He'll be lucky if he gets a thousand. And if it's a good summer, and a good harvest, and trade picks up, next year he'll get none at all.'

And so it was. There were, in fact, more than my uncle's scornfully predicted thousand – twenty-three thousand, Giles Ashburn reported sadly having received the news from my half-brother, Crispin Aycliffe, who had been one among them – but so far short of the expected numbers that, with those special constables poised for the attack, with cannon stationed at the ready on Westminster Bridge, and gamekeepers' rifles sprouting from the windows of the rich and famous, Mr Feargus O'Connor, with true political flexibility, abandoned his march, and instead of leading an army to Westminster in triumph, drove there alone and sedately in a cab, his petition lying in forlorn bundles at his feet.

'I could have told him so,' Uncle Joel announced.

'Aye – so could I,' Mayor Agbrigg added, his meaning, I thought, not at all the same.

'I'm so sorry,' I told Giles Ashburn, thinking of the men who had made that wild goose chase to London, the men who had kept faith, as I tried to do, and who would be wandering now, footsore and disheartened, in an alien city; remembering the undernourished bodies he had himself stitched together, only a few weeks ago, and sent to York.

'It's always the way – people, quite simply, are like that,' he said, and, taking both my hands in his, he bent his head and pressed not his lips but his forehead against them, a gesture of tenderness and weariness that held me quite still, a gesture of need which frightened and fascinated me, and from which I could not turn away.

The fight was over, Chartism, without doubt, was in ashes, its preposterous demands stowed away in some Whitehall archive, best forgotten. The Queen and all her special constables came home again, the English, after all, not being a people much given to wasteful, foreign ideas like revolution, and there was nothing to mar Caroline's wedding-day that June but a slight shower of rain as she left the church, and the indisposition of my sister Celia, who, being pregnant again, was unable to attend.

It was – as had been intended – the most sumptuous wedding Cullingford had ever seen, Caroline an imperial splendour in her satin and Honiton lace, her bridesmaids, myself and Georgiana Clevedon among them, wearing lesser copies of her gown which, as I had suggested they would, made her seem ever more magnificent. And aware of Miss Clevedon standing directly behind me in the bridal procession, and of Nicholas not far away, I felt the stab of panic and saw with disgust that my bouquet was shaking in my hand.

I must not think of her now, should not think of her at all, yet I could think of nothing else, could not forget the fierce protest, followed almost at once by the weakness of pure anguish which had swamped me at the sight of her own wedding invitation, which had reached me some days ago. Just a plain, square card, gilt-edged, my name meaning no more to Miss Clevedon than the several dozen others Aunt Verity had listed for her, Barforth relatives and friends who would expect to see her married; my heartbreak meaning nothing to her since I was draining myself to my very dregs to conceal it. And as my mother handed the card to me, gingerly, pityingly, my senses, very briefly, had escaped their bondage and I had cried out, 'I can't go, mother.'

'Yes, you can,' Prudence had said quietly, barely raising her eyes from her own breakfast-time correspondence.

'I think you must, dear,' my mother had murmured, looking away. And so I replied to the card in my own hand, instructed our coachman to deliver it, and on Caroline's wedding-morning I began to smile and continued to do so throughout the day, as blankly, as brilliantly, as a society hostess who knows none of her guests by name, and cares even less, but is quite determined to impress them all.

There were white roses heavily massed about the altar, baskets of white petals waiting to become a carpet for Caroline's satin-shod feet as she left the church, Lady Chard now, of Listonby Park, a Barforth no longer, although she would be a Barforth in spirit, I believed, until the end of her days. And I heard nothing of the service, remembered little but my Uncle Joel, holding his daughter's hand for a moment with an unlikely tenderness before he gave it to Matthew Chard, and then, stepping aside, taking Aunt Verity's hand, for comfort perhaps, since emotion in this hard man was as rare and difficult as it had always been in Nicholas.

'Is this right for her?' his sudden frown seemed to be saying. 'I've bought it and paid for it, but is it right?'

'Darling – she wants it,' Aunt Verity may well have replied, and as Caroline walked back down the aisle no one could have doubted her ability to fulfil her new role in life.

Celia had been pretty on her wedding-day, Caroline, quite simply, was magnificent; and, as the Wintertons and Floods swallowed their mortification and came to congratulate her, I found myself, for a moment, in the confusion of the church porch, pressed close to Nicholas and understood that all my efforts had been in vain. I could not, after all, endure it – could not – it was as simple as that, and it was as well for me that, succumbing to the emotion appropriate to such a day, Mrs Hobhouse and my mother, Miss Battershaw and Miss Mandelbaum and all the other bridesmaids except Prudence were crying too.

There was a pealing of church bells, and Caroline, her bridegroom looking very aristocratic but somewhat unnecessary beside her, was driven away in a carriage lined with white silk and drawn by high-stepping white horses, to a wedding-breakfast specifically designed to overawe both the manufacturing and landed sections of our community. There was a marquee on the lawn at Tarn Edge, silver trays of champagne served by careful, professional hands, mountains of confectionery, a cake weighing – Aunt Verity had told my mother – a full two hundred pounds, decorated with sprays of white roses bound up with white satin ribbon, surrounding a figure of Caroline herself in gleaming satin, and Matthew bravely attired in hunting pink, an assortment of Cupids cavorting at their feet.

There was Mrs Hobhouse, telling each bridesmaid in turn, 'You'll be the next one, love, it's always the way'; my mother in dainty, springtime yellow, holding out her hand for more wine; Prudence talking quietly to Mayor Agbrigg; Jonas Agbrigg raising his glass to me, his eyes watchful, his mouth sarcastic. There was a certain division of ranks as the landed interest installed themselves at one side of the marquee, the manufacturers at the other, the Floods and Wintertons gravitating naturally towards the Tempests, the manorial family of Bradford, the Ramsdens of Huddersfield, the sporting squires come down from the North Riding and up from Leicestershire, the willowy young dandies and languid ladies from London, while, facing them from the other side of that festive table, the millmasters and brewmasters and ironmasters, the master cutlers from Sheffield, the worsted spinners of the West Riding and the cotton spinners from across the Pennines stood their ground firmly, knowing they could buy out a Tempest or a Flood ten times over, pretending they did not care a fig for any man's pedigree. There was Giles Ashburn, finding his own level too, with Mr Outhwaite, the architect, who was to design Aunt Hannah's concert hall, the vicar of the parish church, the headmaster of the grammar school: a knot of professional men coming between the commercial and aristocratic giants. There was Blaize, moving freely from one group to the other, quite certain of his welcome anywhere, but Nicholas not much in evidence, keeping Georgiana to himself.

There was Caroline – Lady Chard – a plain gold ring on one hand given by her husband, a diamond cluster on the other which had come from her father, circling among her guests with a royal composure, and then dashing upstairs to change into another white gown, embellished with swansdown, which would take her on the first stage of her wedding-journey to London.

And eventually, knowing that I must somehow release the iron grip I had again imposed upon myself, or be crushed by it, I walked off, as others were doing, a simple stroll, in their case, about the garden; in mine, a taking-flight which led me beyond the formal rose-beds, the lily-pond, the lawns falling in smooth, terraced levels down the gently sloping hillside, to the summer-house behind its screen of chestnut-trees and willows. And since a young lady who wanders so far alone in the romantic setting of a summer bridal-day may well be in search of other things than solitude, it was no matter for astonishment that Giles Ashburn chose to follow me.

He stood for a moment in the wide-arched entrance-way, looking at me, seeing, perhaps, the image of me he had himself created, and I at him, seeing little – my eyes unaccustomed to the shade, and with the sun behind him – but the figure of a respectable, respectful man, medium of height and build, medium of colour, a face my memory retained only as pleasant, unremarkable, brown hair touched to auburn by the sunlight, brown eyes, I thought, with flecks of green in them, although for a moment I was not sure. A man who thought he loved me at a time when I was bruised and lonely and so desperately needed to be loved that this emotion seemed altogether miraculous, even though I knew full well that there could be no good reason for it, that I had done nothing to encourage it and, most likely, did not deserve it.

'You looked quite luminous in the church, Faith.'

'Did I? I don't think I know what that means.'

And, coming towards me, instead of saying, 'Will you marry me?', although had that not been his intention I knew he would not have come here at all, he took both my hands once again and said simply, 'I am so very much in love with you.'

It was not the first time I had heard those words. There had been a young Frenchman, and an old Frenchman, a noble Roman who, having transferred his aspirations from my mother to myself, had made me the same declaration.

'How kind of you,' I had replied to each of them, borrowing a whisper of my mother's sophistication, protected from the folly of believing them by my dream of Nicholas. But that dream was over. This man believed what he was saying, whether eventually he would find himself mistaken or not. And the simple, basic need to be warm again, to bask in the devotion he was offering, drew me towards him, the terrible rigidity of my spirit easing as his arms came around me, an almost childlike, entirely trustful nestling of myself against him, the relaxation of a tired body sinking into a healing sleep.

'My darling,' he said, 'I can't tell you – I can't tell you –'; and, closing my eyes because his face, so close to mine, was still unfamiliar, I lifted my own face to be kissed, his mouth resting at first very carefully on mine and then, meeting no resistance, opening, his lips and his whole body still gentle, trembling with a need that thawed my own chilled senses not to passion but to gratitude.

Perhaps if he had made me a formal proposal, if he had listed for me his income and expectations, attempted to explain his feelings in words, I would have remembered a dozen reasons for refusing him, would have thought of my sister, and the sure fact that I – with Nicholas still engraved on my heart – could not be worth this outpouring, could neither match it nor merit it. But instinctively he had said only that he loved me and I had offered him my mouth to be kissed in reply, an unmistakable gesture of consent in our narrow world; and, as I continued to accept his kisses, to remain passively in his arms – the first man who had ever shown his need for me – I sensed beneath his quiet dignity, his quiet endurance, something fragile in him to which both my mind and my body responded.

'I want you to be so happy,' he said. 'That is all I want, Faith – you, and our happiness together.'

And even if I had wanted to reject him – which I did not – I had committed myself too far and could have found no way to do it.

12

I attended Georgiana Clevedon's wedding three weeks later, an ordeal made bearable by the simple fact that my determination never to hurt Giles Ashburn had risen above all else. I had promised to marry him and, whatever my motives had been, it was a promise I would keep. And, far more than that, I would not only give him my hand in marriage, my

517

dowry and my most willing body, I would be the wife he wanted and deserved.

I didn't know why he loved me, but I wanted his love, that much was certain. I respected him, trusted him, admired him, recognized him both intellectually and morally as my superior; I was grateful for him. And, as I watched Nicholas and Georgiana exchange their wedding vows, I closed my mind to them and made a personal, irrevocable vow that henceforth I would not only behave as if I loved Giles Ashburn, I *would* love him, as passionately and tenderly as he desired, in any way that he desired. And to do that it would be necessary not merely to conceal my feelings for Nicholas or suppress them: it was essential that they should be destroyed.

It was no longer a matter of pride, no longer a need to spare Nicholas the embarrassment of feeling he had jilted me. What mattered now was that no one should ever say I had turned to Giles Ashburn as second-best. I must present myself as a girl radiantly in love, not only to Giles – astonishing and delighting him each evening in my mother's hall by my response to his kisses, the eager uptilting of my face, my growing need to fold myself into him, to be warm again, and safe – not only that, of which only he could be aware, but a glow of joyful anticipation which would be apparent to everyone.

Nicholas must be my cousin again, no more and no less, since coolness would be regarded by some – by Jonas – as suspicious; and so I looked him directly in the eye as he came out of church with his bride, took his hand and kissed his cheek as a cousin should, and then kissed his wife, reminding her of our new relationship.

'I hope we may be friends, Georgiana, as well as cousins, now that you are to live in Cullingford.'

And Blaize, standing between us, his smoky eyes seeing too much as always, but not unkindly, advised her, 'Accept the offer, Georgiana, for you may need a friend – in Cullingford.'

There was no great gathering of prestige and power this time, a simple family ceremony in the chapel of Galton Abbey, slices of cold roast beef afterwards on a refectory table, a log fire barely warming the stone-clad hall, the aged Mr Gervase Clevedon delivering up his granddaughter to the Barforths with as much reluctance as she was received. And once again the division of classes began to operate, Uncle Joel stationing himself before the hearth, Mayor Agbrigg beside him, dominating what warmth there was, since the July day had turned unseasonably cold, Aunt Verity and my mother attempting at first to entertain Lady Annabel Flood, who knew this house much better than they, and then drawing as near the fire as they could, to talk among themselves. Aunt Hannah did, indeed, make some attempt at conversation with Sir Giles Flood, who had installed himself in a high-backed oak chair of awesome, if uncomfortable, proportions, but she was too mature, too regal for his taste, her position as mayoress reminding him too sharply of the changing times, while it was soon clear that his talk of horse-racing, of which she did not approve, and of grouse-shooting, which she did not understand, irritated and bored her.

Nicholas, quite clearly anxious to see the end of it, to have done with the drama and recriminations and take up his life again, was standing in the scowling, lounging posture I recognized, talking to Blaize of mill matters, I thought, some crisis at Lawcroft he wished to be properly attended to in his absence, while Georgiana seemed occupied with her own brother, Peregrine Clevedon, the only person, perhaps, who really appreciated her marriage. Mr Gervase Clevedon might never condescend to accept Barforth assistance, no matter how great his need; had, in fact, already gone deeper into debt so that Georgiana could have a dowry of sorts to take with her. But Mr Gervase Clevedon was an old man, and when Master Peregrine came to succeed him at Galton I did not think he would be slow to see the uses of a brother-in-law with money to lend, nor would he be timid in the asking.

But Nicholas's affairs were no longer my concern, and as the awkward celebration came to its close and we went outside to speed the bridal couple on their way, Georgiana having changed her plain white gown for a going-away outfit of light green, a dashing feather crowning her copper-coloured head, only then did I falter for a moment, seeing the stern lines of Nicholas's face soften as he handed her into the carriage, looking at her as his father often looked at his mother – showing me the one thing I had desired in life for myself – his mouth curving into its unwilling laughter as she whispered something into his ear; relief in him, now, I thought, at leaving his father and the rest of us behind, satisfaction at having finally got his way, a snap of excitement at the prospect of the night ahead.

'Good luck!' Blaize called out.

'God bless you!' Aunt Verity murmured.

'Well, that's it, then,' Uncle Joel said sourly. 'I want you down at Lawcroft, Blaize, first thing tomorrow morning, and every morning until he gets home. Your Uncle Agbrigg already has enough to do.'

He was married and gone, his bird of the wild wood caged, if not tamed, willing to feed from his hand; and none of it had anything at all to do with me.

'I see you've taken my advice, Faith,' Jonas said, appearing beside me in the sudden, silent way he had, my enemy, I was sure of it, not because I had once rejected him but perhaps because he needed an enemy, someone on whom to vent his long-stored bitterness.

'Your advice, Jonas?'

'Why yes, Faith – about not staying single. I feel sure that Nicholas will thank you for it.'

'Dear Jonas,' I told him, with my mother's voice, my mother's air-spun laughter. 'Did you really advise me to marry Giles? If you did, then it is I who should be thanking you – believe me.'

I had decided now what the whole course of my life must be. I could not devote myself to a cause, like Prudence, nor to bricks and mortar, upholstery and glassware like Celia, but I could devote myself, I believed, to a man who loved me. And I could see no reason for delay.

'Are you sure, dear?' my mother had murmured on hearing my news. 'Oh yes, I knew he meant to propose and he is altogether eligible – an excellent family and ample means, everything one could wish. It is just that I am surprised to find you so eager.'

'You are providing yourself with a very peculiar son-in-law, Elinor,' Aunt Hannah said tartly, for although Giles's income was more than adequate, he had no vast estates for Jonas to administer, no complicated business affairs for Jonas to entangle, no political connections which could serve Jonas's ambitions when the time came. But he could support me in sufficient comfort. He had a house ready to receive me at the top end – the decent end – of Millergate, where it joined Blenheim Lane. He loved me. How long could it take to apply a coat of paint to the dining-room walls, acquire a trousseau and engage a personal maid, since he already had a cook-housekeeper, and an outside man? Not long. And I was unwilling to remain in my father's sterile drawing-room a moment longer than that.

There were to be no adult bridesmaids. My sister Celia, having miscarried her second child, was too frail in body and spirit, felt herself already too matronly, to oblige. I was uncertain of Prudence, Caroline was still honeymooning in the southern shires, Georgiana unthinkable. And I was grateful to my mother for the provision of some Aycliffe cousins, little girls, all six of them under twelve, who, in pale blue gauze with dark blue velvet sashes, would serve me instead. But, in my urge to give Giles Ashburn everything I thought he wanted, I designed myself a dozen wedding gowns and discarded every one, settling at last for a confection of lace and tulle, fifteen deep flounces from waist to hem caught up with silk ribbon, long flowing sleeves, a coronet of apricot-coloured roses securing my veil, the pretty anonymity which would make me simply 'the bride'.

I was sure of myself, very sure for most of the time, and when I felt unable to ask Uncle Joel to give me away, refusing to admit to myself that I could not walk to the altar with a man who reminded me so strongly of Nicholas, and turned instead to my other uncle, Mayor Agbrigg, no one but Celia felt the need to question my judgment.

'Naturally you must suit yourself,' she told me. 'But I would not care to hurt Uncle Joel's feelings. He is not accustomed to being passed over, and people will wonder why.'

'Nonsense,' Prudence replied. 'What a goose you are, Celia, for there is no cause at all for wonder. Mayor Agbrigg and Dr Ashburn are close friends, that is the extent of it, and Faith will get her bride-gift from the Barforths just the same.'

And when Celia had gone home, having too little trust in her new parlourmaid to remain long away, Prudence said with her habitual composure, 'I had best set your mind at rest, Faith. I have never been in love with Giles, you know – at least, not in the way you understand it.'

'Thank you, Prudence. I wasn't sure, and couldn't ask.'

'Exactly. So now you may be easy. I have thought it over carefully, and to tell the truth I doubt if it is in my nature to feel an exclusive devotion to one person. I believe I resemble our cousin Blaize in that respect – which, of course, is considered delightfully wicked in a man and quite shocking in a woman. Blaize will never settle, because the woman who may be waiting for him in the next room or round the next corner is always more enticing than the woman at his side. And with me – well, I am not lightminded like Blaize, but I am not ready yet to be restricted. Yes, I did think seriously of Giles once, I confess it, particularly when I knew mother was coming home and I would have to play the dutiful daughter again. I was not at all looking forward to it, I can tell you, serving tea and conversation in the drawing-room every afternoon and listening to that silly little clock ticking my life away. I thought Giles would free me from all that. I am fond of him, I respect him; in fact he is worth more than two of you, my dear, and possibly more than three of me, for that matter. But then he saw you, and was so thunderstruck by you, and I found I was not hurt by it, merely concerned that you would let him down. And I found, too, that I could easily manage mother.'

'I shall not let him down, Prudence.'

'My goodness, I should hope not. Why should you? If what you want from life is to be adored, then I know of no one who could do it better than Giles. You will find it so very pleasant that you will soon be adoring him back, make no mistake about it, and will have quite forgotten why you didn't adore him in the first place. And when you move into your house in Millergate, dear, you may invite me to stay with you should Freddy Hobhouse begin to pester me again, or should mother try to take me to France. I am relying on you to be a most convenient chaperone.'

We were married on a grey-gold October morning, the sun spread low across a hazy sky, my mind too occupied with ceremonial details to care that I had not entirely escaped the Barforths, Blaize having been asked to officiate as best man. And I was so grateful for the warmth and gentleness of Giles Ashburn, cushioning me from hurt, that the simple promise to honour him and obey him seemed inadequate when I would have cut off my hair and offered it as a sacrifice on that bridal altar, had he required it.

But later, alone with him in the train going south to the flat Cheshire landscape of his childhood, the fact that I had given my life irrevocably into his keeping, losing my very identity in his, and that my sister was better acquainted with him than I, offered me a brief uncertainty. Yet he held my hand throughout the journey, assisted me from the train with the tender care my father had extended only to his Sèvres and Meissen, shielding me from a few scattered raindrops as if he thought me not only breakable but very likely to melt away, his every gesture a separate act of reassurance, an invitation to lean on him, to offer myself not as a sacrifice but as an object of devotion and cherishing. And few women in the world – or at least few that I have ever known – could have remained indifferent to that.

We spent the first few days in the pretty town of Knutsford, a bedroom and sitting-room tastefully prepared for us at an inn where Giles was known, a log fire crackling in the hearth, a comfortable woman offering us a wholesome dinner, hot chocolate at bedtime, her blessing for our future. And settling down in the vast, herb-scented bed, waiting for my

521

husband who had tactfully allowed me to undress alone, my body, after the strain of the ceremony and the long journey, was too glad of the soft mattress and pillows, the flickering firelight, to be afraid. And I grew so drowsy that, when the door did open, I was startled and sat bolt upright, my heavy hair spilling forward to cover me like a curtain.

'I have never seen your hair loose before,' he said, sitting down on the edge of the bed, a careful hand resting, just for an instant, on my head.

'I suppose not. I was almost asleep.'

'Of course. You must be very tired.'

And, taking my face between his hands, he kissed each corner of my mouth very lightly and murmured, 'Sleep then, darling.'

'Oh – should I?'

'I think so.'

He got in beside me, again with the utmost care, so that no part of me was uncovered, and slid an arm beneath my shoulders, holding me not as I had expected but as if I had been a trustful, vulnerable child whose innocence must be protected, who must be rocked most lovingly and chastely to sleep.

'There is no reason to be in a hurry,' he said into my hair. 'We have all our lives, darling – every day of our lives. I don't want to rush you now, when you are tired and strained and worried, I suppose, about what is expected of you. Just go to sleep now, with your head on my shoulder. I shall be happy with that.'

But I opened my eyes, far into the night, aware, in the confused moment of waking, that something was wrong, that the warmth which had enveloped me and lulled me to sleep was different now, no comforting arms around me but a taut presence, his back turned towards me with what could have been anger, until with the part of me I had inherited from my mother I began slowly to understand.

'Giles? What is it?' And receiving no answer: 'Giles, I'm awake now. I won't go to sleep again.'

I did not expect pleasure from this first encounter, knew, in fact, that this act, by which men set so great a store, was not designed to please women, simply to impregnate them and to make them submissive; but turning to me with something like a groan, his hands were still gentle, his embrace retaining its wondering, almost apologetic quality as if it troubled him that, having been so moved by my body's innocence, he could no longer control his urge to despoil it. Yet I was not, in fact, so very innocent, had been virgin, perhaps, already somewhat too long, and his stroking, enquiring fingertips – ready to withdraw at my slightest movement of protest – released in me a strange, quite feline languor, a great stretching and purring in every limb which, very far from any proper ladylike disgust, was almost impatient with the carefully restrained quality of his desire.

And then it was over. No agony, a moment, merely, of discomfort and surprise. 'Good heavens, so that's it, after all.' Just one brief instant when my body stiffened, drew back, and he, wishing to withdraw, feeling that he should withdraw, could not, taking final possession of me with a long shuddering cry, of despair, it seemed to me, rather than triumph. No agony. Disappointment, perhaps, not in my heart but in my puzzled limbs, which, having been stirred to warm anticipation by his caresses, had found this ultimate act quite inexplicable. After all, it *was* a purely male concern as they had told me, for I failed entirely to see how the piercing of my body by that strange, masculine appendage could give me any pleasure. Yet I had not whined and whimpered as Celia may well have done on her wedding night, nor asked him how he dared, as I could easily imagine Caroline demanding of her Matthew; and feeling I had proved quite adequate I smiled at him fondly through the dark, no thought in my mind of his own adequacy, his own satisfaction.

He got up suddenly and walked naked across the room, allowing me for the first time to see his fine-boned body, the odd fragility of shoulder-blades almost piercing the skin, a fleeting impression of weightlessness that was not angular and awkward, not displeasing, before he covered himself quickly with his dressing-robe and came back to me.

'I am sorry,' he said brusquely.

'Why? Is something amiss?'

'No, no – except that you are only nineteen, with no knowledge of life, and I am past thirty, with enough experience to have done better than this. I should have allowed you at least a day or two of my company before submitting you to a desire you cannot share.'

'Giles, darling,' I told him, feeling a smile begin somewhere inside me, understanding his troubled frown, his anxiety, with the basic female knowledge my mother had bred in me. Yet perhaps because he wished me to be frail, had imagined me frail, he was not consoled, his need for self-punishment surprising me even more than the anguished climax of his sensuality.

'Well, it is done now,' he said. 'It will not always be so difficult, you can believe me. You may bleed presently. It is quite natural. Don't be alarmed.'

'No, doctor.'

'Faith – please –' he said, and seeing that my flippancy had wounded him I leaned forward, feeling suddenly very strong and very sure of my ability to comfort him, although I did not altogether understand why he should be in need of comfort.

'Giles, I have not lived in an ivory tower all my life, you know. I have been to France and Italy, where people are not so reticent as we are – and, in any case, my mother is much more outspoken than is usual in Cullingford. You have not hurt me, Giles – for as a matter of fact I am really very strong – and you have not shocked me.'

'But I have given you no pleasure.'

'How can you know that?'

'Dear girl, of course I can know it. I do know it. You bore it all very stoically and very sweetly, but you had no pleasure and expected none. I imagine you will have been told that women do not, and should not, enjoy these things. And in many cases that is quite correct. It is easier, you see, at such moments, for a man to think only of himself, to do only what pleases him, in the convenient belief that a woman has no sensuality. And I can perfectly understand that a woman who is always pregnant, either recovering from one birth or preparing for the next, must view her husband's demands with utter loathing. I have seen it, Faith, many times in my capacity as a physician – women who would do anything to escape what to them is simply their nightly servitude, women who fall ill expressly to avoid it. And, having seen all that, I have no excuses. I knew I must be patient, knew that I must take you gradually and carefully, little by little. Yet I could not. I have been every bit as self-seeking as the men I have despised, and if you should turn away from me in disgust I could not really blame you.'

What a fuss, I thought, my word, what a fuss! Yet sitting up, strong and sure again, I tossed back my hair and, throwing aside the bedcovers with a steady hand, offered the whole of my body to his eyes, without sensuality but without embarrassment, not desiring him yet but wanting him to desire me, since that was what he wanted himself, and I required, most urgently, to fulfil his every need.

He spoke my name, a strangled sound, his face swimming for an instant before my eyes with an emotion so intense that my immediate instinct was to turn away from it, fearing I could not meet its demands. But I received his light, hesitant body without restraint, knowing that in this, at least, I would not fail him, holding him, learning to caress him – not too boldly, since he did not wish me to be bold – until his honest, generous anxiety had faded away.

'I love you, Faith.'

'Yes. Please love me, Giles.'

And it no longer mattered that I didn't know why. Certainly he had not chosen me for anything I had ever said to him, for any similarities of intellect and outlook, for my wit or my ability to partner him in his labours. Perhaps, at the beginning, it had been no more than the colour of my hair, a trick of light and shade that had given my face the texture of some half-forgotten adolescent dream, so that I had assumed in his mind the identity of that dream. And what could it matter now? I had chosen to spend my life with him, and, as I watched our first morning come slowly peeping through the window, lying easily, contentedly in his arms, I believed I had chosen right.I could make him happy, I was every moment more sure of it. I could be the woman he wanted, whoever she was, whatever she was, even if she was not really me at all. Having lost what I had believed to be my life's purpose, I had found another. Whatever else I might, or might not do, I would not fail Giles Ashburn.

13

My cousin, Blaize Barforth, took us to the theatre on the night of our return, some three weeks later, an evening which in my eyes seemed to mark my new status as a married woman; for, although I had attended performances of Shakespeare in London and of the opera and ballet in Paris, Cullingford's Theatre Royal had always been considered too raucous a place for a young lady. Yet, wishing to prove my sophistication to Blaize at any rate, I settled myself into the first of the dress boxes with no outward sign of curiosity, leaning forward to chat as nonchalantly as I could contrive to a young architect and his wife, to young Mr Rawnsley of Rawnsley's Bank and a lady who was not his wife, who were occupying the box next door.

Taking advantage of my new freedom, I found it entirely delightful to drink cold punch after the performance in the private supper-room at the Old Swan, sitting between my husband and handsome, wicked Blaize, who made no secret now of his tender relationship with a curly-haired, black-eyed comedienne, and his interest – uncertain yet, but promising – in another. It was delightful, too, to learn from Blaize's witty tongue the peccadilloes of so many of our town's founding fathers – that Mr Hobhouse, with his fourteen fine children at Nethercoats, had two or three more, every bit as fine, scattered here and there about the county, while even the worsted spinner, Mr Oldroyd of Fieldhead, had kept an actress of his own, long before his wife died, in a respectable – Blaize thought tedious – area of Leeds.

'But I thought Mr Oldroyd wanted to marry my mother.'

'So he does – which has nothing to do with actresses, Faith. And, while we are on the subject, I must give you a timely warning, for you should know that at least half your husband's female patients are madly in love with him.'

'That does not surprise me, Blaize – not in the least. I merely wonder what is wrong with the other half? Are they blind?'

'Just sensible, I imagine,' Giles said, taking my hand, his slightest touch causing me to sway towards him, lightheaded with offering, wanting him to take more than he already had, to be more demanding, so that I could be more generous.

My new house in Millergate, not new at all, but which had come to Giles with the practice, was not in the estimation of any of my relatives grand enough. It was, indeed, one of the last houses at the confused joining of the ways where steep, stony Millergate became Blenheim Lane, but by no stretch of the imagination could it be considered to stand in Blenheim Lane itself, and Aunt Hannah insisted from the start that it would not suit me to live so near the town.

'Millergate is a shopping street,' she said. 'It is not residential. You are not acquainted with any of your neighbours, nor can you wish for their acquaintance.'

Yet, as she well knew, Millergate, which at its lower end directly entered Market Square by the Piece Hall and the Old Swan, was not so far distant from Simon Street that a frightened man could not reach us in the middle of the night, to beg Giles's attendance on a sick child or a confinement that, having lasted a day or two, was thought even by Simon Street standards to be going wrong. Nor was the doorway too imposing, the maid who answered the bell too dignified, the chair in the hall too daintily upholstered for an exhausted woman who had trudged from the canal bank with an infant strapped to her back, another straddling her hip, to take her rest.

We had a large parlour I could not really glorify by the name of drawing-room, a red-covered sofa and two deep armchairs around the hearth, a cheerful rug, a profusion of flowering plants in pottery bowls my father would have considered undignified. There was a stray cat, brought home one night by Giles; a litter of kittens I had helped him to deliver the night after; my collection of wedding china and silver, displayed, for the time being, in cabinets which were too small and did not exactly match each other. There was a dining-room that also served Giles as a study; a front bedroom with a large, half-tester bed; three smaller rooms; a sinister room at the back of the house, full of glass tubes and bottles, with a small room off, where Giles received patients; attics, and a kitchen which, since plain cooking had not formed part of my education, I could not feel to be my concern.

'I believe your Aunt Hannah is right,' Giles told me at once. 'It is indeed a poky place. I can't think why I never realized it before. Look around, darling, and when you find the house you want let me know. I really can't expect you to settle here.'

But, like the kittens, I was warm in my deep red armchair, unwilling, perhaps, to take on the management of a larger household so soon, since routine domestic matters, I found, did not interest me greatly, my tastes inclining to the decorative rather than the useful. And although, prompted by Celia, I glanced at a smart new villa in Albert Place, talked idly of buying an acre or two of land, even consulted a builder and an architect, I knew that Giles, who cared nothing for houses, wished to move only for my sake, and so I chose to remain in Millergate for his.

Nor did I feel the need to make any sweeping domestic changes. The old woman who had looked after Giles was more than willing to look after me, her chocolate cake being the lightest I had ever tasted, her good humour inexhaustible.

'Just sit you down, Mrs Ashburn, and leave it to me. I know what the doctor likes for his dinner, and what you can do for him is make sure he sits down to eat it. Tell him to let them wait, when they come knocking on the door at dinner-time, because one thing you can be sure of, Mrs Ashburn, is that they won't go away. He'll not lose his customers to Dr Overdale and Dr Blackstone, if that's what he's thinking, because Dr Overdale takes his money in advance, and Dr Blackstone sees none but the quality. Just you sit down and have a big smile ready for him when he comes home.'

And so I obeyed, hurrying into the hall at the sound of his gig, rushing downstairs to open the door for him myself, as obsessive in my care for him as Celia in her constant pursuit of domestic perfection.

It was naturally expected that Celia and I would see a great deal of each other now, for not only were we married ladies, empowered to share our knowledge of life's mysteries, but our husbands were both professional men, a doctor and a lawyer, who should have had much in common. Yet, although they were always very civil, very correct, there was little *rapport* between them, Jonas being too conscious that Giles, with his private income, had not been obliged to struggle for his education nor to marry somewhat against his inclination in order to purchase his practice, Giles mistrusting Jonas's growing habit – prompted, one could not deny it, by Aunt Hannah – of offering his friendship only to those who had something to give him. There was no shrewder lawyer in Cullingford these days than Jonas Agbrigg, to which many others besides Aunt Hannah were ready to testify: a keen, cunning man who could be relied on to spot a loophole in any contract, the contracts he drew up himself being quite watertight, or, when that was impossible, offering a variety of escape routes, skilful, obscurely worded clauses and fine points of law which everyone but himself appeared to have forgotten.

Giles liked people; Jonas, very obviously, liked useful people, cultivating only the rich and influential who could be persuaded to help him, the rich and simple who would be likely to trust him, the rich and slightly sinister who had need of a clever man like himself, his social commitments throwing my sister into such panic that I would often go over to Albert Place and do the table decorations for the parties to which I was not important enough to be invited; or, if she was to dine out herself, would arrange her hair, choose her clothes, attempt to convince her that it was not unbecoming in a matron of eighteen to be just a little vain.

But, more often than not, she would reject the high-piled curls of my devising, would not allow me to spray her with the perfume I still ordered from the Rue Saint Honoré, insisting that a married woman should not embarrass her husband by making herself conspicuous, that a gentleman – according to her father's teachings – required his wife to be self-effacing in public, efficient at home, a model of propriety at all times of the day and, one assumed, of the night.

'You should take care,' she told me. 'Wearing such light colours as you do and such low necks in the evenings, one could be forgiven for thinking you flighty. And how you ever find the time to do your hair so often, and in so many different fashions, I can't imagine. I have never a moment for such things. I am quite surprised at you, Faith, for those cats of yours are everywhere – and it would destroy me, really it would, thinking of those sharp claws anywhere near *my* furniture. You know quite well that father would never have a cat in the house – not even in the kitchen.'

Yet, however much she disapproved of my slovenly habits, the next time some gentleman of awesome importance was invited to dine, a client or a political connection and his sharp-eyed lady, I would heed her distress signals and spend a tedious afternoon draping her candlesticks in ivy, arranging small sprays of moss and roses at the corners of her table, giving her a centrepiece of brightly coloured blooms surrounded by drifts of pink gauze strewn with single rosebuds – any novel thing I could imagine, while she, more often than not, having worn her nerves to shreds, would retire upstairs to be violently sick.

'What does it matter?' I asked her. 'They're only people. Heavens – we've known Mr Fielding for years. And what if he is a Member of Parliament? So was father.'

But nothing could ease her torment, and, knowing full well that her house contained not one single speck of dust, since she followed her housemaid upstairs and down every morning to make sure; that no guest of hers could have found anything, even in the most intimate recesses of her cupboards, but a most perfect order; she would nevertheless fret herself into a raging headache, so that when those guests finally arrived she had nothing to say to them but a distraught 'Good evening', her mind dwelling in agony on the progress of the roast, the French sauce I had suggested and which she knew would never thicken.

'It's all right for you, Faith – you've never cared about such things. You just drift through life in your come-day-go-day fashion – and your husband doesn't seem to care either. A place for everything and everything in its place, that's what father always said, and I agree. I can't bear to see things disarranged. I must have everything just as it should be. I can't help my nature – and I wouldn't expect *you* to understand.'

Yet, in spite of my shabby hall carpet and my inadequate dining-room, I entertained in my haphazard fashion far more, and I believed more successfully, than Celia.

Situated on the road most people took on their way out of town, my house was a convenient calling-place. Mayor Agbrigg – Alderman Agbrigg now that his term of office had expired – stopped in almost daily for a cup of Mrs Guthrie's strong tea, while Giles's bachelor friends, comprising the whole of our town's younger professional men, saw no reason to forgo the comfort of his fireside once they had ascertained that I, like Mrs Guthrie and the easy, well-worn chairs, was perfectly agreeable.

Blaize came too, at unlikely hours sometimes, his high-stepping horses blocking the way, the hem of a satin skirt, the crown of a feathered hat just visible, often enough, inside his carriage, indicating the presence of a female who could not be presented to me. He would occasionally involve me in his escapades, as he had done before, although now that I was married and allowed to know of such goings-on, instead of 'If you should happen to see my father and he should happen to ask, do please say that you haven't seen me here at all,' it was 'Dear Faith – because you understand me so well – if you go to the Assembly Rooms tonight and you should meet Mrs Woodley – yes, dear, *Mrs* Woodley – do make it in your way to tell her I have been called away to Manchester.'

'And how long do you expect to be away?'

'As long as I can contrive. Three days, I think – in fact we'll make it five, and tell her it is London. If it troubles you, you may say you simply think that is where I have gone – since who knows?'

'Should it trouble me?'

'I daresay it should. But you'll tell her, won't you, just the same?'

'I may.'

'Oh, you will. You've always been a good girl, Faith.'

'I daresay, but Blaize – Mrs Woodley. She's such an ancient creature.'

'Thirty-five,' he said, smiling. 'And she has – enthusiasm. You'll know what I mean.'

But quite often he would come alone, spending lazy evenings by the fire, hot coffee and toasted muffins consumed at midnight; Prudence sometimes, having called at tea-time and stayed to dinner, engaging him in verbal combat, demolishing the easy philosophies he invented expressly to tease her, deciding, more often than not, that she would not trouble to go home at all and calmly sending a note to Blenheim Lane claiming her freedom of movement, of speech, of action, in a way which amused and delighted him.

'I believe your poor mother trembles before you.'

'Nonsense. She never notices me now that Mr Oldroyd has started to call so often.'

'So – clever Mr Oldroyd. Does she mean to marry him?'

'She would be ill-advised to do so. And I would not consent to live with them.'

'Ah – you are thinking of getting married yourself then, I take it?'

'Why should you say that?'

'Why, Prudence, my dear – if you will not live with your mother, then you must live with your husband, or with his mother. What else can a young lady do?'

'I will not always be a young lady. I am almost twenty-two. Eventually I shall be thirty and forty – as you will be one day, Blaize, dear – and capable, I imagine, of handling my own affairs.'

'Now why on earth should you wish to do that?' he asked her, his smoky eyes brimming with mischief. 'Why trouble your very charming head with the sordid details of everyday life, when you could easily find a husband to do it for you? I really can't understand your poor opinion of marriage. Believe me, Faith does not share it, and I – well – I will confess, hand on heart, that I envy Giles all this.'

'Nonsense. If you wanted it, you could have it. You could be married tomorrow – except that you would probably fall in love with one of your wife's bridesmaids on your wedding day.'

'Do you know,' he said, as if the idea had just struck him, not at all unpleasantly, 'I believe you may be right. And you have done me a great disservice, Prudence, by putting the idea into my head. It sounds so very apt that, now you have suggested it to me, I doubt if I could bring myself to resist it should the occasion ever arise.'

'Don't concern yourself. It never will. You will chase moonbeams all your life, looking for that one rare creature you are always talking about, who surely doesn't exist – or else you will marry a fifteen-year-old when you are ninety-three.'

'Prudence,' I told her, laughing, although what she had said was not impossible, 'that is not kind.'

'Oh,' Blaize murmured. 'I don't know –' And later, when Giles had been called out and Blaize, making light of it, had accompanied him, declaring he might as well hold Giles's horse in Simon Street as go home and explain his absence at the mills that day to his father, I asked her, 'Prudence, do you think you could ever care for Blaize?'

'Fall in love with him, you mean? No, I could not, and he wouldn't thank me for it should it be otherwise. A man like Blaize doesn't wish to be troubled by emotion.'

'There is more to him than he likes to show.'

'I'm well aware of it. He drove Giles over to Sunbury Dale this morning, didn't he, risking his beautiful sporting curricle on those moorland pathways so Giles could get there in time. Were you not afraid Giles would break his neck? Oh – they didn't tell you. Well, Giles was needed in a hurry, I'm not certain why – a mill chimney had collapsed and fallen into a shed, I believe, and I suppose when Giles got the message it was already too late. Anyway, Blaize drove him there because Giles's horse would have surely foundered in this weather. And when they arrived he made himself useful too – I heard it from Uncle Agbrigg, so there is no call for you to look so put out – which is why Blaize was not at the mill today and is in trouble with his father. Of course, he will not tell Uncle Joel he was at Sunbury. He will let him think what he pleases. And I know it amused him, driving like a madman over the top moor, or he would not have done it. But he did go, he did help, which is more than his brother Nicholas would have done. Yes, Faith – Nicholas may have lent his carriage and paid someone to drive it, but he would not have gone himself. He wouldn't lose a day's business – not for anybody in Sunbury Dale at any rate. I expect you will be calling at Tarn Edge to deliver your bride-gift, now that they have been back from honeymoon for several weeks. We can go together.'

Caroline, Lady Chard, was not expected back until the New Year, having married into a world where a wedding-journey could last a twelvemonth or more, the happy couple returning, often enough, with their first child in tow. But the Barforth mills, unlike the tenant farmers of Listonby, could not be left to take care of themselves, and the new Mrs Barforth had been installed at Tarn Edge for so long now, that I knew my failure to visit her would cause comment unless soon remedied. Aunt Verity had already called on me, bringing me a magnificent matching pair of Sèvres pot-pourri vases, a fortune casually bestowed, and placed just as casually on my altogether unworthy mantelpiece. I had already purchased the dessert service I intended for Nicholas, a dainty, flowery, yet quite impersonal gift that had been standing for weeks now, ready wrapped, on the hall table, reminding me constantly of its need to be delivered. And when a day or so later I encountered Blaize coming out of the Piece Hall, and he, perfectly understanding my hesitation and the need to put an end to it, said quietly, 'Faith, if you should have a moment to spare for my sister-in-law, it would be a kindness, since she is very much alone,' I begged the carriage from Giles that very afternoon.

There had been no question of a separate establishment for Nicholas and Georgiana. Tarn Edge was plenty large enough to accommodate a second family; it was essential for Nicholas to be near the mills; and Georgiana herself, having been brought up to think of marriage as a

530

transfer from one ancestral mansion to another, had neither expected nor wanted one of the smart new villas so dear to acquisitive and possibly, in her view, vulgar middle-class hearts. She had simply taken up residence among the Barforths as she would have gone to the Chards or the Floods, as ready to leave everything to her mother-in-law as if Aunt Verity had been a duchess with three hundred years of domestic tradition behind her.

She was the wife not even of the heir, but of a younger son, a position which, in a noble family, would not have carried great weight. Had Uncle Joel been a Chard, Blaize would have inherited his title, his land, the house that stood upon it, in accordance with the rules of primogeniture, which ensured that ancient estates were not broken up, that ancient names remained tied to the land that for centuries had nurtured them. Blaize's wife would have taken precedence over Georgiana on every occasion, would have become mistress of Tarn Edge at the very moment of Uncle Joel's death, Aunt Verity retiring just as immediately to some dower house or smaller dwelling, leaving little for Nicholas but a younger son's portion – not usually large – and a career of sorts in the army or the Church. And, although Georgiana must have known that in the world of commerce the labours of both brothers would be equally rewarded, the profits divided, that Nicholas could even be a far wealthier man than Blaize one day, while Tarn Edge itself, for which neither of them greatly cared, would probably be sold in due course, its proceeds divided between themselves and Caroline, it seemed very strange to her, her instinctive deference to the first-born amusing no one but Blaize himself.

'She has the quaintest notions,' my mother had told me. 'She talks to her horse more than she talks to Verity. You will find her wildly entertaining.'

Yet there was something almost forlorn about her that afternoon as she received me in Aunt Verity's small parlour – as large and considerably more luxurious than the Great Hall at Galton – and, although she could not at first remember the exact nature of our relationship, I believe she was relieved to see someone of her own age and sex.

'Of course,' she told me, accepting my dessert service with only token enthusiasm, since, I supposed, in that superbly equipped house, where the cupboards were bursting with Wedgwood and Coalport, she could see little use for it. 'I remember now. You are an Aycliffe. Your mother and my father-in-law are brother and sister.'

'Yes, except that I am no longer an Aycliffe. I was married in October, while you were still away.'

'Good lord! October. So you are newer to it even than I. And your husband, does he have a place nearby?'

'A place? You mean an estate?'

'So I do, if that is what you call it. And I am sorry to be so awkwardly spoken, for I suppose he must have a mill or – something of that nature?'

'No. He is a doctor.'

'Really?' she said, honestly surprised, since I suppose the possibility of

531

marrying a doctor had never occurred to a Clevedon. 'Do you know, I haved never consulted a doctor in my life. Not even when I took a tumble out hunting last season and dislocated my collar bone. My grandfather just tugged it back again and told me if I wanted to be sick to get on with it and then go home. Yet the ladies here who call on my mother-in-law seem always to be ailing. There was a Mrs Agbrigg the other day, younger than me, I think, who seems altogether an invalid.'

'Yes, Mrs Agbrigg is my sister. She has always been frail.'

'Oh – I do beg your pardon. I find these names and these relationships so confusing, and I know how important it is to get them right. It was so simple at home, you see. One knew exactly which Tempest had married which Chard, and who was related to the Floods and the Ramsdens and in which degree, because one had grown up knowing it. One had attended all the christenings and the weddings and listened to all the back-stairs gossip. One knew not to mention Lady Winterton in Lady Bardsey's hearing, since Sir Morton Bardsey had mentioned her once too often – that sort of thing. Whereas here, with so many Hobhouses and Battershaws – such strange names – I have no idea what errors I may be committing. Really, sometimes I am quite lost, absolutely at sea, for I was taught never to mention money, never, never, never to ask how much anything cost or to tell what one had paid – never, never. Yet here they talk of pound notes quite openly, all the time. I was quite shocked when I heard a lady just the other night announce how many thousands she had spent on a seaside home, and I expected everyone else to be shocked too. But, in fact, I believe they were impressed. I suppose it is because they *earn* money, as we do not, which makes them so familiar with it.'

Amused in spite of myself by her puzzled manner, her frowning, little-girl concentration, as if all Hobhouses looked alike to her and she despaired not only of learning their language but of ever distinguishing one from the other, I leaned slightly towards her and smiled, feeling older, although in fact I was slightly the younger, feeling that the task I had set myself might prove less difficult than I had feared. I had come here, certainly, to satisfy the conventions, to test the strength of my own resolution, but I had also come – as I did everything else these days – because of Giles. I was not certain how much he knew of my relationship with Nicholas, simply that he must know something, and what better way of easing his mind than to offer my friendship to Nicholas's wife?

'It was all so simple at home,' she had said, quite touchingly, for, although Galton was but a few miles distant, I well knew that in spirit it was another world. And, telling myself that she, at any rate, had not chosen to harm me, was apparently unaware that harm had been done, and must be kept in ignorance of it, I smiled again and said, 'You will soon grow accustomed to us, Georgiana.'

'Do you think so?'

'Oh yes, I am sure of it. If Aunt Verity's friends seem stiff, it is only because they are minding their manners too hard which surely won't last. And if you are bored at dinner-time when the Hobhouses and the

Battershaws – and the Barforths – can talk of nothing but warp and weft, and their lustre cloths and shalloons, well, I have been hearing of such things all my life and I can still neither understand them nor bring myself to care.'

'Oh my word!' she said, flashing me her sudden smile, her pointed face alive with a surge of vitality. 'Can that be true? No, of course not, for I am quite certain you know exactly what constitutes a lustre cloth and are merely denying it to put me at ease. But it was kindly done. Mrs Ashburn – cousin Faith – I believe you are sent to me from Heaven. Shall I ring for tea? At home we are obliged to go and shout down the passage, since we have not a bell in working order, and even then our old Honiman is so deaf, or does not choose to hear, that one can sit and play a guessing game – for money, if my brother Perry is about – as to whether or not tea will come.'

But there were no such games of chance at Tarn Edge, and when she had greeted the silver cake baskets, the trays of muffins and hot bread and butter with a slight shake of her head, as if with the best will in the world she couldn't help finding such over-abundance a trifle vulgar, she frowned suddenly and said, 'Tell me, cousin Faith, what do you do all day?'

'What do I do? I suppose – a hundred things.'

'Then I wish you would tell me their names, for I imagine your husband must go out a great deal, and Nicky is never at home. I simply did not realize that these mills were so greedy of a man's time. I have heard Nicky talk of his managers and I supposed they handled his affairs, as the land-agent at Galton handles ours. But not a bit of it. Nicky must be at the mill every day, all day, and half the night sometimes. Even Mr Barforth spends most of his time there, which my mother-in-law seems to find quite natural. Yet it is very strange to me. My grandfather attends Quarter Sessions, naturally, since he is Chairman of the Bench, and holds Petty Sessions regularly enough in the back parlour at the Abbey, and he is always out and about the estate. But he doesn't live his life by the clock, as they do. How can they bear to shut themselves up in this glorious weather? You do not ride, do you, Faith?'

And when I shook my head she said sadly, 'No. No one does. To the mill and back, to the train and back – Oh dear, Nicky has given me the most magnificent chestnut mare, the loveliest lady you can imagine, and what am I to do with her? He will not allow me to ride out alone. He says it would not be understood. I could not bring a groom from Galton, since we have but the one, and these fellows in the stables here simply cannot keep up with me. So there she stands all day in her stall, just a tame little canter every morning and home again. Well, he must take me to Galton at Christmas, for if I cannot hunt on Boxing Day I shall die of it – especially now that Matthew has succeeded his uncle as Master, for Sir Richard was a dear man but so dreadfully old fashioned. He *would* persist in setting off too early in the morning, before one could hope to unkennel a fox that was fit to run.'

I left soon afterwards, having promised to come again and to escort her to such entertainments as Cullingford could provide, and that evening Blaize called briefly to thank me for the care I had taken.

'It was good of you, Faith.'

Alone with him in the silent house, stung by his accurate knowledge of my situation, I said sharply, 'Why?'

'You know why. I am sorry to see that it still hurts you.'

'You see nothing of the kind.'

'Good. I am delighted to be mistaken. You are married to the best man in the world, you know.'

'I don't need you to tell me that, Blaize Barforth.'

'No. I see. Good-night, then.'

'Good-night. Blaize?'

'Yes?'

'Are they happy?'

'Possibly. She depends on him, since she feels everyone else to be against her, and he is still quite wildly attracted to her. She enjoys that, of course – why should she not? – and I think she appreciates him in other ways and is rather grateful. You should understand that, Faith.'

'Good-night, Blaize.'

'Quite so. And if that means "Don't call again" I shall take no notice. You'll forgive me – you always do. And you need my light touch in this heavy world. Giles won't object to your gratitude. *I* shouldn't. One has to start somewhere, after all, and it's not a bad beginning. Without making the slightest effort I can think of a hundred ways in which a woman's gratitude could be really very agreeable. And you've got all the time in the world, you know, to fall in love with him. Let it come over you gently. It's bound to happen.'

And, kissing my cheek, his mischief entirely without malice, he tipped his hat to me and strolled nonchalantly away.

14

There was a year of peace and quiet content, a year that would serve as a model, I believed, for all the other years of my life, a deep, slow-moving river with no sudden, diamond-scattered cascades, no sharp, unexpected twistings and turnings; but with no stagnant, murky pools, no dried-up, stony places – a clean, deep water.

Caroline, who had been eight months away, came home at the end of a crisp, white January, requiring my immediate attendance at Listonby, so intent on her plans for improving the house and filling it with the grand acquaintances she had made on her travels that when I inquired her husband's whereabouts she said absently. 'Matthew? Oh, I suppose he has gone out hunting. That is what he usually does, at any rate.'

But Caroline, seated before the log fire burning brightly in the massive stone hearth, the stone-flagged pavement of the Great Hall covered with the first of her deep-pile rugs, was intensely happy, showing not the slightest trace of Georgiana's confusion and loneliness.

'That old housekeeper of Matthew's will have to go,' she told me, before the upright little woman, whose breeding perhaps was a shade more genteel than our own, was barely out of earshot. 'He can just pension her off with a cottage on the estate somewhere, which seems to be the custom, and will be a great kindness in her case, for she is far too frail to cope with the way I mean to go on. I interviewed one or two likely persons on my way through London, and I must have someone with style and experience and a great deal of endurance, for the people I mean to invite are accustomed to certain standards, and it won't be enough to merely give them what they are used to. Oh no – I mean to offer something better, something that will really make their journey worthwhile. My father has always operated that way, and I absolutely agree with him. I can do very little at the moment, of course, because it is going to be chaos until the alterations have been made – there is that huge upstairs chamber to turn into a ballroom, which means a new floor, certainly, and new plasterwork, and the Long Gallery to renovate, before I can decently invite anyone to dance; and bedrooms and dressing-rooms to see to – and it seems I am expecting a baby, by the way. But, once all that is done with, I know exactly what I mean to do. House-parties, of course, throughout the hunting season, one after the other, since it is the surest way of keeping Matthew out of Leicestershire. He may think it the best hunting country in the world, but his house there is quite mediocre. I have no mind to sit in it half the year while he goes tally-hoeing about the countryside, and so I shall bring all his friends to do their hunting here. We have stabling enough; carriages with champagne picnics in hampers for the ladies who do not care to ride; everything. I shall give a hunt ball, needless to say, which will attract absolutely everybody – not just provincials, but people from the shires and London – and a harvest ball too, I think, with a marquee on the lawn for the tenants. And my Christmases are going to be altogether spectacular. Naturally I *want* to do all this, but quite frankly I feel it is expected of me in any case. I shall give a servants' dance too, which didn't seem such a good idea to me when I first heard of it, but I attended one in Shropshire and found it rather entertaining. It gives one's staff something to look forward to, at any rate – rather like the bonuses at Tarn Edge.'

'And how did you find Matthew's friends?' I asked her, remembering Georgiana's bewilderment with manufacturing ways, supposing Caroline, in reverse, must have felt it too. But, unlike her sister-in-law, she seemed more inclined to mould her new environment to suit herself and was apparently unaware that anyone could expect her to change.

'They were all extremely civil and glad to know me, which was very pleasant, and put themselves out to see that I was suitably entertained, although, strictly between ourselves, some of them are not nearly so grand as I had supposed. Matthew's aunt in Shropshire is, after all, an earl's daughter, her husband is Lord Macclesworth, which should count for something, and they are not short of money. Yet she has nothing in her wardrobe that you or I would care to put on, and leads a most quiet existence – my word, I was positively dull in her house. Acres of the most magnificent reception rooms and nothing in them but weaponry all over the walls and empty floor space. And some of the others – well, Faith, this is very strictly between ourselves, but at one house I visited it was known, and apparently accepted, that one of Matthew's cousins had been – well – intimately involved for years with a man who was not her husband. My dear, absolutely everybody knew about it. The man was there, welcomed like any other guest, and arrangements had even been made to give them bedrooms on the same corridor, so they might have easy access. Yes, you may well look startled, for so was I when I discovered it, although Matthew laughed at me and said it was nothing to make a fuss about – if the woman's husband didn't mind, then why should he – or I? Goodness! Can you imagine my mother tolerating such a thing at Tarn Edge – or anyone else we know? And I shall not have such goings-on here, I can tell you. Naturally I am not a schoolroom goose. I realize now that such things do happen in the world, but those who commit such indulgences should have the decency, at least, to conceal them. Matthew may call it hypocrisy, but if I gave them adjoining rooms in my house I should call it encouragement, and one has one's standards after all. And some of the younger Chards, and the rest of them, are fearful gamblers – positively silly where money is concerned. I am not at all surprised so many of them are in difficulties. But, apart from that, I have no complaints to make. Well – I must have this baby first, and then we can start talking clothes again, Faith. No baby for you, that is very obvious, for you are really very smart and so slender. I suppose you know that Georgiana is to have one too? Oh yes – and my mother is quite frantic because she will insist on taking that horse of hers over to Galton every Friday to Monday, tearing up the countryside and leaping her six-barred gates, which is very unwise. You should ask your husband to speak to her.'

But Georgiana, intent on making her escape to Galton at every opportunity, had not endeared herself to Cullingford and I – occupied almost totally with Giles – saw her very rarely. I sat a few places away from her on one or two occasions at Aunt Verity's table, large, formal dinners where she, having been warned, perhaps, that neither her hunting stories nor her tales of her brother's rash exploits both in and out of the saddle would be much appreciated, sat quite still, a little girl, I thought, dressed up in finery she found uncomfortable and which did not suit her, listening blank-eyed with boredom to this new language of profit margins, cash flows, the weaving of double-twills and silk warp alpacas, of paramatta cloth and mohair lustres, turning her head occasionally with the startled swiftness of a bird to look at Nicholas for a reassurance he seemed willing to give. But Aunt Verity caught a chill that winter and my uncle, obsessively anxious on her account, whisked her away to the south coast to await the better weather, returning himself only intermittently to clear up his sons' mistakes – as he put it – and to prevent them, in the flaring of their black Barforth tempers, from beating each other to death, Nicholas with his fists, Blaize with his needle-sharp tongue.

Blaize went to America in the spring, a trip which gave him so much personal satisfaction and filled the Barforth order-books with so many remunerative demands for fancy worsteds that a return journey seemed beyond question and would prove, one felt, a standard feature of his life.

'I thought at the very least you would come back with an heiress in your luggage,' Prudence told him.

'Next time,' he promised. 'Yes – it may well be, for some of those girls are quite extraordinary. They sparkle, just like a June morning – very wholesome, very nice. Unless, of course, I should encounter a Red Indian princess. How about that, Prudence? That may even satisfy my craving for originality.'

'I imagine it would kill your father. But you should not stay away too long, Blaize, for I understand your brother has stolen a march on you this time.'

'You understand that, do you?' he said, his grey eyes amused but unusually careful. 'You mean the combing company, I suppose? Yes, I expect it could look rather sinister – as if he had taken advantage of my absence to convince my father. But he has been talking about combing machines for a long time, you know, and all it really means is that this time he has finally got his figures right, or my father would not have listened to a word. Well, it is a dirty business, wool-combing, and I am not on fire to get into it.'

'I understand he didn't ask you.'

'Why, Prudence, how very understanding you are. And how sharp. No, as it happens, he didn't ask me. Law Valley Wool-combers is to belong to Nicholas – and my father, of course – which is a very sensible move, since all our wool needs combing, and Nicholas will be obliged to give us priority over the Hobhouses and the rest. My word, my brother is going to be busy. A new wife, a new venture of his own to get off the ground, and our sheds at Lawcroft and Tarn Edge to manage all by himself whenever I am away, which will be a great deal of the time. But, dear Prudence, if you imagine he is trying to push me out, you may be easy, for I shall have my share of the Barforth mills – oh yes – and keep my hands clean of engine grease while I'm about it. Nicky will probably make a fortune for himself, but he will also increase mine, you know. The new combing machines are speeding up the whole industry: the faster the wool can be combed, the faster we can spin it and weave it, which means there will be more of it for me to sell – no more long faces from the shed managers and my brother when I tell them the delivery dates I've agreed to. Don't worry about me, Prudence. I confess I like it. But there's really no need.'

Nicholas's venture, of which he had spoken to me so eagerly, so long ago, soon became a reality, a low, scowling building not too far from Lawcroft Fold, dominated by a sign which proclaimed it 'Law Valley Wool-combers', an enterprise, like all its predecessors, which brought prosperity to some, great hardship to the hand-combers whose slow, laborious, none too healthy calling would soon be at an end. Some of them, of course – a few – would be employed by Nicholas; others would find work elsewhere, any work; but most of them, quite soon, were simply cast adrift, abandoned, unnecessary, their presence at every street corner becoming so menacing, so inconvenient, that something, it was felt, would have to be done.

'They're hungry,' Mayor Agbrigg said, once again, knowing from his own meagre past that, in work or out of work, the rent had still to be paid, body and soul held somehow – if only barely – together.

'They're impertinent,' Aunt Hannah replied, having received her share of muttered threats and obscene gestures from men who, having witnessed the death of their trade and their hopes for the future, were not concerned with good manners.

'They're a damned nuisance,' said many others, and so Mayor Agbrigg and my sister Prudence formed, almost single-handed, the Wool-combers' Aid Association with the object of placing these men in other situations or, when that proved impossible, of helping them to emigrate; Mayor Agbrigg persuading his colleagues to allocate fifteen hundred pounds from the rates for the purpose, Prudence, for many years after, continuing to receive letters from Australia and Canada offering ill-spelled news – both good and bad – of the families she had befriended.

'I am collecting for the hand-combers,' she told Blaize at the start of the troubles. 'Now then – I am curious to know what the size of your donation will be?'

'Oh – you may put me down for twice as much as my brother,' he told her, those grey eyes wickedly twinkling, frankly admitting that he was offering her nothing at all.

But whatever strife there might or might not be among the Barforths, I was not directly concerned in it. They were rich and would be richer, but I had riches too, a man who needed to see me and touch me, who hesitated, frowning, in the hallway if it seemed to him I was not there, his face warming instantly when he discovered himself mistaken. And if I was anxious about anything it was my conviction that I could not possibly give him enough, the inexplicable failure of my body, which so desired his caresses, to achieve the climax of pleasure he had described to me and wished me to share.

'Giles, I am so sorry. Is something wrong with me, do you think?'

'No, no, darling – don't think about it. Don't try. Just let it happen – there's time –'

But always, turning to him eagerly in the night, my limbs would begin to glow expectantly beneath his hands, everything in me wanting this perfect unity he spoke of, a fluttering at the core of the body, the hopeful wing-beating of a caged bird I wanted to set free, struggled to set free, not for my own pleasure but to please him. Yet always, at the final moment, when I was sure that this time, finally, I would succeed, I could feel it begin to slip away, receding forlornly back to its source, unfulfilled, leaving me so desolate in the face of his disappointment that I could have wept.

'Giles, I'm so sorry.'

'Darling, don't be.'

538

'Does it make your pleasure less?'

'No – my pleasure comes in any case. And the real pleasure is that I love you.'

'Oh yes – and I want to give you everything you want. You *have* to be happy, Giles. I must make you happy.'

'You do make me happy. Don't distress yourself – that alone could make me miserable.'

But the physical pleasure I could not attain became a symbol in my mind of the differences between us. I loved Giles. I was not in love with him in the piercing, consuming way I had been in love with Nicholas. And, in my desire to transfer that total feeling, all of a piece, from one man to the other, I came to believe this physical climax to be not only desirable but essential. If I could experience it, I would belong to him, and he would know that he possessed me. I must give him the satisfaction of seeing me completely enraptured, needing him, my body enslaved by his. I must. And my own determination, my fear of failure, created such tension inside me that night after night I did fail, my body defeating its own purposes.

'It doesn't mean I don't want you, Giles. I do – I do.'

'I know. Just let it happen. Darling – I am asking too much, too soon.'

'No! You're not. You could never ask enough. Why must you always try to take the blame? Don't be so *nice* to me, Giles, when I don't deserve it. If I'm inadequate, then tell me so.'

And there were times when, my teeth clenched with frustration, I would have allowed him to beat me, to force out of me in any way he could the response I was so desperate to give.

But he was unfailingly gentle, and in all other ways I knew we were happy. This was my life – and his – together, inseparable, my purpose, my reason for occupying my place in the world. I had recovered my pleasant pastures, and wanted no other.

Caroline was confined that June, a year after her marriage, bringing forth with characteristic flair not one child but two, a pair of healthy boys who came into the world with no apparent fuss, and were allowed to make none thereafter, lying quietly in their cradles at her bedside while she made out her lists of the furniture, the groceries and the guests she desired to be delivered. Dominic Chard, who would be Sir Dominic one day, master of Listonby and all it contained, just a shock of dark hair at present, on a lace pillow, a diminutive fist reaching out for the sunbeams as they came through her window, looking quite capable, I thought – like his mother – of grasping them. And his brother, his junior by just ten vital minutes, Master Noel St John Chard, who, with no lands and titles to inherit, would have to look beyond Listonby for his livelihood.

'I suppose the young one will be a soldier,' she told me, having accepted my gifts and compliments. 'Yes – a colonel of Hussars. I am not quite sure just what that is, but if it should be as grand as it sounds then that is what I shall make him. Colonel Noel St John Chard – it sounds well, at any rate. We have already had a set-to about the christening, since Matthew has two cousins who are bishops, and my suggestion that we should settle the matter by having them baptize one infant each was not well received. They both expect to baptize the eldest, of course, and unless they come out of their sulks I shall ask the vicar of Cullingford to officiate, which would really put the cat among the pigeons. Well – I am ahead of Georgiana and she is not likely to catch up with me. In fact she is so flat still that one wonders if it is really more than her imagination. She will have the poor mite in a ditch, if she is not careful, with her horse for midwife. Well then, Faith, I shall expect you and your clever husband to the Christening Dinner.'

Georgiana, however, gave birth a month later, luxuriously if not easily in her bedroom at Tarn Edge, her labour, despite her athletic habits and stoical turn of mind, lasting for thirty-six agonizing hours and requiring both the old-fashioned Dr Overdale and the progressive Dr Ashburn to bring about its conclusion.

She was still very weak when I called to see her, still confined to her bed, although I had allowed a full three weeks to pass by, but her face on the pillow looked so spent, her body so boyish and frail, somehow so vulnerable, something about her light green eyes and the tumble-down mass of her coppery hair so touching, that my lurking fear of Nicholas – for this was his bed, his child, his woman – was evaporated by my sympathy.

'Georgiana, was it so very dreadful?'

'Oh yes,' she said, smiling. 'How nice of you to ask me that, for now I can say that indeed it was – quite dreadful. Everybody else has been telling me how well I look – when I know I look a perfect fright – and how brave I was, when in fact I screamed so loud that Nicky must surely have heard me above the racket of his looms or whatever. Yes – dreadful. I was quite angry, really, at being proved such a coward, which made me scream the harder. Your husband was marvellous, Dr Overdale told me to "Hush, hush little woman", but your husband told me to scream if I wanted to and swear too, which I did, I can assure you. Well, there he is – the cause of all the trouble: Master Gervase Clevedon Barforth. He is rather small – one could lose him, almost, among all that muslin and lace they have draped over him – but when he fills out a little I believe he may resemble my brother. He has not much hair now, but you can see that what bit there is will quite definitely be auburn, like Perry's. Would you like to hold him? Most people seem to think it obligatory, but, if you shouldn't care for it, I will perfectly understand.'

I picked him up awkwardly, having no experience of the new born, and, feeling nothing beneath the elaborately swathed shawls more substantial than a kitten, I put him hastily down again, worrying, as I returned to her bedside, that I had somehow injured him.

'I wanted him to be born at the Abbey,' she said wistfully. 'I confess to you that I was quite wicked and went over there as often as I could towards the end, hoping that my pains would begin and I would have to stay. The walks I took – you can't imagine – striding out up hill and down dale with Perry, who even took me up in his curricle to give me a good shaking. Heavens, we drove all the way to Patterswick, hell for leather, to no avail. I did so want him to be born at Galton. I wanted to call him Peregrine, too, but Nicky says one Peregrine is enough, although no one in the world could have objected to my naming him Gervase for my grandfather and Clevedon for myself. It is only right, after all, that he should have our family name, for, if Perry does not marry, then it will be this little Gervase, none other, who will inherit the Abbey.'

'Our cousin Nicholas may not care for that,' Prudence said later when I had made my report. 'I cannot think he has set himself to build an empire with the intention of seeing it squandered by the Clevedons. It is Caroline who wanted the land and the title. Nicholas merely wanted the woman, and Georgiana may as well make up her mind that Master Gervase Clevedon Barforth is destined for the mills.'

The Clevedons, too, had relatives in high ecclesiastical places, but the christening of the infant Gervase was a very private affair in the Abbey chapel, far removed in spirit from the ceremony at Listonby, which seemed more like a launching into society of the future baronet, the future colonel of Hussars, than a baptism. The house, where alterations were still in progress, was crammed with Chards of all varieties, noble, religious, sporting and military, who, having said all that was necessary on the subject of Master Dominic and Master Noel, attended a christening banquet in the eighteenth-century dining-room, a triumph of truffled roast chickens and partridges in aspic, of lobster *au gratin* and spiced sirloin of beef, while outside in the park a whole ox was roasted for the Listonby tenants assembled at tables beneath the sycamores and elm trees.

Caroline's new upstairs ballroom was still littered with carpentry and unfinished plasterwork, but nevertheless there were two dances at Listonby that evening, the Great Hall cleared for family and friends, a marquee erected on the lawn and stocked with several barrels of ale to accommodate the farmers and villagers, the huntsman and his wife, the kennel-huntsman and his exceedingly pretty daughter, who did not seem too alarmed by the attentions of Peregrine Clevedon.

There was a great deal of champagne, the party from the Hall going outside at midnight to toast the sleeping infants yet again, tenants' daughters and gentlemen's daughters, officers and ploughboys raising their glasses side by side, producing the exact degree of mingling, class with class, considered appropriate to the occasion, since the tenantry must be understandably eager to make the acquaintance of their new lady, understandably relieved that she had ensured the continuity of the estate and of their leases, by producing this over-abundance of heirs.

It was an immense success, lavish, yet so efficient that not even the most mercantile, Nonconformist of hearts could have pronounced it wasteful, everyone enjoying themselves hugely, but at the same time minding their manners, gaiety without impropriety – since impropriety would always find it hard to flourish beneath Caroline's eagle eye – a blueprint, one felt, of what she intended to make of her future.

'Well done,' I told her.

'Yes,' she said. 'I believe it was. Not that I mean to rest on my laurels,

541

I do assure you, for the moment one becomes satisfied one has set one's feet on the downward path. My father taught me that. He measures his success by his current trading figures – today's profit, not yesterday's – and I shall do the same. Just wait for my Christmas Eve Ball, Faith dear. I think even my father will be impressed with that.'

The foundation stone of Aunt Hannah's concert hall was finally laid that year, to the hearty accompaniment of Cullingford's own brass band, on the site she had herself chosen off Market Square. The ceremony was performed by a belted earl, an ancient gentleman who appeared uncertain as to the exact purpose of his visit. Yet he made himself pleasant enough afterwards at the reception organized in the Assembly Rooms by my aunt who, although mayoress no longer, appeared to have retained the authority of the office, making light work of comfortable Mrs Hobhouse, who had officially succeeded her. Mayor Hobhouse, indeed, looking portly and complacent despite the persistent rumours that trade at Nethercoats was not good, made no secret of his dependance upon Mr Ira Agbrigg, being himself a man who preferred the afternoon comforts of the Old Swan to a spike-edged tussle with the Cullingford Waterworks.

'Here's my man Agbrigg,' he kept on saying, much to the annoyance of Aunt Hannah and Uncle Joel, whose 'man' Mr Agbrigg undoubtedly was. 'He's got the Waterworks Company by the tail at last, I can tell you. Neatly done, Agbrigg my lad, since, if you're to be mayor again next time, the purchase will come into your term of office and you'll get all the credit.'

'He did all the work,' Prudence said in a whisper that was meant to be heard, and indeed it was no secret that Mr Agbrigg's efforts alone had persuaded the truculent directors of the waterworks company to part with their ailing giant for a sum of a hundred and sixty-five thousand pounds, and that he had not only calmed the fears of a startled Corporation, unaccustomed as yet to handling such large sums of public money, but had obliged them to seek parliamentary consent to the raising of a further four hundred thousand to be used for the construction of reservoirs.

'Such energy!' Mrs Hobhouse had once been heard to murmur, very spitefully for her. 'Only think, Hannah, had it been put to commercial use you might have been a millionairess, not just a mayoress, by now.'

But Aunt Hannah, her own building projects fast becoming a reality, her husband's reputation as a popular hero providing her at last with ample compensation for his lack of social finesse, had replied merely with a smile and an inclination of her handsome Barforth head.

My mother was there too that day, allowing the outwardly respectable but – according to Blaize – inwardly lascivious worsted spinner, Mr Oldroyd, to take her arm, flirtatious and ready as always to enjoy the conquest of any man, but bored, I knew, eager to be off on her travels again, yet not certain this time just where she wished to go.

'You look nineteen, mamma,' I told her.

'My dear – I know, and it is very kind of you to say so. But what is the good of that when everyone else of my generation is looking so old? Darling, where have all the attractive men gone to? I was asking myself that just this morning, for the world used to be full of them and now they have vanished entirely. Well, I have found the answer. They are here, of course, as they have always been, except that they are older – for Matthew Oldroyd was once quite handsome before he became so dry and grey, and Bradley Hobhouse, my dear, when he weighed a mere sixteen stones instead of the ton of him you see today, was a man worth looking at. I confess *I* looked, once; and he at me – merely looked. But now, apart from my brother Joel, they are just a set of bloated or shrunken old gentlemen, and even Joel, you know, is taking on weight. Yes, I may look nineteen, Faith dear, but there are days when I do not feel it. Perhaps I should take to wearing purple satin like Hannah and Emma-Jane Hobhouse, and compose myself for decay. I wonder if it would have been better, after all, to have been born a matron, like Celia.'

Celia had not attended the ceremony in the Square, fearing to stand on her feet so long, fearing to be jostled in the crowd and that the noise of the brass instruments would give her a headache, but Jonas had assisted her up the shallow steps to the Assembly Rooms, provided her with a chair and footstool, opened a window so that she could see something of the proceedings and then closed it again when she declared she would take cold. And, although there was no warmth in the care he took of her, no one could have accused him of being other than unfailingly attentive to the whims of this frail little woman who had always felt the need of her frailty to make herself noticed.

'Jonas, this lemonade you have brought me is much too warm.'

'I will fetch some ice.'

'You know that ice gives me a headache.'

'I beg your pardon. What shall I bring you then?'

'Oh – I don't know. Can't you think of something? There seems to be nothing but champagne, which is not good for me. I don't suppose they would trouble themselves to make me some tea?'

'I will go and inquire.'

'Thank you, – and not too strong, Jonas – for the last time I had tea here it was quite black and bitter, and altogether horrid. Do hurry, Jonas.'

He went off to do her bidding, and, watching his cool, quite passionless retreat, Prudence murmured to me, 'Our little sister seems to have the upper hand of her Jonas. Who would have thought it? I had expected to see things quite otherwise.'

But I was less convinced. Celia, indeed, had always whined and complained, had always been a nuisance, but Prudence knew as well as I that it had stemmed from a combined sense of inadequacy and isolation. If Celia had grown up believing herself neglected, by an all-powerful father who had shown her neither interest nor affection, by her sisters who had openly preferred each other's company to hers, then she had been quite right. Only Miss Mayfield, at the cry of 'My head aches. My back aches', had rushed to attend her, only a hurried summons to Dr Overdale, a darkened room – 'Be quiet, girls, your sister is ailing' – had made her important. And now, the triumph of her early marriage fading, she was using those same ailments, the drama of her two miscarriages, to attract the notice or to punish the man who seemed determined to be a good husband – since it was a requirement of his prickly nature that everything he did should be done to perfection – but who did not love her.

'Well,' I said to Prudence, speaking my thought out loud, 'at least he's not in love with anyone else.'

'Jonas?' she said. 'Of course not. Good heavens, Faith, is that all you can think of? I never thought to see you so besotted with Giles. Well, I am sure he is very glad of it, even if it does make your conversation so limited.'

We left the reception early, Giles having received a call of some urgency, and I drove with him to Simon Street, waiting in the gig while he went down a narrow court, a mere gap, man-wide, between two houses, and entered the house behind them, which my father had built.

Simon Street, which had given its name to the entire area of alleys and back passages cobwebbing between itself and Saint Street, was not the worst place I had ever seen; it was simply larger, its tragedies, its brutalities, its degradations appearing worse because they were more numerous. Built long ago to accommodate the labour force of Low Cross Mills, if offered ample proof to the most casual eye of my father's boasted ability to squeeze in more humanity per acre than any other builder in the West Riding, its damp, flimsy, two-roomed cottages sometimes housing thirty or more lacklustre persons, rarely fewer than eight or ten. The street itself was unpaved, an occasional heap of engine ashes thrown down to drink up the mud, the open sewage channels on either side of it seeping their liquid foulness into the uneven ground. But, in the alleys beyond, I knew there were no drains at all, no more facilities for the functioning of human bodies than was normally provided for stabled cattle, just dung-heaps, rotting and poisonous, in any dark corner, a swill-tub placed here and there overflowing with the festering vegetable garbage for which the pig-men, when they troubled to collect it, would pay a penny or two.

I knew that the woman my husband had gone to visit was dirty, that all women who took up residence in these mean streets, no matter how careful their upbringing nor how precise their early ambitions, were dirty too, not necessarily from idleness or wickedness, but because the stand-pipe in Simon Street was turned on for scarcely more than half an hour a day, few of these women possessing the pans and buckets in which to collect and store the water, nor the strength to carry them even if they had. And I understood too, now that Giles had explained it to me, the impossibility, even for the fortunate owners of buckets and brushes, of scrubbing floorboards that were rotten or walls that sprouted a continual mushroom-mould of damp.

I knew that Giles's patient would most likely be drunk on his arrival, since gin, being cheap and easier to come by than water, was also much valued for its ability to dull the senses of smell, of hunger, of decency, to induce a state of contented apathy – much sought after in Simon Street – a shrug of thin shoulders which said, 'What do I care?' I knew that her children fouled the streets as casually as the packs of mongrel dogs I could see swarming everywhere, because my father had provided no privies, or so few that they were choked with ancient excrement, and the streets were sweeter.

I knew that in the hot weather – down those fearful alleyways – there were fly-swarms, rat-swarms, whores and thieves, murder done for the sake of a shilling, or for its own sake alone, whilst on the strips of wasteland where my father had neglected to build, or his buildings had fallen down. I knew that women washed their infected bedclothes, during the summer fevers, in the stagnant pools where others came to drink.

I knew, too, that the woman my husband had called on could not pay him, would take none of his advice, would continue to drink and breed and moulder her life away, failing, since no one else had ever valued her, to place any value on herself. And, wondering what value the world would have accorded me had I been born in so irrevocable a trap, I was so fiercely thankful for my own life that the sight of Giles coming back to the gig, smiling a little ruefully as he picked his way across the litter, caused my stomach to lurch with gladness, a glow beginning, small but very determined, at the core of me.

We drove off to higher ground, cleaner air, and, sitting very close to him, I said, 'You are a marvellous man, Giles.'

'By no means. I am an ordinary man. There is nothing at all remarkable about me that I can see.'

'I say you are marvellous and don't wish to be contradicted.'

He smiled, quiet and contained as he always was. 'You may call me fortunate, if you like. I believe it would be a more accurate assessment. I have always had sufficient money for my needs and so I can afford to be compassionate. Please don't admire me too much, Faith, for I shall never do great things in the world. I am moved by the misery around me, but I am too content with my own life to be a true pioneer. I did not march to Westminster with the Chartists, as your brother Crispin did, although I believed strongly in every one of their aims. I do what I can in Simon Street, as much as I am asked to do, but I lead no crusades for reform. Basically I am just an ordinary man, concerned with my own affairs, with my home and my wife, and that she should continue to think me marvellous.'

I got down from the gig in Millergate, opened my own front door, crossed my threshold, waiting as he saw the horse put away, my anxieties gone, my whole body dreaming and glowing – waiting for him.

'Giles.'

'Yes, darling?'

And, although I couldn't say, 'Make love to me', since no woman educated by my father could ever bring herself to say that, it was there, unspoken, and more than that: no longer simply 'Make love to me', but 'Giles, let me make love to you.'

15

We spent our second Christmas together in quiet content, Giles's professional commitments obliging me to refuse Caroline's invitation to spend the entire festive season at Listonby.

'You can't miss my ball,' she said, quite horrified, refusing to be diverted even by my discovery of a particularly fine silk brocade which would suit her to perfection, and the detailed sketches I passed on to her dressmaker. 'If your husband can't come then you must come without him. Goodness – he can't possibly want you to miss my ball either. The staircase is an absolute marvel, and even my father has never assembled so many chandeliers together – one directly above my head when I receive at the top of the stairs, seven in the Long Gallery. The Hall is going to be full of candles and Christmas trees, and I'm not even prepared to tell you what I've done with the ballroom. I want to *unveil* it, Faith, like a monument. You *can't* miss it, and you could be a tremendous help to me, since I've never even met half the people who are coming. You don't have to dance with them if you'd rather not, but you could circulate and chat. Naturally your husband wouldn't mind. He'd be glad to see you enjoying yourself – like Matthew.'

And she was still puzzled, still half offended when we met at Tarn Edge a few days before the event, the only afternoon, it seemed, when Aunt Verity could hope to gather her family together under her own roof, Caroline having only that much time to spare and Georgiana being quite determined, no matter what other claims her husband might have on his time, to go over to Galton for the hunting. But even when we were all assembled and had received our gifts, somewhat in advance, from the lavish Barforth tree, our menfolk were called away from us one by one, Giles to a human confinement, Matthew Chard to an equine complication, Nicholas to his combing sheds, where a group of hand-combers were showing every sign of ill-will towards his property. His father went off to assist him, Blaize to see the fun, leaving us with no male company but the infants Dominic and Noel Chard, installed in lonely state in what had been Caroline's nursery, and the infant Gervase Barforth who, carried downstairs by his mother, was tickled and tossed about by her for a while as if he'd been a puppy and then carelessly abandoned on the edge of a sofa, to be rescued by Aunt Verity.

'Poor little soul,' she said. 'You may leave him at Listonby with me, Georgiana, when you go over to Galton, you know. I shall be staying with Caroline until the New Year and would enjoy having my three grandchildren all together.'

But, glancing across at her son settled comfortably in his grandmother's arms – remembering his existence perhaps – Georgiana suddenly clapped her hands in delight and shook her head.

'Do look at the firelight on his hair. I told you, did I not, that it would be red, and so it is – red as a carrot at the moment, but it will darken, just like me and Perry. Oh yes, he is a wild, red Clevedon, that one, there is no mistaking it.'

We saw in the New Year with my mother, who, still saddened by the premature decay of her admirers, talked of returning to France now that it was safe again, the new Republic in fact being destined to fall an early victim to a second Bonaparte, a wily gentleman who, after spending some years of exile in London, would before long win election to the presidency and, like his Uncle Napoleon before him, soon set about the business of making himself a king.

'I think this new France will suit me,' she said, 'for these political adventurers understand the value of gaiety.'

But somehow her journey was never made, only half planned, half prepared, abandoned a dozen times, so that she was with me on the May afternoon that Giles came unexpectedly into the hall, letting the door slam shut behind him, and, when I went out to meet him, said quickly, 'Don't touch me.'

'Giles –?'

'Let me wash my hands first. I'll be with you presently.'

And, as he hurried up the stairs, he called out, 'I have sent a message to Mayor Agbrigg, asking him to call. He should be here almost at once.'

'There is trouble,' my mother said. 'One can always feel it. I shall leave you, Faith. I have little talent for trouble and would only be in the way.'

Mayor Agbrigg came and spent an hour with Giles behind a locked study door.

'It is nothing,' Giles said to me. 'I must go out again.'

'It is nothing,' he said much later on his return. But, when he had scrubbed himself and changed his linen – stowing his dirty linen away, I noticed, in his laboratory at the back of the house – I stood in front of him and demanded, 'Tell me. I am not a child. I must know.'

'There may be nothing to know,' he said, walking away from me, making the brandy-glass in his hand a barrier between us. 'Dr Overdale is sure I am mistaken, and Dr Blackstone has called me a dramatic fool. I hope they may be right. I believe I have seen a case of cholera in Simon Street.'

'But – Giles – there is always fever, surely, in Simon Street?'

'Yes, indeed. Typhus, typhoid, scarlet – any kind of fever you would care to name, and some that have no names at all. You may find them all in Simon Street, any day of the week. I said cholera, Faith, not fever.'

'But you are not sure.'

'I saw it ten years ago in a London hospital. This seems the same. But no, I am not sure, because I want to be wrong.'

'And Dr Overdale?'

'He has seen it too. He is an older man and he remembers the epidemic of 1831. He wants me to be wrong so badly that he is insisting upon it, while Dr Blackstone, who is even older, would like me confined to a madhouse. He takes the common view – as you did – that there is always something amiss in Simon Street.'

'What can you do, Giles?'

'Go back there,' he said, 'in the morning and see how far it has spread.'

Mayor Agbrigg called again, late that night, and, as they sat at my fireside drinking brandy, silence thick all about them, I said, 'What is cholera?'

'I don't know,' Giles answered, his eyes on his glass, his face in shadow. 'Nobody knows.'

'But we have had it before?'

'Oh yes. Our troops found it in India, thirty years ago. Then it appeared in Russia and spread like the plague, which is what they called it at first. So many peasants died in Eastern Europe that for a time they believed the aristocrats were poisoning them, thinning them out so they'd be easier to govern, and there was nearly a revolution. It moved west, until every city of any size had it, and in thirty-one it came to London and killed eight thousand people there – sixty thousand, they say, in England as a whole. God knows how many really died. They didn't know what caused it, or how to treat it, and we still don't. Like everything else, it takes the very old and the very young to begin with, the under-nourished and the weak – the easy pickings. It lives on dirt, breeds in rotting garbage heaps and open sewers such as you can find so easily in better places than Simon Street. And when it gathers strength it seems to take anybody who gets in its way. I don't know, Faith. Some say it comes from the inhalation of bad air. Some say it comes from the drinking of water that has been fouled by excrement, and we've plenty of that in Cullingford. It involves massive vomiting; the bowels open and the body can retain nothing. If it lasted long enough, the patient would starve to death. But it's quick, and exceedingly filthy. We're at the beginning of May. If it *is* the cholera, then you should pray for a cool summer.'

'Aye,' Mayor Agbrigg said. 'And what can I do for you, lad – if it is the cholera? I'll take the council by the scruff of its neck for you, not that I'll need to, for they're old enough to remember the last time, same as I am. What can we do?'

Giles shrugged, refilled the Mayor's glass and his own.

'You can educate them to stop drinking cess-water in Simon Street and provide them with water they can drink.'

'That I can. But tomorrow morning, lad – what then?'

'Chloride of lime,' he said slowly, his eyes still on the warmly swirling brandy. 'The houses in the stricken areas should be limewashed. You could get them to shift the dung-heaps, though God knows where they'll put them. They burned barrels of tar and vinegar, I believe, in the streets the last time. I don't know if it helps, other than to make people feel that something is being done.'

'I'll see to it, lad.'

And when Mayor Agbrigg had gone, leaving Giles still sitting by the fireside, I slipped my hand in his and asked him, 'Are you afraid?'

'Of course. If I could choose between going back to Simon Street tomorrow morning or taking the London train tonight with you, then I'd take the train.'

'I'd come with you, Giles, gladly.'

'I know,' he said, smiling, that great air of quietness still about him. 'What a pity there is no choice.'

He left early the next morning, a beautiful pink and blue day, returning late in the afternoon, the distance he placed between us confirming my fears. In the same family in Simon Street one child had died, three others were ailing; also the woman next door and two more across the street, six people in the same bed next door to that, so that even Dr Blackstone was in doubt no longer.

'I am on my way to the Infirmary,' he said. 'Every bed will be needed, and so I must send home – or turn out – as many as I can.'

And Prudence, who had come to spend the evening with me, said quietly, 'I'll come with you.'

'My dear, you'll do no such thing.'

'But I shall. Do be sensible, Giles. Not one of your nurses will remain when they know what is coming, or the ones who do will be too drunk to be of service. Gallantry is all very well, but you ill need every pair of hands you can muster, and I shall oblige you to take mine.'

'And mine,' I added, with not the least expectation in the world of being refused, since he had never refused me anything before, until he said in a voice that was quite strange to me, 'I think not. In fact I absolutely forbid it.'

'My goodness!' I told him, half laughing. 'Then I shall just have to disobey.'

'No – no. You will do just as I tell you.'

'You must decide that between you,' Prudence said calmly, beginning to fasten her bonnet. 'But you have no authority to forbid me. Only mamma may do that, and I am well able to manage her. I may come and go as I please unless she denies it, and there is every likelihood that she will bolt all the way to France and leave me with Miss Mayfield, who is even easier to handle.'

'I cannot take you to a source of danger, Prudence.'

'You cannot stop me. You must make the best of it.'

But in my case he was adamant. 'You are my wife,' he said much later that night, when I had reasoned and pleaded and threatened to no avail. 'The law allows me absolute authority over you and I shall exercise it.'

'Good heavens, Giles! I had no idea you could be so pompous. You can hardly lock me up. Not even my father ever threatened me with that.'

Yet, when I persisted, finding it unthinkable that I should not be allowed to share his burden, he said simply, 'Help me, Faith.'

'But that is what I want to do.'

'Then do it. I am no hero, Faith. I am uncertain and afraid, and in these next weeks or months, or however long it may be, I shall very likely grow more afraid and extremely tired. I have to know that my wife is safe, or as safe as you can be in these circumstances. I cannot function otherwise. I have never asked you for anything before. I am asking you now for this. Help me.'

And there was nothing more for the moment that I could say.

I remained at our fireside, fretting, through those early summer days, painful with anxiety, as frantic for escape – to get to his side – as a caged bird. Many times I had wanted to make a sacrifice on his behalf, to perform some huge act of courage for his sake in proof of my devotion and gratitude, and, now that it had come to me, this tame cowering in the safety of my chimney corner was harder than any ordeal I had imagined.

'Dear God, there must be something I can do, Giles. I do believe, sometimes, that I am going mad.'

And his answer was always the same. 'I need you now, just as you are. I have asked you to help me. Am I asking too much?'

Within days, it seemed, the Infirmary was overflowing, the vagrants and whores, the lost children of the Simon Street district being picked up nightly in their dozens, drunk and terrified and vomiting their lives away, while in the alleys, the damp, befouled anthills my father had created, every house had its tragedy, the stench of burning tar and vinegar heavy on the air, the stench of fear threaded evilly through it. From one of those back streets alone, seventy-two carts of manure, animal and human, were removed by Mayor Agbrigg's volunteers, the half-rotted carcasses of dogs and cats fished up from the streams and those festering waste-land pools where Simon Street commonly drew its water. Chloride of lime was issued free of charge by a terrified Corporation, aware at last of the marriage between dirt and disease, too late – for those who were to die – to effect its separation.

No one now could really cleanse those abominable hovels, where windows, pasted or boarded up to exclude winter draughts and summer flies, converted each overcrowded room into a stinking oven. No one could even persuade those who lived therein to give up their dead for burial before it suited them, the Simon Street custom of laying out adult corpses on what could be the family's only bed, infant corpses on the kitchen table, continuing to be observed, partly from the habitual delay in scraping together the funeral expenses, partly because undertakers and grave-diggers were increasingly unable to cope.

The illness, as Giles had told us, struck swiftly and was just as swiftly over. A child could be playing in the streets one morning, splashing happily in the sewage channels, and could be dead the same evening. A man could walk briskly to his employment, whistling in the hazy summer dawn, and be on his knees in a retching, malodorous agony in the mill yard by breakfast-time. Yet the Barforth men, the Hobhouse men, the spare, grey-faced Mr Oldroyd of Fieldhead, continued to turn on their engines at five o'clock every morning, to stand at their gates, watch in hand, to admit the punctual and to lock out the latecomers, continued to patrol their weaving sheds and spinning sheds and combing sheds, admitting no reason why their production targets should not be met. The Piece Hall continued to open its doors for the Thursday market-day, the ladies of Cullingford, even, to continue with their tea-parties, feeling this infection of the bowels – somewhat indelicate in itself, even had it not been so lethal – to be largely a matter for Simon Street, until a parlourmaid of the Battershaws collapsed with a horrific clattering of tea-time china and silver, a Hobhouse coachman and then a Hobhouse child began to vomit and excrete and shake without hope of control; at which moment Cullingford began to close its doors.

Prudence moved in with me, my mother, who could not prevent her attendance at the Infirmary, refusing to expose her own person to the 'miasmatic vapours' Prudence might well carry into her house. I received a firmly penned note from my sister Celia requesting me neither to call upon her nor to answer her letter until the danger of contamination should be over. 'You are unable to avoid it,' she wrote. 'But I know you will have consideration for those of us who may.' Caroline remained at Listonby, Uncle Joel and Aunt Verity were already in Bournemouth and wisely chose to stay there. But Aunt Hannah, who did not approve of hospitals, was among the first to march up the cobbled slope of Sheepgate to the rickety converted dwelling house we called the Infirmary and, finding, as Prudence had warned, that such nurses as were available had either taken to the gin-bottle or run away, promptly rolled up her sleeves, donned an apron and set about the boiling of fouled bed-linen, the preparation of turpentine compresses, the constant washing and even the consoling of the dying.

I stayed at home – as a married woman should; obeying my husband – as a married woman should; deciding a dozen times a day that it was impossible, that I was, after all, a woman capable of decision, not a child to be protected and controlled.

'I can't tolerate it, Giles.'

'I can't tolerate it, Faith, unless you do.'

'I am sure you can.'

'I do not know. But what I do know is that I should not forgive you.'

'Do as he asks,' Prudence said sharply. 'Can't you see how weary he is? Dr Blackstone collapsed this morning – no, not the cholera, thank God; old age, I suppose, and the strain. They were obliged to take him home, and Dr Overdale is not young, either. The rest of them are too young, perhaps, and they rely on Giles. Don't trouble him. He has enough to bear, knowing that there's nothing he can really do – having to watch people die, with no real hope to offer them. Leave him alone.'

And, seeing beneath the hard lines of her face a reflection of the horror she had experienced that day – a horror which set her apart from all those who had not shared it – knowing that the foul odours of the sickness were still in her nostrils, the futility of human despair still clawing at her heart, I desisted, fed her and Giles when they came home and could bring themselves to eat, provided clean linen, cool beds in which I occasionally persuaded them to sleep, prayed a little, waited.

My Uncle Joel sent instructions from Bournemouth that beer was to be issued to his operatives in any quantity they were able to consume, a gesture at once philanthropic and sensible, since if the disease was really carried by bad water, as Giles increasingly believed, it was as well to offer an alternative drink. But, if the Barforth mill-hands were grateful and a little more cheerful than some others, they continued to die just the same, and, as that bright, blue and gold June began to merge into a hazy, slumbrous July, it was known that seven hundred people had perished.

I was quite alone now, except for Mrs Guthrie busying herself in my kitchen, with nothing to see from my window but an empty, sun-baked street which had once been the brash, bustling thoroughfare of Millergate – few carriages now, such as there were rushing by closed and furtive despite the heat; an occasional woman, head bowed, handkerchief to her mouth, hurrying on some essential errand, plainly terrified of the poison that must be rising from the very cobbles, seeping like slime down every wall, gathering itself for fresh onslaught in the heavy yellow air. Long, terrible days, appalling nights when Giles, having slept an hour in his armchair, his stomach unable to cope with anything but brandy, would get carefully to his feet, put on his hat again and go quietly away. Hours that stifled me, each one extending itself into an isolation without end, a walking through the empty corridors of an evil dream, so that I was startled one afternoon when my door opened and Georgiana walked into the room.

'Yes,' she said without any explanation. 'I was told you would be sad and sorry, and so you are. I am come to cheer you up, since it seems everyone else is terrified of setting foot across your threshold. Heavens, they do so like to imprison us, these husbands, do they not? Well, I have escaped mine today, but when I called in at the Infirmary to see what I could do, I fell foul of yours, who at once ordered me away. Goodness, he was cross. No place for a lady, he said, which was unjust of him, since Prudence was there – so I can only conclude he meant no place for a married lady unless one carries written permission from one's lord. I cannot understand it. My grandfather would never have forbidden me to be of service if sickness had come to Galton: he would have expected me to do my utmost, since it is one's duty, surely, to look after one's own people? He would have been positively ashamed of me, I can tell you, had I attempted to shirk. After all, if we do not set the example – I mean, if we accept the privilege, then we must also accept the responsibility. That is what I have been taught, in any case, and it sounds very right to me. Well, Nicky does not think so, of course. He has gone to his mill every day because business is business, he tells me, and it is not my business to nurse his operatives. Goodness, at Galton I have always gone into the cottages when there was fever, and so did my mamma and my grandmamma. They are our people, after all – we knew their names and their faces. Yet I have heard Nicky call out "Hey, you there – you with the checked cap", to a man who, it turns out, has been employed at Lawcroft for twenty years. I cannot understand it.'

'Did Nicholas forbid you to come into town?'

'Oh yes,' she said, accepting my offer of tea and settling herself comfortably on my sofa as if she meant to stay as long as she pleased. 'So he did. But he is so cross with me today in any case that a little more will make no difference. I have been spending too much, you see – or at least, not spending, since I am allowed to buy whatever I choose, so long as it is gowns and fans and shawls and trinkets of any imaginable variety. But I am not allowed to give my money away. I have told him, either my allowance is mine or it is not, and he says it is mine, but, whenever I am penniless, which seems to be very often, he requires to know why. What have I to show for it, he asks, and, of course, if I have been over to Galton and bought new pinafores for the little girls at the village school, or have made a little loan to my brother, then I can show him nothing at all. And I wish he would not ask me, in that stern fashion, when I think Perry means to repay me, since he knows quite well that there is no chance of it. Is your husband so particular?'

'No. But I have no brother – at least, I have, but he is far away and has never asked me for money.'

She refilled her cup, standing on no ceremony with me, her slender, abrupt body altogether relaxed, her pointed kitten's face warming to its task – apparently not unpleasant – of cheering me.

'Then you are fortunate, for Perry is always in disgrace. My word, if my grandfather had but a suspicion of the half of it – but I am quite determined to keep it from him. When all this is over you must come again – come often – to Galton, for you would so like my grandfather. He is the very kindest of men, and I know of no one with such perfect integrity. But, of course, his standards are so very high, and Perry has always been a scamp. It is a part of his nature one accepts. It is simply Perry. My father was much the same, and since my grandfather has had a great deal to bear in the past – and takes Perry's escapades far more to heart than I – I do not wish him to be troubled again. I have dozens of new dresses, Faith. One cannot always be buying more of the same thing, and, if I have money in my hands and Perry does not, then how can I refuse him? I could not, even if I wanted to. My grandfather will take nothing from me, and so if I choose to help my brother I cannot think why it should be thought unnatural.'

We talked an hour longer of this and that, her horse, her child, her inability after almost two years as a manufacturer's wife to find the wherewithal to fill her days, and than, as my clock gave warning that the hour of four was upon us, she got to her feet, pulling on her gloves and her perky chip hat with its audacious green feather.

'Heavens – I must be on my way.'

But hesitating, frowning, she held out her hand and then, pausing in the doorway, came back into the room again.

'Faith – tell me – you understand these things better than I, and may be able to advise me.'

And, still frowning, she sat down again.

'Well, this is the way of it. Perry approached me a few days ago, in a great fix as usual. Not a great sum – a hundred pounds merely – not owing to a tradesman, unfortunately, since tradesmen can be asked to wait, but to Julian Flood who has debts of his own and cannot. Oh dear, I did not wish to approach Nicky, since he had scolded me just the day before about not throwing good money after bad, and so – because Julian can be very pressing and has right on his side after all, since it is a gambling debt, and gambling debts *must* be paid – well, I went to Blaize, who was kind enough to oblige me, saying I may repay him when I can. Faith, if Nicky knew of it, would he be – very much put out?'

'Georgiana,' I said, the whole of my middle-class, commercial mind aghast at her rashness, 'he would be furious – and horrified. Georgiana, you must never, absolutely never go into debt.'

She laughed, just a shade nervously. 'Goodness, you are as shocked as if I had confessed to adultery.'

'Georgiana, in Cullingford adultery and debt amount to very much the same thing. In fact debt is probably worse.'

'Yes, I suspected as much. But only a hundred pounds, Faith – from my brother-in-law who seemed ready enough to spare it. And Nicky will never know. I can trust you not to tell him, and Perry will not.'

'No. But Blaize may do so.'

'Faith!' she said, as shocked as I had been a moment before. 'Whatever do you mean? Blaize would not betray a confidence of that nature. No gentleman would do so!'

'Blaize would,' I told her, suddenly very sure of it. 'I am not saying he will, or that he intended it when he advanced you the money. But if it should suit his purposes tomorrow, or whenever – since you will be a long time in paying him back, if you ever do – then he would.'

'But why? He does not dislike me, does he?'

'No. In fact I think he likes you very much. But Blaize is not a gentleman in the way you understand it, Georgiana. He may appear so, and he is certainly very charming and can be kind-hearted – but his code is not the same as your grandfather's. He's a Barforth and, if he can get a return on his investment, then he will.'

'Then he dislikes Nicky – his own brother?'

'No, he doesn't. He may not have taken this affair of the combing company quite so calmly as he likes people to think, because it looks as if Nicholas is going to make a lot of money for himself, and Blaize can't really enjoy that. But it's not dislike. Listen, Georgiana, we were brought up together, and always, if Blaize had something, then Nicholas had to have it too, no matter what it cost him; and if Nicholas had something, then Blaize either had to have it, or spoil it, or get something better to make whatever Nicholas had look small. Their father wanted them to be aggressive and competitive, and so they are. The difference is that Nicholas shows it and Blaize doesn't. But he's exactly the same. If he needs a weapon one day, he'll take whatever comes to hand. And, for heaven's sake, you may owe him a hundred pounds now, but what happens the next time you need money quickly and can't ask Nicholas? You'll go to Blaize again, you know you will, and in the end it could be thousands. What would you do if Nicholas found out then?'

'Shoot myself,' she said, half ruefully, half carelessly.

'I doubt it. Have you actually given the money to your brother?'

'No. I have it here in my reticule. I'm to meet him in half an hour on the outskirts of town.'

'Then give it back to Blaize. I don't believe he'd really allow you to borrow and borrow again until you were in a desperate plight, but no matter. A hundred pounds would be enough to infuriate Nicholas. I can't tell you how angry he'd be. And, apart from that, if it became known that his wife had been obliged to borrow, then the whole of his commercial credibility would be damaged in Cullingford. Blaize wouldn't expect you to think of that, but he's certainly thought of it himself.'

'Oh dear,' she said, looking down at the green velvet reticule in her hands, weighing it, considering, and then with that birdlike movement of her head looking up at me with her sudden smile. 'I do see. Well, never mind, Faith, at least I've provided you with something to think about besides the cholera, which means I have done you good. Good-bye then, I must dash, since my brother doesn't care to be kept waiting – even for money. I'll come and cheer you up again, and if I don't then you'll know it's because we've gone to a debtors' prison, Perry and I together.'

And so it continued, time running slow, an airless July, the burnt-yellow skies of August, my fearful days made bearable only by the demands of Prudence, the occasional hour when Giles would allow me to approach him, a lightning visit every now and then from Georgiana, her raindrop chatter diverting me sometimes to sympathy, often to amusement and gratitude.

'I believe it will soon be over,' Prudence said. 'You will see – by September they will be haggling about the cost of a decent water supply again. There have been fewer cases this last week, and many of them seem likely to recover. It is abating –'

So it continued. Heat, fear, the lethargy of strained nerves that could strain no more and began to atrophy, an enforced idleness that, an instant before it maddened me, engulfed me in a strange, torpid doze, the constant fatigue of doing too little, which was fast rendering me incapable of doing anything at all.

So it continued, until the evening, late, when Prudence came home, not alone, but without Giles.

16

She came into the room and stood by the empty hearth, Mayor Agbrigg beside her, their faces only half visible, since I had not troubled to light a lamp. And, although I could not have said for certain – the next morning, the morning after – whether or not I had guessed their task, it seems to me now that I did.

We looked at each other for a while, and then Prudence said in the crisp tone of every day, which is perhaps the only manner in which one can bring oneself to say such things, 'Faith – Giles was taken ill today while he was out visiting. He drove himself to the Infirmary and wishes to remain there.'

I don't remember what I answered, or if I answered anything at all. I simply remember moving to the door, assuming they would follow me, knowing the Agbrigg carriage must be in the street and that someone would drive me to Sheepgate.

'You cannot go to him,' Prudence said, and I remember quite clearly how my incredulity, my inclination to scornful, nervous laughter gave way to anger as her hand descended on my arm, her arrow-straight body blocked my way.

'You cannot go, Faith. He asked us to keep you away. The Infirmary is dangerous still, and he will not háve you there.'

Once again I don't know what I answered, merely that I went on walking towards the door, fighting her when she tried to stop me, dragging her with me, for I was taller and heavier and crazed, in any case, with my urgency. And I would have struck her, I think, and knocked her down had not Mayor Agbrigg taken me by the shoulders, his hard workman's hands biting through the numbness of me, shaking me – since I was shouting something now – to silence. But even then, shocked by this first experience of male violence, I kicked out at him and hurt him, I think, although he did not let me go.

'I'm going to him, I warn you. I'll walk –'

'Lass,' he said, holding me in his thin, crook-shouldered embrace, the wiry strength of him greater than I had supposed. 'Lass – see the sense to it.'

'There's no sense. He's my husband. You can't keep me away from him.'

'He doesn't want you,' Prudence shouted, bursting painfully into tears, and when I lashed out at her Mayor Agbrigg shook me again.

'Lass – have your wits about you. You know what the cholera is. It stinks, lass. He doesn't want you to see him like that. There's nothing you can do for him. Let him fight it. And then be here, to welcome him home.'

'I can't. You must understand. I know you mean well, but I can't. He needs me – he *must* need me – what good am I if he doesn't need me now?'

'He wants you to be here, when he's well again. You'll weaken him, love, if you worry him now, when he needs all his strength.'

'Write him something,' Prudence said, and they brought me pen and paper and sat me down before it. I began to write, docile, foolish words, and then, as they swam into meaningless hieroglyphics beneath my eyes, I clenched my hands into fists and brought them crashing down on to the table.

'No. You may go to hell, Prudence Aycliffe, and you too, Mr Agbrigg. You will not treat me like a child any longer – none of you, not even Giles. I will go to him and stay with him, and when he is fit to be moved I will bring him home and nurse him here, where he should be, not in that pest-hole. You can't stop me.'

'I can,' Mayor Agbrigg said, his big-knuckled hands biting into my shoulders again. 'Now listen to me. I love that lad as if he was my own – I've wished he was my own. He pleaded with me, not long since, to keep you away – begged me. I promised him. And if I have to knock you out or tie you down, then I'll do it. No matter what you may be suffering, lass, if I'd to choose, I'd sooner be in your place than his. Think on that.'

And when I had written my pathetic scrawl, 'Giles, I love you, I love you', they took it from me and went away.

He died early the next morning with Prudence and Mayor Agbrigg beside him, and when they came to tell me I sat down and saw no reason to get up again. They told me they had given him my letter, that he had read it and understood it, but I didn't believe them. I had said to him so many times, 'Giles, please love me.' I had said, 'I want you. I need you.' But I had never told him that the gratitude, the desire to be warm and safe, the second-rate emotions he had settled for, had started slowly to transform themselves into the total commitment I had longed to give him. And I believed he had died without being aware of it.

He had loved me, and I had not only lost him, I had failed him. I had held back from him. I had been too honest, refusing to say, 'I am wildly in love with you,' until it became the truth, not wishing to insult his integrity with even the whisper of a lie. Now I knew that I should have lied to him, since it would not have remained a lie for long, had already, for months, been very nearly true. And what I felt mainly was a hard anger, a bitter self-disgust. I was worthless. He had been important. There was no justice, nothing to believe in, just the blind, idiot-drooling of Chance, with which I did not care to associate.

A day passed – or so it seemed – and once again Mayor Agbrigg put his hard hands on me.

'I had a wife,' he said, 'a long time ago. We married young and we were poor and ignorant and content with each other. I never looked beyond her, and couldn't imagine a day when I'd be without her. We had eleven children, being young and ignorant, as I said – and lost ten of them, three in two days, something that happens often enough in Simon Street. But it was too much for my Ann. She turned inside herself, and died – of heartbreak, I reckon – leaving me with Jonas and a girl, Maria, who had a look of Ann, and died, you may remember, a year or two after I married your Aunt Hannah.'

'I don't care about that, Mayor Agbrigg. I know I should care, but I don't. I know that you're trying to help me. It doesn't help.'

'No. Maybe it just helps me to talk about it. I've had more experience of losing than you have. But it still hurts me, lass, for all that. I was angry when my Ann died, like you are now, I reckon. By God, I was angry. I lived for her, you see, and she'd never harmed anybody. I hated the whole world the day I buried her. It passes, Faith, little by little.'

'I don't care.'

I didn't attend his funeral. I hadn't seen him die and I refused to watch them put that wooden box into the dry summer ground, refused absolutely to contemplate what it contained. And, when they came back from the churchyard to tell me who had been there and who had not, I wouldn't listen.

I sat in the dark, doing nothing. I put on the black dress Mrs Guthrie got out for me and would have gone on wearing it until it hung in ribbons had she not taken it away from me and handed me another. I left the sheets on his bed and then, unable to sleep with his ghost – the nightmares that asked me was he really dead, since I had not seen him die? – I moved to the cold, narrow bedroom at the head of the stairs, a nun's cell, a place to do penance; and spoke sharply to Mrs Guthrie when she tried to light the fire, to add a vase of flowers, an extra counterpane.

The cholera abated. For a day, a week, six weeks, there were no new cases. Three months passed and no one else died. And I didn't care about that either.

My mother went to France, Blaize to Germany to sell cloth, Georgiana miscarried a child whose conception she had not divulged, and was confined to her bed. Caroline began to issue invitations again. Mayor Agbrigg completed his purchase, on the town's behalf, of the waterworks company and brought me his schemes and plans for the new reservoirs.

'Twenty-five miles of waterworks, lass,' he told me, his craggy face warming as Jonas's never did. 'Eleven reservoirs, when it's all done. A water area of over three hundred acres with a cubic capacity of two thousand million gallons. Think of it, lass. They say I'm crazy, some of those colleagues of mine – plain crazy – but, if I get what I want, and I shall, then there'll be no water shortage in Cullingford, no matter what. A tap in every house in Simon Street. I've said that often enough. The trouble is, they're all gentlemen on the council, lass, and they don't understand. I'm the only one who's seen it from the inside, the only one who's lived in the muck, instead of just turning my nose up at it as I drove by. And my colleagues don't all see the point in spending all this money to provide something they're not short of themselves. But I'll get my way. I'll get my water. I spent the first forty years of my life dragging myself out of the gutter, and the next ten earning my place in the Piece Hall. Now I'll do something worth doing, lass – something *I* want, I reckon.'

I didn't care.

Jonas called, when Celia had satisfied herself that my house was safe again, coming as a brother-in-law to offer his condolences and as Giles's lawyer to assure me that I was well provided for. It was of no interest to me.

My half-brother, Crispin Aycliffe, wrote to me from London, expressing deep regret, suggesting he could come north to see me, or I go south to him, if he could be of use. I didn't answer.

Aunt Verity, remaining in Bournemouth at the insistence of Uncle Joel, who had no intention of taking the slightest risk where she was concerned, wrote a long, warm letter, inviting me to stay with her. I didn't answer that either.

Mainly I sat in the dark, and would have remained there, perhaps, too long, passing the moment when it was still possible to open the door, to walk outside again, had not Prudence entered the room one afternoon, pulled back the curtains with a brisk hand, and said, 'This is quite enough, Faith. He's dead. It was important to him to keep you alive, although if he could see you now he might wonder why. Look at you. Have you brushed your hair this week?'

'Leave me alone, Prudence.'

'I have no intention of leaving you alone, make up your mind to it. You are coming upstairs now. You are going to make yourself respectable, and then we are going to Aunt Hannah's.'

'Why Aunt Hannah's?'

'Because she has invited us, and it is necessary to make a start somewhere.' I got up because, knowing her stubborn nature, it was easier to obey than argue.

'You will have a mare's nest in your hair ere long,' she said, taking a brush to it with a vengeance, hurting me deliberately, perhaps, in order to rouse me, although I was not aroused.

The late October sun was very bright as I went outside, very cruel with no tree-foliage to shade it, dazzling me so that I was not obliged to look at anything as we drove up Millergate and Blenheim Lane, past my mother's house, and turned the steep corner which brought us to Lawcroft Fold.

The mill yard looked as it had always done, my aunt's house still there on the terraced slope above it, the sun glinting on the window where I had stood with Giles, at our first meeting, and watched the Chartists bringing their petition for the factory hands to sign. The Chartists were gone now, defeated, and I was defeated too. It didn't matter.

Aunt Hannah came into the hall to meet us, regal as always in her rustling purple, a handsome Barforth woman who had married a mill-hand and made a mayor out of him, who had laboured at Prudence's side through the days of the cholera, and who must think me a poor, spineless creature, a nuisance. I believed her to be quite right.

'Sit down, dear,' she said, and I sat.

'Will you take tea, dear?' And I took it, accepting milk and sugar, although I did not in fact care for sweet tea, because she had the sugar-tongs in her hand and I saw no point in asking her to put them down.

'Are you well, Faith?'

'Yes, quite well, thank you.'

'Good. You are certainly very pale, but a little fresh air will put that right.'

'I imagine so.'

'You will have heard that Mayor Agbrigg's plans for the reservoirs are progressing well?'

'Yes. It is all very splendid.'

'Your husband would have thought so.'

'I believe he would.'

'I am very sure of it. And, while we are on this obviously delicate subject, Mayor Agbrigg and I were both wondering, in view of Dr Ashburn's undoubted services to the town – well, dear, the fact is that old Miss Corey-Manning is to move to the coast to join her brother, which means, naturally, that her property is to come up for sale. The house is old and small and in a sorry state of disrepair, but the gardens, as you may know, are extensive and extremely attractive. If my husband could persuade the town to purchase it, then it could be most easily converted into a park – the Giles Ashburn Memorial Gardens, we thought. Should you object to that?'

'Not in the least.'

'You are very obliging, Faith,' she said, putting down her cup and saucer rather sharply, allowing me to feel the snap of her impatience, her contempt for all silly females who engulfed themselves in melancholy when the world was so wide, when there was so much to do. 'Yes, most obliging. I regret that your sister Celia is not so accommodating. I had hoped to persuade her to take tea with us today, but without success. You will have heard, I suppose, that she is in a delicate condition again? Well, she will insist on making herself into a recluse at such times, which cannot be good for her. I have told her repeatedly that we are all aware of the facts of life, that women do change their shape in pregnancy, but she has this morbid fear of being looked at – quite ridiculous. She should go about more and keep her spirits high. In fact – and I am sorry to have to say this – she should think of others for a change, instead of dwelling so exclusively on herself. Jonas has his position to keep up, after all, and has as much right to her support as she to his. You did know she was expecting again?'

I did, but I failed to see how it concerned me. I had no child of my own, had been too concerned with loving, or not loving, Giles, to wonder why I had not conceived. Now it was too late.

Prudence made her excuses. She had another call to pay and would come back for me in an hour. I nodded, drank more tea, saw quite clearly that Aunt Hannah, who had never much cared for me, was trying to be kind and, somewhat vaguely, since it could not really matter, I wondered why.

'How is your mother, Faith?'

'Quite well, I believe. She writes that Paris is very gay again. She may be home, she says, by Christmas time.'

'I am relieved to hear it. Her presence will be needed – and yours too – in the New Year. The concert hall is to be opened in April and, if it is to be dedicated to your father, then his widow and daughters must certainly be present. Naturally all building work has been delayed by the epidemic – a great many labourers were infected and the rest too drunk to be of service – but I have the most positive assurances that it will be ready in time. And so it should be. My word, it is a year now since the foundation stone was laid and I have heard nothing since then but excuses – architects and builders attempting to blind me with their expertise, telling me that construction is a slow process and that I must be patient. And now what do I hear? They are building a vast exhibition hall in London, of *glass*, my dear, to house this great international peep-show in Hyde Park we are hearing so much about, and although it was only begun a week or two ago, at the end of September, they mean to have it ready for the grand opening in May. Seven months, my dear, no more, for something of quite colossal proportions, and all this eternity for one relatively modest provincial concert hall. However, one must only hope that Prince Albert and his committee are in possession of all the facts, for the man they have got to build it for them is quite extraordinary – a gardener, it seems, in the employ of the Duke of Devonshire. Yes, you may stare: a gardener. Although he attracted much notice by his construction of the conservatories on the Duke's estate, one can only call him a brave man to undertake a project of this importance. Just think of it, Faith, a giant greenhouse to house exhibits from every corner of the world, and all the hundreds of thousands of men and women who will flock to examine them.'

I thought of it and found that I was not even mildly curious.

'My brother will be exhibiting something, I suppose,' she went on, ignoring my polite but totally disinterested smile. 'He scoffed at it to begin with, as did everyone else, but since there is to be a textile section and a prize to be won I cannot imagine that my brother will let it go to someone else. I imagine we shall all be taking a trip to London next summer to congratulate him. That is something to look forward to at any rate.'

'Yes, indeed it is.'

She poured more tea, stirred her own cup reflectively, approaching, perhaps, the end of her patience.

'When you write to your mother again, Faith, you might mention that we have a slight problem with the concert hall. It has always been my intention that it should be dedicated to your father. His name was clearly stated when I sent out my original requests for subscriptions, and until recently I have considered the matter as being entirely settled. However, since the unfortunate accident to Sir Robert Peel – my dear, you cannot be unaware that he was killed in July by a fall from his horse? Really, Faith! Well, since then it has been suggested to me that the hall should be dedicated to him. There is no denying the extent of his claims. He was a Prime Minister. He *did* abolish the Corn Laws, greatly to our advantage, while your father – as someone quite rudely pointed out – never served in anybody's Cabinet. And recently, of course, even his building work in some areas of Cullingford has fallen into disrepute. But he was our Member of Parliament for many years, he *did* contribute most generously towards local charities, and although it now appears that the quality of some of his lower-priced dwellinghouses left much to be desired – in fact my husband means to use them as an example to persuade his colleagues to introduce building regulations – Well, times were different then. We were not so aware of sanitation, and one cannot doubt that had your father realized the consequences of poor drainage he would not have hesitated to put things right. But I see no point in involving myself at this late stage in arguments as to merit or lack of it. The project from its very conception was mine. The Aycliffe Hall it has always been, and I am quite determined to make a stand. I trust I may rely on your support?'

'Oh – absolutely.' But she couldn't, and she knew she couldn't, for the

561

Morgan Aycliffe Hall, the Robert Peel Hall, even the Giles Ashburn Hall, meant nothing to me.

'Very well,' she said, straightening her back, smiling at me across the tea-cups, the smile I had seen her offer, sometimes, to Mrs Hobhouse or Mrs Mandelbaum, before the delivery of a telling blow. 'And what is your news, Faith? Have you decided to wait until springtime to put your house up for sale?'

'I beg your pardon?'

'Springtime, dear. Much the best season for disposing of property, and that house of yours will not be easily disposed of. I always told you that Millergate was not a residential location and you will be lucky to get a decent price.'

'Aunt Hannah, who on earth can have told you that I wish to sell my house?'

'Why, no one, dear,' she said, giving me that cold smile again. 'No one told me that it is Tuesday today, either, but I am well aware of it. I am merely surprised that you have not already moved back to Blenheim Lane and left your Mrs Guthrie to take care of the property until it is sold.'

'Aunt Hannah, I have not the slightest intention of returning to live with my mother.'

'Nonsense, dear,' she said sweetly. 'Of course you want to go home. And, even if you did not, I cannot imagine any alternative. I have already asked Jonas to look about him for a possible buyer, and there is no reason at all why you should stay in Millergate and give yourself the trouble of entertaining strangers when they come to view. You may leave the management of your money entirely to Jonas, who will invest it most shrewdly and carefully, while the management of yourself must belong once more to your mother.'

I put down my cup, feeling the need to keep my hands free, aware, beneath the fog-bound ice in which my mind had been swimming, of a tiny, healthy spark that would – in a moment or two – be anger.

'I appreciate your concern, Aunt Hannah, but it is entirely misplaced. I shall be staying in Millergate.'

'I think not.'

'Then I am sorry to tell you that you are mistaken.'

'Hardly, dear. You have always been scatterbrained, Faith, but even you could not be contemplating the possibility of living alone. You are far too young for that, and have far too little knowledge of the world. You may have been married, dear, but now your actual situation differs little from that of Prudence, except that you are somewhat the richer. No, no, you must return to Blenheim Lane at once. There is nowhere else for you to go, unless of course your mother should decide to marry again. Mr Oldroyd, I understand, has been most pressing in that direction, and should she decide to take him – which would seem likely and not at all unsuitable – then you will be obliged to go with her to Fieldhead. I think you would find it a pleasant enough house in which to spend the time before you could decently consider a second marriage for yourself.'

'Aunt Hannah,' I said, hands clenched, a quite painful splintering inside my head as the ice gave way to let that spark of anger leap through. 'How dare you say that to me?'

'I dare say anything I choose to you, dear,' she told me, remaining completely calm. 'You were an excellent matrimonial catch in the first place, you know. But, now that you have an additional income and are quite pleasant to look at, you will soon find yourself in demand again. Emma-Jane Hobhouse has already mentioned your name to me in connection with Freddy, since Prudence is so slow to make up her mind. And, although I could not recommend him, the way things are going at Nethercoats, there will be plenty of others. No dear, we shall have no trouble at all in settling you.'

'No,' I told her, shaking with a most uncharacteristic fury. 'You will have no trouble in settling me, because I will not be settled.'

'Really? You mean to be defiant then – and rude?'

'Possibly, and I am sorry for that.'

'And what do you mean to do with yourself then, for I am bound to warn you that, if you continue to sit in the dark and brood, then it is not only your aunt who will recommend your return to parental control – I believe that both Dr Overdale and Dr Blackstone would insist upon it.'

'That will not be necessary.'

'I wonder.'

'Then please do not take the trouble. I am twenty-one years old, Aunt Hannah. I am no schoolroom chit, to be disposed of like a parcel – with no more sense than a parcel. I am a woman who has been married and I will decide what is to be done with me. I shall stay in Millergate, or I shall go elsewhere, but it will be *my* choice. I promised to obey my husband, and I did obey him, but I have never promised to obey anybody else. I am not sure what my rights are, but I am sure they exist and if Jonas will not explain them to me then I shall find someone who will. I don't believe that any of you – any longer – have the power to interfere.'

'Good,' she said, again with the utmost composure. 'I cannot agree with you, of course. You may be of full age, but you are quite incapable of managing either your money or yourself. A widow of twenty-one years, my dear, must be a prey to every kind of malicious gossip, to every unscrupulous male – of which there are very many – and to every possible temptation, which you do not strike me as being strong-minded enough to resist. It is a most unsuitable arrangement, and I shall continue to "interfere" with it as much as I please. If you persist in this folly, then I shall consider it my duty to keep a strict eye on you and shall require Jonas to do the same. However, I shall pardon your rudeness, since even your display of ill-nature and poor judgment is preferable to the poor little drab who crept in to take tea with me an hour ago.'

And she smiled at me again.

'Thank you,' I said after a while and, looking round, imagining I had heard Prudence returning, I saw the sun, flooding through the window again, bringing me not only the memory of Giles, standing there so quietly, explaining to me the six points of the People's Charter, but Aunt Hannah herself walking down to the garden-gate, and my mother telling us, 'Poor Hannah. She is making a pilgrimage. She has gone down there so that we shall not see her cry.' And, taking advantage of her unexpected compassion, which I knew would not last, I asked her, 'Aunt Hannah, my mother told me once that you were to have married Aunt Verity's brother.'

'Edwin Barforth,' she said, understanding why, and how much, I needed to know. 'Yes. He was murdered down there in the mill yard, while I sat in the mill house and made plans for our wedding-day. The old mill house has gone now. It was pulled down some years ago, when Mr Agbrigg and I felt the need for a larger garden to accommodate a carriage-drive. Look – you may see from the window – it stood there, near the gate, just a small house, although it seemed ample to me then, and indeed, oddly enough, Mr Agbrigg lived there with Jonas when he first became manager at Lawcroft. And I spent my first year there too, as his wife. Things turn our very strangely, do they not? I should have gone into that house as Mrs Edwin Barforth: I eventually occupied it as Mrs Ira Agbrigg. And now the house is not there at all. It was used for offices before we pulled it down.'

'Did it trouble you?'

'Demolishing it? I don't think so. Aunt Verity seemed more moved than I, since she and Edwin were both born there. She was sixteen the night Edwin died, and I was twenty-three – Edwin a year older. We had been childhood sweethearts, I suppose one may call it, and I had grown up believing my future could only be with him. It happened a little after supper-time. Verity had gone outside and wandered down to the mill, shocked and upset, of course, since she had seen her father killed by Luddite rioters the night before. Edwin and I stayed at the mill house, telling each other we would soon be married, but I began to be alarmed about Verity and sent him to fetch her. We believed there was no danger. The Luddites had been rounded up, were on their way to be hanged at York. But one had made his escape and had come back to set fire to the mill. Foolish boy! He had brought a kitchen knife with him, a common carving knife, and when Edwin tried to arrest him there was a scuffle. My brother Joel found them, ten minutes later, Verity screaming, Edwin dying –'

'And that is why you went down to the gate when the Chartists were here – to the place where the mill house used to be?'

'Did I? Yes. I suppose I may have done. Quite stupid of me. Is there anything else, of these matters which do not concern you at all, that you wish to know?'

'Do you think of him still?'

She smiled, Aunt Hannah who might not be kind to me tomorrow, who would certainly interfere with my life, would pry and attempt to manipulate me every bit as much as she had promised, but who was ready to help me now.

'I thought of him every day of my life – for a year or two – and I believed it would always be so. And that was hard. But then I came to realize, quite gradually, that I could not exactly recall the lines of his face

564

– that he was slipping away. And that was much harder. I tried for a while to bring him back, but I am an honest woman and I was forced to acknowledge that I had lost him. That was not easy. Other matters intervened, you see – not least a husband and an exceedingly brilliant son. No, I rarely think of him any more. He was a young man of twenty-four; I am a woman well into middle life. What could we have to say to each other now? I would recognize him, perhaps, but he would certainly not recognize me. Come dear, I believe Prudence is returning – and you will not forget what I told you about the concert hall?'

I shook my head, straightened myself, not strong precisely – not yet – but stronger.

'Prudence,' she called out, 'I would like you now – since you seem to have possession of your mother's horses – to deliver a message to Celia. And, since you are bound to pass the Mandelbaums' on your way, you may step inside for a moment and tell them –'

And I knew I would not return to my sick hole again.

17

The Morgan Aycliffe Hall, which in spite of all delays and anxieties as to rising costs had not exceeded Aunt Hannah's original estimate of twenty thousand pounds, opened as promised the following April with a musical festival Aunt Hannah declared should be an annual event.

The hall itself, a solid structure of Yorkshire stone, a soft, mellow shade of brown that April morning, although we knew it would soon be blackened like everything else by its share of Cullingford soot, was a fitting memorial for any man, the entrance, flanked by Corinthian columns, opening into a vestibule from which a much ornamented staircase opened two wide arms, giving access to stalls and galleries where three thousand persons could sit, some of them more comfortably than others, and improve their minds. And here, during that first week in April, I sat every evening, the widow of the deeply regretted Dr Ashburn, the daughter of the now almost forgotten Morgan Aycliffe, imbibing a strong diet of Handel, Bach, Haydn and Beethoven – selected largely by the Mandelbaums – while Aunt Hannah, who was tone-deaf, accepted her personal applause, drawing our attention, since the music defeated her, to the impressive proportions of the organ, the fact that the orchestra contained no fewer than eighty instruments, the choir more than a hundred singers.

My mother, attired in a different pastel-tinted evening gown at every performance – since her mourning, for a son-in-law, had already ended – was presented with a bouquet of spring flowers at the conclusion of the proceedings, and melted most obligingly into tears. Celia, who had miscarried early this time, and was consequently well enough to attend, joined poignantly in the weeping, although I doubted if her recollections of our late parent were either particularly clear or particularly fond. Prudence, in dove-grey half-mourning with a stylish fall of white lace at neck and sleeves, remained dry-eyed, while I, in black, beaded with jet, could see no reason for tears, preferring my mother's speedy return to laughter when Mr Oldroyd of Fieldhead began to ply her with champagne.

'You'll dine with me, all of you, at Fieldhead,' he announced, almost a declaration in itself, since Fieldhead had seen no guests since the day his thin, eternally ailing wife had been carried out of it. And, seated at his table, I concluded that, if my mother chose to make herself mistress of this sombre but substantial house and of the splendid mill just across the way, then it was her concern, and Prudence's concern, not mine.

'If she marries him,' I told my sister, 'then I think we might extract their permission for you to live with me.'

'If she marries him,' Prudence replied, 'then she will regret it, for he is as gloomy and pernickety a man as my father. If she marries him, I will not be the only one obliged to ask his consent every time I wish to cross the street. He will keep a tight hold on her purse-strings, and she will not enjoy it.'

But Aunt Hannah, mistrusting the lightness of my mother's character and anxious to see her settled before she disgraced us all, was more concerned with Mr Oldroyd's finances than with his personality.

'It would be an excellent arrangement,' she told us, having quite made up her mind to it. 'Matthew Oldroyd has no children and no close relatives. The Hobhouses may behave as if they were his kith and kin but in fact Mr Hobhouse was only his first wife's brother, which would count for nothing should he marry again. Depend upon it, if your mother takes him she will inherit a second fortune and Fieldhead Mill with it. My word, I have never spoken to Jonas about the spinning trade, but I do believe that, if Elinor ever found herself with Fieldhead on her hands, Jonas would know how to manage it most profitably. And, since one third of it would be bound to pass eventually to Celia, it could be a very great thing for him – for them both; for between ourselves I have given up all hope of Celia ever making herself into a political wife. I believe the very idea of Westminster would throw her into a fit of the vapours. Yes – Fieldhead – my goodness, girls, I must consult most carefully with Jonas, for if a marriage is to take place then the contract should be very precise.'

But, although Prudence bristled and retaliated in kind, I knew how much my aunt and her husband had done for me and was less susceptible now, in any case, to small irritations.

I was calm now. I brushed my hair again, night and morning, until it shone silver in anybody's candlelight, valuing it again as my only claim to beauty. I wore a black velvet ribbon around my neck at dinner-time, long drops of jet in my ears, scented my skin, listened with smiling attention to anyone who chose to talk to me. But I did it, as I did everything these days, not to please my family, not to please a man, but to please myself. My house was warm now and well-polished, my cat purring amiably in her basket by the fender. I had wine for my guests, and conversation, my windows were open in the good weather, letting in air which many considered unhealthy, and light they thought imprudent, since it would damage my carpet and my complexion. I came and went as I pleased, although in fact I did not venture very far, an occasional visit to Listonby or to Tarn Edge, a weekly pilgrimage to Giles's grave, although I found very little of him there, a stroll in the Ashburn Gardens, which I had myself declared open by unveiling a statue supposedly of Giles, but which could have been any frock-coated, top-hatted gentleman. I was quietly, almost imperceptibly, free, Mrs Guthrie, whose loyalty had been to Giles, having left me to the ministrations of a Mrs Marworth, who was loyal to nothing but the twenty-five pounds a year I gave her. I was not happy. I did not even think about happiness. I was calm. And it was enough.

In June Caroline gave birth to a third son, exactly two years after her twins, a Master Gideon Chard, even bigger and darker than his brothers had been, so noisy and so imperious in his demands for attention that Nurse was soon ordered to take him away.

'I suppose this one will go into the Church,' Caroline told me, receiving me in the lavish, deep-armchaired comfort of the Great Hall, having got out of bed a scandalous seven days after her confinement, since as always she was expecting guests and had no time to play the invalid. 'Yes – that is the way it is done, Faith. The second son for the army, the third for the Church, the fourth for the high seas – and, if there is a fifth, one sends him out to the colonies, I believe, to make his fortune, so that when he comes back one can pretend his money was not got from trade. Well, young Gideon can have the church here at Listonby, to begin with, since our vicar will be quite senile and happy to step down when the time comes. But I think he had best go to Oxford first, to make some suitable acquaintances, especially when one considers that all the fashionable parishes seem to be in the South.'

'In fact you mean to make a bishop of him?'

'Well, of course I do, Faith. Naturally I want to see him at the top of his tree, whatever it is. If one takes the trouble to do something, then one should do it right.'

'Yes. I have heard your father say so many a time.'

'And what is wrong with that?' she asked sharply, ready as always to do battle at the slightest hint that Barforth values could in any way be criticized, so ready, in fact, that I concluded they often were. 'I will tell you this much, Faith. I am extremely fond of Matthew's family, but if some of them would listen to my father they would not suffer for it. One has only to look at the Clevedons. My goodness, it is all very well to be charitable, but Mr Clevedon simply cannot afford it, and if one dared to suggest that Peregrine should give some thought to *earning* a living – well, I have learned not to make suggestions of that kind. Matthew merely smiled when I did so, but Georgiana was quite scandalized. "He is the heir," she said. "There is the land." And that was that. Well, my Dominic is the heir and he will not be required to earn a living either. But our land is not encumbered and if he shows an interest in politics I shall not discourage him – even though he is bound to be a Protectionist and want the Corn Laws back again.'

'You will have a Prime Minister, then, as well as a colonel and a bishop.'

And although we laughed together we both knew that, if Caroline made up her mind to it, it was not impossible.

'I do not see enough of you, Faith, these days,' she said. 'As soon as you are out of mourning, or into half-mourning, then I want you to come on a really long visit. In fact, since widow's weeds go on so long, I see no reason to delay longer than the autumn – and I would be glad of you then. The house will be full to bursting from September to March, and you know how it is in the hunting season – so many women sitting around all day in need of entertaining. And although the men are out from dawn to dusk they enjoy a change of female company in the evenings. One would think so much fresh air might make them sleepy, but not a bit of it. Some of them tend to be quite giddy, and it would be a relief to have a woman in the house I can trust. You will be going to the Exhibition, of course? Yes, so I supposed. Well – I shall not, for Matthew and his friends have made up their minds to ignore it, which seems quite ridiculous since it has spread itself out all over Hyde Park. But there it is. They are all Protectionists, you see, who do not care for Free Trade, and are telling each other that the Exhibition is strictly for the middle classes – an opinion I find hard to understand when Prince Albert virtually organized it single-handed, and the Queen has been going there every day. In fact, Matthew and I have had our very first quarrel over it. If I want to look at industrial machines, he tells me, then I may go and stand an hour in my father's weaving sheds. Naturally he was sorry afterwards – extremely sorry, in fact – and I was sorry too. I could see how hurt he was when I declared I would go with my father. I rather expected him to forbid it, but he actually said, "Please don't," which touched me, I admit it. Anyway, I have decided not to go, so all is well again. Come to see me as soon as you return and tell me how easily my father has won all the prizes.'

To begin with, even Cullingford itself had not thought too highly of Prince Albert's Great International Exhibition, this scheme of displaying manufactured goods and the machines that made them beneath an extravagant glass-house in Hyde Park – Cullingford being more concerned with getting its own manufactures out of the country at advantageous prices than with letting possible competitors so freely in. But, as Aunt Hannah had said, when it became known that there were prizes to be won, at the discretion of a jury half British and half foreign, Law Valley men concluded they might as well win them, and there was no doubt that Barforth fancy worsteds would be most prominently displayed.

The monster conservatory – Prince Albert's Crystal Palace – had been duly completed, its transparent walls covering an incredible nineteen acres of Hyde Park, enclosing within its structure the elm trees which no one had wished to cut down. It was more than three times larger than Saint Paul's Cathedral, was constructed in such a way that it could be dismantled and moved elsewhere at need, and had taken, in all, just seven months to build. It was magnificent, impossible, a brilliant conception, a madman's folly, according to one's point of view. It would not take the strain; it would fall down and shatter, killing thousands; it would be a breeding ground for the diseases, the vice and corruption so many foreigners would be certain to bring with them. Something would surely go wrong with it, and when it was discovered that there were sparrows happily nesting in the branches beneath the glass roof, ready to foul exhibits and exhibitors alike with their droppings, and that shot-guns obviously could not be used to dislodge them, one saw more than a few complacent smiles, a multitude who were very ready to say 'I told you so'. But they, and the sparrows, had not reckoned on the Duke of Wellington, who, stamping irritably from his retirement at the Queen's request, had spat out the one deadly solution: 'Sparrow-hawks'; and within days the sparrows had fled.

The Exhibition opened on the first of May to a salute of guns which did not – as had been predicted – shatter the glass walls and remained open until October, Queen Victoria and her children coming regularly, drawing more stares herself, perhaps, than the acres of industrial and agricultural machinery, the triumphs of engineering and architecture which had given such prosperity to her reign.

Aunt Verity and Uncle Joel, the owners now of a pleasant house near Bournemouth, went south in April, my uncle prepared, it seemed, if only temporarily, to leave his personal empire in the hands of Nicholas and Blaize. And, since the railways were offering cheap rates – Cullingford to London and back for five shillings for the duration of the show – and London was sprouting with lodging-houses where respectable working-men could obtain bed and board for as little as threepence a day, a great many of our mechanics and artisans went south too, for the first time in their lives.

'London is teeming with them,' my mother wrote from the house of an old political friend of my father's, 'so quiet and well-behaved you can't imagine, dressed up in their Sunday best. No drinking, no fighting, such as one sees in Cullingford. Incredible. And, of course, the foreigners, darling – quite sinister, some of them. One sees quite well that they are all revolutionaries come to lose themselves in the crowd, since they are welcome nowhere else. Do come, dear. The Exhibition itself is nothing but a vast bazaar, I must warn you, for one can have a surfeit, quite quickly I find, of gazing at machines, and there is little else to see that one could pick up easily enough in Millergate. However – there are certainly acquaintances to be made, and naturally, if all goes well, there may even be knighthoods to be won. They tell me the Queen is in a mood to be very gracious to certain gentlemen who have offered her husband their support – who have backed his scheme, in fact, when the Protectionist fox-hunting set can do nothing but hope for hailstones, which would certainly tear his Crystal Palace down. Do come.'

And once again I was aware of the division of ranks I had seen in operation all my life: the fox-hunting gentlemen of the Shires, to whom the whole concept of internationalism was repugnant, who saw this princely exhibition as no more than a vulgar display of trade-begotten wealth; and the cool, commercial men of the cities, who regarded no wealth as vulgar, and for whom the world and its markets could not be opened wide enough.

My sister Celia, disliking crowds, disliking heat and noise, disliking anything, it seemed, which would take her from the shelter of her own drawing-room, had no inclination for the journey, but Aunt Hannah, having secured a fortnight's accommodation in the London house of Mr Fielding, our Member of Parliament, was ready to include both Prudence and myself in her party.

'Jonas will explain it all to you,' she told us. 'He will take excellent care of you.' And we believed her, for, although she had not gone so far as to regret the impossibility of his marrying all three of us, she was increasingly anxious that we should learn to depend on his judgment, to submit ourselves, in financial matters at least, to his authority.

Jonas, of course, was no longer a poor man, but both he and his step-mamma were aware that he had still a long, expensive way to travel before reaching that golden pinnacle of which his childhood brilliance had encouraged her to dream. And perhaps because, in Aunt Hannah's view, Celia had let him down, proving too timid, too nervous to suit his needs, she had come to regard it as logical and right that Prudence and I should make up the deficiency.

Should we remain unmarried, we would be very likely to leave what we had to Jonas's children, in the event of Celia managing to carry one to full term, and, if not, to Celia herself. Should we remain unmarried, our social skills, which Celia sadly lacked, could without any impropriety be devoted to Jonas, since the world would have nothing but praise for a woman who graced her brother-in-law's table, entertained his guests, supported his ambitions, disciplined his children, in order to relieve the burdens of an ailing wife. Should we remain unmarried. And so, without meaning either of us the slightest harm – being quite convinced that we would be much better off, much safer with Jonas – she kept a watchful eye on Freddy Hobhouse whenever he approached Prudence, making short work of both Mrs Hobhouse and Mrs Mandelbaum when in turn they offered to take us to London.

'My nieces will be accompanying me,' she told them in a voice that permitted no argument, but in the end only Prudence made the trip, returning to tell me that, although Jonas had treated her as if she had been a schoolgirl, he had been quite informative on occasions, rather more human, she believed, on the days when the monumental splendours of the Machinery Court, the thrust and jostle of the galleries, had proved too much for Aunt Hannah and had obliged her to remain at home.

'It is really not to be missed, Faith, since it is not likely to happen again. You should go.'

But I hesitated, decided against it, and then, as the anniversary of Giles's death approached, I took fright and was persuaded by Aunt Verity to go down to London and visit the Exhibition on the expensive, exclusive Friday and Saturday, and then to be her guest in Bournemouth for a week or two.

It was the hottest part of August, intense in all its colours, all its odours, the richness of grass and flowers pollen-heavy at the summer's end, the park swollen with its excited but orderly crowds, the crystal mansion itself an enormous, many-faceted diamond in the sun, every bit as miraculous as I had expected.

'We will take it in stages, my dear,' Aunt Verity told me, lingering at the breakfast-table of the very cosy little house she had taken for the season. 'It is very vast and very fatiguing. There are pretty things and fearful things, and things which seem to have neither rhyme nor reason. And quite splendid things. My dear, in the civil engineering section they have a model of Liverpool docks with more than a thousand rigged ships – it is quite amazing. Gird yourself, darling, for at the risk of throwing you into a fit of the vapours I had best warn you that there are something in the region of fourteen thousand exhibitors. You will need a good pair of boots, and a smelling bottle.'

Vast indeed and, for a while, exciting to be a part of that international throng, snatches of foreign speech, glances from liquid, foreign eyes returning me to the carefree journeyings I had made with my mother, her 'special time', her butterfly days which she had known even then could not last. But, as my mother had said, once I had marvelled at the twenty-four-ton block of coal at the entrance, the crystal fountain refreshing the nave, the fifteen hundred feet of Cullingford exhibits, dominated, one was obliged to notice, by the Barforths; when I had spent an amusing half-hour watching the medal-making machine with its steady production of fifty medals a minute, the envelope-making machine with its even more impressive output of two thousand, seven hundred envelopes an hour; when I had admired the texture of Aubusson tapestries, of Turkish silks and Indian pearls, the gleaming blades of Bowie knives, made in Sheffield For American Indian-fighters; when I had marvelled at household furnishings and fittings of every conceivable shape and size and ornamentation, and my aunt and I had further amused ourselves by guessing the possible uses to which many of them could be applied, I discovered that machines have a tendency to look very much alike when one has seen several hundred of them, and I was not sorry to go outside.

Blaize, who had spent the winter abroad, escorted us about the Machinery Court on our second day, looking bronzed and handsome and very much in his natural habitat, having so many acquaintances now, both in London and overseas, that he could move through this cosmopolitan crowd with the ease of a man in his own drawing-room. But I had seen little of him since Giles died, his light nature disliking too close a contact with life's harsher realities, and it was Uncle Joel himself who supplied us with lemonade, found us a seat in the shade, entertained us to a prolonged and lavish luncheon and then – unwilling to leave his wife to the mercy of underlings – saw us on our way to Bournemouth.

Their new house, Rosemount, which had been described to me as a 'holiday cottage', was of course quite grand, a white-painted villa in a landscaped acre set high above the pleasant hilly little town, its rooms a shade impersonal, being new and freshly decorated in apple-greens, mossy tints of lilac and rose, but spacious, airy, offering an undisturbed view of a green hillside scattered with poppies, scented with the freshness of blue air and a peaceful, sunflecked summer sea.

'We shall be quiet for a day or so,' Aunt Verity said, 'and I confess I shall be glad of it.'

But the Barforths were never quiet for long, the very next morning bringing a smart, highly polished landau to the door containing a dimpled, mischievous little lady – my mother – peering at us from the shade of an enormous ruched and frilled bonnet and an elaborate, ivory-handled parasol, accompanied by a gentleman I had never seen before, a curly-haired Irishman somewhere in middle life but by no means in the state of decay of which my mother had been complaining. He was well-fleshed, square-cut, with dark eyes that were never still, a smile perpetually tilting the corners of his restless, possibly insolent, but certainly well-formed mouth.

'Good heavens!' Aunt Verity said, scattering the rose-petals she had been gathering for pot-pourri. 'Surely – it is Mr Adair?'

'The very same, ma'am,' he told her. 'Absolutely at your service. You'll pardon the intrusion, I know, for I couldn't resist the temptation of making the acquaintance of Elinor's daughter.'

And feeling that this was perhaps a man not much given to the resisting of temptation – a man, in fact, who liked to be tempted – I held out my hand, finding his grip firm and warm, if a trifle too much inclined to linger.

'Mrs Ashburn,' he said, his merry eyes concentrating totally on my face, inviting me to believe that for as long as his hand was in mine no other woman existed.

'Mr Adair.'

'She's beautiful,' he said to my mother, still gazing at me, a man, it seemed, who appreciated his own charm and knew how to use it, who had relied on it, perhaps, more than once to ensure his survival.

'Of course,' my mother said. 'Could any daughter of mine be otherwise? Faith, this is Mr Daniel Adair who was employed – a long time ago – by your father. You will give us tea, Verity, will you not? And then I am afraid we cannot stay. I simply thought you may care to renew your acquaintance with Mr Adair, and would be interested to see that I had renewed mine. We are returning to London later in the day. Daniel, you may take my arm across the grass, for I declare the sun has weakened me – or something has at any rate.'

And, understanding from the sparkling quality of her laughter, the languorous, faintly wicked but completely joyful glances she had once bestowed on M. Fauret and Signor Marchetti, that she had taken another lover, I was amused at the thought of Mr Oldroyd – who might still become her husband – and I was glad for her.

Georgiana arrived with her maid the following Friday, worn out, she said, and bored to distraction by London, her views on crystal palaces, on internationalism, on this pandering by royalty to the middle classes, exactly matching Matthew Chard's.

'Well, the city was always a poxy place,' she said. 'I must get it out of my system one way or another,' and helping herself, not to the suggested tea and cakes, but to a bottle of red wine, she went out into the garden and remained there, sprawling gipsy-fashion on the grass, drinking and dozing, plaiting daisy-chains with a listless hand, so that when Nicholas and his father appeared she was sufficiently mellowed to throw her arms around her husband's neck and bite him, quite hard I thought, on the ear.

'You've got grass in your hair,' he told her.

'Yes. And I've been asleep with my face in the sun, which is going to make me as brown as a peg-hawker. I've had a glass of wine too, darling, which has made me feel – oh – very glad to see you.'

They went off to their bedroom to change for dinner, my aunt and uncle to theirs, and, spending a moment or two longer in the garden, since my own dressing, with no one to help or hinder me, would take less time, I eventually followed them. My black-beaded evening dress and its half-dozen petticoats were laid ready on the bed, a cheerful, fresh-faced girl of the type Aunt Verity always had about her waiting to assist me. My silver-backed brushes, my black velvet ribbons, the perfume my sister Celia considered too exotic for a lady, scandalous for a widow, were all to hand. And, as I brushed out my hair, peering at myself in the mirror with accustomed concentration, it could not matter to me that in the room next to mine Nicholas Barforth was very probably making love to his wife. It *did* not matter to me. I had not spoken a dozen words to him these past three years beyond the bounds of common politeness. I was better acquainted now with the unusual, annoying, fascinating creature he had married than with Nicholas himself. But I had been obliged recently, by events totally beyond my control, to admit that my body, like my mother's, had acquired the need for a man's caresses and had proved far less docile these past few months than I liked.

Emotion did not trouble me. Emotionally I was cool and serene, indulging myself, as I had always done, with a little humour, a little vanity, remembering, even in these mourning garments, how to make my hair paler by running a black velvet ribbon through it, the effect of dark jet earrings against a fair skin, nothing to break the stark elegance of black and white but a pair of blue eyes which, because they were short-sighted and weak, looked vague and cloudy and – one hoped – mysterious. And I took these pains, resorted to this artifice, not for the admiration of Nicholas or anyone else, but because beneath them I was still the plain, lanky girl my father had despised; and I would not let her show.

Cool, then, in the daylight; composed, even, with a branch of bed-time candles in my hand; less so when my disobedient body woke me in the night, or, worse than that, carried me in my sleep to the brink of an unfulfilled sensation and abandoned me there, the pit of my stomach burning, my limbs aching, straining to grasp that extra moment which would give me the relief I craved, and which was always denied. Relief, not love. Yet, as I well knew, the only relief available to me was in

573

remarriage, and since that was still unthinkable I had no choice but to endure – as my father had taught me – with dignity.

I was the first to join my aunt and uncle in the drawing-room that night, Nicholas and Georgiana lingering upstairs, Blaize not yet arrived, my uncle by no means pleased at the delay.

'He left London two days ago, and in a damned hurry at that. And now where the devil is he?'

But Blaize, who was fond of a good entrance, made one now, heralded by a mighty clattering of hooves and tearing-up of gravel, flinging his hat and cane to an eager parlourmaid and sauntering to greet us already in his evening clothes.

'I changed – *en route*,' he said, the perfection of his attire proof enough that it had not been in a carriage. 'And, if I've kept you waiting, I know you'll forgive me, mamma, since I *am* your favourite son – which leads me to wonder where your other son has got to?'

'He's here,' Nicholas said, coming into the room, Georgiana a step or two behind him, her green silk dress certainly expensive, its lace trim quite exquisite, but put on anyhow, shrugged on at the last moment with laughter and whispering, her body still languorous with pleasure, her bright hair ready at the first abrupt movements to come swishing and tumbling down.

'I presume we may eat now?' Uncle Joel said, and so we ate, a delicious meal, as Aunt Verity's meals always were, Nicholas eating to satisfy his appetite, Blaize with a shade more appreciation than that, Georgiana pecking sparrowlike at this and the other, drinking, 'to drown the memory of London', she said, raising her glass, and then, 'to the memory of green meadows and pastures'.

'To ploughed fields and muddy ditches,' Blaize answered her, refilling her glass, leaning across the table to tuck a loose strand of her hair back into its uncertain, copper-tinted coil, his eyes straying, perhaps only from force of habit, to the low neck of her dress.

'To wet moorland mornings,' she toasted him.

'To wind and foul weather,' he replied.

'Don't you hate London, Faith?' she asked me.

'No. I like it. I like cities altogether.'

'Yes,' she said, considering me, her head on one side, her glass, I noticed, empty again. 'I suppose they suit you – you're so polished and sculptured and poised. I can't even imagine you in a flutter. Oh Faith – Faith – why is it you always do things right, whereas I –? It's not fair. Why do you look like a swan, when I'm such a bedraggled duck? Doesn't she look like a swan, Nicky? Blaize, doesn't she?'

'She does,' Blaize said raising his glass to me. 'A very gracious, clever swan, my Faith.'

'*Your* Faith?' Nicholas said, looking up sharply, scowling through the candlelight.

'Oh my!' Georgiana chuckled, her tipsy face alive with delighted mischief. 'Goodness gracious – wishful thinking, eh Blaize? My brother Perry took a fancy to her too – oh yes he did – he saw her at that dreadful concert hall and very nearly had a fit. Who is she? *How* is she? Possible, likely, not one chance in a million? Get her to Galton, little sister, and –'

'That,' Nicholas said through his teeth, 'is enough. Georgiana, I warn you –'

'Oh lovely, he's angry with me,' she said, bathing us all in her smiles. And then, just as abruptly, her flaunting recklessness changed to a quite touching remorse.

'Oh dear. Faith, I do apologize. I like you so much, and I wouldn't upset you for the world.'

'I'm not upset.'

'You must be.'

'Only if you insist on it. I think I'd rather feel flattered instead, although I can't agree that you look like a duck, Georgiana.'

'Nor I,' Blaize murmured, smiling at me. 'A little bird of the wild wood, perhaps, swimming all bewildered and amazed in a duck pond. How's that?'

We went back into the drawing-room, disposing ourselves suitably, Aunt Verity's eyes watching both her sons with care, ready, as she had always been, to step between them.

'Shall we go for a walk in the moonlight, Nicky?' Georgiana said, offering a reconciliation.

'Presently. Blaize, I met a friend of yours from New York yesterday morning. A Mr Grassmann.'

'Oh yes. A pleasant fellow.'

'So he seems. But before you make promises about delivery dates you could check with me that they're possible.'

'Ah well,' Blaize shrugged. 'It's just that I have such confidence in you, Nicky – never so much as crossed my mind that you wouldn't be able to manage.'

'It should always be possible,' Uncle Joel cut in from the luxurious ease of his armchair. 'I don't want to hear excuses about deliveries that can't be met. I always met mine.'

'Well, you're damn well going to hear them, father,' Nicholas snapped, 'unless you can make him understand that, when the looms are working to capacity, he ought at least to know about it and make his arrangements to suit. I'm not complaining about the orders he brings in. He looks after his side of the business all right, and I look after mine. But we've got to keep each other informed. And you've got to follow things through, Blaize. This Mr Grassmann was looking for *you*, the other morning, not me. And where the hell were you? And what am I supposed to say to him when he tells me what you've promised him, and I know there's no chance of it – unless we expand again.'

'Which is what you want, Nick,' Blaize murmured.

'Do I?'

'I reckon so – unless you're finding it too much, with the Wool-combers on your hands.'

'And what would you know about it?'

'It's so warm in here,' Aunt Verity informed us, intending to be believed. 'Joel, come out into the garden – if we're to expand again there's no need to do it tonight, and I have a most interesting word to say to you about Elinor. Nicholas, do take your wife for that walk in the moonlight. Faith will go with you – and Blaize, one supposes, will do – well – exactly what Blaize supposes.'

'Mother dear,' he told her, laughing, 'you couldn't possibly be cross with me, could you? No – of course you couldn't.'

'Sometimes I think I could make the effort, dear – really.'

But they were smiling at each other, even my uncle – although he muttered that in his case it was no effort at all – looking good-humoured enough as he took his wife's arm and led her outside.

It was an intense blue midnight, velvet-textured, quite beautiful, the grass fragrant with sleeping poppies, the sea moving in a gentle, lullaby-rocking some way below us; a time, it seemed, for steady pathways, for breathing deeply, quietly, for listening. But after a moment or two of strolling, Georgiana, abandoning her little-girl air of decorum, became a restive colt again, impatient of all restraint.

'Let's go down to the sea, Nicky.'

'You said a walk in the moonlight. This *is* a walk in the moonlight.'

'Oh, I suppose it may be thought so in Cullingford. But when there is sand down there, and sea-water and rocks, how can you bear to stay so tamely on the grass?'

'I can bear it.'

'I can't,' she said and, taking up her skirts, she was off, flinging down a challenge as I had once seen her do at Galton Abbey, except that this time nobody followed her.

'It's wonderful,' she called up to us. 'Oh – do come down – it's not living, up there, on the path, it's just doing the right thing. And who really cares about that? Do come down here – we could fetch some wine and fruit and stay up all night to watch the sun rise. Why shouldn't we? It's something to *do*, something we can remember. Not the night we slept in our comfortable beds at Rosemount, but the night we spent on the beach – the night we did something different, that we – well, I won't say it, Nicky, because you'll kill me – but you know what I mean. We'd never forget that. Do come.'

But Nicholas, who may have been excited by her earlier in the day, was moved now to do no more than shrug his shoulders and turn his head away, the better to light his cigar against the wind.

She disappeared, hidden by a curve of rock and, as we paused, Blaize glanced at his brother and said, 'I can see you don't mean to go after her.'

'No.'

'Well, it's none of my business, of course, but she's had more than a glass or two, and she could fall –'

'I doubt it.'

'Or she could wander off and get lost.'

'She'll not do that.'

'Ah well, I don't want to get my feet wet either, but really Nicholas – I suppose the answer is that if it worries me I should go and fetch her myself.'

576

'That's about it. My guess is you won't find her, and she'll be back here before you are. You'll ruin your shoes for nothing – but, as you say, if it worries you –'

Blaize shrugged and walked off gingerly towards the beach, not liking his task at all, since he was a man who cared about his shoes and appreciated their value, leaving us quite alone and for a moment completely silent.

'She will be all right, you know,' Nicholas said.

'Yes, of course.'

'Are you cold?'

'No. I'm perfectly all right.'

'Faith –'

'Yes?'

'I'm sorry – about your husband, I mean. I didn't know him very well but he seemed a decent man. How have you been – since he died?'

'I can cope with it, Nicholas. Georgiana was extremely good to me, during the epidemic.'

'Yes. She can be very kind.'

Silence again, waiting and listening to the night, wishing that Blaize would return, feeling, not awkwardness exactly, not emotion, but something akin to sorrow that even now, when so much time and pain and joy, so much living, had flowed between us, I was still not at peace with him.

'You *are* like a swan,' he said suddenly, making the words into an accusation, and because it was the only possible thing to do I laughed – my mother's laugh – airy, without substance.

'You mean I have a long nose and large feet? Thank you, Nicholas.'

'I have never really seen your feet, and your nose looks well enough to me.'

Silence again, heavier this time, no possible thought now of laughter, no thought either of making any of the dozen pretty excuses that would have obliged him to take me back to the house, to his mother, who would know as well as I that he was unhappy, dissatisfied, angry, that in such a humour he could be dangerous.

He lit a cigar irritably, not asking my permission, inhaling deeply like his father, scowling at the sea.

'Faith,' he rapped out at me sharply, 'I don't have to warn you about Perry Clevedon, do I?'

'Heavens – you certainly don't.'

'Good. I think I have never met a more worthless man. Stay clear of him.'

'Goodness,' Georgiana said, appearing in the unlit dark behind us, the hem of her dress soaked in sea-water, her hair coming down with all the abandon that suited her so well. 'Are you quarrelling with Faith now? I could hear you growling at her as I came back on to the path. What on earth can she have done to make you angry?'

'Nothing,' he answered, and then, tossing his cigar away in the direction of the sea, he said quietly, 'Faith knows what I mean.'

577

18

The New Year at once offered us two events of considerable importance. My uncle, in recognition of his services to industry, his charity, his willingness, no doubt, to support Prince Albert's Exhibition which had meant so much to our Queen, received a baronetcy, becoming Sir Joel Barforth of Tarn Edge, while my mother, taking advantage of the general mood of celebration, announced her forthcoming marriage not to the decaying Mr Oldroyd but to the unknown, excellently preserved Mr Daniel Adair.

He was by no means, it seemed, a stranger to us all.

'Have you lost your senses, Elinor?' Aunt Hannah demanded, striding into my mother's house as if she meant to burn it down, infuriated by the loss of the Oldroyd money, certainly, already mourning the death of her hopes of seeing Jonas at Fieldhead, but considerably shaken at a more personal level too. 'I have never been so shocked in my life and I must give you notice that if you go through with this preposterous marriage I shall disown you.'

'I shall be sorry for that, Hannah.'

'But it will not stop you? No, I feared not. Then I can only hope that Joel may find the means to restrain you. It is an insult to your husband's memory, and to his daughters. You are allowing the man to make a fool of you – again – and, worse than that, you are very likely to ruin yourself. If no other way can be found, then I think that Joel and myself and your children would do well to join together in having you declared – well – unfit to manage your affairs. Insane.'

'Oh dear,' my mother said, smiling at me a little mistily when Aunt Hannah had gone. 'I did not expect them to be pleased, and Hannah had such high hopes of Mr Oldroyd, of seeing Jonas master of Fieldhead. But they cannot stop me, you know, and Hannah will not disown me, whatever she says. She is too fond of me for one thing, and for another there may still be some money left when I have done. Daniel will certainly be expensive, but your father was always a careful man, and his will does not allow me to spend it all. Well, Faith, I had better tell you, since you are the very dearest of my daughters, and neither Prudence nor Celia are speaking to me in any case – Yes, as you will have guessed, I knew Mr Daniel Adair very well, a long time ago, ten years before your father died. Your father was much occupied with politics in those days and appointed Mr Adair to manage his business affairs. While your father was in London, I was here, in this house, a young woman still, and I can only think it unwise, you know, of any man to neglect a young woman of my sort – or of your sort, Faith, for that matter. My word, I fell in love with Daniel quite wildly and was determined to run away with him – well, he ran away, I confess it, but not with me. Your Uncle Joel persuaded him, with pound notes, of course, to leave me, and then persuaded me to return to your father, who did not at all want me but who feared he might lose the next election should there be a scandal. A sorry tale, and perhaps all those years ago I may have wished Daniel had been more courageous and willing to starve with me in a cottage. But he was not, and I would not really have cared for it in any case. Your uncle told me to return to my husband, to serve out my sentence in fact, since he felt I had earned my share of your father's fortune. And he was quite right. I endured ten years longer, and no one can accuse me of being other than a most dutiful, most submissive wife.'

'And you remained in love with Mr Adair all that time?'

'Oh dear no,' she said. 'Life is not like that. And when your father died I was too enchanted by my freedom to be in love with anybody but myself. It was my special time, I told you, and I also told you that I knew it would be quickly over. Depend upon it, if I had not encountered Daniel again, I might well have married Matthew Oldroyd and made myself nearly as rich as Verity. But I *did* encounter him, not at all by chance, since he has from time to time been associated in business with your Uncle Joel. He had informed himself of my circumstances and knew that I would be visiting the Exhibition. He has no money to speak of, of course, since he has just returned from the West Indies, where his ventures have not prospered. Poor Daniel. You must be well able to understand that he needs me.'

'Indeed, but mother, that is hardly a reason for marriage.'

'No dear. Then I will give you one. He deserted me, I suppose, and I should have detested him. I did not. I understood that, having known great poverty, he could not risk it again, and I was forced to admit that the few months I spent as his mistress were the most luminous of my life. I had been a sad little woman with an old, grey husband, and Daniel transformed me. He can certainly be a scoundrel, but that has never been unattractive – Joel has been a scoundrel in his day – and Daniel has a great capacity for laughter. You tell me I look nineteen, Faith dear. When Daniel Adair touches me I *am* nineteen. And I can afford him now. You need have no fear of the consequences. He is not so young as he was, darling, and a time comes when even the most seasoned wanderer is grateful for a comfortable home. And can you think of any reason – really – why he should not be fond of me?'

I couldn't, and when I dined with them some days later – Celia having refused the invitation, Prudence, who had no choice, sitting throughout the meal in spike-edged silence – I concluded that, whatever his faults, and they might well be numerous, his easy, good-humoured charm was beyond denial. He was a man, I thought, who could cheat but who would do it very pleasantly, a man whose roguish smile and all too apparent virility might be compensation enough to a woman like my mother – like myself – for any lie.

Yet Prudence, who was far more intimately concerned in the matter than I, would not be reconciled, could in no way contemplate the sharing of a home not only with Mr Adair but with his son, whose identity had been kept secret from us until now, a young gentleman of six or seven years old whose black eyes and amber-tinted countenance betrayed a hint of something warmer than Irish in his blood.

'If my mother imagines,' she told me, 'that I shall submit myself to daily contact with that dressed-up navvy and his offspring, then she is much mistaken. I shall demand control of my money and I shall come to live with you, or, if you will not have me, I shall make other arrangements. I shall set up a school as I have always wanted and earn my own living, free from encumbrance. In fact I shall go to Jonas Agbrigg at once to ascertain the exact nature of my rights. You had best accompany me.'

But Jonas, when applied to, was quick to point out that Prudence had no rights at all. Naturally he was just as disgusted at our mother's lack of judgment as we were, had as much to lose from it as we had – more, in fact, since the administration of the Oldroyd estate alone, much less its possession, would have made him a decent profit – but he had re-examined our father's will most minutely and could only describe it as unbreakable. The half of his fortune that was held in trust was safe from the assault of even the most skilful fortune-hunter, but could not be paid out to us during our mother's lifetime. The other half was hers – and Mr Adair's – absolutely, while Prudence's dowry could only be made available on her marriage, or failing that at the joint discretion of my mother and Uncle Joel. And we could none of us imagine that Mr Daniel Adair would allow his wife to consent to any such dissipation of funds.

'Had there been a way through it,' Jonas told us, without the slightest change of tone or expression, 'then I would have found it. Had there been a way to twist the meaning to suit our purpose, then I would have twisted it. We are talking of Celia's money too, after all, and my expenses – Prudence dear – are probably a great deal heavier than your own.'

'There's the porcelain,' she said. 'I'll sell it, before that little monster of a Liam Adair sets about the job of breaking it, for I never encountered a more unruly child in my life. Will you handle the sale for me, Jonas?'

But once again my father, with his innate distrust of female judgment, had imposed conditions. The porcelain could be sold as an entire collection or in separate pieces, but only with the consent of Prudence and her husband. Should she attempt to offer it for sale before her marriage or – horror of horrors – without the permission of her spouse, then its possession would revert to that other weak-minded female, her mother.

'I will never forgive him,' Prudence said bitterly.

'I doubt if that will trouble him unduly,' Jonas told her, folding the documents neatly away and slipping them into a drawer of his massive, masculine desk. 'Your father did not mean you to be independent, Prudence. He intended you to be married, and I can see no alternative for you but to obey – unless, of course, you are prepared to wait until your mother dies, which is unlikely to be soon. You had best take Freddy Hobhouse, who will make no objection to your selling the shirt from your back, much less your porcelain, since every penny he can muster is needed at Nethercoats.'

'And is that the best you can do for me, Jonas – with all your cleverness?'

'It is,' he said coldly, getting to his feet as an indication that the consultation was at an end, that his time – being male and free – was of value in Cullingford. 'The absolute best, Prudence, as matters have turned out.'

And they stared at each other, steel-eyed adversaries, detesting each other, since it was in neither of their natures to admit that she would have made him a better wife than Celia, that his intellect and his perseverance could have proved more congenial to her than Freddy.

'Oh yes,' Blaize told me that afternoon, calling in to see me on his way back from town. 'There are no deadlier enemies than those who could have been friends. If Aunt Hannah had not made him so greedy, and your father had not made her so awkward – who knows? But poor Prudence, this is the end of her liberty it seems, for I imagine Dan Adair will keep her very close to home.'

'I don't see why he should concern himself with her at all.'

'No – but then you don't know very much about disreputable men, do you, Faith? He has been a rogue all his life, I imagine, and now, having made up his mind to be respectable, he will be very, very respectable indeed – you may take my word for it. Family prayers every morning, I shouldn't wonder, and no unmarried young ladies of *his* household running unchaperoned about the streets. As I said – poor Prudence.'

'I hadn't thought of that. Why don't you marry her yourself, Blaize? One supposes you must eventually marry *somebody*?'

'Ah – one supposes. Not yet, dear.'

'You are still looking for that rare and special creature Prudence used to tease you about, are you? The one who is always in the next room?'

'It does rather seem so. But in the meantime – it occurs to me – you wouldn't care to dine with me one evening, next week perhaps, would you, Faith? I have a rather pleasant little apartment in Leeds – nothing grand, but worth looking at, and I have very passable dinners sent in from the restaurant across the street.'

'Heavens!' I said, thoroughly delighted, knowing that, although it was not a serious request, merely an exploratory one, he would not have asked at all had he not been tempted. 'What an idea! And you're not even very ardent, are you – asking for next week instead of this week – or tonight –'

'Well, at least you didn't take a fit of the vapours, and with a little re-arranging of my commitments I could manage, shall we say, Wednesday?'

'I really think we'd better not.'

'Yes, now that is just what I expected you to say, but I know you won't blame me for making the attempt. You are looking very well lately, Faith – quite precious, like something cut out of cameo glass.'

'Goodness! First I'm a swan, than a cameo. Whatever next?'

'My very good friend, I think,' he said, moving towards me, his intention to kiss me so obvious that had I not desired it I could easily have turned away. But I remained motionless as his mouth came to rest, butterfly-light, on the corner of mine and then slowly took possession of

581

it, a leisurely, accomplished embrace which stirred nothing inside me but appreciation of his expertise, a certain pleasing blend of amusement and affection.

'Now why on earth did you do that, Blaize Barforth?'

'One takes one's opportunities – and it wouldn't be a hardship to do it again, believe me.'

'No, but think of the inconvenience to yourself. I know that young widows who live alone are supposed to go in for this kind of thing, but in our case, with Aunt Hannah to watch over us –'

'Exactly,' he said. 'How clever of you to think of that.'

And, knowing that he had certainly thought of it himself, I wondered.

It could be no secret to him that, since the Exhibition, Nicholas had called once or twice to see me, exactly as he did himself. And why should it surprise anyone that Nicholas should stop a moment every now and then in Millergate to pass the time of day with his widowed cousin?

He would arrive without warning, always in a hurry – or so it seemed – leaving his horse quite openly at my gate.

'Faith, I've been shouting myself hoarse all morning and the Old Swan is like an oven. Will you give me tea?'

And I gave him tea, sitting a yard away from him, listening, smiling, 'understanding what he meant' and pretending, sometimes, both of us, that I did not, sharing the strain, easing the tension, making no move towards him, refusing to face the possibility that he could approach me, telling myself when he had gone that it was entirely innocent and believing it, because it was what I wanted to believe. He never mentioned Georgiana. I never mentioned Giles. We talked, as we had done years ago, of ourselves in isolation, as if our lives were in no way connected with other lives, certainly not with each other.

'What have you done today, Faith?'

'Oh, mad adventures from morning to evening – my cat on the rooftop wailing to get down, and I think my chimney needs sweeping. And you, Nicholas?'

'Bought myself some new combing machines, although God knows where I'm to put them.'

'Isn't the mill next to yours for sale – the old Barraclough place?'

'Aye – and I've had a look at it.'

'And you could use it?'

'I reckon I could – if I can get the money.'

'Oh, you'll do that all right. Will it take a great deal to put it right?'

And, listening while he offered me his facts and figures, I must have known that I was recreating for him the atmosphere he had once found attractive, that by fulfilling his need I was increasing it.

Uncle Joel, aware no doubt of the contribution his operatives had made to his Exhibition medals, his knighthood, his general altogether stupendous success, entertained them that summer to a grand banquet held under canvas on the lawns at Tarn Edge. He had, it was true, deprived many of their fathers of a livelihood by his introduction of power-looms twenty years ago, but the new machines themselves had given rise in this younger generation to a new class of mechanics, skilled men who, with a trade in their hands, were moving out of Simon Street to cleaner pastures and who, with the aid of the Mechanics Institute my uncle had sponsored, were no longer illiterate labourers, but men who could increasingly lift up their heads and pay their way. He had always been known as a hard master, but there was no job in his factories, however dirty or dangerous, that he could not and had not done himself. He demanded punctuality and self-discipline, both of which he practised himself, but for a good day's work he had always been willing to pay rather more than Nethercoats or Fieldhead, and had been the first man in the Law Valley, long before the law compelled him, to introduce a ten-hour working day.

And now, having proved to the Hobhouses and the Oldroyds that even without exceeding the legal ten hours his factories could make higher profits than theirs, he had invited his employees to dine, spreading before them a gargantuan feast which, Aunt Hannah had informed me, included no fewer than five hindquarters of beef, a hundred and fifty legs of mutton, forty hams and tongues, chickens and ducks and pigeon pies without number, three hundred and twenty plum puddings, a mountain of fruit and nuts, sponge cakes, tarts of every variety and description, washed down with as much wine and ale as every man, and every woman, could decently carry.

There was of course a certain segregation, natural or otherwise, family and friends, shed managers, engineers, designers, skilled men and their families, all in self-conscious Sunday best, keeping themselves a trifle apart from the lower echelons, even the burlers and menders, sedate, matronly looking women for the most part who spent their days repairing faults in the unfinished pieces, letting it be known they felt themselves a cut above the mass of common weavers. But Sir Joel Barforth strolled leisurely that day among them all, shaking any hand that was held out to him, a word and a smile for everyone, a cigar for every man, a trinket in the napkin of every woman, sharing a joke here, a reminiscence there, putting himself and his possessions on display to satisfy their curiosity and to whet their appetites, to increase the ambition of some, the envy of others, although all of them – the ambitious and the envious, the ones who wanted this magnificence for themselves and the ones who wanted no one to have it – were all willing to drink his health that day.

I put aside my widow's weeds for the occasion, not eagerly, but knowing it must be done. I was twenty-three years old. I had worn unrelieved black for two years. It was enough, and so I chose a gentle dove grey, a wide, tiered skirt edged with white lace, slit sleeves showing lace beneath, a grey satin bonnet with a white plume curling behind, a cameo at my throat, a frivolous, lacy parasol, gloves, and dashing, high-heeled boots of white kid.

'My word, how smart!' my mother said, coming to collect me with Mr Adair, since Prudence, who would still barely speak to her, had chosen to accompany the Agbriggs. But after so long in mourning even these neutral colours seemed excessively bright and, as I entered the gardens of Tarn Edge, if Aunt Hannah had rounded on me with a 'Good heavens, girl! You are improperly dressed. Go home and change', I would not have been astonished.

The family table, of course, surrounded by flowering plants and hot-house blooms in copper bowls, was a sight to behold, Aunt Verity – Lady Barforth now – sitting beside her daughter, Lady Chard, and amiable, healthy Sir Matthew. My mother was beautiful as always; Aunt Hannah undoubtedly majestic; Mr Agbrigg a famous man in his own right now that he had brought water, if not to Simon Street, to very nearly everywhere else. Prudence, dressed with her usual quiet elegance, while not precisely willing to speak to Mr Adair, was at least taking pains that it should not be obvious. Even Celia, looking older than either of us, I thought, seemed ready to enter into the general spirit of enjoyment, finding no more than a few, very trivial errands for the impeccable Jonas.

Blaize, as much in his element as Caroline, had clearly been set the task of making himself pleasant and was performing it admirably, far better than Nicholas, who seemed morose and preoccupied, while Georgiana, splendidly attired in honey-coloured silk, her earrings of gold and topaz looking too heavy for her tiny, pointed ears, sat in complete silence, not sullenly but rather, it seemed, because there was nothing she wished to say.

'They have been having a terrible set-to, Georgiana and Nicholas,' Caroline whispered to me. 'So you will oblige me by keeping an eye on her. He was growling at her when I arrived and she was wringing her hands and wailing "Oh what have I done now?", in that way she has, half laughing, half crying – I can perfectly understand why she provokes him. You will have noticed that neither her grandfather nor her brother are here, which may have something to do with it – certainly Perry is head over heels in debt again, which is always a bad sign. Well, they must sort it out later, for nothing must be allowed to spoil my father's great day. I told you, did I not, that he would win all the medals, and so he has. Even Matthew couldn't bring himself to ignore that, and I must say that he has backed down most graciously. If there should ever be another exhibition I shall have no trouble at all in attending it.'

Sir Joel having returned from the grand tour of his property and his personnel, the meal began, and ended, most jovially, my uncle, who had received his share of loyal toasts, standing now to raise his own glass to his wife.

'I have this to say,' he announced, 'and you can all hear it. Without Verity I'd have nothing and I'd be nothing. If I had to choose between all this and her, then I'd throw the lot away. I may be embarrassing her now – and by the look on her face I am – but the only real treasure I have is in her. There'll be men here today who'll look at this house and the mills, and say "He's been lucky". They're wrong. Hard work made the mills, because I was ready to get myself out of bed every morning when others weren't, and ready to labour, often enough, into the night when the rest had gone home. That, and guts I reckon, and a knack of understanding what was needed and how to supply it. There's no luck in that. But if any man looks at my wife and says "He's been lucky" then that man is absolutely right. He could even go further and tell me I've got more than I deserve. So we'll drink now to Lady Barforth – my wife.'

He put down his glass, took both her hands in his and kissed them, not raising them to his lips but bending his head, a most gallant salutation. Nicholas and Blaize pushed back their chairs and, going to her side, kissed her in their turn, then, in a rare moment of brotherhood, hugged each other hard. Caroline, forgetting to be Lady Chard, threw two fierce arms around her father's neck, her hand clasping her mother's behind his back. The brothers kissed their sister, husband and wife embraced again. 'Hannah', my uncle said, reaching out for the sister who was, often enough, a nuisance to us all, but who had helped him through his early, leaner years. And both she and my mother kissed him and each other.

It was a moment of great emotion, of great beauty, this family united by pride of achievement, and, my eyes swimming with tears, I loved each and every one of them, my soaring, splendid uncle, his graceful wife, my annoying, resourceful aunt, my frivolous little mother, artful Blaize and ambitious Caroline – Nicholas. They were my people. But they were not, it seemed, and never could be, Georgiana's; for, lounging in her chair, tapping a fork against her glass with an irritable hand, she was not merely bored, like Matthew Chard, but thoroughly oppressed, the very colour of her hair faded, apparently, by the completeness of her misery. And on such a day, when the Barforth ladies themselves were there to be looked at, when every shed manager's wife would want to count their jewels and the flounces on their dresses, would feel entitled, quite rightly, to a word and a smile, her attitude – whatever its cause – could only give offence.

Yet her attitude itself puzzled me, for, although I had seen her capricious and reckless, I had never before seen her hard, the scornful curve of her lip as she muttered something to Matthew Chard being quite new to me.

'One would have thought a title might have pleased her,' my mother murmured, seeing the direction of my eyes, but clearly my uncle's knighthood was no more to her than an extension of the exhibition she had so despised, a hollow sham as tainted by trade as everything else about him, an insult, perhaps, to the 'real gentry', whose titles had been won on the field of battle or on the tortuous pathways of diplomacy, granted for services freely given, not bought and paid for.

But none of this surprised me. I had expected Georgiana to feel this way and was worried, rather, that she – basically so warm-hearted and who meant so well – should let it show, concluding that some affront must surely have been offered to her own family, that she had been forced once too often into the position of choosing sides; and had chosen.

'Come, girls,' Aunt Verity said, moving towards us, 'I think we should circulate a little and make ourselves known. Faith, dear, there will be a great many, I imagine, who have grateful memories of your husband, and would be glad of a word with you. And Georgiana – I believe Nicholas will be wanting to present his employees to you.'

But, as we began to disperse, Georgiana continued to sit at the empty table, not sulking but totally and quite alarmingly separate, her solitude made more conspicuous by the fact that she herself seemed unaware of it.

But others were not.

'Mrs Nicholas Barforth,' Aunt Hannah inquired, 'are you not well today?'

'Georgiana,' Caroline called out as she took her father's arm, 'you had better come with me.'

'Leave her,' Blaize said to me.

'Georgiana,' Nicholas ordered. 'Get up'; and, staring at him for a moment quite balefully, she suddenly leaped to her feet and raising her hand allowed the fork with which she had been toying to fall with a careless, destructive clatter on to the table.

'Good heavens!' she said. 'Such a commotion! One wonders how you would all behave at a Coronation.'

Pushing back her chair, she gathered her expensive, embroidered skirts together and set off down the garden at a spanking pace, bestowing an ardent, almost hysterical, greeting on everyone she passed, leaving a trail of astonishment – and embarrassment – behind her.

'Dear God!' Nicholas said very low, no anger in him now, a strange, sorrowing note in his voice, the nearest approach to defeat I had ever seen in the sudden droop of his shoulders; and if there had been a decision to make I must surely have made it then.

I stayed late at Tarn Edge that day, later in Blenheim Lane, so late in fact that Prudence, who had planned to return home with me, elected to spend the remainder of the night in her own bed. And so, quite by chance, even my housemaid having gone upstairs, there was only my housekeeper, Mrs Marworth, to exchange a startled glance with me when we heard the gate open and a knock on the door, even that good lady, having some experience, it seemed, of the ways of young widows, melting discreetly away when in answer to my inquiry we were told: 'Nicholas Barforth.'

'Nicholas. What is it? I didn't hear your horse.'

'No. I left her in the Old Swan yard. I'd better warn you I've had a glass or two. You're not obliged to ask me to come in.'

But, without answering, I walked away from him into the parlour, spending a long moment in lighting a lamp, adjusting the candles on either end of the mantelpiece, so that when I had finished he was sitting on my sofa, allowing me to choose the safety of a separate chair.

'Would you like a drink, Nicholas? I think I have some brandy.' He smiled, the unwilling, rueful grin breaking through the cloud of him in a way that had always seemed to me like a reward.

'No – no thanks. How is it you always make everything seem so smooth for me, Faith? I'm here, in what amounts to the middle of the night – when I shouldn't be here at all – and you haven't even asked me why. And, if I got up now and went away without saying anything, you wouldn't make a fuss, would you? I could even come back tomorrow and be sure of my welcome.'

'Yes, you could. But I'd be concerned, Nicholas. I might not ask what was wrong, because if you didn't tell me of your own free will I'd assume you didn't want me to know. But I'd wonder – and worry. There's no doubt about that.'

He swallowed hard, painfully, the slump of his shoulders heavy once again with defeat as he leaned forward, staring at the empty summer hearth, his hands clasped loosely together, his dark face, without its shielding anger, vulnerable to hurt.

'I want to talk to you, Faith.'

'Yes, of course.'

'I mean really talk to you – not about combing machines and tea-parties. Can I do that? I'll leave the instant you tell me.'

'I know.'

'All right. So what do I say? God knows! I'm at the end of myself tonight, I reckon.'

'Yes. I think I know that too.'

'And I'm a selfish swine to come here and pester you with it – which hasn't stopped me from coming. I never really supposed it would. I went down to the Swan to get drunk, which may seem pointless to you – except that getting drunk *would* have kept me away from you. But it hasn't happened. I'm not drunk. Remember – I'll go at once, when you tell me.'

'Talk to me then.'

'About Georgiana?'

'Yes. What happened between you today?'

'Nothing that hasn't happened before. Nothing that should even matter all that much – nothing I didn't expect, right from the start.'

And, throwing himself backwards suddenly against the sofa, he stretched his whole body and gave a long, deep-draining sigh.

'Money, Faith – that's all. And I've got plenty of that. Bills – dressmakers' bills, milliners' bills, that she'd had the money to pay and told me she had paid. Apologetic little women coming to see me and saying they know it must have slipped her mind and they don't like bothering me with trifles, but its been six months now, eight months now – It shouldn't even bother me that she gives every penny she can beg or borrow to her brother – since I must have known she would – or that she can't see what all the fuss is about, since tradesmen are just tradesmen and she's gentry, and nobody called Clevedon or Flood or Winterton, *or* Chard I reckon, has ever been in a hurry to pay his tailor. It shouldn't bother me that the money I work for – and scheme for – buys her brother his place at the Floods' whist table, since a gentleman is in honour bound to settle his gambling debts. I can afford it. I was ready to afford it when it was worth it to me. So I'm to blame. I know it. Shall I go now, Faith?'

'Do you want to?'

'Oh no. I know exactly what *I* want. I won't leave until I'm told.'

'In fact you want me to make the decision. You're ready to accept the blame for your situation with Georgiana, but not for – whatever should come of this.'

587

'That makes me sound very low, Faith.'

'So it does.'

He got up, one hand on the mantelpiece, one foot tapping against the fender, not irritably, merely to release some particle of his tension, and, had I permitted myself, I could have gone to him then and there – guilty as he was, full of wine and self-pity, hurt and hunger – and put my arms around him, making everything smooth for him yet again, telling him that he had no need to coax, nor to plead in order to reach me; telling him, quite simply, that I was here.

'Let me say just this,' he muttered, 'and then I will go away. You may not believe me, but I mean it when I say I'm to blame. Georgiana is now exactly as she has always been. She didn't deceive me by pretending to be otherwise and she never promised to change. I'm the one who has changed. She fascinated me. Christ! – she burned me so badly I couldn't see beyond her. And the only difference between that and being in love must be that it doesn't last. And when it goes it leaves nothing but amazement that it could ever have existed at all. So I've ruined my life and hers too, because she knows I can't put up with her any more. And how can I expect her to understand why? She has a right to believe that I've cheated her, since I once told her that all these things I find so bloody impossible could make no difference between us. She has the right to feel ill-used when the rest of them criticize her and I don't defend her – as I promised – or when I criticize her myself – as I vowed I'd never do. I swear it – whatever she may do to me, I make her so miserable sometimes, so damned miserable I can see the colour go out of her, and because it upsets me it makes me worse. And I believe I understood today that there isn't any cure – that things will always be like this. My father doesn't often stir much emotion in me, but I was proud of him today. I recognized myself in him today, and I recognized what he feels for my mother. I could have had that too – couldn't I, Faith? And so I went down to the Swan because I couldn't stand thinking about it. I couldn't face up to the fact that I was in a trap of my own making and that I couldn't smash my way out of it, couldn't talk my way out of it, couldn't even buy my way out of it. Christ –!'

'Nicholas,' I said slowly, very carefully, 'a moment ago you said you knew exactly what you wanted. You had better tell me what it is.'

He sat down again heavily, a man who had been brought up to believe he could get anything he wanted if he worked for it, fought for it, who had been very sure of himself and who now could not tolerate frustration, a man who could understand the reasons for his captivity but would not accept them. Yet, no matter what fears I entertained, nor how many feeble attempts I made to be resolute, to listen not only to the warnings of shock and shame but to the simple, straightforward urgings of common sense, my body knew, had known from the moment he arrived, that he had only to touch me – a hand, merely, on mine, or not even that much, a hand reaching out for me – and I would answer.

It was completely wrong. There was not even a whisper of right, not the slightest breath of justification, no good to anyone could possibly come of it. He was here in a moment of weakness, knowing – as I knew – that, however much he desired me, however much he might come to love me, he could, in the final instance, only do me harm. And because he was not cruel, and no more self-seeking in love than most men – than most women – by harming me he would most likely harm himself. He knew quite well he should not have come here at all. I knew I should not have let him in. Yet, if we were no more self-seeking than the average, we were no more self-sacrificing either. We were human, imperfect, and I, at least, had stood apart from life for too long. And more than that, perhaps I was still young enough to believe that, what I would have instantly recognized as madness in any other woman, could in my case be otherwise; that I was stronger, possessed the capacity to love more completely – for I was in no doubt that I did love him.

'I want a great many things,' he said quietly, 'and I know it's all impossible. I want to turn the clock back, I suppose – a long way back, years back. It can't be done. I'm sorry, Faith. I'll go now.'

But I had allowed him to leave me too many times in this manner, in those slow, peaceful days when it had seemed right to wait for him to fall in love with me, days when I had remained motionless, believing time to be my ally, and had lost him. Perhaps I had needed only to hold out my hand and push him with the very tips of my fingers in order to pass from one level of feeling to another, from the friendship we had always shared to desire. And perhaps, too, we would all be dust and ashes, mouldering in eternal decay, tomorrow.

'I'll go now.' But he didn't move, and when I didn't answer he said sharply, 'Yes, I'll go, for if I don't – I hurt you once, Faith, didn't I? I can't do it again.'

'That's nonsense, Nicholas.'

'What?'

'It's nonsense, that's all. It just proves that we know the right answers, that we know what we ought to say and do. And it's nonsense. Why don't you say what you mean? You don't intend to leave and you don't think I'll make you. *Say* it, Nicholas. Let's be honest, at least with each other.'

'Faith –' he said blankly, taken off guard for the first time in his life very nearly, and very briefly shy. And then, his hard brown fingers plunging for a moment into his hair as if he required to clear his head, shake it, perform some positive, simple action that was entire and straightforward in itself, he leaned forward and whispered, 'Come and sit beside me.'

'Presently.'

'Now, Faith – please.'

I got up, walked across the room to him and sat down carefully on the edge of the sofa, arranging my voluminous skirts so that no part of them touched him, although his breath was already in my nostrils, filling me with the devasting awareness of a hard, tough-fibred chest behind his shirt-frill, red blood beneath, a powerful, beautiful male body wanting mine.

'All right,' he said. 'I'll be honest. It suits me that way, in any case. I could have been happy with you, Faith, couldn't I? I know it. It's what I should have had – would have had. I cheated myself of it. And that's not the whole of it. I reckon I could live with that. I did live with it, until that night in Bournemouth last year. I wanted you, that night, but I thought it would pass. It hasn't. I want you, Faith – in every way a man could want you – badly. And I've got one life, that's all, and so have you.'

'And do you expect to get me?'

'Yes,' he said, a sudden flash of excitement, of victory in his face. 'I think so – I think I do. Faith, you're shaking –'

'Yes – delirium, I expect. Hold me.'

And although I couldn't really believe I had spoken that last command – 'Hold me' – I heard it, he heard it, obeyed it, his arms instantly around me, his mouth and his hands possessing as much of me as my cumbersome garments permitted.

'Not here, Nicholas.'

'Upstairs, then? I have to take you now, before you change your mind.'

'Darling – that's not romantic.'

'No, I daresay. But, once it's done, it's done, and there's no going back. Once I've got you – when I *know* I've got you – then I'll be romantic.'

He carried me up the narrow stairs, no tender gesture of gallantry but a rough lifting from the ground because it was quicker that way, and I was as conscious as he was of the need for haste. He was not gentle, nor did I require it, for it was urgency alone in those first moments that nailed us together, the need for possession, the need even to punish one another, my whole body burning, wanting him quickly, quickly, so that my petticoats were an irritation to be torn away, his shirt an encumbrance that his hands and mine disposed of together. And it seemed right that his hard, heavy body, emerging from its elegant social wrappings, should crush me and hurt me, too intent on the conclusion of his desire, the simple act of claiming me – since that was what we were about – to think of giving me pleasure. We were as adversaries, bent on taking and devouring the whole of one another, grasping and clutching and biting, a fierce penetration that I answered just as fiercely, until whatever it was inside me that had obscured the source of rapture was invaded, split asunder, and it poured over me, wave upon wave of it, terrifying me and thrilling me at the same time, leaving me docile and bemused and irrevocably possessed.

We lay for a while in silence, recovering, easing ourselves apart, and, when it seemed to me that his breathing had slowed and deepened into sleep, I got up and went to the window, needing, I think, to be a yard or so away from him to experiment with the sensation of shame. Yet, taking a deep breath, waiting for it to start, nothing happened to me with which I could not cope.

I knew, in this cooler moment, the enormity of the social and moral crime I had committed, for which I, as a woman, would be required to pay a far higher price than Nicholas. Discovery, for him, would mean no more perhaps than a personal explanation with his wife and with his father, a certain winking and sniggering among the crowd when he entered the Piece Hall. 'The young devil, he got the Ashburn woman, did he? Good luck to him!', since it was well known that a man took his pleasures where he could find them, and a woman who surrendered was no better than a whore in any case.

But for me the retribution would be terrible and complete, a total casting-out which would oblige even my mother and Prudence to treat me as a stranger, if they wished to retain their own reputations. But – although I did not wish to lose them, had no idea how to face life without them – I had done nothing I could find it in my own heart to regret, had done nothing, certainly, that I would not be prepared to do again. And, having decided that much, I could see no purpose in self-torment.

I am no longer sure if I thought of Giles in that solitary quarter of an hour; it simply seems to me now that I must have done so, for I could hardly have been so calm had I not realized that my feelings for him had been so different that they could still exist, quite independently, alongside my love for Nicholas, which had always been there. I sought no excuses, no justifications. That was simply the way of it. And, if there was a price to pay, then, because I was a Law Valley woman who understood about the settlement of debts, I would pay it.

'Are you awake?' I murmured, and he crossed the room in two strides, his arms coming tight around me.

'Aye – awake and watching you. You'll be thinking about your husband, I expect, and maybe I've been thinking about my wife. And I've got this to say to you, Faith Aycliffe. I reckon you must love me a fair amount or you'd not have let me near you in the first place, and whatever it costs me – whatever it costs you – I've no mind to let you go. Don't whine to me now, and say you didn't mean it to go this far, for I won't take it. It's happened. I've got you and I'll keep you – one way or another – that's one thing you can be sure of.'

'And when did you ever see me whining, Nicholas Barforth?'

'Never,' he said. One hand going gently now into my hair, finding my cheek and the nape of my neck. 'I never did.'

'No – just as I've never seen you romantic.'

He pressed his mouth against my forehead, and I felt his lips curve into their slow smile, 'Yes – well I did promise that, didn't I? Come back to bed then, Faith. What we did just then was need – I expect you know that. So we'll go back to bed now, I reckon, and make love.'

19

It was enough, at least for Nicholas, in those early days to know that his physical possession of me was beyond dispute, to rejoice in his complete mastery of my body's needs; and if he did not precisely wish to see me in a state of abject slavery – and I am not altogether certain of that – he desired, most assuredly, to increase those needs, *did* increase them, so that my body, quite separately from my heart, was famished and painful without him.

I lived through fevered days that should have terrified me and did not, content to take what I could, as if I stood somehow at the very rim of the world, some outer threshold, where I must clutch each moment as it came and live it intensely, to the limits of myself.

And having no experience of the stage-management of adultery, I was surprised how often we could be together.

His horse in the Old Swan yard would cause no comment, and, should anyone look for him in the bar-room and not find him there, there was the Piece Hall across the way, Mr Rawnsley's Bank, the offices of Jonas Agbrigg, who handled the legal complexities of the Barforths – no reason at all to suppose he had taken the brisk, ten-minute stroll to my kitchen door, conveniently screened by a high-walled yard, with no neighbours to bother us. And if he should be seen in Millergate, coming to me or leaving me, what of it? It was a busy, commercial thoroughfare, containing not only the millinery and the bakery he would hardly patronize, but the premises of the architect, Mr Outhwaite, who dealt with all repairs and extensions at Lawcroft and Tarn Edge, the saddlery, the importer of cigars and fine wines, where no one would be astonished to see him.

I could not be certain we were safe. I rather thought that we were not. But that first breathless August, that first mellowing of the year into September, my eyes were too dazzled for caution, my mind lulled, not by recklessness, but by the perilous, languorous philosophy of the opium-eater who, knowing perfectly well that he may die of his addiction, does not even want to resist it.

To begin with he came only in the evening, having purchased the discretion of my Mrs Marworth, who, being too afraid of him to betray us in any case, and worldly enough to rather enjoy this kind of thing, would admit him through her kitchen and then prepare herself to tell anyone else who called that I was not at home. But he required, I think, some further commitment, some act of rashness on my part, and was soon urging me to folly.

'We have a house in Scarborough, Faith. My parents never go there now, and I will confess to you that Blaize has used it, and that I have used it – I'm being honest, you see, like you said. I've done this before, except that I haven't, because it's different now, if you see what I mean? We could stay the whole night together, Faith – two whole nights. I've never made love to you in the morning. Of course you can get away. Yes, yes you can – you can if you want to.'

'But I can't go to Scarborough, Nicholas. I've never travelled alone.'

'You can. You've travelled all over Europe with your mother, who is the most feather-headed female imaginable. If you got her from here to Naples, and back again, then you can find your way to Scarborough. Mrs Marworth can go as far as Leeds with you, which will take care of chance meetings on the platform in Cullingford, and I'll have someone meet you at the other end. *Do* it, Faith. The couple who keep the house open for us won't even remember your face – I'll pay them to forget it. *Do* it. It's October now. Nobody we know goes to Scarborough at this season. You've got a friend, somewhere, haven't you, that you can say you're visiting?'

And so I went to Scarborough, arriving in a state of extreme nervous exhaustion, convinced that every tree I had passed *en route* concealed a prying Cullingford face, that the spare Mr Collins who had been sent to meet me in a closed carriage, and his comfortable wife waiting to give me tea, were spies in Georgiana's or Aunt Hannah's pay. But the house, set high on the cliff-top, was surrounded by trees in full, burnished, Autumn leaf, its garden offering a view of the little grey town climbing downwards to the bay, the castle a stern sentinel above it, the streets empty, it seemed, of anything but the fresh October wind, the stirring of salt-dried foliage, the tang of sea-spray.

'This is the first property my father bought outside Cullingford,' Nicholas told me. 'His first attempt at being alone with my mother.' And for three miraculous days we were alone together, three rain-washed days; grey-tinted mornings which found us still in the same bed, no hurry, no sudden, chilly departures, a slow and lovely reaching out for one another in the moment of waking, free to enjoy this new-found luxury of making love in the uncertain, marine daylight which revealed to me, more exactly than any candleflame, the complex pattern of bone and muscle beneath his skin, the tight-clenching of his jaw in the moment of pleasure, the harsh hands and limbs of conquest, allowing me no quarter, and then the warmth of him afterwards, the cherishing.

'Dear God, Faith! It gets better every time. Doesn't it?'

'Yes, it does.'

'Then tell me – tell me what it does to you.'

'It consumes me – and then it makes me dream about the next time.'

'Now that's what I like to hear. Give me half an hour, will you, then we'll see about that dream –'

There were three blustery afternoons, my hair tangled with sea-wind, walking together through a mist beaded with raindrops, losing ourselves in the grey sweep of sea and sky, laughing as we took shelter from the suddenly slanting rain, running back along the cliff path, giddy with freedom and laughter, to doze on the sofa before a busy tea-time fire.

There were three evenings that could go on forever, until we chose to end them, and which led us warmly, gently, to love and sleep and the new morning. It was the best time, the special time, so good that there was bitterness at its ending, for those three perfect days had shown us too clearly how all the days of our lives could have been, and we were no longer satisfied.

He startled me badly a few days later by striding into my house in the middle of the afternoon.

'Nicholas! Good heavens! – anyone could have been here.'

'Mrs Marworth said not, and I've told her to say you're not at home to anybody else. I was thinking of you. I was there, in Millergate, at the saddler's, and I thought why the devil shouldn't I see you? Why the devil

593

shouldn't I? Give me a kiss, Faith – I've got all of five minutes.'

And so it continued.

'Faith – are you there? I'm just up from the Piece Hall, and I was thinking of you. Come here – closer than that – ten minutes, that's all.'

Until one day, at the perilous hour of tea-time, he strode into my drawing-room, his arms lifting me roughly from the ground.

'I was thinking of you – badly. And why the devil not? I've got half an hour, Faith. Come to bed.'

'Nicholas.'

'Yes, in the afternoon. Scandalous – your Mrs Marworth thinks so too, I expect, but she's ready to stand in your doorway and say you're gone to Leeds, should anyone want to know.'

And I went upstairs, laughing, and locked my door, undressed myself slowly as he lay on my bed, allowing him time to see how the late autumn sunshine, slanting through the chinks in my curtains, dappled my bare skin. I was, I think, half shocked, half excited – since no decent woman made love in the daytime except in Scarborough – and perhaps that in itself was exciting, for, leaning over him, pouring myself against him, I was full of a wicked, tantalizing playfulness that became at its conclusion the purring content of a slumbrously stretching cat.

I watched him dress, loving him, adoring the hardness, the darkness of him, a body that would take on weight perhaps in middle life, as his father's was beginning to do, but which now was wide at the shoulder, narrow in the hips, his stomach taut and flat, beautiful. And sitting down at the bedside, his hands finding me beneath the covers, he said, 'Why don't you stay here, in bed, until I come back tonight?'

'My word, what a sultan you are! You'd like that, wouldn't you, thinking of me lying here all day, ready and waiting for you?'

'I would,' he said, his eyes narrowing, his hands touching me again, awakening so easily the tremor, the faintly expanding glow that was the beginning of wanting him. 'Yes, I'd like that, Faith. By God, I would!'

And although it was a joke – or so I imagined – I was obliged to take him seriously enough on the afternoon when, having accompanied my mother on a shopping expedition to Leeds, I returned, parcel laden, to be told by a smug Mrs Marworth that 'the gentleman' had called.

'Oh dear,' I said, no more than that, disappointed but not seriously alarmed until he strode in, late that night, his jaw tight, his whole body crackling with the anger everybody at Lawcroft Mills had learned to dread.

'Nicholas – darling –'

'Don't make excuses,' he snarled, throwing his hat viciously on to a chairback, although I had made no attempt to do so, having done nothing, I believed, which required it. 'You could at least be here, couldn't you, when I call? That's all I ask. I don't ask you to come to me, do I? I don't ask you to walk up that damned rutted back road, night after night, from the Swan – no, I do that little job myself. I don't ask you to get out of a warm bed in the middle of the night and ride five miles in the rain – well, do I? I don't ask you to snatch every chance you can to get to Millergate and then be obliged to go away again, like as not, because your sister, or some other damned interfering female has got here before me. I just ask you to be here. Can't you do that much for me? Aren't I worth that much? And what else have you to do? Where the hell were you, in any case? In Leeds with your mother. Splendid, Faith – just splendid. All right – I won't trouble you again in the daytime. I'll make a bloody appointment if you like – or I won't come at all.'

And after that my days became, each one, a small earth-tremor of anxiety, shooing callers away from my tea-table before they wished to go, hovering always within sound of the window and the door, refusing, adamantly, nervously sometimes, to go out unless I had first made Nicholas aware of it.

'Oh no, mamma. I don't want to go into town today. No, I am not as bad as Celia – it is simply that I am not inclined.'

'Good heavens, Prudence! If you need a new bonnet I imagine you may choose it without me.'

'Celia – I never expected you to come today, in this weather. I imagine you will not be staying long? Oh – Jonas is to collect you on his way from the office. Well, you had best have your bonnet on ready, for he is always in a great rush.'

And if it was Thursday, market-day at the Piece Hall, and the likelihood of Nicholas in town, I would be on tenterhooks until she had gone away.

I saw no one else. Blaize, who represented my greatest danger, was abroad that Autumn, Aunt Verity in Bournemouth, my uncle joining her whenever he could, which in Nicholas's view could not be often enough. Caroline was occupied with the building of a new servants' wing at Listonby, Georgiana – although I quite deliberately did not think of Georgiana – was rarely in Cullingford during the hunting season. Prudence, blessedly, was busying herself with the progress of Mayor Agbrigg's reservoirs, her attention being diverted from me by such considerations as the transporting of so tricky a substance as water the twenty-five mountainous miles from its sadly porous resting place at Cracknell Bridge to Simon Street. My mother was making ready to embark on her new life as Mrs Daniel Adair, Aunt Hannah intent on preventing it if she could, and, if not, of devising some other way in which Oldroyd wealth – anybody's wealth – might be channelled to Jonas.

Yet there were other dangers besides discovery, not least among them being Nicholas's inability to tolerate frustration, the headstrong, possibly ruthless side of his nature which was fast making him a force to be reckoned with in the textile trade, but which caused him to howl with the rage of a maddened bull sometimes, when it became too clear to him that he could never organize his personal life as logically and conveniently as his weaving sheds. In the world of commerce Nicholas did not walk around obstacles, he smashed them, flattened them, got rid of them one way or another, and if he hurt his own iron fist in the process then he would have allowed for it in advance, made sure that the price would be right. But in the world of personal relationships, the complex tangle of feelings and demands and recriminations, the conventions which governed us, the decencies we were forced to observe, irritated him, goaded him often to recklessness.

'I don't want to leave you tonight, Faith. Why should I? I could stay until morning – couldn't I? – and go to the mill from here.'

'No, you couldn't. Not in your evening clothes.'

'Christ – it won't do, Faith. It's not enough – is it? Well, is it?'

But always – because I was not ready to talk of his wife and his son, because it was too soon, and I was afraid in any case of how I would feel when I faced the reality of it, afraid of the questions I would ask and of his replies – I would hush him, smooth the moment away, pour the length of my body against the length of his to distract him from the future, filling his mind only with me, as I was at that one, irreplaceable, fleeting moment.

And when I had pushed the forbidden images of his domesticity away, I was left to consider the appalling possibility that I might conceive a child I would be able to explain to no one.

Yet, on the first occasion I was obliged to make Nicholas aware that I was not enceinte, his immediate reaction puzzled me. He would be relieved, surely, I had thought; but I had forgotten the solid Law Valley belief that a pregnant woman is a docile woman, who will cling to the father of her child forever – or for as long as he finds convenient – and I was surprised when he pressed the palm of his hand against my stomach and said, 'If it should happen, you know, it wouldn't be the end of the world.'

'It would be the end of mine.'

'Thank you, Faith.'

'Heavens, Nicholas – for what?'

'For telling me you don't want to have my child.'

I took his wrist in the tips of my fingers and moved his hand away, got up, angry and very hurt, striving to push away from my memory the image of Georgiana's spent face, her thin, exhausted body after her son – Nicholas's son – was born, my own terrible hesitation before I had taken Gervase in my arms, my fear, on returning him to his cradle, that I had injured him.

'I wish you hadn't said that to me, Nicholas.'

'Yes, so do I.'

And then, standing behind me, his arms around me, his mouth against my ear: 'I'm sorry. You're quite right to be put out. I am unjust. I am ill-tempered. Anything you like. I love you, you see. I want all of you, and it sours me, sometimes – You'll have to put up with it. But if it happened, Faith – and it's only sense to admit that it could – yes, I know, by rights, we'd have to call it a disaster. But don't be afraid of it. You can trust me, I reckon, to look after you. Can't you?'

'Of course.'

'I'd take you away from here,' he said decidedly. 'Your mother would have to know, but I could fix her. She could go abroad with you until it was over – not that I'd care who knew about it, but I know you couldn't take the scandal and I wouldn't expose you to it. I'd get you a house somewhere and set you up in style. I know you've got money of your own, but I wouldn't want you to use it. To tell you the truth, I sometimes think it would suit me better if you had no money at all. Don't worry, love, I'd look after you.'

But what he really meant was: 'You'd belong to me then. You'd *have* to belong to me, for nobody else would want you'; and, although it was what the purely female part of me craved for, I had a cooler, more rational side to my nature which was unwilling to be so close confined. He would get me a house, a splendid one I had no doubt, but where? Far enough, certainly, from a suspicious, hostile Cullingford; too far for his lightning afternoon visits, too far to leave his horse at the Swan and walk to me those three or four nights a week that now formed the basis of my existence. A secret house where I would bring up a secret child in luxurious solitude, nourishing myself on his visits, with nothing else to do but wait for him, dreading, as I grew older, that eventually he would not come. And, although I loved him enough for that, and did nothing but wait for him in any case, I was still to some extent in control of my life. I might never avail myself of it, but I still had the possibility of choice, and change.

'Am I completely selfish, Faith?'

'Oh yes – but so am I. I expect I would make a prisoner of you too, if I could.'

'Is that what you feel – that I want to imprison you?'

'Yes – I feel that.'

'Christ!' he said. 'You'll have to forgive me, but I believe you're right. All I can promise is that I'll try not to torment you with it – I'll try.'

But the promise, as I suppose we both knew, was in vain, his jealousy proving so acute, so all-consuming, that it often passed beyond reassurance, beyond reason, to a point where nothing less than my actual imprisonment could have given him ease.

'Nicholas – it can only mean you don't trust me?'

'God knows what it means. All I know is I can't help it and I can't stand it. A moment comes in the day – or in the night – when I feel – Christ! – I feel bereft. And when that happens I have to see you, and more often than not I have to make you suffer for it. I know, believe me, how much I hurt you. And what eats into me then is wondering how long you'll put up with it. Please – Faith?'

And, knowing what he wanted me to say, I said it quickly, lovingly, and went on saying it until his need – for that day at least – was over.

'I love you, Nicholas, I understand. It doesn't matter.'

We returned to Scarborough in November, four days this time, shortened from the week he had intended by the exigencies of his combing machines.

'I'm making money,' he told me as we sat by the happily crackling fire, my head on his shoulder. 'My own money, Faith. And I can't tell you what that means to me. I could live easy, for the rest of my life, on what comes out of Lawcroft and Tarn Edge and Low Cross. My father has fixed them up so well that I wouldn't have to change a thing. I could just saunter down there two or three times a week – when he's gone – to interview my managers, which is as much as I reckon Blaize means to do, and the boost they've had from my father would see me through. Well, Blaize may be content to live like that, with nothing to show for himself but another man's money in his pocket. But not me. I said I could do it and I'm doing it. The Woolcomber is mine and it's growing, and I've got plans for Lawcroft and Tarn Edge as well, if my father could just bring himself to trust me or take himself off to Bournemouth and leave me alone.'

'But he's in Bournemouth now, surely most of the time?'

'Oh yes. But he keeps coming back again. One morning my door opens, or I walk into a shed or into the counting-house, and there he is, going through the ledgers, checking up on me. And I've got to admit that the questions he asks are the very ones I'd rather not answer. Eyes in the back of his head, my father – unless, of course, he's had a word or two with Blaize the night before.'

'Does Blaize really know what goes on?'

'Aye,' Nicholas said, chuckling into my hair. 'Blaize knows. It's his money, love, same as mine – the Tarn Edge part of it at any rate – and he don't mind getting his hands dirty when it comes to counting it.'

Perfect days, once again, soon over – too precious to waste by talking of an impossible future – and on my return I was embroiled at once in the fierce opposition to my mother's marriage, which would take place, she declared, at Christmas time.

Celia invited Prudence and myself to dine, a council of war which would have been uncomfortable enough without the tensions of Celia's table. And, after a perfectly served but none too ample meal, Celia's anxieties as a hostess being for the spotlessness of her silver, the perfect arrangement of her plates and dishes rather than the food, we returned to her drawing-room to discuss what might be done.

My sister, need it be said, allowed no tobacco anywhere in her house, obliging Jonas to step outside if he wished to smoke an after-dinner cigar, complaining fretfully on his return that the noxious fumes still clinging to his coat were more than her carpet, her damask wall-covering and her stomach could be expected to tolerate.

'Well,' she said, quickly inspecting the coffee-tray from which I knew we would be foolish to expect more than one cup. 'So here you are Jonas.'

'Yes, Celia.'

'Good – since we are all awaiting your wisdom, and the coffee has gone quite cold while we were about it.'

But Jonas, aware that her habit of measuring out exactly so many coffee beans and no more from her store-cupboards disallowed the ordering of a fresh pot, merely accepted his lukewarm cup and drank it quite slowly, disinclined, it seemed, for wisdom.

'And what have you to tell us, Jonas?'

'Not a great deal.'

'Then I have something to tell all of you. It strikes me you are taking this matter very calmly – so calmly, in fact, that I wonder if my mother is even aware of the repugnancy everyone, absolutely everyone, must feel. She has always been inclined to make herself conspicuous, ever since my father died. And this marriage – Well, she can only have one reason for it – you must know what I mean. Yes, of course you do, and although I don't like to speak of such matters, especially in the hearing of a single woman – Goodness, it is disgusting at her age – at any age.'

'You mean she is in love with him?'

'If that is what you like to call it. No doubt she calls it by that name. I believe there is another.'

'Passion,' Prudence said tartly, irritated as always by Celia's assumption that at twenty-five she must by virtue of her single status be as blindly and totally innocent as Celia herself had been at sixteen.

'Really, Prudence.'

'Really, Celia. I may be without direct experience, but my eyesight is keen enough. I washed and changed dozens of cholera victims during the epidemic and it did not escape my notice that not a few of the girls brought in from the streets – all of them unmarried, some of them too young to be married – were in various stages of pregnancy. I am also aware that in certain areas of our town one may obtain the sexual services of an eight-year-old child, should one be so inclined. Such a child was brought to Faith's door one night, while her husband was alive, somewhat in need of repair. If you don't wish to believe me, Faith will confirm the truth of it.'

'No, she will not,' Celia said, her face frozen, as my father's had often been, into a mask of complete composure, her whole manner suppressing not only the brutality but the sheer untidiness of back-street lust, of any kind of lust. 'If such things exist, then I have no reason to know about them, and neither have you. There is nothing like that in Albert Place, nor in Blenheim Lane. And we have met tonight because we have a real problem to discuss. Jonas – what are we to do about my mother?'

He smiled very slightly, amusement in him being always faint, a little obscure, since one could never be quite certain of just what, or who, had amused him.

'I have already told you, Celia,' he said, his long, pale eyes occupied with the immaculate, empty cup in his hand, 'not a great deal. Your mother is a mature woman in indisputable possession of her fortune. And since there is nothing in our legal system to prevent a widow from remarrying, nor to restrict her choice of husband within the correct degree of kinship, there is nothing to be done on that score. You may not approve of passion, Celia, but it is not yet a criminal offence in our society, nor does it provide just cause for the detention of its victims in an asylum. Admittedly, in certain cases, one may regret that it does not – but it does not. You cannot *forbid* your mother. It did occur to me, however, that it might be possible to *frighten* her, by providing evidence that Mr Adair is not a proper person.'

'Which assuredly he is not.'

'Not in your view, Celia, nor in mine. But my investigations revealed nothing which would be likely to alarm your mother. His background, of course, is very humble, which once again is hardly a criminal matter – even though he is brazen enough to let it show – and in fact his very vulgarity has saved him from certain situations, certain legal ties, which would otherwise have delivered him into our hands. He was married for the first time in Ireland as a young man, but the union was in common-law only – which means, in effect, that they announced their intention of living together and did so – and the woman is dead now in any case, the children adult and dispersed. He has a few debts, but his creditors, very sensibly, have agreed to wait until he is married for settlement, and no one is dunning him. He has no criminal convictions for fraud or theft or anything else – by which I mean he has never been caught. There is a woman in the West Indies, certainly – we have young Liam Adair to show for that – but she is too far away to make a fuss or attempt to claim her rights. Their marriage will not have been legal in any case, and at least he has relieved her of the expense of bringing up the child – a rather gallant action, one could almost say, for a common man. There was an entanglement, some years ago, with a married woman – almost on our doorstep it seems – but it was quickly hushed up. And I believe your mother may already know about that.'

I knew about it too and remembering my mother's vivid face as she made her confession – 'those few months I spent as his mistress were the most luminous of my life' – I found myself unable to meet Jonas's cool gaze, wondering, most uncomfortably, *how* he knew, what else he knew, convincing myself, with a surge of panic, that nothing would be likely to escape him for long.

'You have been very busy, Jonas,' Prudence said, and, smiling again with that faintly malicious amusement, he told her, 'Yes, indeed. Where money is concerned I think you may trust me to do everything one can.'

'So I have always believed.'

'Quite so. And in this case it has also been done in your best interests, as well as the interests of my wife. I am as sorry as anyone else that I could find neither a useful scandal nor the prospect of exposure as a criminal to use against him. The only other method left open to us would be to offer to buy him off, which, in view of the healthy state of your mother's finances, could hardly succeed. And there is always the risk in such negotiations that he would take our money and marry her just the same.'

'Then what is to be done?'

'I have already given my opinion. What do you think, Faith?'

And, with Nicholas's face filling my mind, I said incautiously, 'I think – since she cares for him and we cannot prevent it – that we should leave her in peace.'

'Oh yes,' Celia burst out, 'Of course you would take that view, Faith, for I have never known you when your head was not in the clouds. And it is all very well for you to talk so, when you have a house and an income of your own, and no children to consider. Well, I have no children either, not yet, but Dr Blackstone assures me that there is every likelihood – In fact, since Prudence is so well informed on these matters, I may as well tell you I am expecting again, or so it seems, which gives me every good reason for disliking the idea of that man setting himself up in Blenheim Lane. Oh yes, you may depend upon it, he will take advantage of my mother's foolish generosity. He will spend every penny she has on himself and that ill-mannered child, and any other children he may have hidden away somewhere. And if that does not alarm you – since you are so comfortable already – then you should give some thought to Prudence, who will be obliged to live with him.'

'Not for one moment longer than she must,' Prudence said tersely, and Jonas, looking at her from beneath his heavy, crafty eyelids, gave her a deliberate and very sarcastic smile.

'Indeed?' he said. 'Then I take it we are soon to congratulate you on your forthcoming marriage?'

'I see no reason for that.'

'I see every reason.'

'Well, I hope you do not,' Celia cut in, growing petulant, having tired herself out with her emotions and the fatigue of preparing even this small family dinner-party. 'For, if you are thinking of marrying Freddy Hobhouse merely for the sake of convenience, then I must tell you it would not be convenient at all. Aunt Hannah was here yesterday, and the day before, warning me that you might do that very thing – as if she imagined I could do anything to prevent you – and I am bound to admit she is quite right. Nethercoats would eat up your money in a trice. If Freddy has encouraged you to believe he stands to inherit from his uncle, Mr Oldroyd, then Aunt Hannah says you must bear in mind that he has nine brothers and four sisters. Freddy's portion would not be so splendid, and the inheritance is by no means certain. My word, when I think that my mother could have had it all.'

'You are quite mistaken, Celia,' Prudence informed her coolly. 'I have no intention of marrying Freddy Hobhouse, either for his convenience or mine. I would not insult him nor any other man in that way.'

'Then you will never escape from Blenheim Lane,' Jonas said, a certain bleakness, I thought, in his eyes, an indication that he, too, had not forgotten the loss of Fieldhead Mills and would be unlikely to forgive my mother for it.

'I cannot agree, Jonas.'

'Eventually you will be forced to agree. You are a financial prisoner, my dear, which is the most complete captivity there is. I am in agreement with my wife when she says Mr Adair's cash requirements are likely to be heavy. I think you may safely assume that your mother will not allow you a penny – nothing, at least, beyond the strict necessities of ribbons and toilet-waters and the clothing suitable for a "daughter-at-home". And without money, dear Prudence, believe me – yes, believe me – there is no freedom and no dignity either.'

'Jonas –' I said, glancing at Celia, fearing that he would expose himself too far for her comfort, that his bitterness might wound her. But she was gazing down at her hands, barely listening to him, and, getting up, he walked irritably across the room and stood, one narrow hand on the mantelpiece, looking down at the meagre fire.

'You may talk splendidly of independence, Prudence,' he said. 'But ask yourself – how are you to afford it? Do you have in your possession at this moment even the train-fare to Leeds? And if you had, what could you do there? There is no employment you could possibly take. Employment, for ladies of your station, does not exist. And, if it did, you have no training, nor are there any establishments for females in which training could be obtained. Dear Prudence – you have told me all this yourself many a time. If you have a choice in life at all, then it is simply this – you must either marry a young man like Freddy Hobhouse, who would be easy enough for a clever woman like you to handle, or you must marry an old one like his uncle, Mr Oldroyd, in which case you would be a widow – and a comfortable one – that much the sooner.'

'Must I?' she said through her teeth. 'Must I really?' And it was Celia, oblivious to the undertones of Jonas's voice, hearing nothing but the surface, who broke through what might have been an all-too-revealing altercation.

'Well,' she said. 'I am not so clever, but I can think of another solution. You could come and live here with us, Prudence, for, if I am to start a family at last, both my mother and Mr Adair would be bound to see that I could make use of you. And, since you are always talking about education and how none of us have any idea of bringing up children, you would enjoy busying yourself with mine.'

I returned home, the matter by no means resolved, bringing Prudence with me since Nicholas had left that afternoon for Liverpool. And as she settled herself in front of my cosily flaming fire – since I had not acquired Celia's habits of economy – she said, her eyes as bleak as Jonas's, 'I cannot tell you how much Celia's house, and Celia's life, oppresses me.'

'Yes – but I don't think she is unhappy. Jonas is not satisfied – which may be very clear to you, and to me – but Celia seems unaware of it. She appears to have what *she* wants from her marriage, at any rate.'

'So she does – which may be because she has no more conception of what marriage should really be than he has – except that she is a hopeless case, and perhaps if Aunt Hannah had let him alone he could have been different.'

'And what should marriage really be like, in your opinion, Prudence?'

She smiled. 'Yes, of course, you are about to tell me that I know nothing about it and you are quite right. I merely base my judgment on the marriages I see around me, and none of them fill me with envy. Perhaps I have been single too long. If father had lived, I would have had little to say in the matter. He would have chosen some worthy man for me before I had left my teens, and I would now be making the best of it like everybody else. But I have been free for some years now, Faith, and nothing tempts me to change.'

'You means *no one* tempts you to change. There *are* happy marriages, Prue.'

'Where? Show me. I can think of happy individuals, some of which are married, but it strikes me that in every marriage there is one partner who dominates, one who submits, and I should not like to do either. I can't think it necessary, or right, to do either. Our mother and father lived in peace because she submitted in every way to his will and to his opinions. Mayor Agbrigg lives in peace with Aunt Hannah by stealth – oh yes, he does – by allowing her to have her way so often that when, just occasionally, he does something his way she hardly notices. She dominates and uses and despises him. Jonas tolerates and despises Celia. I don't wish to run the risk of that.'

'Yes, but both Mayor Agbrigg and Jonas married for money. Celia married because she wanted to be married. Aunt Hannah – I don't know – because she thought she could make something of Mayor Agbrigg, and knew she could make something of Jonas.'

'Exactly – because she wanted to do something with her life and, being a woman, could only do it through a man. That is what Aunt Hannah settled for – second-hand glory. I'm not ready to do that. It wouldn't be enough for me to push a man into building an empire. It wouldn't satisfy me to have a clever son and to feed myself on his triumphs. I'm willing to do the work and accept the responsibility – like Aunt Hannah does – but I want the credit as well. I'm not prepared to stand in any man's shadow – at least, not simply by virtue of the fact that he's a man and I'm a woman who shouldn't make herself conspicuous.'

'Not even if you loved him?'

'Faith – I thought we were talking about marriage? I'm not sure about love either. Uncle Joel and Aunt Verity are in love, I suppose, He demands every instant of her time and attention, which she gives him very willingly, as you did with Giles. It seems to make her very happy – and you were not miserable – but I'm not sure I could cope with such total devotion. It occurs to me that I might come to see it as just another kind of captivity. Giles loved you, I know, but he didn't *share* the realities of his life with you, Faith.'

And suddenly, sickeningly aware of the coffin I had refused to look at, the grave I still tended so carefully, knowing it to be empty, I cried out, 'He didn't even share his death with me.'

'Oh – darling – I'm so sorry. I shouldn't have said that. I didn't mean –'

'I know what you meant. He shielded me from life as if I'd been a child. I know it. That was what he wanted, Prudence – and I would have given him anything he'd asked for.'

'I know,' she murmured, looking away from me. 'And I used to wonder how long you could continue to take the strain. It would have stifled me, I know it, very soon.'

'No. I loved it. I needed it. I was safe with him.'

'Good,' she said, her crisp tone instantly drying up the source of my approaching tears. 'Obviously I am not looking for safety. Perhaps I had better find myself a missionary, since at least they have no objection to working their wives, very often to death. Perhaps that would suit me better than sitting at my embroidery in the drawing-room at Nethercoats, listening to Freddy telling me not to worry that the mill is collapsing because he will always take care of me – or sitting at Fieldhead waiting for Mr Oldroyd to die.'

And, swayed by this mood of confidence, and because the need had been growing in me for weeks, because Prudence had shared everything else with me and I couldn't bear to be alone with this any longer, I fixed my eyes on the fire and said very quietly, 'Prudence – for the past six months I have been Nicholas Barforth's mistress.'

'Have you?' she said, no more than that, her voice blending quite naturally with the stirring of the logs, the ticking of the clock; and, as I turned sharply to look at her, she shook her head and smiled, amused by my astonishment.

'Well, and what did you expect me to say? What do you want me to say? I am hardly likely to congratulate you. And you surely don't need to be told you are the biggest fool in Creation.'

'No. You can safely assume I know that.'

'And you couldn't imagine – or expect – that I would assist you or allow myself to be used as an alibi?'

'No. I don't expect it and wouldn't ask.'

'Well, then – am I to urge you to break off with him?'

'No. I won't do that.'

'I imagine you will be obliged to, eventually – but we won't go into that. Are you feeling guilty on account of Giles and Georgiana, and want me to scourge your conscience?'

'Not even that. I manage very well for myself on that score.'

'Yes, I can well believe you might. What do you want, then? You realize, of course, that if you are caught you will have to leave the district in disgrace, whereas he will not. And if you are not caught – well, dear, I wouldn't care to grow old, sitting at this window, waiting for him to come a-calling whenever he can spare a moment or two away from his combing machines, and his wife. Why have you told me, Faith? You must know my character well enough to realize that I wouldn't be prepared to sit here and listen to the tale of how marvellous he is, repeated over and over, to ease your conscience and your loneliness? Faith – what are you hoping for?'

'Nothing,' I told her, knowing she would believe me, knowing, very fully now, that it was true. 'I love him, that's all. That is what I am – a woman who loves Nicholas Barforth. That is all there is to me.'

'How gratifying that must be,' she said, 'for him, at any rate. Poor Nicholas, it must be so very difficult for him now, being obliged to continue his married life – and, of course, he does continue it, for, if he had stopped sharing a bed with Georgiana, the maids at Tarn Edge would have been quick to spread the word.'

And as I gasped at the blow she went on smiling at me as Aunt Hannah had once done, ruthless in the administration of what she hoped might be a cure.

'But you will have thought about that many a time, I would imagine, on the nights he cannot be with you. Certainly it would prey very much on my mind, in your place. But don't worry, darling, for it may not be such a bad thing after all. There is always the possibility that she might conceive another child and die of it.'

'Prudence!' I cried out, aghast, terrified now in case a time would ever come when I could hope for her death – or admit to myself that I could – and, slapping one hand decisively against the other, a schoolmistress calling me to order, she said, 'Let us look at things as they are. He married her. No one expected that the marriage would succeed – or could succeed. But he loved her enough, not so long ago, to break your heart on her account. He could very easily do so again. And if he does not abandon you – either because he has had his fill or because someone forces him to do so, or even because his conscience stirs him to admit that he is doing you immense harm – then what else have you to hope for but her death?'

I bent forward, my head touching my knees, and after a moment she came to sit beside me and slid her cool hand in mine.

'Poor Faith. You are the last person in the world I would wish to hurt.'

'I know. Don't worry about me, Prue, for I am neither stupid nor helpless. He is what I choose to make of my life for as long as I can, and you mustn't blame him for that. It seems very unlikely to me that I could love anyone else – not now. It seems to be a requirement of my nature that I should love him, and I will just have to cope with it. If hard things are said of me – later – I would not expect you to defend me.'

'That, my dear,' she said, her fingers tightening around mine, 'would hardly be for you to decide. I would defend you or not as I chose, just as you are now choosing to put yourself in a position which could require it. Faith – all our lives someone has been telling us what to do, what to say, what to think, and even if it had been done from a sincere desire to protect us, which I doubt, it was always intolerable to me. And I wonder, truly, what credit there is in doing right if one has never been allowed the opportunity to do wrong? I am sick of petty tyranny, Faith. I want freedom for myself – the freedom to make my own mistakes, to make a stand and declare that what is right for you, or anyone else, need not be right for me – and so how can I deny the same thing to you? I have never greatly cared for Nicholas Barforth, but what right have I to say you are wrong to love him? I could not live as you do, nor feel as you feel, but what right have I to forbid you to feel it? I think you are bound to suffer for this and harm others with you, but, if you are prepared for that suffering, what right have I to say you must not? If this is what you choose to do, and can accept the consequences, then do it. I believe you are wrong, but you will not forfeit my affection. I merely hope that you will survive and be given the opportunity to choose better next time.'

But there could be no next time. There could be Nicholas, and I could not see beyond him. Nor did I make the attempt, for he had possessed the whole of me, and I wanted no part of myself back from him. Yet I could not sleep that night, irritated by the thin whimpering of an early December wind, and by morning I knew that I must reserve some small measure of independence, that I must, against the urging of my own nature, retain an area of my life that belonged only to myself, a foundation, however slight, on which to build – whatever I had left in me to build – when it was over.

20

My mother was married on a white winter morning, a swansdown sky streaked faintly with pink, the crackle of new snow underfoot, the parish church dusty and cool in its emptiness, since only Prudence and myself and Jonas sat on the bride's side of the aisle, a quartet of Adairs, fresh from Ireland, occupying the other.

She wore blue velvet, carried a huge white fur muff, and there was a white feather in her hat, a rapturous satisfaction in her cloudy blue eyes. She was marrying the man with whom she was perhaps no longer quite so romantically in love, but whom she most ardently desired. And I could see no reason why he, with his roguish Irish eyes and his rogue's charm, should not desire her too.

'I am going to be so very happy,' she told us, tripping out into the churchyard. 'My word, what a lovely day! Every day is going to be lovely from now on. I will tell you something, Faith dear – it is going to be strawberries and champagne every moment. Yes, as a girl I *did* so long for my strawberries and champagne. And now – you will know what I mean. Perfect content.'

But only our ageing governess, Miss Mayfield, who with young Liam Adair tugging at her hand could count on many years of employment yet, seemed wholeheartedly to agree.

They were to go to London, making no promises to return until the New Year, and, waving them off at the station, I think I was more than ever aware of approaching change, that this Christmas time – this season of sentiment and goodwill, this family festival – would be difficult and dangerous.

Aunt Verity, just back from Bournemouth, called to take tea and to inquire about my mother's wedding, her smile as sweet as it had ever been, sensing no treachery, no awareness that she was face to face with adultery, the mistress of her much-loved son.

'You will come to us, dearest, on Christmas Day afternoon,' she said. 'Caroline has promised me an hour, which is very generous, and Georgiana does not go to Galton until Boxing Day. We are not going to Listonby until the New Year, for your Uncle has not been well and I think we had best be rather quiet. But we shall look forward to seeing you. Faith – it has been much too long.'

And because I could not hide from them forever, because sooner or later I would have to take Georgiana's hand and smile, with Nicholas looking on – because only Aunt Verity's absence had enabled me to delay this long – I chose not to fall ill that Christmas morning, as I might have intended, and sent Prudence a note that I would share her carriage.

There was the usual splendid pine-tree in the hall at Tarn Edge, the lamps already lit in the drawing-room, a mountain of logs blazing and singing in the hearth, their tangy odour blending with the tea-time muffins, the drift of Barforth cigars that had scented all the Christmases of my childhood. Aunt Verity's home, warm and easy, when mine had been cold and difficult. Nicholas, even then, being the hope I brought with me, the memory I took away. And, pausing a moment in the doorway, watching them, my uncle at ease in his armchair, his legs stretched out to the fire, Caroline opposite him in the matching chair, enthroned as became her station, Georgiana sprawled on the sofa, looking out of the window, wishing herself already at the Abbey, I wondered who suspected me, knew, with a surge of blessed relief, that no one did, until a head turned, a pair of smoke-grey eyes flickered over me, and Blaize came across the room to kiss my hand.

'Blaize, how lovely to see you. Caroline – it's been an age, *Georgiana*, how are you?'

And these, I knew, were the bones of adultery, my treacherous hand-clasp, the false smile I gave her as she sighed and stirred herself listlessly to greet me, the criminal ease with which I nodded, through the firelight, to her husband – my lover – and inquired, 'How are you, Nicholas?' as if I had forgotten his dark head on my pillow just a few hours ago. And worse than that – far worse – was the pleasure it gave me to see that she was not looking her best, that boredom, as always, had taken her colour away, that her pointed face, without its vivacity, was quite plain.

'I make her so miserable,' he had told me, and seeing that she was indeed miserable – whether on his account or for lack of the open moorland of Galton – I was obliged to struggle with myself fiercely, to strangle the beginnings of delight, of a most evil-hearted gratitude.

There was a toddling, black-eyed Dominic Chard now to swell the family circle, and his not quite identical brother Noel; a slightly smaller but exceedingly determined Gideon Chard, needing frequently to be restrained. There was an agile little demon called Gervase Barforth, climbing on every chair-back, attempting to mount the fender until his father – my lover – removed him by the scruff of the neck, called out 'Georgiana', and, when she took no notice, strode across the room and dropped the protesting little boy into her lap.

'Can't you do something with that child, Georgiana?'

'Oh', she said, her green eyes only half open, 'What is there to do? I could drown him, I suppose – although it would seem rather a waste of my initial effort.'

'One rings for nanny, surely, at such times?' Blaize murmured, stepping easily – as he so often did – to her rescue. 'Even a poor bachelor like myself knows that much.'

'Faith!' Caroline called out, visibly shuddering at the piercing quality of her nephew's howls as he was carried away. 'Come and sit over here with me. You have been playing the recluse lately and I have started to wonder why. There is no admirer, I suppose, that we have not yet heard about.'

'Why no, Caroline – what an idea!'

'That is exactly what I said to Matthew, when Aunt Hannah inquired. Faith would have told *me*, I said, – didn't I, Matthew? Well, you will come to us for three weeks in February – I am quite set on it. My new servants' wing is quite finished, and I should enjoy your opinion.'

And, anchored to Caroline's side, her interest in her own affairs claiming the whole of mine, I was spared the necessity of talking to anyone else. She had been down to London in November to watch the funeral of the Duke of Wellington, a gentleman who would not be much mourned in Cullingford, since, like Sir Giles Flood and probably Sir Matthew Chard, he had not wished to extend the vote to commercial men. But Caroline had been impressed by the ceremony of his departure, the muffled drums, the military bands playing their dirges, the magnificent black and gold funeral car bearing the coffin draped in crimson velvet, the hero's sword and marshal's baton, his white-plumed hat, set out upon it. She had been touched by the sight of the Duke's poor old horse following on behind, his empty boots hanging, reversed, from an empty saddle; but, rather more to the point, she had made the acquaintance of a certain Lady Henrietta Stone, a woman of decided fashion with a house in Belgravia, who was bringing a party to Listonby at the beginning of March.

'You had best stay on with me for that too,' she said. 'For Hetty Stone is really very smart – city smart, not county smart – and I shall be obliged to put myself out for her a little. And you could cast a glance at my wardrobe, Faith, if you wouldn't mind, for I have brought some new evening gowns back with me from London, and there is something not quite right about them. I told Matthew you would be able to spot it instantly.'

Tea was served quite magnificently. We ate, drank, smiled, made Christmas promises of companionship, solidarity – 'We must see more of one another – my word, how time slips away – do you remember, when was it? Five years ago? Impossible' – and as Aunt Hannah and Caroline began to stir themselves and cast meaning glances at their husbands, both ladies having numerous other demands on their time, the ordeal seemed almost at an end.

'Well, all the best to you,' Aunt Hannah said, getting to her feet.

'Aye,' Sir Joel answered her. 'We'll take a glass of wine, before you go, Hannah, and drink to what we've had, and what's to come. Well then, here's health and happiness to all of you, may you all prosper. Here's to old friends and absent friends and new beginnings – not forgetting our little Elinor.'

And, as we toasted each other, warmed by the easy emotions of the season, Georgina, who had taken a brooding glass or two already, got up from the sofa and swayed forward towards Nicholas, stumbling against him as the trailing hem of her gown caught against the fender, her hair a burnished, beautiful copper in the firelight.

'Oh, dear!' she said. 'Oh, yes – we must drink to that – new beginnings – and forgiving each other our trespasses. Dear Nicky, do forgive me my trespasses, although I expect I shall trespass again.'

And because I couldn't look at Nicholas, I turned my head away and found Blaize's smoky, quizzical eyes watching me.

My mother returned home in February, 'a cat', Prudence called her, 'sitting in a cream-pot', and immediately the resentments that had been so far held in check came bubbling to the surface when it was seen that Mr Adair had every intention of playing not only the devoted husband but the fond, somewhat over-zealous step-papa.

'Family life,' he said, beaming at us as we gathered around my mother's dinner-table – his dinner-table now. 'I never realized, Elinor, in my wandering days, how much I was missing. And here it all is – my little boy and your lovely girls, you and me – there's nothing to beat it, and nothing to beat us, so long as we stick together.'

In his urgent desire to be respectable, to be accepted, Prudence was forced to play a most unwilling part. Gone now were the days when she could eat a solitary breakfast in her own room, spending as long as she liked in perusing the letters and papers brought up on her breakfast tray. Now she was required to eat every meal *en famille*, sharing her news and her correspondence with a jovial but very determined Mr Adair, an easy-going rascal transformed overnight, it seemed, into a patriarch who considered it his duty to watch over his womenfolk, to know at all times their exact whereabouts and their intentions, what they were doing and with whom. Gone now the days when my mother's carriage, more often than not, was at Prudence's disposal, when she had merely to say, 'I'm off now, mamma. I'll be back presently'; for the horses, these days, were in Mr Adair's gift, and he was not generous in their disposal.

'And just where is it you're off to, m'darling?'

'I have visits to pay.'

But young ladies, in Mr Adair's scheme of things, paid no visits that did not include the chaperonage of a mother, did not – most decidedly – concern themselves with reservoirs and the resettlement of unemployed wool-combers. Young ladies were young ladies, motionless and sweet as lilies, proving by their constant presence at their mother's side that they were the products of a happy home, content to share that home with a new, enthusiastic father.

And since 'sticking-together' was very much in Mr Adair's best interests, I soon found my own freedom invaded in a way I had not expected, my time eaten away by 'family teas', 'family dinners', 'family Sundays', in which at my mother's urgent request I was invariably included.

'Just do this for me, darling', she would implore. 'Just let me get settled – I'm so happy'; and since her personal happiness was beyond question, an effervescent fountain of it sparkling in her eyes, her laughter, the eagerness of her whole dainty body – because there was something achingly young and vulnerable in her face, which could not fail to move me – I submitted afresh to the captivity of that drawing-room, my father's black basalt urns still on the mantelpiece, his fragile china figurines still there, in their glass-fronted seclusion, but the whole house fragrant now with Daniel Adair's almost continual cigar, loud with the hearty male presence no Aycliffe had ever possessed, cluttered – as we had never dared to clutter it – by the playthings and the playmates of an untidy six-year-old child. And when Prudence, appalled by the discovery of scratches on the panelling, fearful for her porcelain, inquired of my mother how she could tolerate the antics of young Liam Adair, the answer, with a blissful, languorous smile was, 'Ah – you see, dear, he reminds me of his father.'

I did not believe that Mr Adair intended us any harm, at least not if it could be avoided, for he was a man who took pleasure in women and would have preferred, if possible, to be fond of us and have us fond of him in our turn. But self-interest had long been not only a habit with him but a necessity, and, like any other ageing yet still powerful stallion, he was unwilling to see two well-dowered mares depart from his herd to squander themselves elsewhere.

Like Jonas he could not marry us himself – would not have wished to marry us, since my mother sufficed him gloriously as a wife – but our possessions tantalized him, challenged him, and before long, or so it seemed to us, the Irish Sea was thronging with hopeful Adairs, coming at the summons of their clan-chieftain to the marriage-market.

'Oh dear!' my mother told me, bursting in on me unannounced, to my immense consternation. 'I am afraid Prudence is very vexed, for the house is full again and she declares she is about to take herself off to Aunt Hannah's until they have all gone away, since Daniel has made it very clear he does not approve of her staying here alone with you. Do talk to her, Faith, for they are Daniel's relations, after all – my relations now – and I wish she would not be so sharp. I am sure there was no reason for her to slap Liam, this morning – at least, not so hard – when he picked up that Meissen bowl from the hall table. My goodness, the poor child was just curious to see what was written underneath, for which she was entirely to blame since she had been telling him everything was marked on the underside with the maker's name. Yes, I know the porcelain is hers, but she cannot take it away until she is married, and to box the child's ears so violently was certainly extreme. After all, nothing had been broken, and now she is talking of packing the whole collection away in boxes and storing it in the attic, which I feel sure Daniel will not allow. Indeed, he is the master of the house now. It is *his* attic and if he tells her she may not use it I am sure one must consider him to be in the right. And, since the porcelain attracts so much notice and everybody knows how much it is worth, what would people think should it not be on display? It would cause nothing but gossip and spite. Do talk to her, Faith, for I live in dread of a confrontation between them. I am not quite ready for it yet. Do explain to her that I am really so very happy –'

But my mother's happiness in no way consoled Prudence for the loss of her own freedom.

'The porcelain is mine,' she told me hotly. 'My father spent fifty years of his life collecting it, and if Mr Adair wishes to display it to his friends then he had best keep that little monster under control. Miss Mayfield can do nothing with him, but I am not so delicate, and if I find him just once again playing near the cabinets he will have cause to remember it. So – we have another cousin from Kildare, just arrived this morning. A fine young gentleman, something of a scholar we are told, and so he may be except that he has not yet pronounced a word in my hearing that I could understand. Delightful don't you think? I am to be denied the company of my own friends and forced into his. When Freddy Hobhouse called this morning no one informed me of it. He was told I was not at home and sent away. And I am by no means certain that all of my letters are delivered. How dare he, Faith? Truly – how *dare* he? Well, they are bringing the Kildare cousin to meet *you* later this afternoon, so you had best beware. Perhaps he is to be offered the choice between us, and he will certainly pick you, since you are better-looking and richer.'

And, inwardly trembling, I rushed to Mrs Marworth and begged her to be on the look-out for Nicholas, to warn him, explain to him, to tell me at once if he had seemed put out, if there was any hope of seeing him again that day.

I could not avoid Caroline's invitation to Listonby, enduring three weeks of gruelling activity, gnawing anxiety, since Nicholas had first asked me to cancel, then ordered it, then tried to coax it out of me, and, failing that, had spent a terrible and totally unreasonable hour declaring me flighty and unfeeling, a giddy butterfly like my mother, incapable of denying myself a moment's entertainment.

'If you can do without me for three weeks, then I reckon you can do without me altogether. Of course you must go to Listonby, darling. I perfectly understand it. There's no telling who you might meet there. By God, there isn't! You could even come back with a Matthew Chard of your own. And who am I to stand in the way of that? He might not marry you, of course, but then neither can I. And they say a change does everybody good.'

I should have defended myself, of course, should have grown angry, told him to leave and take his poor opinion of me, and his injustice, away with him; but I threw my arms around him instead and held him, the whole of my body pleading with his, until the rage of his jealousy had subsided.

'I'm sorry.'

'I know.'

'I say things in temper, do things in temper –'

'Yes, I know that too – like the day you wouldn't get on Cullingford's first train.'

'Christ! I'd forgotten about that.'

'I've never forgotten anything you've ever done – at least, the things I know about.'

'She'll have her house full of young sparks from London, Faith, who'll see you as fair game – who'll think that's what she's invited you for. And it maddens me that I have to let that happen. It wouldn't happen if they knew you belonged to me.'

'It won't happen in any case. I love you, Nicholas.'

611

'I'll ride over when I can. It's a big house, and knowing the gentry they'll all be doing the same thing.'

'Not if Caroline catches them. Nicholas – would it be safe?'

'You don't want me? If that's it, then say so.'

'That's not it, Nicholas – you know it couldn't be. It's Caroline. You know she never misses a thing and – and Georgiana is almost certain to ride over.'

'I know,' he said, his jaw set and strained. 'And shall I tell you something? I don't care. I mean it, Faith – I don't care. Oh yes – I should care. I know I'm in the wrong. I'm the criminal – not you, not Georgiana. *I'm* the adulterer. *I'm* the fool. It was my mistake that brought us to this – not yours, not hers. I know. Well – it makes no bloody difference, because I won't accept it. I might get hurt, and so might you. It's the chance I'm taking, and you'll have to take it with me.'

And, after this explosion, Caroline's hectic house was for the first day or two almost a refuge.

I had no reason to believe her other than perfectly happy – for she would have said so otherwise – her relationship with her husband having a definite physical aspect, despite her streak of prudishness, both of them enjoying, I thought, a hard day's work, a hard day's sport, followed by an uncomplicated, energetic bedding about which no one could ever had induced her to say a word. Sir Matthew rose, invariably, at first light, breakfasting, every hunting morning, on slices of red beef and raw eggs beaten up in brandy, which would see him through the excitements of the day. The gentlemen would then set off, not too early – since a fox, being a night-feeder, is sluggish at daybreak, and provides no sport – returning triumphant, ardent, sometimes very frisky, but rarely before dinner-time. And, preoccupied with what she considered as her side of their bargain, her guests, her children, the domestic details and dramas of her tenants, the new servants' wing her father's generosity had enabled her to build, I doubt if Caroline gave him a thought before then.

Like all the Barforths it was her belief that, if one took the trouble to do anything at all, one should do it splendidly, and her new wing – which she showed me the very hour of my arrival – was built in two sections, allowing not only a most efficient grouping of related employments, but a segregation of the sexes. The original servants' hall had been much extended, a giant buffer now between the butler's domain on the left, the housekeeper's on the right, the butler's pantry being surrounded by all the requisite offices where menservants were likely to be found, capacious wine cellars and beer cellars, the plate scullery, the room for the polishing of boots, the room for the polishing of knives, the room where lamps were cleaned and filled, the strong room, the gun-room, the door – in full view of the butler's eagle eye – which led to the single bedrooms where the footmen and valets and assorted, or visiting, menservants slept.

The housekeeper's room was similarly surrounded, by still-room and linen-room, the room where the Listonby china was carefully catalogued and stored, a narrow passage leading to the vast kitchen area where the head chef, whose artistic temperament required a certain degree of privacy, had a small sitting-room for his own use, giving him easy access to the pastry-room, the game larder, the fish larder, the meat larder, and the bakehouse where Listonby's daily bread gave a permanent spicy fragrance to the air.

There was another passage, narrow and dark this time, leading to the steamier fragrances of the laundry-room and ironing-room, where cheerful, sturdy girls worked, rather more bare-armed and bare-bosomed than Caroline liked, at their washtubs and mangles, singing to attract the attention of the stable-boys – or so Caroline thought – as they carried their baskets of linen outside to dry.

And in this complicated, busy household – where Caroline, I felt certain, knew the contents of every cupboard, was as precisely aware of the cost of anything and everything from a full-scale banquet to the replacing of a chipped cup – I was able to lose, temporarily, the keen edge of my anxieties, living from the ceremony of breakfast, the savoury-laden sideboard, the somnolence of newspapers and gossip in the Great Hall afterwards, to the more elaborate rituals of luncheon and five o'clock tea, the ultimate complexity that was dinner. I busied myself in changing my clothes as the occasion and the weather required, flirted mildly with a visiting, non-hunting gentleman or two, talked personalities, dress fabrics, fashionable philosophies with visiting ladies, walked to church with Caroline on Sunday mornings, watching with affectionate amusement as she acknowledged the salutations of her tenantry, the deference of her parson, the slap she administered with her gloves to her children and to her husband when the sermon inclined Sir Matthew to doze, the future Sir Dominic, the future colonel of Hussars, and little Gideon, the future bishop, to misbehave.

Nicholas did not come but quite soon Georgiana appeared, riding over from Galton to join the hunt, vivid and outrageous as she always was in the company of her own people, astonishing those young sparks Nicholas had feared on my account by her daring and endurance in the saddle, her sudden flights of fancy that ended, to Caroline's intense disgust, in a midnight steeplechase from Listonby church tower to Galton church tower, no holds barred, no quarter given, no farmyards and no fences spared, with champagne in the Abbey cloister for the survivors, a great deal of splashing in the Abbey stream, and Peregrine Clevedon discovered in such flagrantly promiscuous circumstances with one of Caroline's married, decidedly tipsy, female guests that my cousin could not be persuaded to overlook it.

'But it's just Perry,' Georgiana explained. 'He's like that, Caroline. He won the race, after all, and you must admit the woman was willing. Matthew – do make her understand.'

But Sir Matthew had taken the measure of his Caroline by now and, shrugging his heavy, lazy shoulders rather apologetically, not only submitted to her judgment but saw that it was carried out. The lady was asked to take her departure. Mr Peregrine Clevedon, who had committed his misdemeanour on his own property, not Caroline's, was severely reprimanded, and for the next day or two Caroline patrolled her guests with the air of a good governess who has every intention of keeping her class in order, a procedure which, rather than giving offence, appeared to provide considerable amusement.

I returned to Millergate exhausted, aching for Nicholas, yet it was Mr Adair, my mother's lover not my own, who came first to welcome me home, his bright black eyes roving merrily around me, shrewd eyes and a shrewd brain behind them, a man experienced in the ways of the world, who, I was quick to realize, could be another threat to me.

'So you're home again, my lovely girl – that's good, since home is where you belong – except that I know how your mother is breaking her heart to have you back in her own nest again. It's not safe, she thinks, for a bonny young thing like yourself to be living here all alone. Fretting she is, which I don't like to see – but there now, what was it I came for? Yes indeed, you're expected at dinner tonight – and she said, now what was it? Yes – Sunday, some little trip she's planning. We'll collect you mid-morning.'

I went to Scarborough again in May, but this time, because Mr Adair had raised a quizzical eyebrow at my explanation of visiting an old acquaintance in York – a friend, it had pained me to add, of my late husband – I was tense throughout the journey, exhausted on arrival, almost sick with nerves when Nicholas, who should have been there to greet me, arrived late. And, instead of the magical days of escape we had planned, we found ourselves compelled at last to admit that there could be no escape, and that one of us, or both of us, would be required to make a sacrifice.

He had a wife and child who might mean little to him just then, but he had a thriving business which mattered a great deal and anchored him firmly to Cullingford. Could he sacrifice that, and possibly his share of the Barforth mills with it for my sake, and start again somewhere else? I had a family who would not easily let me go. I felt love for one sister, a growing feeling of responsibility for my mother and Celia. I had a reputation for which I cared only spasmodically, but of which the loss would be damaging to others. Could I leave them all behind and creep away somewhere to the cloistered existence of a kept woman, a cherished prisoner? Yes, Nicholas, told me, I could. If I loved him, I couldn't hesitate.

But could I forget how Georgiana had flung herself against him that Christmas Day, offering reconciliation, or how wretched she often appeared lately, her spirits and her colour fading, as his temper grew shorter? Yes, he told me. She was his responsibility, not mine. He was the adulterer. His was the guilt and the blame, and his shoulders were broad enough.

Could I ignore the simple, honest truth that so long as I remained in his life there was no hope of peace for any of us? I knew better than to ask him that. But spring is a cruel time for the making of such decisions, an impossible time, and Nicholas refused to be thwarted in any case.

'If Dan Adair suspects you, then he suspects you,' he said bluntly.

614

'And if he comes sniffing around Lawcroft asking me to buy his silence, or around Millergate trying to blackmail you into going back to your mother, then I'll flatten him, and I reckon he ought to know that. I can't see what he'd have to gain by going to my wife or my father, but if he did I'm not even sure I'd give a damn. My father can throw me out of Lawcroft and Tarn Edge but he can't shift me from the Wool-combers, and if Perry Clevedon took it into his head to shoot me I could change his mind with pound notes. It would suit Blaize, at any rate.'

And although the greater part of his nature would have gloried in announcing his possession of me to our narrow world – 'This is my woman and be damned to the lot of you' – I knew beyond the slightest shadow of doubt that, if he lost his share of the Barforth mills to Blaize, a day would surely dawn when he would most bitterly regret it.

The summer drained me that year, shredded my nerves and evaporated my spirit, for, my own anxieties apart, I seemed the constant prey of all those who had cause to complain of my mother, so that I felt besieged day in day out, by Aunt Hannah, who required to know when we could expect my mother's jewellery to go up for auction and then her petticoats; by Prudence, who in her own intense frustration had no thought for mine; by the Irish cousins; by Daniel Adair, whose plans for me were every bit as specific as for my sister; and not least of all by Celia, whose fast developing pregnancy, she felt, was not attracting its share of notice.

'Faith – you will never believe what Jonas has done to me. He has invited the Battershaws to dine. Yes, I know they are among his best clients and we have dined twice with them since Christmas, but how am I to manage? Oh yes – I can order the meal and see that everything is spotless and perfectly tidy, but Jonas should understand that I cannot be *looked at* in my condition.'

'Celia, there is nothing yet to show.'

'No, but I get so fatigued, Faith, by dinner-time, and then the maids are quite likely to bring out smeared glasses and chipped plates unless I make sure of it, and cook is so unreliable about timing, I don't see how I can be expected to sit there with a smile on my face and chat. You must come and do it for me.'

I did, Jonas taking advantage of my presence, I thought, to include our Member of Parliament, Mr Fielding, and his political agent in the party, gentlemen whose good offices would be needed should he decide to embark on a parliamentary career of his own. And so it happened that when Celia, who had quite genuinely worn herself out by a day-long flurry of cleaning and polishing, retired to bed soon after the meal, I remained in Albert Place very late, chatting pleasantly to two gentlemen I had no wish to impress – and so impressed rather easily – and to Jonas himself, who relaxed almost to humanity without the presence of his wife and his mother.

He escorted me home afterwards, a quite natural courtesy, stepped into my hall a moment to thank me, since I had put myself out for his sake, and although the house was perfectly silent, Mrs Marworth's smile

615

quite bland – and although Nicholas had been warned well in advance of my plans – no one could have failed to identify the odour of tobacco betraying a male presence behind my drawing-room door.

'Mrs Marworth –' I gasped, desperately seeking help from anyone, but, having no help to give me, she had already disappeared down the corridor, leaving me with my horrified guilt, and my brother-in-law.

'Jonas –' I said, just his name, bowing my head, I think, as if for execution, since he would be well within his rights to demand the identity of my caller. When I raised it again, I couldn't read the expression – my sentence – in his clever, lawyer's face, had no idea at all what his faint smile might mean.

'Yes, Faith. Thank you for your help this evening. I will leave you, now that I have seen you safely bestowed. Goodnight.'

'Oh Jonas – my goodness!'

And, incredibly, he shrugged his narrow shoulders and touched me, very lightly, with a cool fingertip.

'Good-night. There is nothing for you to be concerned about – except that I believe one of your chimneys may be smoking, and you should attend to it. Celia will be very glad to see you, I expect, should you care to call tomorrow.'

Yet, although he did not betray me, gave no indication when I saw him again that he had observed anything amiss, exerted no pressure on my movements or my activities, the mere fact of his knowledge weighed upon me, burdened me.

An endless summer, hot days, a yellow sky hanging low over Millergate, heavy days spiced with a whisper of faraway excitements, since, in exotic lands I could scarcely imagine, the Tsar of Russia had invaded the territory of his brother monarch, the Sultan of an ailing Turkey, an event in which – for reasons I was slow to understand – we seemed likely to become involved. We could not, of course – or so a dozen people told me – tolerate the presence of Russian aggressors so near to India; but the truth was that we, the greatest military nation in the world, the conquerors of Napoleon, had been at peace for almost forty years now, and even in Cullingford a great many men were eager to hear the beat of martial drums, to show the Russian giant, the Austrian giant, any giant at all, that we had lost none of our vigour. And I found it easier, at tea-time, at dinner-time, at the concert hall and the Assembly Rooms, to ponder the fate of such unlikely places as Constantinople, Sebastopol, the Crimea, than my own.

'There's nothing else for it. We've got to fight them,' Sir Matthew Chard declared, with no more idea than I as to where the Crimea might be found.

'Aye,' Sir Joel Barforth answered him. 'Fight them, and I'll sell you the uniform cloth to do it in.'

'Will it make any difference, Nicholas?' I asked, and he told me, 'No. I almost wish it would.'

I went to Scarborough, most dangerously in June and August, not daring to step out of the garden for fear of the summer crowds; twice in

September, a hunted animal at my arrival and my departure, a few feverish days in between, immense fatigue at my homecoming, a dry-mouthed panic until my first encounter with Daniel Adair, with Aunt Hannah, with Jonas, reassured me that I had not been caught. I became dangerously, uncharacteristically emotional, prone to unexplained tears and sudden bursts of laughter. Loud noises startled me, flickering evening shadows loomed out at me, distorted into fearsome shapes that caused my stomach to lurch, my heart to beat in the wild palpitations to which my robust body was not accustomed. When my sister Celia, who had spent at least half of her pregnancy in bed, gave birth to a daughter that July – Miss Grace Cecilia Agbrigg, a silken little creature with a curl or two of dark hair and enormous liquid eyes – I wept unrestrainedly at my first sight of her, wept when I was asked to be her godmother, stood throughout her christening with tears seeping from my eye-corners, ruining the lace ribbons of my bonnet. There were long nights when sleep would not come at all, other nights of fitful dozing threaded by terrible dreams of myself hurrying through mean streets, a glimpse of Giles Ashburn in a doorway, nothing but an empty room when I ran frantically inside, his figure in the distance, the beloved quietness of him shredding away to mist the instant before I reached his side. A sick tortuous wandering in the dark, a sudden jolting to wakefulness and the certain knowledge that, although my love for Nicholas was deeper and more intense than ever, a change of some kind would have to be made.

A change. Yet, having told myself that I must make it, that it *must* be done, having rehearsed the reasons until they became welded to my brain and gave me no rest, I was unprepared both for the nature and the manner of it when it came.

He arrived very late, the second night of October, restless, ill-tempered, I thought at first, disinclined for conversation, barely listening to the few remarks I made. And then, blunt as he always was in moments of emotion, he snapped out, 'I had better to tell you, before you hear it from someone else. Georgiana is pregnant again.'

'I see.'

'No,' he said, taking me by the elbows, squeezing hard. 'You don't see.'

But I would have none of that, pulling away from him, hurting myself, putting as much distance between us as my tiny drawing-room allowed.

'There is no reason to make excuses to me, Nicholas, because you have – because you have made love to your wife.'

'You knew it,' he said. 'If you were married, you'd have had to do the same. You knew that I was obliged –'

'No. I know no such thing. Be honest with me, Nicholas – that's about all there is left now. When it happened – whenever, how often – you wanted it. Don't insult me, and – just don't insult any of us by pretending otherwise. And don't tell me your reasons – don't – they have nothing to do with me. I'm not angry, Nicholas. I have no right to be angry. Just allow me – a moment or two.'

I stood with my back towards him, willing him to keep his distance, knowing – whatever I really felt, whether I had it in me to endure this, to weather it, or not – that I must not endure it, that I must use it as a wedge to force us apart. And even in that first moment of shock I remembered Prudence telling me, 'She may conceive another child and die of it'; and I knew that that alone was sufficient reason for our separation. I did not want her to die. I must continue not to want it, for, if it should happen and I had the slightest cause to suspect myself, I knew I could not live with it, could certainly never live with Nicholas.

'Nicholas –' I said, and crossing the room he took me by the shoulders, carefully, as if he feared to damage the remnant that was left to us; and even that, I knew, was slipping fast away.

'Don't say it, Faith. You don't want to cause her pain, and neither do I – God dammit, I don't hate her. The child is mine and I'll look after it, as I'll look after the other one – and her. For the rest of my life I'll support her, in style, so she can go on supporting her brother. I'll patch up her Abbey and pay out whatever it costs to keep her land in good order and her brother out of jail. But I won't lose you, Faith. I'll be patient with her now, I'll keep my temper and indulge her whims and fancies until this is safely over. But I won't lose you. I won't throw you away for the sake of the Clevedons. Believe me.'

But it was over. I mourned him all night, dry-eyed, my whole body aching, despairing. I mourned him the next day, my real self locked away weeping and desperate, while the cool shell of my Aycliffe self-control served tea to Aunt Hannah and Prudence, listened and smiled as my mother told me of yet another Irish cousin, and that she was very happy. I mourned him the night that followed and the one after, came downstairs before dawn to wander in sheer desolation from room to room, a burden to myself, which I could not lay down.

It was over; and, when he came the fifth night and rapped a stubborn hand on my window, it was still over. I opened the door to him because it did not occur to me to do otherwise; and, when he came into my parlour, I made some anxious comment about the state of him, since he had walked up from the Swan in the rain. But it was still over.

'You can ask me to leave,' he said. 'I didn't go the first time and I won't go now.'

'Yes, you will.'

'Do you really mean to turn me out in the rain?'

'Yes, I do.' And I believed it.

'Then do it, for I've got nothing to offer you but trouble – I know it. I know all the answers. I'd tell any other man in my position to pull himself together and get over it. I can't.'

He stayed in my bed until morning, a risk we had never taken before. As I let him out through the kitchen before Mrs Marworth was awake, he held both my hands and kissed them, kissed my ears and my chin and the nape of my neck, unfastened my nightgown and kissed my bare shoulders, reckless and heedless, pressing my body hard against the cold, tiled wall.

'I love you, Faith. Do you believe me?'

I believed him.

'We're all right again now, Faith.'

But I could not believe that.

21

I would never go to Scarborough again, at least not until Georgiana's condition was resolved one way or the other, for she had miscarried before, might miscarry again, and, false and treacherous as I was, I wanted him to be with her if she did so.

But by November he had quarrelled with Blaize and with his father, had narrowly averted a strike at Lawcroft for which his own intolerance, his own autocratic temper – Blaize insisted – had been to blame. He was tense and miserable, dreading, as I was, the approaching Christmas season when family festivities would draw us all too close together. We had much to discuss, having parted already a second time, being well aware that we were teetering on the brink of a third separation, and, although our reconciliations seemed powerful enough to propel us from one crisis to the next, we must surely one day reach our limits.

And so I risked myself once again on that solitary journey, Mrs Marworth accompanying me to Leeds, well content with the steady supply of Barforth guineas in her pocket, my happy excitement of earlier times transformed now into a kind of sad determination, since this visit could well – *should* be – my last.

It was a grey afternoon, a high wind churning the sea, the steep little town quite empty as I was driven through it, the house empty too, only the housekeeper standing discreetly in the doorway, telling me, as always, that there was a fire in the parlour, a fire in Mr Barforth's bedroom, muffins for tea. But of Mr Barforth himself she couldn't say, for she was paid merely to make his mistress comfortable, not keep her informed of his comings and goings.

'Muffins?' she said, clearly having reached her own limits, and so I took off my gloves and my fur-lined, hooded cloak, and ate muffins and indifferent gingerbread, poured tea for the sake of giving myself an occupation, and left it on the tray to go cold.

'Dinner,' she told me, 'in an hour, madam, if it's convenient.' And, since it was convenient for her, I went up to the bedroom that contained the most poignant of my memories, allowed the fisherman's daughter they were training as a maid to get out the new gown I always brought with me, a light aquamarine this time, cut low to display the strands of gold filigree Nicholas had given me and which I could only wear here without need for explanations. I brushed and dressed my hair, put his pearl and diamond drops in my ears, his heavily coiling gold snake with its topaz eye around my arm, perfumed my shoulders, threw a lace-edged Cashmere shawl around them, and went down to dine, realizing that, while I had been dressing, the moment had come and gone when he could possibly reach me tonight.

'Crab, madam – fresh-caught this morning,' the placid, disinterested woman told me, meaning perhaps, 'He has jilted you, madam – well, isn't it always the way?'; for she had been with the Barforths a long time and had seen their women come and go.

But there could be a dozen explanations. Simple things, like the destruction of Lawcroft Mills by fire, things I could live with, like strikes and floods and damaged machinery, which had nothing to do with Georgiana. And whatever had happened there would be no way to send me word.

I slept alone, bitter cold all night, listening to the wind – listening for Nicholas – breakfasted alone before a roaring fire, eating heartily of the smoked haddock and creamed eggs because the woman was mildly curious now as to whether or not I might be broken-hearted. And afterwards I went out into the raw November wind, walking as far as I dared – taking the chance we always took that there would be no one here at this season – until I felt as grey and chilled as the weather, could have whined as dolefully as the grey air irritating the surface of the sea.

It was an omen. Nothing had ever kept him away before. I had drifted, as always, allowed my emotions, not my reason, to make my decisions, had in fact made no decisions at all, and now – having known for a long time exactly what I had to do – I had left it too long. Events, other people's decisions, had overtaken me. And even now, although I knew very definitely that he would not come and that I should return home at once to discover the reason, I doubted if I would do it. I would most likely stay here, waiting for him, as I had waited these past eighteen months, as I had waited all my life, straining my ears for the sound of his arrival, telling myself 'Just a little longer. Surely a little longer can do no harm?'

But as I walked back to the house something quickened my step, some impression of activity as I opened the door that caused my stomach to lurch hopefully, eagerly, the unmistakable fragrance of cigar-smoke reaching me as I entered the hall, offering me yet another reprieve.

'Is Mr Barforth here?' I called out.

'Yes, madam, in the drawing-room,' the woman replied, and my joyful, giddy feet took me through the door and half-way across the room before I stopped, comic, I suppose, with shock, and realized it was Blaize.

'I *am* Mr Barforth, after all,' he said. 'My word, Faith, if you mean to faint, then do it gracefully – here, on the sofa, for I have had an abominable journey and hardly feel up to lifting you if you should fall on the floor.'

'Blaize, what on earth –?'

'We'll come to that presently. Yes – yes, I knew you were here. I have come on my brother's business, not my own, and he is neither dead nor dying, merely in the very foulest of tempers because events have conspired against him. Really, Faith, you had better sit down.'

I obeyed, arranging myself very carefully, composing my body and my mind, allowing a moment to pass until I could ask just as carefully, 'Did he – send you?'

The smoky eyes twinkled, his face, which had been quite expressionless, coming alive with the brilliance and mischief of his smile.

'Hardly that. Even Nicholas does not imagine himself to be in a position to *send* me anywhere. But he was in such a blind fury when he realized he couldn't get away that I – well, it wasn't difficult to understand that he had a most pressing engagement. I concluded it could only be you.'

'Have you known for long?'

'About you and Nicholas? Well, yes, as it happens, I have. But you needn't worry about that. I'm fairly certain no one else can have access to my source of information. I use this house too, sometimes, and Nicholas was obliged to check his dates with me. I do apologize, Faith. These practical details may sound sordid to you, but there was no other way it could be done. I knew simply that he was meeting someone here, not necessarily the same person every time, but I like to know what goes on around me and I intercepted a glance or two – of agony, I might add, on at least one occasion – between you.

'That's guessing. It's not the same as knowing.'

'No. And so I inquired. Mrs Collins, our housekeeper here, is a good soul and I asked her to describe you. Naturally she shouldn't have done it, since Nicky pays for her discretion just the same as I do, and his money is as good as mine – it can only be that I have a winning way with housekeepers.'

'I daresay. Does Nicholas know you are here?'

'Ah well – I didn't exactly make the offer, nor admit to knowing of any reason why I should. And, since it was not made, he neither accepted nor refused. But I think you may safely assume that he knows.'

'And there is no chance that he may get away after all?'

'I am sure there is not. There was some crisis at the Wool-combers, and in the middle of it my father descended on him in that quiet way of his – like a bolt from the blue – having made the journey from Bournemouth especially to see him, with a list of complaints and suggestions as long as both his arms. He is staying three days, and Nicky would need a cast-iron alibi to get away from him. Fortunately for me, I was in Bournemouth a week ago, to endure my own inquisition, and my presence was not required. Indeed I rather imagine I might have been in the way.'

I looked at the fire for a while, then at the window, the garden, cowering at the approach of winter, noticed, without knowing why I cared, that a light, persistent rain was starting, washed ashore by the changing tide.

'It was very good of you, Blaize, to come so far.'

'Yes, I think so too. You may take it that when I saw him hurl a spanner at one of his own machines, with my father looking on, I grew alarmed. And it would have worried me, I believe so, to think of you sitting here listening for carriage wheels until Monday.

'Luncheon, sir, in half an hour,' the industrious Mrs Collins announced, her dour face crinkling with smiles as he said, 'Excellent. Crab, Mrs Collins? It's what I came for.'

And so once again I ate crab, drank a dry, well-chilled wine, smiled, with the perfect attention of Morgan Aycliffe's daughter, as Blaize talked of this and that and nothing at all, merely filling the spaces between us until it should please him to tell me at least a portion of the truth. For I did not believe he had made this tedious, inconvenient journey merely to deliver a message from Nicholas – he knew I did not believe it – and, understanding something of the subtle by-ways of his nature, I knew too that, whatever it was, it would not be simple and that I would have to take care.

We took coffee and brandy in the drawing-room companionably enough, and when we had exhausted the gossip of our mutual acquaintances – the clock telling me already that I could not leave today even if I chose – he said, 'Forgive me, Faith, I don't mean to pry, but since we are here and the subject is bound to be on our minds – it has been something over a year now, with you and Nicholas, hasn't it?'

'A year and a half, or very nearly.'

And, rather than an embarrassment, it was almost a relief to me that he knew, for although I did not always trust him he was clever and worldly wise, a man whose vision was unclouded by convention and whose opinions in matters, perhaps not of the heart, but of the senses, might be shrewder, certainly better-informed, than my sister's.

'I find that rather long,' he said, warming the brandy glass in his hand. 'Three months might have been delightful. Eighteen months – well, that strikes me as rather extreme. After that kind of eternity it has either become a habit, or one is very much in love. And remembering Nicky's temper yesterday morning, and knowing you as I do – well, I suppose it has to be love.'

'Of course I love him. Good heavens, Blaize! What are you thinking of? Would I put myself in this position if I didn't love him? I may be behaving like a light woman, but I can assure you that I am not.'

He smiled, raised his glass to me.

'I know, my dear. That is one of the reasons I came.'

'And the others?'

'Presently. Give me your reasons first, Faith – for instance, just what are you hoping for?'

'Nothing – as you well know.'

'Well, then – I have no right to say this, of course, but isn't it time you broke off with him?'

'Of course it is.'

'And do you mean to do it?'

'Yes – yes, of course I do. I know I have to do it. I've already done it twice. I intended to do it again last night – tonight – although I might not have managed it. I might have opened my mouth, determined to tell him, and other words would have come out. It's happened often enough before.'

'Even when you know it would be for his own good?'

'Do I know that? He doesn't think so.'

'Of course he doesn't. He wants you. That's more than enough for him. I believe it would have been enough for my father too, in his day. And you must know that a gentleman's code doesn't allow him to break off with a lady, even in these circumstances. I freely admit that such a consideration would carry very little weight with me, but Nicky is rather

622

more honourable than he seems. The break will have to come from you, Faith.'

'I know – I know – I know all the reasons. I know. It's just that, when it comes to it, none of them seem quite strong enough.'

'I see. Then we shall have to find you another reason, shall we not? – something you'd feel quite unable to justify.'

He got up, poured out more coffee, another brandy for himself, stirred the fire, as attentive to his own comforts as a cat, a light, luxurious man who played life's games so exquisitely that I wondered if he could really be of any help to me after all, since to him it might well be the game itself that counted, and the quality of the playing.

'Can you give me such a reason, Blaize?'

'I can try. I can tell you what I see, from my vantage point on the outside, which is often a very good place to be. I know my brother rather well, Faith, and he is not really the man for adultery, you know. It may not trouble his conscience unduly – at least, not more than he can cope with – but he finds it exceedingly irksome just the same. And adultery, if it is to be successful – if it is to be worth the trouble – must be enjoyed. There are men who can be more excited by the challenge and the danger of clandestine meetings than by the woman herself. There are certain undomesticated men – one of them not a million miles away from you – who find the very lightness of it well suited to their natures. For it should be light, and it should be brief. Nicholas is not that kind of man. I might enjoy slipping in through your back door, Faith, but Nicholas doesn't care for it, and unless you put an end to this the day will dawn when he'll surely come striding in through the front and be damned. If he did that, I believe several people would have cause to regret it.'

I had no answer to give him. What answer could there be? And, allowing me a moment's reflection, he said quietly, 'He should have married you in the first place, I think we must all be agreed on that. But he did not. He married that strange little creature whose caprices no longer enchant him – or very rarely, since he is certainly the father of her child. She is difficult, I grant you. But she has an enormous need for affection – something you should be able to understand – and does very badly without it. I realize how badly he wants you, Faith, but I've yet to be convinced that he couldn't do well enough with Georgiana – if there was nothing to prevent it. Yes – yes, I know. You are going to tell me he doesn't love her, and that she doesn't love him, and you could be right. But if he took it into his head to *behave* as if he loved her, she would certainly respond to it. She is as miserable and down-drooping sometimes as a stray dog, and for the same reasons. If he held out his hand she'd gladly come to heel now, I believe. She'd soon begin to effervesce and sparkle again, which would be an encouragement to him, since happiness makes her very enticing. And he may well find it in himself to forgive her her trespasses.'

I swallowed, quite painfully, and leaned forward to the fire, a chill striking me abruptly across the shoulders.

'You really are Georgiana's friend after all, aren't you, Blaize?'

623

'I believe so. I realize you doubted it. She told me, a long time ago, that you had warned her against borrowing my money. There was really no need, you know, I can't think of any circumstances in which I'd be prepared to call the debt in. And, for once in my life, my intentions were of the very best. I thought it might help her to live, not in peace exactly with Nick, since peace is not really in her nature, and it's a dull little thing in any case, but in the kind of harmony that would suit them both. I'm truly sorry to say this to you, Faith, but there have been times, even this past year, when they *could* have approached one another. You saw her yourself on Christmas Day, offering him far more than a reconciliation. And can you be certain that he would not have taken it – and made the best of it – had you not been standing there? *I* can't be certain. Now then – there's the reason I'm offering. Is it strong enough?'

I got up, walked across the room and back again, making my skirts swirl around me, full of bitterness suddenly, and a desire to hurt him – because he was absolutely right – but with no idea at all how I might punish someone so elusive, so self-sufficient, as Blaize.

'It could be strong enough. But then again, you may have made a terrible mistake. A woman will usually sacrifice herself for the man she loves. She might be less willing to sacrifice herself for another woman – even his wife. You have convinced me that she needs him. Can you convince me that he needs her?'

'Oh – as to that,' he said, getting up too and leaning a lazy arm along the mantelpiece. 'Nicky can find other satisfactions. The keynote of his character is ambition, you must know that very well. He will build himself another Barforth empire and be well content with it. Certainly he wants you, but he wants other things as well. His options are many and various. Georgiana has no option at all but to be his wife.'

'Can you see no wrong in her, Blaize?'

'My dear – of course I can. The whole of Cullingford knows her as a most unsatisfactory woman. She can do nothing right for Cullingford. And, if I happen to find some of her faults extremely charming, I'm ready to admit that she can be perverse and wrong-headed, that her judgment of character, particularly the Clevedon character, is unsound and will continually lead her into trouble. But she was looking very frail yesterday morning, cowering away from his anger, although he was not angry with her and didn't pretend to be. Very frail –'

And he had given me the most powerful reason of all.

We walked in the garden for a while then, and afterwards took tea and muffins and a certain apricot preserve for which Blaize declared Mrs Collins was famous, although it had not been offered to me before. I dressed calmly for dinner, the turquoise dress again, the gold chains, the perfume, smiled with frank amusement at the flower-decked table, the scented candlelight, the richness of the sauces – although I was not delighted to see crab again.

'You are quite right, Blaize. You must have a way with housekeepers. Mrs Collins can hardly be making these attempts at *haute cuisine* on my account.'

'No – she is rather fond of me. But I have to admit that I might have done better not to have praised her crab so highly. We may see it tomorrow morning at breakfast-time, I warn you, and I haven't the heart to complain. But the champagne is very nicely chilled, and not too sweet.' And I could have been enchanted – was, on the surface of my mind, enchanted – by the easy flow of his conversation, his accurate assessment that even a woman with a broken heart retains her vanity and can find pleasure in talking about herself.

In the drawing-room there was a branch of candles on a low table, the leaping firelight answering the candle-flame, the lamps remaining unlit in deep pools of shadow, and, as I agreed against all the rules of Cullingford society to take brandy with him, he warmed my glass in his hands, gave it to me very carefully and said, 'You are an incredibly beautiful woman, Faith, you know.'

'I know no such thing. I take a little trouble with my appearance, that's all.'

'Yes, I believe that is what I mean. I think at some time of your life you must have made a deliberate study of yourself, and I admire that enormously. It was Georgiana who called you a swan, wasn't it? – and she was so right. That long neck with an elegant head at the end of it, turning so slowly and staring, sometimes quite arrogantly, just like swans do. Yes, I happen to know it is because you are short-sighted, and that when you look through people in that rather distant way of yours it is because you actually don't see them – but the effect can be quite devastating. And when the light is too strong for you, instead of blinking and squinting like an owl, as most short-sighted people do, you very languorously close your eyes – I have often noticed it. If, once upon a time, you had to sit and practise it in front of your mirror until you got it right, then I salute you for it. And your perfume is very exotic – really – very nice.'

'In fact I am an enchanting creature altogether.'

'So you are. You are your own creation. You were quite plain once, but no one would notice it now.'

'Thank you, Blaize. You have just told me that I am still plain, and that you have found me out.'

'Which is the greatest compliment I can pay, since I am not nearly so handsome myself as I pretend to be.' We laughed, easy with wine and firelight, well satisfied with our own artistry, colleagues almost, so that when he left his chair and came to perch on the sofa beside me – my wide satin skirts requiring him to keep a certain distance – I was not at all worried by him. He had kissed me before; he might well kiss me again; and, like the last time, it would be no more than an exchange of expertise.

'Yes,' he said, those shrewd grey eyes examining me from the high-piled crown of my head to my décolletage and lingering there, at the separation of my breasts, quite openly, the corners of his mouth tilting into a wry smile. 'You understand your own body perfectly in one sense. You know how to adorn it and how to display it to glorious advantage.

You are not even coy with it. You know I am looking and you allow me to look, quite calmly. You knew in advance that I would be bound to look and would not have uncovered your shoulders had you not felt, even secretly, that you deserve it. I like that attitude too. I am only sorry you haven't yet understood another facet of your nature which seems very clear to me. What would you do if I touched you, Faith?'

'Well, I wouldn't scream for Mrs Collins, who certainly wouldn't help me in any case. But what is this facet of my nature I haven't understood?'

His eyes brushed over me once again, very much amused this time. 'Not yet. Tell me something first. How do you see yourself, Faith – no, not the swansdown and the velvet ribbons of you – yourself?'

'I don't,' I told him, stretching myself a little on the sofa, my posture far too relaxed for good manners, seeing all this as no more than one of his sophisticated, complex games. 'I don't see myself at all. I don't do anything so positive as that. I drift, Blaize. I just float on a lake – like a swan, I suppose, if there is a muddle-headed variety. When the sun shines I fluff out my feathers, and when it doesn't I try to weather the storms. I don't know where I'm going any more than a swan does – except that a swan, I believe, takes a mate for life, and I seem unlikely to do that, the way things are turning out.'

He smiled. 'It will surprise you, then, to be told that in my view you could be a very sensual woman – which must make you unique in Cullingford.'

'Blaize – good heavens! – I don't even know what that means. You are calling me wanton, I suppose.'

'Certainly not. I have encountered wantons in plenty, and it is not at all the same. Wantons will give themselves for a variety of reasons, but rarely for the pleasure of the giving, and the taking. I'm suggesting to you, Faith dear, that you have – or might have – a capacity for that particular kind of giving and taking for its own sake. And that is rare in women – or at any rate I have met it very seldom. But – and I am forced to heave a sigh over it – you are a lady. And because sensuality, as we all know, is not ladylike, you have confused it with romance. You must be madly, wildly in love – or think that you are – in order to give yourself, and you are gaining nothing by it, Faith, nothing at all. In fact you are refusing to acknowledge what could be the most satisfying part of your nature.'

'Blaize, really –'

'Faith – definitely. You love Nicholas and so you may give yourself to him. You lose Nicholas and so your life as a woman is at an end. You believe that no one else could ever rouse you to passion or to pleasure, because you could love no one else. I wonder if the swan believes the same when it loses its mate and sits all forlorn on the riverbank for the rest of its life? It would sadden me if you were to do that, Faith.'

I sat up, straight-backed, angry, uneasy with him for the first time in my life.

'I don't wish to continue this conversation, Blaize.'

'Of course you don't. It's not a proper conversation at all. But the fact that we are here alone together is not proper either. You may relax again, Faith, you know, for I didn't come here intending to seduce you. Not that I wouldn't enjoy it – my word, I'd take you south, I think, to some secret little Italian garden, so you could uncover those splendid shoulders for me all day long in the sunshine. And afterwards we'd still be friends.'

'Blaize –'

'Yes – so we would. But then, you couldn't be stirred by me, or any other man, could you, because we are not Nicholas. And if you *could* be stirred a little, you'd have to fight it, wouldn't you – just as hard as ever you could – because then you'd have to wonder whether you'd loved him quite so desperately after all.'

'Blaize, I shall be angry with you in a minute.'

'You'd do far better to come to bed with me. Now that would be a strong reason – you'd never bring yourself to face Nicholas again after that, you know.'

And because it was preposterous and shocking and because it was true – I leaned my head on the back of the sofa and laughed weakly, a shade tearfully, considerably astonished, beginning to wonder about the part of myself that could understand his sophiscated logic, that could mould itself so easily into his atmosphere. And I wondered, too, what had happened to the part of me that should have been scandalized, should have had a fit of the vapours and demanded to be taken home.

'You wouldn't care for it, Blaize – I'd be far too horrified at myself to be a satisfactory companion.'

'Yes,' he said. 'I know. What a pity.' And leaning towards me he touched the side of my head and my ear, the gesture of smoothing out a stray ringlet I had seen him make to Georgiana, although I knew that not so much as a single hair of *my* chignon could be out of place.

'Yes – truly – what a pity, Faith. You'd feel obliged to hate yourself, and me, afterwards. I know that very well, darling, and I won't tease you any longer. It's just that – well, you may call me a frivolous man if you like, but surely these grand passions don't remain at fever-heat forever? Not unless one nurtures them. And I wonder, my dear, if you might feel obliged to do that too? The same thing applies to what I told you about taking another lover. If one recovers from a grand passion, then was it really so very grand in the first place? Perhaps one could have resisted it – should have resisted it. Might it be more convenient not to recover at all? Believe me, I can perfectly understand how a middle-class lady may feel compelled to cling to her illusions. And now – since you are beginning to dislike me, and those lovely shoulders of yours are starting to prey on my mind – perhaps we should say good-night.'

I got up very calmly and moved towards the door, feeling that I was walking through water, forcing my way through slow but irresistible currents, a sea-weed tangle of impressions and emotions I would need time to unravel. But he reached the door before me, opened it, handed me the branch of bedtime candles on the hall table, bowed very slightly, his smile in no way unkind.

627

'Dear Faith,' he said, 'you have not had quite so desperate a day as you expected. You could even have enjoyed my company if you had put your mind to it. And that should be an encouragement to you, since we are agreed that I am not unique and irreplaceable, like Nicholas. Perhaps I would admit it to no one else, but there are hundreds of men like me.'

22

I set off for Cullingford the next morning at some risk to myself, since I had no real explanations for so early a return, but no accusations awaited me, merely a hastily scrawled note from Nicholas saying he had been despatched to London by his father on urgent business and would be perhaps a week away. And I sat with the letter in my hands for a long time, cradling it, since it was the first I had ever received, and then, again with that strange sensation of walking through slow-rippling water, I went to the fire and burned it, not for reasons of safety but as a test of my own courage.

I had a week then, in which to permit myself the luxury of remaining, if only in spirit, his mistress; a week before I would stand here and dismiss him. And this time I could not say, 'I love you, but it is for your good', since I had said that before and neither of us had believed it. This time I would have to say, 'It is for my good. I'm weary of it. I don't wish to continue'; and, although I didn't believe that either, I must contrive somehow or other to convince *him*.

I no longer chose to dwell on it. I wished simply to *do* it, freeing my mind for the torment that would come after. There could be no more swan-drifting, and if, after all, I found myself marooned in some desolate marshland of the spirit, I would take myself and my grieving elsewhere, so that he, at least, could get on with his life. I would go abroad, perhaps, and take Prudence with me, whatever anyone had to say. For, if I was strong enough to separate myself willingly from the man I loved, whose possessive, autocratic nature would neither accept my reasons nor forgive me, then I could make short work of a dozen Daniel Adairs.

Yet, as often before, I had waited too long, and when Aunt Hannah walked through my door, the third day after my return, perhaps, before she had even taken off her bonnet, I knew it.

'No,' she said. 'Do not trouble yourself to offer me tea. You have troubles enough without that, my girl, and what I have to say to you will not accord with tea-cups and bread and butter. In fact it may well take your appetite clean away – and I confess to you that I have none.'

'Aunt Hannah – what on earth is the matter?'

'You may well ask,' she said, her back so straight that she could have had a poker inside her bodice, her expression confusing me, since, beneath the self-righteous anger which I was accustomed to see in her, lay something else which could just possibly be satisfaction, a certain smugness that some opinion, some guess of hers, had proved correct, presenting her with yet another opportunity of getting her way.

'Is it – my mother?'

'No dear,' she said, arranging her skirts very deliberately, smiling the blank bright smile of social occasions, the one she used before demolishing the clamour of some rebellious committee, the smile, indeed, which she had offered me long ago, before forcing me from my damp fog of mourning for Giles. 'Your mother is as well as one could expect her to be. She is in love, you see, which seems endemic at certain seasons. As her daughter you should understand it. In fact you, have been so bright-eyed and blooming at times, and so jumpy and droopy at others lately, that I could be forgiven for imagining you to be in love yourself. Can you tell me that I am mistaken?'

And, as often seems to happen when one faces the impossible, when one knows oneself overtaken by the ultimate disaster, I experienced no shock, no desperation, only a strange acceptance that may properly belong to the dying, and said quite calmly. 'What do you want from me, Aunt Hannah?'

'Nothing, dear. I am not even sure I shall wish to know you for very much longer. Well, Faith, you were always a feather-brain. Your character has always contained too much of your mother and too little of your father, and I wonder why it should surprise me to find you in this atrocious situation. You may know that your mother once attempted to ruin herself by just such a criminal attachment. I prevented that. I shall endeavour to prevent your disgrace in the same manner. What have you to say to me about that?'

But I could say nothing; and, smiling again, as if my silence seemed quite natural to her – my reaction exactly as she had intended – she continued, not with the accusations and reproaches I had expected, but in another manner entirely.

'At least, Faith, you must be ready to admit the soundness of my judgment? I told you some time ago that you were not fit to live alone, and so it has proved. However, since your mother lacked the authority to compel you to return home, and was too busy about her own affairs to keep anything like a proper watch over yours, I felt it – right, shall we say? – to do what I could in her place. I am an exceedingly busy woman, Faith, and may not have been so vigilant as I would have liked. But my niece, Lady Chard, confirmed my suspicions on your account as long ago as last Christmas, when she remarked you had been playing the recluse and wondered if there was an admirer you had not told us about. You denied it. Lady Chard believed you. I did not. And my observations – dear me, Faith! – the state of your nerves sometimes when I have called here unexpectedly, supposedly to complain of your mother, your little heart pounding and your ears straining for that caller at the back door who must be warned in time and sent away. And these visits of yours to York, to this acquaintance who never visits you in return. Heavens, my dear! not even your mother would have believed you, had she troubled to think about it, and I feel sure her husband does not. Tell me, was the weather fine in Scarborough last Friday to Monday?'

'Cold,' I said incredibly. 'And rather blustery.'

'Good. I am glad you do not feel the need to whine to me or insult me with pleas for my forgiveness. I shall not forgive you. Nor shall I trouble you with a description of how deeply your behaviour has disgusted me, since I imagine all that disgusts you is that you have been found out. I shall occupy myself instead by attempting to remedy the situation, as I once did with your mother, not out of any consideration for you, but because your disgrace must touch us all. You are not just "anybody", Faith. You are a member of a well-respected family, the niece of Sir Joel Barforth and of Mayor Agbrigg, who are both revered, and rightly so, in this town. You are the daughter of Morgan Aycliffe, to whom the most splendid building this town possesses has been dedicated. You are the widow of Dr Giles Ashburn, whose memory is held in high regard by all of us. You are the sister-in-law of Jonas Agbrigg, who is about to take his place on our town council and whose standing in the legal profession demands unblemished respectability. Jonas will be deeply shocked when I inform him of this, since he has appreciated your assistance to Celia as a hostess and had hoped to call on it again – something which now must be out of the question. I have no intention, my girl, of allowing you to damage these worthy men, you can be very sure of that. And I shall not rest until you are decently married.'

I opened my mouth to speak, my whole body leaning towards her in protest, thinking of Irish cousins, Mr Oldroyd of Fieldhead, some husband, any husband willing to take a blemished bride.

'Aunt Hannah,' I said, refusing it, but she held out her hand, palm upwards, in a gesture commanding enough to have silenced a meeting in the Assembly Rooms itself, and said, 'Yes, Faith. There is no other solution. I believe my sources of information to be discreet – certainly they are reliable – but I am not the only interested party capable of making inquiries. There is no time to lose. I have delayed so long only because I was unable to ascertain the gentleman's identity. In the final instance, of course, I would have come to you and forced his name out of you, but that will not be necessary. I believe, my dear, that when you have recovered from your emotions you will have cause to thank me, for I have already been very busy on your behalf. I have just spent a most uncomfortable hour with that rascal of a nephew of mine – uncomfortable for him, I hasten to add – and whether he likes it or not, I shall force him to put everything right.'

Seeing my total astonishment – for Nicholas was in London and could put nothing right in any case – her lips parted once again in a smile of the most complete satisfaction I had ever seen, revealing her cleverness and her superiority to me as a cat must reveal itself to a mouse.

'Yes, you may well stare, Faith, for he is the most complete rogue of my acquaintance and I did not expect him to be reasonable. But he could not deny that he went to Scarborough last Friday and did not return until Saturday. Nor can he deny that you were with him, since you were seen by a certain Mrs Guthrie, who was once in your service and who is now, in a manner of speaking, in mine. He cannot deny that you were alone in that house together, especially since he knows that the housekeeper

630

would be obliged to answer truthfully should her real employer, my brother Sir Joel, put her to the question. She has her place to consider, my dear, and would not risk losing it on your account. Yes, Faith, I believe I have done very well for you. A great many females have attempted to trap my nephew into matrimony, but in this case he overlooked the fact that he would have *me* to deal with. Good heavens, girl, what ails you? Most assuredly I cannot condone your wanton behaviour, but so long as it remains between the three of us it may be brought to a rapid – and highly profitable – conclusion. He has faults in plenty, no one doubts it, but he is a Barforth. I have always believed that family money should remain, whenever possible, in the family, and it has long concerned me that he would encounter some impossible, grasping woman on his travels – someone who would be no good to us at all. Well – it is a great thing for you, my girl, for do not forget that he will be Sir Blaize one day, since he is the eldest son. Joel and Verity may not quite like it, for, although you are not a poor match, you are not the best he could have made. But faced with the alternative scandal there is nothing else to be done. You have made your bed, my dear – both of you – and now you must lie on it.'

I had never lost consciousness before, and did not precisely do so now. I was quite simply and horrifyingly unable to speak, but Aunt Hannah, being well used to reducing her fellow creatures to speechlessness, did not appear surprised at that. She may, in fact, have considered it most appropriate, lingering no more than a quarter of an hour longer, advising me, when inbred politeness tried to force me to my feet at her leave-taking, to remain seated, or rather to go to bed and stay there, since I looked ill, most gratifyingly chastised.

'I have warned Blaize,' she said, 'that I shall require his answer by tomorrow morning. Verity should be here by then, since my brother finds he must remain in Cullingford for some days yet and appears unable to live without her. If my nephew chooses to be stubborn, then she and his father will be informed of it, and Joel will find a way to make him honour his obligation. However – I do not anticipate that things will come to that. I shall call tomorrow then – and if Blaize should come today I must ask you not to receive him. Contact between you at this point would be unwise. If he is looking for a way out, then he may persuade you into fresh folly, and it seems to me that you are all too persuadable. Remember – you are not at home to him.'

But I could not get to Blaize quickly enough, would have sent messages to Tarn Edge and then gone myself had he not appeared, a half-hour later, judging his time shrewdly, I thought, since Aunt Hannah would not be likely to return so soon.

'My word!' he said, throwing down his hat and gloves with great nonchalance. 'I am a trapped man. I have been avoiding this very thing for years, and now –'

But then, seeing my face, the huddled posture of my body in the chimney-corner, he crossed the room quickly and would have taken me in his arms had I not backed away.

'Heavens, Faith! – you will not die of it.'

'Blaize, is there anything you can do to stop her from telling your father?'

'Nothing! She wants me to marry you. It has worried her for a long time that I might dissipate my inheritance or bestow it unsuitably. Like Prudence, she fears I may take a child bride when I am ninety-three, and there would be no hope then of any Barforth money finding its way to Jonas. She disapproves wholeheartedly of what she thinks we have done, but it is manna from Heaven to her just the same. I could leave you an even richer widow than you are already, and who would you have to turn to then but Jonas?'

'It is as bad as it could be, then?'

'It is. She will tell my father, and when she does Nicholas will not keep silent. Mrs Collins will not keep silent either, I'm afraid, so there will be ample confirmation – quite the most explosive scandal Cullingford has ever known, by the look of it.'

'Yes. Then really – do you know – I think I had better die of it. I'm not being in the least dramatic. I can think of no other solution, that's all.'

He smiled, took my hand and, leading me to the sofa, sat down beside me.

'Yes, it had crossed my mind you would feel like that. What weapon would you use? You have no gas in this house, and poison is unreliable. You could jump from an upper window, of course, but it is by no means certain, and before you throw yourself under someone's carriage-horses you should take into account that you might kill the driver and a few passing children as well.'

'There's the railway,' I said and was almost startled when he shuddered, quite violently.

'You are quite serious about it, then. But no, not the railway – please don't think about it again, Faith. It would solve the problem for you, perhaps, but not for the rest of us. Aunt Hannah is really very honest and very courageous, you know. In the event of your suicide she would feel herself very much to blame. She'd say it was because I had refused to make an honest woman of you, and then Nicholas would knock me down and spend the rest of his life believing he had killed you. Really – you had better marry me, you know.'

'I shall have to go away, then, as far as I can, and at once – before your mother gets here. Dear God! she's expected in the morning. I must leave tonight. It doesn't matter where. You can help me to do that, can't you, Blaize?'

And, as panic surged over me again, I couldn't sit still, couldn't stay in this room a moment longer, must go immediately and pack my bags; and, if there was no train, no coach, no donkey-cart to escape in, then I must run.

'Yes,' he said. 'I could do that, I suppose. I could buy you a ticket for the London train and drive you to the station. But what then? I couldn't explain your disappearance to Aunt Hannah, nor to your mother, and the whole sad story would come out just the same. Nicholas would come after you, Faith. He couldn't leave you to fend for yourself. Even I couldn't accept such a sacrifice from a woman.'

I saw my hands clench into fists and come crashing down impotently on my knees again and again, my whole body rocked backwards and forwards by the enormity of my frustration and my fear. I heard my voice moaning, 'Dear God! What can I do then? Whatever can I do?', and the sound irritated me so that my mind said, 'Stupid, hysterical woman – be still! Can't someone make her be silent?' I saw Blaize put his hands over mine, unclench my fingers, smooth them out and hold them steady.

'Oh dear,' he said. 'I wonder if you realize what a blow you have just struck me? I have just asked you to marry me, a request I have never made before. And all you replied was. "I shall have to go away – at once". And that, my dear, is hardly flattering – hardly at all.'

'Blaize, for heaven's sake! Stop playing games. *You* can get out of this the moment you want to; I don't think *I* can get out of it at all. Just don't bother me with nonsense – just don't – when I'm trying to find a serious solution.'

'It *is* a serious solution,' he said; and, releasing my hands, he leaned back a little, apparently at ease, his eyes quizzical and careful, but not without concern.

'It depends on what you really want, Faith. And you have almost no time at all to make up your mind. Aunt Hannah has made a somewhat natural mistake. She knew you were meeting somebody in Scarborough. She sent one of her minions to find out, and the person in question saw me. Well, I have been avoiding traps of that kind for years and when I had got over the shock I could hardly ignore the poetic justice of it. However, we are discussing your feelings now, not mine. Faith, there are several things you can do. You can wait here and allow the storm to break over you, or you can go to London and warn Nicky of it. I have the address where he may be found and you could easily reach him there, or I could even take you there. Either way, my father would be waiting for him on his return. There is absolutely nothing I can do to silence Aunt Hannah, short of telling her the truth, and there's no guarantee she'd believe me. The chances are she'd set it as a trick to get myself out of trouble and land Nicky in it instead – which you must admit I've done often enough in the past – and I'm not sure what would happen if she asked him for confirmation. Obviously the truth *would* come out, because Mrs Collins knows about you and Nicky, but by that time everybody else would know about it too, and the result would be exactly the same. Nicky and my father are not on good terms at the moment, you know, and the explosion would be quite devastating. My father is not precisely fond of Georgiana, but she is his daughter-in-law, she is expecting his grandchild. She's not in good health, and neither, I think, is he, which makes his temper shorter. He wouldn't want to throw Nicky out, and Nicky wouldn't want to go. But this is what would most likely happen. It would cause immense distress to both of them, in the long run, and worse than that to my mother.'

'I know – I know – you don't have to punish me all over again with it.'

633

'I think I do. I think it essential that you should see things very clear. Nicky and I have no legal claim on the mills, Faith. They belong to my father, and can be disposed of as he sees fit. The deeds of partnership are already drawn up, I know. They've been lying in Jonas Agbrigg's desk-drawer for some time now, waiting until my father feels the urge to sign them. It's the golden carrot he's been using to good purpose, but as matters stand we're just employees, and he could disinherit either one of us, or both. So you see, if you allow Nicky to quarrel with him you will be doing me a great service. What you must ask yourself is whether Nicky, in a year or two, would begin to wonder about the disservice you had done him. He has the Wool-combers, of course, but he's short of capital, and when it was known he had broken with my father the bank might not continue to support him.'

'Blaize – I know –'

'And there is Georgiana, and young Gervase, and the new baby. I imagine you must have intended being very discreet until after her confinement. You'll know more than I do about the dangers of shock and distress in pregnancy and I'm sure you wouldn't want to put her at risk – more than she is already. I'm not sure what would happen to Georgiana if all this came out into the open, and you and Nicky went away together. Obviously he'd continue to support her and the children, and, even if he lost the Wool-combers for lack of financial assistance – because all businesses need that kind of help in their early days, you know – then my father would support them anyway. So there'd be no physical hardship. She could go back to Galton, I suppose, although I'm not sure she could, or would, divorce him. An Act of Parliament is required for the dissolving of marriages, you know, Faith – which costs a lot of money and takes a great deal of time – and, since divorced persons don't remarry in any case, it would make no real difference to your situation. No one would ever speak to you again – no one you'd want to speak to, that is – and if you had children I can't imagine that anyone in Cullingford would speak to them either. The discrimination against bastards is really immense, and strikes me as very unjust – but there it is. And there is always the possibility that Nicholas eventually would redeem himself by going back to his wife. The world is very unfairly balanced for a woman. Georgiana would only have to forgive him and everyone else would be glad to do the same. He could come back to Tarn Edge, take his place in the mills – they would even kill the fatted calf for him. But no one would ever forgive you. I suppose he would make you a very adequate allowance – and I might call to see you now and then.'

I got up and began to pace around the room, backwards and forwards, up and down, a great release of energy that took me nowhere, losing myself, at every step more thoroughly, in the maze of my female situation, a dark dream-walking where every door that beckoned cheated me and was no door at all. And in the end – like Prudence, like every other woman – there was no choice but to submit, in this masculine world, to the requirements, the decisions, the mercy of the nearest, most sympathetic male.

'Are you trying to drive me mad?'

'I would prefer not to. Do you want me to take you to London, to find Nicholas?'

'What else can I do?'

'Can you really live with the scandal, Faith – for the rest of your life?'

'What else can I do?'

'Can you cope with the constant strain of pleasing him, which is not the same as loving him, since he will be all you have in the world. And he's not easily pleased. He'll growl and complain sometimes, and, even if he doesn't mean it, you'll die every time it happens because you'll think you're losing him.'

'What else? Dear God – what else is there now?'

'And supposing you *did* lose him? You could, Faith – so easily. He's had money all his life – lots of money – and so have you. Can you cope with poverty? The Wool-combers could eat up your money sooner than you'd imagine, because Nicky has grand ideas. If he lost it he'd be tempted to come home for more. And what then? Every man you met would know about you – men always know these things – and I wonder if you have any idea just how coarse men can be once a woman has lost her reputation?'

'Blaize, for pity's sake! You can extricate yourself. I can't. He can't.'

'Yes,' he said, very casually, 'you can. You can marry me.'

I fell down on to a chair, my head in my knees and began to sob, an ugly, gulping sound that hurt my chest and my ears and such self-esteem as remained to me, and he waited, offering me no comfort, until my body staggered painfully towards composure and I raised my head again, wiping my face with my sleeves, feeling drained and sick and furious because my hysteria had weakened me further and had solved nothing.

'I'm sorry. It's over now.'

But he made no immediate answer, obliging me by his very silence to admit my need of him, to realize fully and finally how alone I would be now, how totally abandoned, without him.

'Good,' he said at last and very quietly. 'Well then, since it's over, may we pass on to more constructive matters than tears? Dear Faith, my proposal startles you, I imagine, because you can see no reason for it. How can I make you understand? A man marries for a variety of reasons, you know that as well as I do. And you must also know that, in our little world, it is very rarely for passion. Faith, I am turning thirty and I have had my share of amorous escapades. Indeed, I now find that I am tending to repeat myself – it is all very pleasant, of course, and the wandering life I lead presents me with ample opportunities. But no man wanders forever – your mother's husband would offer you confirmation of that – and when I do come home, quite frankly, I am no longer comfortable at Tarn Edge. The house is big enough, and the service is excellent, but my nephew is extremely noisy and a new baby is unlikely to add anything to the atmosphere that I shall care for. Moreover, if possible, Georgiana and Nicholas should be left alone. My mother is of the same opinion, and when she is not there I feel somewhat *de trop*. I could take a house of my

635

own, of course, but that would involve me in a mountain of domestic trivia, and apart from that I am a little tired of being so very eligible. It strikes me that every woman in the Law Valley with a daughter to marry has come running after me at one time or another, and I'm sorry to say that my taste doesn't run to young, innocent girls. I show my face in Cullingford, and there they are, put out on display, all tremulous and eager and ready for anything that might succeed in making them "Lady Barforth" one day. They besiege me with invitations to dine with them, to dance with them, anything I like with them. I have to listen to their music, look at their water-colours and their embroidery and anything else they can show me – within reason – that might tempt me. And it doesn't tempt me at all. There are men who very much like virginity, but frankly I have had no experience of it and, even if all these fifteen-year-old dimples and curls succeeded in moving me, how could I ask a mere child to manage my affairs when I am abroad, or to manage me when I am at home? I would be at the mercy of my wife's mother, and that wouldn't suit me at all. The alternative would be to look outside our charmed circle, as Nicky did, but we both know all about his problems, and I may not do any better. I know several attractive women, in London and elsewhere, who might be ready to marry me, but Cullingford is not kind to strangers. I would rather marry you, Faith. We are at ease with one another. You are intelligent and kind-hearted. You have excellent taste. You would be a good hostess and a good friend. You have a lovely body and a more sophisticated mind than is usual in a Law Valley woman. Yet you *are* a Law Valley woman. You understand the way in which I conduct my business and the men with whom it is conducted. And several times I've done more than glance in your direction – I've looked hard and I haven't been indifferent. These seem very adequate reasons for marriage to me. And as for that rare and special creature I've talked so much about – the one who is always in the next room – well, I think I am quite content, you know, to let her remain there. If I ever opened the door, the chances are that I'd be sadly disappointed. She'd most likely turn out to be quite commonplace.'

I walked another step or two and then stood quite still, my head bowed in a brooding silence, wondering what time it was, what day it was, why everything he said to me sounded so logical, so easy, until the moment his voice stopped speaking.

'And you would accept me, knowing that my only motive could be the need to escape from Nicholas?'

'My dear,' he said, 'you married my very good friend Giles Ashburn for exactly that reason, and he had no cause to complain of you. If you decided to devote yourself to me in the same fashion, I wouldn't complain either.'

I sat down beside him, not intentionally, but because my legs had simply released my weight, and he slid his hand into mine, a light, undemanding touch, telling me I could take him, or not, and we would still be friends, warning me, perhaps, that he was no rock to lean on, as Giles had been, that he would never seek to possess me nor allow me to possess him – but that we would be friends.

'It's not possible,' I said. 'Blaize, how can you even think of it? You

636

know that I'm in love with Nicholas and he's your brother – you even look like him.'

'No,' he told me, not the slightest tremor in him anywhere. 'You're quite wrong. I don't look like him at all. He looks like me. And the resemblance isn't really very great. He's blacker and bolder and heavier by at least a stone. And you know quite well I was born believing that, sooner or later, everybody is bound to like me best. What else have you to tell me?'

'That even if I – and I couldn't – that Nicholas wouldn't let it happen.'

'My dear, I'm not planning to ask him. Faith, you spoke of going to London. My bags are already packed. I have to go and see as many of my Continental customers as I can in case this damnable war with Russia, which seems almost certain now, should make travel difficult. I intended to leave at the end of the month, but there's no reason why we can't set off together – tonight. We'd be creating a small scandal, darling, to cover a greater one. Elope with me, in fact. A few weeks in France and Germany, consternation in Cullingford, and we can be married somewhere *en route*. You can trust me, I think, to work out the details. They'd hardly be beyond my organizing capacity. You'd meet with some coolness, of course, when you came home, but my mother will help us with that. If Lady Barforth of Tarn Edge is willing to receive you – and Mrs Agbrigg of Lawcroft Fold – then everybody else will do the same. So – I have brought you to the point of realizing it is not impossible after all. What is troubling you now?'

'Nicholas is troubling me now.'

'Yes, I rather thought he might. But Nicholas makes the elopement necessary, surely you can see that? If he comes back from London to learn we are to be married, he'd be bound to ask the reason why. And I can't see myself explaining it. He wouldn't give you up to me, darling, just to avoid a scandal he thinks he can cope with, and to keep a wife he thinks he doesn't want. And, even if by some miracle he could be persuaded to see reason, could you stand the strain of a family wedding? Could he? He'd be far more likely to shoot me at the altar than act as my best man.'

'And if we go away together he'll think we became lovers in Scarborough, won't he, Blaize? He'll think I fell out of love with him for your sake.'

'Exactly. What else could he think? Aunt Hannah will tell no tales once we're gone. She'd have nothing to gain by it, and my father might accuse her of having pushed us too far, and she wouldn't risk that. As you say, Nicky will certainly think you have jilted him, in a particularly heartless manner at that. And he'll be hurt, there's no doubt about it – baldy hurt even, for a while. He'll be foul-tempered and foul-mouthed and he'll kick his machines, and his operatives, all around Lawcroft mill yard until he's worked it out of his system. I speak flippantly because that seems to be my fashion when something troubles me. But really, Faith – really – the more it hurts him the better, because when he's feeling thoroughly wretched who else is he likely to turn to but Georgiana? He would be miserable. She would be miserable. It would be very natural – wouldn't it? – if they should be drawn together. And that, surely, is one of the things we are aiming for. Very well, I have demolished that objection – give me the next.'

I leaned forward, struggling against the current of his logic that brought me constantly back to him, the warm tones of his voice filling my mind, hushing my panic, easing me, convincing me that this outrageous thing was not only possible but obvious, desirable; that it was right, and could be pleasant, because he said so.

'Blaize, take care. Don't confuse me and persuade me. You are not selling me a thousand yards of Barforth worsted, you know.'

'No, darling – it would have taken me all of ten minutes to do that.'

'I can't believe this is happening to me. You make it sound so simple – and so right – and perhaps it could be. But Blaize –'

'Yes, what is it now? I suppose it must be Nicholas again.'

'Of course it is. He's your brother and he'll probably be your business partner. I could avoid him, but you couldn't. You'd have to see him every day – work for him.'

But my mood was quieter now, my objections more hesitant, his hand on mine much firmer.

'There's that to it, of course. But that's my problem, surely, darling, and there is little love lost between me and Nicky in any case. We don't work together, Faith. We're involved in the same business and we put up with each other. The whole of Cullingford knows it and no one would be surprised to see our relationship take a turn for the worse. People would only think we were bickering over the money, and most of the time they'd be right. And it may not always be so. People mellow. If he finds enough to content him in Georgiana, he may find it easier to tolerate me. And if he doesn't – well – we shall be equal partners in the Barforth mills when my father dies, but partnerships can be dissolved. He could take Lawcroft and Low Cross, and I could take Tarn Edge, and we could go our separate ways. If my relationship with Nicky is the only thing to be sacrificed, then I believe we might come out of this well enough.'

I sat for a long time after that, leaning my head on the back of the sofa, conscious of a gradual draining away of energy, trying for a while to halt the dissolving of my will into his, the slow drifting of my whole self towards the refuge he offered, the submission he had presented to me as inevitable. And then, very slowly, as one flow of quiet water enters another, resistance ebbed away.

'You are going to marry me then?'

'Yes.'

'Good. Then there is one promise you must make me.'

'Only one? I think you are entitled to ask for more than that.'

'Ah well – most of the things I could ask for, you will give me in any case. This one promise will suffice. Nicholas must never know the true circumstances of our marriage. And, since neither Aunt Hannah nor I will tell him, you must not do so either. He must go on believing that you willingly abandoned him, either because you liked me better – which has happened before in his life – or from motives of self-interest, because you knew I had more to offer. You saw the chance of an advantageous marriage and you took it. If he's to think well of Georgiana, he must begin by thinking ill of you. And I'm bound to admit I wouldn't be altogether comfortable otherwise. Will you promise me that?'

'Blaize – that is one promise I would have performed in any case.'

'Of course. So, let's think of you, now, and me. I told you my bags are packed, but I may not have mentioned they are already at the station. We have only your affairs to put in order, darling, and I'm here, at your disposal, until train-time. There's a note to be written to your mother, and a line to Aunt Hannah too, I think, which we'll have delivered in the morning – simply that you have gone away with me and expect to be married when they see you again. You may go upstairs presently to arrange your boxes, and while you're about it I'll have a word with your housekeeper and make it worth her while to be on our side. But I think we might have a moment together now. Come here, darling, for if I am to be blamed for seducing you, I may as well take advantage of it.'

But, with his mouth once more on mine, his hands beginning a gentle, stroking exploration of my shoulders, the curve of my breasts, the outline of waist and thigh, the cool, fresh scent of him invading my nostrils, I felt a new panic.

'Blaize – I can't go from one bed to another – just like that – so quickly.'

'Oh but you can,' he said, his mouth against my neck, his hands delicately parting the folds of my collar. 'Not here, of course – not now – but tonight darling, wherever we find ourselves, I shall manage to provide you with champagne and a good dinner, and a good bed, and I am not at all the kind of gallant gentleman who would allow you to sleep in it alone. You will have to make your full commitment, darling, make no mistake about it. I may not look the part, Faith, but I am a Law Valley man. I expect a return on my investments, just as much, and just as soon, as I can.'

And being a Law Valley woman I could not quarrel with that.

23

It was, of course, a preposterous relationship which should soon have foundered. It did not. Our first night together should have ended in tears on my part, bitter reproaches on his, a mutual embarrassment neither of us could overcome. Incredibly, it ended in laughter, inspired partly, I must confess, by the endlessly flowing champagne Blaize considered an essential part of seduction, but largely by the split in my own nature, the practical Law Valley part of me which understood the reason for this immediate commitment – for once it was done it was done and there could be no returning – the part which said, 'You have made your bed, so now it is only common sense to lie on it as comfortably as you can'; and the other part, the submerged part, released by Blaize's persuasive

639

hands, the woman in me who could enjoy, if only briefly, the languorous, sensual life of a pampered courtesan.

I should have been abominably burdened throughout those early months by the memory of Nicholas and of what he must believe I had done to him. I did not forget it. But I was a woman who had made, if not precisely a decision, a promise my self-respect would force me to keep, had entered into an arrangement the terms of which I perfectly understood and which I was determined to fulfil. I knew exactly what Blaize required in a wife and I saw no point at all – even before we were married – in holding anything back from him.

A good hostess, he had said, and a good friend, but Blaize Barforth's 'good friend' would need to be resourceful, independent, good-humoured, sensual, unfailingly patient; and from the start I became all those things, partly because this was my final opportunity to make something of my life and I couldn't fail it, but also because Blaize himself, who demanded constant attention, expected at all times to be pleased, was well worth the pleasing, a challenge to any woman's ingenuity.

I should not have found pleasure in his arms – not so quickly – and when I did I should have felt soiled by it, betrayed by my own sighing, demanding body. Perhaps if he had been sympathetic and allowed me to be sentimental I would have done exactly that, but the sexual act to Blaize was not so much a matter of need as of skill, a slow appreciation that could occupy the whole of a balmy Mediterranean afternoon – if he had one available – an experience which took on the shades and character of its constantly changing situation, a cosily bolstered French bed, a moonlit terrace overlooking the sea, my back supported by silk-embroidered cushions, a couch in a southern garden, as he had once promised, the spray of a nearby fountain feather-light against my bare skin, a dappled moonlight coming down to us through the chestnut trees. And from the start his expertise defeated me.

'No – no,' he told me that first night, when I turned to him too quickly, knowing it had to be done and wanting it over. 'There's no rush. I have to find out what pleases you, darling. And you have to discover what pleases me. I won't tell you – and I won't ask – because it's in the finding out that we'll have the fun.'

And in full lamplight he explored my body from the crown of my head to the soles of my feet, returning unerringly to the tender places, his hands and his mouth inviting me, persuading me, to pleasure, coaxing it from me and nurturing it into the most acute physical joy of my life, leaving me exhausted but clear-headed, since emotion had scarcely been used at all.

From those first, difficult days when only the iron discipline of my father's teaching enable me to conceal how desperately I was grieving for Nicholas, Blaize intrigued and satiated my senses, filled my nights with pleasure, not infrequently with amazement, my days with a constant flurry of occupations, little errands to run on his behalf, people to meet, dinners to be eaten in gay company or romantically alone, race-meetings and theatres, elegant concert halls and wicked, fascinating pavement cafés, shopping, spending, railway stations, sinister foreign taverns, luxurious hotels. He kept me busy, laughed at me, pampered me sometimes, abandoned me at others for days on end in unfamiliar places while he made lightning trips alone. He indulged me, amused me, entertained me, kept me waiting in strange restaurants without ever making explanations, expected me at a moment's notice to be ready to take a train or a coach, to be as fresh at the end of a journey as I had been at its beginning, expected me at all times – since I had declared myself to be a woman and not a child – to cope alone, to stand firmly on the two adult feet of which I was possessed. And if it was exhausting, sometimes exasperating, it was exciting, leaving me no time to brood on anything else, and I did not dislike it.

We were married eventually in Bournemouth, but it was clear to anyone with the slightest knowledge of mathematics – and there were few in Cullingford who could not do their sums – that we had travelled together on the wicked Continent for several months before he took me to his mother at Rosemount Lodge, and Cullingford, quite rightly, knew just what that meant.

'My mother will help us to put everything right,' Blaize had said, yet oddly enough it was not Aunt Verity who came to our assistance after all, but the irascible Sir Joel himself.

'I don't understand this at all,' Aunt Verity told Blaize on our arrival at Rosemount, having offered me no more than a cool hand in welcome. 'If you wished to get married you had only to say so. Obviously there is rather more to it than that. Are you going to tell me what it is?'

'I shouldn't think so, mamma,' Blaize cheerfully replied, and, instead of the explosion I had anticipated, Uncle Joel, from the depths of his armchair, gave a grim but decidedly humorous chuckle and got to his feet, his face still showing the strain of the chest infection he had endured that winter, but his eyes very keen.

'It strikes me you'll have to be content with that, Verity,' he said. 'There'll have to be a wedding now, no matter who likes it and who don't. And I'm not sure I dislike it. To tell the truth I've had about enough of fancy marriages, and, if he's gone about it in a peculiar way, then your eldest son has always been like that, Lady Barforth – wouldn't you say? I reckon he's fancy enough, our Blaize, without taking himself a fancy wife. And a Cullingford girl was good enough for me. So we'll get you married now, Faith Aycliffe, just as quick as we can, and, as soon as the weather's warmer and I'm feeling up to breathing some bad Cullingford air again, *I'll* take you home and get you settled, where you belong.'

My mother, Prudence, Aunt Hannah and Jonas came down for my wedding, my mother melting into easy tears of forgiveness, Aunt Hannah, her eyes as shrewd as her brother's, telling me that only her sense of loyalty to her family and her Christian duty inclined her to welcome me back to the fold.

'How very enterprising of you,' Jonas told me. 'Obviously there has been no time to draw up a marriage contract, but I trust your husband will see no objection to leaving your personal affairs in my hands?' And, smiling at him, I didn't believe he had betrayed me; for, if Jonas had decided to ferret out the identity of my lover, I felt certain that he, unlike Aunt Hannah, would have got it right.

I took Prudence on a brisk stroll along the cliff top and before she had time to question me said, 'I can't tell you why, I promised not to tell anyone.'

'Ah – you had a reason, then? I imagined it to be just the whim of a moment.' And then, her voice still angry but no longer with me, she said, 'There is no need to tell me. They are calling you a sly minx in Cullingford. Everybody's mamma is pretending to be scandalized, when half of them would have put their daughters willingly on that London train in your place – and Celia is so torn between delight at having you so rich and shame at knowing you so wanton that it has quite made her ill. Well – I believe it has made me ill, too. They have used you, haven't they – one of them or both of them, Nicholas or Blaize – what does it matter? You were manipulated and bewildered, weren't you, and convinced that you had no choice? No – no, don't say anything. I don't know the details, and don't wish to know.'

'Prudence – please. I can ask no one else. Have you seen Nicholas?'

'Yes,' she said, and that was all she would say.

Caroline, who was paying a visit to Lady Henrietta Stone in Belgravia and could easily have come to Rosemount to see me married, declined, expressing herself much shocked at the manner in which I had snared her favourite brother. She was fond of me – in fact she had been very fond of me – but an earl's daughter, she felt, would not have been too good for Blaize, and, when he dined with her in London, she did not scruple to tell him so.

Georgiana, who could not attend, being very near her time, scrawled me a hasty message of goodwill. 'What wickedness! What a lark! What fun! One can always rely on Blaize to do things in style. My brother Perry could not have done it better.'

And although I asked Prudence again, and then again, I could persuade her to tell me nothing of Nicholas.

There was a high, very fragile blue sky on my wedding morning, shreds of cloud blown this way and that by a cool wind which, as I was driven to church, obligingly uncovered a glimmer of sun for me. White satin, of course, even had I not been a widow, would have been inappropriate on this occasion, but Blaize, as Georgiana had said, required things to be done with style, and my dress, ordered in Paris from Monsieur Albertini, was perhaps the most elegant I had ever owned, its cream-coloured skirt filling the carriage, the sleeves a cascade of cream lace, enormous cream silk roses on the waist and the bodice, a silk and lace flower-garden on my hat. Blaize kissed my hand at the altar as tenderly as if he had loved me all his life, I smiled up at him just as mistily, and afterwards, since we had already had our honeymoon, Aunt Verity moved our belongings from the two small spare bedrooms we had been chastely occupying at

Rosemount Lodge into the large, double-bedded one, and we were married.

'Will it be difficult tonight, I wonder?' Blaize said, stretching himself out beside me.

'Yes – you have made an honest woman out of me and so I shall behave like one. I am a wife now, not a mistress, so I shall keep on my nightgown and turn down the lights.'

'Well – that would be something new in my experience, at any rate. But, in fact, my married darling, you will do exactly as I say, for I am your husband now and my authority over you is very nearly life and death.'

'So it is – does that please you?'

He shrugged. 'I've not really considered it. I don't think it matters to me either way. I'd feel myself to be something of a failure, and something of a fool as well, I reckon. And, whatever the law may have to say, you'll only give me what you want to give me, or what you can – and I shall do the same. I think we shall manage well enough with that.'

He went to Cullingford a few days later, leaving me with my aunt – my mother-in-law – who, although she was kind to me again, alarmed me sometimes by the questions she did not ask. And when he returned he had sold my house in Millergate and had brought sketches of another to show me, which, while asking most courteously for my opinion, I suspected he had purchased already.

It was at a spot called Elderleigh Hill, a few miles out of Cullingford on the road to Listonby, not rural precisely, since the low, neatly folded hills were no barrier to those belching chimney-stacks, the lightest of breezes coming smoke-laden across them, but it was still green in patches, still fragrant with blossom in springtime, the house itself, built some fifty years ago in the Prince Regent's day, being an elegant, classical box, a Grecian temple against the medieval cathedral that was Tarn Edge.

'I am sure it will suit you,' he told me and, realizing he had actually said, 'It suits me', and, because, most of all, I desired to be settled, I had few complaints to make.

'You will have a long drive to the mill every day.'

'Darling – I don't go to the mill every day.'

'Well, it seems very nice and quite large. Can we afford it?'

'Oh, as to that, I imagine my father will buy it for us. He keeps Nicholas in luxury at Tarn Edge and is always buying Caroline the odd farm or two. He's bound to do something on similar lines for me. If you're agreeable I will send Jonas Agbrigg word to complete the transaction, for I want to get you settled before I leave for New York.'

'Blaize – you didn't tell me you were going to America.'

'My dear – I'm telling you now.'

'And I can't come with you, I suppose.'

'No, darling. These intensive selling-trips are not suitable for ladies, believe me. I would have no time to spare to be with you, and some of the places I visit are not ones in which I could very well leave you alone. Nicholas may call it self-indulgence, if he pleases, but in fact what I do is extremely hard work. You couldn't possibly enjoy it.'

643

'You saw Nicholas – when you were in Cullingford?'

'I could hardly go to Cullingford without seeing him. He was more or less as I'd expected him to be. I am to buy the house, then? Good. There are some alterations I know you'll be bound to make. The wallpaper is quite appalling throughout, so you will need to be nearby, darling. I shall take you to Listonby before I leave and I expect you'll be so busy that you'll hardly miss me.'

'Blaize,' I said, quite horrified. 'Caroline will not have me.'

'Of course she will. I have already spoken to her and it is all arranged. She may scold you for ten minutes, but she likes to be at the centre of things and is really quite lonely sometimes, you know. She will find you a pleasant change from Hetty Stone, and Listonby is very convenient for Elderleigh.'

'Dear God –' I said, and then, seeing the quizzical arch of his eyebrow, reminding me of our arrangement, that he had warned me from the start that I could not lean on him, I took a deep breath and then another, and smiled.

'Yes, of course. The house will keep me fully occupied. I shall try to have it ready by the time you come back again.'

'Good.'

And, having made his point, won his day, he crossed the room and kissed me.

'I have no choice in the matter, Faith. I plan these journeys well in advance. My customers are expecting to see me, and if I don't arrive they will make it their business to see someone else. And I'm not asking you to face Cullingford alone. I shall be back in plenty of time for that. We will tackle the Assembly Rooms together, and Aunt Hannah's drawing-room, and anywhere else you fancy – that I promise you – but Listonby is hardly Cullingford, after all. Your presence there will be very well advertised. No one will call who doesn't wish to see you. And there will be no reason for you to go into town.'

And that was as much as he would say to me of Nicholas.

I embarked then on a period of my life, lasting almost a year, in which I was continually called upon to do the impossible and somehow or other did it. Listonby was easy enough, for, although Caroline herself was stiff with me for a day or so, Lady Hetty Stone, an almost permanent guest, was a worldly woman, half amused, half bored by the middle-class notions of Lady Chard and more than ready to make friends with any woman who had a husband as charming as mine.

'You will like Hetty Stone,' Caroline told me, a command not a recommendation, and, although her thin, languid body did not please me, her die-away airs and graces were frankly irritating, her intelligence was shrewd enough, her pedigree of the very highest, representing for Caroline, who had so easily conquered the squirearchy, a new challenge. For Lady Hetty was the offspring of no fox-hunting Tory squire living on his rents of one pound per acre, his acreage rarely surpassing the thousand, his influence powerful, perhaps, if strictly local, but of the Duke of South Erin, a Whig grandee of awesome international dignity, whose acquaintance could open new worlds for Caroline. And although Lady Hetty herself had married unwisely, a younger son who had first dissipated his inheritance and then died of his dissipations, she possessed nevertheless the entrée of those glittering Mayfair staircases where the high nobility received their guests, had been received at Court, could drop famous names so casually, yet so thick and fast, that her board and lodging at Listonby was amply justified.

'I have stopped using place cards at dinner,' Caroline told me. 'Hetty Stone says in London no one does. It is up to the butler to recognize one's guests and remember where they are to be seated. Well – Charlesworth is not very pleased about it, and I am forced to agree it must be easier to identify Lord Palmerston and Mr Disraeli than a collection of hunting gentlemen, or commercial gentlemen, who tend to look very much alike, but he will have to do the best he can. You could keep your eyes open tonight, Faith, and give him a little nod in the right direction – since you will be sure to remember everyone.'

Yet she invited no one who could embarrass me, or, if she did, they did not appear, and once again I encountered the impossible and performed it, knowing Nicholas to be but a few miles away, and living, in surface calm, with the dread of turning a corner one day and meeting his anger, his hurt, suffering his reproaches, the temptation of going myself to find him and telling him the truth.

It was impossible now not to think of him. Impossible. I had no way of preventing it, but by then I knew I was expecting Blaize's child, the most binding commitment I had ever made to any man, the ultimate possession, and it was a blessed relief to turn my mind inwards, to the new individual inside me, constantly marvelling at the functioning of my own body, which knew so exactly how to nourish this new life about which my mind, and my inexperienced hands, had no knowledge at all.

I had believed it impossible to drive over to Elderleigh every morning in Caroline's landau, Hetty Stone, who found my company less exacting than Caroline's, more often than not at my side. Impossible to survey those well-proportioned yet ill-decorated rooms, to strip them, in my mind, of some other woman's poor taste and do them up again in a fashion I hoped would be pleasing to Blaize. Impossible to convey my requirements – Blaize's requirements – to a daily procession of craftsmen and tradesmen, impossible to make such sharp inquiries to various establishments in London when the furniture, the glass and the china we had ordered together were not delivered on time. Impossible – when I had not the slightest knowledge of such things – to instal new stoves and boilers, give orders for the cleaning and repairing of chimneys, so that my husband could be warm and adequately fed.

Yet gradually the ceilings were relieved of their ugly, lumpy mouldings and acquired a delicate tracery of acanthus leaves picked out in gold, the cloudy colour of the plasterwork echoed by the flowery pastels of the Aubusson rugs we had shipped over from France. The drawing-room walls lost their busy brown flowers and were covered in honey-gold watered silk, the dining-room in wild rose. The windows, quite suddenly, were clean and intricately draped in muslin and velvet, the marble fireplaces polished, the mantelpieces ready to receive my bridal offerings: a French clock set in the midst of porcelain flowers; pot-pourri vases painted with the pastoral landscapes of Watteau, embellished by the china roses and carnations of Meissen; the classical figures of white biscuit porcelain which my father had so loved. Furniture began to arrive, a Rococo sofa inlaid with mother of pearl, a vast, honey-coloured velvet one, gold-striped brocade chairs, a capacious half-tester bed with curtains and valances in pale lemon silk.

'Impractical,' said Caroline.

'Beautiful,' said Hetty Stone. 'Your husband demands a great deal of you, Mrs Barforth.'

'My husband is that kind of man, Lady Henrietta.'

And before very long there was a cook in my kitchen, a parlourmaid to serve my tea, lay my dinner-table, keep my fine linen in order, housemaids to clean and polish and carry water, a little girl to scour my pots and pans and devote herself bravely to the black-leading of my new, monster stove with its several hot-plates and ovens, to the feeding of its viciously crackling fire and the replenishing of its cavernous, constantly steaming boiler. I had a butler, considerably less grand than Caroline's, to answer my door, take care of my silver, watch over my wine-cellar, wait at my table. I had a footman to clean the boots and polish my cutlery, to deliver my messages and go out with me in my carriage, to mend my fires and light my lamps. I was well-housed, well-served, too busy for the self-indulgence of brooding. I had proved not only my ability but my good faith, so that when Blaize came home he had no more to do than see to the accommodation of his horses.

I had no idea if he had missed me or was glad to see me again – certainly he did not tell me so – but his appreciation of my domestic arrangements was generous, his homecoming accompanied by flowers and champagne and a great many presents: a lace fan on ivory sticks, a lace shawl, an extravagant parasol that could have been a swirl of sea-foam on an ivory handle – exquisite, impersonal things, luxury goods which could have been given by any man to any woman.

But later: 'Oh yes – you may care for this,' he said, and tossed into my lap a cameo heavily framed in gold, the glass cut into the shape of a full-breasted swan, a unique token, the only one, I imagined, in the world, since he must have ordered it to be made specially for me.

'Yes,' he said, 'I thought it might move you – so drift towards me, darling. I may appear dainty in my appetites, but I get hungry – like any other man – when I have been away from home.'

It was to be the pattern of our life together: rapid, casual departures, abandonments almost.

'Blaize – you didn't tell me you were going to London – Germany – New York – the Great Wall of China.'

'Darling – I'm telling you now.'

And always some impossible task to be completed in his absence.

'See to this for me – that for me – why don't you turn the back parlour into a library for me while I'm away?'

And on his return the wine, the gifts, the costly bric-à-brac, and occasionally something to touch my heart, something to amaze me, from a spray of the year's first snowdrops bought for a penny at the roadside, to something as rare and precious as my cameo swan.

But that first homecoming, in its way, was also the end of a reprieve, for now I had not only to face the reality of living with Blaize as his wife, in his home – a far different matter from the nomad existence of hotels, rented villas, other people's houses, we had experienced until now – but I would be forced to take my place in Cullingford again. And that, clearly, was impossible.

I *could* not enter the Morgan Aycliffe Hall on Sir Joel Barforth's arm – my pregnancy, thankfully, as yet not showing – and listen, seated between him and Blaize, to an organ recital given by the willowy young Austrian Rebecca Mandelbaum was determined to marry. But it happened.

'There's no cause for alarm,' Sir Joel said, his smile telling me that he, at any rate, was planning to enjoy himself. 'Anybody who wants to speak to me will have to speak to you, Faith. And I reckon there's not many here tonight who can afford not to speak to me.'

And so it proved.

There was, perhaps, a hushed moment of malice and curiosity, a certain drawing aside of skirts in the vestibule to avoid contamination as I passed. But then: 'Good evening, Faith dear,' said Mrs Mandelbaum, who, having a disobedient daughter of her own, did not wish, perhaps, to throw stones.

'Good evening,' said Mrs Hobhouse stiffly, not really liking it, since none of *her* girls would ever behave in this manner, but too much aware of financial difficulties at Nethercoats to offer a downright snub to any Barforth.

'Mrs Blaize Barforth, how very nice to see you,' said Mr Fielding, our Member of Parliament, sensing the approach of a general election and knowing where a large proportion of his campaign funds came from.

'Ah – here is my niece,' said Aunt Hannah loudly. 'Faith, I believe you are not acquainted with Mrs Birkett, who is new to our area?' And there was no doubt that Mrs Birkett, whose husband was attempting to establish himself as a shipping and forwarding agent in Sheepgate, had no objection to being acquainted.

It was done, and I found, once again, as had been clear to me on my return from France long ago, that everyone considered their own affairs to be far more pressing and interesting than mine. My sister Celia was pregnant again, determined to have a boy this time, since she had been brought up to believe so firmly in the superiority of the male, and when I called in Albert Place she was far more concerned with the insubordination of her nurserymaid, the slovenliness she *knew* went on in her kitchen, than any misdemeanours of mine.

'So you are in the family way at last yourself, are you?' she said. 'Well, I can tell you here and now that you will not like it – just wait until your ankles begin to swell and your head to ache and until you are too stout and breathless to get up from your chair. Not that you will suffer all that much, I suppose. No, you will just sail through it as you do with everything and will probably get a boy first time. Indeed I hope you do, for your husband is to inherit a title, after all, and will want a son of his own to pass it on to. You had best get it right now, and then you may not be obliged to go through it again.'

My mother, having secrets of her own, asked no questions, and in any case was fully occupied with her Daniel, who merely winked a merry eye at me and whispered, 'Clever puss.' Aunt Hannah, now that her husband had been persuaded to accept a third term of office, was engrossed with new building schemes, a town hall, no less, which could not possibly be completed under her husband's aegis but in which Jonas, who had already taken his place on the council, could surely officiate.

And, in any case, there were soon other topics worthy of general discussion, the arrival, for instance, of a certain Mrs Tessa Delaney, a lady no longer in her first bloom of youth but of a most luscious appearance, who had taken up residence in Albion Terrace and was known by some mysterious bush telegraph to be no lady at all but the kept mistress of the widower, Mr Oldroyd of Fieldhead.

Could one receive Mrs Delaney or not? Most definitely not, declared Aunt Hannah. Perhaps one should not be too unkind, suggested Mrs Hobhouse, who had a vested interest in keeping Mr Oldroyd single and was relying on Mrs Delaney to do it for her.

'She gives excellent cream teas,' Prudence said innocently, replying to Aunt Hannah's startled exclamation with a casual, 'So Freddy Hobhouse tells me. And Jonas should be able to give you confirmation, since I believe he advises her on her investments.'

'Jonas,' Aunt Hannah announced with dignity, 'has a great many clients, who rely implicitly on his judgment. But they are not all persons with whom one could wish to take tea.'

And when the burning question of Mrs Delaney became exhausted there was the even more ferociously disputed question of the war with Russia, the appalling, incredible story that, far away in the Crimea, thousands of our soldiers were being murdered, not gloriously on the field of battle but vomiting their lives away as Giles had done, of cholera, dysentery, filth and neglect.

I did not really understand why we had joined the Turks in their fight against the Russians. Perhaps no one really knew. It merely seemed to my weak female intelligence that peace, having lasted so long, had begun to appear stale, so that any war would have been welcome, and we had chosen the first that came to hand. We had grown too fat and too prosperous, it seemed; too bored; ashamed, almost, of our prosperity; and a testing ground was needed, an opportunity for our young men to show us their valour, to replenish the glory of Waterloo which, being forty years distant, was growing middle-aged and dim.

'We must fight them,' Matthew Chard had declared more than a year ago, and when our troops finally sailed eastwards they had gone as conquerors, avenging angels, confident of glory. And since Cullingford had its share of reckless, half-starved young lads who had run off to be soldiers, finding an occasional flogging at the hands of a sergeant no harder to bear than an overlooker's strap in the mill yard, our streets were full of proudly weeping mothers and sweethearts getting ready to welcome the heroes home.

The Chards and the Clevedons were both amply provided with military connections, gallant young captains and high-ranking officers of the stamp of Lord Cardigan, who spent ten thousand pounds a year of his own money to smarten up his Hussars; and they set off eagerly, these gentlemen, some of them taking their private yachts, their wives and their mistresses with them. And because it would all be very soon over, because the men who had beaten Napoleon would have to do little more than display their red coats and their medals to put these insolent Cossacks to flight, a great many civilians went out too, equally encumbered by mistresses and hampers of champagne, worried in case they should arrive too late and miss the fun.

Matthew Chard would have gone himself had Caroline allowed it; Peregrine Clevedon and Julian Flood went off together, returning unshocked and unscathed with gifts of Crimean hyacinth bulbs for Georgiana and Caroline. And I suppose they were all slow to believe, like the rest of us, that courage alone – and there was plenty of courage – was not enough, that the Duke of Wellington, lulled by his own fond memories of Waterloo, had left us an army without reserves, that these glorious men, being immune neither to sabre thrusts nor bullets, had no one to replace them when they fell but raw recruits, illiterate most of them, desperate and juvenile, rushed into battle after a mere sixty days' drill.

But there was far worse than that, for, when our army, already riddled with disease, made the final leg of its journey across the Black Sea, there were transports enough provided for the men themselves, but too few to include their bedding and cooking utensils and tents, such trifling items as bandages, splints, chloroform and stretchers, which were all left behind. And when the battle was won, our wounded – the victors – lay on the grounds, unattended in some cases, until they died.

The ones who were sent back to the military hospital at Scutari lay on the ground too, we heard – a relative of Matthew Chard's among them – since for some unaccountable reason there were no beds; unwashed, since there were no buckets in which to carry water – if there was water; unfed, since there appeared to be no kitchens in working order; unbandaged, naturally, since no one had remembered about bandages. And so they died too, connections of the Chards and the Floods and connections of our mill-hands from Simon Street all together, a fair proportion of wives and mistresses dying with them, since there was still the cholera.

A Simon Street lad limped home from Scutari, having had his leg amputated without even the anaesthetic of a bottle of rum, having lain on the bare deck of a troop ship for fifteen days, waiting to come home, with nothing to shield his mutilated body from the sun, leaving his youth behind him and with nothing in front of him but a bleak apprenticeship to the beggar's trade.

I joined the committee formed by Aunt Hannah to assist him and the girl

649

who had borne his child, and the others who came after him, talking of gangrene and starvation and a woman called Florence Nightingale who had promised to see that their mates were fed. And with the stench of that in my mind, the remembered horror of Giles Ashburn's ending, my present anger and pity, my personal dilemma seemed much reduced indeed.

The day after the organ recital my uncle paid a visit, with both Nicholas and Blaize, to the business premises of Jonas Agbrigg in Croppers Court, where the deeds of partnership were finally signed, converting the private empire of Sir Joel Barforth into the firm of Sir Joel Barforth and Sons, an event which would have been celebrated by a family dinner at Tarn Edge, another impossibility, cancelled only because Georgiana, who had suffered a severe attack of milk fever after the birth of her daughter, was not yet well enough to come downstairs.

Nicholas was not at home when I called to pay my respects to his daughter, Miss Venetia Barforth, named, one supposed, for some ancestress of the Clevedons. Aunt Verity, for reasons I did not care to examine too closely, told me at once that he was not expected back for some time, while Georgiana herself was still too much the invalid either to inquire, or to care, why I had neglected her. The child, lost in her lacy cradle, was the smallest I had ever seen, the merest whisper of a human life, her helplessness touching a certain helplessness in me, so that it was a relief to be told I could not stay.

'Poor Georgiana. She almost lost her life,' Aunt Verity told me as we walked together down the wide staircase, the wide velvet sofa where I had gossiped with Caroline still there on the landing, warmed by the jewelled reflections from the great window. 'In fact at one point Dr Blackstone told us that there was no hope – that it was merely a matter of time.'

'How terrible!'

'Yes,' she said, pausing as we reached the hall, her clear eyes reminding me suddenly of Blaize. 'Terrible indeed. I have never seen Nicholas so frantic. Naturally one would have expected him to be deeply moved, but I really thought – for a while – that he would lose his mind. I found him leaning against the wall outside her bedroom door, not crying precisely but groaning, telling me – or himself – that he didn't want her to die – which, of course, he didn't. No, I have never seen him in such agony, nor so drunk afterwards, I might add, when we knew she would recover. Faith – I beg your pardon. You carry your own condition so well that I had quite forgotten. I have had three children, dear, quite easily, and your mother had no trouble to speak of. There is every reason to suppose you will be the same.'

There remained, after that, the final impossibility of meeting Nicholas again, the unthinkable moment when I would hold out my hand to him and he would either take it, or refuse it. But it was widely known in Cullingford that the Barforth brothers were not good friends, that neither appreciated the contribution the other made to the business, that Nicholas, his looms working to capacity and to order, saw his brother's constant journeyings as self-indulgence, while Blaize insisted that without his self-indulgences there would be no orders to fill. And no one expected to meet them drinking together at the Old Swan, nor in the same box at the theatre with their wives.

I had seen him in the distance often enough those first few months after my return to Cullingford, had turned sick and fled. Aunt Verity, perhaps quite knowingly, had described to me his torment at Georgiana's confinement, having recognized guilt in him as clearly as I had. And if he had been aware of his own guilt, and of mine – if he had understood that it would have been too much for either of us to bear – then would it suffice to clear his pathway to forgiveness and a new beginning? I prayed that it would, selflessly for his sake, selfishly for my own, since I knew my peace of mind depended upon it. And if, at times, I knew it could be no more than a fairy-tale, that life could never arrange itself so neatly as that, there were other times when I believed all might come right because I wanted to believe it, and because Blaize had said so.

But, when the time of our meeting finally came, it was not at all as I had imagined it, rehearsed it, for by then my pregnancy was so far advanced that I was heavy not only in body but in the senses, my emotions lulled, half-dormant, pulse-beat and heart-beat sluggish and expectant, my identity as a woman submerged in my role of breeding female, too placid and patient to arouse or experience any kind of passion. And my condition alone gave him a socially impeccable reason for not looking at me too closely, since Celia was not the only woman in the world to avoid male eyes at such a moment.

I had called for the first time at Blaize's office at Tarn Edge, and, interested in this room where he spent so much of his time, intrigued by this aspect of him as a man of business, by his elaborately furnished desk-top, the huge table where samples of Barforth cloth were set out, the window which gave him so perfect a view of the mill yard where he endeavoured as little as possible to set foot, I barely moved, barely drew a breath when Nicholas came into the room, more samples in his hands.

'Ah – Faith,' he said. 'Are you well?'

'Yes, Nicholas. Are you?'

'Fine, thanks. Look here, Blaize, is this what you want for Grassmann?' And he handed the samples of cloth to Blaize who took them to the window, where they examined them together in the daylight.

'It's not what *I* want for Grassmann,' Blaize said. 'It's what Grassmann wants for himself. What about that piece for Remburger?'

'Christ! It's still on the loom.'

'But you'll have enough ready for me to show? Remburger arrives in London on the twentieth.'

'Aye – you'd better come downstairs and have a look. It's still got a boardy feel to it, to me.'

'Well – it's not my place to put that right. I thought Mayor Agbrigg was supposed to see to it?'

'So did I. And where the hell is he? I should have been at Lawcroft an hour ago. Every time I show my face in these damned sheds it's the same story. If you're coming down, you'll have to come now.'

They walked to the door, warp and weft, delivery dates, profit and loss on their minds, and holding myself very still I said, 'Nicholas – is Georgiana feeling better?'

'Yes – she's mending. Kind of you to inquire.'

And, as in most moments of intense crisis, it was over before it had begun. He had neither taken my hand, after all, nor refused to take it. He had spoken to me. I had answered. The next time we met we would speak again. 'How are you?' 'I am very well.' It had happened.

It was possible after all.

But, as I drove home, my mind once again inexplicably linked with his, it seemed to me – who had always known what he meant – that he would rather have seen me dead than married to Blaize, that he would forgive neither one of us, would make no effort to understand, would not wish to understand, and that Blaize, who knew everything that went on around him, must from the start have known that very well.

24

Blaize, with his usual skill in avoiding times of domestic crisis, was not at home when our daughter was born, returning some days after the event, when she had lost that first crinkled petulance of the new-born, and I was reclining comfortably – even elegantly – among my lace pillows, my wrists and shoulders scented with lavender water, my hair well-brushed, my humour tolerant, since I had not suffered a great deal and could not have imagined him holding my fevered hands and sharing my groans in any case.

'You will have to forgive me,' he said. 'And you must admit you were a little ahead of yourself.'

'So I was. I thought it best to hurry, since there is Caroline's hunt ball to consider, you know. She is expecting me to be up and about in plenty of time for that. She's over there – your daughter – behind that frilly canopy.'

'My daughter,' he said. 'Good heavens!' his enthusiasm for parenthood being only lukewarm, having thoroughly disliked Georgiana's haphazard nursery arrangements at Tarn Edge. But, as he glanced down into the cradle, expecting nothing but red-faced, peevish anonymity, I saw his glance sharpen momentarily with interest, his eyes narrowing as he took a longer look.

'Well – I must say she's not quite the ill-tempered little frog other babies seem to be. In fact she's really rather nice.'

'Of course. But then, you always do things better than other men, don't you?'

'So I do,' he said coming back to my bedside. 'But not too often, darling, in this case. Faith, are you really as well as you look? I *did* come back as soon as I could, you know, and I really thought there'd be a week or more yet.'

'Good heavens! Blaize Barforth, can it be that you are feeling guilty?'

'I wonder.'

'Then there is no need. I did quite well without you. In fact I did so well that I am beginning to wonder what all the fuss is about. And Celia is most upset with me for being so cheerful. She thinks it positively improper.'

'Yes, but then, you see, you don't have to work hard to attract your husband's notice, like Celia – do you?'

My daughter, her birth so physically easy but so emotionally overwhelming, the first unconditional love to enter my life, since no matter what kind of woman she might become – and I had no way even of guessing – we would remain bound together. I would not even need to like her. I would always love her. And the certainty of it gave me peace and purpose, transforming me from a decorative object to a useful one. I had done something of note in the world. I had taken on the kind of total commitment my nature craved, and, even though the nurse and the nurserymaid were of more practical use to my daughter in those early days, I knew that her health, her appetite, the bloom in her cheeks, the growing flesh and fibre of her, had come to her through me.

We called her Blanche in compliment to her pale, quite exquisite colouring, the fair hair and almost transparent blue eyes, the ivory and silver of her.

'She's beautiful,' everyone said.

'She's like her mother,' Blaize replied.

She *was* beautiful. I was deeply content. So long as I remained in my lacy, flowery bedroom, within the four walls of my elegant house, the limits of my garden bordered by its hedge of lilacs and rhododendrons, I was happy. But I was married to a man for whom the world was very wide, who had chosen me not for my breeding qualities but as a partner in the gracious style of living he required, as a mistress, an entertainer, a good friend, and my new role of mother was simply added to these, in no way supplanting them.

'Should you really get up so soon, dear?' my mother asked me, holding my three week's old Blanche carefully on her satin lap.

'Oh yes, I think so. There are some German customers coming north in a week or two – and then some Americans – and they will have to be entertained.'

'Dearest, I never thought to see you so busy. It suits you.'

Remembering the sparse, cheerless nursery of my childhood, I decorated a fairy-tale, upstairs world for Blanche, pastel walls enlivened with sprays of vivid dream-flowers, bright rugs which Caroline thought gaudy and would collect dust, window-boxes crammed with daffodils that first springtime, and china bowls of the Crimean hyacinths Julian Flood had given to me and which my nurse – believing the flowers would use up the air and suffocate my daughter – never failed to remove at night. I dressed her like a princess – better than a princess, since it was my experience that the aristocracy did not spend lavishly on childhood. I pampered her, played with her, placed incredibly costly, incredibly

653

fragile ornaments on her mantelpiece so that she might grow up accustomed to beauty.

'You will make her very soft, and very vain,' Caroline told me, but, knowing rather more of the world, I thought, than Caroline, I believed that every female was entitled to her share of vanity, that it was, in fact, a most useful weapon, a great comfort.

I was the first woman in Cullingford to wear a cage crinoline, delighting in the freedom of movement this light metal structure gave me, for it had taken a dozen horsehair-stuffed petticoats to puff out a skirt even half so far, and if some of my acquaintances – Caroline among them – were uncomfortably aware that this vast, gracefully swaying skirt had nothing beneath it but lace pantaloons, fresh air, and legs – 'My dear, how can you manage to sit down? And what on earth is to happen in a high wind?' – it suited me, and it was not long before others followed my lead.

My clothes became much talked about, not only in Cullingford but in the neighbouring, more cosmopolitan Bradford and Leeds, where Blaize had many friends. And I did not dislike it. I had plain, pastel-tinted afternoon gowns, delicate creams, near whites, with the exotic contrast of a richly patterned crimson shawl draped loosely around them. I had a walking dress – much copied the first year I wore it – of coffee-coloured – *foulard des Indes* trimmed with black velvet, a brown bonnet trimmed with black satin and black feathers, a sable muff Blaize had brought back from some unspecified journey. I had light summer dresses with sleeves of puffed muslin and tulle, wrist-bands of ribbon, pearl and coral, an evening gown – worn for the Listonby Hunt Ball and greatly appreciated by not a few fox-hunting men – in a deep, grape purple, cut scandalously low and worn with no jewellery, contriving to give the impression of a nude body emerging from a dark, gauzy cloud. I was the first of my acquaintance to wear my hair in a net made of strands of pearl, a net of gold chains, the first to order black, military style boots from my husband's bootmaker, to wear Spanish mantillas of black and white lace. And when I persuaded Caroline and Prudence into their first crinolines I had already mastered the little gliding steps necessary to make those capricious cages dip and sway, how to get myself through a doorway and into a carriage without disaster, how to walk across a room without leaving a trail of broken china to mark my passage, how to judge correctly my distance from the drawing-room fire, the bedtime candles, for even I was obliged to admit that, once these colossal skirts were set alight, there would be little for even the most agile of women to do but burn with them.

Blaize gave me a victoria to drive in, far preferable to the more conventional landau, since the victoria, which had no doors, allowed for a better arrangement of my skirts. He abandoned his own curricle for the newer, light-shafted, far more vicious cabriolet which, when he was in residence, carried him from Elderleigh to Tarn Edge at a killing speed. And we became a fashionable couple, as Blaize had intended, giving easy, quite informal dinner-parties when he was at home, the house at all times ready for his return and the reception of anyone he might bring with him.

'Faith darling – this is Mr Remburger from New York.' And I no longer said, 'Blaize – you didn't *tell* me he was coming,' but 'Mr Remburger – I have *so* looked forward to meeting you,' knowing that if it happened to be winter there would be a fire in the best spare bedroom, if it happened to be spring there would be bowls of lilacs and forsythia, roses in the summer, profuse enough to please the most exacting guest. I knew – because I made it my business to know – that my pantry shelves, although minute in comparison with Caroline's, contained at all times their share of delicacies and dainties, that the wine which should be chilled would be chilled, the wine which should be allowed to breathe would already be breathing; for, if my staff was small and my own temperament not exacting, we were all aware that in domestic matters Blaize was very exacting indeed, and my household functioned around a general desire to please him.

When he was at home I existed in a state of pleasant anticipation, of surprise blended sometimes with a mild annoyance, sometimes with an honest delight, a certain stretching of my intellect and my powers of invention, for, although he was never morose, never ill-tempered, suffered no jealous rages as Nicholas had done, no urge to punish me in order to test the depth of my love – since he did not ask me to love him and was not in love with me – he *did* require to be entertained.

He was not in any conventional sense a domestic man. He wanted comfort, certainly, luxury whenever possible; but, although he knew the cost of it and was ready to pay most generously, he did not wish to know the details of how his candlelit dinners, his scented pillows, his immaculately laundered linen, were contrived. Nor did he expect to find me harassed or gloomy – since he was never so himself; expecting no passionate welcome on his homecoming, no questions, no complaints, no demands – since he made none himself; but requiring, instead, the same affectionate companionship he gave to me.

And he was a witty, easy, charming friend, an imaginative lover.

'You might care to wear this for me, Faith,' and he would toss me a peignoir of scandalous transparency or an evening gown that appeared to commence at the waist. And when it transpired that Mr Remburger of New York was also an admirer of bare, blonde shoulders, Blaize was immensely amused, by no means displeased to see that other men desired his wife.

It was, perhaps, not a marriage in the way the Law Valley understood it, since Law Valley men did not encourage sensuality in their wives, being more inclined to fall sound asleep after domestic lovemaking than to lie easily entwined together in the lamplight, drinking champagne and telling each other how very pleasant it had all been. And most Law Valley wives, far from encouraging such nonsense, would have been acutely embarrassed, if not downright horrified by it.

But within the privacy of our bedroom Blaize treated me neither as a sexual convenience nor as a matron who could be asked to do no more

655

than her duty, but as a high-priced courtesan, showing no signs of burning passion and expecting none, quite simply enjoying me, an essential ingredient of his pleasure being that I should enjoy him. And, if the Law Valley would not have understood the black lace peignoir, the velvet ribbon I sometimes left around my neck when all else had been discarded, the leisurely arousal that could begin as he leaned through the candlelight towards me at dinner-time to touch my hand, or brush his mouth against my ear, and might not reach its conclusion until after midnight, then I understood it very well.

'Now then, darling – are you longing for me now?'

'I believe so.'

'Then I think you may long a moment more, Faith, and appreciate me better – don't you?'

'Yes – since you do so like to be appreciated.'

'That's right, darling – drift over me, just melt. You know, I think we do this very well.'

'You mean you think you do it very well.'

'Mmmmm – but you're coming along nicely, Faith.'

He made no inquiries into the state of my emotions. He saw Nicholas daily when he was at the mills and talked of him quite easily when the occasion required it, displaying a lack of curiosity about the past – even as to what my feelings might have been for Giles Ashburn – which I at first mistook for consideration until I realized that he was, quite simply, not curious.

'Blaize,' I asked him, just once. 'Why is everything so easy for you?' And laughing, understanding my meaning exactly, he had replied, 'Because I am shallow, darling, and superficial and immensely self-centred. And it is my firm intention to remain so.'

But it was, of course, less simple than that. He felt no anxiety with regard to me or to Nicholas because, never having been in love himself, he did not really believe in it. He enjoyed what he had, he had everything he enjoyed, and had not spoken in jest of his childhood belief that everyone, sooner or later, must prefer him to Nicholas. We had made an arrangement which was clearly congenial to us both, had sealed it with the birth of our daughter, Blanche. What more was there to be said?

The war with Russia ended, largely, it seemed to me, because everyone had grown tired of it, rather than because anybody had actually won, and we celebrated the peace with fireworks in the park at Listonby where Blaize and I were frequent guests, especially now that Caroline, in hot pursuit of the Duke of South Erin, needed to show his sister and his sister's friends that not all the Barforths were unsophisticated. I continued to sit on the committee, chaired by Aunt Hannah, for the relief of the mauled remnants still dragging their way back from the Crimea, remembering Giles acutely every time I visited one of them in Simon Street, a fine, charitable lady I wondered if he would recognize. I found employment for the wives of men who were now unemployable, gave money to those who had no women to support them, took arrowroot and soup and blankets to sick children, to soldiers' women –

beggars' women – who, despite my aunt's instructions to the contrary, became pregnant again and again.

Yet, when a gentleman who reminded me strongly of Giles as he would have been had he lived to be a little older, gave a lecture in what had once been a church hall at the lower end of Sheepgate on the use of contraceptive sponges, which, of soaked in vinegar and washed occasionally, might be of help, there was a *frisson* of horror among the respectable middle classes, my sister Celia, who had miscarried now for the sixth time, finding it too disgusting to contemplate; others, for vocal if somewhat vague reasons, considering it contrary to the law of God; while Aunt Hannah condemned Prudence soundly for her support of this charlatan, and me for inviting him to dinner.

'There is such a thing as self-restraint,' Aunt Hannah said.

'I have never noticed it,' Prudence told her.

'Not the most romantic suggestion I've ever heard,' Blaize murmured, wrinkling a fastidious nostril when I mentioned the matter to him. 'But, of course, if it could be contrived by a clever woman so that there might be no distinctive odour – so that the gentleman concerned might be quite unaware of it – then I can't really think the gentleman would mind.'

Prudence spent as much time as she could in my house, escaping whenever possible from the restrictions of Blenheim Lane, the Irish cousins, the affectionate but eagle-eyed Mr Adair. She was twenty-eight now, aproaching twenty-nine, a desperate age for a single woman, and although her unmarried status did not disturb her – since Freddy Hobhouse was still willing to put an end to that – she was frequently in despair at the slow frittering away of her time, the bonds with which my father, even from the grave, continued to bind her, and which Daniel Adair had no intention of letting go. She had longed to go out to the Crimea and offer her services to Miss Florence Nightingale, and had been prevented not by the general outcry but by a simple withdrawal of funds which had made her journey impossible. She longed to set up a school where girls of the new generation could be taught – as she put it – to raise themselves above the level of pet animals, but Mr Adair, being fond of pet animals, would not hear of that. Young ladies belonged in their mothers' drawing-rooms. Young ladies did not go out unchaperoned – as Prudence had been accustomed to do. Young ladies did not read newspapers, nor hold political discussions, nor express their opinions on the subject of back-to-back houses, which Mayor Agbrigg's new building regulations were striving to prohibit. Young ladies, on all topics of importance, shared the views of their senior male relative, and the only alternative open to them was to take a husband, who would be selected by that senior male himself. And although Daniel Adair did not really believe a word of all this, and, far from disliking Prudence, was rather fond of her, he was a man who enjoyed a good fight, finding it a pleasant change from a surfeit of conjugal bliss, and could never resist his part in the running battle between them.

'I'm rich,' she said. 'Men want to marry me for my money. I own a fortune in porcelain, and I can't raise a penny.'

And it was Blaize who suggested, 'No, you can't sell your porcelain, of course, but I wonder if there is anything in your father's will which forbids you to give it away?'

'Why should I do that?'

'Oh – generosity, I imagine. There are a pair of Wedgwood urns I have often admired which would look very well on my study mantelpiece, and a porcelain nymph that rather reminds me of Faith. If you should choose to give them to me – or to Faith – I'm not sure anyone could complain. And should it occur to anyone that I might have paid you for them – well, I cannot think Jonas Agbrigg would be willing to take a mere supposition to court.'

'I will check the will again with Jonas,' she said, and when she had gone I told him, 'That was very clever of you, Blaize.'

'Yes – but then we know I am a clever man.'

'It was also very good-natured. Those urns can't be cheap, you know.'

'I do know. But bear in mind that I actually want them – which makes me just a shade less generous. And, if she is suffering from too many Irish cousins, you might care to suggest to her that an engagement is not a marriage, but carries a fair amount of protection. I have it on good authority that Aunt Hannah, in similar circumstances, once engaged herself to a parson with small intention of marrying him.'

'That hardly seems fair.'

'No, but it would give Freddy Hobhouse the boost he needs. I also have it on good authority that my brother is thinking of making an offer for Nethercoats, and if old Mr Hobhouse sells out there will be nothing for Freddy. He is not a partner, and Nicky's offer is unlikely to be generous. There might be enough to keep the old couple in a house on the coast, and to make some provision for the girls, but Freddy and the boys will have to fend for themselves. If he got engaged to Prudence, it might be no more than a stay of execution – but the promise of her money might make Mr Hobhouse less ready to sell, and even if it didn't he'd be bound to put up his asking price. You see, I'm being good-natured again.'

'Yes, I do see. You want to make Nicholas pay more for Nethercoats.'

'Ah – but if it would help Prudence and Freddy – and I'm sure Nicky could find the money. They think the world of him at Mr Rawnsley's bank.'

'It's not a game, Blaize – not to them. Prudence couldn't jilt Freddy if he lost his business. She'd feel obliged to stand by him.'

'I know,' he said, his smoky eyes brimming with amusement and self-knowledge. 'But Freddy is a gentleman, don't you see. He'd release her.'

Yet, whether or not she was inclined to take advice of this nature, I noticed that quite soon a whole series of familiar objects began to appear, the Wedgwood urns, the white biscuit nymph, a pair of Grecian dancers in Meissen porcelain, a biscuit Venus by Sèvres, a bare-shouldered, female figure from Vincennes mounted on a jungle of ormolu foliage.

'How generous you are, Blaize! I believe Prudence is saving hard.'

And, remembering that he had also been generous to Georgiana – that he had a penchant perhaps, for ladies in distress – I wondered if he had once included me among them.

I went to Listonby that autumn on a prolonged visit – Blaize having left for some exotic destination – my presence required there because Caroline, now that her sons were out of the nursery, no longer found the start of the hunting season altogether congenial, fretting a great deal in private that her seven-year-old twins could now take their fences like men – or so their father assured her – and by no means pleased to see them come home to her in so indescribable a state of filth and exhaustion.

But Georgiana, who had taken her own son up on her saddle from his babyhood, determined that like all the Clevedons he should ride before he could walk, had no such qualms, and scant patience with Caroline's heart-searchings.

'Good-heavens! If either of them breaks a leg, it will mend. It's the horses' legs we have to be careful of, darling – one has to shoot them, you know, after a bad fall. And, if there are times when one would quite like to shoot one's children, I'm sure there's no fear of it. I'll keep an eye on your boys for you – and they're both quite careful in any case, they just jog along with the grooms when they're tired – not at all like my Gervase.'

But Caroline well knew that Georgiana, once her blood was up, would keep an eye on no one, would leave her own Gervase in a ditch if he happened to take a tumble; while Hetty Stone, who was no equestrienne, but who regularly drove herself out to the covert-side, would have no time either for little boys, being more inclined to keep her eyes on their fathers. And each hunting day contained its share of misery. No leisurely tea-tray in her bed these days, until the meet had departed, but a strained presence hovering in the hall, her whole nature torn between Lady Chard who must both by rank and inclination have a fine appreciation of such things, and Caroline Barforth, frankly revolted by such recklessness, such waste.

'It's quite ridiculous,' she would tell me as we watched them set out, all dash and clatter in the stable yard as they tasted the air of the fresh morning, the occasional cursing and the laughter as some nervous animal went skittering out of control shredding her nerves to agony as, with outward calm, she ordered the serving of stirrup cups. 'Quite ridiculous, taking children of that age – it can't be good for them. And the language they are exposed to – and the manners. Did you hear Perry Clevedon just now, yelling like a madman? And Julian Flood is every bit as bad. They will go through a dozen horses between them, this season, ruin them – whatever Georgiana may have to say – and I would like to know who pays the bills? Well, in fact, I do know it, for Georgiana is keeping an entire stable over at Galton, for Perry's convenience, and she could only have the money from Nicholas. It doesn't occur to her, one supposes, that he might need his spare cash for something else – that it would suit him better to put it back into the business, or to get another business off the ground. And that animal she has bought for Gervase is enormous – my goodness, I told Matthew at once that, if he had any thought of getting such a monster for Dominic or Noel, then he and I would certainly quarrel. And now he has taken Gideon out as well – to ride with the grooms, he says, since that is what he did himself at that age.'

And, of course, that was the root of her dilemma. She did not really want her children to hunt – did not much care for hunting men apart from Matthew – but the Chards, the Floods, the Clevedons, certainly the South Erins, had always hunted from childhood, and she was determined to fit her sons for their inheritance. She did not really want to send them to Matthew's old school, where they would be required to wash in cold water at a stand-pipe in an open yard, like the lads from Simon Street, and would be flogged when they misbehaved as soundly as factory-boys were strapped by their overlooker – as no schoolmaster had ever dared to flog her middle-class brothers – but young squires had always been treated so, and were sent to school, after all, not to be educated but to be toughened into men who could lead a Light Brigade, armed only with sabres, into the mouths of Russian cannon; who could acquire the passionless hauteur of privilege which had so attracted her to her husband. She did not really want her sons to sally forth, gun in hand, and slaughter with their own not always accurate shot the pheasant and grouse to replenish her larder, would have much preferred to purchase her game clandestinely but safely at her back door, as they did at Tarn Edge. But every young gentleman must know how to handle himself at a *grande battue*, must be worthy of his place in a walking line of guns, must know how to shoot flying and how to shoot well. And, if armed gamekeepers and mantraps were really necessary for the discouragement of poachers, then she, as the wife of a Justice of the Peace who also happened to own the game being poached, could hardly disagree.

'I know they must enjoy country pursuits,' she moaned. 'I know, and they are all so brave. But it seems so wasteful sometimes. Wherever the fox goes, they go, regardless of whose crops they are riding down, and I feel sure the tenants don't like it – except, of course, that since we own the land I suppose they can't complain. Do you know, Faith, really, sometimes I think some feckless lad from Simon Street could understand Perry Clevedon and Julian Flood better than I do. They take every day as it comes, no thought for tomorrow, not the faintest notion of saving anything or planning anything. They don't pay their debts in Simon Street either. And as for the other thing – my word, I have been hearing all my life about immorality in the weaving sheds, but if you had the faintest notion of what goes on in that Abbey cloister night after night – Hetty Stone may smile at Matthew when I complain about it, and imagine I don't see her – and he might smile back, since I know he thinks I am a prude – but it is not *right*, Faith. It is not responsible. Hetty Stone may be a duke's daughter and think it a great lark that her brothers were all sent down from Eton and Oxford, and that one of them is keeping a quite famous actress somewhere off Bedford Square – although I must

660

confess he was a hero in the Crimea –'

'Caroline, your own brothers have not been angels.'

'I wouldn't know about that,' she said, instantly bristling. 'And, whatever they may have done, the business has not suffered by it. They get out of bed every morning and go to the mills, and they pay their bills on time too – right on time or no one in Cullingford would trade with them. Yes – yes – I know old Mr Clevedon wears himself out looking after his tenants, and that they are all ready to go out and fight for Queen and country at a moment's notice, and will govern the country without getting paid a penny for doing it because they think it it their duty. But they don't happen every day, do they – wars and Cabinet appointments? It's not three hundred and sixty-five days a year every year, like the mills. Oh dear, I do hope Matthew remembers about Dominic and Noel – and I am certain he will forget about Gideon.'

But it was young Gervase Barforth who went over his horse's head that morning, landing on his own head on a stony patch of ground from which his uncle Perry eventually retrieved him and tossed him by the scruff of his neck to his mother, the kind of treatment both Peregrine and Georgiana had received often enough themselves at that age. Georgiana rode back to Listonby with him across her saddle, his face quite grey, his posture, when she allowed him to slide to the ground, decidedly unsteady.

'Just put him to bed,' she said. 'He'll be all right. No bones broken, and he'll know better next time.'

And when, having ascertained, as she put it, that he would live, she rode off again, it was perhaps unfortunate that Caroline, alarmed by the child's persistent stupor, took it upon herself to send for Nicholas, certainly unfortunate that he arrived late that afternoon in a black fury, half an hour in advance of his wife.

I had no wish to be present, but could not avoid it when she came striding into the hall, her habit looped up around her arm, mud-spattered and glowing and beautiful as she'd been the first time I had seen her, her boots as careless now of Caroline's carpets as they had been that day of Sir Joel's, that rare bird of the wild wood who had, very briefly, submitted to her captor's hand, but who was flying free again, a lovely lark-soaring of the spirit that halted in mid-air as she saw her husband.

'Good heavens!' she said. 'What brings you here? Are the mills on fire? Has Cullingford burned to the ground?'

'No,' he told her curtly, 'but there could be other reasons just as drastic. Your son, for instance. He had a riding accident earlier in the day, as you are well aware. He may have died – an hour ago – or be on his death-bed at the very least. Since his mother could not be found, it would seem fairly natural that they should send for me.'

I saw the colour drain away from her face, her eyes, against that sudden blanching, a startling, terrified green. I saw her body sway forward a little and then right itself, one hand pressed hard against her stomach, and then, her eyes fluttering from me to Caroline, she said, 'No – no, Nicky – he's not dead and he's not dying. Faith would be crying, and Caroline would be wanting to murder me. It couldn't be true.'

'I think it could.'

She advanced into the room, swishing her crop against her skirt, nervously flexing her free hands, her colour very high now, her temper rising with it, her courage the greater because I could see she was a little afraid of him.

'He took a tumble – it happens, Nicky. It's happened often enough to me. And I brought him home at once.'

'Now that *was* good of you.'

She stood for a moment looking down at her hands, her crop still nervously slicing the air, and then, throwing back her head in an abrupt movement, her light lashes beaded with tears, she said, 'Nicky, don't be hard – please – don't be sarcastic. I can't talk to you when you're like this. There's no harm done. If you think I should have stayed with him, then perhaps you're right –'

'No – no – it couldn't be right to deprive you of a day's sport.'

'Nicky,' she moaned, the note of despair in her voice so piercing that I wanted to cover my ears. 'It wasn't like that. I only did what it seemed natural for me to do. He didn't need me. Caroline was here. Nanny was here. If I'd stayed, they'd have shooed me away. I've been carried home myself like that – worse than that – time and time again and taken no harm. It builds character, don't you see? That's what grandfather always says.'

'I daresay. But you're a Clevedon. He's not.'

'He's my son.'

'So he is. And you have a daughter, I seem to remember, back in Cullingford, who'll be lucky to see you again before Christmas – who won't see much of you at all until she's big enough to sit a horse, I reckon.'

'Oh dear,' she said. 'Oh dear – oh dear –' and she began to pace up and down the room, hands clasped around her elbows, hugging herself, rocking herself almost, in her agony. 'You won't understand me, Nicky – you just won't. I *do* care for the children. Yes – more than you care – yes I do – and you won't see it. You won't let me care in my own way. You want me to be somebody else all the time, and I can't do it, Nicky – I've tried and I'll never do it. You want to think I neglect them – yes, I know it. Nicky, you've hurt me now – it's done – it's enough – don't be hard –'

'Damnation!' he said, swinging abruptly round to the fireplace, his back to us, his hand tight-clenched on the corner of the mantelpiece, and, seeing the opportunity of escape, I fled outside into the fresh air, as far away as I could, hoping Caroline would have the sense to leave them too. And, unaware of the direction I took, feeling his anger as if it had been directed against myself, feeling her misery just as acutely, I was startled by the sound of sobbing, astonished, as I turned the corner of the house, to see Julian Flood slumped against his horse's neck, his shoulders heaving with an uncontrollable anguish, and Matthew Chard standing beside him, white-faced and sick, his own balance unsteady.

'Matthew – good heavens!'

And instantly, because they were gentlemen who did not exhibit their grief before a lady, who had endured their share of floggings in youth to enable them to withstand pain, Julian Flood stopped crying, almost straightened himself, and Matthew Chard came hurrying to meet me.

'Faith, we've had a bit of bad luck, I'm afraid. Perry Clevedon has taken a bad fall – happened just after Georgiana left us – wanted to get back home, she said, to see to her boy –'

'How bad?'

'Oh – bad – his horse reared up, went clean over and fell on him. It's the worst fall there is.'

'And he's – dead?'

'Oh yes – dead when we picked him up. I can't think he knew much about it. Well – I doubt if knowing that will help Georgiana, but I'd better tell her –'

'No. Nicholas is here. Let him tell her.'

'Thank God!' he said. 'Oh, thank God for that! I don't know how she'll go on without Perry – in fact I don't think she'll go on at all.' And, squeezing my hand, his whole body brimming with gratitude, he left me and hurried off to Caroline, and to Nicholas.

Blaize, by some miracle, came home for the Clevedon funeral and perhaps I surprised him – certainly myself – by the extent of my relief.

'I couldn't face it without you.'

'Darling – you flatter me, but I've never seen myself as a rock to lean on. And what is there for you to face? It's Georgiana, surely, who will need a rock. Let us hope she has one.'

But she was most amazingly composed, standing erect and quite still beside her grandfather, her eyes dry, her face chalk-white against her black veil, a fragile figure, supporting an even more fragile, almost visibly ageing man, for Perry had left no sons, at least none that could be acknowledged, and they were burying not only his recklessly broken, carelessly wasted body, but the end of their ancient line. And once more, as at all momentous occasions, there was that deep division of ranks: Aunt Verity and Caroline and even myself, representatives of the manufacturing classes, being ready to shed a tear; the gentry standing like soldiers around the graveside, even Julian Flood, who had been drunk ever since the accident, having sobered himself up that day, his wild, handsome face as expressionless as granite.

The Clevedon tenants, the pensioned-off retainers, the household servants, the village schoolmistress, were all there, knowing far better than I what this death signified, and there was complete silence as he was laid to rest in his own ground, silence as we walked back from the Abbey church to the house, only the October wind stirring the leaves, the crackling of logs in the stone-flagged hall, old Mr Clevedon taking us each one by the hand with perfect courtesy, his whole body quite hollow, his hopes in ashes, but his mouth pronouncing the words he believed it right and proper for him to speak.

We took a glass of wine, arranged ourselves in awkward groupings, Nicholas with his mother and Caroline, Hetty Stone attaching herself to me because Blaize was there, Julian Flood going off suddenly to get drunk again, one supposed, Matthew and those other country gentlemen engaging Mr Clevedon in painstaking conversation. But Georgiana, who had stood so very still – who had surely never been so still in her whole life before – was nowhere to be seen, did not appear, and after an agonizing hour, when everybody wished to leave and no one liked to be the first to go, Blaize put his head close to mine and murmured, 'Where is she?'

'I don't know – upstairs perhaps?'

'No. She didn't come back to the house. Try the cloister, Faith.'

And when I raised my eyebrows in surprise and didn't move he said, 'Yes, Faith – *do* it. Someone should look for her. I can't – not without causing comment – and clearly Nicky doesn't mean to.'

I went outside, unhappy with myself because I didn't want this mission, unhappy with him for asking – uneasy in my heart, in my bones; ready to weep myself for a man I hadn't really known and hadn't liked, because the tears were there, inside me, and needed to be shed; apprehensive and irritable because, if I found her, I had no idea what Blaize expected me to do for her, no idea of what I would have it in me to offer.

But my first sight of her was enough to cancel out any other feeling but compassion.

She was in the cloister as Blaize had foreseen, sitting on the ground, her back pressed against the wall, the arched, fan-vaulted ceiling reducing her to the proportions of a weeping doll. And I had never seen such tears, for they seemed to come not from her eyes alone but from the pores of her skin, a wild fountain of grief more terrible somehow because it was still quite silent, no shuddering, no crying out, just that drowning of her face and her spirit in water.

'Oh, Georgiana,' I said, and sat down on the uneven, stony ground beside her, feeling that words would be of no avail, that I could merely offer her the comfort of another human presence, as one comforts the new-born or some stricken animal.

But she was a Clevedon too – above all she was that – and after a moment she nodded, shook herself slightly, and gave me a rueful, tremulous smile.

'I loved him so much, you see.'

'Yes, I know.'

'Did my grandfather ask you to look for me? No? I'm so glad. I wouldn't let grandfather see me cry. I came over to Galton at once – after it happened – to be with him, and if I'd broken down and cried I'd have been no use to him. So I didn't cry. I couldn't let grandfather down. I'll go back in a minute.'

As she began to dry her face with her hands and her sleeves, I gave her my handkerchief and watched, with great respect, as she restored herself to composure.

'There – am I decent now?'

'Yes – quite decent. But give yourself a little longer.'

'Yes – can you understand me, Faith? I loved him, but it was more than that. I've been sitting here thinking about it, and it seems to me that I've never been alone before. So long as there was Perry I couldn't be alone. He was here, you see – every day of my life. He was older than me and so he was here, waiting for me, when I was born. My father died and my mother went off somewhere and I never saw her again. I don't remember either of them. Just Perry, and grandfather, and the Abbey. I think I was the happiest child in the world. It's here, in these stones, all that fun, all that joy – I left it here for Perry's children, like it was all left here for me.'

She stood up and suddenly pressed her whole body hard against the wall, her hands caressing the uneven surface, making contact with her past, finding and holding the two hopeful, eager children who had played here, their minds so perfectly in harmony that, reaching out for it again, remembering, her face lost its taut agony, and she was beautiful.

'Georgiana –'

'Yes – don't worry. I'm still here. I'm not mad. I know I can't really hear his voice, Faith, but in this place it just seems to me that I can. And that's lovely, you know. Don't look so alarmed, darling. I know what I have to do. It's the Abbey, you see – so long as there's a Clevedon here it doesn't matter which one. We change our faces, but it's always the same person, really, underneath the skin. Grandfather thinks it's over – that's why he's grieving – but the Abbey will come to me now, when he's gone, and I'll look after it for my Gervase. I was never certain that Perry would marry, and I knew I'd better have a son – just in case. I was right, wasn't I?'

'No,' I said, and although she had not really asked me a question she turned to look at me, startled, but still in her fey humour smiling.

'Why, Faith, whatever can you mean?'

I knew it was not the time to speak to her of such things, but there might never be another moment when she would be ready to hear me, another moment when it would be possible for me to speak, and I had let too many of my life's opportunities pass by. I had given Nicolas up for many reasons, but not least among them had been the hope that he would turn to her. He had not yet done so. But now, in her grief for her brother, for the man who had really dominated her emotions, claimed her loyalties, surely, at last, she could turn to Nicholas? Surely something could be salvaged, so that the fairy-tale Blaize had convinced me was a reality might finally come true?

'Faith – you are looking at me very strangely.'

'Am I? Then it is because – because you must take care. Georgiana, this was your world, but it can't be your world now because it's not your husband's. And it may never be Gervase's. He's just a little boy, and you were quite right when you said he would grow to look like Perry – he does – but you married away from here. Georgiana – his name is Barforth.'

She sat down again, with one of her abrupt movements, on the old stone, and, because I could not tower above her, nor appear to dominate her, I sat down too, this hushed, airless place seeming more than ever like a tunnel into the past.

'You are telling me, I suppose, that Nicky will expect Gervase to go into the mills?'

'You must know he will.'

'He has never said so.'

'I believe it must seem so obvious to him that he might not have thought it worth mentioning.'

'And it seems obvious to you?'

'Yes, it does.'

'Just as it seems obvious to me that he should not.'

And for a while she sat perfectly still again, another moment of communion with everything that had a meaning for her, before she startled me with the familiar, bird-like movement of her head, the abruptness of her smile.

'No. It will not happen, you know. If Perry had inherited, and married, even then it would not have happened. I have been feeling very weak, lately, Faith – oh, I told myself it was because I had not recovered from Venetia, but it was not that. I felt overwhelmed, somehow – as if I had failed at everything I had endeavoured. And so I had. I felt that I had nothing to give anyone, and that is a very desperate feeling – so hard to accept that there was nothing in me that anyone could want. You do see, don't you, that now, when I have this great gift – not just the Abbey, but all that goes with it – when I know that Gervase feels as I feel, that he knows it is the land that nourishes us, then I can't hold it back from him. All the rest is just money, Faith – and there's so much of it.'

She stood up, held out her hand to me, and her touch was hot and excited, her face as vivid as I had ever seen it.

'It's the cloister,' she said. 'It does me good. I thought I'd come here to die, an hour ago. I thought if I went on sitting here, very quietly, that I'd just fade away and no one would miss me. But it helped me, like it always does, and now I must go and take care of my grandfather. I'm strong now.'

25

Sir Joel and Lady Barforth did not come north for Christmas that year, my uncle having suffered a recurrence of his chest complaint which could only be aggravated by our damp, sooty air, and so they contented themselves by inviting my mother and Mr Adair, Aunt Hannah and Mayor Agbrigg, to join them at Rosemount Lodge, dividing the generations, not unpleasantly, for the first time.

I spent the greater part of the festive season at Listonby, watching with admiration as Caroline organized her massive household with the same skill and energy her father and Nicholas devoted to their weaving sheds, her unerring eye for detail, her iron discipline, ensuring that one celebration merged into the other as threads are drawn together into some complex pattern on the loom, her guests being presented only with the finished product, a task which, because she performed it superbly, appeared almost effortless.

There was a dinner of seventy covers on Christmas Eve, ending at midnight with carol singers at the door, lanterns and largesse, and even a scattering of snowflakes it seemed quite possible she had arranged herself. There was the manorial progress to church on Christmas morning, the delivery of Christmas hampers to the Listonby poor, an afternoon of children's games in the Great Hall, festooned with holly and mistletoe, everybody's nanny very much in attendance while the gentlemen took their port and madeira and cigars in the library, the ladies gossipped around the tea-time fire.

There was a new pony apiece in the stable yard for Dominic and Noel and Gideon Chard, young Liam Adair, who had been left in my charge until my mother came home, amusing himself by bullying Georgiana's highly strung Gervase, until Dominic settled the matter by knocking Liam down. There was little Venetia Barforth, an auburn-haired Christmas-tree fairy, taking her first excited steps, my pansy-eyed niece, Grace, patiently allowing herself to be kissed by any sentimental lady, her curls to be ruffled by any gentleman, although Celia, who had been invited to dine, found after all that she was not quite well and could not stay. There was my ivory and silver Blanche, lovely and still as a figure carved in biscuit porcelain, aware, it seemed to me, from her infancy that she had no need to make a noise in order to be looked at.

There was dinner itself, another vast spread of geese and turkeys, port jelly and brandied plum pudding, a ceremony crowned by the carrying in of a boar's head, stuffed – I happened to know since Caroline had attended the procedure herself – with fillets of its own flesh, crowned with a forcemeat of rabbit and partridge, tongue and truffles. There was the Boxing Day meet, a ball to follow, when Julian Flood, finding no one else to take his fancy, pursued me with an ardour that amused my husband, but which caused Caroline, when she became aware of it, to give him firm warning that unless he mended his manners he would be sent home.

'Dearest Caroline,' he told her, collapsing in a fit of his wild laughter. 'That is one of the reasons I come here, don't you know, to run the risk of being sent home again.'

But he remained for the full twelve days, was sober enough every evening at dinner to raise his glass and drink most loyally to his Queen, for whom no less than five of his cousins had fought and died in the Crimea. And, remembering that the Floods had always sacrificed themselves in this way, that their family motto was 'Loyalty is its own reward', Lady Chard forgave him.

No one at Listonby was ever aware of work being done. No one ever met a flustered housemaid on the stairs, nor encountered a servant anywhere but in the place he ought to be, correctly attired, impassive, almost leisurely. Yet for those twelve days of Christmas no fewer than thirty guests ever sat down to dine, and every morning, as if by magic, fires were burning brightly in those thirty bedrooms reserved for their accommodation, cans of hot water, warm towels, an array of personal requisites, stood ready on thirty wash-stands, thirty sets of garments were laid out, freshly laundered and pressed, thirty more an hour before luncheon and before tea, thirty more at dinner-time. No matter how early one descended, the logs in the Great Hall blazed out their welcome, the dining-room sideboards groaned with dishes of gammon and kidneys, sausages and eggs, smoke haddock and woodcock, hot bread and cold bread, fruit in and out of season. Newspapers were always to hand, their pages well ironed and clean, writing-paper always available and a liveried footman waiting, unobtrusive but alert, to deliver one's notes. Likes and dislikes were remembered and attended to – written down, I happened to know, most assiduously by Caroline – so that a guest with a preference for turbot found turbot awaiting him, a lady with a passion for whist found a whist table and a steady supply of partners at her beck and call. And every night, no matter how late, an apparently unruffled Caroline, well-versed in the ways of the gentry by now, saw to it that those thirty persons were safely tucked into their *own* warm beds – or cool beds if that was their fancy – assuming, because she expected her wishes to be obeyed, that they would stay there until morning.

Yet the very perfection of it all was a little wearing, and I was not sorry to be home again, nor entirely cast down when my mother returned to claim young Liam Adair, whoses talkative presence at my table was not always pleasing to Blaize. But the Adairs' visit to Bournemouth had given Prudence a fresh taste of freedom, a refusal to relinquish it which ended in the direct confrontation between her and Daniel Adair my mother had always dreaded. There was some rapid, verbal cross-fire, centring eventually on the porcelain, Mr Adair having seen rather too much of it in my hands for his comfort. And, when Prudence defended herself by declaring there were pieces missing that *she* could not account for, they went through the whole collection item by item, and at Prudence's insistence stored it away in the attic.

'That suits me fine,' he told her, whereupon she went through it all again the following morning, having realized, somewhat too late, that porcelain stored in packing-cases would not be so easily missed as porcelain on display.

'Yes, that suits me fine,' Mr Adair said again with a roguish twinkle, making it his business to be seen, on several occasions thereafter, leaving the house with a hastily wrapped bundle under his arm which could easily have been a costly vase, the whole of the Wedgwood dinner service, piece by piece.

'He could take it, little by little, and sell it and I'd never know,' she said, and appalled not only by the possible loss of her property but by the increasing triviality of her mind, she took the most daring, most positive step of her life.

'I feel that I'm drowning,' she said. 'I'm becoming hysterical – that damnable man is turning me into a proper old maid. Unless I do something about it soon I won't be fit to do anything at all.' And telling my mother that she was staying with me, she went instead to Bournemouth to request my uncle's intervention in the release of her money.

Naturally – having recovered from the shock of having his eldest niece appear alone and unannounced on his doorstep – he would not hear of it. Nothing in the world would induce him to put twenty thousand pounds of Morgan Aycliffe's money into the hands of his unmarried daughter, even if he had the power to do so, which he had not.

'Get married,' he told her. 'That's what women do. If you want to teach children their letters, then have some of your own. That's the other thing women do.'

But Prudence, knowing this to be her final opportunity, had her facts and figures, and her objections, ready.

She wished to open a school for girls. There was no proper education of any kind available for females. She was herself ill-educated and consequently unable to teach others, but she could employ those who could, and see to it that the teaching was efficiently carried out. She knew the size of the house she required, its exact cost, the staff she would need to run it, the salaries she would have to pay her teachers. She had already drawn up a list of the subjects she considered appropriate, the fees she would charge for day-girls and boarders, what extras she would include, the hours to be devoted to study and to more recreational activities, the quality of the food she intended to serve.

'Nonsense,' he said. 'Day-dreams – or delirium. Go to bed now. You'll feel better in the morning. And then you may go back to your mother, young lady, where you belong.'

But the next day he asked her, 'And what's the point to this education? I can see no call for it. Girls exist to get married, and I'm not sure I'd like a clever wife.'

'You have a clever wife.'

'Aye, so I have – or I might not be listening to you at all. So where are your pupils to come from? I can think of no man in Cullingford who'd pay you to fill his girl's head with fancy notions – and it's always the man who pays.'

But again she was ready. She would offer not only a rare opportunity for academic achievement, but a degree of polish as well. Her girls would study literature and mathematics, science and philosophy, but there would be music and dancing too, the art of receiving guests and presiding at a correctly arranged dinner table, the art of gracious living which Cullingford was beginning to appreciate: none of that would be neglected. Her girls would be cultured but they would also be polished, and would make excellent wives for this new generation of manufacturers whose horizons were broader, their expectations greater. The world was changing. There was a demand for the type of establishment she was proposing. She could fill that demand.

'Aye. That's your day-girls. What about your boarders? They like to keep their daughters safe at home in Cullingford.'

Indeed. But she had been out in the world long enough to know that there were plenty of girls who were an inconvenience to their parents, girls who could not be acknowledged by their parents, but for whose accommodation and care money could be found.

'Little indiscretions of the aristocracy?' my uncle asked her, to which

669

she replied, 'Exactly. I believe Caroline's friend, Lady Hetty Stone, could be of assistance to me there, since her brother – who will be a duke one day – knows of just such a child.'

'Does he, by God! And you reckon Mrs Hobhouse and Mrs Rawnsley might like their girls to get to know a duke's daughter?'

'It's a start,' she told him firmly. 'I have to make myself known. I have to make a reputation.'

'Do you reckon you can make any money?' he asked, 'I'll say good-night now, Prudence. You'd best be off in the morning.'

But she stayed another day, spent an hour or so walking with him on the sea-front, another hour in his study attempting to get her figures right, and came away with the satisfaction of knowing she had provided him with a great deal of amusement and some food for thought. She had also informed him that, since in her view it was unbusinesslike to make any kind of proposition unless one had more than expertise to offer, she was prepared to hazard her own savings in the venture, representing all she possessed. And she had been honestly delighted at his reaction to the figure she named.

'You didn't save that out of your pin-money, my girl.'

'No, uncle Joel. But it is mine just the same.'

She announced her engagement to Freddy Hobhouse a few weeks later, making his mother very happy, her own mother somewhat less so until Daniel Adair, being a gambling man who knew how to cut his losses with style, shrugged his generous Irish shoulders and wished her well.

'He's not the one I'd have chosen for you, my girl, but if he's what you want – if you *do* want him?' And he appeared far less surprised than most of us when it became known that she had taken a lease on a substantial house at Elderleigh Hill, half a mile away from me, not, as was first thought, as a home for herself and Freddy, but as a school.

'Oh dear!' my mother said, floating into my house at an unusually early hour. 'You must talk to her, Faith, for I cannot understand it. Her dowry has not been touched, and the porcelain is all there, for Daniel has had it out of the boxes again, and checked it over. My goodness! He is not at all angry – he seems to think it a huge joke. It is simply that people are asking me, and I must have something to say. Does she mean to marry Freddy or does she not? For, if she does, and he has agreed to allow her to use her money for any purpose other than Nethercoats, then Emma-Jane Hobhouse will do her best to put a stop to it. Between ourselves I believe they were on the point of selling out and one cannot blame them for wanting to know where they stand. If they should lose their buyer and then Prudence should change her mind, I really don't see how we could be held responsible. But Emma-Jane Hobhouse is one of my oldest friends – and has quite the wickedest tongue of anyone I ever encountered when she is aroused. Do talk to her, Faith. Or ask Blaize. He will know.'

But Prudence was not forthcoming, Blaize, beyond a passing remark that Nicholas might not get Nethercoats so cheaply now, if at all, had nothing to say, and like everyone else I was obliged to wait a few weeks longer until Aunt Verity, paying a surprise visit to Cullingford, announced that she, having wished for some time to make a personal contribution to the town in which she had been born, had finally decided what that contribution should be.

'It came to me,' she said, 'quite suddenly, as if I could hear a voice positively begging me to do it. I had been thinking about it for an age, considering this and that, and then all at once there it was. Yes, I thought, we have our grammar school, which did so well for my boys, but when Caroline became too much for nanny there was absolutely nowhere to send her – nothing to do but fill the house with music teachers and dancing teachers and someone else for French and for drawing, which was such a bother. We had a French governess, I recall, who was quite temperamental and another I would not have cared to inflict on my worst enemy – and another who could hardly take her eyes off Blaize, if you'll forgive me for mentioning it, Faith dear. So, Elinor, I have decided to open a school for girls, and I am relying on you and Mr Adair to allow it. Yes, Elinor – your permission is certainly required – for I have set my heart on having Prudence to take charge of it, and, if you refuse, then of course I shall not proceed – which will be such a pity. Joel thinks it an *excellent* idea, and although I am to use my own money I think we can rely on him to be generous.'

And when Lady Barforth made a request, which Sir Joel clearly expected to be granted, it would have been unwise on the part of any Adair – of anyone at all – to refuse.

'Obviously he has lent her the money,' Blaize said, very much amused. 'Good for her, although he will make her earn it. If she went to him with her tale of wanting some useful work to do, then work is exactly what she will get, for he will expect to be repaid. I can't imagine what private agreement they have made, and clearly she has my mother's blessing, which is more than half the battle with my father, but he will see to it that she keeps her side of the bargain. Well, he must be getting bored in his little paradise – it may do them both some good.'

'And Freddy – was Freddy your idea, Blaize?'

'Now why should you think that?'

'Because her engagement to Freddy could annoy Nicholas – could keep him out of Nethercoats.'

'Really?' he said, his grey eyes completely innocent. 'Do you know, you are not the first person who has suggested that to me. Brother Nick was in my office just this morning, and even he – well, he didn't put it quite that way – he simply dropped into the pool of conversation the remark that Prudence's money could hardly be enough, and unless the Hobhouses stopped shilly-shallying around they might find themselves without a buyer – or with nothing to sell. He may have expected me to pass the message on.'

'So Freddy *was* your idea.'

'Faith – he offers excellent protection for Prudence. If she is engaged to marry him, then she'll have no cause to waste her time fending off anybody else – an end to the Irish cousins. And rather more than that, for if Freddy – her affianced husband, her future lord and master – doesn't object to her playing schoolmistress, then no one else can have anything to say against it. Naturally, if she went ahead and married him it would be a difficult story, since he'd be in honour bound to use every penny she has to try and stop the rot at Nethercoats. But then – will she marry him, or won't she? My bet is she won't.'

But Freddy Hobhouse was a good-natured, hard-working man, his own sound common sense hampered from boyhood by his easy-natured father. He had shouldered as many family responsibilities as he could, made personal sacrifices for his brothers and sisters, had waited a long time for Prudence, and the thought of him troubled me.

'I believe you are using him, Prue,' I told her. 'Is it fair?' But Prudence, these days, was no longer the frustrated woman who had frittered her time away in bickering with her step-father, and fussily, almost neurotically, counting her porcelain. Nor was she the girl who had devoted herself with such unflagging energy to the affairs of Giles Ashburn and Mayor Agbrigg. Now she had work of her own to do, her own decisions to make, being no longer obliged to content herself with carrying out the decisions of others, and, having demolished the objections of Sir Joel Barforth, was certain to make short work of mine.

'Is it fair? Very likely not. But then, you can't be certain what my intentions are with regard to Freddy,' she said crisply. 'If I should seem to be using him, then you must admit he has shown himself quite ready to use me. He may have been patient, but he has not been celibate, you know, all these years. He has made his little excursions to the Theatre Royal, when he could afford it, as they all do. And if he had encountered some other woman with a few thousand a year who had been willing to marry him, then I cannot believe he would have let her pass him by.'

'I suppose not. So you have got everything you want, Prudence?'

'Perhaps I have. I have got my independence at any rate, and, even if you are beginning to think me hard, the truth is that I am sorry to have been obliged to get it by stealth. It would suit me far better to come out into the open and say, 'This is what I have done. This is what I intend. This is what I am – far better if I had been able to claim the money that is mine, instead of selling my vases clandestinely to your husband, and using his father and Aunt Verity as a screen, pretending the school is theirs, when really it is mine. Well – that is the way of it. And as to Freddy, you will have to wait and see, my dear – and so will his mother.'

Opinion, of course, in private was sharply divided, the Hobhouses themselves frankly suspicious, but, as matters stood, unwilling to do anything which could further jeopardize their position. It was not that Mr Hobhouse had mismanaged Nethercoats, rather that he had not managed it enough, for the business, founded by his grandfather, improved by his energetic father, had seemed so secure when it came to him that his naturally easy-going disposition had not received the stimulus it required. Mr Bradley Hobhouse, quite simply, had not been a hungry fighter, not really a fighter at all: a comfortable man of hearty appetites who had married a comfortable wife, both of them so accustomed to live in conditions of prosperity that they could imagine no other. Joel Barforth, until his sons were of an age to do it for him, had continued to descend on his mill every morning, to ensure that his orders were carried out to the letter. Mr Hobhouse, when trade was good, had lingered at home, taken an afternoon stroll to the Piece Hall to enjoy the respect his name commanded, had spent a great deal of his time discussing the wool trade over the punch bowl at the Swan. Mr Joel Barforth had known, at all times, exactly what his managers, and his sons, were doing. Mr Hobhouse knew what they *said* they were doing. Mr Joel Barforth had been the first man in the Valley to mechanize, had ruthlessly abandoned his handlooms for power-driven machines, had been the first man to stop producing the plain, well-nigh indestructible cloth for which the Valley was famous and to develop the lighter, fancier materials which a changing society required. Mr Hobhouse, a heavy man who liked heavy worsteds, had clung to the belief that his customers liked them too. And by the time it became clear to him that, with so many newcomers to the industry, the world was no longer clamouring for Hobhouse goods, no longer so ready to take whatever he supplied because it was obtainable nowhere else, it was too late.

Freddy alone, of course, could not halt the decline, nor, indeed, would Prudence's fortune be enough to restore his credibility at Rawnsley's bank, but a connection with the Barforths could only be seen as a step in the direction all at Nethercoats wished to take – it *might* suffice to tide them over until the miracle they had all been praying for made its mind up to take place – and it was hoped moreover, that it might soften the heart and loosen the purse-strings of the great worsted spinner, Mr Oldroyd, whose late wife had been Mr Hobhouse's sister, Freddy's Aunt Lucy.

Mr Oldroyd, admittedly, was not a lonely man, for having failed to marry my mother he continued to find ample consolation in the scandalous Mrs Delaney, whose charms and whose excellent cream teas were still readily available to him in Albion Place. But – although provision would no doubt be made for her at his decease, as provision would be made for a young lady in Leeds one assumed to be his daughter – the Oldroyd fortune was one of the most important in the Law Valley, and if he approved the marriage of Freddy and Prudence there was no reason why a sizeable portion of it should not find its way to them, instead of to certain Oldroyd cousins who were officiously staking their claim. There was no reason, in fact, why Mr Oldroyd – if suitably softened and impressed – should not take Freddy into his business, should not make him a partner, the beneficiary not merely of a portion but of the whole.

And so Mrs Hobhouse was all love and kisses to Prudence, the desperate quality of her affection moving me to sympathy, and my sister to laughter.

'Poor woman! She will do anything to get me, and if she manages it she will have the surprise of her life. If I ever do go to Nethercoats, then she will first have to move out of it, I do assure you, and take her sons and daughters with her, for I have no mind to play nursemaid and governess free of charge.'

'Prudence, you *are* growing hard.'

'I do hope so – for it is a hard world.'

Yet with Freddy himself she was exacting but occasionally quite tender, commandeering his services most ruthlessly at the schoolhouse – 'Freddy, if you would just fetch me this, carry me that, lend me your carpenter, your glazier, your wagon' – but, since he had his share of the warm Hobhouse temperament, she would allow him to hold her hand under my dinner-table, would go with him quite happily for moonlit strolls in my garden, returning with the air of a woman who had been heartily kissed and had not found the experience unpleasant.

She would be thirty that year, a fine-boned, elegant woman, crackling with energy, compelling in her excitement, her new zest for life. He was thirty-five, heavy and easy, a man, as she said, who had not been celibate, who knew what he wanted from a woman in the moonlight and was clever enough, perhaps, to realize that her brain was keener than his, not too proud to accept it. Would she take him, after all? Would she use him, as men had been trying all her life to use her – to use me – and then discard him? Would she dominate him, instead, and bully him into some compromise that did not include his troublesome family? I couldn't tell.

'She's a joy to watch,' Blaize told me. 'Do what you can to help her, Faith. I won't count the cost.' And I had no need to be told.

Help came to her from many sides.

'Dear Prudence,' Georgiana told her, 'I cannot think why you are doing this, for I believe if you were to shut me up in a house with several dozen children I would end by murdering them all – but do take my Venetia when she is older. Take her now if you like. She is only a girl, after all, and so I suppose I can have my way where she is concerned. They have sent Gervase to the grammar school, didn't you know? Yes, he goes there every morning with the younger Hobhouse boys to do his sums, so that he can work out his profit and loss, I imagine, when the time comes – except that it will not come, for he will not learn. Naturally I wanted to send him to Kent, where Perry and Julian Flood went to school, but I am not breaking my heart over it. In fact I am very much inclined to smile, or would be, if Gervase didn't hate the grammar school so much. Well, he will not have to dirty himself in a counting-house, for he cannot add two and two, poor mite, and it is quite useless for Nicky to stand over him and growl that he is not trying, when it is plain to everyone that it is simply not in his nature. He has only to look at a column of figures and his mind becomes quite blank, which I perfectly understand, since I am just the same. Well, you will not plague my daughter, will you, Prudence, with such things? If she is happy and has good friends, then I shall be content. I have had a word with Hetty Stone and I imagine you may have her relative whenever you like, since no one else wants her in the very least. And Caroline knows such masses of people – she is sure to help.'

Indeed she did, help coming too, rather surprisingly, from Jonas, who, although by no means prepared to fetch and carry like Freddy, had his own academic experience to draw on and, his own Latin being perfect, his Greek flawless, his knowledge of French, mathematics, history, geography, the literature of several countries, enormous, he was not to be deceived by the pretensions of others. And, moreover, for the first time he seemed willing to suggest, rather than tell Prudence what she should do, steering her quite gently away from one very glib teacher of mathematics and directing her attention to another, working out a most ingenious timetable which he submitted, not for her admiration, but her approval.

'Why, Jonas – that is quite brilliant. Why didn't I think of it?'

'Well, it is similar to the one used by an acquaintance of mine from Cambridge. I cannot take all the credit for it.'

And we wondered, Prudence and I, had Aunt Hannah not insisted on making a lawyer, a lord mayor, a Cabinet Minister out of him, whether he would have been happy as a schoolmaster.

My aunt and uncle came up from Bournemouth at the start of the good weather, my uncle still showing the strain of the winter, although, as usual, his descent on the mills was immediate and dynamic, the sharpness of his eye and his opinions quite undimmed. And for a day or so even Blaize was less inclined for laughter, arriving at his office a little earlier, leaving considerably later, while it was widely known that Mr Nicholas Barforth, now that his personal enterprises were prospering, was exhibiting a marked reluctance to do things any way but his own.

Caroline was to leave for London at the beginning of July to spend the summer season with Hetty Stone, her aim very clearly to make the acquaintance of Lady Hetty's brother, now the sixth, or possibly even the seventh Duke of South Erin, and to bring him back to Listonby in triumph as her guest. But she had the time to arrange a dance in her father's honour, knowing how much it pleased him to see her receive the county at the head of her brilliantly illuminated staircase, a duke's sister standing a step or two behind her, making sure she did everything in the correct Mayfair manner, but somewhat in her shadow just the same. And because it also pleased him from time to time to see his family gathered together – and there was nothing Caroline would not do to please her father – she summoned rather than invited us to dine that same evening in the exquisitely frail, century-old saloon she reserved for intimate occasions.

Caroline had changed nothing in this room, leaving the baroque plasterwork, which had once reminded Aunt Verity of gently decaying petals to continue its mellowing from the original white to a blend of musk rose and honey, retaining the fragile chairs with their tapestry covers in the same misty shades, a table polished by generations to the appearance of ebony glass, nothing else in the room at all but hushed space and memory. Yet, despite all her efforts, it was from the start an uneasy gathering, an evening when nothing seemed altogether right.

I had dressed, as always, most carefully, knowing that it was expected of me, that I had a small local reputation by now to consider as well as my husband and my vanity. And, since Listonby was not really Cullingford, I took out a dress I had ordered from Monsieur Albertini in Paris, which I had been reserving for our next trip to London, a tremendous skirt stitched over its wire cage in tiny white frills that had the appearance of feathers, a neck so low that Caroline would certainly raise pained eyebrows over it, my swan cameo pinned on what little there was of the bodice, a pearl scattered velvet ribbon around my neck. Clever, I had thought, checking the finer details in my mirror, something Blaize would appreciate, but when I came downstairs, trailing my shawl behind me, to receive his applause, he merely said, 'Very nice – in fact, *very* nice', quite automatically, and all through the journey from Elderleigh barely said a word.

'Did something happen at the mill today?'

'Dear me no,' he said, stifling a yawn. 'Does anything ever happen at the mill – anything worth mentioning, that is?'

'Well – you are certainly out of humour.'

'I beg your pardon. It is my footloose nature, I imagine, telling me I have been in Cullingford rather too long. I am in the mood to be off again, I think – and really one should take advantage of it, for we are in constant need of new markets. Nicky, of course, can't bring himself to agree.'

'He doesn't want you to go?'

'Possibly not. Perhaps it would suit him better if I stayed and took what he calls my share of responsibility at Lawcroft and Tarn Edge – especially now that Mayor Agbrigg is mayor again and too busy with his building regulations to be much use for anything else. Which sounds quite reasonable, of course, until one realizes that what he really wants is for me to take the weight off his shoulders so that he can do some private empire-building of his own. If I'm in Russia – which is where I'd dearly love to be – Nicky can hardly spend all day at the Wool-combers, can he, nor at Nethercoats for that matter, if he manages to get his hands on it after all. He'll have to spend his time concentrating on Joel Barforth and Sons, as I do – and we really need those new markets, you know.'

Georgiana and Nicholas did not arrive together, Nicholas coming from Tarn Edge, Georgiana from Galton where she had been staying with her grandfather, having taken Gervase with her, I'd heard, to enable him to avoid school.

'Good evening,' Nicholas said to me, giving Blaize no more than a nod by way of greeting.

'Georgiana,' Blaize replied, 'you're looking very beautiful'; but she wasn't, for her extremely expensive ballgown, the kind of over-embroidered creation she bought because she imagined that was how a manufacturer must want his wife to look, did not suit her, the complicated arrangements of ringlets in which she had imprisoned her coppery hair was too heavy for her head, and she herself too much aware of it, holding her neck too stiffly in case it should all come tumbling down. She had emeralds in her ears, bracelets on both arms, a gold and emerald necklace, jewellery she was at the same time too hardy and too

676

air-spun to carry, a woman dressed up against her nature, and more uncomfortable every minute with this false image of herself.

Throughout the meal which Caroline had planned as a joyful family reunion, Nicholas and Blaize addressed not one word to each other; Freddy Hobhouse, unaccustomed to Listonby, talked only to Prudence; my sister Celia, for some reason, seemed unwilling to speak to anybody, which was clearly displeasing to Jonas, creating so tense an atmosphere that everyone around her seemed inclined to whisper, leaving us with the brittle, social chatter of Hetty Stone and my mother, Aunt Hannah's well-meant but heavy-handed determination to 'bring us all out of ourselves', Sir Matthew's vague geniality, Major Agbrigg's clear intention of leaving well – or ill – alone. While even Sir Joel, for whom the celebration was intended, would have preferred, I thought, to have been placed a little nearer to his wife, finding even a yard of mahogany and cut crystal an unacceptable barrier, these days, between him and his Verity.

'I can't think what ails them, Faith,' Caroline muttered as we left the table. 'One puts oneself out, and is it too much to expect that they should do the same – especially with Hetty Stone looking on, thinking that everything she has ever heard about manufacturers must be true. After all, it is for father. And, if Nicholas and Blaize have had a set-to at the mill, then they should have left it there. And Faith – really – what *is* the matter with Celia? She was most odd at Christmas and I declare she is odder tonight. Mark my words, she will start feeling unwell in half an hour and will make Jonas take her home, and if she does then I shall not invite her again. I suppose you know that certain people are beginning to feel sorry for Jonas. I was talking to Mr Fielding and to several of his political associates just the other day – one of them by no means without influence in the party – and they were all saying the only fault they could find with Jonas Agbrigg as a future candidate was his wife. I couldn't bear to hear that said of me. My goodness! I'd hide my head in shame. You'd better talk to her, Faith. Well – I can't feel that this is going to be one of my most successful nights.'

But, positioned at the head of her staircase between Sir Matthew and Sir Joel, waiting to receive her ball guests, Caroline's spirits began to revive, finding the same healing quality in the glittering ballroom behind her, the Long Gallery beyond it, as Georgiana found in the cloister at Galton. And as those august names, one by one, were announced – 'Sir Giles Flood and Mr Julian Flood. Sir Francis and Lady Winterton. Lord and Lady de Grey. The Hon. Mrs Tatterton-Cole. Colonel and Mrs Vetchley-Ryce' – and I knew her mind was already exploring next season's triumphs, when surely, if she made herself pleasant enough and useful enough to Hetty Stone, the Duke of South Erin himself would be advancing up her painted, panelled staircase to greet her.

I danced a great deal, as I always did at Listonby, responding easily to the enchanted world Caroline had created, her lovely, high-ceilinged ballroom panelled at one side in glass so that every drop of cut crystal in her chandeliers was doubled, every swirling, satin skirt had its partner, every soaring violin an echo, everything – as Caroline had always intended – being at least twice as large as life. I went down to supper with Julian Flood, who kissed my shoulders on the stairs and asked me with a composure that was almost off-handed if I would care to meet him one Friday to Monday in London. But I was a fashionable woman who knew how to deal with that, a woman who invited attention and could not complain when she received it. I was Blaize Barforth's wife, too sophisticated by far to dance with her husband, merely smiling, making an amused gesture with my fan which certainly in his opinion signified 'Good luck, darling', when I saw him strolling downstairs with Hetty Stone.

Prudence sat in the Long Gallery, with Freddy, surrounded by portraits of ancestral Chards, no severe school-mistress that night but allowing him rather more liberties, I thought, than holding her hand. Celia, who had been invited with the rest of us to stay the night, went home, a certain friction arising between Jonas and his father when Jonas – involved in serious, possibly lucrative political conversation – had at first insisted that she should remain. And in the ebbing and flowing of the crowd I did not miss Georgiana until Caroline took me sharply by the elbow and hissed, 'Come downstairs – at once. Come and talk sense to her.'

But it was too late. All I saw, through the wide open doorway, were the horses on the carriage drive, two men in evening-dress already mounted, another waiting for Georgiana as she flew down the steps, cupping his hands to receive her foot and throwing her up into the saddle, her expensive satin skirts bunched wildly around her, the lovely, quite fragile line of her profile, her throat, her breasts, fine-etched against the dark as she threw back her head, laughing and crying together.

'Georgiana!' Caroline called out, and Georgiana, looking down raised an arm in a military salute and they were off – Julian Flood, Francis Winterton, Rupert Tatteron-Cole, the reckless, hard-drinking young men who had ridden with Perry Clevedon – and Perry Clevedon's sister – riding off now on some mad escapade, Caroline clapping both hands to her ears as they started their hunter's yelling, their horses tearing past her lodge gates as if the whole world was burning.

'She was bare-legged,' Caroline said, aghast. 'Didn't you see? My goodness! The whole of Listonby is going to see, for she is riding astride. I have never been so shocked – so mortified – in my life.'

'She has gone to look for Perry, I suppose,' Blaize casually offered, when I found him. 'I imagine Perry might seem more real to her than some others she has seen here tonight.'

'She's an original, that one,' Hetty Stone murmured, her hand still on Blaize's arm, her fingers flexing themselves with a feline movement of satisfaction that told him he was original too.

'She'll kill herself,' Caroline insisted, too furious to copy Lady Hetty's Mayfair nonchalance. 'And just where is Nicholas? Obviously he will have to be told.'

It was past three o'clock of a beautiful June morning before the last carriages had rolled away, and although Caroline had declared she would not go to bed until Georgiana returned, having some slight concern for her safety and a great deal for her reputation, Sir Matthew, who could on occasion be firm, eventually led her away, allowing the rest of us to follow.

I slept perhaps an hour, it seemed no longer, waking to an odd sensation of being quite alone, and, raising myself on one elbow, saw Blaize standing against the window, looking down at the carriage drive.

'Darling – is she back?'

'Hush,' he said and, as my head cleared itself of sleep, I could hear in the distance the sound of hoofbeats, one horse, I thought, coming slowly, a hesitant clip-clop that did not convey the speed and dash of anything Georgiana would be likely to ride.

'Hush,' he said again, and as I got up and joined him at his vigil, realizing now that he had not slept at all, I felt once again that careful, feline probing in him, the curiosity but also the concern.

'Now,' he said. 'Here she comes. And I imagine you are about to see a species of destruction. Yes, I knew he'd be there to meet her. Even good old Matthew knew that and had the sense to take Caroline away.'

And far below me I saw the back of a head, the broad, dark shape that was Nicholas, saw the glow of his cigar as he dragged the tobacco deep into his lungs, the taut anger of him as he tossed the butt away.

'I don't think I want to see this, Blaize.'

'You might as well. I intend to.'

She took a long time to reach him, coming as reluctantly as if she were struggling against the tide of air, and, even when the driveway ended and he stood directly in her path, she rode up and down in front of him for a moment, unwilling to dismount.

Her complicated chignon was gone, her hair hanging loose to her waist, lifted from underneath by the early breeze so that it billowed a little and blew forward across her face. And it was clear to me, no doubt clear to us all, that a moment ago, with the sun on her bare shoulders, that delicious breeze under her hair, she had been intensely happy, intensely sad, and that now it was over.

'Did you think I had run away?' she called out, her horse continuing its fretful little promenade on the gravel.

'No. I didn't think that.'

'Well, then – what shall I do now?'

'Take your horse round to the stables, I imagine.'

And, as he turned to go, she pressed the whole of one arm against her eyes and cried out, 'Nicky –! Damnation, never mind. You will have to help me down.'

He walked forward, stood without raising his arms at her stirrup. Putting her hands on his shoulders, she kicked her skirts free and somehow or other slid to the ground, stumbling against him, righting herself with obvious difficulty as he moved away.

'Oh dear! I have lost my shoes.'

'You will have to go barefoot then.'

'Nicky –'

'Yes?'

'Don't you want to know why?'

'No, I can't say that I do.'

She dug her fingers hard into her hair, pushing it away from her forehead, fighting it almost like seaweed, her body brittle, high-strung with desperation.

'Nicky –' and her voice was desperate too. 'Don't walk away. Be angry – knock me down and kick me if you want to – anything – Just don't walk away.'

But he had left her, and a few moments later I heard his step in the corridor as he passed our door, the click of his door opening and closing.

'Very clever, little brother,' Blaize said, speaking in the direction Nicholas's steps had taken. 'Yes – I said it would be destruction, but that was starvation. I didn't know he could be so subtle.'

'Blaize – any man would have been angry.'

'True. And "any man" would have said so. Any man would have dragged her down from that horse and shaken her to her senses. Any man would have lost his temper and let her feel the sharp edge of it – especially a man like my brother Nick, who's known to be well endowed when it comes to temper. I told you – very clever. She was brought up on strong emotions, you see. He could love her, or hate her, and I believe she'd thrive on either. Since he obviously knows that, it would appear he doesn't want her to thrive.'

'Things are very bad, then – between them.'

'As you see. He can be very stubborn, and very foolish.'

'Why? Because he won't always play out your schemes – like the Cullingford train?'

'Yes,' he said. 'The Cullingford train – but bear in mind, before you accuse me of meddling, that he *wanted* to take that train. There was nothing else, that day, he wanted more. Like I said – stubborn and foolish!'

I got back into bed, unbearably chilled although I do not think the room was cold, and lay there shivering, silent, for there was no part I could take in this conflict, and I did not want Blaize to take part in it either.

'You must be tired, Faith,' he said. 'Go back to sleep.'

But I was not tired. I needed him, not to love me, perhaps, certainly not to hate me, but to make some move towards me, to offer me more than his wit and his charm, his skills as an entertainer and a lover, to ask more of me than that. And because he was not a man who wished to be needed, it seemed, for the half hour it took to calm myself, that he too, albeit unknowingly, was starving *me*.

26

There was mutiny in India that year, a screaming, murderous fury against British rule, provoked, it seemed, not entirely by the Enfield rifle, the heavily greased cartridges of which no Hindu, no Muslim, could bring himself to bite, but by a simple fear of an alien religion, a dread, encouraged by dispossessed yet decently Hindu princes, that forcible conversion to the Christian church was just a matter of time.

The princes, quite clearly, were thinking of their principates which had been annexed by Christian governors, the sepoys were thinking of their souls, the British may not have been thinking too keenly at all, so shocked and surprised were they when a small flame of disobedience – just a handful of rebellious sepoys not far from Delhi, a local matter which should have remained so – became overnight a holocaust.

And because there were Chards and Clevedons and Floods serving their Queen in India as they served her everywhere else, there was tension at Listonby and at Galton, a certain well-controlled anger, an even more firmly suppressed sadness.

There was a Chard in Delhi when the hysterical sepoys first flooded into it, leaving a trail of dead Europeans – regardless of age, regardless of sex, regardless of anything but light skin and light eyes – in their path. A very young Chard, in fact, just eighteen years old, who when the Indian garrison joined the mutineers took his stand at the arsenal with the few British fighting men who remained, defended it, until defence became an impossibility, blew it up to prevent the guns from falling into mutinous hands, and then died from a sabre-thrust – Matthew told us – in the groin.

There was an aunt of Georgiana's among the four hundred women and children at Cawnpore who were rounded up by an enterprising princeling and quite literally butchered, their dismembered bodies thrown down a well. There were distant relatives of the Floods and the Clevedons, high-minded, cool-headed ladies, wives of career officers – younger sons ear-marked for military greatness like Caroline's Noel – who found themselves trapped in the besieged Residency at Lucknow, keeping themselves not only alive but in good spirits throughout five months of continuous shelling, the continuous threat not only of murderous sepoys but of smallpox, cholera, rats and starvation, stilling their hunger, when the food supply was failing, by a banquet of curried sparrows.

There were English ladies, products of the fox-hunting shires, who gave birth on the hard ground, in ditches, in bullock-carts, and were murdered moments later when the wail of the new-born betrayed their hiding-place. There was the vengeance afterwards, the sepoys who may or may not have been responsible – since to men who had seen such atrocious female slaughter *any* sepoy would do – tied to the mouths of guns and splattered to eternity.

There was heroism and savagery on both sides, treachery and

681

self-sacrifice. At Listonby and at Galton it was present, vital, real. To the Barforths it was very far away.

In Cullingford, trade was good, Barforth looms were working to capacity and to order, our own streets quieter than they had ever been, and cleaner too, since the water from Mayor Agbrigg's reservoirs at Cracknell Bridge had started to flow. The hand-loom weavers who had once staged a mutiny of their own had disappeared, absorbed by our weaving sheds, our workhouses, or the gold fields of Australia from which no Law Valley millionaires, to my knowledge, ever returned. And every morning the stroke of five o'clock released that patient flow of women, shawl-covered heads bowed in submission to the cold and to their labouring condition, a faceless, plodding multitude going to their ten hours of captivity at the loom, returning to the captivity of fetching and carrying, of bearing child after child in Simon Street.

My sister's school was opened in the autumn by Lady Barforth, who expressed immense pleasure at the brightness of the rooms devoted to study, the good cheer prevailing in the sleeping-rooms, the spacious if somewhat Spartan dining-hall, the pleasant outside acre where the girls could cultivate their own plants and flowers and could take healthy, easily supervised walks.

'Why should we trust our girls to Prudence Aycliffe?' had been the immediate reaction, but her day-girls, comprising the daughters of all those in Cullingford who could pay Prudence's fees and wished to stand in well with the Barforths, were numerous, her most interesting boarder being a ten-year-old Miss Amy Chesterton, who may not have been aware that she was the daughter of the new Duke of South Erin, although everyone else knew it. And for the first month Jonas Agbrigg himself gave instruction to the senior pupils in mathematics, the lady engaged for the purpose having fallen ill, bringing, quite often, his own four-year old Grace to leave in my care, since Celia was again unwell, requiring not merely rest and quiet, it seemed, but total silence.

I would not – before Blanche was born – have described myself as being fond of children, was not, even now, fond of all children, but, having gone through the dangerous agonies of childbirth, I saw no point in leaving the results of it entirely to nanny, contenting myself by playing the mother for ten minutes at tea-time as my own mother had done. I had been Blaize's wife for almost four years now. Within the limits he had set for us, I was by no means unhappy. But in restless moments – when I knew I could not fill my life with lace and ribbons and table-talk – moments when I asked myself uncomfortably, 'What next? What else?', I believed I could find the answer in Blanche.

I had no wish for more children. This one silvery little elf sufficed me, but, from the start, my sister's daughter Grace had always moved me, her dark curls, her solemn heart-shaped face, her wild-rose prettiness offering such startling contrast to Blanche, her response to my attentions sometimes hesitant, sometimes eager, since her mother was too tense these days for caresses, too concerned with grass-stains on her daughter's skirt, mud on her shoes, to take her romping on the lawn, too prone to her sick headaches to endure anything so harrowing as childish laughter.

And so I spent the fine weather, when Blaize was not at home, tying ribbons in my niece's black curls, my daughter's ones, letting them preen themselves in my earrings and bracelets, shawls and bonnets, taking them to pick rose petals for pot-pourri, to find wild blackberries and stray kittens, against Celia's instructions, since roses have diseased thorns, blackberry juice cannot be removed from a dress, kittens have claws to disfigure a child for life and fur to give a child fleas.

We had picnics on the lawn at Elderleigh, braving the earthworms, the moles, the bird-droppings, the general nastiness with which Celia believed it to be infested. We walked in the woods beyond my garden – Blanche astride my shoulders more often than not – trailing our feet through the fragrant October leaves, ignoring the squirrel, that most vicious of beasts, which might descend from its tree to savage us, the quagmire into which we might tumble, the gipsy who, with blandishments and chloroform, could overpower a lone woman and steal two little girls away.

A lovely child – Miss Blanche Barforth – taking her world for granted, knowing herself to be at its centre, the reason for its existence, taking me for granted too, finding me commonplace, I think, in comparison with her far more interesting but frequently absent father. A sedate child – Miss Grace Agbrigg – and a careful child, sensing the atmosphere around her before plunging into it with the caution of a wary kitten, accustomed to be told 'Hush – mamma is poorly. Hush – you will make her worse', so that she was puzzled, sometimes, because I did not suffer from the headaches which, in her slight experience, were the normal condition of women, even more puzzled that such things as gloves carelessly left on a chair, forgotten newspapers in the drawing-room, a cigar butt in an ashtray, did not produce in me the spasms they invariably brought on in Celia.

'Is she really no trouble to you?' Jonas invariably asked me.

'No – no. Please don't stop bringing her, Jonas. I really want her.'

I did not want Liam Adair. I could think of no one, in those early years of our acquaintance, who could possibly have wanted Liam Adair, but increasingly I found him abandoned on my doorstep and, meeting his insolent twelve-year-old eyes with foreboding, was obliged to let him come in.

'Darling – if you could just have him for an hour,' my mother would call out, not even getting down from her carriage. 'I am obliged to run over to the Mandelbaums and, really, they have so many things one can see at a glance are valuable – and breakable. Those harps and violins – you know what I mean – and since he has been sent home from school again in absolute disgrace, and poor Miss Mayfield is having the vapours – Just an hour, darling.'

But the hour would prolong itself to luncheon, to tea-time, to breaking point, to violence on one memorable occasion when Blaize, who had raised a hand to no one in years, took a riding-crop to him in atonement for a stray dog let loose in the stables, which had caused considerable turmoil, and a horse to bolt.

'If I were never to see that young man again it wouldn't break my heart,'

Blaize said, considerably irritated, not only because he had torn a shirt-cuff in the scuffle but because Liam, who was big for his age, had taken not a little holding down. 'In fact, Faith, you could arrange matters so that I don't see him.'

But Blaize was so often away, and on the fine afternoon that Liam tossed a half-dozen live frogs into my kitchen, occasioning so great a flapping and clucking of housemaids that I at first thought my house was on fire, I raised a fist in retribution and then, seeing those pompous, portly little creatures at their hopping, entirely unaware of the havoc they were creating, I suddenly found myself obliged to bite back my laughter. And then, catching the merry Adair sparkle in his eyes, did not bite it back, but laughed out loud, forfeiting my cook's good opinion as I helped him to retrieve the invaders and carry them back to their pond.

'Don't do it again, Liam Adair.'

'Oh no – there'd be no fun in doing it again.'

'Then don't do anything else. Why are you such a nuisance, Liam?'

'I don't know. It's just what I am, that's all – a nuisance. Everybody says so.'

And so he was, a nuisance to my mother, to his father, to his schoolmasters, who sent him home at least twice a week for fighting, so that often, instead of going to Blenheim Lane he would arrive on my doorstep with a torn jacket, a cut lip, blood pouring from his nose, a grin invariably on his lips.

'Liam – good heavens! By the look of it you didn't win.'

' 'Course I did, and there were *three* of them – two Hobhouses and a Rawnsley – that's why I look so beat. But I smashed them all right – Headmaster wouldn't have sent me home otherwise.'

'And what do the Hobhouses look like?'

'Not pretty. But they weren't pretty before.'

'Neither are you.'

But in a way he was, a big-boned, lanky boy as black as any woodland gipsy, a heavy, overcrowded face lightened by the Adair smile, the whip of Adair insolence and humour that would make him one day a man as attractive and possibly as reckless as his father.

'Liam – your coat's in ribbons. Did you get a thrashing today?'

' 'Course I did. The big Hobhouses came looking for me, after I'd smashed their brothers, so I smashed them too – or very nearly. Well, not *very* nearly, but it wasn't as easy as they thought it would be. And then when Mr Blamires came to stop it, and I wouldn't stop – because whatever he says they weren't killing me – he gave me a flogging for good measure. So what I want to know is, can I stay for tea, because my dad's at home this afternoon, and if he catches me he'll give me another.'

And, understanding that three floggings in one day were more than enough for any man, I fed him, darned his coat, and, when he believed the coast would be clear, sent him home.

'Liam – why do you fight so much?'

'I don't know. It's what I do, that's all.'

'I won't have him across my threshold,' Celia told me. 'And my mother knows it. I'm sorry, but there are limits to what one can endure. I have enough with my own child to look after, and my own home to run. I hope you had them scour your kitchen floor with lime after he brought those frogs in – and how you can laugh about it, Faith, I'll never know. It would have made me ill.'

But so many things made Celia ill – so many things had always done so – that I paid little attention until my mother pointed out that she was indeed taking a turn for the worse.

'My dear, she never goes out. She sits in that house and watches them polish it, and it can't be right. If I've invited her once I've invited her a hundred times, not just to Blenheim Lane but to teas and concerts and trips to Leeds, and there's always a reason, at the last moment, why it can't be done. She's not well, or Grace is not well or her housemaid has just given notice – she's had eight girls this year, Faith, and not one of them lasted a month. I declare, I go into her house feeling sometimes a little less than my age and come out feeling a hundred. And Hannah, of course, is far from pleased about it, which is only to be expected since it is bound to affect Jonas, although she does no good at all by lecturing Celia so often and telling her she is letting him down. Of course she is letting him down – one is obliged to admit it – but there is no need to say so quite so often, and so strongly. If it did any good I might not object, but in fact it makes her worse. Well, I never expected to say it, but sometimes I feel sorry for Jonas. There are to be no more children, you know. Strictly between ourselves, Jonas consulted Dr Blackstone and then told Celia that he could not risk her life again, so that is the end of it. Not that Celia will care about that, although I cannot answer for Jonas, since after all he is a man –'

But Celia, when I finally persuaded her to refer to the matter, *did* care, not for the end of her physical relationship with Jonas, which she had always found somewhat inexplicable in any case, but because any kind of domestic failure troubled her, reminding her too closely, perhaps, of a childhood where she had never been placed higher than third. Not only the sex act, it seemed, was difficult for Celia to understand, but life itself, the injustice of a world in which she had obeyed all the rules, and yet had not succeeded in making herself valued. She was the only one of my father's children who had not only obeyed his teaching but had believed in it, had pinned her faith and her heart's hope on the security it had offered. He had told her that if she did certain things and avoided others she would be happy. She had done these things – had made herself a model housekeeper, a domestic angel, devoted herself entirely to hearth and home, had safeguarded her reputation, had never made herself conspicuous, had been innocent, dependent, respectable – yet somehow the formula had not worked. She was not happy, was listless, confused, uneasy. She had done nothing wrong. My father, should he return from the grave, could only approve of her, could only shudder at his frivolous daughter Faith – who had even been scandalous, and got away with it, for a month or two – his strong-minded daughter Prudence, who had flaunted every one of his decrees, laughed in the face of his known

685

intentions. Yet we were well and strong, and she was not. It was not fair.

'Do spend a little more time with her, Faith dear,' my mother asked, and listening to her through those dreary afternoons when I, setting out to cheer her, came away with my own spirits depressed, I understood clearly that after the solitary triumph of her marriage – of beating every one of us, even Caroline, down the aisle – nothing else had lived up to her expectations.

'It's this house that makes me ill,' she said. 'It is far too small and dark – I can hardly see into the corners. If we could move to Cullingford Green, or right away to Patterswick –'

But when Jonas suggested a number of houses she might like to view, her objections were enormous, the difficulties immense – the staff, the furniture, the problems of selling the house they already had – and although Jonas promised to see to everything himself the project was shelved.

'If I could go to Scarborough for the summer it would put me right.'

But to exist in lodgings was unthinkable, a rented house full of hazards, for what would she do if nanny gave notice, what would she do in any case in a town where she had no friends, since she could never bring herself to speak to strangers?

'If Jonas would not always be accepting invitations without asking me, and then looking so put out when I cannot manage it. I am not at all fond of eating in other people's houses as he very well knows, especially since one is obliged to ask them to dine here afterwards – and it worries me to owe hospitality all around.'

But when the invitations ceased she complained that her friends and her husband were neglecting her.

'Oh, so you have come to see me, have you, Faith? Well, no one else has been near me for a week or more, and Jonas can think of nothing to do but spend his time playing schools with Prudence.'

'She's not interested in anything, that's all,' Prudence said, her own interests legion, her vitality a blazing beacon. 'She hasn't enough to do and doesn't want to do anything, anyway. Why worry about it? We know dozens of women like Celia.'

And because it was true, and because she was indeed so very gloomy, I found myself easily distracted on the days I had intended to see her, very ready to drive on past her house and go somewhere else; and when I *did* pay a visit I managed not to linger too long.

I went now and then to Galton with Georgiana, for she knew of no reason why she and I should not be friends, and saw nothing to concern either of us in the growing tensions between Nicholas and Blaize.

'I did not think it possible for anyone to quarrel with Blaize, but I see Nicky has managed it,' was her sole comment, showing no curiosity as to the nature of their conflict, assuming, as most people did, that it was financial rather than personal, Cullingford being very ready to understand why they should watch each other – and their own backs – so keenly, since no Law Valley man is averse to stealing a march on another.

'Never mind them, Faith,' she said. 'It's a lovely day. Let's go and see my grandfather,'; and, bundling her amber-haired Venetia into the carriage – my dainty Blanche usually managing to get more than her share of carriage-space, being careful, at a tender age, not to crumple her skirts – we would set off at the spanking, nervous pace with which Georgiana did everything. And more often than not Gervase would accompany us – far too often – since she would seize any opportunity she could to keep him away from school.

'He hates it. He's not good at it. If Nicky had been willing to send him to a decent school, then it would have been different. What could Cullingford grammar school possibly have to teach him in any case? Heavens – a *grammar* school. He'll profit far more from half an hour's conversation with grandfather.'

And there was no doubt that the squire of Galton's example could do a child no harm, for when I had accustomed myself to the extreme formality of his manners I found that his company had a soothing quality, as if the very nobility of his spirit had somehow extended itself to form a barrier between Galton and a rude, money-grubbing world. He was, I felt, a man who may have been all his life autocratic and narrow of outlook, but never mean, a man who, with the barbarians at his gate, would have changed his coat for dinner, who would, even if his heart was breaking, offend no one by a display of unmannerly emotion. A fine and gallant gentleman, assisting his granddaughter from her carriage as if she were a duchess, shaking his great-grandson by the hand with the courtesy due to the heir apparent of a nation, rather than a few hundred acres of moorland.

'How do you do, Master Gervase?'

'How do you do, sir?' So that even young Gervase, who was tense and excitable, an odd child in many ways, who could chatter with the shrill persistence of a starling or sit for hours on end in an unnatural silence, relaxed in his atmosphere, obeying this august great-grandparent with a readiness he did not display elsewhere.

Yet who, indeed, would not have obeyed Mr Gervase Clevedon?

'Come,' he would say very quietly, and everyone within earshot immediately came. 'We will go now,' and everyone would stand up and follow him. 'We can't have this sort of thing, I'm afraid'; and, whatever it was, from village youths brawling in the market-place to the practice of diluting ale in the Galton taverns, one felt the evil would instantly cease.

He had no money, existing entirely on his rents, no coal deposits, no mineral deposits having been found on his land. It was well known that many of his tenants being elderly, he had not increased his rents for some considerable time. He would take no money from Georgiana – since a gentleman did not impose upon a lady, and he was concerned at the state of her marriage in any case – yet at his advanced age he continued to fulfil all the responsibilities to which his station had called him, sitting in Petty Sessions in his own home, a back, downstairs room being reserved for the purpose, to dispense justice in matters of drunkenness, common assault, falsifying of weights and measures, poaching and paternity. He rode considerable distances, in all weathers, to take his place on the Bench at Quarter Sessions, where more serious offenders would be committed to prison, to Australia, or to the gallows. He spent long, tedious hours in the saddle, busying himself about the affairs of his tenants – his people – making improvements he could not afford, since he believed it his duty to do so. He was, at all times, available to defend the interests of anyone who resided on his land, anyone who had ever eaten his bread and his salt, or whose father had eaten the bread of his father.

'I love him,' Georgiana said, breathing deeply. 'My Gervase will be just like him – don't you think so, Faith?'

Yet young Gervase had another grandparent, the shrewd, indestructible Sir Joel Barforth, a head taller, a stone or two heavier than Mr Clevedon, who had set his own sons to work at an early age in his weaving sheds and his counting-houses, teaching them that, although the gentry may consider service to be its own reward, it was the business of a Law Valley man to buy when prices were cheap and sell when they were dear.

'Aye,' he would say, looking down from a height which his grandson clearly found awe-inspiring. 'His manners may be very pretty, I grant you, but can he do his sums?'

And Gervase, wild-eyed and unsteady as a colt, would turn for protection to his mother, who could not do her sums either, the pair of them more often than not ending in a fit of giggles under Sir Joel's grim eye.

My uncle was ill again that winter – nothing, he said, that he couldn't cope with – but he came north unexpectedly in the spring, several days ahead of Aunt Verity, and immediately there was trouble.

'What the hell's this? What the devil's that?' was heard throughout every corner of Tarn Edge, Lawcroft and Low Cross, while his visit to the Law Valley Wool-combers, in which his financial interest was small, produced such a flare-up between him and Nicholas that the building itself seemed threatened by the blast.

'And what's this I hear about you sniffing around Nethercoats again? You'll overstretch yourself, my lad. Aye – and a little bird whispered to me the other day that you'd been over to Horton End a time or two, going over Sam Barker's dyeworks as if you meant business. And, whatever you have to say to me about it, I'll say this to you. *I* don't want his bloody dyeworks, and *you* can't afford it.'

He cancelled out of hand a trip Blaize had been planning to Russia, refusing to listen to Blaize's explanation that, since war between the northern and southern states of America seemed quite likely, there was a growing need to explore new markets.

'Bloody rubbish! War's good ·for the wool trade – always has been. You just fancy staking yourself to a night or two with a ballerina' – a remark repeated to me by Blaize himself, who found it amusing, although he made no comment as to its accuracy.

On the domestic front, too, nothing could please him. His house at Tarn Edge – the house he had built for Aunt Verity – was going to ruin in

688

Georgiana's hands. The servants, with no one to care what they did, were doing nothing. His bedroom was cold, so was the food, the horses were better cared for than he. Where *was* the damn girl, riding around all day like a lunatic? Why did that boy of hers have to keep on staring at him like a scared rabbit? Why was his granddaughter allowed to make that caterwauling day in day out? Why was no one there to check her?

'Get that lad to school,' he bellowed at Georgiana. 'And then get yourself back here and do something useful – look after your home and your husband, and see he has something fit to eat when he gets back from the mill. Yes, just you do that, my girl, since it's the mill that pays for your fancy thoroughbreds and your Arab stallion. And look pleasant about it – God dammit!'

'I am not an employee in your weaving sheds, sir,' she told him coolly, and, the veins swelling in his forehead, his answer was immediate and damning.

'That you're not, lass, for you'd not have lasted so long in my sheds. I get value for money from my weavers and you'd have been told long since that you didn't suit me.'

And whether or not this was an opinion which Nicholas might privately share, he could hardly allow anyone else to express it, his defence of his wife resulting in the most uncomfortable dinner-time the maids at Tarn Edge – who talked to my maids – could remember, Georgiana drinking glass for glass with her warring menfolk and retiring to bed in a state which even her greatest well-wishers could only have described as drunk.

'It can't last much longer,' Blaize said, having by no means abandoned his Russian trip, whether ballerinas and balalaika-players were included in it or not. 'I don't precisely think of him as an ill wind, but he'll blow himself out eventually, at least as far as Bournemouth. And by the time he realizes I've gone to Moscow I shall be on my way back. I may be late tonight, darling – I promised to call in and pay my respects to the punch bowl at the Swan.'

But he was back in the middle of the afternoon, his cabriolet coming up the drive so fast that I met him in the hall, his distress alarming me the more profoundly because I had never seen it before.

'Faith – get your hat. It's father. He had some kind of an attack in the yard at Tarn Edge. We took him up to the house and the doctors are still with him. It must have been two or three hours ago. Faith – I think he's dying, but I don't believe it. It's not a thing I ever expected him to do. I was furious with him this morning, Faith, ten minutes before it happened. I couldn't wait to see the back of him, and now –'

Aunt Verity was believed to be already on her way to Cullingford, having arranged to join her husband and have a look at her school, but messages had been sent off in case she had delayed, train times had been checked, a carriage already waiting to fetch her from the station. But Caroline was somewhere in the home counties visiting with the South Erins, and there could be little hope of reaching her. Nicholas and Georgiana were already at Tarn Edge when we reached it, Georgiana in her dark green habit, having just come in from riding, Nicholas leaning against the mantelpiece, scowling at the fire, remembering his own explosive desire to see the back of his father, perhaps, and regretting it, knowing that it couldn't now be mended. And a great deal of the afternoon went by, straining towards a cool spring evening, a great deal of clipped, meaningless conversation, mainly between Georgiana and myself, before Dr Overdale appeared and invited us upstairs.

Sir Joel Barforth was in the centre of his vast canopied bed, supported by pillows into a sitting position, the scraping sound of air struggling to enter his diseased lungs dominating the room, dying, there could be no doubt of it, of the same engine fumes, the same factory smoke, the same five o'clock trek to the mill yard which killed so many of his operatives. And because he knew it, and, having believed all his life that time was valuable, was not prepared to waste it now, he gestured to Blaize and Nicholas to stand one on either side of him, refusing – apart from a brief pressing together of the eyelids, which may have been the chasing away of tears – to permit himself the luxury of emotion, since his spending-power was coming to an end and he had need in this extremity to be thrifty of what remained.

'Listen,' he said, 'and pay heed – since it's for the last time.'

And because it was no more than a hoarse whisper rising up to them through layers of pain, they leaned towards him, so that, raising one hand and then the other with enormous labour, he took each of them by the arm and held them fast.

'*Listen* – stick together, lads. You need each other. You, Blaize. You don't understand those machines and never wanted to – don't underestimate the man who does. Nicky – it's not like it used to be. You could have built that business up from scratch like I did – I know it – you're like me, lad, and you could have stood on your own in my day. There was just me and Hobhouse in the Valley with anything worth selling and the world was our market. There's hundreds now, Nick, producing the same, wanting their share of the market. And the world's not getting any bigger. It's getting smaller. Somebody has to go out there now and sell. They won't come knocking on our door like they used to. They had no choice before. Now somebody has to go and tell them we're the best.'

His voice quite suddenly disappeared, a terrible moment, when for a split second there was a panic in his face because he hadn't said enough and thought he could never speak again, but, if death had actually touched him, he snarled at it, shook it away, his knuckles showing white as he clung to Nicholas's arm.

'Stick together. And if you can't, then remember this – you'll need a good man in your sheds, Blaize. You'll need a salesman, Nicky. *Find* one, both of you, before you split the business. Christ – do you understand me?'

'Yes, father,' Blaize said. 'It's all right – we understand.'

'Nicky?'

'Yes,' he said. 'Oh God – yes.' And, having fought each other, exasperated each other, loved each other so well, I don't know why it surprised me that they were crying.

'Look after your mother,' he said. 'Whatever you do to one another,

690

and to anybody else, keep her out of it. See to it that she's all right. Georgiana – you'll not be sorry to see the back of me, I reckon, but do the best you can. Now then – they tell me I've got to rest, so leave me to get on with it. Faith – you can stay. The rest of you go downstairs. I'll see you again, I reckon – presently –'

'Faith?' Nicholas said sharply, but Blaize simply nodded 'Of course,' and went out, taking Georgiana's arm, Nicholas following, leaving us alone.

'Come here,' he said and I moved to his bedside, not knowing what he wanted of me, aware only that his power, his glorious fighting spirit was dying far more slowly than his body, and whatever it was I would perform it.

'I'll need you closer than that,' he said, reaching out a hand that, from weakness and failing vision, missed mine by several inches. 'No – I've no mind to pry out your secrets, if that's what you're thinking. Just come here, and hold my hand.'

And I was amazed by the strength of his grip, the cruel effort of will that fastened his hands to mine and kept them fastened, a man raising himself by agonizing inches from a quicksand, knowing exactly what must befall him should he let go.

'Hold on to me, lass,' he said, 'for I can't go before my wife comes. And I'll have to work at it – concentrate – and by God I'll do it! I reckon you know something about loving, Faith – so hold me fast – rouse me if it seems I'm slipping away, for I'll not go before I've seen her again. And keep the damned doctors away from me, lass. They'll be in here in a minute, earning their fees, fretting me and giving me something to make me sleep, I reckon – which won't do, because I might never wake up again. Can you do that for me, Faith Aycliffe?'

'Oh yes. Yes, I can.'

And for those next hours I sat and held him – as I had not been allowed to hold Giles – joining my spirit to his as death very slowly began to lay claim to his body, paring him down, stripping away one layer of life after another, until there was little left but the fierce whispering of his will, forcing those exhausted lungs to take another breath and another, that failing heart to take another beat, dragging enough of himself away from extinction each time it threatened to engulf him so that there would be something left of the man who had loved her when his wife came.'

'How long now?'

'Not long.'

'I can't feel your hands, Faith. Are you still holding me?'

And I dug my nails into his flesh, pinched him, strained every muscle I had to jolt him just a moment or two nearer to train-time.

'How long now?'

'Just half an hour. They've gone down to the station. *Now*, listen, there's the train – she's on the platform. *Now*, Joel Barforth – she's in the carriage. *Now* – she's coming.'

But I had heard no train, the carriage had left but not returned, the doctor had leaned over me, pursed his lips a dozen times. 'I think, Mrs

Barforth, that the rest of the family should be called. His sons will expect to be with him at the end.'

And when the man persisted and would not obey me when I ordered him to leave us alone and said that the responsibility would be mine, it was the remnant of Joel Barforth himself that raised a head somehow from those pillows and spat out a last obscenity that chased the doctor away.

'I'll make it, lass – by God, I will! And if I don't, if the train should be late, tell her –'

'I'll tell her nothing. You'll do so yourself.'

But I had believed him dead twice already, had shaken him and screamed at him, had grown hysterical with his need, her loss, the strength and beauty of their combined passion, and exhausted bone and muscle, ached, sweated, bitten my lips until they bled, before I heard the carriage and she came running across the room to him, his wife of thrity-five years, to throw herself into his arms with the passion and despair of a girl of seventeen. And there was nothing for me to do but close the door very quietly and walk away.

They were, as before, in the small drawing-room, Georgiana in the big armchair, Nicholas leaning against one corner of the fireplace, Blaize at the other, both of them smoking, empty tea-cups and brandy glasses on a tray, Georgiana's riding crop carelessly abandoned on the hearth-rug, and it seemed a hundred years since I had last met them, another place, their taut, untidy lives having no bearing on mine since they had not witnessed the suffering I had just shared, had not been privileged to see that outpouring of devotion.

They had moved, in one sense, a little ahead of me, in another had fallen far behind, for they had had time now to come to terms with bereavement and were already making room for other things. They had shed their tears, had their tea; to them their father was already dead, and whatever they might privately feel about his loss – and I think they each felt a great deal – they were faced now with the task of living without him, and with one another.

Nicholas threw his cigar into the fire and immediately lit another, his face full of the scowling anger he always used to screen emotion, his voice curt, aiming itself at Blaize rather than addressing him. And because I had entered the room in the middle of their conversation, with no idea of what had gone before, it seemed doubly strange to me.

'So – you'll be Sir Blaize Barforth, second baronet, tomorrow, by the look of it. How does that suit you?'

'I imagine I can handle it.'

'You'll have seen the will, I reckon?'

'Yes. I had my half-hour with Jonas Agbrigg. I expect you did the same.'

'So I did. And you understand the implications?'

'Do I?'

'I reckon so. Fifty per cent of the business to you and fifty per cent to me.'

692

'Which seems reasonable enough, brother.'

'I'd say so – provided we're both ready to earn it.'

I walked past them, ignoring them, feeling their unspoken questions in the air behind me: 'What did he ask you – tell you – give you? Is he dead?', ignoring them too, and stood at the window looking out – away from them – aware mainly of my own hands clasped tight together, the knuckles as white as my uncle's had been when he had clung to me a moment ago, his voice, still in my ears, infinitely more real to me than the voices behind me, which were no more than the shrill twittering of birds, incomprehensible, irritating.

'In certain circumstances,' Georgiana said, 'Blaize would have everything, since he's the eldest son.'

'Ah yes,' Nicholas told her, 'the good old rule of primogeniture. But that's in good society, darling. This is Cullingford, and we all know a title doesn't pay the rent.'

'But just the same,' Blaize drawled, 'you think he could have left you a little something extra in compensation, do you?'

'Maybe he did. He left me the sense to know that unless we pull together – now that he's not here to stand between us – we're going to waste a lot of time, and a lot of money, getting nowhere.'

'Ah – I take it then that I'm to pull in *your* direction. Is that what you're saying to me?'

'I might be – and then again I might just be telling you not to pull against me for the sake of it, because it tickles your sense of humour.'

'*Telling* me?'

And their bird-twittering got inside my head, senseless little noises cheapening the real words I had heard upstairs, my aunt throwing herself across that room, her whole body saying 'I love you, Joel', knowing that she had fulfilled his whole life's purpose, and he hers; and I couldn't bear it.

'Stop it!' I said. 'Stop it – now!' And my hands became fists crashing down on the window-sill before I swung round and shouted at them again, 'Stop it!'

I saw Nicholas's brows come scowling together, Blaize make a movement of surprise, and, as I backed away from them, although neither had attempted to touch me, my legs gave way and I fell down on the window-seat, appalled not so much by the violence of my tears as by the knowledge that I could not control them. I was a grown woman who knew that no grief lasts forever, yet, huddled there, I was a child sobbing and howling in the dark, beyond the reach of my adult logic, alone and terrified until Georgiana flung herself down beside me and took me in a thin, nervous embrace, her slight body shielding me as best it could from those keen Barforth eyes. And even then I continued to weep, releasing the pain of my entire lifetime against her narrow shoulder, the inner chamber in which I had stored it wide open, the flood-gates broken.

'Poor Faith,' she said, her small, hard hands accustomed to the handling of mettlesome horses holding me fast. 'You are breaking your heart, and it is not for Sir Joel either. Oh no, it is for something else, someone else – Oh dear, I am so sorry – I didn't know – I thought you so happy with your lovely clothes and your cool, elegant life. I thought it suited you. How sad to be so mistaken, for you *are* miserable, aren't you? As miserable as I am –'

I heard the door slam as Nicholas left the room, heard his step behind me on the gravel as he walked past the window, and then other sounds, other voices which would make it easier for me to raise my head, as I would have to do, and look at Blaize.

But when I did look up all I saw of him was the back of his head through the open doorway as he bent to kiss my mother's cheek, and then Aunt Hannah's, his courteous, quite graceful shepherding of them upstairs to the wide landing where the doctor was waiting to greet and console them.

I was gracious and graceful as always, and quite alone.

27

Aunt Verity shut up her house in Bournemouth and moved back to Tarn Edge, mainly because this house, of all others, contained her most cherished memories of her husband, partly because the state of her younger son's marriage was causing her serious alarm. But, if Georgiana had neglected her domestic obligations in the past, Aunt Verity's return enabled her to abandon them completely, for the house was Aunt Verity's personal property in any case, and Georgiana had never concealed how much she disliked it.

'An absolutely first-rate hotel,' I heard her tell Julian Flood one evening as they sat in the Hall at Galton, a pair of retrievers scuffling companionably under the table, Georgiana's greyhound bitch curled daintily in her lap, the level of the brandy bottle much reduced. 'Yes – that's Tarn Edge. My word, now that my mother-in-law has come home one can see how it is that Caroline does so well at Listonby – if one cares, that is, for first-class hotels.'

But Georgiana's barb seemed always to wound herself, would turn almost immediately to a laughing, flaunting self-reproach.

'Well, thank goodness for my mother-in-law, since I can do nothing right, and at least now the fires are lit when they should be, and there are muffins at tea-time. How is it that I could never manage muffins? She simply orders them and they appear, but she remembers to interview Cook every morning, you see, and tells her what will be required – whereas I – well – I can never remember tea-time, let alone muffins. I am a sorry creature, Julian – come and drown me in the stream. It's all I'm fit for.'

And, as that sad year merged into the next, she was rarely seen in Cullingford, riding off very early in the morning before Aunt Verity – or anyone else – had time to pack Gervase off to school, or, failing that, going herself sometimes to snatch him from his academic prison under the startled eye of a headmaster who could refuse nothing to a Barforth.

694

'Why not?' she told me. 'He learns nothing in any case. He just sits there wishing himself at Galton, so I may as well make his dream come true just as long as ever I can.'

Yet, although he showed no aptitude for the manufacturing life, I was by no means certain that Gervase's enthusiasm for country pursuits matched his mother's. He could, indeed, ride the tall, spirited roan she had bought him, looking, with his auburn hair, his sharp-etched profile, for all the world like a miniature Perry Clevedon, but I wondered if the excitement in his face was perhaps occasioned not so much by a dash of his late uncle's recklessness as by the over-straining of his nerves, a spice of something that could be akin to terror? He could trudge out with Georgiana across the dry August fields, a gun across his arm, to attend the annual slaughter of grouse on Galton Moor, but I – a frequent guest at Galton in those days – couldn't help noticing that he was often sick the same evening, feverish and chilled the morning after, apologetic when he was told to stay behind, but happy enough, I thought, to allow Liam Adair to go in his stead.

Gervase Barforth, in fact, was a child who belonged nowhere, a boy who, wishing to please his mother because he loved her and to please his father because he was afraid of him, seemed unlikely to please either, torn by a conflict which did not exist at Listonby where the young Chards were being raised in the belief that it was their duty to please only themselves.

'He's soft,' said Liam Adair, a boy no longer but a young man approaching fourteen, with all the insolent swagger of a guardsman. 'He never hits anything when he comes. Georgiana hits everything, and I don't do so bad – we got a hundred and twenty brace last time we were out. But Gervase just dithers and shuts his eyes. And I'll tell you this, he don't much like the dogs.'

But when a pair of hound puppies ran off, one of them to a mangled death in a man-trap in Galton woods, the other only barely surviving an encounter with some sharp-toothed woodland predator, it was Gervase who resisted Georgiana's immediate intention of putting the bleeding, whimpering little creature down.

'Darling – it's merciful.'

'But it might get better, mamma.'

'Oh no, darling. And, even if it did, it could never chase foxes, which is what hounds are made for. It would not be fair to it, Gervase.'

'I think it should be given its chance.'

'Well,' she told him, her face very serious. 'If that's what you want to do – if you think it's best – then I think you should do it. But if you take the decision, darling, then you must take the responsibility as well – all on your own. That's what people in command, or in office, have to do, and if it goes wrong they have to take the blame.'

'Yes, mamma.'

I sat up with him half the night on a bale of straw, sharing the vigil which Georgiana felt – perhaps rightly – he should have endured alone, because I could see no empire-builder in him, rather a glimpse of Giles Ashburn, who as a boy might well have done the same.

Georgiana came once, lantern in hand.

'Are you sure, Gervase – quite sure?'

'Yes, mamma.'

'He's going to die, you know, darling.'

'You can't really know for certain. I understood about taking the blame.'

And, nodding her head, courteous and friendly as her grandfather, she went away.

'You don't have to sit up with me, Aunt Faith – unless you want to.'

'Well – I'll stay a little longer.'

And, having done what we could for the ailing pup, we buried it at two o'clock of a cool, damp morning, Georgiana's child ashamed that he had lacked the good sense, the guts, to shoot it in the first place, Nicholas's child scowling, telling himself it was a dog, that was all – a damned dog – and refusing to cry.

'He'll know what to do next time, at any rate, the poor lamb,' Georgiana said. 'Don't think me hard, Faith. He had to *choose*, you see. He knows now that he chose wrong and made the poor dog suffer longer than it need have done. He made that decision – a gentleman's decision – and he's faced up to it like a gentleman. He'd never have learned that lesson, you know, at the grammar school.'

Caroline had taken her father's death very badly. She had set off on her visit to the South Erins, believing him safe and well in Bournemouth, had been called from the ducal breakfast-table to be told he was dead in Cullingford. And she was haunted by the confusion, the shock, the terrible disorientation she had suffered. Caroline had always known where she was, what she was doing there, what she intended to do next, but his loss had disturbed her sense of direction, set her askew, and she could not entirely right herself. He had left her enormously well provided for. She could continue to dazzle the county with her receptions, could extend her house and improve her estate as much as she desired, but, without her father there to see, without the deep satisfaction it had always given her to please and impress him, that desire was considerably diminished, arousing in her a melancholy which not even gifts of venison from the Duke of South Erin's deer-park, nor Lady Hetty Stone's firm promises of luring her brother to Listonby, had the power to dissipate.

Sir Joel, not Sir Matthew, had been the audience before which she had played out her life; his applause, not Matthew's, her chosen reward; and she was bewildered at its loss.

'He liked it here, at Listonby, Faith. He didn't want it himself but he liked to see me have it, doing it all so much better than Hetty Stone could manage in a thousand years, even if she was born to it. And do you remember, the last time we were all here together, how sulky everybody was – how nobody would speak at dinner, and how Georgiana went tearing off in her ballgown? I'll never forgive her for that. I'd planned it all for him, and I wanted him to be proud. I wanted him to see what I was doing with his money – because it *was* his money – and that night before he went to bed he walked me down the Long Gallery and kissed me, and

696

he said, "I'll say this for you, lass, you've always been a good investment. One of the best I ever made." And he was telling me he loved me. Oh Faith, I didn't know how ill he was. I wouldn't have gone near the South Erins if I'd known. I'd have gone straight to Bournemouth. I'd have stopped him from coming up here, tiring himself out for those brothers of mine, who could do nothing but plague him. Look – you remember the portrait I had done of him last year? I've moved it from the dining-room and put it in the Gallery – I don't care what the Chards may say.'

And when the future Sir Dominic Chard, home from his exclusive public school for the holidays, was heard explaining to a friend, 'Oh no, that is not a Chard, that is my manufacturing grandfather', he was no doubt amazed at the violence with which his mother fell on him and boxed his ears.

'Don't ever let me hear you say that again.'

'What have I said wrong? He wasn't a Chard, was he? He wasn't born at Listonby?'

'No he wasn't,' she shrieked, raining haphazard blows on him with every word, an assault, I might add, which his public school training enabled him to withstand like a rock. 'And if it hadn't been for him there wouldn't have been a Listonby. Just you remember that, young man – just you remember it.'

'Dearest –' Hetty Stone murmured, as always slightly amused if a little pained by her friend's occasional breaches of good conduct. 'The servants, dear – one really doesn't give them cause to gossip.' But Lady Chard – Caroline Barforth now, in full fury – pushed her astonished mentor away, ruining, perhaps, all hopes of that ducal visit, and, aiming a final, most accurate blow at her son, screeched contemptuously, 'The servants! They eat my bread and they'll do as they're told. And so will you.'

I had never been very close to Aunt Verity. She had been kind to me, in my girlhood, as she had been kind to most people, but she had been too radiantly happy in her own life, perhaps, to require any affection from outside, and I knew she had been suspicious of my marriage, worried, quite naturally, on her son's account rather than mine. Yet, in those first months of her widowhood, I was increasingly drawn to her, finding, even in her bereavement, that she was the most complete woman I knew, knowing very definitely that her marriage was the only one I had ever envied. I knew that everything I had ever desired for myself had been shown to me, very plainly, during those hours I had spent at my uncle's bedside. I had witnessed the kind of love of which I believed myself to be capable, the intense, exclusive emotion which I had glimpsed between them in my girlhood, had wanted then, wanted now. But I had failed to give it to Giles, had been prevented from giving it to Nicholas – largely by Nicholas himself – and Blaize did not much care for intensity. There were times that year when I suffered a great hollowness of the spirit, when I looked at myself and saw a graceful, beautifully adorned, empty shell.

Had I been born a citizen of Simon Street, my anxieties could not have

697

extended beyond rent-money, porridge-money, the stark necessities of shelter, a blanket, a cold-water tap, a few pennies desperately hoarded to pay a doctor for a sick child. Had I lived in Simon Street, I would have been too exhausted to care. But life had given me the leisure and the luxury to contemplate the condition of my heart and soul, and to understand that, once again, the pleasant pastures of my existence were not enough.

In the eyes of Cullingford I had everything any right-minded woman could possibly desire: a place in society and the income to maintain it; a fascinating if somewhat footloose husband, who had even given me a title, his father's death, which had made him Sir Blaize, having created me the second Lady Barforth of Tarn Edge. But I could not recognize myself in that title, could hardly remember myself as Faith Aycliffe, had failed to live up to the expectations of Faith Ashburn. What was I? The wife of a man who shared less than half his life with me. The mother of a girl who would become a woman entitled to a life of her own, which might hardly include me at all. And, increasingly aware that the silk and champagne atmosphere of my marriage no longer sufficed me, I took the false solution many women find in similar circumstances. I gave more dinner-parties, ordered more clothes, dressing Blanche, as she became five and six, in miniature copies of my gowns, a child with her father's cool stare, her mother's vanity, accepting quite naturally that a father was someone who took the train and came back with presents. I tended my garden, made vast indoor arrangements of daffodils and forsythia, white and purple lilacs, roses and ferns, polished beech leaves and dried grasses in season. I joined this committee and that committee, all of them chaired by Aunt Hannah, for the improvement of this, or that, evil. I took care of Liam Adair, of Grace Agbrigg, of Venetia and Gervase Barforth when no one else was inclined to do it, my house – when Blaize was away – being a depository for inconvenient children, harassed women, occasionally of a hopeful gentleman whose advances I resisted, since Blaize allowed me to be flirtatious only when he was there to see. I did what I could for Celia, removing from her shoulders the burden of Jonas's ambitions by inviting them both to dine as often as possible with me, always including in the party those people who could be of most use to Jonas. I visited the Lady Barforth Academy for Young Ladies whenever Prudence would have me, even *my* services being appreciated during an outbreak of measles, an occasional bout of homesickness among her boarders. I went to Leeds with my mother, to London now and then with Blaize, occasionally to Paris. I should have been happy.

Perhaps I could have been. Blaize had not slept the night his father died nor even tried to, remaining alone downstairs, smoking, brooding, refusing both my comfort and my company.

'Darling, do go back to bed,' he had told me. 'I'm restless and wide-awake, and – really – I can manage very well.' And I supposed that Nicholas might have said much the same, if more bluntly, to Georgiana: 'Leave me alone. I don't need you.'

They had stood at their father's funeral as granite-faced as any Flood, any Chard, and had gone, both of them, to the mill that same day, Blaize returning very late, his face unusually strained and grim. Yet which particular thing had worried him, angered him, hurt him the most, he would not say.

'Brother Nick is preparing to be unreasonable, it seems.'

'And will you be unreasonable too?'

'I imagine he will think so.'

I was still very careful of Nicholas, a relationship resting entirely on 'Good evening, are you well?', not even listening to the answer, a dryness in my throat even now when I encountered him a chair or two away from me at the Mandelbaums' dinner-table, a refusal to discuss him at those gossipy, feminine tea-times which – in view of the known hostility between him and Blaize, and of Georgiana's supposedly scandalous conduct – won me an undeserved reputation for family loyalty.

'Faith will not say a word against any of her relations,' they said of me in the better areas of Cullingford, but I was obliged, often enough, to hear others speak those words for me, to learn – from Mrs Mandelbaum, Mrs Hobhouse, Mrs Rawnsley – that the Nicholas Barforths, far from living in peace, were scarcely living together at all.

'My dear, there's no point in inviting them to anything, since she's always at Galton and he's always at the mill. If she bothers even to come, the chances are she'll come abominably late and unsuitably dressed. And if he comes without her he never has a word for the cat – just scowls and makes cutting remarks, and drinks. Well – she drinks too, there's no doubt about it, for the maids at Tarn Edge make no secret of it. She can match him glass for glass, I hear tell, which is more than my poor husband – Mr Rawnsley, Mr Hobhouse or Mr Mandelbaum – has ever been able to do. Poor Verity – my heart goes out to her. It can't be easy, when she's brought up a family of her own, to be saddled with those grandchildren while their mother goes a-gallivanting. And they're not *easy* children. That little Venetia is a handful – anyone can see it; and I wouldn't want a boy of mine to look so peaky and so over-strung as that Gervase – which is not at all to be wondered at, since, when she has him at Galton instead of sending him to school, he's allowed to sit up until all hours of the night, playing cards and drinking her brandy too, if the truth be known.'

I heard – in Blenheim Lane, at Nethercoats, at Albert Place – of the terrible evenings at Tarn Edge when husband and wife would not exchange a word. I heard of the glass a frantic, probably tipsy Georgiana had hurled at her husband's head, the fork she had hurled after it, both missiles striking the back of his chair. 'Speak to me, dammit!' she had shrieked at him. 'Curse me to hell if you like, but say something.'

'I'll say good-night, I reckon,' he had told her, calmly brushing the splintered glass and the drops of brandy from his sleeve. 'I'm expected at the Swan and I ought to change my jacket. Sleep well.' And he had left her.

I heard about her screaming rages; the slap he had once been seen to administer, not passionately, but merely to silence her; the night he had dragged her upstairs, pushed her through her bedroom door and locked it, remaining himself on the outside, his motive once again no passionate revenge – no passion at all – but simply to prevent her, at a late hour of the night, from taking Gervase to Galton. I heard of the night she had returned from Galton wet through, having driven herself in her brother's old curricle.

'Nicky, I came – It occurred to me – in fact. I've come to say I'm sorry.'

'And you've driven ten miles in the rain to tell me that?'

'Yes.'

'And you've left Gervase behind you at the Abbey?'

'Oh – yes.'

'Then how is he to get to school tomorrow? Isn't that the very thing you should be sorry about?'

I heard it all, and all of it, every word that was spoken, every word that was implied, hurt me. I had cared for Nicholas all my life. He had been my hero in childhood, the tremulous dream of my adolescence; as a woman I had loved him. I had committed myself to another man and would fulfil that commitment to the letter. But there was no magic ingredient in my marital fidelity, my maternity, to obliterate that caring. Most of the time I cared for him only at a submerged level. I did not burn for him, no longer thought of him in that way – managed, for periods of varying lengths, not to think of him at all. But I continued to care, to be concerned, to suffer acutely, at unguarded moments, from a surge of guilt against which I had no defence. I wanted to ask, 'Am I entirely to blame for his bitterness, his stubbornness? And if so what can I do to mend it? But, since Blaize was the only person I could have asked, and I was not certain I could cope with his answers, I kept silence.

Yet in other ways Blaize talked of Nicholas quite freely, enjoying the fast-accumulating tensions which he, from time to time, quite deliberately set himself to aggravate.

Nicholas had always been ambitious but now, with no one to restrict his management of the mills, his appetite for expansion became keener, his requirements more exacting. With Blaize so often away, he was the Barforth Cullingford knew best, the man who commanded instant attention when he entered the Piece Hall, the man his operatives looked out for in the mill yard, since he was known to be a hard master – as autocratic and shrewd as his father had been, not always quite so fair – and nothing went on at Lawcroft or Tarn Edge, at Low Cross or the Law Valley Wool-combers, or at Sam Barker's dyeworks either, now that it was his own, that he wasn't aware of. He worked long days, long nights, taking the escape, perhaps, of many men who are not content at home, and the feats of endurance he performed himself he expected in others.

Joel Barforth, to ensure punctuality, had locked his factory gates at half-past five every morning, obliging the late-comers to stand outside, patiently or otherwise, until breakfast-time, considering this loss of three hours' earnings to be punishment enough. Nicholas Barforth continued to lock his operatives out, but, finding that the saving of three hours' pay did not compensate him for his loss of production, fined them as well, a practice which improved the time-keeping in his sheds but won him no popularity. Joel Barforth, to some extent, had been approachable, capable of exchanging a word or two with a familiar face in a loom-gate, capable, if reminded in advance, of offering congratulations and an appropriate ribaldry to an overlooker who was to be married. Nicholas Barforth was not concerned with personalities, only with efficiency, did not wish to be acquainted with the private lives of his operatives nor to recognize their faces. He came to his sheds for the sole purpose of work. He paid others to do the same. That was the extent of the relationship between them and he would tolerate no other. He understood the machines. He knew exactly what they could produce and exactly the time needed to produce it. And, if his targets were not met, his shed-managers would be warned no more than once that others were waiting to take their places. Yet, for those who could survive his demands, his tempers, his sarcasm, his refusal to accept any excuses, his apparent conviction that everybody enjoyed hard labour as much as he did, although he gave no praise, no thanks, his financial rewards were good. He wanted value for money, but when value was given he would pay, and it was a constant thorn in his side that the man he valued least was the only one he could not dismiss, and who made sure of paying himself most handsomely.

'Brother Nick was in good form today – do you know, he's a year younger than me and I believe he looks ten years older. My poor mother. She'll have a miserable dinner-time with him tonight, for he'll plague her half to death about my Russian trip.'

'Are you going to Russia, Blaize?'

'Of course I'm going to Russia, darling – a week on Tuesday as it happens – and he'll growl, I imagine, until I'm back again. Poor mother, and poor Nicky too, because he tried so hard to stop me and couldn't manage it. We had the whole gala performance – my word, he could have been father, except that father *would* have stopped me, I suppose. And since we both knew that, and I said so in any case, it hardly improved his temper.'

'*Must* you provoke him, Blaize?'

'Yes, I think I must. It makes him that much more anxious to get rid of me.'

'Can he get rid of you?'

'He's not sure. He could buy me out, of course, but the cash for one half of Joel Barforth and Sons is too steep for any man I ever heard of. Even if he did find it, or came up with some scheme to pay me off over a number of years – to give me a good living and nothing to do for it – there's no guarantee I'd accept. The only thing he can do is to split the business – give me my share and send me on my way, if I'd agree to go. And he's tempted to ask me. Not that he likes the idea of parting with a fraction of the business, but then, if I'm really such an incompetent fool as he likes to think, I'll make a mess of it, won't I, and might be glad to sell it back to him at a price he can afford. But – and it's quite a substantial but – he may be well known in Cullingford, but the only face the Remburgers and the Grassmanns know is mine, and it must have crossed his mind that if I leave I'll be likely to take my customers with me.'

'Wouldn't it make your life a little harder, Blaize – if you split?'

'You mean, wouldn't I have to go down to the sheds rather more, and stay at home a bit more often? So I would – but darling, don't join with my brother in underestimating me. I may not understand the machines but I do understand commerce. I can add and subtract and work out my percentages every bit as fast as Nicky.'

'Then why don't you try to get on with him?'

'Ah,' he said. 'Yes. Why indeed? If you can give me a reason, darling, I'd be grateful, for I'm running out of mine.'

He left for Russia even earlier than he'd planned, giving me no exact idea of when I might expect to see him again. I knew I would hear no word from him unless there should be a little task he wished me to perform, or should take it into his head to have me meet him in London or in Paris, where, on arrival, I might discover from some casual comment that he had already spent a week in Berlin or in Rome, with no explanation as to why he had gone there. But, far more likely, I would be taking tea with Aunt Hannah one afternoon and she would say, 'I understand from Mr Agbrigg that the Russian trip was worthwhile after all.' And it would transpire that Blaize had arrived in Cullingford that very day, on the morning train, gone straight to the mill, eaten his luncheon with Mayor Agbrigg at the Old Swan or at Tarn Edge with his mother, and when I unpacked his treasure chests that night there would be something among the trinkets, the luxuries, the costly little toys for Blanche that could not possibly be Russian.

'Good heavens! – I didn't realize they had such exquisite glass in Moscow.'

'No, darling, they don't. It's Venetian.'

'And how was Venice?'

'Perfectly lovely. Gondolas floating in the moonlight just as one imagines it.'

And I couldn't suppose for a moment that he had floated in a moonlit gondola alone.

I took tea with Aunt Verity the day he left, finding some slight suggestion of tears about her, an unusual frailty that prompted me to ask her if she was unwell.

'No – dear. Merely tired. To tell you the truth I have been indulging myself. My husband wrote me very few letters, since we were rarely apart, but naturally the ones I did receive I have kept – quite curt little notes, some of them, reminding me to do this and that – not love letters at all. But, reading them just now, I could see him scribbling away with not a moment to spare, probably growling out instructions to somebody or other while he was doing it. And – well – I allowed myself to realize that I shall never stop missing him and that there is nothing I can do about it. I began to dwell on the finality, and to frighten myself with the idea that I couldn't cope – which is nonsense, of course, since one can cope with anything. But I was rescued from my misery – before it had gone on *too* long – by Nicholas. He came up from the mill to make sure Gervase had gone to school – which unfortunately he had not – and he spent an hour with me.'

'Is he well?'

'No,' she said gently, 'I am sure he is not. Oh – his health is good, of course. But I would not say he was well.'

'I'm sorry.'

'Yes. I believe he is in danger of becoming a very hard man and I shall regret that. People say my husband was hard, and so he was in many ways. But he had areas of great warmth. He loved me, and Caroline, and he loved the boys too – and would have made great sacrifices for any one of us. Nicholas is growing hard in quite another way – a very cold way, and I am afraid that quite soon all that will matter to him is the accumulation not so much of money as of the power it conveys. He tells me he will own the town and then the Valley, and I am ready to believe him. I can even understand it. I have lived all my life surrounded by ambitious men, and I have seen ruthlessness often enough before. I have even appreciated it on occasions, when there was a purpose to be served. But lately Nicholas has shown himself to be ruthless without cause, as if he took pleasure in it for its own sake – and he can do himself no lasting good.'

She paused, looked at me for a moment very reflectively, and then, shaking her head, she sighed.

'I may as well tell you, Faith, since you will eventually hear it, and in fact it must be of great concern to Prudence. We all know that the Hobhouses have been struggling for a long time to keep their heads above water. Just as we all know that Nicholas has offered several times to buy them out – and has not increased his offer, I might add, after each refusal, but quite the reverse. Well – he has now done something which must surely sink them at last. Oh dear – I don't know if it is commercial practice or downright bullying or calculated fraud, but whatever one may call it I seem to be caught in the cross-fire and don't much like it. Some time ago Mr Hobhouse was – as Mr Hobhouse often is – quite desperately short of cash. His borrowing from Mr Rawnsley's bank had reached its limits. Mr Oldroyd of Fieldhead – his brother-in-law – is not famous for generosity, and in any case it has always been Hobhouse policy not to upset him, because of his will. Mr Hobhouse looked around him and saw Nicholas, or Nicholas put himself in Mr Hobhouse's way – I don't know – but what I do know is that when Nicholas advanced him the money he must have been well aware that it could never be repaid. Yes – yes – Mr Hobhouse is very rash and much too hopeful. I know it. The tide, in his view, is always on the turn – that is his way – we all understand him. I suppose he was relying too much on your sister's dowry, and since he is kind-hearted himself he felt that Mr Oldroyd, deep down, must be the same and wouldn't really abandon him with his back to the wall. Well – my son Nicholas is demanding his money. Mr Hobhouse cannot pay.

Mr Oldroyd will not oblige. Mrs Hobhouse came to me in tears, for she has a large family and is a woman I have known all my life. I spoke to Nicholas and I could not reach him. The law is on his side. He wants Nethercoats. He has found not only the way to get it, but the way to get it cheap. He didn't ask me to admire his cleverness. He simply shrugged his shoulders. It was not easy for me to hear Emma-Jane Hobhouse describe him as heartless and greedy – especially when there was no defence I could make. Yes – I could lend Mrs Hobhouse the money to repay him. I could easily afford it, as she wasn't slow to point out. But to do that would be to damage my own relationship with Nicholas – and, whether he values that or not, it is about the only thing he has left.'

'Aunt Verity –?'

'Yes, Faith. You know as well as I do that he has no relationship with Georgiana, which is not entirely her fault. I have told him so and he agrees with me. I have told him that if he made the first move she would probably be ready to make the second – glad to make it. He agrees with that too. Nicholas was very close to me, Faith. All his life he has done things in temper, in stubborn pride, and then regretted it. You have cause to know that, I imagine. Even his temper is different now. It burst out of him, once, quite spontaneously – a true, snarling, red-blooded rage, a true emotion. Now he uses it when he needs it, manufactures it almost to order, which is not at all the same. And gradually, this past year or so, I have felt him moving away even from me. It has been like entering a familiar house and finding that all the doors are closing one by one. Well – I am sorry for that, and even sorrier that he has felt the need to shut out his children in the same fashion. Yes – they have a great deal of Georgiana in them, Venetia even more than Gervase. Nevertheless, they are his children – my grandchildren, like Blanche and Caroline's boys. And I think I would like to tell you, Faith, that, if I seem to give more of my time and attention to Venetia than I give to Blanche, it is because – well, who else is here to do it?'

'Aunt Verity, please don't worry about Blanche.'

'Oh, but I don't worry about her, Faith dear. She has you, and if Blaize is something of an absentee father I imagine he gives her good measure when he is at home. And besides, she has enough of Blaize in her to be able to cope with life very well on her own, when the time comes. Venetia is very different – the wildest little girl I have ever known – not wilful and headstrong like Caroline or like Nicholas himself. No – altogether Georgiana's child. It is Venetia, believe me, who most resembles Peregrine Clevedon, not Gervase, and because she is enchanting and open-hearted at the same time, so eager and hopeful, my heart bleeds for her. Nicholas will always take care of them, of course. He will pay their bills, and very handsomely. They will have the best of everything money can buy, there's no doubt of that. Quite simply, he doesn't wish to be personally involved with them. He doesn't want to know them and he doesn't want them to know him. It worries me dreadfully.'

The calling-in of the Hobhouse loan became common knowledge soon enough, causing all the resentment my aunt had feared; for, although Mr Hobhouse had been foolish, and there was usually little sympathy in Cullingford for a man who could not hang on to his money, he was popular, had been with us for a very long time, while Nicholas Barforth, a much younger man, had shown himself too devious, was not much liked in the Piece Hall in any case, where it was felt that he already had too much and had got it both too easily and too soon.

Cullingford, with the exception of Mr Rawnsley of Rawnsley's Bank and the astute Mr Oldroyd, believed that Mr Hobhouse should be given time to pay. Nicholas Barforth would not make that time available. Mr Oldroyd was applied to again, Mr and Mrs Hobhouse, Freddy, Adolphus and James spending the best part of an afternoon at Fieldhead, reminding him perhaps of his wife, their dear Aunt Lucy, who had come to him from Nethercoats with a considerable dowry in her hands.

Mr Oldroyd was seen in Lawcroft Mill yard the following day, in conversation with Nicholas, and dined with him at the Old Swan that night. The next morning Mr Oldroyd conveyed his regrets to Nethercoats, declining to throw good money after bad, a decision for which Nicholas Barforth was blamed, since his purchases of Oldroyd-spun yarn were considerable enough to allow him to exercise a little persuasion.

And it was largely to escape the gossip, in which Prudence was inevitably involved, that I packed Blanche's boxes and mine and went to Galton with Georgiana, looking for quietness and finding instead that I was soon infected by her restlessness, the impulses which drove her on her wild, midnight riding, that caused her suddenly in mid-sentence to take flight, splashing across the Abbey steam, scrambling up any stony hillside which seemed steep enough, dangerous enough to challenge her reckless spirit, moving so as not to stand still, shouting so as not to listen, running without direction, unless it was towards Julian Flood's equally restless arms.

I was not sure of it. 'Julian, darling, I have stones in my shoes', and, flopping down on to the grass, she would stretch herself full length while he undid her shoe, pulled off her boot, his fingers curving far too easily around her ankle, as if he had done it all too many times before for any outward show of passion. It was not flirtation. They simply touched each other a great deal, jostling and back-slapping in the stable-yard. 'Help me over this fence, Julian.' 'Lift me down from this gate'; and she would lean against him as frank and affectionate as she had been with her brother.

'*You* love me at any rate, don't you, Julian?'

'Of course.'

'That's good – we're alike, aren't we, you and I? And although she had talked in exactly the same fashion to Perry, Julian Flood was not her brother, and in his case the barrier of comradeship, which had been fragile enough with Perry, could easily be crossed.

'Faith, darling, I'm going off with Julian this morning – over the hills and faraway – God knows where! You don't mind seeing to Venetia until

I get back, since my nanny is half-witted and yours so supercilious that I daren't for the life in me ask her myself.' And, while she roamed the hillsides, the highways and by-ways of her beloved outdoors and of her own nature, I found myself for the first time involved with a girl-child who had no time for my stories and my games of make-believe, a tiny red-haired imp who found nothing to amuse her in my trinket boxes, an agile little creature who did exactly as she pleased and was impossible to catch. One moment she was there, passive, her face, like her mother's, growing plain with the ebb of her vitality. The next moment she had vanished from the face of the earth, no one had seen her go, no one could find her. Consternation, my pulses fluttering, my mind full of that perilous Abbey stream, the quarry a mile away, the shaft of some ancient, worked-out mine; my sympathy going out to my sister Celia, who experienced this terrible anxiety, needlessly perhaps, but every day. No trace of her anywhere and then, in the very place one had looked a moment ago, she was there, her woodland green eyes blinking in amazement at the fuss, the sorry spectacle of Aunt Faith on the brink of nervous tears.

'I went outside,' she would tell me. 'Just out –' And no more than that could I ever discover.

Gervase was with us too, playing truant again from the grammar school, his presence another bond between Georgiana and Julian Flood, for, failing Perry, what better example than the future lord of the manor of Cullingford could she find for the future squire of Galton to follow?

'Julian, do show him how to load that gun. No – no, darling, you have to really make your horse *work* to get him over that gate – watch Julian. There, you see, he did it with a yard to spare. No, darling, you're too stiff in the hips and the knees, sit *easy* in the saddle, like Julian. And Gervase, look at Julian's feet – straight forward, darling, not sticking out like yours. Do look, Faith. Isn't he coming along splendidly?'

One morning, as they were all three riding up and down the stream to accustom Gervase's nervous animal to the fast-flowing water, and I was leaning on the bridge taking a final breath of Galton air, since I was going on to Listonby that day, I looked up and saw Nicholas walking towards us from the house.

'Georgiana!' I called out, conveying, against my will, a warning; and, seeing him too, 'Damnation,' she said, and, turning her horse's head, sent it careering out of the water and up the hillside, turf and stones flying, and was off across the open fields, Julian Flood behind her.

I waited until Gervase got his horse up the bank, and taking his bridle walked him back along the path where Nicholas was waiting.

'Father,' he said, very pale, that wild look in his eyes again, clearly expecting to be blamed. But Nicholas merely nodded and told him, 'Take your horse to the stables and then tell them to clean you up and get your things together. It seems to me you should be at your lessons.'

'Yes, father.' And he rode away, his toes turned sadly outwards, slouching in his saddle, smaller than he had been a moment ago.

We were quite alone, the whole of the Galton estate spreading around

us, the bare hillsides, the empty fields, a vast, smoky autumn sky, Mr
Gervase Clevedon away somewhere at his Quarter Sessions, two little
girls – his daughter and mine – safely indoors in the care of a few
indifferent maids, six years separating us from the last time we had been
together and he had persuaded me, against my own judgment, to go and
wait for him in Scarborough. I didn't know him now. He had been the
boy who had defied his father and refused to ride on Cullingford's first
train, who had said so often 'Faith will know what I mean'. He had been
the young bridegroom who had told me, 'They will say it is for my money
on her part, and because I am stubborn. It is more than that.' And later
he had said to me, 'Faith, I won't let you go.' He was a stranger now, the
man who was about to ruin the Hobhouses, who had shut the doors of his
nature to his mother, his wife and his children. The man who would ruin
his own brother – my husband – if he could. I didn't know him.

'Good morning, Lady Barforth,' he said, and I laughed quite easily.

'Heavens! Don't call me that. Every time I hear it, I look over my
shoulder expecting to see your mother.'

'I daresay. She's at Listonby. I've just come from there. I understand
you're to join her.'

'Yes – with Blanche, and with Venetia too, if you don't mind. Are you
taking Gervase back to Tarn Edge? Nicholas – I don't know how long
Georgiana will be –'

'Don't you? She'll be back as soon as she sees me leave, I imagine. I
just came to pick up the boy. She knows that and knows she can't prevent
it – so what point is there in starting a battle she can't win?'

We walked in silence up the narrow little track and into the cloister
that would lead us to the Abbey house.

'And how are you, Faith? Well?'

'Yes – very well.'

'I'm glad to hear it. How long have you been here – five days? Six
days? And how long has Julian Flood been with you?'

'Nicholas, I don't think you should –'

'What? Ask you to betray a confidence? Darling, you don't have to tell
me. He's been here night and day, I imagine. And why not? What else
has he got to do? These things happen.'

I walked a step or two ahead of him, stung by his familiarity, which had
been intended to sting me; embarrassed by his mention of Julian Flood,
which had been intended to embarrass, the word 'darling' having come as
coarsely from his tongue as if I had been a music-hall dancer. And I was
aware again of the silence around us, nothing but my angry footsteps to
break it, that vaulted roof arching away into a timeless, treacherous
distance.

'Come, Faith. You're a sophisticated woman. You understand how it
is.'

'Yes,' I said, turning to face him, meeting the granite wall that was his
anger. 'I understand. As you say, he's been here all the time, and so have
I. I've seen nothing to suggest that there is anything between them but
friendship.'

'Then he's a fool,' he said bluntly. 'And so is she. So far as I'm concerned, it couldn't matter less. You have my permission to tell her so.'

'I don't want to know about it, Nicholas.'

He stopped and lit a cigar, the fragrant trail of tobacco in the air somehow very wrong in this place, a quite deliberate desecration.

'No. I imagine you don't. I merely mention it in case you should feel uncomfortable – adultery does have that effect on its spectators.'

'Nicholas, there *is* no adultery.'

'So you tell me. In which case I'll tell you again – he's a fool. I took him for a man who could recognize his opportunities.'

I walked on again, and then came to a halt somehow facing the fluted, crumbling stone of the old wall, my hands clasped tight together, my whole mind remembering him, knowing he was still there, unwilling, perhaps, but painfully present behind the hardness, the coarseness, the grim-textured façade.

I could neither hear him nor see him. I could simply feel him there, know him there, one part of me finding it ridiculous that I could not turn around and touch him, the rest of me anguished, terrified that I might do it. And already there was a whisper inside me, a warning that said, 'Be very careful'; for his will had vanquished mine often enough, easily enough, in the past, and I had no greater resolution than before.

'My dear sister-in-law,' he said, a certain harsh amusement in his voice. 'You seem very agitated. I do apologize if I have given you cause.'

'There's no need to apologize.'

'Good. Nevertheless, you *are* upset?'

'Yes.'

'And is there anything I can do?'

'You could believe me about Georgiana and Julian Flood.'

'Could I? I'm not so sure of that. Belief, you see, implies a measure of trust and, I really don't think it would be wise. I imagine you know what I mean.'

'Yes. I know. And you're quite wrong.'

'Really? I should need to be convinced of that. Could you convince me?'

'No,' I told him, sighing out the words, despairing over them. 'Because there are things I can't tell you.'

'And have I asked any questions?'

'No. I almost wish you had.'

He came to stand beside me, heavier than my body remembered him, his nearness creating an imbalance in my reasoning, so that at the same time he was the man I knew best in the world and a total stranger.

'In fact you'd like me to shake the truth out of you to ease your conscience, so that afterwards – like most women – you could say "he made me do it".'

'I would not.'

'I'm glad to hear it, because I couldn't oblige you. And is there even a mystery? You saw the chance of a good marriage. You took it.'

708

'No.'

'You mean it's not a good marriage?'

'No. I don't mean that. But it didn't happen – as you suggested – from self-interest. You must know that. You *do* know it.'

'I know nothing about it, Faith. I was away at the time, if you remember, and when I eventually got to know about it your motives seemed plain enough. If I'm wrong, then tell me so. But I shouldn't ask that of you, should I? Let's forget, as I did, because I expect you've promised to keep quiet and it doesn't pay to break your word every time. We'll say no more about it.'

Yet I knew, very clearly, that he intended me to say a great deal, that every word he spoke was pushing me harder against that stone wall, driving me into a corner the better to search out the source of my caring, the source of my guilt. And, if he needed to know the truth, there was no doubt at all that I needed to tell him.

'We'll say no more,' he repeated softly, firmly, and weak with relief I took a step away from the ancient stone, imagining myself free, until I understood from the glimpse of satisfaction in his face that he had done no more than loosen my reins and had found a sure way to bind me again.

'That brooch on your shoulder,' he said with false indifference. 'You wear it a great deal, I notice.'

'Yes – yes I do.'

'And so you should, for it's a pretty compliment – a cameo swan. A present from Blaize, I reckon.'

I nodded, dry-mouthed, afraid again, wondering what he could find in a brooch to use against me, knowing, in his present mood, that there must be something; and he smiled.

'Of course it is. It's got his stamp all over it. And he'd put himself to a lot of trouble to get it.'

'I believe he may have done.'

'There's no doubt about it. He'd go a few hundred miles out of his way to find a jeweller who could design it and cut it, time and money no object. That's Blaize.'

'Yes.'

'Whereas I'd never think of such a thing. I'm not ungenerous. My wife has a diamond or two and some good emeralds, but there's no particular finesse about that. Any man with a decent bank account could manage it.'

'Does it matter?' I asked, meaning, 'Where are you leading me?'; and it was to the unspoken question he replied.

'It doesn't matter to me because I'm not a man for personal relationships. Oh yes, one tries a little of this and a little of the other as a young man, but in the end a man with any sense at all finds out what he's good at and where he can best make his profit. And the truth is that close relationships don't suit me. My mother sometimes gets upset about it, but if I am hard, as she says, then I find it quite natural.'

'I don't.'

709

'I daresay. But then, you knew me best in my younger days, when I was still trying out a few sentimental notions.'

'Such as marriage – and love?'

'Well, marriage at any rate. And adultery, I suppose, from which I must exonerate you, since you were not married at the time and betrayed no one – well, not a husband –'

Self-pity perhaps, and bruised conceit, the Barforth inability to accept that he could not have everything his way. And, forcing, myself to remember the weight of his jealousy, his temper, his injustice, I tried to take refuge in anger. He's selfish, a part of my mind insisted. He's hurt, another replied, both were true. It was the hurt that mattered.

'Nicholas – you may find this hard to believe – you may not even want to believe it – but I never deceived you. Blaize didn't deceive you either. He came to Scarborough that week-end for no other reason than to tell me you couldn't be there. He didn't touch me. He didn't try to touch me. I don't think he particularly wanted to. Certainly I didn't want it.'

And even these few words scorched me, took my breath away, hurt my throat and my tongue in the speaking, caused my will to flicker into its last feeble resistance, pleading with his will. 'Please Nicholas, let that be enough. Don't make me say any more.'

But having waited so long he was not disposed to be merciful. 'Faith – dearest Faith – I have four mills to run. How much time do you imagine I spend wondering just when, and how, you got into bed with my brother?'

But he had wondered, had tormented himself with it, and, pressing my back to the wall, turning my face away from him, the cold stone easing my burning cheeks, I knew I was about to give him the answer. I had been wrong about everything else, very likely I was wrong again, but I had contributed more than my share to his load of bitterness and this much, at least, was owing. It was the only promise Blaize had ever asked of me. I didn't want to break it. It was against my nature to break it. I understood why it should not be broken. It made no difference.

'Listen,' I said, closing my eyes, pressing my face harder against the stone, each word leaving me with great effort, great labour. 'We were seen together in Scarborough, Blaize and I, by someone who informed Aunt Hannah. She assumed that we were lovers. She was going to tell your father. You were in London. Georgiana was expecting Venetia and you were as worried and confused as I was about how you'd feel if she should die. I was terrified. I'm terrified now.'

And it had been waiting for me a long time, this cloister, where nuns had walked barefoot in penitence, a right and proper place for the scourging my spirit required. I felt his hand clench on the wall above my head, a feeling of unbearable strain communicating itself from his body to mine, tightening the air around us until I could scarcely breathe, and then suddenly he threw back his head and gave, no groan of pain, no string of curses or reproaches, but a short, quite savage peal of laughter, showing me at last the true meaning of punishment, since nothing could have wounded me so much as this.

'Christ!' he said. 'So that's how he did it. The clever bastard. He convinced you that you were saving me, did he? Yes – I could have worked it out, I reckon. It's like him. It's like you.' And he laughed again, the sharp, ugly sound of it stripping me bare and flaying me.

'Stop it, Nicholas. You've hurt me – it's enough.'

'When I'm ready,' he said. 'When I'm good and ready.'

And then, the mirth vanishing, whipping out of him and leaving his face granite hard again, he took me by the shoulders, his face very close to mine.

'But it didn't work, darling, did it? He played God once too often, didn't he? And don't you ever ask yourself why? Oh yes, he gave you his reasons, plenty of them, and they'd seem good to you at the time, because he can talk the birds from the trees, we all know that. But what was he really after? It wasn't done for my sake, Faith, and it wasn't done for yours, you can rely on that. It's the Cullingford train all over again. I wouldn't play then, and I won't play now. He should have known that.'

I got away from him, ran down the cloister into the house, and he drove off a half-hour later with his son, leaving me to face Georgiana, who appeared as if she had been awaiting the signal, just as his carriage went out of sight.

'He's gone then?'

'As you see.'

And she stood for a moment staring in the direction he had taken, too deep in her own thoughts to notice that I had been crying, that I was very near to tears again.

'He thinks I'm having an affair with Julian,' she said. 'It's not true – of course, it's not true. Heavens, if he really thought about it – wanted to think about it – he'd know it couldn't be true.' And then, her voice very low this time. 'Ah well – he has a mistress in Leeds and another in London – did you know that? No, of course you didn't, and I shouldn't know either, except that one always knows. Yes – one knows and one should be able to accept it with resignation, and dignity. One should make no more of it than a simple "My dear, men are like that", which I've heard so many women say. I can't say it.'

She turned away as if she meant to go inside and then turned slowly round again, drawn against her will to the empty road he had just travelled.

'If it hurts me, then you'd think I'd be able to tell him so – wouldn't you? Just go to him and tell him? I can't. He wouldn't answer, you see. And when he won't talk to me it hurts me so much that I can't risk making it happen. So I just go on pretending there's nothing I want to say to him.'

She turned away again, her narrow hand making a gesture of finality.

'Well, so much for that,' she said. 'There's always the Abbey – always my blessed cloister. At least nobody can take that away from me.'

711

28

The calling-in of the Hobhouse debt was still the subject of every tea-time, every dinner-table, when I returned, my sister Prudence walking up from Elderleigh schoolhouse the moment she became aware of my carriage on the drive, for now she must either marry Freddy or break off with him, and the decision was harder than she had anticipated.

Freddy had waited more than ten years for her, not, as she continued to insist, very patiently and certainly not without diversions. He had gone regularly to Bradford every Tuesday and Friday for years to treat himself to the supposedly medium-priced charms of a lady who kept a tobacconist's shop in Darley Street, had paid brief court to Rebecca Mandelbaum before her Austrian musician won her heart. But, at this crisis in his family's fortunes, circumstances had placed him in Prudence's hands, and, in the prevailing mood of sympathy, Cullingford would expect Prudence to do her duty by the Hobhouses or would condemn her as a heartless jilt.

'Not that I care for that,' she said. 'Why should I care what anyone thinks of me?'

But she was fonder of Freddy than she had intended, attracted in spite of herself by his weighty, lazy charm, his constant good-humour in adversity, the sheer hard labour he had given to Nethercoats, his lack of rancour when all his efforts had been defeated, one by one, by his father. And she could no longer deny that she had used him.

'Of course I did. And why not? No one thinks ill of a man for using a woman. It is what men are supposed to do, and women are supposed to put up with it. If I had lost *my* money, it would have been taken for granted that he would break off with me, and they would have called him a sentimental fool if he hadn't. But it is not the same for me. I am a woman and so I am expected to sacrifice myself and everything I have for the sake of his incompetent father. And, if I don't, I run the risk of losing my reputation and my school – for no Law Valley man will allow his daughter to be educated by the heartless woman who jilted Freddy Hobhouse, in case my pupils should follow my example, in case I should take it into my head to teach them that a woman has as much right to be considered as a man. I've laboured hard for my independence, you know that. Dear God! how I've laboured – and it didn't please me that I had to lie and scheme for it, and hide behind Sir Joel Barforth in order to maintain it. But I'm succeeding, Faith. I'm gaining the reputation I set out to gain. I'm being taken seriously, not as the daughter of Morgan Aycliffe with twenty thousand pounds and expectations, but as myself – for what I've made of myself. And I can't lose it. I might share it, but I won't lose it. I won't sink my money and my identity in Nethercoats. If Freddy wants me, he'll have to break off with his family first. He'll have to choose my business instead of his own.'

But such an idea would have been considered preposterous, downright criminal, in Cullingford, and Freddy, who was no revolutionary, who was kind-hearted and easy-going and extremely attached to his even easier-natured father, would not listen to it in any case. He would marry Prudence if he could. He would plough every penny she brought with her and every penny he could raise elsewhere into his ailing Nethercoats. And, if he failed, then he would take any man's wages and work himself to death to provide for her. He would give her the shirt from his back, the last crust from his table, and go cold and hungry himself; but nothing would induce him to see what in her opinion was reason, in his opinion treachery, nothing – absolutely nothing – would persuade him to allow her to provide for him.

A woman's dowry and her inheritance belonged by right and custom to her husband, since wealth of this kind had been earned and accumulated by a fellow male – her father – but there was an ugly name for a man who lived in the fruits of a woman's labour, and Freddy Hobhouse would not be called by that name.

'Good heavens!' my mother said. 'What a diverting notion! He would have to do exactly as she told him – can you imagine it? No more "Darling, may I have a new bonnet?", but "Unless you mend your manners I shall not buy you a new coat". Really – one can see the advantages to it. Daniel has explained to me that by law even a woman's earnings belong to her husband, but I can see that it is not at all the same. A man knows in advance the size of the dowry he is getting and once he sets his hands upon it no one can have it back again. But earnings – well – all she needs to do is threaten to stop earning, and if he depends upon her income he will be obliged to let her have her way. Yes, so he will, just as we are obliged to let our husbands have their way, for the same reason. My dear, it is revolution, and although I am perfectly happy with my Daniel – indeed I am – I think the idea of such power could quite turn my head, were I a younger woman. Earnings. Good heavens! – your father would turn in his grave. Quite suddenly I am able to understand why he was so careful to teach you nothing. What a dangerous, tantalizing notion – to earn a living of one's own.'

But others were less tantalized, and perhaps it suited me to rush to my sister's aid, doing my very best to defend her actions and her name, since I could no longer defend my own.

I had made my confession to Nicholas in good faith. Like his mother, I had felt that bitter shell hardening around him and had wanted to pierce it, however slightly, to reach the part of him that could still find joy in life, not necessarily with Georgiana, certainly not with me, but somehow, with someone. But once again I had blundered. I had not reached him. Possibly there was nothing left to reach, and I had done no more than lay myself, and Blaize, open to his malice. I had dredged deep into my store of courage, drained it and myself with it to make that revelation, and he had laughed at me. What would he do now? Would he keep it to himself, or, appreciating its worth, would he toss it casually at Blaize the next time they quarrelled. And how would Blaize react to it? I had rarely seen him angry, never with me, but how could he live in peace with a woman who had put such a weapon into his brother's hands, a woman who understood full well how lethal that weapon could be, and that Nicholas would not hestiate to use it.

I had no defence. I had wounded Nicholas long ago before the granite had encased him and he was still vulnerable to pain. The wound remained, if only in his pride, and he would hurt me now if he could, not in anger but in calculation, as a lever to dislodge Blaize from Tarn Edge. He would use me as he had used the Hobhouse debt, a few thousand pounds well spent to bring Nethercoats to its knees, a cheating woman to do the same with his brother, and, waking suddenly in the middle of one tormented night, it seemed to me that I had nothing more to lose, that I might as well go to him and beg, as abjectly as he liked, for mercy. I was in his power, as I had been all my life in the power of one man after another. I was a female, one of Nature's penitents. I would accept the role assigned me and plead. But by morning I knew that by doing so I could only drag myself further into the mire, for, knowing him as I still did, the dark side of him as well as the light, I knew he would take my pleading and anything else it pleased him to extract from me, would play cat and mouse with me for as long as it suited him, and would still betray me.

I would not wait then, and, delving inside myself once more for my feeble content of courage, decided that I would tell Blaize myself as soon as he came home. I would prepare him so that he could have his defence ready, and I would accept whatever retribution he chose to inflict, aware that the punishment itself could hardly be worse than my dry-mouthed dread of it. But, when he arrived with the fur cloak, the Russian boots, the gorgeous Oriental robe, the icons, the samovar, his cool quizzical gaiety, it was easy to convince myself that, after all, he would not take it hard, that he would shrug this off as lightly as everything else.

'My word!' he said when we had dined and made love, when he was lounging easily among the pillows, and I, the encrusted Eastern robe draped around my satiated body, fear again in my heart, had told him about the Hobhouse debt as a means of introducing Nicholas's name.

'Yes – I quite see your sister's dilemma. Shall I solve it for her? Nothing prevents me from lending Hobhouse the money to pay Nicky, and I doubt I'd require any better interest-rate than the look on my brother's face.'

'No, Blaize. Don't do that. Please don't.'

'Darling –?' And, leaning forward, supporting himself on one elbow, he turned his cool, grey eyes full on my face. 'Is there any particular reason why I shouldn't?'

'Yes. Yes, of course. There'd be another great explosion, you know it, and – well, I think your mother has had enough to bear. She was telling me just the other day how concerned she is about the pair of you.'

'Yes, I believe she is. Well then, I shall try not to aggravate her fears – although she could lend Hobhouse the money herself, of course. I doubt if even Nicky would do too much snarling at *her*.'

'Blaize, for goodness' sake! Can't you leave things alone – just for once?'

714

'Darling,' he said, with his unique smile, 'are you accusing me of meddling?'

I didn't know what I was accusing him of, didn't know what he was thinking or feeling, what he wanted, cared about, if, indeed, he cared for anything. I had lived pleasantly, sometimes very happily, with the surface of him and had no idea what lay beneath it. I had worn my lovely clothes for his entertainment, had given him my body in every mood and manner his imagination could devise. I had laughed with him, enjoyed with him, preened myself with him, had not precisely trusted him but had believed he could trust me.

I spent five days of silent agony, an earthquake stirring beneath my feet each evening when I heard his carriage, the qualms subsiding only when his smile told me that all was well. I went to Aunt Verity, determined to make my confession and ask her help, and could not. I made up my mind to lie, when the blow fell, to brazen it out by declaring that Aunt Hannah herself – or Jonas – had said something to make Nicholas suspect the truth, and I had merely confirmed it. I doubt if I could have done either.

'My brother has been making himself very pleasant,' Blaize said on the sixth evening as we were dining alone, a bowl of late roses on the table between us, the curtains drawn against the chill of the November night. 'I wonder why? I agree, the orders I brought back from Moscow are altogether stupendous, but why, I ask myself, is he so pleased about that? It merely proves I was right to go in the first place, and gives me an excellent reason to go again.'

And, throwing down my napkin, my eyes fixed on the candle-flame, I said harshly, 'I'll tell you why. He knows about Aunt Hannah and Scarborough.'

A long time went by. The candle-flame got into my eyes, filled them, and when they had regained their focus I saw his hand lifting the wine bottle from its ice, filling my glass and his own, his face so entirely without expression that for a sickening moment I wondered if I had actually spoken at all.

'Blaize, did you hear what I said?'

'Oh yes,' he said, raising his glass and sipping reflectively, his face telling me nothing. 'I heard. Thank you, Faith. That was splendid – absolutely splendid.'

I got up, impeded for the first time by my crinoline, walked to the window and to the fire and back again, alone, it seemed, in the room, although he still sat there at the table, drinking his well-chilled wine, enjoying, for all I knew, the excellence of its bouquet, the effect of the candlelight on his silver and his crystal, these things adequately consoling him, perhaps, for the betrayal of his silly, sentimental wife.

'Blaize – say something to me.' And perhaps my voice reminded me of Georgiana's. 'You must want to know how – and why. At least that much.'

'Darling, if he knows, it can only be because you told him.'

'Yes – yes I did. And, if you want to know, I have bitterly regretted it.'

715

'Well – that's something, at any rate.'

'He came to Galton while I was there, to fetch Gervase away. He was upset –'

'And you consoled him.'

'I broke the only promise you ever asked of me.'

And once again a Barforth male, from his height, or his depth, had it in him to laugh at me, although this time there was no cruel explosion of mirth, merely a chuckle that had a wry sound to it, his amusement directed at us both.

'Ah well – as to promises and their making and breaking, perhaps I am not the man who should complain. Faith – do sit down. Now that you've just stabbed me in the back, don't add to my discomfort by all that nervous pacing.'

'Blaize, don't you care at all?'

'Yes, as it happens, I do. I think I'll just step outside and smoke my cigar in the garden, if you don't mind. I'll join you for coffee presently.'

I had them clear the table, ordered coffee to be served in the drawing-room, sat by the crackling autumn fire and drank one cup, then two, aware, I think, of the beauty of the room, the light-green silk walls, the creamy Aubusson rugs, the discreet elegance which had marked our lives together, which had contented my nature almost completely, as Blaize himself had almost contented me. And, although I was no longer afraid, I was inexpressibly saddened, the misty, quite gentle sorrow one feels sometimes at the summer's end, the first glimpse of age in the face of a woman who has lived by her beauty.

'I am sorry,' he said, coming in through the long windows, 'I've kept you waiting rather a long time, haven't I, for the pronouncing of your sentence.'

And, knowing the qualities he most admired in a woman, I answered calmly, 'Shall I send for more coffee?'

The tray was removed, another brought in its place. I filled his cup, adding sugar, no cream, in the way he liked it. He drank, replaced the fragile Wedgwood cup on the tray and, since we were alone, lit another cigar.

'I find,' he said, 'that we have evolved a very agreeable way of life together. Am I right in assuming that you value it too?'

'Yes. I value it.'

'Well then – what more is there to say? I'm very loathe to lose anything I find pleasant, Faith, you must know that. I was inclined to be rather put out, half an hour ago, but then, thinking it over, I'm bound to admit that, had you been my mistress in the first place and then eloped with him, I'd soon have found a way of persuading you to tell me why. So I can hardly be surprised that Nick has done the same.'

'And you're not – disappointed?'

'In you?'

'Of course in me.'

'I shall get over it. And at least I'll be ready to defend myself when Nicky mentions it – if he ever does. Really – it makes very little difference.'

716

'I'm glad you think so.'

'Faith,' he said, leaning as near to me as my skirts allowed. 'Did you expect me to throw the soup tureen at your head or brain you with the candelabra? That's not quite my style, you know. I'm altogether the wrong Barforth for that sort of thing. And, in any event, that's not the way of it – is it, my love? – between us? If you want to make amends you can treat me with very obvious affection the next time we are all together – it won't hurt to let him think you like me best. It won't hurt me, that is –'

And, although it was not forgotten, although from time to time I saw, or imagined I saw, a certain coolness, a certain watchfulness, we did not speak of it again.

Mr Oldroyd of Fieldhead died very suddenly that November, his demise occasioning an inevitable if discreet rejoicing at Nethercoats, where it was assumed that Freddy at least, who had been a favourite nephew, must surely benefit, if not in entirety, at least substantially enough to settle the Barforth debt.

'Only think,' my mother breathed, quite ecstatically, 'If Freddy should get it all, for I cannot think what else Matthew Oldroyd can have done with it. Prudence could then be mistress of Fieldhead, which even *she* would find most agreeable. And just think, too, darling, that it could all have been mine. Well – I would have given it up twice over for my Daniel, but, I confess, I would be well pleased for my daughter to have it in my place. Do give her a little push, Faith. Earning a living is all very well, but Matthew Oldroyd was very rich, you know, and if it all comes to Freddy there will be a hundred young ladies ready to share it with him. Tell Prudence that.'

But Prudence had no need to be told, for, although Freddy himself was still her devoted slave, his mother, in the interval before the will was read, made it plain that, with the Oldroyd millions at his disposal, Freddy would have no need to settle for a self-willed schoolmistress no longer in her first youth, whose opinions were, to say the least, peculiar.

'She thinks he may help himself to a biddable little chit of fifteen,' Prudence said. 'One of my pupils, in fact, rather than myself. Well I do not at all blame her for disliking me. I merely hope that if Freddy is to be so rich he will have the sense to keep it away from her, and from his father – for if he does not we shall see Nicholas Barforth at Fieldhead as well, five years from now. Poor Freddy, he will allow them all to impose upon him, you know. He will give his father the means to ruin Nethercoats all over again, and provide so handsomely for all his brothers and sisters that they will be too busy spending it even to thank him. Poor Mr Oldroyd too. They say he was very mean, very careful with his money, and it must have saddened him to know how recklessly the Hobhouses would throw it away.'

A prophetic utterance, certainly, on my sister's part, for it had clearly saddened him so much that he had, in the end, found himself unable to give them the opportunity, the Oldroyd will providing a scandal which contented Cullingford for many a long day, acting as a stone flung into murky waters, its ripples spreading wide and, to some of us, most painfully.

As expected, provision had been made for a certain Miss Jamison in Leeds, a few trifling bequests to household staff, an insulting five hundred pounds apiece to his brother-in-law, Mr Bradley Hobhouse, and to Emma-Jane Hobhouse, his wife. To his favourite nephew, Mr Bradley Frederick Hobhouse, he left the sum of ten thousand pounds, with the suggestion that it be used for the setting up of some personal enterprise; but the bulk of his estate, his spinning mill at Fieldhead and Fieldhead mill-house, his railway shares, his brewery shares, his substantial bank deposits, were to become the property of one Mrs Tessa Delaney, who, it appeared, was not Mrs Delaney at all, but for the past year had been the second Mrs Matthew Oldroyd of Fieldhead.

'Oh dear,' my mother said. 'I fear there will be trouble. My poor Celia.'

And, although it was not immediately clear to me why my sister Celia should be involved, I was soon enlightened by the visit of a distraught Mrs Hobhouse who, with nothing more to hope for, nothing more to lose, would have been glad, I think, to see the whole of Cullingford consumed in flames. She was not herself to blame for her family's ruin. She would not blame her husband. Who then? A conspiracy, no less, the greedy, evil-hearted Barforths standing solidly behind Nicholas to rob her of her home, to put her and her children out in the street. She was no fool. She could recognize criminal practice when she saw it, and what had it been but that? Who had persuaded Mr Oldroyd to change his will? Nicholas Barforth. Who had drawn up that new will? Jonas Agbrigg, who happened to be married to Nicholas Barforth's cousin, whose father, Mayor Agbrigg, was a Barforth employee, whose mother was Nicholas Barforth's aunt. And who had suggested that Mr Oldroyd should marry his disgusting hussy in the first place, who would have thought of such a thing but the lawyer Jonas Agbrigg, since he would know how easily they could otherwise have overset the will? Who had attended that abominable ceremony of marriage? Jonas Agbrigg, she announced, her soft bulk quivering with fury, for she had inquired, had been informed, had found him out in all his perfidy. Who had dined at her table, looked her in the eye and smiled, knowing all the while of the dagger he had helped to thrust in her back? Jonas Agbrigg. Who, in his capacity as the Hobhouse family lawyer, had advised her husband time and time again to sell out? Jonas Agbrigg. Who was brother-in-law to Prudence Aycliffe? And what had he told her that had prevented her from marrying Freddy years ago? How much had Jonas Agbrigg been paid for his treachery? What bribes had he taken from Nicholas Barforth and from the whore Delaney? And what had happened to the first Mrs Oldroyd's jewels? Could we expect to see her diamonds in that trollop's ears, and her pearls around the scrawny neck of Mrs Jonas Agbrigg, who had been Celia Aycliffe, another cousin to Nicholas Barforth?

'Yes, you have carved me up, all of you, carved me up nicely, and I hope you are satisfied. But I still have my tongue, Lady Barforth – Faith

718

Aycliffe that you were – and I shall let it be known what you have all done to me.'

'Mrs Hobhouse, you must not say these things. You will only hurt yourself.'

'No,' she said, her mighty chest heaving, her breath as laboured as my uncle's had been in the hour before he died. 'I shall hurt *you*. And don't imagine you can get your tame lawyer Agbrigg to buy my silence, for I will not be silent. I know what I know, Faith Aycliffe, about your aunts and your sisters and your cousins, and your precious mother, who is no better than she should be and never has been. I know what I know, and I shall say it.'

And so she did, at every tea-table to which she was invited – and who could fail to invite her now? – and at her own tea-table at which every lady who kept her own carriage, whose husband was well placed enough to have an interest in such matters, eagerly attended, offering the stricken Mrs Hobhouse the utmost in sympathy and understanding, patting her hand quite tearfully as they made their escape to my mother's equally busy drawing-room in Blenheim Lane, or to the court Aunt Hannah had long established at Lawcroft Fold.

'I will silence her,' Aunt Hannah said grimly, 'I will sue her.'

But Jonas, maintaining his habitual cool distance, would consider no legal action. The woman was hysterical. Women, in his experience, often were. Certainly he was well acquainted with Mrs Delaney, since for several years he had taken care of her investments, and had negotiated the purchase of her house in Albion Terrace. Certainly he had known of the marriage, since he had attended it, and of the will, since he had drawn it up, but no sane person could have expected him to divulge such information to anyone. To do so would have been a serious breach of professional conduct, of which he had never – neither in this case nor in any other – been guilty. In view of her obvious afflictions one should extend to Mrs Hobhouse the leniency due to all those of an unbalanced mind.

But, as my mother had foreseen, the effect on my sister Celia's already ailing nerves was of a very different order. Mrs Hobhouse, even at the height of her dementia, had not quite dared tackle Georgiana, but Mrs Jonas Agbrigg – little Celia Aycliffe – had seemed a natural and easy target. She had spent twenty raging minutes in Albert Place, reducing Celia to such a state of palpitating, choking hysteria that even Mrs Hobhouse had been terrified by it and had rushed away, leaving her shawl and gloves behind. They had put Celia to bed, heavily dosed with laudanum, and Jonas, at last compelled to action, had written a cold letter to Mr Hobhouse warning him of the consequences should he permit his wife to molest Celia again. Aunt Hannah, without Jonas's knowledge, had gone to Nethercoats herself to return the shawl and gloves, but had been denied an interview with Mrs Hobhouse, who had also taken to her bed.

'You may tell her I shall call again,' she informed the interested parlourmaid who, uncertain as to her next month's wages, could be relied on to let Mrs Hobhouse know how angry and how very determined Mrs Ira Agbrigg had seemed.

But Celia, who had been unwilling to venture out a great deal before, would no longer go out at all, maintaining herself behind drawn curtains in a state of siege that reminded me strongly of my own behaviour after Giles died. I too had sat like this in the half dark, doing nothing, staring at empty shadows on a black wall; but whereas I had been angry, Celia was deeply, most distressingly afraid, displaying as much alarm at the sound of her own doorbell as if she believed an avenging army had made its camp outside her door.

And indeed, in a way, she did, for was not the whole of Cullingford talking about her, would they not whisper about her behind her back the moment she showed her face? Well then, she would not show it. She would stay in her own home, lock her door, keep her curtain tight closed, and unless they chose to stand and scream abuse at her through the window, or climb on her rooftop and hurl it down her chimney, she was safe.

But was she? What of the servants? What of that parlourmaid with the shifty eyes, and Cook, who had never liked her? What were they saying about her in the kitchen? Oh yes, she knew, muttering that her husband had taken money from Nicholas Barforth to persuade Mr Oldroyd to change his will, that he had taken money from Mr Oldroyd himself, suggesting that there was even something between Jonas and Mrs Delaney – oh yes, she knew – making up these vile stories because Jonas had attended Mrs Delaney at her home once or twice with documents to sign. And because Cook knew, and the maids knew, that she and Jonas were obliged now, because of Celia's health, to sleep apart – yes, they had assumed the worst, believed the worst, and were spreading it, whispering it at the garden-gate to the maids next door.

And what of Grace, who was at school now with the two younger Hobhouse girls? What was she being made to suffer? What were they saying to her about her mother? Grace had better stay at home and be safe too.

'No,' Jonas said. 'No – darling.' And, although it was the first time I had ever heard him use such an endearment to Celia, it produced nothing but a storm of tears. Had he no consideration for his own child? Did he want them to poison her mind against her own parents? After all, he had exposed them both to this, and Grace was delicate too. Yet, oddly enough, in spite of Grace's still dainty appearance, the wistfulness of her pointed face and her huge dark eyes, she had a surprising resilience, a tendency to spread her wings in fresh air and sunshine that I recognized from my own too-sheltered childhood, and I was glad of Jonas's insistence that she continue her lessons with Prudence.

'Then she will have to come to you, Faith, after her class, and wait until Jonas can fetch her,' Celia told me. 'For, if it is seen that I can afford to send the carriage for her every day, they will think Jonas keeps his own and will wonder where the money is coming from. Except that they will not wonder – they will say it is from Nicholas Barforth or Mrs Delaney.'

Mrs Hobhouse's venom, it seemed, had no power to make itself felt at

Tarn Edge, where Georgiana and Aunt Verity, and Nicholas, continued to live their separate lives, Nicholas calmly continuing his negotiations for the purchase of Nethercoats, his offer considerably reduced, it was believed, now that the Hobhouse resources were at an end; and shortly before Christmas it became his property, to be used for the weaving of silks and velvets, the existing orders for worsteds to be transferred to Lawcroft.

The Hobhouses departed with a suffcent income, one hoped, to support their younger children in a small house in Bridlington, leaving the older boys to fend for themselves, and since there is always a tendency in a commercial town to forgive a rich and powerful man, it was considered generous of Nicholas to employ Freddy and James at Lawcroft, even finding a niche of sorts for Adolphus at Low Cross. But I was frankly astonished to be told by Liam Adair, who still called regularly to show me his black eyes and to boast of his prowess with a shot-gun, that my mother's beloved Daniel had also taken service with Nicholas.

'Oh no – no surprise at all,' Blaize murmured, looking amused, no matter what his exact feelings may have been. 'He needs someone to sell his silks and velvets, after all, and, since he can hardly do it himself and I'm not likely to do it for him, Daniel Adair is just the man. Not exactly my calibre, need it be said, but he'll do well enough, and Nicky is only following my father's advice. He's preparing for the day when he can buy me out, or throw me out – if it ever comes – and from Dan Adair's point of view it's no more than common sense. Your mother won't live forever, and if she goes before him the Aycliffe money comes to you and Prudence and Celia, not to him. He needs something to fall back on. Well, good old Nick, he's got the Wool-combers, and the dyeworks, and Nethercoats to call his own. If he goes on working his eighteen hours a day, he'll be able to pay my price before too long.'

'Will you sell?'

'I wonder?' he said. 'Let's keep him wondering too.'

And I knew his light, cynical eyes were saying to me, 'Yes, darling, just wonder, for what you don't know you can't tell.'

29

Freddy Hobhouse had been too occupied by his family's tragedy – in consoling his mother, moving her to Bridlington, finding places for his brothers, settling his own ten thousand pounds on his four sisters so that they could get themselves decently married, by the collapse of his father into total, often drunken helplessness – to have time to consider his personal affairs. But once the sale of Nethercoats was completed, his parents safely installed in their new home – waiting, as Mrs Hobhouse put it, to die – he came to see my sister and released her from their engagement. He had nothing now to offer her. He was a shed manager in the employment of her cousin, and no one in Cullingford would expect a

721

Miss Aycliffe to descend to so lowly a station. Cullingford, in fact, was now entirely on her side and would think her a fool if she did. But, knowing her contrary nature, her sneaking fondness for Freddy himself, I was less certain.

She walked the half mile from her house to mine immediately after the interview, her eyes red, she told me at once, because of the cold east wind.

'Well,' she said, sitting down very straight-backed, sniffing slightly as if the wind had affected her nostrils too. 'I have been properly punished for my independence of mind. I have asked a man to marry me and have been refused. I am probably the only female of our acquaintance to whom such a thing has happened, and it is not at all pleasant, I can assure you.'

'You asked Freddy to marry you?'

'I did. I could see nothing against it. That octopus of a Nethercoats is gone now. We are in no danger of being strangled by it. I am doing extremely well, especially now that my financial arrangement is with Aunt Verity, rather than Uncle Joel, and although she accepts my repayments she usually manages to find a way of giving me the money back again. With what I earn, and with what Freddy can earn, we would be well above the level of starvation. I have a good house – a very good house – and marriage would release my dowry and all my lovely porcelain, which would enable me to pay off my debt to Aunt Verity and to extend my premises.'

'And Freddy –?'

'He wouldn't have me. He is being manly, you see, and gentlemanly too. He would really have liked to put his head on my shoulder and have a good cry, I could tell. And I wouldn't have minded a bit. But no – it's not manly to cry, so he just rode off to those terrible lodgings in Gower Street he thinks I don't know about. And I expect he'll send just about every penny he earns to his mother. His shirt was not quite clean either, and I can't tell you how much that distressed me. He's never had to think about getting his laundry done before.'

'You had better stop feeling sorry for him, Prue. You may begin to enjoy it, and then we shall see you doing his laundry yourself.'

'And why not?' she declared, her back straightening even further. 'If I decide to ask my laundry maid to put his linen in my tub, which stands in my scullery, in my house, I know of no one who could prevent me.'

But we both knew that Freddy himself would prevent her, and I, at least, assumed there was no more to be said.

With the departure of Mrs Hobhouse, interest in Nethercoats began to wane, the most pressing problem that winter being whether or not one could acknowledge and eventually receive the second Mrs Oldroyd, now established very cosily, one supposed, at Fieldhead. And on the whole, since it was assumed that the Oldroyd mill would now be offered for sale and the lady would soon remove herself and her ill-gotten, or hard-earned, gains elsewhere, it seemed hardly worth the trouble.

I saw her, very occasionally, driving out in her silk-upholstered landau, once in the parish churchyard when I made my weekly pilgrimage to Giles's grave, and she, presumably, was performing the same office for Mr Oldroyd, a tall woman with the kind of timeless profile I had seen among Italian peasants, walking like barefoot queens to the grape-harvest, erect and commanding, yet, like all women who have lived in life's shadows, instinctively discreet, taking an opposite pathway so I would not be obliged to greet her.

But she had done me no harm and, waiting until our paths crossed, as was inevitable in that small space, I said, 'How do you do, Mrs Oldroyd?'

'How do you do, Lady Barforth?' she replied, her voice a rich contralto, her self-possession absolute, no surprise in her, no gratitude, no satisfaction, at my willingness to acknowledge her, a faint suggestion that she had chosen, not rushed, to acknowledge me.

Yet, during those early months of her widowhood – presumably her first, since no one believed there had ever been a *Mr* Delaney – she made no attempt to thrust herself upon our sensibilities, making no changes at Fieldhead and restricting her hospitality to the few who had been accustomed to her famous teas in Albion Terrace.

'A clever woman,' Blaize said. 'If Freddy Hobhouse had the sense to make himself pleasant in her direction, he might end as master of Fieldhead after all. She can't be much on the wrong side of forty, and it strikes me she's in no hurry to pack her bags and leave. She has the money; Freddy could give her the respectability which is about the only thing it can't buy. And I understand that when someone, who may have been Nicholas Barforth, inquired the asking price for Fieldhead, not even Jonas Agbrigg could explain the lady's intentions. Unless, of course, he knew and wasn't telling, which one could bring oneself to believe of Jonas. Why don't you ask your sister?'

But Celia, at the very mention of the new Mrs Oldroyd, was apt to stiffen like an animal at bay, to lower her voice and glance swiftly around her, so terrified of being overheard that it was an effort to catch her muttered opinions at all. Mr Oldroyd, quite naturally, had seen the necessity of appointing someone to look after his widow's concerns, to see to his investments, to keep the business going until it could be sold and then to wind the estate up profitably, in exactly the same way as my father had appointed Uncle Joel. In the Oldroyd case, since the lady had no relations, or none she cared to speak of, the obvious person had been Jonas, a choice which would have caused no comment at all had he not been named, by Mrs Hobhouse, as an arch-conspirator. And I was totally unable to convince my sister that the gossip had abated, that every visit Jonas made to Fieldhead – since no one expected a lady to attend her lawyer in his chambers – was not noted down and conveyed to Mrs Hobhouse by some evil-wisher, that Celia's household expenditure was not checked by servants and shopkeepers and tradesmen for the tell-tale increase that would proclaim Mrs Hobhouse to have been right.

She would not, that winter, purchase so much as a new bonnet for Grace and was thrown into a state of intense anxiety when, among my several Christmas presents, I gave the child a fur-lined, velvet cloak.

'Heavens, Faith, must you be so extravagant? I can't let her wear a garment like that. Everybody would want to know where it came from – how I could possibly afford it.'

'Tell them Blaize brought it back from Russia, since Blanche has one just like it.'

'But I can't tell anybody anything, don't you see? They won't ask *me*. They'll just tittle-tattle and make up their minds it came from Fieldhead. And, if they get the idea that Mrs Delaney is giving presents to Grace, they'll all think they know the reason why.'

'Really, Celia – such a fuss.'

'Oh, it's easy for you – you just sail through your life. Nobody has ever accused your husband of malpractice, nobody is going to ask you to receive that woman.'

'Celia, surely Jonas has not asked you to invite Mrs Oldroyd?'

'No,' she said, her hands clutching at one another, holding on to one another as if every part of her body was independently afraid. 'He has not. Not yet. But he will. She wants to stay in Cullingford, I know she does. The mill is not sold, is it? The house is not sold, certainly, and is not going to be sold, for she has ordered new curtains. I know because Jonas's clerk came here with some documents the other day and said something about Fieldhead looking more comfortable, as if he imagined that I *knew* what Fieldhead looked like, that I had actually been there – which is what they must all be saying. And when I asked Jonas he just said, 'Good lord! new curtains, no more –', which I think is quite sufficient. And, if she is to stay, then she intends to be received, and someone must be the first to do it. I lay awake all night thinking about it, for, if he forces me to have her, who am I to ask to dine with her? How am I to manage it? In fact I cannot manage it, and I told him so. He doesn't realize the implications. If we are seen to be living in that woman's pocket, then it won't be long before somebody starts saying he forged that will.'

'Celia – Celia – nobody could think that. Not even Mrs Hobhouse could think that.'

And, stiffening again, glancing furtively around, she muttered, 'Oh yes, they could. You just don't know how wicked people are, Faith – how very wicked. And that woman – Mrs Hobhouse – sitting there in Bridlington, waiting – like a spider – just waiting. And that other woman at Fieldhead, who doesn't care – who'll just swallow us up to get her way – They could say anything.'

Yet, although her misery touched me very deeply, my own life had its claims. I could, more often than not, think of many things I would rather do than sit in the dark with my sister, an opinion shared by the majority of our acquaintance, so that she was left increasingly alone.

'She saddens me,' my mother sighed, her own life, now that her Daniel had found something interesting and profitable to do, being sunnier and easier than ever.

'She makes me feel inclined to give her a good shaking,' Aunt Hannah declared, her fingers clearly itching to make a start. 'I am sorry to say this

724

to you, Elinor, but she should not have put my son in this difficult position. He will be mayor of this town, ere long – would, indeed, have accepted office already had he not been so overburdened at home – and a lady mayoress cannot sit in her parlour and hide, you know. I shall allow her until after Christmas, and then, if she has not righted herself, I shall tell her so.'

We spent Christmas once again at Listonby, returning to find an official letter from Nicholas informing Blaize that, in view of the difficulties they experienced in working together, it would seem advisable that their partnership be dissolved. He was prepared to purchase Blaize's half of the business at a stated figure, a sizeable down-payment and the balance to be taken as a percentage of his profits over a number of years, an arrangement which would provide Blaize with an easy living.

'My word, he's richer than I thought,' Blaize said and, leaving the communication unanswered, calmly proceeded to make plans for a second Russian visit in the spring, which the profitability of the first, and the war-clouds menacing the unity of the northern and southern states of America, amply justified.

'You must answer him, Blaize.'

'Yes, I imagine he must think so too.'

And sitting down at my writing desk he penned a casual note of thanks for the letter which, he declared, he had safely received.

'You could leave this at Tarn Edge, Faith, some time when you happen to be passing. Just put it with the calling-cards on the hall table. He'll find it.'

Nicholas called at Elderleigh for the first time a few days later, his height and breadth filling the doorway as he came into the drawing-room, an invader in my house, too big and abrupt for the dainty, cabriole-legged chairs on which he declined in any case to sit, preferring to plant himself on the hearth-rug as his father used to do, his anger well under control but too fierce, just the same, for the pale silk on my walls, the muted atmosphere of my life.

'You could give your husband this,' he said, handing me a long brown envelope. 'I imagine you know what it contains. It's a good offer. He won't get a better, and he may not get another. Tell him that.'

'Shouldn't you tell him yourself, Nicholas?'

'No. I can't talk to him, and he won't talk to me. Until now I've used my mother as a go-between, but it's not fair to her – the poor woman happens to be fond of us both – and I reckon we've caused her enough distress. You'll have to serve instead.'

'I see. Are there any other messages you'd like me to deliver?'

'Not at the moment. Does he discuss his affairs with you?'

'Is that any of your business?'

And it surprised me how much easier it was to meet him at this level of cool hostility, to speak only to that granite shell, forgetting the man it had once contained.

'Very likely not. But, if he *should* ask your opinion, then think

725

carefully about your own position before you advise him. There are two ways of doing this. He can sell out or we can split the business. Lawcroft and Low Cross together have about the same asset value and profitability as Tarn Edge. I can take one and he can take the other. I might be persuaded to it. But he'd have a mill to run then, wouldn't he? All of it, not just the bits and pieces he fancies, and if he ran it into the ground you might just find yourself living in Bridlington, next door to the Hobhouses. He doesn't like work, Faith. He never did. You could be Sir Blaize and Lady Barforth very comfortably – in London for instance – on what I'm offering.'

'Oh – so we're to be banished to London, are we?'

'Not necessarily. There are other places. If you persuade him to sell and move away from here, I can only feel it would be to your advantage.'

I picked up a small object from the table in front of me, a paper-weight, a fan, a posy of porcelain flowers – I was never certain, afterwards – replaced it, moved it an inch or two on the polished surface, and then, looking up at him, smiled.

'Heavens! We are talking of *my* advantage, are we? I do beg your pardon, Nicholas, for I have been very dull-witted. I thought it was *your* advantage we were discussing.'

'Indeed,' he said, biting off the word at its final letter, his jaw muscles clenched tight. 'So we are. I wouldn't be here at all unless I had something to gain, for I am not much given to social calls these days. However, in this case, the advantage could be mutual.'

And once again, speaking only to that hard shell, I looked him full in the face and smiled.

'Are you playing the squire with me, Nicholas – ordering me off your land? Will you set your dogs on me if I disobey?'

There was a brief silence, the familiar tightening in the air.

'You seem intent on quarrelling with me, Faith. I really wouldn't advise it.'

'No – but then, I'm not sure that I consider your advice to be very sound, Nicholas. I can't know what your financial resources are, but I imagine this offer must stretch them quite considerably – if it is accepted.'

'My word,' he said. 'Lady Barforth has a commercial mind after all. Yes, I would be somewhat over-spent, which you may take as a measure of my determination. I have had enough of carrying passengers. Blaize is a passenger. The more I think of it, the more it strikes me that London would be the ideal destination for him.'

The afternoon was drawing in, winter shadows filling the garden, entering the room to stand thickly around us, a bird somewhere, far away, winging homeward across the thin, grey air of this sad season, a great void inside me, a sense, suddenly, of futility, for what would it all matter next year, or tomorrow, a deep regret that so much inside me had been wasted.

'Would you like some tea, Nicholas?'

'Of course not.'

726

'No. Then will you tell me why you cannot work with Blaize? He's not a passenger, and you know it. Your father told you not to undervalue him and I don't believe you do, since you've been careful to get Daniel Adair to take his place. I thought for a while it was because of me. But it's not that, is it?'

And, turning my face towards the window, the expanse of dead garden, the grey, nervous wind, I closed my eyes to await the answer I knew would come.

'No, Faith. It has little or nothing to do with you.'

'Well?'

He crossed the room and stood beside me at the window, looking out for a moment in silence at the dark trees, sketched in February charcoal in the distance, the wind rising now, scattering the remaining corpses of last year's leaves across the sleeping lawn, tossing against the window-pane a peevish handful of rain.

'I don't deal in personalities,' he said quietly. 'I told you that once before. I gave up personalities – people – a fair while ago. A sensible man stops playing the games he can't seem to win, and goes in for something more suited to his nature. I want the Barforth mills, Faith, simply because I want them. I shall most probably do anything to get them. Blaize is just a hurdle in the course I've set myself, an extra dash of spice to the challenge, if you like – no more than that. And when I can call Tarn Edge and Low Cross and Lawcroft mine, I know damned well I won't be satisfied. It won't be long before I'll find something else – need something else – to go after, another hurdle to cross, and when I've crossed it all that is likely to matter to me is the next. Some men feel like that about women. Blaize feels like that about women, as you must know. Frankly, I prefer my satisfactions to his. Take him to London, Faith, and go on looking pretty for him as long as you can. If he stays here and tries to force my agreement to a split, then something may happen to sour his temper, which would make your life no easier.'

'My life is not difficult, Nicholas.'

'Of course it isn't. And I'm sure we're all anxious that it should continue to be just as pleasant. Give him my letter. Try to convince him that his marriage to you is no thorn in my side. You could even let him know that his support of my own wife against me is something I can tolerate without much trouble. He's always been meddlesome, and I'm quite accustomed to it. Georgiana can always visit him in London when she feels the need of his advice, or when she's run through her allowance by the second of the month and doesn't feel she can tell me. She may find it marginally less convenient than running to his office at Tarn Edge, but I'm not disposed to worry about that. You should take care, Faith, for knowing his whimsical turn of mind he must find her dependence on his judgment – and on his generosity – very appealing.'

I walked away from him, moving very slowly through the darkened room to the table where I had put down his letter and, picking it up, I passed it from one hand to the other, studying it carefully, no anger in me at all, nothing but a deep, calm sadness.

'May I go through the points you have raised with me, Nicholas?'

'By all means.'

'Yes – first of all, then, you are telling me that Blaize is incapable of running a business and that unless I prevent him from making the attempt I could find myself destitute?'

'I reckon there's a fair chance of it.'

'Yes. That is what I thought you meant. And then, in case that should not frighten me enough, you dropped a little hint about Blaize's past reputation with women – a slight suggestion that it may not really be past at all.'

'Did I really go so far as to suggest that?'

'Oh yes – indeed you did. Is it against the law, Nicholas, to destroy a letter addressed to another person?'

'I believe it may be.'

'Ah well – I cannot imagine you will see any profit in bringing me to justice.' And, holding the letter with the tips of my fingers, I dropped it quite daintily into the fire and stood very still, blocking the hearth with my wide skirts until it shrivelled at its edges, spurted with a brief flame, blackened to a heap of ash and then to nothingness.

Behind me, Nicholas made no movement, no sound, and when the small murder was done I turned, still calm enough, to meet his eyes.

'You have declared war on me, have you, Faith?'

'Oh no. Whatever was in your letter you may write again. If you send it, I will make sure Blaize receives it. He is no more likely to ask my opinion than you would ask Georgiana's, but, if he should ask, then I will answer in the best way I can. I don't really know how I would advise him. I haven't decided yet. But when I do, it will be for my reasons, Nicholas, not for yours.'

He walked towards me, his face, with the light behind him, almost invisible, so that he was very close to me before I could see the familiar tight-clenching of his jaw, which seemed for just a moment to be painful rather than angry, the fine lines around his eyes, the deeper ones from nose to chin etched by a weight, not of temper, but of disillusion, that made him a harder, older, wearier man than he should have been.

'So be it,' he said very low. 'I'll have it on his desk when he gets back from London.'

'Oh – he's going to London, is he?'

'Yes, on the evening train.'

And, incredibly, he smiled at me.

There was a storm later that day, a cloudburst, it seemed, directly overhead, releasing a slashing torrent of rain that soaked my hapless laundrymaid to the skin in the two or three minutes it took her to empty her washing-line. And within half an hour the garden was water-logged, each pathway a separate rivulet rushing to its mainstream, which was the Cullingford road. I went to bed early, cold, besieged by the weather, threatened all night by the growling of thunder, the spikes of lightning on the other side of my curtains, waking to an awareness of rain still falling, an uneasy sky.

And I was instantly embroiled in the kind of domestic drama which, that day, was not unwelcome. The fires would not light, the stove would do nothing but lower and sulk. Blanche, who had slept soundly all night oblivious of the tempest, was demanding her breakfast, and there was no breakfast to be had. There was no hot water; no milk had been delivered; and when a stable-lad was finally dispatched to the farm to inquire, his returning tale was one of pure disaster. The countryside had been reduced overnight to a bog, Cullingford itself was drowning; it was useless, the farmer's wife had said, to milk her cows when the end of the world was clearly nigh. Far better, it seemed, to spend the time remaining in prayer and so, while the lightning continued to flash across the sky and the rain to fall, they abandoned, in my kitchen, all attempts to boil water and draw fires, and went down on their knees, remembering that the wise-woman of Knaresborough, Mother Shipton, had long ago predicted this.

'Nonsense,' I told them, not altogether certain of it myself. 'She said the world was destroyed by water last time – which everybody knows – and that it would end by fire this time. I don't see any fire. I only wish I did.'

But the moaning and the sobbing, the 'Our Fathers' from my Protestant cook and the 'Hail Marys' from my two Irish housemaids, continued, and in the end, abandoning my crinoline for an old woollen gown and a few petticoats, I managed the drawing-room fire myself, having seen it done often enough in happier conditions, and huddled over it, reading stories to an indignant Blanche, until Prudence came.

Not one of her day-girls had arrived at school that morning. Her boarders were in varying states of disarray. Her competent teacher of mathematics had locked herself in the broom-cupboard and, in view of the panic she had been spreading, could remain there indefinitely so far as Prudence was concerned, telling her beads and muttering of sins which, in other circumstances, would have been most entertaining. Prudence herself had come only to check on my safety, at some risk to her own, and with a houseful of girls in her charge could not stay. And I suppose we were both aware that every stream in the hills with which Cullingford was surrounded must by now have transformed itself into a fast-flowing cascade, pouring into the city streets; that by now, in the low-lying districts, every cellar, every warehouse, would be awash; that the level of the canal, encircling one half of the town with its murky waters, would be insidiously rising.

I put on the Cossack boots Blaize had brought me from Moscow and walked with Prudence to the end of the garden, determined that my courage should match hers, and returned, soaked and soiled and exceedingly apprehensive, to find a drowned apparition on my doorstep that was Liam Adair.

'Well, I *am* your brother,' he said cheerfully, amazed at my concern, since I should have had the good sense to know that no lightning in the world could ever have the nerve to strike him, no thunderbolt could be strong enough to block his way. 'I thought I'd best come and rescue you since Blaize is snug and warm in London.'

And even the fact that I had managed, so far, to rescue myself, occasioned him no dismay. He had been up before dawn, except that really there had been no dawn, and had had a fine time. Sheer panic, he told me, and what fun it had been to watch people splashing ankle-deep, knee-deep, in flood-water, cursing and struggling and yelling about their carpets and their cats and their grandmothers; what fun to see packets of raw wool come floating out of the Mandelbaum warehouse, the milliner, at the bottom of the river that was Sheepgate, baling out her shop like a boat, water, hat-moulds, feathers and all. He had rescued a litter of puppies from a cellar and almost been drowned for his pains. He had tried to right a brewer's cart in Market Square and had held any number of screaming horses. He had gone down to Low Cross mill, the only low-lying Barforth property, where his father and Nicholas were salvaging what they could from the sheds, and then, growing bored, had fought his way through falling tree-branches, a tidal wave of nameless dangers, to Elderleigh.

'Your mother said I was to go to Celia, but I thought I'd rather come to you. Celia's got Jonas, after all.'

But had she? Jonas, I knew, had gone to Manchester some days ago and I had not heard of his return, nor could I ignore the fact that Albert Place was not on high ground, was, indeed, constructed in a marshy hollow where water could collect. And there was not only Celia, there was Grace.

My coachman refused, rudely, explicitly, to get out the horses. He valued his job but had no mind to commit suicide for it, since there was no man alive who could control horses in this weather. And even when the lightning had abated, leaving only the perils of rutted tracks turned into bog and slime, branches and boulders and the incessant rain, he continued adamantly to disobey.

'Do you think we can get there on foot, Liam?'

'Well, I can. I don't know about you.'

But we set off together, my skirts a sodden encumbrance, my cloak so heavy that quite soon it served no purpose but to delay me, and I took it off, finding a strange exhilaration in this exposure to the tormented sky, the slashing yet somehow cleansing attack of the rain. I had never been outdoors without a bonnet before, but now, striding bareheaded towards real issues, towards real danger, a lifetime of convention was discarded as easily as my cloak, tossed aside into the nearest puddle, leaving me clear-sighted and resolute.

Yet Celia, if we succeeded in reaching Albert Place, would not be so resolute. And although I had never felt stronger in my life, I knew I was driven mainly by determination, that my pampered body would not enable me to get back to Elderleigh with Grace in my arms. Nor could I put my sister and her child in a cart and pull them to safety as others were doing, women frailer in build than I, who, having laboured at the loom, were using that strength now, that gritty endurance, to make their escape.

A moment came when my chest seemed torn apart, my breath deserted me, whipped out of my body by the wind, and for an instant of

730

sheer panic I knew my ability to breathe again was shattered. I was choking in cold air and rain-water, dying in some alien place, since nothing in these terrible streets was familiar to me, and had it not been for Georgiana I would have had no choice but to turn and struggle home again.

No man, my coachman had said, could control horses in this weather, but he had reckoned without a woman, for suddenly there she was, driving the Barforth landau, her drenched hair hanging like seaweed about her shoulders, her familiar green riding-habit black with rain, a trio of children clutched together on the silk cushions, three more like a tangle of kittens on the carriage floor.

'Georgiana!' Liam called out, his face blazing with excitement and with pride. 'Good old Georgie. I knew you'd do it.' And, setting her passengers down, dispersing them with instructions to run to the nearest house, she leaned her whole body against the wind and laughed down at him, her face beautiful as always with animation.

'My God! there's no lack of water in Simon Street today. I've made a dozen trips already, and on the last one a woman almost gave birth right behind me. Come on, Faith, if you'd care to risk it, for these brutes are likely to bolt at any moment. They'll do one more journey, I think, before they're finished.'

'But you're not finished,' Liam said, scrambling up beside her.

'Oh no,' she told him, one rope of her seaweed hair blowing hard across her face, her hard, narrow hands firmly managing the reins.

'Come on, Faith, they're rescuing wool down at Low Cross, which is all very fine, but I come from Galton and I reckon we're more inclined to rescue the sheep before the shorn fleece. Celia! Lord yes, we'll do something about her, and then let's have an adventure, shall we? Or break our necks. Either way it leaves them with something original to put on our tombstones.'

We took Celia and Grace back to Elderleigh – Celia cowering and silent in the landau, her eyes tight shut – deposited them with Prudence and then, Georgiana having exchanged her spent animals for mine, we set off again for the dips and hollows of Cullingford, where people well accustomed to living without water were now dying of its surfeit. Georgiana, at considerable peril to herself, somehow controlled Blaize's fractious horses, while I waded into the mean, porous dwellings my father had constructed, where Giles Ashburn had met the seeds of his death – and brought out those who were too young or too old to walk away, and when we were threatened by men and boys and strong, desperate women who saw no reason to walk when they could ride, Georgiana used her driving-whip as the best argument.

My arms may have ached, and my back. I was not aware of it. Nor would Georgiana permit me to be aware of it.

'Come on, Faith, we've got room for that little ragamuffin over there – we'd best have a look at the next street– Faith, that poor woman looks likely to jump out of her bedroom window if you don't restrain her. Come *on*, Faith – *noblesse oblige*, you know. I may not be good at paying

731

my debts, but I do understand that I have to pay for my privileges.'

And so I half struggled, half swam through heaps of liquid foulness, up rickety staircases and down again, a child on my back, another straddling my hip, and then, with an unlikely assortment of humanity crammed all around me, closed my eyes as Georgiana flourished her driving-whip and somehow forced those quivering beasts to move sensibly forward to the upper reaches of Blenheim Lane and Horton End, where Cullingford's more public-spirited ladies had opened their doors, their blanket boxes, and their soup tureens.

'Come on, Faith. One more journey. When you reach the point where you know you can't endure, it really means you can endure just a little longer – that's what grandfather says.'

But the very moment she judged the horses were approaching their limits, she shook her head, shrugged her narrow shoulders. 'That's it then. They're not people. One can't ask them to make sacrifices,' and drove carefully home.

And I was at once too exhausted and too exhilarated, too indescribably filthy, too much aglow with kinship for Georgiana, to have any time to spare for Celia.

30

The sky cleared, the waters receded, exposing an atrocious litter of splintered wood and broken glass, dead dogs and cats and rats, the dray-horses which had fallen and been shot where they lay, the old man who sold matches and drank gin at the bottom of Sheepgate, a young man who had been struck on the head, it was thought, by a falling beam and had drowned in an inch or two of rain.

Damage to property had been immense. The old warehouses on the canal bank behind Market Square had sagged, in some cases, like damp paper, while even the more substantial property of the Mandelbaums, in the same area, although it had kept its roof intact, had received its share of flood and cess water in the cellar, occasioning a total loss of the bales there stored.

Everybody, in fact, lost something. Not a few lost all they had, and overnight the Workhouse and the Infirmary were bursting at their seams, every available church-hall overflowing with the homeless. Aunt Hannah occupied herself completely with the collection and distribution of food and clothing and medical supplies, her husband devoted himself with equal efficiency to the question of where these unfortunates were eventually to be housed when the churches reclaimed their halls for parochial purposes. Jonas, in pursuit of his civic ambitions, assisted him. Prudence and myself and even my mother had similar work to do. We were busy. Too busy even to glance at Celia.

Her house had not suffered irreparable harm. A half-inch of water had entered her front door, ruining her carpet and making a certain amount of decorating advisable, but her furniture, her china, her personal bits and pieces, had escaped damage, her upper floors were altogether unblemished, neither she nor Grace nor any member of her household had been hurt or even taken cold. And, in the midst of such appalling destruction, she found no one, including myself, with the patience to understand why she was so reluctant to return to Albert Place, remaining at Elderleigh long after the new paint was dry, the walls re-papered, a cheerful, busily patterned carpet laid in place, insisting that, beneath it, the floorboards still retained the foul, flood-water smell, while in her cellar strange things brought in by the deluge still lingered.

The cellar was swept clean, limewashed, swept clean again. She would not venture inside it. She could smell something, she insisted. Jonas, for all his thoroughness, had missed something.

'Will you keep her another week or two?' he asked me, and the cellar was limewashed once more, to no avail.

'It smells,' she said flatly. 'And this carpet is the colour of slime. I cannot think what possessed you to choose it, Jonas.'

'Largely because you would make no choice yourself, Celia. I will have it taken up and replaced.'

'Yes – yes – do that. Two new carpets in two months, so that everyone will wonder where the money is coming from. Except that they will not wonder – they will imagine they know.'

'Celia!' he said sharply. 'This is all nonsense. You have a home and a child, and you cannot trespass on Faith's hospitality forever.'

'Oh, there is no trespass, Jonas. She may stay as long as she pleases.'

'Naturally she inconveniences you,' he said as I walked with him to his carriage. 'Naturally – but if you could keep her a while longer – well – quite frankly I cannot feel I am the best person to be with her when she is in this humour. I believe I once told you that my mother suffered from an affliction of the nerves. Poor woman. I could understand her sufferings, I could even suffer for her – but I couldn't cope with it. I feel that I am coping badly now. I try to be patient – in fact I am patient – but she senses the effort it costs me and I believe it adds to her strain. You have an easier nature, Faith, which might be of more help to her.'

'Don't worry about it, Jonas. She's my sister, after all. She may stay as long as she pleases.'

But, although Blaize was unfailingly polite, her continued presence could only be irksome to him, her stilted dinner-time conversations depriving us both of the opportunity for any real discussion at a time when it was badly needed; and, although he never asked me to hurry her departure, I felt that he expected me to do it, knew that he had intentionally delayed his return from a recent trip to London in the hope of finding me alone. And so I was inclined to agree with Aunt Hannah when, walking unannounced into my breakfast parlour one morning, she declared, 'Now look here, Celia, this simply will not do. You have had a shock, but so has everyone, and if you remain here much longer people will begin to ask the reason why. And no one is likely to believe it is because of an imaginary odour in your cellar. They will say you have quarrelled with your husband because of Fieldhead, my dear, and will rake up all this nonsense about a conspiracy to defraud the Hobhouses. It amazes me that you, who are so afraid of gossip, cannot see that.'

'There *is* an odour in my cellar, Aunt Hannah.'

March became April, Celia remaining like a little mouse in my chimney corner, asking nothing in this world of large tabby cats but to be left alone, and eventually it was Blaize himself who dislodged her by the simple announcement that he was taking me to Paris.

'I expect you will want me to go away then, Faith?'

'Darling – you can hardly stay here alone. How could you do that?'

'No,' she said. 'I couldn't. And, getting up, she left the room, walking like a young girl in disgrace, who fearful of adult anger has been sent to bed.

I accompanied her the next day to Albert Place, where Jonas, deserting his clients and his commitments, was waiting. The house, very obviously, had been spring-cleaned, an odour, not of slime nor of any other foulness, but of beeswax, greeting us as we went inside. A large bowl of daffodils stood on the hall table, late hyacinths perfuming the drawing-room, the tea-table covered in immaculate white damask, freshly baked scones and gingerbread daintily arranged on white, gold-rimmed china. The brass fender gleamed, the ornaments on the mantelpiece were arranged so perfectly that even my father could not have faulted them, a matching pair of flowery Coalport vases, the ormolu clock with its fat cupids spaced precisely between them, a tapestry firescreen at each corner of the hearth, her favourite chair and footstool ready to receive her, her embroidery frame to hand.

'How beautiful!' I said.

'Yes,' she replied.

'Are you quite comfortable?' Jonas asked.

'Yes,' was her answer.

And when we had taken tea together, I, with packing to do, was obliged to hurry away; Jonas, with a business to attend to, could not linger; Prudence, who had taken temporary charge of Grace, would have no time to call; my mother would be too occupied with the culinary and amorous demands of her Daniel to look in for more than a moment; Aunt Hannah too concerned with the still unsolved plight of the town's homeless to worry overmuch about a woman who could sit all day in idleness by her own fireside, drinking her tea from fine china.

She remained, perhaps, for some hours quite cosily installed in her chair, stirred far enough to ring her bell and give orders for Jonas's dinner, lamb cutlets in onion sauce, curd tarts and then, changing her mind, rang again to say that apple tarts would do better, and that Cook should remember to add an egg-white to the accompanying whipped cream. She made some inquiries into the state of her linen-cupboards, some slight complaints about the starching of Jonas's shirts and Grace's petticoats, appearing, to both her cook and her parlourmaid, a little tired, a little dazed, which was in fact very much as usual.

But when Jonas returned that evening, she was, quite simply, not there, had not been heard or seen to leave the house, to go upstairs, or even to move at all; but was not there. And it was only after Aunt Hannah and Mayor Agbrigg had been called and much frantic searching had taken place that a maid, sent to bring up more coal, drew their attention to the cellar door, jammed, it seemed, by its new coat of paint; and, levering it open, they found her huddled at the bottom of the stone steps, dead from the fall, or from fright.

I could in no way accept it. 'There *is* an odour in my cellar,' her voice whispered to me all through those first unspeakable nights, and she had gone down, candle in hand, not to investigate, I was sure of it, but because she had been compelled to it, drawn by the very things which so repelled her. And there, in the half dark, she had finally encountered them, no slimy debris of the flood-waters, but her own fears and futilities lurking in the shadows. She had seen her own face, perhaps, on the freshly limewashed cellar wall, and, running from it, finding herself shut in with her own sad image, a woman who could find nothing to replace the values of her childhood which had failed her, what had she done then? Surely, she had needed only to call out and someone would have heard her? Had she panicked, stumbled over the hem of her gown and fallen? It was possible. But a panic-stricken woman might have been expected to make some sound, to beat frantic hands on that unyielding, new-painted door, would not – perhaps – have placed her candle, still burning, on a shelf at the cellar-head as Celia had done. A hysterical woman would not have been so neat, so thoughtful. What then? Had she turned at the cellar-head, looked down into the perilous shadows and thrown herself into them, choosing not to come out again? And all the time, while she had been staring at that blank wall, I had been filling my boxes with armfuls of lace, my windows wide open to the April day, planning what I would wear and what I would buy in Paris.

And, together with Prudence, I could find no comfort, no escape from the stark knowledge that we had never taken her seriously.

I had not credited my mother with the strength to attend the funeral, but she was there, hiding behind thick mourning veils, supported by an honestly grieving Daniel Adair and by Aunt Verity, who, like my mother herself, looked old that day, and very weary. Caroline, puzzled but defiant, privately thinking Celia a madwoman but ready to challenge anyone else who dared say so, had brought Dominic and Noel and Hetty Stone, thus demonstrating to Cullingford that, if the Chards and the South Erins believed the tale that Celia had accidentally stumbled, then everyone else would be well advised to do the same. Freddy Hobhouse arrived late, having begged an hour's leave of absence from Nicholas, and stood with a self-conscious arm around Prudence, while, at the very last moment, as the coffin was being lowered into the eager spring ground, I saw Nicholas himself on the fringe of the crowd and knew with what unease my sister would have viewed his presence.

'Go away, Nicholas Barforth,' her memory pleaded, its eyes furtive, terrified. 'If you show sympathy to my husband, they will say it is because he helped you to get the Hobhouses out of Nethercoats and Mrs Delaney into Fieldhead.'

And perhaps Jonas, standing in chalk-white, painful rigidity at her graveside, heard her dead voice too, a thin whisper in his mind teasing him as she had never done in life with her dreadful riddle. 'Did I fall by accident, Jonas – playing the good housewife, checking the soundness of my cellar? Did I do that? Or was my life – our life together – so burdensome to me that I was glad to throw it down? Did you kill me? Or did my father, and your mother, and Mrs Delaney, do it for you? Guess, Jonas. Forever go on guessing.'

We returned to Albert Place in silence and sat, equally silent, in that immaculate drawing-room, my eyes checking the tea-tray as Celia's would have done, for smeared silver, a less than perfectly laundered napkin, my heart somehow swollen inside my chest, straining against the inner wall of my body as if it would burst. Joel Barforth's death had moved me, but he had been a man of another generation who had lived, not long enough, perhaps, but fully. Giles Ashburn's death had deeply grieved me, but he had seemed too admirable, too complete, to be compared with myself. But with Celia the comparison was all too dreadful and too easy. Celia – my younger sister – could have been myself, a woman who had lost her life before she had started to live it, who had achieved no more than I; and, beneath my shock and my sorrow, I felt an appalling restlessness, the stirring of needs, of hopes I did not wish to recognize, a sense of time rushing away from me and myself reaching out for it, my body and spirit aching to fly forwards and upwards, my feet anchored firmly in muddy ground.

My mother and Daniel Adair drank their tea and went away.

'Dear Jonas,' Aunt Verity said, her mind full of her own loss. 'Will you really be all right, staying here – alone?'

'Perfectly, Aunt Verity, thank you.'

And she went away too.

'You're welcome to come back with us, lad,' Mayor Agbrigg said gruffly. 'Since we're keeping Grace a night or two we may as well all be together.'

'No thank you, sir. I'm better in my own home.'

And perhaps it surprised me that Aunt Hannah did not insist.

'I'm sorry Sir Blaize could not be with us,' she said to me in passing, her voice dwelling, heavy with sarcasm, on his title.

'Yes. I'm sorry too.' But I saw no reason to explain that Blaize, who had gone urgently to Leeds that morning, had promised to be back in time for the funeral, should have been back, and that his absence did not in the least surprise me.

Aunt Hannah and her husband took their leave, only Prudence and myself remaining in what seemed to be an empty house, Jonas so remote in spirit that, my mind sliding over the edge of reality, I had a brief, nightmare impression that he was not there at all, a shadow merely, standing with one foot on the fender, one hand on the mantelpiece, staring unblinkingly at the fire.

'We had better go now,' Prudence said, but grief had taken her angrily, and before I could intervene she muttered, 'Yes – what is there to stay for? What else can we say about what must surely have been the most completely wasted life –'

'Thank you, Prudence,' Jonas said without stirring.

'Please don't thank me. I'm not in the mood for social niceties.'

'You're feeling guilty are you, Prudence?' he said, his head turning very slightly, his long pale eyes opening and then closing again rapidly to shut the living man away.

'Yes. I'm feeling guilty. Aren't you?'

'Jonas –?' I murmured inquiringly as Prudence went into the hall to get her bonnet, my hand moving forward instinctively to touch his shoulder, and then somehow retreating.

'Yes?'

'I'm not sure. I know you're suffering. I don't ask your reasons. How can I help you?'

'Take your sister home.'

'Jonas – she doesn't really blame you. If she blames anyone, then it must be my father, I think, more than you.'

'Really? It was your father, then, was it, who loosened the hem of Celia's gown so that she caught her heel and tumbled down the steps? You amaze me.'

And catching a fleeting glimpse of the anger, the horror, the pain of that cruel riddle inside him, I turned and fled.

I returned Prudence to her school, myself to my shrouded house, the windows deeply curtained in mourning, nothing to greet me but my butler's professional sympathy, the curiosity of my parlourmaid who, believing tea to be a certain cure for all ills, brought me a full pot accompanied by the even surer comforts of hot scones and gingerbread.

'You'll feel better with that inside you, madam.'

'Yes, I expect so.'

And I made no inquiries as to the possible whereabouts of Sir Blaize.

He arrived an hour later, bringing an impression of cool air and spring rain with him, ruefully smiling an apology he did not expect to be denied.

'Darling – you'll have to forgive me –'

'Yes, I expect I shall.'

'Faith, I'm really sorry. I tried to get here on time –'

'Of course.'

'Faith – it was hardly my fault that a goods train came off the rails at Hardenbrigg Cross, half an hour ahead of me.'

'Really? How terrible. You had better change your clothes, for you are quite wet through.'

We ate a solitary meal: no guests, since we were in mourning; no visitors from abroad, since we should have been ourselves abroad, in Paris; no word spoken beyond the strict limits of civility – 'May I refill your glass? Please and thank you. This sauce is excellent. I will tell Cook'; for, although I believed every word of his ride from Hardenbrigg, that for once he had not tried to evade an irksome duty but had considerably inconvenienced himself to perform it, his absence at my sister's graveside seemed a symbol of the inadequacy of our relationship,

737

and I could not forgive him for it.

My mother had collapsed with perfect trust and confidence against her Daniel's shoulder and had been almost carried from the cemetery in his arms. Aunt Verity had been supported by the ever present awareness of her husband, a memory in many ways more real and vital than the living presence of her eldest son. Aunt Hannah, iron-faced, iron-willed as she was, had nevertheless put a grateful hand on Mayor Agbrigg's arm, while he, looking more deeply shaken than anyone, had placed his gnarled, unsteady fingers over hers and squeezed hard, each one drawing strength and stamina from the other. Even Prudence had rested her head briefly against Freddy's shoulder and, stumbling on the stony pathway from the churchyard, had found his hand instantly on her elbow, steadying and guiding her. Only I – and Jonas – had stood alone, not merely for the half-hour it had taken to bury my sister, but for a long time before, and a long time after, bearable, perhaps, to Jonas, who had always been alone, whose very nature was steeped in solitude, but unbearable to me.

'Faith,' Blaize said as we drank our coffee, sipped our brandy in the muted light and warmth of our drawing-room. 'Are you not being a shade unreasonable?'

'I daresay.'

'But you don't mean to forgive me?'

'Lord – what is there to forgive? The train was late. It happens often enough. It's not as if I'd been relying on you –'

'No – you'd hardly have been doing that.'

'Shall I give you some more coffee?'

'Please. Was my mother much distressed? If you can't believe I meant to come for your sake, then at least you must see I was concerned for her. The last funeral she attended was my father's and it must have reminded her.'

'I don't suppose she wants to forget. She looked very sad, but she wasn't alone. Nicholas was there for part of the time – and even if he hadn't come she wouldn't have been alone. I don't think she ever is.'

He blinked, not shutting away tears, of course, since Blaize did not cry, but perhaps a possibility, a memory, of tears.

'Quite so. And what did you make of Agbrigg? He was wearing his usual dead-pan lawyer's face when I called.'

'Yes. But what does that signify? Jonas never shows his feelings in any case, and he certainly wouldn't show them to you, Blaize. Not after the beatings you've given him.'

He blinked again, this time with frank surprise.

'Faith, I do assure you, I've never laid a hand on him.'

'Oh yes you have – all of you. He was the only boy at the grammar school – surely – who'd come out of a weaving shed, the only one whose mother wore clogs and a shawl, and whose father had a cloth cap he had to doff to your father. And you all let him know it. If he'd been tough and strong I suppose he could have thrashed you all. But since he was puny, as well as being poor, the only thing he could do was pretend he didn't care. I think he's been pretending ever since. I think he's been pretending so long that most of the time he convinces himself.'

He leaned forward, took a cigar from the intricately embossed silver box I had given him several Christmases ago, raised his eyebrows in automatic enquiry as to whether or not he might smoke – yet another request he did not expect to be denied – although when I nodded he kept the cigar unlit in his hand.

'How is it you know so much about him, Faith?'

'Oh – heavens! – because I think he was fond of me once. For about half a minute he let me see it and then it disappeared, so quickly that I could never be sure. What I *am* sure of is that he's suffering now. I felt it today and if I can help him –'

'Can you help him?'

'Probably not. I can look after Grace sometimes, since she gets on well with Blanche, and I can show him sympathy, at least – can't I?'

'Darling – are you asking my permission?' he said, his voice light, one eyebrow raising in faint sarcasm, definite amusement. 'I wouldn't dream of interfering with your sympathy. At the very most I might advise you not to be too liberal with it. If he was fond of you before, there's always the danger that he could grow fond of you again, especially now that he's lonely and nobody else seems to care much about him.'

'And would you object?'

'My dear,' he said, leaning back against the sofa cushions, his subtle face mischievous and relaxed, his intention, I thought, to fend off my mood of introspection with laughter, 'why should I mind? I have the most perfect confidence in you, and if you chose to bask in his adoration for a while – well, that's natural enough and I'd see no cause for alarm.'

I should have laughed. The mere idea of Jonas openly adoring me – or anyone – and of myself basking in its glow should have provided ample cause for mirth, as Blaize had expected. But instead of the unwilling smile, the pathway to easy reconciliation – because I couldn't bring myself to tell him, 'I needed you, Blaize. I'm afraid and uncertain. I need you now' – I looked at him for a moment, quite coldly, and astonished myself considerably by asking, 'And you, Blaize? You do your share of that particular kind of basking, I know. Do you do more than that?'

'I beg your pardon?'

And, though I heard an inner voice very clearly urge me, 'Stop this. Change this dangerous, foolish topic now, while you still can. You have nothing to gain by it,' I could not obey.

'I said do you do more than just bask?'

'I wonder.'

But even then, aware of the cool cynicism that would make him a formidable opponent for any woman, I was compelled to continue.

'You wonder? Well – that is a very clever answer, Blaize, and I am sure you can think of a dozen just as clever. Obviously I am not so subtle, because I don't know what you mean.'

'Perhaps I don't know what you are asking.'

'This – are you unfaithful to me?'

'Oh dear – I – really – I do wish you hadn't said that, Faith.'

'Yes – so I imagine.'

He got up and stood for a moment half turned away from me, one long, beautifully preserved hand – not the hand of a Law Valley man at all – resting on the mantelpiece, his face extremely careful.

'Shall we say – no, I am not.'

'I don't believe you.'

'Faith – perhaps you should.'

'I don't.'

He sighed, his fingers flexing themselves against the polished marble before he turned to face me. 'Then shall we say – occasionally, briefly, and never in Cullingford – in fact a long way from here. Faith – this is all nonsense, you know. It can't be a shock to you.'

'Did I say it was? I didn't say I cared, either.'

'No – you didn't. I hardly expected you to. But I didn't begin this conversation, Faith, and I'm not eager to go on with it. You've had a very difficult day –'

'So I have. Shall I go to bed with a headache, like Celia used to do, so as not to be a nuisance?'

'*Faith*!' he rapped out, the first threat I had ever received from him. 'I think that is more than enough. Is there a point to any of this? I have never pretended to be other than I am. I accepted you as you were. I don't believe it would help you – and it would considerably annoy me – to go over that old and painful ground again. I *am* sorry, Faith. If you are having an emotional crisis, then I may be able to understand it, but I'm not ready to share it. In fact it will be far better for us both if I go down to the Swan until it's over.'

He looked down at the cigar still unlit in his hand, replaced it carefully in its silver box, straightened the sleeve of his jacket.

'I don't want to hurt you, Faith. I refuse to be hurt by you. We have had a pleasant life together so far. Do you deny that?'

I shook my head, still obstinate and miserable, a danger to myself and to the very fabric of that pleasant but artificial life – that sham – more willing, in that moment, to have endured a beating at his hands than the cool logic of his mind, the sharp wit of his tongue.

'Good. I'll leave you then.'

But he paused an instant in the doorway and, looking at me as I sat, hands clenched in my lap, said quietly, 'I give you everything I can, you know – as much as it is in my nature to give. Which is rather more – in fact a great deal more, Faith Aycliffe – than you give to me.'

31

We made our trip to Paris as soon as circumstances allowed, a delightful round of gaieties during which our relationship appeared, on its surface, to be unaltered, except that he was much more considerate than usual, a shade less affectionate, and that he went out alone two evenings and one afternoon without the flimsiest of explanations. I bought dresses from Monsieur Albertini, went to theatres and to amusing little suppers afterwards, drank a great deal of champagne, conducted light-hearted, very temporary flirtations, because, in this sparkling Paris of the new Napoleon and his Empress Eugenie who had brought the first crinoline to England as I had introduced it to Cullingford, flirtation was an acceptable means of passing the time. I drove out in the Bois de Boulogne as I used to do with my mother, acknowledging masculine admiration with a sidelong glance, a half smile, as she had. I allowed a gentleman – on the afternoon Blaize so mysteriously disappeared – to kiss the palms of my hands and the nape of my neck, a pastime of which I soon tired. I was pleasant, talkative, brittle, uneasy. I was a woman turned thirty who, beneath her carefully acquired poise, was no longer certain of her direction. While Blaize, beneath his witticisms, his teasing, his social chatter, would not talk to me.

The American war, as Blaize had foreseen, was now raging, a circumstance which provided ample justification for his expensive exploration of new markets, and would send him off to Russia again before long. But on our return to Cullingford he was subjected at once to pressure from Nicholas, who considered he had been kept in ignorance of his brother's intentions quite long enough.

During our absence there had been trouble at Low Cross, the smallest and oldest of the Barforth mills, Mayor Agbrigg – who was famous for his caution – having noticed a series of fine cracks in the soot-blackened, weather-beaten walls. Nicholas – at once – had emptied the mill, absorbing as much of the work-force as possible elsewhere, even paying compensation to others, while the old wooden beams, never intended to take the weight of power-driven machinery, could be replaced with cast iron, winning himself a certain amount of grudging respect, since everybody knew of masters who had ignored such warnings until shattered floorboards, falling machinery and crushed bodies had proved their architects right. But 'shoring up and making do' not being in Nicholas's nature, he would have much preferred to knock the old building down and start again on a far grander scale, an operation which – since it required Blaize's agreement – brought the question of their partnership to the forefront again.

A long brown envelope made its appearance on my hall table, delivered this time by the coachman from Tarn Edge, followed, a few days later, by another.

'I'm glad to see Brother Nick keeping himself so busy,' Blaize murmured, and I learned, not from my husband but from an irate Caroline that, although he would not agree to sell, he was prepared – if properly persuaded – to split.

'Either way would considerably upset me,' Caroline announced, having driven over very early from Listonby, her intention to recruit me to her service being very plain. 'They have the best business in the Valley, they are both clever men – or so they would have us believe – yet they are worse than Dominic and Noel used to be at five years old, ready to murder each other for the biggest slice of apple tart. Well – they have been squabbling all their lives, those brothers of mine, and it is high time now that they grew up and learned to get on together. You should tell

Blaize so, Faith, and keep on telling him until he believes you. Georgiana is hopeless, of course, and doesn't care what happens, but I am relying on you. I should certainly never allow Matthew to be so foolish. My father devoted his life to those mills, and I refuse to see his efforts wasted. Goodness – if he had left the mills to me there would have been none of this futile wrangling. Remember, Faith – talk sense to him and let him see you won't take "no" for an answer.'

Yet, in reply to my cautious enquiry, 'Caroline says you want to split the business?', Blaize merely lifted a nonchalant shoulder. 'Ah well, if Caroline says so – But of course there is always the chance I may change my mind tomorrow.'

And it was hard to face the truth that my husband did not trust me.

'Blaize, is it decided yet? Which way is it to be done?'

'Darling, why do you keep on asking? Is Caroline pressing you for an answer?'

Even Georgiana was better informed than I.

'Are you not sick to death of it?' she demanded, walking into my breakfast parlour and helping herself to toast and coffee. 'I declare, it is the most vexing thing I ever heard – especially since I hear nothing else. Blaize will not sell and Nicky will not split. Caroline, I believe, has lost her wits, since she seems to think there is something I can do about it. Even my mother-in-law spoke sharply to me the other day. Well – they may do as they please. And while they are making up their minds I shall do as I please, and go over to Galton to stay with my grandfather.'

The Duke of South Erin was finally enticed to Listonby that winter, happy to escape a London made gloomy by the death of the prematurely aged Prince Albert.

'You'll adore him,' Caroline told us, a command rather than an opinion, and indeed he proved amiable enough, an older, slightly more sophisticated version of Matthew himself, requiring no more complex pleasures than a spot of good hunting and shooting, and a handsome woman to laugh at his jokes at dinner-time.

I attended the ball Caroline gave in his honour wearing a vast confection of black chiffon that entirely filled the carriage, a diamond on my hand which Blaize had tossed into my lap that morning because he thought Caroline would expect us to look our best. Georgiana had a new diamond too; Caroline wore the whole of her not inconsiderable collection; and Aunt Verity was not very far behind.

'Very civil of you to take so much trouble,' the Duke told her at the end of the sumptuous celebration.

'It is something of a family tradition,' Caroline replied, blinking hard, her firm chin for just a moment quivering, so that I knew she had actually said, 'I haven't done this for you at all. I've done it for my father.'

The Lady Barforth Academy for Young Ladies was also honoured by a ducal visit, the noble gentleman wishing to check the progress of his natural daughter, although his paternal impulse was soon replaced by another impulse, of amusement this time, of curiosity and a definite if grudging admiration for Prudence.

'Never met a governess like her,' he said. 'Clever women always did make me uncomfortable and that one terrifies me.'

Yet from then on the school was a regular recipient of game from the ducal deer parks, pineapples from the ducal pine-pits, hampers of strawberries and other exotic fruits from the greenhouses the designer of the Crystal Palace had built, and a steady stream of enquiries from titled gentlemen – or their legal advisers – to whom my sister's school had been most highly recommended.

My daughter Blanche became a pupil there on her seventh birthday, an arrangement, it must be said at once, from which she obtained no academic distinction, having decided even then that her silver curls and cloudy turquoise eyes, a dash of her father's elusive charm, would be more than enough to win the prizes *she* desired from life.

'She's not stupid,' Prudence told me. 'And she's not lazy. In fact – in her way – she's rather clever and quite determined. It's just that – well – she doesn't see the point to education. After all, whenever we have a distinguished visitor, he may have a dutiful look at Grace Agbrigg's mathematics or Amy Chesterton's handwriting but then he'll take a very long look at Blanche. So why should she take the trouble to work at her copperplate, or do her sums?'

And I understood that my beautiful Blanche was of far less interest to Prudence than her other niece, the intellectually promising Grace Agbrigg, or Georgiana's impish Venetia who, when she could be restrained from making her escape through the nearest window, had an entertaining, if totally undisciplined, mind.

'Blanche will marry well,' Prudence said. 'There's no doubt about that. Venetia could marry a prince or could elope with a chimney-sweep. Grace – I don't know – I think I love Grace. I would like Grace to do something quite extraordinary.'

Jonas, too, maintained his interest in the school, coping admirably at the same time with his depleted household and his daughter, their relationship being in no way demonstrative, yet certainly of great importance to them both, based, it seemed, on mutual respect, the interest and sympathy of a clever man for a clever child.

'They manage so very well together,' my mother enthused, but there was no doubt that Aunt Hannah, although she had felt sincere grief for Celia, had no intention of allowing her son to be alone for long, His marriage to Celia had been the very best, at the time, he could have possibly hoped for, but his circumstances had vastly altered since then. He was a man of substance and distinction these days, whose opinions carried weight with our town council and were not disregarded by our local politicians of the Whig persuasion. He was the master of a fine house in Albert Place, kept his own carriage and a smart suite of offices in Croppers Court, and, although Celia's share of the Aycliffe money would pass now, when my mother died, to Grace, this – although initially disappointing – was not altogether a bad thing, since it would prevent the child of his first marriage from becoming a financial burden to his second.

The world of matrimonial opportunity was suddenly wide open again for Jonas, and, as his period of mourning – so much shorter for a man than for a woman – reached half-way to its close, Aunt Hannah began to give serious thought as to who this second wife should be. Naturally he would marry again. A woman – certainly our own widowed queen – might be allowed to bury her heart in the grave of her departed husband – in fact it was considered right and proper that she should – but a man, especially a man with a child to raise and his way to make in the world, had no choice but to be practical. And in Jonas's case, according to Aunt Hannah, perhaps the time had come to be magnificent.

Most men in his position, of course, would have been thinking along the lines of some sober, sensible woman of mature years, a lady, certainly, of some gentility and a little money, but selected mainly for her skills as a housekeeper, her patience with motherless children. But Aunt Hannah, who had been obliged to take what she could get for him last time, acquired, quite suddenly, what seemed to be a new lease of life, all her old ambitions rekindling to such a fever-heat that his frequent visits to Prudence's school, where several ladies of the mature and sensible type were employed, caused her immense alarm.

'I do not care to see him hob-nobbing quite so much with those schoolmistresses,' she told me. 'And I am relying on you, Faith, to keep your eyes open. You are a woman of experience, as I am, and it can be no secret to you that men have certain requirements which often lead them into great foolishness. I have no intention of allowing Jonas to be trapped by one of Prudence's spinster ladies, I do assure you, since there is no doubt that each and every one of them would give their eye-teeth – and very likely their virtue – to have him.'

Prudence herself, of course, had she not been placed within the forbidden degree of kinship, would have been an ideal choice, being richer than Celia, infinitely more energetic, her very independence of mind a quality which would have been of great use to a man embarking on the political life. But, failing Prudence, there was Rebecca Mandelbaum who, having been deceived by her Austrian musician, was still languishing at home, a virgin of thirty-three summers and large financial expectations, who could find consolation for her own loss, perhaps, in a man who had also suffered. And if she could not, then there was the youngest Battershaw girl, not yet in her twenties but old, it was felt, for her age, and – perhaps best of all – the daughter of Mr Fielding, our Member of Parliament, an alliance in the grand Whig manner which rejoiced Aunt Hannah's heart.

At her suggestion I invited these ladies, suitably chaperoned, to dine with me in their turns, seating Jonas beside them at table, letting it be seen, in accordance with my aunt's specific instructions, that any arrangement with the Agbriggs would include the Barforths too. But Angelica Battershaw, I felt, was too giddy, the twenty-five-year-old Miss Fielding too plain, Rebecca, although sweet-natured enough, handsome enough, still dwelling on her departed musician, and – quite fiercely and irrationally – I wanted Jonas to have some warmth in life, some joy, a little gaiety.

744

'It could well be Rebecca,' I ventured when my aunt pressed me, having learned that Jonas had spent a comfortable evening at the Academy, thrashing out some knotty philosophical problem in the staff sitting-room over red wine and ratafia biscuits.

'He seems to enjoy her company, Aunt Hannah.'

'Good,' she said. 'I confess I would have preferred Maria Fielding, but the Mandelbaums are well placed and I shall not complain. I shall leave Rebecca to you, Faith. Flatter her and coddle her a little, show her some new way of doing her hair and lend her one of your lace shawls – that sort of thing. And while you are about it, I shall get to work on the parents. Naomi Mandelbaum is a good soul who has always been easy enough to manage, and George is a sensible man. His daughter may be rich, but she is no longer young, and after that unfortunate attachment if he can get her decently settled he'll be glad of it. You could introduce her to Grace and work on her sympathies, and then, if Jonas makes his intentions clear around Christmas-time, they could be married as soon as his full year is up. After all, she'll be thirty-four by then and no one would expect her to delay. Really – it will be very suitable.'

So it was. A sizeable dowry, a sedate, healthy woman who would do her duty and cause no trouble, who was not brilliant yet perfectly able to entertain his guests without strain, and be kind to his daughter. Yet I too had been present that evening in Prudence's sitting-room when Jonas had entertained us with wine and philosophy, had seen him relax easily into the academic atmosphere of his youth, and, having taken more than a glass or two myself – enough to remind me of lost loves and opportunities – I flung my arms around him at parting and told him, 'When you marry again, Jonas, I want her to be beautiful and generous and madly in love with you. I want you to adore her –'

'How kind,' he said smiling, steadying me, since it must have been apparent to everyone that the second Lady Barforth was well in her cups. 'But I think I may have passed the season for such things, you know.'

'Oh dear – is it winter already? Then I'd best invite Becky Mandelbaum to dinner again, I suppose.'

'Yes,' he said very quietly, a man, I thought, who had never allowed himself to neglect his opportunities, however burdensome he had known they would prove. 'I believe you should.'

In the spring, Mayor Agbrigg's final term of office came to its close, an event deemed worthy of some expression of gratitude and respect, since he and Aunt Hannah between them had been responsible for the Concert Hall, the reservoirs, the Giles Ashburn Memorial Gardens, the passing of an Improvement Act which had resulted in the lighting and paving and, in some cases, the widening of streets, the knocking down of old, dangerous buildings, and a set of building regulations = at which my father would have shuddered – to oversee the more solid, more hygienic construction of new ones.

The Agbriggs had brought both water and culture to Cullingford, had concerned themselves with both public health and public buildings, had worked hard and often successfully to transform what had been little more than a mass of humanity huddled together in one place into a community with a sense of civic pride. A debt, clearly, was owing, and since we paid our debts in Cullingford a banquet was held in honour of our Mayor and his lady at the Assembly Rooms, followed by speeches and praises, the presentation of a silver salver that would not have disgraced a baronial hall, and of a gold mayoral chain, twenty-eight ounces in weight, worth a lordly two hundred and forty pounds, which Mayor Agbrigg wore for the first, if the last, time that night.

Every gentleman who had held civic office since the date of our incorporation was present, with the exception of Mr Hobhouse, who had rather tactfully declined, every industrialist, members of all the professions, several politicians of several parties, Jonas, who would soon have that chain of office around his own neck, sitting beside Rebecca Mandelbaum who would soon be his wife, Aunt Hannah, showing, at the only public banquet in Cullingford for years which she had not arranged herself, the face of a woman who is seeing not all, perhaps, but a sufficiency of her dreams come true.

There was still the Town Hall to build, with its banqueting hall and mayor's parlour, where she herself would be unlikely to hold court, her husband having firmly announced himself unwilling to stand for re-election. There was the art gallery and museum to be completed in the Ashburn Park, the growing need for a library now that so many people were learning to read. But Jonas and his placid Rebecca could do all that for her – because she had made it possible for it to be done at all – and I had never seen my aunt so gloriously, almost girlishly happy as on that night.

I took Blaize to the station in my victoria some five days later, presented my cheek to be kissed as he boarded the train, smiled, pronounced my calm good-byes – asking no questions so as not to be reminded that he would give no answers – and, walking out, chilled suddenly, into the station yard, I found myself unwilling to go home, could see no reason, no use in being there, and drove instead to Lawcroft Fold.

It was a calm, commonplace day, nothing, as I drove in at the top gate – wishing to avoid the mill yard and the possibility of Nicholas – to disturb me, nothing to surprise me at the sight of the equipage I believed to be Jonas's standing outside the door, until Jonas himself appeared and drove off without greeting me, his wheels almost shaving mine on the carriage-way, the glimpse of his face telling me something was awry.

Mayor Agbrigg was in the drawing-room when they announced me, standing at the window looking down into the mill yard, his hunched shoulders frailer than I had realized, the lines of his face deeper, dustier somehow, like crevices in old stone.

'Faith, lass –' he said.

'Uncle Agbrigg – what is it?'

And in reply he gestured towards the old lady scarcely recognizable as my aunt, a grey face with two raw streaks of crimson beneath the cheekbones, grey hair – why had I never noticed her hair was so grey? –

escaping in impossible disorder from its pins as if she had tugged at it in fury or despair, shaken her head and screamed out some total protest. 'Never! I will not have it.' And Jonas – for it could only be he – had walked away from her, leaving her to grapple with her first defeat.

Had he refused to marry Rebecca Mandelbaum after all, since I well knew nothing had been settled, much less announced? Had he decided to sell his practice and go into some rash academic venture, some scheme that would relax and humanize him, even if it made him poor? I hoped so. Fervently I hoped so. Yet Aunt Hannah and her husband had helped me once, and I too had a debt to repay.

'Aunt Hannah,' I said, kneeling on the floor by her chair. 'Let me help, if I can. Or if you would like me to go away again –?'

'No,' she said, the movement of her lips hard and painful, as if she feared they would crack. 'Stay a while. You will have cause to avoid me soon enough. Tell her – Mr Agbrigg – what has been done to me.'

'Not I. I'll have nothing to do with it.'

'He's your son, Ira Agbrigg.'

'No,' he said, turning to face her, the bitterness in him shocking me, amazing her. '*Your* son, Hannah. You had the moulding of him. That was the condition you made when we married, and I accepted it. *Your* son – not mine and not his mother's – *yours*.'

She got up slowly, her body aching, I thought, from some inner violence, some grievous wound that, because she was Hannah Barforth, she chose to ignore, and *would* ignore even if it killed her.

'Quite so, Mr Agbrigg. I feel sure that my niece, Lady Barforth, cannot wish to be bothered with that.'

And, turning to me, her face a mask of false, quite painful cordiality, she said brightly, 'You will be interested to learn, Faith, that Jonas is to be married.'

'Yes, of course – but we supposed, surely – in the spring.'

'Ah yes. Then let us suppose no longer. He is to be married the very minute he is out of black arm-bands – an eager young bridegroom of something over forty, a blushing bride of forty-five, or fifty, or sixty beneath her paint, for all one knows. Yes – he is to marry the second Mrs Oldroyd, the luscious Mrs Delaney, the widow of a dozen husbands and not a single wedding ring to show for it, if the truth be known. And I warn you, Faith, if you ever allow her across your threshold, then I shall not have you across mine.'

She sat down again. Mayor Agbrigg returned to his silent scrutiny of the mill yard. I stood between them, uncertain as to what consolation I could offer, what they would be willing to receive, seeing, with Aunt Hannah's eyes, the tarnishing of that gold mayoral chain, that princely salver, feeling her bleak conviction that she would be remembered now, not as the woman who had built the Morgan Aycliffe Hall, but as the mother of a man who had made himself master of Fieldhead by marrying a whore.

'Your sister Celia was not such a goose after all,' she said, her voice harsh, her face very cold. 'The mill was not sold, the house was not sold.

747

Celia knew why and none of us would believe her. She said the servants were whispering about Jonas and Mrs Delaney – yes, so she did – and perhaps they had good cause.'

'Aunt Hannah, I don't believe that.'

'Why not? He called on her often enough, didn't he? And when Celia complained we said it was natural for a lawyer to call on his client. But now you may as well believe the worst of him, Faith, since everybody else will. He used to call on her before Matthew Oldroyd died – before Matthew Oldroyd married her – to advise on her investments, or so he said. But can you prove to me that they were not lovers even then? They could have worked together to persuade Matthew Oldroyd into that scandalous marriage, for which I was the first to condemn him, and still condemn him. Why not? Emma-Jane Hobhouse *said* there was a conspiracy, and we ignored her just as we ignored Celia. Well – I must write to Emma-Jane and give her the good news. If it crosses her mind that Jonas may have pushed your sister down those cellar steps, I wouldn't be the one to blame her.'

'Aunt Hannah – no! I won't listen to that –'

'Then you'll be the only one who won't listen to it, and gloat over it. It fits – it's a good story – and who asks, who cares, for the truth of it?'

'Aunt Hannah, you can't believe such things of Jonas.'

But, getting up again, her fists clenched, those raw red spots once more mottling her cheeks, she took a quick stride to her work-table and back again, and staring straight at me, hissed through clenched teeth, 'Yes, I can.'

'No, Aunt Hannah.'

'Oh yes, Faith Aycliffe. Yes. You don't know what he is capable of. He would sell you, or me, or his own daughter to the highest bidder, and now he has sold himself to a brothel-keeper. He is going to live on the earnings of a whore, for what else is Fieldhead now but that? He is going to marry a woman I cannot receive; and when I pleaded with him, reminded him of all I have done for him – of all I still could do for him – he answered me – he said, "Such a fuss, mamma! For when all is said and done I am only following your teaching." Yes, he said that to me.'

And after a moment of anguished silence, her breast heaving with her poisoned emotions, she said hoarsely, 'I used to love him – just an hour ago,' and sat down again.

There was nothing I could say to her. There would have been no point at all in telling her she would eventually forgive him, since most probably she would not; no point in suggesting that the rumours and the gossip would soon die away, since even in commercially minded Cullingford there was a dividing line between good money and bad, and Jonas's reputation would never recover. Men would do business with him, of course, would even dine with him eventually, and privately, at the Swan. But that gold chain of office, that splendid Town Hall with its stained-glass windows and Doric columns would pass now to others; and what would happen to Grace?

An hour ago my aunt's life had been full, her intentions plain. There

748

had been Jonas's wedding to arrange and then his election. There had been his term of office, during which the Town Hall would have been completed, the grand opening banquet with herself beside him, encouraging his taste for public life so that he might at last make that momentous journey to Westminster. There had been the possibility of more grandchildren, and, failing that, there had been Grace's début into West Riding society, another marriage contract, in due course, to negotiate. And now, at one stroke, he had taken away everything she cared for, had tarnished her respectability by tarnishing his own, had robbed her of her committees, her functions, her grandchild; had broken her heart.

'What am I to do?' she said, not with Jonas, I thought, but with herself, for her days now would be long and empty, shrinking one after the other to the dimensions of a 'woman at home' who was not much needed anywhere else.

'I'm not well,' she said, pressing her hands to her head, the first time I had heard her speak those words, or seen her make that gesture – my mother's gesture – of feminine frailty. And, rushing for the door, the strongest woman I knew and the stateliest collapsing before my eyes, she disappeared, going upstairs to hide, as my mother and Celia used to do.

'Shall I go up to her, Uncle Agbrigg?'

'Nay lass, it's not you she wants. And Jonas won't be going up those stairs again.'

'Someone should.'

'Aye. I'll go myself presently. There's nobody left but me now, I reckon – whether she likes it or not.'

'Uncle Agbrigg – you don't mean to forgive him either, do you?'

'Nay, lass,' he said, his craggy face relaxing into a brief smile. 'And that surprises you, does it, since all he's doing is marrying for money, same as he did before, same as I did myself. No – no – I'll not hold that against him. I could even admire him for it, because even when a man recognizes himself as a callous, scheming devil it takes guts to say so. And as to the woman, yes, she's a whore all right, but I take a different view of that to your Aunt Hannah. I reckon poverty can make a whore out of any lass – when it comes down to whoring or starving there's not much choice at all – and we don't know what Mrs Delaney was like at her beginnings. A lass from Simon Street, maybe – or somewhere like it – abused by her mother's husband one night when he was drunk and pushed out of the door the morning after. And when that happens to a lass she'll be sure to find the brothel-keeper waiting. Nay – it's not Mrs Delaney who troubles me. Maybe I got to thinking just now of another lass from Simon Street and wondering what she'd make of her Jonas now. Maybe it crossed my mind she'd tell me it was all my fault.'

He crossed the room and sat down heavily, closing his eyes in pure weariness. 'I reckon you don't know how I came to be acquainted with your Aunt Hannah, Faith. It might ease me now to talk about it, and you're a good lass. I clawed my way up from the very bottom of the muck-heap, Faith – a muck-heap neither you nor your aunt can even

749

imagine. And by the time I met Hannah I'd got as far as Low Cross, from mill-hand to overlooker to shed-manager to manager of the whole lot, doing Joel Barforth's dirty work for him when he had any – and there were times when he had. Sickness came. I lost three bairns – nearly lost my wife – I *did* lose her, I reckon, because she couldn't bring herself together. And Miss Hannah Barforth helped – found me a woman to clean the house, saw to it that Ann, my wife was fed, had a look at Jonas and made up her mind he was wasted on me, and on my Ann. And it was Hannah who put the shame into him – shame of his beginnings and his mother. I saw it happen and I let it happen because, even if I didn't like it, I thought it would spur him on, making him fight that much harder – and I knew how hard he'd have to fight. You don't mind if I smoke, lass?'

'No. What happened to your wife, Uncle Agbrigg?'

'She died. I once told you how, and what it did to me. But men don't grieve for long, they can't afford it. Well – this was the way of it. Hannah was turned thirty by then. She'd lost the man she'd wanted and she'd been let down by another. She was sick of living in other women's houses and the choice was between a fancy parson she reckoned would never make a bishop, and me. The parson had his hundred a year and his gentility, I had Jonas, and she picked me. Her brother didn't like it, but when Hannah wants something there's no stopping her. What she says she'll do, she'll do, and so we got married – Hannah and me and Jonas. And that was always the way of it. She could run the town through me, she reckoned, but she could run the world through Jonas. Well, I let her have her way and I saw him grow into a man I didn't like – which has nothing to do with loving. He's my lad, Ann's lad, and I don't have to like Ann's lad to love him. She wouldn't much like him herself, I reckon, although she'd fret herself into her grave all over again in case the woman should make him unhappy.'

'And it doesn't worry you?'

'No,' he said, quite decidedly. 'That it doesn't. He knows what he's going into. He's made a mathematical calculation of it and he finds that the embarrassment is outweighed by the gain. In fact she's worth it to him, and there's no more to be said. It's Hannah who worries me now.'

'What will you do, Uncle Agbrigg?'

'With Hannah? Well, first of all, lass, I'd best get myself upstairs and convince her I'll not be mayor again, because that's what she'll be wanting now. No – I'm getting on in years, Faith, and so is she. She'll take the loss of Jonas hard – I can understand that – but he's gone, and maybe that could suit us now, Hannah and me. Maybe it's time – well, my Ann's dead, there's no denying it, and the man Hannah fancied has been long gone too. And if there hasn't been love between us, we've grown accustomed to each other – we respect each other, I reckon. Maybe we even like each other.'

'*I* like you, Uncle Agbrigg.'

'Well, that's a feather in my cap and no mistake. So you'll come and see us in Scarborough, will you, when I've convinced her that Scarborough's where she wants to go – a little house on the cliff, away

750

from the smoke, on account of my bad chest, which I'd never noticed until she pointed out to me how bad my breathing was –'

'Oh yes, Uncle Agbrigg, I'll come.'

'Good,' he said, getting up and rather awkwardly patting my cheek. 'Good. I was nobody when she met me, Faith. Just a man who wanted to better himself and didn't much care how. But now – well, I built those reservoirs, I reckon – I got the water in. She's got no reason to be ashamed of me now. And, do you know, Faith, I think we could even be happy.'

32

I drove for a while quite aimlessly about the streets, knowing that I should go home, yet absolutely unable to turn myself in the direction of Elderleigh. Already it was late afternoon, Blanche would have returned from school by now, and I had left no clear instructions about dinner. Yet, despite the urgings of common sense and duty, 'home', whatever it might mean to me, whatever it consisted of, was the one place in the world I could not – at that moment – tolerate.

I drifted an hour longer, half thinking, dream-thinking, letting the familiar streets go by with nothing in any one of them to detain me, nothing to distress me or to please me – just space and time with myself caught up in the crowded void of it, making the best I could of every quiet water, every ebb-tide, ever stony wasteland in which it stranded me. Space, and time, and a slow-dropping, soft-penetrating sadness.

And then I went to Albert Place and asked for Jonas.

He was dressed to go out, to Mrs Delaney I was forced to imagine, but when I began to apologize for my intrusion, insisting I had looked in only for a moment, since I didn't really know why I had come at all, he told me, 'Do sit down. I am in no hurry, Faith – and not grealy surprised to see you. Have you come straight from Lawcroft Fold?'

'Yes – in fact, no, since I have been driving around a little – going nowhere –'

'Composing yourself to face up to my villainy?'

'Is that what it is? I don't think I care about that.'

'But you must be – shocked?'

'Yes. Indeed I am. And sad – so terribly sad that I don't know how to explain it. Jonas – is this right for you?'

He sat down in the chair facing mine, his face, in shadow, looking tired, not creased and dusty like his father's, but somehow quite hollow.

'Well,' he said, 'thank you at least for that, Faith.'

'For what? Because it worries me that you could be miserable? I suppose it worries Aunt Hannah too, although she wouldn't say it. She will miss you cruelly, Jonas. And she will never be reconciled.'

'I know,' he said, giving me once again the impression of hollowness, as if the living impulses that had filled him had all been carefully reduced and put away. 'Had she calmed herself by the time you left?'

751

'Oh no. I don't think she knows how to calm herself, but I believe your father might do it for her. He wants to retire and take her to Scarborough, or allow her to take him there.'

He smiled, his long eyes still hooded by their heavy, shielding lids.

'Well, there would have been no chance of that had I married suitably and taken office as Mayor. So I may have done him a service with my perfidy.'

'I can't think you perfidious.'

'Why ever not? Miss Mandelbaum will surely not agree with you. Celia would not agree with you either.'

'I don't know that I want to talk about Celia.'

'I don't see how it can be avoided. You tried to comfort me when she died. I realize you would like to defend me now, and in that case you should know the truth. Faith – whatever you may have glimpsed in me these past months – a little more humanity than you had supposed, perhaps – then don't deceive yourself. Yes, the capacity exists. I have even toyed with the idea of developing it. I would like to be happy. I would like to care for a woman who cares for me. It has never happened. It never will happen.'

'Jonas – it could happen. You haven't looked – you haven't tried –'

'Nonsense,' he said flatly, a lawyer once again, demolishing my immature logic, my foolishness. 'We are talking of marriage – an exceedingly tight contract which requires obedience from one party and supportiveness from the other, happiness, so far as I am aware, from neither.'

'Jonas, that is legal jargon and you are hiding behind it.'

'Faith, it is the truth. I married your sister for a down-payment of twenty thousand pounds because I was desperate to buy out old Corey-Manning. On the very day I buried her I *knew* the way to Fieldhead Mills was open to me if I chose to take it. Walking back from the cemetery I knew I *would* take it. I have no excuses, Faith. I am no longer a poor man. I could live comfortably on my present income, here, in my pleasant house with my very charming daughter. We have a great deal in common, Grace and I. We could read together, travel abroad together. We could talk together. I could become very scholarly and possibly very content. The thought of it, even now, gives me a whisper of pleasure. And, failing that, I could marry Rebecca Mandelbaum, who would suit me well enough, and buy myself a seat in the House of Commons with her dowry. Political power interests me. For many years I wanted it rather badly. I believe I could have it now. So – there you see my choices. Contentment, power, or cash. It took me moments, Faith – no more – to decide. Do you still want to defend me?'

'Yes.'

'Knowing how miserable your sister was with me?'

'Yes. Celia carried her misery inside her. You were not to blame.'

'Once again, she would not agree with you. I'm not sure I agree with you myself.'

'Then you should. My father crushed her, Jonas. You should know

752

that. He took everything that was real and special out of her and filled her up again with the trivial little bits and pieces he thought proper in a woman. And so she was never a woman at all. I don't know why Prudence and I escaped without too much damage. Perhaps it was because we never really believed in him. And in that case – if that is true – then Celia must have loved him. Poor Celia – that was her misery – not anything that happened to her afterwards – not you. You wanted more than she knew how to give, that's all. Any man would have wanted more.'

He turned his head sharply, a moment of emotion to be concealed instinctively, as he had always concealed such things, an act of self-preservation in a world which did not encourage the finer feelings in a lad from Simon Street.

'Yes, Faith. I wanted more. Six months before I married her, a house in Albert Place, an income, a decent working capital – all that – seemed beyond my wildest dreams. Six months later and it was – well – inadequate.'

'And now, Jonas?'

'What now?'

'Will Fieldhead suffice you any better?'

'Probably not. But I could never live at peace with myself if I let it pass me by. It will make me almost as rich as Nicholas Barforth – certainly as rich as Sir Blaize. Now ask yourself, Faith, how a man of my origins could turn his back on that?'

'And Mrs Delaney?'

'Yes – Mrs Delaney?'

'Is she – agreeable to you?'

He smiled at me again, wryly.

'You mean do I desire her? Not particularly.'

'Then how can you commit yourself – Jonas? You can't force yourself – surely – not all the time – not forever –?'

'I could,' he said. 'If I had to. Fortunately it is not quite so bad as that. Mrs Delaney is experienced enough in that direction to know how to please any man – she does please me, in fact, since we have already consummated our intentions, at her suggestion, not mine. I believe her motive was kindness. She could see I had been somewhat deprived – frustrated would have been my description, famished was hers, and no doubt she was right. She satisfies my appetites most thoroughly – and pleasantly – and I am grateful. It is not the same as desire.'

'You mean it is not the same as love.'

'Yes, I suppose that is exactly what I mean. I hesitate even to use the word.'

'Is Mrs Delaney in love with you?'

'My dear – hardly that. She has a weakness for intellectual men and a hankering, not for respectability, since she recognizes it to be beyond her, but for stability perhaps. She has led a wandering life and, like Rebecca Mandelbaum, she feels the need to be settled. Oh yes, I have been obliged to serve my apprenticeship to her cause. She has allowed me to manage Fieldhead since Mr Oldroyd died and has kept an eagle eye on my methods. She required very definite proof of my commercial acumen, I do assure you, before expressing herself willing to place her fortune in my hands. She is a sensible woman, who accepts my limitations, and her own. Naturally she realizes I can no longer make her a mayoress, since the city fathers will have none of me now. She understands that my mother, and your mother, and a great many other ladies, will never receive her. But in her own eyes and in the eyes of her past acquaintances she will be a married woman. She trusts me in so far as it is in her to trust any man. And my presence beside her spares her the attentions of other fortune-hunters. Small matters to you, perhaps, but then you have never been much exposed to the coarser side of the great world.'

'And Grace?'

He sighed.

'Yes. Grace. She may, I imagine, entertain some doubts as to my rightful place in her estimation, but at the same time she will be one of the greatest heiresses in the Law Valley. She will have Celia's money, Matthew Oldroyd's money, Tessa Delaney's money, my money, all in due course – and I shall make a great deal of money now, Faith, in addition to all the rest. Fieldhead will be her official home, of course, but I think I may leave her with Prudence for a while – Monday to Friday. Remember, Faith, I *am* a lawyer. My new will is already drawn up and waiting to be signed after my marriage. In the event of my death, the guardianship of my daughter will pass to you and Blaize, if you will accept it. You may be sure that where Grace is concerned I have left nothing to chance.'

The maid came in to light the lamps and check the fire, glanced enquiringly at us and went out again, her interruption conveying to me the lateness of the hour but inducing no inclination whatsoever to take my leave.

'You may lose her, Jonas.'

'I know. But I would lose her in any case. She will marry, sooner or later, and at least now I can give her the freedom of choice I lacked myself. With Fieldhead behind her she can afford to marry where she pleases. She can even afford not to marry at all.'

'It is all decided, then?'

'Yes, quite decided.'

'What can I do for you, Jonas?'

And for just a moment, caught unawares by my offer of help when he had anticipated condemnation, there was pain in his face.

'Should Grace turn away from me, you could offer – such consolation as occurred to you and which she might be ready to accept. You could express the opinion, at Cullingford's tea-tables, that my daughter's reputation cannot suffer from exposure to such a step-mother.'

'Jonas, I would do that in any case.'

'Of course you would. I have simply allowed myself the pleasure of asking, since there is no one else I would wish to ask.'

'Prudence –?'

'Of course. There is Prudence, who may never forgive me, but who will help me just the same. Nevertheless it is you I wish to ask. That is the place you hold in my life. You must know why. It seems pointless to deny it, just as it would seem equally pointless, at this late stage, to put it into words.'

He got up and moved away from me, quite deliberately putting distance between us – allowing me a moment to realize that he had almost said he loved me, that, in other circumstances, I could almost have welcomed it – and then he resumed his seat, composed, neutral as always, his face serious but gentler, I thought, than before.

'You should not worry about me, Faith. You should think of your own affairs, which may need thought.'

'Why do you say that, Jonas?'

'Because I am a devious man, an expert in the deciphering of motives and meanings, and the drawing of conclusions. And it is no secret that the Barforth pot is about to boil over. I see you in the midst of it and it troubles me. Faith, I have no right to ask and you are not obliged to answer, but there is something amiss with your life, is there not? It gave me pleasure just now to ask for your help. It would mean a great deal to me if you would allow me to help you.'

And, having accepted for so long his own personal judgment, that he was indeed devious and calculating and self-seeking, it amazed me that I could now turn to him with the perfect trust I had previously extended only to Giles. All my life I had seen him through other people's eyes, through Prudence's hostility for the brother-in-law who could cheat her of her inheritance, through Aunt Hannah's driving ambitions, her almost pathetic desire to fulfil herself in him, through Celia's fretful complainings, through Caroline's frank contempt for 'the Agbrigg boy'. I had believed him to be cold and crafty, and so on occasion he was. Only recently had I come to realize that in gentler circumstances, like those which had moulded Giles Ashburn's character, he would have grown differently. Only now did I realize it fully and my heart ached for the waste of him.

'I don't know what is wrong with me, Jonas – only that something is.'

'Blaize?'

'I don't know anything about Blaize. I thought him my dearest friend, but I seem to have rather lost him, now. We are beginning to lead our own lives, except that I am not physically unfaithful –'

'There are other kinds of infidelity.'

'Yes. I believe he may think so. But I don't know how to defend myself. I don't really know what I am guilty of. Our marriage was bound to be difficult. Blaize himself is difficult. But it isn't that. Something, at some point, came between us, something large and definite and quite invisible. There's nothing to grapple with. And if Blaize knows what it is, then he won't tell me. He won't tell me anything at all.'

'And have you asked him?'

'No. I can't ask him.'

'In fact you have allowed the silence to fall and now you can't find your way through it.'

I shuddered. 'Well, I shall just have to go on as best I can.'

The maid appeared again, hovered, her agitation reminding him that he had ordered his carriage an hour ago, reminding me of the woman whose claims on him were far more valid than mine.

'Heavens! It must be getting late.'

'Yes, I fear so.'

I got up shakily, against my will. 'I don't want to go home, Jonas.'

'My dear, where else is there for you to go?'

'I know – I know.'

'Faith – listen to me. I understand the art of being alone. I have always lived separately, and inward – and I shall simply continue so to do. You are not made that way. When the conflict in your family comes to a head, and if you are forced into a position of choice, you will have to choose Blaize. You must know that. My hope for you is that you will want to choose him.'

I could find no member of my family willing to accompany me to the wedding of Jonas and Tessa Delaney. My mother and Aunt Verity, at Aunt Hannah's urgent request, declined, feeling that their loyalty was to her rather than to her adopted son. Prudence, fearing the effect of the marriage on Grace and bitterly disappointed in Jonas himself, declared that wild horses would not drag her to see the foul deed done. Blaize was out of town. 'I'll come with you,' Georgiana offered. 'I don't care a scrap for Mr Agbrigg or Mrs Delaney, but if you want my company you shall have it.' But her grandfather, who had been ailing for several months, took a sudden turn for the worse, so that instead of a wedding she was called to a death-bed; and I went to the parish church alone.

It was a heavy morning of late August, a yellow sky pressing down upon the city, a tight, dusty quality in the air that promised heat, and, even as I got down from my victoria and walked across that familiar churchyard, I hoped to see Aunt Hannah, grim and resolute, hostile and bitter, but present, in the church porch. I even waited a moment, not seeing her carriage, hoping for the sound of her unsteady nags, or at least the heavy footsteps which might bring Mayor Agbrigg, coming alone to offer a measure of reconciliation. But the church was almost empty, just the law clerks from Croppers Court, the managers from Fieldhead, who knew which side their bread was buttered, and Nicholas Barforth, come, one supposed, to pay his respects to a new power in the Valley.

'Good morning, Lady Barforth.'

'Good morning, Nicholas.'

And I stepped into a pew beside him, knowing how conspicuous I would seem should I sit elsewhere, the entrance of the stately, timeless bride preventing further conversation between us, bringing me an unwilling image of Celia, coming down this very aisle to this very bridegroom, beautiful – for the first and only time in her life – a breathless, delicate bloom that had soon perished. And behind her came Giles Ashburn's bride, on fire with gratitude, running – although she didn't know it then – from Nicholas Barforth to Nicholas Barforth, determined to keep faith with him yet losing it, keeping faith in the end not even with myself. 'I give you everything I can,' Blaize had told me, 'which is rather more – in fact a great deal more, Faith Aycliffe – than you give me.' Yet was he asking for my love or simply telling me to be satisfied? 'I give you everything I can – everything it is in my nature to give.' Surely that could only be a reminder of our agreement, a warning that I should content myself within the limits he had set and to which I had consented? Certainly I had overstepped those limitations by questioning him about his infidelity, and had lost his trust long before that by breaking the one promise he had asked of me. 'I give you everything I can, which is rather more than you give to me.' Did he want more? Could I give it? Assuredly I could, for I had indeed thought of him as my dearest friend – as Nicholas and I, in spite of all the love, the pain, the need, the rich complexity between us, had never been friends – and I had missed Blaize acutely since he had withdrawn from me. Did he want more? It was the hope with which I tried to nourish my bleaker moments, a pale, hesitant little hope which soon failed. For Blaize, above all, was an opportunist, who had never to my knowledge practised self-denial. If he wanted something from me, from anyone, he would ask. And there was no denying that, since Celia died, and my own needs had somehow sharpened, whenever I tried to approach him I encountered nothing but cool air and my own sadness.

We came out of the church into full sunshine, the second Mrs Agbrigg taking her husband's arm with authority, her handsome head, beneath its relatively modest bonnet, held high, a smile of composure only faintly tinged with satisfaction on her full, dark red lips.

'Lady Barforth, how kind of you to come,' she said, by no means overwhelmed at my generosity, understanding it had been done for Jonas, and considering herself a match for Lady Barforth any day of the week. 'And Mr Barforth too – how kind. You *will* come back with us now, to Fieldhead, I know, and take a glass of champagne.'

'So we will,' Nicholas said, kissing her hand, amused, I thought, at meeting someone whose presence was as commanding as his own, and who took it for granted she would be obeyed. 'That is – I'll come if my sister-in-law will give me a ride in her carriage, since I left mine at the Swan.'

'But of course –' murmured Mrs Delaney-Oldroyd-Agbrigg, and, although a visit to Fieldhead was the last thing in the world I intended, the memory of Nicholas's horse left in the Swan yard the last thing I could bear on such a day, we drove off together to be greeted on arrival by the new master of Fieldhead himself, alighting from his own carriage to escort us into the house I had last entered in the days when Mr Oldroyd had wanted to marry my mother.

The new mistress of that house had as yet made few changes beyond the crimson velvet curtains which had so grieved my sister, but her casual offer of a 'glass of champagne' was, of course, more elaborate than that, a well-garnished spread of galantines and pâtés, the angel cakes and

757

chocolate cakes for which she had become famous, a sure indication that I would be obliged to stay far longer than the quarter of an hour I had allowed.

'Dear Lady Barforth – do take a little of this – and that – another glass'; and, because I was tearful again, thinking of Celia, wishing Jonas well with all my heart yet not certain that he would be well – that Grace would be well – I meekly accepted her food, her wine, strolled into her garden to admire her plants, a glass of champagne in my hand, too many, already, in my head, so that when I found myself alone with Nicholas, in view of the others but separated from them by low box-hedges, several yards of roses, I was not sure if she – with her harlot's knowledge and complicity – had arranged it.

He had a glass in his hand too, a cigar in the other, his skin and his hair darker, it seemed, each time I stood close to him than the time before, the resemblance between him and Blaize growing smaller with the years as he became heavier, more dominant, Blaize lighter, more elusive.

'You'll be glad to see your brother-in-law doing so well for himself,' he said, not asking me but telling me in the grand manner of Jonas's new wife.

'I shall be very glad, if she can make him happy.'

'Oh, there's not much doubt of that, surely.'

'I do hope not.'

'I'm sure not. She keeps a good house and a good table. She's given him the best business in the Valley after mine – and I imagine she's accommodating in other directions. She knows what she wants, our Tessa Delaney, and since it happens to be Jonas I reckon he's set for life. I just hope she'll give him time off to handle one or two little matters of concern to me, since he's still my lawyer.'

And the fact that he had mentioned these matters which were of concern to him was a clear indication that they must also be of concern to me.

'I'm sure she will.'

'Yes. Well, I'd best finish my drink and take my leave, for by rights I shouldn't be here at all. I've had word from Galton that Mr Clevedon died in the night, so I should get over there, shouldn't I?'

'Nicholas – you should have gone at once.'

'I do know that, Faith. But I was already on my way here when Georgiana's messenger caught me and I thought – well – since Mr Clevedon was beyond any help of mine, I might as well carry on and give my support to the living. And, in fact, since I *am* here, I may as well remind Jonas that the estate can now be properly valued, and that he should start looking around him for a buyer – if he hasn't found me one already.'

It was, perhaps, the strong sunlight, the wine which, curdled by shock, dazzled me, causing the rich colours of the garden to rush away from me into a pale obscurity and then back again, their impact crushing my stomach to nausea. But it was essential to right myself, for I knew he had followed me into the garden on purpose to tell me this, that my knowing it had some significance that I must be calm enough to understand.

'Nicholas, you *can't* sell Georgiana's Abbey.'

He took the glass from my hand and set it down on a low wall, his own

758

beside it, the sun making diamonds of what had probably been the first Mrs Oldroyd's – Miss Lucy Hobhouse's – wedding crystal.

'As it happens,' he said quietly, 'you are quite mistaken. It is not even Georgiana's Abbey. The Galton estate is not held under entail nor under any kind of settlement whatsoever. The reigning Clevedon has always been able to dispose of it as he thought fit – which, admittedly, has always been to the next male Clevedon in line. My wife's grandfather has decided differently. He could have left the property in trust for my son, but in fact, and very sensibly, he has left it to Georgiana. And since, as you well know, anything a married woman inherits belongs automaticially to her husband, then we can safely say that Galton is mine.'

'Are you trying to kill her, Nicholas?'

'Are you not being a trifle melodramatic, Faith? I am disposing of a few hundred barren acres and a house that would take thousands I can't spare to put right. I am disposing of what could be a future millstone around my son's neck, and a present distraction from what he ought to be doing in life.'

'Does Georgiana know?'

'No. Until we find a buyer – which may not be easy – there's no need for her to know. She may as well enjoy the grouse moor as long as she can. You could mention it to Blaize, if you like. He knows so many people, and, as I said, a customer could be hard to find. The bare market value would satisfy me, and it can't be high.'

'You want me to tell Blaize, and you don't want me to tell Georgiana. Is that it?'

'I'm not aware that I want you to do anything.'

But what his voice spoke to me was not of market values and purchasers, but of destruction, not only the ruin of Georgiana's bright childhood, the very essence of herself, but a doing to death of the last shred of our remembered emotion, a final hardening of his nature for which I was probably to blame, and couldn't bear.

'Good-bye then, Faith. I'll just have a word with our bridegroom and kiss the bride, and be on my way.'

But I had to say more, he expected more, for the slight intake of my breath before speaking halted him, caused him to turn and face me.

'Nicholas –' And it was the ultimate opportunity. There would be no other.

'Nicholas, I've already lost you twice –'

'What are you talking about now?'

'You know very well. If you do this cruel thing –'

'I fully intend to.'

'Then it will be like losing you again.'

'There's nothing in me for you to lose.'

'Nicholas – I don't want to go through it a third time.'

'You survived before.'

'Yes, of course I did. I had to, and meant to. But you owe me something for that survival, Nicholas. Oh yes – you came to me, knowing

759

I was in love with you, and told me you were in love with Georgiana, and I wished you joy. I didn't cling to your coat-tails and embarrass you with my silly broken heart. I wished you joy. I tried to mean it, and I certainly behaved as if I meant it. Don't you remember that?'

He glanced quickly across the box-hedges, where the new Mrs Agbrigg was still plying her guests with cake and champagne, and, taking my arm, his hand hot but very hard, very steady, he drew me even further down the garden, to the deep, spreading cover of a chestnut tree.

'I remember it, Faith. I hurt you. You crucified me. If there was a debt, I paid it.'

And it was more urgent than ever now, more vital, for the time allowed us was running out.

'I paid it too, Nicholas. Listen to me – please, please – and just hear what I'm saying to you, not what I've said before, or what you think I might have said. I could have tolerated the scandal, Nicholas. I could have tolerated the isolation. I could have tolerated the risk. I loved you so much and I'd loved you for so long. I was ready to grow old waiting for you – or so I thought – and it was then that I discovered the one thing I couldn't tolerate. When Georgiana was ill with Venetia, I had to wonder how I might feel if she died, and I knew I couldn't live with myself if what I actually did feel turned out to be glad. Nicholas – I was ready to spend the rest of my life waiting for you. I *couldn't* spend the rest of my life waiting for her to die, wanting her to die – and if we'd stayed together, openly or secretly, I couldn't have avoided wanting it. I know what it would have turned me into – and you. There'd have been nothing but bitterness left between us in the end – which is all there seems to be now. But at least she's alive, and intact – something was salvaged. Nicholas – don't waste that.'

I could see the tender green of the chestnut leaves waving above me, dappling the sunshine, an intense blue sky, the richly overburdened earth of high summer. I could see my own hand offering itself to him with the shaky, groping movement of an old woman, although my skin, amazingly, was still smooth, my flesh still firm, only my spirit, it seemed, having aged a hundred, difficult years. I saw his hand, the square, workmanlike palm, the long, brown fingers, a heavy gold ring on one of them catching the sunlight as they closed very briefly, very painfully around mine.

'Harden yourself against me, Faith. When they say I'm a callous devil, agree with them. The evidence is plain to see.'

'I know. I see it, and know it to be true. Somehow I can't believe it.'

'I'm sorry,' he said, releasing my hand. 'Really, Faith – if I could change it – but I know myself too well. I knew how you felt, and I shared it. I didn't want her to die either. But in the end I reckon something in me got twisted instead, or something you obviously don't much care for took root – I don't know. Either way, I'm not likely to change now. I don't dislike the way I am. It's easier, Faith – easier for me, at any rate. You'll understand what I mean. And don't forget to ask Blaize if he can find me a customer. He'll understand me as well.'

33

Blaize returned home in time for Mr Clevedon's funeral, accompanying me to Galton and then to Listonby, where we stayed for a subdued Friday to Monday, respectful of the dead and marvelling that Georgiana should be so calm. And, although I opened my mouth a hundred times to tell him of Nicholas's plans for the Abbey, a clamp descended on my tongue, a paralysis took hold of my throat, releasing me only when my brain had consented to speak of something else. Why? I couldn't be certain. Was it my great and growing reluctance to speak of Nicholas to Blaize, to speak of Nicholas to anyone, an inexplicable difficulty in so much as pronouncing his name which caused me, when it could not be avoided, to refer him as 'my brother-in-law', 'my cousin', 'him'? Or was it merely suspicion, a notion that Nicholas's motives had been other than they seemed? He had wanted me to tell Blaize. And in that case perhaps it would do Blaize no good to know. Yet whatever the rights and wrongs of it, the motives and manoeuvrings, I could not bring myself to tell him; and, as that tense August turned amber with September, the days quickening into the smoky pulse-beat of autumn, I felt treacherous without understanding the nature of my treachery, uneasy and overburdened with a guilt which surely was not mine.

I saw a great deal of Georgiana. I stood beside her in the churchyard as Mr Clevedon was laid to rest, walked with her afterwards in the cloister, meeting Nicholas's eyes as we went into that timeless passage, and meeting them again when we came out, unable to recognize either satisfaction or disappointment in him when her strange serenity made it clear I had divulged no secrets.

'It doesn't matter so much about grandfather,' she told me. 'It was different with Perry, because he hadn't even started to live his life. Grandfather had nothing else he wished to do, and it's only our faces that change, after all. We're still here. You must have heard me say that before, since it's the creed I live by.'

And, crushed by pity and anxiety, remembering the Georgiana who had comforted me on the night Joel Barforth died, the Georgiana who had driven her horses through the flood, the vivid, lovable, laughable Georgiana of her better days, I went straight to Blaize and announced, 'There's something I must tell you.'

'Well, darling – if you must.' And that first quizzical lift of his eyebrow froze me, forced me, after a moment, to produce a trill of light laughter, a careless, 'Oh, never mind. It doesn't signify.'

Yet every time I heard her step I clenched my nerves in agonized expectation of disaster until her face told me she was still, in her own mind, the possessor of her ancestral acres, their rightful guardian for future generations as her grandfather had been, her unusual calm arising – I well knew, from the deep satisfaction of believing she was now empowered to pass them on intact to her son.

I lay in bed one night deluding myself with the nursery tale that Nicholas had changed his mind, that he could not after all perform this act of extreme cruelty. I awoke far into the night, cold and horrified, recognizing my delusion, my mind refusing any other function but to repeat over and over, 'How will she bear it? How will she survive it?' And I knew, of course, that she would not.

It was a very fragile morning towards the end of September, a thin, pale sky, a light haze slanting across thirsty grasses and flowers blanched by the long summer heat. My daughter was at school, my household quiet after the bustle of rising and breakfasting, the lull before anyone need think of luncheon. Blaize, who had travelled overnight from London, was somewhere in the house, having made no appointments until the afternoon. My windows were open, a scent of full-blown roses drifting through them, the scent of pot-pourri within, a huge, over-burdened bee expiring on my window-sill, birdsong in the elm trees at the edge of the garden, nothing to distract me from the sound of a sporting carriage driven at speed, nor the sight of Georgiana's face as she brought it to a perilous, shuddering stop and came running indoors.

She looked very much as I had anticipated. I was prepared for it. And I had seen grief before. I had seen women from Simon Street who had lost eight out of ten children. I had myself lost a husband. I had seen the agonized collapse of Mr Hobhouse as he had handed over the keys of Nethercoats, and of his children's future. I had never seen a woman facing the loss of everything she possessed, everything in which she believed, her creed, her immortality; and the sheer savagery of it, the sheer nakedness, was overwhelming.

'Blaize?' she said as I ran to meet her, his name jerking itself out of her with the uncoordinated movement of a marionette, and, understanding that she needed to conserve every drop of her self-command, I nodded and made a gesture of assent. But Blaize too had heard the approach of that aged curricle which had once belonged to Perry Clevedon, had recognized the wild, rake-hellish driving, and came quickly into the hall, sensing alarm with the fine, far-sighted sensitivity of a cat.

'Georgiana?'

And, as she began to speak, her face once again was the face of a tormented doll, the terrible effort of wooden features forcing themselves to emit human sounds when the only sound perhaps in her mind was a scream of raw hate and vengeance.

'I met a man on the road to Galton – a tenant of ours – how ridiculous!'

'Yes, Georgiana?'

'A man – as I said – who asked me if there was nothing I could do to stop the new master from –'

'What is it, Georgiana?'

'Nothing.'

'Yes – what is it you can't say?'

'To stop the new master from selling the estate.'

'Dear God!' Blaize said.

'And so I told him what nonsense, and he said everyone in the village was talking of it – which couldn't signify because people do talk so in country places – so I went to the village – yes, I went to the village –'

'Georgiana, will you sit down?'

'Not yet. Blaize, if it should be true, you do know that I couldn't bear it?'

'I know. Have you seen Nicholas?'

'No. I knew that's what I had to do. So I got the curricle and came back here as fast as I could. I drove right into the mill yard at Lawcroft and right out again. Blaize – I *couldn't*. My hands burned on to the reins and I couldn't let go – couldn't get down. Blaize – I have to know.'

'Yes. I'll go and see him right away.'

'Thank God for you, Blaize!'; and, swaying forward, as if, like a soldier dying of wounds, she had endured only until her message had been delivered, she collapsed against him, allowing me to see this man who had warned me he would never be a rock for me to lean on, standing firm as a rock now for Georgiana, his body supporting hers to my drawing-room sofa and then holding her, rocking her like a child, the caressing note of his voice whispering comfort against the dishevelled head she pressed against his shoulder, so that abruptly painfully, my mind was flooded by sharp-etched memories of all the other times he had helped and protected her: Blaize stepping in adroitly to shield her from malice and backbiting in the early days of her marriage; Blaize going to fetch her from the sands at Bournemouth, worrying for her safety when Nicholas had remained on the path with me; Blaize waiting up the whole of one summer night at Listonby, watching from the window until she had ridden home; Blaize making the journey to Scarborough that fateful Saturday to persuade me, harass me, frighten me into giving Nicholas up, not for my sake, but for hers, seeing me, perhaps, as no more than a threat to Georgiana's peace of mind; Blaize – so many years ago – leaning forward in his mother's carriage, saying to Caroline, 'She is exactly the kind of girl a man might come to love quite foolishly, without at all wanting to'; Blaize *then*, his voice continuing, cool, unforgotten, 'She could get inside a man's head and his skin and he could find himself quite unable to get rid of her, no matter how much he tried'; Blaize *now*, offering her the strong shoulder for her tears, the warm, protecting arms for her reassurance as he had never offered them to me. And through the layers of my pity, my remorse, my toleration, something stirred, heaved, made its long-subdued protest so that the only clear thought in my head was, 'Take your hands off that woman.'

I left the room quickly, gave instructions that my husband was not to be disturbed, mentioned the word 'discretion' to my butler, who interpreted it correctly as keeping as many people as possible out of the way. I walked back to the drawing-room door, stretched out a hand towards it and could not move any further, caught painfully and perhaps ridiculously in a nightmare panic. I had stood in dreams, many times, exactly like this, in a familiar house, nothing to threaten me but the knowledge that somewhere, on an upper floor, was a room I must not enter. And so I would not enter it. There were other rooms in my dream,

763

pleasant rooms, no reason at all for my feet to mount the stairs – although they mounted them – no reason at all to find myself standing at that one forbidden door, hypnotized by the nameless terror behind it.

I stood at that door now, waiting, as the fear took shape. I went inside and there it was, my own blindness, my own inadequacies, the futile knowledge that I had entered far too late. And, as I crossed the threshold, Blaize did not even raise his head to look at me.

Georgiana was sitting alone, a brandy glass in her hand, Blaize leaning on the arm of the sofa, not touching her, but alert, intuitive, *there*, to anticipate her need.

'Promise me,' he was saying, 'that you will stay here while I'm away – no running off in that crazy curricle, Georgiana, no wild schemes. I don't know how long I'll be, since Nick could have gone to any one of the mills, or the Piece Hall, anywhere. And when I do find him it could be over in ten minutes or it could last all day. I must know that you'll be here when I return.'

She drank off her brandy, set down the glass, and sat for a moment staring down at her own narrow hands, the tension in her slight body so piercing that it got into my own nerves and sinews, drawing them out in subtle anguish.

'I'll stay,' she said, her voice no more than a hoarse whisper, her eyes still fixed on her hands which now had coiled themselves into fists. 'And Blaize – he must want something – surely? Something more than it seems?'

'Oh yes – I do believe so.'

'Then tell him, please, that I'll do anything. Yes – it's not businesslike, I know, to make offers before one knows the asking price. I've learned that much from being so long a manufacturer's wife. But, you see, when something is beyond price, nothing one offered could be too much. You have *carte blanche* –'

'I know,' he said quietly, and, pressing his hand lightly against her shoulder, he got up and went out into the hall, asking me with a glance to follow him.

We stood in the open doorway waiting for his carriage to be brought round, my arms folded as if against the cold although the sun was shining, the air still and heavy with the fragrances of summer's end.

'You don't seem much surprised about this, Faith.'

'No. I'm not surprised,' and I was smiling, in the way sacrificial victims are supposed to smile on their way to the altar, as my voice continued, 'I already knew.'

'I beg your pardon?'

'I already knew. Nicholas told me on Jonas's wedding day.'

'You will have a reason, of course – and I do hope it is a good one – for not telling me?'

'No. No reason at all.'

'And is that all you can say?'

He walked down the shallow steps to the carriage-drive, leaving me in the doorway, my arms still folded, taking with him the first flare of his

764

annoyance, so that when he returned his voice was curt, his eyes not angry, I thought, but disappointed, disdainful.

'Faith – there's no time now to have this out. But let me explain this – if you'd told me the estate was to be sold – as you should have done, as any woman without a personal axe to grind would have done – then all this unpleasantness could have been avoided. I don't know what Nicky's up to. Possibly he does want to get rid of his wife. Possibly he does see the Abbey as a bad influence on his son. Those may, or may not, be his reasons. I don't imagine for one moment he'd sell the estate to me, but if I'd known in advance I could have used an agent and no one the wiser. However, since there's no chance of that now, I shall just have to find another way.'

The carriage was driven smartly round from the back of the house and I went with him to the step, hugging myself tighter, the cold which seemed to be attacking me from within making me shiver.

'Faith,' he said, wanting, I think, to give me a second chance. 'Her roots are so deep in that soil that if they were taken up she might just wither – not necessarily die, although one can't be certain – but just wither. If I can prevent it – however I can prevent it – then I will. You must understand that.'

'Yes, of course.'

'And you'll help? You'll look after her now?'

'Of course.'

'Thank you,' he said, and, because his eyes were still careful, asking me, 'Can I trust you?', I gave him such reassurance as I could, not being myself quite certain of it.

He stepped up into the carriage, drove off, and I went back inside to help him as I had promised, smoothing out the tangle of detail he had neglected. I sent a note to Prudence asking her to keep Blanche and Venetia until they were sent for, another, infinitely more cautious message to Aunt Verity explaining that Georgiana was with me and that all was well. I conferred somewhat apologetically with my cook about the luncheon we had not eaten, making no firm promises about dinner. And when it was done I went back into the drawing-room and sat down in a thick silence, waiting for the blast which must alter the course of both our lives, which had already shaken mine.

For a long time we had nothing to say to each other, Georgiana being not really present in the room at all, but far away in the meadows and moorlands of her childhood, the long summertime of her adolescence, reliving those eager days with Perry drop by drop – Perry who could never be lost because Galton could never be lost – and, although I struggled hard to pity her as I should, to love her as I believed I did, I couldn't rid my memory of her trusting head on Blaize's shoulder, nor my own anguished cry, 'Take your hands off that woman,' although I knew he had never really touched her.

Yet what did touching matter? He had touched other women, beautiful women, I supposed, made anonymous by distance and by his own nonchalance. I had accepted it as an essential part of his nature. But tenderness, concern, the ingredients, surely, of love for Georgiana, all

765

that was, quite simply, beyond acceptance. I could neither tolerate it nor even contemplate it with anything approaching reason. Yet I had seen it. I forced myself to look at it again and, as I did so, jealousy assaulted me, left me gasping and sick, left me foolish and astonished and bitterly cold.

'Blaize must have found him by now,' she whispered at last.

'Yes. I imagine so.' And there was coldness in my voice because coldness was all I had.

She got up, paced a moment, sat down again, her hands on her knees.

'I didn't know he hated me so much.'

'Didn't you?' And I had spoken harshly, to punish myself for all the things I hadn't known.

'Faith?' she said, her start of surprise clearing my head enough for me to realize my own strangeness, and that she was not to blame.

'Georgiana – do forgive me. I can't think why I said that, since it can't be true.'

'Don't you think so?' she said, and as she leaned towards me her pointed face was almost eager.

'I wouldn't mind hatred, Faith. I understand it. If Nicky had been with me this morning when I heard about the Abbey, I could have turned on him so easily with my driving-whip and killed him, I believe – really – if I'd managed to hit him hard enough in the ten minutes before my head cooled. It's not a pleasant feeling, perhaps, but at least it's alive. At least it's not silent. And if he wants to punish me like this, then he must hate me – surely? What else could it be? There's no profit to be made from selling my land, and the money I'd need to keep it going would be nothing to him. It has to be for my chastisement.'

'You sound as if you want him to hate you.'

'Oh dear,' she said, pressing the palms of her hands against her eyes. 'I believe I do. How terrible – except that if he can still feel so strongly – I don't know. Perhaps we could just *talk* again. A little thing like that would be a great deal.'

'And the Abbey? Could you forgive him if he sold it?'

'No,' she said, suddenly on her feet in one knife-edged movement, her body so rigid with terror, reminding me so strongly of myself face to face with that nightmare door, that I threw my arms around her and held her fast, not with the comforting assurance of Blaize but as one drowning woman might cling to another, both of us separately floundering.

'Faith – what is it?'

'Nothing. Pay no attention to me. Don't worry. Blaize will be back soon. He means to buy the Abbey and give it back to you, somehow or other, and he'll find a way – truly he will –'

'And you wouldn't mind that?'

'Of course not. Why should I? Why *should* I?'

'I wouldn't claim it for myself,' she whispered, her lips very pale, 'If he could keep it for Gervase, that would be enough – and it might satisfy Nicky. I'd agree never to set foot on Galton land again if I could be sure it was still there, for Gervase. I hope Blaize has thought to tell him that.'

But Blaize returned by mid-afternoon having achieved nothing, having

766

made the mistake, in fact, of going first to Lawcroft, so that by the time Nicholas's whereabouts had been ascertained he had already boarded the Leeds train.

'I left a message with the stationmaster asking him to come here,' Blaize told me, still watchful. 'We can do nothing now but wait, which gives him an advantage I don't like. Faith – when he arrives take Georgiana upstairs and stay there.'

And I was not to blame – although perhaps Blaize did not immediately agree – when my butler, either from a surfeit of curiosity or an attack of nerves, blundered, showing Nicholas directly into the drawing-room and allowing Georgiana no time to escape.

She shot to her feet, alert and desperate, her breath catching on a low moan, but Nicholas merely glanced at her, her attitude of defence telling him all he needed to know, and turned instead to Blaize.

'I understood you were looking for me.'

'Yes. I expect you know why.'

'I expect I do.'

And already the conflict was between the two of them, as it had always been, the Barforth males who could submit to no authority but their own, who had fought each other since their nursery days for anything and nothing, and who were closing in now, on the battleground of my drawing-room carpet, to put an end to it. And I started to shiver again.

'You took your time,' Nicholas said. 'If you'd come to me sooner I reckon we could have spared the ladies.'

'I didn't know about it sooner.'

'You mean she didn't tell you?'

'She didn't tell me.'

'Didn't she, by God!' he said, his mouth twisting into a smile that was deliberately sardonic and unkind. 'Now that *does* surprise me, and it's a pity. But never mind. I didn't want this to happen so publicly, but there's no help for it.'

And sliding a hand inside his coat he took out a familiar brown envelope and set it down with a brisk slap on the table.

'That's my new offer for your share of the mills, Blaize. I've had to slightly reduce the down-payment, I'm afraid, since times are getting so hard. But I'll tell you what I'm ready to do. I'll throw in the Abbey to make up the difference. How does that suit you? Otherwise, of course, the estate goes under the hammer.'

I heard a strangled sound beside me which must have been Georgiana, and then, for a dreadful moment, could hear nothing but my own pulse-beat, my own protest, for I had suspected it could be something like this and had wanted, most acutely, to be wrong. Hate and punishment would have been a beginning. Reconciliation a possibility. But, as always – and I *should* have known – it was hard cash, ambition, the limits he had chosen for himself, the limits within which he felt powerful and safe, and which he had no desire to cross. 'Personal relationships don't suit me,' he had once told me and I had not believed him. But he had wanted it to be true, had forced it to be true, and I believed him now.

767

'You clever bastard,' Blaize said, sitting down, I think, because his legs in that moment of shocked revelation failed to support him, looking for the first time older than Nicholas, his frame leaner, more brittle, too light in substance to combat the bold, tough-fibred bulk of the younger, far more ruthless man.

'Yes – you clever bastard. You used Oldroyd's whore to get Nethercoats, and Galton to get me.' And, as his words ended, heralding a deep silence as chilling and insidious as sudden drifts of snow, I continued to shiver. If Blaize accepted this offer, if whatever it was he felt for Georgiana proved strong enough for him to make his sacrifice, then I knew our marriage would be over. Yet if he refused it, and harm came to her as a result, then we could have no real future together either. Guilt, I thought, or solitude. Which is it to be?

I saw Blaize only from my eye-corner, Nicholas not at all, Georgiana standing chalk-white, arrow-straight, her hands clenched, the taut concentration of her face telling me she was well aware of the sacrifice which had been demanded, the implications of its acceptance. And already, for me, it was over. This morning I had been aware of a few vague sorrows. This fine, early evening I knew I had been my own sorrow, my own disaster. All I wanted now was to go back to the evening Blaize had given me my cameo swan, to relive that homecoming and the next, to make sure there would be another; and I could see no real chance of it.

'I reckon you can give me your answer straightaway,' Nicholas said, obviously in no doubt of it, and as I made a half turn, intending to leave the room – since I could not doubt it either – Georgiana suddenly lifted her head, her cheeks flooded with colour, and, crossing to Blaize's side, looked directly at Nicholas and said, 'It won't be necessary for him to give an answer at all.'

He began, I think, to tell her to be silent, but she made a gesture of quiet command that I had seen before, a gesture the squires of Galton, perhaps, had made from time immemorial, so that now it was bred into their heirs. And, although she was young and slender and very certainly a woman, it could have been her grandfather standing there, or his grandfather, a line of upright, honourable men whose code it was to sacrifice themselves at need for the good of others, rather than allow others to be sacrificed: a line of men – and women – who could be narrow and overbearing, but could also be very true and very strong.

'Please don't say anything, Blaize. There is absolutely no need. For, even if you could be persuaded to agree to this monstrous coercion, I would not allow it.'

'Georgiana,' he said, 'You shouldn't –'; but she silenced him too, with that same movement of calm authority, a woman I had not seen before, who had been badly hurt, assuredly, but who seemed able to meet and to overcome this new pain as bravely as the madcap girl in her could gallop home from the hunt with a broken bone or pick herself up bruised and laughing from a stony ditch.

And the whole room was completely full of her.

'Oh Nicholas, how very like you,' she said. 'I have been sitting here all day trying to decide just why you hated me so much, whether you wanted me dead so that you could marry again, or merely wished to drive me insane so that I might be locked up out of your way, or whether, perhaps, there could still be a spark of a quite different insanity left between us – such romantic notions. I thought you were doing it all for passion, when really – oh, my goodness! – I see now it couldn't possibly be that. It's just a matter of business, isn't it? What else? And really, Nicky, it won't do, you know. Don't you think we've embarrassed your brother, and poor Faith, long enough – and to no good purpose? I think we should leave them in peace.'

'Be careful,' he said. 'Be very careful, Georgiana –'; but, although the threat was there, the anger of a man who had forgotten how to be thwarted, it was less than I had supposed, an indication that even he was aware of the change in her, the sudden deepening of her nature, a moment of growth and self-knowledge leading her to a threshold it should be our privilege to watch her cross.

'You must think very poorly of me, Nicky, if you imagine I would lay claim even to my rightful inheritance at such a price.'

'I'd think you a fool if you didn't,' he told her, recovering from his initial shock with the speed of a seasoned campaigner, his body alert now with the stalking caution of a predator circling her defences, certain of breaching them, since he no longer believed in the existence of a woman – or a man – who could not be bought or bullied or otherwise persuaded.

'Georgiana,' Blaize said, with quiet pleading. 'Indeed, you must be careful. This is no game.'

'Oh – I think it is. What else can one call it? Nicky wants your share of the mills. He has the money to buy, but no weapon to make you sell. But then my grandfather dies, and, gambling on his belief that I cannot live without the Abbey and that you will not allow me to be destroyed, he decides to use me as that weapon. A very simple game – and very effective – except that I will not be so used. Good heavens, Nicky! you have not the slightest chance of success. I have only to say I do not want the Abbey and all your cards fall down.'

'Then say it, Georgiana,' he told her, menacing her quietly, almost casually, since he still believed her to be incapable of any such thing. 'Say it, and mean it.'

'I –'

'Yes, Georgiana?'

'I don't want the Abbey – not on your terms.'

He swung away from her, his back briefly turned, and when I saw his face again he was actually smiling.

'Ah yes – I see you qualify your statement. You don't want the Abbey on my terms – which doesn't convince me that you're ready to give it up.'

'I believe I am.'

'I doubt it. What you really believe is that I won't go through with the sale. And, if that's the hope you're clinging to, then you couldn't be more mistaken. I'll do it, Georgiana. Ask Blaize.'

'He'll do it,' Blaize said, still strangely brittle, very pale.

'Ask Faith.'

'He'll do it,' I answered, my mouth stiff and awkward to manage. 'He'll really do it, Georgiana.'

'I know,' she told me almost kindly. 'He'd have to, I realize that, to save his pride and ease his temper. I know – strangers walking in the cloister, riding in the stream – I'll say it for you, Nicky, to save you the trouble of taunting me. I know.' She made a small gesture with her hands, pushing some unseen object away and smiled, shakily, but with resolution.

'Nicky, I would like to make you understand. This morning I believed no price could be too high. I was wrong. The Clevedon land nourishes the Clevedons – you've heard me say that often enough, too often I suppose – but only if we deserve it. No, no – I'm not talking fairy-tales. If I accepted your quite shameful terms, then the crops wouldn't fail and the cows wouldn't abort, I know that very well. But if I lost my self-esteem I could hardly consider myself a Clevedon and I'd have no right to the Abbey then. I'd be the stranger in my own cloister and I would prefer not to be there at all. There's no need to take the Abbey away from me, Nicky. I'll give it to you freely, even if the law says it's not mine to give – for it seems to me that, in this case, the law is showing very little common sense.'

She paused, her hands clasping themselves jerkily together, the great strain in her face sharpening every feature to a heart-rending clarity, her eyes a darker green than I remembered, her eyebrows a deep copper, a dusting of freckles across her resolute, patrician nose, a beading of sweat above her lip, the merest suggestion of tears blinked fiercely away whenever she felt them threaten. And she had not yet done.

'Yes, Nicky – I'll give it away, and let me tell you what it is I'm giving – since you see everything in terms of what it could fetch in the market-place. I don't understand such things, but I can tell you what my gift is worth to me. Every happy day of my life is in that house. My father and my grandfather are in the churchyard, and my brother, who was not a good man – but I loved him. To you it is a heap of stone. To me every stone has a voice. But it doesn't matter. Take it all, Nicky, and sell it, because if it has become an instrument of harm – a weapon – then I can't wish to keep it. My grandfather would not have kept it himself on those terms. My son, if he grows to be the man I am hoping for, would not wish to receive it from me at such a cost to others.'

He said, 'How noble. Perhaps you'd care to visit your tenants tomorrow and explain why they're to be dispossessed.' And I could have slapped him, hurt him.

'You can't turn them off – surely?'

'Some of them, yes, I can. The choice is yours.'

'Then do it, Nicky.'

Once again he turned away, allowing the silence to fall, Blaize and myself remaining on the edge of it, Georgiana standing with her hands neatly folded now, her head high, waiting with at least a surface calm for the next blow.

'What now, Nicky?'

'Just this. Don't stand in my way, Georgiana. You'll surely regret it.'

And this conventional threat surprised me, caused me to glance at him keenly, half afraid of seeing defeat in his face, although I wanted him to be defeated. But there was not even a spark of anger in him now, nothing so warm nor so weak as that, nor even any great coldness. Calculation, certainly, and shrewdness, a perfect readiness to manipulate his wife's finest feelings as if they had been figures on a balance sheet, not from greed or jealousy or any kind of passion, but for the sake of the manipulation itself. And for a moment Georgiana allowed him to look at her in silence, her body relaxing now beyond calm to a strange and moving serenity.

'I believe you are right,' she told him. 'I will regret it. But not for the reasons you suppose. I have been so afraid of you sometimes, Nicky, and now, quite suddenly, I can see no cause. What can you really do to me? The law allows you full control of my body and my spirit, we all know that – but I have already told you that the law, in these matters, is sadly lacking in sense. All I need to do is refuse – and go on refusing. And if that is a very alarming step to take, at least the first time – and it *is* very alarming – I would get used to it. Eventually I would be bound to prevail. The Abbey is the only real cord you had to bind me, and now it's gone I do believe I'm free. How very astonishing, but really, Nicky, what else can you take away from me?'

'I wonder,' he said smoothly, almost as if this unexpected resistance, this stretching of his ingenuity, was giving him enjoyment. 'Let's see. There are the children –'

But even this – which I anticipated with dread – did not dismay her.

'Yes, indeed. The children. In law you are their guardian and I am nothing – I realize that – just the brood mare that gave them birth. And who ever heard a brood mare complain of ill usage when one takes her foals away? Yes, Nicky, the law allows you to treat me in just that fashion, for I have made enquiries as to my exact rights, and have been correctly informed that I have no rights at all. But, for all that, I am not sure you can do it. My children are no longer babies who can be locked away in a nursery with a nanny to bar the door. You could keep me out of Tarn Edge, but you can hardly keep Gervase and Venetia in – not all the time. And your mother would not help you to do it in any case. If they love me and want to be with me, then they will come to me, whatever I have done, wherever I may be. It may not be in accordance with the law, but it accords well with reality. I am not afraid of it.'

'I take it you are thinking of leaving me, then?'

'Yes,' she said without hesitation, but without hurry, as if it was the most natural thing in the world. 'I have been thinking of leaving you for some time.'

And when I made a flustered movement of escape, a muttered plea that they must wish to be alone, Blaize silenced me with a gesture, while neither Nicholas nor Georgiana appeared to notice my interruption at all.

'It can hardly surprise you, Nicky.'

771

'It doesn't. I suppose you had planned to live at the Abbey.'

'Yes. I had planned to be discreet, as a woman should. I thought if I went over there for a month, three months, six months together, then there would be no gossip when it became a year – forever.'

'You could still do that, Georgiana.' But even before she shook her head I doubt if he expected to be taken seriously. For the Abbey, as a weapon, had lost its cutting edge. Whether in the end it would be relinquished or not, she had shown Nicholas that she could live without it, and I understood, with a mixture of respect and sorrow, a touch of grudging amusement, that he had put it out of his mind. The Abbey had been a possibility. It was so no longer. And his acute, deliberately narrowed brain would soon be leaping forward – if it had not already begun – to explore other possibilities, some other way of settling his –differences with Blaize. I had been reluctant to witness his defeat. He was not defeated. He had simply put the matter into abeyance.

'No, Nicky. I wouldn't like to do that now.'

'What would you like, then?'

And, lowering her eyes, she said, almost in a whisper, overcome even in her new-found strength, by the enormity of the request she was making. 'I think – in fact – is it possible for us to be divorced? There have been some new laws, have there not?'

'Yes.'

'Then what must I do?'

'Please – not here,' I said in anguish, for divorce, although possible now in law, and in London, was unknown in Cullingford, was as shameful, as unforgivable, as great a casting-out as it had ever been, and I didn't want that for her. But, turning to me, half smiling, she said, 'Oh Faith, I am so sorry, but please don't stop me now, for if you do I may never find my voice again. And it must be said. I can't live with you again, Nicky, and it is for your sake as much as mine. We have not been good for each other. No – *that* we have not. To begin with, I was foolish and inexperienced and easily hurt, and you were never altogether sure you loved me. Sometimes it was to distraction – although that was long ago – sometimes hardly at all, even from the start. You confused me, Nicky, and by the time I gained some understanding of the things you needed in a woman I rather imagine you had discovered them elsewhere – and I was very lonely. I was not self-sufficient, you see, when we married. I had never needed to be. I had grown up among people who loved me and who told me so. We lived *together*, not separately each one in his private egg-shell. And silence terrifies me. Sometimes I had to get to Galton just to convince myself that I wasn't dying. I could feel the blood turning sluggish in my veins and I had to keep it flowing. Well, I am a little more in command of myself now, and a good deal older. I have learned, really, that what I must do is the best I can, and our remaining together would not be for the best. It would not be honest. We have damaged each other enough. And I think we have failed each other enough. I have seen your father, sometimes, as hard as you. But what he

772

felt for your mother always came through it. I have never been able to do that for you, Nicky. And you have never learned to accept me as I am. You have wanted me to be myself and different from myself all together, and it has been too much to ask. I have soured you and you have stifled me. And why should we continue to spread the misery of it through our lives, and our children's lives, so that the Cullingford tea-tables might not be shocked? I suppose they will call me a whore when I leave you, but I shall not feel like one, and you will know I am not. Will it be very difficult?'

For a moment I thought he couldn't answer, but then he spoke gruffly, gratingly almost, as if the words had been forced through some blockage in his throat.

'To leave me? No – no difficulty except that you have no money and I would not be obliged to support you. Divorce? Relatively simple nowadays – if you are ready to support me with proof of your adultery.'

'I have not committed adultery, Nicky.'

'No. I never thought you had. But if you wish to obtain a divorce there is no other way.'

'You could not –'

'No. Adultery on the part of a husband is not a ground for divorce unless it is accompanied by other offences of which I am not – and couldn't be – guilty. I'm sorry. I don't make the law. In this instance I simply benefit from it. I would have to track you down like a criminal – which is how the world would see you and treat you. I would have to catch you with your lover, like a thief caught with his loot. And then I would have to take action against you. If I succeeded, then it could only be because the charge of adultery had been proved, which would allow the Cullingford ladies to call you whatever names they liked. I am not squeamish, Georgiana, but I wouldn't enjoy doing that to you. And even then you would not save the Abbey. Should our marriage be dissolved, you could take nothing away with you. Your Abbey, your children, the few hundred pounds your grandfather left you, would still legally belong to me – unless I chose to be generous.'

'And would you?'

'I don't know.'

'We'll talk about it, shall we?'

And when he quite clearly had no answer, she made it for him, 'Yes, I believe we will. My goodness, how strangely our prayers are sometimes answered. What I hoped for – even a day ago – was that we could somehow begin to talk to each other. And now – Ah well, I am no schoolroom goose. I won't live with you again, Nicky. Oh no – I haven't altogether displeased you tonight, have I? I may have spoiled your scheme, but you don't really mind that. You'll soon concoct another. And I've been bold, at least, and interesting. I've struck back at you, which you can't quite help liking. I know. And I know it wouldn't last. There'd be silence again very soon, and it's far better for us to live apart and learn to talk. Oh dear – I think – yes, really, Nicky – I would like to go back to Tarn Edge now. Faith, if I may use your mirror a moment?'

And as I made a move towards her I had no need of Blaize's restraining glance to tell me she needed to be alone.

34

I didn't believe that anything more could be said; certainly I could not have spoken. But after a moment Blaize got to his feet and, looking at Nicholas, nodded and smiled wryly, almost wonderingly, his face plainly showing the stress of the day.

'It occurs to me that the lady may have won herself an Abbey all on her own,' he said.

'It could well be – or not. Who knows?' and picking up the long brown envelope Nicholas looked at it for a moment and then tore it neatly into two even pieces.

'All right, Blaize. So much for that. I don't see the point in suggesting we could work together again. Do you still want that split?'

'I'm not sure I want it, but I'll take it. I think it's the best we can do.'

'We'll see Agbrigg in the morning and get the figures right. And then you can set yourself up as a manufacturing man. I'm not usually free with advice, but I'll tell you this much – you'll need somebody reliable to look after your sheds.'

'Yes, I know. Are you starting to worry about me, Nick? I thought I might take Freddy Hobhouse off your hands. He's reliable enough, and he might feel easier about taking my money than yours.'

'He might at that. I wouldn't stand in his way – since I don't need him. And, if you should happen to sell the sheds back to me in a year or two, it would help to know they'd been properly managed.'

Blaize smiled, nodded again, a swordsman, I thought, accepting a challenge.

'I'll have a word with him, then. Who knows – it might even boost his confidence so high that he'd marry my wife's sister and make himself a rich man again – rich enough to buy his own sheds back, I reckon. And Nick – since we're exchanging advice – don't rely too much on Dan Adair. He's good, but he's not young, and it's hard out there on the road – harder than it used to be.'

'I know. I've got a lad or two coming up. I wouldn't waste your time worrying about me, Blaize. There's no reason for it.'

'No reason at all. I notice you can't say the same for me.'

And this time it was Nicholas who smiled. 'I reckon not – but we'll see how it goes. And if it goes downhill, Blaize, then I expect you'll have the sense to pull out before it's gone too far. Because even for Tarn Edge I'm not the man to throw good money after bad.'

'That's what you're hoping for, is it, Nick? That I'll pull out at the first slump in trade or that I'll get bored?'

'No. I don't deal much in hope. It's what I'm expecting.'

'I'll see you in Croppers Court then, first thing tomorrow – if Agbrigg's wife allows him to practise law so early in the day.'

'Aye. And after that we'll meet in the Piece Hall – if you can remember where to find it.'

Georgiana came back, not entering the room, but hovering in the hall, wanting urgently to be gone, an air about her of a woman who has been very ill, resolute in spirit but still bodily frail.

'Is the carriage coming, Blaize? I need a breath of air.'

And, as they went outside to await the arrival of Nicholas's horse and the ancient sporting curricle which had been Perry Clevedon's, I stood at the window and looked out at them, no longer shivering with that inner cold, but far distant, yet, from any certainty of warmth and ease.

I saw Georgiana lean down a moment as she drew on her driving gloves to say a word to Blaize and then drive off, steadily, skilfully, her destination apparently clear. I didn't know if she would succeed, or could succeed. I was proud of her. I loved her.

I saw Nicholas lift himself briskly into his saddle, a powerful silhouette in the twilight, quite certain of his own success, as I was certain of it too. And, as I watched him ride away I knew, with the relief one feels at the ending of physical pain, that he had no need of my anxiety, my remorse; no need, in fact, of me at all. I had seen him change and had believed myself responsible for it. I realized now that he had not changed, but simply progressed quite normally to the man his nature and his ancestry had always intended him to be.

Had Georgiana never come his way, had he married me instead, I would not have contented him. He would still have required Nethercoats from the Hobhouses, Tarn Edge from Blaize, anything and everything that challenged his ingenuity, any woman, perhaps, who – like the widowed Faith Ashburn – had said 'we must not'. And although, had I understood all this a dozen years ago, I would still have married him, I had not done so. I had taken other directions, opened other doors, so that now I could look back at him, from their various thresholds, and understand that neither of us had been to blame.

I had sat, long ago, by my fireside and told my sister, 'I am a woman who loves Nicholas Barforth. That is all there is to me.'

That woman had meant what she said. For her it had been true. But that woman very gradually had become a chrysalis for someone else, who for a long time had been painfully, sometimes eagerly, emerging. It was no longer in me to love with that overwhelming, self-destructive intensity. I was no longer capable of submerging myself in another person, nor did I wish to do so. I had indeed loved Nicholas Barforth, but there was far more to me now than that. What I wanted now was to love, with clear eyes, a man who saw me clearly, who would allow me air to breathe and space to grow, who would not need to prove his manhood by reducing me to a state of slavish adoration or childlike dependence, a man, in fact, who was strong enough and sure enough to value me as a woman. And there was only one man who had ever offered me the enormous gift of freedom.

'Faith,' Blaize said, somewhere in the room behind me, my first

775

awareness of him being the warm odour of his cigar, the fresh citrus of the toilet-water he wore.

'Yes.'

'I was sharp with you earlier. I'm sorry.'

And for a few moments we talked around ourselves, of other people, other aspirations, approaching each other slowly, and with care.

'Will Freddy Hobhouse come to you, Blaize?'

'Oh yes – not that Nick will worry about that, since, whatever Freddy can do, he can do it better. He'd be hard pressed, perhaps, if I took Dan Adair.'

'But you won't?'

'I can't. I've asked him already and he'll use me, I imagine, to push up his value with Nick. But he has the sense to stay where he's needed – which is hardly with me. Even Freddy knows that much, or if he doesn't then Prudence will soon explain. If she marries him she'll learn how to drop me a hint occasionally that he's thinking of starting up on his own with her capital – knowing I'll be inclined to change his mind with pound notes.'

'Prudence wouldn't –' I began and then, meeting his quizzical eyes, 'Yes – so she would.' And, although he was smiling at me, the time had gone when I could have leaned towards him, surrendering into laughter. It would not suffice.

'And Georgiana?'

'Yes?' he said, cautious now and very intent; and, sensing the change in him, remembering acutely the comforting arch of his arm around her, I shivered, feeling a sharp stab of pain, a swift upsurging of hope – of excitement almost – when I saw he understood the reason why. And I knew I could say anything to him. Here was the man who knew me best, the friend, the lover, who expected me to be neither better nor worse, nor anything other than myself. Here was the man who required to maintain his own individuality, but would allow me to keep mine, and I was at ease with him, warm with him, stimulated by him; I was adult with him.

'What shall I tell you about Georgiana, Faith?' And I knew he would tell me anything I asked, even if it hurt me, since I was no household angel to be protected and petted, but a woman capable of judging the amount of hurt she could withstand.

'She was the rare and special person you used to talk about, wasn't she? The one who was always in the next room. You said you'd stopped looking, but, of course, since it was Georgiana all the time – It was Georgiana, wasn't it?'

'Yes,' he said, quite gently, not out of kindness for me, but because it was a gentle matter. 'So it was. And you must see that she remained rare and special precisely because I left her in that other room.'

'Yes – but then, would you have parted with your half of the mills for *me*?'

'I can't believe,' he said, looking at me very steadily, 'that you would ever have placed me in the position of having to do so.'

776

'No, I suppose not, which would be a compliment –'

'It is a compliment.'

'I daresay – except that it makes me sound so very boring.'

And once again we were close to that easy, pleasant laughter, that companionable surrender, until he took my hand, pressed it and said, quite ardently for him, 'I have never – absolutely never – found you boring.'

'Then tell me –'

'Yes. Faith, I was twenty-three or thereabouts when I first met Georgiana, and it was too soon for me. If I'd been ten years older, perhaps, but I really don't think so. I wanted her as she was that first Christmas – do you remember? – with mud on her skirt and blood on her cheek, trampling her dirty boots on my father's carpet, because to a frank, free spirit like hers what could carpets matter? There was a skylark inside her sometimes, and I didn't want to see it crushed and caged. Nicky tried to do that, as perhaps any man would have done who really loved her – since what man could feel safe with a skylark. It escaped today and took flight. I'm glad – very glad for her, and for myself too, because it was a lovely thing to watch.'

'And will it last?'

'Possibly not. She's not Prudence, who can stand alone. She may come to earth and find herself tied to Julian Flood, for I believe he loves her – certainly he needs her – and if she goes off with him to provide grounds for her divorce he'll be unwilling to release her. He'll marry her if he can, which will make her our lady of the manor – I doubt if Nick will put any obstacles in her way. He'd rather see her settled, I imagine, with Julian Flood, than wandering alone a prey to any man. But on the other hand she may fly very high and very far. I wouldn't wish to follow her. I find myself somewhat firmly attached to the ground and – all that apart – I have lived with you now, Faith, for a long and valuable time. I couldn't welcome anything which might spoil that.'

'Why?'

'My word!' he said, but whatever easy, witty remark had risen to the surface of his mind was immediately suppressed as he saw the necessity for my question. Why indeed? And it must be stated, not masked by humour, but very clearly. The old limits we had set ourselves, which had long been crumbling, were now almost broken down, the old restraints abandoned. We were almost at liberty, had almost disentangled ourselves from the past. And there was no doubt it was a big step we were taking.

He got up and crossed, characteristically, to the fireplace, leaning one arm along the mantelpiece, looking reflectively, ruefully, at the arrangement of tulle roses I had placed in the empty hearth.

'I think I can tell you why. But I would like you to tell me something first. When you heard about the plan to sell the Abbey, why didn't you come to me?'

And, although it would not be easy, it was certainly fair; for, if I had needed to know about Georgiana, I could not refuse to talk to him of Nicholas.

777

'I think – really – it was because I knew he wanted me to tell you. And I concluded, in that case, that it would do you no good to know.'

'You didn't trust him, in fact?'

'No.' It had to be the truth, or else he would know it; and indeed it was the truth. 'No, Blaize. Perhaps I never have trusted him. I thought otherwise, but now it seems to me that I never really did. I don't mean it unkindly. I think I mean, not that I didn't trust *him*, but that I never trusted his judgment. There is a difference.'

'Yes, indeed. You mean that his judgment would always be heavily weighted to his own advantage?'

'I suppose I do.'

He looked down at the flowers a moment longer and then, raising his head, gave me his brilliant, quizzical smile. 'Faith, I must warn you that my own judgment is invariably weighted in the same direction.'

'I know that. Perhaps I feel that your advantage is bound to be mine.'

'Thank you,' he said and, coming to sit on the sofa beside me, took my hand. 'I'll answer your question now. You asked me why I didn't want to spoil our life together. I should be able to make you a lengthy and beautiful reply. I can't. I find, in this one instance, that my salesmanship deserts me. I had occasion to wonder, some time ago, how I would feel if you left me. I found myself unable to contemplate it. I have never been able to contemplate it.'

'Blaize – I have never thought of leaving you.'

'Of course not. I realized that, which indicates – surely –? Now what does it indicate? That I suspected your reasons for remaining beside me were not so strong as I would like? That I wanted to make them stronger? Good heavens! must I make a declaration? You know perfectly well what I mean – perfectly well – but if it pleases you to see me stumble –'

But he was very far from stumbling, was treading as surely as he had ever done and, squeezing my hand once again, he got up and crossed to the window, making a great and totally false display of impatience.

'Dammit, Faith. I have had a very difficult day, you know. I hardly slept a wink in the train last night. I am greeted this morning by my sister-in-law swooning in my arms, and, when I pick her up, my wife can do nothing but glare at me, claws out, like an angry cat. I am then obliged to dash off on a wild goose chase into town in search of my brother, who was in none of the places he should have been, and then home again to find my wife in no mood to care that I had a raging headache and had missed both my luncheon and my tea. Tomorrow morning I have to get up early to go and sign my freedom away, and I have just had the devil of a job to persuade my wife that it is her duty – and ought to be her pleasure – to honour and obey me, and should she care to cherish me as well I'd hardly complain – and would be well-pleased, exceedingly well pleased, to cherish her in return.'

I crossed the room to him, my throat tight with tears, and put an arm around his shoulder, one hand under his chin to turn his subtle, mischievous face into the light.

'Blaize – such a declaration –'

'Indeed – such as I have never made before, and sincerely meant.'

And then, as his weight seemed greater than I had expected: 'Darling – you really are tired, aren't you?'

'I really am. My head really does ache. On such basic issues you have no reason to doubt me. I think it is high time you sent me to bed.'

He went upstairs while I, lingering a moment in the hall, gave instructions for his early breakfast, named the hour he would require to see his carriage waiting on the drive, and then walked slowly, one step at a time, delighting in my body's every movement as it took me, not in the direction which had been chosen for me, or which I had accepted as a compromise, but in which I truly desired to go.

I reached the landing, turned down the hushed, deep-carpeted corridor, remembering my past desires without regret, with the affectionate amusement that can only arise from self-knowledge. I had wanted to be adored, and Blaize would not adore me, since adoration is given to idols, the passive objects of men's imaginings. And a man cannot share his warm, imperfect humanity with an idol. I had wanted to be needed, but Blaize, self-contained and elusive as he was, would never need me as Giles and perhaps even Nicholas had once done, refusing to weaken either of us by dependence. I had wanted a rock to lean on, but he had paid me the compliment of allowing me to stand alone; and, when circumstances required it, we would lean on one another. I had wanted to trust him: I did trust him. I had wanted a homecoming: I stood already at the door.

He was waiting in a room that was darker than usual, a single lamp, well-shaded, on my toilet table, showing me a mere outline of his head and shoulders, very little of his face.

'I thought,' he said, 'that – perhaps – you might have something to tell me.'

'Yes. I love you Blaize.'

And although he smiled – wishing to make a show of lightness, of accepting it merely as homage due – I couldn't miss the tremor in his face, the flicker of relief as his arms came around me, holding me with all the warm assurance I had required, and then passing through trust and cherishing to an intensity I had never shared with him, no familiar ease now but an emotion new-born, uncertain as yet but ready to grow.

'Thank God,' he said, the words whispered so lightly against my ear that I could have missed them, although I seized them and held them fast, knowing he could not sustain himself much longer at this high key.

'How very pleasant,' he said, 'to be so consistently in the right.'

'Yes, darling?'

'Well – you can do no more than agree. I have been saying all my life, have I not, that sooner or later the Barforth one prefers is bound to be me? And if you have taken a great deal of convincing, then at least –?'

'You have convinced me now.'

And it was all I had ever needed to say.

The Sleeping Sword

To Marjory

who was with me every step of the way

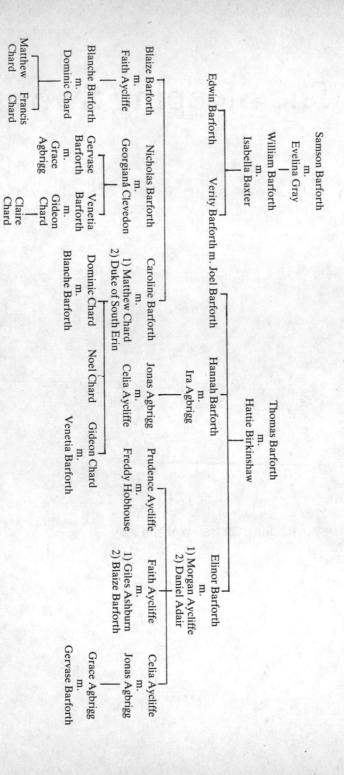

Samson Barforth
m.
Evelina Gray

William Barforth
m.
Isabella Baxter

Thomas Barforth
m.
Hattie Birkinshaw

Edwin Barforth   Verity Barforth m. Joel Barforth   Hannah Barforth   Elinor Barforth
                                                      m.   m.
                                                      Ira Agbrigg   1) Morgan Aycliffe
                                                                         2) Daniel Adair

Blaize Barforth   Nicholas Barforth   Caroline Barforth   Jonas Agbrigg   Prudence Aycliffe   Faith Aycliffe   Celia Aycliffe
m.   m.   m.   m.   m.   m.
Faith Aycliffe   Georgiana Clevedon   1) Matthew Chard   Celia Aycliffe   Freddy Hobhouse   1) Giles Ashburn Jonas Agbrigg
                                         2) Duke of South Erin   2) Blaize Barforth

Blanche Barforth   Gervase   Venetia   Dominic Chard   Noel Chard   Gideon Chard   Grace Agbrigg   Gervase Barforth
m.   Barforth   Barforth   m.   m.   m.
Dominic Chard   m.   m.   Blanche Barforth   Venetia Barforth   Gervase Barforth
                   Grace   Gideon
                   Agbrigg   Chard

Matthew   Francis   Claire
Chard   Chard   Chard

1

It would have been easier, perhaps, had my father's wife been a truly wicked woman, in which case I could have detested her with a whole heart and a clear conscience. But her villainy was of a mild enough variety, the result, mainly, of her desire to be my father's wife rather than the mother of his child. And, in all fairness, it must be said that I made no great effort to be lovable.

Her name, when first we knew her, was Mrs Tessa Delaney and she was a handsome woman of large proportions, very smooth and wise and persuasive; not virtuous, of course, in any conventional sense since she had first taken up residence in our thriving factory city under the protection of one of its most distinguished aldermen, the elderly, childless and reputedly self-indulgent worsted-spinner, Mr Matthew Oldroyd of Fieldhead Mills. Yet their affair had been so discreetly conducted that even the Oldroyd relatives came to regard it on the whole as a good thing, the keeping of so sensible a mistress being preferable in their eyes and working out much cheaper than the greedy sixteen year olds to which his aging fancy had hitherto been prone.

Indeed, the Oldroyd nephews and nieces who certainly expected to inherit his money would have been much inclined to offer Mrs Delaney some material token of their gratitude at the end – allowed her to keep his watch or even the lease of the house he had taken for her – had not his last will and testament revealed that for the twelve secretive and shameful months before he died she had been no mistress at all but Mr Matthew Oldroyd's second and decidedly legal wife.

Clandestine marriages, need it be said, did not suit the taste of our plain-spoken, strait-laced town of Cullingford in the County of Yorkshire, and there had been immediate talk of breaking the Oldroyd will. And even when the Oldroyd lawyer, my father Mr Jonas Agbrigg, declared himself unable to place any legal obstacle in the lady's way when she proceeded to move into the mill-house at Fieldhead, it was felt that she would not reign there long. After all, she had cheated the Oldroyd nephews – Cullingford men every one – out of their rightful inheritance and if the Law as represented by Mr Jonas Agbrigg could not touch her then surely a Greater Law might be relied on to prevail? Surely – and Cullingford men were deeply moved by this – Fate could not allow any female so rapacious, so cunning, to actually *enjoy* her ill-gotten gains?

But the proud, easy carriage, the clear skin and excellent white teeth we had seen in Mrs Delaney continued to flourish in the new Mrs Oldroyd to such a degree that my father, who had won a reputation for shrewdness rather than kindness of heart – although he was always kindness itself to me – married her as soon as he was able, thus making himself absolute master of her fortune and creating a scandal of a magnitude rarely seen in the cautious, conventional Law Valley.

No-one thought any the worse of a man who married for money, since most men did so, and a widower with an eleven year old daughter to raise and whose ambitions had always been larger than his pocket, could not afford to be too romantic when it came to matrimony. But my father's hasty union with Mrs Delaney marked him not merely as a fortune-hunter but as a conspirator. And Cullingford had a thing or two to say about that.

He had been Matthew Oldroyd's lawyer, after all, and Cullingford well remembered how completely Mr Oldroyd had trusted him. He had certainly been aware of the secret ceremony which had transformed Mr Oldroyd from Mrs Delaney's lover, who might have left her a few hundred a year, to a doting husband who had bequeathed her everything. Even more certainly he had been aware of Mr Oldroyd's new will, signed in my father's office on that furtive wedding morning, when the decaying bridegroom had virtually disinherited every one of his relations, his first wife's family it was true, not his own blood kin, but decent Yorkshire folk just the same who had deserved better of him than that. And afterwards my father had moved quietly through Cullingford's dining-rooms and drawing-rooms, a close-mouthed man accustomed to secrets, listening as the Oldroyd nephews hinted at their plans for Fieldhead Mills, for the railway shares and brewery shares, the coal deposits and bank deposits of which Mr Oldroyd had been so amply possessed.

He had listened without comment, without encouragement, but when the awful truth burst upon them the mere fact that he had listened at all was enough to condemn him. He was marrying the whore Delaney not for her money but for *theirs*; for the fortune which he, with his lawyer's cunning, had helped her to steal from a bemused and senile man. They had conspired together – *of course* they had – Mr Jonas Agbrigg and Mrs Tessa Delaney, the cool fastidious man of law, the mature and sensible Jezebel, and Cullingford did not intend to countenance treachery such as that. No Cullingford woman of any standing would ever receive the new Mrs Agbrigg, at least so they said and probably believed, while Cullingford men would be interested to see what use the Cambridge educated Jonas Agbrigg might make of his Latin and his Greek in the spinning-sheds at Fieldhead.

My father's own mother, my outspoken and unbending Grandmother Agbrigg and my grandfather, who had several times been mayor of Cullingford, would not attend the wedding and retired soon afterwards to Scarborough unable to tolerate their son's disgrace. My mother's mother, my dainty and sentimental Grandmamma Elinor, could not bring herself to attend either and she too, with a rapidity I could not help associating with these painful nuptials, soon lost her taste for Cullingford, exchanging her house in imposing but narrow-minded Blenheim Lane for a villa in the South of France. Only my mother's sister, Aunt Faith, was present in the Parish Church on my father's wedding day among the Fieldhead managers and their wives – proving they knew on which side their bread was buttered – and a handful of others, Mr Septimus Rawnsley of the Cullingford Commercial Bank, Mr Outhwaite, a local architect who could not afford to ignore the rumours of repairs and extensions at Fieldhead; a few ecclesiastical gentlemen who believed in the forgiveness of sinners, a few commercial gentlemen for whom the only real sin was poverty and who could detect no trace of it in the regal bearing of my father's bride. While I, banished to the seaside for the duration of the honeymoon, felt my solid, reliable world turn suddenly to an uncertain angle and then start to slip away – as my grandparents, my home, my father's good name, our shared and precious affection had slipped away – between my hands.

My memories of my mother at that time were recent and uneasy for she had died only a year before my father's second marriage and it was a matter of great concern to me that I did not really miss her. She had been an invalid since my birth, tense and timid and often very low in spirits, the tumult of her nerves demanding drawn curtains, hushed voices, a great walking-on-tiptoe on my part through her sufferings which oppressed me, sometimes annoyed me and then instantly filled me with guilt. And I knew two things about her relationship with my father; that he was not happy with her and that he had been lucky to get her.

My father was the academically brilliant son of a man who had risen from great poverty to become a mill-manager, a rise quite astonishing in itself although never quite enough to satisfy the social ambitions of Grandmother Agbrigg who had decided very early to make at least a cabinet minister out of her son. And since a mill-manager can earn so much and no more and political careers are notoriously expensive, it had been essential for my father to marry well, his choice falling on my mother – Miss Celia Aycliffe – I suspect because she had been very young, exceedingly innocent, and so crammed full of romantic notions that she had been ready to fall in love with the first person who asked.

She had brought him a substantial dowry for her father had been a master-builder, responsible for the erection of most of Cullingford and its environs, and he had left his widow – my pert little Grandmamma Elinor – and his daughters very well provided. But the dowry had been sufficient only for the purchase of a suitable house and a partnership with a local solicitor, my mother's interests had all been domestic, her disposition retiring – not at all the stuff that cabinet ministers' wives are made of – and they had not been content together.

Perhaps he felt she had given him less than he deserved. No doubt, in her view, he had received more than any man in his position could reasonably expect, for, money apart, she had brought him family connections worth their weight in gold. Her own family, the Aycliffes, were themselves people of enormous local consequence. Their cousins, the Barforths, were the most powerful industrialists the Law Valley had ever known, the Barforth brothers, Nicholas and Blaize – who had married Aunt Faith, my mother's sister – appearing to own outright or to have a controlling interest in everything of value in Cullingford. While the Barforth sister, my Aunt Caroline, being unable to compete on the battleground of commerce on account of her sex, had chosen to devote her quite formidable energies to the pursuit of social advancement, becoming Lady Chard of Listonby Park, thus widening our horizons by allying us to the landed gentry.

With connections such as these my mother was at a loss to know what else she could offer her husband. She concluded it should be a son, miscarried eight times to produce a daughter and devoted herself thereafter to the supervision of her servants – by no means so numerous as those of her sister, Aunt Faith – fretting over specks of dust, smears on silver, stains on linen, wearing out her nerves and my father's patience until the day she died. And exactly one year later her well-dusted, well-polished house was sold to strangers, the daughter whose birth had cost her her health believed herself to be unwanted and lonely, while her husband was a poor relation of the mighty Barforths no longer but the master of Fieldhead.

Fieldhead mill-house was a square, sombre pile built at the start of the Oldroyd fortunes, large, high-ceilinged rooms, functional and plain, a vast, stone-flagged kitchen equipped with a strict eye to efficiency, no eye at all to comfort, not even a rocking chair by the hearth on the day I was invited to inspect this new setting for my life. 'A very handsome house' the Law Valley called it yet the only concession I could see to beauty was the profusion of polished wood, each room oak-panelled, fragrant with beeswax and the winter hyacinths set out everywhere in copper bowls, a combination of odours which even now returns me to the afternoon I first stood there, tall for a girl of not quite twelve, long legs, thin shoulders that were too wide, dark brown hair Aunt Faith had brushed and plaited for the approval of my father's wife, although for my part I could not see the necessity for that approval, feeling, I believe, that she should have been anxious to gain mine. And had I been old enough to cope with the hostility she at once aroused in me – for he was my father, *mine*, and not even my mother had expected him to love her better than me – perhaps I would have admired her.

They had called her the whore Delaney and now – Aunt Faith had explained to me – in order to be considered respectable at all she would have to be very respectable indeed. Her housekeeping, if it was barely to satisfy her ill-wishers, would have to be superb, her manners altogether beyond anyone's reproach. She had far more important things to do, in fact, than cater to the whims of a green and awkward girl, having made up her mind to take the entire fortress of polite Cullingford society by storm. And when she received me that first time in the Fieldhead drawing-room she had not only the air of a woman born to these surroundings but of one at whose christening all the virtues – honesty, chastity, industry and the rest – had attended. She wore a dark silk dress, jet beads, narrow gold chains, her black hair smoothly parted at the centre and drawn down in two modest wings to frame a countenance of placid dignity. She walked erect and very slow, sat straight-backed, her large brown hands quietly folded. She spoke words of authority, her voice low, gentle, inescapable. She had presence and power and she was very handsome. I detested her and for the five years that remained to me

786

before childhood officially ended and my upswept hair and long skirts proclaimed me a young lady my life was marred constantly and foolishly by our mutual resentment, the thoughtless cruelty of my youth, the anxious cruelty of her middle-age, which caused us to struggle for the same not always happy man.

At no time did it occur to me that he might be fond of her. He had married her for money, *only* for money, I insisted upon that, and although privately I did not think it worthy of him I justified it all on the grounds of his frustrated brilliance, the long bitterness I knew he had felt on seeing other men succeed – the Barforth men, for instance – not because they surpassed him in intelligence or energy – who, I wondered, could surpass him in that? – but because they had been born to fathers who could pay. And although my faith in him had wavered I soon learned to be proud of him again. He had come late to the spinning trade, a soft-skinned lawyer in middle life, and the thoroughness with which he mastered each technical process, the determination which took him to the mill-yard at the grim morning hour of five o'clock and kept him there, often enough, until midnight won him not only my regard but the grudging respect of many who had firmly intended to despise him. Cullingford might never again consider him a good man. He was beyond question a fortune-hunter. He may even have tipped Mr Oldroyd's scales a little in the direction of matrimony and that scandalous will. But, very soon, he was *making a profit* and after a year or two it became the considered opinion of the Piece Hall and the Wool Exchange that much could be forgiven a man who did that.

The new Mrs Agbrigg, who had been the new Mrs Oldroyd, who had been the whore Delaney, had won her battle and all might have been peace and countentment at Fieldhead had I not been there to question her slightest command, to pick disdainful holes in her explanations, to neglect no opportunity of letting her know that the bond between father and daughter – or at least between *this* father and daughter – was of a far higher order than anything that might exist between a man and his second wife.

'You see it all through such young eyes,' Aunt Faith murmured once or twice, attempting – as my mother's sister and therefore my closest female relation – to console and advise me. But youth is not compassionate and at fourteen, fifteen, even at sixteen when I found my eyes on a level with hers, I could see nothing in the new Mrs Agbrigg to arouse my pity. She had wanted wealth and security. They were hers. She had desired, from the colourful remains of Tessa Delaney, to create a new woman of intense, heavy-textured respectability. She had achieved that too. Yet this same woman who assembled her servants each morning for prayers, who served tea and charity to this clergyman and that each tedious afternoon, had also retained a weapon I had not yet learned to call sensuality. Her sombre dignity, her suave piety stifled me, but the sight of her hand on my father's arm at dinner time, the voluptuous curve of neck and shoulder she offered him through the lamplight aroused in me a prickly sensation I recognized as shame.

'Jonas darling, it is late,' and to avoid the hush that fell around them whenever she spoke those simple words I became an almost professional guest in other people's houses, lingering with Aunt Faith and her daughter Blanche from Christmas to Easter, spending easy, if well-chaperoned summers at the sea with my other Barforth cousin, Venetia. A guest, a close friend, not quite a member of any family not even my own, so that growing sharp-eyed, self-contained, careful of how and where I might tread, it was no hardship to me to go abroad to Italy and Switzerland, to acquire the accomplishment thought appropriate to the heiress – no less – of Fieldhead.

I was as tall as my father when he came to Lucerne to fetch me home, my hair piled high and swept back in a cascade of curls, my skirts most fashionably tight in front, most fashionably and intricately draped behind over a bustle I had learned to manage with style, having acquired by studious practice the art of kicking my train aside in order to turn smartly around, the equally precise art of sitting down. And as I demonstrated my knowledge of Italian and French and German Swiss, of painting and sculpture and as much philosophy as they had thought safe for a young lady – my flair for mathematics being considered quite unladylike – I found him far less exacting, an easier or perhaps just an older man than I remembered. I had gained not only an understanding of art and science but of humanity – or so I imagined – and now that my father was no longer the centre of my universe, now that I was the polished Miss Grace Agbrigg whose experiences had ranged far beyond the confines of Cullingford, I believed I could be at peace with him.

'You see it all through such young eyes,' Aunt Faith had said, but my eyes were kinder now – I thought, I hoped – while my tongue might even school itself, in the interests of domestic harmony, to call my father's wife 'mamma'.

She was on the carriage drive to greet us, smooth, impassive, her gown of chocolate coloured silk drawn into a modest bustle, nothing but a fall of lace at neck and hem to relieve its housekeeper's plainness. But the fabric itself was very rich, the cross at her throat was of massive gold, there were rings of great value on her patiently folded, housekeeper's hands, her voice speaking its soft welcome, her eyes going beyond me to my father, wryly conveying to him, 'So she's home again. Ah well – we must make the best of it, you and I.' And everything was the same, exactly as it had always been and as I had known it would be.

There were great things astir in Cullingford. My cousin Blanche was to be richly married, which was the destiny Blanche Barforth had always envisaged. My other Barforth cousin, Venetia, was believed not for the first time to have involved herself with an unsuitable man. While as to myself, for all my new found philosophy and compassion, it was very clear to me from the hour of my return that the only way I could ever restore harmony to my father's house was by leaving it.

2

My cousin, Blanche Barforth, was married on a sparkling summer morning, her veil of gauze embroideries mistily revealing the silver and ivory tints of her hair and skin, her long, quiet hands clasping their bouquet of apricot carnations and white roses. She looked fragile and mysterious, passive as a lily, the prize men seek for their valour and expect for their cunning. A most perfect bride.

She was not, of course, in love nor did she wish to be. She was merely following to its logical conclusion her personal and undeniably excellent strategy of doing the right thing at the right time and doing it magnificently. In the manner of Queen Victoria and Prince Albert she was marrying her first cousin and in true imperial fashion appeared to believe that her own role in the proceedings was simply to be looked at.

For the past six months she had been 'the fiancée' offering herself up tranquilly to the world's admiration and envy while her harassed mother and her Aunt Caroline, who was soon to be her mother-in-law, arranged her wedding around her. Today she was 'the bride', offering herself once again with that air of cool serenity to a bridegroom who, by the untimely death of his father on the hunting field, had recently been transformed from a supercilious and, in my view, not entirely good-tempered young man into an extremely eligible if no better-humoured Sir Dominic Chard of Listonby.

Without his lands and titles it would not have occurred to Blanche to marry him. Had she been obtainable to him in any other way he would not have married her, since a gentleman of only twenty-four summers with health and wealth and boundless opportunity on his side rarely feels the need to limit himself in matrimony so soon. But pale, silvery Blanche *had* her loveliness and her calm, infinitely challenging purity. Dominic *had* his baronetcy, his three thousand ancestral acres, his beautiful, quite famous ancestral mansion. There was no more to be said.

'I am to be married,' Blanche had written to me in Switzerland. 'I am to be Lady Chard of Listonby, just like Aunt Caroline – except, of course, that I am taking her title from her. You are to come home and be my bridesmaid.' And so, feeling the moment opportune, I returned to Cullingford to divide my time, as I had so often done, between my Barforth cousins, Blanche who was to be splendidly married and Venetia who would quite like to be married but would much rather fall intensely, no matter how unwisely, in love.

I had, of course, envied Blanche from time to time as most people did, not only for her looks, her composure and her placid, sometimes comic, belief that she could always get her way, but for the possession of so affectionate a mother as Aunt Faith, so generous a father as Uncle Blaize who was not, perhaps, the richer of the two Barforth brothers but certainly the more agreeable.

'That child is the image of her mother,' they had been saying in

Cullingford ever since the days when a fragile fairy-tale Blanche had first taken her daily airings in the Barforth landau, her gown a miniature copy of Aunt Faith's, each silver ringlet bound up with silver ribbon, exhibiting even then a certain cool graciousness far beyond her years which came, perhaps, from an inbred knowledge that her abundant pale silk hair and startling blue-green eyes would be quite enough to open any door *she* might be likely to choose in life.

And what she chose at the tender age of seventeen was to be Lady Chard of Listonby Park, a decision which had disappointed her mother who believed ardently in love and was saddened to see that her only daughter did not, and which had infuriated the existing, dowager Lady Chard – Aunt Caroline – who, having been the absolute ruler of Listonby Park for the past twenty-five years did not feel at all inclined to abdicate her authority, her keys, her place at the head of the baronial table to lovely, lazy, self-indulgent Blanche.

So strongly, in fact, did Aunt Caroline Chard feel that, at the merest hint of an engagement she had despatched her son Dominic to London, hoping at worst that he would find distraction, at best the earl's or the cabinet minister's daughter she believed *his* breeding and *her* ambition deserved. For although Lady Caroline Chard had once, long ago, been Miss Caroline Barforth, a mill-master's daughter just like Blanche, she had shed that commercial identity and very nearly forgotten it. Barforth money, indeed, had enabled her to shine at Listonby, her own share of Barforth energy, tenacity, the urge all the Barforths felt to pursue success had enabled her to place it among the most luxurious and hospitable houses of the North. The Barforth in her had caused her to break down, trample underfoot, or simply to ignore all obstacles in her path, but that same Barforth driving force, even as it had swept her on from triumph to social triumph, had, by some strange act of metamorphosis, converted her entirely into a Chard. And in her heart of hearts she did not believe that Blanche Barforth, who was beautiful and rich and her own brother's daughter, could really be good enough for her eldest son.

But Dominic had always been stubborn. Blanche had made up both his mind and her own, and here they were, an exquisite bride, a handsome groom, with myself and Venetia standing behind them in our bridesmaids' finery of apricot silk, thinking, I suppose, that next time – quite soon – eventually – we would be brides and wives and mothers ourselves.

Venetia was the daughter of the second Barforth brother, Mr Nicholas Barforth, a gentleman whose restless ambition and overwhelming shrewdness had not allowed him to be content with the fortune his father had left him and which he and his brother had divided between them. Blanche's father, Uncle Blaize, had taken good care of his money, making absolutely certain that it amply sufficed for the very pleasant life he enjoyed with Aunt Faith. But Venetia's father had set himself, with a singleness of purpose rare even in the Law Valley, to increase his inheritance, had extended and diversified it to become the owner not only of the original Barforth mills of Lawcroft Fold and Low Cross where worsteds of the very finest quality continued to be woven, but of such gigantic undertakings as the Law Valley Woolcombers, the Law Valley Dyers and Finishers, and, more recently, a brand new structure of Italianate design built on the site of an old mill at Nethercoats where the weaving of silk and velvet was making Mr Nicholas Barforth's fortune for the second, the third, or even for the fourth time.

Yet his acute judgment in the field of commerce had not extended to his private life and even his well-wishers – relatively few, it seemed, in number – were forced to admit that none of his personal relationships had prospered. He had quarrelled violently and unforgiveably with his brother and no hostess in Cullingford would have dared invite both Blaize and Nicholas Barforth to her table at the same time. He had quarrelled with all his mill-managers in turn, making no secret that although he paid high wages a man needed nerves of steel and the stamina of an ox to earn them. He was known to live in a state of bitter discord with his son, to have little time for Venetia, his daughter, while his relationship with his wife had been a source of gossip and speculation in Cullingford for many a long day.

Unlike his brother who had chosen Aunt Faith from the manufacturing middle-classes, Mr Nicholas Barforth, following his sister Caroline's lead perhaps, had married into the landed gentry. But while Caroline Barforth's marriage had brought her Listonby Park and the title that went with it, Nicholas Barforth had received nothing but a fine-boned, high-bred, quite penniless lady and – it was rumoured – a great deal of trouble. For once, long ago in Venetia's early childhood, her mother had run away from her father and had been brought back again – or so we believed – a mystery Cullingford had never solved to its satisfaction, the gentleman in the story being unapproachable, the lady well-nigh invisible.

'How is your dear mamma?' Cullingford's matrons, unwilling to be cheated of so promising a scandal, were fond of asking Venetia.

'Very well indeed,' was her only reply. But the fact that her mother lived almost exclusively at the house in the country, the ancient estate of Galton Abbey with its few hundred scrubby acres and its decaying mansion – a far cry from Listonby Park – which had been in Mrs Barforth's family for generations, while her father resided permanently at *his* house in Cullingford, troubled Venetia deeply. And this pall of scandal hovering around her parents – for if they *were* separated then there must have been a mighty scandal indeed – had drawn us together; Venetia about whose mother strange things were whispered, nothing proved, and myself, Grace Agbrigg, motherless daughter of a man who, by his marriage to a rich and disreputable woman, had invited scandal and for the most of the time managed to ignore it.

Venetia was not beautiful like Blanche, her figure being of an extreme, quite boyish slenderness, something sudden and brittle about her movements, an air – every now and then – that was both vulnerable and eager; for whereas Blanche had always known what she wanted from life

Venetia quite simply wanted everything life had to offer, its joys and sorrows, triumphs and disasters, as soon as she could lay her hands on them and in double measure. She had a thin, fine-textured face, a delicate skin, eyebrows that flew away at a wide angle, hair the rich colour of a woodland fox, her pointed auburn looks owing nothing to her tough-grained Barforth father but coming entirely from her mother, the lady who had been the subject, or the cause, of scandal. And although Venetia herself had done nothing of a scandalous nature Cullingford believed, on the whole, in the saying 'like mother like daughter' and many would have advised Mr Nicholas Barforth, had they dared, to get his daughter married while he was able.

But today, standing meekly behind immaculate, triumphant Blanche, we were shielded from past gossip, being simply 'the bridesmaids', anonymous girls in pretty dresses provided like the icing on the cake, the lace frills around the bridal posies simply to decorate. It was, of course, a lovely wedding, somewhat to the surprise of the bridegroom's mother, Aunt Caroline, who, with her vast enthusiasm for entertaining, her twenty-five years experience of balls and dinners, house parties, hunting parties, parties of all shapes and sizes at Listonby had found it hard to leave to Aunt Faith the planning of so vital an event as the wedding of Listonby's eldest son. But, despite her predictions that Aunt Faith would forget this and neglect that, nothing had been overlooked, nothing left to chance.

The horses which brought the bridal procession to church were all high-stepping, glossy with good health and good grooming and – as Aunt Caroline had insisted was essential for a wedding – all perfectly, correctly grey. The carriages were lined with white satin, the church transformed into a flower-garden of white and apricot blossoms, the aristocratic Chards on one side of the aisle, a sprinkling of baronets and Members of Parliament, at least three bishops, half a dozen generals and one real duke among them; the manufacturing Barforths on the other side, millmasters, ironmasters, bankers, builders, although the differences between them were less marked than they had once been. A commercial gentleman of a generation ago might have felt a sense of achievement, of having breached a stronghold hitherto impregnable to men of his station had he succeeded in bestowing his daughter on a High Church, High Tory squire. But now, although all three of those Chard bishops still preached the doctrine that God, having called all men to the position he had selected for them in life wished them to stay there, the Barforths knew better than that, my manufacturing Uncle Blaize escorting his daughter to her noble bridegroom with grace and good humour, perfectly at ease among the 'ruling classes', especially nowadays when, in many cases, their power to go on ruling depended on the co-operation of his – and his brother's – money.

A lovely wedding. There was a flood of golden sunshine as we left the church, a cloudless summer sky, no need at all for the huge marquee spread like the palace of an Arabian prince on the lawns of Aunt Faith's home in suburban Elderleigh. There were bowls of pale roses on every table, in accordance with Aunt Caroline's oft repeated suggestion that in Aunt Faith's place she would be *lavish* with the flowers. The menu-cards – printed in silver and in French – had the additional extravagance of silver lace borders. The cake, which Aunt Caroline had feared would never be big enough to conform to Chard standards of size and grandeur, was immense, intricate, surrounded by sprays of the same white roses and apricot carnations which made up the bridal bouquet and which would be distributed later to each female-guest.

There was champagne, violins concealed romantically by the swaying summer trees, curiosity, a little mild envy, a few sentimental tears. 'A handsome couple' everyone was saying and so they were, Blanche looking more fragile than ever among the dark, large-boned Chards, her bridegroom and his two brothers with whom I was not well acquainted, for unlike the young commercial gentlemen I knew who had all been educated at our local grammar school, the Chard boys had gone away to school at an early age, returning at midsummer and Christmastime when I had found their loud, drawling voices irritating, their manners condescending. And they had looked so much alike – Dominic, Noel, Gideon – that they had seemed to me to be quite interchangeable; self-opinionated boys who would grow to be haughty men of the kind one encountered on the hunting field, in fashionable regiments and fashionable London clubs or half asleep on the benches of the House of Commons.

Dominic's future, of course, had been mapped out for him at birth for he was the eldest, the heir to his father's lands and titles, Squire of Listonby, Master of Foxhounds, Chairman of the Bench of Magistrates, while his twin brother Noel – born ten vital minutes too late to claim the inheritance – and Gideon, 18 months younger still, were simply the extra sons who – unless some tragic fate should befall the heir – would be obliged to make their own way in the world, their father having no secondary titles, no spare estates to bestow on them. Following the family tradition of service Noel – it had been decided as Aunt Caroline first looked into his cradle – would go into the army, Gideon into the church where, having completed the preliminaries of promotion their mother saw no reason why they should not join the prosperous ranks of Chard generals, Chard bishops and make advantageous marriages while they were about it. And Aunt Caroline had expressed these aims so often, with such total certainty, that in my half-attending mind they had become aims no longer but realities. Noel *was* a general, Gideon *was* a bishop so that I had been mildly surprised on my return from Switzerland to meet a very gallant Lieutenant Noel Chard and to hear some very strange rumours indeed in respect to Gideon.

'I suppose one can feel for Aunt Caroline,' Blanche had informed me airily. 'For she has never liked her plans to be upset, and first there was Dominic who was supposed to be a bachelor until his fifties, or so she hoped, so she could go on queening it at Listonby. And now there is Gideon.'

And when I had expressed a degree of interest I did not feel, she went on, 'Yes, indeed. Poor Aunt Caroline. She had set her heart on making Gideon a bishop and he has turned her down flat. He says there is no money in religion, which surprises me since all the clergymen we know seem to live very well – except that I think Gideon means a *lot* of money and spending it on things clergymen don't have, or shouldn't have. I expect you are dying to hear what it is he means to do?'

'I expect you are dying to tell me.'

'He says he will go where the money is – heavens, I can picture Aunt Caroline's face when he said that – and so he has made an approach to my Uncle Nicholas Barforth with a view to joining him in his mills. Yes, you may stare, indeed you may, for I stared too. A Chard in trade! Whatever next? The Barforth blood coming out, I suppose, and Aunt Caroline cannot bear to mention it – not to her London friends and her foxhunting friends at any rate. But since we all know the trouble Uncle Nicholas Barforth has with Cousin Gervase – although Venetia, of course, will not hear a word against her brother – well, I think he may be glad of Gideon. Poor Aunt Caroline, indeed. For if Gideon does well with Uncle Nicholas he will surely try to marry Venetia. Well, of course he will, Grace. In fact he *must* marry her in order to secure his position, for if he does not then someone else surely will. And that "someone", if he has the sense he was born with, will be bound to cut Gideon out of the business. It absolutely stands to reason.'

So it did, and remembering it now on Blanche's own wedding day, I shivered, for I was an heiress too – like Venetia, like Blanche – who might be so easily married not for the pleasure of my company but because marriage to me brought with it the eventual ownership of Fieldhead Mills. Naturally my father would take care in his selection, would look for a bridegroom who was sound in business, high of principle, even kind-hearted. But I knew that the dread of it, the sheer humiliation of being courted for anything other than myself, had made me aloof and suspicious of men since I first understood the size of my fortune and its implications. I could not accept it. I did not think Venetia could accept it either and, watching Blanche for whom it all seemed perfectly natural, who considered her money a fair enough exchange for Dominic's title, I shivered once again.

Aunt Faith received her guests with enormous tact and skill, necessary accomplishments in a family gathering such as ours where the Chards were uncompromisingly Tory and High Church to a man, the Barforths Liberal in politics and Nonconformist in religion; where it was vital that my father's wife and my father's mother should be kept apart; where my father himself must not be allowed to stray into the company of anyone connected at all closely with the Oldroyd nephews; where Mr Nicholas Barforth, the uncle of the bride, had not spoken a civil word to his brother, the bride's father, in twenty years; where Mr Nicholas Barforth's wife, if she came at all, would only come under suffrance, to 'keep up appearances' and must be sheltered from the curiosity of Cullingford's ladies, the occasionally ribald speculation of our gentlemen.

On Aunt Faith's instructions my Grandmother Agbrigg was at once surrounded by a screen of elderly ladies, my Stepmother Agbrigg just as swiftly introduced to one of the Chard bishops – since what in the world could convey more respectability than that? – and to a merry little gentleman who happened to be the Duke of South Erin, neither particularly rich nor particularly important but a *duke* just the same, and a frequent visitor of Aunt Caroline Chard's at Listonby. But no skill of Aunt Faith's could halt the sudden whispering, the turning of heads, the eyes that pretended not to look and the eyes that looked openly, avidly, when Mr Nicholas Barforth's carriage was seen on the drive, a lady in a tall green hat beside him, for this was no local scandal, no simple tale of prickly middle-class morality but was of interest to everyone. Mrs Tessa Delaney had been notorious in Cullingford. Mrs Agbrigg was still somewhat suspect there. But the whole County of Yorkshire, or the sporting, landed portion of it, was acquainted with Mrs Georgiana Barforth who was usually to be found not under her husband's imposing roof but in her decaying manor house at Galton Abbey. All three of the Chard bishops knew her. The Chard generals and colonels had served in the same regiment or played cards at the same clubs as her father; the Duke of South Erin had shot grouse over her moor at Galton many a time. And if these gentlemen were inclined to take a broader, easier view than Cullingford, she remained nevertheless a woman who did not appear to lead a regular life, who might be socially very dangerous, or very interesting, to know; who could, in fact, be approached with a familiarity and with an intent no man would permit himself with a lady who was *known* to reside safely in her matrimonial home.

And, of course, it was the uncertainty which everyone found so intriguing and so maddening. Were the Nicholas Barforths separated or were they not? Did she live in the country for her health, as had once or twice been hinted, or was that just a part of the charade they were playing to make things *look* right; so that their conflict might not damage their unmarried and consequently very vulnerable daughter? Had Mr Nicholas Barforth banished his wife from his hearth and home unable to support her aristocratic freedom of manner, which had never been greatly to the liking of Cullingford in any case? Or had she fled away from him in protest at his money-grubbing, middle-class ways? Had there been misconduct, which in Cullingford could be taken to mean adultery, and if so whose adultery, when, with whom?

Mrs Rawnsley of Rawnsley's Bank felt certain that there had been cruelty and adultery on the gentleman's part which the lady had probably deserved. Mrs Sheldon, the devoted wife of Mr Thomas Sheldon MP tended, without actually saying so, to take the deserted husband's part since the wife, as a woman, had no vote and could therefore be no serious loss to Mr Sheldon at election time. Miss Fielding, the spinster daughter of our other now very elderly MP condemned no one, such an attitude being contrary to her Christian principles, although having done her own duty unstintingly all her life she was bound to feel that Mrs Georgiana Barforth, by this desertion of her husband and her home, had lamentably failed in hers. And the rest of Cullingford, sifting through these divers views, concluded that, like everything else of importance in the Law Valley, it had simply been a matter of money.

Mrs Barforth had been well-bred but extremely poor. Mr Nicholas Barforth had been common, as Cullingford itself was common beneath its prosperous veneer, but extremely rich. 'She got what she came for and then she left,' Cullingford gleefully pronounced, finding it pleasantly ironic that Mr Nicholas Barforth who used his money so ruthlessly to manipulate others should have been so blatantly married for it.

Yet whatever the true facts of the matter, Mr Barforth had retained the power to call his elusive lady to his side whenever it suited him, producing her annually at the Christmas concerts in the Memorial Hall, escorting her, always splendidly dressed, to the anniversary dinner of Cullingford's Charter, the gala opening of a new hotel, a fashionable wedding, so that no one, however inventive or malicious, could ever be sure.

But to Venetia's frank and eager nature these parental deceits were insupportable and I heard the sharp intake of her breath, saw how painfully she bit her lip, as she watched her mother get down from the Barforth carriage and take her father's arm.

'I told her not to come,' she whispered, 'for she cannot bear to see these Cullingford hens cackling and staring whenever she shows herself. I told her *I* wouldn't come, in her place. She just smiled and said that at my age she wouldn't have come either. And I can't tell you how much that startled me – to think she was once like me and has lost her nerve. How terrible.'

She came slowly across the grass, her hand still on her husband's arm, trailing her elaborately draped skirts behind her with a regal disregard for the frailty or the cost of apple green satin and Brussels lace. Her hair, which had the same auburn sheen as Venetia's, was fashionably curled, her fine-etched, pointed face fashionably gay, a quick smile flitting on and off her lips in automatic greeting, her green eyes unwavering, nothing in her manner to indicate how much she had dreaded coming here, except that everyone knew it and many were hoping she would finally reach the end of her aristocratic tether and let it show.

But there was an added flavour to the spectacle today since Mr Nicholas Barforth was not merely parading his wife to a hostile public but was on uncertain ground himself, having last entered this house over ten years ago with a legal document in his hand terminating his association with Blaize Barforth, his brother. And I heard, behind me, a collective sigh of anticipation as these two powerful men at last came face to face.

Cullingford, quite naturally, had hoped for emotion. But such hopes were instantly dashed.

'Nicholas,' said Blaize Barforth with a crisp, quite impersonal nod.

'Blaize,' Nicholas Barforth replied in kind.

Clearly there was no more that could be usefully said.

We took our places at table soon afterwards, partook of rich food and old wines, laughed and applauded the witty easy speech of the bride's father, admired the few well-chosen words of the groom – chosen, one could not doubt, by his mother Aunt Caroline. We drank toasts as we were bid, grew sentimental, or languid, or even a trifle bored. And when Blanche had floated away upstairs to change into the travelling dress Monsieur Worth had made for her in Paris, I watched my father's wife, Mrs Agbrigg, rise from her place and skilfully reclaim her bishop, saw my father join the group of serious gentlemen who, on the paved terrace, were discussing wool prices, share prices, wondering when trade with France would be likely to pick up again now that so free-spending an emperor as the third Napoleon had been chased off his throne. I saw Mrs Georgiana Barforth get up too and launch herself into the crowd like a blind swimmer, her progress impeded at every step by an ingratiating Cullingford smile, an inquisitive Cullingford eye, her own eyes constantly darting to her husband seeking his reassurance that she was saying the things he had brought her here to say, playing the part he had designed for her in the manner he had intended. I saw Aunt Caroline – the *Dowager* Lady Chard now – grimace in an unguarded moment with visible pain, her eyes on the chair Blanche had just vacated, her mind certainly dwelling on the beauty and prosperity of Listonby which she, who had created it, must now relinquish to a careless seventeen-year-old girl.

But the weather-beaten little Duke of South Erin moved quickly to Aunt Caroline's side. Venetia's brother, Gervase, came strolling around the corner of the house, glass in hand, to join the mother he so resembled, a wild young man who was far more at home, one heard, among the aristocratic pleasures of the hunting field and the gaming table than in his father's counting-house. The day was almost over. The Blaize Barforths had creditably married their daughter. Lady Caroline Chard had lost her life's work at Listonby as well as her son. The Nicholas Barforths had demonstrated that they were, in a manner of speaking, sufficiently united to stifle the worst of the rumours which might wreck the matrimonial prospects of *their* daughter, Venetia. Mrs Agbrigg, my father's wife, had made the acquaintance of a bishop.

I had gained nothing, lost nothing. But remembering that tomorrow morning and the morning after I would be obliged to sit in Mrs Agbrigg's drawing-room and dine at her table, I got up too and began to move aimlessly through the throng, recognizing myself to be as complete a captive as Mrs Georgiana Barforth and for the same reasons. We were women. We had no money of our own and no means of earning or otherwise obtaining any. We were dependent, luxuriously but completely, and had the freedom of choice, it seemed to me, merely between the authority of a father or of a husband.

I found Venetia as I had expected surrounded by her admirers, swaying slightly towards this one and that, almost taking flight in her eagerness to offer them her quick gestures and quick smiles, her swift ripple of laughter, giving a little of herself to each one and then, I soon noticed, turning back – for approval, for pleasure, to make sure he was still watching her – to the same man. No one, of course, of whom her father could possibly approve but a certain Mr Liam Adair, a relative of mine by marriage, who had long been classified matrimonially as a bad risk.

I had not consciously thought of Liam Adair for a long time but watching him now, the dark, heavy-featured face I remembered, the merry almost insolent black eyes, I was not surprised. He was the son of an exceedingly witty and resourceful gentleman, now deceased, who had had the great good fortune in middle life to marry his employer's widow, my pretty little Grandmamma Elinor. But my late grandfather had tied his money up in so shrewd a fashion that no predatory second husband could touch it and Liam Adair had been required to make his own way in the world, an erratic way I'd heard which no lady could be asked to share. He had travelled, gambled, taken chances which, more often than not, he had lost and although for the past year or two he had been employed by Venetia's father to sell worsted cloth abroad I had heard no rumour that he had settled down. And that alone, coupled with his height, his breadth, his swagger, would be more than enough for Venetia. Was this, then, the 'unsuitable involvement' my step-mother's tea-time ladies had hinted at? Yet Venetia had spoken to me of Liam Adair only a few days ago warmly but too easily as a 'dear friend' and perhaps I hoped – since it would have been far better that way – that it was the presence of Gideon Chard that was making her so excitable and flirtatious.

I did not feel my best in the pretty apricot silk which had been Blanche's choice, but I looked well enough I suppose and there were a few among Venetia's following who, rating their chances of her favour very low and considering my fortune to be every bit as interesting as hers, began at once to pay me attention, a young member of Rawnsley's Bank saying all that was needful about my stay in Switzerland, the nephew of Mr Sheldon MP requesting my opinion of Venice and listening, quite intently, while I gave it.

'Bit of a pest hole, Venice, if you ask me,' drawled Gideon Chard from the fringes of the crowd, and although I had not asked him and would have done better to ignore him entirely, the self-assurance of his manner, that accumulation of three hundred years of Chard authority and Chard arrogance at Listonby stung me badly, stirring a certain arrogance of my own that came from another source entirely. For if his ancestors had been privileged and powerful mine had been tough-fibred and long-suffering, had fought hard for their prosperity not tamely inherited it, releasing themselves from the trap of poverty by their own stubborn refusal to stay there. And in actual terms he was only the third son of a baronet while I was the heiress to the whole of Fieldhead.

He had not changed greatly in the two years I had been away unless it was that he had simply become the man I had always expected of him. He was the youngest of the Chards for whom the estate could make no provision and who would not be needed by that estate for the purposes of procreation or management unless accident or disease – which seemed unlikely – should carry off both his brothers. And perhaps it was because he had been so carefully taught to respect the claims of primogeniture and to acknowledge the superior rights of those brothers that he had turned out to be a slightly better shot, a keener horseman, a rather more perfect example of his creed, his public school, his class, than either. Yet despite his pedigree, his expensive education, his exquisite manners, his air – and his conviction – of enormous superiority, he was every bit as much an opportunist and a fortune-hunter as Liam Adair, the kind of young gentleman – I was absolutely sure of it – that I had always dreaded, who believed that middle-class heiresses like myself and Venetia were not only fair game and ripe for the plucking but should be glad to pay for the privilege of marrying his noble name. And instantly he inspired me with a great antagonism, a most irrational desire to topple him from his aristocratic height into a puddle of real, industrial, Cullingford mud.

'Venice did not meet with your approval then, Gideon?'

'I can't say that it did.'

'Poor Venice.'

But, nevertheless, a moment later and without knowing exactly how I had submitted to it, I found myself strolling beside him among Aunt Faith's roses, Venetia and Liam Adair a few paces ahead of us, my humour worsening by the moment since I knew I had been 'managed', as Mrs Agbrigg sometimes 'managed' me, and I did not like it.

'What a lovely day.'

I agreed that it was.

'In fact a very fine summer altogether.'

I was not disposed to quarrel with that. But there was no doubt that I wanted to quarrel with him about something, being eager to let him know that there was at least one Cullingford heiress who had 'seen through him', who could never be flattered and consequently never deceived by him.

'How well Venetia is looking,' I said, indicating as clearly as good manners allowed that she was much admired – for *herself* not for those Barforth millions – and that even with her father's backing he would have his work cut out to get her. But the sight of her vivid face upturned to Liam Adair could be of no consequence to a Chard – since Liam would not be allowed to have her in any case – and, disliking him the more for not being jealous, I transferred my attack to his self-esteem.

'So you are going into the mill, Gideon.'

And I believed – hoped – that few things could be more galling to even the third son of a baronet than the necessity for that.

'Am I?' he said, toying with the remark and all too obviously amused by it. 'Is that what you call it? I rather imagined I was joining my uncle's business – or might be doing so.'

'Which happens to be a mill, or rather several of them.'

'So it does. With room for several more, I imagine, if this boom lasts.'

'My word, Gideon, I have never thought of you as a commercial man.'

'Ah – then you *have* thought of me, Grace?'

'Have I? I imagine I must have done, at one time or another.'

'Bu not as a millmaster?'

'Hardly.'

'How then?'

'As a Chard, I expect, among Chards.'

'And you have quite forgotten that my "other grandfather" as my brother Dominic calls him – my mother's father – was Sir Joel Barforth, that prince of commerce?'

'Well, I have hardly thought of you in such detail as that, Gideon. But, of course, if you are modelling yourself on a prince.'

'It would seem a reasonable place to begin, would it not,' he said, smiling with a dry humour, 'for a Chard?'

But instead of laughing with him as I should have done I felt my own humour desert me entirely to be replaced by a quite absurd notion that I must be on my guard, must not – absolutely *must* not – allow this man to win me over.

'I take it, then, that you are an expert on the worsted trade?'

'No – no – I cannot pretend to that. I have an appreciation, merely, of how things are bought and sold and some skill with mathematics. I imagine my Grandfather Barforth would have made his fortune equally well with whatever came to hand. The product might have varied but his methods, and his results, would have been the same.'

'Yes, and the necessity of working eighteen hours a day in the dust and heat and the quite abominable racket of the weaving sheds – *every* day, of course, even in the fine weather – even in the middle of the hunting season … That would have remained the same too.'

'Of course.'

'And you would have enjoyed that, Gideon?'

'I wonder. Fortunately I shall be spared the necessity of finding out since my Grandfather Barforth was kind enough to put in all the spadework somewhat before my time.'

'You think hard work to have gone out of fashion, then?'

But if I had believed him cornered, or had hoped to expose his weakness – to find him lazy, which was a considerable crime in Cullingford, rather than just greedy which was not – I was disappointed.'

'Did I say so? Surely not. My grandfather did everything himself because there was no one else to do it, or no one else who could do it. the machine age was in its infancy then and one had simply to manage as best one could. It is not so today. We have progressed to an age of experts, you see. And nowadays not even a man like my Grandfather Barforth, nor even my Uncle Nicholas Barforth, could maintain and repair his own very complex engines, design his own cloth, oversee its production, go out into the world and sell it, as the old millmasters used to do. We have professional engineers and designers, salesmen, accountants, a whole tribe of specialists.'

'I do have some knowledge, Gideon, of –'

'Do you really?'

'Of course I do. My father, after all, is master of Fieldhead.'

He smiled, giving me a slight bow which reduced the knowledge I had claimed to the level of knitting needles and embroidery frames, pressed flowers and charcoal sketches, the trivial occupations of femininity.

'Why yes, of course he is. I had not forgotten. And so you will know better than to underestimate the value of the man who decides what policy those specialists should pursue – since he takes the risk and the responsibility.'

'He takes the risk,' I snapped, 'because he invests the money.'

'Quite so.'

And because even in the blackest of my rages I was still far too well brought up to hurl at him, 'And you are preparing to sell that aristocratic profile of yours for the money to invest', I increased my pace to catch up with Venetia.

She had come to a halt some way ahead of me, waiting with an unusual quality of motionlessness about her as her mother and father, her brother and several others came walking towards us. And as our groups met and mingled, displaying the polite veneer of our intricate civilization, I felt suddenly overcrowded, hemmed in by an array of quite separate hostilities; ambitious, cool-eyed Gideon seeking the means, through Venetia, to support in appropriate style his aristocratic birth and breeding; Venetia's moody, unmanageable brother who might despise his rich inheritance but would surely not give it away so tamely to Gideon; Venetia's admirer, Liam Adair, who had neither inheritance nor breeding, an even more typical adventurer than Gideon Chard except that his heart, I thought, might be rather warmer. And Venetia herself, eager, vivid, hopeful, standing on the rose-strewn pathway looking once again poised for flight, ready to soar upwards and magnificently, cleanly, away from the ambitions, the greeds, the conflicting pressures around her as she smiled a very private welcome to a young man I had never seen before.

'Grace,' she said so very quietly, imparting to me a precious, still fragile secret. 'You are not acquainted with Charles Heron. Charles, this is my cousin, Grace Agbrigg – my dear friend.' And it was all there in her voice, her radiance, that quality of stillness so new to her which now formed an aura of light and air around her, separating her and this pleasant yet for all I could see unremarkable young man from the rest of us, the commonplace herd of humanity who were not in love.

3

He was, so she told me the next morning, the son of a clergyman whose religion was both harsh and self-indulgent, the very kind she most despised, a man who preached the virtues of poverty and self-restraint with a glass of vintage port in his hand, so that she had understood from the first moment why Charles had found the parental vicarage unendurable. He had run away from its cloying hypocrisy at a tender age and had kept on running until he grew too old to be apprehended and fetched home; and now – since without paternal assistance few young men can prosper – he was a teacher of Greek and Latin at a local school

801

where the Spartan regime, the narrow belief that the mechanics of language counted for more than its poetry, were deeply offensive to him. They had first met at Listonby where Mr Heron, who was perfectly well born, was sometimes invited to dine, and since then they had seen one another, oh – here and there, a concert at the Morgan Aycliffe Hall, Aunt Caroline's hunt ball, a shooting party at Galton Abbey where his lack of expertise with a gun, his preference for absorbing the scents and shades of the autumn moors rather than slaughtering its winged residents – which was so favourite a pastime of her mother and brother – had not displeased her. And if she had flirted a little with Liam Adair – and of course she *had* flirted with him – it had been absolutely necessary, to conceal just for a short while the direction her interest was really taking; and Liam, who was worldly and extremely flirtatious in any case, would not mind.

'I have always known what I was looking for,' she told me simply, quietly, still enveloped in her unnatural stillness. 'I have always wanted to *feel*, not at all in moderation but so strongly that it tests me and stretches me, *demands* my utmost of me. And now I do.'

But love, now that she had encountered him, had proved frailer than she had supposed, no bold and adventurous wayfarer like Liam Adair but a young man of sensitivity whose spirit bruised more easily than her own. And she was herself astonished and a little afraid at the depth of her desire not only to love him but to protect him, the sudden and acute need of her body not only to be touched by him but to shield him from harm.

He had no money, but what could that matter when she would have so much and when his needs, and hers, were very simple? She required from her father no more than the means to open a school of their own where Charles could put into practice his theory that young people should be taught first of all to enjoy learning rather than have it beaten into them, as nowadays seemed to be the case. While Charles himself would be unwilling to accept even that much.

'He does not approve of large fortunes,' she told me, wrinkling her nose. 'He believes they cannot have been made honestly or without great exploitation of others.'

'Well, he is quite right. But he had better not say so to your father.'

'Lord, no! – but there is far worse, for he will have nothing to do with religion and he is something very like a republican ...'

'Perhaps your father will not mind so much about that.'

'No, but others will mind. He was dismissed from his last school, in Sussex, because the parents objected to his advanced views, and he came north because he thought people would be less hidebound up here. But they are not. At least, the ones who can afford the fees at St Walburga's School are not, and he will not bring himself to compromise.'

'In fact he is even more honest and straightforward than you are, Venetia.'

She laughed, tossed her head in a gesture designed to banish anxiety.

'So he is. Well, never mind, for if my father should cut me off without a shilling there will be that much more for Gervase. I will come to see you again, Grace, tomorrow – the next day –'

But there remained the question of Gideon Chard, of family convenience – for the more I thought of it, the more convinced I became that Mr Nicholas Barforth would find it convenient. And although as yet this marriage could be no more than a possibility, depending very largely on how well Gideon might adapt himself to the manufacturing life, I felt absurdly threatened by it, being so much aware of the frailty behind Venetia's rash courage, of how easily hurt she really was and how very slow, once hurt, to heal, that when she did not appear on the tenth day I borrowed Mrs Agbrigg's carriage, altogether by stealth, and went to Tarn Edge to find her.

I should not, of course, have paid this visit, since Mrs Agbrigg had forbidden it, and should certainly not have gone alone, but the old Barforth house in its several acres of elaborate, impersonal gardens, had no mistress nowadays who might be offended by my impropriety and there would be no other callers, no Mrs Rawnsley or Miss Fielding to carry tales to my stepmamma, no Mrs Thomas Sheldon MP to smother me in sweet and serious tones with her advice. There would be no one, indeed, but a housekeeper, her courtesy largely reserved for Mr Nicholas Barforth, who paid her wages; an indifferent butler who did not encourage callers; and hopefully there would be Venetia.

The house, built by the founder of the Barforth fortunes, Sir Joel Barforth, at the pinnacle of his success, was many times larger than Fieldhead, its Gothic façade a marvel of carved stone, its walls rising to ornamental turrets and spires, with a stained-glass window on the South side that would not have disgraced a cathedral. When Sir Joel and his wife – my mother's Aunt Verity – had lived here, no house in the Law Valley had contained such luxuries nor entertained its guests so royally. But Sir Joel had died, Lady Verity had moved away, and only the Nicholas Barforths had remained at Tarn Edge.

For a while, I suppose, nothing had appeared changed, Lady Verity's well-paid and competent servants continuing to function in the old ways without need of supervision. But the new mistress – who had been Miss Georgiana Clevedon of Galton Abbey, a squire's daughter – had not cared for manufacturers' houses, new houses built with new money, and inevitably her lack of interest in Tarn Edge had infected her staff so that the work became slipshod or was not done at all; a careless mistress being carelessly served until the day she went away.

A series of housekeepers had followed her, none of them staying long, for Mr Barforth was exacting and quick-tempered, his son, Gervase, extremely troublesome, while it had not occurred to Venetia, as it would probably have occurred to Blanche, certainly to me, that she was old enough now to take things in hand. But Aunt Faïth, I think, was grieved by the neglect, enquiring whenever I visited there as to the progress of a decay she was unable either to witness or to prevent. Was it true that the bronze stag which had guarded the hall since her early childhood had lost an antler after a party, a most unruly gathering she'd heard, held in his father's absence by Gervase? Had someone really chipped the tiles of the drawing-room fireplace which her Aunt Verity had had specially sent over from Italy, and scorched the priceless rug where, every Christmas of her youth, Sir Joel Barforth had stood to drink his family's health? No; the stag, I discovered, was intact, larger than life, magnificent, the drawing-room too perfect if anything, a cool air of disuse about it, the Aubusson rug Aunt Faith had described no longer there, its disappearance casually explained by Venetia: 'Oh *that* – oh yes, Gervase set fire to it one night, I don't know how and he can't remember. Threw his cigar into the fire, I expect, and missed.' And so the house, when I first knew it, had acquired the air of an expensive but somewhat mismanaged hotel.

Venetia and her brother were still at breakfast when I arrived at a little after eleven o'clock that morning, a circumstance less shocking in her case than in his, and as I entered the small breakfast-parlour – no servant troubling either to warn them of my arrival or to show me the way – I saw that they were quarrelling and had no intention, for my sake, of concealing it.

The room was small only by Tarn Edge standards, a table in the centre which could have comfortably seated two dozen, sideboards on two walls, one of them presenting a bare, none too well polished surface, the other set out with a princely array of hot dishes – princely, that is, in the massively embossed silver of the dishes themselves, since not one of them was more than a quarter full, being too large for the family they now served, and no one, very clearly, having thought of buying new. There was a large silver coffee-pot at Venetia's elbow, a stain on the damask cloth beside it where she too had aimed badly – today? yesterday? – the odd blending of luxury and neglect one came to expect in that house and for which Venetia, had she noticed it, would have felt no need to apologize. For after all what did a torn napkin, a chipped saucer *really* matter when there was a vast, sparkling sky above her windows, living green earth beneath. When there was Charles Heron.

'Darling Grace,' she said, pushing a cup and saucer towards me with scant ceremony, 'we are having a little tiff, Gervase and I. Do come and join us.'

'Do you think I should? Is it safe?'

'You mean is it proper? Oh heavens, yes – don't turn out to be like Blanche who can do nothing unless it *looks* right. Gervase is being selfish, not for the first time, and thinking he can get away with it because he is a man – thinking *I* should take the consequences because females don't amount to much. Why on earth should you be shy, Grace? It's only Gervase.'

'Thank you,' he said, his voice light yet rather hoarse, his eyes narrowing as if the quite muted daylight hurt him. 'But perhaps – before we go on – surely one ought to say how very nice to see you, Grace, after all this time. May one hope you had a pleasant journey home?'

'Yes I did, thank you. Very pleasant.'

'And you are very well?'

'Yes, I am. And you?'

'Absolutely splendid!'

'No he's not,' Venetia said, wishing to be cool and cutting, but biting back a chuckle. 'He drove his cabriolet off the path last night and ploughed up about half an acre of father's roses. Yes, yes, I saw it all, Gervase, from my window, and how you stopped from overturning I shall never know. I felt quite proud of you, or would have done if you had not been drunk – since getting drunk is so shameful and silly – like that time you went steeplechasing after dinner at Listonby with a broken arm. I suppose that was silly too.'

'I suppose it was – except that I won.'

'Yes – I know,' and rippling with her sudden laughter she brushed her hand lightly against his, a swift reminder of shared affection, unconditional support, two of them against the world, an attitude I envied since in my case there had only ever been one.

Gervase Barforth closely resembled his sister, the pointed, auburn looks of his mother's family, which in him had an extra leanness, green eyes that were almost always narrowed as if against strong sunlight, a thin, hard mouth tilted by a not altogether compassionate humour. And although I had known him, at a distance, all my life, I understood no more of him than the plain facts which were available to anyone.

He was twenty-four years old and so far as I knew had never performed what anyone in Cullingford would consider a hard day's work in his life. He had an office at Nethercoats Mill, a desk, a portrait of his mother on the wall, but what he actually did there no one in Cullingford could rightly say. He was neither physically lazy nor mentally slow as rich men's sons sometimes seem to be, possessing on the contrary a restlessness which made him uneasy company. Yet even his queerness of temper, his ability to touch raw nerves in others, would have been tolerated had he bothered to conceal his contempt for the values which had made Cullingford – and his father – great.

'Reckons himself too fine a gentleman for the textile trade, yon lad,' Cullingford had decided, secretly pleased that Mr Nicholas Barforth, who had succeeded in everything else, should have failed so dismally with his wife and son.

'Takes after his mother, young Master Gervase.' And so perhaps he did, not merely in those finespun, auburn looks but in his disgust for factory cities, his intolerance of the middle classes into which he, unlike his Clevedon mother, had been born.

'The young squire' they called him at the Barforth mills, and indeed he rode to hounds, shot grouse and pheasant in season, drank brandy and claret, played cards in low company, associated, I suppose, with low women, pastimes by no means unusual among the squirearchy but which in Cullingford – where manufacturers required their sons to devote a fair amount of their time to the processes of manufacturing – were considered to be not so much sinful as unprofitable, definitely not to be encouraged. And since he had been christened Gervase *Clevedon* Barforth and was the last male survivor of that proud line it was generally believed that he might one day drop the name of Barforth altogether, that like his mother before him he was simply awaiting his share of the Barforth fortune in order to turn his back on Cullingford and the manufacturing side of his ancestry altogether.

If there was more than that to Gervase, then I had not discovered it; and would be unlikely to do so now, I thought, for as Venetia, having reassured him of her affection, began not so much to quarrel with him as to urge him to action, he gave a faint shudder and closed his eyes, conveying the impression that his constitution this morning was exceedingly fragile, his head painful and his stomach sour, his sympathy with his sister's troubles at a low ebb.

'*Must* it be now, Venetia?'

'Of course it must, for I am obliged to deal with you when I can catch you, and unless we have this out now you will be off again. Do pay attention – and there is no need for you to look so pained about it. You may put your head in the sand as often as you please, Gervase, but – I warn you – *I* will not go away.'

And in a rush of words and gestures and exclamations she presented him with her impression of the visit she had made the day before, the two or three rooms at Galton Abbey kept open by her mother, the stone-flagged hall with its array of family portraits and ancient weaponry, the small sitting-room with its rag rugs and tapestry chairs, a long, low-ceilinged kitchen, its door standing open to wind and weather, the air that came spiced and sharp from the moor, the movement of a clear, fast-running stream.

It had been an enchanting day of sun and wind and glorious liberty, nothing in her mother's manner to indicate discontent, except that Venetia *knew* she was discontented; no hint of frustration, except that Venetia could sense it as clearly as one can sometimes divine the presence of hidden water. And indeed the life of a woman living apart from her husband was both sad and strange, for although she was deprived – albeit at her own choosing – of his status and his protection, she was still as subject by law to his control as if she had never set foot outside the matrimonial front door. Mrs Barforth may well have retired to her family estate but in fact that estate, which had come to her in her grandfather's will, did not really belong to her at all but to her husband. Separated or not separated, she remained his wife and as such could own no property apart from him. What she possessed he possessed. What he possessed was his absolutely. He could claim Galton as his own, could sell it or knock it down as he chose, without her consent, and there was no authority to which she could realistically complain. A married woman, we all knew, assumed her husband's name and was absorbed into his identity. A separated woman appeared to have no identity at all, and no protection, being obliged to depend financially, legally and every other way on the whim of the man who was still her legal guardian. If Mrs Barforth had tried to run away, she had not gone very far, her bolt for freedom – if such it had been – ending in a fresh captivity which, however irksome it might or might not be to herself, was the cause of much honest indignation to her daughter.

'They should be together or they should be separate – one thing or the other,' was Venetia's deeply held opinion. 'And she should stand up to him and tell him so, for he is not so terrible and she is brave enough in other ways. *I* would tell him ...'

Her mother, in fact, despite her outer layer of cheerfulness, had reminded Venetia of nothing so much as a woodland creature tethered in its natural habitat on a very long chain which, while permitting an illusion of freedom, could be drawn tight at any moment to suit the purposes of its master. And although she knew her father's hand was on that chain, she believed the cause of it – at least partly – to be Gervase. Left to her own devices, her mother – Venetia was sure of it – would have evaded all restraint long ago and flown away. But she remained; and since daughters, in the Clevedon tradition, had never counted for much, the reason for her enforced docility could only be her son.

'Ah yes,' he said, outwardly very languid now. 'Do blame me – do follow the fashion.'

'So I will, because she is sitting on that land guarding it for you – you know she is.'

'And rightly so, since I am the last of the Clevedons.'

'And do you know that every time father tells her to do something she does it, however much she loathes it, because she's afraid he'd sell the estate if she disobeyed him?'

'Yes, Venetia. I am a little older than you, if you remember, and none of this is news to me. But she cares about the land, Venetia – she *wants* to be there.'

'Exactly. But do you?'

'I beg your pardon?'

'You know what I mean. She wants the land – yes, more than anything – but she doesn't see the estate as hers. It was her grandfather's and her father's; it was going to be her brother's. And when he was killed she started to think of it as yours. But I don't know, Gervase – really I don't. You used to run off to Galton when we were children, and she'd keep you there when you should have been at school, until father came to drag you back. And now sometimes you can't bear to keep away – you run off there now when you should be at the mills – but there are times when mother hardly sees you at all. And when she does you're not always sweet.'

He paused, smiled, moved one very weary hand towards the coffee-pot and smiled again, evidently deciding that, since neither of us showed signs of coming to his assistance, the effort of picking up the pot and pouring would be too much for him.

'Oddly enough,' he said, still smiling, 'there's really no need to be sweet with mother. That's the great thing about her, you know. She actually likes the kind of man I am. In fact, I'll go further than that, and say she rather thinks that's the way men *ought* to be.'

For a moment there was a heavy silence, Venetia leaning forward perplexed and frowning, while Gervase, his eyes half-closed again, seemed very far away.

'Do you want that estate?' she suddenly flung at him. 'Are you going to let her down? I'm not so sure.'

He got up and crossed to the sideboard, glancing with dislike at the overcooked sausages cowering in a corner of their dish, the congealed eggs and bacon, and then, helping himself rather gingerly, came back to the table.

'I feel I should eat something,' he said. 'In fact I absolutely must ... So you don't think I'm cut out to be squire of Galton, Venetia?'

'I didn't say that. I said I'm not always sure you want it.'

'Mother's sure.'

'I know.'

'So we'll consider it settled, shall we – since if you imagine I'm cut out to run those mills, then you haven't been listening to father. And is it really all my fault, Venetia? We know why mother keeps up the illusion – to protect Galton for me. I'll grant you that. But why does father do it? What does *he* want out of it? He wants you safely married and off his hands, Venetia – that's what he wants – before the illusion cracks and the gossip starts. So if your heart is really bleeding for mother, then use that to bargain with. Tell him you'll get married and he can pick the groom.'

'That's terrible –' she began, her mind on Charles Heron, her face as pale as if she were already a captive bride. But almost at once, with the lightning shifts of mood common to them both, her colour came flooding back, he smiled.

'Idiot!' she said, her own mouth trembling into unwilling mirth. 'They'd have to drag me down the aisle ...'

'No, no – no need for that. I'd shoot you if it came to it – much kinder.' And when their father came into the room a moment later they were still laughing, reconciled, joining themselves instinctively together in mutual defence against him.

He was a very large man, as dark and solid as they were light and fine, a man of substance and presence who had been very handsome once and would have been handsome still, perhaps, had he been less morose. A silent man, accustomed to issuing orders rather than holding conversations, who did nothing without a purpose or the expectation of a profit, and who in my father's informed opinion was the hardest and shrewdest of the very many shrewd and far from tender-hearted gentlemen in our Law Valley.

'Sir?' Gervase murmured by way of greeting, a slight question in his voice.

'Oh –' said Venetia, biting her lip, a child caught in a guilty act, although there was no reason why she, at least, should not be breakfasting at this late hour.

But Mr Barforth ignored both his children and, turning to me, said quietly: 'Good morning, Grace.'

'Good morning, Mr Barforth. May I apologize for calling so early?'

'I wouldn't call it early,' he said, his eyes straying to Gervase, implying, I knew, that he and the greater part of Cullingford had been at their work for some hours already. 'And you are always welcome. You could give me some coffee, miss.'

And although this last remark was certainly addressed to Venetia, she had become so strangely downcast – remembering, no doubt, that this awesome parent would never appreciate Charles Heron – that I took the pot myself, ascertained Mr Barforth's requirements as to cream and sugar, and handed him his cup quite steadily, feeling that if I had managed to contend with Mrs Agbrigg all these years I should not be intimidated by him.

He smiled, drank deep as men do after an hour or so in the weaving-sheds, and without really looking at Gervase, said, 'You're back, I see. It occurred to me as I was shaving this morning that I hadn't seen you for a day or two – five or six, I reckon. But then on my way out I noticed a certain amount of destruction that told me you might have come home to roost again.'

'Well yes, sir – bad penny and all that.'

'Quite so. It's the end of the month, isn't it? And you'll be overspent.'

'That's about it, sir.'

And what surprised me was not the hostility of their relationship but the lack of it, the absence, almost, of any relationship at all, which was not often seen in an area like ours, where mill masters thought nothing of chasing their sons to the factory yard with a horse-whip if necessary and of keeping them permanently short of money to make sure they stayed there. It had been the boast of Sir Joel Barforth that he could usually make his first thousand pounds of the morning while his competitors were still cooling their porridge. Mr Nicholas Barforth, his son, whose business was even larger, could probably do better than that. Gervase Barforth had never by his own ingenuity made a single penny, and would not be asked to try, it seemed to me, because Mr Barforth quite simply, quite coldly, did not think this difficult, almost alien son of his to be worth the trouble. He had written him off, I thought, as he would have done a bad debt, dealing with the consequences, resigning himself to the loss, and it did not escape me that Gervase – who from the moment of his father's arrival had become more languid, more dissipated and trivial than ever – was fully aware of it.

'Badly overspent, Gervase?' Mr Barforth asked, naming in an outstand-ingly casual manner an offence any other Cullingford father would have dealt with as a major crime. To which his son, still lounging at ease – although he seemed to have turned rather pale – replied in like manner, presenting so complete a picture of an expensive, useless young gentleman that I glanced at him keenly, finding his portrayal too perfect and wondering if he was attempting, as I often did with Mrs Agbrigg, to see just how far he could go.

'Much the same as usual.'

'And is there a chance this month, do you think, of my getting a return on my money?'

'It rather depends what sort of return you had in mind, sir.'

'Oh, nothing much – I wouldn't ask much.'

'That's good of you, sir.'

And now the atmosphere between them, although I could still not have called it anger, chilled me, warning me that, whatever name they gave to it, it was tortuous and hurtful and unpleasant.

'I want somebody to go down to London and take a man out to dinner. You could manage that, I reckon?'

809

'Well, yes, I could,' agreed Gervase, his drawling accent belonging so accurately to the public school he had never attended that once again I glanced at him, recognizing his intention to provoke, to enrage, to demonstrate that his father's opinion of him was if anything not bad enough. And what hurt him and strained him – as I had so often been hurt and strained in my combat with Mrs Agbrigg – was that his father would not be provoked, had no need to be enraged, being possessed absolutely of the power and the authority that would ensure him, every time, an easy victory.

'I know where London is, sir – there'd be no trouble about that. But this man you want me to meet – does he understand the wool trade?'

'No,' Mr Barforth said, smiling grimly, 'he does not. He understands horses and guns – the American variety of both – and I reckon you'll find other things in common. You could take him to a tailor and a music-hall – and a few other places of entertainment I expect you'll know about – if you feel up to the responsibility, that is.'

'One tends to rise to the occasion.'

'Good. Tomorrow, then. The morning train. I'd planned to send Liam Adair but he's needed.'

'How very nice for him,' Gervase said sweetly, 'to be needed.'

And now at last there was anger, just a moment that contained the possibility of a bellow of rage, a box on the ear, the easy, healthy curses which any other father would already have been hurling at any other son. But – since anger implies a degree of caring, or hoping, and is a warm thing in any case – the moment froze, or withered, and with a casual 'I'll make my arrangements, then', Gervase got up and walked away, brushing a hand lightly against Venetia's shoulder as he passed.

'Doesn't it occur to you, papa,' she said, staring down at her hands, folded tightly before her on the table, 'that one day perhaps he won't come back? In his place I don't think I'd come back – not every time.'

But her father chose neither to hear nor to reply, asking me instead for more coffee, which he accepted with a smile of amazing charm, his grim contempt giving way to an altogether unexpected cordiality.

'I hear you did very well in Switzerland, Grace.'

'As well as I could, Mr Barforth.'

'Aye – which put you so far at the head of your class as to set your father wishing you'd been born a boy. He reckons you could run Fieldhead mill, if you were the right gender, without much trouble.'

'I am very pleased he should think so.'

And offering me once again that astonishing smile he submitted me to a moment's scrutiny, examining me as carefully as if he had never seen me before, a keen mind assessing not only my appearance, my character, but the uses to which they might be put, as if – like Gideon Chard – I had come to him for employment.

'Didn't you know,' Venetia said when he had left the room, 'how charming he can be?'

'Why, yes – I suppose I did.'

'I suppose you did not, because he has never taken the trouble to be

810

nice to you before. Lord, he even charms me sometimes! Well, Grace, you had better watch out, because he must want something from you, or from your father. I wonder what it can be? Perhaps he wants to send me abroad, out of harm's way, and thinks you'd be the one to keep an eye on me. Or perhaps he's just picked you out as the right wife for Gervase. Heavens! I didn't mean to say that –'

'Then please don't say it again.'

'I won't, for there's no hope of it. Gervase won't get married for ages yet. He's enjoying himself too much. And when he does he'll go to one of the foxhunting set – Diana Flood, I suppose, if she keeps on making eyes at him in that odious fashion.'

'I gather you don't much care for Diana Flood.'

She shrugged, her mind probing beyond Miss Flood, who was known to me only as the niece of Sir Julian Flood whose family had held the manor of Cullingford as long as there had been Chards at Listonby and Clevedons at Galton Abbey; a gentleman, in fact, who intrigued me rather more than the equestrienne Diana, since it had long been rumoured that if Venetia's mother had ever had a lover, then most assuredly it had been – might still be – the impecunious, unsteady, yet undeniably well-bred Sir Julian. Yet if these rumours had reached Venetia she made light of them now, displaying no more than a mild irritation towards the girl who might well become her sister-in-law, a young lady whose aristocratic notions and athletic habits must surely appeal both to Gervase Barforth and to his Clevedon mother.

'Oh, there's no harm in her – at least, if she'd leave Gervase alone she'd be as bearable as the rest of them, with their eternal hunting stories.'

'You go hunting yourself, Venetia.'

'So I do. But that's not all I do. It's not all I think about. It's not all Gervase thinks about either – except that when he spends too much time with the Floods and the Chards and the rest he becomes so like them that really one can hardly tell the difference.'

'Do you see much of the Chards?' I asked cautiously, hoping against all the odds that she might blush, turn coy, make some fond reference to Gideon which would reassure me that Charles Heron had not really absorbed the whole of her heart and her mind. But she only shrugged again, her gesture tossing the very substantial Chards quite easily away.

'From time to time. Dominic and Noel never come to town, but Gideon is here sometimes, talking textiles to father and talking down to Gervase. He doesn't talk to me.'

'Don't you like him?'

'Gideon? He's well enough. Clever, of course, and very good-looking, and my word doesn't he just know it! But all the Chards are like that. I believe I envy them. It must be very pleasant to have such a good opinion of oneself.'

'Ah – I see. You have a poor opinion of Venetia Barforth, do you?'

She laughed and shook her head. 'I suppose not. It's just that sometimes I'm not too sure who Venetia Barforth really is – or Gervase. It has never been easy, you know, with a father who is so very much a Barforth and a mother so much a Clevedon that all our lives what has been right for her has been wrong for him. And because we could never please them both, we were always in a state somehow of having to choose. Well, I suppose for me those days are over. I'm a female and females don't inherit. No one is going to make me squire of Galton or master of the Barforth mills. Gervase is the one who has to make that decision. I just hope he lives long enough.

'Now what on earth does that mean?' She smiled, shook herself a little.

'Oh, well – the Clevedon males tend to burn themselves out rather soon, you know, or they get themselves killed. The graveyard at Galton is full of them, most of them cut down or shot down in battle, but others not – My mother's father fell an early victim to the brandy bottle and there was her brother, of course, our Uncle Perry, who took one fence too many and broke his neck. The wild red Clevedons – you must have heard the country people call us that? It appeals mightily to Gervase, until he remembers his name is actually Barforth.'

'And then?'

'Yes – then he takes a higher fence or a wider ditch. Whatever the Floods or the Chards or the Wintertons can do, he can do it better or more of it. He can, too – so far.'

'And you, Venetia?'

'Yes,' she said, her face softening, richly glowing as always at any reminder of Charles Heron. 'I have my own fences to jump too, do I not? I am not naive, Grace. I know my father will never consent to Charles. It makes no difference at all to the way I feel. I think Gervase could fall in love too – I really think so.'

'And you wouldn't like it to be with Diana Flood?'

'No,' she said, frowning, concentrating hard, as if, quite slowly, she was working something out, reaching a long-suspected conclusion. 'No, I wouldn't. I know mother wouldn't agree with me, because Diana likes all the things mother likes and can do all the things mother can do, and of course she'd make a splendid new mistress for Galton – and that matters tremendously to mother. But Galton is made of stone and he's not. What I'm saying is – oh dear! –'

'That you don't want to lose your brother to the foxhunting set?'

'Oh, that's part of it – a big part. But there are two sides to him, you know, and whatever he says, and whatever mother says, I'm not sure the Clevedon side is the strongest. He's a Barforth, after all, and what's wrong with that? Why shouldn't he be a Barforth? Oh Grace, I don't know why I never thought of this before, and of course I shouldn't say it and I know it won't happen – nothing so marvellous *could* happen. But if I could have a wish – just one – since I already have Charles, then I'd –'

'Venetia, if it's what I think it is, then please –'

'Then please just let me say it, just once, in case a good fairy should be listening. If I could have that solitary wish, then I'd wish for Gervase to marry you.'

4

'Mr Gervase Barforth,' Mrs Agbrigg remarked sweetly the following morning across the breakfast table, 'is a young man of a most unreliable disposition. It is a connection I do not wish to encourage and must ask you to co-operate.'

'He will be very rich, Mrs Agbrigg.'

'And very spendthrift. On the other hand, Mr Gideon Chard has a most pleasing manner ...'

'And nothing much to be spendthrift with, Mrs Agbrigg, I imagine, since he is only a third son.'

'But of such an excellent mother,' she said, still very sweetly smiling, demolishing my insolence by ignoring it.

'So we are to encourage the Chard connection?'

'If we have the sense we were born with, dear Grace, we must endeavour to do so.'

'You have not heard the rumour then, that he is being held in reserve for Venetia?'

'I have,' she said, stately, imperturbable. 'But rumour is often at fault. An ambitious man requires a woman of sense to partner him – which Venetia is not. A man who enjoys material possessions rather than philosophical concepts – and I believe Gideon Chard to be that kind of man – needs a wife of a practical rather than a whimsical turn of mind. Venetia may be fascinating and affectionate, but a young man with his way to make in the world might not feel safe with her, no matter what promises were made to him by her father.'

'Heavens, Mrs Agbrigg, how dull you make me sound! Am I really so safe and sensible and thrifty?'

'Sensible enough,' she said quietly, 'to get yourself creditably married. Tell me, dear, do you see any particular reason for delay?'

I did not expect either Gideon or Gervase to pay me any further attention, for Gideon's best interests were certainly with Venetia, while Gervase, who despised commerce, could hardly wish to ally himself to one of its daughters. But Mrs Agbrigg's next 'at home' day brought first one and then the other, Gervase accompanied by his father, who may, for all I knew, have dragged him to that stuffy gathering of teacups and bread and butter by the scruff of his neck. The two young men came separately and did not meet each other, remaining no longer than the correct quarter of an hour, Gervase replying very languidly, almost without opening his lips, to the few remarks which Mrs Agbrigg, aware of his father's powerful eye upon her, addressed to him.

'Yes, ma'am.'

'As you say, ma'am.'

And when her back was turned he gave me an almost imperceptible wink, an exaggerated grimace of dismay which inclined me – for the first time in that hushed and hallowed drawing-room – to giggle.

But Gideon Chard was received with an enthusiasm I found distasteful, an eagerness to display our worldly goods to him and hint at the existence of more which covered me with shame.

'Pleasant house you have here, Mrs Agbrigg,' he told her, rather, it seemed to me, as if he owned it and was thinking of increasing her rent.

'Pleasant enough, Mr Chard – only a mill-house, of course, although I do my best with it. I have had my little notions of moving into the country, but my husband – as yet – cannot bear to be separated from his mill.'

And there, in those few words, she had placed it all before him, had sown a tempting seed to convince him that the Agbrigg daughter had not only good sense, a safe disposition and a prosperous business to offer her husband, but the possibility of a country estate, which would be regarded as a most enticing bonus by the sporting Mr Gideon Chard.

'No, I cannot persuade my husband to leave the view of the mill we have from this window.'

'Indeed?' he said, striding to the window she indicated and staring keen-eyed down the slope of lawn and flower-beds and over the hedge to the mill-yard. 'An excellent view – and a splendid building, if I may say so.'

'How kind! Should industrial architecture be of interest to you, my husband would be delighted to show you around.'

'I should be very much obliged to him.'

'Then please consider it settled.'

'It is not so large,' I said, my mouth very dry, 'as any one of the Barforth mills.'

But, involved with their own thoughts and with one another, they ignored me.

'Shall we say the day after tomorrow at three o'clock? I will tell my husband to expect you, and if you should care to walk up here afterwards and take tea …?'

'I should like that enormously.'

I did not like it at all.

'What an exceedingly fine vase,' he said, his landlord's eye carefully assessing our treasures. 'Meissen, I think?'

'Oh goodness!' Mrs Agbrigg fluttered. 'I am always confused by the porcelain. Grace will tell you.'

'Meissen,' I said shortly, rudely, receiving a raised eyebrow from the lady, a slight bow from the gentleman.

'We will see you the day after tomorrow then, Mr Chard.'

'With the greatest of pleasure.'

He came, inspected the mill from top to bottom as if he had the means to make an offer for it, fired sharp, pertinent questions at my father and then sat for a full hour at ease in the drawing-room – too much at ease for my liking – and paid court not to me but to Mrs Agbrigg, recognizing her at once as the source of authority.

'What a charming young man, Grace!'

'He's a fortune-hunter, Mrs Agbrigg.'

814

'Well, of course he is, dear. All men are hunting for something or other. It is in their natures – and when one has a fortune, what else can one expect? The great thing about it, my dear, is that a fortune, if placed in the right hands – unlike youth and beauty – has no tendency to fade but can even be made to grow.'

But Gideon Chard did nothing to commit himself, biding his time in true commercial fashion until the climate of the marriage-market should be exactly right. And when later that month it was made known to us that he had become an official Barforth employee, I believed Mrs Agbrigg's game to be lost. He would try to marry Venetia now, I was sure of it, and would probably do anything to get her, since he could hardly enjoy the prospect of investing his time and energy in the Barforth business to let half of it go with Venetia to someone else.

He was often to be seen in Cullingford accompanying his uncle on his daily round of the mills – splendid Lawcroft, smaller but thriving Low Cross, brand-new, awe-inspiring Nethercoats and the rest – or at the Piece Hall, the platform for the London train, the Wool Exchange; sometime with Gervase in attendance and sometimes not. But it was not generally expected that he would long endure the discipline, the sheer physical discomfort of the textile trade; the factory hooter which every morning shrieked out a demand for punctuality which he, like the meanest operative, would be expected to obey; the heat, the dust, the grinding, monotonous toil of the sheds. 'Come the first taste of autumn,' they said, 'and he'll be off, riding down some poor farmer's crops to catch those blasted foxes. They're not *steady*, the gentry. They're only glorified farmers themselves, after all, used to following the seasons instead of the clock. And if Nick Barforth can't handle his own lad, what chance has he got with Lady Caroline's?'

But it was Gervase, as I had known it would be, who disappeared in mid-August, called to Galton Abbey by the early grouse, while Gideon could still be seen strolling towards the Piece Hall on market-day and afterwards in the bar parlour of one of our new commercial hotels where deals were often finalized, a most perfect man of business in his black frock coat and light grey trousers, plain grey silk waistcoat and immaculate linen, only the pearl in his neck-cloth and his own very superior manner marking him as the son of a baronet, albeit the third.

'My father is very pleased with him,' Venetia offered, too deep in her dream of Charles Heron to take the effect this might have on her own life in any way seriously. 'Although I believe our managers dislike him, which is not to be wondered at, for they have been expecting an easy time of it under Gervase when father retires. And although Gideon cannot yet be sure of himself and has so much to learn, they can see that he means to be *hard*. No, they really don't like him at all but I doubt he cares a fig for that, since he has not come to us for affection, simply to get rich.'

'Venetia –' I said, wanting to say more, but she shook her head in the coltish movement that was so impatient of restraint, and smiled.

'Oh yes, I am not such a goose as you seem to think. I know they are all expecting him to marry me. But that is all nonsense, you know. It is just my father and Aunt Caroline thinking that everything must be arranged their way. And in any case I believe I have seen Gideon looking at you.'

I replied very calmly that I had not noticed it, but her remark sent me out into the garden when she left me, needing solitude in which to ponder the growing trouble of my mind and body, which had both endured the restraints of total dependence, of the 'young-lady-at-home', for too long.

I had returned from Switzerland feeling myself to be a woman, my chaperonage abroad having consisted of governesses and paid companions, who although by no means careless of my reputation had been for the most part reasonable. And while I had done nothing disgraceful nor even particularly adventurous, I had at least been allowed the dignity of choice.

In short I had been trusted, my own judgement of what I could or could not do, with whom I might or might not associate, had been respected. And since I had not abused that trust I had not anticipated its withdrawal. But from the day of my return Mrs Agbrigg had shown a determination to keep me as cloistered as a flighty fifteen-year-old, not, I suspected, out of any concern for my virtue or my safety, but quite simply to drive me away.

I had made a scene the first time she asked to read a letter of mine, had thrown it at her feet and vowed to take up her excess of zeal – her excess of spite – with my father. But he had come home late from the mill that night, weary and dispirited and coughing, a pain in his chest, a pain in his head, glad of the mulled wine she had ready, his chair with the cushions placed just so, the warm sympathy of *her* voice, not the shrill protest of mine; and watching her smooth the tensions out of him, I had found nothing to say.

The immediate solution, of course, would be to go abroad again, to Paris, perhaps, now that the war with Prussia was over. It would be interesting, I thought, to watch the new republic emerge from its troubled infancy, to hear at first hand those elusive, tantalizing ideals of liberty and fraternity which had been born in France a century ago. It would be fascinating to watch and to hope that this time, after so many years of bloodshed, so much pain and sacrifice, they had been able to get their formula right. But in the end I would be obliged to come home again, to find these same conflicts waiting for me unresolved, and catching sight of the mill below me, a charcoal sketch of rooftops around it, a damp, grey sky above, I knew that no matter how long or how frequent my journeyings I would always wish to return.

I had seen splendid cities, the heart-rending, crumbling elegance of Venice, imperial Rome, the opulence of Vienna, sparkling Lucerne. I had seen towering blue-white mountains, the extravagant massing of southern flowers, the rich profusion of the summer vine. I had seen the outpouring of artistic genius in paint and in marble, the jewelled and silken interiors of churches and ducal palaces. And Cullingford had none of these. But there was something in these narrow, grimy streets climbing so tenaciously up hill and down which moved me; some force of energy and resolution, a blunt refusal to submit to blind authority, or blind fate, of which I felt myself to be a part.

I knew there was injustice here, and oppression, knew that my father's sheds were full of women who, labouring the ten hours a day which the law allowed, returned each night to hovels built back to back in dingy rows and the further drudgery of an everlasting maternity; I knew that in all the streets around Fieldhead, around Lawcroft and Low Cross and every other mill in our town, small children were turned out of doors in flocks and left to roam unattended from early morning until the murky evening hour when the factory gates were unlocked to release their mothers.

Yet I was a part of that too, for if my Grandfather Aycliffe had made his fortune by building these hovels, my other grandfather, known to us all as Mayor Agbrigg, had lived in such places himself; my father had been born there, and the memory perhaps had been bred in me. Mayor Agbrigg had been a pauper brat, sent north by the overseer of a poorhouse at so young an age that he had no recollection even of his proper name, being called 'Agbrigg' – since, like a dog, it was necessary to give him a name of some sort to answer to – by an overlooker of the mill where my grandfather had slaved for seventeen hours a day until he turned twenty-one, eating and sleeping on a pile of waste in the corner of a weaving-shed. Yet this remarkable grandparent of mine, who might never have reached that ripe old age of twenty-one, had not only survived but had prospered, had risen by the dogged endurance I so ardently admired to a position of authority, to be Mayor of Cullingford and to send a son to Cambridge. And he had survived, not bitterly and harshly, but with the compassion of true courage, a conviction that all men – and all women – were entitled to basic human dignities.

Grandfather Agbrigg was a plain man, hard-handed, grey-visaged, blunt-spoken like Cullingford itself, yet his strength, to me, was magnificent and at the same time quite familiar in our steep, cobbled streets where so many of our men – our patient, labouring women – also possessed it. He had suffered and overcome, as not everyone could do, but I believed that Cullingford itself, which he seemed so accurately to personify, could overcome its blights, its cruelties, its greeds, could – now that the first mad fever of industrial expansion was over – grow graciously, kindly, with care for all. And that was the challenge – not the agony of the Paris barricades – in which I felt entitled to participate.

Yet my participation, as I well knew, was hampered by three things: my sex, my single status, and by Mrs Agbrigg. I had never set foot in the clamorous sheds of Fieldhead, prevented by my female gender from concerning myself as to the means by which my family fortune, my dowry and my inheritance were made. But watching the mill-girls file into the yard on many a cold morning wrapped in their blankets, clogs sounding painfully on the frozen cobbles, I knew that, had my grandfather failed in his endeavours, I might well have been among them; knew that, had I been a boy, I would already have been set above them as the 'young master' of Fieldhead.

My father's son would have been in no way subject to the interference of his stepmamma, escaping daily from her cloying world of manners and morals to the realities of work and responsibility, the challenges to which my father's daughter felt equally suited to respond. My father's son would have had his own horses by now and his own carriage, would have taken the train to Leeds or London when in his own judgement his circumstances required it. My father's son would have had opinions, commitments, obligations, aims, would have taken risks and made decisions, would have suffered, perhaps, a diversity of blows and failures, but would have been equipped at all times with the glorious weapon of freedom.

My father's daughter, who may not have differed greatly from her unborn brother in temperament and ability, had but one obligation, to be virtuous and obedient; while the only real choice open to her was simply to be married or not to be married. And sitting in my father's garden that day, the hushed, well-polished house behind me, the sprawling, unpolished town below, I rather thought I would be married.

I cannot say that I was consciously looking for love, for although a barely acknowledged part of myself might have gone eagerly towards it, the side of my nature with which I was most familiar had acquired a cautious view of emotion. As a child, made solitary and serious by an invalid mother, I had adored my father, and although in his view he had not failed me – having given me riches, which in Cullingford were looked on as the very warp and weft of happiness – I had known desolate moments since his marriage, a loneliness far colder than my childhood solitude, which did not incline me to build my life once again around another person. Certainly I did not wish to make a marriage of convenience, but while I could appreciate, could almost envy, the rapture which was the breath of life to Venetia, it seemed to me so dangerous that I had small inclination to hazard myself in that direction at all.

A marriage, then, neither of convenience nor of passion, but of mutual trust and liking, an ideal arrangement which in a recess of my mind I was forced to colour with gratitude since it offered me escape both from Mrs Agbrigg and the limitations of spinsterhood. And if no suitable gentleman should immediately present himself, then I would not be foolish – or so I imagined – but would endeavour, within those iron bands surrounding a 'young-lady-at-home', to find some congenial occupation. For my father's daughter was Agbrigg enough to detest failure, and what could be more humiliating, more destructive, more inescapable than a bad marriage?

Not that I could have named, offhand, more than one or two that I envied. Mrs Rawnsley, I knew, had married for the simple reason that at the age of twenty-three she had no longer been able to support the shame of remaining Miss Milner. Mrs Agbrigg had married for respectability, Mrs Sheldon from a desire not so much for the person of Mr Thomas

Sheldon MP as for his political standing. The girls I had met at school appeared with few exceptions to be scrambling into matrimony just as soon as they were able, some of them honestly finding domesticity and motherhood alluring, some of them because 'what else was there to do?', others quite simply to get away from 'papa'.

Yet, on the other hand, I saw nothing in the lives of the maiden ladies I knew best to inspire me with enthusiasm, being frankly irritated by the self-effacing Miss Fielding – daughter of our senior MP – whose fluttering devotion was given not really to God but to his servant, our vicar, whose willing slave she had become; while only the example of Miss Rebecca Mandelbaum offered me a little hope, a little entertainment.

Miss Mandelbaum was unusual for a number of reasons, not least among them her talent as a pianist, which could have taken her to the concert stage had not her parents – for what seemed to them the best of reasons – opposed it. Following the deaths of those parents some years ago, she had taken up residence alone in the no longer fashionable but still very genteel neighbourhood of Blenheim Lane, her independence made possible by her mature years, a substantial inheritance and the understanding of her brother, who as head of the family might well have preferred to keep her at home.

She was a rounded, stately woman who passed her days talking to friends on such thoughtful topics as art, music and philosophy, the nature of truth and justice. Miss Mandelbaum did not care in the least for the triumphs and heartbreaks of an Assembly Rooms Ball; nor, I suspect, did the inadequate drainage of large areas of Cullingford enter her mind other than rarely. But the respective merits of Botticelli and Andrea del Sarto could arouse her to excitement, a Beethoven sonata could leave her mesmerized, while the National Society for Women's Suffrage inspired her, quite rightly, with passion.

'Forgive me, Miss Agbrigg,' she had murmured to me on my third or fourth visit to her quiet house, 'I do not care to speak of personal matters, but I wonder if you have considered how very wealthy you might be one day?'

And when I had assured her that I had, she still seemed compelled to apologize. 'I mention it merely because I am myself very adequately provided for. And do you know, Miss Agbrigg, it has often seemed strange to me that the man from whom I purchase my groceries, any man, in fact, who can, however meagrely, be called a householder, is entitled to his vote at election time. Whereas I, who own this house and another by the sea and a street or two of rented property in Cullingford, am allowed no vote at all. Is it any wonder that so many laws of our land are unjust to women, or simply take no account of women at all, when no woman has had a hand in their making?'

'You are a suffragist then, Miss Mandelbaum?'

'My dear, I believe I am, for I made the acquaintance on a recent visit to Manchester of Miss Lydia Becker, a founder of the Society for Women's Suffrage. Should I succeed in persuading her to visit me and speak a few words, perhaps you would care to attend?'

819

Miss Becker, as it turned out, was unable to oblige but sent instead her lieutenant, a dry and rather angry Miss Tighe, who explained to our select gathering certain matters which seemed to me so obvious and so right that I understood – with the force of a revelation – that I had been born believing them.

I knew – as who did not – that the Reform Bill of 1832 had given the vote to all middle class gentlemen, a privilege which had hitherto belonged exclusively to the aristocracy and any others who possessed property and connections enough to number themselves among the 'ruling classes'. The Reform Bill of 1867 – considerably overdue – had fallen far short of the universal male suffrage which had been demanded, but had granted 'household suffrage', a phrase, Miss Tighe told us, in which a loophole had been spotted, nearly four thousand women in Manchester alone – Miss Tighe among them – who owned houses and income far above the minimum property qualification the bill required, having attempted to place their names on the electoral register.

Miss Tighe had taken her claim to court, where it had been defended by the dedicated and philanthropic barrister Dr Richard Marsden Pankhurst, a man so devoted to the many facets of social justice that he had declared his intention of remaining unmarried the better to pursue them. But the law had declared Miss Tighe's claim to be invalid, maintaining in effect that although the right to vote depended on the amount of property one possessed, that right – like most others – was automatically rendered null and void by the sorry accident of having been born a woman.

Miss Tighe had been present in 1868, immediately after the passing of the Second Reform Bill, at the first public meeting of the newly formed Manchester National Society for Women's Suffrage in Manchester's Free Trade Hall, and had since then associated herself closely with Miss Lydia Becker and those male champions of the suffragist cause, the Quaker politician Mr Jacob Bright and the lawyer Dr Pankhurst. Nor had they contented themselves with public meetings, having agreed – in the very appropriate setting of the Free Trade Hall – to adopt the tactics of the Anti-Corn Law League which a quarter of a century ago had done successful battle against import controls and had given us Free Trade.

It was the aim of the National Society for Women's Suffrage, Miss Tighe went on, to attract attention to the female cause by presenting regular petitions to Parliament as the Anti-Corn Law League had done, Miss Lydia Becker herself having produced a pamphlet entitled 'Directions for Preparing a Petition to the House of Commons' which Miss Tighe would be glad to distribute among us. In 1869 alone, she said, without once referring to any notes or figures, two hundred and fifty-five petitions, requesting the vote for women on the same terms as it had been granted to men, had been presented. The flow of these petitions would continue, the flow of Private Members' Bills must be encouraged to flow with it. Mr Jacob Bright having introduced such a bill two years ago which had passed its second reading in the House before being annihilated by that great enemy of the Women's Cause, the leader of the

Liberal Party, Mr Gladstone, who like numerous others believed female suffrage to be a serious threat to family life.

Mr Gladstone, it was very clear, believed in the concept of woman as domestic angel, his reluctance to burden her with electoral responsibilities stemming from his oft-expressed fear that her fine and gentle nature might be damaged, the delicate structure of her mind distracted from her rightful worship of hearth and home. And if it had occurred to him that the population of England numbered rather more women than men, which would – if enfranchised – make the female a mighty power to be reckoned with, he had not said so.

But the Women's Cause had few other champions in high places. The Conservative leader, Mr Benjamin Disraeli, had expressed cautious sympathy in his younger days when speeches on controversial issues had been very much his style. But once he had taken office and had no need of controversy to get himself noticed, little more had been heard from him on the matter. Nor could the movement rely overmuch on the support of famous women, the great Florence Nightingale having heartily condemned her own sex as being narrowminded, uncooperative and unsympathetic, while it was no secret that Queen Victoria, although a reigning monarch, enjoyed nothing better than the domination of the male, having always insisted in private – during her husband's lifetime – on regarding herself as his 'little wife'. And so strongly was she opposed to the notion of women's rights that she believed any lady – titled or otherwise – who spoke openly in their favour deserved a good whipping, presumably by a dominating male hand.

Women, in Miss Florence Nightingale's opinion, were too feeble. In Queen Victoria's view they could not be feeble enough. What did Miss Mandelbaum think, or Miss Fielding and Miss Agbrigg, Miss Tighe wanted to know?

'You might care to consider getting up a petition of your own,' she said, her keen eyes passing speculatively, a little scornfully, from Miss Mandelbaum's enthusiastic but somewhat flustered expression to Miss Fielding who, as the daughter of a Liberal MP, had not liked the reference to Mr Gladstone, and who furthermore had suspected from the start that the Church, with its creed of submission, could not possibly approve of this. And then her sharp, rather stony gaze resting on me, Miss Tighe smiled.

'The future of the movement – perhaps the fruits of it – must belong to you,' she told me, coming to sit beside me as we partook of Miss Mandelbaum's scented tea and ratafia cakes. 'Why not pay a visit to Manchester, Miss Agbrigg, and make the acquaintance of Miss Lydia Becker and Dr Pankhurst? I could ask my friends the Gouldens to invite you – a perfectly respectable manufacturing family whose daughter Emmeline must be about your age.'

And even had I been less convinced by her explanation of the Women's Cause, the mere fact that I wanted badly to accept her invitation and knew I would not be allowed to do so would have converted me.

Mr Nicholas Barforth invited us to dine that autumn, a circumstance astonishing enough in itself, since for a very long time his entertaining had been done expensively but impersonally in hotels, a necessary if tedious part of his business which he delegated whenever possible to Liam Adair or to Gervase. But his invitation now was most specific and most correct, gilt-edged, gilt-lettered, designed to fill Mrs Agbrigg's heart with joy had she not been too well aware of his intentions.

Mr Nicholas Barforth, it seemed, had decided to take a hand in his son's affairs, to give him, perhaps, one final opportunity. For after all, blood was notoriously thicker than water, and knowing that Gervase would one day have to stand alone against the ambitions of men like his cousin Gideon, Mr Barforth would certainly bring him up to the mark if he could.

'Steady yourself down,' I could imagine him saying, 'and get a steady woman to help you – a sensible lass with money of her own behind her.' And it could be no secret that I was the 'good catch', the strong-minded, steady Law Valley woman of his choice.

'I see,'my father said, the invitation in his hands.

'Precisely,' Mrs Agbrigg answered him. 'I have been dreading this approach, for with the best will in the world I cannot discover one shred of evidence to alter my opinion of that young man. And considering the irregular position of his mother, the rumours by which she is surrounded, I wonder – well, perhaps Grace might have a convenient headache that evening and find herself indisposed?'

But the knowledge – conveyed by Venetia – that Gideon Chard would be among the guests confused Mrs Agbrigg's tactics to a point where, on the evening in question, she failed to make the objections I had been expecting to the rather scanty bodice of my peach-coloured silk, nor to the skirt cut very straight in front and very full behind, the folds of the bustle and the train studded with black velvet bows. She was herself in cinnamon brown, a shade much darker but not unrelated to the tint of her skin, my father narrow and correct in his evening clothes, his face wise and sad as he helped me from the carriage, his own opinion of this almost-proposed marriage – his desire to dispose of me or his fear of losing me – remaining unspoken.

'A historic occasion,' he said as the huge, carved oak door of Tarn Edge was opened to us by the indifferent Barforth butler, who announced our names and abandoned us to a considerably amused Venetia who, having never played hostess before, could not bring herself to treat it as anything but a game.

There was a huge fire in the marble fireplace, costly treasures of Sèvres and Meissen on the mantleshelf, a clock sprouting Cupids and acanthus leaves of a metal which appeared to be gold. The Aubusson rug – repaired, one presumed – was back in its place by the hearth, Mr Barforth standing firmly upon it, his back to the flames, Mr Gideon Chard standing, too, at the corner of the fender, his feet not yet on the precious rug but not too far away, while Gervase, lounging in a red velvet armchair, took a moment to rise, as if his body, after an arduous day of pleasure, required care.

'We have just ridden in from Galton,' Venetia said, as vibrant wih energy as her brother was listless. 'Or, at least, no more than an hour ago, so if I am not immaculately enough turned out for you, you will know the reason why. We were out with the Lawdale at five o'clock this morning, when even the foxes were sleepy.'

'Too sleepy,' put in Gervase, his eyelids drooping. 'There's no sense – and I'll keep on saying it – in disturbing a night-feeder at that hour, when he's still too full of his dinner to run. An afternoon fox, that's the thing – not that Noel Chard would take notice of it.'

'I expect Noel knows what he's doing,' said Gideon, drawling out the words as if none of them could matter less, although we understood quite well that he would allow no criticism of his brother's mastership of the Lawdale Hunt, an office which his family had held for generations.

'You must miss your sport, Mr Chard, in this fine weather,' murmured Mrs Agbrigg artfully offering him an opportunity to demonstrate his worth – since he *was* a sportsman by birth and breeding and *had*, unlike Gervase, spent this glorious afternoon at the mill.

'I miss it enormously,' he said, his voice suave and serious. 'But then, one is obliged to put first things first, after all.'

'Oh lord!' Venetia exclaimed. 'Do you know, Gideon, when you talk like that I wonder if you might have done better as a bishop.'

To which Mr Gideon Chard, without the slightest hint of ill-humour, gave her a slight bow, and smiled.

We ate gamebirds, as I remember, as was appropriate to the season, and various over-cooked vegetables unworthy of their massive silver dishes. The crystal was magnificent, the wine highly satisfactory to the gentlemen, who all drank a great deal, the chocolate cream a decided failure, being of a most uneven consistency and far too sweet. Nor was the conversation more evenly blended, my father and Mr Barforth talking warp and weft, profit and loss, Gervase refusing deliberately and impudently to speak one word that was not connected with foxhunting, while Gideon Chard maintained an attentive and rather careful silence, appalled, I imagine, by the food, which would never have been permitted to leave the kitchens at Listonby, and by the haphazard service, which as his mother's son must have amazed him.

I was silent too, feeling stiff and awkward and false, and it was a relief to me when, the meal over, Venetia finally remembered her duty and escorted her female guests back to the drawing-room and installed us in deep armchairs by the fireside, Mrs Agbrigg placidly partaking of coffee and cakes while Venetia, her cheeks flushed wih wine and firelight, lost herself at once in an apparently blissful dream.

There was a long silence, Mrs Agbrigg and I having nothing to say to each other, Venetia and I nothing that could be said in Mrs Agbrigg's hearing, and noting her sharp eyes seeking out the flaw in the Aubusson rug, her satisfied smile when she found it, I was reminded of her objections to Venetia as a friend, to Gervase as a husband, and felt my colour rise.

He was not, of course, attracted to me, I felt absolutely certain of that. But should sufficient pressure be brought to bear I thought he might well find it easier, safer, to succumb; might shrug those lean, mischievous shoulders and say 'Why not?', thus making me mistress of this grand, neglected house and sister to Venetia. And because Venetia, already, was closer to me than any sister, I allowed that imaginary future to ease itself into my mind, my fancy restoring Tarn Edge to its former splendour, my voice speaking sharply to that supercilious butler, that disastrous cook; taking my breakfast with Venetia in the back parlour, declaring myself 'not at home' when Mrs Agbrigg came to call; and then I found myself smiling, because in this pleasant, schoolroom fantasy of marriage I had entirely forgotten the husband – Gervase.

One could not, of course, forget Gideon Chard. He would take and maintain his place anywhere, in fact or in fantasy, by his simple refusal ever to be overlooked. But I had no reason to believe he had ever thought of me with anything warmer than self-interest. Mr Nicholas Barforth was the wealthiest man in the Law Valley and Venetia's share of his fortune would be considerable, but her inheritance was encumbered by the existence of a brother who *might* – how could one ever be sure? – discover within himself a sudden interest in commerce. Whereas I, although I did not know the exact terms of my father's will, could expect my share of his worldly goods eventually to consist of the whole. And I had no brother to stand between my husband and complete possession of Fieldhead.

Yet Fieldhead itself suddenly oppressed me – Mrs Agbrigg's house, never mine – and I knew with a fierce and persistent certainty that I must marry a man with the means to take me away from there. No husband of mine must ever depend entirely on Agbrigg favour, reducing me from the sorry position of 'daughter-at-home' to the even more unbearable level of 'married-daughter-at-home', the young mistress forever subservient to the old. I must have an establishment of my own, must have some measure of authority and freedom; and no fortune-hunter, however noble or shrewd or desirable, could give me that.

'You seem very comfortable,' Mr Barforth told us from the doorway, crossing the room to stand on the hearthrug again, his son and his nephew and my father following behind.

'Sit down by your wife, Jonas,' he said, and my father, with his sad wry smile, obediently sat. 'Venetia, you can give us our coffee. Gideon, sit there. Gervase – there.' It was done.

He had arranged us to his own satisfaction and for as long as it suited him, for life perhaps, Venetia, still in her blissful dream of Charles Heron, inattentive and uncaring, but sitting nevertheless by Gideon Chard; Gervase, his mother's son, sitting just the same by me; Mr Barforth himself still planted on the hearthrug, dominating the room, his wide back absorbing the warmth of the fire, his keen eyes well satisfied. He had arranged us, and knowing his disposition to be both autocratic and vindictive, I wondered how he would bear his disappointment, so certain was I that it could never be.

824

5

It was an autumn of petty and intense frustrations, of officious supervision and an unremitting, heavy-handed control. Aunt Faith's sister, Mrs Frederick Hobhouse – my Aunt Prudence – the owner of a flourishing school for girls in Ambleside, invited me to stay with her and was told, with scant courtesy, that I was too young to travel in such wild country alone. Miss Tighe sent a correct little letter from Manchester wondering if Mrs Agbrigg could 'spare' me for a week or two and was refused in terms which humiliated me, although Miss Tighe, when I met her again, seemed amused by them.

'Poor lamb,' she said, her shrewd, hard eyes atwinkle. 'You are bound hand and foot, I know it. And although the bonds, if you examine them well, are made of nothing but convention, we have been so thoroughly trained, have we not, to obey mamma and papa, that it seems impossible to break free. Yes, dear, a strong-minded mamma can be a great burden. You may find a husband somewhat easier to manage.'

And I was in no doubt that, day by day, Mrs Agbrigg was forcing me towards that same conclusion.

My cousin Blanche returned home at the start of the winter, looking as lovely and – one could not avoid noticing it – as virginal as ever, and immediately Aunt Caroline, who had been living quietly since the wedding, awoke to her accustomed activity, organizing an ambitious programme of winter events which one could only assume to be her swan-song. The house once more was full of guests, fox-hunting gentlemen from London availing themselves of the well-stocked Listonby stables, ladies with double-barrelled names and flat, high-bred voices who sat about all day – like Blanche – in the Great Hall, where tea and muffins, hot chocolate and gingerbread, chilled white or hot, spiced wine were in constant supply, served by footmen in Listonby's blue and gold livery who seemed possessed of the ability to materialize from thin air.

'Wonderful, is it not,' Blanche asked me, stifling a contented yawn, 'how it all happens, as if by magic?'

But the magician – as Blanche well knew – had been up since dawn setting these luxurious wheels in motion and would not retire that night until the last of her guests had been escorted ceremoniously to bed.

'Aunt Caroline must work extremely hard,' I suggested, but Blanche only smiled.

'She loves it, Grace – simply thrives on it. She wouldn't be without it for the world. And as for me – well, I haven't the least notion of depriving her. It would be too unkind.'

Yet, although Blanche seemed content to remain a pampered guest in her own home for ever, there would be times, surely, when Sir Dominic's wife must take precedence over his widowed mother? And I wondered, with some amusement and a certain sympathy, how Aunt Caroline would come to terms with that.

There was a change of guests that first fine November Saturday, one house-party being carefully conveyed to the station to catch the morning train, the next one not due until Monday, making dinner that night a family occasion in the small, early Georgian saloon, an apartment the colour of musk roses where Aunt Caroline – who had 'improved' so much else at Listonby – had retained the original century old Baroque mouldings, the elegant, satin-covered Regency chairs, the impression of great age and the gradual, heart-searching decay of great beauty.

'How nice to be *en famille*,' she said, smiling very brightly as Blanche sat down at the head of the table opposite her bridegroom, not troubling in the least as to where anyone else should sit; claiming, in fact, the privileges of the lady of the manor while not even appearing to notice the responsibilities. But the Duke of South Erin, very much *en famille* at Listonby, automatically took the place of honour to the right of Blanche, Aunt Caroline to the right of Dominic, Gideon Chard and Venetia finding themselves side by side, an indication, one supposed, that Aunt Caroline had abandoned her hopes of an earl's daughter and decided to 'see reason'; while Noel Chard, not receiving any instructions, hesitated, his eyes on the empty chair beside Blanche, wondering perhaps if he should be paying attention to me until his mother deposited me to the left of Dominic and released him.

Unlike Tarn Edge, the food was superb, the service miraculous, the conversation dull, I thought, but without strain, Sir Dominic and the weather-beaten little duke confining themselves to hunting and shooting stories of a technicality which rendered them incomprehensible to me, although Gideon and even Venetia from time to time joined in, having all of them in their day jumped a wider ditch in pursuit of a craftier fox, confirming my belief, as the brandied oranges and champagne syllabubs were brought in, that a sportsman will discuss his sport with the same fervour as an invalid listing his symptoms, and to the same stultifying effect.

Noel Chard, who had served as master of the Lawdale Hunt during Sir Dominic's absence, made small contribution to these equine enthusiasms, his attention absorbed by Blanche, his solicitude arousing in her an even greater helplessness than usual, a total inability to manage her napkin or reach her glass which clearly convinced Noel – if few others – of her frailty and her need, at all times, to be handled with care. Aunt Caroline too was silent, not really listening to the strident voices of her sons, not even calling them to order when one of them let slip an audible 'damn', a sure indication that her thoughts were very much occupied.

'When does Aunt Faith return from France?' she asked me, although Blanche had mentioned the date not an hour before, and when I said that it would be the week after Christmas, she sighed and muttered: 'How inconvenient, since they could join us –', without specifying who or where.

The dessert over, there was a pause, my eyes and Venetia's going automatically to Aunt Caroline for our signal to withdraw, Dominic too glancing sharply at his mother, who had never before kept the ladies in the dining-room so long, depriving the squire of his port and cigars and the freedom to say 'damn' and worse than that if he had a mind.

'Mamma?' he said, puzzled and rather put out, revealing himself already as a gentleman who not only expected to get his own way but to get it at once, the very moment – as any fool could see – that he desired it.

'Yes, Dominic?' she replied.

'Shouldn't you –'

'No,' she said. 'Not I, dear – not now.'

And even then there was a moment before Blanche, catching her husband's irritable eye, exclaimed, 'Oh goodness! Are you waiting for *me*?', and started to her feet, her movement clearly requiring the assistance of Noel Chard if it was to be successfully completed.

But Aunt Caroline, having scored her point and proved her daughter-in-law to be incompetent, shook her head, turning imperious again.

'In a moment, dear. First there is a word to be said, and a toast to be drunk, I think.'

'Oh yes,' Blanche agreed, sliding back into her chair, assuming the toast was to be 'long life and happiness to the bride', so that she was unprepared and completely vulnerable when Aunt Caroline announced: 'Dominic, as the head of the family, already knows what I have to say. I have his approval and am in no doubt of yours. The Duke of South Erin has aked me to be his wife – and I have agreed to it, which should surprise no one.'

And through the sudden scraping back of chairs, the exclamations and the laughter as the little duke was shaken by the hand and the tall duchess kissed in turn by each of her tall sons – all three of them keenly alive to the advantages of a ducal step-papa – I heard Venetia's clear voice say 'Lord, what a lark! You've always been a duchess, Aunt Caroline', while Blanche, feeling the weight of Listonby already on her shoulders, howled out her dismay. 'You didn't *tell* me, Dominic.'

The match, of course, was altogether splendid, for while South Erin was not a great political duke, his family no older than the Clevedons and the Chards themselves, he was of the nobility, not the simple landed gentry as they were, and even Sir Dominic, whose view of his own worth must have been a great comfort to him, was impressed.

There would be a tall, somewhat dilapidated house in Belgravia for Aunt Caroline to renovate, an estate in Devonshire for her to 'improve' in her unique fashion, a presentation at Court, for although our Queen did not approve of second marriages, considering that the heart of any decent widow should belong, like her own, in her husband's grave, she could hardly refuse audience to the new Duchess of South Erin.

Aunt Caroline, in fact, had done far better than anyone had expected for the second time in her life, and there was no doubt that her sons – Dominic already contemplating a flirtation with politics, Noel eager for military promotion, Gideon ready to pick up power and influence wherever he found it – were very pleased with her. They remained a long time in the dining-room with the pleasant, nut-brown little duke, to tell him so; and finding Blanche's indignation hard to bear – having no answer to her 'How am I to manage this great barracks of a place when everyone knows I have no head for figures and cannot remember names – when I just want to be peaceful and *comfortable*' – I soon made my escape.

From the painted, panelled staircase rising out of the Great Hall one reached the ballroom, the darkness of a winter evening not really hiding its gilt and crystal splendour, and beyond it came the Long Gallery, lined on both sides with massively framed Chards, their stern faces registering no surprise, in this cheapjack modern world, that a tradesman's daughter had first married one of their descendants and had now snared herself a duke.

But I had seen these portraits too many times before to play the old game of deciding which ones reminded me most of Dominic, or Noel, or Gideon, and walking briskly from end to end, it seemed to me that in Blanche's shoes I would have welcomed this marriage. In Blanche's shoes I would have resented so powerful a mother-in-law as Aunt Caroline, would already have acquainted myself with every linen cupboard and china cupboard at Listonby, with the guest book and the menu book, with the staff and the tenants, with the formidable expertise of my predecessor, so that hopefully and in time I might do even better. But Blanche's shoes – alas – included the sporting, self-centred Sir Dominic, and smiling as I realized how little I desired to acquaint myself with him – how little, indeed, there was in him with which to be acquainted – I turned to retrace my steps and encountered Gideon, amazing myself by the lurch my stomach gave at the suspicion – I would not call it the hope – that he had come here not by chance but to look for me.

Amazed. And then, because it was absolutely necessary to be cool, I said coolly, lightly, 'What exciting news!', deliberately setting a tone of insipid and safe formality.

'Yes indeed – although Blanche does not seem to think so.'

'Oh well, there is no need to worry about Blanche She will find someone else to look after her.'

'I daresay – except that my brother Noel will be obliged to rejoin his regiment in the New Year.'

And not wishing to answer this, finding it too personal, too apt to lead to other things, although I could not have named them, I turned back to the portraits, chancing on the one gentleman in that gallery who was not a Chard, a saturnine and undoubtedly handsome face reminding me strongly of Mr Nicholas Barforth, although it was Sir Joel Barforth, his and Aunt Caroline's father.

'My manufacturing grandfather,' Gideon said, half-smiling. 'Do you know, I believe Dominic will take that picture down when Mamma has gone to South Erin. We were made to suffer, somewhat, at school because father had married into "trade".'

'But Dominic has done the same.'

'Yes. But Blanche is a generation away from the more sordid side of it. And she *is* very beautiful.

'Yes.'

'And very spoiled.'

'Yes. And I am very fond of her.'

'So are we all, for there is nothing of the heavy woollen district about her. One could take her just about anywhere. And, of course, she has such a lot of money.'

I should have been very angry with him then. He had spoken, I think, with that intention. But there was something behind his words which caught and distracted my temper, something directed against himself which, instead of the sharp retort I could have made, caused me most astonishingly to enquire, 'Is Dominic – displeased – that you have gone into trade yourself? Does he feel –'

'What? That I am a traitor to my class? Very likely.'

'Well – I am sorry for that.'

'How kind. But there is no need. He may well call me a money-grubbing tradesman the next time we quarrel, but if anyone else dared to do so you can be sure my brother Dominic would knock him down.'

'And you would do the same for Dominic, naturally.'

'Naturally.'

'Gideon –', and I did not at all wish to ask him this question, did not wish to offer him what he would see as sympathy – which *was* sympathy. 'Gideon – have you found it very difficult – I mean, in the Piece Hall and the Wool Exchange?'

'Oh yes,' he said, very nonchalant, negligent almost. 'To tell the truth, I find Cullingford difficult altogether. But then, difficulties exist to be overcome, don't you know?'

'Yes, I do know.'

'I rather thought you might.'

And having no answer ready – because he should not have been thinking of me at all and I should not have been so very pleased, so cat-in-the-cream-pot smug to know he had – I looked up into his face and for what seemed a long time could not look away again, held by something I was unable to name but which my body recognized as desire. And not his desire alone, not merely the narrowing of his eyes in sudden concentration, the faint air of surprise about him, his attitude of listening to his own body, the quickening of his own pulse-beat, the stirrings of heat and hunger. Not that alone but my own response to it, the feeling of new blood being somehow released inside me and flowing vigorously, rhythmically, towards an awareness not only of my own body but of the dark, hard, beautiful body of Gideon Chard, rushing me headlong towards the recognition, the *expectation* of physical pleasure.

I had grown accustomed to thinking of myself as a young woman of sense and moderation, but what had awakened in me now – and how could I doubt it had always been there? – was a most immoderate sensuality. And although I had known of the existence of this phenomenon – natural, I had been led to believe, in men but wanton in women – I was unprepared for the sheer force of it, the enormity, this tempestuous arousal not of the feminine side of my nature but of the *female*; the deep-rooted, primitive urge to submit. How glorious! How appalling! How total the self-betrayal! How complete the self-fulfilment! How perilous! Yet that spice of fear was in itself desirable, and nothing in my glowing, expanding limbs nor in my dizzy head held me away from it. He had only to touch me – only that. I could not resist him, no matter what it cost me – *could* not – until the moment I did so and said in a quick, cool little voice: – 'It is very dark in here and rather chilly.'

'Yes,' he said, 'so it is,' his voice telling me nothing, a man not without experience of women, who knew when his moment had passed.

It was over. I had come to no harm. But as I walked back down the painted staircase I was as careful on my feet as an invalid, aware that I had escaped not by my own resolution alone, for if he *had* touched me, if – And my thought could extend no further, cut out, veered aside, refusing, like a fractious horse at a ditch, to hazard itself.

We were to drive to Galton Abbey the next morning, Blanche's satisfaction in being a married woman who could now act as chaperone to Venetia and myself altogether swamped by her gloom at Aunt Caroline's desertion. And as we negotiated the bare November lanes she had much to say on the subject of her mother-in-law's ambition and duplicity.

'She does not care a fig about the poor little man himself, you can be very sure of that. All she sees is a ducal coronet and being a society hostess in Belgravia. Not that she will even stay in London once she gets there. Oh no, she will be forever coming back to Listonby to satisfy herself that things were better in her day. And it is not my fault, for if she intended running off like this – as I am sure she did – then she should have *said* so. Dominic thinks it a small matter. Just carry on, he tells me, as mother does. Well – Dominic Chard has not the faintest idea of how those stupendous meals arrive on his table four times every day, and neither have I.'

Nor much intention, I thought, of finding out, since by the end of the first mile she was considering how a secretary, a companion, and her cousin Grace Agbrigg, might be pressed into her service.

'You could come over every Friday to Monday and stay on until Tuesday, or not go home at all. You would be glad to get away from Mrs Agbrigg, and I would be glad of you.'

But Venetia, dismissing this suggestion out of hand, made her own designs on my future very clear by declaring, 'Nonsense, Blanche, you must manage your own life as best you can, for Grace – if she would like it – could soon have a life of her own.'

The house at Galton was quite small and very old, older indeed than the date of its construction, the first Clevedon having come here as a conqueror, a supporter of King Henry's breach with papal authority which had allowed him, an English Protestant, to pull the Roman Catholic abbey down and use its ancient stones to build himself a manor. I had been here only once before in childhood, when the house had seemed dark and eerie, an emptiness about it of which I could not be sure, which did not seem, somehow, to be empty at all, so that I had spent a night of terror in a low-ceilinged chamber, a heavily curtained bed, plagued by the creaking of old wood and the unaccustomed noises of the open countryside, convinced that the room was dangerous, yet not daring to venture into the passage outside, that airless, pitch-black tunnel which might have taken me anywhere.

But today, although the house was certainly low, its colour a shade darker than the November sky, its situation, on what in another season would be a leafy bend of the river, was very beautiful; the parlour where Mrs Barforth awaited us furnished with over-stuffed chintz, a good fire burning, an ageing dog and cat lying on the rug in pleasing harmony.

It was not a tidy room, the pewter jugs on the mantelshelf brimming over with odds and ends of letters and bills, a button-hook, a scrap of leather, a pair of riding gloves thrown down on the sofa, the sofa itself showing traces of animal hair. Nor was Mrs Barforth a tidy woman, having come indoors, I thought, when our carriage wheels had reminded her she was expecting guests, leaving herself no time and probably no inclination to change her riding-habit for a morning gown.

'Darling,' she said, giving Venetia's cheek a companionable kiss, 'and Lady Chard – good heavens, Blanche, how very grand that sounds! Is it not altogether too heavy for you? And Miss Agbrigg –'

And although her smile and her swift, light green gaze were as frank as Venetia's her handclasp firm and honest, my suspicion that her husband must have told her to consider me as a possible bride for Gervase stiffened my manner and my tongue, making me formal and cold.

'What an interesting house, Mrs Barforth.'

'Oh, do you think so? Then allow me to show it to you.' And while Blanche dozed by the fire, displaying the same purring delight in her creature comforts as the cat, I was taken on a tour of the house which meant far more to Mrs Georgiana Barforth than any riches the Barforth mills could provide, for which she had been prepared to sacrifice her liberty and her peace of mind – one supposed – so that she might pass on this noble heritage of the Clevedons to her Clevedon-Barforth son.

There was a Great Hall here too, minute when compared to Listonby, being only twenty feet square, a bare stone floor, a few battered oak chests, a long oak table set out with bowls and tankards of dented pewter. There was a high stone fireplace, weaponry and family portraits on the walls, stone steps leading to the upper floor where that creaking rabbit-warren of passages awaited, those low, stone-flagged bed-chambers with their tiny mullioned windows, their impression of peopled emptiness which comes from great age.

'That,' Venetia said, indicating a picture of a narrow-gowned Georgian lady, 'was my Great-grandmamma Venetia, who was an earl's daughter no less, although I have heard that the noble earl was not pleased to be connected with us, mamma.'

'He was not,' Mrs Barforth cheerfully agreed. 'So little pleased that he disinherited her, or would have done so had there been anything to inherit. She was very poor, alas, like the rest of us –'

'Are we poor, mamma? I had not noticed it.'

'Ah,' Mrs Barforth said, smiling, meeting Venetia's clear, slightly accusing eyes without flinching, 'I believe I was speaking of the past, when we were truly poor, my brother and I and Sir Julian and everyone else we knew, and one forgets – Miss Agbrigg, do tell me what you think of this picture over here.'

It was a large canvas, prominently displayed above the hearth, showing a young man the same age as Gervase, the same sporting jacket and flamboyant neck-tie Gervase often wore, the same nervous, whipcord energy that could just as easily ebb or flow, the pale pointed face and auburn hair that for some reason she wished me to mistake for Gervase, although I knew it could not be he.

'It is my Uncle Peregrine,' Venetia said flatly, denying her mother this small satisfaction. 'You were supposed to take him for Gervase. Everyone else does. But it is the famous Perry Clevedon who could bring down eighty grouse wih eighty shots any day of the week –'

'My brother,' Mrs Barforth said, smiling at her daughter sadly, although she was offering the explanation to me, 'died some years ago, unmarried. We were very closely united, for we had been brought up here together without any other company and needing none. We were, I believe, perfectly happy. A dangerous gift, I admit, for any child, such happiness, since one tended to think the whole of life would be like that, and learned only slowly otherwise. His death was not only a great and lasting grief to me but it left Galton, for the first time in three hundred years, without a direct male heir. I wonder, Miss Agbrigg, if you realize how much that matters to people like us?'

'Very likely I do not, Mrs Barforth. I know the name of my great-grandparents but beyond that I am uncertain as to just who, or what, my family may have been.

'Yes – forgive me, Miss Agbrigg, but I believe the word "inheritance" as used in the cities tends to imply money, or property which can be readily converted into money ...? With us it is not quite like that. What this estate of Galton means is not profit, not material gain of any kind, but a tradition of service to the land that has supported us these three hundred years, service to the tenants who farm it, and to the village communities settled upon it. It is a very hard life, Miss Agbrigg, a very dedicated, specialized existence – not so much an inheritance, I think, as a *trust* with which the men of my family have always kept faith.'

And being in no doubt at all that, albeit gently and with considerable embarrassment, she was nevertheless warning me that my middle-class values could accord neither with Galton nor with her son, I made some non-committal answer and moved away from the fire to the narrow mullioned window, seeking a distraction and instantly finding it in the sight of horsemen approaching at speed down the hillside.

They came splashing across the stream and into the courtyard, Gervase Barforth and all three Chards, mud-spattered, wet through, and quite magnificent, shaking off the physical discomforts of November wind and weather with a lordly nonchalance proper to the squirearchy. And instantly Mrs Barforth, whose house had seemed ill-equipped for the serving of tea to ladies, broke free from the restraints my presence had imposed upon her, her face glowing with the uncomplicated joy of being among her 'own people' as she served them strong ale and mulled wine, standing companionably among them as they crowded to the fire and drank deep, their coats steaming. And while Noel Chard did briefly say to her 'You may have heard that mamma is to be a duchess', to which she replied 'Oh yes – I have a maid who talks to the maids at Listonby …', her attention was not diverted from these young men who in their insolent, unruly splendour were a thousand miles away from Cullingford.

Yet they were not a contented band, having found no sport that morning, so little prospect of it that afternoon that in disgust they had decided to ride home, the scarcity of foxes inclining Sir Dominic to believe that some villainous gang of farmers, in order to protect their miserable chicken-runs, had been shooting the beasts or poisoning them, instead of leaving them to be properly slaughtered by gentlemen.

'Not on my land they haven't,' said Gervase.

'What land is that?' enquired Sir Dominic who, as a first-born son, liked to be precise in matters of inheritance.

'This land.'

'Oh – I beg your pardon. I thought *this* land belonged to your father.'

Perhaps no real slight had been intended, Sir Dominic feeling quite simply a little peevish and knowing no reason why others should not suffer for it. But for an instant there was an ugly flaring of tempers, Gervase tensing himself like an angry, wary cat, the Chards closing ranks, three hounds, I thought, of high and disdainful pedigree who would turn as one and rend to pieces all who threatened them. But it was Blanche, or rather her voice drifting lazily from the doorway, which put out this spark of combat, drawing all eyes towards her as she came into the room and simply stood there, allowing herself to be looked at, rosy and a little dishevelled from her sleep, her whole body languorous, still purring with the pleasures of idleness.

Noel Chard succumbed at once, wanting nothing now but to gaze at her.

'Heavens,' she said, 'such a racket! – I thought we had been invaded.' And now it was Gideon who, grinning suddenly, relaxed and gave her a slight bow.

'I had forgotten you would be here,' said Sir Dominic, a man who rarely remembered his wife until bedtime in any case. But looking at her now, the silver and ivory of her, the dreamy, slumberous quality which was not sensuality but which he perhaps had mistaken for sensuality, I saw him swallow hard, his quarrel with Gervase, his irritation with his gamekeepers and with the foxes shrinking to a proper childishness before the instinctive, eternal wisdom of a beautiful woman.

'I have been asleep,' she said, her manner, her tone, everything about her conveying that this simple remark of hers – if one really listened to it – was not only of great importance but exceedingly profound.

Noel Chard smiled at her fondly; Gideon Chard smiled too, not fondly but with amusement and speculation, and Gervase smiled with him. Dominic Chard, her husband, continued to look at her with the same

833

acute concentration I had seen the night before in Gideon, calculating the extent of his desire.

'There now,' she said, stretching herself a little. 'I believe I am awake.' And with none of the book-learning Venetia and I had so diligently acquired at school, she had disarmed them all.

A simple country luncheon was set out on the hall table, bread and cheese and pickles, jugs of milk and mugs of ale, a huge plum cake, sweet red apples. And afterwards, the sun having made up its mind to shine, the gentlemen strolled outside, having drunk themselves through their ill-humour and back again, to an even greater restlessness.

'I shall go back to the parlour, Aunt Georgiana, if I may,' said Blanche, 'or they will be making wagers ere long, and doing foolish things – one can read the signs. You had better stay with me, Grace, and keep warm.' But half an hour of renewed complaining about her mother-in-law wearied me and as soon as her eyelids began to close I took my cloak and went outdoors, responding gladly to the onslaught of the raw, damp wind, delighted by the very greyness of the sky, the sweep of the bare brown land.

Venetia and her mother were standing by the dry-stone wall of a nearby field, both women watching intently as Gervase came cantering across the rough grass and took his horse cleanly over a long pole supported between two posts which had been cut quite roughly so that the jump could be lowered or, as seemed the present intention, made higher still.

There had, quite naturally, been a wager, Gervase having declared his chestnut mare capable of jumping higher than Dominic's roan or the two sleek Listonby bays of Noel and Gideon. And since he had offered twenty Barforth guineas to back his claim – a sum which Noel, at least, would find hard to raise from his army pay, or Gideon from whatever salary Mr Barforth paid him – they had set up the practice fence which, as apparently all Galton and Listonby knew, the legendary Perry Clevedon had jumped regularly, drunk or sober, day or night, to a height of seven feet.

I could see no real danger except to someone's pride or someone's pocket, for I was no horsewoman and had nothing but imagination to tell me of the terrors and exhilarations, the cool nerve and fine judgement that propelled each animal in turn into that fierce-arched leaping and safely to the wet, uneven ground again.

'Higher?' said Gervase.

And since Mrs Barforth's two elderly grooms had enough to do elsewhere without catering to the whims of gentlemen, Noel Chard and Gervase were obliged to lift the pole from its groove and slot it into the one above, Sir Dominic disdaining so menial a task, Gideon quite simply ignoring it.

Noel, predictably, was the first to go; a moment of insufficient determination, or the habit perhaps of never taking first place, which caused his horse to pull up short in stubborn refusal, sending Noel over the animal's head and into the mud from which he emerged smiling, a good sport and a good loser.

'Higher?' said Gervase.

And a quarter of an hour later it was Sir Dominic who hit the ground, demonstrating, as he got up, that although he was furious and had *expected* to win – felt that a man in his position *ought* to win – he had the good manners not to say so.

'Well, Gideon –' he ordered curtly, not wishing to make too much of it, but implying, just the same, that the honour of Listonby was now at stake and must not be sacrificed to this mongrel Clevedon-Barforth. And Gideon, responding to the appeal of the family loyalty – although he may also have been thinking of those twenty guineas – rode his tall bay horse forward at the gallop and lifting himself in the saddle cleared what amounted to the height of a man with apparent ease.

'Well done,' said Noel.

'Not bad,' said Sir Dominic.

'Higher?' said Gervase.

'Oh lord!' called out Venetia, 'do we have to stand here all day?' But she did not move, her eyes fixed on her brother with an intensity which forced me to look at him too, and after a long scrutiny to see what Venetia may always have seen in him and which their mother – the sister of Peregrine Clevedon – might not care to contemplate.

There had from the start been something in his manner which I felt certain I had remarked in him before, and it took time – more time than was readily available – to understand the similarity between this lithe, keen-eyed rider and the young gentleman who at eleven o'clock one morning had lounged at the breakfast-table playing a languid but very dangerous game with his father's temper.

That young gentleman had been malicious, provocative, foolhardy. He had also been afraid. And his fear had not only been of his father – who was a frightening man – but of his own compulsion to put himself so continuously to the test. He had deliberately and skilfully aroused his father's wrath that morning. *This* morning it had been Gervase, not the Chards, who had flung down the challenge, Gervase who seemed determined to see it through to a possibly bitter end. And watching his lean figure astride that fretful, difficult horse, his resemblance to his uncle, Perry Clevedon, now so marked that the portrait in the hall might have come to life, I knew, with a great, complex pang of surprise and sympathy and irritation, that he was afraid of this too. And I had no need of Venetia's frowning anxiety to tell me that if his nerve should suddenly snap – as it might, as eventually, I supposed, it *must* – then he would grievously hurt himself.

'Higher?' he said.

'As high as you please,' answered Gideon. And with a spitefulness quite alien to my nature I concluded that Gideon – that country gentleman of impeccable pedigree who believed he might find the way to pick up a manufacturer's fortune without soiling his hands – lacked the imagination to be afraid.

At their first attempt both horses refused, snorting and wild of eye, steaming with effort. But at the second try both Gideon and Gervase cleared the seven-foot pole by an inch apiece, which should, I thought, have been more than enough.

'We could leave it there,' said Noel. 'What about it, Dominic?' But

835

before the baronet could pass judgement, Gervase, demonstrating that he was not subject to the laws of Listonby, shook his head.

'We need a clear decision, don't we – if you're up to it, Gideon?'

Gideon Chard shrugged his wide shoulders, nodded his head, and once again, with far less than an inch to spare this time, he got his sweating mount over the jump, inelegantly I thought, with more force about it than finesse, demanding more from the horse than it had wanted to give and offering only a casual pat on the neck as a reward.

But he was clear for the second time. He had completed his course and whatever happened now he had made his profit.

With every breath in my body I wanted Gervase to win. My muscles strained for him, my own city-bred spirit flinched with him as his horse began to churn up the mud again, the smell of steaming horseflesh and the animal's laboured breathing remaining in my memory long after; a remnant of it lodging there still.

I never understood the technicalities of what occurred. I thought for a moment he had jumped clear, but the pole was knocked loose and the horse – they told me afterwards – came down hard upon it with a front hoof. I think I heard the crack of splintering bone – perhaps not; certainly I heard that terrible screaming and the crash as they fell to earth together, horse and rider and that murderous wooden structure; the thud of feet and the short, bitten-off curses as the Chards flung themselves from their own saddles and came running.

'Dear God!' I heard Mrs Barforth mutter as they dragged Gervase clear of the lovely, ruined chestnut body which made no attempt to rise with him.

'No –' said Venetia, pushing some invisible menace away with a clenched hand. 'Gervase –'

But although he stood erect for a moment, his neck, his spine, his legs unbroken, having escaped once again the fate of his uncle Peregrine, he suddenly sank down on one knee and remained there, his face lowered and hidden, his hand on the neck of the horse which lay quivering and, even to my inexpert eye, dying on the muddy ground.

Get up, I thought, Gervase get up, for although it would have seemed natural enough to me – and touchingly human – had he flung his arms around the horse's head and wept, I knew the Chards would not find it so. For there were rules now, of custom, of breeding, of good manners, which must be obeyed. The horse was dying and must be put out of its misery. And since it belonged to Gervase and he was to blame for the position in which it found itself, then what – three pairs of disdainful Chard eyes wanted to know – was he doing kneeling beside it, his head bowed as if he were praying over it, instead of stirring himself to do the decent thing?

'You should go and fetch a gun, shouldn't you,' said Gideon, not really asking a question.

'And you'd best be quick about it,' ordered Sir Dominic, 'for that animal is suffering. Good God, *Gervase* –'

'Should I –?' began Noel, and was instantly quelled by the baronet who believed, quite rightly, that the disposal of a man's horse was no one's business but his own.

They were, of course, quite right about everything. The horse must be shot. That dreadful, quivering agony must be ended, and quickly, by the man who had caused it, or the whole of the county would hear of it – and condemn it – by tomorrow morning.

But Gervase did not lift his head, could not expose whatever it was he might be feeling to anyone. And realizing that neither Venetia nor his mother – who certainly would have gone to fetch that gun by now – knew how to help him, I took a step forward, looked without seeing the mess on the ground, and said, very tart and prim and city-bred: 'Well, whatever is to happen, I can see no reason why we should all stand around and watch. I have never owned a horse, but I can well imagine that its loss must be a private matter. In any case, I am cold and would like to go indoors to that glorious fire of yours, Mrs Barforth, if I may? I told Blanche I would only be a moment and she might be growing concerned.'

'Yes – yes, of course,' Mrs Barforth answered absently, her face very white, and then suddenly understanding. '*Of course* – let's all go in, shall we? I had quite forgotten Blanche.'

And so we talked of Blanche as we made our way back to the house, the men leading their horses, my voice continuing to exclaim about the cold weather, the hope that my cousin had not ventured outdoors and lost her way, any commonplace remark my tongue could find to speak, while at some tunnel at the end of my mind I watched that kneeling figure made smaller by distance and by solitude; a man grieving for what? Because he was not Peregrine Clevedon, nor even Nicholas Barforth? Because the conflict around him and within him did not allow him a true identity at all? Because he wanted, and did not want, the same things at the same time? I couldn't know. It was not my concern. It would be better, I thought, to leave the conclusion to Venetia, or to Miss Diana Flood.

6

We heard the shot as we sat drinking tea in the chintzy, firelit parlour, and although Venetia winced and Mrs Barforth looked as if she badly wanted to rush outdoors, she sat down again while Blanche continued to pour and to murmur 'Sugar and cream?' as if nothing had happened at all.

'The afternoon is drawing in,' she said brightly, 'we must soon be on our way. I have had such a pleasant afternoon, Aunt Georgiana.'

'I am so glad, dear.'

But Venetia, as always, disdained these social posturings.

'I must see Gervase before I leave,' she declared and, since the Chards had already gone, I soon found myself pressed into her service.

'He will not be in the house. I will look in the stables, Grace, while you look in the cloister.' And when I began to protest that I would not know what to say to him and should one not respect his evident wish to be alone, she stamped her foot and almost flew at me. 'Heavens, Grace, how stubborn you are! All you need say is that I want to see him, and I am sure he will not bite you for that.'

'But Venetia – the cloister?'

'Lord – what is there in the cloister to bother you? I don't ask you to go to the stables because I know you are nervous of the horses and ladylike about the muck. But there is nothing in the cloister except, one hopes, Gervase – and even that is not likely.'

And so, trusting her, I hurried to the little side door she indicated and the short covered walk which took me to the cloister, the only part of the original abbey to remain intact, a hushed and airless place, too old for comfort, where I found Gervase – as she had known I would – leaning against one blank wall and staring at another.

There was no point in prolonging a silence that could only be awkward and, realizing he had seen me, I called out at once, 'Gervase, I am so sorry but we are leaving now, and Venetia is looking for you.'

'Is she?' he said, his voice, to my great relief, perfectly under control, the lounging, drawling young squire again, hard and insensitive, although still rather pale. 'I imagine she knows where to find me.'

'Well – she has gone to the stables.'

'Then that means she wanted *you* to find me.'

'Oh – well then, since I have found you, shall I go and find Venetia and tell her so?'

'How very busy that sounds. Have you nothing to ask me about the horse?'

'What should I wish to know?'

'There must be something – if only how I am to raise the twenty guineas I have lost to the Chards.'

'You are not short of money, surely?'

'No,' he said, a ripple of nervous laughter running through him. 'I surely am not. Twenty guineas might have been a problem to Gideon Chard, but hardly to me. You think me a coward, I suppose.'

'You might be.'

'How kind –'

'But not because you disliked shooting a horse. It would have upset me greatly.'

'Ah yes, but in your case, you see, you would have been allowed your emotions. It would even have been expected of you. It was not expected of me.'

'Does it really matter, since you did it in the end?'

'Did I?'

'I heard the gun.'

'Which proves what? Only that a gun was fired. But did I fire it? Or, once the coast was clear – once you had cleared it for me – did I fetch one of the grooms to do the dirty deed in my place?'

'Gervase, does *that* matter either?'

There was a pause, the silence of the ancient walls closing in on us, creating a strange distortion of time and distance, a little space, perhaps, where time overlapped and we stepped forward, without knowing it, to a moment which might never come to pass, a threshold of familiarity we might never actually cross, but which enabled us somehow to speak freely.

'It matters to me,' he said. 'One thinks of oneself as a certain type of man, and it is rather galling to prove oneself so wrong. The Chards would not have behaved as I did. Whatever they may have felt, they would have concealed it admirably, as old Etonians have been trained to do, so that no one need have been embarrassed by it. Our great public schools specialize in the building of "character", you see. After today the Chards will feel entitled to say that I – as a mere product of Cullingford Grammar School – have none.'

'Do you care?'

'Yes, I care. Feeble of me, perhaps, but I care both for their opinion and for my own estimate of myself.'

'You mean, I suppose, that if you are not the man you thought you were, then who are you?'

'Is that what I mean? How very profound of me!'

'I also think you did shoot that horse.'

'Do you indeed?'

'Yes, I do. And the Chards will think so too – because they lack the imagination to think otherwise.'

He bowed very slightly, hardly easing his body away from the wall, and meeting my gaze – because it has always seemed best to me to look people straight in the eye at awkward moments – I found his eyes so light a green that they seemed quite transparent, the fine skin around them crinkled by his habit of keeping them half-closed, something in his regard which was not open and frank like Venetia's but which – for just a moment – seemed every bit as vulnerable.

'What do you think of this place?' he said abruptly, settling his back once more against the old stone, making contact with it, I thought, or possessing it.

'Of Galton? Well, I –'

'You may speak the truth.'

'I shall. When I came here as a child it scared me. I expected to see a ghost at every bend of the stair. When we arrived today I thought it – austere. And so it is, but I am beginning to think it *should* be like that.'

He nodded very lightly, his eyes skimming along the passage, the pale grey walls, the fan-vaulted arch of the ceiling, before coming back to me.

'Yes, it has something about it, this place – some power ... My mother once tried to leave my father, you know – really leave him – and it was Galton that held her back. She really thought she could do it, I suppose, but when it came down to it, when he actually told her "Do as I say or the estate goes under the hammer", she couldn't let it happen.'

'Gervase, should you be telling me –'

'Yes,' he said, his eyes showing that bitter, transparent green again, his thin mouth very tight. 'There's no "should" or "should not" about it. I'm

839

a spoiled and vicious young man, everybody knows it, and it's what I
want, not what I *ought*, that counts. If Uncle Peregrine had lived, it would
have been different. The estate would have passed to him and he – well,
he'd have been in his fifties by now, just about ready to take a
fifteen-year-old wife and get himself an heir, so there'd have been no
need for me. My mother could have left my father if she'd wanted, or she
might have settled down with him and given Uncle Perry her pin-money
every month, which is what she used to do when he was alive. But Uncle
Perry broke his neck –'

'Doing what you were doing this afternoon.'

'Quite so – or something very like it. And instead of leaving the estate
in trust for me, as he could have done, my mother's grandfather left it to
her – which, as Miss Grace Agbrigg will be sure to know, was the same as
leaving it to my father.'

'And your father wished to sell it.'

'No – *threatened* – to sell it – used it as a lever, a weapon, whatever
seemed useful to him at the time. One day, according to their agreement,
it comes to me. But until that day dawns – and it will be of his choosing –
he has her and can hold her fast. For if he sells Galton – well, Grace
Agbrigg, there are three hundred years of Clevedons in the graveyard
over there. How can we let him dispose of that?'

He paused, from indignation or pity or the sheer weight of that
three-hundred-year-old burden I couldn't tell, although it gave me time
to ask the question that was uppermost in my mind.

'Your father is very determined to keep your mother by him. Why is
that?'

'My dear girl!' he threw up a hand in mock astonishment. 'You cannot
be suggesting he should allow her to leave him? Women are very grateful
to the men who marry them – or ought to be. Certainly they fight hard
enough to get a man to the altar. And having endowed a woman with all
his worldly goods, and rescued her from the shame of being a spinster to
boot, it must be embarrassing – wouldn't you say? – if she throws it all
back at him. People would talk, Miss Agbrigg. They would say he must
have been very wicked, or very peculiar, for a woman to give up all that.'

'Gervase, I asked you a serious question.'

'I answered it. I answered it. I don't really know. Venetia has
something to do with it, I suppose. He *is* her father, after all, and he can't
wish her to be involved in an open scandal. No one could accuse him of
doting on her, but he's never been one for shirking his responsibilities.
The Barforths are like that.'

'So am I.'

'Yes, I believe you are. So he may want to avoid a scandal for
Venetia's sake. He may even want to protect my mother from herself –
or from Julian Flood. He's not likely to tell me. We don't stand on such
friendly terms as that. Gideon Chard may know, of course – perhaps
you'd care to ask him?'

But I was unwilling to be distracted.

'If those really should be his motives, then I don't think you could call him either wicked or peculiar – really, I don't.'

He grinned, the first real amusement I had seen in him.

'You approve of my father then, do you, Grace Agbrigg?'

'I am not in the habit of making judgements –'

'Are you not? I thought quite otherwise. You seem so very determined and so positive to me. And I would know, wouldn't I – being so negative myself.'

'Being so full of self-pity, you mean.'

'You don't pity me? I rather thought you might. After all, you were very efficient and very prompt just now, out in the long meadow – taking them all away in case I couldn't manage to pull myself together and they should begin to laugh at me.'

'Gervase – was it only the horse?'

'My word, are you a philosopher too, besides all the other marvels I hear of you? No – since you ask – not only the horse. I was – tired. There are times when I do tire rather easily – rather suddenly. A little instability of temperament, perhaps, which you might find interesting?'

'I don't believe so. In fact I am beginning to find this whole conversation quite pointless.'

'Then you shouldn't linger, should you, Grace, in lonely places with strange men.'

'You are not a strange man.'

'Am I not?' He threw back his head and laughed, as delighted as any other far less complicated man would have been with the trap he had set for me and into which I had fallen. 'Well – at least in one respect I am not strange. I can prove it, if you like – in fact I really think I ought –'

'You'll do no such thing.'

But as he moved away from the wall and took a step towards me, I was not afraid of him as I had been afraid of Gideon Chard. It had nothing to do with weight or size, for although Gervase was lighter and smaller, he was strong enough to hurt me and more likely, I thought, to offer me violence than Gideon, who would not see the need for it. It was simply that nothing in Gervase's lean, over-wrought body menaced me as Gideon's had done, the very absence of fear – which I had too little knowledge to recognize as the absence of desire – unchaining my curiosity, my eagerness to participate, to experience, to grow; for with Blanche already married and Venetia so rapturously in love, it was irksome to me that, at eighteen, I had still to receive my first kiss.

And having made up my mind to it, I remember quite distinctly willing him to stop talking and to *get on*, surprised, when his hand brushed my cheek and slid to my neck to find his touch so cautious and so cold, having expected a deliberate coarseness in this wild young squire, a mouth which demanded or took by force instead of asking so hesitant a question. I made no response, no answer, simply allowing his lips to touch mine, his tongue to part them, remaining calm and still, no pulse-beat leaping inside me but no awkwardness, a rather pleasing consciousness at the back of my mind that, although this was very pleasant and rather daring, I was still very much in control.

841

'Grace Agbrigg,' he said, his mouth against my ear, his quick, nervous laughter making my spine tingle. 'I have misjudged you. I thought you a schoolroom innocent, and now I am bound to ask myself what did they teach you in Switzerland?'

To which I replied, with studied composure, 'Good heavens! Gervase, at eighteen years old I am not likely to swoon on account of a kiss.'

When he rode over to Listonby the next morning and asked me to marry him, my first reaction, quite simply, was to wonder why, so that my answer, far from being romantic, sounded even in my own ears like a scold.

'Really, Gervase, if it is because of what happened in the cloister, I can tell you that I do not feel in any way compromised. If you have come out of a sense of obligation or because you imagined yourself committed –'

But he would not allow me to continue, his odd, light eyes slitted with anger. 'So – I kissed you in the cloister and what of it, Grace Agbrigg? I'd not be here, asking this, unless I wanted it, even if I'd done far worse than that to you.'

And when he was calm enough to accept my refusal and went away, I was obliged to endure, an hour later, the recriminations of his sister, whose heart, she insisted, I had also broken.

There is no question of broken hearts, Venetia. Gervase is not in love with me.'

'How do you know?'

'Because I know. And anyway, he didn't say so –'

'Of course he didn't. He wouldn't know how. But what *I* know – absolutely and beyond question – is that it was not done because father told him to. That in itself would be enough to make him *not* ask you. And the fact that he *did* ask means he wants you – and I want you – and father wants you. And the reason I know how much he wants you is because mother doesn't – simply doesn't at all – and he hardly ever goes against her. You could do so much for him, Grace.'

'And what could he do for me?'

She smiled and tucked her hand into mine.

'Well – first of all he could make you my sister. And then, of course, he's very rich. And don't you think he's rather beautiful?'

'I suppose I must say he is, since he looks like you.'

'Thank you, darling. And will you say yes when he asks you again?'

There was no danger of that, I decided. It had been a whim on his part, no more, some quirk of his complicated nature which had picked up my sympathy that day at Galton and converted it into something which had briefly attracted him. Certainly he would not ask again, would be more inclined, I thought, to thank me for my good sense in refusing him, and if he still felt the need of a wife would already be gravitating towards Diana Flood. Yet it was Miss Flood herself who showed me my mistake, for when I met her a day or so later, having extended my visit to Listonby at Blanche's request, her manner was taut and miserable and she had no more to say to me than a forced 'Are you well, Miss Agbrigg?'

Miss Flood herself clearly was not well, and I felt myself wince slightly

842

at Venetia's casual, 'Oh – Diana. Well, she'll just have to find herself a real squire, won't she – the genuine, beefy variety – and make the best of him.'

I returned to Fieldhead and to the centre of a storm, a glacial Mrs Agbrigg losing no time in enquiring why I was so little to be trusted, for Gervase, it seemed, had not only informed his mother and possibly Miss Flood of his intentions, but had ridden home to Tarn Edge that same day and asked his father's help. Mr Barforth had driven at once to Fieldhead and made his proposition to my father. I was the girl he wanted for Tarn Edge. My father might have some reservations about Gervase but the marriage-contract could be as tight as my father liked. I could have, in the way of pin-money and housekeeping money, anything I desired. Mr Barforth was ready to be generous, and although he would expect my father to be the same, he made it clear that my welfare would be his personal concern. Gervase Barforth, in fact, would make me happy or would answer to Nicholas Barforth for it. And feeling the need to finalize the matter in case Gervase should change his mind, he went next to Galton and warned his wife – to my everlasting regret – that she would be well advised to be pleased about it too.

'You should not have told your father,' I reproached him when next we met.

'I know that. But a desperate man will stoop to anything.'

'I wish you would not describe yourself as desperate. It sounds very foolish.'

'My father seems highly delighted with the state I am in. And I can't quite get over how natural it seemed to turn to him.'

'Perhaps you should make a habit of it.'

'Do you think so?'

'I think you would be happier if you could.'

'I'd like to. I need you to show me the way.'

'What nonsense, Gervase –'

'No,' he said, his eyes turning that wild transparent green again. 'No – not nonsense at all, I'm afraid. Grace, you won't stop me from coming to see you? I'll be calm. I'll behave –'

The only ally I found was, of all people, my father's wife.

'This is all quite ridiculous,' she said. 'Jonas – you must put a stop to it.'

'It is for Grace to decide,' my father told her sadly. 'I will neither force her nor persuade her in any direction. This is the most important decision of her life – perhaps the only real decision she will be called upon to make. I cannot interfere with her right to make it.'

But although I declared firmly and frequently that I had already decided, that I had refused him once and would do so again, no one appeared to believe me, being too involved with their own desires to notice mine.

I should be sent abroad again, Mrs Agbrigg decreed. I would be gone soon enough, my father replied and for the first time since his marriage stepped firmly between us and ordered her to leave me alone. I was not to be rushed, Mr Barforth agreed. I was young and it was a big step to take. I could take it, thought Mr Barforth, in my own good time, provided I made haste, saw reason, bowed – as a woman should – to the highly convenient workings of Fate. And quite soon, each time I opened my mouth to say no, there was no step to take, I couldn't marry him, I had a nightmare sensation that no one heard me, that I was voiceless or that my words were somehow being converted into a foreign tongue.

'An excellent match,' wrote my Grandmother Agbrigg from her home in Scarborough, for she had been a Miss Hannah Barforth herself and liked the idea of the Barforth money remaining in the family.

'I said you would be our next bride,' Grandmamma Elinor wrote enthusiastically from her winter retreat in Cannes, for she too had been a Barforth, a pretty, dimpled Miss Elinor who had married once for money and once for love, and was still exceedingly romantic.

'You would be very rich,' said Blanche, 'with more pin-money, I daresay, than I have, since Listonby seems to cost a great deal and Westminster – now that Dominic seems set on having a go at politics – will cost even more.'

But Mr Nicholas Barforth, taking my measure more accurately, sent Venetia to assure me that the position awaiting me at Tarn Edge would not be without its element of authority and freedom.

'I know you hate the whole idea,' she told me, dropping down beside me on my bedroom sofa, 'and will probably end up hating me for talking about it. But my father says – if you come to us – that you should pay no heed to me at all. I am just the daughter-at-home who has nothing to say to anything, and since mamma is never there you would be as much the mistress of Tarn Edge as if it already belonged to Gervase. Father says you could engage servants or discharge them as you wanted and make changes to suit your fancy – the house is so badly run, he says, that *any* change must be for the better. And Mrs Agbrigg, you know, would never, absolutely never, be able to get past father. We just wondered if you realized that no one at all would stand in your way –'

I had not wished to realize it, suspecting how much it would tempt me. And now, being tempted, I was forced to consider it, my desire for a free and independent existence stirring me to a considerable discomfort. It would not, of course, be total freedom, for at the end of every road I would have a husband and a father-in-law to answer to. But within the confines of four very splendid walls I would have as much authority, as much liberty, as any woman could expect; more of it, perhaps, than I would ever be likely to find elsewhere. And, my mind leaping from one idea to the next, as Mr Nicholas Barforth may have known it would, I was quick to see the scope of what he was offering, its potential and its extent; quick to realize that, since marriage was the only career open to me, I would be unlikely to find one more advantageous than this.

Of course I had no intention of marrying Gervase, since there was far more to be considered – far more – than advantage. But just supposing I did marry him, then I saw no reason why the two sides of his nature, his double inheritance, could not be reconciled, I saw no reason, in fact, why

844

he could not enjoy both the sporting estate of Galton, the Barforth mills, and Fieldhead besides.

Someone, in fact, must take care of Tarn Edge, for Mr Barforth eventually would grow old and Venetia, I was sure of it, would not marry Gideon Chard nor anyone else of whom her father would be likely to approve. Her choice would be idealistic, soft-spoken, sweet-natured, a dreamer like Charles Heron who would fare no better in the mills than Gervase. When the time came someone would have to be there with a level head and a practical disposition, someone who knew how those mills had risen from the ground and did not want to see them sink back again.

Naturally, it would not be Grace Agbrigg, but Grace Agbrigg could do it if she wanted to, could make a life for herself with that commodity so rarely available to females of her station; some *real* work to do. And although these pressures, these enticements, would not in themselves have swayed my resolution, they moved me, step by slow-moving step, in their chosen direction to a point where the challenge of Tarn Edge seemed matched by the challenge of Gervase's complex nature; to a point where I began to ask myself, with a decided loss of composure, why he wanted me.

It was not money, as with many men – perhaps with most men – it would have been; and I was ready now to admit how much the dread of being courted for my fortune, used and subsequently set aside, had haunted me. Perhaps I was even ready – although I am not sure of this – to admit a certain disappointment at the rapidity with which Gideon Chard had withdrawn from me, having made up his mind, I supposed, that if he obstructed Mr Barforth's plans on my account he ran the risk of losing his employment and his chance of Venetia with it.

No, Gervase Barforth did not want my money. What then?

'Darling, you're beautiful,' cried Venetia.

'Nonsense – utter nonsense!'

'Oh, yes you are. I've always envied you that mass of dark hair and those blue-grey eyes, you know I have – and you have *presence*, Grace, simply heaps of it. When you come into a room people look at you, and when you talk they listen. And in any case, none of that really matters. You're beautiful because I love you.'

'Gervase doesn't know me well enough to love me.'

'Now that,' Venetia declared, 'really is nonsense. Lord! It took me all of half an hour to fall in love with Charles, and now – only look at me – I love him more and more by the minute. And it's *good* for me. I actually think it makes my hair curl and even Princess Blanche, who never notices other women, asked me the other day what I was using to give my skin such a glow. Not a jar *she's* likely to dip into, I can tell you, or perhaps I should tell poor Noel. But, Grace – don't you want to be loved?'

Yes. Yes, of course. For even studious little girls who grow to be sensible, efficient young women have indulged in a little romantic dreaming, especially when, as in my case, childhood had been cool in terms of affection, girlhood sometimes quite barren.

845

'My dear,'murmured Mrs Rawnsley, who badly wanted to be the first to know, 'that poor young man is so smitten that, really, one would need a heart of iron not to pity him. And when one remembers how wild he was – my dear, you have scored a triumph.'

'He loves you,' Venetia told me again. 'Don't ask why, just be glad of it. What else in the world can compare with *that*?'

And quite soon it came about that, although I still maintained I had no emotion to give him, I was fascinated by his.

He did not give me the easy assurance of 'I love you, I cannot live without you', but, pacing Mrs Agbrigg's drawing-room with the taut, nervous step of a caged feline, carrying from one corner to another his chagrin that once again I had turned him down, he told me: 'I'll wait. I was too hasty before. Don't say anything now, Grace – please don't say a word. Just consider – *Please*.'

'I *have* considered. I think you are mistaken in me, Gervase. I believe your mother cannot approve of this –'

'She will forgive me. She will see that, with you, I will be steadier and easier – because I will be happier. She will see that everything will turn out to her satisfaction just the same. Grace, they were equally my parents. Is there any reason in the world why I shouldn't please them both?'

'I think it can be done.'

'I believe you. I thought it altogether impossible, but now I believe you. I have to have you, Grace.'

And so, due to the highly organized communications system of Mr Nicholas Barforth, it became known in Cullingford and in Scarborough, in certain areas of London and the South of France, that in fact he did have me; that I had become the exclusive property of the Barforths upon which any other aspiring male would be ill-advised to trespass.

Annoying, of course, when the other men I knew kept their distance, or when Miss Mandelbaum murmured to me softly: 'My dear, it seems you are to be congratulated, although I fear Miss Tighe will be disappointed. She was relying on you to organize our petition for woman suffrage and you will have no time now, of course – and no inclination.' Annoying to feel myself manipulated by the powerful Mr Barforth, yet exhilarating too, sometimes, to realize that his approval was not easily won and to wonder if I had the skill to retain it.

And increasingly, almost daily, there was Gervase, *present* in my life, absorbing more and more of my time and my attention, confusing and exasperating me, making me smile, warming me, sometimes touching me, sometimes making me cruel and sometimes kind – but present.

'What a nuisance you are, Gervase!'

'So I am.'

So he was, casting me those looks of mute reproach across everybody's drawing-room; but if, the next day, he did not come to find me, did not appear in some doorway just a little dishevelled, a little pale, that transparent look in his eyes, quite soon I began to wonder why, to watch for him, to expect him, to miss him.

There was an evening of acute misery, an Assembly Rooms Ball, when, in a low-cut dress of white lace draped up over black silk roses, I danced with a flattering variety of young men, aware at every step – when I had been so determined not to notice it – of a silent, suffering Gervase leaning like a spectre in the buffet corner, his face drawn and strained by his inexplicable burden of wanting me. And when we did dance together I could feel no flesh on his hands, simply the bones crushing my fingers, wanting to hurt me.

'You have no right to be jealous, Gervase – no right to be so miserable.'

'There is nothing you can do about it, Grace. I am jealous. I am miserable.'

I made up my mind, with great firmness, that I would not be influenced by his misery. I would be pleasant and reasonable but cool, until this strange emotion of his, which had risen, like fretful summer fires, from nowhere, should burn itself out. But when he strode from the ballroom, leaving me, as he said, to my pleasures, I worried, wanted him back again, not because I actually wanted *him* – of course not that – but because he had looked so pale, so reckless, so very likely to bring down his horse on the cobbles or get into a fight, and already I was beginning to feel responsible.

There was a sparkling December afternoon of hard frost and brilliant sunshine when he escorted Mrs Agbrigg and myself on a tour of the new mill at Nethercoats, an occasion when every possible attention was paid to us, beginning with glasses of sherry served by Mr Nicholas Barforth himself and ending with an inspection, not of the whole mill, which since it extended over a full six acres would have been too exhausting, but of the finer points of it, the elaborate Italianate façade, the chimney stack, two hundred and fifty feet high, the suite of offices with their opulent oak-panelling, the extensive warehousing, six floors in all, where Barforth expertise was storing away the silks and velvets and all the other soft, luxurious fabrics which had come into demand since fashion had abandoned the crinoline.

'You have a stupendous inheritance awaiting you, Mr Barforth,' said Mrs Agbrigg as Gervase assisted us to our carriage. And, almost a stranger in his dark coat and trousers, his plain white linen, he glanced swiftly around the bustling mill-yard, the enormous chimney directly behind him, four other factory chimneys, very nearly as huge, dominating every corner of Cullingford's horizon, each one forming part of that stupendous, that crushing birthright.

'So I have, Mrs Agbrigg,' he said very quietly. 'And unfortunately I have no natural aptitude for it. I must simply do the best I can. Grace – may I come and see you tomorrow?'

'Yes – tomorrow.'

And instinctively, because it seemed the right thing to do – the only thing to do – I held out my hand and ignored Mrs Agbrigg's sharply drawn breath when he kissed it.

Lady Caroline Chard became the Duchess of South Erin in the small village church at Listonby, two days before Christmas, in the presence of her mother, Lady Verity Barforth, who had come over specially from the South of France; her brothers, Mr Nicholas Barforth and Sir Blaize; their wives, Mrs Georgiana Barforth resplendent in the emerald and diamond finery she kept for these occasions, Aunt Faith her sweet and lovely self in soft shades of amber and aquamarine; and a few other carefully selected guests.

Sir Dominic gave his mother away. Blanche drifting forlornly into the church to take her place between Gideon and Noel, who looked extremely handsome in the full dress uniform of a hussar, while I sat with Mrs Agbrigg on one side of me, Gervase and Venetia on the other, Gervase taut and silent, Venetia flushed with a triumphant ecstasy since she had somehow procured an invitation for Charles Heron.

She had, I knew, seen a great deal of him lately, her father, intent on arranging his son's affairs, having accepted her explanations of afternoons with her mother or with me when in fact she had seized any opportunity, rushed any distance to spend an hour with Charles.

'I am in the process,' she told me gaily, 'of losing my reputation.' Yet I knew, quite definitely, that nothing improper had occurred. She may, in the first rapture of meeting, have rushed into his arms – very likely she had – and, indeed, the mere fact of being alone with a young man by assignation was quite enough to condemn her. But Venetia was too deeply and too idealistically in love for impropriety, her embrace offering trust rather than sensuality, conveying to him no tale of urgent passion but a slow and lovely building of her hopes for the future, the strength and devotion of her whole life.

I hardly knew him; a fair, sensitive face, a quiet, hesitant manner of speaking, although his habitual themes of social justice, atheism and republicanism were strident enough. Yet he had abandoned God, I thought, because he had confused him with his own harsh father, while his revolutionary principles, when compared to some I had heard abroad, seemed relatively mild. He believed in one man one vote, with which I heartily agreed, and he had not flinched when I suggested 'one vote one woman'. He believed in education for both sexes, and although he seemed to know more about knocking things down – like churches and royal palaces – than building things up again, there seemed every likelihood that in time he would settle down to be a responsible and, apart from his blue eyes and enchanting fair curls, quite unremarkable schoolmaster.

Charles Heron's republicanism – inspired mainly by the refusal of our sad little Queen to show herself in public – would probably go the same way as his disregard for money, his unrealistic, if undoubtedly Christian view, that the world's bounty should be equally shared. I smiled, knowing word for word how Mr Nicholas Barforth would reply to that, and then in great confusion turned my head away, for in trying to locate Charles Heron at the back of the church I had found instead the dark, dissolute face of Sir Julian Flood and the tightly controlled misery of his niece Diana.

The new duchess and her merry little duke were not disposed to linger, having a mountain of Christmas engagements awaiting them in London. There was a lavish but by Listonby standards hurried wedding-breakfast, a great deal of champagne, the Duchess looking resolute and triumphant, Blanche rather smug since she had discovered a way of avoiding the social and domestic responsibilities of Listonby and of rather overshadowing her mother-in-law by announcing, the night before, that she was pregnant.

The Duchess put on her sable-trimmed coat and feathered hat, the Duke distributed handshakes and kisses as if they had been medals. There was a sudden scramble for carriages as the bridal party left for the London train, Blanche melting gracefully into tears, Venetia – glimpsed through a window-pane – holding out her narrow, boyish hand to Charles Heron, her face suffused with a joy that caused me a sharp stab of pain; and then there was Gervase, taking me out into the fine, frosty weather, to a pink winter sky above charcoal trees, a bare, empty sweep of parkland.

He had nothing to say, striding out in the sharp air at a speed somewhat beyond the capacity of my elaborate skirt and dainty shoes, his humour frowning and grim.

'Gervase, I am quite breathless.'

'Yes, I see.'

'Then do you mind –'

'Yes,' he said, 'yes – I do.' And coming to a halt by a screening circle of evergreens, he took me by the shoulders with a hard, horseman's hands and kissed me more with his teeth than his lips, a painful embrace from which I quickly broke free.

'I think that's quite enough –'

'I can't wait any longer, Grace.'

'Then don't wait. I told you before –'

But once again he took me in that spiked embrace, except that this time, although he hurt me, I felt pain in him and a response in my own female body which had been conditioned through the generations to offer itself, in love and in healing, on all occasions such as these.

There was an ornate iron bench close to the hedge and we sat down, his shoulders hunched, his head bowed, hiding his face as I had seen him do before, the tension in his lean body so great that it vibrated through the air between us as sharp as needles. And remembering him kneeling in the field at Galton – that treacherous memory of him weak and vulnerable – I put my hand on his shoulder, startled by the tremor that went through him, by the wild, hurt face that looked up at me, the thin mouth spitting out the words: 'I need you, Grace. God dammit, can't you see that? Grace – *please*.'

And still I thought, why me? But I was breathless now, not only from walking, and a little dizzy, feeling that I could just as easily laugh or cry; and I had no resistance when he took both my hands, rather more gently, and kissed me again.

'I need you, Grace.'

I shook my head. But I was expecting his kiss this time, leaned forward

849

a little to meet it, the coolness and the lightness of him pleasing me, nothing at all to fear in his hard, hurt body as I put my arms round it and held him, the scent of lavender and lemons rising to me from his skin, delighting my nostrils as the texture of the skin itself, so paper-fine across his cheek bones, delighted my lips.

We got up and walked back to the house without saying anything of importance, and wherever there was a tree or a shelter of any kind, we paused and I stood as if mesmerized while he kissed me, lifting my face towards him more readily each time, growing more and more obedient to the impulses of my body, those sweet, yielding sensations which pressed me ever more closely into his arms, holding me there longer, so that before we reached the prying windows of the house, I was kissing him too with curiosity and with a freedom from restraint which enchanted me. It was as if I had shaken my hair loose from its pins, kicked off the confining weight of petticoats and bustle and my long, trailing gown, and was basking for the first time in fresh air and sunshine. It was, I suppose, very wanton and I did not care.

I had not agreed to marry him. Nothing had been decided. But as we entered the house there were several people still drinking champagne in the hall who, seeing us, fell silent without meaning to, as people do when they have been told of 'something in the air'. And as we came forward to join them, walking a respectable distance apart, my hair no more dishevelled than could be accounted for by the wind, Gervase deliberately caught his father's eye and then, very slowly and firmly, reached out and took my hand.

'Good lad,' Mr Barforth said. It was done.

7

We spent the first weeks of our married life in Cumbria, in a low-beamed slate-roofed cottage not far from the village of Grasmere, overlooking Rydal Water, relieved, I think, quite simply to be married and that the fuss was over.

There had been no open opposition, Mrs Agbrigg being so glad to be rid of me that she was soon reconciled, while if Mrs Georgiana Barforth reroached her son for what she must have seen as a class-betrayal, she reproached him privately and made nothing but polite murmurings to me.

Yet this alliance between two important commercial houses could not take place without its share of pomp and splendour. On such an occasion money – like justice and the sad little face of our Queen – must not only be spent but must be seen, very copiously, in the spending. The self-respect of both the Barforths and the Agbriggs required it, the same mountain of bridal trivia I had seen around Blanche piling up so rapidly at Fieldhead that the ceremony itself began to appear more than ever as a release from bondage.

The night before the wedding my father, in his capacity as a lawyer, called me into his study to explain what my new status as a married woman would be, in fact no status at all since when I left the parish church the next morning I would no longer exist, my identity absorbed entirely into the identity of my husband. There had been a Grace Cecilia Agbrigg, but the law would not recognize a Grace Cecilia Barforth, merely a Mrs Gervase Barforth who could not, in any legal sense involving matters of finance, contract, or inheritance, be distinguished from the man whose name she bore. Mrs Gervase Barforth, being the property of her husband, could not own property herself. Her dowry, her body, and in due course her children were all irrevocably his. She would be as absolutely dependent on his judgement and his authority, in fact, as if she had herself been his child; indeed, rather more so, since a son, on his majority, could claim his independence, a daughter, on marriage, would be transferred to the control of another man.

The Married Women's Property Act of 1870 – now entering its third year – had not amounted to much, my father thought, its provisions going no further than to allow a married woman to retain her earnings. Useful, perhaps, in the case of some famous literary figure or of some fabulously talented prima donna or prima ballerina, of which there could not be many. Less appropriate in what could be seen as the real world, where women of even moderate means did not *earn* money, and could not earn it, since there was no paid work for them to do, the services of women being required at home by their men, who would reward them with food and shelter and, in fortunate circumstances, with love.

Nor, my father declared, had the Act of 1870 made any difference to the class below our own, where from early childhood both men and women were obliged to go out and scratch a living wherever they could, no labouring man in the poorer areas of Cullingford disputing the right of his wife to keep her earnings when every penny was needed for the purchase of their daily bread.

But, my father told me, none of this need greatly concern me, since the law – which had been made by men of property to serve the interests of property – provided, in cases such as mine, for the drawing up of a marriage contract, a settlement which by allowing me a most generous and untouchable allowance, and by a complicated series of trusts and restrictions imposed upon the property which would one day be mine, made it certain that I would never be in want.

My father, in addition, had obliged Mr Barforth to be specific in the matter of Gervase's salary and in the provision he intended to make for Venetia and any husband and children she might acquire. My father, as my legal guardian, had felt entitled to know where I stood. Mr Barforth had been most obliging, the financial position of my future husband no longer depending entirely on the whim of his father but on certain firm guarantees. However – and my father thought it wise to tell me this – when Mrs Barforth had attempted to take advantage of her husband's good humour by suggesting to him that the time had come to make over to Gervase the ownership of the Galton estate, Mr Barforth had merely replied, 'Not yet.'

When the explanations were over, my father took from a drawer of his desk a small, flat case and placed it gently before me, my throat instantly tight since I knew this was my mother's jewellery and I was not certain – if my father should become emotional – that I could bear it.

'You may not care for these,' he said coolly, opening the lid and indicating a strand or two of gold and coral, a locket, a cameo, coral and turquoise ear-rings, a brooch of blue enamel. 'Trinkets merely – not valuable. I was not a rich man in those days, you see, and your mother was not – not much given to display. There is no reason why you should wear these things, but perhaps you would like to have them – indeed, I can think of no one else to whom they could go.'

'Thank you, papa.' And as he gave me the case I caught his hand and held it, my throat aching now, longing to ask him, 'Father, are you happy?', despairing because I could not say to him, 'Father I love you', although I was brimming over with love.

I had wanted us to be quite alone on our honeymoon night, no grand hotels, no complicated menus, no after-dinner conversations with knowing strangers, and the house at Grasmere, which belonged to my father – a book-lined, leafy retreat, a cottage garden, a discreet housekeeper – offered the warmest, most perfect solitude.

I had imagined, too, that we might use this quiet time to tell our secrets, to talk of his mother, the conflicts we had both known in childhood, our hopes now for the future which we could map out together. In fact we hardly talked at all. We made love, which I had not realized could be a conversation until he brought the lamp to our bedside that first evening and, with an almost idle hand, touched me, just touched me from the curve of my eyebrows to my breasts, to the hollows of my ankles, and then touched me again, his hand whispering gently into my skin, his body trembling so that he seemed once more to be vulnerable. And although I knew he had done this before with other women and should not have been uncertain, he was uncertain until I touched him too and heard, with astonished delight, the harmony of my hands and his fine-boned, fine-textured leanness, the lovely auburn skin that had so delicate a bloom as my mouth tasted it.

An hour, perhaps, of bemused caresses, a few moments to dispose of my virginity, no anxious questions afterwards as to if he had hurt me, but his head on my shoulder, his body sinking in my arms into his fretful sleep which rarely lasted, I was to learn, for more than two hours, so that at some far reach of the night I was kissed to a dreamy half-waking and being totally relaxed took his body into mine this time without pain.

We walked the lake path the next morning and paused every step or two to touch hand to hand, cheek to cheek, forehead to forehead, simply to touch, and there was nothing else we wished to do but that, to savour this communication of the senses, his need arousing mine until, at some imperceptible moment, the pleasure of being loved flowed into the pleasure of loving and became one with it, the same. I love him, I thought, and it took me by surprise. He needs me. How wonderful that he needs me. And it was but a breath away from confessing that I, too, needed him.

We made love or we looked at each other and imagined it. We dreamed of it, sighed out our longing for it, we did not speak of it. Our bodies said all that was needful, and very soon I did not wait – as a woman should wait to be loved – but, when I desired him, reached out and took him, to his delight and to my eventual, slow-building but quite devastating rapture.

'I need you, Grace.'

'You have me.'

With his hands upon me I was entirely his, unwilling, during that fragile spring, to stray a yard from his side, parched with the thirst of any half hour in which he had not caressed me; while he – I knew it – had delivered himself to me body and soul. It was a peak of intensity I had never expected to discover. I did not know how long such exaltation could be expected to last and perhaps I would have been fearful even then had I realized that Gervase desired it to continue, unabated, forever.

'I don't want to go home,' he said, sounding so much like a child at the end of a party that I laughed and kissed him.

'I mean it, Grace. We could go down to London – why couldn't we? – and I could buy you a diamond.'

'I have a diamond.'

'Should you object to another?'

But we returned to Cullingford because, without being aware of exerting pressure upon him, it was what I wished to do, arriving on an afternoon of rain which could have accounted for his ill-humour, although once in our huge, luxurious yet not quite immaculate bedroom at Tarn Edge, he seized me as the dinner gong was sounding and made love to me as if it had been an act of defiance.

He went to the mill at a reasonable hour the next morning, not quite so early as his father or mine, but early enough, considering his past performances, to please Mr Barforth, leaving me to what I recognized with apprehension and a little pride as my first day as mistress of Tarn Edge.

But before I could make myself known to my staff, I spent an hour with Venetia who, having welcomed me rapturously the night before, had nevertheless warned me that great things were afoot, and that all would be revealed, in true sisterly fashion, the very moment we could be alone at breakfast-time.

'You need not be alarmed,' she told me, perching on the edge of her chair and wrinkling her nose, 'for I shall not ask you for the details of the "great wedded mystery". I have spent too many hours in the stables at Galton to be entirely ignorant and I can see that you have taken to it in any case. Darling, I *knew* you would love each other and I am so happy or would be if such positive disaster had not struck me –'

Yet this disaster, however positive, did not appear to have broken her, for, leaning both elbows on the table, her pointed chin resting upon them, she spent a moment smiling and shaking her head, perhaps at her own folly, but by no means in despair. Like her mother, it seemed, she had hoped to take advantage of her father's unusual good humour and had introduced him to Charles Heron. The occasion had not been a success, Mr Barforth finding a schoolmaster of radical opinions not at all to his liking, while Mr Heron had been so overcome with shyness that her father, scorning the excuse of sensitivity, had declared him to be – in addition to everything else – a half-wit.

It was not Mr Heron's poverty in itself to which my father-in-law objected, for, in certain circumstances, a poor man would have been very acceptable to him, someone like Gideon Chard who was shrewd and ambitious, or even Liam Adair who might not be quite respectable, but who knew how to put in a hard day's work for his pay. But Charles Heron had ideals in place of ambition, and Mr Barforth, knowing of no market where ideals would be likely to fetch a profit, had simply declared: 'That young man will not do.' And when Venetia seemed disposed to argue he had threatened to pack her boxes and ship her off to her grandmother in the South of France.

'And so now,' she wailed, 'I am forbidden to see Charles and – of all things – Gideon Chard is courting me, which is quite ridiculous.'

'Not really. Everyone expected it when he took employment with your father. You are not so innocent as all that, Venetia.'

'Lord, yes, of course I knew people would say it, for it would have fitted in so neatly. But Grace, we are talking about *life* – the only life I shall ever have – my only chance to get it right. And *Gideon*, my goodness! Grace, ten years from now you will not be able to tell him from my father, except that he will be grander than father and more self-indulgent. Mark my words, he will make his fortune, Gideon Chard, and he will let it *show*. He will live like a king and you must know very well that I am in no way cut out to be a queen.'

I asked them to clear the breakfast-table a little earlier, I think, than was usual at Tarn Edge and – armed with the knowledge I had acquired in Switzerland and my observations of that immaculate housekeeper, my father's wife – I spent the rest of the morning interviewing the upper servants one by one in the drawing-room, a procedure I deemed necessary in order to banish any notions that, because I was young and the wife of the son of the house not its master, I could easily be disregarded. This career of marriage, after all, now that I had embarked upon it, was of vital importance to me and I intended, with the full force of my Agbrigg nature, to make of it an immense success.

Mrs Winch, the housekeeper, I had marked down as a careless woman, but once it was established that I had my own ideas as to how things should be done and that, of the two of us, my will was the stronger, I believed I would soon get on with her. She was in her mid-fifties, at an age when she would prefer to keep an old situation rather than hazard herself in the market-place for a new, and seeing many more useful years in her yet, I was inclined to be hopeful, although her reaction to my first command was less co-operative than I might have wished.

'The serving dishes in use at present are far too large, Mrs Winch, and I would like you to put them away. Have you nothing smaller?'

'Nothing at all, madam. I believe Sir Joel and Lady Barforth were accustomed to do things on a large scale, and with so many splendid dishes in every cupboard new purchases seemed unjustified –'

'They seem quite jusified to me. There is nothing more unappetizing at breakfast than to see three sausages cowering in the corner of a dish a yard square. And a smaller coffee-pot would avoid the disposal of a pint of cold coffee each morning, and would thus pay for itself, quite soon I believe, by the saving of coffee beans.'

'Very good, madam,' she said, straightening her shoulders, and went away I believe not too unhappily.

I fared less well with the butler, Chillingworth, who had, I imagine, found life very easy in what had become a masculine household; an occasional rumpus, perhaps, in the smoking-room, glasses and cigar butts and a drunken young man or two to clear away but no ladies with their 'at homes', their constant demands for fires and fresh tea, their callers and dinners, their endless comings and goings. But now, instead of accepting the fact that my presence would make all these annoying duties inevitable, he made an ill-advised attempt to treat me like a starry-eyed child, hoping to intimidate me with his imposing male presence as a clever manservant can sometimes do with an inexperienced young mistress or a timid old one.

And thinking it wise to let him know right from the start that I was not timid and although inexperienced would be quick to learn, I gave him a detailed list of my intentions. The door-bell, I made it clear, would be increasingly demanding from now on and must be answered not merely promptly but at once. There would be the possibility of callers, as in all households where the mistress goes out into society, from Monday to Saturday at any hour between mid-morning and four o'clock in the afternoon. There would, every day of the week, be five o'clock tea, a meal not much partaken of by gentlemen but to which I had always been accustomed and which would delay the serving of dinner to a more fashionable if – for Chillingworth – more inconvenient hour. And since I had a large number of relatives and friends who would invite me to dine and must be invited in return, there would be formal dinners with a great deal of elaborate table-setting, a great polishing of silver and crystal, deft carving and serving of complicated dishes; every opportunity in the world for an enterprising butler to shine.

'Yes, madam,' he murmured with the utmost deference, wishing me, I imagined, at the farthest corner of Far Cathay; and I was not certain whether or not I could rely on his goodwill.

I liked, at once, the head parlourmaid, a wholesome, capable-looking girl, assured in her movements and her manner without putting herself too much forward, although it seemed that the cook, Mrs Loman, would be a thorn in my side for many a day. Like Chillingworth she had done very much as she pleased in the service of a family where no one seemed greatly interested in food, Mr Barforth not caring what was on his plate

855

so long as it was hot and plentiful, both he and Gervase being away a great deal in any case, while Venetia would have been happy enough on a diet of apples and cheese. The ample, rather peevish Mrs Loman, I imagined, had fed herself rather better than the Barforths, dishing up a slight variation of the same thing day after day, and was not pleased to know that I would require her attendance in the back parlour every morning, as was quite usual, so that she and I could discuss the day's menus together.

'When Mrs Nicholas Barforth was here she always left it up to me, madam.'

'I daresay. But new brooms sweep clean, you know, Mrs Loman. I feel sure you will be able to rise to the occasion.

But remembering the disastrous chocolate cream she had once served to me in this house, I was not convinced of it.

I had brought my own maid from Fieldhead, cheerful, pretty Sally, who was used to me, and I thought it best merely to assemble the others, chambermaids, kitchenmaids, assorted menservants, in the hall and say a few words of introduction, not wishing to usurp the duties of Mrs Winch, Mrs Loman and Chillingworth, there being no point in calling a woman a housekeeper and paying her a housekeeper's wages unless she can control her maids, no point in keeping a cook or a butler and then concerning oneself with the daily routines of footmen and bootboys or kitchen skivvies.

And having done all that, thinking that at least I had made a start, I awarded myself the supreme satisfaction of ordering the carriage and paying on Mrs Agbrigg my first call as a married woman.

All had gone well so far – very well indeed. I was busy, happy, more pleased than otherwise to receive a note from Lawcroft Mills to the effect that my father-in-law could not dine at home that evening, having been called to Leeds, since his presence would be bound to impose restraint. But by dinner time Gervase had not come either and, having delayed as long as I decently could, I was at last compelled by pride and the sheer indifference of Venetia, to eat without him.

'Could he be working late?'

'Oh lord, I doubt it. He's never worked late before – father thought himself lucky if he could get him to work at all.'

'Could he have gone to Leeds with your father?'

'Did father's note say so?'

'No.'

'Then he hasn't.'

We had coffee together in the drawing-room, a smaller pot I noticed, the pleasure I should have felt unable to break through my anxiety, and leaning towards me Venetia chuckled knowingly, her eyes bright with mischief.

'Grace Agbrigg – I beg your pardon, Grace Barforth – admit now that I was right. You thought you didn't want him and now look at you – unable to spare him for an evening.'

'Venetia, for heaven's sake! – it's not that.'

'What then?'

'I should have thought it obvious. I am worried about him.'

For a moment she quite simply did not understand.

'Worried? Oh lord! you think he's dead in a ditch, do you? Be easy. He's no such thing. If you ask me, he could have gone to see mother –'

'Without letting me know?'

'Oh dear! Yes, Grace, he *could* have forgotten about that.'

We sat an hour longer, Venetia's mind floating away somewhere with Charles, mine angry sometimes – because if he had gone off to Galton, or anywhere else without the easy courtesy of a message then I believed I had a right to be angry – and then, at other times, for most of the time, frightened, remembering that he drove too fast, that there was rain again and no moon, wanting only – or so I thought – to know that he was safe.

I heard the door and froze as Chillingworth moved sedately across the hall to answer it, willing him to hurry, restraining myself from leaping to my feet as the double doors were smoothly opened – Chillingworth putting himself through his paces – and Liam Adair came into the room, with no air of tragedy about him, having come to deliver some documents to Mr Barforth, which – since he must have known Mr Barforth would not be here – meant that he had come to see Venetia.

She received him with open friendship, warmly jumping up from her chair and tripping to his side, her narrow, outstretched hands disappearing into his, looking very slight and fair beside him.

'Liam, do come and cheer us up for we are both in our miseries.'

'We can't have that now, can we,' he said, his voice still touched with that faint green memory of Ireland, his smile as roguish as I had ever seen it and his eyes as merry, although he must have known quite well that if she was suffering it was not for him. But Liam was the oldest of our generation, a man approaching thirty now, who before his father's marriage to my Grandmamma Elinor had lived precariously and afterwards had seen and survived so many changes of fortune that perhaps Charles Heron did not seem so great a threat to him.

'So what is this misery then?'

'Oh, I am being bullied, as usual, by papa and Grace is afraid Gervase may have run away – No, of course she is not and I didn't mean to say it. It is just that he did not come home for dinner and sent no word. Have you seen him today, Liam?'

'I have indeed – or rather the dust he was making along the top road – It struck me at the time that he'd be on his way to Galton.'

'Well,' said Venetia flatly, 'I can think of nowhere else he'd get to on that road.'

'So that's one misery settled,' murmured Liam, knowing it was no such thing. 'But what I *did* want to tell you, Grace, is that I've had the oddest little letter from Cannes from Grandmamma Elinor, and it wouldn't surprise me to hear by the next post that she's in love again.'

And so, easily, mercifully, we discussed the whims and undeniably the fancies of that enchanting little lady, now entering her sixty-third year, and her generosity to Liam when his father died, although the Aycliffe money – unfortunately for Liam, fortunately, pehaps for me – had been tied up so well that Grandmamma Elinor could not dispose of too much of it. And he had been glad, he said, to go on the road and sell cloth for Mr Nicholas Barforth. It was the steadiest job he had ever had and it suited him. Far better, he thought, selling the high quality finished product which could be easily carried in his sample-case than shearing the raw wool off the sheep's back, as he'd once been obliged to do for a spell some years ago in Australia.

'Australia,' breathed Venetia, her eyes shining, and immediately his rich, lilting voice took her there, showing her the parched, brash, perilous, thrilling country she wished to see, making her gasp with excitement and shake with incredulous, wholehearted laughter.

'Liam Adair, you never did that. Never.'

'Now would I lie to you?'

'Yes. And I don't care – just go on telling me – *do* go on.'

She was still laughing when he kissed her hand to say goodbye, having stayed far longer than her father would have allowed, and saying my own careful good-night, I went upstairs for the first time in a month alone, finding the bed huge and cold, while sleep, without the restless tossings and turnings of Gervase, was quite impossible.

I did not expect him to return that night and, even had I done so, I would not have waited up for him. I had made no provision for his return. I had not asked that a light should be left burning or a door unlocked, or that any servant be given the task of admitting him. Nor did I intend to spend the night straining my ears in the hope of his arrival, although lying in that chilly bed I soon realized that my determination not to listen only made me listen the harder, my mouth going dry when I at last heard a carriage, which proved to be my father-in-law.

Obviously he had gone to see his mother and there was nothing surprising in that. I had gone to see my father that afternoon and Mrs Barforth was every bit as entitled to a visit from her son. Yet suddenly, in the cold and sinister night, the whole of the Galton estate, the wild moorland tangle of it, the thin, rapid waters rushing down its stony hillsides, the dark house built from those ancient stones, loomed large in my mind, recognizing me – since those weathered stones must surely know how to see and feel – as an enemy and an alien. And, having detected my animosity, how could I doubt their ability to defend themselves?

But there was nothing new in this, nothing I had not pondered a dozen times. And in marrying me, surely, the conflict of his double inheritance had been resolved? Certainly his father thought so. But his temperament, like Venetia's was mercurial, a summer's morning abruptly changing to a winter midnight, and supposing – supposing – he already regretted it? Supposing, having hated his day of confinement in the mill, he had taken his habitual lifelong escape, not to me who believed men should be so confined, but to his mother who did not?

I had started to love him for the vain and selfish reason that he loved me, but now I had gone far beyond that. Now I needed him to love me. I

858

had grown accustomed to it, to depend upon it, and would not easily let it go. And although I was possessive, certainly, I was more than ready to give him what I thought he had asked for, to keep the vows I had made him, since I would not have made them otherwise. I was brim-full of good faith and good intentions, and I wanted him here now, with me, to take advantage of them. was hurt and unhappy, which had happened to me before. Most of all I was afraid, for I had not expected it to happen again.

I fell asleep at last, as one always sleeps in the end, and woke to find him in the room pulling a wet shirt over his head and letting it fall to the ground where his other garments already lay. It was around three o'clock in the morning, rain lashing against the window, a high wind blowing.

'Lovely driving weather,' he said, stripped now and shivering.

'Is it really? I was sleeping.'

'Ah – so I wasted my time, did I, driving through the storm just to get to your side?'

'I didn't expect you. I assumed you were at Galton and would stay there.'

'So did I. I could have gone from there to the mill in the morning, but my mother said no, it wouldn't do, it was my duty to come home – and the Clevedons are very particular when it comes to duty. I told her she was probably sending me to my death but she reckoned a spot of rain wouldn't melt me, and if I went into the ditch – well, I've done that before.'

It was the Gervase I had known in other days, Venetia's difficult brother, a stranger in my bed, keeping his distance so that it was to his naked back that I delivered my crisp reproach.

'You should have sent me a message.'

'Saying what?'

'That you would not be home.'

'Yes,' he said. 'I know I should.'

And rising to the provocation, wanting it settled once and for all, I snapped: 'Then why didn't you?'

He sighed and, turning, lay on his back for a moment.

'You do realize, don't you, Grace Barforth, that nothing obliges me to answer.'

'You can suit yourself.'

'Exactly. I didn't send a message because until I was on the road for Galton I wasn't sure I was going there.'

'I see.'

'I very much doubt it. I expect you had a splendid day, Grace, putting the house in order, making old Chillingworth mend his manners – my word, he was even polite to *me* just now when he let me in.'

There had been tears clenched very tight in my throat from the moment of waking and now, horrified to feel them stinging my eyelids, I sat up, knowing merely that since I was being attacked it was necessary to defend, to let him know once and for all that I would not be downtrodden. But what had I done to deserve this cool hostility? What had I done that he had not expected me to do, had not known I would do? I was exactly the same as I had been in Grasmere, exactly as he had said he wanted me to be. Nothing in me had altered except the depth of my love for him and surely he could not be displeased with that? I was bewildered and hurt but determined – in order that it could be put right – to know why. And because there were still a great many tears in me which I was firmly resolved not to shed, my voice, straining to hold them back, sounded cold when I asked: 'How is your mother?'

'Splendid – absolutely first-rate. Busy with her hound pups just now, of course – sends you her very best.'

'Gervase, I think it is high time I asked you this, and I think you should answer. Your mother was not pleased, was she, about our marriage?'

'No, Grace. My mother was not pleased about our marriage. Good-night, Grace.'

'That is no answer. Will she be reconciled?'

'I believe so. My father pointed out to her that, whatever happens now, even if he should throw me out of Tarn Edge by the scruff of my ungrateful neck, there will still be money enough – your money, that is – for Galton. How can she quarrel with that?'

I had not thought it possible that he could so wound me. He had said 'my father pointed out to her', not 'I married you for your dowry and your expectations', the very fate, in fact, which I had so dreaded. But it made no difference. He had intended to hurt me. He had done so. And for a long time, while he appeared to sleep, I lay winded from the blow. If he had beaten me with his fists I could not have felt more shocked, more bruised, more completely bewildered, and in fact would have coped better with physical violence, being strong enough and determined enough to strike back very hard. But against his spite – whether he meant it or not – I had no defence and was obliged, quite simply and in a strangled silence, to endure.

I knew I could not fall asleep again but I slept, waking as I had done in Grasmere to find his arms around me, his desire already far advanced, and in that first moment I pushed him roughly away, revolted at the thought of being so used, refusing, no matter what the cost, to be an object of pleasure without identity, a wife who was required by law and custom to submit. But his face, in the light of early morning, was pale and tense as I had seen it in the garden at Listonby, his body trembling as it had done on our first night together, nuzzling and thrusting against me with the hurt and puzzled intensity of a child to which my own body responded, opened, enfolded him and held him long after his brief pleasure, until the trembling had ceased.

'Darling, what is it?'

'God knows – just hold me – and don't blame me too much. Just hold me.'

So fluent in other ways he had no words for tenderness, the sighing relaxation of his body as he settled his head on my shoulder was my sole indication that, whether he was sorry or not for having hurt me, he appeared to love me again. And I believed I could be content with that.

8

Blanche had her baby that July, giving birth as effortlessly and as correctly as she did everything else, the confinement being without drama and the child a boy, the new heir of Listonby.

'So you have got it right first time,' said Venetia when we called to congratulate her, to which Blanche serenely replied: 'So I have – which means, with a little contriving, that I shall not be obliged to do it again.'

'How feeble of you,' Venetia told her. 'I believe I should like a dozen.'

But Blanche, draped in white lace, surrounded by lace pillows and pink roses, smiled her infinite superiority and shook her head. 'You know nothing about it, my dear. I would advise you to have *one* and see how you get on with it before making plans for a dozen. And in any case it is considered – well – a little over-enthusiastic to have such large families.

'The Queen has had nine children.'

'Yes, but then the Queen, of course, is so very enthusiastic.'

'Of course,' said Venetia, winking at me behind Blanche's exquisite, indolent back, for Blanche – since her mother-in-law had become a duchess – had started to assume a familiarity with Court circles which both irritated and amused us. Not that Aunt Caroline had succeeded in penetrating the seclusion of so ostentatious a widow as our Queen who, having chosen to spend the rest of her life in mourning, expected others to do the same. But there was, in London, a gregarious Prince of Wales and his beautiful princess, the Danish Alexandra, a lady who, although her own temperament was placid and domestic, seemed prepared to understand that a prince – especially when his mother refuses to give him employment – must be amused. And to this prince Aunt Caroline had been drawn as a moth to a flame, being ready to declare to anyone who cared to listen that for all the scandals and half-scandals that surrounded him Victoria had no one but herself to blame.

It was taught, after all, in every charity school, board school and Sunday school in the land that 'the devil finds work for idle hands to do', and in consequence it was most unwise of Victoria to exclude her son from all responsibility. And, having done so, it was more than unwise, it was downright foolish to set up such a caterwauling when, from sheer boredom, he got into mischief.

But the Queen, alas, could not trust a young man who reminded her far more of her uncles, the dissolute sons of King George III, than of her saintly Albert, who – it was widely believed – having gone virgin to his own bridal bed, had been heart-broken when it became clear to him that his son could not do the same. The Prince was now a man of thirty-two who wanted to work, all his efforts to obtain work having been frustrated by his mother's conviction that he was not fit for it. What, then, did the Queen expect? But Blanche, repeating to us Aunt Caroline's question, was not really interested in the answer – not much interested, I thought, in the new-born Matthew Chard – her fancy having been taken by the recent engagement of the Queen's second son, Prince Alfred, Duke of Edinburgh, to the Tsar of Russia's daughter, and the fuss it had created.

'Imagine,' she said, very obviously quoting the Duchess of South Erin, 'the Tsar has refused to send the girl over to Balmoral for the Queen to have a look at before the wedding, as was done even with Princess Alexandra. And then, to top it all, they are asking that their Grand Duchess Marie, who will only be the Duchess of Edinburgh after all, should take precedence over the Princess of Wales and all our Queen's daughters, even the one who is Crown Princess of Prussia.'

'How very interesting,' said Venetia, stifling a deliberate yawn.

'I think so,' replied Blanche, settling down among her lace pillows, the baby luxuriously but quite definitely neglected at her side, no clouds now on her horizon since it had already occurred to her that by dividing her time between Aunt Caroline's house in Belgravia and country house visits in the southern shires, returning to Listonby only when Sir Dominic's sporting activities demanded it, she could enjoy the pleasures of high society with almost no effort at all.

'So much for Blanche,' Venetia said as we drove home. 'She will be off to London before that poor little mite is weaned, and she will leave him behind, just mark my words, with nurserymaid and nanny, until he is old enough to be sent away to school. If a mill woman treated her baby like that they would say she had abandoned him. But when Lady Blanche does it – well – that is the way things are *done* in good society. I see no point in having children if one means to leave them to strangers. In her place I'd want to curl up with him and snuffle him like a cat in a basket of kittens.'

'Venetia, I didn't know you were so fond of babies.'

'Neither did I, because I'd never been close to one before. But when I held that little scrap just now I felt so – so – lord, I don't know what I felt except that I was bursting with it. And if I can feel so strongly about him – because, after all, he's half Blanche and half Dominic and I'm not wildly enthusiastic about either – then how would I feel about a child of my own, half me and half – well – some special, lovely man? Grace, can you even *imagine* the bliss? Don't you just long for it?'

I was not quite sure about that. It would happen, I supposed, in its own good time, since I knew of no way either to hasten or to prevent it. But for the moment Gervase occupied my ingenuity, demanded my attention and my time as fully as any child, and indeed I could not really imagine him a father.

We had been married for almost half a year now and I believed we were happy, were succeeding, little by little, in consolidating our uncertain foundations. I was the stronger, the steadier, the more determined – we both knew it. Perhaps that alone had first attracted him to me and there were still times when it was all he wanted. He had knelt in a field at Galton that winter's day, an injured horse beside him, unable either to administer the swift *coup de grâce* a gentleman's training and tradition demanded or to contain the remorse and pity which even his mother and sister would have seen as weakness. He had felt at that moment a dreadful alienation from his chosen surroundings, his chosen role in life, from his uncle, Peregrine Clevedon, whose physical likeness he bore and whose nature he had desired to stamp upon his own. But I – a city-bred girl from the other half of himself – had spoken out, offered help which he had taken grudgingly, then gladly. That had been our beginning, and it seemed as sure as any other. He had seen in me something he wanted and I had not deceived him. He had seen my true likeness and now, being sure of it, could draw strength and comfort from it as he chose, or could sometimes – not too often – strike out a fretful, a teasing, always a glancing blow, to test me or to assert himself.

'I can't tell you what a comfort it is, Grace, to know you are always right. So very pleasant, don't you see, no longer to be burdened by decisions.'

'My dear wife, if you say I must then I must. Unless, of course, you would care to force me? In fact – yes – *do* force me –'

But it was said with his arms around me, his mouth nibbling at my shoulders and the nape of my neck, his body – in the act of love – stronger and more knowledgeable than mine. It was light, pleasant, erotic, part of our love-play which, if resentment was there even in some small measure – and I must have known it was there – love would be sure to cancel out.

He went to the mill every day – or very nearly – but when I enquired as to what he did there and the degree of his success he would merely reply: 'Oh, I am not much use, you know, for I have no head for machines and mathematics. The only percentage I can arrive at with any certainty is ten, and I will readily admit that many things which appear quite obvious to my father and to Gideon are not at all obvious to me. But do persevere, Grace. You may make a business man out of me yet, one day.'

'Do you get on with Gideon?' I carefully enquired.

'Is it necessary,' he said coolly, "to get on" with one's employees?' And I was to reproach myself bitterly – most bitterly – for not heeding the warning contained in his reply.

Yet he continued to get up – most mornings – and make his appearance at the mill, which so pleased his father, who was anxious at this stage merely that he should *try*, that he willingly allowed him a week's shooting at Galton that autumn and a further week with the Lawdale, a concession which was either not extended to Gideon Chard or of which he did not take advantage, since he continued, through the fine, sporting weather, to attend to his labours. And gradually our lives fell into shape, or so it seemed, a pattern of my own designing which was therefore bound – if nothing else – to satisfy me.

The housekeeper, Mrs Winch, and I were soon on terms of understanding, and to my surprise and pleasure the butler, Chillingworth, chose to accept the sensible view that, if I was a shade too exacting for my years, I was neither mean nor capricious and might be worth serving after all. Unfortunately Mrs Loman continued to send in dubious sauces and soggy vegetables, talked down to me at our morning interviews – knowing that I had never with my own hands so much as boiled an egg – so that finally, when apple tart had appeared at dinner five nights in succession, I went to Manchester and found myself a Mrs Kincaid who brought her own kitchen-maids with her, thus putting an end to Mrs Loman.

'Poor soul,' said Venetia, reminded of Mrs Loman by the excellence of Mrs Kincaid's soufflé. 'I daresay she has ten starving children somewhere and a husband who takes all her wages for drink.'

'Nonsense. No husband at all and one child, fat as a pig, who lives with her sister in Huddersfield.'

'Venetia,' said Gervase in mock reproach. 'You should have realized that Grace would *know*.'

The house became warm again and reliable. There were fires laid every morning in rooms where fires should be, hot water in constant supply, warm towels, maids who, because they were told what was expected of them, did it at the appointed hour and for the most part did it well. No one waited now at the front door of Tarn Edge while Chillingworth read the sporting papers he should have been ironing for Gervase. Callers were admitted promptly and then most carefully looked after. Meals were served punctually and beautifully, beds were well aired, linen immaculately pressed. I had set the wheels in motion as I had seen Aunt Faith and Mrs Agbrigg do, and if Venetia scarcely noticed and Gervase did not seem particularly to care, I knew my father-in-law was pleased with me.

I had been apprehensive at the thought of sharing a home with him, knowing his nature to be both exacting and domineering, but it was soon clear to me that Mr Barforth's main interest in life – perhaps the only true one – was work. He worked, certainly for money and for the authority it gave him, but he worked also for the sheer pleasure of the work itself, which like tobacco had become essential to him. He rose early, returned just in time for dinner and would then disappear to his library to be visited by one or other of his managers, his lawyer, his architect, by Liam Adair or Gideon Chard, sometimes by my father when business would be discussed and a great deal of brandy consumed. On three or four nights a week he went out, going, one supposed, to drink brandy in some other man's library, and from time to time he would spend a night or two away, making a point of letting me know when he expected to return and notifying me, usually through Liam Adair, of any change of plan. He was uncommunicative but considerate, at least where I was concerned, so that when I realized how much his children and his wife were afraid of him I could not really see the reason why.

'Wait,' Venetia said. 'So far he has been kind to you, amazingly kind for him. But just wait until you want something and he doesn't want you to have it, and then you'll know. Because nothing can move him, believe me – nothing. Most people give in eventually. They get tired, or frightened, or it stops being important. Not father. He never gives way. And when you realize that, when you feel it, it wears you down. I think

864

that's why Gervase used to run off so much. He knew if he stayed near father he'd give in to him, no matter what it cost him, because a moment comes – *believe* me – when you'll do anything just to end it. So Gervase used to run. Not that it did any good because father would only bring him back again.

'And you?'

'I can't stand up to him either, Grace,' she said very seriously and sadly. 'No one can.'

And before I could ask her about Charles Heron she shook her head and raised a finger to her lips, hushing me.

'Grace, what you don't know can't grieve you – can it, darling? I won't burden you now with my secrets – it simply wouldn't be fair.'

Mr Barforth had issued no precise commands with regard to Charles Heron other than that his presence at Tarn Edge would be unwelcome, his aspirations with regard to Venetia unthinkable. If there was to be a chosen suitor, then, unless Venetia could provide someone of like calibre, Mr Barforth decreed that it should be Gideon Chard. And perhaps it was her docile acceptance of that decree which stopped him from forbidding her to see Charles Heron elsewhere. Venetia, we all knew, had had her fancies before. Charles Heron could well be as fleeting as the rest, and I think Mr Barforth would have been more alarmed by a man like Liam Adair, whose attractions – being more similar to his own – he could more easily understand, than this gentle young revolutionary, so different from himself in every way.

But, whatever his reasons, he did not issue the general prohibition which would have barred Charles Heron from any house where Venetia was likely to be a guest, so that when he scraped acquaintance with Aunt Faith she had no reason to send him away should Venetia happen to call nor any reason to warn Mr Barforth – even if she had been on good terms with him – that they had spent half an hour in her shrubbery, within sight of her drawing-room windows, but technically alone.

Yet when Gideon Chard was mentioned, when the man himself strode into the house to smoke cigars and drink brandy with her father, Venetia greeted him cheerfully, even pertly, as she had always done.

'My word, Gideon, I never thought to see you so industrious.'

'When something is worth working for, one does one's best.'

'But such a pillar of virtue you have become.'

'Hardly that, Venetia.'

'Oh, absolutely, for you have been out with the Lawdale no more than twice this season, and I am constantly besieged by young ladies asking your whereabouts.'

'And what do you tell them?'

'Oh – that you have taken up residence in my father's counting-house and will not emerge until you have made yourself a millionaire.'

But when at my father-in-law's suggestion I tried out the paces of my new cook by giving my first dinner party, she placidly accepted Gideon as her partner for the evening, offering him the sudden ripple of her laughter in exchange for whatever it was he whispered to her at table, while Dominic, no longer interested in flirtation, pronounced the *suprêmes de volaille* rather better than he had expected, the chestnut purée interesting, the Chateau Yquem altogether to his liking, paying no attention to Blanche as she regaled us with the preparations for the Duke of Edinburgh's Russian wedding at which, if one had not known better, one would have assumed she was to be a guest.

'Well done,' Mr Barforth told me, and I was inclined to agree wih him. I was, on the whole very happy. My marriage would not be perfect, but who has ever heard of a perfect marriage? Who could even imagine or sustain such perfection? Yet, quite soon, when simple freedom of movement, the right to come and go as I pleased, no longer seemed so miraculous and when Tarn Edge no longer required my constant presence to keep it from falling down, I felt the need of other things to fill my days. There was a by-election to be fought that year, due to the collapse of Mr Fielding from a congestion of the lungs, in which Miss Mandelbaum and her suffragist group took a strong interest, the new Liberal candidate having declared himself sympathetic to the female cause. Yet when I accepted Miss Mandelbaum's invitation to meet him – although I had already dined in his company both at Tarn Edge and at Fieldhead where he had gone to assure himself of the Agbrigg and Barforth vote – I found that my own position as a suffragist had greatly altered.

The candidate, Mr Colclough, and his colleague Mr Sheldon both made themselves very pleasant, enquiring most attentively as to the health of my husband, my father, my father-in-law, my grandfather Mayor Agbrigg, my grandmother's stepson Liam Adair, and any other male relative of mine who might be likely to vote for them. But the possibility of my own vote, which had never been great had now, I was given to understand, been rendered null and void by the simple act of matrimony.

'My dear,' Miss Mandelbaum said nervously, glancing at Miss Tighe, who had lately taken up residence in Cullingford, 'we have only ever asked for the vote for widows and spinsters – never for married women.'

'And why is that?'

'If you had given serious thought to the matter, Mrs Barforth,' said Miss Tighe, 'you would have found it obvious. At our first public meeting in Manchester, six years ago, a resolution was passed asking for the vote on the same terms as it had been, or would be, granted to men. It is the view of most of us, I believe – certainly it is the view of Miss Lydia Becker and her many supporters, including myself – that this resolution should not be tampered with.'

'Why, Miss Tighe?'

'Because, Mrs Barforth, the vote – the Government itself – is about property, not individual personalities.'

'I do understand that, Miss Tighe.'

'Then you will also understand that although some men have holdings large enough to entitle them to two votes, or more, there are others – something approaching half the male population of this country, my dear – who have so little property that they are not entitled to vote at all.'

'And you think that right?'

'I have not said so. I am simply stating the facts. The vote concerns property, Mrs Barforth, and since a married woman's property, on marriage, passes to her husband, what claim can she make – what justification – to the vote? A married woman has her husband to speak for her. To allow her to vote would be to allow the same piece of property to be represented twice.'

'And does the whole of the Manchester Suffragist Society share your view, Miss Tighe?'

'No,' she said tartly. 'One does not expect any view to be universally accepted. There is an element of dissent. There have always been those who have advocated the extreme doctrine of one man one vote for which – however attractive – I cannot believe we are ready. Presumably these same extremists would offer the vote, if they had it, to married women. Our own Dr Pankhurst and Mr Bright, I believe, are among them. Ah well, I imagine Mr Bright must have his own wife to answer to, although I am at a loss to comprehend what Dr Pankhurst's motives may be in this.'

'And you, Mr Colclough?' I aked the new candidate. 'How do you stand?' But if I had hoped to embarrass him I was disappointed, Mr Colclough possessing, like Mr Sheldon, and Mr Fielding before him, the career politician's ability to produce an opinion to suit every occasion, a quick glance around the room assuring him that he would do better tonight to support Miss Tighe, who knew more people and could do him more harm than I.

'Mrs Barforth,' he said with great solemnity, going through the motions of taking me seriously, just in case, by some Act of God or revolution, I should one day be enfranchised. 'It is a many-sided question of enormous complexity. Perhaps I can do no better than quote the view of our leader, Mr Gladstone, whose regard for women and the sanctity of marriage is such that he fears the vote would weaken the female situation rather than strengthen it. You are not burdened by the necessity of earning a living, Mrs Barforth, as we men are. You are free to serve in many positions of influence, school boards and the like, where by making your views known you could bring in many votes. And by accepting such posts, which are unsalaried, you would enable the men who now hold them to take up paid appointments, thus easing their financial anxieties and liberating their energies for the benefit of *our* Party. When a woman can do all this, Mrs Barforth, without losing one shred of her femininity or exposing herself to the slightest embarrassment – by remaining a *woman* – then one wonders why the vote should be at all necessary to her? I know Mr Gladstone takes this view. While the Queen, you know, is most uncomfortable at the idea of women hazarding themselves in politics. No place for a woman, she declares, and one must admit she is in a position to know. Have I answered your question, Mrs Barforth?'

'I believe so, Mr Colclough.' ·

And it was Venetia, who had seemed content to drink Miss Mandelbaum's tea in silence, who put an end to it, her low chuckle dispersing my gloom and making me smile.

'This is really no place for you at all,' she told me. 'You had best leave the government to Mr Sheldon, Mr Colclough, Miss Tighe and myself. Run home, Grace Barforth, to your husband and get on with your knitting!'

My first Christmas as a wife was spent at Listonby in a gathering of the whole family except for Mr Nicholas Barforth, who remained at Tarn Edge, and his wife, who remained at Galton, although Gervase, Venetia and I spent a day with her. The Duke and Duchess of South Erin came up from London; *Captain* Noel Chard had leave from his regiment to celebrate his promotion; my father and Mrs Agbrigg came over for the ball on Christmas Eve; while Blanche put herself and her son attractively on display and then sulked an hour or two when her father told her he was taking Aunt Faith abroad in the New Year and would therefore be unable to have the infant Matthew at Elderleigh while Blanche went to London.

Gervase gave me diamond ear-rings, galloped off on Boxing Day morning with the Lawdale and was back before noon, alone, his horse having gone lame, he said, although it looked sound enough to me, and we spent a glorious afternoon of winter sunshine in Listonby Woods, watching the squirrels frenziedly searching for the nuts they had hoarded in such careful hiding places, now forgotten.

I was happy. I believed Gervase was happy too, to the extent his complicated nature allowed. Blanche, I felt, was rapidly arranging matters to her entire satisfaction. And although Venetia burst into a characteristic blend of tears and laughter on Christmas Eve when the toasts were drunk, thinking, I supposed, of Charles Heron sampling the sparse festivities of nearby St Walburga's School, she flirted most obligingly throughout the holiday with any young man who offered, including Gideon, allowing him to kiss her under the mistletoe in a way not entirely pleasing to his mother, who since her elevation to the peerage had started to wonder, once again, if she might do a little better than a manufacturer's daughter for her handsome younger son.

There was a charity ball at the Assembly Rooms in Cullingford in the New Year, an ambitious affair which I had helped to organize and which Gervase, at the last moment, was unable to attend, having been sent on a little tour of Barforth interests in the home counties which – although disappointed about the ball – I could only feel to be a step in the right direction. And wishing to believe what I wanted most to believe – as we all do – wanting Gervase to improve his commercial capacities and his father to trust him, it did not occur to me that, as the one person likely to resent the Chard connection, he had been deliberately sent out of the way.

But from the day of his departure Gideon was a much more frequent visitor to the house, calling regularly in the evenings to see Mr Barforth, who instead of taking him into the library would casually invite him to stay to dinner – 'I reckon Grace can manage another one' – and afterwards would contrive, if only for ten minutes, to leave Gideon and Venetia alone.

Mr Barforth, in fact, had made up his mind with regard to his daughter's future and expected her to prove every bit as amenable – as biddable – as had his son. Yet Venetia herself, who should have been rebellious, furious, contemptuous, remained suspiciously untroubled.

'Do you mean to refuse him?' I asked her bluntly.

'No, for he will not ask.'

'Venetia, he *will* – believe me.'

'No, he will not, you can believe *me*.'

And I heard her singing to herself as she went tripping around the house, her dreaming face enraptured.

Gideon Chard dined with us on the night of the charity ball, very handsome in the stark black and white of his evening clothes, the jacket fitting without a wrinkle across his wide shoulders, his shirt elaborately tucked and pleated, a heavy gold ring on his hand; a fastidious young man who took far more care of his appearance than either his millionaire uncle or his own elder brother, the baronet. And even then I did not realize what his marriage to Venetia might mean to me, and to Gervase, because I did not believe – and Gervase did not believe – that she would marry him.

She kept us waiting after dinner while she went upstairs to make some adjustment to her dress, leaving me to carry on the kind of stilted conversation with Gideon that people make when they know the carriage is at the door, their cloaks are being held ready in the hall, and the hour is late.

'I'll go up and fetch her, shall I?'

But then there she was, hovering in the doorway, her gauzy skirts floating around her like the wings of a green butterfly, that air of blissful expectancy about her, of an immense, secret joy she could not quite suppress.

'Venetia – you're beautiful,' Gideon said, as if he was both surprised and rather pleased about it.

'Am I really? I'm so glad.'

And as he held out a hand to her, she came with little dancing steps to meet him, her own hand outstretched, and then stopped abruptly, her hand falling to her side, her attitude one of almost comic regret.

'This is all nonsense, you know, Gideon.'

'What is nonsense, Venetia?'

'All this – all this – you know what I mean, for you do not want me at all, and you know quite well that I very badly want someone else.'

'Ah,' he said, and, his eyes never leaving her face, he smiled. 'Shall we leave it – for now – at that?'

But Venetia, having wound herself up to this pitch, could not endure even a moment's silence and, clasping her hands together, began dancing a few more little steps up and down, jerky ones this time, which took her nowhere.

'Gideon – please believe me. I *do* want someone else.'

'Venetia, I *do* believe you. But these things happen, we all know that, and we are not talking about wanting, my dear. We are talking about marrying.' And perhaps because it seemed best to him, he was still tolerantly, easily smiling.

'It is the same thing, Gideon – for me it is the same.'

'Then there is only one thing to be done. I shall have to see to it that you do want me.'

'Gideon,' she said, half exasperated, half shocked, unable, as she met his eye, to hold back her laughter. 'Such an idea – really!'

'Yes – really! And you will do well enough with me, you know. I am not so terrible.'

'Indeed you are not, not terrible at all. In fact if you did not remind me so much of my father I would very likely find you fascinating. And if he were not my father, I do believe I would find him fascinating, too. But you do see, Gideon, don't you, that all this is *his* idea, because you are doing so well at the mills? And *your* idea because if you marry me he will probably make you a partner, and when he dies half of everything will belong to you – and because if you don't marry me somebody else will get what you have started to think of as *your* share. I perfectly understand all that, and in your place I could even see the sense to it. But it would not *do*, you know. I would be a terrible wife to you, Gideon, without meaning you any harm, simply because I am not at all the kind of wife you *should* marry. And you are not at all in love with me. I am so glad of that, for if you cared –'

'I *do* care, Venetia.'

'Oh,' she said, considerably taken aback. 'No, you do not. I made sure of that, for otherwise I would not have given you the slightest encouragement ...'

But he shook his head, allowing her voice to peter out before he smiled again.

'Then you have been in error. I do care for you, Venetia. Who would not? You are thoroughly exasperating – everyone says so.'

'Do they really?'

'Yes, indeed. And I absolutely agree. But you are just as thoroughly amusing.'

'How very nice!'

'I think so. You are very nice altogether, Venetia.'

'Gideon, I could almost believe you.'

'You *do* believe me. Shall we go now and dance at Grace's ball?'

She smiled, offering yet another glimpse of that lovely, inner joy.

'Yes,' she said. 'I'll dance with you, Gideon.' And reaching herself towards us, she slipped an arm through mine, the other through his, and went out with us into the frosty night.

9

I slept late the next day, very late, Gervase not being there to disturb me with his tossing and turning, and it did not surprise me when I reached the breakfast parlour to find myself alone. It was a dull, February morning, a low grey sky over the chimney-stacks, damp clinging air, an occasional peevish handful of rain, a day to make up the fire and doze, perhaps, like Blanche, over a book, a cup of chocolate, a day when I could almost agree with Mr Colclough and Mr Sheldon that it was pleasant to be spared the burden of earning a living.

And thus idling my time away it was not until luncheon, when I sent up a tray for Venetia, that I learned she was gone.

Yet, gone where? She had staggered to her bed at four o'clock that morning and had told her maid she would probably sleep 'for ever'. No one had disturbed her. If Miss Venetia wanted breakfast she would ring for it. Her bed appeared to have been slept in, her gauzy dress placed over a chair, awaiting attention, since she had torn the hem. Could she possibly – and I prayed for it to be true – have got herself up and dressed and gone out for a breath of air? No, of course she could not. Or, at least, not once the servants were awake. Far more likely that she had allowed her maid to undress her, had sent the girl away, had waited until Chillingworth had made all secure for what remained of the night, and then, putting on a travelling dress and a warm, dark cloak, had let herself out through the side door Gervase had used for his night-prowlings and had run off somewhere to meet Charles Heron.

I knew it and would not believe it, worked hard to convince myself otherwise – for this was not the unique destiny I had imagined for her and I would miss her terribly – until her maid picked up her ball gown, thinking she might as well get on with her mending, and from its green gauze skirts fluttered Venetia's letter to me.

'Darling, you did not think this of me, did you? And believe me, I would have preferred the parish church and all the family, and father to give me away. But you must know he would never allow it and I have told you I cannot stand up to him. Darling, I wanted to tell you. I even wanted to tell Gideon last night and to apologize to him because I have used him rather, to throw sand in father's eyes – not that Gideon will care for that. Gervase will understand that this is right for me, that I don't mind about the money should father decide to disown me. Dear Grace, I told you once before that this is the only life I have, my one chance to get it right. And this *is* right. Please tell Gervase and learn to be happy for me.'

I sat down on her bed and let a long time go by while I prayed, fervently yet without too much conviction: 'Venetia, I do hope so'; then more time while I indulged myself in a few tears and a great deal of slow, brooding anxiety. And then I wrote a note to my father-in-law stressing how urgently I required to see him and had them take it to the mill.

I had no idea what I could say to him and, in fact, said nothing, simply handing him the note and waiting, not daring to look at him, while he read it. But no thunder bolts came crashing over my head, just a curt voice saying to me: 'The man's name?'

'Charles Heron.'

'The schoolmaster?'

'Yes.'

'And where do you suppose they have run off to?'

'To Scotland, surely – to be married?'

He glanced down at the letter, tapped it against his hand and then slid it into his pocket.

'Scotland? Yes, that would seem a possibility. Grace, would you kindly send to Lawcroft Mills and ask Liam Adair to come here?'

I heard, of course, only later and very gradually the details of what next occurred, piecing together from the varying accounts of those most closely concerned a picture which seemed to be exact. A lesser man than Mr Barforth, a warmer man, would, I imagine, have set off post haste for Gretna Green, where Scottish law so obligingly allowed runaways to be married. It was the obvious place to go, too obvious to Mr Nicholas Barforth, who all his commercial life had sat straight-faced and keen-eyed while men far shrewder than Charles Heron and far more devious than Venetia had tried to hoodwink him.

'Ah, Liam,' he said, greeting him in the hall with a brief handshake, 'a word in your ear, and then a little job for you'; and twenty minutes later, while Mr Barforth remained smoking a cigar in his library, Liam rode off to St Walburga's School, where with the inbred charm of the Irish he acquired enough snippets of information to conclude that Charles Heron had probably not taken Venetia north to a speedy and foregone conclusion, but south where the implications were less obvious and rather more sinister.

North was a declaration of certain intent, marriage at any price, a race to the altar after which the irate father might do his worst. North shouted out loud: 'Disinherit us if you must. All that matters to us is being together.' North was where idealistic Charles and headstrong Venetia *should* have gone, for once the matrimonial knot was tied, what could her father do to her except stop her money? And she had declared often enough how little she cared for that.

South was not quite so outspoken. South, in fact, might just be the direction in which a man might take a girl to be seduced rather than married, knowing that, since there is no place in the marriage-market for damaged goods, the father of a girl so damaged must be glad to take any man – even her seducer – as her husband, at a price the husband will feel entitled to dictate. Except, of course, that Charles Heron was not that kind of man.

'Well, Liam,' said Mr Barforth, having ideas of his own on that score, and very soon the carriage stood at the door to take them to the train, Mr Barforth stern and quiet, Liam serious and concerned but with a flash of excitement in him too, for if a husband should be required for Venetia in a hurry this might be his golden opportunity.

They experienced no difficulty in finding Charles Heron's father, since Vicars are not notably anonymous, and the reverend gentleman proving susceptible to the temptation of golden guineas and rather intimidated in any case by the generous muscular endowment of Liam Adair, they were soon apprised of all that was needed. And less than an hour later they had located the runaways sharing the one upper room of a singularly unattractive inn, Venetia's eyes terrified, not, Liam thought, of her father but of her own disillusion. For this was not what she had expected.

872

This was not right. She had trusted Charles Heron implicitly, feeling him so much a part of herself that it would have been impossible not to trust him. To go north, he had said, would be too great a risk. North was the direction in which her father would first look with an excellent chance of finding her before the ceremony had taken place. And so she had put her hand in his and kept it there as they headed south, to that sure hiding place which had turned out to be a meagre inn, a narrow bed where he, two nights ago now, had asked her with tears to prove her love.

She had been most reluctant to comply, having cherished for a long time a dream of her wedding night which was very far removed from this. But the loss of her virginity, being the key to Charles Heron's whole plan, could not be delayed, and using the strength of her emotions as his best weapon he had somehow made her feel that to refuse him her body would be the same as withdrawing her love. And since he couldn't live without her love, she would be killing him.

Yet, having longed for months for his embraces, she found that she could not now enjoy them, her distaste being so apparent that she felt compelled to apologize for it and was persuaded by his show of hurt feelings to go through the sorry performance again. It was to have been a magical experience, a slow progression towards perfect physical harmony. It was, in fact, quick and clumsy, as half-baked as his revolutionary theories had really been, a mere stumbling along a road that had Charles Heron's orgasm at the end of it; and when, on the second night, he pressed his hand against her stomach and said: 'Only think – you have very likely got my son in there by now', she turned away from him and wept.

She had expected him to cower with fright when they saw her father striding across the inn yard and up the stairs, but he had remained perfectly calm, his composure – or so she thought later – increasing her suspicions that he had wanted to be discovered.

'Mr Barforth,' he said.

'Mr Heron,' my father-in-law answered him. 'And would this, by any chance, be Mrs Heron?'

'You might think it desirable that she should be. Perhaps we could step downstairs to discuss how best it might be contrived?'

'No need for that, young man. It's straightforward enough, I reckon. You've seduced my daughter, by the look of her, and I'd like to know how much you think that ought to cost me. I assume you have the figure in mind?'

'If we could step downstairs, sir,' said Charles, somewhat embarrassed. 'I see no reason for Venetia to be obliged to listen to this.'

But although Mr Barforth had never doubted his ability to find his daughter and bring her home, it was no part of his plan to have her spend the next few months of her life pining for a scoundrel and he shook his head.

'I see every reason for Venetia to listen. And because it won't be pleasant for her and she's looking out of sorts, I'll make it short. There's no money, Mr Charles Heron. Marry her, if she'll have you. But there's no money.'

873

'I can't believe that, sir.'

'Believe it. She thinks you can live on love. I reckon you know different. There's no money.'

A braver man than Charles Heron might just have taken the gamble. Cullingford was a small town, thirsty for gossip, where a scandal of this magnitude could never be lived down. Surely Mr Barforth could not run the risk of taking her back there as if nothing had occurred? Charles Heron had been brought up to believe in female virginity, in the enormity of its value, the tragedy of its loss. So had I. So had we all. He knew that a girl who lost it would – unless her seducer consented to marry her – be better off dead. He knew that an unmarried girl who became pregnant had no real alternative but to die, and apparently always did so, since none of us had ever encountered such a person. But Mr Nicholas Barforth seemed unaware of his own desperate situation, ignorant of the disgrace, and would do nothing but repeat, 'Marry her, if you like. But there's no money'; while Venetia herself, instead of falling to his feet and begging him to save her from ruin – as she *ought* to have done – simply turned her face to the wall and said not a word.

'Marry her, if she'll have you.' And glancing at her taut, poker-straight back, Charles Heron was no longer sure she would. And when he muttered something to the effect that his heart was broken, Mr Barforth, in order that Venetia should be in no doubt at all as to her lover's true character, offered to compensate him for any damage to that organ with the sum of a thousand pounds. That, Charles Heron declared, was paltry, ridiculous. Possibly, Mr Barforth agreed, but nevertheless his offer would hold good until three o'clock that afternoon, at which hour it would be reduced by half. And since the time was then approaching five minutes to three, Charles Heron, so as not to come away empty-handed, took his thousand.

'Don't think I didn't love you,' he said to Venetia's blind back. 'Don't think that. I never pretended to be strong. And you don't know – you just can't even imagine what it's like to be poor.'

'Perhaps now you'd care to step downstairs with my friend here,' said Mr Barforth, 'who will explain to you exactly what I want for my money – which is exactly nothing, no words, no letters, no boasting one night when you've had a glass or two – nothing, Mr Heron. Mr Adair will make it plain to you.'

And whether or not it was done on Mr Barforth's instructions, Charles Heron tripped and fell down those inn stairs with Liam Adair's boot behind him and was kicked out into the inn yard to be paid off and sent, slightly bleeding, about his business.

'Come on, love,' Mr Barforth said to Venetia, 'let's go home'; and that was all he said to her, leaving Liam to distract her as best he could throughout the difficult journey, which passed for her in a confused haze.

She had been wrong about everything. She had believed completely in Charles and, having lost faith in him, she had lost faith in herself. The world had moved, somehow, out of focus, distorting her vision so that objects she had thought solid became thin air between her fingers,

874

objects she had thought soft and yielding seemed suddenly possessed of the power to scratch and burn her hands. Yet her loss of faith had not, to her unbearable distress, brought with it a loss of love, for the clumsy stranger of the last two days had not really been her Charles Heron. She had lost *her* Charles and certainly she would never find him again – since he had never really existed – but she had loved him with her whole heart and now, totally disassociating him from the commonplace fortune-hunter, the commonplace trap into which she had fallen, she grieved for him. She could see no hope for herself, and had her father proposed some convenient, undramatic way of self-destruction she would have been glad of it.

She could not face me when they finally brought her back to Tarn Edge, hiding her face in her father's shoulder when I came running out to the carriage-drive, clinging to him with such desperate, drowning hands that I kept my distance as he lifted her up like the child she had suddenly become and carried her upstairs.

'Liam?'

'She'll be all right,' he said. 'She'll mend.' And we went together into the drawing-room, Liam answering my quesions absently, listening for Mr Barforth's return so that the first steps on the landing took him out into the hall again.

'Ah, Liam –' said Mr Barforth, descending the stairs slowly, a vigorous, healthy man who even in the fiftieth year of his age made nothing of a sleepless night or two in a train. And Liam Adair answered him, 'Yes, sir?', his whole body alert, excited yet cautious, knowing that his own future, which lay in the hand of this powerful man, had already been decided.

'I believe I am in debt to you, Liam.'

'There's no debt, sir.'

'That's what I thought you'd say. Good lad, Liam. But I've made myself free with your time. You'll be wanting to get home now.'

'Is there – nothing else I can do for you, Mr Barforth?'

'That's very civil of you, Liam. If there should be anything I'll let you know.'

'I'll be off then, sir.'

'Yes – take the carriage.'

And as Liam accepted his dismissal and turned to leave, Mr Barforth said: 'Chillingworth, have this note sent round to my nephew, Mr Chard.'

Once again my father-in-law had not only made up his mind, but had succeeded against all the odds in getting his way. Yet I wondered, as I went meekly back to the drawing-room, if he would find Gideon as biddable, as grateful, perhaps as greedy as he clearly expected. The seriousness of Venetia's position required immediate marriage. Everyone wold agree on that. Liam Adair would have taken her with nothing but promises for his future and the present security of her dowry. Three days ago, Gideon Chard might have done the same. But now, with these new cards in his hands, he would drive a harder bargain and Mr

Barforth would probably think him a fool if he did not. He was being asked, after all, not only to avert a scandal with the power of his noble name but, just possibly, to give that name to another man's child. And, to that end, surely, important financial concessions would be required, specific guarantees which, as I contemplated their possible nature, gave me a sharp reminder of my duty to Gervase.

I heard Gideon's step in the hall, Mr Barforth walking firmly to meet it. I let them talk an hour, the half of another, and then, realizing with some surprise that it was still only four o'clock in the afternoon, I went upstairs for my hat and gloves and ordered the carriage. Until now I had thought only of Venetia, but Gervase was even more entitled to my loyalty, entitled, most definitely, to know what plans were being made for his sister's future, which must affect our own. And since he was not here to enquire and Mr Barforth would be unlikely to explain himself to me, I would go to my father and ask him to take whatever steps seemed necessary on Gervase's behalf.

But Mr Barforth, who could not have heard the carriage from his library, had evidently instructed someone to keep an eye on me, for I had barely set foot on the drive when he appeared, the inevitable cigar in his hand.

'Grace, may I have a word with you?'

'Of course.'

And putting an arm around me he walked me a little way down the garden, leading me gently yet very decidedly away from the carriage.

He had never touched me before, but now the very bulk of him, which had often seemed so menacing, comforted me, that wide chest wreathed in cigar smoke, the square, brown hands with their powerful, competent fingers, the habit of authority. And I had hardly slept for three nights. I was anxious and uncertain and very tired.

'Where were you off to, Grace?'

'I thought I should see my father.'

'Quite right. But I'd be obliged if you'd put it off until morning. If it's Gervase you're thinking of, then think carefully, Grace. We'd do well to keep him out of this, you know. If he found out about it too soon, before we get it properly settled, then I reckon there's a chance he might just go and take a shot at that young scoundrel. That's what Venetia's afraid of at any rate and it wouldn't help matters. Duelling has been against the law for some while now, you know. They call it "murder" these days, not "honour". And in any case it wouldn't help. Talk to Venetia about it when you see her presently – I reckon she might be asking for you ere long.'

We walked back to the house and I saw that the carriage had gone and my resolution with it, for how could I go to Fieldhead when Venetia needed me, how could I take the risk that my father might telegraph to Gervase and that he might then go looking for Charles Heron with a gun, as Peregrine Clevedon would have been sure to do? Mr Barforth, no doubt, had manipulated me – I quite saw that – but it seemed to be not only to his own advantage but to mine and Venetia's. It seemed right.

'Will you be dining?' I asked, taking off my gloves.

'Possibly.'

And it was then that I caught a glimpse of Gideon Chard as the library door opened and swiftly closed to admit a servant with a tray in his hand.

'Yes, Gideon is still here,' Mr Barforth said. 'And I reckon he'll stay just where he is for some time yet, since he has a little problem to solve. Should he enquire for me, I shall be upstairs with my daughter. Have them fetch me down.'

And I turned and hurried away, my skin suddenly cold, for there had been nothing at all in Gideon's scowling, brooding countenance, nor in the fastidious, almost pained set of his jaw to indicate a happy bridegroom.

The engagement was announced the next morning and caused no sensation, a great many people – knowing that Mr Barforth wanted it – being mildly surprised, if anything, that it had not happened sooner. Venetia came herself to tell me of it, very early, sitting on the edge of my bed, her eyes dark-shadowed, her manner that of a quiet and docile stranger. She had no wish to speak of the past. It would be better, indeed, never to speak of it again. She simply wanted me to know that she was to marry Gideon. 'And it is good of him,' she said, 'very good – you must never forget that. One would have expected him to find me distasteful – lord knows I am distasteful to myself. But he says not – silly merely. *Silly*. Good heavens, such a little word! I have been a silly little girl, but that is not how I feel. Poor Gideon, I don't know how he can bring himself to do it – even for the money. He must hate being poor, in his degree, every bit as much as Charles. Grace, will you do something for me?'

'Of course I will.'

'Promise?'

'What is it?' And, naturally, it could not have been too much.

'Just this. Don't tell Gervase. *Please*. Grace, I am so ashamed. I don't want him to be ashamed of me too. Just let him think that Gideon asked me and I said yes – just that. Father says I am to tell myself over and over that it did happen like that, until I believe it – that I *must* believe it, for Gideon's sake, since I owe him so much. Grace, please let me keep my brother's good opinion.'

'You would not lose it. He is not so narrow as that.'

'But I have been such an idiot, you see. I have been mistaken in everything. I thought Charles right and my father wrong, yet my father has been so kind. I thought he would murder me if he caught me and instead of that he was kind – *kind* – and *right*. I am not fit to decide anything any more. I don't want to decide anything. The whole world seems upside-down to me and strange – and I am the strangest thing in it. But please, Grace, you know how little it takes for Gervase to quarrel with father, and I couldn't stand it – not now. After all, marriage is for life, and since it is the only thing women are supposed to do, then somehow or other I must manage to do it properly – I must work hard and be good at it. That is what father says.'

They were married very splendidly and very quickly, using a forthcoming business trip to America and the well-known impetuousness of youth to account for their haste, for although she had discovered by now that she was not expecting Charles Heron's child, she was still most touchingly anxious to carry out her father's wishes, having abdicated her will, it seemed, entirely to his. She was still docile, listless, easily tired, her attention apt to wander, so that one had to ask her the same question several times and even then she could not always answer. 'Did I order the carriage? Heavens! I must have done. Do I want to drive to town? I don't think so. Surely – isn't there something I ought to be doing?' She had become obedient, as she had never been in childhood, wanting to be guided, wanting to please, a little girl again who could escape from the world and all its ills by hiding her face in her father's broad chest and murmuring 'Yes, papa.' She looked very small that morning in the parish church, overwhelmed by a sumptuous bridal gown of white satin stitched all over with clusters of seed pearls and crystal, the skirt extending to a train of imperial proportions, decorated not with the common orange blossom but with orchids, her father's wedding gift of diamonds in her ears, a strand of them round her throat. She carried orchids in one lean, boyish hand, the other hand, bearing a diamond of great size and ostentatious value, resting on the arm of her large, handsome father as she entered the church, and of her large, handsome cousin as she left it.

'What is that lace on her sleeves?' whispered Blanche, 'It looks like Valenciennes. Heavens! what does that cost per yard, Grace, and I declare there are yards of it – and those diamonds! Mamma said diamonds were too old for me on my wedding day, but only *look* at that solitaire. Lord – if this is her trousseau, one wonders what the dowry may be.'

'She looks very pale,' said Aunt Faith. 'I suppose it is the excitement.'

'She was always excitable,' the Duchess of South Erin replied, no better pleased with Venetia as a daughter-in-law, no matter what the size of the dowry, than she had been with Blanche.

The wedding-breakfast was not unduly prolonged, the bride and groom wishing to take an early London train, and when it was done I returned with Mrs Barforth and Gervase to Galton where we were to spend the night, Mrs Barforth changing for dinner that evening somewhat in reverse, discarding her emerald green satin – her Barforth clothes – as soon as she could for a dress of brown foulard that had no particular style about it, her hair brushed out of its elaborate Barforth ringlets and coiled none too securely on the nape of her neck. 'There now,' her manner seemed to say, her ringless hands happily greeting her dogs. 'I am *myself* again.'

The meal was served in the stone-flagged hall, candlelight and firelight leaving their crowded shadows in every corner, a sudden burst of flame showing me the ancient weaponry on the walls and that host of gold-framed Clevedons, sharp-etched and light-boned like Gervase and his mother, like Venetia, a fine vein of recklessness, a free adventurous spirit extending down the years from one to another, with a flaw in it somewhere – surely – which caused them in times of crisis to droop, sometimes to give way; their courage blazing out like that brightly crackling fire yet lacking the dogged persistence of the Barforths or the Agbriggs, the undramatic heroism of every day.

'Well, mother,' said Gervase, filling his glass from the claret jug at his elbow and holding it up to the light. 'You have married your daughter to a Chard. Do I raise my glass to celebrate or to commiserate?'

And with a gesture that appeared to salute the portrait of Peregrine Clevedon hanging directly above him, he tossed down the wine and reached out for the claret jug again.

'Well, mother, what do you make of it? And what does Grace make of it, I wonder? I should dearly like to know.'

And feeling his eyes upon me, I said hastily, unwisely, in answer to the question he had not asked and which I ought not to have understood, 'There is no reason at all – *none* – why Gideon should not adore her.'

'Which means, Grace dear, that you know perfectly well that he does not adore her, that he has taken her for her money and for as much of mine as he can lay his hands on.'

'Then you must make sure he doesn't lay his hands on it, or on anything else that is yours.'

'Ah yes,' he said, once again taking up the claret jug, his lean face turning away from me to his mother. 'You see how concise Grace is, mamma – how very certain. You can imagine her, can you not, standing her ground when the Chards begin to advance and commanding "Hands off" – or the ladylike equivalent?'

'Gervase, is it necessary?' she said, leaning towards him, their similarity of face and feature, texture and colour excluding me. 'You have a most decent income already. Is the rest even important?'

'There is a great deal of it, mamma.'

'Oh yes, a mountain of it. A mountain of gold – I know.'

'And why should I leave it all to Gideon Chard?'

'It would not come to that. Your father has given certain guarantees which would enable you to –'

'To what, mamma? To live here like a gentleman?'

'Only if you want to, Gervase – although I have always believed you did want that.'

He got up, the claret jug in his hand, and stood with one foot on the hearth directly below the portrait of his uncle, two sharp-etched profiles, two pairs of light green eyes that seemed permanently narrowed from days on horseback in strong sunlight, nights among the smoke and wine-fumes of the gaming tables, two lean, light bodies stretched to their limits of nerve and muscle and endurance. And I knew neither one of them.

'Shall we set wanting aside for the moment, mamma,' he said, his hooded gaze on the flames. 'Yes, father has made certain guarantees, but do you imagine that Gideon will abide by them a moment longer than necessary? Will he really be content to work seven days a week as father does and then pay out half his profits to me? If he can find a way to force

879

me out, or cheat me out – even to buy me out – do you think he will not take it? Yes – there is a mountain of gold, mamma. There are times when I grow very jealous of my share of it.'

She stood up too, arrow straight, her hands palm down on the table, the firelight deepening the red of her hair, shading the years from her pointed face so that she could have been Venetia.

'I wanted it for myself once,' she said, 'for Galton and for my brother – I saw it as nourishment for our soil, prosperity for our tenants, an extension of our land to what it used to be. I saw it as ease for my grandfather in his old age, and security for Peregrine and the children he should have had. I saw it as a bright future for all of us, and not even the whole mountain, not even the half. I was not greedy and would have taken nothing that could not be spared. It did no good. Give it up, Gervase, for it belongs to *them*. Don't burden yourself with it as I have done. Dear God, if I could only be free of it –'

And now, in that treacherous firelight, she *became* Venetia, crying out to me down the years to come, her bright, eager hopes long vanished, their shadow absorbed into this single yearning – that she had neither hope nor brightness – for liberty.

'Oh dear,' she said, pressing both her hands to her cheeks. 'Oh dear! I am being very frail and foolish – quite unforgivable. Whatever will Grace think of me?'

'She will forgive you, mamma.'

'Yes, of course she will. I must go and tidy my hair and then, perhaps, I will say good-night.'

She hurried away, giving me a quick apologetic smile, and we sat for rather too long in silence, Gervase continuing to brood by the fireside – continuing to drink – while I, with some amusement, some small annoyance, tried to decide whether or not she had wished to offend me. For the income she had spoken of was my income, those guarantees had been made on my behalf, the future of her estate – very evidently – was to be secured at my expense, and she had not even consulted my wishes, had simply assumed that, as a woman, I existed to serve the best interests of my men. She had assumed, in fact, that my marriage would purchase Galton for Gervase as hers had not succeeded in purchasing it for Peregrine. How dare she? Yet my indignation lasted no more than the moment it took me to realize that she was not so much unfeeling as disappointed, not hard-hearted but simply a woman of her class and her time, obedient in all things to her training.

Once, in a previous generation, she would have been sent out to win political connections for Galton, to settle – with her hand in marriage – a disputed boundary; her purpose, as the daughter of one noble house, being not to inherit but rather to breed heirs for another. But in her day it had been hard cash – the substance her grandfather had thought demeaning to carry on his person – which had been lacking and with that inbred, female impulse of self-sacrifice she had attempted to provide it. She had accepted the inferior status of womankind and had sold herself, not for her own profit, but for the benefit of her grandfather, of her

brother, and of Gervase. And how terrible now if he – her son, *my*
husband – should declare her sacrifice to have been in vain. How terrible
for *her*. But I, with my own future to consider, did not feel so greatly
inclined for sacrifice. Nor, having escaped one captivity, was I anxious to
enter another, and although her cry for freedom had moved me I did not
feel called upon to give up my own. After all, she had not sacrificed
herself for me but for pale, auburn Peregrine, and I was not yet certain
that Gervase wished, or felt able to accept, her complex and weighty
bequest. But one thing I knew beyond the slightest question. If he
decided to come here, then I would be obliged to accompany him, as all
women are obliged to follow their husbands, but I would come not as a
mild-mannered daughter-in-law but as mistress. If my money was to be
spent here, then one way or another I would have my say in the
spending.

He came back to the table and dropped irritably into his chair, pouring
out the last drop of wine and then pushing the jug away from him so that
it slid perilously along the polished surface, to be retrieved just in time by
my careful, commercial hand.

'It's empty,' he said unnecessarily.

'Yes.'

'And I've not had enough. What do you suggest I do?'

'I suggest that you've had enough.'

He began to rise rather unsteadily, gave me an exaggeratged bow and
fell back into his chair again.

'Then of course you must be right, since that's what you're good at,
Grace – being right.'

'If I have done something to offend you, Gervase, then you had better
say so.'

'Good heavens, no – the very idea! How could one be offended by
perfection?'

'It apears *one* has managed it. Obviously you intend to quarrel with
me. May I know why?'

'I don't know why. Perhaps I'm just bad-tempered. Perhaps I didn't
enjoy seeing my sister walking down the aisle today wearing those
diamonds as if they were shackles.'

'Gervase –'

'Perhaps I wondered why it needed quite so many diamonds as that to
dazzle Gideon Chard.'

'I don't know what you mean.'

'I hope not, Grace – I hope there is no meaning. I hope, as I said, that
I'm just bad-tempered.'

'Then I won't be the whipping-post for it. Either I have done
something to displease you or I haven't. If I have, then say so. But I
won't bear the brunt of your temper unless I have caused it.'

'Bravo,' he said, his face sharp and spiteful. 'Perfect – and absolute
rubbish, my dear. You have done nothing to displease me. I wouldn't
dare be displeased.'

'What nonsense –'

881

'No, Grace, the living truth. You have your feet so precisely on the ground. Wherever we happen to be going, you know how to get there. I don't.'

'So – is it my fault if you are a spoiled –'

'What? A spoiled child? So you make me feel.'

'How can you say that?'

'Easily. Shall I say it again?'

'I don't care what you say. If you behave like a spoiled child, you must expect to be treated like one.'

He got up and stood by the fireplace again, his face no longer spiteful but sombre and brooding, his body, even with the table between us, so taut that I could feel the strain of it.

'No one has ever really spoiled me, Grace, you know – except you.'

'Obviously I have done wrong.'

'No – no. Perhaps you are just too good for me.'

'That is a dreadful thing to say.'

'Yes. I suppose it is.'

But as I got up, to run for cover, I think, before the tears started, he spun round and threw words, like stones, across the room to me. 'That's not the same as saying I don't want you.'

I stopped, my breath laboured as if I had been running, tears clasped so tight, held so fiercely in check that I feared they would choke me.

'Grace – for God's sake!' And he reached me with a rapid stride, to throw hard, urgent arms around me.

'I have been drinking all day, Grace, you know – all day and last night – and it turns me sour sometimes. This business of Venetia – and *Gideon*. Christ, I have to see him as it is every day at the mill. I don't want to live with him.'

'Surely there is no need for that? *Surely* they must want a home of their own?'

'Not a bit of it. Venetia has no care for such things. And Gideon will not move from Tarn Edge, mark my words, until he can afford to build himself something better. He will take care never to come down in the world, Cousin Gideon, you may be very sure.'

'Then we can move away.'

'Where? Here?'

'There are other houses, Gervase.'

'Are there?'

And when I had made a movement of impatience, having already started to lay the foundations of some elegant new villa in my mind, his arms tightened their grip, his cheek pressing hard against mine, his body whispering to me, coaxing me, talking to me as his voice alone could never do.

'I have to get this house settled first, Grace. And if I do and if it seems right to live here – will you live here with me?'

'If it seems right – yes.' But even then I believe I qualified that promise, in my mind, to 'Yes – if it seems right to *me*.'

'I really am quite drunk, you know,' he said into my ear, his familiar scent of citrus and lavender reaching me through the wine.

'Yes, I do know.'

'And I have been a brute?'

'Yes.'

'And a bore?'

'Very boring.'

But the pain and the man who had inflicted it were both gone. The man in my arms continuing to make a direct apology with his body to mine, his forgiveness being quickly granted.

'Did I hurt you, Grace?'

'Yes – you did.'

'One strikes out, I suppose, at one's nearest and dearest. I'll be very good to you from now on.'

'Every day?'

'Well – that's a tall order, but I'll do my damndest. I need you, Grace.'

'You most certainly do, if you are to get up those stairs without breaking your neck.'

'I'm forgiven then?'

'It would appear so.'

'Thank God for that!' he said fervently, and as we began to negotiate the stone stairs, his arms around me, laughing and easy and expecting to make love – my husband now far more than her son – I glanced down into the hall, at the portrait above the hearth, and thought, 'To hell with you, Perry Clevedon. Go to hell!'

10

The honeymoon was not a success, for although Venetia was still docile and grateful, humble in a way which broke my heart, she was quite simply unable at certain precise and crucial moments to believe that she was married at all.

For months past she had felt herself to be Charles Heron's wife in every aspect, which to her had seemed essential. With Gideon she had submitted to the rites of religion and sensuality and the law, but she could not during those tense honeymoon nights convince herself that all this had really made him her husband. Try as she might, and she tried very hard, he remained her supercilious Chard cousin whose naked presence in her bed horribly embarrassed her.

They spent their first few days in an expensive London hotel, indulging Gideon's appetite for complex food and fine champagne, his manner towards her indulgent, teasing, not unaffectionate. But when he began to make love to her, all she could really see was the stranger with Charles Heron's face who in that squalid bed had hurt and humiliated her, her body becoming so rigid that her husband's lovemaking deteriorated into a mere act of possession, after which, to his unconcealed disgust, she had been unable to stifle her tears.

The next morning he was curt and businesslike, inclining to sarcasm as the day progressed, but he took her to the theatre that evening and to a rather famous restaurant afterwards, and later, her body full of guilt and champagne, she threw herself into his arms and endured as best she could, pushing the ghost of Charles Heron away until it was done. He made love to her every night after that, being a man whose temperament required it and having been brought up to believe, like the rest of us, that honeymoons were intended solely for that purpose; but his satisfaction could only be quick and solitary, and although Venetia, far from refusing him, was almost too anxious to please, she knew that it would not suffice. By the time they returned to Cullingford she had read his nature accurately enough to know he would probably make up the deficiency elsewhere and felt she had no right to blame him if he did.

Gervase displayed all the delicate watchfulness of a cat on the day of their return, smiling at the bridegroom's insistence, before his bags had been carried upstairs, on going off to the mill.

'It's all right, Gideon,' he said soothingly, maliciously. 'It's all right – we managed to put the fire out.'

He was very quiet at dinner-time, not even appearing to listen as his father and Gideon discussed market trends, the growth of foreign competition, the demand, nowdays, for 'soft' goods of silk, velvet, plush, the constant need to develop new products and designs now that the demise of the crinoline had put an end to the manufacture of heavy lustre cloths, causing severe embarrassment to such Cullingford manufacturers who had not moved with the times. Neither Gideon nor Mr Barforth so much as glanced aside as Venetia and I withdrew, and when they eventually joined us for coffee Gervase was not with them. Nor, it seemed, had they noticed him leave. He came back long after everyone else had gone to bed, reverting to his old nocturnal habits of slipping in by the side door, having drunk himself to a pleasant state of unreason in which my reproaches, like lustre cloths and percentages and Peregrine Clevedon's wild horses, could only amuse him. But I made no reproaches. 'I'm cold,' he said and I threw back the covers, put my arms around him, warmed him and indulged him, made up my mind that now, in these altered circumstances, I must be watchful too.

Gideon left for America three weeks later with Liam Adair – a trip I thought Gervase should have taken – and although the journey was a commercial success Liam came back with the same cautious air about him I had seen in Gervase and almost immediately presented Mr Barforth with his resignation.

'So much for Liam Adair,' Gervase said, far too quietly.

'But he resigned, Gervase – surely – no one asked him to go.'

'I absolutely agree. No one asked him to go. But "someone" may have made it clear to him – on that long transatlantic crossing, perhaps – that he had no reason to stay.'

Liam called to see me on the day he cleared out his desk at Nethercoats, his step as jaunty, his manner as carefree as ever as he told me that he had just bought a small printing firm which had cost – I assumed – just about every penny he had.

'What do you know about printing, Liam?' and he smiled broadly, not in the least dismayed.

'Nothing. That's the beauty of it. I couldn't shear sheep or drive a goods wagon or sell textiles until I tried.

'You could lose everything, you know.'

'So I could. But then "everything" in my case doesn't amount to all that much, Grace. And I could just as well end up a millionaire.' But when it also became known that he had heavily involved himself and his printing presses in the production of the ailing *Cullingford Star*, I doubted it.

For as long as I could remember, the only newspaper of any significance in Cullingford had been Mr Roundwood's *Courier & Review*, Mr Roundwood himself being a frequent dinner guest at Fieldhead, where throughout my girlhood I had heard him express the same Liberal and Methodistical views as his editorials. The *Courier*, in fact, was designed to please the commercial gentlemen who purchased it, approving what they approved, demanding or condemning whatever the Barforths, Agbriggs, Mandelbaums and Rawnsleys demanded or condemned. To the Liberal leader, Mr Gladstone, it gave unlimited praise and maximum coverage, extending only a cautious hand to his opposite number, the flamboyant Mr Disraeli, whose heart, the *Courier* would have us believe, was in the keeping of our natural enemy the squirearchy. The *Courier* reported no royal scandals, informing us instead of the success of our own charity balls, the weddings and christenings and glowing obituaries of our neighbours and friends, considering a concert of sacred music at the Morgan Aycliffe Hall of far greater social significance than the glittering receptions of the Prince of Wales at Marlborough House, the war between France and Prussia interesting only for its effect on the worsted trade, rumours of coming conflict between ourselves and Russia for control of the East noteworthy for the amount of uniform cloth likely to be required.

Such violence as we had in Cullingford was not to be found in its pages, Mr Roundwood having no interest and assuming us to have none in the rough and tumble of our back alleys on Friday nights. *The Courier*, in fact, was a publication which a gentleman might safely leave on his hall table, the picture of solid well-being and conventional values it presented being more likely to bore his wife and children, should it fall into their hands, than corrupt them. The *Courier* acknowledged virtue, ignored vice, in the hope perhaps that it would go away. It spoke to prosperous people about prosperity – assuring us that we were rich because we were industrious, that the poor had only themselves to blame for their poverty – while the *Star*, on the other hand, spoke to very few people at all, operating from a ramshackle first floor and basement in unkempt Gower Street, its circulation, which had never been robust, limping now to a halt.

It had been founded in the 'bad old days', almost fifty years ago now, by a group of radical intellectuals, a member of my own family, my mother's half-brother, Mr Crispin Aycliffe, among them, who had wished to shatter Mr Roundwood's complacent middle-class dream. The *Star* had not ignored vice, although it had located it in places far removed from our gin-shops and our unlit, unpaved alleys. It had reported violence in our streets but also in our weaving-sheds, where, before the legislation the *Courier* so abhorred, five-year-old children had been regularly beaten to keep them awake at their labours. It had reported the filthy condition of our working classes, and pointed out the unpalatable fact that they were unwashed largely because they had no water; ignorant because education was either not available or beyond their means; of inferior physique because their employers, the readers of the *Courier & Review*, were in the habit of keeping wages so low that they did not always get enough to eat.

But the readership of this volatile little publication, which now appeared only once or twice each week, had always been small, the excessive stamp duty on newspapers in its early days putting it beyond the purchase of the working man for whom it had been intended. And now, although it was cheap enough to be within anyone's reach and it was estimated that at least half of Cullingford's population could read, it had somehow not 'caught on', deteriorating from its crusading fervour to mere peevishness, one of its main obstacles being the odd but undoubted ambition of a large proportion of the working classes to be middle class, and consequently to take the *Courier & Review*.

'What do you know about newspapers, Liam?' I asked him.

'Nothing,' he cheerfully replied to that as well.

'And can you tell me just who reads the *Star*.'

'Well now, Grace, I reckon *you* might if I started to advocate votes for women.'

'Do you believe in woman suffrage, Liam?'

'I don't see why I shouldn't. It never crossed my mind to give it a thought before. But now I do think of it – well, I can't say that I *believed* in Barforth cloth, when it comes down to it. But that never stopped me from selling it – thousands and thousands of miles of it, all over the world. So I think it might pay me to drink a pot of tea one of these days with Miss Mandelbaum and Miss Tighe.'

'It seems to me you'll need more than Miss Tighe.'

'It seems to me you're right. I'll need – well, there's our mutual relative, Grandmamma Elinor, and her good friend Lady Verity Barforth. I've never known either of them refuse to support a worthy cause. And then there's Grace Barforth, of course, my stepmamma's granddaughter, who might care to invest her pin-money.'

'Liam Adair, you are preying on women.'

'I wouldn't put it quite like that. But if I should be, then at least I'll make sure they get some enjoyment out of it.'

'Liam – do you regret leaving the mill?'

'Well now, whatever your reason for asking me that question, Grace, I reckon you'll know my reason for thinking it was time I moved on. And I expect you'll have your hands full now, won't you, Grace, with an extra appetite to feed – and a fine, fierce appetite at that.'

It had entered no one's head, with the possible exception of mine, that Gideon and Venetia should look for a home of their own. Tarn Edge was an enormous house. It suited Mr Barforth's convenience to have Gideon in it. There was no more to be said. A large front bedroom was prepared for them and an adjoining dressing-room with a bath-tub in a tiled recess. I had the wide, canopied bed aired and scented with herbs and lavender. I put daffodils on the broad window-sill, a bowl of fragrant pot pourri on the toilet table. I had the brass fender polished, a small fire laid in the grate, and wondered, not for the first time, about the inevitable tensions of a house with two mistresses and two – possibly three – masters.

But Venetia had so little interest in domesticity that my suggestion of shared responsibility positively amazed her. She could have responded to the challenge of keeping house for Charles Heron on a limited income, the sheer novelty of scrimping and saving, the satisfaction of seeing each economy, each effort, as a brick in the building of their life together. But Tarn Edge – her father's house – held neither challenge nor novelty and had always functioned adequately with no effort of hers.

'Heavens! Grace, I don't mean to interfere. You do it all so beautifully and we all know I can do nothing right in any case.' And she sank back quickly, perhaps gratefully, into her position of 'daughter-at-home', shedding her garments and leaving them where they lay, ordering her tea without the slightest notion of how it was purchased or prepared, littering the hall table as she had always done with her riding gloves and crop, her tall shiny hat, coming and going with no explanation and no regard for either the weather or the hour, the only real change in her circumstances being that now she went to bed every night with a man.

But – as I had known, as I had feared – the house could not absorb Gideon's presence so lightly, for his nature, like his mother's nature, was definite and precise in its requirements, his temperament exacting. When he entered a room one became instantly aware of him, the tone and temper of one's conversation altered to accommodate him, one realized – at once – that he was not a person who could be taken for granted, the more so since the past eighteen months spent in his uncle's employment had not been easy for him.

He had come late to the textile trade from a world where trade itself was held in contempt, so that he had encountered prejudice from all directions, from his old schoolfriends and hunting friends who were puzzled and a little embarrassed by him; from the Barforth managers who thought he was getting too much too soon and too easily; from the weavers who laughed at his accent and made jokes about his masculinity, since no *man* ought to talk like that. And although his brother the baronet and his mother the duchess both loved him and would have defended him to the death, they had made it plain that when he was a visitor at Listonby or South Erin or Mayfair they would prefer him not to be too explicit about what he did for a living.

It was a difficult time for him. I knew it and although I thought him mercenary and predatory and kept a sharp look out at all times for the dagger I believed him capable of stabbing into my husband's back, I could sympathize too, knowing that in his place, had I been ambitious and poor and a man, I might have fought just as hungrily and with as little scruple. He had told me that he had no particular knowledge of textiles, merely some appreciation of how things were bought and sold. Mr Barforth had insisted from the start that he should learn – as Gervase had never been made to learn – every process of cloth manufacture, scouring, combing, spinning, weaving, dyeing and finishing, not merely by observation but by his own toil, his own sweat, so that he would know the skills, the snags, the tricks involved, without relying on the explanations of mill-managers who might know a trick or two of their own.

'If they tell you it can't be done and you want it done, then you've got to know how,' Mr Barforth decreed. '*I* know how. My brother Blaize only thinks he knows That's why he's got one mill and I've got half a dozen. He can sell cloth. I can spin it and weave it, mend my own looms if I have to, and then I can sell it too. Nobody can cheat you, lad, if you know their job better than they do.'

Alien notions these, perhaps, to a Chard of Listonby Park, who would not dream of enquiring into his tenants' affairs so long as the rent was paid, nor his gamekeeper's so long as the grouse and the pheasant were plentiful. But Gideon, nevertheless, applied himself with stern calculation and unflagging energy to this task for which, after all, he had been hired, enduring his employer's often unreasonable demands and tempers, enduring the sheer discomfort a man brought up in the open air was bound to feel for those close-confined weaving-sheds, the screech of machinery, the heat, the dust, the stench of raw wool and engine grease – enduring the painful hesitations of a wife who, despite all her efforts, could not love him – enduring the whole of it not patiently. not meekly, but with a deliberate purpose, since he had long recognized Mr Barforth as a grand master of his chosen craft: that of becoming and remaining a wealthy man.

Long working hours, frequent absences from home in those early months, relieved or delayed the tension I had feared between him and Gervase, yet Gideon, who might never be the owner of Tarn Edge, knew exactly how he and everyone else ought to be served within it, and I was soon to feel the strain of his demands.

He had survived the harsh discipline of his public school, had been obliged to wash every morning of the winter term in cold water at a stand-pipe in the school-yard, had been flogged and bullied and humiliated, the better to force his character into the sparse, unyielding mould of an empire-builder. He had followed the hunt since he was five years old, and when he took a tumble had learned to bother no one with such trivialities as cuts and bruises and a cracked ankle. He had learned to control both his lusts and his emotions, to appreciate the importance of good taste and good manners, the underplaying of anything from a spear-thrust in his side to a broken heart. But his mother's drawing-room and the drawing-rooms of her friends were all luxurious, their tables superb. At Listonby he was accustomed not only to the highest quality but to the utmost variety, no dish appearing twice among the hundreds

Aunt Caroline presented every month, no wine ever leaving her cellars that was not merely old but venerable, unusual; her cuisine a delight both to the palate and to the eyes. These were his standards. He had not expected to lower them, and although he made no complaints, being far too well-mannered for that, he had a way of toying with the food when it displeased or bored him, prodding it gingerly with a fork in a disdainful manner that once or twice caused Gervase to look up sharply and say, 'What is it, Gideon? The food not to your liking?'

'The food?' Gideon replied, the faint question in his voice so clearly implying 'Food? Good God! is *that* what it is?' that I winced, while Gervase's eyes – as always in moments of suppressed emotion – lost their colour. And determined that there should be no conflict if I could help it, my interviews with my cook, Mrs Kincaid, became every morning more difficult.

'No, no, Mrs Kincaid, not haddock and certainly not cod – nothing so commonplace as that.'

'Turbot then, madam?'

'Oh yes – turbot is very well, I suppose. But since we had it twice last week it will have to be done in some other fashion than a lobster sauce.'

'Salmon then, Mrs Barforth.'

'Yes – but how might it be served?'

'Oh – with mushrooms and truffles in béchamel sauce.'

'Why yes, Mrs Kincaid – how clever!'

'And as to the haddock, madam, I could make it into a mousseline and wrap it in slices of smoked salmon.'

'Excellent, Mrs Kincaid. Please do that.'

'Yes, madam, but hardly for luncheon since – as you will know – a mousseline takes time.'

'Oh, not for luncheon, Mrs Kincaid. Mr Chard will not be here for luncheon. You may please yourself as to luncheon.'

'Thank you, madam.'

'So we have settled on the salmon with mushrooms and truffles, and the sauté of lamb in *sauce chasseur*, and a really good rich *crème Chantilly* for dessert, do you think? And a strawberry syllabub? No, perhaps not, since they are too much alike in consistency – both creamy.'

'Pears marinated in brandy, madam. Or a *mille-feuiles* with strawberries and whatever else is available and of good quality?'

'Yes, Mrs Kincaid – the *crème Chantilly*, and the pears – and yes, the *mille-feuilles* too – all three to be on the safe side.'

'Very good. and the soup, Mrs Barforth? Will you leave that to me?'

'Oh yes, but something *different*. Or at least something that cannot be easily identified.'

The wines, of course, were beyond my province, Mr Barforth stocking his cellars to suit his own preference for the heavier clarets, a taste which Gideon shared but not exclusively, Gervase quickly seizing the opportunity to express his wonder at the extreme sensitivity of the Chard palate and the amount of titillation it required. There was trouble too about Gideon's linen, the pressing of his trousers, the polishing of his boots, trouble not violently but fastidiously expressed, his attitude reminding me rather of the Englishman abroad who, with the best will in the world, cannot always quite understand the natives.

'Is it possible to have something done about this?' he enquired, indicating with that faint, infuriating curl of distaste what looked like a perfectly respectable shirt.

'Lord! I don't know,' answered Venetia. 'Ask Grace.'

'I wouldn't dream of troubling her.'

Yet he did trouble me, his insistence on being well served, well valeted, well nourished, on observing what he considered to be not the luxuries of life but its common decencies, offering me both a challenge and a practical method of keeping the peace.

'Are you protecting him against me, Grace, or is it the other way round?' Gervase wanted to know.

'I am trying to be a peacemaker so that I might inherit the earth.'

'Ah – if we are talking of inheritance and if you are doing all this to watch over mine, then I suppose I cannot complain.'

Yet his own behaviour, quite soon, became less watchful and perhaps – although who can say? – had I spent less time fretting over lobster sauces and cambric shirt-frills I might have noticed it, might even have understood it in time.

Every morning Mr Barforth and Gideon left early for the mill, Gervase sometimes accompanying them, sometimes not. They returned late and separately each evening, dined and retired to Mr Barforth's library, where Gideon would invariably stay the course and Gervase would more often than not slip away to drink his brandy in the bar parlour of the Station Hotel or the Old Swan. And because he would have the appealing air of a naughty schoolboy on his return – and perhaps because his very absence had made the evening glide by much smoother – I made no greater fuss than could be turned to other purposes when he had pesuaded me to forgive him.

'I know it's past midnight, Grace – an hour or two past, I daresay. But look at it like this – if I never did anything wrong then you couldn't scold me and I couldn't coax you into granting me a pardon. And you do enjoy that, you know. Don't you?'

Yes, I enjoyed it, particularly at the end of a tense evening when the beef had been too rare, Venetia too flippant, when I had just – and only just – managed to keep Gideon and Gervase apart. I enjoyed his comic but slightly anxious apologies, my own grudging forgiveness quickly turning to laughter, his head nuzzling into my shoulder, those teasing, tender, enraptured conversations, his body still held with mine. I enjoyed it, even the taste and smell of the bar-room about him not displeasing me, bringing me a glimpse of a wicked, masculine world which – like many an indulgent, affectionate woman before me – I could not feel to be as wicked as all that.

He came back to me, we made love, and when he took himself off to Galton without warning and his father complained of it, I defended him, insisting I knew his whereabouts – for my own pride's sake, perhaps – when I did not.

'Well, then, Grace, since he keeps you so perfectly informed perhaps you can inform *me* when I'm likely to see him again?'

'Tomorrow morning at the mill.'

'Can you guarantee it?'

'Oh –'

'Good girl, Grace Barforth. Goes against your commercial instincts, doesn't it, my lass, to give guarantees when there aren't any. I'm glad to see you understand that.'

Yet his absences, even in that first year, grew longer, and an evening soon came when he strode into the house white with anger, his father a menacing step behind him, their quarrel locked in the library for half an hour before I heard the door slam, Gervase's step in the hall, and ten minutes later the sounds of a carriage going fast and precariously down the drive.

'It would appear that your husband will not be dining,' Mr Barforth told me, looking like a thunder cloud at the drawing-room door, his massive body still so full of rage that an outlet was clearly required.

'Oh? Why is that?'

'Because your husband, by his incompetence, has lost me a certain sum of money. Not a great deal – not by his standards at any rate – but that is not the point, is it?'

'I suppose not.'

'No, because money lost is money lost, and worse than that, for it involves an order, a contract – God dammit it involves a reputation. Because your husband was not where he should have been *when* he should have been, a certain gentleman who has done business with me for years has placed his order – his trifling little order – elsewhere. And if he gets good service and good quality he may do likewise with the next one – which may no be so trifling. Do you follow me?'

'I do.'

'Apparently your husband – my son – did not.'

'Where has he gone?'

'Gone? To his mother, I suppose. To his bolt-hole in that damned abbey cloister. He can stay there – believe me – for as long as he pleases.'

'Then perhaps I had better join him.'

'I beg your pardon?'

'If he is to be at Galton for any length of time, I should go there too. I will set off in the morning.'

He crossed the room, lit a cigar and stood for a while with his back to the fire, frowning, the anger that had been spilling out of him in almost visible sparks subsiding now, the eyes he eventually turned on me losing their ferocity.

'He has a treasure in you, Grace. I hope he appreciates it.'

'Oh – as to that –' And then, approaching him carefully, for even in this softer mood he was still a very awesome gentleman, I said quite hesitantly: 'Father-in-law, he has no natural aptitude for business as you have, as Gideon has. It is not easy for him – perhaps sometimes he needs to get away. And he has tried. Until recently I think he tried very hard.

He listened as my voice, lacking the resolution at the last moment to complain of Gideon, trailed away. And then, drawing deeply on his cigar, he smiled at me with his rare, astonishing charm.

'Until recently? You mean until Gideon came? Yes, I know he doesn't like Gideon being here. He was never intended to like it. He has to learn to compete, Grace, if he hopes to succeed. You know that. And if he can't learn – if he can't cope – then at least he has to make up his mind. Had he convinced me he was ready to take on the management of his mother's estate, I might have released certain sums of money which have been set aside for him. He has not convinced me. Has he convinced you?'

I shook my head and, his own head wreathed in smoke, he leaned towards me and gave what in any other man I would have called a grin.

'There is a lot of money, you see, Grace. And if he parted company with me now, who knows where I might leave it? In his place I'd be inclined to wait for me to die. But if that's his purpose, you'd oblige me by telling him this – he can't have it all ways. Sooner or later he has to make up his mind, and if I were you, Grace – since I know you don't want to live at Galton – I'd set about making it up for him. I reckon you'll know the way.'

Perhaps I still believed that I could and so – short-sighted if not entirely blinded by self-confidence, by faith in my own future – it was Venetia, under my eyes all day and every day, who worried me more than Gervase.

Her docility had survived her honeymoon and had changed, very gradually, to a passivity I could not like. She had been eager and vivid. Now she seemed always half asleep and very far away. In her swirling apple-green silks she had been quite lovely. In her tall shiny hat and the mannish cut of her riding-habit she had been an enchanting madcap, worthy of any man's admiring eye. But her charm had stemmed from her fierce joy in living, her tumultuous eagerness for the future, and now, with that joy removed, her future irrevocably decided, she seemed unlit and empty.

She had no interest in the wedding-gifts which, her father's commercial reputation being world-wide, continued to arrive by every train.

'Heavens! what use are they? The cupboards here are full of such things.'

Nor could she be persuaded to apply herself to the writing of letters of thanks.

'Venetia, I can't do it for you.'

'Of course not. I'll make a start tomorrow.'

'Why not now? Here is your pen, Venetia, and paper.'

But although she sat down with a good will, I found her an hour later fast asleep at the table, the one letter she had started crumpled in her hand.

'Oh dear! I just couldn't *concentrate*. I don't know why. And then this wave of absolute weariness came over me.'

It was a wave which swamped her very frequently, washing her away to some hidden, comfortable shore each evening after dinner, so that even when our menfolk joined us in the drawing-room she would remain curled up in her chair, dozing and yawning and rubbing her eyes.

'I'm so *sleepy*.'

'Then go to bed,' her father told her.

'Oh –' and her eye would dart nervously to Gideon like a little girl who was asking 'May I?'

She was still so pathetically anxious to please him that her very eagerness became a source of irritation, and ere long there were tenser moments, for Gideon's notions of how a wife should conduct herself were as exact as his notions of *haute cuisine*, whereas Venetia on both these issues had no precise notions at all, believing the sole purpose of food to be the keeping of body and soul together, the sole purpose of marriage to be love.

'Venetia, I happened to see Mr Rawnsley today and he happened to mention that his wife had been expecting you to tea and was – shall we say puzzled? – at your non-appearance.'

'Lord! – oh lord! – next week, surely?'

'No, Venetia. This week. Yesterday, in fact.'

'Gideon, I am so sorry. And one day is so much like another.'

'I daresay. Mrs Rawnsley, however, had gone to some trouble, I believe. She had other guests – not local people – who were expected to meet you and who must have taken offence. Naturally you will be able to put matters right, won't you?'

'I shouldn't bother,' said Gervase from the depth of an armchair, barely lifting his eyes from their perusal of the sporting press.

'Wouldn't you?' enquired Gideon, his jaw tightening.

'I reckon not. Mrs Rawnsley don't rate so high in my book, nor in my sister's either, for that matter. And as for those other guests who were not local people, don't trouble about *them*. Venetia. Businessmen's wives from Manchester, stout old bodies whose husbands might be of interest to Gideon, I grant you, since he's rather new, after all, to this sort of thing. But we've met them all before, Venetia, you and I, and we've never cared for them.'

'Oh –' she said quite helplessly, sensing, as I did, the snap of Gideon's temper, which we had not yet seen but assumed to be monumental. And for a moment my own voice speaking against his pent-up anger – against the pent-up resentment of Gervase – sounded hollow and false.

'I don't think much harm was done. I met Amelia Rawnsley this afternoon and she seemed happy enough with my invitation to dinner. If we step in to see her for a moment or two tomorrow, Venetia, and admire the silver she worked so hard to inherit from that great aunt of hers, then –'

'Please *do* that, Venetia,' snapped Gideon Chard to his wife and strode out of the room.

'Well done!' drawled Gervase Barforth to *his* wife, withdrawing himself from the scene as effectively as Gideon by closing his eyes.

We made our peace with Amelia Rawnsley the next morning, Venetia becoming very quiet on the homeward journey, very listless as she drifted into the hall at Tarn Edge, totally disinclined for the task of sorting out the drawers of her writing-desk as she had promised, in case other forgotten invitations should be hidden there.

'I believe I will go to bed for an hour before luncheon.'

But a great many notes and cards had been delivered to her of late, many of them, I suspected, unread, and since it was easier to give in to me than resist me, we went together into the back parlour where both our writing-tables had been placed and set to work.

'Venetia, how can you find anything in such a muddle?'

'I can't. That seems to be the problem.'

'Good heavens! There is a note here from Miss Mandelbaum asking you to bring Gideon to meet Miss Tighe. Did you ever reply to it?'

'I don't think so.'

'And this letter from the Sheldons has not even been opened.'

'Tom Sheldon is a pompous ass.'

'I know, but a talkative one, and a Member of Parliament – which always has its uses. Why do you think we contribute so heavily to his campaign funds? Obviously there are things we want him to do. And this note could be about anything.'

She shrugged her shoulders.

'Don't you even mean to open it and find out?'

Again she made that odd, jerky movement of the shoulders, her head turned abruptly away, and then, quite shockingly, two fierce hands swept the desk clear of all it contained, scattering pen and ink and sealing-wax, letters opened and unopened, all of them unanswered, to the floor while she threw herself across the desk top in a storm of grief, beating her forehead and her fists against the wood in a deliberate search for pain. And when at last it subsided, all she could say, her face drained and pinched and horrified, was: 'What happens to me next, Grace? What next?'

But she knew the answer, and getting up unsteadily she began to pat her face and her hair, making an effort to be as brave and sensible as her father had told her to be, and as she had truly intended. She had been in a state of shock and terror from which now she was most painfully emerging. Her speedy marriage, designed to screen a pregnancy which had not occurred, had removed the terror. And now the shock which had numbed her and cushioned her from reality was receding too, opening her eyes fully to her exact condition and the knowledge that it could never change. She had herself told me, many times, that she had one life and but one chance to get it right. The chance had come and gone and she had neither taken it nor refused it. Others had decided for her, manipulated her, moved her this way and that, and having submitted she had no choice now but to submit again.

'Nothing else will happen to me,' she said. 'I see that. This is all there is.' And I could have told no one how deeply her words and her calm, sorrowing figure moved me.

'Venetia –'

'Yes, I see that. And I shall manage, I suppose.'

894

'Do you care nothing at all for Gideon?'

'Lord, yes! He is very clever and tries to be patient, and I fail him in everything. He will end up by detesting me.'

'I cannot believe that.'

'Oh, but you may as well believe it for it is the exact truth. Poor man – he has a man's needs after all, and I cannot – Grace, let me tell you this for it is eating me away.'

'Yes, of course.'

'It will shock you, I know.'

'That doesn't matter.'

'Grace – when he touches me – in the dark – oh lord! what a state I am in, for sometimes he becomes Charles Heron, which I suppose is natural enough, but sometimes – and this is horrible – sometimes it seems to be my father lying there.'

'Venetia – oh, Venetia, how dreadful!'

'Yes. Quite dreadful. It makes my skin crawl. It freezes me. And how can I explain to him? How can I tell him why I have to turn away – how can I ever tell him that? And then I forget invitations from his friends and don't trouble to read their letters. Poor man! He has a sorry wife in me.'

'Darling, it will pass, surely?'

'Do you think so?'

'I do.' And struck suddenly by her air of contrition and apathy, I found myself urging her: 'Venetia, there is no reason to be so humble. He is not perfect.'

'Heavens no! But I –'

'*Venetia*, don't put so little value on yourself.'

'Oh darling, what real value have I?'

'Enormous value. Indeed you have. You are generous and kind and quite lovely when you are in good spirits.'

'Oh no – not now.'

'Yes. Now as much as ever. And in any case he did not take you from charity – *never* think that. He wanted to marry you, Venetia, right from the start. And whatever your shortcomings – and they will not last – he has done well enough in other ways. He *wanted* you, Venetia. You should not forget it.'

She smiled. 'Oh Grace, we know very well what he wanted and I do hope it will content him. Because – as you say – he was no gallant knight, was he, galloping to my rescue? Oh no, *that* was Liam Adair. And do you know, I still wonder how he could bring himself to take me – a Chard of Listonby condescending to such a prodigal, such a poor little drab as I was then. Liam would have done it for my sake alone, which would have been noble, you know. But it was not noble of Gideon, I quite see that, nor even compassionate. It was just for the money And when one looks at it like that, then perhaps we have both got as much – or as little – as we deserve.'

She was a little more wide-awake at dinner that night, talking mainly to Gervase, but at least saying something. She wrote a few letters the next day, had her hair done differently, began to smile rather often and in a new, perhaps brittle way that was at least better than her vague, disquieting stare. She was just possibly mending, or, if she remained unhappy, had begun to learn – as so many women must – the futility of letting it show.

A year passed and the half of another. I was purposeful, successful, had established myself as the mistress of an impressive household, as a hostess and as a wife. I had achieved, within the limits of my sex and my class, my cherished measure of authority and freedom. My father and my father-in-law were pleased with me. My mother, had she been alive, could have held me up as an example to other women's daughters. And how can I say just when it was, in those busy, commonplace months, that I lost Gervase?

11

I saw less and less of Blanche. She had returned to London shortly after Venetia's marriage to participate in the festivities occasioned by the arrival of a number of Russian 'Imperials', a state visit which had a distinctly family flavour about it, Queen Victoria's second son, Prince Alfred, having recently married the Tsar's only daughter, Marie, whose brother, the Tsarevitch, heir to the Russian throne, was the husband of Princess Dagmar, sister of our own Princess Alexandra of Wales.

There was, of course, the possibility that we would have to fight Russia ere long to safeguard our interests in India, but the next Russian tsar would be the brother-in-law of our future king, the tsar after him would be our king's nephew, and until hostilities broke out – if they ever did – London was prepared to be very gay.

The Duchess of South Erin served caviar that season, discovered a balalaika player to serenade her guests and procured invitations to a costume ball at Marlborough House, where the bare-shouldered, enticing but altogether untouchable Blanche had been noticed by no less a person than the Prince of Wales. Had she been of a warmer or more adventurous disposition, the degree of his interest was such that she might well have become a royal mistress as famous as Mrs Langtry, Lady Brooke or Mrs Keppel. Perhaps the offer was made and Blanche, in her cool, vague fashion, pretended not to understand it. Perhaps – and this seems rather more likely – the Prince was far too experienced in the ways of women to look for passion where quite cleary there was none to be found. But, just the same, my cousin pleased his eye, and when it was realized that he would be far more likely to accept a dinner invitation if Blanche was invited too, then her place not only in society but in her mother-in-law's heart was irrevocably secure.

With no greater effort than the dressing of her silver-blond hair, the displaying of her magnificent bosom and her sleepy smile, Blanche had filled Aunt Caroline's drawing-room with the world's élite, and transformed herself in the process from the little manufacturing niece who had not been quite good enough for Dominic to the Duchess of South Erin's pride and joy. There could be no question now of those arduous domestic duties at Listonby, no question of playing the hostess, the chatelaine, or even the mother, when all these matters could be delegated to others, leaving Blanche free to practise her supreme art of attracting the rakish heir to Victoria's throne.

But in the October of 1875 the Prince set off on a six months visit to India, and the Chards, whether by mutual agreement or separate inclination, decided to use this time as profitably as they could by making a more prolonged autumn visit than usual to Listonby, where Sir Dominic could attend to his stock and his estate, the Duchess to her son's house and his larder, and where Blanche could produce another child, preferably male, no gentleman being able to feel himself secure with only one heir to his name.

There was, of course, a dance, the ballroom having been redecorated in white and gold for the occasion, the chairs in the Long Gallery re-covered in oyster satin, every chandelier in the house dismantled for cleaning, every item of plate, linen and china got out for the inspection of Aunt Caroline, while Blanche, installed by the fire in the Great Hall, took it upon herself to acquaint me with the details of upper-class adultery which she seemed to find not so much immoral as unnecessary.

'Naturally,' she said, 'Aunt Caroline would not hear of it in this house, nor at South Erin, and she appears not to notice it in the other houses we visit. But in fact there is a great deal of it about. No one seems to mind so long as one obeys the rules.'

'And what are the rules, Blanche – in case I should ever need to know?'

'Oh, quite simple really. If Lord A and Lady B decide to fall in love, all may go swimmingly unless his wife, or her husband, should decide to make a fuss, in which case one cancels immediately, since it would be embarrassing to do otherwise. After all, one could hardly expose one's friends to jealous scenes or oneself to the Divorce Court.'

'I should think not.'

'Exactly. Which is why the Prince and Princess of Wales get on so famously. When he takes a fancy to someone or other, Alexandra simply looks the other way. She keeps herself busy with her knitting and the children and leaves him quite free to please himself.'

'How convenient!'

Blanche pouted and shrugged. 'For those who care for it, I suppose it is. You have seen the new skirts, have you, Grace? Very tight in front with almost no bustle. They will suit you this winter far better than they will suit me, for I am already three months in the family way, although I am determined to have it over and done with by March. Yes, a boy in March, April and May to recover, and back to London in June. I feel I shall have earned that.'

But I was no more confident of my ability to wear the new tight skirts than Blanche, having experienced, these past few weeks, the symptoms of a pregnancy I could not quite bring myself to admit. I knew of no contraceptive practices in those days and had not sought to discover any. I belonged to a society where women were expected to bear children. I was a woman. I would probably bear children. It should have been as simple as that. Indeed, being already in the third year of marriage, I should have been glad of it, and only too anxious to rid myself of the stigma of sterility. But every morning since the start of my suspicions I had awoken not only to nausea but to a burden of unease which grew heavier throughout the day.

I was neither physically afraid nor emotionally ill-equipped. Women died in childbirth in their thousands, I well knew it, but I did not expect to be among them, nor to shirk in any way this supreme responsibility. I knew exactly how a nursery should be staffed and furnished and had my own notions as to the care of the young. I would be a good and conscientious mother. I had quite made up my mind to it. Yet somehow, for all my good intentions, I could not contemplate my condition without panic, and quite soon could hardly contemplate it at all.

Three times I drove to Elderleigh to tell Aunt Faith. Three times I failed. A hundred times, with stiff lips and a tight, dry throat, I began to tell Gervase who had, after all, a right to know. A hundred times I heard my voice inform him instead that the night was fine, that dinner would be late or early, that it would probably rain by morning, and on the night of the Listonby ball he was still – perhaps happily – unaware of his approaching fatherhood.

It was from the start a difficult evening, Gervase arriving home late and in an odd humour, out of sorts and disinclined for company.

'Do we have to go, Grace?'

'Of course we do.'

'Why? Because Princess Blanche is expecting us? Listen – take off that ball gown and come to bed with me. And then pack a bag and we'll go off to Grasmere until Monday. You'd like that, wouldn't you?'

'Yes, I would. And you know quite well it can't be done – not tonight.'

'I know quite well *you* can't do it tonight, Grace. That's not the same thing.'

And when I had told him how unreasonable he was, that he should have taken me to Grasmere two weeks ago when *I* had suggested it, instead of going off with the Lawdale, that in any case one simply could not please oneself in these matters when it involved letting other people down; when I had said all that and he had grudgingly, sourly, got into his evening clothes, it was Venetia who delayed us, losing first an ear-ring and then a glove, dashing upstairs again when the carriage was already at the door, to put another comb in her hair, so that Gideon's impatience, never well concealed, became black enough to feel.

'We shall be very late, Venetia.'

'Lord, yes! But does it matter? After all, it is only kings who are obliged to be punctual – or queens. And Aunt Caroline is hardly that.'

'Quite so. But she is my mother, to whom courtesy – I should have thought – is due.'

'And Listonby, after all, is where you belong, Gideon, wouldn't you say so,' drawled Gervase, leaning against the mantelpiece as if he had all the time in the world at *his* disposal.

And for a moment, before he gave his answer, Gideon stood and measured us all with an angry but careful eye, accepting both the challenge of Gervase's hostility and the reasons for it, calculating with a swift glance that, although he was outnumbered, he might just as well take up that challenge now as later.

'I might say that,' he agreed looking directly at Gervase. 'I was born at Listonby, which has to mean something. But I believe a man belongs where he decides to belong – where he can carve out a place for himself.'

'Or take somebody else's place?'

'Yours?'

'If you like.'

'Are you making me an offer, Gervase – or a gift?'

'I might be stating a fact.'

'That's very civil of you, Gervase. If I had a place ready carved out for me, I doubt I'd let another man step into it.'

'Then you've no need to worry, have you, Gideon, since there's not much competition in the world to be the third son of a baronet.'

It was the moment I had dreaded, the confrontation I had made up my mind must not take place, but which now, when I needed to be strong, touched my already uneasy stomach to nausea, reminding me of my condition – my frailty – precisely when I could not afford it.

'Oh lord –' Venetia said, her hands clasped tight together, her voice trailing off into a faint, nervous breath of laughter. And then – because it was the very best I could do – I said tartly: 'Well, if it's to be pistols at dawn perhaps you'd have the good manners to wait until dawn. There's no sense in spilling blood on the drawing-room carpet.'

'I beg your pardon,' said Gideon, bowing stiffly.

'Ah,' said Gervase, 'it goes against your commercial instincts, does it, Grace?' And although he had said much the same thing to me often enough before with the wry teasing humour of our love-games, I heard the insult in him now – the distance – the deliberate separation of his values from mine, and turned cold.

He did not speak to me through the drive, did not help me to get down from the carriage, walking ahead of me into the house where he tossed his hat and cloak irritably down. But he made his greetings pleasantly enough, kissed Aunt Caroline on her hand, Aunt Faith on the cheek, Blanche, to her great distaste, on the corner of her mouth, a procedure designed, I thought, not only to upset Blanche but her brother-in-law, Captain Noel Chard, who during his frequent leaves of absence from his regiment rarely strayed from her side.

'Gervase – really!' she said, pushing him away. 'Why must men carry on so?'

'Men are made that way, Blanche, don't you know? Or *don't* you know?'

I walked quickly into the ballroom, making a point of not looking behind me to see if he was following, simply assuming – hoping – that he

899

would, although, as a husband of three years' standing, no one could expect him to remain long at my side. He would go to the billiard room or the smoking-room, I supposed, as soon as he could, where, in his present childish humour, he would drink too much, play cards for stakes I thought scandalous, wasteful, and lose, which would sour his temper tomorrow when we had been invited to Galton, thus increasing the difficulties of what I expected to be a difficult visit. What a nuisance he could be, now irresponsible!

'Gervase –' I commanded.

'Yes,' he said, 'I know. You are telling me to behave.'

'I am asking you, since we are here, to make the best of it. And as to what happened between you and Gideon – well, it wasn't the moment.'

'My word!' he said. 'Can I believe my ears? Are you actually apologizing to me for not leaping to my defence?'

'Gervase, that is nonsense –'

But he was gone.

All around me were faces I recognized, my everyday neighbours transformed by those mirrored walls, those rivers of candle-lit crystal, into glamorous creatures of silk and satin who, just the same, would chat very cosily to me. And although as a younger matron I did not expect to dance, since it was neither the duty nor particularly to the advantage of any gentleman to dance with me, there was a great deal to observe, and a decided pleasure in the company of Aunt Faith, who so long as the Barforth family feud endured could nót visit me at Tarn Edge. And so for a pleasant hour or two we talked quietly together of Blanche, who was so serenely content, and of Venetia, who was perhaps not made for contentment, although she seemed better that night, dancing a wild polka with some London stranger, than I had seen her since her marriage.

'She is recovering her glow,' Aunt Faith murmured, 'and her madcap spirits. Just look at her now, with her skirts flying – what a pity we married ladies are not supposed to enjoy ourselves quite so much as that. I fear her mother-in-law is about to call her to order.'

And sure enough Aunt Caroline, appearing purposefully on the edge of the dance-floor, extracted her third son's wife from that frenzied polka with a single wave of her hand.

'Venetia, you are *breathless*.'

'Lord, yes! Aunt Caroline – and loving it.'

But Aunt Caroline, for whom a ballroom was no place for enjoyment but for the serious business of social advancement, shook her head.

'No, dear. Sit down *there*, by Grace and Aunt Faith, and compose yourself. We have certain "politicals" here this evening who could be useful to Dominic and may wish to speak a word to his brother's wife. A *word* dear, no more – and should they enquire as to the extent of your father's commercial reputation, all that need concern them is that it is *vast*.'

'And my brother's part in it?'

'Really, my dear!' Aunt Caroline said vaguely, drifting off, her nonchalance telling us very clearly that, so far as Dominic's political friends were concerned, Venetia had no brother, the whole of Mr Nicholas Barforth's commercial empire being destined – they had been given to understand – for Gideon, who in true feudal fashion would not hesitate to place it at his brother's political disposal.

'So Dominic is to be Prime Minister is he?' Venetia enquired pertly of Aunt Caroline's retreating back.

'Hush, dear,' murmured Aunt Faith, 'for the sad thing, you know, is that Aunt Caroline would do the job of Prime Minister far better herself.'

I did not expect to see Gervase in the ballroom again and it was not until my generous Uncle Blaize offered to dance with me that I glimpsed his reflection in the long mirrored wall, lounging beside a chair that contained Diana Flood. There was nothing in the sight to disturb me. I was very definite about that. She had been married a year ago to a military, rather older cousin, thus changing her status but not her name, and I had attended her wedding without any particular feeling of involvement. She had been a thin, excitable girl who three years ago had wanted to marry Gervase. Instead he had married me, Diana had married her Major Compton Flood and had increased neither in weight nor in composure, retaining the nervous but not unattractive restlessness I had often remarked in her thoroughbred uncle. There was no more to it than that, no reason at all why Gervase should not be sitting with her and her foxhunting friends – *his* friends until the demands of commerce and matrimony had made such friendships inappropriate. And in acknowledgement of the rightness and naturalness of it all, I smiled at her very civilly as I danced by, receiving in exchange a startled movement of her head, a trill of nervous laughter which told me I had been the subject of their conversation. They had been whispering together, intimately, unkindly, enjoying their own high-bred malice, their own wit; and I had been the subject of it. I stared for a moment aghast, recoiled, and then, taking a deep breath, drew myself together with an almost cruel resolve, my back very straight, my head high.

I had received my first lesson in the defence I was to practise so skilfully and for so long; the proud but painful art of pretending not to care.

I went down to supper with Uncle Blaize and Aunt Faith, keeping up a flow of reminiscences and observations to which they calmly and easily replied. I ate what it was proper for me to eat and in the right quantity, refusing to notice that my husband, in a corner of the same room, was entertaining another woman; refusing to wince at the consistent, high-pitched note of her laughter; refusing, absolutely, to wonder how much of that giggling was directed at me. And to make my performance complete, when her mirth became too persistent to ignore, I turned and smiled indulgently in her direction, letting it be clearly seen that what did not alarm me need trouble no one.

Pride? Very possibly. But there was bewilderment underneath it too, the numbing sensation of a blow not really felt because I could not quite believe in it. And perhaps my fresh awareness of physical unease, and ache at the small of my back, the return of nausea, was a relief to me.

A few hours before and I would simply have found Gervase, told him I was unwell and gone to bed. Now I could not. Nor could I get up and take my leave without loss of self-esteem. If I did so then he would think me jealous. *She* would think me jealous. There was nothing to be done but sit and chat and smile – nothing at all – and it was not until the ballroom crowd was growing thin and I had seen Sir Julian Flood take his niece away that I accepted Aunt Faith's advice and went to bed. And then, half-way up the stairs, it struck me most unpleasantly that I had perhaps erred in the opposite direction, exposing the jealousy I resolutely *would* not feel by lingering too long.

But as I entered one of Listonby's spacious, rose-pink bedrooms a fresh assault of nausea erased such considerations from my mind, and when it became necessary to ring for assistance and two worried maids had brought me a clean water jug and basin and installed me gingerly between clean sheets, I was too weak for anything but a few self-indulgent tears.

I drifted into a shallow sleep, my head filled with racing, half-coherent thoughts, my body still unreliable, and I was too feverish and confused on waking to find it strange that Gervase should not be there. And when I understood, a while later, that it was very strange indeed, I was too weary, too sick and too unaccustomed to sickness to feel any real alarm. I fell asleep again, beyond anxiety, waking this time to panic, for he had still not come to bed, would surely not come now, and what could I do about it? Was there, in fact, anything that should be done? Of course not. *Of course* not. He could quite simply have fallen asleep in the smoking room, a brandy glass at his elbow, as happened to some gentleman or other at every party. And, failing that, there would certainly be a card game in progress somewhere in this house tonight and no reason why Gervase should not be involved in it. He played cards. He drank brandy. He also rode fast and ill-tempered horses over dark fields, high hedges, to settle some stupid wager. And as a pang of terror twisted my stomach – for he could be lying dead somewhere in a ditch, there was no doubt about it – I swung myself out of bed and was sick again, as neatly as I could contrive, in the basin.

I took the quilt from the bed and spent what little remained of the night in an armchair by the window, shivering and sweating in turn, yet not trusting myself to lie down or close my eyes; crushed, in that crowded house, by an appalling isolation, my world shrunk to the dimensions of the jug and basin, regulated by the heaving of my tormented belly. And it was when I was empty, my energy and my will all spent, that I thought of him with Diana Flood and burst into a storm of hot and exceedingly foolish tears.

I had seen her hands on him, plucking at his sleeve as they sat in the supper room. I had seen her fingers touching his as he gave her her glass. I had seen her thin figure swaying closer to him than was proper and then withdrawing, laughing, swaying forward again. I had seen hundreds of women – hundreds of them – go through the same flirtatious performance with hundreds of men. And what did it signify? Who remembered it, even, in the morning? But supposing, when her uncle came to fetch her, she had called out to Gervase: 'Why don't you ride home with us? What a lark!', would he have refused? Could he, in fact, have answered: 'Let's ride to Galton on the way and drink champagne in the cloister.' Of course he could, for there had been champagne parties often enough in the cloister in the days when I had been warned against him, and she was no virgin now but a married woman who went about without her husband.

Yes, quite definitely they could be together, for he had been angry enough to hurt me, had started the whole shabby nonsense on purpose to hurt me, and it would be like him to carry it on too far. And once again that persistent wave of nausea made it impossible for me to decide in any detail what ought to be done, what *could* be done.

I was resolute enough by breakfast-time and, determined not to be the first downstairs, entered the crowded dining-room with a smile, although the smell of so much fried food revolted me, and there was still that gnawing ache at the bottom of my back. I had toast and coffee, spoke a few words to strangers – Blanche and Aunt Faith being still in bed, Venetia, it seemed, in the billiard room, where no lady had any business to be, the Chards and other kindred spirits out long ago with the hunt. Could Gervase be with them? And the realization that I could not possibly enquire jolted my tired brain a fraction away from reality to a confused nightmare sensation of frantic hurry, of constantly opening wrong doors.

'My dear,' a London lady told me, 'you are looking very pale.'

'Yes, I think I need a breath of air.'

And it was then that I found him, coming across the grass with half a dozen others, young bloods still in their evening clothes moving with the careful step of men who, emerging from their drunken oblivion, are finding the world a very loud and very garish place.

'Good morning, Gervase.'

'Good morning, Grace.' And he would have walked on had I not put out a hand as imperious as Aunt Caroline's and detained him, seeing no reason to wait a moment longer for an explanation.

'Later, Grace –'

'Now.'

'Grace – I'm not up to it.'

But seeing the set of my jaw he sighed, shrugged, and turning to his waiting friends – all strangers to me – he made a grimace that said 'Good God! – women –'

I was too hurt to speak. My throat seemed stiff and all my terrible anxiety – my dread of finding him with his neck broken like his uncle Perry Clevedon – seemed converted, now that he was safe, into a fierce anger. And striding forward around the corner of the house, my whole body trembling, so hurt – so hurt – that I had to find release, I spun round intending to be glacial, dignified, to insult him certainly, but with propriety, and hit him instead, hard, across his cheek.

Perhaps I expected him to hit me back. Perhaps I wanted him to hit me, was ready for it, needed his savagery to match and encourage my own, but my blow seemed to have taken the malice out of him, stunning him so that he could do nothing for a long moment but stand and stare.

'Christ!' he said at last, 'Oh, Christ!', and even with my vision blurred by outrage, I could see he had not the least idea how to cope with me. 'Grace, for God's sake! Whatever you may have been thinking, it wasn't all that bad, you know –'

But nothing he could have said just then, no apology, no threat, would have made any difference, since I could not bear to listen to it. Nor could I bear to look at him or stand beside him, and having fretted over his absence for so many tortured hours, all I now desired was for him to go away again. And since he seemed unwilling to move, I set off myself, still trembling, going anywhere so long as it was far away.

'Grace –'

'Just leave me alone.'

'Good God –'

'Leave me alone! Don't follow me. Just leave me.'

'All right,' he shouted after me. 'All right. If that's what you want – I will.'

But one does not carry one's personal conflicts into the homes of one's closest relations and when we met at luncheon I was outwardly very calm. Nor did I feel able to cancel that long-arranged visit to Galton Abbey, my relationship with my mother-in-law being too delicate to risk a misunderstanding, and I set off as arranged in the early autumn afternoon, the small portion of roast chicken and *crème caramel* I had managed to swallow pressing like a dead weight against my stomach.

I made the journey in one of the Listonby victorias, Gervase on horseback very far ahead. Although we had only five miles to go, they were all uphill and then, quite sickeningly, down again, narrow lanes and jolting, rutted tracks that jarred my back as they descended, through a sharp, spiteful little wind, the slope that led to Galton. And although I knew, because everyone had told me so, that it was a glorious day, a vivid blue sky streaked with hurrying cloud above the deep reds and golds of October, I was too intent on ignoring the remainder of that *crème caramel*, that infuriating ache in my back, and did not notice.

'What a glorious day!' my mother-in-law called out, lifting her pointed face with keen enjoyment into the spicy, smoky air. And because there were other horses standing beside Gervase's bay on the drive, I kept the smile on my lips as I walked through the hall and into the untidy, chintzy parlour where Diana Flood, pushing a cat from her knee, got up and held out to me a well-bred, ill-manicured hand.

Her uncle, Sir Julian, was with her, and another man, somewhat younger but very much like him, thin and dark and nervous like all the Floods.

'Mrs Barforth, you will remember my husband?'

'Yes indeed – Major Flood, how do you do?'

'What a glorious day!' he told me.

'Yes – very fine.'

'Downright criminal, I call it, to stay indoors on a day like this.'

'Oh, yes – yes, indeed.'

'Oh, come now!' Diana Flood cut in. 'Mrs Gervase Barforth is being polite, darling, for she does not care for the countryside. Is that not so, Mrs Barforth?'

But all I cared for just then was to sit down, somewhat speedily, before the weakness of my legs became apparent, and my only answer was what she may have taken for a frosty smile.

Tea was served, for no one's benefit but mine, the gentlemen seeing the appearance of the tea-kettle as a signal for escape into that glorious outdoors, Diana Flood and my mother-in-law remaining only because it would have been ill-mannered to leave me alone. But conversation was stilted, quite painful, constantly broken by such exclamations as 'Oh, listen! I believe they have brought out the new black mare – I would know that whinny in a thousand', so that when no second cup was offered and Mrs Barforth suggested 'A breath of air? Shall we walk to the bridge?' I got up at once, declaring myself very willing.

'I fear Mrs Gervase Barforth is not dressed for walking,' remarked Diana Flood, glancing at her own stout riding-boots, 'real walking, that is.' But I could think of nothing worth saying to that and went outside again into the crisp amber day, unable to suppress a shiver as the wind, coming fresh from the moor, struck me its first blow.

'Exhilarating,' said Diana Flood.

'Yes – quite so.'

But as we walked to the unsteady wooden bridge spanning the little stream, her faint contempt meant nothing to me compared with the enormous effort of moving and continuing to move one leg after the other, of keeping that aching back erect, of forcing that taut, uneasy stomach to obey my commandment that, come what may, I would not – absolutely *would* not – vomit in a public place.

'Oh, yes! Look! There is Gervase on the mare. My word, Aunt Georgiana, she is absolutely first-rate!'

'Is she not? And brave and willing into the bargain. Grace, dear, come off the bridge or you will get rather wet as they ride across.

We had been all three on the ramshackle bridge together, looking down at the stony river-bed and the clear, rushing water. They had moved away and I had barely noticed it. I followed them meekly, stood beside them, their conversation, which seemed mainly to be of hocks and withers, defeating me; and clenching my teeth to conceal a sudden, brief pain – a gesture they may have mistaken for sullenness or bad temper – I watched as Gervase and the two Floods rode their horses into the stream and up the bank beside us.

I no longer knew if I had forgiven him. I could not even judge how much or exactly what there had been to forgive, so urgently did I now require to concentrate on the basic function of keeping on my feet. And when he swung out of his saddle, his beautiful black mare – just a *horse* to me – momentarily screening us from the others, his evident ill-humour seemed far less menacing to me than the claw which had embedded itself somehow at the base of my spine.

'Is it necessary to look so peevish?' he hissed from the corner of his mouth. 'Whatever it is I am supposed to have done to you does not concern my mother. You will oblige me by not making her pay your price for it.'

But I couldn't answer him.

The black mare was now the object of their most minute attention. They looked at it loudly, ecstatically, touched it, picked up its hooves and examined its eyes and teeth, arguing at length which one of its many qualities should be counted the best. And when that was done, all that remained was for them to put it through its paces, to match their own mounts against it somewhere where the hedges were high enough, the ditches wide and deep, where there was sufficient flat ground for a good gallop.

'Stargate Meadows,' announced Major Compton Flood, naming a stretch of land belonging to Sir Julian, not far from the Flood manor, and as Diana waited for her own horse to be brought she smiled at my mother-in-law and said: 'Aunt Georgiana, won't you come with us?' knowing full well that only my presence prevented it.

'Hardly, dear –'

'Please,' I said quickly. 'If you would like to go, please do. I shall be perfectly comfortable.'

But the Clevedon code did not permit the abandoning of one's guests, even such tiresome city-bred creatures as myself who – in this glorious weather – did not ride.

'No – no, dear. We shall be very comfortable together.'

'Goodbye, mamma!' called out Gervase, leaning down from the saddle to kiss her cheek. But if he made a deliberate attempt to slight me – and of course he had – then his effort was wasted, for I was incapable by then of resentment or jealousy or any human emotion at all. All that concerned me was that something inside my body appeared to be breaking and I needed peace and solitude, a corner in which to hide, and if possible to mend myself.

They rode off. I turned, moved, went inside, my mother-in-law's voice behind me still murmuring of the fine weather. And then the stone fireplace in the Great Hall which had seemed quite far away came suddenly towards me, or I to it, so that I put out both my hands to push myself clear of it and encountered nothing at all against my fingers.

'Oh, my dear!' Mrs Barforth whispered urgently. 'My poor dear!' And as her strong, horsewoman's hands took hold of me, I felt myself to be bleeding and understood I had started to lose my child.

12

Perhaps I had expected her to be efficient, for she was accustomed to mares in foal, to hound bitches and their litters, and had none of the squeamishness of the city-bred. I had even expected her to be kind, or to go through the motions of kindness, since she had always tried to like me and had done her best to behave as if she did. I had not expected to believe in her kindness, to need it, had not thought I could cling to her in that desperate fashion, nor find such reassurance in her lean, firm hands. I had not expected to be so afraid, but in the half-hour before the doctor came I was terrified of death, assaulted by the rushing memories of all those thousands of women who every year must bleed away their lives in this fashion. I couldn't end like this. Until not so very long ago I had believed I could never end at all. That illusion had faded, but even so I could not bear it to be like this, not now; and as the futility of it, the waste of it, reduced me to helplessness, she put her arms around me and held me gently but in a manner which conveyed her very definite intention of not letting me go.

I suppose there was nothing the doctor could really do, and being accustomed to a country practice where there were no great fees to be earned, he said so quite bluntly, assuring me that nature, which had put me in this predicament in the first place, would now take its course. He would make me as comfortable as he could, and after that there would be some days in bed, how many he was not yet prepared to specify, and with proper rest and food I would soon be up and about again.

'Beef tea,' he said. 'Herb tea. Red wine and raw eggs. Anything you like. If you believe it's doing you good, then it probably will be. No reason to make a fuss. It happens every day.'

And I was calmer after that.

'My dear,' Mrs Barforth said, bringing me the hot milk and cinnamon I had requested. 'I really didn't know –'

'I hardly knew myself.'

'Gervase?'

'No. I didn't tell him. I wish there was no need to tell him now.'

'Dearest, how can we avoid it?'

'We can't. Where is he?'

'I imagine he must be at the Floods' by now, for they will surely have invited him to dine. I have sent word.'

But she must have known as well as I did that he would not come soon. She had also sent word to Listonby, for, not long after, I heard a carriage and there was my maid with my hairbrushes, my bottles of toilet water, my clean linen, a note from Blanche saying all that was needful, promising she would come when she could, telling me that Venetia who would have come then and there, had returned to Cullingford directly after luncheon with Gideon. And unaware until that moment of how much I had been longing for Venetia, I was ashamed of the tears in my eyes and considerably annoyed by this strange new tendency to weep.

I no longer felt any pain. I was simply weary to my very bones, drowning in the weight of it, the effort of saying 'No, thank you' to offers of food and drink and nursing becoming so tremendous that I closed my eyes, not to sleep but to escape. And I supposed it to be far into the night when I heard the sound of hooves below me and Mrs Barforth, hastily rising from her chair, hurried downstairs to meet Gervase who only later – *much* later I thought – appeared in the doorway, looking at me and trying not to see me with an expression I vaguely recognized.

'Are you – all right?'

'Yes. Quite all right.'

'You should have told me – shouldn't you?'

'I wasn't really sure. Do come in.'

He came, gingerly, treading like a cat unsure of its ground, ready, I think, to avert his gaze from the many things around me and within me which he thought might alarm or disgust him. And abruptly I remembered when I had seen him like this before and pressed my eyelids together to shut away yet another onslaught of those feeble, irritating tears.

'When did it start?'

'Does it matter?'

'No, I suppose not. I – I'm sorry.'

'Yes.'

And I knew that, whether or not he wanted to take my hand, he would not take it, that he was as helpless now, faced with my pain, as on the day he had knelt beside an injured horse in the paddock just beyond this bedroom window, holding himself responsible for those injuries as now he was accepting the blame for mine. He was suffering and I knew it. Yet I was suffering too and his anguish, in my present weakness, did not console me.

'They say you should rest.'

'Yes – as much as I can.'

'So – do I disturb you?'

I shook my head.

'Grace –'

'Yes?'

But, whatever it was that he wished to say, it could not be said. It may have been some expression of tenderness or self-reproach, the things one hopes a lover might say at such a moment. 'I could not bear to lose you' or quite simply 'I love you'. Very likely it *was* something like that, and anything would have sufficed. But it was beyond him. He swallowed hard, took a nervous step up and down the room, said nothing, and was very glad, I suppose, when he glanced at me, to find I had apparently fallen asleep.

He came to see me the next morning very early, hovering once again in my doorway.

'They say you had a good night.'

'Yes.'

'Grace – you don't need me for anything, do you?'

'No.'

'Then – look here – the thing is I'm supposed to be at the mill this morning.'

'Then you'd better hurry.'

'If you'd rather –'

'I'm *all right*. Your mother can look after me.'

'Of course.'

He crossed the room, possibly disliking the part of himself that could barely wait to be off; disliking, too, the effort it cost him to brush the back of his hand against my cheek. And because I was stung afresh by the memory of that dying horse and was yet again close to tears, I said tartly: 'You'd do well not to keep your father waiting.'

I heard his voice and his mother's in the yard below and then, when my breakfast tray had been brought and Mrs Barforth, coming in behind it, had persuaded me to a cup of hot, fragrant chocolate, she sat down beside me and sent the maid away.

'You do know, my dear, that Gervase feels terribly to blame?'

'I know.'

'Is he to blame? He says you quarrelled at Listonby and that he was – difficult. But he did not realize – I did not realize – yesterday afternoon, that you were ill. We thought –'

'You thought I was in a sulk.'

'Oh, dear! And if you had been a sulk I wonder if I should be surprised at it, knowing how difficult Gervase can be? But to have inflicted that drive on you – and that walk to the bridge –'

'I inflicted all that on myself, Mrs Barforth.'

'I wonder if you can convince Gervase of that?'

'Should he ever ask me, I will try.'

The doctor came soon after, expressing himself well satisfied, and then there came a note from Mrs Agbrigg murmuring her regret both at my misfortune and my father's absence in Manchester. But she would visit me herself that afternoon. Blanche too, I thought, might well stir herself to drive those few miles from Listonby and would perhaps bring Noel Chard with her. But I soon became aware, as the slow, sickroom hours passed, that I was simply waiting for Venetia.

Gervase, I calculated, would have reached Cullingford by eight o'clock, and even if he had gone straight to the mill, he or his father would have sent a note which could bring her here by mid-morning. Gervase would know I wanted to see her. She would know it. She would drop everything – naturally she would – and come. But one always recognizes the final moments when if something does not happen *now*, it will never happen at all. And struggling with a disappointment enlarged by physical weakness, I failed to notice the change in the weather and was surprised when Mrs Barforth murmured: 'I cannot think anyone will have set out from Cullingford today. The sky has been black in that direction since luncheon, and Blanche will not risk herself even from Listonby in this rain. I fear there is a storm coming.'

'She could have been here by now.'

'Who, darling? Mrs Agbrigg? I doubt it, for if she set off at all she may have thought better of it, since she will wish to get home again.'

'No – no – Venetia –'

'My dear – oh heavens! is it Venetia you have been pining for?'

'Of course it is.'

Light and quick in all her movements, she got up from the window-seat and slipped her narrow hand into mine.

'Dearest, I am so sorry. Naturally I should have sent a message to Tarn

909

Edge first of all, I suppose. But I did not. She cannot have heard, unless Mrs Agbrigg – which seems unlikely.'

'But she *must* have heard. Gervase will have let her know.'

'Gervase?'

'Of course. He went to the mill this morning and must have arrived in time to – he may even have gone by Tarn Edge, surely? And his father, or Gideon – or Mrs Winch –'

And as my voice trailed off into those damnable, ridiculous tears, my mother-in-law looked, for just a moment, as if she might weep with me.

'He did go to the mill, didn't he, Mrs Barforth?'

'Oh, my dear, he may have done. That is what he *said*. Grace, if it eases you to cry, there is no shame, you know – no shame at all. I will not look, and I will never tell.'

I slept for perhaps an hour, waking to a late afternoon sky black with rain, a wind, risen from the moor, howling in cold anger about the roof tiles. Mrs Barforth was not there, my maid, Sally, sitting alone as close to the fire as she could, and for a long time I lay without speaking, staring at the small mullioned window and the desolate prospect it offered me of dark sky and naked, wind-raked trees.

I was alive and would apparently remain so. My personal danger was over, and with its passing there was now room inside me for the despair I had so far held at bay, the terrible realization that what had oozed so painfully out of me yesterday afternoon and evening had been a human life, an individual, unrepeatable being, deprived by me of the future.

Gervase might well blame himself for the distress he had caused me. I might blame him too. But I – who had known of my condition as he had not – had taken no care of it. I had attended the Listonby ball and had stayed up half the night, my body clamouring for rest, in order to demonstrate to Gervase that he had not succeeded in making me jealous. I had followed him here the next day in that bitter wind, enduring those bone-shaking miles, for the same reason. I had obeyed the demands of my pride and my self-respect, and in so doing had violated the most basic and most profound instinct of the bearing female. I had failed to protect my child. And grief for that child so overwhelmed me that I turned my face into the pillow and sobbed helplessly, dreadfully, releasing now the tears I had suppressed from all the other griefs of my life.

But my maid Sally was accustomed to finding me rational and calm, and had so little idea of how to manage me in this extremity that her alarm in itself restored my composure

'Oh, my!' she said, round-eyed with fright, 'and Mrs Barforth not here –'

'Where is she, Sally?'

'Oh – gone to Tarn Edge for Miss Venetia – or Mrs Chard, as I suppose we must call her, although it never sounds right.'

'Sally. She has gone to Tarn Edge *herself* – in this weather?'

'So she has, ma'am, the weather being the cause of it, since nobody else could handle her horses in a storm, or should be asked to. That's what she said, ma'am. She'll be back before nightfall although its been night all day today, I reckon. Chicken broth she said you were to have for dinner. Shall I fetch it, ma'am?'

I heard the storm break half an hour later, a great crack of thunder that shook the lamps and set the candles flickering, and then a great lashing of rain as if some floodgate had been opened directly above us.

'Here it comes, ma'am.' And there it was, the lightning flash that could induce panic in horses far less nervous and flighty than my mother-in-law's, the wind, the blinding rain, the pitch dark, the rutted, pock-marked roads. I had not liked her and had believed she disliked me. Perhaps she did. But it no longer mattered. She had seen my need, had understood that Gervase had not supplied it, and so, recklessly but quite suddenly, she had gone herself. I was terrified for her, proud of her, more than ever ashamed of my tears.

She would – or so I hoped – have reached Tarn Edge before the storm. Naturally she would not set out again but would spend the night there and return with Venetia in the morning. Even if she was foolhardy enough – magnificent enough – to make the attempt tonight, neither Mr Barforth nor Gideon would allow it. And knowing full well that both mother and daughter were magnificent enough – mad enough – I prayed that my father-in-law had indeed been there to prevent them, straining my ears at the same time for the sound of their carriage.

'She is gone in the cabriolet, ma'am.'

Dear God! such a light, flimsy equipage, a young man's carriage stripped down for sport and speed.

'They are saying in the kitchen, ma'am, that there is a tree struck by lightning on the Cullingford road – quite blocking the way, ma'am.'

'They seem very well informed, in the kitchen.'

'And if the river rises, ma'am, as it usually does, there will be no way to get across and every chance of her wheels bogged down in the mud.'

'Sally, I don't really care to know what the kitchenmaids are saying.'

'Will you take chicken broth, ma'am?'

'Yes– and I would like anybody who is able-bodied in that kitchen to go out with lanterns to make sure she is not bogged down by the river.'

But there was no need for it. I heard the horses, the burst of welcoming laughter, the gruff voice of the groom trying to hide his thankfulness, those tears again – which I had determined to control – welling up behind my eyelids as the door flew open and the room came alive with the exuberance of Venetia, soaked to the skin and frozen to the marrow, but glowing once again with the simple, joyful excitement of being alive.

'Darling, I am too wet to kiss you, for there is no sense in coming all this way just to give you pneumonia – and how lovely you look! That *must* be the wrong thing to say, but it is quite true. Oh dear, Grace – how terrible! How sad! The poor little baby! But I have come to cheer you, not depress you. Thank goodness father was not home from the mill when mamma came to tell me – nor Gideon. Well, now that I am here they may be angry with me for coming through the storm, but I am *here* and they can hardly fetch me back again. I shall stay, of course, until you are well.'

911

And, knowing the answer, I did not ask her when she had last seen Gervase.

There were more visitors the next few days than Galton had seen in years, my father the most frequent among them, although his visits were less satisfactory than I had hoped. My mother had miscarried, I remember, several times before my birth and several times after, undermining her health in her determination to give him the son he had not particularly desired, and it troubled him so much to see me like this that he could hardly contain his distress. Yet, since Jonas Agbrigg had believed all his life in the rigid control of emotion, he did contain it, permitting himself to do no more than press my hand and say quite tonelessly: 'There is no hurry, you know. You are still young enough, and for my part I cannot subscribe to the theory that a woman's worth is measured by her fertility. And as to this instinct of maternal devotion we hear so much about, I imagine a woman may lavish that kind of thing equally well on a dog.'

And because I knew he was really saying 'I love you, Grace. For my sake, don't put yourself in danger again', I smiled and murmured 'Yes, papa.'

Aunt Faith came often; Uncle Blaize, pleading the excuse of business, although in truth he was ill at ease at Galton, which was, after all, his brother's house, sent me out-of-season flowers obtained, I knew, at great effort and expense. Grandmamma Elinor, being in the South of France, was not informed, but my grandmother Agbrigg sent me pages of good advice, while my grandfather, the Mayor, came himself from Scarborough and spent a day at my bedside, entertaining me in his broad, West Riding accents with reminiscences of his younger days. Mrs Agbrigg, whose visit I had not welcomed, came once, assured herself with her usual, smooth efficiency that everything was being properly done and thereafter, with unexpected tact, allowed my father to come alone, sending with him some nourishing and invariably delicious concoction she had made herself. Blanche came, accompanied by both Dominic and Noel, although her husband, who was easily bored, soon rode off on business of his own, leaving his brother – his natural second in command – to take Blanche home.

Aunt Caroline and her husband spent an hour with me, the Duchess jollying me along, telling me, in effect, to take my disappointment like a man; the Duke, with embarrassed kindliness, wishing me better luck next time. Mr Nicholas Barforth looked in and instructed me in the curt tones which made his managers tremble to take care of myself. I felt surrounded by friendship and affection and was grateful – once again with those absurd tears – that my welfare should be of concern to so many. I ate up my broth, drank my chocolate and the red wine my mother-in-law insisted was good for me, and promised them all – when they required it of me – that I would get well.

Gervase, of course, came too, but contrived adroitly never to be alone with me for very long. I never learned where he had spent the day of the storm, except that it was neither at the mill nor at the Floods', as became

912

clear when they called to pay me their respects. He offered no explanations. I did not enquire, which was in itself a sure sign of danger and
decay. Once – just a week or so ago – when I had believed he loved me and
needed me, when there had been trust between us, I would have
demanded to know his exact whereabouts and expected a quick and
convincing answer. But now, when the trust had gone, I did not ask. For
now – until I was stronger – I could not risk the truth. I was still too weak to
quarrel, too weak to make demands or decisions and it seemed safer –
while the weakness lasted – just to be polite.

I got out of bed after five days or so and into a chair, a feat considered
unworthy of admiration by my village doctor, who informed me that a
peasant woman or a mill woman would have been back in the fields or at
her loom long ago. But I soon graduated to the parlour sofa and almost
immediately became available to the ministrations, the sympathy, the
curiosity of Cullingford's ladies – Miss Mandelbaum, Miss Tighe, Mrs
Sheldon and the rest – who felt unable to visit me while I remained
upstairs. And, when all this feminine gentility began to cloy, there was
Liam Adair, dividing his attention so neatly between Venetia and myself
that not even the lady's husband – had he condescended to notice it – could
have complained.

Liam had not, of course, grown prosperous, his flirtation with the
Cullingford Star satisfying his instincts as an adventurer and winning him a
certain notoriety which he frankly enjoyed, but by no means filling his
pockets. The *Star*, for all his efforts, remained a shoddy and irregular
publication, its continued existence depending largely on money borrowed from my Grandmamma Elinor, Liam having made the journey to
the villa she shared with Lady Verity Barforth near Cannes on purpose to
acquire her championship of this cause.

'I coax what I can out of her,' he frankly confessed, 'and she enjoys it.
Better me, I reckon, than the casino or that black-eyed violin player she
had about her the last time I was there. And when I printed that piece
about the houses her first husband built being unfit for pigs to live in, she
near died laughing. In fact she offered to put her own name to it to give it
an extra dash of spice. I tell you – she enjoys it.'

I believed him, for if the air he brought into my sickroom was not
precisely fresh, being too heavily laced with tobacco and Irish whisky for
that, it was at least bracing and had a far greater chance of stimulating my
still-flagging energies than Miss Fielding's gentle committees for the relief
of the not-too-wicked poor, Mrs Rawnsley's obsession with her neighbours' social and sexual peccadilloes, even Miss Tighe's oft-repeated
conviction that the vote should only be given to women of property and
militant virginity like herself.

Liam Adair was not much interested in the Prince of Wales's visit to
India nor in the recent atrocities in far off Bulgaria, being more concerned
with atrocities in the poorer areas of Cullingford, in those dingy streets and
verminous dwellings which had made my Grandmamma Elinor's first
husband his fortune. The Turkish empire, no doubt, *was* crumbling. The
Russians, equally without doubt, *would* take advantage of it to strengthen

their position – and weaken ours – in the East unless we sent a few timely gunboats to prevent it. But Liam, nonchalantly dismissing those gunboats as something designed to please the readers of the *Courier & Review*, was far more impressed by the astuteness of our admittedly very astute Prime Minister Mr Disraeli in purchasing, before the ruin of the Turkish empire came about, a majority shareholding – 177,000 shares out of 400,000 – in the Suez Canal company, thus ensuring without bloodshed our passage to India no matter which empire – Turkish, Russian or British – should gain effective control of Egypt.

'I believe Mr Disraeli to have great influence with the Queen,' murmured Miss Fielding, who was uncomfortable with share manipulations but perfectly at ease with royal widows. And indeed the artful Mr Disraeli appeared to show the same skill at coaxing the Queen little by little from her seclusion as Liam himself when it came to increasing his allowance from Grandmamma Elinor, although there were few in Liberal Cullingford with a good word to say for this exotic, imaginative Tory whose greatest claim on the affections of Liam Adair lay in his legislation to control the purity of our daily bread and of the butter with which – if we could afford it – it was spread.

The practice of increasing the bulk, improving the appearance or simply reducing the price of foodstuffs by the addition of odd and in some cases downright lethal substances was as long-established as the poverty of those who purchased them, and their need to fill the mouths of hungry children with anything that was cheap and could be made to 'go round'. All my life I had been hearing whispers of brick-dust in cocoa, sand in sugar, flour whitened with chalk, red lead used to colour the rind of cheese. I had heard of brewers who added green vitriol or sulphate of iron to put the froth on their beer and improve, with deadly results, its flavour, while as a child I had been warned never to accept sweets from strangers, since these tempting little confections might well be coloured with copper and lead. One learned to purchase one's tea with care, for the green China variety *could* have been doctored with verdigris, the black Indian variety with black lead. All the world knew that water was frequently added to milk and no one expected a cow-shed to be clean.

But the *Cullingford Star*, from its squalid little offices in Gower Street, expected it, and availing himself of the services of a chemist – paid for, one supposed, by Grandmamma Elinor – Liam Adair had purchased loaves from every baker in Cullingford and its environs, sent them for analysis and published his results, naming the place of origin of all bread in which traces of chalk or alum or any other dubious ingredient had been found.

The ground-floor windows of the *Star* had been broken a night or two later, and for the sake of expediency had been roughly boarded up again, since the following week he had printed a tale of dried ash leaves added as a makeweight to someone's tea, and mentioned the sour welcome he had received in certain ale-houses, which had caused him to suspect that their landlords had *something* to hide.

He had, of course, increased the circulation of his paper and thoroughly enjoyed himself, but Liam, while not for one moment forgetting either his profits or his pleasures, had the Irishman's instinctive sympathy for the oppressed, and Disraeli's Act to control the sale of food and drugs had pleased him at a more personal level than he cared to admit. He had no real conviction that it would be adequately enforced, no real convictions about anything, or so he insisted; but sitting at ease in my mother-in-law's parlour, his long legs stretched out to the fire, he could easily be persuaded to tell us, with a chuckle, about the shopkeepers who put up their shutters rather than sell him a pound of tea or coffee, and of the landlady who, as the sister of a local baker, had felt obliged to ask him to return the keys of his lodgings and move on.

'What next, Liam?' breathed Venetia.

'Oh, something will turn up. There's always a crusade.'

'A crusade? I hadn't thought of that. Now *I* would have gone on a real crusade, Liam – sold all my possessions and set off without even a map to rescue the Holy Land. But not you.'

'No, not I. I'd get myself a map all right, which would make me a useful man to meet in the desert. Because one has to get back, you know.'

But Venetia laughed and shook her head. 'Oh no, Liam, if one thought about getting back safe and sound that wouldn't be a *crusade*, don't you see – just an expedition. The whole point of a crusade, surely, is that one gives everything – one just goes forward and does what must be done, without a thought for what happens after? *That* is what I call a crusade. Had I been a knight in the Middle Ages – yes, do you know, I would have been very comfortable with that. I would have been right for it – don't you think so?'

I did, and for just a moment I felt a prickle of unease, a premonition, perhaps, which began to take shape and was then scattered by her frank, wholehearted laughter. She had been constrained and silent with Liam for a long time after her marriage. She had been constrained and silent with everyone, but now, in her mother's house, it was a delight to see the return of her vivacity.

I asked her no questions, for the facts of her life remained the same. She, who had believed so ardently in love, had married for convenience, and it would have been too much to expect that Life, or Destiny or whatever one might, choose to call it, should now arrange by way of compensation for her to fall in love with her husband. But human nature finds its own compensations, acquires the good sense to compromise – at least *my* nature intended to do so – and perhaps she too was learning now to live with herself and with Gideon. I hoped so, and was dismayed to be so soon proved wrong.

There was a day of strong sunshine and sparkling frost, glorious holiday weather which had Venetia and her mother out of doors by early morning, so that I was alone when Gideon came, his arrival producing in me a condition I could only describe as flustered, an enormous reluctance to admit, even in the veiled phrases of good society, the physical and sexual nature of my malady. At Tarn Edge I concerned myself with his dinner, ordered his carriage to take him to the station, kept his bed well aired for his return, and was as remote from him as the owner of a good hotel is remote from her guests. But here, where we were both guests together, it was not the same. Here I was obliged to meet him not as a brother-in-law or a second cousin, but as a man whose presence, for reasons I saw no sense in examining too closely, embarrassed me so much that I was glad when the excited yelping of a dog advised us of the approach of Venetia.

She had been heaven knew where, following the wind and weather like a gypsy, her arms full of heather gathered for good luck, the tangy fragrance of the moorland all about her; unkempt perhaps – for the hem of her dress was splashed and stained, and her hands clutching the purple heather were not clean – but enchanting, a woman, surely, who was like no other?

'Good God, what have we here?' said Gideon, by no means displeased with her, looking, on the contrary, as if this gypsy charm could please him enormously, could please her too if she would allow him to show her the way. But it was not to be.

She had not seen him for ten days and now – taken completely unawares – she stared at him aghast, as if she had forgotten his very existence and was now most painfully remembering, her vivacity draining from her and leaving her no longer a captivating woodland nymph but a rather awkward young lady who no longer knew what to do with that armful of heather.

She put it down on the table and spent a moment retrieving the sprigs which fell to the ground, the dog which had come in with her yapping around her heels in shrill excitement, leaping on and off the chintz-covered armchairs, treating us all to the antics of a half-trained, muddy and extremely boisterous pup until Gideon, who was no longer smiling, said coldly, 'Should that dog be allowed in the house?'

And when, looking as flustered as I had felt ten minutes before, she failed to retrieve the playful little hound, he eventually took it by the scruff of its neck and dropped it none too gently through the parlour window.

'Until a dog can behave, it should stay outdoors.'

'I suppose it should.'

'There are no dogs allowed inside, ever, at Listonby.'

'Well, you country people don't really care for animals. You eat them, or ride them, or train them to retrieve your game-birds for you – *work* for you, in fact – but you don't *like* them.'

'Really?'

'Yes, really. And of course you kill them too. But never mind. Have you been here long, Gideon?'

'No,' he snapped. 'Not long. And I cannot stay long either. I thought you might care to come home with me now, since Grace comes back tomorrow.'

'Yes, of course,' she said, because those were the words assigned to the role she had been given to play in life. 'That seems a good idea. I will tell them to pack my things. How long before we must leave?'

'An hour.'

'Yes.'

And smiling, she turned dutifully away, her manner telling me that there had been no compromise, no adjustment, that these ten happy days had been, quite simply, a reprieve which now was over.

13

I remember no precise moment, no single event, no threshold between the condition of a woman who, having once been happy and loved, believed she could be so again and a woman in true emotional disarray, whose marriage – like so many others – was no more than a financial and physical convenience, a hollow but indissoluble sham. The two conditions, it seemed, had blended together, had perhaps always simultaneously existed, the condition of failure gradually becoming the stronger until it had absorbed the other.

I had allowed the silence to fall between us because I had been too weak to break it and when I regained my strength I could think of nothing to say. Gervase brought me home from Galton. He enquired carefully as to the progress of my health, ate his dinner more often than not at my table, slept in my bed. He gave me his escort and his company when the social niceties required it. He behaved, in public, as a husband and I as a wife, and in private we remained polite.

We even became lovers again, or rather he reclaimed his conjugal rights, since I could not glorify what passed between us by the name of love-making; his body, which had turned its fastidious back to me all night, being drawn to mine sometimes in the moment of half-waking, a performance part duty, part need, which any nameless female could have satisfied and during which I lay quite still, as nameless females do, despising myself for this submission, despising him for accepting it. But the law, which called me his wife, forced me to give him free use of my body whenever he required it. He was not even obliged to ask, simply to take, and gradually, as the rift widened, I learned how to insult him with my passivity as his hurried satisfaction insulted me. And when we had reached that dismal stage I was no worse, perhaps, than those many thousands of other women for whom this side of marriage had always been a burden, or those many thousands of others who prided themselves on their skill in avoiding it altogether; except that it had not always been so with us.

Nor could I recall any single moment when I became certain of his infidelity. I merely anticipated it, so that by the time I became aware of it I understood that it had already been taking place for some time; and although I suffered I was not surprised. He was not, at the start, unfaithful to me with Diana Flood, as I might have expected, nor with anyone else I could identify. I simply knew that there was someone, and then someone else, learning with a delicate species of self-torture to read the signs, an indefinable but to me quite unmistakable air about him that fluctuated from wariness to nervous gaiety, from a brooding self-disgust to a bruised and satiated fatigue, his humour varying with the woman who – for the days or the hours these affairs lasted – had tempted him, amused him, consoled him, briefly delighted him, left him only half satisfied, or who had revealed, in a few cases, some new aspect of his carnal nature which in the clear daylight appalled him.

And I did nothing.

Even on the summer night when, strolling into the cloister at Galton, I saw him at the far end of the tunnel kissing the bare shoulders of a woman I vaguely took to be one of Blanche's London friends, I did nothing. I simply turned and hurried away, thankful he had not seen me, hoping the woman had not seen me either. I did nothing because I was proud, and afraid, and for the stark and simple reason that I could think of nothing to do. I was a betrayed wife. So were hundreds of thousands of others. Woman was, by nature and by necessity, a faithful animal. Man was not. Brood mares stayed peacefully with the herd. Stallions ran wild. 'My dear,' I could imagine a dozen female voices murmuring to me, 'men are simply made that way. You must forgive him and understand.' And above the other voices would be Mrs Rawnsley's shrill, smug whisper; 'Make him buy you something, Grace, to apologize – something really expensive. I always do.'

I could not tolerate those whispers.

There was, of course, the time-honoured and possibly effective method of running home to my father. But I could not do that either, knowing as I did what my happiness meant to him. He had had few joys in his life. His main concern now was that I should have joy in mine, and I was determined above all not to let him down. He desired to see me happy. He *would* see me happy. He *did* see me happy. It was the least I could do for the man who had done so much for me. And even had I been tempted to weaken – and I was not tempted – I could never have contemplated the possibility of sharing a home with Mrs Agbrigg again.

But even so, had I retained just a small measure of hope, I might not have been so scrupulous. Had I believed it possible to be truly reconciled, I might have turned to anyone, resorted to anything which might have brought it about. But I well knew that Gervase's neglect of me and his infidelity were in themselves only symptoms of the disease. The real tragedy – and so I named it – lay in the one simple fact that my husband, who had thought he loved me, no longer did so, no longer found me desirable nor even interesting. And how could I, or anyone, remedy that?

There had been no physical violence, no public humiliation, no tangible insult with which his father or mine could grapple. He was not, after all, keeping a mistress in style and leaving me to starve. Nor did he flaunt himself and his women in local places of entertainment as Mr Rawnsley had been known to do. He had never subjected me to any unnatural form of lust, nor infected me with any form of disease. He 'pleased himself', as Cullingford put it, rather too often, but so did plenty of others, and although it was all very regrettable no one would really have thanked me for making a fuss.

I did not make a fuss, for my own and for my father's sake. I had chosen to marry a difficult man and those who had warned me against him – Mrs Agbrigg the chief among them – had been right. I had believed in his love and it had not lasted. And I preferred to suffer the lack of it rather than make any attempt to force him or shame him into some feeble pretence.

The love and the need, then, were both over, but the marriage would last for the rest of our lives. The shell remained. I could leave it empty or I could fill it with venom, but either way I became obsessed with my determination to keep that shell intact. No one must know. And when I realized the impossibility of this – since the women who received Gervase's attentions knew, and their friends, and their maids – I once again adopted the shameful device of pretending not to care.

What did not trouble me need trouble no one else – I had learned that on the night of the Listonby ball and had lost my baby – and I became an expert at the indulgent smile, implying, 'Heavens! of *course* men are made that way, the poor darlings. What can it signify?'; expert too at the unruffled greeting, making no more and no less of the suspected mistress, the current fancy, than of anyone else, introducing Gervase's name into my conversation no more and no less than I had always done and keeping myself busy – busy – busy, so that it could be said 'Dear Grace, she is so occupied with her organizing and her entertaining that it is hardly surprising she does not notice –', or 'Grace Barforth – good heavens! of *course* she notices. What of it? She has that mansion to live in, hasn't she, and what does she care for the man so long as she can have the spending of his money?' and if the rumours climbed the hill to Fieldhead, then I knew that Mrs Agbrigg – who could not be eager to share her home with me either – would have the good sense and the skill to keep them from my father.

Naturally I suffered – naturally and abominably – for these decisions which sound so cool were not taken coolly, and although logic was certainly employed I was often obliged to wring it out of myself through layers of heartache. There were times when I ordered the carriage to go to Fieldhead and could not complete the journey, telling my coachman to take me anywhere, out of the city streets and the prosperous suburbs to a country lane where no one knew me or pitied me or thought I had got as much as I deserved; where no kind soul was anxious to tell me – in case I didn't already know it – that my husband had been in dubious company in Manchester last Friday night; where I was not obliged to be bright and busy and brittle, but could indulge myself with silence.

There were times when my own suppressed emotions threatened to break free and the urge to throw myself weeping against Gervase's lean, fastidious chest – or to put a knife into it – became almost too great to resist. I resisted it. My nature was constructed and moulded in such a way that I could do no other than resist, although these urges, turning inward, caused me much solitary grieving and bitterness.

There was jealousy too – how could there not have been? – of women I barely knew, acquaintances of the Chards who, visiting Listonby for a Friday-to-Monday might never come again; and of women I did not know at all, strangers from Bradford and Leeds and the Theatre Royal who briefly aroused not so much his appetite, since he was not prone to enormous sexual hungers, but his curiosity, the need of a man who does not know what he is searching for to try everything. And although logically it was wrong to hate these women, since it was Gervase, not they, who was doing me harm, I could not always be logical. There were times when I murdered them all, quite horribly, in my imagination and was sickened afterwards by the violence I had done only to myself.

But all this took place, as I have said, little by little, and on my return from Galton that autumn of my miscarriage, Venetia's affairs appeared more urgent than mine. She had had her period of mourning, her period of humbleness and gratitude. She had endured fear and shame and a kind of despairing lethargy. She had regained her physical strength and with it a portion of her self-esteem. What now? And because she had not found the answer, because she suspected there was no answer – and because the role of good, obedient, contrite little girl no longer sufficed – she grew subject to abrupt swings of mood that winter, troughs of despair and peaks of nervous elation which made her as unpredictable and often as difficult as Gervase.

'Grace, I absolutely must *do* something. I really don't want to waste another day. There must be something – something important – that has to be done?'

But none of the activities I discovered or invented for my own diversion could hold her attention for long, her initial frenzy of enthusiasm soon giving way to a shrug, a sigh, a sudden drooping of her spirits.

'Oh lord! – what's the use of it? What is it really good for?'

And the dinner-party invitations I had asked her to write would not be finished, the recipes of a famous French chef I had found in a borrowed magazine would remain uncopied, the flowers she had been arranging with a flair I did not myself possess would be left half done and wilting.

'What's the good of it? When I die will they put on my tombstone that I wrote an excellent copper-plate and could arrange a very pretty vase of carnations? Why trouble to be alive for *that*?'

And one day, after an hour of restless silence, she startled me badly by saying without any warning, 'I wonder if it would be possible to discover what has become of Charles Heron?'

'Possible, I suppose. But it could hardly be wise.'

She gave a short, rueful laugh, and jumping to her feet began pacing up and down the room, picking up small objects as she passed and setting them down again.

'There is no need for you to look so sour, Grace. I am not in the least in love with him now, you know.'

'Then why should you care what has happened to him?'

'Because –' she paused, shrugged her fine-boned shoulders, her pointed face taking on a dreaming, very disturbing quality as her eyes became focused on the past. 'Because – oh, yes – because to tell you the truth I believe I am in love with – yes – with myself as I was in those days.'

And because it had been a bad day for me, because Gervase had done me some small, stinging injury and she resembled him, I said tartly, 'You would do better to fall in love with Gideon.'

She came to a halt, not angrily but rather as if the mere sound of his name acted as a brake, or a weight which slowed her down.

'How very tidy that would be.'

'Venetia, I am sorry to have mentioned it, but since I have, then – really – I would be very glad if you could grow to love him.'

'Do you know, Grace – so would I. Very glad indeed.'

'Then, surely –'

'What? You think wanting is half-way there?'

'Yes. I do think so.'

'Then you are quite wrong.'

She moved again, just a step or two, almost sedately, with a composure and a certainty I had not seen in her before.

'Gideon would have to want it too,' she said. 'And he does not.'

'Oh Venetia – surely? He *must*.'

'There is no must about it. You should know quite well, Grace, that one does not tell Gideon what he *must* do. He doesn't want me to love him. He wants me to be his wife.'

'I should have thought the two might easily go together.'

She shrugged.

'Not in our case. And, of course, the sad thing is that perhaps I could love him if he would allow it. I realize now that love is not so very exclusive as I thought. It simply exists in the body and one needs to release it. One even needs to feel loyalty and devotion and sacrifice – to go on crusade a little – at least I do. I suppose there are dozens – hundreds – of men I could love and be faithful unto death should I happen to meet them, so why not Gideon?'

'Yes – why not?'

'Because it is not what he wants. Does Dominic want Blanche to love him? I doubt if it has even crossed his mind and never will so long as she is in his bed when he desires her and at the head of his table when it suits him or flatters him or is to his advantage to have other men desire her. Gideon would like the same from me – exactly that – and no, it is not too much, don't you see? The terrible thing is that it is not enough. If he'd ask something more of me – something real and that I could see the sense of – then I'd try. I'd respond to the *challenge* of him, because after all he's good to look at and the very circumstances of our marriage are a challenge in themselves. It would be magnificent to make something lovely and lasting out of our appalling start, to get to know each other and forgive each other, and then to be friends, and lovers. Just think of the range of emotion one would need for all that.'

'You have the range, Venetia.'

She smiled, her eyes twinkling with a rueful humour, laughing not without affection at herself.

'I know. It's the one thing about myself that I'm sure of and that rather pleases me. I'd be very good at nursing him through some near-fatal illness, you know, and if he lost his money I'd manage to be brave about it. If there should ever be a riot at the mill I'd be more inclined to stand by him than not. And should he ever be disgraced and sent to prison I'd be rather splendid about waiting for him and doing my utmost to clear his name – can't you just imagine it? I don't even require quite so much drama as that. I'd be perfectly willing just to rejoice with him whenever he scored a triumph, or help him to overcome his disappointments if he'd just let me know what his triumphs and his disappointments are. But I have no talent for sitting about the dining-room in a low-cut dress so his colleagues can see what a lucky fellow he is, and wearing his jewels so they'll all know he's doing well at the mill. And as for the other thing – as for the desire – well I don't mind it now as I used to, but one can hardly build one's life around it – at least, I can't.'

'Venetia, are you really sure?'

'About Gideon? Of course I am. Wives are for drawing-rooms and bedrooms, my dear, and by that reckoning I rate very low. After all, I suppose a wife can only measure her success by the effect she has on her husband, which definitely places me among the failures. It's women like Blanche, I find, who do best. She knows what's expected of her. She even likes what's expected of her. She understands the rules and knows how to get her way without breaking a single one of them. She was a silly girl, I always thought, but she's a clever woman. And I suppose I'm the ninny now.

But she was not always so humble, nor so inclined to measure herself on the yardstick of Gideon's estimation, the docility to which she had accustomed him giving way quite often now to bursts of nonchalance, amusement, and the beginnings of defiance.

'Lord, Gideon, does it matter whether we go or not? It is only to Miss Mandelbaum's.'

'Miss Mandelbaum's brother, Mr Jacob Mandelbaum, is a wool merchant – as you may know – who does a great deal of business with me.'

'The Mandelbaums have always done business with *us*, of course I know. Is that a reason to spend this lovely evening listening to Rebecca Mandelbaum thumping her piano?'

'Your father may think so.'

'I daresay. But I see he does not feel obliged to go himself.'

'Why should he?' Gideon said with a tight, sarcastic smile. 'He has me to do it for him. If Gervase should ever be available, perhaps I might be excused. But until then you will have to accompany me.'

'Take Grace. She understands about Mozart.'

'You will not be required to understand Mozart, Venetia, merely to behave as if you do.'

'Oh, I see. In that case you had better take Blanche.'

They went together to Miss Mandelbaum's recital, returning in a state of mutual irritation which quickly, as Gideon slammed down his hat and gloves on the hall table, flared into their first open quarrel. Neither, it seemed, had appreciated a note of the music, Gideon being more concerned in making the acquaintance of a gentleman from Hamburg who had some importance in the wool trade and of a merchant banker from Berlin, instinctively obeying the rules his mother had taught him that these personal contacts, if carefully nourished, were often worth their weight in gold.

'May I present you to my wife,' he had said, but his wife instead of assuming a graceful pose and allowing herself to be looked at, as Blanche would have done, or of asking a few safe if uninspired questions about the German landscape which might have been my solution, ignored these worthy gentlemen altogether, devoting herself entirely to the praise of Miss Mandelbaum's performance, her enthusiasm increasing in proportion to the guilt she felt at not having really listened to it.

'Miss Mandelbaum, I have heard nothing better on the concert stage.'

'My dear, as a girl that is where I longed to be.'

'Then why did you not –'

'Oh, naturally, my parents would not allow it.'

'What nonsense. You should have defied them, you know – for your art's sake.'

'Oh no, dear. That would have been impossible.'

'Not a bit of it. We must stand up for ourselves, Miss Mandelbaum, indeed we must. Miss Tighe would say the same.'

And Venetia, in a spirit part mischief and part genuine compassion for these wasted talents, began to urge a considerably startled Miss Mandelbaum to abandon the gentle, comfortable life in Cullingford and to adopt the vagabond and – Venetia insisted – thrilling status of an artiste.

'Just think how gloriously free! Goodness, it makes me wish I had learned the piano myself, or at least the violin.'

The two foreign gentlemen may well have been amused. Their wives were not. Venetia – it was abundantly clear – would not be remembered kindly in the commercial circles of Hamburg and Berlin, and neither Frau Grassmann nor Frau Goldsmith would be likely to resist the temptation of conveying the poor impression she had created to their numerous cousins in every business centre of Europe.

Gideon, who had been with the firm of Nicholas Barforth for over four years now, was by no means content either with his progress or with his lot. He was determined, as his mother the Duchess of South Erin would have been determined, to carve out for himself an international reputation and take his place eventually among Europe's industrial élite, thus casting doubt on the sound judgement of the man who had married her.

'Lord!' she now declared. 'What a pair they were, those two foreign women – one of them like a dressed up stick and the other with a moustache – you can believe me, Grace – beneath her ringlets.'

'Mrs Goldsmith,' said Gideon coldly, 'is an extremely intelligent woman. She speaks five or six languages fluently, I believe.'

'And what is the use of that if she has nothing interesting to say?'

'Venetia, did it not occur to you that Goldsmith could be very useful to me?'

'No,' she said very clearly, looking directly up at him. 'It did not. I am not accustomed to judging people by their usefulness, nor by the profit I might expect to make from their acquaintance.'

'Then you are very naive.'

923

'Naive? Or honest – don't you think so?'

'Naive. Or stupid – that might come a little nearer.'

'Ah,' she said, making the sound insolent, provocative, and then swiftly repenting. 'Heavens, Gideon, and just what damage have I done? This is not Listonby or Mayfair or South Erin, you know, where everything depends on being invited to dinner by the right people and having the right calling-cards on one's hall table. This is Cullingford. If you have something to sell and your price is right and the other person wants it, or needs it, then he buys. It can make no difference whether or not I am on good terms with his wife.'

He stood by the fire, on the centre of the hearthrug as her father often did, looking at her with a fine-drawn, entirely Chard disdain that seemed, despite its muted quality, to fill the room.

'I am indebted to you,' he said, 'for the information. But the world has grown somewhat larger, I fear, since your grandfather founded these mills – larger and faster and infinitely more complicated. Your grandfather had very little competition from other manufacturers – since there was no more than a handful of them able to compete – and he could sell undisturbed in any market he liked. The markets are still there, but the manufacturers have increased a hundredfold. And what is a man to do – Mr Goldsmith, for example? – if he encounters a dozen, or a hundred manufacturers whose prices and whose delivery dates are equally convenient? I imagine he would turn to the manufacturer he knows best, whose character he judges to be sound – a manufacturer whose personal standards are high and whose wife can be trusted to behave. Don't you think he might do that? And one's horizons need not necessarily be bound by Cullingford – at least, mine need not.'

I saw her chin quiver very slightly, her eyes cast down as she murmured, 'Does it matter? There is so much money already – more than one could ever spend. Why this fever for more of the same thing? Why'

But her answer was the slam of the door as he strode from the room, his patience at an end, leaving her to bite her lip for a moment, half afraid of her defiance, for Gideon in his anger had looked more than ever like her father.

The Goldsmiths, the Grassmanns, Rebecca and Jacob Mandelbaum dined wih us some days later, my efforts to convey the impression that Venetia was their hostess being defeated by Venetia herself who, as each course was brought in, made some remark of delighted but tell-tale surprise. Ye she made herself very pleasant to the shrill Mrs Goldsmith, sitting beside her in the drawing-room after the meal and listening with an almost mesmerized attentiveness – in fact the daze of a crushing boredom – to that lady's particular theories on the culinary and domestic arts, agreeing with eager nods of her auburn head each time Mrs Goldsmith paused for breath or demanded 'Is that not so?'

Miss Mandelbaum played and sang for us, Mr Jacob Mandelbaum, a cultured and worldly man, talked music and landscape, and managed, with a fine discretion, to prevent his sister from asking me why my husband was not present, since it must have been clear from the odd number at my table that he had been expected.

The gentlemen from Hamburg and Berlin remained in the drawing-room for a very long time with Gideon, smoking cigars and discussing, almost with love, the intricacies of finance at an exalted level where money was not for spending but for manipulation, a world-wide chess game which Gideon, with the Barforth fortune behind him and his own fierce ambitions driving him towards the making of another, might one day be invited to play.

'When you are next in Berlin –' Mr Goldsmith said, taking Gideon's hand in both of his at parting.

'You will find much in Hamburg to interest you,' said Mr Grassmann.

'Lord!' said Venetia when they were all safely gone. 'Do tell me – am I not heroic?'

And meeting Gideon's cool eyes, the lift of his eyebrows that plainly said, 'Heroic? Just barely adequate, I'd call it', I saw her own brows come together in a frown, her pointed face flush with a rare loss of temper.

'All right,' she said, squaring her slight shoulders, her back very straight. 'You have no need to tell me. I have not been heroic. I have simply been a hypocrite. Is that what you want from me?'

She had never allowed herself to be really angry with him before, had been too quick, if anything, to agree with his every opinion, to accommodate his least desire, but now, after a slight start of surprise, he merely sighed as one does when dealing with a troublesome child.

'Venetia, must you be so enthusiastic?' And we were in no doubt that he had used the word in its Listonby and Mayfair sense of 'brash', 'melodramatic', 'middle-class'.

'Oh, don't play the squire with me, Gideon,' she told him, 'although truly it is what you are.'

'Is this necessary, Venetia?'

'Indeed it is, for I wish to know if I have pleased you. I have spent the evening flattering a woman I dislike and who dislikes me, for the purpose – if I understand aright – of procuring you an invitation to her house in Berlin. Not because you care two straws for her or for her husband, but because he might be of *use* to you. Is that what I have been doing?'

'Is it? I rather thought you had been giving a dinner-party, or that Grace had been giving one on your behalf. Why all this fuss, Venetia?'

'Because I want to know if I have done well. Have you got your invitation? Is this what you want from me?'

And for what seemed to me a very long time, during which I longed to leave the room and frankly dared not desert her, he did not reply.

'Ah well,' he said at last and taking a cigar lit it, inhaled with calm enjoyment, his attention apparently caught by the gracefully curving spiral of tobacco. But the silence was too much for Venetia – as he had intended – and taking a deep breath she raised herself on tiptoe, attempting, I suppose, to match his height and suddenly threw at him, 'Damnation – yes, I mean *damnation!* Do you know, Gideon, I believe I would think better of you if you wanted to make love to that woman, if you found her desirable instead of just a stepping stone to her husband's good graces. Yes, if you desired her, I could understand it. You see – you wrinkle your nose at the thought of it, don't you, which means you don't like her either.'

'It means I am appalled by your manners – or lack of them.'

'No, it does not. It means I have made you look at her and admit she is an old harpy – for so she is. But I ask myself, does that matter to you: Would it matter if –' and I could hear on the tip of her tongue – as he could surely hear them – the words that must never be spoken: 'If you had to make love to her, Gideon, to get what you want, would you go so far? Would it be no more and no less a hardship to you than making love to me?'

No one, of course, in the complexity of human relationships can ever be entirely right or wholly wrong. Gideon was a hard, ambitious man – qualities much valued in Cullingford who expected no more than he had been brought up to expect from a wife. He had seen his mother devote the whole of her formidable energies to creating at Listonby an atmosphere which attracted influential men like bees to clover; men, need it be said, who could be of service, not to Aunt Caroline herself, but to her husband and to her sons. He had seen Aunt Faith drop everything at the sight of a telegram from Uncle Blaize and, not caring what engagements she cancelled nor whom she offended, set off on the hundred- or thousand-mile journey to join him. He had seen Mrs Sheldon force herself, entirely against her nature, to make public speeches in her husband's praise, giving up her own friends and her own occupation as a landscape painter to devote herself to the humdrum work of the constituency in order that Thomas Sheldon MP might be at liberty to bask in the delights of Westminster. He knew that Mrs Rawnsley, who was neither particularly kind nor particularly clever, would nevertheless defend in any drawing-room or at any tea-table the interests of Mr Septimus Rawnsley, her not particularly faithful husband, and had sense enough to make herself very pleasant to all those who transacted their business through Rawnsley's Bank. And these ladies were not making sacrifices. They were simply doing what they *ought* to be doing. They were keeping their marriage vows.

In the beginning he had been surprisingly patient and even now, when patience was growing fragile at its borders, remained conscious of his responsibilities. He would, I believe, have been ready to give Venetia every conceivable luxury, would have enjoyed seeing her swathed in sables and dripping diamonds, not so much as evidence of his generosity but of the fact that he – the third son of a baronet – could afford them. He would have allowed her to travel too, as often as she had a mind, since he lacked the middle-class notion that husband and wife should never be apart. He would not have objected too strenuously had she acquired her mother's passion for the hunt, so long as she hunted with 'decent' people and took care always to be well mounted and well dressed. He would have turned a blind or an indulgent eye to the

926

occasional card-party, since useful acquaintances can be made at a fashionable whist table, providing she took the trouble to wear an expensive gown and did not lose too much. She could have stayed in bed all morning, like Blanche, while he went to the mill to earn their daily portion of caviar and champagne, had he been able to rely on finding her, vivacious and hospitable, at his dinner-table at night.

But Gideon's ambitions, while not incomprehensible to Venetia, irritated her, increasing her feeling of alienation. She understood money and knew there was plenty of it. Why, then, should she devote her one, precarious, already blemished life to the task of making it grow? What concerned her was the *quality* of life, not its luxury. What she most desired was an intense and demanding relationship which would test her ingenuity and stretch her resources to the full, an emotional crusade requiring the investment of her whole heart. And she could see no similarity between these fierce longings and the driving force of Gideon's ambition which could not be content with the fortune his uncle and his wife had brought him, which goaded him into a crusade of his own.

Grand in his ideas, lavish in his tastes, it pleased his vanity – that touchiness of a younger son for whom no provision has been made – to consider the splendid Barforth mills as no more than a starting point. He had not been born a manufacturer. The rules of primogeniture had forced him to it and from the first he had determined to conduct himself with style, to lift himself by his own efforts from the confines of grubby, middle-class Cullingford to a plane where business was conducted by gentlemen. After all, it had been a Rothschild – a prince not of the blood but of commerce – who had enabled the British government to purchase its controlling interest in the Suez Canal, and although Gideon had no interest in politics himself, his brother Sir Dominic was soon to take his seat in the House of Commons behind the flamboyant Mr Disraeli, and there was no reason why the Chards, if the game was played aright, should not attain influence in the land. Blanche would play her part in that game, Aunt Caroline would glory in it. But if Venetia could be brought to understand it at all, she would be very likely to enquire, 'What's the good of it? What does it matter? It's not even *real*.'

She may well have been right. I did not set myself to judge, merely to perform, each day, the tasks I found to hand, the building of a façade which screened us all but which only Gideon seemed to appreciate.

'That menu was exceedingly well chosen, Grace.'

'Thank you Gideon.'

'Tell me – how did you get on with Frank Brewster's wife over coffee?'

'Famously. She believes she will never survive the journey to New York next week.'

'So they are going to New York, are they? Now why – I wonder – did Brewster forget to mention that?'

'Well – they are staying with the Ellison-Turnbulls.'

'Are they, by God? Thank you, Grace.'

And so it continued.

I became, that year and the year after, an obsessive housekeeper and

927

hostess, a great compiler of lists and designer of domestic routines. I kept files in date order of my menus and my invitations, so that no dish was ever served to the same guests twice over. I kept files on the guests themselves, their gastronomic and personal preferences, the names of their children, their enemies and their friends. I made it my business to know which notable would be arriving in Cullingford, having found a reliable informant at the Station Hotel, and if Gideon wished to meet them I never failed to find the correct approach, or to make the impression he desired. It became a challenge, finally a compulsion, my pride in discovering the favourite wine of a total stranger, his wife's favourite flower, and having both in plentiful supply when they came to dine, outweighing by far its object.

My aims had reduced themselves perhaps – in fact, they were much reduced – but were altogether 'in keeping' with my status, a perfect dinner-party, the organization of a charity ball at which I walked roughshod over any lady who dared to question my authority taking on the importance of the Balkan crisis, not because I cared about charity balls but because this – unlike my relationship with Gervase – was a matter in which I could be certain of success. The reality of my marriage was a hollow sham. The illusion it created was still very widely admired. It was the illusion which, of necessity, counted.

I sat at my dinner-table one summer evening, enjoying the rose-scented air through the open windows, knowing that everything in this huge, ornate house that should be polished had been polished most thoroughly, that every item of linen requiring starch was starched to perfection, every inch of upholstery meticulously brushed. I knew my larder shelves were full, my drawers and cupboards scented with sweet herbs and lavender, my staff respectful and respectable, even the beds where the kitchenmaids slept supplied with good mattresses and warm blankets.

I was surrounded by order and efficiency, I was at the centre of a beehive of ongoing tasks which I knew would be well done. And if the running of this house was a small matter compared to the running of the Barforth and Agbrigg mills – to the affairs of the real world outside – then at least no one, I believed, could have done it better. I was making a constructive effort of my life – as some others were not – and whenever it troubled me that the effort was really very small, that Grace Agbrigg, surely, with her flair for mathematics and languages, had been capable of far more than this, it seemed wiser and safer to belittle that flair, to shrink my capabilities, to narrow myself down to fit the reality of my situation, and be content.

There was no conversation at the table that night, Venetia staring listlessly at the white brocade wall, Gideon's mind on facts and figures, Gervase leaning back in his chair, eating little, saying not a word. And when their silence oppressed me I began to tell them whatever came into my mind, Aunt Faith's return from Paris, a dinner at Mrs Rawnsley's the night before, when her parlourmaid had spilled a decanter of wine on a brand-new capet.

'What rotten luck!' said Gideon whose training as a gentleman always enabled him to produce some sort of reply.

'Mmmmmm,'said Venetia.

'Yes, terrible luck, for the carpet is pale green and the wine, as you might imagine, was red. I am not at all sure the stain can be removed.'

Gervase leaned towards me, his face very pale in the twilight, his eyes carefully narrowed, his mouth touched by a smile that deceived me, since he was not much given to smiling these days.

'Grace,' he said very distinctly, 'what a bore you are.'

To which I coolly and to no one in particular replied, 'Do you know, I believe this sauce is much improved by that dash of tarragon. I must remember to tell cook.'

14

One night the following autumn, my maid, Sally Grimshaw, who had been given permission to attend a wedding, did not return, her absence being only grudgingly explained to me by Mrs Winch, my housekeeper, who did not seem to think it my concern. The girl, while walking back to Tarn Edge alone at what could not be called a respectable hour of the night, had been 'set upon' by some unknown male, and as a result of her injuries had been taken by a constable to the Infirmary. The constable had then been kind enough to inform Mrs Winch, who for her part saw no reason to trouble me. Sally would be missed, of course, but either Mary-Ann or Martha-Jane would be able to do my hair and mend my linen and should they not give satisfaction Mrs Winch knew an agency which could be trusted to supply a proper lady's maid at short notice.

What injuries? Not serious. Shock, mainly, thought Mrs Winch, and the cuts and bruises one would expect after such an affray. But I must remember that she had been 'set upon', after all, by a man she said she had not recognized, although there was no way to be sure of that.

'You mean she has been raped?'

'Yes, madam, I do.'

And she was very angry with me, I could tell, for using the word, even angrier when I ordered my carriage and went off to see for myself.

Cullingford's Infirmary, at the top of steep, cobbled Sheepgate, was an old and inconvenient building, clean enough since Miss Florence Nightingale had taught us that, if hospitals could not always cure the sick, they should not by their filth and squalor actually do them harm. But it was equipped as sparsely as a workhouse, black iron bedsteads pushed close together against a stark white wall, cheerless, not intended for the affluent who would be nursed at home, but for the poor, the vagrant, the disgraced, who for one reason or another were homeless. And what disturbed me most about Sally was not the evidence of a brutal beating but her fear.

I was interviewed with barely adequate courtesy by the physician in charge, an elderly, ill-tempered, possibly over-worked man who, like

Mrs Winch, did not really know what I was doing here and had no time and certainly no patience with my indignation. There was in his view no need to make a fuss. After all, these things occurred with enormous, in fact with tedious regularity and he had seen worse – far worse – than Sally, who had had broken no bones and lost no teeth.

'My dear lady,' he said finally, his tolerance at an end, 'one must take a rational view. Your sympathy does you credit, but the young woman *was* alone in a questionable area of the city at an advanced hour of the night. In such circumstances any woman must expect to be molested. Her assailant no doubt mistook her for a prostitute.'

'I see. It is permissible, then, to rape a prostitute?'

He raised a dry, somewhat disgusted eyebrow.

'Madam – I would consider it to be something of an impossibility.'

'I cannot agree.'

'Indeed? It astonishes me, Mrs Barforth, that you – as a gentlewoman – should have any views on the matter at all. And I will give you a further piece of advice. You would do well not to trouble our constabulary with a sorry episode such as this, for if that young woman's assailant was really unknown to her, she cannot name him; and if he was not the stranger she claims, then she *will* not name him. These incidents are best left to settle themselves. Good-day to you, Mrs Barforth.'

I took Sally back to Tarn Edge in the victoria, Mrs Winch greeting me with tight-lipped disapproval. Did I realize, she wondered, the extra work involved, the trays to be carried upstairs, the hot water, the bed linen? And when I reminded her that we had had sick maids before who had not been turned outdoors like stray kittens, she folded her hands, drew a deep breath and compressed her lips even further.

'I wonder, madam, if you have considered the effect of this on – well – the others?'

'Why should there be any effect at all, Mrs Winch?'

'Because she is not suffering from influenza, madam, or a sprained ankle. In fact we cannot be sure what she *is* suffering from.'

'Mrs Winch, what do you mean by that?'

'I will tell you, madam. I keep these girls well under control. I think you will agree with that, and it is essential they should be controlled. But most of them are naturally flighty, and a thing like this can only arouse their curiosity. They will be around her bed, mark my words, like bees round honey, asking their silly questions, letting it all go to their heads and neglecting their work. And we have men-servants too, Mrs Barforth, please do not forget that. It is difficult enough, at the best of times, to preserve the decencies in these large households, and one cannot expect these young footmen to treat a girl who has – well, they will not treat her as they treat the others, you may take my word for it. I cannot think it right to take her back and I believe you will find the girl herself does not wish to stay.'

'If she is treated as something between a leper and a Jezebel, then most likely she will not.'

But Mrs Winch, armoured by her self-righteousness, did not lack

930

courage and, quite calmly, had something more to say.

'Mrs Barforth, that girl should be discharged at once for the sake of your own peace of mind. She may well be pregnant, Mrs Barforth, and since you would *have* to discharge her then, it is better to do it now, when no one can be sure. That way she will have time to make her arrangements and your conscience will be clear. I was forced to dismiss a pregnant thirteen-year-old in my last place, madam, and it was most distressing. Sally Grimshaw is older, has more sense, and she will be far better off now with her mother.'

I had never thought of Sally in terms of a mother, family, or in any terms whatsoever that did not involve the dressing of my hair, the laying out of my clothes, the cleaning of my brushes. She had been present, the plump, pink and white face glimpsed behind me in the mirror, the quick, capable hands wielding a button-hook, her cheerful gossip of disaster on the night I had lost a child of my own. I was neither fond of her nor otherwise. I was simply used to her. But I was appalled, now, by the callousness her plight had aroused in the normally well-meaning Mrs Winch, and made it my concern that very afternoon to go and see her mother.

I had come with sad tidings and expected them to cause distress, an honest show of indignation, a desire for revenge, and I was badly shaken by the indifference with which the gaunt, grey woman who was Sally's mother lifted her shoulders, displaying a body which I at first thought to be misshapen by accident or disease but which was in fact pregnant.

The house was small and dark as I had expected, one room downstairs and one above, a bare floor and a kitchen chair or two, mattresses rolled up and stacked in corners, a flat stone sink, a steep, littered staircase leading to the upper floor, stone steps leading down to a dank, open cellar. All this I had expected to see, but even Liam Adair's fluent denunciations in the pages of the *Star* had not prepared me for the smell of damp and poor drainage, of the overflowing privy a yard or two from the door, the sweat and the urine soaked into those splintering floorboards, a smell which, at this our first encounter, stung my eyelids and took my breath away.

'It happens. She'll get over it. She'll have to,' said Mrs Grimshaw, one hand on her swollen belly, another child no more than two years old straddling her hip. 'And she knows not to expect anything from me.'

Mrs Grimshaw, I discovered, was the mother of seventeen children, a large family she was ready to admit but not unusually so in a district where the men were mostly unemployed and, as she put it, 'had nothing else to do'. She herself worked in the weaving-sheds – anybody's weaving-sheds – when her health permitted, and when it didn't she took in washing for anybody who could afford to pay her a penny or two, since her husband was not, she said, 'reliable'. She had married at sixteen, when she had already given birth to her first child, and had been recovering from one pregnancy or starting another very nearly ever since. And she had alleviated the squalor of nineteen persons in two dingy rooms by the simple procedure of pushing each child out of the nest as soon as, or even a shade before, they had started to fly. The boys were welcome to stay as long as they were earning and could bring something in, although two had gone to sea, another into the Army, and unless trade picked up she supposed the rest would follow. But her one prize possession was a sister who had done well in the service of a clerical gentleman at Elderleigh, and, as each of her daughters approached the age of eleven or twelve, this sister had never yet failed to place them as kitchenmaids, maids of all work, skivvies; after which Mrs Grimshaw rarely saw them again. They moved on, or, if they succeeded and became parlourmaids or lady's maids like Sally, they grew proud. Her eldest girl had taken employment so far away that Mrs Grimshaw had been unable to attend her death-bed and, far from complaining, had simply been relieved that the girl's employer had agreed to bury her.

'I'd stopped her funeral club payments, you see,' she told me in her flat, monotonous voice. 'And it would have been awkward having to borrow. Because they won't put a nail in the coffin unless you can pay cash down.' And as for Sally, she had given her the best start in life she could and had not received so much as a shilling from her ever since. Nothing, on either side, was owing. And there was nothing to spare.

She shrugged her shoulders again, her hollow eyes asking me, 'What can I do? I feed them, and clothe them after a fashion, until they're big enough to see to themselves. And after that I have to think of the babies – the babies – until this wretched body of mine is too old for babies.'

I knew from that first meeting – although indeed I never met her again, merely hundreds like her – that I could not judge her, and leaving behind the few coins I had on me, ashamed at this easy gift of money and her lethargic acceptance, I went home with the smell of her so deep in my memory that my bath-tub of scented water, carried upstairs by girls who could have been her daughters, gave me no comfort. And even when I had explained to Sally that she need not be afraid, that in any eventuality she would be looked after, I saw that neither her fear nor my discomfort had subsided.

She was a victim, but I seemed the only one able to believe it. She had been forced to the ground and held there as dogs hold bitches, her whole life possibly ruined to satisfy a drunken caprice, a fit of madness, a 'poor fellow's mistake'. A woman alone after dark must expect to be molested, they had told me, and I could not accept it. He mistook her for a prostitute, the doctor had said, considering this sufficient justification. I could not accept that either.

'My dear, the girl probably knew him and led him on,' murmured Mrs Rawnsley, who had been something of a 'tease' in her younger days.

'If it should come to the worst,' Mrs Sheldon told me in her sweet and serious manner, 'I may be able to arrange for the adoption of the child.'

'She will not feel the disgrace as we should,' Miss Tighe insisted stoutly. 'They have their own morality, these girls, you know, and a mishap of this nature can make little difference. She will find somebody ready to marry her, I expect – especially if you should feel called upon to make her a decent wedding present – and all will be forgiven.'

932

'Lord! What does it matter?' said Venetia. 'She's only a woman, and what's a woman for, after all?'

But Sally had done nothing wrong. A crime had been committed against her by a man for whom these ladies, with their talk of 'leading on', the eternal, discreetly whispered 'My dear, men are made that way' seemed ready to supply with excuses. 'It is always the woman who suffers', they said, finding this state of affairs if not precisely desirable then at least quite natural. And of all my acquaintance only Liam Adair seemed able to comprehend my indignation.

'Aye, these women are the very devil,' he told me cheerfully, 'especially when it comes to tearing another woman to pieces. Fear, I reckon, in this case, because some of them dread it happening to them and some of them are plain terrified they might like it. So if they can blame the girl it makes them feel safer and better. Grace – I know there are men who do these things, but we're not all the same. Come now, you don't really think I'd force my attentions on some poor helpless soul, do you?'

'Oh, you wouldn't have to, Liam. With your famous charm how could it ever be necessary? Quite the other way round, sometimes, I'd say'

But, just the same, the spectre of male violence clung to me, giving me a wariness of the men I knew, an unwillingness to take my coachman's muscular arm when he came to assist me at the carriage-step, a positive discomfort in the presence of Gideon Chard, for although he was a gentleman to his fingertips, fastidious in his tastes and his manners, I knew that in the most private areas of his life he did not need the refinement of affection. And from there it was an easy step to ask myself what remained of affection in the few early morning encounters that had become my own marriage? Why did I submit to it? To what degree of compulsion was I myself subjected? Or was I in fact playing the prostitute to secure my way of life, to keep the peace, in simple obedience to the way society – but not my nature – had fashioned me? I was not certain, but the next time Gervase touched me my body could not endure the insult and turned rigid with disgust.

'I beg your pardon,' he said coldly, and although I had probably given him the excuse he needed, I had salvaged some minute part of my self-esteem.

It was not merely Sally but her mother who haunted me, and I was grateful to Liam Adair for including in his paper an article on the brutalizing effects of poverty and constant childbearing, describing as if it had happened to himself, my interview with that apathetic and defeated mother of seventeen.

'You did well by me there, Grace,' he told me, 'for she'd never have talked so freely to a man. Why don't you pay the *Star* a visit one of these days and see how it's done?'

And perhaps my own need for diversion and my even more pressing need to divert Venetia inclined me to accept.

'What does it matter?' she still sometimes enquired, but increasingly her phrase would be 'I don't care whether it matters or not', or even

933

more positively than that, 'I don't give a damn. Yes – I mean a *damn*'. And no doubt it was to provoke Gideon, to see how far she could go, that, on her way back from Galton with Gervase a week or so later, she stopped on the outskirts of town to attend – of all things – a cock-fight.

It had been very nearly criminal of Gervase to take her there. I knew it and could not defend him, for, impropriety apart, she had been in real danger among such rough company. I was shocked and furious, yet just the same profoundly grateful that he was not in the house the following evening when Gideon strode into the drawing-room and spat out the one word 'Why?'

I had never seen him so angry, had never felt such a boiling of wrath in any man, but Venetia, instead of shrivelling in the heat of it, jumped to her feet and flew at once to the attack.

'To see how men pass their time – to see what pleases them.'

'Have you any idea who saw you there?'

'Oh I don't care about that, although I know *you* care. And whoever saw me must have been there himself, so what does it signify? If *he* could be there, why shouldn't I? Have you ever been there yourself, Gideon?'

'Yes,' he said. 'Oh yes, I've been cock-fighting many a time, Venetia, with the whores and the thieves – the rabble – yes.'

'And did you enjoy it, Gideon?'

'I may have done – once. What's more to the point is did you enjoy it, Venetia?'

'I hated it,' she shrieked at him, her control snapping. 'It was cruel and degrading and disgusting. I loathed it and I loathed *them* for enjoying it – even Gervase. It was foul. But don't take that to mean I won't go again – or that I won't do something else men do, just to find out why they do it, and why they tell me I must not. That is – if I feel inclined. You follow your inclinations, don't you, Gideon, so why should I not follow mine?'

If she had planned to take his breath away I think she had succeeded, for he seemed momentarily unable to speak, an incoherence which, had he not quickly mastered it, would probably have led him to strike her. And watching as she swayed a little towards him, her pointed face trying hard to be insolent, I saw that she wanted him to strike her and thought – perhaps – that it might be a good thing if he did. But what he gave her was not the hot flaring of anger which must have contained some spice of emotion, but his silence, his back turned towards her in a gesture of cool and fastidious dismissal. A bitter thing for them both.

We visited Liam Adair the morning after, Venetia and I, my coachman showing serious displeasure when I gave him the address of the *Star*, not, I imagine, out of any consideration for me but because it was not a neighbourhood in which he cared to venture his horses. And so from the start it was an adventure, the broad paved thoroughfares we knew giving way first to warehouses and old, half-used mills sagging listlessly by the canal bank, and then to the dingy row of lodging-houses, alehouses and cheap shops that was Gower Street.

The lower windows of the *Star* were still boarded over following Liam's dispute with the baking trade, there being no sense, he thought, in replacing the glass when he would surely offend somebody else ere long, and had we not glimpsed his printing presses on our way upstairs I suppose we could have been in the office of some small and slightly shady lawyer, a vast quantity of papers, documents, odds and ends, covering the surface of two battered desks, spilling from half-open drawers and spread in haphazard piles all over the floor; an air of comfortable confusion, a smell of cigar smoke, beer from the pot-house next door, dung from the street, and gas.

'How very thrilling!' said Venetia, meaning it, needing quite badly to be thrilled, so that I glanced sharply at Liam, who had once been in love with her and who would surely not be unmoved today by her straight, fine-boned little body in its sheath of amber silk, her upturned face vivid with curiosity. Liam would have married her in place of Gideon. I wished he had. But her father had chosen otherwise, and catching my eye – reading my thought – Liam nodded to me as if in agreement, then shrugged and smiled.

'Aye, so thrilling in fact that when the landlord comes knocking at the door I'm obliged to pass the hat round to pay the rent.'

'Oh Liam, I fear you'll never get rich.'

'Why should he wish to?' enquired a voice from the corner of the room, a head which had been bent – decidedly 'at work' – since the movement of our arrival looking up now to reveal a dark, by no means handsome face, thin and intense, and at first acquaintance without humour.

'Why not?' Venetia said, startled, having taken the man for a clerk, a menial, and being clearly taken off guard to hear an accent as pure and privileged as Gideon's.

'Because we are not in the business of getting rich, Mrs Chard. We are in the business of giving information or education or such assistance as we can – of giving. Naturally there is no money in that.

'Lord!' she said, rippling – as I had not seen her do for a long time – with laughter. 'And just who are you? A saint?'

'He's Robin Ashby,' Liam said easily. 'My assistant – my conscience. He doesn't believe in money.'

He stood up, revealing an angular, slightly awkward body, and we shook hands, telling each other we were 'delighted' although he was clearly not pleased at this interruption to his work.

'I was at school with your husband, Mrs Chard,' he said coldly. 'No, he will not remember me, although I believe he is acquainted with my cousin, Lord Macclesworth.'

'Good heavens!' said Venetia, as we drove home, having spent the rest of our visit dutifully examining Liam's presses. 'Lord Macclesworth's cousin, and did you see his threadbare coat and the state of his shirt collar? And his bones all sticking through as if he had not eaten for a week? He may not believe in money, but Liam should still pay him.'

'He is probably the kind who gives it all away.'

'Yes,' she said, still laughing. 'And he is as ugly as a monkey too, poor thing.'

935

Gideon, when applied to at dinner that evening, did not at first recall the name. 'Ashby? Don't ask me – Yes, just a minute, there *was* an Ashby – the *Wiltshire* Ashbys. Good family but if he's the one I'm thinking of, I can't recommend him. He was expelled from school, and it strikes me they locked him up later on for debt or libel or breach of the peace, or some damned political thing. No, I'm not keen to renew acquaintance. Nor, I imagine, is he.'

We of course returned to the *Star*, my own interest claimed by the greater reality I found there than in Miss Mandelbaum's genteel petitions for the voting rights of middle-class spinsters; Venetia because she had discovered a new game in the baiting of Robin Ashby, a game she did not always play with kindness and did not always win.

Dressed in her elaborate and costly best, a diamond on her hand, emeralds swinging in her ears, a feathered and beribboned hat perching among her curls, she amused herself by flaunting a deliberate and quite false extravagance.

'Come now, Robin Ashby, since you don't believe in money, what else is there to believe in?'

'Freedom, Mrs Chard.'

'Nonsense. No one is free. *You* are not free.'

'As free as possible. I own nothing. I have a coat and a change of linen, a few other necessaries which will easily fit into a small bag. Nothing detains me – anywhere.'

'Yes, and that sounds very grand, but you are one of the *Wiltshire* Ashbys – Mr Ashby – my husband has told me so. It is easy to preach poverty when you have all that prestige and wealth behind you.'

'I have no expectations from the Ashbys, Mrs Chard. I long since cut myself adrift from all that.

'You can't be sure. Supposing they called your bluff and left you a fortune?'

'Then I should make the best possible use of it.'

'You mean you'd give it away?'

He nodded and, suddenly disgusted with him, she rapped her parasol smartly against his desk.

'What nonsense! What you really mean is that you don't want the responsibility. Is it true you were in prison once?'

'Yes,' he said as calmly as if she had aked him the time of day.

'And I suppose you are proud of it?'

'No.'

'Well then, I expect you enjoyed it – because you thought it made a martyr of you.'

'There was nothing about it to enjoy.'

It had, of course, been a political matter, an inflammatory speech which had caused a riot in a cathedral town, six months of acute discomfort for Robin Ashby, who had suffered not only from degradation but from attacks of bronchitis and a severe fever which had nearly killed him.

'Serves him right,' said Venetia when Liam explained this to us. 'Insufferable creature that he is. Lord! Why do I talk to him?'

But talk to him she did, of freedom which she insisted to be impossible, of equality of opportunity which aroused her derision, of social justice which she declared to be a fool's dream, all these discussions taking place beneath the watchful eyes of Liam Adair and myself, who could see no threat in this shabby revolutionary, our idea of a crusader – and we both knew Venetia was ready for a crusade – being someone tall and bold and handsome like Liam himself.

'What an idiot he is – what a child!'

But when I decided to give a ball at the start of the winter and wondered if Robin Ashby should be invited, she flew at me in a quick burst of temper, caused not by her unreadiness to see him at Tarn Edge but by the embarrassment my invitation might cause him.

'Grace, have you no tact? You must know that he can have no evening clothes.'

'Well, he is a Wiltshire Ashby and will know where such things may be obtained.'

'*Grace*, he is not striking attitudes, you know. He means what he says. And why should we ask him to waste his time borrowing evening clothes, which would not fit, I daresay?'

But nevertheless he was an acquaintance, and a gentleman. He should, I decided, be given the opportunity to refuse. But the next time we visited the *Star*, Venetia, marching ahead of me, walked straight up to him and burst out: 'Grace is having the dithers because she wants to invite you to her dance.'

'And you do not.'

'No. I don't.'

For a fleeting moment there was something beneath the studious intensity of his face, his habitual concentration on the task in hand, which could have been hurt.

'Well then, since you do not wish to see me in your home, Mrs Chard, there is no more to be said.'

'Yes,' she told him, her face drained of its mischievous sparkle, looking very small beneath her dashing, high-brimmed hat. 'You would not like my home, Robin Ashby. I think you would find it rather a poor place.'

I had chosen to give a ball for no better reason than that the ballroom at Tarn Edge had not been used for its proper purpose for years. The time seemed opportune, for Blanche, who had produced her second son the year before with the same gracious ease as his brother, was at Listonby for the season, the Goldsmiths were once again in our area, staying with cousins in Manchester who would be delighted to cross the Pennines. And since the Goldsmiths *were* coming, since the affair was not to be confined to our local industrialists and our local squires, it crossed Gideon's mind that a certain Monsieur Fauconnier of Lyons and a Mr Ricardo of New York were both in London with their wives and might appreciate an opportunity to travel north.

'In fact,' he said, coming into my breakfast parlour one morning and handing me a list of names and precise directions as to where their

937

owners might be located, 'you might care to consider these. Merely suggestions, of course, but if one is to give a ball one may as well make the most of it.'

And I understood at a glance that his 'suggestions' would involve me, not merely in a larger and more formal dance than I had intended, but in a considerable house-party, since the Fauconniers and the Ricardos, the Goldsmiths, the Brisbane Matthewsons and the Auckland Faringdons, could not be asked to stay at the Station Hotel.

There would be bedrooms which had not been used for years not merely to be 'got ready' but to be made inviting, accommodation for foreign maidservants and foreign manners, trains to be met, gallons of hot water available at any hour of the day, the transformation of my home, for a day or so, into a luxurious, well-managed hotel.

It was a feat which Aunt Caroline had reglarly performed for twenty-five years at Listonby, which she continued to perform at South Erin and at her elegant house in Mayfair. For me it was a challenge flung down by Gideon, and for his own good purposes, to which I eagerly responded, planning the whole affair, as Venetia said, like a military operation, immersing myself for days on end in railway timetables, dinner menus, breakfast menus, place settings, supplying Mrs Winch with lists of everything I expected to find in each guest-bedroom when I came to inspect, lists of the dinner services I wish to be used, of the lace and damask table-linen I wished to be got ready, lists of who must be sent to meet which train and of the type of refreshment I wished to find awaiting each guest on arrival.

There would be a dinner-party before the dance, a shoot the following morning at Listonby for those who cared to sample the English sporting life, a tour of the Barforth mills for those who did not. There would be a house-party from Listonby – a small matter Gideon mentioned to me in passing – containing a few 'politicals', no one *frightfully* important, of course, or so Gideon said, but one or two of them better placed than they might seem. And in view of Sir Dominic's budding career at Westminster, Gideon supposed I would have a quiet room ready with some decent brandy and a few good cigars in case anyone should want to have a quiet word.

'Yes, of course, Gideon.'

'Good – and a card table or two, since these fellows don't usually dance. And by the way, I hear the Fauconnier son and daughter-in-law may be in London on the seventeenth. Would it be too much to write and extend a friendly hand?'

I wrote. Fauconnier *fils* accepted my verbal handshake gladly, assuring me that the journey north would in no way tire his very delicate wife. I ordered another room to be prepared, then two rooms when Gideon happened to mention that the young Madame Fauconnier's nerves were too fragile to permit the sharing of a bed.

'She drinks goat's milk too, for some reason,' he said, and I went off at once to make arrangements for a goat.

I worked hard and long, to the exclusion of everything else. I got up at

938

dawn with Madame Fauconnier's invalid diet in my head and sank exhausted into bed long past midnight with the violins I had hired from Manchester singing in my ears And when the evening came, when the house was filled with light and fragrance and music, when the chrysanthemums I had pillaged from every available greenhouse were massed in my hall and on every step of my stairs, when my supper-table groaned wih every kind of roasted fowl and game, with two dozen different kinds of savoury tart and two dozen different kinds of sweet, with ices and sorbets, soufflés and creams; when my champagne was chilled, my musicians in their places, my dinner guests mingling happily together and my ball guests eagerly arriving *then* I became as taut as any fine-strung violin and would have been glad to send them all away again.

But such poor spirits could not last as I began to feel that the evening would be a success. There were partners in plenty for those who wished to dance, comfortable chairs for all who wished to sit, a convenient back staircase where a young lady could escape her chaperone. There was conversation for the serious, gossip for the frivolous, cards and fine wines, acquaintances to be made. There was Blanche, in gleaming blond satin, royal secrets and scandals whispering in the hem of her gown, and the Duchess of South Erin setting herself – on Gideon's behalf – to fascinate both Mr Goldsmith and Mr Ricardo. There was Sir Dominic, who paid me the compliment of treating my home as if it belonged to him, looking worthy of a seat in any man's Cabinet. And if Mr Disraeli himself was not present, there were among the Listonby party one or two who knew him well, somewhat to the disgust of the Sheldons, Rawnsleys, Fieldings and Mandelbaums, who were Gladstonians to a man.

I even remember the dress I wore, a fine apricot silk cut straight and tight with almost no bustle, draped at the back of my knees with lace frills and falling into a fluted train. I was bare-shouldered, my hair dressed very high, not by Sally, who, finding she was not pregnant, had left my service, but by a French maid aunt Faith had lent me. I had seed pearls and apricot silk roses in my hair, pearl ear-rings, the diamond ring Gervase had given me four years ago and the sapphire my father had given me the previous Christmas. I thought I looked composed, not beautiful like Blanche nor striking like Venetia, but elegant enough to be interesting, forceful enough to be noticed in a crowd.

I remember Venetia in a green gown so vivid, cut so tight and so low that Gideon had raised a sardonic eyebrow at the sight of it; a guest as always in her own house and a very gay one that night, dancing, laughing, chattering, flirting, not with the younger Fauconnier, which might have served a purpose, but with a young lieutenant of Hussars, a young clergyman, the young squire of Winterton Park who was known to be just a step away from bankruptcy.

I remember her well. But most of all I remember Gervase and the exact moment when our relationship, which had been shredding away from me like mist for so long, finally evaporated, was dispersed as mist can be dispersed by a sudden wind, blown away, and gone.

He was not very much on my mind that evening, for I had a multitude of names, faces, last-minute details to remember, so many introductions to make, so many conversations which looked like flagging to bring to life again, so many wallflowers for whom partners must be found, so many tours of inspection to check that all was well, that no one would have cause, tomorrow, to feel neglected. And I remember – quite distinctly – my start of surprise when I saw Gervase in the supper room, not because he was with Diana Flood but because he was still in the house at all.

They were not touching, nor even standing very close together. They were not flirting, not even talking very much. And it was their stillness and the stillness they had created around them which struck me the first warning blow, for had I been a stranger entering the room I would have known, instinctively, that I must not speak to them, must not disturb them, must make no sound that might spoil their deep and blissful concentration on one another.

They did not notice me. But I saw her bold face grow timid, her eyes cast down, Gervase's eyes turning almost transparent with feeling as they had done long ago when he had cast his puzzled, despairing glances at me. I walked quickly away, upstairs, opened the first door I came to and sat in the dark until I could stop trembling, sickened and shocked with the certainty that what I had seen was no sexual caprice, no London socialite easing her boredom, no provincial actress earning her fee, but the giving and the acceptance of love.

How long he had been in love with her I didn't know. Nor could I tell how long it would last. But he loved her now, I was sure of it, and I was just coherent enough to be surprised that the pain should be so deep-rooted and so terrible. His promiscuity had been bearable – just – because it had been faceless and because I had grown accustomed to it. But Diana Flood's face was engraved on my mind, and how was I to accustom myself to that?

But one does not sit in a darkened room and shake when there is work that must be done, a house full of curious, not always kindly, eyes and plenty of spiteful tongues. One does not give way to private sorrow when one's services are urgently required by others. A woman worth her salt – thank God! – gets on her feet and, having invited these guests in the first place, attends to their needs. She tidies her hair, walks down the stairs and smiles, and should anyone question the state of her health or her heart she answers 'Very well', which is as much as anyone really desires to know. And when it was over and the carriages were already rolling away, the house-guests preparing for bed, I stood on the terrace, the empty ballroom behind me, the thin light of a winter morning already in the sky, unable to release the hurt I had clenched so tight, unable – for the rest of my life it seemed – to shed a tear.

Silence; in which to think of failure, of sterility. Silence; in which to contemplate the futility of all my efforts, the petty little tasks which I had welded together into a life. Silence; in which to confront myself with solitude. And then, very suddenly, Venetia apearing beside me, perhaps looking for silence too, one ear-ring missing, I noticed, and, incredibly, a cigar in her hand.

'Ah, yes,'she said, holding it aloft with a flourish. 'You might well stare, for everyone else did so. I have won fame tonight, Grace, as the first woman in Cullingford to smoke a cigar.'

'Have you really?'

And she was too deep in her own disillusion to see that I did not care.

'Yes, really. Here on the terrace with a dozen people watching – with Gideon watching.'

'Whatever for?'

'For freedom, Grace – because I remembered a remark someone made to me about the petty restrictions with which women are shackled. Why – this person wanted to know – is it improper for a woman to smoke when all the men we know do so? Why?'

'I haven't a notion.'

'Neither have I. Just a petty, futile shackle, I thought, and I decided to break it.'

'And did you?'

'Of course not,'she said, 'of course not. Oh yes, I smoked a cigar all right and had a fine time shocking a few old ladies. A fine time – like the cursing and the cock-fighting – and what's the good of it? I'll tell you what I've achieved. I've made myself sick – that's all – like *they knew* I would – like Gideon *said* I would.'

She threw the cigar down into the garden and went away, my voice too weary to say good-night, my head too weary even to turn and watch her go. Yet there were things still to be done, lamps and candles to be seen to, a final check that no gentleman – or no footman – had fallen asleep in some unlikely corner with a cigar burning in his hand. There were things to be done. practical things, necessary things, safe things that would not shun me or hurt me. And crossing the ballroom and turning down the corridor beyond it, I saw Gideon at the smoking-room door, doing my work for me.

He had been, all evening, a careful but unobtrusive host, for he was not the owner of this house and he had borne that very much in mind. But he had been *there*, ready to step into any conversational breach, had danced a great deal and taken at least a dozen happy women, one by one, to supper. He had known – as I had known – the exact atmosphere of every grouping, had removed very adroitly a certain gentleman from the vicinity of a certain lady and introduced her to another gentleman whose attentions had proved more welcome. He had watched – as I had watched – had seen what was required and had supplied it. And now, being as full of brandy and champagne as anyone, he was still watchful, had remembered as his mother always remembered – that servants, if left to their own devices, will put off until morning the many things which he, and I, wished to be done tonight.

I had a word to say to Mrs Winch about the arrangements for breakfast. Gideon wished to be assured that Chillingworth knew exactly who to call at what hour in the morning, and their eventual destinations. We settled everything to our liking and then, finding ourselves in the smoking-room, he drew up a chair close to the fire, handed me into it, poured out two glasses of brandy and held one out to me.

'You will rest better for this – for I believe you have gone beyond sleep.'

'I believe I have.'

'Then shall we drink to your success? It has been splendid, Grace.'

'Thank you, Gideon.'

'It is I who should thank you.'

'Oh, no –'

Yet no one else had thanked me, no one else had cared whether I gave a ball or not. And now they had all gone off, happily or otherwise, to their beds, leaving me with the remains – and Gideon.

'I am so glad,' I said hesitantly, for, after all, I had not done it for him, 'so glad you enjoyed it –'

He raised his glass to me and smiled, his teeth flashing very white in his dark face, a wolf's smile I had often thought, although it seemed gentle enough now. 'I did. And you did not. But a hostess never enjoys her own dances – at least so my mother tells me. She always took a brandy or two with my father – in the old days – when all was over.'

Aunt Caroline? I had not thought her so human. And imagining her now, kicking off her shoes as I longed to do, holding out her glass to her husband, asking him 'Matthew, did it go well?'; imagining him reassuring her – as Gideon had just reassured me – 'It has been splendid, Caroline', I realized that this was his fantasy of how a marriage should be.

I had not believed him capable of fantasy. Now I recognized it, entered into it, for it had been my fantasy too, and in order to break the silence which was settling around us – dangerous because, astonishingly, it was so comfortable – I said quickly, 'I hardly knew your father.'

'Oh, he was a fine fellow. I suppose of the three of us Noel is the one most like him. I believe he and my mother did very well together.'

Aunt Caroline? And once again I saw her through the fatigue and the brandy in my head, smiling at her Matthew as he refilled her glass.

'Come, darling, drink up – you have earned this.'

'Oh Matthew, did you see? – did you notice? – heavens! I nearly died laughing when –'

'Yes, I saw it all.'

The fantasy beckoned to me again and, blinking, I pushed it away, swallowed the last drop of the spirit and set down my glass.

'I am very tired now, Gideon.'

'Yes, so you should be. Grace, would you accept a gift from me?'

'Why on earth should you wish to –?'

'To show my appreciation of all you have done. You have worked like a slave these past weeks, and although it was not on my account I have certainly benefited from it. It would please me enormously if you would take this. It is nothing of value –'

It was, in fact, quite beautiful, a bracelet of fine chains, each one a different shade of gold, coiled together into a delicate, intricate web sprinkled here and there with tiny amethysts. And it was exactly right. Not valuable enough for a husband to question it – and I did not really have a husband in any case – but so very tasteful, so different, that

942

whenever I wore it some woman would exclaim 'My dear, how exquisite. Where *did* you get it?' And every time that question was asked – had he been my lover – I would indulge myself by remembering.

He was not my lover. But he *could* be my lover. In this huge house, where we were thrown so much together, it would be possible – had he thought of that, did he want it? Had he understood – or had I – that the distance between us could be so easily crossed, should we ever wish to cross it? The thought struck out at me, held me for a moment in a kind of fascination, appalled me, and then – blessedly – became ridiculous, for this was Gideon Chard, the materialist, the opportunist, the fortune-hunter, who would not risk his share of the Barforth inheritance for a folly such as this.

'Gideon – how exquisite!'

'I felt sure you would like it.'

Perhaps his father had always made his mother a gift on these occasions. In my fantasy it would have been so.

We walked together up the broad, richly carpeted stairs and then went our separate ways with a brief good-night. It was almost morning, and my bedroom seemed very muted and very cool, the winter sky behind the curtains letting in a pale grey light, Gervase lying on his back, his eyes closed, although I knew he was not asleep. I got in carefully beside him, leaving a chilly space between us, and lay there for a while watching the daybreak, listening to his shallow breathing, sensing his misery. What could I say to him? Nothing. How could I approach him? I could not. How could I bear it? I *would* bear it. I felt myself stiffen, a tremor starting somewhere inside me, a movement of distress, and then, breathing deeply, slowly, the rigidity of my body eased again. I had things to do. Work – that was how I would bear it. I had guests all day tomorrow, a luncheon, a dinner, a tour of the mills, a dozen farewells at the station. I would survive.

15

Gideon went abroad the following spring on a tour of Barforth interests in Germany, Austria, Italy, Belgium and France, in search of the personal contacts which the state of trade and his own instincts required, winning golden opinions, we heard, as a shrewd man of business and a gentleman, a combination very pleasing to Europe's commercial élite.

Venetia had not wished to accompany him. I do not think he had wished to take her. But – perhaps at her father's insistence – she set off in low spirits and returned with a great many new clothes and an air of dejection which did not augur well. They had been to Paris, to Rome, Vienna, Brussels, a dozen other famous cities. She had seen nothing, she said, but over-furnished drawing-rooms, grand hotels, expensive, identical women who were married to pompous men. She had seen nothing *real*, nothing particularly foreign, just Cullingford with a

943

different accent, and worse than Cullingford, since she had not once been allowed out alone.

She had been bored to death, she told me, tolerated only as Gideon's wife and even then not always gladly.

'Oh, they all adore Gideon,' she said. 'He could have his pick of those foreign women and probably does. In fact I know he does. Well, good luck to him, for what difference can it make to me?'

She meant what she said. She had been grateful to him once but it had not escaped her notice that he had done very well for himself out of her folly, that he was successful and fulfilled, that he enjoyed his life, while she remained a frustrated, often desolate woman who had paid dearly for those two nights in Charles Heron's arms. The price was becoming too high and she had reached a point where she felt she owed Gideon no more gratitude and very little loyalty.

She spent the first days after her return at home doing her hair and changing her clothes, and when she did go out it was not to the *Star* but tamely to Fieldhead to take tea with Mrs Agbrigg, to Elderleigh to visit Aunt Faith, to Miss Mandelbaum's where, after listening in moody silence as Miss Tighe explained the progress of the women's cause, she suddenly and very crisply announced, 'You will not get your vote, Miss Tighe.'

'I beg your pardon, Mrs Chard.'

'You will not get it, and I will tell you why. What notice do you imagine they take at Westminster of these genteel petitions of yours? None, you may be sure, expect to smile and shake their wise heads and say "These dear ladies are at their tricks again". You have no power, Miss Tighe, to make them pay heed to you. They know you hold your meetings here, around your tea-table, all nice and polite and proper, and what have they to fear from that? Some enterprising young politician may make a speech in your favour now and again to get himself noticed or to make his name as a "progressive", but once they *have* taken notice of him – once Mr Gladstone or Mr Disraeli takes him up – he will turn his mind to more profitable issues than yours. He will just put your petitions away and forget about them, and why not, since you have all the time in the world to write him another? No one who has privileges wishes to share them – I am not clever but that much I *am* certain about. The Duke of Wellington didn't want my grandfather to have a vote back in 1832. My grandfather didn't want his foreman or his shed manager to have it when their turn came in 1867. The shed managers don't want the agricultural labourers or the men who live in lodging-houses to have it now. And there are no more than a handful of men anywhere in the world who really want to give the vote to a woman. And if you did get it, Miss Tighe, then you certainly wouldn't want to share it with me. I should have to go around with a banner crying out "Votes for *Married* Women. Give us the same rights as widows and spinsters". And unless I can *demand* those rights – unless I have a weapon – then I won't get them.'

'Oh dear!' said Miss Mandelbaum, and I have wondered if either she or Miss Tighe were ever aware that Venetia's sentiments were a direct quotation from Robin Ashby's latest contribution to the *Star*.

I don't now when she first saw him again nor how often they met thereafter, only that they did meet, for whenever she encountered him at the *Star* offices or elsewhere it often seemed to me that they were continuing, not starting, their conversation. Yet I said nothing, felt no particular alarm, did not in any case feel competent – having failed so abysmally myself – to advise her.

I believe I respected Robin Ashby in the sense that he was sincere in his aims and realistic about their chances of success. He was a clever, very separate man, compassionate towards the suffering masses but impatient of individuals and hard on himself, who would surely regard the intense personal commitment Venetia craved for as a burden, to be shunned like the property and possessions which in his youth had weighed him down. He might fall in love with causes, I thought, but hardly with a woman.

'I make no claims on anyone,' he said, and surely that was the same as saying 'I allow no one to make claims on me.'

She was not enraptured by him as she had been by Charles Heron. Whatever existed between them caused her no outward joy, tending rather to sharpen her tongue and blacken her humour, making her touchy and unusually unkind.

'Grace, you amaze me – you used not to value yourself so low.'

'I beg your pardon?'

'Oh, you know very well what I mean. Will you be content forever, just being polite?'

'I manage very well, Venetia.'

'Lord! so you do. And you have your dignity, of course. I suppose you can warm yourself on that.'

The Chards came early to Listonby that year, arriving for the August grouse, Dominic and Gideon spending long hours together charting their political and financial future, while Noel escorted Blanche on her country house calls, his face, which was a paler, better-tempered version of Dominic's, lit by her presence, indulgent of her whims and fancies, and a little amused by them but careful of her, *enjoying* her, his attitude not so much one of desire but of cherishing. He loved her, there was no doubt about it, everyone knew it and accepted it and found it quite delightful, taking their lead from her husband, who saw it as downright useful, particularly now that his Parliamentary duties were proving so greedy of his time.

The Listonby estate had always been large, the generosity of Aunt Caroline's father, Sir Joel Barforth, had increased it, and a property of this size required a capable and conscientious man at its head. Tenants were apt to encroach on manorial privileges when the squire was so often away; gamekeepers tended to rear birds for sale to city shopkeepers instead of preserving them for the guns of the squire's guests. There had been a shortage of grouse on Listonby Moor for the last two seasons; farmers had been shooting foxes, to the great annoyance of the Lawdale

Hunt; while stewards, as everyone knew, were expert at falsifying accounts. Dominic, whose tastes and ambitions never left a penny to spare, believed he was being cheated, Gideon was too busy and a shade too grand these days to make a good second-in-command, and there was a move afoot that year to persuade Noel, whose military career had not greatly prospered, to resign his commission and take charge of affairs at home, a scheme enthusiastically endorsed by Blanche.

'Noel is so devoted to the land,' she told us – and him – repeatedly 'The tenants adore him, and is it any wonder, for he has patience with them, as Dominic does not.'

And one afternoon when she had refused, with a lovely drooping air of sadness, to listen when Noel mentioned that his regiment seemed likely to be posted abroad, and had then sent him off on some errand of her own, Venetia leaned towards her and said, very loud and clear, 'Do you know something, Blanche? I wish with all my heart that Noel would rape you.'

'My dear,' Blanche replied in her best Marlborough House manner, 'I am sorry to disappoint you, but he never will.'

'Of course he will not, the poor devil. So why don't you do the *decent* thing, Blanche – the honest thing – and give yourself?'

'Because – Venetia dear,' she said, smiling very serenely, 'it is simply not necessary.'

Venetia left us soon afterwards, having arranged – or so she said – to see her mother at Galton, and calmly pouring out more tea Blanche asked me thoughtfully, 'Grace – is she having an affair?'

'I don't know. Are you having an affair?'

'With Noel? My dear, as I said just now, it is really not necessary.'

'And if it became necessary?'

'Then I suppose one would have to think again. But about Venetia – if she should be having an affair, I do hope she will manage to conduct it – well – *suitably*. There is really no need for her to set the world on fire. Fortunately both you and I understand that.'

So we did, for the Chards were very often apart, Blanche in London, Dominic on some political country-house visit. He went to Newmarket and she to Cowes, he holidayed *en garçon* each winter in Scotland, every summer in Baden, separations which encouraged his casual infidelities, her long basking in Noel's devotion. Their marriage retained a sound financial, legal and social base. She had given him two sons and they had done their duty by each other. Indeed, they considered themselves to be very definitely married, even though in real terms they did not live together.

And since Blanche neither expected nor wanted her husband to be faithful, she was not surprised by the conduct of mine, which could be no secret to her. Clearly, like herself, I had chosen the path of discretion, of compromise, the turning of a blind eye, which she considered a small price to pay for domestic harmony. She had her compensations in plenty; so, presumably, had I. And she seemed very glad – for my sake – to welcome me to this charmed circle of the worldly-wise.

I had my dignity, as Venetia had pointed out to me, and I had Tarn Edge. I had also a great fear of the future, which I managed more often than not to suppress to a bearable proportion. But the constant need for self-discipline often made me appear distant and cold, so that the younger maids were nervous in my presence, the menservants sullen. I became sharp-spoken and sharp-eyed, and having picked a quarrel with Miss Tighe and found it enjoyable, I went on, spasmodically, to quarrel with everyone except Gervase.

We said nothing to each other now beyond the bare civilities, knowing, I suppose,that if we began to talk it would have to be of Diana Flood. And since she had a conventional husband, he a virtuous wife, what could usefully be said? Major Compton Flood might tolerate a discreet flirtation, but he would not take kindly to an affair so intense, so passionate as to transform his wife's face with wonder whenever my husband entered the room. He would not sit idly by discussing the state of the nation and of the weather while my husband's eyes fastened themselves upon her, transparent in their desire and their longing. Care would be needed, for Major Compton Flood would know the way, and certainly had the right, to grievously punish an erring wife. And care was taken. Gervase went out with the Lawdale throughout the winter, but he came home often enough to put an end to any rumours that he and I were living apart, lying beside me sleepless and taut with misery; sick, I suppose, at the thought of his mistress in her husband's arms and the knowledge that his initial lack of judgement in preferring me to her had placed her there.

He was suffering, and although I was not saintly enough to pity him, I was well able to understand. He could have married her and had not done so. She could have been his, but his volatile emotions had played an atrocious trick on him, had convinced him that he needed an entirely different kind of woman, and he had let her go. Now, after straying through that wilderness of haphazard sensuality, he had fallen in love with her as desperately as he had once loved me, seeing in her the salvation I too had represented. And she belonged to Compton Flood. He was wretched, could neither eat nor sleep nor sit still for five minutes together, so that, having watched him prowl the confines of Tarn Edge like a caged animal, it was a relief to me when he rode away again.

He went to the mill too, more often than I had expected, partly to avoid trouble with his father, partly to be seen there so that Major Flood might be aware of no tell-tale changes in his way of life. But he did little more than hang about the mill-yard, seizing upon any excuse to break free, and I believe it was his father's acceptance of this turn of events which caused me finally to lose heart.

Mr Nicholas Barforth, once again, had given up on his son. For a time he had hoped that marriage might bring about a change for the better, and would anchor him to the industrial side of his inheritance. But that hope had failed. And recognizing that he had set me an impossible task, my father-in-law did not blame me for that failure, choosing instead to make my life as comfortable as he could. After all, I could have made the

947

house hideous with jealous scenes, could have lost my health and my nerves and publicly washed a whole laundry-room of soiled Barforth linen. Instead, I was mindful of my dignity and my duty – for what else is left to a failed wife but that? – and in gratitude Mr Nicholas Barforth restrained his temper when Gervase was present and refrained from questioning me as to his whereabouts when he was not. I was a good girl. There was no scandal. And, as for the rest, we would just have to wait and see.

It was not the life I desired. A year and a half ago I would not have believed myself capable of bearing it. I bore it – just – at some times better than others and was infinitely relieved when my father-in-law, perhaps to ease my strain, sent Gervase abroad that summer.

I went – of all places – to Galton on the afternoon of his departure and lay on the summer grass, exhausted, greedy for rest, and spent ten days eating the new bread and the herb dumplings my mother-in-law set before me, sleeping in the sun and in the great bed where I had lost my child. I was an invalid again who could only be healed by quietness, by lying down – until he came home again – that sorry burden of pretence. And when I had energy enough to walk the leafy borders of the stream with Mrs Barforth and her dogs, she talked to me about her brother, Peregrine Clevedon, of their happy childhood in the days when her world had been shielded by the Abbey stream, and by her love for this brown, stony land. But for most of the time we walked silently in the warm air, listening to the rippling of the water, a drowsy bee in the clover, birdsong, the busy life of the summer hedgerows and trees, two women who had failed at the great career of marriage – the *only* career – yet being obliged to remain bound within it, had no choice but to adapt themselves, in their different ways, to that captivity.

She would have told me all I burned to know about Gervase. Would he force me, as her husband had forced her, to spend the rest of my life observing the conventions, safeguarding my reputation, conducting myself in such a manner that people would not talk about me and so *could* not talk about Diana Flood? Or might he lose his nerve one day, and his head, and throw her reputation and mine to the winds in a desperate bid for happiness? But I asked no questions, being too weary to grapple with the answers, while she, understanding my need for repose, told me no tales.

Oddly enough it was at Galton that I heard of Robin Ashby's imminent departure from Cullingford, Liam Adair riding over on purpose to tell me.

'Cullingford's not grim enough for him,' he said, making light of it, although I knew he was uneasy. 'He's going north to have a look at the Scottish mining villages. Somebody told him they still use women in the pits up there instead of ponies and he's off to put a stop to it.'

'Did he resign, Liam, or did you discharge him?'

'Now why ever should I do a thing like that? He'll work all hours God sends, high days and holidays – it's all the same to him. And he's clever. And cheap, too. Why should I want him to go?'

'Have you told Venetia?'

'I imagine he may have done that himself. Grace, it's the truth, you know, that I don't *want* him to go. But that's not to say it's a bad thing that he goes – if you see what I mean?'

I went home a day early but found Venetia perfectly composed.

'Have you heard about Robin Ashby?' she said. 'Not that I ever expected him to stay in Cullingford. He could be comfortable here, you see, and that would never do. So he's going to work in a Scottish coalmine just to see how long it takes him to choke on the dust. Then he'll write about it and after that, who knows? I expect he'll be off to India to find himself a bed of nails.'

We went to the *Star* the next morning to say goodbye and drink his health in Liam's champagne, Venetia once again in her extravagant feathered hat with its emerald buckle, a frilled parasol in her hand, a great deal of gold and emerald jewellery about her neck and wrists, marking her as the wife of a successful man.

'Goodbye, Robin Ashby,' she said brusquely, 'and good luck – unless you should be crushed to death in a rock fall, or choke – or starve –'

'Or be hanged.'

'Yes – there's always that. I didn't like to mention it.'

And I understood not only that they had been lovers, but that I had actually known it for a long time.

He left an hour later on the Leeds train and she came home dry-eyed to dress for a dinner-party her husband had asked me to arrange.

'I'm going to London in the morning,' Gideon said, 'and if it turns out that I have to bring Bordoni of Bordoni and McKinlon back with me, Grace, can you cope?'

He departed, returned, Mr Bordoni being joined by a Mr Chene, the one a most gregarious gentleman, the other something of a gourmet, both of them requiring to be lavishly entertained. I entertained them, aware, as I asked the questions they expected and made the answers they wished to hear, of Venetia watching me, her expression no longer indulgent or friendly as it had always been with me, but one of cool mockery, her pointed face, for the first time in her life, hard.

Messrs Bordoni and Chene, after effusively kissing my hand, went away; and a morning or two later, at breakfast, Gideon looked up from his correspondence and said: 'Damnation! I shall have to go down to Sheffield on the first train. And Grace, it looks very much as if I shall have to bring my trip to New York forward by a week or two. In fact next Friday would suit me, if you could have them get my things ready by then? And Venetia had better come with me. From the tone of this letter I think the Ricardos are expecting it.'

'Yes, Gideon,' Venetia said, getting up from the table, and it seems to me that, in a manner of speaking, we never saw her again.

There was no elopement this time, no note hidden in the folds of a ball gown, no ecstasy. She walked calmly upstairs, packed a small bag, ordered the carriage to take her to the station and – while I was busying myself about the arrangements for her journey to New York – got on the train for Leeds. A dozen people saw her on the platform at Cullingford, half of them saw her walking towards the ticket office in Leeds and idly wondered why Mrs Gideon Chard should be travelling alone, without even a maid. But she had the reputation of an unsteady woman – Cullingford being unable to forget that sensational cigar – and no one questioned her, although the booking-clerk did remember afterwards that he had sold her a ticket to Glasgow.

'I'll get up there by the next train,' said Liam Adair, who had been called in by me before the final pieces of the puzzle became clear.But Mr Nicholas Barforth shook his head.

'You'll do no such thing. It's not your place, Liam, nor mine, to fetch her back. That's her husband's privilege and his alone, if he chooses to take it. I'll be in my study, Grace, when Gideon gets back from Sheffield. I expect you'll be glad to send him straight in to me.'

I sat in the drawing-room alone and utterly appalled as I had done on the night they had rescued her from Charles Heron, the double doors open so that I could not miss Gideon's arrival and expose him to the risk of servants' gossip. The day had been fine, but hearing the patter of rain on the window, sharp and cold as summer rain can be, I shuddered, thinking of rain in the far north, remembering the watchfulness and the scorn in Venetia's face this last week or so, and grieving because in the end she had turned against me. She had gone at the last because there had been nothing in this house nor in her life here that she valued. She had rejected us all, and I knew how cruelly I would miss her.

Gideon came, received my message with raised eyebrows, went into the study and remained there a long time – an hour and a half, I think – before I heard his steps once again in the hall and his voice curtly informing Chillingworth that he required his carriage.

'Will you be dining, sir?'

'I will not.'

'Very good, sir.'

I got up and walked very carefully down the corridor and, tapping on the door, giving him time to compose himself should he require it, went inside, finding my father-in-law as I suppose I had expected him, sitting at his desk, cigar in hand, the butts of several others beside him, two glasses on a silver tray, the traditional comforts men offer themselves in times of stress.

'Ah, Grace – yes – you had better sit down.'

'Thank you.'

And, his movements a little heavier than usual, he stubbed out his cigar and lit another, refilled his glass and drank, reflectively and very deep.

'Well, Grace – you are entitled to know. What can I tell you?'

'Has Gideon gone after her?'

'No.'

'But he will be going?'

'No, he will not.'

'Then you will go – surely?'

'No, Grace.'

'*Father-in-law*.'

He inhaled, narrowed his eyes against the smoke, closed them briefly as if the light hurt him, and shook his head.

'For what purpose, Grace?'

'To see that she is safe – at least that.'

'I doubt if she would welcome the intrusion. And there are a great many mining villages in Scotland, Grace. How could I find the right one?'

'If you wanted to find it, you could.'

He sighed, contemplated for what seemed an uncomfortable time the drift of cigar smoke, and then once again shook his head.

'You are remembering the episode of Charles Heron, Grace. I was her legal guardian then. Her husband is her guardian now. The decision is his. I intend to respect that decision and so will you. That is an order, my dear daughter-in-law – and believe me, it is the very least you can do for him.'

'For Gideon?'

'Yes, for Gideon,' and with the force of a whiplash his hand came smashing down on the table. 'Damnation, Grace, what excuses can you find for her? I could find none. He has every right in the world to call her a whore, every right – and not a clever one either, by God, but an idiot, a lunatic. And what man in his right mind would be willing to live with a mad whore? Yes, Grace, she may *want* to come home some day, for she has gone off with another lunatic, it seems, who will not look after her, and I think we can safely take it that she cannot look after herself. When that day comes I might have a few hundred pounds a year to spare for her – I might – but what I cannot and will not do is ask her husband to live with her again. Grace, in his position – the position she has put him in – I would not live with her. And let me make it very clear that for as long as Gideon remains under this roof – and I see no reason at all why he should not remain here – I expect him to be shown every consideration by you and by everybody else – *everybody*, Grace. I think you will understand me. And now, if you will excuse me, I have a call to pay on my wife.'

Nothing could have persuaded me to stay in that empty house, and had there been no carriage available I would have walked down the hill to the town and found my own way to Gower Street. But the victoria, as always, was at my disposal, Liam Adair looking rather as if he had been waiting for me, his hat in his hand, a travelling bad standing ready by the door.

'Liam, you are going to Glasgow after all, aren't you?'

'I am that. I don't work for Nick Barforth these days and if I decide to go north, then it's no business of his.'

'They don't want her back, Liam.'

'Did you expect they would?'

I paused, frowned. 'Yes, I thought Gideon might *need* to.'

'Why? To stay at Barforths? By God, Grace, but you're an innocent.' And sitting down rather heavily he too reached for a cigar.

951

'He doesn't need to do anything now, Grace, that he hasn't a mind for. He's got Nick Barforth exactly where he wants him, which only goes to prove, my girl, that they're two of a kind, since nobody else has ever been able to put one over on old Nick. But now Venetia – God love her – has played right into Gideon's hands. He runs no risk now of being cut out of the business. How could Uncle Nick ever do that to him when he's the injured party, when Nick's daughter has given him such a raw deal? And if Gideon goes on playing his cards aright – as he will – he could even get Mr Barforth to offer him something fairly substantial as an inducement to stay. You'd do well to warn your father to keep his eyes open, because if he *does* decide to pay Gideon some sort of compensation, it could be something that he'd have to take away from Gervase.'

'*What* compensation?'

'I know what I'd ask for. A limited liability company – Nicholas Barforth and Company Limited in the modern fashion instead of a private firm belonging to Nicholas Barforth Esquire. Mr Barforth as chairman, of course, with a majority shareholding. Gideon Chard as managing director with a share or two. Gervase Barforth with a seat on the board and equal shares with Gideon, of course, a least to start with – I expect your father would make sure of that. But I can't see Gervase putting up with it for long. He'd sell out and go off to Galton, I suppose, which may not suit you, Grace. And if Gideon wants that company – which is the same as getting himself officially recognized as heir apparent – now's the time to make a push. If I can see that, then so can Gideon.'

But Gervase, I thought with a cold, shuddering sensation at the pit of my stomach, would probaby go to Galton in any case. I was in danger of losing nothing that I could still call mine; and I had not come here to talk about myself.

'Will she be all right, Liam?' And it was this that I wanted to know.

'With Robin? Christ! I shouldn't think so. It depends what she's hoping for.'

'Did he even ask her to go with him?'

He smiled, remembering Robin Ashby, in spite of himself, with affection.

'No, no, that wouldn't be his way. He believes too much in freedom to make a request like that. She probably found him packing his bag one day and when he'd told her all about the Scottish miners he'd casually wonder if she might care to come and see for herself. And if not, then no hard feelings.'

'Dear God, Liam – does he even love her?'

'Do you know, Grace, I can't think of one single reason why he shouldn't.'

'And you knew?'

'Of course I knew. And if there was anything I could have done about it, then I'd be glad to hear of it – short of telling her husband – and even that crossed my mind. I expected it to run its course I reckon I didn't realize she was so near the end of her tether. Well, she's gone on her crusade now. God help her – God bless her!'

'Liam, tell me the plain truth. What chance does she really have of any kind of happiness?'

He glanced at his watch again, took his coat from a peg behind the door, thinking carefully, trying perhaps, to rid himself of the hope that he might find her already disillusioned and willing, at last, to accept a compromise; to let Liam Adair love her since no one else would. But the memory of Venetia herself forced him to be honest.

'Just what was she leaving?' he said. 'It may seem a lot to most people, but it was nothing to her because she didn't want it. She was sick of her life and of her husband long before Robin came. No – she won't regret anything she's left behind. And yes – he does love her. Yes – he is sincere in his aims. It's quite true that if he went home to Wiltshire they might not kill the fatted calf, but they'd give him a decent allowance so as not to be embarrassed by that threadbare coat. He won't take their money because he doesn't need it. I don't think he'd take it if Venetia needed it. He might not even notice she was in need. Money is excess baggage to him. It clouds his vision and makes it harder for him to see the truth. He's not a religious man – he calls that excess baggage too – but that bit about it being easier for a camel to pass through the eye of a needle than a rich man to enter the Kingdom of Heaven – that reminds me of him. He believes in that. I don't know what happens to men like him when they get old. Perhaps they never do.'

I shivered, badly feeling the cold.

'Do you know where he is?'

'No. He didn't tell me and I didn't ask. I'll just go up there, in the general direction, and let it be known who I'm looking for, since a pair like that won't be anonymous. And if I make it worthwhile, somebody will let me know. If that's your carriage down there you'll be wanting to take me to the station.'

We walked downstairs together, his large warm hand under my elbow, and drove in silence to the cobbled station yard.

'If you see her, will you tell her that I – that I am still the same – that she can rely on me – for whatever –'

'Aye – if I see her.'

And this sudden wavering of his confidence caused me such evident alarm that he put an arm around my shoulders in a companionable hug and kept it there, despite the astonishment of our stationmaster.

'All right, Grace, let's look on the black side. I reckon the worst that could happen is that I don't find her at all.'

And looking down the track at the panting approach of the train, he smiled into the far distance and sighed.

'Aye, that's the worst.'

'And the best?'

'Well – I reckon the best we can hope for is to find her living like a coalminer's wife. And I doubt either one of you can even imagine a kind of life like that.'

16

My father appeared at Tarn Edge the following day and for several days thereafter, was instantly admitted to Mr Barforth's study, to be joined at various intervals by Gideon, by the Barforth and Agbrigg lawyers, by Sir Dominic and the Duke of South Erin; by the males of the family gathered together in judgement upon one of our women to condemn her sins and to reapportion her wealth.

Gervase came home, furious, hurt and spoiling for a fight, grieving for the loss of his sister yet unable to suppress a pang of malicious pleasure at seeing Gideon in the sorry position of a deceived husband. But the confrontation Gervase attempted to provoke was prevented by his father, by that solemn conclave of family lawyers and by the dignity with which Gideon seemed determined to conduct himself, Gervase's belligerence giving way in an abrupt swing of mood to a contemptuous rejection of the proceedings and all who took part in them.

'To hell with it!' he said, slamming the study door behind him and very nearly pushing me aside when I tried to intercept him. 'They're carving it all up very nicely in there. But don't worry, Grace. You've got your father to make sure they don't carve you up, too. And as for Venetia, I believe she's better off where she is.'

I sat in the drawing-room again, not alone this time but with the other women who had strong interests in the negotiations taking place, with Aunt Caroline who insisted that Gideon's position must now be clarified, with Mrs Agbrigg who did not intend to allow the Barforths to swallow Fieldhead, with Blanche who, to my everlasting gratitude and slight surprise, was obviously saddened and alarmed for Venetia. Even my mother-in-law, who was so rarely seen in that house, kept vigil with us, looking, one supposed, for an opportunity of freeing Galton and herself from Barforth control, she and Aunt Caroline facing each other like a pair of spitting cats when, after several hours of polite whispering and several dozen cups of tea, the Duchess could no longer contain her indignation.

'It is my son who is the victim, Georgiana. And it is your daughter who has wantonly betrayed him.'

'I suppose that is one way to look at it, Caroline. But it might also be said that your son had driven her away.'

Opposing points of view which would never be reconciled, although they both did agree wholeheartedly that something must be done about it. In Aunt Caroline's view, Mr Nicholas Barforth, her brother, must now make a legal and binding statement of his intentions with regard to Gideon's future. In the natural course of events Gideon had expected to inherit one half of Mr Barforth's assets and holdings, but that inheritance had depended on his marriage to Venetia. Mr Barforth's existing will, Aunt Caroline believed, covered the possibility of Venetia's death, but no provision had been made for her adultery. God alone knew what might happen to her now, and those family lawyers must stir themselves and devise some scheme which would make it impossible, no matter what the circumstances, for Robin Ashby to touch a penny that might even loosely be called Venetia's. In fact Mr Barforth, however painful, must in his new will strike out the name of 'Venetia' altogether and substitute 'Gideon'.

'Really?' said Mrs Georgiana Barforth, for although she genuinely wished for no more than her widow's portion when her husband came to die, she was ready to do battle for her daughter. 'Are you not being a little premature in your judgement, Caroline? It may seem unlikely at the moment, and *you* may not consider it even desirable, but it is surely not impossible that they might be reconciled. And before we cast my daughter once and for all into the pit, may I remind you of your Christian charity? I am not religious myself but I have seen you on your knees many a time, Caroline Chard, in the church at Listonby. And with all your preaching of morality and decency, it seems a pity you have not learned anything at all about compassion.'

'I have never liked you, Georgiana Clevedon,' said Aunt Caroline, her eyes blazing, to which my mother-in-law responded by tossing an aristocratic, auburn head.

'I shall lose no sleep over your opinions, Caroline, for I must tell you that when you married my cousin Matthew Chard you were so gauche and your views so narrow and middle-class that you provided amusement for the entire county. I suppose you entertain London just as thoroughly now that you have started to play the duchess.'

I believe they could have come to blows had not Mrs Agbrigg inserted her persuasive, velvet voice between them, Blanche being far too amused by the possibility of their combat to intervene, while I quite simply did not care a rap. And when their grudging truce had been declared and I had sent yet again for more tea, it was not long before the study door opened and those sober, dignified gentlemen emerged to inform us of our various fates.

Mr Barforth, certainly, had been subject to a great deal of pressure, but he was accustomed to that and I think all the Chards had really achieved was to hurry him a little in the direction he had already decided to go. There was to be a limited liability company, the previously separate mills of Lawcroft Fold, Low Cross, and Nethercoats being welded together and given the commercial identity of Nicholas Barforth and Company Limited. Mr Barforth, naturally, would hold the position of chairman and a hefty eighty per cent of the shares, while Gideon and Gervase would each occupy a seat on his board and divide the remaining twenty per cent shareholding between them, a concession which in itself made them independently wealthy men. But Mr Barforth, for the time being – and he did not specify how long that time might be – would serve as his own managing director, and furthermore would retain the immensely profitable Law Valley Woolcombers and the Law Valley Dyers and Finishers as his own. And when this had been settled, not entirely to Chard satisfaction but a step at least in the way Gideon had determined to take, they turned their attention to Venetia.

Perhaps – I am not certain of this – but perhaps Mr Barforth did not want to change his will, being accustomed to the fact of a married woman's property passing automatically to her husband who, when all was said and done, remained Gideon Chard whether she was sharing his roof or not. But it was pointed out to him by the lawyer representing the Chards that there was a growing inclination in the land for legal reform, that it might one day be possible for a married woman to inherit no matter what vast fortune in her own right, to administer it, spend it, give it or fritter it away without so much as asking leave of the poor husband, who would have no claim on it whatsoever. And when he had digested the implications of this, when heads had been shaken and they had all wondered at the state of a world where such things might come to pass – while Gideon stood silent, I suppose, looking if not disinterested then certainly not greedy – Mr Barforth gave a curt nod.

'See to it, then.'

And for the purposes of his last will and testament Venetia was no more. The bulk of his fortune – after due provision had been made for his wife – was to be safeguarded for his son and his son-in-law, while if his daughter was to be mentioned at all – and he made no promises either way about that – it would be in some codicil among the bequests made to his staff.

Aunt Caroline was jubilant. My mother-in-law asked for her hat and gloves and went away, although her distress over Venetia must have been to some extent offset by the new independence of Gervase.

'There'll be no profit to anybody in talking to me about this matter again,' said my father-in-law and went out to dinner with Gideon at the Station Hotel, to discuss, in a more congenial atmosphere, the details of Gideon's trip to New York.

And there began a sad, slow year, a wasteland in my memory. There was gossip, of course, but no information was ever forthcoming, and Cullingford was obliged to content itself with the bare and eventually boring fact that Venetia Barforth – Mrs Gideon Chard – was no longer in residence at Tarn Edge. But where she was, and with whom, Cullingford could not say. Probably she had absconded with a man, but there again it was possible she had lost her flighty wits and been expensively confined somewhere, out of harm's way. How dreadful, they said, for her husband. But the romantic aura which settled on Gideon for a while was soon dispelled when he made it abundantly clear that he did not welcome sympathy. He went to America as planned, then to Germany and France, spent long days at the mills and two or three nights a week away from home, finding consolation, one supposed, in approved bachelor fashion, since no one expected him to live celibate.

I kept the house and waited, one day following another, faceless, lacking colour and flavour. Waited for something to crack the thin but nevertheless restricting ice which had overgrown my capacity to feel. Waited for something to move me nearer or further away from Gervase. Waited most of all for news of Venetia. I wanted to hear that she was well and happy, that her decision had been right for her. I wanted to hear she had not been mistaken in herself, that Robin Ashby was truly the kindred spirit she had always craved, that his values really were hers, that this was indeed her crusade.

Our lives went on. I heard that Liam Adair had involved himself romantically with a widowed lady who might make a substantial investment in the *Star*, unless of course she should discover that he was equally involved with her niece, also widowed but ten years younger, who shared her home and had no money at all.

I heard, with a polite smile, that Colonel Compton Flood had gone with his regiment and his wife to India, and responded with the same smile – having gone far beyond hope – when I was told some months later that Mrs Flood, unable to support the heat, had returned to Cullingford Manor. Her husband would join her in six months, a year. How very interesting, I said and was appalled to realize how little I could manage to care that she had come back to Gervase.

My waiting ended the following autumn on a day of high wind, a hurrying amber sky, when Liam came at last to see me, having just got off the train he said, hungry and thirsty – yes, muffins and gingerbread and hot, strong tea would go down a treat – his manner as jaunty as ever, his eyes tired.

'Have you an hour to spare for me, Grace?'

'Of course.'

'Then ask them to bring a fresh pot of tea and tell them you're not at home. There's no chance of Gideon walking in, I suppose – or old Nick?'

'They're out of town, both of them. Is it Venetia?'

'It is.'

And my whole body turned cold, so badly did I want her to be well, so completely did I doubt it.

I waited just a little longer until he drank his fourth cup of scalding tea and ate several quick slices of gingerbread, as if his hunger had been with him all day, all night in the train and he had only now become aware of it.

'Grace, can you get away for a day or two?'

'Yes.'

'Without anybody knowing?'

'I could say I was going to Scarborough to my grandmother. Where will I be going?'

'Glasgow. And one way or another you've got to bring her back with you.'

I heard the story little by little, first, as he sat still swallowing that scalding tea, the things he knew, the framework of facts with the substance left out; then, as we boarded the northern train, the things he had guessed, the conclusions he had drawn, the things he wanted to believe and the things he could not avoid believing.

He had first found her ten months ago, standing in a cottage doorway, thin and pale but with a kind of taut resolution about her that had reminded him of a young knight undergoing the exhausting but ecstatic process of initiation. She had been neither glad nor sorry to see him, had treated him politely but with her mind very obviously elsewhere, her interest in him entirely without depth, as if they had been twenty years apart and now discovered themselves to be strangers. His visit, he believed, had seemed irrelevant to her. He wondered if she would bother to mention it to Robin, or even remember it herself. She was living in a small mining town, in a rough community where violence was commonplace, yet she had smiled when he had asked her to promise that she would contact him in case of need. And having promised, she had smiled again, waiting politely for him to leave, so distant and somehow so pure that he had not dared to offer her the twenty guineas he had brought with him but had sent the money on to her later, and had never learned what she had done with it.

She had been, not happy exactly – not in the sense he understood it – but exalted, yes, that was the word – *exalted*. And although he wrote her several letters in the following months, he had received no answer, her silence confirming his impression that she was in need of nothing he could give.

But her situation had altered. She had called him and he had gone to her, not quite at once, since there were other demands on his time, but within the week, at the address she had given in Glasgow.

'Well, you'll see for yourself, Grace. It's a bad place, but that's not the worst of it. I reckon I was prepared for that.'

The facts then – the points of which Liam was certain – were these. She had joined Robin Ashby in that pit-head cottage and had remained there until the local coal-baron, who was also their landlord, had discovered Robin's intentions, branded him a troublemaker and made it impossible for him to get work anywhere in the district. They had moved first to Glasgow, then Newcastle, Liverpool, back to Glasgow again, living by his itinerant journalism, which meant very meagrely, Liam thought. Shortly after their return to Glasgow, Robin had met a man – another thin, intense, exalted individual like himself – who had spent some time among the sweatshops in the East End of London where poor immigrants were herded into the tailoring trade like cattle, fifteen or twenty to a steamy, insanitary room, and forced to labour for considerably longer hours than the law allowed. Factory inspectors, this man alleged, could rarely gain admittance to these 'sweaters' dens' – in fact the reforms for which men like Robin and himself had fought so hard were not being carried out. It was the spark of another crusade.

By morning Robin Ashby had already made up his mind to travel south and no doubt expected Venetia to go with him. But he believed a woman should be an independent individual, entitled to think and decide for herself, not merely a possession who must automatically follow her man. They were comrades, partners, together because they wished to be together, not because the law or the Church or some intricate financial settlement insisted they should. And so – overestimating her strength or believing her to be as strong as she wished to be, overlooking the biological and social conditioning which had created her weakness – he asked her if she was ready for this new venture. She replied that, on the

958

contrary, she had decided to return to her husband. And when he left, a few days later, she did not tell him that she was expecting his child.

I had never entered a common lodging-house before, but imagination had prepared me for the smell of damp and vermin, the peeling walls, the fouled staircase where those who had not even the price of a bed in such a place as this would huddle for warmth on winter nights. But at least – as Liam informed me – there were worse places, kennels not fit for dogs, where one did not rent a room but a *place* on a straw mattress thrown down on bare boards with a dozen others, men and women all together. And it was not until I had picked my way through the filth and litter of those stairs and entered a narrow, foetid corridor, that he said gruffly, 'You'll find her much changed. Some women bloom in pregnancy, others don't. As I say, you'll find her – different.'

She had asked him to bring me, and after a moment he left us alone together, Venetia sitting on the hard plank bed while I took the only chair. There was nothing else in the room but a low table, a high, uncurtained window, a cracked water jug, one small bag in the corner, and my own great astonishment at Venetia's calm. She was extremely thin, without any colour, her skin a dull chalk-white, her hair faded from its deep auburn to light brown, her dress, from which all the trimming had been removed, too big for her and not clean. She looked as I had sometimes felt, like a woman sitting an inch or two away from reality, no longer entirely in the world but conscious of its garishness and its clamour, too numb to feel pain but still able to recognize it; watching herself bleed, in fact, with a faint surprise, a certain cool pity.

Had she sent Robin away in a spirit of self-sacrifice? She shrugged her brittle shoulders and smiled. It may have seemed so to her at the time, but what else could she have done? Naturally, if he knew of her condition he would look after her, as he would care for anyone else he called comrade. She did not want that. Were she to write to him now and tell him the truth, then he would return, she knew. And if it became necessary, he would ask help from his family in Wiltshire and accept the terms on which they chose to give it. She knew that too, and refused to be the cause of his surrender.

They had never discussed the possibility of children. Neither Charles Heron nor Gideon had impregnated her and certainly Gideon had tried hard enough, she told me in her cool, toneless manner, since he had believed motherhood would steady her down. She had considered herself to be sterile. The mistake had been hers and now she must take the responsibility. She could not avoid becoming a mother. But she would not be the means of forcing Robin Ashby back into the conventional mould which had so nearly destroyed him. Her own female biology had trapped her. She would not allow it to trap him too. So she had thought to begin with, and for a little while she had felt herself to be quite heroic. But very soon she realized that there was no self-sacrifice – no heroics – involved at all. Her decision was the only possible one to take, which made it inevitable, easy, and absolutely right. 'What happens to such men when they get old?' Liam had asked of Robin Ashby and had answered his own question. 'Perhaps they never do.' And a man whose own future was so limited, so soon to be burned out, perhaps in its own fierce flame, could have no place in the future of a child.

She had never known freedom herself, merely an illusion of freedom in her younger days, and she accepted now that she never could be free. She was a woman, and as such could only escape from one captivity to another, not the least of these being her own unwelcome fertility. But she had desired freedom all her life, she desired it still, so intensely that she could not deny it to another. She had failed at everything else in her life but now – for the first and final time – she would succeed in this.

Yet there remained the question of the child, and she had had plenty of time these last few weeks to contemplate the helplessness of her situation. She was acquainted now with the raw facts of poverty and knew that the moment her condition became apparent she would be turned out of her lodgings and into the street to wander and to beg – there being no work she was fit to do – and then to give birth and lose her child among the faceless infant multitudes of a workhouse.

Her intentions were very clear. She had no hopes and no desires for herself. Her own mind was, strangely enough, peaceful. But nevertheless she *was* pregnant, her child – in this masculine world – might well be a girl and she had seen – oh yes, she had seen at close quarters, the drudgery, the squalor, the exploitation of a working woman's life. She had herself been bred as an ornament for a man's pleasure and the propagation of his name, and had suffered for it. She had been imprisoned by trivialities until she had felt unable to breathe. But in the pit villages she had met old women who had been harnessed to coal-carts in their youth like brute beasts and forced to crawl down black underground passages where no beasts could be made to go. She had seen for herself other old women of nineteen with four or five infants trailing at their skirts and nothing in their futures but the prospect of four or five more. She had met cheerful young harlots in Glasgow of twelve or thirteen years old, and then seen them again six months later, eaten alive by the harlot's disease. She had seen death by violence and by starvation, death by the desire for death which had caused a woman on the floor below to drown herself only last week, and, in the lodging-house before this, a girl – a child, in fact, no more than fourteen – to strangle her new born baby and then hang herself. And they had died partly from ignorance and poverty, mainly because they were women.

She had seen it. She knew. Women *were* weak, as everyone had always told her, not in their spirits but in these fertile, female bodies which continued year after year to give birth, and in these fertile, female emotions which caused them to love each unwanted child. Theirs was the crusade she had wanted to fight, but she was a woman too, her body draining itself to produce another life, and she believed the fight to be hopeless in any case. Once, a long time ago, she had wanted to have a child, had seen it as 'half me and half some wonderful man'. It was not so for the women of the pit villages and the workhouse hospitals, the mean streets of Cullingford, and she asked herself now what relevance such lofty ideals as the vote could have for them? What mattered was food and shelter, a blanket in winter, a few coppers to call a doctor to a difficult confinement and something put aside to pay for a funeral.

And if a woman must either be an idle ornament or a beast of burden, then she would rather condemn her own daughter to a life of frustration than of endless, brutalizing toil. I had money of my own, she knew, and Gervase did not interfere with my spending. Would I take the child when it was born and make the necessary arrangements? I could afford it, she said, raising her shoulders once again in a listless shrug, and if the child could be placed in some school, some establishment which would give it a measure of respectability, then she would be content. She had once scoffed at respectability, but she was tired now and she no longer scoffed at anything. She accepted her error. She had overstepped the limits of her femininity, of the role men like her father and Gideon had designed for women to play, and she knew now – had known for some time – that she could not win. *They* would always win – her father and Gideon, Charles Heron, the men who exploited women, the men who feared women, the men who desired women – and that being the case she wanted her daughter to be the kind of woman men desired, the kind of woman who did not threaten them and so did not require to be punished by them – a woman like Blanche.

She supposed I would be glad to help her and she would put herself entirely in my hands. She had discovered in herself these last few days a growing inability to concentrate, a buzzing in her ears and a loss of balance whenever she tried to fix her mind in positive thought.

I picked up her bag, wrapped her in a cloak, Liam paid what was owing to her landlady and together we took her to the station, both of us appalled by her weightlessness, her dreaminess, the way she drifted between us, passive and insubstantial as a curl of mist. I had no immediate plan beyond getting her to a warm, dry bed, a hot dinner, a doctor.

'Where?' said Liam, as we boarded the train for Leeds.

'I'll let you know.'

And we were nearing the end of our journey before I told him to take her, as a temporary measure, to her mother at Galton.

She went with him, willing, it seemed, to be taken anywhere, while I found my way back to Tarn Edge, changed my clothes and thought – as Venetia did not appear to have done – of next October and the October after that, when she would have had her child and recovered at least something of her spirits. She was in a state of grief and shock, I knew, overwhelmed by a sense of failure, exactly as she had been on her forlorn return from Charles Heron. But she had overcome that, and she would overcome now. Her child would be born, her body freed of its obligations. Life would still be there, stretching ahead of her, to be lived, endured, enjoyed, and any arrangements I made for her now must take account of that. She no longer believed in the future, had given up all her desires, but the future existed and I had no intention of allowing her to produce her child as a cow drops her calf and then go drifting off again to

961

certain disaster. I made up my mind that she must give birth to her baby in comfort, which was easy enough to contrive, but I was also determined that it would be no furtive, hole-in-the-corner confinement, no hurried whisking away of the child afterwards to some secret destination, never to be seen again.

She would love her child when she saw it, not because it was Robin Ashby's but because it was her own, and although I was not yet certain how to go about it, I was adamant that she and her baby would not only live together but would live in peace.

Left to himself, I did not think her father would stand in the way of anything I wished to do for her. My own father would support me. Aunt Faith would do her part. But Aunt Caroline would surely oppose the return of so disastrous a daughter-in-law, Sir Dominic would see no sense to it, now that Gideon had shown he could manage his affairs very profitably without her. And what might Gideon feel? But I could not think of Gideon in terms of feeling or sensation, could not even contemplate the possibility of his distress, preferring to regard him – certainly in this instance – as a survivor, a victor, an adversary. For he was Venetia's guardian and the decision would be his.

I ordered the victoria and drove to Nethercoats Mill, my carriage in the yard occasioning no comment, the clerk who showed me to Gideon's splendid, oak-panelled room being more concerned with the details of my dress – presumably in order to tell his wife – than with the nature of my business. I was, after all, the 'young squire's wife', and so I walked boldly through the double doors, drew off a glove and smiled with far more composure than I was actually feeling as I saw how much I had taken Gideon by surprise. For we had kept very separate from one another while Venetia had been away – very separate, elaborately polite – and I could not expect the next half-hour or so to be easy.

His vast, polished table was in excellent order, nothing in evidence upon it but an embossed silver cigar-box, a silver-banded inkstand, a sheet of expensive parchment elaborately stamped and sealed, a contract, no doubt, worth many thousands of pounds, which he now replaced neatly in its folder. The room was fragrant with beeswax and tobacco, good quality wood and good quality leather, his panelled walls bearing a heavily framed picture apiece, dark landscapes borrowed, I thought, from Listonby. There were several high-backed leather chairs, a smaller writing-table, a wine cupboard which I knew – since I had placed his order for him – contained the finest of old brandy and cut crystal.

'Good afternoon, Gideon,' I said, 'or is it a little later than that?' And as he came round his desk to draw up my chair and to ask me if I had had a good journey from – where was it I had been visiting? – I wondered, with a terrible inclination towards nervous laughter, how best I might tell him that I had been to Scotland and brought him home a pregnant wife.

But one way or another it had to be said. The fact that I was here at all proved the matter to be serious, and once he had resumed his own seat I began to tell him as concisely as I could all that had occurred, my voice taking on the passionless tones Venetia herself had used, my eyes fixed on a corner of the cigar-box and his hand close beside it, square-palmed and long-fingered, a scattering of black hairs disappearing inside an immaculate shirt-cuff, a beam of late sunshine slanting across his arm, glinting on his plain gold shirt-studs and the heavy gold ring with the Chard crest upon it.

I told him the 'facts' as Liam had told them to me, then I told him what I had observed and what conclusion I had drawn, watching his arm stiffen as I did so, the beam of sunlight moving slowly away from him so that the room seemed to darken. And when I had finished he said, 'How dare you come here and tell me this!', speaking not in anger, not in condemnation, but because he wanted to know.

'Someone else would have told you, Gideon.'

'Ah yes, I see. You are merely saving me from the curious and the malicious.'

'I am doing what I believe to be necessary – and right.'

He snapped open the lid of the cigar-box, let it fall shut again, tapped his fingers irritably on the desk-top and then rapped out at me, 'Quite so. And what am I to do about it, Grace? What "right" am I to believe in? Are you suggesting I should play the Christian gentleman and take her back?'

'I could not make that suggestion.'

'No,' he said, throwing back his head so that I could see the tight clenching of the jaw muscles, the long dark glitter of the eyes, the brows drawn together in a scowl, his whole face a mask of suppressed anger and disgust. 'No, I suppose you could not – not in words at any rate. But your attitude – your attitude, Grace, says it. And I ask you again how you dare?'

He got up, pushing back his chair, and stood at the window staring down at the mill-yard – the Barforth mill, the Barforth daughter – the line of his back still taut with anger, his fingers still tapping out their frustration against the window-sill, although gradually his wide shoulders seemed to haunch a little, the rhythm of his fingertips to assume a more measured pace.

'Very well, Grace,' he said, making a half-turn towards me but remaining by the window. 'What are you actually saying? Are you telling me that, since I married her in the first place to give my name to a child which never materialized – and for money – that now, when there *is* a child and I've made sure of the money, I should be willing to do the same? Is that it, Grace? If it is, then say so.'

It was. And recognizing the need, I said it, word for word as he had expressed it himself, looking straight at him – because it would have been cowardly to have done otherwise – but not really seeing him.

'I am extremely sorry, Gideon. I am not insensitive to your position. I know – believe me, I *do* know – how very dreadful it must seem. But –'

'But what? My position has its inconveniences, but on the whole I have done very well out of it? Is that what you think, Grace?'

'I have said I am sorry, Gideon. And I think it only right to tell you that whatever you decide – or whatever anyone else decides – I shall not desert her. If no one else will look after her, I will find a way to do so.'

'Should that surprise me? It does not. It is like you,' he said, returning slowly to his desk and sitting down again, his brows still drawn together in a frown, but of concentration this time, his defences, which had been shaken by anger, now altogether intact.

'Has she expressed a wish to return to me?'

'I don't think it has even crossed her mind – either to come back or that you might agree to take her. She is here only because I brought her. She would have gone anywhere she was told to go. She is really – very unwell, Gideon. All she wants is to have her baby in safety and she has given no thought at all to what comes after.'

'What seems strange to you about that? When did she ever make allowances for tomorrow morning? Have you spoken to her father?'

'No. But I am sure he would accept your decision – as he did when she went away.'

'My decision not to follow her, you mean – to let her go and be damned? Yes, he accepted it. But did he *like* it?'

'One assumes so.'

'Why? Because he formed a limited liability company as I'd been urging him to do for a long time? One should beware of assuming too much in one's dealings with Mr Nicholas Barforth, Grace. He did not give me the managing directorship which I felt I had earned and which I had been promised – merely a seat on the board, like Gervase. And the limited company does not include Law Valley Woolcombers, nor the dyeworks – both highly prosperous concerns over which I have no control whatsoever. Nor have I the faintest notion as to what his plans might be for their eventual disposal. So perhaps he was not altogether delighted by my readiness to let his daughter go. Perhaps he may have an Achilles' heel after all. Who would have thought it?'

I had nothing more to say. I had asked a man whose wife had left him because she disliked him to take her back now that she was pregnant by another man. What else could I say? He would make his own decision for his own reasons. I had simply placed the matter before him, and for the moment it was out of my hands. My bones were aching from the discomfort of the train, my stomach hollow and uneasy from scanty meals taken in dubious places. I was tired and from sheer weariness sank readily into the silence that fell between us, the sky darkening now towards evening, the mill-yard emptying and then filling again with shawl-clad figures as the night-shift came on; the screech of a hooter, doors banging, carts laden with wool-sacks grinding the cobbles, and Gideon Chard sitting at his desk, staring at his inkstand, his eyes unwavering in their concentration, thinking, planning, working it out.

'Thank you, Grace,' he said, startling me. 'I suppose you have been kind.'

'I can hardly think so.'

'Well, we will not argue about it. Let me see you to you carriage.'

I put on my gloves, allowed him to take my arm as we walked downstairs and across the yard, his manner courteous and unhurried, although his glance was keen, checking, perhaps automatically, that everything was as it should be, letting it be seen that he was not the 'young squire' like Gervase but the 'young master'.

964

'Take the top road,' he told my coachman, 'to avoid the wagons. And go steady. I shall not be home to dinner, Grace.'

'Are you going to Galton?'

And in the twilight, his smile seemed to flash at me, his skin very dark, his teeth very white, a hungry, healthy man whose humour took me by surprise.

'We'll see about that,' he said. 'I reckon I'd do well to have a word with my chairman and managing director – and our father-in-law – first of all. Well now, Grace – and wouldn't you?'

I returned to Tarn Edge and immersed myself gratefully in hot water, feeling bruised now in body and in spirit and totally unprepared for the slamming of my door, an hour later, as Gervase strode into my room. I had ordered a tray to be brought up to me, soup and bread and cheese, chocolate cake, a wholesome, almost nursery, supper which did not require me to move from my bedroom sofa; and neither his arrival nor his too obvious temper could be welcome.

'You have been very busy, have you not?' he almost spat at me. 'Yes, very busy – traipsing off to Scotland with Liam Adair and all the way back again with my sister – yes, *my* sister. I was at Galton this afternoon, which might have occurred to you had you given it any consideration. And what was I to feel when she arrived like that – with Liam?'

'I just hope you didn't make a fuss.'

'Christ! And if I did?'

'I just hope you didn't. She's been upset enough already.'

'She's my sister,' he said, coming to stand over me, his fury blanching and shaking him, my response to it being fierce and immediate since at last we had found a reason to abuse each other that had nothing to do with Diana Flood.

'She's my sister. Did you think of that? She's my sister and I have a right – damn it! – to help her.'

I jumped to my feet, dislodging the tray as I did so, its contents scattering with a mighty clatter, no thought now in my careful housewife's mind of coffee stains on my rose-pink carpet, the soup bowl upended, the crumbs.

'She's your sister,' I yelled at him 'and what does that mean? I'm your wife. That means nothing either. Just words – like company director, when you never direct anything. Like husband, when all you do is come home twice a week. Like brother, when – God dammit, Gervase Barforth, what help could she expect from you? Like son –'

'That's enough.'

'Like son, when you live like a parasite on your father's money and lie to your mother. Yes, lie to her, Gervase, to keep her on that wretched estate so you can take your whores into the cloister –'

'That *is* enough.'

'I'll decide that.'

'I don't give a damn what you decide, Grace,' he said, hating me. 'And as for my whores, it strikes me you've never cared overmuch about that, so long as it meant I was leaving *you* alone.'

It was enough then. Had I remained in that room I think I would have

965

tried to kill him. I believe he felt the same. I walked out on to the landing and down the stairs. 'Mrs Barforth,' my housekeeper said, intercepting me. 'What has happened to your dress?'

'An accident with the supper tray! Please see to it.'

And I walked past her and Chillingworth, not even acknowledging the discreet rapidity with which he opened the outer door for me, not caring what conclusion he might draw and I went out into the cold October air, and a blessed solitude.

17

It was not really Venetia who came back to us, but I had great faith in the healing processes of time, in letting nature take its course, and did not despair.

I had played no further part in her restoration to the family fold and had been acquainted with only a bare outline of how it had taken place. The gentlemen, in fact, had assumed control and I had been sent, as so often before, into the drawing-room to wait. Gideon had spoken to his father-in-law. Mr Barforth had then driven over to Galton and had returned very late that night. The following morning – a Sunday – he had called Gideon, and then Gervase, then Gideon once again, into his study where he had spoken to them at length, both separately and together. Mr Barforth had next made his second journey to Galton Abbey, and Gideon, an hour later, had set out to join him. Gervase rode off, one knew better than to ask where. Mr Barforth and Gideon returned for more discussions. Gideon rode off, not to Galton, I thought, but to Listonby to make his explanations to his mother, and a few minutes later my father-in-law sent for me.

'Grace – if you would see to the domestic arrangements. The room adjoining Gideon's might serve for the time being. And you might drop a hint to the servants that there's been a reconciliation in the offing these past three months and more, and they've been together a time or two to discuss it. You understand my meaning? Good girl – then you'll realize the importance of stressing that they have been *together* – secret meetings in hotels and the like, you'll know the score. She's been in the South of France, by the way, with my mother. People may not believe it, but if I say so, and you say so, and my mother says so, then I reckon it will suffice.'

Gideon came back looking grim, having endured a gruelling interview with Aunt Caroline, who had never liked Venetia in the first place and would certainly never abide her now. We had dinner, and soon afterwards Venetia arrived with her mother, drank her coffee in the drawing-room and went up to bed, her luggage having been delayed, I told my housekeeper, by the vagaries of Continental trains.

'What a nuisance!' said Mrs Winch, who did not believe a word of it. 'Might it not be wise to wash and press some of her old things, since really, with foreign travel, one never knows?'

966

'Please see to it, Mrs Winch.'

The separate room, a lovely bay-windowed apartment adjoining Gideon's dressing-room, I did not attempt to explain and was thankful, when Mrs Rawnsley and Miss Mandelbaum came to call, that if they had heard of it from their maids, who assuredly gossiped with ours, they would consider it a subject too delicate to mention. Nor did I try to conceal the fact that Venetia was a prodigal returned. Certainly – and in the strictest confidence – I was now ready to admit that she had absconded from her husband and her home. But Gideon had pursued her, which was exactly what one would have expected him to do, had shown himself masterful and persuasive, and now one must simply hope and pray for the best. The child – the result it was implied, of his persuasions – had certainly influenced her decision to return, but all the world knew that children held a couple together, and one could only look upon it as a blessing. And because this was a more romantic version, a better story, than the truth, it was gradually accepted, while even those who continued to insist that there had been a lover somewhere in the story were thinking of some Gallic or Latin charmer safely abandoned in the South of France, not of a pit village and Robin Ashby.

She was home again, and that was all I cared for, and when, a month later, her father resigned his position as managing director and appointed Gideon in his stead, there was no conclusion I wished to draw.

'You see,' said Venetia with her astonishing calm. 'I have been sold for silver once again – or is it gold? A great deal of it, I imagine.'

But there was no animosity in her voice and no humbleness either. She was not meek as she had been at the beginning of her marriage, nor grateful, nor anything else to which I could easily give a name. Neutral was the only word I found for her, the state of un-feeling which had enabled Sally Grimshaw's mother to accept her daughter's rape with a shrug. 'It happens.' Not apathy precisely, but an impenetrable resignation. 'It happens.' And she seemed to be quietly, rather sweetly amused by women like myself who still believed that there was something to be done about it.

I don't know how much conversation Gideon had with her, if any at all, but since I lived with a husband to whom I rarely addressed a word, I could not be astonished at that. He had won his directorship, she had won respectability for her child. For the time being that would amply suffice. No entertaining was done at Tarn Edge that winter, Gideon making use of the Station Hotel, Mr Barforth dining more often than not from a tray in his library. Christmas was bitter cold and almost friendless, Gervase at Galton, Gideon at Listonby, my father-in-law, as usual, at his mills, my father in Eastbourne with his wife. Only Blanche drove over to see us on Boxing Day, grieving a little because Noel, after all, had followed his regiment abroad to Africa of all places, where everyone knew the Boers, or the Zulus, or both, were spoiling for a fight. But one glance at Venetia's face caused her to forget both her sorrow and her curiosity as to whose child this actually was, a piece of information which not even Sir Dominic had been able to prise out of his brother.

967

'Venetia, you do not look well.'

'I suppose I do not. You look very splendid, Blanche.'

'I daresay. You will come to London, won't you, when this is over – you and Grace? It will take you out of yourself and will help me too, since I am worn out with worry for Noel – It is all right for him, having a fine time playing soldiers. He *knows* he is not wounded or dead. But I don't. And by the time I got a letter telling me he is not killed – well, heavens! by then he could be.'

But as I walked outside with her to her carriage, she said quickly, 'She's not well, is she? What beasts they are, all of them, Dominic saying straight out to Gideon that he hoped the Barforths had made it worth his while, and Gideon smirking and saying he wasn't complaining. And Aunt Caroline going on – and on – about how it had best be a girl, because a girl can be packed off with a dowry, whereas a boy would expect to inherit his fair share – and had he considered how best to protect the interests of his own children if he – and presumably Venetia – ever have any? And then I look at Venetia and it all seems so terrible. Oh dear! Noel would not have behaved like this. Would he, Grace? Noel would have been kind. Well, I shall just go and write to him and tell him never mind his regiment, he is needed at home.'

Venetia was not well. Her ankles, from the very early days, had swollen, her hands become so puffy that she could not wear her rings, and there had been recurring bouts of dizziness, a buzzing in her ears which increased her air of vagueness. Her abdomen became hugely distended, her arms and shoulders, her face, remaining very thin, so that instead of the bloom one often sees on expectant mothers, the whole of her health and strength, her substance, seemed to be draining away into that monstrous belly, and being absorbed by it.

By January she was too heavy and too uncertain of her balance to walk without difficulty and was forbidden to come unaided down the stairs. February sent her to bed and kept her there for three of its sleet-grey weeks, sleeping, waiting, smiling at the cradle with its spotted net draperies we had already placed in her room, and the minute garments of embroidered linen I had purchased ready-made in Leeds.

'I have never seen anyone so spent,' her mother told me, 'unless – dear God, I wish I had not thought of it! I have seen birds in cages like that, wild birds no longer trying to get out, which is the saddest of all. What did he do to her, Grace, to exhaust her so?'

'Nothing that he knew would harm her. I think he treated her as the kind of woman she wanted to be.'

'Are there such women?'

'I hope so. But Venetia is not one of them. I think it was understanding that, that broke her heart.'

She talked of course, sometimes a great deal but always of the distant past. She never spoke of Robin Ashby nor of Charles Heron but of herself as she had once been, that vivid, hopeful self she had believed in and to whom she now referred with affection and regret, sparkling madcap Venetia running from one Galton summer to another, completely

968

unaware of the limitations of her sex, her class, which her family would so soon impose upon her. It had taken her a long time to understand that she could never be an explorer, a doctor, a lawyer, an architect, a *participator*, could not even ride a horse astride. And when she was asked to contort her body into a side-saddle and a corset, she had responded with that lovely ripple of laughter, only half-believing that anything so ridiculous could be true.

'Lord! Do you remember the trouble they had lacing me into those stays – me flat on my face on the carpet and Mary-Jane with her foot in the small of my back pulling away at those laces until I let out my breath and they snapped clean away? And what was the point to it when I was as flat as a pancake in any case and my waist only measured eighteen inches? Nobody could tell whether I was wearing stays or not – except that "no respectale female every goes without them". Lord, how I laughed at that!'

But the tight-fronted bustle skirts had obliged her to wear her corsets like the rest of us; she had given up riding not, she insisted, because of the side-saddle but because her sympathies in the hunting-field were increasingly with the fox. And the days were gone when she could simply shin up one of the ancient oaks at Galton and lie for hours stretched out like a cat among the branches, savouring her laughter.

She came downstairs at the end of February and sat in the drawing-room, her body so grotesquely swollen that it seemed impossible she had still two more months to endure. I engaged a nursemaid and a wet nurse on the doctor's recommendation, kept the cradle and the baby-linen aired, sent notes almost daily to Aunt Faith, whose assistance now I would have greatly welcomed.

'Two months,' Venetia said. 'Lord! I shall be a mountain by then.'

But on the night of the fourteenth of March, her pains began, she was assisted by Mrs Winch, the nursemaid and myself to bed, the doctor, the husband, the mother, were all sent for, hot water was kept simmering at the ready, while I found myself brimming with a strange excitement, that feeling of childhood Christmas which can easily be accompanied by tears.

I had no real expectation of bearing a child myself. For a long time I had not wanted a child. Now – at this inopportune moment – I was consumed with the longing to hold my own child in my arms, to feel it tugging at my hand, needing me; and I was glad to be reminded that, for the time being, Venetia needed me more.

She was in labour the whole of that night, the next day and the night after. Not unusual, said the doctor, at a first confinement, although he conceded, when Mrs Barforth pressed him, that her pains were close together and clearly very sharp. There was really nothing to do but wait.

'My dear lady,' Dr Blackwood said, venerable and easy and infinitely reassuring. 'This is one little task which cannot be done without pain, you know.'

'Yes, Dr Blackwood, I do know – my memory retains this particular pain very well.'

'Then perhaps, Mrs Barforth, if we all remain very calm we will do her more good?'

Mrs Barforth and I sat beside her, giving her such encouragement as we could, but by the morning of the sixteenth her pains were so rapid and so severe that she could scarcely draw breath between them, her cheeks had sunken into dark hollows, there were black rings around her eyes, she was exhausted, barely conscious, and the doctor had called in a colleague, a younger man with a less compassionate, more businesslike manner.

'Perhaps if you would leave us alone for a while,' the new doctor said, and I went downstairs to confront the faces in the drawing-room, all of them – even Gideon's – showing evidence of lack of sleep, of strain, of the helplessness and the guilt men feel on such occasions.

'It is not going well, is it?' snapped Mr Barforth, as if he held me to blame for it.

'They're giving her something now. I don't know –'

'Giving her something?' he shouted. 'I should bloody well hope so! If this goes on much longer you can send that sanctimonious Blackwood down here to me, and I'll have something to give *him*.'

'There are other doctors,' said Gideon. 'My mother would know the best. I'll get over to Listonby.'

'I'll do it,' said Gervase, leaping to his feet like an arrow, his face chalk-white and desperate. 'You go to your mills, Gideon. Leave this to me.'

I do not intend to dwell on the agony of childbirth. One has either given birth oneself and knows, or one has not, in which case it is useless and presumptuous either to describe it or try to understand. She slept an hour or two that morning, whimpering in her drugged sleep, her face swallowed by black shadows, her nose standing out sharply against her hollowed cheeks, giving her head the appearance of a bird. And when her pains began again at noon with great violence and the child was still not born, the younger doctor declared that it had gone on long enough and that a forceps delivery should be tried; the old one decreed that nature was best left to go its own slow, sure way; and I had begun to be terrified.

I stood in the corridor outside her room, pressed against the wall while the two men of science expounded their theories to my mother-in-law.

'There is the danger of strain to the heart,' said the younger man. 'And, of course, one might also take the view that she has suffered enough.'

'Indeed,' Dr Blackwood replied, his manner as avuncular as ever. 'But forceps, my dear fellow – yes, we might spare the mother a little pain that way, but these instruments of yours have been known to damage the skull of a child, you cannot deny it – and it would be wrong to conceal the possibility from these good people – wrong indeed.'

'Do it,' said my mother-in-law.

But the younger man raised his shoulders in the direction of Dr Blackwood, whose case this was, while Dr Blackwood shook his head and smiled his 'favourite uncle's' smile.

'Dear lady, naturally you are moved by your daughter's agony, but she is young enough to bear it – in fact it is well known that these pains and the instinct of maternal devotion are most definitely bound together – most assuredly they go hand in hand. And neither your daughter nor her husband would thank us if any rash surgical intervention resulted in harm to her child. The child, madam. Above all, one must consider the child. Her husband may not care to take the risk of injuring what, after all, might well be his son and heir.'

'Do it!' shrieked Mrs Barforth.

'On whose authority?'

She turned, erect as a soldier on parade, and marched away down the corridor, returning some minutes after with her husband.

'You,' said Mr Barforth, indicating the young doctor with a jerk of his irate head. 'Get in there and do what you can. And you, Blackwood, go with him and *assist* – if he needs you.'

'The husband,' Dr Blackwood said smoothly, accustomed to childbed hysterics. 'It is my policy to consult the husband in such cases.'

'The husband,' thundered Mr Barforth, 'will do as I tell him – and so will you.'

They administered slow, blessed drops of chloroform, Mrs Barforth kneeling at the bedside to hold her daughter's hands. 'Darling,' she said, 'not long now – not long.' And I caught Venetia's face in my eyes and my mind as the nurse ushered me from the room, that bird-skull surrounded by a wild tangle of auburn hair darkened by sweat, her lips flecked and bitten, immersed in pain as an ember immersed in fire, nothing left of her nature, her individuality, her civilization, just a female body engrossed in its labour.

I pressed myself once more against the wall, closed my eyes and listened to the sounds of combat behind me, the footsteps, the haste, the sudden exclamations, the rapid instructions, a murmur of encouragement. And then, when I had stopped hoping for it, the thin wail of the new-born, releasing my tears, a whole floor of them running unchecked down my face in sheer thankfulness. I had lost track of time, could not have said with any certainty what day it was, much less the hour, but it was over. She could rest now, with her baby beside her in its spotted net cradle, could be pampered and spoiled, surrounded by sweets and flowers and gifts, as new mothers ought to be. And I was excited again, eager to tell her how clever she was and how brave, eager to say 'How beautiful! What a darling! What a treasure!' so that I forgot both my anxiety and my fatigue.

'It's a girl,' said Mrs Barforth, staggering in the doorway like an old woman. 'Go tell them.'

But as I moved forward, wanting to see – wanting to touch – she shouted: 'Grace – go and tell them,' her slight body barring my way until something called her back into the room and she slammed the door violently shut, excluding me.

But her wish to protect me, for such it was, was unnecessary, for I would not have dared to enter that room. There was some horror inside, I knew it, and my immediate instinct was not to intrude upon it – in no way to draw myself to its attention – but to escape.

971

I heard the sound of sobbing through the wall, nursemaids who sob easily and my mother-in-law for whom it came hard, her voice raised in a sudden howl of grief and anger. 'Go and tell them,' she shouted. 'Go and tell them you lost the mother but saved the child – and expect to be praised for it. GO!'

And it was Dr Blackwood who obeyed her command and hurried downstairs. His younger colleague came next, still in shirt-sleeves, and then there were a great many comings and goings, the nurse, Mrs Winch, both doctors again, Mrs Barforth herself with a lacy bundle in her arms at which I no longer wished to look, and then the pretty net-draped cradle being taken away to another room by the wet nurse, leaving the room empty since Venetia had gone – when? – could it already be an hour ago?

I wandered to the landing, every joint aching, leaned against the banister rail beneath the great stained-glass window and looked down into the hall where the maids were standing in huddled conclave until Chillingworth appeared and with a flick or two of his agile wrists sent them all away. The drawing-room door was slightly ajar. I knew Mr Barforth and Gideon, possible Gervase, were standing within. I knew I should go down to them and could not. My duty was clear. Mrs Barforth was fully occupied with her grandchild and could not be expected to do the many things which must be done. Somebody must stand firm, must speak to the servants, must offer comfort to those men down there who were surely – and differently – in need of it. And for the first time in my life I shirked utterly, *could* not, for if I should detect the faintest glimmer of relief in Gideon – for the child was a girl, the woman was dead, the money irrevocably his – I would want to kill him, and I had no strength left and little inclination to stand between him and Gervase. But perhaps most of all I could not cope with the grief of a man like Mr Nicholas Barforth, who was unused to grief, did not wish to see him break, especially now when I was breaking myself.

And so I stayed at the head of the stairs leaning against the banister, my mind fastening upon such trivial details as the high wind and the clock in the hall which told me we had reached late afternoon. The sixteenth of March, I thought. We were twenty-four years old, Venetia and I, and soon I will be twenty-five. What does it matter? What's the good of it. I began to walk slowly downstairs – because what *did* it matter – and I have never known what miracle, at that moment, brought Aunt Faith into the house, what passing servant told her coachman as he waited for her outside the new shops in Millergate, what chain of gossip had carried the news so far, so that she bade him turn his horses and bring her to Tarn Edge.

She had not crossed this threshold for twenty years and for an instant I thought my need of her had transformed itself into an illusion.

'Grace,' she said. 'Is it true?'

'No.' I told her. 'Oh yes – yes it is,' and flew into her arms. But the sound of the drawing-room door brought me alarm, for there had been a bitter quarrel between the Barforth brothers and even now I could not be sure my father-in-law would permit her to stay.

Nor, perhaps, could she.

'Nicholas?' she said, the question plain in her voice as he appeared in the doorway, his face looking as if it had been carved out of dusty granite.

'Faith.' For an instant he could scarcely believe it.

'Oh Christ! Faith –' And she moved quickly towards him, as if she could sense the approach of his tears and wished to shield him, to throw a screen of concern around this man who had perhaps never wept in his life before. They went into the drawing-room together and shut the door.

I was left alone in the marbled hall with Gideon, and after standing in a frozen silence for a minute or two, I sat down on the chair by the bronze stag, knowing there was nothing in the world I could say to him. Tomorrow and for a long time hereafter he would be told by the well-intentioned and the sentimental, 'Bear up, old fellow. At least you have your daughter to console you.' But she was not his daughter. She could be no consolation, but no great encumbrance either. He was free now to take another rich wife and have sons of his own to inherit Venetia's money. And because, once again, his destiny had brought him out on the winning side, and because hate was easier, less complex, than grief and even soothed it a little, I sat for quite half an hour and hated him, accusing him and condemning him in my mind for everything. I had feared him, years ago, as a fortune-hunter when he had hesitated briefly between my wealth and Venetia's, and I had been so right – assuredly I had – to keep my distance. He had taken Venetia readily from Charles Heron's soiled hands and then, not content with the money alone – and notably discontented with the woman who came with it – he had tried to change her, as he had changed this entire household, to suit his precise requirements – *his* tastes, his desires, not hers, not ours. Fortune-hunter then, opportunist, seeing nothing but his own advantage; sensualist too, I supposed – yes, certainly that, although not with his wife. Widower now, of impeccable demeanour, looking not grief-stricken but saddened, very much moved beneath his patrician self-control. It was a sham, I was certain, and as I went on glaring at him, quite balefully I suppose, his eyebrows drew together into their black scowl and he came striding the step or two towards me.

'Well – and what have I done, Grace Barforth?'

'What do you mean?'

'You know very well. And you are not usually so sqeamish when it comes to calling me a scoundrel. Come on, Grace – out with it – what are you thinking of me?'

'I am not thinking of you at all.'

'Oh yes – yes, you are – and if the very worst you are thinking should be true, then tell me this, what have I done that your own father has not done – except that the Delaney woman was older, and faithful, and had stolen the money in the first place?'

But Aunt Faith intervened, appearing suddenly from the shadows, her gift of compassion enabling her to throw both arms around Gideon's unyielding neck and to tell him. 'No one would think it odd if you went to Listonby to be with your mother.'

'Am I in the way, Aunt Faith?'

'No, darling. You are suffering and don't know how to show it, like Nicholas. I am giving you the opportunity to hide.'

Suffering, I thought. Never. She's giving him the chance to go and tell them he's free and that Aunt Caroline can advertise him on the marriage-market again. And my heart felt like a stone.

'Grace,' Aunt Faith said, 'please come with me'. and slipping her hand into mine she took me upstairs, tears flowing gently down her cheeks. I thought, for a moment, that she wanted to see Venetia and started to tug my hand away from her, knowing I could never enter that room again.

'No, dear,' she said, and we went up another flight of stairs to the nursery wing, which I supposed she remembered from her own childhood when she had come here to play with Aunt Caroline.

The nursemaid sprang instantly to her feet and dropped a curtsy, beaming her relief that some older woman was here to take the responsibility, for the child was very small, the wet nurse a clumsy fool, and the poor dead lady's mother had been put to bed now, on the doctor's orders, with a dose of laudanum inside her strong enough to knock out a donkey.

'She'll not wake till morning, ma'am.'

'Good,' said Aunt Faith. 'I think we shall manage very well, nurse, until then. Grace, dear, do come here and look at this lovely little elf.'

It took me a long time, a dreadful time, to cross that room; and when I did reach the cradle, I could not bring myself to look down but bent my head, at first, with closed eyes.

'Look, dear,' she said, her voice telling me those tears were still pouring from her eyes, and eventually, her hand on my rigid shoulder stroking me, urging me, I obeyed and saw the tiny dark head, eyelids already long-lashed peacefully closed, the shallow but even breathing, the fingers of a minute hand delicately curled in perfect innocence.

When I left the room my tears were flowing as freely as Aunt Faith's, my head clearing sufficiently to admit the thought of Gervase, a realization that my protective impulses towards him were far from over. If I held out my hand to him now – for he would need a hand – would he take it? Did I want him to need me again? Could I need him now? Was this our final opportunity? I heard his voice in the hall and ran, finding him face to face with Gideon, the precarious balance between them almost visibly tilting in an atrocious direction. And having dreaded this confrontation for years, having held myself for so long in readiness to prevent it, I stood now aghast with some kind of fog in my mind, and watched it happen.

'What should I offer you, Gideon? Congratulations?'

And although I had the same thought an hour ago, the terrible mockery in Gervase's voice chilled me.

'You can go to hell, Gervase.'

'I shouldn't wonder. And where are *you* going, Gideon? To Listonby to tell them the good news?'

'Get out of my way.'

'Oh – I reckon you'll make sure of that.'

'I reckon I might.'

And with an accompanying obscenity I had not heard before but easily understood, he put the flat of his hand on Gervase's chest and pushed hard.

I shook my head, cleared it, and somehow put myself between them, relying not on strength to keep them apart but on the fact that as boys they had been trained not to hit girls, that gentlemen did not strike ladies. And even then there was some more pushing and shoving, Gideon rockhard, his eyes completely blank, Gervase like some kind of cold flame, my intervention merely making it harder for them to get at one another.

A scandalous, ridiculous performance in any circumstances, appalling in these. 'Stop it!' I shrieked, becoming ridiculous too, striking out with my fists in all directions, this feminine violence which ordinarily would have amused them reducing their own to a point where insults began to seem more appropriate than blows.

'You didn't know what you had in her,' hissed Gervase, shaking now with hatred and hurt. 'Talk about pearls before swine – and you were the swine all right, Chard.'

'I don't have to defend myself to an idle parasite – and a bloody alley-cat, like you.'

'Then try defending yourself to a hanging judge – that's what I'd like to see.'

'I told you, Gervase – get out of my way and out of my sight – *now*.'

'And out of *your* house too, I reckon. Is that it, Gideon?'

There was no answer.

'I see,' said Gervase. 'Then listen here, Chard, and I'll tell you what you can do with this house, and those mills, and everything else that goes with them.'

He told him, explicitly, obscenely, and with a total and damning contempt. And when he had done – when he had entirely slaughtered the Barforth side of himself – I ran after him down the long, stone steps into the garden and caught him on the carriage-drive, walking fast towards the stable block.

'Gervase – oh Gervase, not like this – just a moment –'

But his nerve had snapped now, he was wild and very close to tears, and shook off my hand with a shudder as if it burned him or soiled him.

'Leave me alone.'

And when I would not, he stood for a moment in front of me, took my shoulders in hands that hurt and shook me just once, but very hard.

'You heard me, Grace. I told him what to do with the house and the mills and whatever else goes with them. That includes you, Grace. You ought to know that. *Now* will you leave me alone?'

I watched as he disappeared around the corner, and then turned and walked back to the house, each step taken as if through water, my skirt an impossible weight around my legs, the sensation one has in dreams of movement impeded by unseen hands, of running through a barrier of weariness and going nowhere.

Gideon was standing in the open doorway, the light behind him outlining the powerful set of his shoulders, the extent of his self-assurance and his authority; Gideon, controlled and immovable, the natural leader of the herd thriving on his power to drive his rivals away. Fortune-hunter no longer, since the fortune was assured, but the dominant male of the clan, the old man in the house behind him no longer desiring to challenge him, the young man who might have challenged him having proved unwilling and unequal.

'Let him be,' he told me calmly, in no doubt that I – a woman of the clan – must obey him. 'Let him go to earth for a while – it can do no harm. And you, Grace, come back inside.'

18

She had made many mistakes in her life, which had, in the end, proved fatal to her. In her place I would not have been deceived by Charles Heron, and had I consented to a marriage of convenience I would have accepted its limitations far better than she had done. I would not have gone away with Robin Ashby, but had I done so I would have been less easily broken and quicker to mend. Being made of tougher, coarser stuff, I would have survived where finespun Venetia had not. Being less hopeful, I was less prone to disappointment. Being less honest, I was better able to compromise. But I expected no one, when my time came, to mourn me with the intensity so many of us mourned for her, no one to feel, as I now felt, that the world had grown cooler and dimmer, infinitely impoverished, for the sorry waste of her.

I had been unable at first to contemplate her funeral, but the mundane requirements of mourning had occupied my mind and I managed to stand at her graveside on the blustery March day without dwelling too closely on what the coffin contained. I had not looked at her, had refused all blandishments to try from those who assured me she was only 'sleeping', that she looked 'so very beautiful' when I knew she was dead and could find nothing beautiful in that.

I stood in stony immobility, irritated by the tears of Miss Mandelbaum and Mrs Rawnsley, by the stately gesture with which Mrs Sheldon lifted her veil and dabbed a wisp of cambric to her eyes, by the hushed and overblown condolences of Thomas Sheldon MP, who always attended the funerals of his richer constituents; irritated most of all by the vicar, a great favourite with Mrs Agbrigg, who appeared to find it a matter for rejoicing that she had been too good for this world and was now a resident in a 'better place'.

The funeral was, of course, a major event, all five of the Barforth mills being closed for the day, so that the steep slope of Kirkgate leading to the parish church was lined six deep with Barforth employees craning their necks to watch the spectacle of upper-class Cullingford on parade; the black silk gowns beaded with jet, the hats with their black satin bows and black feathers; the women of the immediate family in knee-length mourning veils; the black-draped carriages and the black horses; the fun,

I suppose, of identifying each party as it arrived, Aunt Caroline's coach with its ducal crest proving a firm favourite.

There were mourners, too, from far afield, coming to pay their respects not to Venetia, who was unknown to them, but to her husband, her father, her grandfather, Sir Joel Barforth, whose name lived on and whose widow was here today, standing for the first time in twenty-five years between her sons; Aunt Faith clinging to Sir Blaize's other arm, my mother-in-law standing up very straight and then suddenly leaning – for the first time in years – against her husband.

The widower stood among his own kin, maintaining a grave but otherwise impassive countenance, Aunt Caroline scarcely knowing what expression to adopt since she had not liked Venetia but was troubled by so young a death, Blanche looking tearful and out of sorts, Sir Dominic, who was probably very bored, looking every inch a baronet.

I stood with my own family and with a tightly controlled, not quite sober Liam Adair, my hand on my father's arm, glad even of Mrs Agbrigg to shield me from Gervase, for I had not seen him since the night of Venetia's death and refused to demean myself by looking too closely at him when he appeared on the fringes of the crowd, his face as sickly and unreal as candlewax.

We walked away, all of us in the same direction, except Gervase who, remaining at the graveside a moment, went off down a path which would lead him nowhere but away from his family, and from me. We got into our carriages and drove back to Tarn Edge, where I served tea to the ladies, spirits to the gentlemen, conferred with Mrs Winch about luncheon for those mourners who, having some distance to travel, might require it; functioned, in fact, like the machine I had become.

But the animosity to which I had become accustomed among my relations was absent today, Sir Blaize Barforth taking and holding his brother's hand for a long moment in the churchyard and thereafter staying closely at his side, while Aunt Caroline had no wish to pursue her feud with a woman who had lost her only daughter. They sat all together by the drawing-room fire when the guests had gone, the three children of Sir Joel Barforth, Blaize, Nicholas and Caroline, with their spouses and their mother, united if only imperfectly by distress, and talked quietly among themselves of neutral subjects, happier days.

'What is to become of the poor infant?' said Aunt Caroline, sensing a threat to Gideon, since this was not his child and already it was paining her to be obliged to pretend otherwise. But Mr Barforth, never one to brook interference in his affairs, merely shook his head, and instead of informing her that the child, whatever else she might be, was *his* grand-daughter, said wearily, 'No need to fret, Caroline. There's enough to go round – more than enough, I reckon.'

'I should hope so, Nicholas, considering the healthy state of the business my father left you. But I was not only referring to that. The child must be looked after, "brought up" – Grace, dear, should you need advice at any time, I shall be very happy, for babies are not quite so simple as one supposes.

'Grace will manage all right,' said my father-in-law, and there was an immediate chorus of family aproval. 'Of course she will.' 'Grace does everything so well.' 'How fortunate you are, Nicholas, to have her here – what a comfort to you – how very convenient!' 'Grace is so fond of children.'

Was I fond of children? What difference did it make? Here once again was a female task that must be performed. I was the obvious female person to perform it. It had occurred to no one that I might object, that I might have some other plan – some other hope or dream or desire – for my unique and unrepeatable life.

'I suppose you will be expecting to use the Chard christening gown,' Aunt Caroline said to me with extreme reluctance a few days later, assuming already that I had taken on the authority, the responsibility of a mother.

'Of course she will,' Blanche answered for me, being far less subservient to Aunt Caroline than she used to be. 'I have brought it with me in the carriage. It was made for *giants*, Grace, I warn you, and you will have to stitch it around that little mite.'

The christening was very painful. Blanche and I were the godmothers, still in our funeral black, Gideon, who should, I thought, have insited on using the chapel at Listonby, looking just faintly embarrassed in this parish church of Cullingford, where he had married the wife who had left him and was now baptizing her child, not his. While Gervase, who was a blood relation and should have offered himself as godfather to his sister's daughter, was not there. Nevertheless the ceremony was performed, the duty done. We took an anonymous little creature wrapped in costly lace to church that day and brought home with us Miss Claire Chard, riding in the victoria with her Aunt Blanche – who had chosen her name – her Chard cousins, Matthew and Francis, and her Aunt Grace; the man who had agreed to call himself her father riding alongside with the man who would allow her to call him Uncle Dominic, while behind them, in his own carriage, there came the man with a sudden sprinkling of grey in his hair who was most decidedly her grandfather.

I had dinner that night with my father-in-law, the two of us alone in the high, panelled room among a splendour of crystal and silver, served as deferentially as if we had been at a banquet. The child was upstairs in her nursery, expensively tended. Gideon had taken the London train and would be back the day after tomorrow. Gervase was not there.

I left Mr. Barforth to his brandy and cigars and sat alone in the drawing-room, drinking my coffee and glancing with resignation at the pile of letters of condolence to which I must reply. This was my life. Gideon would return with his fine cambric shirts to be laundered, his well-cut coats to be pressed, and before long there would be his friends to entertain again, his recherché little dinners, his sophisticated appetites. I would visit my father on Sunday afternoons and go to London occasionally to see Blanche. I would argue mildly the tea-table issues of the women's cause as understood by Miss Mandelbaum and would be mildly irritated by the narrowness of Miss Tighe, the noble insistence of Mrs Sheldon in considering herself not as a person in her own right but as

978

Thomas Sheldon's wife. The child would grow. Gervase would not be there. Eventually Gideon would marry again, a woman whose wealth and solid family connections would make her a power at Tarn Edge. My father-in-law would not live forever. Where would Gervase be then?

'Grace, are you not well?' Mr Barforth said, coming into the room and sitting down heavily in the chair opposite mine.

'Oh yes – quite well.'

'Aye – so you would tell me even if you were in agony. Grace – there is something I ought to tell you.'

'Yes?' But I was suddenly very tired, my eyelids aching for sleep and could muster no curiosity.

'It concerns the Galton estate.'

And even then, knowing how closely it must also concern Gervase, I could not stir myself to more than a faint interest.

'I have made the Abbey over to my wife, Grace, in such a manner that it is hers absolutely, to be disposed of at her wish, not mine. I wonder if you know what that means?'

'That you have set her free.'

He smiled. 'She may see it that way. But there is rather more to it than that.'

'I know. It means she can give it to Gervase and that he, with the income from his ten per cent of your business, can live like his Uncle Peregrine, except that Gervase has turned thirty now and I believe Peregrine Clevedon never got so far.'

'And you feel I've let you down?'

'Why should you concern yourself with me?'

'Don't talk like a fool, girl,' he said brusquely. 'It can't suit you to have that estate in your husband's hands. I knew that very well when I took my decision. My choice was between what suited you and what suited my wife, and I chose my wife. Something was owing to her. I paid – and since you may have to pay too – well, Grace, I rarely feel called upon to explain myself but I think you'd best listen to me for a minute or two. You haven't lived in my house all this time without knowing how matters stand between me and Georgiana. It might make things easier for you to know why. She married me for my money. That's no secret and it seemed fair enough at the time. I married her because I wanted her, and I suppose it wasn't all her fault that I got more than I bargained for. The fascination didn't last and I'm a poor loser – always have been. It struck me that I wasn't cut out for close relationships and so I made up my mind to keep to the things I was suited for – running the mills and making a profit. There's no reason to be ashamed of that. Well – I could have kicked that lad of mine into shape, I reckon, if I'd got myself involved with him. And when he didn't shape up on his own, I gave up too soon. I can train my managers and my son-in-law – by God, I can! The training I put them through is so damned hard that the job itself seems easy by comparison. But I can keep my distance, you see, from them and it would have brought me too close to Gervase. So – if you feel the need to blame somebody for the way he is, you can start by blaming me. You can

979

call me a fool too, if you like, Grace – a damned fool. I kept my distance from Venetia, too. I denied myself all the things she could have been to me and what have I gained by it? It hasn't made losing her any easier – by Christ it hasn't!'

We sat for a moment in a strangling silence and then, gruffly, quite painfully, he demanded: 'What else could I have done when she went off that first time? And I didn't drag her down the aisle to Gideon. Damnation! I even thought she'd put up more of a fight than she did, which was no fight at all, just "Yes, father – if you think that's best" – just that, no argument. And it *was* best. I had my own reasons for wanting him but I knew he'd look after her, do the right thing – I knew he *could* look after her, for he's got a head on his shoulders and an eye to the main chance – And what's wrong with that? So – when she didn't argue – it struck me that, at the bottom of her, she probably fancied him. He's a good-looking man – why shouldn't she have fancied him? What else could I have done?'

'I don't know.'

'Then I'll tell you. I could have made more of an effort with my own wife in the first place, I reckon. If I'd handled my business like I've handled my marriage, I'd be a pauper now, Grace, and no mistake.'

Once again we sat in a tense silence and then, leaning suddenly towards me, an undemonstrative man who resented the occasional necessity to demonstrate his feelings, he said angrily, 'God dammit! Grace, you are valued here with us. You know that, don't you?'

'Yes, I know.'

'I'm glad to hear it. See that you don't forget it. We need you here. In fact I'll go further and tell you straight that I don't know how we'd manage without you. This house is yours, Grace, for all practical purposes – entirely yours – and I shall allow no one to interfere with that, whoever they may be.'

I let a few more days go by, coped with the small upheaval invariably occasioned by Gideon's return, and then chose a bright blue and white morning to drive over to Galton.

Mrs Barforth was walking by the Abbey stream, two young retrievers splashing excitedly in the water, a black and white sheepdog puppy hesitating on the bank, one cautious paw extended to test the ripples; and I was glad to see no sign of Gervase.

'Grace, dear – I was hoping to see you. I suppose you have heard my news?'

'About the estate? Yes. Do you feel differently, knowing it to be yours?'

She smiled, shaded her eyes against the sun to check the progress of the young dogs who were chasing last autumn's leaves now on the opposite bank.

'Do you know,' she said, 'it is the oddest thing – I have lived years of my life for this moment, longed for it and taken every opportunity I could to bring it about. It seemed of the most desperate importance – truly the difference between life and death. Now I have it, and nothing

980

seems really changed. I suppose I must have known deep down, all the time, that my husband would not really sell me up lock, stock and barrel as he used to threaten. Yes, that must be it. How very nice to know that, in a way, I have always trusted him.'

She slipped her arm into mine and we walked across the ancient, unsteady little bridge, the gentle sheepdog at our heels, the two retrievers greeting us with boisterous rapture at the other side, leaping all muddy and eager against our skirts.

'What will you do now, mother-in-law?'

'Do? Must I do anything? Well – I might spread my wings and fly away. But I don't think so. Twenty years ago my husband thought I might fly to Julian Flood, which is why he clipped my wings and put salt on my tail – not from jealousy, you understand, but because he believed Julian would not be good for me.'

'Would you have gone to him?'

'Oh yes,' she said, smiling at the stony track ahead of her, seeing beyond it to a wealth of contented memory. 'Yes, I would have gone to Julian had my husband allowed it. And I might even have been very happy. If I have a talent at all, it is for friendship. These storms of passion, you know, these truly gigantic desires – well, I fear they are a little outside my range. But I am very comfortable with friendship. And next to my brother, Peregrine, Julian was the best friend I had. When Peregrine died, he often seemed my only friend. That was the ingredient I found lacking in my relationship with my husband. We were never friends.'

She bent down to murmur a word of encouragement to the timid collie bitch and to restrain the gun dogs who had begun to root ferociously in the ground.

'Yes,' she said and then, as if suddenly making up her mind, took a deep breath and muttered rapidly, wanting it to be over and done. 'You have asked me what I mean to do. What do you mean to do, Grace? For I must tell you that, for the time being, I do not think Gervase will return to Tarn Edge. Nor do I think he will stay here, either.'

'Where will he go, then?' And my voice was sharp, very cold, hurtful to my own ears.

'Dearest – I don't know – what can I say –?'

But her concern, her affection, her hand coming to rest gently on my arm, were all intolerable to me and I shrugged her away.

'You can tell me nothing I cannot see for myself, and indeed you should be obliged to tell me nothing at all, since Gervase ought to be here to say it for you. But I already know. He married me, as your husband married you, on an impulse that did not last. I believed he loved me, as you believed your husband loved you, and I relied on that. I feel cheated now, as you did. Can you blame me?'

'No. I do not blame you. I do not blame him either.'

'Naturally you would say so.'

'Why? Because I am his mother? And because I have always defended him? Grace, I do not defend him blindly and I am ready to accept my own share of blame. When he was born and they first put him into my arms, I looked at him and saw my own son, a fine, red-headed Clevedon, and I forgot that his name was Barforth. And when he gave every sign of being a Clevedon, with no inclination for business and a downright aversion to that foul machinery of theirs, I encouraged him. I shielded him from discipline, told lies for him when he ran away from school, because it was a school for manufacturers, you see, not a school for gentlemen such as my brother and the Chards attended. When his father and I separated, his loyalty was all for me, such a little boy as he was then, saying he would always look after me – And I was always here, to hide him from school, from his father, from the mill. My only excuse is that I sincerely believed that the whole of his heart was here, at Galton.'

'And it is not?'

'How can it be, Grace? He would not have married you had he been certain of his true inclinations. He had the mills within his grasp on your marriage, for my husband would have known how to tame Gideon had Gervase remained constant – had he continued to try. He did not remain constant. He let the mills go. He has Galton now, if he chooses to take it. I am not sure he will. Grace, if he felt the need of a breathing-space, a trip abroad, perhaps, alone, so that he could think, make a decision on his future – would you allow it?'

'Could I prevent it?'

She shook her head, her cheeks very flushed, her manner hesitant and embarrassed in a way which was unlike her.

'Oh, not physically or legally I suppose. I am simply asking if you could bring yourself to understand his need – oh dear, how very hard this is!'

'Yes, very hard and I imagine it will become harder still. I believe you are trying to tell me he has already decided to go abroad, and you are asking me not to make a fuss. Is that it?'

'My dear, I suppose it is.'

'And he is running away from me as he used to run away from school, is he not? Well – is he not?'

'Oh dear, yes – yes, he is. Grace, it is so easy to view him as no more than a spoiled and worthless man but you saw far more than that in him once, and I cannot believe you to have been mistaken. We have asked too much of him, his father and I – pulled him in too many diverse directions, and now he *must* have time and solitude if his conflict is ever to be resolved. Failure – yes, of course he feels he has failed – at everything, not least as a husband. Enormous confusion – yes, of course. But Grace – my dear – I do not think he is running away from you, nor even from himself. He is trying to *find* himself. Please allow him to try.'

And once again I saw her flush with embarrassment, sensed an uneasy movement of her mind, warning me that although her words were no less than the truth they were not the whole of it.

'He wishes to leave me, then – for good?'

'He has not said so. In his present state of mind he could not risk a decision of that magnitude.'

'I see. And so I am to wait, am I – how long? Six months, a year or two? I am not to bother him – is that it? – until he feels able to make up his mind?'

We walked on for a while in silence, my anger extending my stride, quickening my pace and then gradually evaporating in its own futility. He had left me years ago and what was being asked of me now was perfectly in keeping with the conventions. Blanche and Dominic did not live together in any true sense. Certainly my parents-in-law did not. My own mother had withdrawn from her marriage by the gradual but complete process of making herself an invalid. It had not escaped my attention that ladies from such different walks of life as Mrs Rawnsley of Cullingford and Mrs Goldsmith of Berlin were content to live almost separately although under the same roof as their husbands. They had made an 'arrangement' as I was now being asked to do, had retained the status, the protection, the *responsibility* of marriage without the man himself. They had not made a fuss. They had obeyed the rules and had done their duty. And my own duty was clear. I had a position to keep up, a home to run, Venetia's child to raise. I had a life of my own. 'One life,' Venetia's voice whispered in my memory, from the days when she had believed her own life would be glorious and she had still trusted me. 'This is the only life I'll ever have and my one chance to get it right.' Was this my one chance too? Or had the choice been made for me long ago by my upbringing, my conditioning, bred into me by those generations of women behind me who had submitted to the limitations of their bodies and their easily aroused, easily exploited emotions; who had believed without question that their own claims on life must always be inferior to the claims of their children and of their men?

I was a decent woman and decent women made sacrifices. It was the basic instinct of womankind to protect the young. I possessed that instinct, and who would raise Venetia's child if I did not but a procession of governesses working not for love but for wages? And how could I explain myself to my father? 'One life,' Venetia whispered, 'one only', and then, with sudden mockery: 'But at least you will have your dignity.'

We walked back down the hill and across the bridge, the air sparkling and clean, the dogs still playing around our feet, even the little collie exhilarated now by the scent of the new grass and the rich burden of the earth, forgetting her timidity at this promise of a fragrant springtime.

'You must see the kittens, Grace,' and dutifully I went into her parlour to kneel by a cat-basket overflowing with minute tortoishell bodies, as dutifully drank my tea and ate the muffins she seemed anxious to serve me, aware, as I did so, that through her talk of cats and chickens and apple-preserves, she was acutely uneasy, badly troubled in her conscience.

I took my hat and gloves, and prepared to go outside again, my carriage at the door.

'Will Gervase agree to see me – here, if he cannot face Tarn Edge?'

'My dear, I believe it is *you* he cannot face.'

'Ah – I thought he might *have* to see me, to tell me himself whatever it is that you – quite clearly – are holding back.'

She bit her lip, her face flushing again a most uncharacteristic crimson, tears starting in her eyes.

'Oh dear, I could wish you less astute –'

'There is something else then?'

'I am obliged to deny it.'

'You mean you have been instructed to keep it from me. I shall find out, you know.'

And for a long while she could not bring herself to speak but stood nervously clasping and unclasping her hands, her loyalty visibly and hurtfully torn, until finally she gave a deep sigh and raising her head gave me a look that held both determination and compassion.

'I should not tell you, Grace. There is no need for you to know.'

'I am not a child to be kept in the dark.'

'It will hurt you, Grace.'

'I am hurt already. And if it is of such great importance, perhaps I have a right to know. If there are decisions to be made, then I think I *must* know.'

'Very well. Diana Flood is to have a child five months from now, and since she and her husband have been apart for something more than a year … My dear –'

'Yes,' I said, the high pitch of my voice taking me by surprise, my words rising straight up from a deep source of bitterness I had never before acknowledged. 'Gervase, of course, is the father. Good. I am glad – yes, I am so glad – that he can do at least one thing that I cannot, that he can have children, whereas I must make do with other people's, with waifs and strays and orphans that are not wanted. Oh – pay no attention to me – none –'

I righted myself after a while, Mrs Barforth standing quietly beside me, subduing her own feelings while I brought mine to heel and leashed them with a hard hand, seeing no profit to anyone in allowing them to escape again. And when I could, I asked her curtly. 'What steps do they mean to take?'

'My dear, the usual ones – the sad things which are always done on such occasions. Julian will send her away somewhere to give birth in secret, for it is not the first time such a thing has occurred in his family, nor in mine, nor in the Chards either. It has all been done before, and *must* be done, for her husband will be Lord Sternmore when his uncle dies, and when there is a title to inherit a man must be very sure of his eldest son.'

'You do realize that this is – *dreadful*?'

'Yes I do.'

'And Gervase?'

'He will accept financial responsibility, and then I imagine Diana will go off to India to brave the climate and her husband. The baby will be looked after and then, perhaps nine or ten years from now, I may offer a home to an orphan child, a distant relative, perhaps. Or Diana, even, may find it possible to offer that orphan a home, particularly if in the meantime she has supplied the colonel adequately with heirs. It appears – usually – to work well enough in the end.'

'And Diana Flood accepts this?'

984

'She does.'

'Why does she? You say Gervase will accept financial responsibility for the child. Has he not offered more than that? You tell me he wishes to go abroad. Has he not asked her to go with him?'

'I believe the offer was made – yes – yes, he did ask her to go abroad with him and live there as his wife. Yes, he did.'

'And she? Please tell me the truth.'

'Shall I? Yes, I see that it is only right. She seemed, at first, inclined to accept. But in the end – and after consultation with her family – she declined to place herself in so precarious – so very perilous – a situation. She has, after all, a great deal to lose. The Sternmore title is a very old one and although there is no great fortune to go with it, the land being somewhat encumbered, the house upon it is very noble – even rather famous. Lady Sternmore of Sternmore must always be a person of consequence. The adulterous wife of Colonel Flood living openly with her lover and their bastard child must be considered as one socially dead. And lovers, you know, do not always remain faithful. No one could guarantee her that – certainly not Gervase. He is in love with her now but it was pointed out to her that, not too long ago, he was in love with you. Forgive me, dear, but you asked me for the truth.'

'You are saying she is a conventional woman who will play the game. Gervase is not a conventional man.'

'In this case he is obliged to be.'

'And who else knows of "this case" beside ourselves?'

'My husband. And your father. We felt it only right that he should be informed.'

'How scandalous that no one felt it right to inform me.'

'I have just informed you, Grace, and you have not thanked me for it.'

What had actually changed? I had known of the affair and had taken no action against it. I had already grown accustomed to the sterile existence of a woman separated from her husband. What had changed except that our separation, which had been known only to ourselves, was now to be acknowledged by a few others, by my father-in-law who had already reassured me as to my position at Tarn Edge, and by my father who would pretend he knew nothing of it to protect my feelings, just as I had tried to protect his. What difference? None at all except the hardening, or perhaps the recognition of a resolve to win for myself an identity, to put an end to this eternal legal childhood which added me to the sum total of a man who did not care for me. Perhaps that – and the dangerous, disturbing memory of Venetia.

She had looked at me sometimes, during her last few months, in an odd manner, her eyes clear and cool and pitying, picking out each one of the deceits by which I lived and shaking her head over them sadly but with a hint of amusement that said: 'Poor Grace. She is just like the rest of them – she will endure any insult, any hardship, any wrong, so long as it *looks* right.' But would it comfort me on my dying day to know I had obeyed the rules, had shown myself at all times to be a dutiful and reasonable woman?

'What has he done to her?' Mrs Barforth had asked me, speaking of Robin Ashby and Venetia, and I had replied that he had treated her as the kind of woman she had wished to be.

'Are there such women, Grace?'

'I hope so.'

Were there, indeed, women who did not simply allow things to happen to them – as we had been taught women should – but who took action on their own behalf, who *made* things happen in accordance with their own judgement and their own desires? Was I such a woman? Most fervently I hoped so.

There had been in my mind, in my conscience, a mountain to climb, an enormous, outrageous decision looming on my horizon, an impossible decision and a frightening one since I knew of no one who had ever taken it before me. Yet, as I drove back alone to Tarn Edge, it struck me that I was very calm – too calm – and at some point on that familiar journey the decision which should have crushed me and torn me apart and from which in the end I should have retreated, to slide meekly – almost gratefully – back into my feminine mould; that decision was somehow made without conflict, even without much awareness, an imperceptible passing from a state of desperate uncertainty to a state of being quite sure. Venetia had known, when she sent Robin Ashby away from her, that there had been no other course to take. I now understood and was comforted by the same complete assurance. There was nothing else I could do.

Chillingworth greeted me in the hall with some tale of calling-cards, a note from Mr Chard, some crisis in the nursery. I glanced at the cards and at the few words in Gideon's large, bold hand, warning me he would require an earlier dinner. I went to the nursery on the second floor and then came down again without going inside, afraid, perhaps, that Claire Chard, with her mother's fine sensibilities, would guess my intentions and accuse me of treachery.

I packed a small bag, no bigger than the one Venetia had taken when she went away, and leaving instructions for the week's menus and a few, quite false words of explanation with Mrs Winch, had myself driven to Fieldhead, where I enquired of my father, in our cool, restrained Agbrigg fashion, how best I might obtain a divorce.

19

My father was a man of acute perception, of a brilliant and clear-sighted intelligence, accustomed throughout his life to the untangling of complex problems and situations. But even he, in his aloof manner, seemed stunned by my request and not at all disposed to treat it seriously.

'You have had a shock,' he said. 'Yes, I am acquainted with the circumstances in which your husband finds himself with regard to Mrs Flood. And however deplorable it may be, I am bound to inform you that it is not unusual. Yes, you have certainly had a shock. I deeply regret it and can only suggest you remain here at Fieldhead for a day or so, to compose yourself.' And when I assured him that I was already very composed he added sharply. 'Good heavens! Grace, it is a sorry business and I let my displeasure be felt when Nicholas Barforth came to tell me of it. But these things do happen, you know. Of course you know, and one must retain a sense of proportion. Perhaps it is the Floods one should pity the most, for either the woman must give away her child or the husband must tolerate a cuckoo in his nest – unpleasant for both, whatever they decide.'

'I see, father. And all that is required of me is to forgive and forget?'

'Ah,' he said, his long, pale eyes glinting with a wry humour. 'You are a woman, my dear. Surely that is what women are made for?'

He let two days go by without another word and then on the third evening he called me again into his study, the same dark, panelled room where he had explained to me the terms of my marriage contract and had given me my mother's jewellery.

'Sit down, Grace.' And for a few moments he barely glanced at me, occupying himself with the heavy, leather-bound volumes on his desk, his manner quietly efficient, thoroughly professional.

'You made a certain request to me the other evening. After thirty-six hours of reflection, I would like to know if you are of the same mind?'

'I am.'

'You amaze me. Very well. No doubt when you have heard what I have to tell you then you will change it.'

He had not practised the law for a very long time, had never in the whole of his experience handled a case of divorce and had therefore been obliged to return to his books. What did I know of my own rights in this matter? Nothing. He had thought as much and having made a thorough study – his intellect responding to the challenge after so long – he was in a position to inform me that, until some slight changes in the law a mere twenty years ago, I would in effect have had no rights at all. Divorces, of course, were granted before then, but only by the passage of a private bill through Parliament and almost exclusively as the result of a husband's complaint against his wife, the House of Lords in particular taking the view that a nobleman unlucky enough to have married an adulterous woman should be allowed to free himself from the entanglement so that he might remarry and provide himself with heirs.

In two hundred years, my father told me in his precise, neutral tone, only four women had been granted divorces against their husbands, a certain Mrs Dawson having had all six of her petitions refused only so short a time ago as 1848, despite her conclusive proof that her husband had not only committed adultery but had beaten her with a horsewhip. The law, my father said, shrugging cool shoulders, had never regarded adultery on the part of a husband as being in any way so serious as adultery in a wife. And if one could not applaud the morality of such a view, my father thought one could bow to its logic, since a married man could be so easily tricked into believing himself the father of a bastard child who would inherit his property, while a married woman, who had no property in any case, could not.

But the high cost of the Parliamentary divorce had placed it far beyond the reach of all but the wealthiest in the land, and even among these few the fact that a woman who separated herself from her husband invariably lost sight of her children tended to make women submit more readily to the domestic yoke. And even for a woman who did not greatly care for her children, or who had none to lose, there remained the question of how and on what she might live. She could not take away with her any moneys she had possessed at the time of her marriage, since the very sacrament of marriage had made such possessions her husband's. She could not, by any act of separation, acquire a legal identity of her own, but remained so far as the courts were concerned an appendage of the man who had been her husband. She could not make a will, even if she had anything to bequeath, could not earn a living since there had never been any work for gentlewomen to do, and would have the greatest difficulty in denying her estranged husband's claim on anything she might herself inherit unless it had been settled on her separately in a most watertight manner. It was not unknown for a husband to live apart from his wife for twenty years and then to return, sell her valuables and her furniture, possess himself of her savings, and then to abscond again. Nor was it unknown for a man to remove his children from his wife's care and place them in the home of his mistress, the separated wife having no right of appeal against him and no hope of seeing her children again, unless he graciously allowed it.

However, in 1857 some few changes had been made, divorce being taken away from the ecclesiastical courts and the Houses of Parliament – a move bitterly opposed by Mr Gladstone – and given a court of its own, these new proceedings being much simpler and cheaper, and having the decided advantage, from a feminine point of view, of restoring the divorced wife to the status of a single woman.

Under this new form of divorce a woman could retain without encumbrance any money earned, inherited or otherwise acquired by her *after* the date on which her marriage had been dissolved. Her legal identity was now returned to her. She could enter into contracts and take legal action if they were broken, she could defend herself if necessary by suing anyone who slandered her or anyone who owed her money, matters which previously could only have been handled through her husband. She could even make her own will and leave her property where she chose. And, of course, it had for some time been possible, if the court thought fit, to grant the divorced wife access to her children, and in some cases even to award her custody of any infants under the age of seven years. Had I followed him so far, my father wished to know?

'Yes father. And how may this divorce be obtained?'

'I will tell you. In the case of a man it is amazingly simple. He has only to prove his wife's adultery and the thing is as good as done. A woman, however, is obliged to prove her husband's adultery coupled with another offence.'

'What offence?'

'One of a number. I have them all listed here. One of them, no doubt, will serve to use against Gervase. In fact one of them *must* serve or you

988

will have no case at all. Shall we proceed? Well then, has he been guilty of adultery coupled with incest – that is a physical relationship with a mother or a sister?'

'Good heavens! father, you know he has not.'

'You are shocked, I see.'

'I am revolted.'

'Quite so. It is a revolting business, Grace, and if you go on with it you must be prepared for a great deal of unpleasantness. I would do you no service if I attempted to conceal it.'

And taking up his pen he neatly and coolly crossed out the words 'incestuous adultery' from his list.

'So much for that. Bigamy, I suppose, is not a possibility?'

'No father.'

He raised an eyebrow, crossed out the words 'bigamy with adultery' and gave a slight shrug.

'Sodomy, Grace. Do you know what that is? And bestiality?'

'*Father*.'

'My dear, I am not speaking to you as a father but as a legal adviser. I am interpreting the law as it stands, and I must ask you – as someone else could well ask you – if your husband has been guilty of adultery coupled with either of the above. And you would do well to restrain your quite natural repugnance and answer me calmly.'

'Are there really men who do these things?'

'Grace, that is not a calm answer. *Of course* there are men who do these things. There are other men who despoil eight-year-old virgins, and women who offer their little daughters to be despoiled. We are talking of Gervase.'

'No – no, of course he is not guilty of that. Is there nothing else?'

'Yes. There is rape, which I suppose we can dismiss – rape, need I add, not of yourself but of some other woman, since no man can be said to have raped his wife, who is not entitled to refuse him. And then there is adultery coupled with desertion –'

'Why, yes, that will do, surely, for his mother has told me he will not return to Tarn Edge and he has not asked me to join him anywhere else.'

'– with desertion, Grace, that has lasted a minimum of two years.'

'Oh, father – so long?'

'Yes, Grace.'

But, having allowed me to suffer this acute disappointment for a moment or two, he neatly folded his list, placed it in a drawer and gave me his faint smile.

'However –'

'So there is something else to be done?'

'Yes, I do fear so. The adultery is well established, there can be no difficulty about that. Consequently, if you were to obtain a court order – or rather were I to obtain one on your behalf – instructing your husband to return to you and to restore to you your conjugal rights, and if he did not comply with the order within a period of six months, then divorce proceedings could be instituted against him.'

'And would that order be difficult to obtain?'

'Apparently not. The difficulty – and I must warn you of this – is that your husband might obey it. For if he should return to Tarn Edge or invite you to live with him in any other home he may provide, then you will have no case against him. The adultery alone will not suffice and the desertion, my dear, could be made null and void at his choosing – any time he chose to make it so. You must keep that firmly in mind.'

'I cannot think he will come back to me.'

'My dear – and it pains me to say this – he may feel obliged to come back to you for Mrs Flood's sake. He may see it as an act of gallantry towards her. I understand she wishes to conceal the affair and return to her husband. If you sue for divorce she can have no hope of that. And your husband might wish to spare her the social ruin it would entail – or pressure might be brought to bear on him to that effect. Have you considered that?'

I had not considered it. I considered it now and then shook my head, recognizing it as the first of many painful obstacles which would be put in my way. It was the first risk I was to encounter, the first occasion when I was required to choose between the interests of another person and my own. I would take the risk and I would choose myself.

'Father, I have made up my mind, you know. All I am asking you to do is legalize something which actually happened a long time ago. There is no marriage to dissolve. The marriage dissolved itself. It slipped away, little by little, and perhaps there never was very much of it to begin with. Gervase does not want me. I do not want him. There is no need for him to take any legal action to free himself. He can simply walk away, go wherever he chooses, live in the manner he thinks fit. I cannot. I am bound to him – shackled to him. He is not bound to me. And I will not – believe me, father, I will not continue to lead so false and futile a life. I am not afraid of the scandal. I would prefer to be the subject of Mrs Rawnsley's gossip than the object of her pity.'

'Do not dimiss the Mrs Rawnsleys of this world so lightly, Grace, for however trivial they may be when taken singly, when they come together they have great power.'

'As I said, father – I am not afraid.'

Once again he gave me his pale smile and carefully stacked his books away.

'Very well. We have established that you are not afraid and that you have made up your mind. Only one more question remains and I must insist that you answer it very carefully. How much of this, my dear, are you doing for yourself and how much for Venetia?'

I lowered my head for just a second and then raising it slowly met his eyes.

'You are very perceptive, father.'

'Of course I am. I have an excellent mind, as you should know since you have been fortunate enough to inherit it.'

'Fortunate? Do you think so? Surely it is better for a woman to be a little stupid and immensely good-natured. Surely that is best?'

'Easier, perhaps, But we are not concerned with ease. Nor are we concerned with avoiding the answers to awkward questions – at least, I hope we are not.'

'No, father. I think Venetia would understand what I am doing and would want me to do it. She valued honesty and what broke her was being obliged to live a lie.'

'No, Grace. What broke her was her discovery that she lacked the strength to live the truth.'

I looked down again, my eyes filling with tears which, knowing his aversion to weeping, I hastily blinked away.

'Yes, father, I do know that. I believe I have that strength. And Venetia, you know, was not weak. There were times when she had great courage – greater than mine – although she could never sustain it. She felt more joy or sorrow than I feel, and consequently her disillusion went far deeper. What she lacked was resolution. I do not.'

'I am well aware of that. I wish merely to be sure that you are fighting your own campaign, not hers. She was an enchanting young lady, I willingly concede it, but I cannot help thinking that her troubles were largely of her own making.'

'No, father. She handled them badly, but she did not make them. No, no, please let me finish – I am not suggesting anyone treated her with deliberate cruelty or wished to do so. Her father and Gideon behaved as fathers and husbands are supposed to behave. They obeyed the rules society has laid down for men and women to follow – rules, like our laws, which were made by men and so *must* suit men rather better. Venetia was simply not the kind of woman society envisaged when those rules were made. Neither am I. For a long time I have been able to compromise. Venetia could neither conceal her unhappiness nor live with it. Her death has made me see the futility in living with mine. Father – I would say this to no one else – but I almost believe her elopement with Robin Ashby was a deliberate act of self-destruction. I almost believe she knew she could not survive it but chose to have something – just a year – that *mattered* to her.'

I was trembling violently, and to my suprise he let his hand rest on my shoulder and pressed it just once, evenly and firmly.

'Very well. We shall proceed then – shall we? – with caution. And for your first move, my dear, I would like you to leave Cullingford for a week or two. Go to Scarborough to your grandmother or to my cottage at Grasmere, it makes no difference. Take long walks in the fresh air, consider your situation from every angle, and on your return you may instruct me again. I need not tell you, I suppose, that you must have no communication of any kind with Gervase, since the merest hint of collusion between you would entirely destroy your case. A husband and wife may not conspire together, my dear, to end their marriage, indeed they may not. If the case of Barforth v. Barforth ever sees the light of day, one Barforth must be shown as guilty, the other as entirely innocent, and there must be no hint or suspicion that you encouraged him in his guilt or in any way condoned it. These are criminal proceedings and must be treated as such. I trust you can be ready to leave tomorrow?'

I went to Grasmere, to test myself perhaps, since I had spent my happiest days with Gervase among these lakes and hills. But walking through the fine spring days as I had been instructed, I found myself thinking mainly of Venetia, acknowledging her as the source of my decision but not of my determination to follow it through. I would do the things she should have done. I would find the steadfastness of purpose she had lacked. I would be the woman she had dimly perceived in the mind of Robin Ashby, a woman strong enough to live the life of a man, to bear his responsibilities and thus lay claim to his privileges. I would be free, not to smoke a cigar or attend a cock-fight, but to think, decide, take charge of my life. I would carry my own burdens and choose my own pleasures. I would suffer the consequences of my errors and reap whatever reward I could on the occasions when I happened to be in the right.

I would be resolute. I *was* resolute, even on those treacherous evenings when the air was warm and scented with all the enticements of April, rendering me sleepless and forcing me to think of Gervase. He may well have deserved the blow I was preparing for him, but that did not make it easy to strike. And so I allowed my mind to proceed, as my father had said, with caution, no more than one step at a time. We had failed each other. My action now must hurt us both, but surely it would allow us in time to start afresh? Surely? But it did not seem the moment to dwell too closely on that.

My father wrote to me, setting out once again in grave language the procedure for divorce, its consequences, its dangers, neither forbidding me to proceed nor advising it, simply laying the facts before me in correct fashion. I replied that I had not changed my mind, and when I returned to Fieldhead three weeks later nothing had occurred to alter my decision.

'Very well,' my father said, 'I will apply to the courts for an order commanding your husband's return. And you, my dear, may sit here as quietly as you can and wait for the storm to break.'

I expected unbridled anger from my father-in-law and when, on his first visit to Fieldhead, he sat for a while in Mrs Agbrigg's hushed drawing-room, staring fixedly at her green and gold carpet, I interpreted his silence to mean the worst. But eventually he got up and stood on the hearthrug, his favourite vantage point, his back to the fire, his broad shoulders a little hollower than they used to be, not only the grey at his temples ageing him, and said in his abrupt, autocratic manner, 'I suppose you realize that I could put a stop to all this – or at least your father and I together could put a stop to it. All we'd have to do, my girl, is to cut off your money – the allowance we've both been good enough to pay you all these years – and that would be the end of it. You'd be forced to come back to Tarn Edge then and play at being my son's wife whether you liked it or not, and whether he was even living there or not. That's the reason, I suppose, why thousands of women stay with husbands they don't care for and who don't care for them – for the sake of a roof and a blanket and a bite to eat. Now then – do you understand that?'

'Yes, I do.'

'And if I was really set on it, young lady – if I really put my mind to it – I reckon I could persuade your father to clip your wings, since at the bottom of him he doesn't like the way matters are turning out any better than I do. He might be glad to see you back at Tarn Edge – glad of me to show him the way to get you there. Do you understand *that*?'

'Yes, I do.'

'All right – just bear it in mind. And now I'll tell you what I *am* going to do. You brought money with you when you came to Tarn Edge and I'll see every penny paid back to you before you leave. There'll be no trouble about that.'

And because I knew he was thanking me for the effort I had made, expressing his affection in hard cash because that was the only way he could express it, I felt tears in my eyes.

'Thank you.'

'Have you anything else to say to me – anything you'd like me to do?'

'Mr Barforth – you do understand, don't you, about this court order? You do realize that I don't want Gervase to obey it?'

He smiled, sat down and shook his head, ruefully I thought, amused in spite of himself.

'There's no need for alarm, Grace. If you think I might drag him back to you by the scruff of his neck, then you can be at ease. I've got more sense than that. I reckon I've interfered in other people's marriages for the last time. He can sort himself out now, that son of mine, the best way he can.'

'Mr Barforth, I wouldn't want you to punish him. I wouldn't want him to lose – I mean, to be made poor because of me. Really, I wouldn't.' He lifted his dark, still handsome head and looked at me keenly.

'He has ten per cent of my business, Grace. He can live well on that.'

'And he couldn't lose it?'

'He could sell it, although the only customers he'd get would be me or Gideon. And you'll have to wait, like the rest of them, Grace, to find out what I mean to do with the Woolcombers and the Dyeworks and my eighty per cent of Barforth and Company. Aye – I reckon you'll have to wait until the time comes to read my will.'

But he was not offended and smiled when I replied, 'That will be soon enough.'

'I'll be off then, Grace. I just wanted you to know you'd be getting back your dowry.'

And I was acutely grateful that he had not mentioned tiny, helpless Claire, and his own deepening solitude.

Knowledge of my exact situation was reserved, of course, for a very few, but speculation as to the cause of my prolonged sojourn at Fieldhead grew quickly rife.

'My dear,' Mrs Sheldon murmured to me in her sedate manner, 'I cannot avoid the impression that something is troubling you, and there is a great deal of truth, you know, in the old saying that a trouble shared is a trouble halved.'

993

'I do not at all blame you for taking a holiday from Tarn Edge,' Mrs Rawnsley told me. 'Doing one's duty is well enough but I have often thought it scandalous how everything in that house is left to you. I would not wear myself out in their service, I can tell you, for it is not your house, after all, and not your child, and you will get small thanks for any of it when Mr Gideon Chard brings home a new wife. I am entirely on your side, Grace dear – entirely in sympathy.'

While those ladies who were not sufficiently acquainted with me to hint or to pry came regularly to see Mrs Agbrigg and to shower me with invitations to this and that which invariably contained the words 'and do, my dear, bring your husband.'

In these circumstances it was unwise of Sir Julian Flood to visit me at Fieldhead, the sight of his horse glimpsed through my window causing my stomach to lurch most painfully and my breathing to become far too rapid so that I had to walk downstairs very slowly to avoid the appearance of a woman badly flustered.

He was standing, as my father-in-law had done, on the hearthrug, a lean, dark, undeniably handsome man, the manorial lord of Cullingford whose family had dwelt here for three hundred years – when my family had been peasants or vagabonds or worse – and who now, although he was known to have gambled away what little money his spend-thrift grandfather had left him – still had an air of distance about him, the disdain a man of high pedigree cannot always conceal in his dealings with his inferiors. Yet he was the man my mother-in-law had spoken of as her best friend, her salvation in the dark days after her brother had died, and I refused, in fact I could not afford, to be afraid of him.

'Mrs Barforth. I trust you are well?'

'Quite well, thank you.'

'And wondering what I'm doing here, I imagine. Although, really, there's not much cause for wonder.'

'Sir Julian, I must tell you I think it improper of you to have come at all.'

He laughed, his dark eyes brushing over me with the automatic appraisal he bestowed on horseflesh, womanflesh, particularly – and the suspicion caused me to flush with welcome indignation – women who had lost their caste or their reputations.

'Improper? Now that's not a word I'm much used to hearing, Mrs Barforth. In my part of the world we tend to call it "bad taste".'

'You live ten miles away, Sir Julian.'

'So I do, but it could be another world, m'dear, for all that – different manners, different values. I hope that we may manage to understand one another?'

'What is it you wish me to understand?'

'Well, I wish to put an end to this nonsense for one thing, m'dear. No need for it, you know. Shocking business – won't attempt to deny it – and nobody in the world could blame you for being peeved about it. But we can settle it in a civilized manner, surely?'

'Yes, of course. That is my intention.'

His brows flew together in a frown, his face half suspicious, half ready to believe he had so easily got his way.

'You mean you've dropped this litigation?'

'I do not. I mean I intend to follow it through. *That* is the civilized solution.'

He took a pace or two about the room, shooting at me from time to time a look of pure contempt, his nostrils dilating with it, his whole manner expressing regret that he had been born too late to settle this dispute, and any others, by having me flogged at the manorial cart-tail.

'I see. I see, Mrs Barforth.'

But eventually the realization that he could not evict me from my cottage nor refuse to renew the lease on my farm, that he had no real power over me at all, took the edge from his anger and he returned to the hearthrug, doing his best to calm himself, one hand restlessly clenching as if it missed the feel of a riding-whip.

'Civilized, is it, Mrs Barforth, to drive a woman to her ruin? I wouldn't call that civilized.'

'Neither would I.'

'Then you'll be obliged to drop these proceedings, madam, unless you intend to make yourself responsible for the ruin of my niece. That's the plain truth, madam, and don't try to deny it.'

A moment of silence, his anger snapping around me and something more than anger, for after all he had come to protect his own kin, his brother's daughter whom he had raised casually, perhaps, but as his own child, and no one could blame him for that. Silence, and then my own voice dropping cool words into it one by one, speaking slowly because I had dreaded this, and was not finding it easy.

'You are quite right that my petition for divorce will do harm to Mrs Flood. I do not consider myself to blame for that.'

'Who then?' he snarled, very nearly at the end of his tether.

'That is not for me to say.'

There was another moment of silence, badly needed by us both, and then, remembering that he was here to defend his niece's reputation not to give himself the satisfaction of blackening mine, he overcame his temper and smiled.

'Come now, Mrs Barforth, we will gain nothing by quarrelling. Have you really considered, I wonder, what this could mean to Diana? I don't excuse her, but you can't put her through this agony, you know. Public exposure of a very private matter – the newspapers having a field-day, the poor girl branded an outcast, which is what would happen to her afterwards. It could be the end of her, Mrs Barforth, and I don't see how you could live easy with that on your conscience. And then there *is* her husband to be considered. He has his feelings, too, you know, and he at least has done you no harm. Very decent fellow, Compton Flood – absolutely first-rate – ambitious too, which would make it pretty well impossible for him to take her back after this sort of thing. With the best will in the world he'd be bound to feel that his career couldn't cope with the scandal.'

'What do you suggest I should do then, Sir Julian?'

'Be charitable, m'dear – and sensible. I daresay you can't forgive, and I suppose women never forget. But be sensible. You know the fix Diana is in. Don't hound her, Mrs Barforth. Let her have her child in peace and whatever arrangements are made for it afterwards – well, there's no reason why you should be troubled by them. That's the way these things are done, believe me. No need to go to extremes. And afterwards she'll be off to India to make her peace with her husband. No fuss, no mess, no proof, Mrs Barforth – no scandal. That's the thing. Water under the bridge next year, or the year after. It's the only way.'

'I almost wish I could agree with you.'

'I beg your pardon?'

'I am sorry, Sir Julian. I fully realize the seriousness of Mrs Flood's position. But I have my own position to consider and intend to do so. It seems to me a great pity that Mrs Flood failed to realize the consequences of her actions before it was too late – or before those actions had taken place at all. I repeat I am sorry, but I do not hold myself in any way responsible.'

He gave me a look of the most complete loathing and then, still restlessly flexing his hand, his lips drew apart in a grimace that was intended, but did not succeed, as a smile.

'So that's it. Vindictive, eh? – want your pound of flesh, do you? But I won't have it, Mrs Barforth. I won't stand idly by and see you ruin a thoroughly delightful girl for your sanctimonious whim. I warn you, madam, this shopkeeper's morality is not to my liking and I shall not tolerate it.'

I could have said, How dare you speak to me like that? I could have ordered him from the house, or I could have burst into tears. I believe I wanted to do all these things, but instead I remained quite still, hands folded, back very straight, rigid with my determination that I would not flinch. For, if this was the first abuse I had ever received, it could not be the last and I must school myself to meet it.

'Sir Julian, you may call me whatever names you choose, but the plain fact is that I have committed no offence against Mrs Flood. When she became my husband's mistress she was surely aware of the risk she ran. She must have known what the consequences might be to herself and to Colonel Flood, and I do not feel called upon to bear those consequences for her. This divorce is of the utmost importance to me. It is the only possible course I can take in order to lead what I believe to be an honest life, and I will not sacrifice that for the sake of Colonel Flood's career nor Mrs Flood's reputation. Would they put my interests before their own? Of course they would not, and neither would you. It is quite useless, Sir Julian, to bully me or intimidate me or to make me feel guilty, for I will not change my mind. I am prepared to take full responsibility for my own actions and Mrs Flood must do the same.'

He stood and glared at me for what must have been a full minute, his mouth a thin line, his face taut with anger, although suddenly and quite shockingly there were tears in his eyes.

996

'This could kill her you know. Damnation, woman, can't you see that?'

And when I made no answer but continued to stand as tall and straight as I could, he clenched those nervous fingers into a fist, smashed it hard into the palm of his other hand, and rapped out: 'Self-righteous bitch!'

'Good-day, Sir Julian.'

'Not for you, madam – there'll be no "good-day" for you, I promise it.'

He took his thunderous departure and I sat down on the nearest seat, my legs trembling, my whole body, as it relaxed from its awful rigidity, full of little aches and pains, my mind far too distracted in those first moments to realize that this attack could only mean that Gervase had refused to put an end to the matter by coming back to me.

Beyond the window, the spring afternoon continued to sparkle, daffodils tossing their bold heads in the fresh breeze, new green on the trees and a hint of pink and white blossom; an impulsive, passionate season, more adapted to the making of light-hearted promises than the grim keeping of one's resolve. I heard a bee, the first of the year, new-born and boisterous on the window-sill, a voice in the hall saying something about tea, a deeper voice answering 'Presently', and then Mrs Agbrigg came into the room and sat down in the chair opposite mine, choosing her moment well, I thought, since I was still too exhausted by my confrontation with Sir Julian to engage successfully in another.

'Grace, I think it is time we had a word about your situation,' she said, and I looked across at her, the dragon of my childhood, velvet-pawed now but still very powerful, and smiled.

'Yes. But you must not be afraid that I have come to seek permanent refuge here, you know. You will not be troubled with me forever, Mrs Agbrigg, for it is my intention, when everything is settled, to live alone.'

She returned my smile, her large, handsome face hardly creasing, folded her smooth hands, her rings catching the light in the way I remembered, the heavy gold cross still at her throat.

'Your father has explained all that to me and I have every confidence in your ability to keep your own house in order. It is the, shall we say social, aspect of the matter I would like to take up with you.'

'My goodness, Mrs Agbrigg – you mean Mrs Rawnsley will cross the street to avoid meeting me and Miss Mandelbaum may feel uneasy about asking me to tea?'

But she shook her sedate head with an unruffled, almost placid motion.

'No Grace, I do not mean that at all. I would not expect you to value the good opinion of Mrs Rawnsley and Miss Mandelbaum since you have never been without it – as I have. Tell me, Grace, was Sir Julian very rough with you?'

'Yes.'

'In fact he spoke to you as no gentleman has ever spoken to you before?'

'Yes, he did.'

'I wonder if you know why? No, not entirely because of Mrs Flood, but because you had placed yourself in a situation where he was no longer

997

obliged to consider you a lady. Men have a keen nose for these things, my dear. And when a woman ceases to be a lady, she is just – well – just a woman and consequently fair game for anything a gentleman may have in mind. For a gentleman, you know, will do what he likes, or what he can, with a *woman*.'

I moved uncomfortably in my chair, surprised not only by her words but by the sincerity and the concern with which she expressed them.

'But Mrs Agbrigg, why? I am not an adulteress – I have done nothing to lose my reputation.'

'My dear, indeed you have. You have flouted convention, don't you see? You have shrugged off the authority of your male relations and are setting yourself up in an independent fashion – your own home, your own income, keeping your own carriage – while your husband and your father are still living. You are a threat to society, my dear, for what would happen if the rest of society's wives and daughters were to follow your example? Domestic chaos, dearest, and – which is a far more serious matter – *financial* chaos too. No, no, you cannot be allowed to live free and happy, for that would be an inducement, would it not, to other women. And so what can society do but shun you, impose a total ban on you, fill your life with as much insult and irritation as possible? My dear, they would find it easier to forgive you if you *had* committed adultery. And that apart, what man, meeting you in the years to come, will enquire into the exact circumstances of your divorce or even care about them? You will have a label, "Divorced Woman", that is all he will see. And what it will mean to him is "Woman of Easy Virtue". Once your divorce is granted – if it ever should be – no man who desires you will feel obliged to restrain himself from telling you so. You will be subject to the most positive advances, my child – to a degree of aggression which I doubt you capable of imagining.'

'Mrs Agbrigg – I believe you are afraid for me.'

She sighed and unclasped her hands a little, looking fondly down at her rings.

'And of course that surprises you? You do not know me very well, Grace. I wore a label too, you see, from the start which said "Wicked Stepmother" in bold letters, which was natural enough. You had made up your mind to dislike me and I saw no real harm in it. My maternal instinct is not strong. I wanted to be your father's wife, not the mother of his child, and beyond the physical comforts of good food and good shelter I had nothing to offer you. You had your Aunt Faith and your friends. I had your father and intended to keep him. You know that. But your Aunt Faith cannot tell you how it feels to be treated like a whore. I can. Will you listen to me?'

'Gladly.'

'I made my first money, Grace, by satisfying the perverse appetites of a man who – well – let us say I was thirteen years old at the time and he was at least fifty years older than that. And if it shocks you that there are women – and children – who do these things for money, may I remind you that it is only men who do them for pleasure. When he died I found another "protector", which is an excellent description, since that is what a woman of my old profession most needs – protection. And not only from the lusts and hazards of her clients and of the streets but protection from the self-righteous, who are rarely charitable, and from the "godly", who more often than not have no imagination and not much compassion. I soon understood that the only real protection was respectability. I earned money. I learned to speak and dress like a lady. I tried, when my circumstances allowed it, to live a decent life among decent people. It always proved impossible. I was always "exposed" and suitably punished. Eventually I came north and one night, at a music-hall in Leeds, I met Mr Matthew Oldroyd of Fieldhead Mills, another old man of the type I was used to, although I was myself no longer thirteen nor even thirty. He brought me to Cullingford and set me up in the kind of little "love-nest" I had inhabited often enough before – my last, I thought, considering my age and my competition, and so I was determined to make the most of it. I was warm and comfortable. I had gold rings and more than enough to eat. But the ladies of your town still drew their skirts aside, still looked down their noses as if I had sprayed myself with their own foul sewage water instead of the most expensive perfumes of France. Well, you will not find yourself in quite those circumstances, Grace, but once you step outside the charmed circle of respectability you will enter a jungle – believe me – where the hunters are very far from gentlemen.

'But not all beasts, surely, Mrs Agbrigg.'

'No,' she said, looking into the far distance. 'Not all. There was Tom Delaney, for instance – yes, there *was* a Mr Delaney, who was my husband, if only in common law, until he died in prison, at twenty-five years old, of the fever. And Matthew Oldroyd was not a beast either, just old and sour and fool enough to marry me to spite his relations. And your father – dare I mention your father?'

I nodded, and for the first time since I had known her she leaned back in her chair, her large, handsome body arranging itself with less grace than comfort, a woman of a certain age who, having found a secure refuge, no longer felt the need to be young.

'I like your father,' she said, a simple statement of which no one could have doubted the truth. 'Indeed I do. I made up my mind from the start, when we were both employed by Matthew Oldroyd – your father as his lawyer and myself as his mistress – that I would get him one way or another.'

'And he?'

'Oh no – he was still half in love with – well, with a dream he once had, I suppose. But he found the reality – my reality – very comfortable. He wanted my money, of course, and I wanted the respectability I knew he would somehow contrive to give me. That was the bargain he thought we were striking and he expected nothing more, for his life had been meagre and at the start he was shy of taking. But I am very determined, Grace – as you are – and I made up my mind that if I'd survived what I *had* survived, if I'd kept body and soul together on fresh air and cold water

999

sometimes, *and* made myself a fortune out of Matthew Oldroyd, then surely I could make my husband like me. He does. There now, I've got more than I deserved, but I came here to talk about you. Do you mean to go through with this, Grace?'

I nodded.

'I thought so. I don't like it, child, because it hurts your father. He doesn't know, you see, just how long it's been hurting you – as I know – and he's afraid you might not stay in Cullingford when it's done.'

'I hadn't thought of it.'

'Think of it now. Much easier, of course, to go away – a clean start where no one knows enough to tell tales. You could lose yourself in a big city, go abroad, buy a cottage in a country town and call yourself a widow.'

'Yes –'

'It would ease his mind if I could give him the impression that you mean to stay here, where he can keep his eye on you.'

'Yes,' I said once again, and, smiling, she leaned forward and put her smooth, brown hand over mine.

'You see, Grace, there is no real freedom – not until the last person you care about is gone. I believe you were planning, were you not, on that fresh start?'

'I think so. I suppose a man would just get up and go, wouldn't he – regardless of anyone else?'

'Not your father.'

She stood up, having achieved her purpose as she always had, but I understood her now and it seemed right to me that she should go and lay my promise to remain in Cullingford at my father's feet as another gift of love – *her* love, she would make sure he realized, and not mine. And that seemed right to me too.

'Mrs Agbrigg.'

'My dear?'

'Is there a name I can call you? Mrs Agbrigg no longer seems appropriate and I think we have gone rather beyond stepmamma.'

'My name is Tessa,' she said. 'Why not? Call me that, dear, the next time Mrs Rawnsley comes to tea, and when you see her pinched lips and her accusing eyes you will know that your apprenticeship in independence has begun.'

20

'But what is it all for?' Blanche asked in great perplexity. 'I am broadminded enough I believe – good heavens! with the company I keep how could I be any other? – but I really cannot see the point of these extreme measures. Ask yourself, Grace, is it necessary? I will tell you plainly that it is not wise.'

And when I merely smiled she gave an impatient little shrug and sighed.

'Ah well, if you are set on it you had better come back to London with me until it is over, for these old tabby cats up here will claw you to pieces once the news is out. Oh yes, they will, for they may have abused Gervase soundly so long as you were a poor, brave little woman who put up with his philandering. But once you are known to have turned against him they will all turn against you, for he is a *man* after all, and these dear ladies would rather have a wicked, attractive man any day of the week than a good woman. There is no need to worry about Aunt Caroline, if you should be worrying about her, for she is obliged to stay at South Erin, very likely for the whole season, to nurse the Duke's bronchitis. We shall have the house to ourselves.'

It would be a quiet season, she said, since she was still officially in mourning for Venetia, but Blanche's idea of a mourning gown was a cascade of black lace frills which turned her shoulders to marble, her hair to silver; her notion of a 'quiet season' involving her immediately in the complexities of calling-cards and invitation-cards with which, every morning, her hall-table was littered several inches deep.

Her friendship with the Prince of Wales which had launched her into society no longer occupied a great deal of her time, the Prince having turned his realistic eye on such ladies as the incomparable Sarah Bernhardt and Mrs Langtry, that most enduring and enterprising of Jersey Lilies. But Blanche's reputation had been made, and every year now, from April to late July, she could make her selection of lunch-parties and afternoon teas, could be sure that her carriage, whenever it appeared in the Park, would occasion a great raising of tall silk hats and quizzing glasses, a great many curious and envious stares. She could make her selection, too, of grand formal dinners any night of the week or could dine out in a smart restaurant, dash along to the theatre afterwards with a supper-party to follow, and then go on to catch the last hour or two of Lady So-and-So's ball. She would certainly attend Ascot and Goodwood and the Henley Regatta, would go to Hurlingham from time to time to watch a polo match, would visit whatever art galleries and exhibitions were being visited that year, would fit in, somehow or other, a garden party, an afternoon concert, put in an hour's enthusiastic shopping, sit at least one night a week in Aunt Caroline's box at the opera, a programme of events which would keep her fully occupied from nine o'clock in the morning, when she breakfasted, to four o'clock in the morning after, when she would be driven home in the clear summer daylight from a dance.

She saw little of Dominic, who had his own invitations and his seat in the House of Commons, which kept him busy, although not too strenuously, from February to August, all government conveniently closing down to accommodate the shooting of the early grouse and not reopening until very nearly the end of the hunting season. And in the spaces between his sporting and his political activities he maintained a friendly but very casual relationship with his wife.

No, Blanche admitted frankly in reply to my question, she would not say they actually lived together any more than Gervase and I had lived together this last year or two, but neither she nor Dominic felt inclined to make a drama of it. In Cullingford perhaps – and here she raised a pointed eyebrow – it may not have been so simple, but in London it was quite the thing and no one thought it worth a mention.

'You should spend more time in London, Grace.'

'I have not the stamina, Blanche. The hours you keep would kill me.,'

'Nonsense. One easily gets accustomed to that. You know exactly what I mean. If you have this fancy to live alone, then take a house here for three-quarters of the year, while Gervase stays at Galton. The first year or two our good ladies might gossip but eventually they would find something else to gossip about – something they could prove – and would be delighted to see you whenever you came north, as they are always so delighted to see me. Grace – it would be *exactly* the same as divorce, except that you could keep your reputation.'

'And I would still be married to Gervase.'

'And what difference can that possibly make unless you should want to marry someboday else? You don't wish to do that, do you?'

'No.'

'Then really, Grace – why make such a fuss? When one sees a chance to get the best of both worlds – to have one's freedom and still be married. Good lord! one doesn't just take it, one seizes it with both hands. Why ever not? Unless, of course – oh dear, Grace, I do hope you have not filled your head with notions of looking for a grand passion, like Venetia.'

But there was a drop more passion in Blanche's own nature than she cared to admit, a certain very human anxiety and need for reassurance which sometimes succeeded in penetrating even the gilt and glitter of her 'Season'. In early January that year, five thousand British soldiers, Captain Noel St John Chard among them, had marched into Zululand, supported by some eight thousand native troops, to confront, under the leadership of Viscount Chelmsford, the forty thousand warriors of the Zulu king Cetewayo. On the twenty-second of that month, Chelmsford having split his forces and ridden off with half his men looking for battle, ten thousand Zulu warriors fell upon the British camp at Isandhlwana, spearing all but fifty of our eighteen hundred British officers and men to death.

Noel Chard, it transpired, had not been at Isandhlwana, nor was he at Rorke's Drift where, that same day and the following night, a minute British garrison of eighty-five fighting men endured six ferocious Zulu attacks, losing only seventeen of their number. But as skirmish succeeded skirmish, as more British soldiers were hacked to death, here and there, by those fanatical Zulu spears, Blanche's fears for Noel grew, giving rise to sudden lapses of memory, sudden demands, through the bird-twitter of society's tea-tables, for news from Africa.

The Prince Imperial, the only son of the late, deposed Napoleon III of France and his Empress Eugenie, who had gone out as a volunteer, was killed that June in a Zulu ambush, a sad end for this young descendant of Bonaparte who had been popular in London, much liked by the Prince of Wales.

1002

'How terrible!' said Blanche, speaking of the Prince Imperial, thinking of Noel Chard, who even now could be bleeding somewhere in the dust, the mud, on some foul bullock-cart, who could have been speared by a Zulu assegai or fallen victim to some filthy African disease.

'What a waste!' she said, 'I don't even know what they hope to gain by it. If only he had stayed at Listonby as I told him.'

On the fourth of July, Chelmsford, with a force of over five thousand men, caught Cetewayo at Ulundi and there, after hard fighting, slaughtered a sufficient number of spear-throwers to proclaim himself a victory in fitting retribution for the massacre of Isandhlwana. Cetewayo fled. The war was over.

'What of the casualties?' Blanche moaned, turning white when the news was brought to her with the morning's invitations. And the dead? Are there no lists published as yet? Dominic must go and ask Disraeli, for surely the Prime Minister will know. And if he is listed as wounded, then Dominic had better go out there to fetch him home – or Gideon. What do you think?'

I couldn't be sure. Were her affections disturbing her or simply her conscience? But in either case once Dominic had made all possible enquiries there seemed nothing to do but wait, to continue the suddenly monotonous round of balls and dinners and drives in the Park. And it was there, some days later, during the hour before luncheon Blanche devoted to carriage exercise, that I saw Gideon Chard some way ahead of us, standing by a silk-lined victoria, in conversation with a lady.

He had, quite definitely, seen our approach – he could have done no other – yet neither he nor Blanche gave the slightest sign of recognition, Blanche, who had been planning to send him out to Zululand two days ago, looking through him now as if she had never set eyes on him before, while his expression remained polite but completely blank.

'Blanche, surely that is Gideon?'

'Don't stare,' she whispered, and as the two carriages came abreast and we could both easily have touched him, she bowed to a passing acquaintance on the other side and adjusted the handle of her parasol.

'Really Blanche – if he does not wish to speak to me –'

But she clicked her tongue with rare impatience and snapped her parasol tight shut.

'Don't be such a goose, Grace. It has nothing to do with us at all. You have been out in the world long enough by now, surely, to know that a gentleman does not embarrass a lady, nor a lady a gentleman, by acknowledging one another – no matter how well they are acquainted – when he is with his mistress. Good lord! Grace, I would have died if you had spoken to him – and so, I expect, would he. For goodness' sake do not look back – what are you thinking of?'

'Mistress? Already?'

She shrugged, pouted.

'Well, she may not be his mistress now. In fact she probably is not, for it must be all of three years since I first saw them together and these affairs do not often last so long as that. But come, Grace, you know the terms on which he stood with Venetia. One can hardly blame him. And Venetia would not have cared. She is an actress, or dancer, or some such thing and we could not be asked to meet her in any case.'

'So we did not see him?'

'We certainly did not. And we will not mention it when we do see him. I wonder when he arrived and why he is not staying with us? Perhaps he is, for we have been out since breakfast-time and Dominic would not necessarily mention it to me. I suppose they were both out on the town last night and slept until noon, for he does not look as if he has just got off the train in those clothes.'

I had not seen him since my departure from Tarn Edge and experienced now so powerful an aversion to sharing, even for one night, a roof with him that had it been possible I would have gone to a chance acquaintance, an hotel, anywhere to avoid him. I could not have said why. The fact that he had a mistress did not surprise me. Had it occurred to me to wonder I would have assumed he had. Nor did I anticipate any interference from him in my own affairs. He had no right to interfere. I had no right to be disturbed by his visit to his brother. Yet I *was* disturbed. Irrationally, idiotically, I did not wish to see him or hear him, and was considerably put out on our return to see two silk hats in Blanche's hall, two pairs of gloves, two large, dark-skinned Chards, not one, lounging by the drawing-room fireplace, requiring fresh tea with *lemon*, for God's sake, not cream and sugar; is there nothing else, Blanche, for my brother to eat but these odd little rout cakes, and does that doorbell never stop ringing?

He had come, as we supposed, for news of Noel, the Zulu war providing discussion enough for that uneasy tea-time hour, Sir Dominic taking his brother to dine at his club while Blanche attended an engagement of her own and I had my supper on a tray, my mind back in Cullingford among my familiar anxieties. The court order requiring Gervase to return to me had been obtained. My father had written informing me of the date, the implications, what I must and must not do. Mrs Agbrigg had written enquiring after my health and reporting on my father's, asking me to send her a special brand of clover honey from an address in Chelsea which, when taken with milk and cinnamon, would do wonders for his cough. Aunt Faith had written saying, 'Darling – if this is what you want then God Bless you.' My Grandmother Agbrigg had written from Scarborough supposing I had learned this kind of behaviour from Mrs Agbrigg. Mrs Barforth – did she still think of herself as my mother-in-law? – had written of her daily round at Galton, her joy in the fine weather, the progress of that timid collie puppy. Aunt Caroline had written to Blanche from South Erin without once mentioning my name.

But no one had written or spoken to me a word about Gervase. I knew nothing of his whereabouts – except that he was not at Tarn Edge and did not seem to be at Galton – nothing of his plans, except that he would probably have made no plans; nothing of his fears, except that he would probably be afraid. I didn't know his reactions to the divorce itself, whether he wanted it, intended to contest it, or did not care. I didn't know if he still wished to go abroad, nor how much Diana Flood's decision not to accompany him had hurt him; whether in fact, now that her ruin seemed unavoidable, she may even have changed her mind. I didn't know, at the start of every morning, if the day might bring him to Blanche's door demanding my return to our matrimonial home in compliance with the court order I had myself obtained. I didn't know what pressure Sir Julian Flood, or Diana Flood herself, may have put upon him to that end, nor how much – or how little – her desperation might move him.

The last time I had heard his voice he had ordered me to leave him alone. The last time I had seen him he had been standing like a wraith at Venetia's graveside with no more hope – it must have seemed to him – in his hollow, fretful life than she had found in hers. I couldn't help him. I knew it and I had been very careful, for a long time, not to love him. But he worried me – just that – a faint but ever-present anxiety hovering at the edge of my mind, leaving me in no doubt that it would have been far easier had I managed to hate him.

He worried me. Yet Gideon Chard worried me too, for reasons I seemed unable to bring to the surface of my mind, so that I was far from pleased when, returning sooner than I had expected, he found me still in the drawing-room with the coffee-tray.

'They have left you alone, have they?' he said, although I believe he had expected to find me so.

'As you see. Is there any news of Noel?'

He shook his head.

'We know Chelmsford lost a hundred men and Noel does not seem to have been among them. The chances are he is perfectly fit and well, and has won medals and promotion – which pleases me enormously when one considers he is the least warlike of the three of us.'

'Yes. But if you will excuse me, Gideon, I am rather tired.'

Again he shook his head and smiled a little wryly but with a great deal of studied charm; the smile, I thought, of a man who wishes to persuade, or who has something to sell.

'I am sorry for that. I came back early on purpose to speak to you and would be grateful for just a moment –'

'I am really very tired – perhaps tomorrow?'

'I may not be here tomorrow.'

'Then I am sorry but I must say good-night.'

'No, Grace.'

'I beg your pardon?'

'I have something to say to you. I intend to say it.'

'Oh – do you catch the early train tomorrow?'

'My plans are uncertain. Sit down, Grace. Please.'

'No – no – I simply wondered if you would take a package for me to Mrs Agbrigg – something she asked me to buy for my father?'

'With pleasure – when we have had a word.'

'I will let you have the parcel in the morning then, at breakfast –'

'*Grace.*'

1005

And as I moved to the door, pushing the air away from me in my haste, he rapped out: 'Grace, I will follow you upstairs if I must, which will do nothing either for your nerves or your reputation.'

I paused, my hand on the doorknob, willing myself to turn it and walk up the stairs without looking back; willing myself to shrug off the claims he was about to make, the restraints he was about to impose, like the free spirit I wished to be. I paused – for how dare he speak of *nerves*? – and hesitated, feeling, in fact, as nervous as I had ever done.

'Grace,' he said, no hesitation anywhere within him. 'Unless you wish me to shout my questions through your bedroom door for all to hear, you will remain in this room and you will tell me why you are set on this folly.'

'You have no right to ask that question.'

'I daresay. But I insist upon an answer and you should know me well enough by now to realize that I will go on asking until you give it to me.'

I knew him. I knew him far too well. I walked back and stood on the hearthrug before the empty summer grate in the favourite vantage point of authority, the spot where he and Mr Barforth and my father and all the other masters of households and fortunes and destinies were accustomed to stand, my hands neatly folded, my back straight, the posture I had adopted for my confrontation with Sir Julian Flood, telling myself – without believing – that this confrontation could be no worse.

'By "folly", Gideon, I presume you mean my divorce. And what I have to say to you on that score is quickly done, since it does not concern you in the very least.'

'You are quite wrong, believe me.'

And now, forcing myself to look at him, I saw that the charm was gone, leaving his face careful, serious, very determined.

'Grace, when all is said, and done, we have shared a roof these past few years. I have come to value you very highly and cannot keep silent when I see you embark on this course of self-destruction. Whether you realize it or not, you have lived very sheltered and somebody must tell you what the world is like.'

'There is no need for you to take the trouble, Gideon. Mrs Agbrigg and Sir Julian Flood have done it for you.'

He made a movement that was both contemptuous and irritable, dismissing Sir Julian as an older man and consequently out of touch, Mrs Agbrigg as a woman of dubious reputation herself, who, being unreliable in her morals, could be trusted in nothing else.

'I daresay – in fact I heard something of your interview with Flood. But he has his own axe to grind.'

'And you do not?'

'Yes, if you like – if concern for you can be called an axe, then yes, I have one. I do not mean to stand idly by and see you go to your ruin.'

'Good heavens! Gideon, your knight-errantry does you credit, but I do not expect to find myself entirely beyond the pale. I do not intend to set up house with a lover, you know.'

'You intend to live alone,' he said, his jaw clenching as if the words made him very angry, 'which is just as bad.'

And his loss of temper where there should have been nothing warmer than a faint irritation, this smouldering anger when all that was required of him was to be mildly disappointed, alarmed me, for I did not feel very composed either, having far less inclination than usual to defend myself.

'There is no need for this, Grace,' he said, speaking quickly while I still seemed disposed to listen. 'What do you really have to gain by it? Yes – I know, I know – I have seen the difficulties you have had to face. I know what Gervase is, and what he does. I have seen your courage and feel no surprise that your patience is at an end. But why give up your home for his sake? And Tarn Edge *is* your home, Grace. If he could be persuaded to leave you alone – and he *could* be so persuaded – there is no reason why you should not continue to live there and enjoy the same respect, the same authority – the same *independence*, for who has ever attempted to restrain you? You are valued at Tarn Edge. Why cut yourself off from that? And for what? The pleasure of setting up in some poky place of your own and enduring the insults of those who – well, for want of a better word, those ladies who cannot hold a candle to you, and of those 'gentlemen' who will come swarming like bees around clover. Surely, Grace – since you would be free of Gervase either way – what is the sense in deliberately exposing yourself to harrassment and injury? I see no sense in it.'

'Ah – and *I* see that you are not satisfied with the way they have been laundering your shirts since I went away.'

He could very easily have thrown back his handsome head and laughed. I hoped rather earnestly that he would. But instead his heavy eyebrows flew together, his face not flushing but darkening with a rush of temper which would have gone ill with me had I been in his employ or had I been his wife. Yet when he spoke again his voice was low and even.

'Grace, since we are speaking plainly – I know there are times when you dislike me. I am not sure I merit it, not every time.'

'Probably you do not.'

'Very well. You believe I married for money. You are quite right, of course.'

'Gideon, it has absolutely nothing to do with me –'

'*Grace* – will you leave off this constant side-stepping of every important issue, for God's sake! If I wish you to be concerned in it, then you are concerned, and I am entitled to defend myself. Yes – it was for money. But I wonder if you realize what small provision is made in families like mine for younger sons? We are all brought up to be princes, but in the end everything, the land, the title, such money as there is – everything – is for the eldest son, the heir. I don't quarrel with that. It is the only way an estate can be kept intact. If every son took his share there would soon be no great estates at all, important houses would fall into decay, and no man would have the means to support his title. I know that. Younger sons are obliged to do the best they can within the limits custom permits – and the one thing custom positively encourages is the making of a good marriage. Grace, I saw my way to the kind of life I desire by entering the mills, for my tastes are luxurious and exacting, I

1007

cannot deny it. And nothing – *nothing* – either in my upbringing or my education told me I was wrong to marry my employer's daughter.'

'Of course not.'

'Yet you have accused me, in thought, I know it, and now you will listen to my defence. Was I cruel to her? She believed I took her solely for the money, insisted on believing it, and it is perfectly correct that I would not have taken her without it. But the truth is that I found her attractive to begin with and if she had allowed it I would have – Damnation! Grace, you know exactly what I mean. You saw me today with that woman in the Park. You must know how little that sort of thing can matter –'

'Of course – just a woman for your convenience, at your convenience. What can it mean?'

'It means,' he snapped, 'a woman who gives me what I pay for and no more, and with whom I know exactly where I stand. Not an ideal arrangement, but businesslike – the best, from time to time, that one can manage – and which has the advantage of hurting no one.'

'Yes. I beg your pardon.'

'Will you agree, then, that my intentions were not wholly callous – that I may have had *some* fondness for her when we married, and that when I took her back I may have felt some pity? Do you think it was done entirely for the sake of that managing directorship?'

'Venetia thought so.'

'Yes. Venetia thought so. What does Grace think?'

'I think you asked for your promotion, or made it clear you would expect it.'

'Yes,' he said unexpectedly, somewhat disarming me. 'I did.'

'*Gideon.*'

'Why not? Mr Nicholas Barforth, in my place, would have done the same. He knew what I wanted and how long I had waited for it. He also knew that I had earned it. When Venetia left me he gave only half of what he had promised – the limited company. When she came back I had no need to tell him I wanted the other half – to be managing director of it. He knew. I sat in his office and waited for his offer. And then I made sure it was exactly the offer I required before I took it. But he can't know – and you can't know, Grace – what I would have done if the offer had not been made.'

'It can make no real difference now.'

'Yes, it can, if I can gain your good opinion. And if not then – listen, Grace, if I am the reason you cannot return to Tarn Edge then *I* will leave, not you. A man can live anywhere, and I am away a great deal in any case.'

'Yes Gideon – and for how long?'

And feeling suddenly hemmed-in with him in this large, high-ceilinged room, too close to him, impeded by him, although we were a yard apart, I knew I must end it as quickly as I could and walk cleanly and decisively away.

'I ask for how long because in fact once I was safely back at Tarn Edge and had rendered my divorce impossible, you would come back too.'

'I would hope to do so – at your invitation – I admit it.'

'And if I did not invite you, you would come back just the same.'

He grinned, quite boyishly, my stomach lurching at the display of his charm in an altogether dreadful fashion.

'I imagine I might try that.'

'I am sure of it. And I quite understand why. A house the size of Tarn Edge needs an efficient mistress, for even the best of housekeepers grow slack after a time. I suppose things are sliding already and my return would quickly put that right. I know, Gideon – there is a house to run and even a child to educate. I also know that sooner or later you will marry again. My presence at Tarn Edge would be less convenient to you then, and possibly most unwelcome to your new wife.'

He came quite close to me, his feet on the hearthrug only an inch away from mine, the frilled hem of my skirt touching his polished evening shoe; his hand, on the mantelshelf behind my head, allowing his body to lean forward, not touching me but *over* me, my own awareness of his breathing, the movement of pulse and muscle and vitality beneath his skin, the skin itself, a great trouble to me; my own senses, which I had allowed to grow sluggish, stirring now to curiosity and excitement, for those senses, after all, were barely twenty-five years old and had once been very strong.

'I will not marry again,' he said.

'Nonsense!'

'*Grace* – I will not marry again and for a very good reason which you should understand – which you *do* understand.'

And leaning closer, his eyes seeming to bore into my skull as if he meant to inject his meaning inside it, he repeated his words over again, his face grim and hard with concentration, the force of his will taking me prisoner so that my breathing came no longer at my own pace but at his, my pulse catching the rhythm of his pulse, quickening to meet it and match it and be absorbed by it. Yes, I understood. And how could I be shocked by the desire which had existed for so long, dormant yet terribly present, in all our dealings with one another? All he was asking me to do was call that desire by its proper name, to receive it, to *accept* it, now that the obstacles to its fulfilment – my husband, his wife – no longer stood quite so visibly in our way. He was asking me to do what the very root of my body longed for and which only a portion of my mind resisted. I was not ashamed of my body. I was glad of the joy it had once brought me and could readily admit how urgently I often craved that joy again. But if Gideon was desire then he was also captivity, strong arms to enchant me and bind me; demands that would obliterate my own demands; needs that would soon swallow up my needs; an identity that would overshadow mine. And I did not trust him.

His hand tightened on the mantelshelf, his face hardening still further, not with anger but the sheer effort of his control.

'I should not speak to you now, I know it, and would have said nothing, except that you leave me no choice. If you had stayed at Tarn Edge as I expected, there would have been no need for this. I could have bided my time – chosen a better moment.'

'Gideon –'

'Yes – and even now, when I am driven to speak, what can I say that you will listen to? How can I make you understand the necessity – that this is *right* for you, Grace? I am saying come back to Tarn Edge, not to keep the house nor raise the child, but to make your life there.'

'With you?'

'Yes – in time. *Yes* Grace, look at me – if you had not married him in such a rush I believe you would have married me. You ought to have married me, and I think you know it.'

'You did not ask me to marry you, Gideon.'

'I was given no opportunity to do so. Suddenly you became the property of Gervase Barforth – or so his father would have me believe – and I was warned off. And it has not been easy, Grace, believe me, these past years, living in that house with you, seeing the evidence, every day right beneath my eyes, of how perfectly we would have suited each other.'

'And now you want me to remain married to Gervase so that I can stay at Tarn Edge and continue to suit you perfectly – to be your mistress, in fact?'

'Yes,' he said, bowing his head. 'In time – I said in time. Put like that – and so soon – it can only shock you, I know. But I could hardly take the risk of keeping silent and allowing you to go on with your present plans, Grace, believe what I say. It would be right for us.'

I shook my head, compelled to deny it, and with great audacity – foolhardiness – force of habit. I couldn't tell, he put a hand on the nape of my neck, a large, warm hand as unlike Gervase's cool, narrow touch as it could possibly be, and let it stay there just long enough to be sure of his welcome before he began to stroke reassurance into my shoulders and the length and the small of my back, reminding my body – which had not forgotten – of hunger and pleasure, of the healthy need for a man's caresses.

'Yes, Grace, it is right. We know each other. You understand the life I lead and I understand the life you should be leading. I can give you that life. Gervase will be far away and will not trouble us. I want you, darling, and I think – I know – you want me.'

Of course I wanted him. I had stood years ago in the Long Gallery at Listonby and wanted him so much that it had terrified me and driven me to what had seemed the lesser peril of Gervase. I wanted him now and was no longer afraid of the physical consequences, indeed I was only too well aware of how glorious those consequences could be. I had only to take one step towards him and at once – tonight and in this house – he would possess me, claim me, take the whole course of my life into his capable, challenging hands. I could wake in the morning as his mistress, replete, perhaps, and purring like a satiated cat but entirely dependent on the duration of his desire, on how long and how much I could continue to please him. And what greater risk, what greater humiliation could there be for any woman than that?

I needed anger to combat that dreadful, wonderful melting of my limbs, disgust to subdue that quick, hungry stirring at the pit of my stomach. I needed a weapon. I found it, hurt myself a little against it, and then pointed its keen, cutting edge straight at him.

'Why don't you ask me to marry you now, Gideon?'

But perhaps he had expected this and had taken thought what to say.

'How can I do that?'

'After my divorce I believe you can?'

'If it were so easy I need not have spoken to you now. I could simply have waited and then, when the time was opportune, come a-courting in the proper manner. I should have enjoyed that, Grace. But a man may not marry his deceased wife's sister, that much I do know. What the law says in the case of a sister-in-law who is divorced from a deceased wife's brother, I don't profess to know. But it has an illegal ring to it, somehow. One would have to make very sure.'

I needed scorn now to match my anger and disgust and, catching my breath – taking note of his smooth, easy manner, his confidence in his ability to persuade me – I found that too.

'I think such enquiries would be a waste of time in our case, Gideon, and had you thought otherwise you would have already made them.'

'Come, darling – really, I had to seize my opportunity and could hardly equip myself with every detail –'

'Oh yes, you could – and did – for the truth is that you do not wish, whatever the law may say, to marry a divorced woman, do you?'

'Darling –'

'And I think you will never call me darling in public, Gideon, because – well, because your mother, the Duchess, would be likely to throw a fit at the very idea, and your brother, the baronet, would not like it. And moreover – and far more to the point – I think your own sense of good taste and expediency is rather revolted by it too.'

'Grace – that is not kind.'

'No. But true, I think, because – Listonby and Westminster apart – the Goldsmiths and the Fauconniers would not care to associate with me either. A divorced woman is a social embarrassment. I have been warned of that often enough, and that would not do for you, Gideon. After all, my skills as a hostess would be no good to you, would they, if no respectable – *useful* people could be persuaded to accept my invitations. But if I remained your sister-in-law, safely married to Gervase who would never be there, *then* I could be a social asset, I quite see that. And if at the same time I discreetly shared your bed, your friends would not mind that at all and – well, how very much more convenient to have a mistress waiting in one's own home than to be obliged to pursue one in the Park. I see that too. Yes, I could be of great use to you, Gideon, until your mother found you the earl's daughter or the merchant princess she has always dreamed of.'

I saw the colour leave his face, felt his body harden and turn cold, and then, stepping away from me, he bowed, not, I thought, accepting defeat but disdaining to make any defence.

'I am sorry your opinon of me should be so ill,' he said curtly. 'If you would care to give me the parcel you spoke of, I will see that it is delivered to Fieldhead.'

But there could be no question now of parcels for Fieldhead or anything else. If Gideon remained in this house tomorrow, then I would be obliged to leave it, for I could face him neither as the man I had insulted nor as the man I had desired and might – very probably – desire again. But I came downstairs in the morning to find all changed, for news had been delivered in the night that Noel Chard had indeed been wounded at Ulundi, how seriously was not known. Blanche was in despair, had already sent a flurry of telegrams to her father in Cullingford who, she said, would have contacts, would know what to do; while both Dominic and Gideon were arranging to leave for Natal at once.

I remained in London with Blanche through a stifling August, a September that was wet in patches, hot and overcast in others, my own concerns oveshadowed by her agonized waiting for telegrams, letters, casual, unfeeling gossip that prostrated her on her bed, struggling with the first passion of her hitherto passionless life, terrified as a child because, like a child, she believed it would go on hurting forever.

I gave what comfort I could, sat with her and shared her vigil, the Season being over now and all her acquaintances gone to their shooting-parties, their country estates, escaping her demands only rarely to walk alone in the empty autumn streets. And it was on one such solitary outing that I came face to face with Gervase.

It was not, of course, by chance, and seeing my shock and my inability to conceal it, he came hurrying forward, light and pale and thinner, I thought, than I remembered, the skin at his eye-corners crinkling as he smiled, his hat tilted at the rakish angle he always wore it, carrying himself with all the accustomed young man's dash and swagger but his face hollower somehow, and a little older.

'Grace, you look as if you had seen a ghost. Don't worry. I know the court order has nearly expired, but I have not come to comply with it and ruin your life all over again.'

'They said we should not see each other.'

'I know. But we shall not tell.'

And for the first time in our lives the hand he put on my arm was firm and purposeful while mine was trembling, the strength of his will the greater, since I was too shaken to have any strength at all.

'One moment only, Grace. I am in London on other business and it seemed ridiculous to go away without seeing you, since there may not be another chance.'

And to avoid the certainty of bursting into tears I would not ask him what he meant to do, could only question him by a glance, a movement of the hands, the whole of my mind overwhelmed not by pain but by a deep sadness. There was no bitterness left, no need to strike out, no sense of outrage, no sustaining anger. I felt like the parkland and the trees all about me, waterlogged, fog-bound, wet and weary.

'It seems I have a son,' he told me, and through the mist which seemed to have settled around me I smiled weakly, knowing full well that I was here, wide awake, hearing this and believing it, yet feeling myself to be in a dream.

'Yes – and what now, Gervase?'

He shrugged, smiling too, his eye-corners creased again, those first marks of age sitting oddly on his boyish face, a mask he might suddenly remove and throw away.

'Well, I shall see Diana settled first, one way or the other. And then I shall go abroad if I can.'

'Settled?'

'Yes. Compton Flood is to be Lord Sternmore any day now, and Diana is still rather keen on that. At first he said no, wouldn't hear of it. But the title has no money to go with it you see, and at the moment he's having a long good think about that. If Diana goes abroad for a bit after you've done with her, to let the talk die down, and comes back a little richer, then he might forgive her. I expect he will. But if not she'll have to go abroad again, with me.'

'Gervase, are you still in love with her?'

'No. I'm not in love with anybody, Grace.'

And feeling misty still and far away, I nodded and smiled.

'Do you understand why I'm going through with the divorce?'

'I do. Otherwise I would have come back to you, wouldn't I, like the court order said, and saved Diana. That's what they wanted me to do. I didn't – for what it's worth to you.'

'It's worth a great deal. Where are you going?'

'Oh – sheep-shearing in Austrialia, perhaps – or herding cattle in America. It doesn't really matter. Not running, as I suppose you think. Searching might be nearer the mark. But why I'm here now is to put your mind at rest. I'll raise no sudden obstacles in your way, Grace. That's all.'

He took my hand and pressed it, the cool, light touch I knew, the sad smile I had not met before, my own sadness settling around me like a cloud, insubantial but impenetrable, weighing me down.

'Goodbye, Grace – and good luck.'

'Gervase – take care.'

'Well, I don't know about that.'

He walked away and the cloud was all over me, a soft barrier dimming my sight and my senses, making it impossible for me to cry out since all sound must have died away in that thick, sorrowful air. And I walked back to Blanche's tall, tense house, tears dripping from my eyes like raindrops from those sodden trees, remembering that he had had no cloak, thinking of the dust and dangers of cattle stations, sheep stations, his eyes that betrayed lack of sleep, his fancies and his fears; his tendency to take cold.

21

And so it was done. I entered a bare court-room in the company of lawyers whose main concern was for their fee, and placed before a judge who did not like me the better for it the evidence of servants and of a new-born child that my husband had committed adultery with the wife of Colonel Compton Flood – Lord Sternmore any day now. I proved conclusively that the guilty pair had lived openly together for some months at Cullingford Manor and before that had been seen in the most compromising of situations, quite regularly, by Mrs Flood's maid. I proved that my husband had abandoned me and refused to return. I tore to pieces the reputation of the aforesaid Mrs Flood, causing her to seek refuge abroad. I broke the heart of Colonel Compton Flood who, while the trial was in progress, finally became Lord Sternmore, leaving his uncle's death-bed a nobler and, if he chose to compromise, a richer man.

I forced my own husband to abandon his home, his inheritance and his mistress, to hide his disgraced head in rough colonial pastures, very likely never to return. I branded a tiny baby boy with the stigma of bastardy. Or so a certain section of the Press implied, finding more drama and consequently more sympathy in the plight of the disgraced but evidently warm-blooded Diana Flood than in the cold-hearted wife who had taken her revenge. Had I plunged a jealous knife into Mrs Flood's heart perhaps I would have been more easily forgiven. But my vengeance had been cool, calculating and very mercenary, since far from making any sacrifices I had actually gained by it. A little womanly compassion, the newspapers thought, would not have gone amiss among so much self-righteousness; while certain among them suggested – in general terms – that when a husband went astray it might only be realistic to assume that he had his reasons.

The judge, in the moment of pronouncing the decree, could not conceal his distaste for it. The barrister who had represented me, although an old college friend of my father's, treated me with great caution, feeling, perhaps, that a woman who could divorce her husband might be capable of anything, while his clerks and the officers of the court stared at me speculatively, rudely, and did not always drop their eyes when I caught them at it, as they would have done had they still considered me a lady.

Our marriage had taken a whole day to perform, flowers and white horses, organ music, champagne, two hundred happy guests. A few caustic words accompanied by a bad-tempered sniff ended it. But I knew that our divorce had really taken place on a wet afternoon in Hyde Park when he had made no excuses, asked no pardon, but had simply said 'Goodbye – good luck,' and I had replied 'Take care'. He had brought me a gift that day, not of love, for I believed him when he said he loved no one, but of understanding, and I had wept – could still weep – with gratitude and with loss.

I walked from the court a single woman again, an adult with a legal identity of my own. Mrs Grace Barforth now, no longer, Mrs Gervase. I went to bed, slept the rest of the day and the night, and the next morning came North again to Scarborough where my Grandmother Agbrigg, who had decided she was too old now either to understand or to criticize, was nevertheless deeply shocked when she noticed I had taken off my wedding ring.

'I am being honest, grandmamma.'

'You are asking for trouble, my girl. There is a mark, plain for all to see, where the ring has been. And since no one will take you for a spinster, one must assume the worst. Since you insist on travelling alone you will oblige me by not removing your gloves on the train.'

Blanche was appalled by my decision to remain in Cullingford.

'Darling, are you entirely mad? They wouldn't know what to do with you. There's simply nowhere to *put* a divorced woman in Cullingford. You'd do far better to get that little house in London we talked about – and it won't be easy even there.'

But her mind, and Aunt Caroline's mind, the attention of most of the family, was blessedly distracted from my affairs by the needs of Noel Chard, who, crippled by an assegai-thrust at the base of the spine, had seemed at first unlikely to walk again. He had been discovered by his brothers in exactly the fevered, squalid conditions Blanche had feared, plagued by flies and heat and overcrowding from which they had deftly extracted him, bringing back a yellow, hollow-cheeked man who could have been their father.

But the clean air of Listonby, the determination of Aunt Caroline, the devotion of Blanche, who was herself embarrassed by the extent of it, soon restored him. He would not walk again without a limp or a stick, would no longer spend whole days in the saddle, but he would remain now on the land where Blanche could keep an eye on him, enabling Dominic to go about his Parliamentary duties in peace. He would be at Listonby when Blanche was at Listonby, which would be rather more often from now on. He would come down to London when she needed him, or would suddenly appear at South Erin during those duty visits she found every year more tedious. He would be here to supervise her growing sons, to teach them to ride and shoot and know their manners, as Dominic had no time to do. He would be here to *talk* to her, to understand that there were days when she felt less beautiful – less cheerful – than others.

'You see, Grace,' she told me, 'or at least you *should* see how it is. If one can arrange one's affairs sensibly – if one can get what one wants without hurting others – then why not bend a little? Why be strictly honest and lose, when by just making it *look* right – It did Venetia no good, being honest, you know, and sometimes, Grace, I am quite afraid for you.'

I stayed at Fieldhead for a while, accustoming myself slowly to insolence, treading wearily like an invalid after a long and weakening disease, until the averted heads and pinched lips of Cullingford's carriage trade no longer troubled me. I entered the draper's shop in Millergate to find myself suddenly invisible as Mrs Rawnsley's glance passed straight through me. The first time it was painful, then awkward, quite soon it meant as much to me as she did, which was very little. I saw the timid Miss Fielding risk a trampling to death by carriage horses as she scuttled across the street to avoid me, and I stood in embarrassed perplexity, since I too had reason to cross over. The first time I remained on the opposite side of the street until she was out of sight, greatly to my own inconvenience. The third or the fourth time I strolled nonchalantly over to the shop I wanted, bade her a good morning, made my purchase and went away. I accepted Miss Mandelbaum's invitation to tea with surprise and gratitude, yet found her so jittery with nerves, so overwhelmed by her own daring and so fearful for her reputation that I did not go a second time. I returned Mrs Sheldon's bow, made when her carriage was at a safe distance, in the knowledge that the distance would be maintained until her husband had calculated the number of votes he might lose by permitting his wife to acknowledge me against the loss of favour at Fieldhead. I endured a short, sharp lecture from Miss Tighe who, caring for no one's opinion but her own, marched up to me in broad daylight and made me aware that, although I might now choose to consider myself a single woman, she did not, and hoped I would make no attempt to claim the voting rights which might one day be granted to the truly unwed.

But it hurt me immeasurably to be cut dead by Mrs Winch, the housekeeper from Tarn Edge, when I happened to meet her in Market Square, although the butler, Chillingworth, was not ashamed to raise his hat to me and stood one Sunday morning for fifteen minutes beside my victoria, regretting both my departure and Mrs Winch's now all to evident incompetence.

She did her best, of course, he didn't doubt it, but Mr Chard was difficult and Mr Barforth gloomy. Ah no, the child would make no difference, for yesterday morning they had sent the little mite to Listonby to be brought up with her cousins, Sir Dominic's boys, which seemed an excellent idea to Chillingworth. The nursemaid, it seemed, had got above herself, the wet nurse had twice had to be changed, Mrs Winch had declared herself unequal to the responsibility and Listonby, where the nurseries were well-staffed, well-organized, well-supervised by Mr Chard's mother, the Duchess, appeared a good and permanent solution to one and all. Unless, of course, Mrs Nicholas Barforth should take it into her head to leave Galton Abbey after all these years and return to her rightful home, a suggestion much favoured in the servants' hall, since Mr Barforth had been spending a fair amount of time at Galton lately, he and his wife having lost both their children in a manner of speaking, the daughter in the graveyard and the son gone to the devil, for ought they knew, in Australia, begging my pardon. A fair basis for reconciliation, thought the servants' hall, although, between ourselves, Mrs Winch was already looking for another situation, and if Mr Chard continued to make those scathing remarks about his dinner, no one expected Mrs Kincaid to last long either. As for Chillingworth himself, yes, he would very likely stay on until they pensioned him off, and in any case, although I was sorely missed, his work was easier now. No mistress meant no visitors and he need hardly stir from his pantry in the afternoons. Mr Barforth was rarely seen, while Mr Chard could always get himself upstairs to bed whatever state he might be in, not at all like Mr Gervase.

1016

My hands were shaking as I drove away, my parasol unsteady against my shoulder, images inflicting themselves like small wounds upon my memory; the tiny, elf-face of Claire Chard who was not really a Chard at all, the child I had not wished to touch because I had known how easily love for her could have detained me at Tarn Edge; and then Gervase, who had been very much my child, wending his uncertain way upstairs in the small hours of the morning, humorous and somehow gentle in drink, the sharp edges blurred from his vision. I didn't know what had happened to his son. No one would be likely to tell me and I could not ask. My own miscarriage came back to me, not the fear or the pain but the sense of failure, for there had been no sign of pregnancy since then and could be none now. I felt defeated, sterile, and then – to complete the agony – I began to remember Gideon.

But I was not always so feeble. It was spring again, an excellent time to make changes, and having examined the state of my finances and found them healthy, I shocked Cullingford further by quitting my father's house, where it was felt I might have had the good taste to languish, and purchased a home of my own in Blenheim Crescent, a short, curved terrace of houses designed for those who aspired to gentility but could not quite afford the greater elegance of Blenheim Lane.

It was a narrow building with a long front garden, a flight of shallow steps to a door with a fluted, many coloured fanlight somewhat too grand for its surroundings. The hall was narrow too, accommodating a thin staircase which led to two large bedrooms on the first floor, three small ones above. I had a drawing-room with a dining-parlour behind it on the ground floor, a square, dark kitchen behind that, more steps, very steep this time, leading to a stone-flagged yard which offered me a view of houses very much like my own.

'Something of an ugly duckling, is it not?' Mrs Agbrigg said, and so I set to work – badly needing employment – to create a swan. The dark and decidedly ugly kitchen was stripped of its bottle-green paintwork and repainted in cream and pale blue. I threw rugs in cheerful, possibly vulgar colours on the stone floor, placed a rocking-chair by the hearth, purchased a new stove, a brass fender, acquired a stray but rather disdainful cat. I took out the paltry little fireplace in the drawing-room and replaced it with cool, amber-veined marble, stood a porcelain clock in the centre of my mantelshelf, a Sèvres vase on either side. I hired a cook and a parlourmaid, a man to do the outside work and look after my carriage. I bought a carriage too, a brand-new, smart-as-paint victoria, although I allowed my father to provide the horses and see to their stabling.

I opened my first completely private and personal account at the bank, spending an hour with a considerably embarrassed Mr Rawnsley, who, although well-versed in the financial requirements of widows and spinsters, had never been alone before with a divorcee.

I moved into my house, alone with three servants and a cat, closed my door, went to bed, got up the next morning, sat in my drawing-room, waited – saw the afternoon and the evening come on, ate my dinner, went back to bed – waited, between some hours of light sleep, for morning. Aunt Faith called, bringing flowers and reassurance, the promise that her house was always open to me and should I wish to accompany her to Venice next month I would be more than welcome.

There was a weekly letter from my Agbrigg grandmother urging me to find something useful to do, and from my Grandmamma Elinor in France offering me asylum there where 'nobody would know' and hinting that, whatever I might have heard to the contrary, I would soon find another man to marry me.

Gervase's parents surprised me by coming to see me together, Mr Barforth looking older, although perhaps he was not ageing so much as mellowing, Mrs Barforth covering the many good things we could not speak of by her talk of good weather and good harvests, sunshine and fresh spring pastures. But, before coming to me, they had been to the churchyard to take flowers to Venetia, and her memory inhabited the air around them.

'If there's anything you want, Grace –' he said gruffly as they were leaving. 'Anything I can get you?'

And when he had gone to fetch his hat, Mrs Barforth pressed her cheek against mine and gave me what they both knew I most longed for.

'Gervase is in Mexico, darling. Don't ask me why, for I thought it was to be Austrialia, but no, Mexico. Good heavens! how very *far* that sounds. But he says he is well. Diana is still in Nice but Compton Flood – Lord Sternmore – is to call and see her on his way home from India, and Julian is very hopeful. Dearest, may I come and see you again?'

She came, sometimes alone, sometimes bringing that gentle, nervous sheepdog with her to the disgust of my imperious tabby cat. Mr Barforth came too, usually at teatime when he would eat large but absent-minded helpings of sugary foods and drink several cups of strong tea, a sure indication, I thought, that Tarn Edge no longer provided fruit cakes and gingerbread, no longer served scones hot from the oven and muffins freshly toasted and rich with syrup; and even surer indication that he was lonely.

My father came every day on some pretext or other, but these family visits occupied a mere fraction of my time and I could see no way of filling the rest. Cullingford society was closed to me and I did not care enough about it to attempt a breach in its ranks. Only one woman among my new neighbours would speak to me, for the very good reason that her husband was employed by my father at Fieldhead. I had expected all this and had prepared for it, yet now, when the decisions had been taken and the struggle was over, when each day opened out before me with nothing to distinguish it from the next, I was bound to ask myself, as Blanche had done: 'What is it all *for*?'

What I required was work and there was none available. I had decorated and furnished my house and did not mean to spend my life obsessed with the need to be constantly changing my wallpaper for lack of better employment. Yet what else was there? Such few public appointments available to women specified above all, that the women

1018

must be of good character, and I had lost my character altogether. I could not open a school, since no right-minded parent would entrust me with the instructions of the young. I could not sit on a school board nor on the administrative committee of the workhouse as Miss Tighe did. Indeed, I could not sit on any committee, charitable or otherwise, since no respectable woman would be willing to serve with me. I had no musical talent like Miss Mandelbaum, no interrupted artistic career like Mrs Sheldon's which I could take up again, no particular religious faith like Miss Fielding's to which I could devote my time and ingenuity. What had it all been for?'

I began to lose energy, to wonder about joining Aunt Faith in Venice, travelling as widely as I could and coming home just often enough to keep the promise I had made through Mrs Agbrigg to my father. Running away, in fact, and it was Liam Adair who rescued me from my gloom, taking my house by storm one bright, windy morning, a dozen copies of the *Cullingford Star* under one arm, a bottle of champagne under the other, an enormous bouquet of white and purple lilac which he flung down on the hall table with his hat.

'Well, now – if you can bear a visit from a gentleman of the Press after what some of my colleagues did to you. But you must admit that both the *Star* and Eustace Roundwood's *Courier & Review* left you alone – me because I love you dearly and Roundwood because he can't afford the wrong side of your father.'

And seeing the sharp, interested eyes of my maid as she closed the door behind him – for a man with flowers and wine and pretty speeches at ten o'clock in the morning was the kind of thing she had been hoping to see when she entered my service – I laughed, let him kiss my cheek, and invited him inside.

'Champagne, Liam – at this hour of the day?'

'Why not? When one visits an unusual woman one hardly expects to be fobbed off with tea. Miss Mandelbaum and Miss Tighe give me plenty of that.'

And for one hour I indulged myself with champagne and great bursts of laughter, as fallen women do, while he regaled me with the up-and-down fortunes of the *Star* and his own literary and amorous endeavours; the widow who had almost succeeded in marrying him; his exposure of bad housing in the neighbourhood of Gower Street, which had caused some irate landlord or other to put a brick through his windows again; his old landlady's daughter, who had taken it into her head to get into bed with him, which had necessitated yet another change of address; his concern at the rate of infant mortality in Cullingford's workhouse; the damnable little brats who raised havoc all day in Gower Street so that he was undecided whether to advocate shooting them or sending them to school; his new landlady who went to chapel three times every Sunday and looked like a martyred missionary, but who had started giving him some very odd glances lately from her eye-corners.

'Come and see us at the *Star*, Grace, and meet my new assistant. I can't think why you haven't been before.'

His new assistant, since the old one had been Robin Ashby, was the nearest he came to mentioning Venetia, my appearance at the *Star*, as he well knew, having been put off because I had not wished to be reminded of the happier days when she and I had gone there together. But his visit had warmed me, offered me a reason to get out my new victoria, to put on my new hat and gloves for something other than a visit to Fieldhead or an excursion among the stony stares of Millergate. I went, my mind on Venetia every inch of the way, my eyes misting over as Gower Street came into view, the unwashed, underfed urchins scuffling in the gutter, the stench of dung and garbage, those boarded-up windows. But it was not my intention to forget Venetia and I got down resolutely and quite calmly from my carriage, walked briskly upstairs, past the aged printing-presses, into the cluttered upper room, to be enclosed at once in a hearty, just faintly alcoholic embrace.

'So you've come to look us over? I thought you would.'

'Nothing seems changed.'

'I don't know about that. I'm older – you're bonnier. There's my new assistant – at any rate, *that's* a change for the better. I've been wanting to see the two of you together. Grace, this is Mrs Inman – Camille, this is Grace Barforth, my stepmother's granddaughter, that we've spoken of.'

'Mrs Inman.' And through my amazement that she should be female at all – any kind of female – I realized I was holding out my hand to one of the loveliest women I had ever seen.

She was, as I learned later, in her early thirties, a perfect oval face, glossy black hair and a great deal of it in a huge coil high on her head, eyes which should have been dark, too, but which were an astonishing amethyst, long-lashed and altogether entrancing. She was tall and very slender, plainly dressed but extremely neat, a bunch of violets pinned on the lapel of a pale blue bodice, a fall of white lace at the throat, a warm smile and a firm handshake, a friendliness of manner which was one of her greatest charms.

I sat down in the chair by her desk, fascinated, and we began a conversation which lasted in fact for several days, my curiosity about this woman who had once shared her life with a man who sounded very much like Robin Ashby and who had not only survived to tell the tale but could tell it with affection and humour, proving insatiable. She was a missionary's daughter who had spent her girlhood in the wild places of the world where propriety – although her mother had made the effort – did not seem to matter. Her parents had been killed, she did not say how, and she had lived 'here and there' for a while, finally settling with a spinster aunt who, among other things, had founded a shelter for wayward girls in the East End of London. No one had ever really protected Camille as Venetia and I had been protected. Her father had been too busy caring for his heathen flock to concern himself with his daughter. Her mother had trusted in God and hoped for the best. The spinster aunt had put her to work, at an age when Venetia and I had been ignorant of life's basic facts, among child prostitutes and the victims of household rape. She had married at eighteen and gone adventuring with her husband, a journalist ten years her senior who, like her father and Robin Ashby, had been more deeply touched by the sufferings of the masses than of the individual. But she was used to that. When her husband fell ill, she wrote his pieces for him. When he recovered, they continued to work together. When he died five years ago, she had gone on supporting herself as, for the six months of his final malady, she had supported them both.

She had a slender income of her own, barely enough to keep a roof over her head, and when Liam Adair, who had been a good friend for years both to herself and her husband, had offered her employment she had been glad of it. She did not live well, she was ready to admit, but she found life interesting. Sometimes very interesting indeed. No, she saw nothing alarming in walking about the city streets alone. She took a cab when she could afford it, which was seldom, but mostly she came and went as she pleased without too much hindrance. No one had ever told her she was frail and in need of care, and she had seen no advantages, therefore, in fragility. Her husband would have been irritated by it, her father would not even have noticed. Women, she had found, were very rarely frail in any case. As for herself, she was always busy. At the moment she was investigating housing conditions in a nearby street, selected at random, and Liam would publish her survey in weekly instalments in the *Star*.

'Why don't you lend a hand?' Liam said, leaning an arm along the back of my chair. 'It's a job worth doing and, unlike Camille here, who costs a fortune, I know would wouldn't expect any pay.'

'Liam, you are still exploiting women.'

'Yes – yes, I know. But these printing-presses of mine won't last forever, my darling, and neither will Grandmamma Elinor. Think it over. Camille could do with the help, and she'll tell you what a jewel I am to work with.'

Camille Inman came to tea with me the following Sunday, stayed, at my urgent request, to dinner and told me, among a great many things, that although Liam was assuredly no 'jewel' she was not ashamed to be in his employ. The *Star* in his hands would make no one rich, but its readership was extending now from the few radical hot-heads who had previously purchased it to the more thoughtful members of all classes. There was no denying that, because of the *Star*, it was somewhat safer to eat Cullingford's bread than it used to be and she had great hopes for her survey of overcrowding in St. Mark's Fold.

She was no missionary like her father. She simply wished to investigate and inform and would be content to leave the moralizing to others. Could she not tempt me to lend a hand? I would need a strong stomach, of course, for she had known many a well-intentioned and truly compassionate soul who had been quite unable to cope with the *smell* of human poverty and distress.

I drove to the *Star* the following morning dressed plainly, without jewellery of any kind, as she had instructed, and together we took the ten-minute walk from Gower Street to St. Mark's Fold, Camille once again with a bunch of violets pinned to her lapel, her startling amethyst eyes expressing no shock, no disgust, no anger, but remaining in all circumstances perfectly serene and friendly.

A pleasant enough sounding place, St. Mark's Fold, reminiscent of some cloistered cathedral city, a green lawn and tapering ecclesiastical spires. I had never heard the name before, although I was Cullingford born, and discovered it to be a dank alleyway among a hundred others just like it, a filthy cobweb of streets built by Grandmamma Elinor's first husband, my Aycliffe grandfather, around the Barforth mill at Low Cross. It consisted of ten squat two-roomed houses on the right hand side of a narrow, muddy street, with ten more built behind them, a further twenty houses on the left-hand side constructed in the same back-to-back fashion, the houses at the rear being reached by passages that seemed no larger than arrow-slits cut into the walls.

And in these forty houses, with their total of eighty rooms, Camille expected to find between three and four hundred people living, her calculations being difficult to make not from any unwillingness on the part of the inhabitants to be counted but because of their habit of taking in lodgers and throwing out wayward daughters; and because only one in two of all infants born here would be likely to reach the age of five. She had done these surveys before, she told me, her composure unruffled. She knew.

I was not to suppose that the whole of Cullingford's working classes lived in such squalor. Far from it, for the Law Valley produced a most enduring breed of men and women who, by hard work and good management, and a kind of shrewd, down-to-earth humour Camille found most appealing, organized their affairs in a much better fashion. She knew many houses where there was not much money but where the women were scrupulously decent and the men hard-working and philosophical. She had encountered in other houses a kind of realistic, almost sardonic nobility, a grudging respect between husband and wife, and a gruff-spoken affection, a family united against all comers, facing the insurmountable and somehow – without making too much of a fuss – surmounting it. But these were the ones who paid their rent on time and put something aside for a rainy day, who sent their children to school and who had the resilience, the nerve, the stamina, to pick *themselves* up whenever Life or fate or the state of the textile trade knocked them down. I would meet very few of them in St Mark's Fold.

It was slower work than I had expected, for we visited only five houses that day, Camille sitting herself down on whatever chair or packing-case or heap of shoddy seemed available, taking whatever stray urchin or stray dog or cat on to her lap that wished to go there, with no particular demonstration of affection, no grimace of pity, but as a matter of course, something quite natural. She had no money go give, no cast-off clothing, no basket of goodies, she made that clear from the beginning. There was no use asking her to pay a doctor's bill or find shoes for the children. She was hard pressed, often enough, to get her own shoes mended and could show the worn leather to prove it. But what she could do was tell other

1022

people, who might have something to spare or who, better still, might tell the landlord it was high time he did something about those roof-tiles and those ugly damp patches. 'Now then, Mrs Ryan – Mrs Backhouse – Mrs O'Flynn – how many beds did you say you have? – and how many sleep in them?'

Mrs Ryan had one sagging double bed in her upper room where she slept with her husband and her three younger children, two girls and a boy. Her four elder children, 'two of each', slept downstairs on the kind of mattresses I had seen at the home of Sally Grimshaw's mother. There was another daughter who 'came and went' but had not been seen for six months and more now. Mrs Ryan and her elder daughters worked sometimes at Low Cross Mill, sometimes elsewhere, for the girls, she said, were 'flighty', prone to 'answering back' the overlookers and spending their wages on themselves every Thursday night before she could get at them, while her boys could get no work and her husband was unfit for it, suffering so badly, as so many ageing mill-hands did, from bronchitis – the disease of smoke and damp and raw northern mornings – that he seemed unlikely to get through another winter. He had been a good man once, earning good wages as a wool-sorter at Low Cross which he had put straight into his wife's pocket, not across the bar counter. They had even managed to save a little, had got together some decent furniture, had been in a 'fair way of carrying on'. But the bad winter six years ago had finished him. He had lost his job at Low Cross for 'breaking time' on those icy mornings when he had scarcely been able to breathe, and that had been the end of it. No job, no wages, and the doctor's bills had soon taken care of their savings. He could hardly drag himself to the end of the street now, her man, and had no interest any more in trying. Her boys and one of her girls were turning out troublesome – because, after all, they needed a man's hard hand sometimes and *he* wouldn't stir himself these days – the lads hanging about the streets all day, the girl loitering on her way home from the mill. No, the children never went to school. It was too far and in any case she had to be in her loom-gate at Low Cross by half-past five every morning and was not at home to get them out of bed and see them off. So far she had managed to pay her rent every week, although often enough it meant taking her decent shawl and her husband's boots to the pawn shop on a Tuesday morning and redeeming them on a Friday, as best she could. But if there should be any more doctor's bills this winter, then she might not do so well.

'Thank you,' said Camille and as we went outside she sniffed the violets at her lapel and translated for me. 'The eldest daughter, the one who "comes and goes" is a prostitute, of course, and the other one who "loiters" is serving her apprenticeship to the same trade. The boys she calls troublesome are starting to steal, there can be no doubt about that. They will go to prison sooner or later, I suppose, and their little brothers will be awfully proud of them. Oh yes – for in St Mark's Fold, you see, it is thought quite bold and dashing to be in a House of Correction, and when they are released they will strut about like peacocks and take their pick of the girls – a fine old time until they are sent back again. Poor Mrs Ryan, for it is poverty that does it, you know, and she can't help that – just as her husband can't help his bad chest. I wonder if she knows she will be better off when he is dead?'

Mrs Backhouse did not get out of bed to greet us, having recently given birth to a child, a wailing little scrap wrapped in a corner of her blanket who looked no more likely to survive than the mother. She had no interest in us nor in herself, nor in the baby whose persistent crying she seemed not to notice. She had no man of her own and pregnancy had stopped her earnings. She was in arrears with her rent and when the landlord threw her out she would have no choice but the workhouse where they would take her baby away from her in any case. So far as she was concerned it couldn't happen soon enough.

Mrs O'Flynn had eleven children in her two rooms and four lodgers in her cellar. She kept a pig in her yard, which, she cheerfully admitted, did not please all her neighbours. She had been brought over from Ireland as a girl because the potato crop had failed and people were starving. They had been set ashore at Liverpool and had walked to Cullingford in slow stages, her parents and their six children, pushing everything they possessed on a hand-cart, obliged to keep moving in order to avoid being picked up for vagrancy and shipped back to Ireland again. But her parents, being country-bred, had been unable to withstand the impact of the city. Cullingford's foul air and smoky skies had withered them quicker than the famine, their children being saved from the workhouse by the intervention of several large-hearted neighbours who had absorbed a child apiece into their own families on the principle that there is always room for one more. But these kind neighbours had long since moved away, taking Mrs O'Flynn's brothers and sisters with them, she didn't know where, and would be unlikely to recognize them now in any case. She had given birth to her first child at fourteen or thereabouts – younger rather than older – and, like Sally Grimshaw's mother, had been pregnant more or less ever since. Her fertility was a nuisance, of course – certainly she could not comprehend how anyone could call it a blessing – but although she did not understand it, she accepted it, like menstruation, as one of the drawbacks of womanhood. She had kept her family decent because she was hard-handed and foul-mouthed when she had to be. Any man who molested a daughter of hers would have the mother to deal with and she had dragged her husband out of the ale-house by the scruff of his neck on many a Thursday night. She worked in the weaving-sheds at Law Cross and so did her girls as soon as they were ten years old. The only one among them to have lost her job had not dared face her mother and had run away from home. She had one son who had lost the use of his legs in an explosion at the local ironworks and yes, her husband was 'chesty', so were all the men, what of it? Women had babies, men who had worked in the mines or the mills and who smoked cheap tobacco coughed in the winter and were short winded in the summer time. The future? What did we mean by that? If she could get herself from Monday morning to Friday night and back again without coming a cropper, then she wouldn't complain.

1024

'Four houses,' Camille said, when we had interviewed a bustling, cheerful Mrs Clough, eighteen years old and two years married, her husband holding down a steady job, only one child in her cradle, her manner briskly assuring us that none of the misfortunes of these old women – her neighbours – could possibly happen to her.

'Four houses. Thirty-six more to go. Thank heavens Liam picked a short street!'

I accompanied her every day for a week after that, uncomfortable at first at being in the vicinity of Low Cross where I might possibly encounter my father-in-law, who would certainly enquire the nature of my business in this rough locality. But both the work and Camille's reaction to it absorbed me. No, she was not shocked by what she saw in St Mark's Fold. It was not vice to blame, after all, but hardship, just people adapting themselves to poverty's rules as I had adapted to affluence. When there was no work and no hope of work the result was always the same. The boys stole and the girls took to street-walking. Her aunt in London had calculated years ago, when Camille herself had been a child, that there were upwards of six thousand brothels in the city alone and easily eighty thousand prostitutes, girls, in many cases, who were not so much wayward as extremely hungry. Naturally, even at her aunt's London shelter she had met girls who found nothing distasteful in offering their bodies for whatever such a body might fetch, finding the work less arduous and rather more profitable than the sweatshops of the tailoring trade. But mainly, she had found, a girl went on the streets because her choices were between that, the workhouse or starvation. And what, she wondered, in those circumstances would I myself have done?

Camille had encountered none of the great stars of the profession. Doubtless there were women who received pearls and diamonds and racehorses for their favours. In fact she knew quite well that there were. But they had never required the comforts of her aunt's soup and bread, nor her protection from an outraged, short-changed pimp. Camille's experience had been confined to girls like the daughters of Mrs Ryan who, having grown up sharing a bed with several brothers found promiscuity a natural extension of their family life; or the little fifteen-year-old mothers one could find ten a penny in Gower Street and who had to feed their babies somehow.

Doubless there *were* brothels furnished with silk draperies and couches of rich velvet, at least she hoped so for the sake of one's friends who had had recourse to them. But she had seen nothing of the kind. The brothels she had visited had been dreary establishments, not much better than the house of Mrs O'Flynn, where an old bawd offered for sale her own and her neighbour's daughters.

She had luncheon at my house the following Sunday, her glossy hair still dressed in its single massive coil which made her neck seem very supple and very long, her gown of light forget-me-not blue with its high frilled collar bringing out the wonderful amethyst of her eyes. She had pinned flowers on her shoulder again, having no jewels, and her manner was easy and cheerful, her appreciation of my house and my possessions without envy. She was not, she confessed, cast in the domestic mould herself, tended to get her own cupboards and drawers in a frightful muddle, but how comfortable all this was, how enjoyable. We relaxed, became easy, almost frivolous, and were giggling like schoolgirls when the doorbell rang and my father-in-law appeared.

'Camille,' I told her, feeling oddly flustered, 'this is Mr Nicholas Barforth. Mr Barforth – Mrs Inman.'

'How do you do,' she said and knowing of no reason why she should be intimidated by him she continued to chat of one thing and another, receiving from him the most monosyllabic replies. She smiled, talked on. He became quite forbidding, I thought, very much the master of the Barforth mills, a man of his class and his time who would instantly have assessed the cost per yard of the pretty but inexpensive fabric of her dress, the reason for that spray of tiny yellow flowers on her shoulder, the unusual freedom of her conversation, and would have judged her by that.

'I must be going,' she said as the teacups were removed, shaking her head and making light of the distance when I offered to send her in my carriage. She would just put on her hat and could be safely at her own door by the time they had got out the horses. She was used to walking. There was no need to make a fuss. She was pleasant, amused, determined to have her way.

'How far?' snapped my father-in-law.

'Prince Albert Road, just down the hill.'

'Yes – and across the centre of town and up the other side, on a Sunday when the streets are full of mill-hands drinking their wages. It won't do, you know.'

'I beg your pardon.'

'Now look here, young lady,' he said, very exasperated, 'you'll either take Grace's carriage or you'll take mine. In fact you'd better take mine, since it's standing there ready and it's time I was off. I'll set you down on my way.'

For a moment her eyes met his in a level stare and then her lovely oval face dimpled with mischievous laughter, her magnificent body bent itself forward into a swift, parlour-maid's curtsey.

'Certainly, Mr Barforth, sir,' she said.

'Good,' he told her, smiling grimly but broadly. 'Then you'd better put on your hat.'

22

I encountered a world I had never suspected but which had been there all the time, running parallel with mine, Camille Inman's world of tolerance and good humour, of undemonstrative, unsentimental caring, of sound common sense; an atmosphere in which Venetia would have blossomed and flourished. I had started life as Miss Agbrigg, heiress of Fieldhead. I

1026

had become Mrs Gervase Barforth of Tarn Edge. The Cullingford I knew now regarded me not as a divorced woman but as *the* divorced woman, since Cullingford had no other. Camille and her acquaintances saw me as Grace who helped at the *Star*, an entirely new and separate person to be assessed on her own merits or lack of them, not on the bank balance of her husband or father, nor the immaculate condition of her linen cupboards and her reputation.

She took me, one evening, to the house of a Dr and Mrs Stone, the younger of the two physicians, as it turned out, who had attended Venetia. He did not remember me. I did not remind him, being content to drink his wine, a rough, red vintage in heavy glasses, and enjoy the conversation of a man who saw no reason to treat me like a half-witted child. When Dr Stone found it necessary to refer to pregnancy he referred to it, no vague suggestions of being 'in an interesting condition' or 'in the family way' but pregnant – just that – an expression which had not endeared him to Mrs Rawnsley and her like who had great admiration for those women who, rather than expose their naked bodies to a male eye, preferred to suffer and eventually die in chaste silence. If Dr Stone felt obliged to mention legs or breasts or buttocks he mentioned them, and consequently was rarely consulted by those ladies – and we knew many – who did not acknowledge possession of such things.

He was a square-shouldered, blunt-spoken man who had been something of a radical in his younger days and – as he freely admitted with a twinkle in his eye – had made himself very unpopular in his first practice by advocating the use of such contraceptive methods as were then available, among patients in a rough labouring area of Liverpool who had an abundance of nothing but children. He had seen, as one saw in St Mark's Fold, the squalid overcrowding, the grinding poverty, the inability to feed even the mouths one already had, and he had thought, in his innocence, that the knowledge of how not to increase those mouths must be welcome. He had reckoned without the virtuous, the narrow-minded and, very often, the sterile, who saw these large, undernourished families as proof of the lustfulness and general inferiority of the poor. The remedy, for such people, was extremely simple. The sexual act was intended only for the procreation of children. A decent man fathered the number of children he could afford, and, when his limit had been reached, abandoned the act for ever. A couple who mistook its purpose and indulged in it for pleasure must accept the consequences of their over-breeding, must wallow in the mire they had themselves created. Dr Stone, who by this time had made the acquaintance of a young school-teacher and fallen deeply in love with her, had not agreed and had aroused so much ill-feeling by his recommendation of the contraceptive sheath – this device being normally used by gentlemen in their dealings with whores, not to protect the woman from maternity but themselves from venereal disease – that he had been obliged to leave Liverpool, taking his schoolteacher, now Mrs Anna Stone, with him.

They had lived in London for a while, in the notorious Seven Dials district where they had first met Camille and her crusading aunt, and had come north some years ago, first to the fashionable spa town of Harrogate, where Dr Stone's brusque manner had not succeeded, then to Cullingford to join Dr Blackwood, who had been impressed by the younger man's qualifications and unaware until too late of his opinions. Dr Blackwood, the senior and considerably more popular partner, lived in some elegance at the top of Blenheim Lane, where, despite the grubby out-thrusting of our growing town, it remained leafy, hushed, exclusive. Dr Stone's house stood at its lower end, a yard or so from the point where residential Blenheim Lane deteriorated into commercial Millergate, bustling with shoppers, idlers, urchins, carts and carriages, clattering down the cobbles to Market Square, the raucous, often indecorous centre of our town.

Dr Blackwood was a member of our town council, chaired several charitable committees, dined out a great deal. Dr Stone had no time for committees and was suspicious of both organized charity and those who dispensed it. He had been asked to leave meetings many a time in his Liverpool days because of his impatience with those who expected a St Mark's Fold mother to send her children to chapel every Sunday in starched white pinafores and expressed self-righteous disappointment when she did not. He had derided the maxim 'cleanliness is next to godliness' in circumstances where soap was a luxury and hot water rarely available. He had suggested that the children of the ragged poor so rarely came to Sunday School because the children of the prosperous had been trained not to sit beside them, for fear of catching fleas; and he had fallen foul of the congregation. Now he tended to keep his own counsel or dispense it discreetly, and I had been a regular visitor for several weeks before Mrs Stone showed me the hut in their back garden and explained its purpose.

Anna Stone was as quiet as her husband was explosive, a face as smooth as Camille's although it lacked Camille's beauty, having nothing remarkable about it but a pair of steady grey eyes. She was a competent woman who would stand firm, I thought, in a crisis, accustomed to the panic that often accompanies sickness, to hysterical men and women pounding at her door at midnight in search of medicines or miracles, or simply needing to be told that everything would be all right. She was assured, patient, gave herself slowly, and like Camille had never learned to rely on male protection, having been brought up by an older sister who, through two happy marriages and two widow hoods, had taken an active part in matters of education, woman suffrage and the 'rescue', whenever possible, of girls from the city streets.

This 'rescue' work was not uncommon, such notables as the very serious and very high-minded Liberal leader, Mr Gladstone, having participated in it, somewhat to the disgust of Queen Victoria, it was said, who, disliking Mr Gladstone personally, was inclined to think the worst. But the provision by Dr and Mrs Stone of a shelter in their garden, four narrow beds, an old table, a wash-stand with a metal jug, a mirror on a nail above it, pretty chintz curtains and a vase of garden flowers, seemed to me a sensible way of doing good.

Their aims were modest, their expectations of success extremely light. They were not reformers in the sense that they hoped to make sweeping changes. They could, in fact, see little chance of lasting change at all. Conditions, for perhaps four-fifths of humanity, were very bad and seemed unlikely to get better. They were simply a practical couple who knew that sometimes a girl's whole life could take a disastrous turning because for a vital night or two she had nowhere to go. When they met such a girl they offered her an alternative, not much, of course, just a hard bed in that garden shelter, a decent breakfast, medical treatment if required, a little sound advice which usually was not regarded. Not much, and usually after a day or two, when the cuts and bruises were healed and the hunger-pains gone, when the miscarriage had been tidied up and the swelling in the groin seemed not to be syphilis, the girl was gone too. Usually – not always.

Mrs Stone would not allow me inside the shelter to begin with, not wishing to give its occupants an impression, as she put it, of being monkeys at the zoo, and she entirely agreed with Camille that, although poverty was the usual and most powerful motive, there were girls who enjoyed this undoubtedly old-established profession and others who did extremely well out of it. I had myself seen Gideon Chard lounging beside the carriage of a woman whose favours would certainly not have come cheap. I had seen women gorgeously attired in satins and towering plumage strolling up and down the Haymarket when I had visited the theatre with Blanche, none of them among the first rank of courtesans, perhaps, like Gideon's, but well fed, cheerful, looking as if they had the means to pay their rent.

But Dr and Mrs Stone did not interest themselves in such as these. Nor were they concerned with the little girls of eight and nine years old who could be purchased easily in any of our cities, since such children were offered up by their mothers, more often than not, who would take care of them afterwards. And if it shocked me that there could be such mothers – as, of course, it must shock me – I should remember that these women, in many cases, had been compelled themselves, before the introduction of our various Factory Acts, to labour from the age of five for seventeen hours a day in woollen-mills, cotton-mills, coal-mines, had been deflowered by overlookers, foremen, workmates, their brothers, sometimes their fathers, in those hovels where they slept six or seven to a bed. To such women the loss of virginity for cash in an eight-year-old child could not seem so terrible as it did to me.

Terrible enough, of course. But sharing a practical disposition, Dr and Mrs Stone preferred to offer their assistance to the slightly older children, the girls of twelve and thirteen and fourteen one could find in abundance any day of the week at the railway stations of any city, girls from the country sent off to fend for themselves, particularly in these days of agricultural depression, because there was no room at home, or girls who had left home respectably to take up employment and had not given satisfaction, little nursemaids and kitchen maids discharged without a reference for the crime, sometimes, of being too young to understand what was required of them, and with nowhere to go.

'Good' girls, of course, and usually quite innocent, unlike the urchins we bred in our cities. And Mrs Stone was in a position to assure me that every train, in every city including our own, was met regularly by sharp-eyed, soft-tongued women who traded not in simple prostitution but the highly profitable marketing of virginity.

'Really?' I said and Mrs Stone smiled, realizing I had believed virginity to be of importance mainly to husbands desirous of producing an heir they could be sure of. But no, for virginity, she told me, within her working memory had been valued as high as sixty or seventy pounds, a sum which had shrunk in recent times to a discreetly proffered five pound note, not for want of customers, she hastened to add, but because the commodity was now so much easier to come by and had lost the value of its rarity.

And why should it be so valuable in the first place? Well, of course, there *were* men who found the deflowering of virgins moving and mysterious, others who required it as an added titillation, but mainly it was seen as a sanitary precaution, a virgin being presumed free from venereal disease. There was no cure for syphilis, she told me, clearly wondering if I had heard the word before, and, as any doctor would tell me – or, at least, any doctor like Patrick Stone – there were times when it reached the proportions of an epidemic. It was a terrible, shameful way to die, but, men's needs being what they were, the risk continued to be taken, and since supply is created by demand she had met several women who had dealt for many years, and very lucratively, in virgins, procuring for some of their regular customers as many as two a week.

The girls were picked up, hungry and frightened, at the stations and in the public parks, persuaded, or in some cases given an entirely false impression of what would be required. Just a kiss and a cuddle, they would be told, a deceit which necessitated the use of rather isolated houses for such transactions, since when the truth dawned some girls would kick and scream, while others – suspected as likely trouble-makers by the procuress – would have been so heavily dosed with laudanum in advance that they would have to be carried inside.

An evil trade, necessitating a rapid turn-over, since the same girl, obviously, could not be used twice. And when the damage was done she would be bungled back into a closed carriage, driven away from that very secret address and abandoned somewhere in an alien street, with perhaps a guinea from that purchase price of £5 in her hand. Sometimes the Stones would find her. Sometimes a more conventional brothel-keeper who did not deal in maidenheads would find her first. Often enough some man would pick her up and take her home with him for a night or two, which would lead, of course, to the brothel in the end. Sometimes, if she was badly torn or badly shocked, she would spend a longer time than usual in the Stones' garden, performing small tasks about the house, and even then the final reaction varied. Some girls would hang their heads in shame and creep tamely away, others would shrug their shoulders and realize they had now learned a trade. And so long as these disease-conscious gentlemen were willing to pay, neither Mrs Stone nor my friend Camille could see an end to it.

I worked throughout the spring and summer almost obsessively, my enthusiasm and my indignation marking me, I knew, as an amateur, although Liam – professional to his fingertips – made full use of it, sending me, when the St Mark's Fold survey was done – to equally appalling dens elsewhere in the city, thus proving the evil to be widespread. I listed the sordid details of every house in Commercial Close and the older, rat-infested Silsbridge Street, cowering a mile away from the splendid, Italianate façade of Nethercoats Mill; checked and cross-checked, with a novice's determination to get it exactly right, so eager to inform the world of these injustices which everyone in Cullingford, including myself, had always known and not wished to think about, that personal relationships – the stuff of which my life had hitherto been made – became slightly blurred, faintly unreal. And so it was that the sudden dreaminess of Camille escaped me, or, if it did not, then I had no time to think about it, and consequently missed the choicest scandal to hit Cullingford since my own, which had been going on right under my zealous nose.

'Do you know,' she said to me one warm and, for me, extremely busy afternoon, 'Mr Nicholas Barforth is a very attractive man.'

'My father-in-law? I suppose he must have been.'

'But he still is, you may mark my words. That type of man improves with age. The ruthlessness mellows and the – well – the *attractiveness* remains. And he is not so old.'

Of course she had been giving me a clue, worried – as Liam told me afterwards – that her unlikely yet obviously very satisfactory affair with my father-in-law might shock me; as indeed it did. Not for any reasons of morality but simply because he *was* my father-in-law, because she was beautiful, whimsical, adorable and because I had rather hoped to see him reconciled to his wife.

It had happened very quickly, taking her so much by surprise that she had told no one, being herself barely able to believe it. They had met at my house and she had been a little irritated and very much amused at his insistence on taking her home in his carriage. They had measured each other, and although she acknowledged his attractions – power, shrewdness, toughness and wealth being a potent blend in any man – she knew they could have little in common and did not expect to get on with him. And they had not got on together. She had sat in his carriage for over an hour, outside her front door, while he poured disapproval – scorn almost – on the life she led, shredding her ideals to pieces while she, just as quickly, patched them up again. The horses had grown restless and he had simply driven off with her to the station, and since it had been nearly dinner-time by then and they had not eaten – well – they had gone to Leeds and dined, she couldn't – or wouldn't – say where, except that it had been extremely elegant and probably outrageously expensive.

They had met again twice that week and on the Friday she had gone with him to Scarborough – yes, so soon – how very shocking! – and had stayed with him until Sunday night, at a house right on the cliff-edge

1031

where they had – and here she swallowed and blushed, not from guilt, I thought, but from some quite blissful memory – where they had found themselves in harmony in every possible way. She had been seeing him since then as often as she could, which turned out to be very often, and yes, it was altogether a fit of madness, she would readily admit it, but the mere thought of him caused her to glow and tingle – how utterly insane, yet so *wonderful* and to feel shivers down her spine – caused her to *long* for him, and she wasn't ashamed of it. She had been to Scarborough almost every weekend since then, surely I had noticed her unseemly haste, the way she had rushed to catch the train? And what of Mr Barforth, my father-in-law – whom to my amazement she now called Nicholas? Did he long, too?

'Don't be unkind,' she said. 'I know you can't believe it of him, but he does. He's beautiful, Grace. Perhaps you can't believe that either. But he is.'

I could hardly bring myself to face him when next we met, not because I blamed him for desiring Camille – how could any man be blamed for that? – but because her blissful, sighing ecstasies had forced me to think of him not so much as an elderly relative but a potent, sensual male, and it embarrassed me. But, whatever his ultimate intentions might be, he made no secret that at present he could not have enough of Camille and had called to see me solely for the pleasure of talking about her to someone who knew just how desirable she was.

'Why not?' said Liam Adair, finding me alone in the office the following Thursday morning. 'So she's gone a day early this time, has she? Well, I didn't think the affair could get much hotter, but it seems I'm wrong. And why not? Every rich old man deserves a young woman to round off his life – or so most rich old men will tell you. Good luck to her.'

'I rather though that you and she –'

'Ah well – I rather thought myself, at one time, that she and I – But no, she's met too many men like me, and at least Nick Barforth is *different*. I reckon we might send our congratulations to Gideon Chard, for if old Nick's in Scarborough every Friday to Monday – or every Thursday to Tuesday – with Camille, he'll hardly be troubling Gideon overmuch at the mills.'

The story, as yet, was by no means common knowledge, Cullingford needing to be sure of its facts before spreading rumours about its most powerful resident, but I knew they must have been seen together, the gossip would be bound to start, and it would have been a kindness to go over to Galton in case my mother-in-law – his wife – had heard. But I delayed, shirked, fearing to be confronted by a too visible memory of Gervase, and in the end she came to me, bringing fern-scents and tree-scents in the folds of her plain green skirt, her hair spilling out of a hat she had crammed on her head at a rakish and very becoming angle.

'Now then, my dear,' she said, sitting down and taking off her driving-gloves. 'I know you are much occupied and very businesslike these days, so I shall not give you reason to accuse me of beating about the bush. I have come to enquire about this gorgeous Camille I have heard so much about. Yes, yes, don't look so astonished, Grace, for we are none of us children, and it is my husband himself who has told me. Now then, the fact that she *is* gorgeous I do not dispute. I can trust Nicky to be accurate about that. But what else is she, Grace? That is what I want to know, for to tell the truth, Nicky has been very disappointed in his women, including myself, and I should not like him to be disappointed again – not now when time is no longer quite so available. So tell me about this paragon.'

I told her and she listened, her head on one side, concentrating hard, and when I had finished she nodded, brisk, assured, a woman who, against all the rules, appeared well content.

'Well, I did not expect to see him with a social reformer, which sounds a humourless breed, but you tell me she has a great deal of laughter – and generosity. Good. And she is quite besotted with him?'

'She is in an absolute trance.'

'That is very good. I think he has always needed that.'

'Mrs Barforth, I rather thought that you and he –?'

And, as Liam had done when I asked him a similar question, she gave what amounted to a roguish smile.

'Yes, I could see you did, and I confess it crossed our minds. When Venetia died we realized how much we had wasted, and we were able to approach each other again, but not as lovers, darling. Yes, we *did* think about it, but the time had gone by for us and it would have been foolish to pretend. Yet Nicky has worried me lately – how strange, for I always thought him so self-sufficient and strong, so distant by his own choice, which of course he was. But since Venetia died I think he has been lonely. He never spent much time with her but I suppose he knew she was there – poor Nicky! – and because she was so frail in spirit he knew she might need him. He wouldn't admit it, and perhaps doesn't know why, but he has been lonely. I have been very far from that. And now that this wonderful thing has happened to him I find that I am glad. I confess to you – and only to you – that there was a moment when I *could* have felt quite otherwise, but no – on the whole I am glad.

'And you?'

'Yes, that is something else I have to tell you, and you may not be pleased with me. Please remember, dear, that men – and women – who can afford what they want do not *wait* for it at our age – Nicky's age and mine. Do you understand that, Grace?'

'I do.'

'So – what my husband intends is to take his Camille off quite permanently, to Scarborough, I suppose, which is where Blaize and Nicholas Barforth used to take their lady-friends in the old days. He is comfortable there and it is time he got away from the mills. If she will give up her freedom – give up *everything* for him – and if they are happy, then I – yes – I shall be happy too, not alone, of course, and not, my dear, in wedlock, for I am a woman of my own generation and divorce is far too extreme for us. But I shall be happy, just the same, with my dear

1033

friend Julian Flood – he in his house and I in mine, of course, but happy. Do I disappoint you?'

And when I did not answer she leaned forward and patted my hand, very brisk again, a vital and energetic lady with her mind made up.

'He is my friend, Grace. I realize he was rude to you but he was defending his own kin, which is what one would expect of him, and he was most distressed afterwards at the things he had said to you. He is loyal, you see, in the way I am loyal myself – and he is not so dangerous now as he used to be. Even the wildest of men settle with time and there is no denying that he has waited twenty years – not celibate, of course, but single – for my sake. He has denied himself the heir he should have had and which his ancestry demanded of him – all because of me. Nicky says he is the nearest I could ever come to my brother, Perry, and perhaps he is. But what is wrong with that? Perry was so close to me that it was difficult, sometimes, to tell ourselves apart, yet nothing took place between us that should not have taken place between a brother and sister. We simply belonged together, fitted together. Julian, of course, is not my brother. We can love each other differently, yet almost with the same belonging. It contents me, my dear. It is Nicky who needs the total devotion, the grand passion, not I. Be happy for me. And as for you, dear – well, to begin with, there is a place now vacant, is there not, at your so enterprising *Star*.

Liam's articles on St Mark's Fold, Commercial Close and Silsbridge Street had appeared in consecutive weekly issues, liberally peppered with the facts I had supplied him, and had caused a great deal of angry murmuring, his judgement of callous landlords who expected men to live in worse conditions than pigs and callous millmasters whose wages were too low to permit them to live any better giving offence to some, satisfaction to others, fanning the resentment that had always smouldered very near the surface in Cullingford. Letters came pouring in thick and fast, indignant, self-righteous, abusive, offering threats or congratulations, provoking, when we printed the best of them, a controversy on social justice and responsibility that seemed to be raging fiercely enough to carry us through until Christmas. Letters began to arrive in direct reply to our readers' letters, arguments, we heard, began to flare up in common beer-houses and the saloon bars of our better hotels as to who was to blame, who ought to put it right. Who were the demon landlords of Silsbridge Street and St Mark's Fold and Commercial Close in any case? Would the editor of the *Star* name them? The editor made no promises. One would have to buy the next week's edition, and perhaps the week after, to find the answer to that.

'This is all very inflammatory,' Mrs Agbrigg said, 'and very dangerous. Jonas, dear, do you own any property in that area?'

But Liam, I believed, was merely intent on selling his newspaper, for those guilty landlords could have been anyone, my Grandfather Ayecliffe having built his workmen's houses in many areas of the town, throwing them up, in fact, and tacking them together in the interests of speed not durability; somewhere to put the mill-hands and fill the

1034

factories until something better came along. But that work-force, rushed in from anywhere when the new, power-driven machinery had sparked off the industrial boom, had doubled it size eight times since my grandfather's heyday, his terraced cottages – never substantial to begin with – sinking beneath the weight, their walls dripping damp, their floorboards rotten, their sanitary facilities so haphazard as to be virtually not there at all. Who owned them? Dozens of people, hundreds, Grandmamma Elinor very likely among them, with not a few held in trust for Aunt Faith, Aunt Prudence and myself since one had solicitors, after all, to arrange the collection of one's rents and a lady was not expected to know exactly what she owned nor to concern herself with damp walls and doorless, overflowing privies.

Cullingford owned them. We were all their landlords, guilty because of our indifference.

'That's a very good line, Grace,' Liam said. 'I might use it presently. Now then, what about these peaky little bairns in the workhouse? Our Miss Tighe has got herself elected as a Poor Law Guardian again, so if you could make it in your way to have a word with her? She'd talk easier to you than to Camille – even if Camille could take an hour or two off from Paradise.'

I saw Miss Tighe, who told me so firmly to mind my own business that the workhouse, the low, grey building which had scowled down at me all my life from a patch of wasteland above Sheepgate, began at last to cross the barrier between the things I saw without observing and the matters which had lately begun to prey on my mind. I visited Patrick and Anna Stone at least once or twice a week. I accustomed myself to the smell of unwashed humanity until it became bearable, then hardly noticeable. I passed from the burning, crusading fervour which Venetia had never lost, to an uneasy suspicion that I should give my money away, and from there to a calm realization that it would do no good. Charity, Anna Stone had said, was a crutch, a dependency like alcohol or opium which, when removed, like any other crutch would cause the addict to fall down. The answer, she said, was education, the widening of opportunity, some sure and just system in which men and women would be helped to help themselves. She did not believe her theory to be possible, simply right.

I was alone in the office one September day – Camille in Scarborough, Liam heaven knew where – when a man dressed with almost painful neatness came stepping into the room with the air of one who feels certain of encountering something nasty underfoot, his pinched expression and the curtness of his tone making no concession to the fact that he was addressing a lady.

'Mr Liam Adair?' he enquired.

'As you see – I am afraid not.'

'May one enquire his whereabouts?'

'One may. But unfortunately I have not the faintest notion.'

'Then would you be so good as to tell him – miss? – that Mr Gideon Chard requires to see him at his office at Nethercoats Mill this afternoon at three o'clock?'

'I will tell him if I see him. But Mr Chard might do better to come here.'

'Oh, no, Mr Chard will not want to do that,' Mr Chard's clerk told me, pained by my effrontery in suggesting that his employer should risk his beautifully polished boots on this most dubious of floors. 'Three o'clock then. Good-day to you – miss?'

Liam's employees in those days, besides Camille and the men who operated his ancient presses, consisted of an elderly, extremely scholarly man, Mr Martin, and a young lad, Joss Davey, learning the trade. And, as three o'clock came and went, then four and five, I left messages with them for Liam and went home, no longer inclined to make a fuss if the sauce on my fish was not thick enough or if there should be a coffee stain on my napkin, now that I had so much else to interest me.

I had no idea why Gideon should wish to see Liam. The arrogance of the summons had both amused and offended me, and I was sorry, I think, that Liam had not been there to inform that officious little clerk that if Mr Gideon Chard – fine leather boots, silk waistcoat, curly brimmed beaver and all – wished to see him, then he knew where he could be found. But so little did it seem to concern me that I was taken completely unawares when, an hour or so after dinner, my doorbell sounded and Gideon walked into my drawing-room, three or four copies of the *Star* under his arm.

I had not seen him since last summer when he had asked me to be his mistress, but, like me, he had clearly decided to put that folly behind him, for there was nothing amorous in his manner now, his well-shod feet treading firmly, his eyes taking in without the slightest embarrassment every feature of the room, automatically assessing not merely the value of my furnishings and fittings but whether or not they were tasteful and well-chosen, and perfectly ready to inform me of it if they were not.

'Good-evening, Grace,' he said calmly, apparently feeling no need to mention why for the past year we had avoided one another.

'Good-evening, Gideon.'

'You are very comfortable here, by the look of it.'

'Yes. I have been here now – oh, six months and more.'

'Have you really? How time goes by! I believe you saw my clerk this afternoon?'

I nodded, not asking him to sit down since I preferred to remain standing myself, thus signifying that I expected his visit to be short. And understanding this, he too nodded and smiled.

'I take it then that Adair did not return?'

'As it happens he did not, but he may have been unable to see you in any case. He has a great many calls on his time.'

He raised those strongly marked eyebrows in a movement of false surprise, anger only just beneath the surface of him, cool sarcasm above it, prepared to be as cutting as the circumstances – whatever they turned out to be – required. But this was the Gideon I knew – the adversary rather than the lover – and I had no intention of being intimidated by him.

'I am to make an appointment to see Liam Adair nowadays, am I?'

'I can think of no reason why you should not.'

'I can think of several. However, you can probably tell me what I wish to know, since you are so closely associated with him.'

And, his expression remaining perfectly calm, he let those rolled-up copies of the *Star* fall on to my table with a sharp, slapping sound of contempt.

'These articles about which there has been so much hot air expended – these surveys of St Mark's Fold and Commercial Close and Silsbridge Street – can you tell me how these particular streets were chosen?'

'Yes. They were chosen at random, I believe.'

'Indeed? And by whom? By Liam Adair?'

'Yes, of course. Good heavens! Gideon, he had dozens and dozens of streets to choose from. One had merely to take a map and a pin.'

'Exactly,' he said, his jaw set at a hard angle. 'Exactly, Grace. And so it would seem somewhat contrary to the law of averages, would it not, that with such a multitude of streets available his pin descended on the three which belong to Nicholas Barforth and Company Limited, and consequently – in a manner of speaking – to me?'

I heard the intake of my own breath, for, in my intense preoccupation with the tenants of those houses I had given no thought to this, did not really wish to consider the implications of it now, not with Gideon standing there, at any rate, his inquisitor's eyes fixed on my face, his mouth grim and sarcastic. But he had no intention of letting it go.

'We own a great deal of property, Grace,' he said, 'most of it in very decent order. I presume you must be aware of that?'

'Yes, I am.'

'And is it not a fact that every mill in this town, in this valley – every mill and any mill – has a number of near-derelict cottages attached to it? *Every* mill, Grace, of which there are sixty or seventy in this town, including your father's business at Fieldhead. And not one millmaster implicated, among so many, but Gideon Chard. Could I be forgiven for suspecting that Liam Adair is not conducting this survey in the interests of humanity but as a personal vendetta against me?

It was possible. I turned my head slightly away from his so that he should not see my growing realization that it was quite likely. The evil existed and needed to be remedied, Liam would not have lost sight of that, but if he could grind a very personal axe while he was about it, I rather thought that he would. It had been Gideon, after all, who had ousted Liam from the Barforth mills, Gideon who had married Venetia, Gideon who had gained, it seemed, from everyone else's loss. And Liam might easily have decided to exact a price. It was possible.

'I – I am sorry, Gideon. I can make no comment.'

'Can you not? Your loyalty to your employer does you credit – if that is what he is to you.'

'I don't know what you mean by that, Gideon – or rather I don't choose to know. What I can tell you is that *I* was not aware of the connection between those streets. If it was done deliberately, then – yes –

it was unfair and I shall tell Liam so. But those houses really are an abomination, Gideon, you know – we have been absolutely exact about that. And surely, if Liam is criticizing anyone, it could just as well be Mr Nicholas Barforth as yourself?'

'I think not. I am in charge of affairs at Lawcroft and Nethercoats and Low Cross. Mine is the name Adair will use, which is just as it should be – I am not complaining about that. If one accepts the privileges, then one accepts the responsibility that goes with it. I simply wish to make him aware that I know I am being singled out and that I know why. I am able to defend myself – should the need arise – without assistance from my chairman or from anyone. Our father-in-law, in any case, is too occupied at the moment with his new woman to care –'

I swung round to him, ready to be angry now that he had given me a safe outlet.

'Camille Inman is a friend of mine, Gideon, and I am not prepared to hear her spoken of with disrespect.'

He smiled, the sophisticated, disdainful smile of Blanche's London drawing-room, of Listonby and South Erin.

'My dear, I have the greatest possible respect for Mrs Inman, who not only keeps my chairman thoroughly distracted but is decidedly one of the most gorgeous creatures –'

'So she is. But now you are talking about her as if she were a thoroughbred mare for sale at Appleton horse-fair. I cannot allow that either.' He gave me no answer. I could think of nothing more to say. Silence came dangerously between us.

'Can I do nothing right for you, Grace?'

'It is not my place to judge what you do – or to be concerned – as it is not your place –'

And, hearing my voice trail off into a lamentable, tell-tale confusion, I was glad to hear the doorbell again, and then appalled when Liam came breezing into the room, his eyes – which had certainly recognized Gideon's carriage outside – resting on those rolled up copies of the *Star*, his mouth smiling its jaunty, Irish smile.

'Now then – and doesn't this turn out to be handy? I hear you were looking for me, Gideon?'

'So I was, Adair, and I reckon you'll know the reason why.'

But still smiling, Liam walked past him and to my complete horror put one large, warm hand on the nape of my neck and kissed me, just a light brushing of his mouth against mine; the assured, almost casual greeting of a lover of long standing.

What happened then was over in a moment, never actually happened at all, since we drew back, all of us, from the brink of it.

'Now then, Gideon, what *was* it you wanted to see me about?'

'Information, Adair. But I have all I need to know.'

'I'll see you out then.'

And so he did – the man of the house escorting a casual caller, leaving me to grapple with the ferocity I had seen in Gideon's face, the murder I had felt in him, and, far worse than that, my own wild impulse to deny it, the urge I still felt to run out into the hall, to the gate, and call after him that it was not true.

Liam returned, smiling no longer, and I launched through the air towards him a fist that fell far short of its mark, my whole body trembling.

'How dare you use me like that, Liam Adair? How *dare* you?' And he pulled me firmly but gently into his arms and held me there until the trembling had ceased, giving me time to remember that Gideon Chard, by my own choice, was nothing to me.

I moved away from him when I could, calm now but sharp and bitter.

'There's no need to hold me any longer, Liam. If Gideon happened to look through the window, he's already seen us – and he's gone now.'

'That wasn't the reason. And if it's bothering you how I knew he *would* be jealous, then – well – I don't suppose many other people know it. I'm sorry, Grace, but whenever the opportunity comes for me to scratch him a little beneath that aristocratic hide of his, I can't help taking it.'

'You *did* choose those streets then, as part of a vendetta?'

'Is that what he called it? Very classy. You'll just have to bear in mind, Grace, that the survey needed to be done, that some good might come of it, like the adulterated flour and those workhouse brats. I think you ought to forgive me, Grace, because Camille has just given me her notice and the truth is I need you.'

I walked to the window, stared out at the gathering dusk, putting myself carefully together, every piece snugly if a little painfully in its proper place, and then turned back to him.

'Yes, Liam. I'll take Camille's job, since I've been doing it for the past two months in any case, for the same wages you pay to her.'

He laughed, jaunty and debonair again, nothing about him to suggest the merest whisper of passion or revenge.

'Now as to that, Grace, I was rather hoping –'

'That I would work for nothing? Of course you were. And of course I shall not. We're friends, Liam, although I sometimes wonder why, and distant relations. And I am not in need of money. But none of that gives you the right to ask me to work without pay. We'll be businesslike about it, shall we – and fair? I am ready to do Camille's work for Camille's wages, and in exchange for that I will be at my desk every morning at the hour you tell me and will stay until you permit me to leave. If you value my services, you must pay me for them, and I will earn far more than anything you are likely to give me. Agreed?'

He shook his head and grinned broadly.

'You're a hard woman, Grace Barforth.'

'Yes, and you are not the first man to tell me so. But it is a hard world, is it not? Agreed?'

'Agreed,' he said and held out a hand which I clasped in firm businesslike fashion.

'Tomorrow morning then, Grace, at eight o'clock.'

'I shall not be late,' I said, and those simple words transformed me. I was a dainty, useless lady no longer, dispensing soup and milk-and-water

1039

charity to the poor. I was still shaken, still bruised a little in spirit. But I was employed.

23

Camille gave up her lodgings in Prince Albert Road and went off to Scarborough, ecstatic as a young bride of seventeen. She was not a bride, of course, and might never be so again, but clearly and quite magnificently she did not care. All she wanted was to be with her Nicholas; she had cheerfully sacrificed her independence, her reputation, had given up everything to that end, and I was not the only one to be surprised at the speed with which he now abandoned his commercial empire to other hands, quickly adding his beloved Woolcombers and his dyeworks to the sum total of Nicholas Barforth and Company Limited, the better to concentrate on his love.

'How romantic,' said Mrs Agbrigg, smiling slightly. 'I only hope he will retain the stamina –'

'How these men do make idiots of themselves!' declared my Grandmother Agbrigg, having made up her mind not to call on Camille unless she was married and possibly not even then, although her own house in Scarborough was only a mile or two away.

'What is she like?' Aunt Faith asked me, rather tremulously I thought. 'Is she very lovely? *Dark*, you say? Is she really?'

'Shall we wish them happy?' enquired Uncle Blaize.

'Oh yes, darling,' she told him, reaching for his hand. 'As happy as we are – since no one could be happier than that.'

'Well, it makes Gideon very powerful, I suppose,' was Blanche's opinion, 'and gives him a house of his own at last, since Uncle Nicholas can hardly be thinking of bringing the woman back to Tarn Edge. And now that Aunt Caroline is so busy getting Gideon married again it may turn out very well, for no second wife could possibly want to live with her husband's first wife's father.'

But Aunt Caroline, although well pleased to see Gideon in complete charge of the mills and in sole residence at Tarn Edge, was so incensed by her brother's behaviour that she made the journey to Scarborough to tell him so, installing herself at the Grand Hotel and sending him word – since she could not set foot in any house which contained a 'loose woman' – to attend her there. He went, Camille told me, and entertained his sister to a lavish dinner, after which he advised her quite cordially that she would do well to leave him alone. But Aunt Caroline, from her suite at the Grand, had caught a glimpse of Camille strolling along the cliffs, the fresh and youthful appearance of my friend suggesting at once an additional and exceedingly unwelcome complication.

'That woman is young enough to bear children,' she announced accusingly, as if we were all to blame. 'And it would be most unfair to Gideon, at this stage, if Nicholas should get himself a son.'

'My husband already has a son,' said Mrs Nicholas Barforth when this remark was conveyed to her.

But there was no news of Gervase.

I sat down at my desk every morning now at eight o'clock, a point of honour, although Liam quite often did not show his face until after ten; and I would work throughout the day and often enough into the night, talking to anyone about anything which might interest the readers of the *Star*. Had anyone asked me if I was happy I would not have welcomed the question. I was busy, which had always been a necessity to me, but in some ways I was still only playing at independence, and was uncomfortably aware of it. I earned Camille's wages but I had never tried to live on them, retaining my allowance from my father, the security of my capital in Mr Rawnsley's bank, the lure of my inheritance. Not happy, then. Not even particularly content once the keen edge of my enthusiasm had blunted. But busy, willing to learn and interested in what the Stones and Liam Adair had to teach me. Busy and interested – and as an alternative to sitting in my house in Blenheim Crescent and wondering if Mrs Rawnsley would ever call on me, it was good enough.

I was twenty-six and became twenty-seven, paring down my ideals as I did so, to make them functional rather than sentimental. I could not burn for long with a crusading fervour like Venetia's, being quick to see that even in the most ideal conditions many would never learn to stir themselves on their own behalf. Yet through the apathy of those without hope – those who had lost it and those who had been born with no capacity for it – I saw, often enough, courage working like yeast, fermenting to bring some hard-eyed, bright-eyed girl, some canny, curly-haired lad to the surface. There were lads in those streets around Low Cross who after their day-long stretch in the sheds would walk briskly home to wash off the engine grease at a cold-water tap and then, eating a slice of bread and dripping on the way, would spend their evenings in study at the Mechanics Institute; lads who, when brought to the notice of Gideon Chard or Nicholas Barforth or Jonas Agbrigg, pulled no humble forelock but looked the 'gaffer' straight in the eye. There were girls who kept themselves decent not so much for virtue's sake but because they could see what haphazard pregnancy might lead to, tough-fibred girls, fiercely independent of mind and free of tongue who when they became wives went clandestinely to Dr Stone for the means to limit their fertility to a life-saving two or three, and kept their offspring – and their husbands – in order with a wry good humour and an iron hand.

These – as Camille had told me – were the survivors, lads like my Grandfather Agbrigg had been, girls such as I might have been myself. But there were others, like the aged, the sick, the feeble-minded – like the middle-class married woman – who could not speak out for themselves, thousands of them in a state of neglect or oppression, the recipients of cold charity or downright exploitation which I – like Venetia – could not ignore.

I paid rather less attention to my house and had trouble with my maids who, being respectable girls themselves, did not really approve of me and left my service as soon as they were able. I developed a crisp manner, a shell which concealed the occasional pinpricks of hurt I still felt from time to time, a brief but very sharp reminder that I had not succeeded as a woman, the restlessness – quite terrible sometimes – that overcame me when I saw the rich, slumbrous glow of Camille, the deep contentment of Aunt Faith, the perfect companionship of Anna and Patrick Stone, Mrs Georgiana Barforth's vivid face as, with her close and loving friend, she set about the rebuilding of her life. I was at my desk every morning at eight o'clock. When I gave orders they were usually obeyed. I had friends and a few enemies, brief bouts of sorrow and sudden enjoyments. I was busy and interested. It was a life.

I did not meet Gideon Chard again and saw no point in thinking of him, although I did not always take my own advice. On the night he had asked me to live with him I had understood his motives, or so I believed, and told myself that I had hurt nothing but his pride. I preferred to think so, for I was used to his pride and could cope with it, as I was used to my own stubbornness which often made me unwilling to recognize the unease I sometimes felt at returning to my empty house each evening, a house where nothing awaited me but a cool, neutral order, each one of my tasteful possessions in its allotted place with no one to help me cherish them or break them, with no one to cherish or to break me.

And so, when this mood was on me, I did not return home, finding plenty to occupy me at the *Star*, plenty to interest and tax me at the Stones's garden shelter, where I met girls who had been truly crushed and broken in body and in spirit; and occasionally one who had fought back and would sit there, among her bandages, bright-eyed and pugnacious and ready, when the bones were set and the splints removed, to get up and fight again.

I liked such girls, recognized myself in them, although their willingness, sometimes their downright eagerness to return to the men who had maimed them truly appalled me.

'He's jealous, miss – that's all. Fair mad with it. He'd kill me before he'd lose me.'

'If he killed you, he *would* have lost you.'

But logic had no part of passion and the bruised little face would take on a certain smugness, the swollen lips curve into a superior smile, the undernourished body flex itself with a sensuality that I – presumably a spinster since I was not married and Silsbridge Street had never heard of a divorce – could not be expected to understand.

'He loves me, miss – that's what it is.'

And for the year or two that it would last, until poverty and childbearing wore it away, it was a very decided – and for me very disturbing – glory.

Blanche was very often at Listonby these days, since Dominic, having lost his seat in the Liberal landslide, had taken it into his head to travel abroad, to the wild places of the world where a man could shoot something more exotic and dangerous than grouse and pheasant, and where wives could not be included. Blanche gave him a farewell dinner, kissed him goodbye and came north to Listonby, her children, and to Noel.

'I believe I am a far more scandalous woman than you are,' she told me, descending on my house in a dress the texture of sea-foam, roses of every shade of pink in her hat, 'yet Mrs Rawnsley almost fell out of her landau just now in her eagerness to greet me. I have always told you there was a right way and a wrong way, my darling.'

'So you have allowed him to rape you at last, have you, Blanche?'

'My dear,' she said, her serenity never for one moment wavering, 'if I have – and I do not say so – then it is not a subject for conversation.'

But on other matters she was more forthcoming and in a single afternoon I learned that Lord Sternmore had taken back his wife, the penitent and now very devoted Diana Flood, who was already expecting his child. I had news of Claire Chard, now two years old, the darling of the Listonby nurseries where she was in the process of being moulded – as Venetia had desired – into a perfect little copy of Blanche. What would happen to her when Gideon married again Blanche could not say, for neither the younger Mademoiselle Fauconnier nor a certain Miss Hortense Madeley-Brown, both apparently in the running, seemed very motherly to Blanche and would probably not wish to burden themselves with a first wife's child.

Did Gideon spend any time with Venetia's daughter? She shrugged. It was hard to tell. He came over to Listonby often enough, rode to hounds with Noel and stabled some excellent horses there for the purpose, better mounts than Noel could afford. He walked about the estate a great deal with his brother, or took out a gun, and in the evenings they would play cards together. He was *there* and how could one tell how much attention a man paid to a child? Dominic had always appeared totally oblivious of young Matthew and Francis, but would fall on them like a ton of bricks at the slightest hint of bad manners or if he caught one of them slouching in his saddle. In any case, the boys would be going away to school ere long, would be polished strangers when they came back again, and she would rather like a little girl about the house, to dress up and titivate, if Gideon did not object.

Tarn Edge was no place for children now in any case, since Mrs Winch and Mrs Kincaid had left and Chillingworth had been pensioned off – had I not heard? – and Gideon had got himself a French chef and a very suave butler, definitely a gentleman's gentleman, in their place. Had I not heard? Goodness, had I no interest any more in what was going on around me – in the *news*?

My work with the *Star* prospered and my respect for Liam Adair with it, his easy, amorous disposition, the fact that he was unreliable both with money and with women, no longer blinding me to the generosity – more often than not – of his intentions. He was vain and promiscuous and thoroughly enjoyed his notoriety, yet on the whole his opinions were fair and honest, fearlessly expressed, unless they concerned Gideon Chard, in which case they would be heavily weighted with his memory of

Venetia. He had wrung from the derelict housing of St Mark's Fold every drop of gall that he could, managing, without naming Gideon, to make it very clear who was to blame, and since then every time a shuttle came out of a loom at Low Cross, Nethercoats or Lawcroft Fold, and struck a weaver with its pointed end, every time a woman's arm was broken by a picking-stick, every time a man was turned off for no better cause than he had not 'suited' his overlooker, mention of it was made, discreetly but plainly, in the *Star*. Such accidents were common in all our factories, and far fewer than they used to be, now that we no longer employed children under the age of ten, but when a woman was struck by a flying shuttle at Nethercoats and lost an eye, the *Star* was as shocked as if such a thing had never been heard of before, while Liam had quite forgotten to mention that the Barforths had paid the doctor's bills.

'Must you do this?' I asked, receiving in answer his jaunty, Irish smile.

'Well, Grace, look at it another way and you'll see I'm doing him a favour. What else has he got to worry about? And unless I keep goading him on a little, he'll get fat and complacent sitting in that big house all by himself, drinking his Napoleon brandy. He ought to thank me for it.'

And I have not forgotten the glee in Liam's handsome, dark eyes when it was discovered that the whole area around St Mark's Fold – or such of it as did not belong to the Barforths already – was being purchased by them, and that the houses which came empty were not being let again.

'I'm on to something,' he said, and so he was, a month of ferreting and foraging for news informing him that these mean streets, hemming in the thriving but cramped Low Cross Mill were to be demolished, the mill considerably enlarged and its work-force housed in new accommodation nearby.

'Liam – we said ourselves those houses were unfit to live in.'

'Not all of them, Grace. St Mark's is a pigsty, but there's St Jude's. There's nothing wrong with St Jude's. Good houses, good neighbours, people still living in the houses where they were born and where their parents were born. They won't take kindly to this, you know.'

'I know. I expect you'll make sure of that.'

And so he did, explaining to St Jude's Street and others like it that their plight was no different to that of an agricultural labourer turned out of his tied cottage – which which was, in fact, quite true – to suit the whim of the squire. New houses, indeed, were being provided, but where were these houses to be? Nearby, said the squire, but he had measured the distance from the saddle of his thoroughbred gelding, or at the reins of his spanking, speedy cabriolet. The *Star*, however, had walked those three miles from the squire's new houses at Black Abbey Meadow to his mill at Low Cross and had found them long, particularly on a raw winter morning with the five o'clock hooter to beat, even longer at the end of a day's hard labour, especially if one happened to be very young or rather old, or a woman with infant children to hurry home to. And if the residents of St Jude's Street could afford the rents of these new houses, which were bound to be high, the *Star* heaved a sigh at the suspicion that the people of St Mark's Fold could not. Was it beyond the bounds of possibility that the people of St Mark's Fold were no longer required at

Low Cross, being largely the unskilled, the weak, the ones who coughed most in the winter and caused the most trouble, having the most – let it be said aloud – of which to complain?

A larger mill meant more jobs, certainly, but not, it seemed, for the tenants of St Mark's Fold, and once their insanitary hovels were gone, what remained for any of them but the workhouse?'

'Do you hope to stop him?' I enquired.

'Of course not. The mayor and half the corporation either work for him or do business with him. Every magistrate in the county is either related to him, dines with him, or would like an invitation to Listonby. Our Member of Parliament will be careful not to offend him and the *Courier & Review* can do nothing but sing his praises. Of course I can't stop him. I am making mischief, that is all.'

'Then be careful, Liam, for if you go too far he may sue you.'

'I hope he may. But he is far more likely to knock me down, which would sell me a great many newspapers, you must admit. And I shall know how to pick myself up again.'

'Just take care.'

But he would heed no warning and as the area around Low Cross began to simmer, its anxieties and the certainty of its doom made plainer with each new issue of the *Star*, I began myself to grow uneasy, waiting, I think, for that pompous little clerk to appear again, or a more official gentleman coming to tell Liam he had broken the law.

'You can't afford litigation, Liam. It's expensive. I ought to know.'

'Then you'll lend me the money, Grace, won't you, my darling – out of the splendid wages I pay you? Unless he simplifies matters and has set me upon and murdered one night in an alley.'

'If you go on like this he'll do something.'

But I was not prepared for the afternoon that the office door was kicked open and Gideon himself strode into the room, every inch the squire whether he had intended it or not, from his immaculate leather boots to the crown of his shiny hat, driving whip in one hand, kid gloves in the other, nostrils wrinkling their distaste of these mean surroundings, and of the mean, sordid little people who inhabited them.

Liam, blessedly, was not there, just myself and the scholarly Mr Martin, stooping over his desk, and glaring around him a moment Gideon allowed a pair of hard and angry eyes to rest on my face before he rapped out the parade ground command 'Come with me.'

'I beg your pardon?'

'Just *do* it.'

I saw Mr Martin, from the corner of my eye, raise a weary shoulder and glance at his watch reminding me that Liam was already overdue and could return at any time. I understood that Gideon would not go away until at least something of his demands had been satisfied – *could* not lose face by going away with nothing at all – and so I got my hat and my gloves, my mouth dry, terrified of meeting Liam on the stairs, and submitted – telling myself there was no alternative – when Gideon put a hand under my elbow and almost threw me into his carriage.

He drove very fast, the cabriolet swaying so alarmingly at each tight, narrow turning that I closed my eyes and pressed one hand against my stomach, fearing not only for life and limb but that I would lose the last remnants of my dignity by being sick. There was a final, terrible jolting, a rutted track, the smell of dust and earth, his body still snapping with anger as he drew in the reins not a moment too soon and shaved a heap of bricks with nothing to spare.

'Get down,' and roughly he took my elbow again and set me down on the uneven ground of Black Abbey Meadow where the foundations of his new dwellings were under way.

'Over there,' he said, his hand in the small of my back pushing me towards a hut at the far end of the site, and kicking open the door with that expensive boot, thrusting me – there was no other word for it – inside towards a table littered with drawings and maps.

'Here it is,' he said. 'So just damn well look at it – every hovel I pull down I'll replace – every damnable, miserable one. And this is what I'll replace them with – five hundred cottages with dry cellars and good sculleries, gas and water, a stove and a boiler – will that do for you, eh? Some with two bedrooms and some with three, and not back to back either, but in separate rows with back passages wide enough to drive a cart through, so they can take out the night-soil and empty the privies. And you won't blush to hear me mention that, I know. One hundred and fifty pounds apiece they're costing me, and the overlookers' houses eighty pounds more because they've got a parlour sixteen feet by sixteen, four or five bedrooms and a nice little yard. How does that suit you? And I'm not asking more than ten shillings a week for any one of them – and as little as two shillings and ninepence. I'm building washhouses and bathhouses, and a school to keep the brats off the street while their mothers are at the mill. I'm building shops so they don't have to carry their potatoes and their bacon or whatever else they eat the three miles from town, except that it's not three miles and nowhere near. A mile and a quarter, or it will be when the new mill goes up, since I'm building out in this direction. Have you understood that?'

I nodded, but his temper was not yet done and, his hand descending like a clamp on my arm, he took me outside and marched me like a hostage up and down his building site, making no allowances for my thinly shod feet, nor the chill of the March day.

'This,' he said, giving my arm a shake to be sure of my attention, 'is where the school will stand. The baths over there. There are plenty of beer-houses already, not too far away, and I doubt anyone will object to walking a mile to them. And should religion be needed there is a chapel over there of some Nonconformist persuasion or other, and another just beyond it. I went over to Saltaire to see what Titus Salt had done – well, he's built himself a monument and a damned fine one – no beer or spirits of any kind to be sold in *his* village, no washing to be hung out across *his* streets. Well, I don't claim to be either a temperate or a religious man. I just want somewhere to put my workers, that's all.'

And for more than an hour, while the sky darkened and the wind grew colder, he fiercely propelled me over every inch of the ground, showing me and making sure I looked at his drains, the distance between his privies and his kitchen doors, the quality of his building materials, the substantial walled yard around his school so that the children would have somewhere to play without risking death every moment under somebody's horses.

'Not my idea,' he said shortly. 'My architect suggested it. I merely mention it because you'll be unlikely to read it in the *Star*.'

And when he considered I had seen enough – although it seemed to me I had seen everything twice over – he bundled me up into his carriage again, my feet so frozen it was hard to tell if they were scratched or bleeding, although I rather thought they ought to be, and drove me at the same killing speed to my door.

I did not ask him to come in. He simply came, slammed down his hat and gloves on my hall table, walked uninvited into my drawing-room and threw himself into a chair.

'I'm hungry,' he said.

'What?'

'I'm hungry, which should surprise no one since it must be dinner-time. Have you forgotten how to treat your guests?'

Perhaps I found his effontery amusing. That was the excuse I made. But, although I was in no mood to tell myself the truth just then, the truth was – as I was soon to discover – that the whole tumultuous proceedings had exhilarated me. Of course I could have resisted him. Of course I could have got away from him. Instead I had allowed him to make off with me and had thoroughly enjoyed it. I had felt, and still felt, alert and eager, curious and adventurous, bold and rather better-looking than usual. What kind of creature was I? What kind of creature, indeed, could possibly set such store by independence and yet thrive on this bullying? Even now I had only to speak the word and he would leave. I knew it, and, somewhat more to the point, he knew that I knew.

But I had lain fallow for so long, involving myself in dramas which were not my own, that this personal flesh and blood confrontation was not to be missed. I might tell myself that I must settle this issue for St Mark's Fold, but just then St Mark's Fold seemed very far away. Something real – whether it might be good for me or not – was actually happening to *me* – not to Camille nor to Blanche nor to some battered hopeful girl from Silsbridge Street – but to me, and I could not resist it.

And so I went tamely to enquire what might be found in my kitchen for this fastidious man to eat, knowing that the oxtail soup, the cutlets in mushroom sauce, the treacle tart my cook eventually produced could not hope to gain his favour.

'I gather you are less interested in *haute cuisine* than you used to be?' he said, examining the treacle tart with faint surprise before he covered its plebeian countenance with whipped cream.

'We cannot all of us afford a French chef, you know, Gideon.'

'Ah – you have uncovered the secrets of my kitchen arrangements have you? No doubt your employer finds you a useful source of tittle-tattle.'

I ignored his rudeness, offered him port which he refused, although he would take brandy – assuming such a commonplace was to be had – and would drink it, with coffee, in the drawing-room as he had always done in the past when we had dined alone together. But in those days, with the well-peopled splendours of Tarn Edge about us, we had not really been alone. We were alone now, my drawing-room appearing suddenly very small and rather frail as he took possession of it, helping himself to the brandy I kept mainly for Patrick Stone and Liam Adair.

'You admit, then, that although I am no philanthropist like Titus Salt, I am no ogre either?'

'Yes – I admit you are neither.'

'And that I am building good houses?'

'You would hardly put your name to anything that was not of the highest quality, Gideon.'

'Exactly. Then what are you complaining of?'

'Gideon – please understand that Liam, whatever personal rancour he may have against you, really does care about those people. You cannot accommodate all of them. It was never your intention to do so. These houses are being constructed solely for your work-force, you will not deny that.'

'Certainly they are for my workers. We have agreed that I am no philanthropist. I do not feel called upon to make myself responsible for the sleeping arrangements of the whole town.'

'Of course you do not – I realize that. I suppose our grandfathers did not feel responsible for the hand-loom weavers when the power-looms came in – nor Mr Nicholas Barforth, thirty years ago when his combing-machines made so many hundreds of hand-combers destitute. They were casualties of progress too, and of course we must progress.'

'I am glad we agree on that.'

'But those people in St Mark's Fold are not your workers, Gideon – or very few of them. And even if you have any of your new houses to spare, they could not afford your rents. What is to become of them? I thought one could not sink much lower than St Mark's Fold, but perhaps one can. There is the workhouse, of course – of which I know very little – but Liam seems to think death by starvation would be preferable to that. However rash he may be – however wrong-headed – he does care.'

'Believe me,' he said, clenching a hand and leaning towards me, 'I don't give a damn for Liam Adair and his opinions. I feel no need to explain myself to him. I want *you* to know what I'm doing – that's all.'

And leaning closer, he flexed his hand again and placed it deliberately on my knee, his presence completely filling the room, his touch penetrating the fabric of my dress, burning through to my skin and the bone and beyond it, to the pit of my stomach where I could feel a pulse-beat starting.

'*Gideon.*'

'Yes,' he said, 'Why else am I here? And I should have come a long time ago. I've wanted you for years, Grace – years – and I see no reason now to deny myself what other men –'

1048

'There are no other men.'

'I *saw* you – with Liam Adair – in this room. I saw you.'

'You saw nothing.'

'I saw him kiss you. I've never kissed you. Are you going to refuse me?'

'Of course!'

I fought him. I had to fight him. I struck out with hard fists at his head and shoulders, pounded them into his back as he caught me and dragged me forward against his chest; did everything, in fact but the one thing that *would* have stopped him, the simple calling out to my maid for help. His mouth hurt mine, his tongue parting my lips was an invasion, his teeth sinking into my tongue seemed to draw blood, his hands, taking in possession whatever they could, maddened me. I fought him and the plain truth is – oh yes, and I was well aware of it – that I was fighting not to make him stop but because the battle itself was exciting, splendid, a rich and rare feast in itself for my starved senses. And so I fought on until his hands and his mouth had already possessed so much of me that to deny him the rest seemed pointless – or so I convinced myself – my resistance petering out to a feeble, vanquished plea that the maid might come in.

He got up, leaving me winded in my chair, and I heard his voice saying calmly into the corridor, 'Your mistress will not be needing you again tonight. You may retire', and then the sound of the key turning in the lock as he came back into the room.

He walked towards me, shrugging off his jacket, loosening his neck-tie, and then, kneeling down on the hearthrug, he carefully made up the fire and stirred it into a blaze.

'Dear Grace, I can't tell you how often lately, usually at this time of day, I've thought of you. Yes, when I've eaten my gourmet dinner, I've sat many a time with my brandy and wondered how you'd look naked, in the firelight. Come here to me now, Grace. I'll fetch you if necessary – but come to me.'

I got up – entranced as I had seen Camille entranced – and sank to my knees on the rug beside him, wanting him so badly that it *was* unavoidable, my body telling me that he was air and water to me, my powers of logic – which knew better than that – being laughed to scorn by the unashamed urgency of my desire. I wanted him. Everything else was unimportant, unreal. No matter what he did to me, no matter what violence or shame he offered me, while that fire remained inside me – like the women of Silsbridge Street – I should want him still.

'Yes, you looked like this, Grace – a hundred times. You trembled too, and moaned how much you wanted me. Do it, Grace.'

But for answer I kicked away the few garments which remained and fell against him, his chest as hard, his skin as supple and fragrant as *I* had imagined it, the clamouring inside me so urgent now that he felt it, laughed in triumphant excitement at it and then, without more ado, descended full upon me and inside me with great purpose.

'That's the first time – for possession,' he said, but our excitement had not abated and we remained pressed close together in the firelight, a time

1049

of exploration, of long sweeping caresses that set me purring and glowing, offering my body to his eyes and to his hands, stretching myself against him, my own hands delighting in the firm, flat muscle of him and the hard angles, my nostrils luxuriating in his odours, my mouth tasting his skin until desire came again and, in this new frenzy, I wanted not merely to be possessed but to be swallowed whole and alive, unable to give enough to take enough until fulfilment thudded through me, retreated and came again as intense as before, causing me to bite my lips and cry aloud.

We slept then, my head on his shoulder, waking, when the fire burned low, to the chill of the March night. And when I shivered he got up, pulled me to my feet, and smiled.

'I want you again,' he said, 'but in your bed this time'; and so we went upstairs to my virginal bedchamber which, once again, he filled and transformed so that it was his room, his bed, as I was his woman.

The excitement was less this time, the possession deeper. There was more leisure, more caressing, an arousal not only of the senses, his mouth brushing with closed lips over my face, my fingertips tracing the heavy arch of his eyebrows, the high-bridged line of his nose, the length of his firm, full lips which kissed my exploring hand playfully, gently, then my wrist and the inside of my arm, the sensitive angles of neck and shoulder and thigh. There was no haste, no urge to devour this time, a joining together that seemed to happen of itself, quite naturally, my body flowing into his happily; opening itself readily and with a simple, wholehearted joy, to pleasure.

He lay for a moment on his back staring at the wall and then, decisively, he said, 'I'll marry you if I can. It may not be legal because your marriage and mine made us close kin. But if it *is* legal I'll marry you. And if not then, I'll take you back to Tarn Edge and be damned! You don't mind if I smoke, do you?'

And having made his decision – having decided when and where to 'take' me – he smoked his cigar and fell asleep abruptly, both of us having good reasons for exhaustion, although I lay beside him very far from rest, watching the sky lighten to a cool dawn behind my curtains, passing from a state of bitter conflict – not with him but with myself – to an attitude of stubborn but grievous resolve.

I wanted him. The fire in my limbs had subsided now and still I wanted him. I had wanted him long before I had wanted Gervase, had been so overwhelmed by him that even complex, unstable Gervase had seemed safe by comparison. And so it had proved, for although Gervase's light-weight, auburn body had delighted me, it had never possessed me as Gideon's had just done; had given me pleasure which had rippled over me and left me free, not the pleasure I had just known, which could weld me irrevocably and quite slavishly to the man who had created it.

I had wanted Gideon and feared him. I wanted him now and I still feared him. I could go to Tarn Edge and be the woman he wanted, the woman I had been before. But did that woman still exist? And if she did not, then could I recreate her? Did I even *like* that obsessive housekeeper, that efficient hostess, with all her brilliant, irrelevant skills? But she was the woman Gideon wanted and yes – if I desired it – I could bring her to life again, could place myself entirely under his protection – sacrificing my independence as Camille had done – and, little by little, could be completely possessed by him, for I knew he was the stronger and had always known it. I knew he would expect me to want only what he wanted, act only as he acted, think only as he thought, not from any conscious need to dominate me but because, like his mother, he sincerely believed only his own way to be right. He would possess me, absorb me, that was why I feared him, but what frightened me most was the part of myself that even now, in this cool dawn of logic and common sense – of survival – would have submitted joyfully to that possession, asking nothing in return for the whole of my ingenuity, my will, my brain, every drop of my energy and my time but the pleasure of moaning and sighing in his arms every night.

I wanted him and feared him. For an hour, while he slept, I hovered precariously balanced between the two, wanting him so keenly at one moment that the submerging of my identity in his seemed a small price to pay, terrified the next moment and furious with myself when I remembered the implications of that price, the captivity I had struggled so hard to escape and to which now I was so mindlessly eager to return. And unlike Gervase, Gideon would hold me fast whether he continued to desire me or not. Once I was his, once I had committed myself, then his I would remain.

I wanted him. It was all that mattered and if the time ever came when I found myself neglected – as Gervase had neglected me – then at least I would have lived through who knew how many years of bliss. I wanted him as Venetia had wanted Robin Ashby and, like her, was prepared to offer myself, if necessary, as a sacrifice. But, as dawn came slanting through the window, my fear was greater, the risk too terrible and the price too high. We were too alike. I would resist too bitterly and, in the end, I would not be possessed, I would be broken. Fear prevailed – that, and the acute, heart-rending memory of Venetia. I could not do it.

He woke and, finding me sitting on the edge of the bed, leaned over and kissed the base of my spine, his hands very warm and very sure as they travelled the length of my back and reached my shoulders.

'*My* bed next time, Grace, on my satin sheets,' he whispered against my skin which responded exactly as it should have done, and as he had intended, with the frisson that anticipates pleasure.

'Ah – you have satin sheets now, do you?'

'I do. I have every conceivable luxury that money can buy. I indulge every whim, give way to every extravagance – you should know that, my darling.'

'I am not a luxurious woman, Gideon.'

'But you are – you are. You are a rare woman – altogether unique – and what has more value than rarity? What would the *Mona Lisa* be worth if there were a dozen? I find everything I want in you, which makes you very luxurious indeed.'

1051

'And the things I want?'

'You shall have them, better and more of each one than you imagined. You'll want me gone, I suppose, before the maid comes in?'

'Yes.'

'Then I'll go. I'll obey the conventions for now, at any rate. Remember – I'll marry you, Grace, if I can.'

'That's very good of you, Gideon.'

But my tone did nothing to dispel his easy, tolerant humour, the content of a man who is well satisfied both with himself and with his woman, and pulling me against him he began to kiss the nape of my neck and my ear.

'Don't play the independent female with me, Grace Barforth. We know better than that now, don't we?'

So we did. I leaned back against him, surrendering to his hands, the warmth and strength of his body and his will, letting his odours wash over me, indulging myself just once again, just once – But he was not inclined to be amorous, for morning was fast approaching, he had many things to attend to and must go home, change his clothes and shave before showing his face at the mill.

'I have appointments until half-past ten,' he told me, dressing quickly, knowing exactly what he wanted from those appointments and how to get it. 'And then I'll drive down to see my lawyer and find out if, and how soon, we can be married. I'll be back here at half-past eleven or thereabouts.'

And already my time was his time. He would come back at half-past eleven if he could, but if not, if other matters should delay him, then I must wait cheerfully, sweetly, since what activity of mine could possibly compare in importance to his?

'I shall not be here at half-past eleven, Gideon. I have my own employment to go to, remember.'

But instead of the impatience I had expected, he remained warm and indulgent, not in the least inclined to take me seriously.

'Lord! as to that, just send Adair a note saying you've made other arrangements. He doesn't pay you, does he?'

'He certainly does.'

'Really? But never mind, I doubt he'll expect you to work your notice. Just send a note, that's all.'

'I can't do that, Gideon.'

'Of course you can.'

And defeated by his good humour I swiftly changed direction.

'Gideon, I don't want to go back to Tarn Edge.'

'Yes you do – to begin with, at any rate. There's nothing wrong with Tarn Edge that *you* couldn't put right. Nobody may want to visit us for a while but we can eat our little dinners together, drink our brandy in the firelight – make love on those satin sheets of mine. And when I can afford it I'll built you a palace. I'll buy a couple of hundred acres one of these days and put a house the size of Listonby on it. You could play hostess to the county then and you'd like that. You'd be splendid –

first-rate, my darling – you'd do it as well as my mother and a damned sight better than Blanche. And whatever you may think, they'd scramble for your invitations, once they'd got used to the idea of us, because propriety is all very well but it's money that counts – the right sort of money – and I've got that money now. I can *afford* to please myself now, Grace – I can afford the life I want and the woman I want to go with it.'

'Gideon, I can't –'

But, without waiting to know what it was I could not do, he slid his hands under my shoulders and bent over me.

'Darling, there's no reason to worry. There'll be talk, I know, and what of it? My mother won't like it, and Dominic won't be pleased, I know that too – and yes, all that influenced me before, when I spoke to you in London, I admit it. I don't give a damn now. My shoulders are broad enough and my position in this town secure enough. I can look after you, Grace.'

'I can look after myself.'

'There's simply no need for that now. And where's the fun in it, my darling, anyway?'

'But, Gideon –'

'Just leave everything to me.'

I began to say no, there was more to consider, and he kissed the words away. I implored him to listen, to understand, and cradling me in his arms he told me not to be afraid, that he would allow no malicious tongues to hurt me. I tried again, tearfully, to resist, and, smiling, he replied that my bare shoulders, in this first light, were so enticing that he wondered if he might sacrifice another half-hour and come back to bed. He shrugged off his clothes again and made love to me, convincing me that I couldn't live without this raging joy, that if I *did* leave him and he came to find me, he would only have to put a hand on me and I would follow him anywhere.

'Now just what is it that is worrying you?' he whispered into my hair. But lying in his arms in those vulnerable moments after pleasure, all that worried me was how to stay there as long as possible, how to be there again just as soon as ever I could.

I stood in my window and watched him drive away, knowing, since I could not withstand his presence, that I must not allow him to come back again. I remained, my cheek pressed against the glass, for a long time and then, stony with resolution, went downstairs to my writing-desk and penned the most difficult letter of my life.

'Dear Gideon – You want me to be the woman I was before. I could not even if I wanted to, for I am no longer that woman.'

But this was not enough, these were the words he had kissed from my mouth an hour ago and so, with a heavy, aching hand I wrote: 'As you supposed, I am already somewhat committed to another man and in the cold light of day I find myself unwilling to give up a relationship of such long standing and which suits my present way of life so exactly.'

I signed my name, folded the paper, handed it to my maid who, bustling into the room, was surprised to see me up and dressed.

1053

'Lord, ma'am, you fair startled me!'

'Yes. Have this delivered to Mr Gideon Chard at Nethercoats Mill at once. And tell Richards to hurry since I shall need the carriage at half-past seven to take me to Gower Street.'

It was the letter of a cool and promiscuous woman, the kind of letter polite society expected a woman of my sort to write, and I did not think he would answer it. For I had raised the one objection he could neither demolish nor forgive. I had told him I preferred Liam Adair.

I waited until my coachman had set off, walked stiffly upstairs, speaking to my maid as I did so about the badly polished mirror in the hall. I went into my room, fell face down on the bed in a storm of weeping that lasted until I feared it could not stop, and although eventually I got up and dried my eyes, put on my hat and went to Gower Street, and although no one else was aware of it, I knew that I was ill for days – and days – thereafter.

24

I turned gratefully to work as one turns, in great thirst, to water, and found it in plenty, for the circulation of the *Star* was growing, our advertising revenue with it, enabling us quite soon to put out two weekly editions instead of one, to take on more staff, more enthusiasm, and eventually perhaps to replace those ailing presses which had seen service in my Grandfather Aycliffe's day. But, in that far off time when Aunt Faith and my mother had been young, the stamp duty on newspapers which had made them too expensive for the working man to buy had been less of a hardship than it seemed, very few of those working men being able to read. Now, in these enlightened times of Mechanics Institutes and public libraries, when the Act of 1870 had decreed there should be a school within walking distance of every child and the Act of 1880 had just, with the heartfelt approval of the *Star*, made school attendance compulsory, a few hours a week, for all children between the ages of five and ten, literacy was spreading, the craftsmen, the artisans, the workmen at whom the *Star* was aimed being able to purchase it now with the same nonchalance as Gideon Chard purchased his *Times*, his *Yorkshire Post*, his *Cullingford Courier & Review*.

I worked, all day and every day, not only at the amassing of sordid or sensational facts, the uncovering of human dramas and injustices, but the small doings of a small community which enjoyed hearing about itself. I sat in draughty church halls on hard wooden benches and listened to interminable lectures on 'improving', artistic, or scientific subjects. I drank weak tea in those same halls when some fund-raising activity was in progress, admiring both the examples of fine needlework which were for sale and the charity for which their proceeds were destined. I watched amateur theatricals, operas, dancing displays, remembering to note the name of every single player and the number of flounces on the organizers' dresses. I attended weddings, not of Blenheim Lane or

Elderleigh, but of skilled workmen, weaving-onlookers, shopkeepers, schoolmasters, clerks, publicans; and their funerals, finding an appropriate mention for each one. And on the evenings when the *Star* could not detain me I went to the Stones and talked to women whose basic need for food and shelter should have made my own needs seem irrelevant – or, for an hour or two, more bearable.

I left my house by half-past seven every morning and was rarely home before midnight to a supper of cold meat, bread and cheese, some kind of cold pudding on a tray. I lost weight and colour and a great deal of sleep, and suffered for a short while after my letter to Gideon from a strange imbalance of mind, a feeling half dread and half desire that I had conceived his child. Three painful weeks convinced me otherwise and even then, my reactions remaining considerably off-key, I wept first for sheer, blessed relief of it, and then wept again at my own continued sterility.

I acquired a professional manner, pleasant yet cool, a woman not easily pleased and who did not care to please everyone. I wore plain but stylish cut gowns in good quality fabrics and dark colours which made me taller and thinner, did my hair in a low chignon since I had no time now for ringlets, although I did not abandon a certain musky perfume which had its uses in Silsbridge Street. I was acutely miserable for some part of every day, then less so, for the decision to part from Gideon had been mine and, having taken it, it would have been senseless to waste my cherished independence grieving for him. He lingered in a raw place at the back of my mind, a guarded area quick to bleed when one prodded it but bearable if left alone. I know now that his feeling for me went deeper than convenience and that had I married him before making my dangerous acquaintance with freedom we would now be living happily together. But I had married Gervase. Gideon had married wonderful, maddening, enchanting Venetia and had not been enchanted. It was too late. I knew it and the fact that he had neither answered my letter nor thrown it in my face proved that he knew it too. I began to busy myself with the affairs of the workhouse, falling foul once again of Miss Tighe, for whom I was not a competent adversary.

'There is nothing wrong with the administration of the Poor Law,' she told me.

'Not for those who administer it,' I replied, 'although one has yet to learn the opinion of those it is supposed to benefit.' And I concentrated throughout the next few months on gathering those opinions together and repeating them, with my own reactions to them, in the pages of the *Star*.

I had never – as Miss Tighe reminded me – seen the inside of Cullingford's workhouse and while she remained on the Board of Guardians would be unlikely to do so. But it took little imagination to picture the bare, whitewashed wards, the narrow wooden beds like coffins all in a row, the conviction that in this bleak place Charity was not only cold but cruel. And I found many who had been obliged to suffer that Charity to agree with me.

This system of Poor Relief had come into being in my grandparents' day, based on the assumption that, except in the case of the old, the infirm or the juvenile, poverty was invariably the result of laziness, lustfulness or strong drink. And consequently a committee of frock-coated, silk-hatted gentlemen had decreed that outdoor assistance on the old parochial system be abolished and that those who could not maintain themselves must be maintained in workhouses – 'Bastilles' their inmates called them – where the conditions were so harsh that the able-bodied would do anything – presumably even go to work – in order to avoid them.

The diet was of the most meagre, little more, it seemed, than water-porridge, dumplings, and thin gruel, the paupers being obliged to eat all their meals in total silence and to pay for them with their labour, the men being set to stone-breaking, bone-grinding, the picking of oakum, the women to housework and coarse, monotonous sewing. There was, in all workhouses, the strictest segregation of the sexes, husbands and wives being separated on entry and allowed no contact with each other, a precaution thought necessary by the Poor Law Commissioners to prevent the breeding of infants who would be a further drain on the rates, although this same rule was applied to old couples, long past child-bearing age, who had lived together for fifty or sixty years and were often much distressed at being so roughly torn apart.

In fact old couples thus separated quite often died soon after. Infants removed from their mothers and placed in the children's ward as soon as they were weaned tended to do the same. And since no account had been taken by those original Commissioners of the fluctuating state of trade, the fact that a man thrown out of work by bad weather and bad conditions could, if given a little something to tide him over, soon find employment again when things picked up, many were forced into the Bastilles who need never have been there at all.

One heard of mothers who were not told of a child's death until after the funeral, of men in their seventies forced to hard labour; of unruly children punished by being locked in the mortuary for a night or two with corpses for company. One heard of overseers who sexually abused young girls and young boys, of strange outbreaks of disease, and other deaths which, being unexplained, were presumably suicide. One did not, I must add, hear of these things in Cullingford where our Board of Guardians, at the direction of Miss Tighe, was most vigilant, making regular inspections of the wards, employing a qualified teacher for the children who, in their natural habitat, would have received little or no education at all; ensuring medical attention for men and women who had never in their lives possessed the wherewithal to pay a doctor's fee.

But there were abuses of a more subtle nature and it had come to Liam's attention that the superintendent was a very sleek little man, rather better dressed than he should have been when one considered his wages; that the matron had a cool air of competence which had pleased Miss Tighe but a greedy mouth and crafty eyes, quite capable, Liam thought, of further watering down that eternal porridge, of reducing the five ounces of meat allowed each adult pauper four times a week to four ounces, the twelve daily ounces of bread to ten, and thus, with the dreadful patience of a spider, building a profit.

The workhouses, of course – as Miss Tighe was quick to point out – were not prisons, only infirmity, extreme old age or extreme youth obliging anyone to stay there. But since entry to the Bastille meant the breaking up of homes and families, the sale of furniture and pots and pans, of anything one had that would fetch a copper or two, the meagre treasures of a lifetime all gone to purchase that wooden bed, that bowl of gruel, it was not easy, once incarcerated, to get out again. We all knew that in the area around St Mark's Fold there were old husbands and wives who preferred to starve or freeze *together*, rather than apply for the workhouse test; young women who would go to the brothel before the Bastille; we knew of the desperate young man, quite recently, in Simon Street, who, crippled in some accident for which no one felt the need to pay him compensation, had watched his furniture sold, his wife and small children led away, and then hanged himself. I had, to my shame and distress, heard an old woman pleading with her daughter: 'Just hold a pillow to my face, Lizzie, when I'm asleep, so I'll not wake again. It's kinder.' But Lizzie had eight or nine children of her own, a husband who was violent in drink, pains in her chest and dizziness in her head, the fretful cough and wasted cheeks of the consumptive.

'They'll look after you, ma. I can hardly look after myself. And I'll get you out when I can.'

'It's a pernicious system,' Liam decreed. 'I think I'll make a little mischief again.'

But when the *Star* printed a sketch of an unnamed but easily identifiable Bastille, portraying the superintendent as a fat tabby cat, the matron as a weasel, the inmates as tiny skeletons of mice, Miss Tighe, who would not visit the *Star* and could not set foot in the lodgings of so notorious a bachelor as Liam Adair, brought her complaints to me.

'Good-morning, *Mrs* Barforth,' she icily greeted me, a martial light in her eye. 'I have one thing to say to you. I have here Miss Mandelbaum's copy of the *Star*, since I do not take it myself. It will have to stop.'

'The *Star*, Miss Tighe?'

'Preferably. But I am referring to these attacks not only on the workhouse, which I believe to be the most efficiently managed in this union or any other, but on its employees, Mr Cross and Mrs Tyrell – for that is what they are, Mrs Barforth, just employees. I would have thought such attacks to have been beneath even so dubious a publication as your own.'

'I will convey your opinions to my editor, Miss Tighe.'

'I daresay. And while you are about it you would do well to note my further opinion that while your editor, as you call him, is moralizing about the Poor Law and hinting that my superintendent is somehow making his fortune out of it he turns an entirely blind eye to the scandalous conduct of his friends, Dr and Mrs Stone.'

I was, for a moment, astonished.

'I know of no scandal concerning the Stones.'

'Do you not? Then regretfully, Mrs Barforth, I must tell you that you cannot be speaking the truth. Come now, my house is directly opposite theirs in Blenheim Lane, Miss Mandelbaum's a few doors above, and we have *seen*, Mrs Barforth, the use to which they put their garden shelter – it is the talk of the neighbourhood. Can you deny that Dr Stone, if indeed he *is* a doctor at all, goes on the prowl at night and brings home – well, I shall not say the word – *persons* of the lowest character, diseased minds and diseased bodies too, I shouldn't wonder –'

'Miss Tighe, you must know as well as I do that Dr Stone's purposes are the very opposite of immoral.'

'I know no such thing. What I do know is the evidence of my own eyes. I have seen that man set off alone and return accompanied by some creature who quickly disappears with him into that shed. I have heard cries and screams on many occasions, and the unmistakable sounds of drunkenness. I have seen girls who had no business to be in Blenheim Lane and would never have come there had he not brought them, running out of his gate and past my windows in a state of terror. And I have asked myself what it is that could terrify *them*. What is going on in that garden, Mrs Barforth? Is it a shelter for vagrant women, as he declares, or is it a bordello to accommodate the perversities of his friends?'

'How *dare* you, Miss Tighe – especially when you know it to be entirely untrue?'

'Are you accusing me of lying, Mrs Barforth? How dare *you*?'

'This is all nonsense, Miss Tighe.'

'Really? Then the whole of Blenheim Lane is nonsensical, for I am not the only one to watch and complain – not the only one by a long way.'

'Dried up old stick,' Liam said, grinning broadly when I reported the interview. 'She enjoys it. There's nothing she can do.'

Yet I was uneasy and mentioned the matter that evening, hesitantly, to Anna Stone.

'Poor Patrick!' she said calmly smiling. 'They broke our windows in Liverpool and threw stones at his horse. He is quite accustomed to it. But the really sad thing, you know, is that if Martha Tighe would only broaden her views a little she could be most useful. She really believes that her workhouse is humane and orderly – certainly it is clean. And if it is ever proved to her that Liam's suspicions are true, then that superintendent and that gimlet-eyed matron will have a very angry Miss Tighe to deal with. There was a girl here last week who lost her baby in Miss Tighe's Bastille. There is an allowance of two pints of beer a day given to nursing mothers until their infants are weaned, not only for the extra liquid to make the milk but because the hops and malt are strengthening. It was never given, although one assumes it was charged for. The girl lost her milk, other forms of feeding did not succeed, and the child died. Well, perhaps it would have died anyway, for the mother was very undernourished, somewhat beyond the remedy of two pints of beer, nor was she too badly grieved by her loss, for a baby would have

1058

been an encumbrance to her and would have obliged her to stay longer in the Bastille. She went off quite cheerfully, knowing just how to get another baby whenever she wanted one. But Miss Tighe, had she known the truth, would have been very grieved indeed.'

I returned home preoccupied as always by the extent of Anna Stone's tolerance, to find two notes awaiting me, one from Mrs Barforth, the other from Aunt Faith, both telling me that Gervase has returned to Galton.

'Will you be dining, ma'am?' the maid asked, and for an instant I could barely understand the sense of her question, much less answer it. Would I be dining? I had not the faintest notion. But there was something I must do, although exactly what it was eluded me. I must hurry. But where? And why? I must make arrangements. But for what purpose?

'Yes, Jenny. I will be dining.'

But even then, seated at my plainly set table, eating the kind of food servants choose when left to themselves by a mistress who does not care – the kind of food which would have revolted Gideon – I could not lose the feeling that there was something I had neglected or forgotten, something to which I absolutely must attend.

'He is looking well,' Aunt Faith told me the following Sunday. 'Very well indeed. I was at Galton on Wednesday and he had walked in quite unannounced, half an hour before me. Georgiana was in ecstasies of course, for she had feared never to get him back again. Well, he is here, very bronzed and healthy, and I believe on Friday he went over to Scarborough to see his father. My dear, if he means to stay you must be prepared to meet him.'

A letter from Camille reached me on the Monday morning.

'Grace, I was terrified, for if he had come to accuse me of blighting his mother's life what could I have answered? What he actually said was: "I believe you have become, more or less, my wicked stepmamma?" We laughed and I could have wept with relief. "I suppose you have come a-begging?" Nicholas said to him, which sounds ungracious except that it was said with a twinkle in his eye and that unwilling little smile, as if he didn't really mean to smile at all. We dined very pleasantly, Gervase telling us his traveller's tales, which made me laugh until I ached and even made Nicholas grunt once or twice in the way he has when he is actually very amused but doesn't want to show it. He said he wishes to settle at Galton and farm the land and I suppose there is some suggestion that if he sticks to his plan Nicholas will buy him more land in compensation for the fortune he could have been making in the business. I certainly hope so. He is much quieter than I supposed. And of course we talked a great deal of you.'

I waited, still prone to that sudden need for haste when nothing required it, until another letter was delivered to me, and holding it in a carefully steady hand it seemed incredible that I had never seen Gervase's handwriting before. It was pointed and slanting, rather fine, suggesting that, since we certainly would meet, it might be easier for both to meet by arrangement rather than chance, and in the privacy of Galton, without danger of observation by any Mrs Rawnsley, any Miss Tighe. Did I agree? I did. He wrote again appointing a day and an hour he hoped would suit me. It suited me. I informed my coachman, begged a day off from Liam, and found that my mind had wandered rather foolishly to the subject of hats, a certain blue velvet confection veiled with spotted net and topped with a pile of blue satin roses which I had glimpsed in Millergate only a day ago.

I bought it that evening on my way home from the *Star*, knowing as it went into its box that it would not do, that it was a hat for high days and holidays, for garden-parties and fashionable churches, fashionable promenades; a hat for the life that used to be mine.

In the end I put on a smart but not extravagant cream straw with a black velvet ribbon, a cream silk dress draped up to show an underskirt patterned in cream and black and hemmed by a black fringe, a cream parasol with a black handle, cream silk gloves and cream kid shoes. And as we drove away from town, up Blenheim Lane, past Lawcroft Fold and Tarn Edge, past Aunt Faith's suburban Elderleigh to the narrow crossroads which led one way to Listonby, the other to Galton, I was pestered by a fly-swarm of senseless anxieties, the probable muddiness of the Abbey grounds that would spoil my shoes, the specks of soot which could ruin my silk gloves, a conviction that I was too smart – or not smart enough – which occupied my mind and helped me not to admit that what really ailed me was cowardice.

It was early June, the sky a soft, light blue streaked here and there with gauzy cloud, the hillsides around Galton fragrant with new grass, the hedges dotted with unexpected flowers. The house looked empty as I approached, the river which almost encircled it sparkling and hurrying in the sun, the massive oaks just coming into leaf, since spring had been late and cool, a tender, delicate green running riot now on those vulnerable branches.

I busied myself a moment with gloves and parasol, the cream velvet reticule embroidered in black which I had picked up from my toilet table without checking what it contained. I should, most assuredly, have brought an extra handerchief. Had I done so? I opened the reticule, saw that I had, closed it with a snap, and there he was, waiting to help me down from the carriage, looking – and that first impression remained with me every after – quieter than before, as Camille had said; not a quietness of speech or movement, but *quietness* for all that, an absence of restlessness which, for a moment, since restlessness had been the deepest shade of his nature, made him almost a stranger.

'Grace, I am glad you could come.'

'Yes. How are you?'

'I am extremely well. You are looking very smart.'

And to ease our way carefully through those first vulnerable moments we employed the device of etiquette, making the enquiries one can make with such perfect safety as to the state of the weather and of the Listonby road, the convenience of living in Blenheim Crescent so near to town, the extent of his journeyings, how long it had taken him to get there, and how long to get back again. I took off my gloves, smiled at him, asked my courteous questions, made my courteous replies, so that a listener would have taken us for casual acquaintances who were suffering no particular strain.

The stone-flagged hall was cool and dim as it had always been, the family portraits so dark that, after the strong sunlight, it was hard to distinguish one Clevedon from another. There was no fire today, branches of purple lilac standing on the hearth in great copper jars, the long table, more scarred and battered even than I remembered it, set with wide copper bowls full of blossom, their perfume blending pleasantly with the scent of beeswax, the dusty odours of old wood and stone.

'What can I give you, Grace? Tea – or a glass of wine?'

'Is your mother not here?'

'No, she has gone down to Leicestershire with Sir Julian, I believe.'

'You don't mind, then – about Camille and Sir Julian?'

'No. I don't mind. And Venetia would have been glad. Grace, will you take some refreshment now or shall we walk a little first? The ground has dried up wonderfully already after yesterday's rain.'

We went outside again, walking towards the stream, the old wooden bridge, the stepping-stones leading across the water to a gentle green hillside, a dog I had not noticed getting up from the chimney corner and padding after us, the black and white collie, so nervous last year, who now kept correctly and closely to heel.

I had not yet discovered just what had so changed in him for in appearance he was remarkably the same. His auburn hair had faded, perhaps, or been bleached lighter by the sun, certainly his skin was browner than I had ever seen it, the cobwebbing of lines around his eyes much deeper, the eyes themselves keen somehow, as if they had grown accustomed to scanning horizons far wider than one found at Galton, or in Cullingford.

'What a lovely day!' he said and took a heavy breath, inhaling the moist green land, the heavy earth, the hint of moorland on the brow of the hill, the warm air bringing the fragrance of small, pastel-tinted flowers, newborn oak leaves, no tropical flaring of violent colour but the slow and gentle unfolding of an English June.

'How very lovely!'

'You missed Galton then, Gervase?'

'Yes – happily I did.'

'And now you are going to live here and look after the estate?'

'I am. And if you are wondering why I could not have taken that decision years ago and spared myself – and you – all this trouble, then that is why I asked you here today. To explain myself and to tell you that I am sorry.'

We had reached the bridge, the dog still closely to heel, looking up at Gervase enquiringly, wagging a hopeful tail.

'Yes,' he said, 'go'; and daintily, almost cautiously as a cat, she went down the river-bank to take a well-mannered drink, looking back at him from time to time to make sure he was still there.

'That dog was not so well behaved when I last saw her.'

'No, my mother never manages to train her dogs. However, this one appears to be my dog now. Grace – I went away to find out what it was I *would* miss, and had it turned out to be nothing I would not have come back. In the end it was Galton. It struck me that I really was a Clevedon and that what had caused the trouble before was that I was trying to be the wrong Clevedon. Do you understand?'

I nodded, my mind releasing the memory of his taut, white face years ago as he had forced his horse over a fence beyond its stamina and his nerve, and his shame afterwards at the distress Perry Clevedon could never have so much as imagined. And suddenly I felt, not love, not even affection but *akin* to him – closely akin.

'I understand. I think you would have been afraid of that Clevedon.'

'My dear, that Clevedon – Peregrine Clevedon – *was* frightening. Unfortunately from my early childhood I thought it absolutely necessary to be like him. I have only one clear memory of him. My mother had taken me and the Chard boys out with the Lawdale, when we were all six and seven years old, the Chards on reliable ponies because Aunt Caroline was nervous about them breaking their necks, and me on a brute about sixteen hands high because I was a Clevedon and wasn't supposed to bother about trifles like that. No hanging back and keeping out of the way for me, as Aunt Caroline had told her boys to do. I had to *keep up* like my mother and my uncle had kept up at my age – they weren't asking me to do anything they hadn't found easy and enjoyable themselves – and, of course, because I was scared, I couldn't. I did take a tumble that day, head first into a ditch, and at first I thought they hadn't noticed and would just leave me lying there – damned uncomfortable and freezing cold, of course, but at least I wouldn't have to go on sitting that terrible horse. The Uncle Perry came at me at the gallop, heaved me out of the ditch by the scruff of the neck and threw me at my mother – what seemed to me a mile away. And she just tossed her head and laughed, because they'd both had plenty of rough treatment when they were cubs and taken no harm. I remember how very splendid they both looked. Poor Uncle Perry! His horse reared up and fell over backwards on top of him that same afternoon, and neither of them got up again. They buried him over there, in the Abbey churchyard, and my mother brought me here after the funeral and explained that the land and the house would be mine now. The trust that would have been Perry's when old Mr Gervase Clevedon died would now come to me, the family traditions, the holding of the land for future generations, the responsibility of making sure there would be a future generation. And every time I went into the village or round the farms some sentimental old woman would start telling me I was the "image" of Master Peregrine.'

'And so you simply thought you had to *be* Peregrine, and do the things he used to do.'

'So I did, which would have been bad enough even if I'd had the nerve, as well as the face, for it. But unfortunately there was somebody else I was expected to be, was there not? A second Perry Clevedon at Galton.

Another Joel Barforth at Tarn Edge. I loved my mother the best and so I tried harder for her, but there were times when I couldn't have said what scared me most, riding one of Peregrine's wild horses or standing in those weaving-sheds and in the counting-house knowing I was supposed to understand those machines and those columns of figures and give orders to men who *did* understand. And it wasn't merely a question of courage. It was the sense of failure that really troubled me. I stood between two splendid inheritances and was not fit for either. Consequently what was I fit for? Not a great deal, perhaps. It has taken me all these years to find out and I have hurt you and some others in the process.'

'You said when I arrived that you wished to apologize. For what? For marrying me?'

'Dear Grace, how could any man be sorry for that?'

'Yes – well, that is the *right* answer, of course. Now tell me the truth.'

'That I regret marrying you? For your sake I must regret it. I treated you abominably. I was like a wilful child constantly seeing how far he could go, except that I was playing adult – and very cruel – games.'

I sighed, remembering.

'Yes, I know. You thought I could make everything right for you – as if I had some kind of magic formula. And when I hadn't – and couldn't – you were angry with me. You resented me, I think.'

'Yes. And when your magic failed me I turned to Diana, thinking she could do the same. I had formed the habit of clinging to strong women, you see. My mother – then you. The failure was entirely mine and I reacted as I always did, by running away. Not far, just into other women's beds to start with. I believed, for quite a long time, that those casual affairs were as much as I was capable of.'

'Until Diana.'

'Yes,' he said quietly. 'Until Diana. I was in love with her, and it turned sour like everything else I had attempted. I was so full of self-disgust when I went away that I hardly expected to survive it. After all, how could I possibly survive without my father's bank account to draw on, or my mother to provide me with a bolt-hole? Or without you to blame for all my shortcomings? I found that I could. And for a while the blessed relief of being with total strangers who had never heard of Perry Clevedon or Joel Barforth – of Galton or Tarn Edge – was the most marvellous experience of my life. For a while all I wanted to do was relax into it. For a while. Then I stood still and found that, after all, I could look at myself squarely and coolly and live with what I saw. I hadn't been cut out to run the mills. My mother was right about that. And my father would have accepted it – as he's accepted it now – if I'd been able to show him something else I wanted to do. But I was never sure. I needed first to discover that I really was a Clevedon, but of an entirely different breed to Peregrine.'

He smiled once again into that far distance, quietly, easily, the hectic rhythms of his nature slowing, it seemed, and mellowing, no longer driven by his old, fast-burning uncertainties but at the gentle pace of the seasons.

1063

'If you came here with Venetia, Grace, when you were children, then you must have met my great-grandfather, the old squire? He was a man who occupied the one place in the world which suited him best. He had never been rich, because a life of service in keeping with the Clevedon code is no way to make a fortune, but he understood the land, as my mother understands it – as Peregrine did not – and he understood the needs of those who farm it and graze their beasts on it. I don't know if he could bring down eighty grouse with eight shots like Peregrine – certainly I can't – but he looked after his fields and his moor and he looked after his people. That is the kind of Clevedon I am. Not in the least exciting like Peregrine but – amazingly – quite solid and rather sound. Who ever would have thought it?'

We turned to retrace our steps, smiling and easy with each other, the dog, aware of Gervase's slightest movement instantly leaving her game in the water to follow after him, and then, recognizing the path he must take, frisking ahead of us into the cloister, our quickest way back to the house.

'How peaceful it is,' he said, breathing in once again the scents of his heartland, the perpetual dusty twilight of this strange corridor where nuns had once walked with bowed head and folded hands. Yet I had never been at peace here, and quickening my step had almost reached the far end – the strong uncomplicated daylight of every day – when I heard someone call out, a quick burst of laughter, and a child, presumably escaping from the house and with his nursemaid in hot pursuit behind him, came toddling towards us.

I stood quite still for a moment because I was unable to move, watching the sturdy little legs, the self-important step of a child already three years old, the eager, explorer's hands outstretched, expecting to encounter nothing in the whole world but affection and pleasure, as mine had done at that age.

'This is my son,' said Gervase quietly.

'Yes, of course,' and I bent down as any other woman would have done and reached forward to welcome him as anyone – certainly the child himself – would have expected me to do. He looked like no one in particular, light brown hair in soft, loose curls, a rounded, rosy face, light eyes which could have been green but which reminded me far more of two bright little buttons than of Gervase or Venetia, or Diana Flood. There was nothing there of the sharp-etched, auburn profile, the birdlike delicacy which could have disturbed me – which *my* child might have had – yet to my complete horror I knew that I could not touch him, that even if he stumbled I could not put out a hand to prevent his fall.

I straightened up swiftly and turned my face to the wall, tears spilling from the corners of my eyes, utterly ashamed, while Gervase retrieved the little boy, gave him back to his nurse, and then put a cool, steady arm around my shoulders.

'Grace, I am so sorry. I should have warned you.'

'Heavens! I can't think why I am being so stupid.'

'Can't you? When you lost your own child here, in this house – our child? I grieved for him too. I couldn't tell you then. May I tell you now?'

1064

'No. Tell me about *him* – the child you have. Please. It's better.'

He gave me a moment to dry my eyes and then, understanding that I could not bear to speak of my own loss, he shrugged and smiled.

'Very well. He is called Peregrine, I fear. My mother's choice, of course, and since it seemed, at the time, that she would be left to bring him up, one could not complain.'

'I thought he had gone abroad with Diana.'

'No. Diana did not wish to grow accustomed to him, for she knew Compton Flood would never take him. Had he been a girl possibly, but with a title in the offing a boy was out of the question. She understood that and once she had made up her mind to be Lady Sternmore she planned accordingly. She wanted that title badly and now she has another son. My mother was to have had this one, but, like the sheepdog, I seem to have acquired him. Will you take that glass of wine now?'

I took, in the end, rather more than a glass, sitting at the scarred oak table beneath the portrait of Peregrine Clevedon, Gervase, who still looked so like him, lounging beside the hearth telling me once again his traveller's tales, easing our way from the past, where love had been difficult and had not succeeded, to a future that might offer us friendship.

'I must go.'

'Must you really? May I come and see you in Blenheim Crescent and scandalize your neighbours?'

'Please do.' And I knew I would be very disappointed if he did not.

He had changed, and as I drove away, my head pleasantly confused by his excellent wine, I knew that I had no need ever again to feel anxiety or guilt on his behalf, no need to worry on sharp, raw nights if he had found a place to lay his head, no need to concern myself with his tensions, since he was not tense, nor with his nervous rages, since he was neither nervous nor angry. He had changed far more than I – had done better, perhaps, than I had done, at picking up his pieces. Who ever would have thought it? And I could not deny that this assured and steady Gervase Clevedon intrigued me.

25

These fresh outbreaks of scandal in the Barforth family rather surprisingly made my own social position no easier. Mr Nicholas Barforth, defying all conventions, had gone off to live in open and apparently most enjoyable sin with a woman half his age. But Mr Nicholas Barforth had always been a law unto himself. Mrs Georgiana Barforth was known to be, if not precisely living, then spending far too much of her time with Sir Julian Flood. But Mrs Barforth had simply transferred her affections from one gentleman of distinction to another, a procedure which Cullingford might abhor but was well able to understand. And it was I, who had not abandoned my husband for a lover but for a solitary and unseemly independence, who remained

1065

Cullingford's true disgrace; the woman who had betrayed her sex and her class by shunning the charitable duties and the unsalaried employments appropriate to a lady and selling her services, like a common housemaid, for money.

And I suppose it was only natural when, the better to account for my perversity, it was whispered that I must surely be the mistress of Liam Adair.

'They flatter me,' Liam said. 'And they tempt me too – I'll not deny it.'

But Liam, whatever else he lacked, could find temptations – and mistresses – in plenty and had more than that to occupy his mind just then. There was the eternal problem of finance, or the lack of it, the printing-presses which he still could not afford to replace, the salaries – including mine – which had to be paid, the advertisers who could not always be convinced they were getting value for money. But more pressing than that was the problem of the demolition of the streets around Low Cross, and, as the first hammers began to fall, Liam was quickly aware that he had unleashed rather more than he had, I think, intended.

I knew that the houses in St Mark's Fold had not been fit to live in. I knew that those who can help themselves must be allowed and encouraged to do so. I knew that progress in all its forms had always displaced and often destroyed the weak, the sick, the unnecessary, and that enough of them had survived each fresh catastrophe to implant its memory in their children. The power-looms introduced into this valley by Joel Barforth had thrown a whole generation of hand-loom weavers out of work. The combing-machines, brought in twenty years later by Nicholas Barforth, his son, had made the occupation of hand-comber a thing of the past, causing some to starve and thousands to emigrate. I knew that Gideon Chard, who could not comprehend poverty in any case, did not expect and was not expected to make himself responsible for the hundreds who had been living in debt and near destitution in St Mark's Fold.

Millmasters built houses, as landowners built farm cottages, for the simple reason that they required workers who in turn required somewhere to live. That was the extent of the obligation, and if the farm labourer or the mill-hand turned out to be idle or ill-tempered, fell ill or in some other way failed to give satisfaction, then he was turned out of his job and the cottage that went with it. Everybody in Cullingford understood that and few were prepared to dispute it, taking the view that, when employment and accommodation were tied together, a man with any sense at all took good care of both, and in the case of an accident or sickness or a slump in trade, well, these were hazards which all working men must face and, however much one might sympathize in some cases, no one could expect a landlord to find alternative accommodation for his tenants. Cullingford's landlords did not expect it. The *Courier & Review* did not expect it either. By far the greater part of Cullingford stood solidly behind Gideon Chard in his plans for expansion and improvement, well aware that he was about to dispossess only those tenants who had been undesirable in any case, those who would take no care of their squalid cottages even if they were allowed to remain in them, and who, quite often, could not pay their rent.

Eviction notices for rent arrears which should have been issued months ago had been held in abeyance pending demolition, thus giving the families in question a far greater respite than they had been entitled to. Gideon had made a charitable gesture which had not, in fact, cost him a great deal and, for the rest, he paid his taxes, a part of which maintained the Poor Law which in its turn maintained the poor. He had been taught, as I had – as we all had – that poverty was a sin that brought its own punishment, and I knew there were those in St Mark's Fold who were idle by nature and would always remain so. But I had seen courage and intelligence and humanity there too, and the seeds of it, which would not come to flower in the workhouse. And I had no thought in my mind of attacking Gideon when I tried to share my horror of that grim establishment with the readers of the *Star*.

I hated the Poor Law with all my heart. Liam hated the Poor Law and Gideon, and although we told St Mark's Fold clearly that it had society to blame for its desperate condition – those Poor Law Commissioners who believed they could cure poverty by making it too unpleasant to endure – there were times when Liam could not resist apportioning a hefty share of that blame to the new squire of Low Cross.

'You should stop this, Liam,' I warned him.

'Yes,' he said, 'I know I should.'

But society was an abstract concept somewhat beyond the grasp of St Mark's Fold. The Poor Law Commissioners were very far away. Gideon Chard was there, visible and tangible, riding every day to the mill on his glossy chestnut mare, immaculate in tall hat and perfectly tailored coat and trousers – different ones each morning – which fitted him without a wrinkle. And the night after St Mark's Fold was finally reduced to a heap of smoking rubble, the mill at Low Cross was attacked by a gang of youths, resulting in broken glass and broken heads, a watchman knocked unconscious, a lad of sixteen severely mauled by a Low Cross dog; and a tremendous increase, throughout the whole area, of bitterness.

We condemned the attack in the *Star* as unnecessary, foolhardy, but some days later an old woman from St Mark's Fold who, after a lifetime at the loom had been obliged to sell the few sad possessions she had saved and enter the Bastille, hanged herself there. A month after that, a young family who had gone on the tramp to avoid the workhouse test, and who had been considerably under-nourished to start with, were found dead, presumably of starvation, in a derelict barn. Liam condemned that too. The attacks continued.

Additional dogs and men with sticks and possibly shot-guns were stationed in the mill-yard, but boys in their teens are agile and far too brave and almost nightly one would climb a wall and throw a stone which, with luck, would result in nothing more serious than broken glass. And when enough of them had been bitten, and a few had been rounded up and despatched to the House of Correction, attention was diverted to

Black Abbey Meadow where damage was done and building materials stolen, with the result that houses for which tenants were waiting could not be finished on time.

'You should tell them to stop this, Liam, before one of them gets killed. They might just listen to you.'

'Yes,' he said. 'I know.'

But he did nothing, and in the end the person who could have been killed was the squire of Low Cross himself, when half a dozen youths who had been painting obscene slogans on the mill wall early one morning decided to wait for him, presumably to observe his reactions, and then, when he appeared, took it into their heads to throw lighted paper at his horse.

I was not there to see what happened, but many were, and I heard how the thoroughbred animal quivered, reared up in panic and then, as fire came at it from all directions, went completely out of control, the very devil, they told me, screaming and snorting and trying to do murder with those thrashing hooves, with another devil on top of it, cursing, spitting blue flame, until the pair of them went crashing to the cobbles and only the human devil got up again.

He must certainly have been winded and bruised, and there had been blood on his cheek and on his hand, staining an immaculate shirt-cuff, greatly – I well knew – to his displeasure. But the horse, the only completely innocent party in the whole affair, had broken its knees, for which death was the only remedy. The wiser, or the softer-hearted of the lads, ran away. The fiercer, or the more foolhardy, waited while a gun was fetched from the mill – why, Liam was to ask later, had a gun been there in the first place? – and watched as Gideon, without any visible tremor, put it to the animal's head and fired the one merciful shot and then, whipping round to face his assailants, caught two particularly skinny little urchins and thrashed them with his riding-whip until they bled.

'Don't print it,' I told Liam. 'You *shouldn't* print it.'

'I know,' he said, but the next day the *Star* carried not only the words but the picture of the deed, a millmaster at least eight feet in height, dripping gold chains and fobs and rings, with two bleeding children cowering at his feet.

'You forgot to include the horse, Liam.'

'Yes, I should not have forgotten that. There are some who used to live in St Mark's Fold who'd be glad of the carcass to eat. Are you very angry with me, Grace?'

'I'm trying not to be.'

But a day or so later, after months of painstaking detection, some bribery and bullying and not a little risk to himself from the burlier characters in the story, he was finally able to supply the evidence that the workhouse master, Mr Cross, had indeed been falsifying his accounts, and gave Miss Tighe and her Board the choice of dismissing him forthwith or facing a scandal. Not, I suppose, that the scandal would have been very great, Mr Cross's habit of serving meat only twice a week

1068

instead of on alternate days – and very suspicious meat at that – not likely to shock those, and there were many, who wondered why paupers should eat meat at all. But Miss Tighe's reputation as a shrewd woman of impeccable judgement was at stake and she so abhorred any kind of fraud or theft that she almost chose scandal for the pleasure of sending Mr Cross to jail. Her Board, for the first time, defied her by deciding otherwise. The guilty man and his matron were sent packing, a comfortable couple selected in their stead, largely at the recommendation of certain voices on the Board of Guardians which had not been heeded in Miss Tighe's heyday. Miss Tighe retained her position, but her authority was no longer quite the same, and we knew she would blame Liam for that.

'You are not quite so angry with me now, are you, Grace?'

'No. But have a care for Miss Tighe. She will harm you if she can.'

'I daresay she will. But you know me by now, Grace. There's always some woman coming after me,. wanting to harm me in one way or another. I reckon you'll stand by me when the time comes.'

The summer was intense and overcast that year, heavy yellow skies, airless nights, a perpetual taste and smell of dust as one by one the streets around Low Cross disappeared, reducing the area in which I spent my working days to a wasteland. Gower Street itself remained intact but half of Simon Street was gone. Colourful if by no means aptly named Saint Street, with its pawnshops and lodging-houses and brothels, was a memory by August, and unrest generally was so rife that, even in the streets where poverty had not been condemned, people were on the move, packing up as fast as they could and leaving as if from a beseiged city, unable to be certain of what Gideon Chard might buy up and knock down next.

The new factory buildings were already growing outwards, the same handsome, Italianate façade as Nethercoats, containing – because Gideon was in charge of it – everything of the very latest and best.

'Yes,' Gervase said on his first visit to me in Blenheim Crescent, 'I came by Low Cross and I can only be delighted to see that Gideon is increasing our fortune so grandly. *His* fortune rather more than mine, these days, I imagine.'

'I know nothing about that.'

'Well, I don't know all the ins and outs of it myself, for I believe he has a sideline or two that perhaps even father is not aware of. But I have no cause to complain. Do you remember the meadow where we used to jump the young horses? I have put cows in it now. Why don't you come and see?'

'Why on earth should I want to look at a field of cows?'

'To watch them pleasantly grazing on the place where you first saw me cry.'

'I'll come.'

I went, and we had a long, warm afternoon together strolling the leafy little pathways around Galton in the sunshine. I went again, walking farther afield this time, even daring to risk myself on the stepping-stones bridging an admittedly very narrow and very shallow stream. And when I was safely across he found me a seat in a grassy hollow and, stretched out beside me, spent a lazy hour telling me the names of the grasses and the delicate wild flowers, of the trees and birds which he could identify, to my surprise, by their song.

'Wherever did you learn all these clever things?'

'Grandfather Clevedon taught me when I was a boy. I never mentioned it before because –'

'Because you thought it wasn't the kind of thing Uncle Perry would have been likely to mention. But he must have known all about it too.'

'I suppose he did.'

'Then what a bore he must have been, with nothing but his fast horses and his fast women.'

'Ah – so I bored you, did I?'

'Oh no. Almost everything else, but not that.'

I met Noel Chard on that second visit, waiting near the new cow pasture as we came back to the house, his resemblance to Dominic and Gideon diminished now not only by the assegai-thrust he had received at Ulundi, which still caused him to limp slightly, particularly in damp weather, but by the same weather-wise, earthbound calm I had noticed in Gervase.

'Blanche wouldn't care for cows so near the house,' he said, merely stating a fact without the slightest hint of criticism, being a man, these days, who could recognize the nucleus of a prize herd when he saw it.

'Grace wouldn't mind,' said Gervase and indeed, although I had never consciously thought of cows before, the sound of their lowing, coming with the scented breeze through the window as we drank our afternoon wine, had a gentle monotony that was not unpleasing.

Whenever Blanche was at Listonby, which was almost all the time since Dominic went abroad, we met the first Sunday of every month in the parish churchyard to take flowers to Venetia. And that first hot August afternoon, having arranged the wonderful roses Blanche had brought from Listonby to our satisfaction, Blanche ran her fingers along the marble of the elaborate headstone and murmured, talking to me but actually telling Venetia, 'My husband has written to say he is thoroughly bored with Africa. But don't worry, for I am in no danger of seeing him again. He thinks he may go after tigers in India next. He believes a man may really live like a lord in India and consequently is bound to stay there.'

'I suppose he must come home sometime, Blanche.'

'I suppose he must. But I am relying on India to call him back again – all those tigers to shoot and elephants to ride and beautiful brown girls in plenty, I expect, who are very willing. He is a perfectly happy man.'

'And Noel?'

She smiled, gave what for her was almost an ecstatic sigh and suddenly pressed her living, blushing cheek against the cold tombstone.

'What else could I do, Grace? He had loved me for such a long time and I – oh yes, I admit it – I made sure he kept on loving me. I stopped him from loving other people, didn't I? Of course I did! Which is why Venetia said she wished he'd rape me, which *of course* he never would. I started to wish the same myself so that I could make the excuse – only to myself – that he'd forced me and that afterwards I'd thought, oh well, what's done is done, and allowed it to continue.'

'How like you, Blanche!'

'Yes. That is exactly what Noel said when I told him. And that very same night – quite a long time ago now, as a matter of fact. It was not rape, of course, although according to the law it seems to be incest. Well, what Dominic did to me on our wedding-night and for a year or two thereafter seemed more like rape to me than this – and as for the incest, I sometimes try to worry about it, without much success.'

She remained for a moment, her cheek against the stone, her face as finely chiselled and serene as a porcelain angel, her pale hair pure silver in the sunshine: beautiful, surprisingly competent Blanche who had always meant to have everything her own way and who now that she had it was quite hesitantly asking our approval – mine and Venetia's.

'Well, I only wish Venetia had realized that, in our dishonest fashion, we are all three of us very happy. I can't help thinking she would expect me to bring it all out into the open, as she did – and as you did.'

'Blanche, I only decided what was right for me. You are the only person who knows what is right for you. Don't allow anyone to persuade you otherwise.'

'Oh, Grace, do you really think so?'

'I do, since you are ready to take the responsibility for your choices, and are hurting no one else.'

We rearranged the flowers once or twice again as we usually did and then drove off quietly to take tea with Aunt Faith, an essential part of our pilgrimage, finding, as we approached Elderleigh, that there was already a carriage on her drive.

'Oh lord!' said Blanche disgustedly, 'it is Aunt Caroline. Yes – I did forget to mention it – she has come up again from South Erin to plague the life out of me and has brought a house-party with her. I expect she has driven over to show Gideon's new fiancée to mother.'

'Oh –' And then, because whether Blanche knew it or not, my silence was very strained, my breath gone clean away, I said with a blessed coolness, 'I did not know Gideon was engaged.'

'Well, perhaps he is not, but his mother is certainly very keen on it and the girl is willing. It is an excellent match, but of course there can be no need to tell you that. She is thoroughly tedious but very rich and, I must admit, rather beautiful. Gideon came over to dinner last night and spent quite an hour with her alone in the Long Gallery, so I imagine we may expect the announcement at any time.'

They were sitting in the garden screened from the sun by Aunt Faith's wide-spreading chestnut trees before a table set with a lace cloth and the expected tea-time apparatus of silver tea-kettle and sugar-tongs, wafer thin cucumber sandwiches on flowery china plates, scones and chocolate cake; Aunt Faith, like Blanche, in a gown of soft white silk, Aunt Caroline in a robust shade of magenta; another white dress at which I only glanced as I walked slowly across the lawn.

Chairs were awaiting us, and Aunt Faith welcomed us into them, talking easily, ignoring the awkwardness she knew was coming, presenting Miss Hortense Madeley-Brown to me with the simple explanation that she had come with Aunt Caroline, until the Duchess herself, who had not forgiven me for introducing Camille to her brother and had piled up other grievances against me since then, announced crisply: 'Well, Grace, I had not expected to see you here today, since Blanche does not acquaint me with all her plans, and I find it most awkward. My son Gideon is to join us presently to escort us to Tarn Edge and I am not sure he should be asked to meet you.'

'I beg your pardon,' I said, not quite so sharp-spoken as I might have been, since, for a shocked moment, I thought she was implying knowledge of our tempestuous, night-long affair. But of course it was my connection with the *Star* that troubled her and which, as she quickly informed me, raised doubts in her mind as to the suitability – even to herself – of my company.

'Caroline,' said Aunt Faith smoothly, since in her view this was simply 'Caroline being Caroline', 'that is very harsh.'

'I believe it to be just. Forgive me, Hortense dear, for speaking of these matters in your presence. I regard you quite as one of the family already, from whom no secrets should be kept. And, like all families, we do have our little difficulties. Grace can hardly deny that she has been disloyal –'

'I most certainly *can* deny it.'

She smiled at me with the same total self-assurance which exasperated me so thoroughly in Gideon.

'Nonsense, my dear, of course you cannot. Is it not disloyalty to ally yourself with a man who has deliberately slandered my son – your own second cousin – a man who has whipped up so much ill feeling that my son might have lost his life only the other day as a result of it? If that is not disloyalty, then the world must really be changing.'

I did not wish to lose my temper, partly for Aunt Faith's sake, partly because I considered it essential to be composed when Gideon came, and so I answered rather quietly, 'Aunt Caroline, it is a very complex situation and I am truly sorry about the accident to Gideon's horse. But Liam Adair is not my ally. He is my employer. I am not responsible for his opinions and, after all, he too is a member of my family.'

'Good heavens!' she said, diverted, as I had intended, into matters of genealogy. 'He is no such thing.'

'Indeed he is,' Aunt Faith said quickly, understanding my motive.

'Faith, he is no such thing. Her grandmother married his father, and what sort of a relationship is that? But on our side of the family, her mother was your sister and my first cousin. She married my brother's son, although the least said about that the better –'

'Do you really think so?' murmured wicked Blanche. 'For my part I find Gervase much improved. I am sure Grace does too.'

'And what would Grace know about Gervase?' Aunt Caroline snapped, her eyes, bright with the dawning of a new suspicion, flashing from one politely smiling face to another. 'You surely haven't been *seeing* him, have you, Grace?'

1072

And although she was both deeply mortified and deeply shocked – for how could I be so shameless and what effect might it have on Gideon's inheritance? – at least it distracted her sufficiently from Liam to enable us all to drink our tea, while I took my first uninterrupted stare at Miss Madeley-Brown.

She was, indeed, the kind of girl who, in her first appearance in London's drawing-rooms is acclaimed a 'beauty', a tall, in fact a very tall girl with fine, broad shoulders, a bosom which even now, in the seventeenth or eighteenth year of her age, was magnificent, a lovely if rather vacant face and a haughty manner, coils of bright gold hair doing exactly as they had been bid beneath an expensive, much beribboned hat.

'You will be pleased with Tarn Edge,' Aunt Caroline told her. 'It is not a palace, of course, but for a town house, and for this part of the world, I do not think one could do better. My father built it for my mother and I must confess it has been sadly neglected since she left it. My brother's wife, Mrs. Nicholas Barforth, took no care of it, my niece Venetia even less, and now, although my son has made many improvements since Mr. Barforth retired to sea, it is sadly in need of a woman's touch. I know it will please you.'

Hortense Madeley-Brown smiled, a dazzling exposure of strong, pearl-white teeth which did not waver for one moment when Blanche, who had raised pained eyebrows over Aunt Caroline's deliberate failure to mention my own meticulous housekeeping, now lazily enquired: 'I dare say it will. But tell me, Aunt Caroline – for I am often puzzled by it – to whom does Tarn Edge actually belong?'

She received no answer, Aunt Caroline detecting a bee somewhere in the branches above her head; Aunt Faith quickly handing round more chocolate cake, which Miss Madeley-Brown, with the keen appetite of youth and something not too much under six feet of thoroughbred blood and bone, began placidly to consume.

She would look superb, I thought, on horseback, her riding-habit cut so tight that her maid would be required to stitch her into it every morning. She would be a luxurious adornment to any man's table, that creamy bosom half-revealed in the candlelight. Those pale, slender limbs of hers – I could not dismiss the image, no matter how hard I tried – would look more than enticing on the satin sheets Gideon now used to cover his bed. She was the kind of girl I had expected him to choose when Venetia died, the kind his mother had always wanted for him, rich, conventional, not too bright, who would obey him and please him, produce for him a pair of healthy, uncomplicated sons; a girl who would bring out the worst side of him and stifle the rest. Vapid creature, I thought, sitting there sipping her tea with nothing in her head but how pretty she looked, a bosom like a Renaissance Venus and a brain no bigger than a pea – how could he demean himself by wanting a girl like that?

I must not think of it. I drank my tea too quickly and too hot, burning my tongue in my determination not to think of it. It made no sense. I had

1073

given him up and in order to do so effectively had hurt him and made him despise me. Now, because of the increasing bitterness between him and Liam Adair, he must despise me even more. I had known quite well I must face him sooner or later. The time had come. And if it was to be made more painful by the presence of his mother and his recently acquired fiancée, then I would have to grit my teeth a little harder and bear it. What else could I do? Certainly it was not the moment to begin examining my own feelings towards him, and as Blanche – more perceptive than she used to be – drawled: 'Here comes Gideon now', I arranged myself carefully and decided to model my own behaviour on his, whatever it turned out to be.

If he had really wanted me as much as he had said he did just six months ago – *if* – and if I had hurt him as much as I had intended, then the situation might have been difficult for him too, although nothing in his manner, trained first by Lady Chard and then by the rigours of a particularly harsh public school, betrayed it.

'Aunt Faith,' he said easily, kissing her cheek with the degree of affection exactly appropriate to a nephew. 'Have I kept you waiting? I do apologize.'

'No. You are just in time,' Aunt Caroline answered instead, squeezing the hand he held out to her across the table in vigorous welcome. Blanche received no more than a nod from him, a smile and an almost imperceptible wink, a familiar, friendly greeting quite suitable for the woman who, as he must know quite well, was making both his brothers happy. And then: 'Hortense. How are you?' he said very quietly, the whisper of the accomplished, successful lover who can create a moment of intimacy while still permitting others to hear. And taking her hand he kissed it lightly but so near the wrist – bringing his head too close, in fact, to that splendid bosom – for casual gallantry.

'I am very well,' she told him, which so far was the longest sentence I had heard her speak.

And it was not until Aunt Faith, fearing he did not mean to speak to me at all and hoping to cover the gap, had placed a teacup in his hand; and even then not until he had slowly helped himself to milk and sugar, stirred his tea, replaced the spoon in his saucer, that he glanced in my direction, nodded curtly, and said, 'Grace.'

'Good-afternoon, Gideon.'

'Do you know,' Aunt Faith said brightly, 'I believe it is the warmest afternoon we have had this summer.'

'Oh, I don't think so, mother,' murmured Blanche. 'Last Sunday was scorching and the one before it. What do you think, Hortense?'

'Oh, absolutely,' she said, 'scorching – quite.'

And thus we settled it.

He took his golden young Amazon strolling in the rose garden soon afterwards – the same roses, I supposed, which Venetia used to admire with Charles Heron – no sooner were they out of sight than Aunt Caroline leaned towards me and said crisply, 'Well then, Grace, I was not prepared to speak of this matter in Hortense's hearing, since it could concern her very closely, but I suppose you are in a better position than most to have some inkling of my brother's intentions. Does he intend to remain in Scarborough, which is quite bad enough, or is he so lost to reason as to contemplate setting that woman up at Tarn Edge?'

And turning to Aunt Faith she made a wide gesture, half anger, half distress. 'You understand me, Faith, I am sure of it. Here is my poor Gideon, after all he has done – the work, the responsibility – and all he has suffered – yes, here he is without even a home to call his own. Tarn Edge, as you well know, belongs to Nicholas and I cannot tell you how much I regret making over my share in it to him when my father's property was divided. Yes, I know, I was paid handsomely, or so I thought at the time, but those few paltry thousands – I forget how many – would be no compensation at all for seeing that woman in the house my son has *earned*. Yes, Faith, earned – not only by his labour, and he has laboured very hard, but by the insult he has endured there. The Madeley-Browns are great people, Faith – this is the best marriage I could have made for him – and he must have somewhere decent, somewhere fitting, to take his bride. And you, Grace, I cannot tell you how deeply it shocks me to learn you have been in contact with Gervase. He has been over to Scarborough too, I hear, making up to that creature, so one must assume his travels have taught him on which side his bread is buttered. He has just bought three hundred acres of Winterton land adjoining his own, my son Noel tells me, and since I have not heard that he has sold any Barforth shares to pay for it – and my son Gideon would be sure to know – one may safely assume that the money was a gift from my besotted brother Nicholas. Certainly the world *is* changing.'

For Aunt Caroline it was and for that reason I found it easier to be patient, accepting her scolding as I would not have done in the days of her social glories. But her husband, the Duke, had declined rapidly this last year or two, and when he passed away his land, his title, his property, would pass with him, placing Aunt Caroline in the same dilemma from which on her first husband's death she had extricated herself. A new duke would take possession of South Erin the very day the old one was carried out of it, bringing a new duchess to preside at his table, giving Aunt Caroline nothing to do but hand over her keys and the family jewels and take her leave.

She would have been surprised to know how well I understood her bitterness. She was a strong-willed, intelligent, forceful woman who had nevertheless accepted one of the roles traditionally assigned to her sex and had played it brilliantly and to the full. She had devoted herself entirely to the ambitions, interests, property of others, living her life not through her own achievements but at second-hand through theirs, and was now beginning to find that one by one those who had depended on her to create an atmosphere in which they *could* achieve were in their different fashions leaving her.

She had raised Listonby from the dust to create a splendid home for her husband and a fitting inheritance for her eldest son, had surrounded herself for years with influential, possibly quite boring men, who might one day make a Cabinet Minister, a Prime Minister, of Dominic, only to find that he preferred tiger shoots and polo games and – she surely knew this – brown-skinned women. And then there was Noel, who should have been a general by now – *she* would have been a general by now in his place – content to roam about the farms with none of the dash and swagger she had bred into him, refusing, for all her coaxing, to restore the Listonby Hunt Ball because it would be 'too much' for Blanche. Only Gideon remained and I knew how fiercely she would defend him against all comers, against Camille who, apart from the luxuries which would be lavished upon her, might further complicate the Barforth inheritance by producing a bastard but much-loved son; against the existing son, Gervase, who might worm his way back into his father's favour; against that son's former wife who, if she became his wife again, might claim Tarn Edge and more besides.

I understood and so, following Aunt Faith's example, I drank tea, smiled, made sympathetic noises or indignant ones as required, said, 'Really?' 'How very provoking', while Blanche, sitting between us, fell gracefully but deeply asleep.

'Wake up,' said Aunt Caroline, prodding her with the handle of her parasol. 'Gideon is coming back and Hortense would be very surprised to find you in that condition. They are very well-connected, Faith. She has one uncle a bishop, another who is very high up at the Treasury, and one who has some kind of a place at Court. How very gratifying to find a girl with all that money who has breeding too, and who is young enough to be *adaptable* – who will allow herself to be moulded, for she has a most pliant disposition. Gideon will have not one moment of anxiety with her. Hortense, dear, did you enjoy your stroll?

Hortense agreed that she had enjoyed her stroll, Aunt Caroline beaming at her fondly, her good spirits entirely restored as she contemplated this rare find, this biddable, beautiful girl who – unlike her other daughters-in-law – would run her home and raise her children as Aunt Caroline told her, who would even be glad of her advice.

'We must be off now, Faith,' she said, drawing on her gloves. 'For we are to make quite a little tour with Gideon – the estate at Black Abbey Meadow, the mill of Low Cross and the new property beyond –'

'New property?' said Blanche, asking the question which burned the tip of my tongue. But for once Aunt Caroline was not being astute or malicious or inquisitive, simply talkative in the manner of ageing aunts, and looked vaguely for assistance to Gideon.

'Why, yes – there has been some more property investment. Where did you say it was, dear?'

But he was not at first inclined to be very precise.

'It seemed advisable,' he said, smiling beyond his mother at Miss Madeley-Brown, who seemed intent on examining the lace flounces on her sleeve, 'in view of recent difficulties, one wished to be certain of one's hold in the neighbourhood, should one wish to expand again or to house an additional work-force. And so as certain properties became available, it seemed pointless to let them go elsewhere.'

I looked pointedly at Blanche and, knowing as well as I that he was up to something, she asked obediently: 'Which properties, Gideon?'

'Oh – whatever came to hand, here and there around Low Cross – and Gower Street. A buyer's market certainly, at the moment. In fact I have seen nothing like it. If one judged by the willingness of landlords to sell, one might think the hordes of Genghis Khan were encamped about a mile away – that or the Black Death. One can have just about any house one wants at the moment, for a very decent price, around Low Cross – and Gower Street.'

But I had endured long enough and taking up my gloves to give my hands an occupation, I said with a calm I at least thought creditable, 'What is it you have bought in Gower Street, Gideon?'

And I did not need his voice, merely his faint, malicious smile and the glint of satisfaction in his eyes to tell me it was the offices of the *Star*.

26

'So he is our new landlord, is he?' said Liam. 'Well, well, I suppose we must look for a hefty increase in our rent.'

It came heftier than we had supposed, and we knew there would be worse to follow.

'Well, I reckon there's just about one thing left for me to do,' said Liam. 'I'll give him a run for his money. But while I'm about it you might look around, Grace, and find us another address before he puts me and my old presses into the street.'

But rehousing the *Star*, as Liam – and Gideon – had foreseen, was no easy task, for the healthier buildings in Sheepgate and Kirkgate and the new business premises which were raising their handsome heads these days, from Market Square to the fringes of Blenheim Lane, were either beyond Liam's price range or their owners – quite often friends of Miss Tighe – did not view our tenancy with favour. While in the poorer quarters of the town everything I inspected was too small or too squalid, a verminous tenement in Leopold Street where the rotting floors could not have supported our presses, a slightly less flea-bitten address a street away but directly alongside a slaughterhouse where the stench of death and panic, the squealing of sheep as their legs were broken to render them easier for butchery, was unacceptable; in fact, nothing at all.

'You'd best have a word with our advertisers,' Liam told me, 'in case they've heard rumours – which wouldn't surprise me.' And so, in my smart blue velvet hat, wearing enough jewellery to inspire confidence, I made the rounds of the small business men and tradesmen whose services were publicized, playing Miss Agbrigg of Fieldhead Mills to those who might respond to it, flirting discreetly with some others, calling a spade, in some quarters, a plain shovel; assuring one and all that, whatever they may have heard to the contrary, Cullingford's *Star* would continue to shine. Nevertheless, a certain amount of business was not renewed and it seemed certain we would soon be obliged to retrace our steps to a single edition a week.

'I'd best be off to Cannes for a word with Grandmamma Elinor,' said Liam. 'That is, Grace, if you can manage a week or two without me – and if you can lend me the fare?'

'I could save you the journey altogether, Liam, and pay your rent.'

'So you could. And when I'm desperate enough no doubt I'll ask you. But I reckon I can manage till then.'

'As you like. But at least you can forget about my salary for the time being.'

'Now that's very sporting of you, Grace,' he said, easy and debonair as always, although I couldn't miss the occasional wariness in his face. 'But considering the pittance I pay you – well, you may as well have it as not, for I know what it means to you. In fact, while there's still something left, how about me taking you to the theatre in Leeds tonight, and then to supper?'

We saw a melodrama, as I recall, from the splendours of a stage-box, his arm resting on the back of my chair more from force of habit, I thought, than real interest, his eyes on my *décolletage* from time to time as we ate our discreet and very expensive supper largely because that was the correct way to behave in a private supper-room. He even enquired in a roundabout but extremely good-humoured fashion if I would care to spend the night and expressed a pleasing degree of equally good-humoured disappointment when I decided it would not be wise.

'They say you are my mistress already, you know.'

'So they do. But you have mistresses enough, Liam. I think you have more need, just now, of a friend.'

'And I think you may be right. We'll drink to it.'

We drank deep, returning to Cullingford on the last train at a scandalous hour when no decent woman should have been abroad.

'Of course you'll not let me in?' he said as we reached my door.

'Of course not.' But I had no objection to the kiss he lightly planted on the corner of my mouth, and went inside still smiling at his assurance that if Miss Tighe happened to be awake – and it could surprise no one to learn that she *never* slept – and if she happened to be standing on a footstool at her back landing window, she would, with a certain acrobatic skill, be able to see us in an embrace about which she would draw her own conclusions.

A pleasant evening, a happy time, but, as the summer progressed, each day hotter and more malodorous than the next, the game of baiting Low Cross Mill continued nightly, any tenement lad who could break a window or steal a few bricks, who could show off the tooth marks of a Barforth dog, a cut lip or a black eye received from a hard-handed navvy, being declared king of his own particular muck-heap the next morning.

'They wear their scars like medals,' said Liam, who would have done the same at their age. But this constant raiding of the newly cleared site was a serious nuisance to the building contractors, who needed to take advantage of the good weather to complete their schedule. If the walls were not up and the roof not on by October, then Mr Chard would be out of temper and everybody else out of pocket. The tenement lads decreed that the roof would *not* be on by October. The building workers, with their bonuses at stake, decided otherwise. Threats were made and ugly scenes ensued, one of them in the street directly below my office window when a gang of navvies, strapping Irishmen for the most part, encountered an equal number of our local breed, smaller and perhaps not quite so fierce but wiry and cooler, more reasoned, so that the battle was even matched and most unsightly.

'Appalling,' thundered the *Courier & Review*. 'Unfortunate,' said the *Star*, without adding for whom, and I suppose it was not to be wondered at when some days later our office was not so much entered as invaded by a man, well-dressed yet somehow not a 'gentleman', huge not only in girth and muscle but in the anger that was mottling his heavy cheeks and his thick, bull-neck, who, even before a word was spoken, had curved his big-knuckled hands into fists.

'Tom Mulvaney,' he said, considering this sufficient explanation, since we would be sure to know that the firm of Charlesworth and Mulvaney had won the much-coveted contract for the building of the new houses at Black Abbey Meadow and the new mill at Low Cross. And, after making his announcement, Mr Mulvaney remaining at his vantage point in the doorway, glanced swiftly around the room, assessing the fighting strength against him and seeing just old Mr Martin, sorting through the morning telegrams, the boy, Davey, the printers on the floor below, who were as elderly as their presses, myself, and Liam.

'Good morning,' Liam said without getting up, very sensibly keeping his desk between himself and this very obviously superior adversary. 'And what can I do for Mr Mulvaney?'

'Call off your rat-pack, Adair.'

'Which particular rat-pack did you have in mind?'

The desk was reached in two long strides, an iron fist smashed down upon it, oversetting the inkstand and the water jug Liam always kept there, the pool of ink and water doing a small violence of its own among his papers.

'*Mr* Mulvaney,' he said, and leaning back in his chair clicked his tongue reproachfully, an act of provocation which brought me to my feet, my presence as a woman, which might appeal to Mr Mulvaney's sense of decency, the only support I could offer.

I was not sure just how old Liam was. There was no grey in his hair, no apparent lessening of vitality, certainly no sign of the sobriety men are assumed to acquire with age. But he was older than Gervase and Gideon, had seemed a man to me when I had still been at school, and could not, I thought, be much short of forty, while this murderous, mountainous Tom Mulvaney might at a guess be twenty-nine. I doubt if Liam could withstand him. I saw that Liam doubted it too, and I did not wish to see him try.

'Call off your bloody rat-pack, Adair.'

'I have no rat-pack, Mulvaney.'

'This is the last warning you'll get.'

'You're threatening me, then? Would you care to be more explicit? And would you watch your language, old fellow, in front of a lady?'

'I see no lady,' snarled Tom Mulvaney, darting me a glance as vicious as any he had bestowed on Liam, and, having been drawn to his attention, I came forward to the side of the desk, unable to stand between them but positioning myself so that he would have to push me aside to get at Liam.

'Then I must bring one to your notice,' I said, my voice emerging very cool although in fact I was quite terrified. But Liam, for all his possible forty years, could not consent to shelter behind a woman, and as he got to his feet, exposing himself to attack for his pride's sake in a manner I found most exasperating, there was an ugly moment when I felt myself to be physically holding them apart as once – in another world it seemed – I had stood between Gideon and Gervase.

I had lost my head that night. I must not do so now. 'Mr Mulvaney,' I told him, 'you may not see a lady but I am sure I see a gentleman. And certainly you have a grievance –'

'A grievance? Is that what you call it? As fast as we put the windows in at Black Abbey those louts of his have them out again. And who pays? Not Chard, who can afford it. *I* pay. And if it goes on then I'm telling you –'

He was right, entirely right, and I told him so, repeating at such length and with such conviction how right he was that at last his killing rage turned sullen, smouldered a while and then hardened to a point where he would be more likely to sue for damages than extract blood for them.

'You think you're a clever woman, don't you, Mrs Barforth? I've heard about you.'

'She *is* a clever woman,' said Liam.

'Aye. Maybe so. But I'm not much taken by cleverness in women. And I warn you, Adair, if this goes on, then the next time we meet she'll not talk me out of a thing.'

'There's no need to wait, Mulvaney. I'll meet you any time you like.'

But Tom Mulvaney, in his full green prime, could recognize an older man's bravado when he heard it, and making a gesture of contempt I had seen often enough by now in Gower Street, he turned and went down the stairs, a victor who condescends – until it suits him to do otherwise – to leave the field.

'My goodness, gracious me!' said Mr Martin returning to his telegrams.

'You can't do anything about it now, can you, Liam?' I said, feeling suddenly very weak about the knees.

'Of course I can't. But I reckon that bog-trotter in his Sunday suit could do something about me any time he had a mind. So it looks as though you'll have to guard me, Grace, day *and* night, my darling – I can see no help for it.'

Was he afraid?

'Of course,' said Anna Stone later that evening, adding with her habitual gravity: 'There can be no courage without fear.'

'Which means,' said the Doctor, with a twinkle in his eye, 'that if one measures on that scale then Liam is probably a very courageous man indeed.'

But the Stones themselves had come increasingly under attack, a campaign of hostility being waged against them which, although admittedly genteel, was nevertheless as virulent in its way as anything likely to be devised by Tom Mulvaney. It was no new thing in their experience. In Liverpool, people had risen against them as once they might have risen against a coven of witches and warlocks, and made it physically unwise for them to remain in the city. Cullingford's hostility, taking its character, I thought, from Miss Tighe, was a more silent matter, no vicious stoning of the culprits to the town gates, but an ostracism, a withdrawal of all those who considered themselves decent, which was designed to smother them out. Mrs Stone found herself ignored in the better shops of Millergate, all of them patronized by Miss Tighe, who had far more money to spend. Dr Stone found the more lucrative side of his practice dwindling away, no respectable woman likely to openly consult a man who was known to advocate contraception in case there might be talk that he was advocating it for her; few gentlemen caring – with Miss Tighe's drawing-room windows directly across the way – to risk their reputations at a house where such dubious characters were known to frequent the back garden.

The Stones reacted in their separate fashions, Anna Stone becoming more preoccupied, more intense than ever, the Doctor whistling a great deal as he went about his business, continuing to prescribe as he thought fit and to bring home with him such waifs and strays as he believed might best profit from his attention, arriving one September night with a young woman who had a child of two or three years old fastened to her side by a shawl.

There had been heavy rain, an early autumn cloudburst so violent that within moments the gutters had been overflowing, the streets transformed to muddy, narrow streams, everyone, rich and poor alike, soaked instantly to the skin. And running for shelter, Dr Stone had found the woman half-collapsed in a doorway, willing – despite her obviously weak condition and the child strapped to her hip – to go anywhere with him, for any purpose, and for as much or as little as he might care to pay.

She was very thin and dirty when he brought her into the garden shelter, the child knotted so tightly in the sodden shawl that we were eventually obliged to cut him loose, this bondage being necessary, we understood, to prevent him from crawling away, down some squalid alley or through the mire of some cheap lodging-house while his mother slept. And occupied with hot water and hot broth, soap and towels, milk and bread for the whimpering child, I did not immediately recognize this gaunt, suspicious, flint-eyed woman as cheerful Sally Grimshaw who had once been my personal maid.

She had recognized me at once, of course, but had not particularly cared to make herself known to me. If she had fallen on hard times, so had thousands of others, and she could see no point in discussing it, since talk, although cheap, made things no better. But, with a plateful of beef broth inside her and her child washed and wrapped in clean, warm blankets, she shrugged her shoulders and, in the spirit of one who is paying for her supper, allowed me to question her.

She had left my house because she had been uncomfortable there, with people who knew her circumstances. She had been raped, true enough, but she had lost her virtue just the same, or so everyone had told her, and there were plenty of others who had said, behind her back but loud enough for her to hear, that rape was impossible and all it meant was that she had not fought hard enough. At any rate, she *knew* more than she ought to know, whether one called it rape or seduction, sin or folly, and the others knew she knew. The maids kept on asking her questions, the menservants – or some of them – tried to take advantage, because what was done was done, and what more had she to lose by doing it again? She had moved on to get away from her reputation, but it had followed her on the below-stairs grapevine and eventually – well – if you give a dog a bad name, sooner or later it will probably earn it. There had been a baker's boy who had coaxed her into folly for a week or two, succeeding mainly because she had been very lonely. And then, in her last place, she had fallen in love with the butler, a man of dignity and authority, older than herself, who had first taught her to enjoy her body and had then impregnated it.

The mistress had dismissed her the moment her condition was discovered – very early, since speed was to her lover's advantage – and he had stood nearby, impassive and slightly disdainful, while she was turned off without a reference. She had worshipped him and even then had seen no sense in implicating him so that he would have lost his job too. He had told her from the start that he could not marry her, but she had not really believed him, had thought he was testing the strength of her feelings, which had been – she admitted it – powerfully strong. And she knew he had been considerably annoyed with her, had called her a little fool, a damned nuisance, when she had turned down his offer to pay for an abortion, refusing to be mutilated for his convenience by some old woman with a knitting needle. No, she had made no appeal to the law, for no court in the land would award her more than two shillings and sixpence a week for the support of a bastard child, and in any case her lover needed only to bring other men before the judge – the menservants directly in his employ – to swear they had had her too and the case would be dismissed.

He had made only one other approach to her. He had found a woman who specialized in these things who was ready to adopt the child, no questions asked, as soon as it was born, for a cash payment of ten pounds, which he – to be rid of the obligation once and for all – was prepared to supply. But knowing what this meant, that these baby-farmers would keep a child in misery for a year or two and then let it die, handsomely insured, or, failing that, would sell a girl to a brothel-keeper, a boy to a gang of thieves, she had again refused. She would manage, one way or another, on her own and had expected it to be hard. Domestic service being no longer possible, she had gone to work, first as a trouser-hand at a sweatshop in Leeds, stitching all day and into the night, until her fingers were raw and her eyes smarted with strain, for as little – when she had paid for her thread and her share of the lighting – as three shillings and sixpence a week. And since it was impossible to live on those wages, much less put something by for the few days after her confinement when she would earn nothing at all, she had taken the only course that had seemed available.

It was not unusual, she said, in the sweated trades for girls who had neither parents nor a man to support them, to supplement their incomes by some part-time street-walking. And Sally was not unusual. She had gone out for the first time with a friend, another trouser-hand, and thereafter alone, transacting her business in dark corners and back alleys since she could not take men back to her lodgings. But she had earned just enough, before her pregnancy became too cumbersome, to enable her to stay in those lodgings – such as they were – while her baby was born.

Had she felt disgust or shame at her new trade? She could not afford disgust, and whose was the shame? She had stood many a time with her back to a wall and marvelled at the filth men were ready to pay for. And if they despised her for supplying it, then she had nothing but the most complete contempt for them. And as for the moralizers, the churches, the police, the law, if they really wanted to sweep the streets clean, they should discourage the demand, surely, not the merchandise? And as for the respectable ladies who drew aside their skirts and averted their eyes when she passed, she would be interested to know how many of them had ever been hungry or unable to find an honest penny to buy milk for a child?

She had gone out again after her baby was born, too soon, and had suffered an illness which had nearly killed them both. But she had made up her mind not to die, had not died and had taken up with a man soon after, a former, very minor champion of the illegal bare-knuckle prize-ring, an unstable character – even Sally admitted it – but the kind of companion her trade required. They had looked after each other, the woman contributing her earnings, the man the protection of his muscle, but he had been caught at a race-meeting relieving a gentleman of his wallet and had been given twelve months' hard labour.

It had not been an easy year for Sally. The very week of his sentence she had been badly beaten by a customer, an occupational hazard to which the loss of her man exposed her, and had recovered slowly. She had lost her regulars, then her lodgings, and had been reduced once again to doing business in back passages, coal-sheds, a man's jacket on the hard ground, and to living where she could, in constant danger of being picked up as a vagrant. She had taken refuge for a while in a navvy camp, a law unto itself, and had been travelling recently with a tinker

1083

who after a quarrel had dumped her in Leicestershire. She had been on the tramp since then, making her way north again since her man was soon to be released and she had agreed to meet him in Leeds. He would not have a penny piece in his pocket and neither had she, and she did not expect his stint at the treadmill, on prison rations, to have sweetened his temper; but two, she found, were better than one. He had lost an eye, she'd heard, in a prison brawl, which in a way could be counted a blessing since it meant that his thieving days were over. What future did she see for herself and her son? Future? She lifted her head from her mug of hot, sweet tea and gave me a look of frank contempt. Future? She had not thought me so simple-minded as that.

'You could come and work for me again, Sally?'

'I doubt it, ma'am. Your other servants would walk out of the door in a body the moment I came in.'

'I daresay. But I have a very small house these days and do no entertaining. You could manage it yourself, Sally, with a girl to do the rough.'

'And my boy?'

'I am seldom at home and there is no reason why he should inconvenience me. It's a future.'

'Yes,' she said, no more; but when I returned the next day intending to take her with me, she had gone, had left very early that morning, her child knotted to her side, refusing to take anything but a packet of bread and cheese to sustain her until she got to Leeds, some time that night.

'Why?' I asked, and Anna Stone sighed and shook her head, her husband clicked his tongue, irritable with pity.

'It has gone too far with her, I suppose,' he said. 'When a woman suffers some gross physical deformity from an accident which was no fault of her own, she will usually hide her face, partly to spare decent people the pain or the embarrassment of looking at it, and partly because she does not wish to be seen. Perhaps your Sally feels much the same. And after all, with this man of hers – she has no need for any kind of embarrassment. He is vicious and inadequate and has lost an eye. She had no reason to feel inferior to *him*. Poor woman! It could happen to anyone.'

It could have happened to Venetia. I went home, haunted afresh by the memory of her slight figure in that dingy, rented room, unable to face the hopelessness of her situation and so retreating from it, gathering just enough of herself together to do what was necessary for the child. And I had done nothing for that child, could do nothing now but send expensive, impersonal trinkets to Listonby at Christmastime and make occasional, rather guilty enquiries of Blanche. But what I could do, for what it was worth – and I was uncertain as to its exact value – was to write a thinly disguised account of Sally Grimshaw which Liam included, with my signature, in the following Friday's *Star*.

I made no judgements. I did not even question the wisdom of the law which, considering a bastard child to be a fitting punishment for the sin of sexual depravity, regarded that punishment to be an entirely female matter, according maintenance settlements that would have been insufficient to feed a sparrow. I did not ask why one partner in a crime should go unscathed while the other paid the penalty for two. I merely stated that it was so. I did not ask who was responsible for this woman's downfall, whether it was her attacker or her seducer, the mistress who had coolly dismissed her, knowing full well the misery that awaited her; whether it was the owner of the sweatshop who had not paid her a living wage, or the narrowness of a society which allowed only half its members – the male half – to possess realistic emotions and desires which in the other, female half were condemned as vice and lust. I did not ask, but the answers came thick and fast, letters of abuse some of them, others of mild reproach, suggesting to me that such things should not really be spoken of and certainly not by a lady. But there were other letters bristling with honest indignation, a few with compassion, a few more declaring stoutly that Sally Grimshaw was a victim of circumstances beyond her control but not beyond ours, and asking what could be done.

'We'll have some more of this,' said Liam, and I had only to visit the Stones two or three evenings a week to find all the material he required, managing at the same time to show the work of Patrick and Anna Stone in an entirely different light.

I did not wish to moralize, having met too many self-indulgent moralizers far too fascinated by their own 'goodness' to be of use to anyone. I did not wish to force my opinions on others, nor even to persuade, being myself suspicious of persuasion and hostile to force. I wished simply to speak my mind, and, if nothing else, my controversial opinions helped to sell a great many copies of the *Star*.

'Keep it up,' said Liam, 'and we may just pull through this little contretemps.' But that was the day before we received yet another increase in our rent, intended to remind us that, when all was said and done, power lay only with those whose standing was highest at Mr Rawnsley's bank.

'Liam, will you allow me –'

'No,' he said, very sharply for him. 'No, Grace I'll not borrow your money. I thought I could do it when the time came, believe me – I fully intended to do it. You were a kind of insurance, I suppose, at the back of my mind – always there and always willing. But now – well – no, Grace. I won't borrow your money. It turns out that I'm too fond of you – quite a bit too fond of you – for that.'

27

'It makes no real difference,' Camille told me, speaking of her uncertain status. 'Nicholas would marry me if he could, because then he could give me things and leave me things without interference from Duchess Caroline. But what exists between us could be made no deeper by a legal document. I wish you would fall in love, Grace.'

'No, thank you. Is that all you can think of now, Camille?'

1085

'Do you know, I believe it is. It leaves me no room for anything else. One day you will see.'

'I very much doubt it. I don't think I would care to build my life entirely around another person. Yes, I know women are supposed to give themselves completely in love and marriage, and I have seen some women dissolve themselves in their menfolk with obvious fulfilment. You, for instance, and Aunt Faith. It is certainly what Venetia *wanted* to do, and it would probably have saved her life had she succeeded. It seems dangerous to me. Perhaps it is not in my nature.'

But Camille dismissed my objections with the smile of a woman who no longer uses the word 'perhaps' – a woman who *knows*.

'I used to think that too, and I did not dissolve myself in my husband, you may be very sure. We were colleagues and companions, which was pleasant enough, and we thought it daring and very progressive to tell everyone we were no more than fond of each other. And "fond" was very nice, you know. Life was busy and various, quite complicated sometimes, and full of concerns and necessities, battles to fight and problems to solve – like your life, I suppose. Now there is Nicholas. I wonder, sometimes, what all the rest was really about.'

'Camille, you are not so blinded as all that.'

'I am.'

I did not entirely believe her, but no one, after two minutes in her company, could have been unaware of her bliss. Her house, set high and very lonely on the cliffs looking down on the Spa and, across the grey sweep of the bay, offering a view of the steep little town and its ancient castle, was not large, a square box merely of four rooms downstairs and four rooms up, but set in a shady, high-walled garden and furnished with a blend of luxury and cosiness that was essentially Camille.

'A perfect little love-nest,' my Grandmother Agbrigg described it, although she had never been inside and in any case her experience of such establishments could only have been slight. Yet so it was, over-abundant in its splendours, the typical retreat of an elderly millionaire and a penniless woman, who apart from youth and beauty had also, surprisingly, brought him love.

Nor was she shy of expressing it whenever the mood overcame her.

'I adore you, Nicholas,' she would tell him, leaning through the evening firelight or suddenly taking his arm and squeezing it during an afternoon stroll, a declaration made as naturally as a remark about the weather.

'Excellent!' he would answer gruffly. 'See that it continues.'

'Oh, it will, for it does you so much good. Your sister thinks I shall very likely kill you, but in fact I have never seen you look so well. And I have not heard you cough once all winter, not even when you have been obliged to go to Cullingford.'

But his vists to Cullingford grew fewer and fewer, Gideon being called to Scarborough instead at regular intervals to give an account of himself, occasions which Camille found difficult, for although he was always charming and even treated her sometimes with the same teasing gallantry she found very acceptable in Gervase, he was nevertheless Aunt Caroline's son and she felt certain he shared his mother's belief that her involvement with Nicholas Barforth was solely for money.

'He kisses my hand sometimes,' she told me, 'and admires my dress, and he has a look at my shoulders while he is about it and I know he is thinking what a clever little minx I am to have got myself so many diamonds and furs and a snug little place in Nicholas's will, but that when the time comes I had better watch out, for he will not let me have everything my way. Well, when *that* time comes I shall be too stricken to care or even to notice how they carve up the mills. They will have no trouble with *me*. How dreadful, Grace! Gervase never makes me feel like that, although I believe Duchess Caroline has accused him of worming his way into my favour. Heavens! I never expected to see the day when my "favour" counted for anything, although Gervase certainly has it and I am not ashamed to say so. What absolute hell these families are, for, as Nicholas says, there is plenty to go round and all we ask in return is that they leave us in peace.'

Yet, despite her understandable reluctance, she entertained Gideon and Miss Madeley-Brown to a celebration dinner shortly after their engagement was officially announced, Gideon considering it politic to introduce his chairman and his bride, although Aunt Caroline – who had brought Miss Madeley-Brown to Scarborough under her chaperonage – remained adamantly at the Grand Hotel.

'She is very splendid to look at,' Camille told me, 'and has a diamond solitaire quite as big as mine. She sat and watched it sparkle in the candlelight for most of the evening, being too refined, I suppose, for conversation. Certainly she thought herself a cut above me. When I took her into the drawing-room after dinner I was not at all sure what I would do with her, for I knew our gentlemen would stay a full hour over their port and cigars. But I had no need to worry. She looked at her ring again and arranged the flounces of her skirt and was perfectly content. She rides – that much I *did* discover – and Nicholas says she will be very accommodating in bed and what more can a Chard want in a wife than that? Caroline would not come here to dine, of course, but I am afraid Nicholas forced her to take tea with me at the Grand – told her absolutely straight that unless she did he would not even *discuss* Tarn Edge, which just goes to show what money can really do. Oh dear, that dreadful house! I wish Nicholas would just give it to them as a wedding present and have done, for I shall never live in it.'

But Tarn Edge was a valuable property not to be parted with lightly, and further complicated by the fact that if half of it might reasonably have been expected to pass to Venetia – and consequently to Gideon – the other half might equally well be considered as belonging to Gervase. Aunt Caroline made another journey to Scarborough, alone this time, abandoning her husband on his sickbed at South Erin in her determination to do her duty by the son who most resembled her. Gideon was to make a splendid marriage and needed a suitable home for his bride. He had lived at Tarn Edge now for nine years, had maintained

1087

and staffed it at his own expense this last year or two. Rent free? How dare her brother suggest such a thing. Or if he did suggest it, then perhaps he might like to consider his granddaughter, Claire Chard – who was no granddaughter of hers – and who had been maintained, rent-free, at Listonby virtually since her birth. Mr Barforth did not wish to consider that. He did not wish to remind Aunt Caroline that her son's entry into the Barforth mills – bringing nothing with him but his ambitions – and his eventual shareholding had depended entirely on his marriage, in full knowledge of the circumstances and ramifications, to Venetia. He did not wish to remind her of any of these things, although he forced himself to do so.

For a moment brother and sister faced each other across a gulf which seemed likely to widen into a final breach, and then, because in their way they were fond of each other, they backed down, Aunt Caroline hastily, Mr Barforth deliberately, having led her, I suppose, to the point he had intended. There might be a measure of right on her side, he conceded. Gideon had worked very hard and certainly his efficiency had made Mr Barforth's own life much easier this last year or two. Yes indeed, it was a great relief to see the business in the hands of a man whose commercial acumen he could trust. But, looked at another way, where would that man be today without Nicholas Barforth? A country parsonage, perhaps? Some minor administrative appointment in India? And Mr Barforth wished to make it very clear that, if Gideon Chard ever became the owner of Tarn Edge, it would be because such an arrangement was pleasing to Mr Barforth, not on account of any pressure whatsoever from either his sister, his managing director or even from Camille. Mr Barforth, as always, would decide for himself and when he had reached a decision he would let his sister, his managing director and any other interested party know.

A valuable house, then, full of valuable furnishings, silver, pictures, porcelain, built fifty years ago by Sir Joel Barforth to astonish the Law Valley with its grandeur. If Gideon wanted it, no doubt he could afford to buy it, since he drew healthy dividends every year, was the possessor of a princely salary and engaged in various profitable little trading ventures of his own from time to time of which his uncle – and his managing director – was supposed to be unaware. All circumstances considered, perhaps the best thing would be to have a proper valuation, after which Mr Barforth could name his price, half the market value perhaps, which he would then most likely pay over to Gervase. That way Gideon would be getting Venetia's half of the house for nothing, which seemed fair enough. Mr Barforth had felt obliged to provide a home for his daughter and for his son, but hardly for his son-in-law's second wife. And if the dowry was as handsome as one had been led to believe, then Gideon would be in easy street in any case.

'How absolutely splendid!' remarked Gervase when I next visited Galton to inspect the progress of his prize Friesians. 'I shall invest my share in land, of course. And then I shall buy our lovely Camille a rather ostentatious gift to convince Aunt Caroline more than ever that we have been conspiring against her. Perhaps we could go somewhere rather expensive, you and I, and choose it together?'

'To convince Aunt Caroline of *our* conspiracy?'

'No, Grace dear, for the simple pleasure of your company.'

'I have no time for shopping trips, Gervase. I am not the squire of Galton with nothing to do but plant my crops and then wait for them to grow. I must be at my desk every morning, Monday to Saturday, at eight o'clock.'

'Who says you must, Grace?'

'I do.'

It was a rule I strictly kept, arriving so early sometimes that I was greeted only by the foraging of a hungry mouse, or, on one occasion, by a rat grooming himself serenely on my desk-top. I was becoming a strange woman, Miss Tighe said so, and I was to annoy her further that winter by a renewed interest in the women's cause. I had already stated on several occasions in the *Star* that women caught up on the treadmill of the factories and overburdened by large families could not be expected to care one way or another about the franchise, an opinion with which Miss Tighe definitely agreed, since she did not mean them to have it in any case, sticking to her belief that government, having been created to serve the interests of property, automatically excluded all those who, for whatever reason, did not possess it. Married women did not possess it, and I became aware that winter of the propsals for a new Act which, it seemed to me, would alter the entire concept of matrimony.

Former legislation – now over ten years old – had made no *real* difference, simply giving a married woman the right to keep her own earnings, which in most cases would be nothing at all or would be eaten up every pay-day by the demands of hungry children and a persistent landlord. But this new Act made the revolutionary and thrilling proposal that any women who married after the date of its passing should be allowed not only to keep, but to administer without the interference of a trustee, the money she brought with her; while as a concession to husbands who had long since spent or invested their wives' dowries, women already married might claim similar rights over any money acquired by them in the future.

It excited me and I transferred my excitement to the *Star*. What hope for fortune-hunters now? Doubtless the breed would continue to exist but at least, after the passing of the Act, they would be obliged to behave themselves, for the fortune they married would no longer be *their* fortune but would remain attached to the woman who came along with it. Never again would a man be able to spend his wife's money on himself and his mistress and leave her to starve. Perhaps few men had ever gone so far as that. One would be quite enough. But now, surely – if this new Act ever reached the Statute Book – a husband and wife would be able to look at each other differently? Surely the removal of total female dependence and total male dominion must imply that there was space for two individuals in a marriage, that it was no longer a question of master and servant but of two responsible and – if possible – loving adults? And moreover, if the vote was about property and married women were about to hold on to theirs, what objection could Miss Tighe and her party raise against their claiming the vote, on equal terms with those widows and spinsters so dear to Miss Tighe's heart? None, I declared and went on declaring it until Liam, harassed by yet another increase of rent, no nearer to finding new premises and increasingly uncomfortable in the old, requested me to devote at least part of my time to other things, such as a wedding in the family of one of our principal advertisers, who had little interest in votes for women.

I attended that wedding on a chill December Saturday and spent the evening cheerlessly writing all the flattering, tedious details of white silk and orange blossoms, describing the extreme elegance of the mother of the bride, the dignity and substance of the father, a saddler whose patronage was not only desirable but necessary to the *Star*. And when it was done – when I had tried to see the bride as a lamb going to the slaughter and had been forced to admit she had looked extremely happy about it – I wrote a letter to Camille putting off her invitation for Christmas, since I knew Gervase would be in Scarborough then and I was reluctant – by fits and starts – to grow any closer to him.

There was a keen frost that Saturday, a long, cold Sunday to follow, a high wind the next morning that woke me earlier than usual and sent me – since I had nowhere else to go – to the *Star*. I expected the office to be unwelcoming and empty, Monday morning never finding Liam at his best, and I was mildly surprised – no more – to see his horse among the crowd which seemed to be gathering around our door. What of it? Liam might well have been at the office all night, not necessarily alone, and when was there not a crowd of idlers in Gower Street?

'Oh good lord, Richards!' I said to my coachman's indifferent back. 'I believe someone has put out our windows again.'

'Yes, madam,' he said, probably not in the least surprised, helping me down and then, quickly withdrawing his valuable horses and his own superior person from too close contact with the mob, leaving me on the pavement to contemplate the gaping holes where the windows and the window-frames had been, and the havoc inside.

I cannot remember, in those first moments, any feeling whatsoever. I simply walked through the crowd and went inside, through the space where the door had been torn off its hinges and into the ground-floor rooms which had contained our printing-presses. There was nothing there now that I recognized, just a litter of wood and metal, the junk of a scrap dealer's yard, and I understood that this was how the first power-looms had looked when the Luddite hammermen had worked over them. The whole of some millmaster's investment gone in a single, violent night, the *Star* lying in inky, rusty fragments about my feet, and Liam – who had no insurance, no capital, no credit – standing among the ruin, haggard and unshaven yet managing to smile.

'I reckon I can give you the day off today, Grace. You'd be better at home in this cold.'

I picked my way across the debris to his side, my skirt catching and

1090

then tearing on something that had once formed an essential part of our livelihood – something else, sharp-edged and probably very rusty cutting into my shoe – and stood close to him, closeness being necessary, I found, in the face of such total disaster, the proximity of a sympathetic body offering more than the empty indignation of words. He was ruined and he knew it. He had no need of me to tell him so. A senseless and brutal thing had been done to him – a foul thing – for which no one but himself would ever pay the price. He knew that, too. And when I could speak it was simply a name.

'Tom Mulvaney?'

'Well, I doubt Miss Tighe to be capable of it, so yes, I reckon it was Tom Mulvaney. He got his roof on but he was late, and I hear Cousin Gideon cut up rough about the bonus. So yes – Tom Mulvaney – with or without instructions from Gideon Chard we shall never know.'

I put my hand on his arm again and pressed it, seeing no point in telling him that Gideon would have been most unlikely to involve himself in this massacre, not from any moral scruple or lingering kindness of heart but because he had no need of such crudity. He had only to sit in his luxuriously appointed office at Nethercoats or in the splendid boardroom at Lawcroft Fold, had only to despatch, at regular intervals, those notices of increased rents, in order to bleed Liam dry; a procedure, I thought, which would suit Gideon's nature far better than this. But if it eased Liam now to blame Gideon, or anyone else, then I would not quarrel with it.

'When did it happen?'

'Sometime in the night. They sent a lad to fetch me about two o'clock this morning, but it was over then, of course –

'Liam, that was six hours ago.'

'So it was.'

'And you've been here all the time since then?'

'I reckon so. I sat and looked at it for a while, and thought about it. It's much the same upstairs. No machines to smash, of course, and the furniture wasn't worth much, so they tore the floorboards up and knocked a few holes in the walls. It's a wreck, Grace.'

The staircase was a mess of fallen plaster and splintered wood, hatchets, it seemed, having been used to attack the roughcast walls, while the upper room was a battleground, the door thrown down, desks and chairs overset and shredded as if for firewood, the partition wall between office and storeroom knocked clean through, broken glass and builders' rubble underfoot, papers – papers – churned and scattered everywhere, and, in case there might be anything we could salvage, soaked in whitewash and green paint – the colour they had been using at Low Cross – which had been thrown down by the bucketful and left, most foully, to congeal.

Total devastation which must have taken several large and noisy men at least an hour to perpetrate. No one had intervened. No one, thank God, had sent for Liam until it was over. Now, as the shock abated, it seemed that something, however futile, had to be done and so, without making any visible headway, we began to go through those soiled and scattered papers, a task so very much akin to emptying the North Sea with a ladle that I knew it would either break my heart or make me very angry. And so, kneeling there among the sodden litter, in the bitter cold of that December day, I grew very angry indeed.

We sent the boy for bread and cheese and beer at noon and worked on, sorting, discarding, achieving nothing, while on the floor below us the helpers Liam had recruited from the street were sweeping up the corpses of his printing-presses, to carry them away by the barrowload and bury them in the nearest midden.

'There goes the *Star*,' he said, raising the brandy flask he always carried with him as the unkempt cortège trundled by. And by this time, still on my knees on that loathsome floor, I was crying with the sorrow of true bereavement and my terrible fury. I had needed the *Star*. I loved her, and I wanted blood for her now.

'What are you going to do, Liam?'

He remained silent for a moment, staring after those funereal barrows, and then, raising his flask again, he took a rapid swallow.

'That's not a question you should be asking me now, Grace. Give me until tomorrow.'

'Mr Liam Adair?' we heard a dry little voice calling, and, through the gaping doorway came stepping a painfully, neat, self-important figure I recognized, a clerk from Nethercoats Mill, hastily taking a handkerchief and pressing it to his nose and mouth with the gesture of one who enters a plague spot.

'Mr Liam Adair?'

'Who wants him?'

'Mr Gideon Chard presents his compliments –'

'Does he, by God?'

'– and asks me to deliver this letter, sir.'

A long brown envelope changed hands, the pompous little man smirked, seemed disposed to linger and then, catching a hint of his peril in Liam's eye, moved hastily away.

'Will there be an answer, sir?'

'Get out of here.' And the simple command was followed by so explicit an obscenity that the precise little gentleman turned tail and fled.

I gave him a moment to read and then went to stand beside him again, my skirt, smeared with paint and damp, filthy patches, feeling heavy against my legs.

'What is it now, Liam?'

He folded the letter, replaced it carefully in its envelope, his hands steady, his face grey.

'Aye, what now? News travels fast in Cullingford, it seems. Mr Chard has heard of my misfortune and wonders when it would be convenient for someone to call and assess the damage to *his* property.'

'Liam!'

'Yes – damage to his floorboards and his walls, his doors and windows, for which, naturally, I am liable.'

'How much?'

He shook his head as if to clear it and blinked hard.

'God knows! More than I can afford, at any rate, which wouldn't make it very much. Enough to bankrupt me, I shouldn't wonder, which would mean I couldn't carry on this – or any other business – again. Enough to silence me once and for all, should Gideon decide to take legal proceedings against me. And I'm not in much doubt about that, Grace, my darling. Are you?'

His eyes closed again, just for a moment age touching every feature, until his sudden grin sent the years, but not all the greyness, away.

'I'll have to make a run for it, I reckon. The world's wide enough. How about coming with me, Grace? I wouldn't be the first man who went out to the colonies to escape his creditors and came back a millionaire.'

'There's Grandmamma Elinor.'

'So there is, except that I've got nothing for her to invest in, and whatever else I am, I'm no beggar. I wouldn't feel right about taking her money now, Grace, and I hope you know better than to offer me yours. I think we've done all we can for today. Go home now, my darling, you look done in.'

'Come with me.'

'Later. I'll call and see you this evening, a little after dinner maybe. Right now I'm going to do the only rational thing I can think of. No – no – there's no need for alarm. I'm not considering blowing Chard's brains out, nor my own. I just want to get quietly drunk. It won't solve anything, I know, but – whether you approve of it or not – it won't hurt.'

I watched him walk down the stairs and pause for a word or two with the men who were still sweeping the lower floor, take another swig from his flask, and then go out into the street. I had never been so angry in my life, had not even realized anger could be so burdensome and so painful. I went out into the street myself, speaking to no one, went home and kicked off my soiled clothes, refusing to answer the foolish girl mouthing at me questions to which she knew the answers.

'Lord! ma'am, whatever have have you been doing? Paint, ma'am – and the state of your shoes – it won't come off –'

'Burn them – everything. Now shut up and get me my hot water.'

I washed, dressed, brushed my hair and did it up again, that load of anger still pressing hard against my chest.

'Tell Richards to bring the carriage round again.'

'But he's just taken it away.'

'Should that be of any interest to me?'

He brought it back again and I got into it, feeling as if I was made of granite. I had hoped, by the delay of changing my clothes and making myself presentable, to reduce my anger to manageable proportions. I had not done so, and since one way or another I would have to unleash it before it suffocated me, I was going now, not tomorrow morning as I had first intended, to see Gideon. I still did not suspect him of ordering the attack on Liam's presses, but I wanted to ascertain the extent and the nature of his complicity, whether his letter had been the result of a malicious impulse or part of a cruel plan. And what else did I want? To save the *Star* if I could and to strike a blow for Liam, to keep him from bankruptcy and out of jail in some way that did not oblige him to borrow money he could never repay from his female relations? Certainly I wanted that. But there was something else, at the very root of my nature, which I wanted too.

I had desired Gideon as I had desired no other man, to a point where it had become difficult for me to desire other men. One day, if I ever found the courage to face the truth, I might well find that I had been very much in love with him and unable to love anyone else because of him. But that day had not yet dawned and since he was committed to marry Hortense Madeley-Brown and I was committed to independence – and since neither one of us would be likely to deviate from those commitments – it would be easier for my peace of mind if I could think ill of him. I wanted to eliminate the slightest possibility that I might ever again – for no matter how fleeting a moment – long for him. I wanted to greet his wedding morning with a detached amusement – dear God, not another wedding! – to report in the *Star* on the astonishing beauty of his bride, the splendour of her jewellery, which *would* be very splendid, and then casually to remark: 'Vacant little fool – pompous opportunist – they deserve each other.' I wanted him to mean nothing to me, and to achieve that blessed state of indifference I would have to hate him first. I would have to hurt him again and give him the opportunity to hurt me.

I knew his habits. In the morning and the early part of the afternoon he was difficult to trace, dividing his time among the four other factories in his care, but in the days when I had had charge of his social engagements, his travelling schedules, his recherché dinners, a note sent to Nethercoats at this hour had usually reached him. I was kept waiting, as I had expected to be, sitting with several curious strangers in the ante-room through which he passed twice, a flurry of clerks about him, without even glancing at me.

'Mr Freeman, if you'd care to go in now, sir?' the clerk said, the same smirking little man who had twice delivered messages to Gower Street. Mr Freeman went in and half an hour later came out again. A Mr Porter did the same. I was still very angry.

'Now then, who's next?' said the clerk. I was alone, and without answering him I got up and walked away into Gideon's room unannounced, letting the heavy door swing shut behind me.

I had last come here – was it almost five years ago? – to ask him to take back his wife who was pregnant by another man. It had been painful then. It would be painful now and for both of us. I was determined to make sure of that.

'Good afternoon, Gideon.'

'Yes?' he said curtly, dismissively, the tone of a man too busy for any woman's arguments, since he is always in the right in any case. And I understood that he was very angry too.

'You have not asked me to sit down.'

'I beg your pardon. I merely thought the length of your visit unlikely to warrant it.'

1094

'Are you asking me to leave unheard? I should be inclined to take that for a sign of defeat you know – or of a troublesome conscience.'

'Then you have the advantage of me, Grace, for I have not the faintest notion as to what you mean.'

I sat down, carefully arranging the folds of my skirt in the manner of Miss Madeley-Brown, took off my gloves and placed them, with my muff and reticule, on his immaculate desk-top, a gesture calculated to annoy. For I had come to engage him in battle and it was essential now to strike hard, to strike first if I could, and after that to stand firm against the returning blow.

'It occurred to me, Gideon, that your letter came very promptly.'

'And you see some significance in that?'

'I am not sure. Perhaps you can enlighten me.'

He leaned slightly towards me, assured and sardonic, a man in his own territory, abominably at ease.

'My dear, you have worked for the gutter press until it has affected your judgement. Can you seriously imagine I would hire a gang of drunken navvies to break into my own property and smash a few machines which would have fallen apart ere long in any case? It would make a good headline in the *Star*, I admit – except that the *Star* is no longer with us, it seems.'

'You have missed my point, Gideon.'

'Then do please correct me.'

'I shall. It is my opinion that you did hire those navvies. Not as Luddites, of course, but as building workers on your sites at Black Abbey and Low Cross. And if you cannot keep your employees in order, it is my further opinion that you have no claim against Liam Adair or anyone else for the havoc they create.'

He leaned forward again, a great deal of incredulous amusement, even a very faint, very grudging respect in his face. But then, perhaps, he too remembered the purpose of my last visit here and all tolerance was gone.

'Unfortunately the law does not share your opinions. You might advise Adair to cast a glance at the terms of his lease. I understand the damage was very extensive.'

'Yes. I understand it would be in the interests of anyone who did not entirely approve of Liam Adair if the damage should be very extensive indeed. So – by that reckoning – Tom Mulvaney has done a very good job for you.'

'How very ably you defend your – well – what shall we call him? – your friend?'

'Yes, you may call him my friend. And the reason I defend him is called loyalty.'

'Whatever one calls it, my dear, it will not suffice. I did not order his machines broken, as even he must know. I would have arranged it differently, but one way is quite as good as another.'

'I am not so sure he is finished.'

'Oh, yes. He may extricate himself from the worst of it with the help of some foolish woman or other. But he knows now how vulnerable he is and he will not be quite so brave, you can be very sure, if he ever acquires a platform again. I must offer you my commiserations, I suppose, on your loss of employment. You will no doubt find some other way of passing your time.'

'You have intended to close down the *Star* for some time, have you not, Gideon?'

'Naturally.'

'I see nothing natural about it.'

'You were not the subject of Adair's slanders.'

'There was more to the *Star* than the slandering of Gideon Chard – my dear Gideon Chard.'

'Yes, tales of whores and thieves and child-molestation – titillation for perverse appetites – vice made available and interesting to the general reader by the pen of a lady –'

'How *dare* you say that to me?'

'I dare say anything I like to you. If you choose to lead a man's life, then you must take the rough with the smooth. One feels obliged, often enough, to curb one's tongue when dealing with a lady. One expects a man to be *man* enough to handle the truth.'

'Very well,' I said. 'Yes – very well.'

For it was this I had come for. He was hurting me, goading me, giving me every reason I needed to strike him a foul blow. It was just as it should be.

'You call it a man's life, Gideon, because I earn my living?'

'You do not earn your living. Your living comes to you from your father. You are supported by a man as women are and should be. The pittance you *earn*, as you call it, would not pay your own servants' wages.'

But I had expected this, for in his place it was the line of attack I would myself have used; and I was prepared for it.

'I take nothing from Fieldhead to which I am not entitled, Gideon. My allowance comes from money left in trust for me by my mother. And you are in no position, you know, to dispute my right to that, since so much of your own good fortune has been willed to you by a woman.'

It was done. I had struck hard and foul, and it should have been enough. But that heavy, angry boulder was still there in my chest, pressed tight against my lungs. The remnants of what I had once felt for him had not been wrung out of me yet. I would have to strike again.

'Bitch!' he said very quietly, rather pleasantly, as if it pleased him to call me so. I understood that it did please him, that he wished to abuse me as much as I desired to be abused. His need was exactly the same as my need, his aim identical to mine. We were playing the same game by the same rules, and if we were harsh enough and hateful enough we might succeed in making the next half-hour too painful to remember, and in consequence would have good reason never to think of each other again.

'So we are to exchange insults are we, Gideon?'

'Why not? I imagine Grace Barforth of the *Star* might know a filthy name or two.'

'She might. However, all I really want to say to you is that I find your conduct towards Liam Adair astonishing.'

'*My* conduct? Would I have done better to break his neck?'

'I think you would have done better to remember this famous public school training we hear so much about. I thought it contrary to the code of a gentleman to strike someone in a weaker position than himself, or to hit a man when he was already down?'

'Very clever, Grace. But a gentleman does not allow himself to be stabbed in the back. And when he deals with a scoundrel he deals acordingly. Adair began this.'

'He had his reasons.'

'Yes. He was in love with my wife.'

'She was a lovable woman.'

'I don't deny it. And I was the brute, in his opinion – and I suppose in yours – who did not deserve her?'

'You did not understand her.'

'Did she understand me? I am not so hard to please.'

'I know. You take the view that women should be seen and not heard – like children – which is easy enough for a woman who has nothing to say.'

'I take the view that women should be women –'

'Ah yes – gentle and sensitive and clinging –'

'I see nothing wrong with that. Women who *are* women seem to thrive on it.'

'Domestic drudges.'

'Domestic angels, cherished and respected in their own homes, as any woman would be, if she could –'

'One does not respect a dressed-up doll who might open her mouth occasionally to say "Just as you wish dear, how very clever of you dear." '

'One might prefer her to a woman who talks too much and to no good purpose, to prove what? – that she cannot face a woman's responsibilities and is only playing at taking a man's.'

'So I am irresponsible, am I? Well – of course I am. For I refused to devote my life to the care of your shirt-cuffs and the temperature of your bathwater, did I not? How terrible!'

'I shall survive it. I may even consider myself well out of it.'

'I do hope so, Gideon, for let me ask you this. What makes you – or any man – imagine he has the right to a servant of my calibre? What makes you think yourself entitled to the lifelong obedience of a woman – another human being – who has a brain every bit as good as yours and whose talents may be different from your talents but just as valuable?'

'Because I pay for it,' he snarled, a very dangerous man now.

'Pay for it?' I snarled back at him, feeling dangerous, if a little dizzy, too. 'The devil you do! You take it. You have made laws that allow you to do as you please.'

'I?'

'Yes – and the rest of you – and you have been able to do it because you have the physical strength and you do not bear children.'

'Ah yes – I have read something to that effect in the *Star*.'

'Then pay heed to it. You admire gentleness and sensibility in women because it flatters you and because it is easy to use against us.'

'Easy? Perhaps. But expensive too, you know, for the very gentlest of women, in my experience, are never averse to life's little luxuries. And one needs a generous man, my dear, for that – any gentle woman will tell you so.'

'I daresay. And what about the women you employ in your mills because they will work for lower wages than the men and are easier to handle? And why are they easier to handle?'

'I feel sure you are about to tell me.'

'I am. Because you – and the rest – have informed yourselves in advance as to the nature of motherhood and you know a mother will put up with anything, for as little as you are inclined to pay her for it, so long as her children can be fed.'

'Forgive me for mentioning it, but I seem to have read something about that too – one is obliged to conclude in the *Star*.'

'If you wish to make me lose my temper, then you have succeeded very well, you know. There is no need to continue, Gideon.'

'Ah – but I suppose one can hardly hope that *you* have done?'

'Assuredly not. You call those women who accept your pathetic wages weak and foolish. You ought to call them victims of exploitation. You make laws to prevent your wives from owning property so that they are obliged to depend on you and obey their marriage vows. And I wonder – if you are really so lovable and wise – why you need the power of the law to make your women honour and obey you? You talk about women who *are* women and you know nothing about it. You just want a silly sheep to bleat at you and breed for you, and that – my dear Gideon – is not a woman. It may, of course, be called Madeley-Brown, but what sort of a brood-mare is that?'

'His hand shot out and fastened around my wrist – his attack now as crude and brutal and childish as mine – dragging me forward so that the desk bit hard into my legs.

'That is quite enough.'

'When I say so.'

'When *I* say.'

'You have no authority over me, Gideon Chard.'

'And want none.'

'I am delighted to hear it.'

'In fact I will tell you what it is that I do want. I want a woman called Hortense Madeley-Brown, who is beautiful and much younger than you are –'

'Oh, fresh from her schoolroom, Gideon – that is very clear –'

'– who satisfies me most perfectly in all of my appetites –'

'I hope you may satisfy hers – for they seem hearty to me.'

'– who will give me beautiful children and plenty of them, being of an age and a disposition for maternity – *that*, Grace Barforth, is the sum total of my desires.'

'Then let go of me.'

'When it pleases me – for I have the physical strength, as you pointed out just now, and do not bear children. But then, neither do you.'

I tried very hard to hit him with my free hand, this being no time at all for dignity, but he caught it and held me fast, exultant now that he had located my most vulnerable spot – the one wound that did not seem likely ever to heal – and had used it so ruthlessly against me. Perhaps I had expected him in the final instance to be merciful. I had been wrong. I must show no mercy either.

'You had better wait nine months after your marriage, Gideon, before you taunt me with my sterility, for we may be in the same boat together since I know of no child you could *honestly* lay claim to.'

And although the words meant very little, were on the same infantile, foolish level as the rest of it, their intention to insult and to maim, to probe and reopen the very rawest of wounds, was enough.

'One day, Grace,' he said, his voice only a whisper, 'one day – if I could contrive it – I would like to see you helpless and penniless and –'

'And what Gideon? Pregnant and *manageable* – like Venetia?'

It was done.

'Get out!' he said, dropping my wrists as if suddenly he was aware of their contamination. 'Get out! *Now.*' And it was part threat, part plea, for he could no longer bear to be in the same room with me. It was done.

There had been no victory and no defeat, not really a battle. I had performed an amputation, had destroyed one unreliable, troublesome part of myself for the benefit of the whole. It had been essential. 'Get out!' he said, and he was right – quite right. I must go now and quickly, so that I might heal myself cleanly, and fast.

28

I went through the outer office quite blindly and then, turning right instead of left, going up instead of down – I am not certain – missed my direction, the sound of machinery, the rancid smell of raw wool, warning me I was approaching the weaving-sheds when I should have been leaving them behind.

'Can I help you, ma'am?' And a puzzled junior clerk escorted me back to the imposing main staircase, the marbled and panelled walls, and then to my carriage.

'Where to, ma'am?' Richards asked me and I could not tell him.

'Home ma'am?'

'No, not home. Not yet. I told him to take the road to Elderleigh and then, when the town was far behind me, I got down and entered a little wood, just an acre of naked, winter trees, leaves silvered and crunchy with frost underfoot, a pink December sky feathered with white cloud, approaching twilight. I felt the cold and welcomed it, drawing it into my lungs, its sharpness awakening me to other sensations. I had been a stranger to violence but I understood something of it now. There were lads in Gower Street who would batter each other until they bled, who would get up no matter how many times they were knocked down, no matter how tough or how numerous the opposition, and come back for more. I understood now that while the killing rage lasted they felt no pain, did not care how much damage was done to them so long as they could continue to damage their adversary. But when the rage had cooled, when the lad finally crawled away to count his wounds, he would find them to be many and grievous.

Face to face with Gideon I had felt no pain. I felt it now, accepted it, allowed it to run its course, took hold of it when it became manageable, parcelled and tied it and stored it away. I felt the cold again, a damp icy blast reminding me that women who live alone with only indifferent servants to care for them cannot afford to fall ill.

'Home now, Richards.' And throughout the journey I thought carefully and deeply about the *Star* and Liam.

He came to see me quite late that evening, freshly shaved and presentable despite the odour of whisky and tobacco he brought with him.

'Have you dined?'

'I seem to remember that I have.'

'Then it was probably a long time ago and more likely to have been liquid than solid.'

I ordered him a supper tray, cold beef and pickles, custard tarts, a great deal of sweet tea which he accepted with a grin.

'What's this? A good meal for a condemned man?'

'You'll survive.'

'I'm honestly beginning to doubt it.'

'I shouldn't if I were you. You're far too old to go back to sheep-shearing in Australia.'

He ate his supper, asked for more tea, finished his second pot and then smiled across at me, tired – bone-weary by the look of him – but determined, somehow or other, to live up to his reputation as a carefree, come-day-go-day Liam Adair.

'Do you want to tell me where you went to this afternoon, Grace?'

'No, since you obviously know. Did you get very drunk?'

'It sufficed. Listen, Grace – it's not the money. I can lay hands on enough to settle the damages bill – my grand relatives won't want to see me in court for debt. But – well, as far as the rest of it goes, I reckon this has taken the heart out of me.'

'Nonsense. You mean you've lost your nerve. Gideon Chard said you would.'

'Now, Grace –'

'Yes, Liam, *you* declared this war on Gideon and we both know why. You were wrong and we know that too. I think you'd have been glad to put a stop to it a long time ago, if you could. You couldn't. So now you'll just have to put up with the consequences. He's beaten you because he has more money than you. He didn't get Mulvaney to smash your machines. He'd have had much more fun starving you out. You know you can't fight money, Liam – nobody can – unless you've got money to do it with.'

'So I'm a damned fool – I'll be the first to admit it.'

'And I'll be the second. But I can forgive you that. What I don't want to do is lose the *Star*. It's worth more than your feud with Gideon Chard – to me and to plenty of others. So you'll just have to get back on your feet and build it up again.'

He sat for a while looking down and then slowly – heavily for him – shook his head.

'I know what you're leading up to and it's no good. I'll not borrow money from you, Grace.'

'I'm not about to lend. But I might invest.'

'In me? I couldn't advise it.'

'No, not in you. In myself and you together.'

He frowned, started to say something; but the time had come for me to be businesslike – brusque if necessary – and I quelled his objections with a gesture I copied exactly from Gideon.

'I've given it a great deal of thought, Liam, and this is what I propose. I am not the wealthiest woman of your acquaintance, but I have some capital and a fairly decent allowance. Put another way, I have a great deal more than it would take to get the *Star* in production again – unless, of course, you object to an equal partnership with a woman?'

'Not if I had anything to contribute.'

'Oh, for heaven's sake! Liam, why must you be so feeble? You know quite well that it can't be done without you. The *Star* was nothing when you took it over. All money could have done then would have been to make it another *Courier & Review*. But you put your signature on it and made it something – not perfect, of course, but perfection is hardly human, after all, and whatever else the *Star* lacks it does have humanity. Do you want to lose it?'

'No, Grace – by God, I don't!'

'Very well. We have established what you want. What *I* want is to earn my living – really earn it. I can't do it without risk, and I can't do it if I remain an employee. My money and your expertise might serve us both. But I warn you, if you take me as your partner I will *be* a partner. I will do my share of the work and take my share of the responsibility – that goes without saying; but I will make my share of the decisions, too. If I take the risk, then I am entitled to the authority. What do you think?'

'I think you are a fine and lovely lady, Grace Barforth.'

'I daresay. But do we have a bargain?'

His hand reached out and took my arm just below the elbow in a hard, unsteady grip, his emotion very evident and very burdensome to him, weighing heavily on his tongue.

'I believe we do.'

And it was a bargain I did not intend to regret, the final seal on my liberty and which had the additional merit of convincing anyone who wished – or needed – to think ill of me that I *was*, indeed and almost in broad daylight, the mistress of Liam Adair.

New premises became quickly available once it had been established that we could pay the rent, and having selected a square, solid three-storey building at the top end of Sheepgate, I saw no reason to disabuse the landlord of his notion that we had the power of Fieldhead Mills behind us. Our partnership became a legal reality amidst the disapproval of my father's lawyers, who also believed him to be supporting yet another expensive and decidedly improper whim of his wayward daughter. Liam saw to the installation of the new presses. I equipped and furnished the offices with the meticulous attention I had once bestowed on the kitchens and larders of Tarn Edge. We interviewed staff, took decisions, not always with immediate agreement on our policies, and it became quickly apparent that Liam was the true journalist, the investigator, the innovator, the schemer, while I was the organizer of his creativity, the co-ordinator of his efforts and the efforts of our employees, the woman of business. I was harder than Liam and found it easier to refuse, to dismiss, to discard excuses. But it was his personality, his flair which moulded the *Star*, and each one of us recognizing the contribution of the other, we worked well together.

I set out at once to win back our advertisers and to pursue others, with a fair degree of success. I sought to increase our circulation by broadening the appeal of what we had to offer, delegating, each morning, our town's humdrum social and cultural events to young reporters who, however bored they may have been by Temperance Meetings and Philosophical Societies soon learned the folly of neglecting my requirements. I invited our readers' opinions on the issues of the day and printed them with the signatures prominently displayed, recognizing any controversy, from the annexation of the Transvaal to the correct preparation of a suet pudding, as the stuff of which our profits were made. And, with my mind on suet puddings one day and the amazing ignorance of even basic cookery I had often encountered in the streets around Low Cross, I organized a group of sensible, thrifty women to supply me with cheap and simple recipes which could be prepared at the open fire and the narrow coal-oven of a small kitchen range.

I went on to include as a regular feature the daily happenings of an imaginary Gower Street family, a vehicle for general sanitary precautions and the recognition of the symptoms of various children's ailments which I put together with the help of Patrick Stone. And for readers of a different order I supplied such details of the London and Paris fashions as were passed on to me by Blanche; discovered herbal 'remedies' for beautifying the hair and the skin which need not be called by that disreputable word 'cosmetics'; suggested dinner-party menus that were within the reach of any young married couple with five hundred pounds a year, a maid of all work and a cook, and, to whet the appetite and stimulate the ambitions of such couples, some other menus which would have required a fully staffed kitchen and the expertise of Gideon Chard's French chef.

1102

We followed the progress of Gladstone's new Liberal Government very carefully, assuming that the Conservative influence on the Queen had been lessened by the death of Disraeli almost a year ago, that colourful gentlemen having refused a visit from his grieving monarch as he lay dying because he thought she would be all too likely to ask him to take a message to her departed husband, Prince Albert. We applauded Gladstone's bill to allow Dissenters to bury their dead in parish churchyards, and supported his move to abolish punishment by flogging in the Army, although, of course, no one suggested that this leniency should be extended to our public schools. There had been trouble in the Transvaal, where the Boers, whose territory had been added to the sum total of the British Empire by Disraeli in the face of strong Liberal opposition, rather thought that Gladstone might give it back again, his failure to do so resulting in the slaughter of British soldiers at Majuba Hill. There was trouble brewing in Egypt, where a certain Colonel Arabi seemed intent on spreading the notion that Egypt should belong only to Egyptians, thus threatening our prized passage to India. There was, as always, trouble and tragedy, murder and bitter misunderstanding in Ireland, culminating in the imprisonment of the Irish leader Parnell and in the stabbing to death of the Irish Secretary, Lord Frederick Cavendish and his Under-Secretary, Mr Frederick Burke, in Dublin's Phoenix Park.

In March that year an attempt was made to assassinate Queen Victoria – the seventh, so far, since her coronation – when a Mr Roderick McLean, known to be but half-witted, took a shot at her carriage as it stood outside Windsor Station, and was instantly set upon and overpowered by two schoolboys from Eton; Her Majesty faring much better than the Tsar of Russia, who had been virtually blown to pieces by a bomb the year before, leaving as his successor his son Alexander III, who was the brother-in-law of the Prince of Wales.

There was a royal wedding, the Queen's haemophiliac son Prince Leopold marrying Princess Helen of Waldeck and being created Duke of Albany for the occasion, although his mother continued to call him 'Prince Leopold', since in her imperial opinion *anyone* could be a duke.

In Cullingford, trade remained stable; those who set themselves out to make profits usually made them, and those who did not were considered to be unenterprising rather than unfortunate. The wool merchant, Mr Jacob Mandelbaum, went into retirement, handing his business over to his son and setting off, in the company of his sister, Miss Rebecca Mandelbaum, on a series of extensive foreign travels. Miss Tighe became an active member of the Temperance Society and acquired a paid companion and a pedigree cat. The Cullingford Bicycle Club and the Cullingford Photographic Society were formed, the names of their founder members recorded for posterity in the *Star*. The new mill at Low Cross was completed that summer, a splendid six-storey building five hundred feet long and seventy-five feet high, covering fourteen acres of what had once been Simon Street and Saint Street, and in which four thousand people would produce an estimated thirty thousand yards of cloth each day. The main weaving-shed was over eight thousand square yards and would hold over a thousand looms. There was a reservoir with a capacity of five hundred thousand gallons of rain-water, every drop of which would be needed for the scouring of Low Cross wool. The opening celebrations would include a banquet at which, among other delicacies, a baron of beef weighing two hundred and fifty pounds and eighty hindquarters would be served to the upper two thousand or so Barforth employees, the Lord-Lieutenant of the West Riding, our Mayor and Corporation, members of Parliament and magistrates, the Duke and Duchess of South Erin, the board of directors of Nicholas Barforth and Company Limited and their wives and families, and such other guests as those directors chose to invite.

And if this was not enough – and for my part I thought it was more than enough – it was suggested by no less a person than Lady Verity Barforth herself that as a further tribute to the memory of her husband, Sir Joel, the banquet be followed by a general exodus of upper and middle Barforth management to Scarborough, where they and their wives might be offered a day at the sea and a night at the Grand Hotel.

'The dear old lady is trying to patch things up between her sons,' Camille told me, having arrived somewhat unexpectedly at my door while Mr Barforth went on to Low Cross to confer with Gideon. 'The idea is for Blaize and Faith to come too, and certainly Nicholas has no objections to it. Indeed, I shall be glad of Faith, for she has been very sweet to me, and if I am to contend with the South Erins and the Chards *and* the Madeley-Browns, I shall need every friend I can get. Would you prefer to stay with us, Grace, or with your Grandmother Agbrigg?'

'Camille, I shall not be there at all.'

'Ah well,' she said, 'that is what you think, and no doubt what you intend, but you will give in, my dear, there is no doubt about it, for Nicholas, who is chairman of the company, and Gervase, who is still a director, are both determined to have you.'

'I daresay, but –'

'But nothing, darling, for there is too much against you. Lady Verity has expressed a wish to have *all* her family about her, and since she is old and getting rather frail one can hardly refuse her that. She wants Nicholas and Blaize and Faith and, very kindly, she also wants me. She wants Caroline and her duke; Grandmamma Elinor is coming from France; your Grandmother Agbrigg is already here. I daresay she would also like to have Georgiana and I should not mind – except that it would probably kill Caroline. And of the younger generation there is to be Blanche, Gervase, Noel – and Grace.'

'And Gideon.'

'Ah yes, but one can hardly think of him as part of the younger generation, since he is organizing the whole proceedings with what Nicholas calls a typical fit of Chard grandeur. There is to be a special train, a dinner and a ball on the Saturday night, heaven alone knows what else, and you cannot abandon me to the tender mercies of Duchess Caroline, who would certainly like to murder me. Oh yes, she would, for Nicholas has issued warning that unless *everyone* is very kind to me he

1104

will very likely cancel the whole celebration and evict Gideon from Tarn Edge. Now Grace, you cannot leave me to face Duchess Caroline alone after that.'

'Somebody must cover all this high life for the *Star*,' Liam told me, 'and *I* can't do it, Grace.'

'What are you going to wear?' asked Blanche. 'White for me, I think, although I will check first with mamma, for she is fond of white, too, and there is no need to encourage people to tell us how alike we are. The Madeley-Brown will cut a dash, of course, with that quite stupendous diamond Gideon has given her, and I have no intention of being put in the shade. I think, between us, Grace, we can make short work of her. So – white for the journey and the luncheon and the walking about the promenade they are sure to make us do, and for the dance I really wondered about black, cut very low since my shoulders are still worth looking at – and pearls. Yes – that's exactly right. Now what about you, Grace? Something the Madeley-Brown will remember.'

'You will naturally want to stay with me,' my Grandmother Agbrigg wrote from Scarborough. 'I shall have your room ready.'

'Please come,' Gervase wrote on the corner of my official card of invitation.

'I can't think of any reason why you shouldn't,' said Liam. 'Can you?'

There was no reason I would admit and that evening I forced myself to take out my 'London' clothes and selected an ice-blue taffeta walking-dress that would exactly suit a warm July day, a pale blue velvet parasol with white lace edging, the blue velvet hat with the blue satin roses and the spotted net veil I had bought for my first visit to Gervase. I had an evening gown I had never worn, cream tulle over pale gold silk, and another, worn only once, a cream satin skirt embroidered here and there with a single crimson rosebud, a crimson velvet bodice with tiny puffed sleeves. Either one would take me creditably to the Grand Hotel. And in my jewellery box, in the lower drawer that I never opened, I had a diamond too, given to me by Gervase, and the bracelet of fine gold chains scattered with tiny amethysts from Gideon.

But that bracelet and that ring were a world away and I must make it my business to see that they stayed there. I would go to Scarborough in fitting fashion, as the guest of my former husband, and as Grace Barforth of the *Star*.

29

The banquet at Low Cross was held on the second and warmest Friday in July, all the Barforth mills, including the one belonging to Sir Blaize, being closed for the occasion; and the following morning early we boarded that special train to Scarborough, to the accompaniment of Cullingford's brass band and the good wishes of her Mayor and Corporation. The journey, which I made in the company of Gervase,

Noel and Blanche, was unexacting, even rather pleasant – the train being amply provisioned, in accordance with Gideon's grandeur, with hampers of cold chicken, little savoury delicacies and champagne – until we reached our marine destination, where my Agbrigg grandparents, another brass band, and – by express command of Mr Nicholas Barforth – Camille, were waiting to greet us.

Camille had not made the journey to Cullingford for the opening of the mill, fearing, she said, to give Duchess Caroline an apoplexy, but as her august lover got down from the first compartment she came forward to greet him with the composure of an empress, a performance she had been rehearsing for weeks in front of her mirror and which, for all her good intentions, lasted but a moment, melting clean away in her gladness to have him home again; a show of emotion which wrinkled the nostrils and quite visibly curdled the sensibilities of Aunt Caroline. Yet because Mr Nicholas Barforth required it, and because his was the power, the authority, the title-deed of Tarn Edge, she forced her mouth to smile, her tongue to pronounce a stiff but audible 'How do you do, Mrs Inman', choosing, as she had always done, to sacrifice her own beliefs, her own pride, very nearly her own moral values, in the best interests of her sons.

We were driven to the Grand Hotel in solemn procession, Sir Blaize and Mr Nicholas Barforth in the first carriage with their mother and their sister, Aunt Caroline, the Duke of South Erin being now so frail that it was thought unlikely he would ever make the journey north again. Camille and Aunt Faith came next with my dainty little Grandmamma Elinor, who had been Sir Joel Barforth's sister and was worldly enough to appreciate that a mistress could be every bit as valuable and powerful as a wife; while behind them came Sir Joel's other sister, my Grandmother Agbrigg, my grandfather, who had been Sir Joel's mill-manager and Cullingford's first mayor, followed by my father and my very good friend, his wife. The next carriage should have carried Gideon, Miss Madeley-Brown and Gervase, but finding a large and determined *Mrs* Madeley-Brown occupying her own place and half of the one reserved for him, he gracefully withdrew and got in with Noel, Blanche and myself and a delightfully frilled and beribboned little doll called Claire Chard who had just been retrieved from her nurse. And so we set off, the Barforth managers and their well-dressed, self-conscious wives coming behind us, their quick, keen glances leaving us in no doubt as to how much we, the Barforth women, were on display. We were served a light but delicious luncheon, the menu certainly chosen by Gideon, who I knew would have come over to the Grand several times in person to make his requirements known, although the rather casual arrangement of the small tables which allowed us to seat ourselves was not to the taste of his mother, Aunt Caroline, who clearly felt that even at so informal a meal as this some distinction should be made between her son, who was the managing director of this company, the man responsible for the continuing prosperity which we had come to celebrate, and her brother's son, a director in name only, accompanied by his former wife who, in Aunt Caroline's further opinion, should have had sufficient good taste not to come at all.

'I trust we shall be more formally arranged at dinner,' she said, intending to be heard, her sharp eyes rapidly calculating that the table occupied by Gervase – and, to her intense indignation, by me – was at least six inches nearer to Mr Nicholas Barforth than the table where Gideon had calmly seated himself with his golden young fiancée.

'Poor Aunt Caroline!' murmured Gervase. 'She believes the most arduous task I perform in a twelvemonth is to go down to Nethercoats on the due date to collect my dividend.'

'But you are always there, I suppose – on the due date?'

'Ah yes, with not a moment to spare. But let me remind you, Grace, of the hard life of a working farmer. Noel here will confirm it.'

'My son's position is most awkward,' I heard Aunt Caroline explaining to Mrs Madeley-Brown, 'for when father and son are present he feels unable to put himself forward.'

Nevertheless, when the meal had reached its coffee and brandy stage and neither father nor son seemed inclined to make a move, Gideon got up and went from table to table speaking an appropriate word to every manager and his wife, the length of time he devoted to each one being regulated by the fine social instincts of Listonby, so that all were satisfied. He spent a longer moment with my Agbrigg grandparents, paying his respects to my rough-grained but mayoral grandfather with a warm double handclasp, exchanging a brief but pleasant word with my father, a slight inclination of the head and a smile conveying a different sort of respect entirely for my father's wife.

He kissed Lady Verity Barforth, his grandmother, on her hand and her cheek, and seeing that Grandmamma Elinor, with her notorious fondness for tall, dark, youngish gentlemen, expected the same treatment he kissed her too. He took Camille's hand and held it long enough to prove himself a man of the world who could well understand – could even envy – his employer's obsession with this luscious woman. He whispered something in Aunt Faith's ear that made her smile, chatted with Uncle Blaize and Mr Nicholas Barforth pleasantly but without the slightest hint of subservience to these two powerful men of affairs, letting it be seen that, although he respected their opinions – which had made them several fortunes apiece – he had opinions, and perhaps fresher ones, of his own.

He came to our table too, slapping his brother Noel companionably on the shoulder, ruffling the hair of pretty four-year-old Claire Chard who after all was supposed to be his daughter and who tugged at his sleeve with more familiarity than I had expected her to show.

'How goes it, Gervase?'

'Not bad – not bad at all.'

'You're managing to rear your young stock, then?'

'So I am.'

He sat down, took brandy, discussed stirks and heifers with Noel and Gervase, told Claire to be a good girl, told Blanche she was looking beautiful. He stood up, lingered a while longer with his hand on the back of Noel's chair, describing the arrangements for the rest of the day. He ruffled Claire's curls again, made some remark to a passing waiter, walked away. And he had not spoken one single word to me.

At Lady Verity's request there were to be photographs after luncheon, a camera having been already set up on the terrace, and knowing how awkward this might be – for Aunt Caroline was not the only one to feel surprised at the sight of Gervase's hand on my arm – I would have made my escape, as Camille swiftly made hers, had not my Grandmother Agbrigg detained me with an imperious command to 'Come here, my girl, and sit beside *me*', and an equally imperious request that I should put an end to the rumours about my involvement with Liam Adair.

'You would do well to go back to France with Elinor,' she told me. 'In fact I have had a word with her and she is more than willing to take you. I have had a word with your father about it, too, which may surprise you – the first word I have had with him in many a long year – and he gave me his gracious permission to put my suggestion to you for your consideration. Now what sort of an answer is that?'

But luckily she was called away by that other imperious lady, Aunt Caroline, to have her portrait taken, the first group consisting of the older generation, Sir Joel Barforth's wife, Lady Verity, and his two sisters who were both my grandmothers; just one male survivor of those harsher, elder days, hollow-chested, hollow-cheeked Mayor Agbrigg, the pauper brat brought up to Cullingford in a consignment of a hundred half-starved little factory slaves, who, from such meagre beginnings, had outlived both of Grandmamma Elinor's husbands, my refined grandparent, Mr Morgan Aycliffe and the charming Mr Daniel Adair; and Sir Joel Barforth himself.

Lady Verity was next positioned between her two sons, then alone with her daughter, then all four of them together. Her eldest son's wife, Aunt Faith, was next added, a perfectly proper procedure until Lady Verity, her sweet and knowing smile passing from her daughter Caroline to her son Nicholas, said very clearly, 'If this is to be for daughters-in-law, then surely we should include Camille, who is my daughter-in-law in everything that matters. Yes, certainly we must have Camille. My other daughter-in-law, dear Georgiana, who could not be present, would say the same.'

'Mother!' Aunt Caroline muttered, much shocked, hoping the Madeley-Browns had not grasped the significance of this, trusting she could plead her mother's age and long sojourn in France if they had. But Camille was sent for, placed between Mr Nicholas Barforth and his brother, Uncle Blaize, Aunt Faith greeting her warmly, Aunt Caroline obliged – as she so often was obliged these days – to make the best of it.

Lady Verity's grandchildren were then required to come forward, or such of them as were available, Noel, Gideon, Gervase, Blanche in her cascade of lace-edged white frills with a flower-garden of pinks and apricots and mauves in her hat, biting her lip as she remembered Venetia – as I remembered Venetia – and then frowning, biting her lip even harder when Aunt Caroline, not thinking of Venetia at all but simply wishing to compensate herself for the effrontery of Camille, called out

'Hortense dear, do come and pose for this – here, between Noel and Gideon, with Blanche on Gideon's other side – and Gervase, oh – at the other side of Noel, I suppose. Yes, Hortense, do come – you don't mind, mamma, I know, since after all she will be your granddaughter quite soon now. And since Dominic cannot be here – simply could not get away – we are one short.'

Miss Madeley-Brown got up, parting her lips in her wide, brilliant smile and came forward, quite splendid in a yellow gown that might have been painted on to her full-breasted, long-limbed figure, her shoulders as broad, her back as strongly arched as an Amazon queen. Her hair, beneath the chrysanthemum colours of her hat, looked like spun gold, she had swinging drops of topaz on her ears, that huge diamond on her hand, no idea at all of the hornets' nest into which she was so obediently and so elegantly stepping.

'Blanche!' Aunt Caroline said sharply, expecting no defiance from this quarter. 'Move over to make room for Hortense.'

'I thought this was to be grandchildren only, Aunt Caroline – that's what you said a moment ago.'

'Blanche, don't make a fuss!' Aunt Caroline gave warning.

'Oh, I am not in the least inclined to do that. I am just trying to be helpful, Aunt Caroline – just trying to get it right – and since we are rather more than *one* grandchild short, I suppose Claire is the best person to take the place of the other one we are missing. Claire darling, do come over here – yes, nurse, just give her ringlets a little shake and straighten that ribbon. Oh, good. Now then, Aunt Caroline, where would you like little Claire Chard to stand?'

She stood, in the end, beside her Uncle Noel, having found his presence the most reassuring, her rosy little cheek pressed against the hip he had damaged at Ulundi, Blanche still most uncharacteristically scowling, Gideon looking as if he had noticed nothing amiss, Miss Madeley-Brown, who really had not noticed anything, smiling until she was told to stop, Gervase, who had been pushed into the background by Aunt Caroline and then dragged forward again by Blanche, appearing much amused. Yet Venetia had been his much-loved sister and it was no doubt in tribute to her memory that when the photograph was taken he shook his head and told Aunt Caroline: 'We have still not got it right, you know, for we did not include Grace.'

'Oh, Grace – come on,' said Blanche.

'Good heavens!' said Aunt Caroline.

'Who is Grace?' Miss Madeley-Brown's fixed smile seemed to enquire.

'Of course we must have a picture of Grace,' Lady Verity agreed, settling the matter. 'I was just about to say so.'

'Grace,' said Gervase, holding out a hand to me, and so we were captured for posterity, Blanche and Noel side by side now, with Venetia's child happily between them, Miss Madeley-Brown with her hand on Gideon's arm, her diamond showing to advantage against his coat-sleeve, Gervase holding me by the elbow, his fine-etched profile

quizzical, my face looking puzzled and by no means at its best, only my hat, I thought, doing me credit beside the stupendous Madeley-Brown.

We escaped soon after – Blanche, Noel, Gervase and I – to stroll along the cliffs, enjoying the salt breezes and the bright sunshine, in suprisingly easy harmony, Gervase still holding my arm, Blanche and Noel, with Claire skipping between them, behaving openly now not as a pair of lovers but as the married couple they felt themselves to be. We sat for a while on a shady wooden seat, Blanche, who was careful of her complexion, making full use of her parasol, while the men took Claire to look at the sea, Uncle Noel and Uncle Gervase taking it in turns to carry her shoulder high, stopping every now and then to explain the sand and the shells, the busy population of a rock-pool, a sail hurrying across the horizon, the purposes of the noisy, greedy gulls.

'I shall never let her go back to Gideon, you know,' Blanche told me, her eyes on the dark, sturdy, serious child who bore so little resemblance to Venetia.

'I didn't know you were so fond of children, Blanche.'

'Well, and neither did I – but, oh heavens! I may as well confess it, I cannot stop myself from pretending she is mine and Noel's – can't you see that? The boys belong entirely to Dominic and are as remote from me now as he is. When they come home from school we are no more than polite to each other, and Matthew is already talking of spending his next long vacation in India. So she is the nearest I can ever come to having Noel's child – I take good care of that. Why not, Grace? Nobody else wants her. The Madeley-Brown will set about breeding, one can see that, as soon as he consents to ask her – which will be as soon as he has finished his negotiations for Tarn Edge – and Claire will not be welcome in *her* household then.'

We met Gideon and Miss Madeley-Brown on our way back, Blanche having no need at all to bristle like a mother cat, since no one threatened her kitten, Miss Madeley-Brown merely glancing at the child, perched on Noel's shoulder and saying 'Was it fun on the beach, little girl?', a remark designed to draw Gideon's attention, Blanche thought, to the sand on Claire's shoes and the hem of her dress, which prompted him, although not without humour, to warn his brother: 'You'll ruin your coat, Noel.'

'Oh – we farming men don't pay much heed to things like that,' Gervase murmured wickedly.

'Luckily he has another,' declared Blanche, in a great huff. 'But come along, Noel, that child must have her tea and be put to bed. Come along, for nurse is waiting.'

And once again Gideon had not addressed a word to me.

I wore the dress with the crimson velvet bodice and the cream satin skirt that evening, largely because Blanche told me it was elegant and unusual and cut low enough to give Aunt Caroline the vapours.

'And you have rather a lovely bosom, Grace – which is most unexpected since the rest of you has got so thin. And if you take your hair a little higher and lift it off your forehead just there, your eyes –

1110

which are quite big enough anyway – will look simply enormous. Have you nothing better than that gold chain to put around your neck? Oh Grace – you had heaps of jewellery once.'

'Yes – that was once. I have put it all away. I don't wear it any more.'

'Well, I am sorry, but that gold chain will not do. It should be rubies, of course – big ones surrounded by pearls and set in antique gold. Your friend Camille has just the thing. But since Aunt Caroline would be sure to recognize it and draw all the wrong conclusions, you had better borrow from me instead. Luckily I have my black velvet ribbon with me and it has enough pearls stitched on it to make a decent show. It will look well enough.'

It did, or so Gervase told me as he took me in to dinner, it having been found convenient, for the purposes of the seating arrangements, to restore to me for the duration of the evening my position as his wife, an arrangement which, astonishingly enough, appeared to offend no one but my watchful Aunt Caroline. And so I sat beside him, allowed him to unfold my napkin and place it on my knee, to touch my hand as he gave me my menu, to lean over me, breathe on me, to remind me – as several people present wished me to be reminded – how easy it would be, how *restful*, to turn back to him, to restore myself truly and finally to this family which had never really meant to relinquish me.

We had a lengthy, complicated meal, a great many toasts and speeches, both Gideon and Gervase saying a few accomplished words, Mr Nicholas Barforth making a dignified reply, Sir Blaize Barforth, who had been something of a ladies' man in his day, raising his glass to his female relations with a witty salutation. It was all very pleasant and very civilized, extremely well done, each lady now being invited to open the little trinket box beside her plate amidst squeals of delight, gold lockets of very adequate value being provided for the managers' wives while each Barforth lady received a pendant of heavy gold set with her birth-stone, a diamond for Miss Madeley-Brown, I noticed, a pearl for Blanche, a ruby for me, the very thing my outfit required.

Gervase fastened the clasp for me, adjusted the jewel to a correct central position on its chain, the back of his hand brushing the tops of my breasts as he did so, the precious metal very cold against my skin when he took his hand away.

'Uncle Nicholas – thank you – how lovely!' trilled Blanche, who knew the market price of pearls and was very pleased with the size of this one.

'You'd best thank Gideon,' he told her, 'for it was his idea, and he took the trouble to find out what month you were born.'

'Thank you, Gideon,' she said and, as everyone was getting up now in preparation for the dancing, she went up to him and, being rather tipsy by then, stood on tiptoe and gave him a reasonably flirtatious kiss.

'Yes – thank you, Gideon,' smiled Camille, an amethyst sparkling around her throat, kissing him too, without any need for tiptoe. Aunt Faith, his grandmother, my ˙ grandmother, followed suit. Miss Madeley-Brown, no doubt, would thank him later and privately. Only my thanks remained to be said and there was no doubt at all that I would have to move forward, to attract his attention, to say 'Thank you, Gideon'; and if he snubbed me or brushed me aside, I would have to carry it off somehow or other and pretend to anyone who had noticed – to Gervase who *would* notice – that it was solely on account of the *Star*.

I walked forward. He did not appear to see me coming, but started to turn away. I put out a hand to touch his sleeve and withdrew it as sharply as if the fabric had scorched me, and for a moment, as he looked down at me with no expression, almost no recognition on his dark face, I did not think my voice could penetrate the sudden, quite total dryness of my throat and my tongue.

'Thank you, Gideon.'

He nodded sharply, gave me a smile that was a brief parting of the lips, obeying his training as a gentleman far more than his inclination, which would have been – I thought – to order me from his premises, his sight, his hearing, from the quota of air he wished to breathe. And I understood, with horror and a futile quite terrible distress, that his silence was intended neither to punish nor humiliate me, but had come about quite simply because he could not bear to speak.

I went into the ballroom where the Barforth men were dancing with their lovely ladies, Mr Nicholas Barforth with Camille in her floating amethyst gauze, Noel with Blanche in her sensational and very daring black lace, Uncle Blaize and Aunt Faith, who had chosen her favourite blonde silk, Hortense Madeley-Brown in gold satin and not too much of it at that, going twice round the floor with Gideon and then sitting placidly beside her mother and Aunt Caroline while he did his duty by his managers' wives. I danced with Gervase, my hand going gratefully into his, my body taking shelter in his arms, for I was shaken and disarmed, most unusually defenceless, and no longer cared what speculation our being so much together might arouse, no longer cared what I should or should not do when he was the only person I *could* be with just then, the only person who could accept my silence – and my suffering – without question, the only one who could give me time to gather myself together. Yet when that much was achieved, I had been in his arms for rather a long time, admittedly in full view of most of our relations, but nevertheless in an embrace that was not polite but familiar and affectionate – *companionable* – and which, if allowed to continue, could give rise to a companionable desire.

'If we were meeting for the first time,' he said, 'I would be quite thrilled with you by now, do you know that?'

'Then it is perhaps as well we are not meeting for the first time.'

'Well – and if we were, I wonder how much you would object to me? I *am* the father of a bastard child, but the enlightened and liberated Grace Barforth of the *Star* should be able to forgive me for that.'

'Gervase, I do – in fact I never really blamed you.'

'I am not speaking of the past, Grace. I am telling you of my life *now*, as I would have to tell you if we had just become acquainted. The boy and the estate are an essential part of what I am. They make up the sum total of me. I can present myself to you now as a whole man – which I

1112

could not do before. I am not altogether displeased with that man. If we had just met tonight I would be doing my best to make you like him too.'

'With a very fair chance of success.'

'Why, thank you, Grace. Had I known, long ago, that you had it in you to like a very ordinary farmer with a quite moderate estate and a delightful but probably – in anybody else's eyes – a very ordinary son, then I wonder –'

'Don't wonder. Everything would have been just the same.'

'Unless, of course, I had shown any real aptitude for business, in which case you would have been the hostess here tonight – and far better at it, I must say, than the luscious Madeley-Brown.'

'It does no good to wonder about that either.'

'Then I wonder if you could care to drink some more champagne with me? That seems a reasonable occupation for those who *were* married – and *are* not.'

We drank rather more than I had intended, his new occupation having in no way lessened his taste for fine wines, and returning to the ballroom an hour later, seeing Hortense Madeley-Brown seated beside Aunt Caroline, too placid and too pleased with herself to know she was being neglected, I asked him: 'What do you really think of her, Gervase?'

'Miss Madeley-Brown? Well – I would very much enjoy a night or two in her bed, for her physique is awe-inspiring, there is no use in denying it. One would begin with the feeling of paying homage, almost, at a shrine of Aphrodite, which would make – if nothing else – a delicious aperitif.'

'Gervase, that is not the language of a working farmer.'

'No. But I was a wild young man, if you remember.'

'I remember.'

'No longer, Grace – believe me. Not dull, I hope, but quite dependable, if you can credit it.'

'Perhaps I can. Gervase – what do you think of me?'

He took my hand, companionably, and, not caring who saw us, brushed a closed and friendly mouth against my cheek.

'I like you, Grace. I think one can build on that.'

And so one could. All day I had been surrounded by the faces and figures and attitudes which had peopled my childhood, formed me and moulded me and had never for one moment lost hope of my return. Warm affection awaited me here on a dozen faces; and one man who hated me. The affection was like the thin vapours of an autumn morning glimpsed in the distance. The hatred was real to me.

I left, some time after midnight, with my Agbrigg grandparents, Gervase escorting us gallantly to their house half a mile away.

'I do not pretend to understand this,' my grandmother told me when he had strolled off along the cliff-top. 'I presume he wants you to return to him as his wife, since I can think of nothing else he has a right to want from you.'

'I think he might want that – yes.'

'Well then, I have no right to interfere – your father has assured me of that – but it would seem – *suitable* – would it not?'

'I suppose it would. But it will not break his heart, you know, if I refuse him. I think he would quite like me to say yes, but he will not really mind if I say no.'

'Good gracious! I have never heard such coolness.'

'Not coolness, grandmamma, just good sense. He is so remarkably self-sufficient, you see – whoever would have thought it? He likes me but he doesn't need me. Well – at least *that* has turned out all right. Grandmamma, you will not be pleased with me, but I am going back to Cullingford on the early train tomorrow.'

'Ah – and do you imagine there is somebody in Cullingford who needs you?'

'I simply think it is where I belong.'

'Hannah,' my grandfather said sharply, 'leave the lass alone. She knows what she's doing.'

But I could not share his confidence, for I was not leaving Scarborough for any high-minded principles of self-sufficiency, independence, who needed me or did not need me. I was running away from Gideon.

30

My grandfather took me to the station the next morning, found me a compartment – in accordance with my grandmother's instructions – in which two elderly ladies were already seated, and asked me no questions. I had left a note in his care for Camille and one for Blanche, explaining that 'pressure of business' had required my early return, and although neither of them would believe me I did not really care for that.

'This is not a good train,' my grandfather said. 'You will have to change at Leeds and there might be a long wait. Now take care, lass –' And it was as I began to reassure him of my ability to travel alone, my understanding of the dangers of rape and kidnap to a life of sexual slavery in a warmer clime – although I did not use these words – that Gideon Chard came striding along the platform, a leather document case under one arm, a newspaper under the other, and, raising his hat to me with an automatic gesture, got into a compartment as far away from mine as he could.

'Now what the devil –?' my grandfather began, for no matter how deep a grudge Gideon might bear the *Star* it was discourteous, it was ungentlemanly, it was downright peculiar of any man to refuse his company and his protection on this hazardous Scarborough to Cullingford line to any lady of his acquaintance – unheard of, if she happened to be a relation.

'Grace, lass, what *is* all this?' But the doors were slamming now, the train getting ready to pull out of the station, I was already on board, and there was nothing to do but stand at the window and wave to him, and then, feeling considerably shaken, to sit down and defend myself against the curiosity of my two elderly travelling companions by closing my eyes.

I had thought, in that first numbing moment of recognition, that he

1114

had come to meet the train, not travel on it, and I spent the first thirty or forty miles telling myself the many reasons he might have for doing so. The festivities, as such, were over now. A special train would be waiting that afternoon to convey his employees back to Cullingford, suitably provisioned with those luxurious little hampers of chicken and champagne, but few if any of the Barforths would be on it.

Uncle Blaize and Aunt Faith were to stay in Scarborough for the rest of the week and perhaps another with Lady Verity, who wished to bask for as long as possible in the renewed friendship of her sons. Blanche and Noel would not be leaving until Wednesday, perhaps longer if the weather should hold, and Gervase had declared himself in no hurry to get away. I had not been informed of Aunt Caroline's plans but it seemed unlikely that she would neglect this opportunity of persuading her brother to finalize the transfer of Tarn Edge to Gideon and might well stay at the Grand with Miss Madeley-Brown in tow until she had. And in that case it was not surprising that Gideon, who would have appointments tomorrow morning, should wish to avoid the special train, preferring to travel alone with his newspaper and his documents than in the effusive company of his managers' wives.

He could not have known I would be here. I had not known myself until last night and had told no one. He had been as shocked to see me as I was on seeing him, yet what real difference could it make? I would not have stayed in Scarborough even had I known he meant to leave it. What I needed was to return to my own home, my own atmosphere, my own life, and his presence, although awkward, could not hinder me in that. Yet throughout that hot, tedious journey I spoke not a word to those kind, well-meaning ladies, who whenever I closed my eyes began at once to tell each other how ill I looked, how pale; and by the time we arrived in Leeds I could not deny that I was feeling wretched indeed.

The station was busy enough, I suppose, and people who wish to avoid each other can usually manage to do so. I remained in my compartment until he had passed the window, walked slowly down the platform, giving him time to get far away with his long strides, and went at once to the waiting-room reserved for ladies. A half-hour passed – a dreadful half-hour – before I got up and went to find the Cullingford train, hoping that he was staying in Leeds or going to London, anywhere, since the small station-yard at Cullingford would be difficult; but he was there, as far down the platform as he could get, irritably pacing, irritably smoking – he was there – and it was then, in that moment of distraction, that something struck hard against the backs of my knees and aware of wheels and shouts and, oddly, the shapes of boxes, cages, canvas, I realized to my complete horror that I was falling down.

I know what happened only because other people were there to tell me so, a great many of them, it seemed, in those first dizzy moments of returning consciousness, bending over me and arguing quite ferociously with one another as to whether the porter who had run into me with that trolley of bags and baggage had been drunk or just malicious, or whether *I* had been drunk or deaf or just plain slow-witted not to have got myself out of his way. But although I had certainly not been drunk a moment ago, I felt very drunk now, helpless and incapable and bewildered, and very willing to abandon myself to Gideon when he parted the crowd, helped me to my feet and then, when I found I could not stand erect, picked me up and carried me somewhere or other – did it matter where? – to remove my shoe and give orders that something was to be done about my ankle, which was swelling.

A capable-looking woman bathed my foot in cold water and applied a bandage, while I drank the brandy Gideon had sent for – all of it, every drop – although it made my head no clearer. And realizing dimly but with a weak inclination for laughter that he had obliged them to hold up the train, I allowed him, with complete docility, to lift me into the compartment of his choice and to place me exactly to his liking, my back supported by the pillows he had by some means acquired.

I was suffering, perhaps, from a slight concussion, certainly from a sprained ankle and a drop more brandy than I was used to at this hour of the day, and as the train began to ease its way out of the station – Gideon, no doubt, having told the driver to go slow and be damned to anybody who might be in a hurry – I began to wonder why I did not feel more ashamed.

'Heavens, Gideon, what a ridiculous thing!'

'Accidents happen.'

'Oh – my bag –'

'There, in the corner.'

'Yes – or lord, where *is* my hat?' For I had just realized it was not on my head.

'Ruined, I'm afraid. The railway company will buy you another.'

'Oh – *damnation*!'

'What is it now?'

'I don't know – I just feel so –'

'Don't feel anything. Just be glad you were not alone.'

I drifted then, partly because it was easier to drift placidly, docilely, spinelessly, easier just for a little while to leave everything to him, to let him decide – since he so much enjoyed deciding – than to gather my cloudy wits together and decide for myself. And when I recovered sufficiently not merely to wonder where I was but to care what I was doing there, we were approaching Cullingford.

'Will there be anyone to meet you, Grace?'

'No. I am not expected until tomorrow.'

'Then I will take you –'; and I allowed myself, like a dreaming child, to be 'taken' in his carriage to a destination he did not name but which I knew, quite soon, must be Tarn Edge.

The butler, whose extreme elegance had long been the talk of Cullingford, greeted us without the faintest hint of surprise, as if he was accustomed to see his employer arriving home every day of the week with a bareheaded, bedraggled and probably slightly tipsy woman in his arms.

'Sandwiches and coffee in the drawing-room, Sherston, and a bottle of Chablis if you have one chilled.'

'Certainly, sir.'

1116

'And Mrs Barforth, I imagine, will first wish to attend to her dress.'

'Certainly – at once, sir.'

Two parlourmaids and a housekeeper with the bearing of a dowager duchess assisted me to a dressing-room, brought me hot water and warm towels, combs and brushes, and then returned me, no longer quite so bemused although still dangerously passive, to the armchair their master indicated. The drawing-room was cool and fragrant, a haven from the heat and dust of the long day, roses and carnations standing in very professional arrangements in silver-rimmed bowls of exquisitely cut crystal I had not seen before. Two nymphs in white biscuit porcelain, a foot high, were poised in graceful flight at each side of the hearth, more nymphs in costly groupings by Sèvres on the mantelshelf above them, the mirror I remembered replaced now by the portrait of a dark-eyed, curly-haired lady clad in the scanty muslin draperies of the Regency, unmistakably a Chard.

The sandwiches, when they came, were of smoked salmon very daintily garnished, the wine ice cold in its long, fluted glasses, delighting my tongue and rising at once to join the pleasant confusion in my brain.

'Well, I wanted you weak and helpless, Grace,' he said, raising his glass for me. 'And now I have you.'

'Yes.' Not for long, of course, but for the moment I had, not surrendered precisely, but certainly ceased to struggle. My grandfather's fears for me had all been realized. I had exposed myself to the risks of travelling alone and a man had kidnapped me. Astonishingly, I laughed.

'What is so amusing?'

I told him, and received a slow, almost unwilling smile.

'Unfortunately it is not so simple.'

'Unfortunately?'

'Yes, Grace. If I took you away and locked you up and made love to you often enough, you would eventually stop trying to escape and then you would stop wanting to – or so the theory goes. I can't do that.'

'Would you even want to?'

'Oh yes. There was a time when I might just have succeeded. My misfortune has been that I wanted you to come as a willing captive. I have not been able to achieve that.'

'Oh Gideon – *Gideon* –'

Never in all the years I had known him had I seen him look so weary. Never in the whole of my life had I felt such a desire to reach out, in body and in spirit, to another person. Never before had I lost sight of my own needs, my own futile, fussy dignity, my own most precious common sense, very nearly my own identity, in my need to give whatever I could give – whatever he would take. And it seemed to me advisable that this impulse of quite overwhelming devotion should not last long either.

'I thought I had made you hate me, Gideon.'

'You did. I understood why and played the same game. I have hated you very well – by fits and starts.'

'Yesterday you couldn't bring yourself to speak to me.'

'I do not forget it.'

1117

'That is why I took the early train today. I was running away from you.'

'Is there anything new in that? You have been running away from me, have you not, ever since –'

'Ever since I was eighteen and you came to have a look at Fieldhead as if you might buy it and me with it – or so I thought – and made yourself pleasant to my father's wife instead of arranging to meet me at the bottom of the garden and trying to kiss me, and telling me – telling me – lord, why am I prattling on so?'

'Telling you that I loved you? But I didn't love you then, Grace. That happened later – would have happened no matter what the circumstances. But before I say another word – since I retain my pride in these matters, or such of it as you have left me – I must know that you have loved me too.'

'Yes. Yes, of course I have.'

'That will not suffice me, Grace. If you came upstairs with me now and gave yourself to me in the most slavish fashion I could devise, it would not suffice me.'

'How, then?'

'You have taken every opportunity you could to hurt me and humiliate me, have you not?'

'Yes – I am afraid so.'

'Now make atonement for it. You are a clever woman. You will find a way.'

'Will it serve a purpose?'

'At this stage I don't much care for that. You are very accomplished when it comes to wounding me. I think you must now show me your skill as a healer. I need that much from you, Grace.'

'Yes.'

I had been asked only the night before if there was anyone in Cullingford who needed me and I had not expected it to be Gideon, yet now, although I could never have spoken the words and would be very likely, I believed, to deny them tomorrow, my thought urged him: 'Yes, need me and go on needing me. Need me so that I am filled to my capacity with it and strained even beyond the limits of my need for you. Ask more of me than I can possibly give and see – just *watch* – how I shall find the means to give it.' This was the consuming emotion Venetia had felt for Robin Ashby, the crusade of which I had not believed myself to be capable. I loved him. *Naturally*, I loved him. I had lived in the shadow of it for years. The only difference now was that I wanted to tell him so.

'It was fear,' I said slowly. 'A physical fear to begin with because I desired you – quite acutely – and didn't understand it. How could I? Young girls of eighteen are not supposed to understand desire. They are not even supposed to feel it. And I am not going to take all the blame, Gideon, for you were older and you were not a virgin. You could have understood and helped me get over it – couldn't you?'

'No,' he said, smiling slowly, sadly almost, as if at a very distant memory. 'I was behaving as I had been told a gentleman ought to

1118

behave, you see – with a virgin. I was a little older, and had a little more experience, yes, but not enough – believe me – to know that I'd have done better to drag you off somewhere by the hair. That kind of knowledge came much later. And even then, Grace, when you were eighteen, there was more to your fear than that. My dear – I *know* you didn't trust me in those days and I know why, but you are going to *tell* me.'

'Yes. I knew you needed a rich wife and I understood that. I had money and I had been told, at an early age, that men would want to marry me for it. I understood that too. My father had educated me to believe that marriages should be made with a cool head. I couldn't name my feeling for you at that time but it was not cool, and we have all seen the pathetic spectacle a woman makes when she has married for love but has been married only for her money. That was my fear and you did nothing to alleviate it. Your marriage to Venetia suggested to me that I had been right.'

'You had married Gervase by then, Grace. I certainly did not jilt you.'

'And you were not in love with me then either, were you – not really?'

He shook his head, still sadly, I thought, and slowly, a movement – like every movement he had made since entering this room – which was full of regret.

'I fear not. If I had really fallen in love with you when you were eighteen and ripe for the plucking, then you would have known about it, my darling, for I would have been far less gentlemanly, with far greater success – But even so you were the reason I hesitated as long as I did in marrying Venetia. I didn't want to share a house with you. I wasn't sure why. I simply thought it would not be wise. Quite soon – too soon – that house, *this* house, in fact, would have been unbearable to me without you. Those were not easy days for me, Grace. I had a trade to learn, prejudice and hostility to overcome on both sides, for my own people thought me sadly *déclassé*, and any one of the managers we had then would have put a knife in my back given half a chance – and it's a weary business when a man has to guard his back all day and every day. You were the only person who understood the effort I was making, except Nicholas Barforth, for whom no effort could ever be enough, and even he failed to realize just how damned distasteful I found those sheds – this town – any town – to begin with. I didn't *want* to be a manufacturer, Grace. I simply wanted to be rich. If I could have made my money in land or on the high seas or in any other clean and clever fashion, then I'd hardly have condemned myself to twelve hours a day shut up in those mills. I think you understood that too. I think, in my place, you would have done the same.'

'I understood. And I admired you enormously for it.'

'Admiration? Is that all you had for me?'

'Possibly not. But it was all I was prepared to admit, and I am very stubborn. You were married, Gideon, and I loved your wife like a sister.'

'I know,' he said, his smile once again heavy with regret. 'I know. Oddly enough, so did I. Oh yes, you may look startled and surprised, but it is the plain truth. That is exactly what I felt for her, the exasperated kind of affection I would have given to a sister, and which in her case was sadly inappropriate. When she left me for Robin Ashby I made no attempt to get her back. Well, I was not slow to spot my own advantage, I never am. But the truth is that I wished her well. If it was what she wanted, then I had no mind to spoil it for her. I thought her reckless to the point of madness, but I hoped just the same that she might succeed.'

'Gideon – I am so glad you told me that.'

'Yes, I thought it might please you. What I am about to say now will not suit you so well. Venetia was gone, with my blessing, although she didn't know it. I knew how Gervase was situated with Diana Flood. I can't be certain how much Nicholas Barforth suspected but he watched me like a hawk those first few months, and so I had to keep away from you. But you were the woman I wanted and I was going to have you, my dear, as soon as ever I could. We were going to live together in the way we actually *had* been living together for several years, except that when the dance was over and the dinner guests had gone we were going to walk up those stairs hand in hand and get into the same bed. I was going to take you abroad with me, bully you and rely on you, spoil you and make sure you spoiled me. I was going to *have* you, Grace – and then suddenly there you were, asking me to take Venetia back. Once again my sense of timing had been at fault.'

'I would have asked you to take her back, Gideon, even if we had already been lovers.'

'My dear, I know. There is nothing I want to say about her death. But, yes, as you guessed, I was appalled when I heard of your intention to divorce Gervase – appalled and furious, and quite determined to put a stop to it. Your assessment of my motives, that night in London was quite correct. The social stigma of divorce was more than I could stomach, especially when I could see no need for it. One way or another I was going to make you abandon it and come back here with me, where I was certain you belonged. No one raises any objection to Noel and Blanche. Why should anyone have objected to us? I would have been faithful to you, you know – far more scrupulous in my behaviour than if you had really been my wife, just like Noel has to be. A man assumes his wife will forgive him. In most cases she has very little choice in the matter. But he is obliged to tread rather more warily with a mistress, who can make up her own mind. I believe Grace Barforth of the *Star* may have said something like that. Will you admit that I could have made you happy?'

'Yes, perfectly happy – once. The life you planned for me was everything I desired and would have given me complete fulfilment – once. By the time it became possible I had moved on – forwards or backwards I don't always know – but *moved*, anyway.'

He came very swiftly to sit on the edge of my chair and leaned over me, sliding one hand beneath my shoulder-blades, gathering me up in an act of possession into which my body nestled with gratitude and content.

'Grace, listen carefully, for I cannot think I shall ever say this to you

1120

again. This is all I know how to give – this house and the luxury inside it, the gracious way of life we could make for each other here. This is what I have worked to achieve and to maintain, and I shall achieve much more – much more. I can afford, by my own efforts, to surround you with ease and beauty. I can offer you protection and security. I can provide for you. These are the things I understand – the things I have always believed women wanted. Will you take them, Grace?'

I leaned forward, my head against his shoulder, my arms around him, holding him like a woman drowning, for this was our final chance and we both knew that, once again, Time had cheated us, had forced us along parallel but separate roads, at varying rates of progress, so that we could glimpse and hope and strive but never really meet.

'What must I give you in return?'

'Yourself.'

'Which is everything I have. You would not give me everything, Gideon. Would you allow me to continue my association with the *Star*?'

'Of course not.' But it was spoken sadly, no rancour, no disgust, no jealousy, just a simple statement of self-knowledge and regret. He *could* not.

'And would you allow me to continue my work with Anna and Patrick Stone?'

'No.'

'Would you receive them here?'

'Grudgingly.'

'Would you expect me to break off with them entirely?'

'Yes, I would expect that. I would try not to enforce it, but if you delayed then I probably would enforce it.'

'Oh, Gideon –'

'Yes, I know,' he said, his mouth against my hair. 'You see how very carefully I have thought it over, for I am indeed a calculating man. But in this case I am as much a prisoner of my own nature as you are. I cannot rid myself of the belief that if you loved me you would willingly give up your friends and associates for my sake. I know you will not agree, but I cannot feel I am asking too much, or even anything very much at all. I am asking you to be my wife and I am entitled, surely, to my notions of what a wife should be? I am ready to be your husband, which also entails a measure of sacrifice, for if you take me there is every likelihood that my mother – of whom I am very fond and who is getting no younger – will never speak to me again.'

I had no wish to move from the shelter of his arms, would have been grateful, I think, if he had forced me to stay there. But I had asked for freedom of choice. He had given it to me. And I knew by now that the liberty for which I had struggled and on which I would not relinquish my hold could be a cruel burden indeed.

'I love you, Gideon.'

'I wonder what good that is going to do me?'

'Very little, I suppose, unless you can accept me just as I am.'

'Yes, I knew you would say that. I am prepared for it. Go on.'

1121

'And what good will it do?'

'None, I suppose, for you cannot accept me as I am either. But say it.'

'Gideon – you once told me I did not earn my living, that I had rejected a woman's responsibilities and was not fit to take a man's.'

'I remember.'

'Now I *do* earn a living, or at least now I can see the way to earn it. I can see where my living is and I have the ability – I know I have – to go out and fetch it in. I have taken the risk. I have done the work and continue to do it, whether I feel inclined for it or not; and I spare myself nothing. I may send home my clerk if he has a bad cough or a bad headache, but I do not go home myself, not matter how unwell I might feel, until the work is done. And I want you to respect me for that, Gideon, not for my dinner-parties and my dances, which are only life's frills, after all, and come nowhere near its substance. You could not fill your life with menu cards and invitation cards and small-talk, you know you could not. Neither can I. I want you to believe in my ability, Gideon, and to value it, instead of trying to dismiss it like a child's toy. You have told me of your own early days here in the mills and how difficult it was for you to gain acceptance because they thought your accent too refined and your hands too clean – because you were not a Cullingford man. Can you imagine what it has been like for me – a woman – to gain even a hearing? I have to work ten times harder than a man, I can tell you, just to convince some people that I am actually working at all. And even now I waste hours a day sometimes – hours I cannot spare – with men who are too small-minded to take me seriously, and with women whose peace of mind I seem to threaten. I am ambitious – which is considered unwomanly – and I am not ashamed of it. Whatever I promise I perform, and since women have a reputation for light-mindedness and are generally supposed to break their promises rather freely I have to be very certain of keeping mine, not only to the letter but on time. And in any case I prefer to call these promises "commitments" which cannot be casually abandoned. You would not abandon yours. I have employed men who have wives and children to feed, and I am responsible for that. I cannot put those families in jeopardy. Neither could you. Could you?'

'I could not.'

'And if I can respect that in you – and find it pleasing – then why can you not respect it in me? I love you, Gideon. If you had married me when I was eighteen I would have been your adoring wife ever after and would never have cast a glance beyond you. For years I wanted exactly the life you wanted, and if we had become lovers before I left Tarn Edge, then – yes – I am sure I would have been here still, with no sense of frustration or regret. I would have made your life my life – would have considered you to *be* my life – and the sad thing is that I know I would have been happy. I cannot do that now, however much a part of me may still want to – and a part of me does want to – *I* know that I cannot. I am ready to share your life but not to live it at second-hand. I want you to share my life but not to live it for me, not to absorb it into your own or to deny that it even exists. The last time I came to your office I said terrible things to you – it makes me shiver when I remember them – but there was some truth there. I believe men and women should be equal if they are fit to be equal, and I think I am fit to equal you, Gideon, to complement you, to live with you independently but in harmony, to trust you and to deserve your trust – to live together as two *people* who love each other. It should be possible, Gideon – oh, really it should.'

'Yes,' he said, his face almost hollow now with fatigue and strain. 'I know. And it pains me – I can't tell you how much – to realize that I cannot –'

He got up and went to stand by the fireplace, my body turning cold without him, but before I could follow or call him back to me the door opened and his butler informed him: 'The carriage, sir.'

'Thank you, Sherston.'

The man withdrew, and across the spreading, splintering gulf between us Gideon said, 'I ordered the carriage to be ready in an hour. I had no hope, you see, and I thought an hour would be long enough. I took the liberty, too, of sending a message to your house, warning them of your arrival and of the accident to your foot, and they will have all ready for you – even your friend Dr Stone to attend you.'

'Gideon –'

'No more. At least, just this, although I have no right to say it – absolutely none at all. I would not like to see you married to Liam Adair. It has nothing to do with his treatment of me – nothing –'

'I am not going to marry him. There has never been any question of that.'

He nodded curtly, his head bowed, half turned away from me, my own face wet, I suddenly realized, with tears, although I could not recall the moment they had begun. Nor could I force any kind of voice at all through my tight throat to ask him when or if or how he could bear to marry Hortense Madeley-Brown. But he heard my thought and gave what looked like a dismissive, impatient shrug.

'I have gone rather far along that road now to be able to withdraw with honour. You may think her vain and slow, but in fact she is very young and shy and has a good heart. She will – she will *do*. Excuse me, I must say a word to Sherston –'

He did not come back. The butler and two impassive underlings assisted me to the carriage, the housekeeper getting in beside me and giving a masterly performance, all the way to Blenheim Crescent, of a woman who has not the slightest idea that her companion is crying. They helped me down, took me inside, bowed, made some impeccable murmurings, and went away.

'What ails you?' said Patrick Stone, not referring to my swollen ankle.

'God knows!'

But I knew. And this time, no matter what anyone told me, I did not expect to recover.

31

I was *busy*. That was the only thing I thought about and spoke about. I was frantically, permanently busy.

The Duke of South Erin died that summer, thus further delaying

Gideon's wedding and somehow, when the mourning period was over, the engagement was over too, Miss Madeley-Brown or more likely her mother having got wind of a better offer and feeling she had waited for the Chards long enough.

'Poor Gideon has been jilted,' Blanche told me, 'for the Madeley-Brown has got herself a baronet.'

But I had nothing to say about that.

He went abroad soon afterwards, to stay with the Fauconniers in Lyons, the Goldsmiths in Berlin, undoubtedly, Blanche thought, to have another look at the younger Mademoiselle Fauconnier, to cast an appraising eye at a supposedly very promising Goldsmith niece.

'And he had better be quick about it,' she declared, 'or he will have Aunt Caroline moving herself into Tarn Edge now that the new duchess has moved her out of South Erin.'

I had nothing to say about that either.

I was busy. I had so much to do. I had my bright new *Star*, my plans – endless plans – to make it brighter, my desk, my decisions, my authority. *My Star*, increasingly mine, as Liam, who had always preferred a battle to a victory, began somehow to keep his distance.

'There's nothing wrong, Grace,' he told me in answer to my sharp enquiry. 'Nothing at all. It's just that I'm an odd sort of character, and to tell the truth there are times when I miss the life we had in Gower Street.'

'You mean this is all too easy now – too civilized?'

'Is that what I mean? You could be right. You usually are. Yes – I've often thought I'd like to climb a mountain, one hell of a big one, just to prove I could. But the chances are I'd be wondering what the devil to do with myself when I got to the top. I reckon the mountain next-door, or the one next-door to that, might look very good to me.'

But if he preferred to remain Liam Adair of the Gower Street *Star*, I could only respect him for that. And if Monday mornings rarely saw him in the office these days and he took frequent, unexplained trips away, then it suited me just then to be over-burdened, to have more work than I could possibly do and then, by a total concentration of energy and will to do it, so that I had no time to think of other things.

'My dear, you are losing weight,' both Anna Stone and Tessa Delaney told me. I had not noticed it and when I did I had no time to care.

'Dearest, we never see you,' gently complained Aunt Faith. 'Could you not come to tea on Sunday?'

Of course I could not. Good heavens! Sunday was a working day like any other, the only day when I could really sit down and plan my schedules and the schedules I imposed on others for the week ahead. I would have no time for tea.

I suffered a severe chill that November from which I recovered slowly and, succumbing to the combined pressure of my father, Patrick Stone and Camille, I agreed to spend a week in Scarborough. And, having agreed, instantly regretted it, for Mr Martin was getting too old, Liam too careless, the rest of them had too little experience and too little sense, and I believed their chances of getting along without me to be very slight. Liam took me to the station, laughed at me, kissed me, saw to the bestowal of my luggage and myself in a compartment where – and I knew how poor a safeguard this could be – another lady was already sitting. I wore a sealskin coat with a grey fur trim, a huge fur muff, a dashing Russian hat. I felt cool and purposeful and pleasant. I looked poised, I thought, and expensive, which, in my case and unlike my travelling companion, did not mark me as the wife of a rich man but as a successful woman. I was my own person, in charge of my own life and responsible for the welfare of others. And on the whole, despite an occasional tightness in my chest, a weakness in my legs – the remains of my influenza – I was pleased with myself.

I received a rapturous welcome from Camille, the usual gruff affection from Nicholas Barforth, who entertained us to a spectacular dinner that evening at the Grand, not quite managing to conceal his surprise, which gave way to wry amusement, when he understood I had not known Gervase would be there.

'Did I forget to mention it?' Camille murmured. 'Yes, of course I did. I am a disreputable woman, after all, and one can expect no better of me. But since you are both here, then – well – here you both are. You must simply force yourself, Grace, to enjoy it.'

Force was by no means necessary. Dinner was exceedingly pleasant, Camille vibrant as always with her happiness, Mr Barforth entertaining us royally but waiting, just the same, to be alone with her, Gervase smiling his quiet assurance at me as if he knew why I required it. And as the evening drew to its close I did require it, for by my own choice, the complexities of my nature and of my past, I had rejected my own chance of tasting Camille's bliss and did not always care to be reminded of it.

'Nicholas,' she said, 'it is late –'; the same words, the same spoken caress Mrs Agbrigg had used to my father and which had threaded themselves so uncomfortably throughout my childhood. But now I understood the joy they offered, the physical harmony I had briefly experienced, and the more complete harmony of the spirit which had always eluded me. And abruptly I was calm and poised no longer, but seemed – among the most substantial glitter of the Grand Hotel – to be falling into a void, a fading away of reality, so that I stood like a wraith, invisible and insubstantial, on the fringes of Camille's humanity, aware of her emotion, her joy, her deep personal fulfilment, the very heat of her body, without being able to touch her; feeling nothing distinctly but a chill air blowing, not around me but through me. And I was horrified.

I managed to walk outside, glad of my expensive fur coat and my dashing Cossack hat to anchor me to the ground, since there seemed nothing heavy enough inside me to withstand the high sea-wind.

'Home now,' said Camille, since there was nowhere else in the world she wished to go.

'Grace and I would like to take a walk,' Gervase told her easily. 'The night is so fine and the stars quite exceptional.'

And once their carriage had gone, I collapsed against him as we stood in the shadow of the hotel and burst into tears, not with the ugly, convulsive sobbing of pain but the fast-flowing, unrestrained weeping that brings relief.

'Is this for the past, Grace?'

'I think it must be.'

'And for our child?'

'Gervase, I can't speak of that – really, I can't speak of it –'

'I think you must, for it has been inside you too long. Let it go, love – let it go.'

And until it was over and I had dried my cheeks and adjusted my hat, and we had strolled away hand in hand along the cliff-path, he had nothing more to say.

'Are you strong enough now, Grace, I wonder?'

'For what?'

'My confession?'

'Lord! I don't think so.'

'But I am going to make it. Listen to me, darling – if I could have crossed the room to you that day at Galton instead of hovering in the doorway, and knelt at your bedside – as I wanted to do – and held you and cried a little and asked you to forgive me – because I did blame myself – If I could have done those things, you would have forgiven me, that terrible silence would never have fallen between us, and you would still be my wife –'

'Gervase, you are always telling me what might have been.'

'I think I am trying to make amends. I am happy, Grace, and I see that you are not. I am *satisfied* – thoroughly satisfied – with the life I lead, because every facet of my nature is involved in it. I feel that I am using myself to capacity, and it is a rather marvellous feeling. Forgive me, Grace, but it strikes me that you are concentrating all your energies on one side of yourself – which is a most interesting and provocative side, a very challenging side, I admit. But there is another side to you which you seem to have put into some kind of cold storage, my darling. And that saddens me.'

'Really?'

'Yes, Mrs Barforth – really. And there is no point, you know, in taking that brisk tone with me, for I am a gentleman of independent means and not in the least inclined to tremble before the proprietor of the *Star*.'

'I suppose you are telling me I need a lover.'

'Possibly you do. But what I really wish to say is that if I have hurt you so badly that you are too afraid to risk yourself again, then I must find some way of healing where I have harmed.'

'You are taking a great deal upon yourself, Gervase.'

'I would take *you*, altogether, if you would have me.'

I came to an abrupt halt, finding myself somehow face to face with the cliff wall, a sharp salt wind across my back, my answer coming as naturally and easily as my tears.

'It would not be fair to you, Gervase. If you were in love with me, then perhaps you might be ready to put up with me, but since you are not –'

'Am I not?'

'No. You like me, and I like you, probably better than anyone. But it would take a very grand passion to shift you so much as an inch from your way of life – or me from mine – and you are not a man for grand passions, Gervase.'

He smiled and kissed me, very lightly, on the mouth.

'No, thank God! Venetia was the Barforth for grand passions – and Nicholas, as it turns out. I am entirely a Clevedon in matters of the emotions, with my mother's fondness for friendship and – hopefully – something of her talent for it. She is divinely happy with her good friend Julian, you know. Do I not tempt you?'

'From time to time – but not to be mistress of Galton.'

He laughed, kissed me again, we laughed together.

'Very well. I accept your refusal. And at the risk of sounding decidedly unromantic I will even confess that I expected it. But I wanted to ask you so that you would know there was an alternative – that you could if you would –'

'I am very glad you did ask me, Gervase.'

I was calm again, or calm enough to contemplate our return to Camille's warm and welcoming home, the sight and sound of her joy and the reasons for it, calm enough to endure both her bliss and my own rejection of it – calm enough. And when I came downstairs to breakfast the next morning Gervase had gone.

I stayed the whole week as I had promised, restraining myself from sending more than half a dozen telegrams to Cullingford, marooned in Camille's snug little parlour by the weather which had turned steel grey and intensely cold.

'Let us sit by the fire and keep warm,' she said. 'That's the great thing.' But I had not chosen to live safe and warm, and could not be dissuaded from setting off for Cullingford the following Sunday, despite a heavy fall of snow.

It was from the start a terrible journey, the train bitter cold and sluggish, the changes, first at York and then at Leeds, chilling me to the point of numbness, the Cullingford train departing from Leeds an hour late and then proceeding to exhaust and alarm me by its shuddering, unexplained halts among desolate snowfields, freezing rock-hard as night descended, to receive another burden of snow. The sky, which had been overcast and menacing all day, darkened entirely, robbing me of any sense of time or direction, the world and its ills and injustices reduced ere long to my own physical discomfort, my total isolation, since my compartment had emptied a very long time ago and no one since Leeds had been rash enough to get on board this train.

There would, of course, be no one at the station to meet me – supposing I ever reached it – for no one would expect me to travel on such a day, and if my coachman had stirred himself so far, he would by now have gone home again. There would be no other vehicle available, and unless the roads were blocked with drifting snow, which seemed quite likely, I would have to send the station boy with a note to Blenheim Crescent and spend another freezing, tedious hour in the waiting-room until someone came. And if the roads *were* blocked, then – with the resolution of a woman who has chosen to live alone – I would have to grit my teeth, wrap myself a little tighter in my sealskin coat, and walk.

It was a dark and dangerous night when I reached Cullingford, the snow falling in fine, slanting lines, driven by the wind, the stationmaster, who had not really expected the train to arrive, cross and confused, taking charge of my luggage but waving me away towards the yard where, miraculously, through the gloom, I saw a solitary carriage waiting. Liam I thought, for who else would dare risk himself and his horses for me in this storm? And hurrying forward, grateful and glad, I was defenceless when Gideon said curtly, 'Get in.'

'I beg your pardon?'

'Get in. Get in. I've been waiting here since God knows when and I'm frozen to the marrow. Get in. Don't stand and argue.'

Where to? I didn't ask him and there was nothing more he seemed inclined to say, his concentration and his skill being required in full measure to handle the reins, for the snow was very deep, Cullingford's steep cobbled streets very treacherous, and I was always passive, it seemed, whenever he chose to kidnap me, or to rescue me. I closed my eyes and went with him, as I had done when he had marched me around his building site at Black Abbey Meadow, when he had carried me to the Leeds train and then to Tarn Edge; as I would have done in my far away girlhood if he had then understood his need to master me. I went with him, not for long, not too far, but pleasurably, almost slavishly, for this was my very secret, my very precious fantasy, my sole indulgence, and would last no longer this time, I supposed, than the others.

Where to? My own front door, my own servants waiting – was I surprised, or disappointed about that? – and then, as we stood in the hall, his face tight and strangely guarded, he said curtly but somehow without anger – with something in his voice I did not recognize, 'When you have changed your shoes and whatever else you wish to do, I would appreciate a word.'

There was a good fire in the drawing-room, and seeing him installed before it, a brandy glass in his hand, I flew upstairs and down again, seriously incommoded – there is no use in denying it – by the persistent thumping of my heart, that gave rise to a breathlessness I could not hope to conceal.

'Gideon, I must thank you –'

'Must you? There is no need.'

'But there is – and I am sure you are wet through. I only hope you will not take cold.'

'I shouldn't think so,' he said, his faint air of surprise indicating that the Chards did not take cold so easily, if at all. But in fact he looked extremely chilled and I was full of concern for him.

'Well – do have some more brandy, just the same.'

'Thank you. I will. Grace – there is something I must tell you.'

'Yes?'

But as I waited dry-mouthed, preparing myself to face some new injury

– my heart not for a moment abating its giddy, quite painful thumping –
he said nothing, set down his glass, picked it up again, refilled it but did
not drink, the movements, so very unusual in him, of a man who could
not bring himself to speak his mind.

'I knew this would be difficult, but really – indeed it is very hard,
Grace, very awkward –'

And looking at him keenly, almost with disbelief, I said, 'Gideon – I
do believe that you are *nervous*.'

'I believe I am – very nervous.'

'Lord – what have you done?'

'I have put myself in a damnably difficult situation – a very delicate
one. I have only myself to blame.'

'Is it very serious?'

'I fear so. I have staked, perhaps not everything, but a very great deal,
on one card, which is not at all my habit. And the truth is I hardly know
which way to turn.'

But he had turned to me.

'How can I help you, Gideon?'

'Are you sure you want to help me?'

'For goodness' sake! Of course I am. It involves money, I suppose?'

'Money is concerned in it – yes.'

'And since you do things on such a grand scale, I suppose it must be a
great deal more than I have available. I shall have to try and raise the
difference from my father.'

He picked up his glass again and drank the spirit straight down this
time, his head turned away from me so that I could see only his heavy
Chard profile and could not read his expression.

'Grace – have I understood aright? Have you just offered me what
amounts to everything you have and as much as you can borrow?'

So I had. And what was astonishing about that? It had seemed the
most natural thing in the world.

'Well, I shall not go hungry, you know. And I have the very greatest
confidence in your ability to pay me back.'

'And if I do not?'

'Then you will have a very good reason. And I shall still not go
hungry.'

'My dear – that is not a businesslike answer. One does not accept these
"good reasons" for the non-payment of a debt in business.'

'No. But had it been a simple matter of business you would have gone
to Mr Rawnsley's bank.'

'Quite so. And you have not yet asked me why.'

'Then tell me.'

'I think I am afraid to tell you.'

'Gideon – *tell* me. Nothing could be so bad as that, and if it is, we shall
just have to look harder for a solution. If it is failure, and you are afraid
of failure, then I can understand, because so am I. And if you have been
unscrupulous, then at least I shall not be surprised about it.'

'And if I have cheated?'

1129

'Yes. You may have cheated. But I do not think you have done anything mean.'

He swung round towards the fire, remained a moment with his back to me, and then turned to face me again.

'Very well. I am entirely in your hands, Grace. I have made Liam Adair an offer – a very substantial offer – for his half of the *Star*. He would be glad to accept it but will not proceed – and neither will I – unless we have your full agreement. Now then – you may pronounce my sentence.'

I felt so many things, so acutely, all of them crowding me and filling me, each separate feeling clamouring to be heard above the others, that I was – most uncharacteristically – speechless, could do nothing but stare at him, almost deafened now by my thunderous heartbeat, and by so many other things inside me which seemed to be stirring, rising to the surface, preparing to take flight. I was about to lose my head, I knew it, to be deliriously happy or to agonize with despair, to do something huge, something stupendous, some magnificent, gigantic thing which would alter the whole course of my existence, and I needed just a moment more of that breathless quiet before it came.

'Adair really wants my offer, Grace,' he repeated belligerently, striding forward and putting hard hands on my shoulders. 'I did nothing to force him or intimidate him. In fact I behaved so well I amazed him – and me. He wants to go off and find himself another Gower Street somewhere – he says you know that.'

'Yes.'

'He says you practically run the place without him now anyway.'

'Yes. I do.'

'Then come out of your trance, for God's sake, and listen. You said you were ready to share your life with me. If I buy into the *Star*, then I can share it. Grace – I know nothing about running a newspaper and care even less. I haven't the very slightest intention of interfering in what you print or don't print, whose battles you fight, what you condemn – all that is entirely up to you. All I want is a link between us that people – ordinary people – can understand, something to salvage my pride, I suppose, and satisfy the conventions, because I *am* a conventional man most of the time, and it would be easier for me this way. Rawnsley and Mandelbaum and Goldsmith would assume *I* was supporting you – indulging your whim – instead of your father. And why should you refuse me a harmless compromise when the people you care about would know different – and when there's always a chance that, given time, I might be able to accept it and admit it? I understood you, Grace, when you talked about two people who loved each other living together in harmony but retaining their separate identities. I understood all right, but I could see no way to make it work. It needed a link, a key – something *else*, something I couldn't name, to bind us, however loosely together. I have it now. It's not ideal but I can see the way to make it work. Grace, for God's sake, don't just stare at me. Say something, if only to damn me to hell –'

1130

'Yes, Gideon.'

'*Grace*. Everything I said to you that day at Tarn Edge is still true. I would prefer you to give all this up and devote yourself to me if I thought there was a chance of it. You may call me jealous, insecure – anything you like – but if I could choose, then I'd choose that – by God, I would!'

'Yes, Gideon.'

'And everything you said is still valid too. It won't always be easy. I'll try, Grace. That's the progress I've made – I'm willing to try and I shall expect you to try damned hard too. And if you say "yes Gideon" to me once again I may take it very much amiss. Do we have a bargain?'

'How clever you are, Gideon!'

'Yes. But do we have a bargain?'

'In fact you are quite brilliant.'

'I won't deny it.'

'Don't ever deny it, for I mean to tell everybody. You have absolutely overwhelmed me.'

'Ah yes – and for how long? Let me tell you this, Grace Barforth. You have talked a great deal about clever women and how only a strong man is able to cope with one. Very well, I am a strong man and I will readily admit you to be a clever woman. Let us see, shall we, just how you will cope with me?'

'Let us see how we cope with each other – shall we?'

Bemused and tremulous, I put my arms around him, so unaccustomed to this pure joy that it easily took control of me, my whole being luxuriating in it like a sudden burst of sunshine, my spirit altogether triumphant, desiring only to sing his praises, my fear all gone, so that for the first time in my life I was truly at liberty.

'You will take me as your partner then, Grace?'

'Yes, I will.'

'And your lover?'

'Oh yes.'

'And your husband, in due season?'

'Yes. I will even say please to that.'

'And will you trust me?'

'I will.'

'And obey me?'

'Whenever it seems right to me – which may be rather more often than you suppose. Will you obey me?'

'Ah well – it is a little early, I think, for that. Should it ever seem right to me, then I will give it my consideration.'

'I suppose that is something.'

'It is a very great deal.'

'But you will trust me, will you not?'

'That I will. And should I ever be facing bankruptcy, as I led you to believe a few moments ago, then I shall know exactly who to turn to.'

'Gideon – how did you know I would come home tonight? You had waited a long time at the station and you were not at all surprised to see me. Yet it would have been more natural – surely – considering the weather, to have stayed in Scarborough. How did you know?'

He lifted me just an inch or two from the ground and we sat down together on the sofa, cosily installed before my good fire, our arms about each other, my heart almost bursting now with the release of that other side of myself which I had so carefully encased in ice.

'How did I know? Because, my darling, I knew you would have "commitments" tomorrow, and that no matter what the weather or the inconvenience you would wish to be at your desk by eight o'clock – as I shall be at mine.'

'Gideon – I think that is probably the most beautiful thing you have ever said to me.'

'Ah yes – except that I have flattered you a little too much, of course, since I am usually at my desk by seven.'

'How convenient! I can take you to Low Cross in my carriage, can I not, and have plenty of time to go on from there to Sheepgate – in the morning.'

He had indeed found a way for us, not an easy one, but what did that matter to us when we both knew that difficulties existed to be surmounted, problems to be solved, mountains to be climbed and then, when one reached their summits, not to be abandoned but cultivated, guarded, nourished. And we would do all these things together, two very individual people who loved each other. It was the only direction in which either of us could go. It was our beginning.